Wanderers Eastward, Wanderers West

BY *Kathleen Winsor*

FOREVER AMBER

STAR MONEY

THE LOVERS

AMERICA, WITH LOVE

WANDERERS EASTWARD,
WANDERERS WEST

WANDERERS EASTWARD, WANDERERS WEST

Kathleen Winsor

RANDOM HOUSE NEW YORK

FOR
Paul

"I long ago lost a hound, a bay horse, and a turtle dove, and am still on their trail. Many are the travelers I have spoken to concerning them, describing their tracks and what calls they answered to. I have met one or two who had heard the hound, and the tramp of the horse, and had even seen the dove disappear behind a cloud, and they seemed as anxious to recover them as if they had lost them themselves."

—*Henry David Thoreau*

Part

I

I

STRANGERS who arrived during the week supposed they had come to a large city, recently deserted. Few women were to be seen on the streets and fewer men, apparently no children lived there at all, and only an occasional dog or horse gave some reassurance that Virginia City had not been abandoned.

But empty or not, there were restaurants and stores and saloons enough for the camp's reported population of fifteen thousand. Some of the houses were new and tidy, although the favored architecture was a lopsided cabin, and there were still many tents and wickiups of braided willow twigs, using whisky barrels for chimneys and flour-sacks for windows. And there could be no doubt that the population had been there lately and energetically at work, demolishing the countryside, for alders and willows had been burned along the creek banks, and there were vast wandering mounds of earth and crumbled rock, where early summer wildflowers had taken root on the raw surfaces.

On Sundays, however, this illusion of emptiness and quietude was abolished, for by early morning those men who had been invisible, at work on their claims, descended with eager excitement upon the saloons and hurdy-gurdy houses, the stores and gambling halls and brothels, or stood about the streets looking restless and uneasy, rambled aimlessly, and kept alert watch for the first distraction. Children appeared, to sit gossiping on the edges of board sidewalks, and the women, too, came out of hiding.

Men went rattling in hacks from one end of town to the other, or charged about the hills on their squat Indian ponies. They roved singly and in groups, and whether they had been there for several months or had just arrived, they all looked alike, for the conglomerate nature of this population had been lost in the general disguise. Their beards and hair were long, their faces darkly sunburned, their black hats dusty, and each man carried his arsenal of pistols and a knife stuck into his boot-top, as if he must momentarily defend his life or, at least, seem ready to. One looked as fierce as another, their eyes flared with the same delirious excitement, their faces showed the same keen curiosity and alert vigilance, and only an occasional pilgrim could be recognized by his quick, nervous step and apprehensive glances, as if he had happened into some crazy carnival and was hoping to pass through before the fever possessed him, too. But of course, he seldom did—in another week or two he would be gathered for this Sunday revel, as ravenous as anyone else for the new sights and experiences of a mountain mining camp.

Bullock carts crept along, their wheels squawking and screeching on ungreased axles. Wagon trains drawn by teams of oxen passed, their drivers walking beside them and cracking their whips, making a sound like the report of a pistol. There was an occasional Indian to be seen, now and then a Chinese passed, his pigtail wound about his head to keep it out of the way of small boys armed with jackknives, or a Mexican with a string of mustangs went careening by, yelling and maneuvering swiftly among the wagons; but most of the population consisted of those bearded men in their black hats and black trousers, their red or blue flannel shirts, who spoke with the accents of Missouri and Vermont, Georgia and Louisiana and New York, and some few from more distant places—Australia, Germany, Wales, or Ireland.

Barrels were piled to the eaves before store fronts, fresh lumber lay wherever its owner had chanced to leave it, blocking the streets or sidewalks, and weekday miners, turned carpenters and millwrights, set up a din of sawing and hammering. Men were carrying mining tools to be sharpened, window frames to be set into houses, tables and chairs and mattresses, holding them above their heads as they scurried along, weaving their way through this dense traffic with the ceaseless busyness which overcame them the day they arrived, and only the women and children seemed impervious to the general exaltation.

Now and then a well-dressed whore drove by, but the respectable women kept their eyes fixed on the sidewalk, and the traffic parted before them as if a plow had been run through it, for a woman in the mountains still had some of the charm of novelty, and even a young girl walking alone was shown such deference that she might not have been there at all, for she passed among the men like an inquisitive wraith and they fell away from her path with guilty haste, averting their eyes for fear she might catch them looking at her with some of that hungry sentimentality which overcame them at sight of a child.

And this one seemed little more, though she was perhaps fourteen or fifteen years old—a thin young girl with a sorrowful face, moving softly in her low black slippers. She was looking for someone, or pretending to, and every now and then she paused, peeked into a store or a hurdy-gurdy house, and continued on her way. Once she was asked if she wanted help, if she was lost, but she scarcely glanced at the man who spoke to her, though she smiled vaguely and shook her head and walked on, still with the same aloof, wistful expression.

A street auctioneer had drawn a crowd, and this brought her to a temporary stop while she listened to him shouting his wares— horses, wagons, household goods, oxen and tobacco and lumber— and giving from time to time his triumphant yell: "Sold again and got the money!"

She soon glided around the edge of his audience and went a little farther, threading the maze quite easily, until she peeked into another hurdy-gurdy house, and at that moment one of the dancers was slapped by the proprietor and sent spinning onto the floor and into the arms of a customer, who caught her eagerly and took her bounding about the room with him. The young girl shuddered, as if the blow had been intended for her and had luckily landed on someone else, and moved quickly on.

She passed livery stables and grocery stores and restaurants sending out rank smells of frontier cooking, and on the next corner a preacher had drawn a few men who watched him seriously or cynically as he waved his arms and shouted, "Be composed, brother! Be composed! There's no composure in hell or damnation!" Sunday, they liked to say, had been dropped into the Missouri River, and there was no God west of St. Louis, and yet some of them scowled and shifted their feet, and seemed concerned their sins might have followed them here, after all.

She did not wait to hear any more of hell and damnation but kept walking and, at last, discovered someone she knew, and though she might have preferred to meet almost anyone else she nevertheless smiled submissively and looked into the woman's face as she passed her, murmuring her name in a tone of superstitious deference. "How are you, Mrs. Honeybone?"

Mrs. Honeybone made no reply to the greeting, only gave her a menacing grin and a gesture of one raised fist, and the girl began to run. When she looked back, Mrs. Honeybone was far up the street, distributing her ominous signals as she went, striding along in her rusty black cape and carrying the telescope valise from which she peddled beads and pins and harmonicas.

"Does Rick know where you are, Miss Nella?" A man stood before her, easily smiling. She glanced up, startled, gave a petulant shrug and went pacing slowly on her way, but he fell into step beside her, as affable as if she had welcomed his company. "Are you sure your brother would like you to be down here all by yourself?"

"I'm looking for Rick," she told him crossly. "I have something to give him."

He laughed at that, seeming to find it an unlikely explanation, and the laugh was full of healthy good humor and mockery, for he had an advantage of some eight or nine years and was, furthermore, so big that she looked more childish than ever beside him. "Then maybe I can help you, because I saw him not long ago."

"I can find him without your help, Zack Fletcher."

He was spoiling her walk, and surely he knew it, but this did not trouble him either, and he was still beside her when they paused at the next corner and found themselves confronting a man and woman who looked down at them from a stalled hack.

The woman wore a yellow satin dress, cut low enough for a ball gown, and as she sat exposed to the hot sun her face and shoulders glistened with moisture, and the translucent mountain light turned her red hair almost pink. In spite of the day's heat, the man beside her wore a black bearskin overcoat and, while their driver swore and belabored his horses, he drummed his knuckles upon his knee, drew down his tufted black brows in a fierce scowl, and nodded brusquely in reply to Zack Fletcher's greeting.

"Good afternoon, Mrs. Matches. Afternoon, Mr. Flint."

Mrs. Matches gave Fletcher a confiding smile and was about to speak to him, but at sight of the young girl, solemnly watching her, the smile disappeared and she turned her head, refusing to look at them as the hack drove off. Nella started on her way again and he still kept beside her, and must have decided that she needed a guardian whether she wanted one or not, for after she had told him quite sharply to stop following her, he fell back a few steps, but each time she glanced around there he came, loitering along with his hands in his pockets, pretending to be interested in something that was going on across the street.

A black buggy turned the next corner with a reckless dash which made men leap, and Nella discovered another acquaintance—though not one she had ever dared speak to—and watched her go by with a concerned and sympathetic frown, wondering what could be troubling Mrs. Danforth today. For she seemed almost angrily preoccupied and, wherever she was going, quite ready to overrun whoever got in her way, though Nella never doubted that if this should happen her victim would only spring nimbly to his feet again, thinking it sufficient honor to have been knocked down by this severe and imperious beauty.

On every other day Mrs. Danforth's expression was abstracted and indifferent, but it seemed that something had disturbed or destroyed her composure today, and Nella fell to musing over what it might be. She followed Mrs. Danforth's progress through the traffic as she went deftly cutting in and out, and observed with care the clothes she wore—dark red silk with white lace collar and cuffs and a red velvet hat—for they were what she would like to have herself, once she had outgrown blue cotton smocks and white stockings.

And even after she could no longer see her, Nella stood thinking of the house Mrs. Danforth lived in—which she had often stopped to admire: a white frame house with green shutters surrounded by a low white fence—which was pointed out to arriving pilgrims as evidence that the camp was becoming civilized. She had been told that it had a wooden floor with a carpet, and walnut furniture, and although she liked to believe that some day that arrogant lady, the wife of one of the camp's few doctors, would come out and find her standing there and invite her in, Mrs. Danforth had never taken any notice of her, and no doubt the invitation would have sent Nella skipping away, too awed even to mumble an answer.

All at once there were shouts, men ran pelting by, and someone raised a Rebel yell that made Nella cringe and cover her ears. A crowd had gathered outside Troy's Casino, and the shouts grew louder, uncanny yells of rage and excitement. Then the crowd shifted as a man staggered a few steps and collapsed on the sidewalk, and another stood over him, rocking uncertainly on his heels, gave him a last sharp kick in the ribs, and reeled off down the street. He had not gone far before he pitched over and lay on his belly. A smaller crowd drew around to discuss what they should do with him, and at last both men were lifted up by heels and shoulders and carried back into Troy's Casino, while Nella shook her finger at Zack Fletcher, telling him once again that he must stop following her

"Go away," she scolded. "Before you make me mad."

He shrugged, then bowed and begged her pardon for having troubled her, and presently he disappeared inside Troy's Casino. But as she approached the door, intent on finding out what had become of the two men, there he was; and this time it was Zack who wagged his finger and gave a shout of joyous laughter which sent her running as fast as she could go in the opposite direction, to get away from him.

She stopped after a block or two, made a careful survey which convinced her she was free of him at last, and strolled on, lingering where she liked and peeking into one building and then another, but presently she stood at the edge of the sidewalk and looked with a listless indifference at the men who passed, and was telling herself that none of this had anything to do with her, so many strangers parading by, when she was pleased to see two men she knew riding slowly toward her.

Their cabin was not a quarter of a mile from where she and Rick lived, and she had seen them often during the past several months, walking by in the early morning on the way to their claims. She had come to look forward to those meetings and to wait for them, and always felt reassured by their smiles and their habit of raising their hats and giving her slight formal bows, with as much gravity as if they were acknowledging an introduction to a renowned beauty. She knew their names—Matthew and Peter Devlin—and knew that they were brothers and that they had come from New York, for occasionally they had talked to her and had seemed concerned that a young girl should be left so much alone.

Both men had the same bright black eyes, the same black hair and close-cropped beards, and both were tall, almost of a height, although Matt was robust and muscular, while his brother she had sometimes thought looked a little somber, not so quick to smile his morning greeting when they found her picking wildflowers or spreading Rick's shirts to dry over bushes near their cabin. Matt was the one she had selected for her favorite, and she always looked at him first, to get his comforting, warm smile, but she felt a secret link of sympathy with Pete, and wondered what it was he had to think about which made him so quiet and preoccupied.

She watched eagerly now as they advanced toward her, lifting one hand to be sure they did not overlook her in that crowded place, and when Matt noticed her and smiled in his usual way, removing his hat, Pete saw her, too, and smiled, and Nella made them a curtsy and felt a glowing pride to have been recognized by these imposing men.

They were followed by two boys, also on horseback, who looked about her own age, one very much resembling Matt, the other with light brown hair and eyes and a merry, humorsome face, and directly behind them came two boys some years younger who rode with scowling concentration and were plainly determined to make a dignified and manly entrance into this camp; for, as she now realized, they must have come from Fort Benton, where the early boats were beginning to arrive and several men had gone to meet their families. And all four boys, though they looked as pilgrims always did, dazzled and disbelieving, had an air of meaning to take things as they found them and not let themselves be intimidated, and as she watched them pass she wished she might assure them they would soon learn to accept this place and to forget more settled towns.

This troop on horseback was followed by a wagon loaded with barrels and crates and driven by a pretty young woman, and beside her, to Nella's incredulous delight, sat a girl about her own age who held a tortoise-shell cat on her lap, clutching it so firmly she must have suspected its loyalty.

The girl glanced down and smiled at her, a smile of such bright eagerness that Nella gazed back in helpless surprise, but before she could return the smile the wagon had gone by and the procession continued on its way toward Nevada City, where recently three men had been at work building a big cabin near the one where Peter and Matthew Devlin lived. She had gone there a few times to watch its progress, though even after its completion it had remained empty, something she had pondered over from time to time as a mystery in this place where every tent and cabin and wickiup was occupied. And now the mystery was solved.

She watched for a few moments as their caravan got stuck in the traffic and worked its way free, proceeded a little farther and was stopped again; and at last she set off slowly and at a discreet distance to follow them, sure that the girl's flashing smile had been meant to tell her they were friends who would come to depend upon each other, and that she must have been as glad to see a girl her own age waiting there for her in this strange town as Nella had been to see her.

She was so intent on not losing them that she did not see her brother until she collided with him, and then she gave him a sheepish, apologetic smile, for he was obviously angry.

"Now what the hell are you doing here? You know I told you to stay home." ·

"I was just taking a walk, Rick."

He seized her wrist and started off, dragging her with him and looking as belligerent and exasperated as he always did when she disobeyed him. "Come on. You're going home and, by God, you're going to stay home."

She tried to hang back, but Rick jerked at her arm, scowled at her, and walked so fast she was forced to skip now and then to keep up with him, and as he went he muttered about the burdens he bore and the trouble she was.

She had begun to be afraid that at the rate he was going they would catch up with her friends and she would be disgraced before she had even met them, but they came to his pony nodding at a tie-rail, and in another moment Nella was seated sideways behind him, her arms clasped about his waist, and they were jogging slowly through the traffic.

Presently they came abreast of the wagon. The girl smiled at her again and she looked, Nella thought, with her thick dark hair and tanned skin, gay as a gypsy, but although Nella replied this time with a smile of her own, it was shy and rather hesitant, and in the end she had to look away. Still, it seemed the girl had spoken to her and said quite plainly that they would meet again soon.

As they passed the four boys, Nella looked intently in the opposite direction, and presently she heard Rick saying respectfully, "Afternoon, Mr. Devlin. Afternoon, sir." Their pony began moving at a quicker pace and when they were some distance away she grew suddenly bold enough to wave, and that gesture seemed to make their friendship actual.

"I wonder which of them is the girl's father?"

"They're all Matt's kids, somebody said."

"And now they'll live near us and I'll have someone to talk to, won't I?"

"Don't count your chickens."

They rode on without talking, Rick sullen and preoccupied with whatever schemes he had nowadays—and they seemed worrisome ones, for they took most of his time and spoiled his disposition. Presently, they turned off the main road and started up the hillside where cabins and tents were scattered at random among the pine trees, and in a few moments had come to their cabin. Nella slid down and stood in the deep grass, looking up at him.

"What shall I do now, Rick?"

"Clean the house."

"But I cleaned it this morning."

"Read your book, then."

"I've read it until I know it by heart."

"Then don't read it, god damn it—but stay at home!" He pointed his finger at her and squinted, another habit he had acquired these past few months, as if he might be imagining himself peering down a gun barrel. "Do whatever you damn please but stay here and mind your business. Go on, get inside." He made an impatient gesture. "Do I have to lock the door?"

"Of course not. Shall I get dinner for you?"

"I'll eat downtown."

"When will you be home?"

"How do I know? When I get here."

"When you get here," she repeated, gently chiding.

He looked thin and rather helpless to her with his self-conscious scowl and the black hat that was too big for his head, and she smiled with affectionate pity for the brave figure he imagined himself to be. But he was jerking at the bridle, hauling his pony back on its haunches and sending it forward with a springing bound, giving her a wave as he went tearing down the hillside, and when he had disappeared she sighed, relieved to have him gone but disconsolate at being alone again. Then she sat on the doorsill and fell to dreaming of her new friend, although it was true she was a little afraid to meet her again, for the girl had seemed so lively, so full of an audacious confidence, that Nella felt herself grow small and humble by contrast.

Even so, the girl would be kind to her, once she knew how eager she was for her friendship, and knew that she brought her no rivalry but only admiration. And so as she sat there, her eyes closed and her head resting on her arms, Nella tried to imagine she had passed through the first awkward moments of speaking to the girl, telling her where she came from and how she happened to be living here with only her nineteen-year-old brother, and pretended that she was established among them, able to participate in their lives when she needed to and free to draw away when she must, and was convinced they would give her great prizes, whatever they might be, from their own vast stores and without even the necessity of asking, only because they would know what she longed to share and would offer it gladly.

The next morning, she decided, when the men had left, she would go down and introduce herself, but she was somewhat dismayed to find what a sense of dread and stifling timidity the prospect gave her, and foresaw that when the moment came she would be stricken dumb by some fear she could not name, and would turn and run away, and so lose the girl's friendship, after all.

She jumped up, suddenly bold and decisive, determined to run down there and announce herself to them, step up to their doorway and tell them she was a neighbor who had come with her greeting, to welcome them to this mountain city; but then as she set out she walked slowly and, presently, cut off the main road and took a circuitous route which might, eventually, if she did not lose heart, bring her to the vicinity of their cabin.

She passed cabins which sent out smells of wood smoke and cooking, heard men talking and the occasional voice of a woman, now and then the sound of a banjo or fiddle, and after a few minutes could see, from what seemed a safe vantage point, hidden among a stand of pines, the two Devlin cabins—the small one where the brothers had lived, and the large, new one she had explored only recently. The wagon was drawn up before the new one and the men and older boys were at work hammering barrels and crates apart; the younger ones ran between the house and the wagon, carrying chairs and lamps and rolls of bedding, but neither her friend nor the woman was anywhere in sight.

She roamed about restlessly, approaching and then retreating, wishing the girl would come out, for then she might find courage to go up and speak to her. And then, as if by some providential grace, their tortoise-shell cat went streaking by and she began to chase it, coaxing and calling to it, creeping toward it as it crouched in the grass, staring at her with yellow eyes and switching its tail, and when she was ready to touch it, it sprang away again, darted up a tree and clung there, peering down as she reached toward it, and was gone. They played together for several minutes, the cat skimming away each time she seemed about to catch hold of it, and Nella grew more and more distracted, for surely this was meant to be her first test, to retrieve their cat and bring it to them. At last she threw herself down in the tall grass, ready to cry with exhaustion and despair, and the cat came stepping through it, advancing warily, permitted her to stroke it, and after a time crawled into her lap and set up a contented rumble, its sides heaving and its heart fluttering against her hand, while Nella cradled it close and murmured words she hoped would serve to reassure and mollify it.

But just when she and the cat seemed to have achieved some harmonious understanding, she heard the girl's voice calling and she held the cat fast, bending lower in the grass while she watched her running about, clapping her hands and crying, "Shekel, Shekel, come here, kitty-kitty-kitty. Oh, just wait until I catch you—"

The cat began to stir restlessly and Nella held it closer, stroking its ears and head and begging it not to scratch her, then jumped up and walked forward, still clutching it against her and asking in her high light voice, "Is this your cat?"

The girl ran up to her, snatched the cat away and shook it, giving it a smart slap, scolded it and then hugged it fiercely, her lips touching its ear tips. "How did you ever catch her? This cat is worth one hundred dollars in gold, did you know that? Before we left my father wrote that whatever else we forgot, for God's sake don't forget the cat. Those were his exact words." For the first time she turned her attention from the cat and looked at Nella, and gave her once again that dazzling smile. "Oh, I'm sorry. Thank you. I was so scared and mad I was ready to kill it."

They regarded each other carefully and then Nella took a backward step, as if to escape from the girl's intense black eyes, for they searched Nella's face as if she expected to discover a secret. And she was so animated, her expression changed so quickly, passing from anger at the cat to relief at its rescue, from joyous laughter to vigilant attention, that Nella grew confused and embarrassed, lowered her eyes, and felt that the girl's gaiety and strength had defeated her. But the girl continued to talk with an eager and confiding manner, as if she wanted Nella to like her and was ready to coax her into admiration.

"My name's Lisette Devlin. That was my family you saw me with. We just got here today, as I suppose you could tell. Pilgrims," she added, and gently rocked the purring cat and scratched behind its ears. "At least, we're all pilgrims but my father and Uncle Pete, and they've been here almost two years." She gave her another quick intent look, slightly smiling.

Nella had decided that this girl was prettier than she was and that she was, furthermore, used to having her own way and no more willing than any other absolute monarch to let others tell her what to do, and these discoveries made her feel a little easier. For if her friend was prettier than she, then Nella might be proud of having her friendship, and if she was arbitrary, so much the better, for that meant she would make the decisions for both of them.

Nella had said nothing, and Lisette went on. "My father came out here when he was discharged from the Union army after he was wounded. He went to war because he said that if the South was to be a separate state there would be perpetual anarchy—and the country would never amount to a hill of beans." She laughed proudly. "What are you? Yankee or Rebel?"

"Why—I'm neither one."

"Neither one? You have to be one or the other. Where did you come from?"

"St. Louis," replied Nella meekly, and wished that her father or uncle had told this girl that in the mountains no questions were asked about the past.

"That's a Rebel state," cried Lisette, and took a few steps away, apparently ready to leave this pale little traitor without another word. "My father was almost killed by a Rebel."

Nella sprang forward, so afraid of being deserted that she reached out and touched her arm pleadingly. "Please don't go. Please talk to me."

"How many slaves did you have?"

Nella laughed, spreading her fingers over her face, and Lisette looked at her in alarm. "We never had any slaves, we were poor."

"I'm sorry," Lisette said reluctantly. "You're not crying?"

Nella dropped her hands to show that she was not. "My father was killed by a Yankee three years ago." She said it in a tone of vague detachment, for it seemed to have happened so long ago she might never have known him at all.

"That's why you look so sad," Lisette whispered. "How you must hate us," and her expression became so anguished and sympathetic that Nella hoped she would never find out he had been killed in one of the guerrilla raids across the Kansas border, for then she would probably think he had been justly punished for his sins.

"No, I don't hate the Yankees. It would have happened to anyone else who had been where he was."

"What a philosopher you are," Lisette said, a little scornfully. "If my father had died I'd have wanted to tear every Rebel apart with my own hands." She clenched one fist, but quickly relaxed it. "Let's not talk about the War." She smiled. "You haven't even told me your name."

"Nella Allen."

"Nella Allen, that's pretty." She considered it a moment. "Why, Nella is Allen spelled backward. How clever of your parents." She seemed delighted to have made the discovery, but Nella was staring at her in as much terrified confusion as if she had been accused of a crime. "Hasn't anyone else ever noticed it?"

"Oh, yes. Now and then. Does it seem strange to you?"

"Why, not at all. What's strange about it? I like it." From the direction of the Devlin cabins came the sound of a fiddle beginning to play and they listened attentively, Lisette's face growing thoughtful and serious. "That's my Uncle Pete. How I've missed his music."

"I've heard him play before, sometimes when I've gone for a walk in the evening. His music is beautiful—but so sad."

Lisette stroked the cat, and gave a soft sigh. "He is sad. But he has reason to be." She looked at her again. "I'm thirteen. How old are you?"

"I'm fifteen."

Lisette seemed impressed, and then skeptical. "You are? You don't look it."

"I know," Nella agreed apologetically.

"I wish I was fifteen, or older, anyway. But I'll be fourteen this October. Was that your brother I saw you with today?"

"That was Rick. We've been here since last July." Nella felt that by now she must have earned the right to ask a question of her own. "Were all those boys your brothers?"

"They're all my brothers," Lisette assured her, and tapped her fingers, one after the other, reciting, "Morgan's sixteen and Jonathan's fifteen. I come next and then Douglas, who's nine, and Robert's only seven. I haven't any sisters." She gave a triumphant little laugh. "Aren't they handsome?"

"Oh, yes. You all are," she added, although she thought it unlikely this girl had much need for flattery or even subservience, and all at once she wanted to go away, back to her cabin where she could sit alone and try to absorb this meeting, which seemed so greatly significant, try to remember what lies she had told and to guess where the next challenge might come from. "It's almost dark."

"Lisette," a man's voice called. "Where are you?"

"That's my brother. Come meet him. Let him take you home. Here I am, Morgan!"

"Oh, I can't," Nella protested and started away, scampering off so quickly that when she turned she could see Lisette only dimly, and a taller form beside her, but which of the two older brothers it was, she could not tell. "Good-bye," she called. "I've got to go home. Rick will be looking for me."

"Come see us tomorrow." Lisette raised her arm in reply to Nella's wave and they set off down the hill while Nella paused, listening, and heard Lisette laugh, quite tenderly, saying, "The strangest girl, nervous as a rabbit—but so pretty."

II

Jenny Danforth leaned back to study the picture, a cluster of white and purple violets in a pewter cup, partly closed her eyes as she compared it with some imaginary bouquet, then dipped the brush into water and made a few deft strokes. As she worked she glanced out the window occasionally, though there was nothing to be seen but the bull trains which passed through Virginia City in a steady procession all summer long, bringing supplies which must last through the months when the roads were blocked by snow.

The little parlor was crowded with walnut furniture upholstered in black horsehair, there was a patterned carpet, a center table had a neat arrangement of books, and the window was hung with two layers of white muslin curtains, so that the room was as dim as if it might be late afternoon, rather than the middle of the day.

The door to the one bedroom was closed and the house had no dining room, but it had a kitchen and, in back of that, a lean-to which was the Doctor's office, with its operating table and an assortment of instruments and bottles. But she tried to imagine the office was in some other part of town and went there infrequently to clean it—taking care not to breathe deeply, for the smell of chloroform made her queasy—and left before the job had been properly done, feeling each time as if she had escaped some near disaster where she might have been forced to lie on the table and subject herself to his earnest, clumsy attentions. For the Doctor was careless and the blood of one patient mingled with that of the next on the sheet which covered the operating table and on his instruments and on the floor; but there were few doctors in the mountains, and since most of those preferred to work the placer mines, Dr. Danforth was regarded with superstitious affection for his ability to set a broken bone, lance a boil, deliver a baby, sew up a wound, pry out a bullet, or prescribe any of the mysterious medicines which composed his pharmacopoeia.

Now, as if upon some impulse, Jenny laid the brush aside and went to look at herself in the mirror over the sofa, consulting that face which startled everyone who saw it, and which very often seemed not to be her own. Her eyes were a light green, with black brows which slanted slightly at the outer corners, her skin was remarkably clear and white, and her straight black hair was parted in the center, brushed smoothly over her ears and twined into a knot low on her neck, and she looked, when she was not smiling, supercilious and aloof, so that strangers who glanced at her expecting that here was only another pretty face found, instead, this relentless young woman who offered them no rewards for their admiration, often refused even to notice it, and left them perplexed and mystified. Dr. Danforth's wife was known all over the mountains—by those who had seen her in one or another of the towns where they had lived and by those who liked to build legends, whether of murders or Vigilante hangings or of a beautiful woman—but she was not very well consoled by their envy and, after a moment, she turned from the mirror with a shrug.

She went back to work on the picture again and was, for some time, engrossed and nearly content, almost persuaded that neither the bull trains nor Virginia City itself was more real than the Doctor's operating room, for they seemed equally a penalty she must pay for her earlier mistakes.

If she had been more prudent, or luckier, Jenny Danforth thought, she would not be now, at the age of twenty-seven, condemned to this western limbo—a fugitive, like so many others who came here, from her own misfortunes, which she believed had been manufactured by some malicious fate and only incidentally suffered by herself. For here, of course, what had happened eight years before in that small Ohio town made no difference because it was not known, or was known only to the Doctor, and he had forgiven her long ago.

She had gone to ask him to perform an abortion because her husband, as she called him, had left her. But he had refused, saying it

would be criminal to kill the child of so beautiful a girl, and after a
few weeks he had married her. They had given the child, a girl, to
his sister to care for and had started west, first to San Francisco
where they had lived for nearly five years and then, when the Doctor
decided his fortune was waiting for him in one of the new gold
camps, they had gone to Florence and Oro Fino and Bannack and on
to Virginia City, after the strike a little more than a year ago. But
she was no better reconciled to this turn her life had taken than she
had ever been, although she felt obliged to be grateful to the Doctor
who, she knew quite well, had not married her only in a fit of quixotic
infatuation.

For in fact his practice had begun to disappear as he drank more
heavily and, when they met, she supposed he might have regarded
her as a kind of savior, someone he could help and be helped by, a
woman he adored who must be grateful to him; a much better arrangement in many ways, she had often thought, for Andrew Danforth than it had been for her.

She sat there, engrossed and slightly smiling as the picture began
to emerge, touching the pewter vase to heighten its luster, deepen-
ing the shadows, and all at once she leaned forward as at a warning,
parted the curtains, and caught her breath in a little angry gasp as
a buggy stopped before the gate and she saw a red-haired madam
who called herself Milly Matches, and a girl in a purple silk dress with
a green shawl over her head. They talked for a moment, and perhaps
the girl was reluctant to see the Doctor, for they seemed to be arguing, but at last she climbed down, Milly Matches drove off, and
Jenny opened the door, crying, "You can't come here in the daytime!"

The girl unfastened the low gate and walked quickly toward her,
and Jenny retreated into the house, but then hesitated, for the girl's
face had a trail of blood from her forehead to her chin, and as she
held out one hand in a pleading gesture, the palm was smeared and
wet. "Is the Doctor home? Please let me come in."

The girl passed her and stood staring distractedly about, trembling
and whimpering, and Jenny, murmuring that she would get the Doctor, went quickly into the bedroom and closed the door. Andy lay on
the bed, still dressed in his trousers and shirt, still fast asleep, and
did not awaken easily as she shook his shoulder but began to moan
softly, as if in sympathy with the sounds which came from the other
room, and as Jenny wiped his face with cold water he at last opened
his eyes, but promptly closed them again and gave a deep, sorrowful
sigh. "What time is it, Jenny?"

"Nearly one o'clock." Jenny was brushing his coat and talking in a
soft, urgent voice as he began to make tentative efforts to get up.
"There's a girl out there from Milly Matches' house who's been badly
beaten. You've got to see her, Andy——" She held the coat, pretending
not to notice the sheepish and apologetic glance he cast her over his
shoulder, and went back to where the girl knelt on the floor, clutch-

ing the green shawl which covered her head and rocking to and fro.

Jenny approached her, whispering, "Oh, I'm sorry, I'm sorry," but the girl did not glance at her, perhaps did not know she was there, and after a few moments Andy came out, somewhat unsteadily, but wearing his black frock coat and with his cravat neatly tied. "I'll get you some coffee," she told him, and went to the kitchen, poured a cup, and spilled some as she picked it up, for she had begun to tremble, and heard the Doctor, in his low reassuring voice, begin to talk to the girl.

"I'm Dr. Danforth, my dear. Let me see you. What seems to be the trouble?"

He gestured the cup away and Jenny set it down, but when he approached the girl she scrambled away on her hands and knees and huddled across the room, watching him with such terror she might have been expecting a new attack. She went on moaning, chattering incoherently, but at last she let him come nearer, and began to talk. "He said he only wanted something to remember me by, just a little keepsake, and I thought he was teasing me, but then he began to cut—" The shawl dropped to the floor, showing a crescent-shaped gash on the crown of her head. "I tried to get away but I couldn't, I couldn't move, the son of a bitch had hold of me—"

Jenny turned and ran through the kitchen, out the back door, and on toward the town, never stopping once or glancing back. The street was more or less empty, as it was during the week, but still it was always surprising to see the numbers of men who, even in the midst of a gold rush, had nothing to do but stand on street corners whittling, apparently engaged in some deep meditation, and she looked into their faces as she passed them, silently asking each one: Which of you did it?

At last she went into a livery stable, hot and dark, with a thick dust of manure and a bright flame at the forge, and a man approached her. "I want my buggy. I'm in a hurry. Please."

"Yes, Mrs. Danforth. Right away."

He looked at her curiously, and while she waited Jenny paced around, walked to the door and stood staring out, and from time to time shut her eyes to obliterate the image of a naked girl struggling with a man who held a knife in his hand. And then there came a vision of Andy, seated in his office, smelling strongly of mountain whisky and stitching at a young whore's scalp with all the solemn concentration of a woman working over an embroidery hoop, and at that she longed to shriek with crazy laughter.

She set off at her usual heedless rate, and at the next corner turned away from the main part of town and started up a steep road, where cabins stood in a disorderly line and mounds of overturned earth meandered among them. Some distance farther she came to where men were at work, digging or trudging behind wheelbarrows, with others shoveling dirt into the flumes or pitching rocks out with forks, talking little and sweating in the hot sun, for placer mining was hard physical labor, to the surprise of those who came here intending to pick up golden nuggets like a stroller on the seashore selecting only the prettiest shells.

When she had gone nearly a mile she stopped and sat with her eyes closed, sick and weak, and still unable to stop trembling. But finally she looked up, toward a hillside some distance away, discovered him there working with several other men, and seemed to see him as plainly as if he were very close. After a few minutes she called softly to a young boy at work nearby, pecking at the ground like a chicken on top of a grain pile, the way pilgrims always did.

"Will you come here for a moment, please?" she asked, with so much tenderness that in one motion he dropped his pick and came floating dazedly toward her.

"Ma'am?"

"It's hot, isn't it?" He gave her a foolish smile, nodding. "May I ask you to do something for me?"

"I'd be glad to, ma'am."

"Do you see where those men are working, several of them together just beyond this near rise? Now, do you see the man in the red shirt with the black hat and trousers who is throwing rocks out of the flume? Will you go to him and say that I have something I must tell him?"

"Yes, ma'am," he agreed, as if this request was an unusual favor she had done him, and started off at a trot.

He jogged along, leaping nimbly over the rock piles, and was soon there. They talked together briefly, and as the boy started back she got out of the buggy and stood beside it, feeling as much frightened apprehension over this meeting as she had ever felt over their earlier ones.

"He's coming," the boy told her, and Jenny gave him that smile which changed her face so remarkably, making it momentarily gay and candid.

When he was quite near she started impulsively forward. "Matt, oh, I'm sorry to come here, but something has happened that's so dreadful I think I'm going insane. One of Milly Matches' girls just came to the house to see Andy, and there was a cut on her head—like this—" She raised one hand, describing the wound. "Someone had tried to scalp her."

He was staring at her with horrified disbelief. "Hostile Indians near Virginia City?"

"It wasn't an Indian, Matt." She became all at once as calm as if the news was inconsequential, or imaginary, some invention she had contrived to give her an excuse to see him, and she had thought of others nearly as strange these past few months; and she grew so engrossed in watching his face, darkly tanned with black, shining eyes and thick brows, a strong, keen nose and sensually molded mouth, that the questions he asked her might have concerned some disaster

she knew nothing about, although at last she inquired, almost listlessly, "Will they hang him? I hope so."

He smiled at her with a sad humorousness, and shook his head.
"Now, Jenny, you've lived in the mountains long enough to know better than that. They won't do a damn thing—because that little whore
is no one's responsibility."

"But what happened to her is. They hang a man quickly enough for
stealing a can of gold dust, or even because they suspect he did." He
made no reply to that and they stood watching each other, both their
faces wary and sorrowful, and at last she sighed, touched his arm,
but then quickly drew her hand away. "Oh, Matt, I'm so unhappy."

"I'm sorry, Jenny."

"If I hadn't come here today—when would I have seen you again?
It's been two months and a half."

"You told me you didn't want to see me after they got here," he reminded her gently.

"But you must have known I didn't mean it. A woman in love has
no idea what she says." She tipped her head to one side, looking up
at him with a slight, wistful smile, though her eyes still watched
him with the same intent anxiety. "You're glad to have them?"

"Yes," he said slowly. "Yes, Jenny, I am."

"I saw them that first day. Erma Finney tells me she and your wife
are good friends—she's very pretty, Matt."

Matt smiled. "Erma was there the next morning."

"And suppose she decides that your wife must know about us?"

He smiled more broadly. "What could she say, after all? No,
Jenny, it won't happen, you know that. Her husband has too much interest in my friendship."

"I should think he has. An eighteen percent interest, to be exact."
All at once she seemed angry, and turned and started away. "I'm
sorry I came." She paused, looking at him with the grave and
thoughtful expression which appeared so naturally, and which, for
all its seriousness, served to enhance that singular face. "I'm
ashamed to say it, Matt, but it's true—it's myself I've been feeling
sorry for all this time, not Marietta."

She lowered her head as she spoke, glancing away, and, as she did,
it seemed he could see her walking toward him once more through
the trees the early morning nearly two years before when he had
gone to their cabin looking for the Doctor, found it empty, and a man
passing by had pointed, saying, "There she is, that's Mrs. Danforth."

He had run forward, asking her urgently, "Can you tell me where
I can find the Doctor? My brother's been hurt. I think his ankle is
broken."

She had looked at him for a moment and then bent her head in a
gesture which seemed to him so graceful, and so poignant, that he
believed it would be the last thing he wanted to remember in life.
"I'll show you." He followed her, feeling a sense of shock and excitement, and had almost forgotten Pete waiting at their diggings, swear-

ing and drinking mountain whisky. She walked lightly and quickly, without glancing around or speaking to him, and her long skirts swayed with the movement of her hips.

They passed among the shabby tents which at night looked like so many blocks of luminous marble, and at last she stopped and raised her arm. "He's over there, just at the edge of that clearing, do you see?"

He took a moment to find him, squinting his eyes and pretending to be more puzzled than he was, then looked swiftly back just as she glanced away from his face, furtively, he thought, as if she was ashamed of her interest, and she walked away. "Thank you, Mrs. Danforth," he called, then with a guilty start went running toward the clearing, cupping his hands to his mouth and shouting, "Dr. Danforth, Dr. Danforth," as if to assure himself that was really what he had come there for. He turned once more and looked back, but she had disappeared.

He began to watch for her and was chagrined to find that, although he had imagined himself at the age of thirty-six to be a sober and stable man with responsibilities and ambitions enough to keep him very well occupied, and had thought it unlikely he would ever be taken by surprise again—whether by a woman or by any other experience—whenever he saw her or expected to, he was overcome by a kind of boyish confusion which disgusted him. They passed now and then in what was called the middle of town, where a few shacks had been thrown together by the owners of grocery stores and gambling halls and whorehouses, but she was always with her husband or another woman, and though each time he was alertly ready to take off his hat and speak, she seemed not to remember him. She rode by one day where he and Pete were working, for Pete had stubbornly insisted on strapping his leg and keeping about his business even though the pain tormented and preoccupied him steadily, and glanced at him, but neither smiled nor nodded.

He was perplexed and a little angry, but it did not occur to him that perhaps she was being deliberately provocative, until he saw her one day at Josiah Webb's cabin.

He and Pete had met Josiah Webb and Lemuel Finney in St. Louis, by that infallible western chance which drew together men of similar purposes, they had taken the same boat up the river and, when they arrived in Fort Benton five weeks later, had formed a partnership and decided to go to the new camp of Bannack, rather than their first destination of Florence, and there they found several hundred men panning gold and building sluices and a few were reported to have gotten rich.

She came in with her husband as he and Webb and Finney sat smoking cigars and drinking the Mormon whisky which circulated through the mountains, talking of their various plans, to dig ditches and sell water, to buy up several claims and form a corporation, to start a bank, and all three had their hats on and their boots propped

on the flour barrel which served as a table. It was early Sunday afternoon and both she and the Doctor were dressed as if they had been
to church in any eastern city. She looked very fashionable in a black
silk dress and black straw hat with roses clustered under the brim,
and held her gloved hands clasped lightly at her waist, as if to receive an offering.

The three men jumped up, setting down their glasses and cigars
with guilty haste, sweeping off their hats, and as Lem Finney made
the introductions her green eyes went from one face to the next and
she smiled, as if she were amused and pleased by their consternation.
"Yes, I've met Mr. Devlin. How is your brother, has he recovered?"

Matt found himself giving a longer description of Pete's troubles
than it seemed likely could interest her, then stood watching resentfully as she made small talk with Webb and Finney, and was blaming her for his own confusion when she glanced at him and her face
was whimsically mocking, telling him she wanted him to feel foolish
and was glad to see that he did, and that glance all at once put him
at ease.

He saw her occasionally during the next several weeks, but had no
other chance to speak to her and could not invent one, and it was December before he saw her at the camp's first general ball, to which
everyone was invited who might expect to be welcome and who was
willing to pay five dollars in gold dust. He had gone in the hope she
would be there, but when he arrived she was not.

He had had his hair cut for the occasion and was wearing, like
most of the men, a blue flannel shirt and black tie, black trousers
and boots, and he stood against the wall with Pete and smoked a
cigar. The hall had a hard-packed dirt floor, and was dimly lighted
and smoky from the tallow candles stuck into tin wall sconces. Two
fiddlers sat on stools at the far end, stamping their feet and playing
with excited industry, while the dancers spun about, the women's
skirts floating and skimming, and there was an atmosphere of exultant gaiety, as if they were proud of having organized this civilized
entertainment in the wilderness. But the men outnumbered the
women by at least twelve to one and so most of them stood along the
walls, watching with wistful or sullen expressions and quite often
went outside to have another drink or left in discouragement to go to
a part of the camp where women were available.

Little girls, ten or twelve years old, were gravely approached by
bearded men and humbly requested to honor them with a dance.
Some of them went readily, composed and smiling, as if they had
been dancing at balls all their lives, but others were bashful and
hung back, though eventually they would all be dragged onto the
floor and whirled through the schottische and the mazurka.

Matt stood silently, watching one pretty brown-haired girl who
looked about twelve being spun around in expert style by a miner
who moved through the steps with devoted seriousness, and he grew

homesick thinking of Lisette and then of Marietta and began to wonder again, as he often did, if perhaps he had been dishonest to leave them. He had gone to the War out of conviction, though Pete had called him a damned fool to fight in a war which could never be won by either side and where the reasons for fighting were wrong, whichever side you were on, but Matt had made reference to some large patriotic sentiments, most of which he thought he believed, and had enlisted almost immediately. Four months later he had been wounded and, when he was well enough recovered, he and Pete had set out for the Territories, where men were going at an increasing rate, as if the War itself had made them restless and dissatisfied and unable any longer to keep tamely at home.

Their law practice had been successful, they had money to invest, and Pete, at least, had no reason to stay in New York, for his wife and young son had died several years before and he had not remarried. And when they left, Matt had promised Marietta they could come out later, if he had any luck and if he thought they would like the country, or he would be back in a year. That had been seven months ago and he was thinking that Lisette looked something like that little girl with the springing brown curls who pranced with such confidence from one end of the floor to the other, delighting them all with her poise and grace.

The door opened, a gust of wind swept the room, blowing the women's dresses and putting out several candles, and four people came in, Jenny Danforth first, shivering but laughing with more animation than he had ever seen her show, as if this might be the self she kept for special public occasions, then Erma Finney, doubtful and suspicious as she paused to sniff out the atmosphere, determining whether there was too much hilarity in the room and too little decorum, Lemuel Finney and the Doctor stepped smartly in together, and the door slammed shut. The little girl had lost her audience, though the dance continued, and the men now covertly watched as Mrs. Danforth let the Doctor take her coat, touched the back of her hair where she had fastened a spray of cedar, and moved forward with the same bright smile to join the dancing.

Matt looked at her with guilty longing as she went gliding across the floor, giving her hand to one man and then another, and might have begun to feel some jealousy had she not seemed so gaily impersonal, smiling, but never looking directly into their eyes, engrossed in the complex figures of the dance but not at all aware of her partners.

He was thinking, as if it might be some significant discovery he had pursued a long while, that for all her air of remoteness and formality, Jenny Danforth was ready to accept unhappiness with joy, knew as much about sorrow as she knew of pleasure and was as well acquainted with regret as with anticipation, and since he knew this much about her, he decided they were strangers no longer.

"What the hell is a woman like that doing out here at the fag-end of creation?" Pete mumbled.

Matt turned to look at him with quick disapproval, but could find nothing in Pete's face but curiosity and admiration, and surely, Matt told himself, amused by his own combative rivalry, Pete was entitled to that much of Jenny Danforth. "You noticed the Doctor wasn't quite sober when he set your ankle?"

"That's why he's here. But why is she?"

"Loyal wife," Matt assured him, and went back to watching her, pleased by her gracefulness and taking an almost defiant pride in the attention she attracted and the numbers of men who gathered as there was a pause in the music, surrounding her so effectively he could not even see her.

"The undisputed belle of mountain society." Pete was skeptically smiling. "Do you imagine it means anything to her?"

Matt did not answer but looked preoccupied and somber as he asked himself if it was possible that Pete was interested in Jenny Danforth. And as the next dance began, he fell to studying Pete's face, observing the look of preoccupied sadness which had become his most usual expression since Lorena and his young son had died, and told himself confidently that Pete Devlin was an honorable man, almost ferociously committed to his principles, and owning a great many more scruples than he could claim for himself. And it was not at all likely that Pete, who accepted virtuous women as virtuous and naughty women as naughty and had no expectation of combining the two into one more satisfactory female, would imagine that another man's wife was his own logical prey—and would furthermore suppose it would not occur to Matt, either.

Pete, however, was not yet done with Mrs. Danforth, but now answered his own question. "I don't think it means a damn thing to her. She despises this place, she despises those guys she's dancing with, and no doubt she despises the Doctor, too. The poor son of a bitch is at least twenty-five years older than she is." Matt listened with a sense of outraged indignation, for he had not supposed Pete would have given her so much thought, felt his face and neck grow hot and his collar tight and began to feel an urge to move quickly, dash out there and dance with her himself, or leave and drag Pete away with him. "She sets quite a value on herself and, with her look of threatening splendor, maybe she's entitled to."

"Maybe she is," Matt agreed sullenly.

They watched the rest of the dance without speaking, while Matt wondered if Pete had meant to tell him, in the oblique way he sometimes had, that he was aware of his interest in Mrs. Danforth and disapproved of it. For although it was quite natural to Pete that they visit Milly Matches' house from time to time, he would not think it at all natural if Matt were to show a keen if only sentimental admiration for a woman who would expect to be taken seriously. But he decided that his own greedy curiosity about Jenny Danforth was giving him strange notions, for he knew well enough that in spite of Pete's protective love for Marietta he was no more likely to take charge of his brother's conscience now than he had ever been.

All at once Matt went striding onto the floor, made his way without ceremony through the group which surrounded her, and spoke to her with an air of grave formality, as if he delivered some official message, news of distant battles, governments overturned, and was imploring her to send out a rescue committee. "Mrs. Danforth, I hope you haven't forgotten that you promised me this dance?"

"I did? I had forgotten. But yes," she added, glancing at the others, "Mr. Devlin's memory is better than mine."

A slow Spanish waltz began, a saraband, and she lifted her arms but did not look at him; her face had again become still and secretive, and they circled several times about the room with Matt watching her anxiously and almost beseechingly, but whether from confusion or malicious obstinacy, she refused to look at him. They were near the door when it flew open again, the accompanying gust of wind caused them all to turn to see who had come, and they found Milly Matches smiling confidently at them, while behind her stood Jeremy Flint in his black bearskin overcoat, drunk and belligerent.

The music stopped, and after a few moments of astonished silence, the women began to twitter indignantly.

"What is she doing here?"

"She must leave. Whoever invited her?"

"I knew something like this would happen."

"Jeremy Flint has lost his mind."

Jeremy Flint had announced to friends that he would not only bring Milly Matches to the ball but would dance every dance with her himself if they were too cowardly, and now he was dangling above his head a pouch of gold-dust containing the price of their admission and swinging it suggestively to and fro, though Milly Matches looked less confident than she had a moment ago, and all at once four or five men, who might have formed a spontaneous posse to handle this crisis, started forward.

They talked to Jeremy Flint in reasonable undertones and Jeremy answered them in the same cautious way, but then spoke up in a voice which carried over the room. "I've got no god-damn intention of going quietly. This is a public hall, here's your bloody entrance fee, and Mrs. Matches is as good a woman as any—" The posse moved nearer, easing him backward, other men approached the group, and presently Jeremy Flint was so densely surrounded by his friends that neither he nor Milly Matches could be seen. Their voices rose and fell, Jeremy shouted from time to time; the women kept close watch on the proceedings, as if they expected Mrs. Matches to slip through the cordon, and the little girls seemed filled with marveling delight at these grown-up antics.

Matt turned to Jenny. "Mrs. Danforth, please let me come to see you."

She did not answer, but continued to watch the group at the door, where now at least twenty men had gathered, and he was surprised to see that she looked amused and a little cruel.

"Go to hell, you pack of god-damn hypocrites," Jeremy Flint shouted. "I'll remember this, by Christ, I'll—" He continued to mutter as the door was opened and the group moved through it, guiding Mrs. Matches and Jeremy Flint ahead of them. The door slammed shut and the women broke into sharp cries, demanding how such a thing could possibly have been allowed to happen and why someone had not had the foresight to post a guard at the door.

"Didn't you hear me?" Matt asked her.

"Come to dinner on Sunday at one o'clock," she murmured, and turned in response to her next partner.

Matt had been waiting with a suspenseful anxiety so acute his muscles ached, and now he swung about and walked toward Pete but paused partway, surprised to see that Pete's face had a sardonic grin, and, for a moment, supposed he must be laughing at him. But then he realized it was Jeremy Flint's predicament, not his own, which had caused Pete's grin, and said, "Come on, let's get a drink."

They found that Mrs. Matches and Jeremy Flint had disappeared, although the posse still lingered about the door, passing a bottle from hand to hand in celebration of their night's work, and Pete gave a burst of laughter, slapping his leg. "Good for Jeremy, the bastard's got guts."

They started walking, not very fast, for Pete was still hobbling, and Matt glared at the darkness, furious to think of his meek humility, begging her to see him and being told to come to dinner with her and her husband, and from time to time Pete laughed aloud and seemed more pleased by the incident than by the best day's work they had had.

Matt was assuring himself he would not go on Sunday and would never give her another chance to entertain herself at his expense, when Pete said, "The sight of Erma Finney's face is something I'll treasure all my life, the most perfect image of righteous intolerance I've ever seen. But then, respectable women," he added philosophically, "seem to have all sense of mischief killed in them at an early age." And hearing that, Matt felt a little easier and smiled to himself, reflecting that perhaps Jenny Danforth's sense of mischief was still quite lively.

When Sunday came he dressed in the same blue flannel shirt and black trousers, got into the heavy officer's coat he still wore, and set out for the Danforths' new cabin, which stood with several others that had been completed just in time for the winter, and as he walked was wondering at his own arrogance ever to have imagined she might suggest anything else.

It occurred to him as he approached the cabin, which, unlike any other in the camp, had a balcony across the front of the second story with a small outside staircase leading to it, that the Doctor might, after all, not be at home, might have been conveniently sent for by one of his patients, or perhaps would be called away during dinner. But Dr. Danforth was there and met him at the door, looking so much the distinguished professional man that it was not easy to remember how he looked when he was drunk.

Jenny was not in the room and as Matt grew hungrily appreciative of the smells of venison roasting and coffee brewing, the Doctor poured him a drink, casually remarking, "Another man died this morning, did you hear about it?"

"No, I hadn't. How did it happen?"

"Another of those quarrels among themselves." The Doctor nodded. "But we're mistaken if we suppose they'll be content only to shoot one another. I know some of them, knew them in Florence and Oro Fino, and I know why they're here. They follow the strikes, and they're waiting until it becomes worth their while to kill other men."

Matt and Dr. Danforth sat for a moment regarding each other solemnly, for the Doctor was not the first who had made this prediction, and then Jenny appeared, wearing the same bright green taffeta dress, its wide white linen collar tied with a black velvet bow, that she had worn at the ball, shook hands with him and smiled, but seemed uneasy and almost embarrassed, and left again quickly, saying that she would have dinner ready in a few minutes.

"What are we going to do about it?" the Doctor asked. "Expect each man to protect himself?"

Matt looked somber and perplexed and was displeased to realize that this discussion of criminals might as well apply to him as to anyone else, since he had certainly come here with robbery in his heart and was only chafing at the Doctor's watchful presence, and wondered if this was Andrew Danforth's way of letting him know that a man with a beautiful wife was as subject to depredation as a man with a cache of gold dust. He glanced up after a moment and stared at him suspiciously, but Dr. Danforth was plainly concerned about what they were discussing and had intended no parables.

"I suppose each man will have to protect himself, sir," Matt agreed. "We're a long way from any organized authority."

"And we have no way of knowing which man we can trust—and which would murder us for a trifle." Dr. Danforth looked into his glass. "It's happened in other places and it will happen here. We should all try to discover our friends. But of course, that isn't easy."

Matt became aware of the beating of his heart. "No," he agreed, watching the Doctor earnestly, as if he might be trying to make that same discovery himself. "That isn't easy."

III

The winter was mild and men continued to work their claims as long as the water was not frozen and, when it was, spent the time building sluices, repairing their cabins, and planning new projects.

Matt and Pete, with Josiah Webb and Lemuel Finney, explored their partnership in as many ways as they could discover or invent, and were so occupied with plans and so elated by their good fortune that it was easy to persuade themselves the constant quarrels and shootings were no concern of theirs, and they confidently predicted that by spring there would be no desperadoes left to trouble them, if only they had the luck to keep out of the path of stray bullets in the meanwhile. They bought and sold claims, made grubstake arrangements with prospectors who went dashing off on random ventures and usually disappeared, but sometimes came back to say the rumors had been false, after all; they bought a pack team and sent it to Salt Lake City for supplies; Lem Finney opened a grocery store stocked with those four necessities of mining-camp life, whisky and flour and coffee and bacon; they organized a company to bring in machinery for a quartz mill, and started an informal bank in a corner of Finney's store where they loaned money at five percent interest a month and, more often than not, took over the property when their debtor lost his money at faro or spent it in a whorehouse.

And in all these ventures they were so successful that Lemuel Finney several times remarked, "A man's got to be unlucky or a fool not to get rich out here."

Lemuel Finney, who had been a storekeeper in a small town in northern Connecticut, was a spare man, not very tall, with a beard which did not conceal his shrewd, clever face. He had a habit of blinking his blue eyes, as if in recognition of an idea which flashed upon some screen in his head at regular intervals and, when the flash came, would smile and rub his hands together with a crisp, dry sound. Whenever Matt and Pete saw him, usually two or three times each day, Lem Finney had another idea, a new adventure they must undertake at once before someone else thought of it, and their discussions ranged over irrigation systems, extensive strings of flumes to which they would control the water supply and, thereby, the miners, schemes for chartering a new city or lighting Bannack with gas; but however far Lem stretched his imagination, Matt and Pete and Josiah Webb listened politely and discussed it earnestly, for although some of Lem's projects were impossible of accomplishment, others were as neat and precisely efficient as Lem himself.

"You've got to admire the son of a bitch," Pete said. "He's a true

New Englander—makes more use of his ignorance than other men do of their knowledge."

And Erma Finney, who looked to Matt as if she had been meant for a spinster's life, although they had two children in school in the East, was Jenny's constant companion and possibly considered that she was her guardian, as well, for no doubt in Erma Finney's opinion a woman like Jenny Danforth needed protection and surveillance, and might be in as much danger from her own impatient and demanding nature as she was from any man.

Jenny had not invited Matt to dinner again, but whether this was because of some objection the Doctor had made or because the afternoon had been a trying one, he could not guess.

He passed their cabin quite often and sometimes saw her talking to Mrs. Finney or another woman, and once, when there was an unusually warm day, she was seated on the little balcony at an easel, so absorbed in whatever she was painting that he had bowed two or three times from horseback, grinning very obsequiously, he thought, before she glanced up, smiled and raised one hand, waving casually, and returned to her work. Matt continued on his way, pleased to have seen her, then angry because of her manner, perfunctorily dismissing him, as it seemed, and finally amused because this woman he scarcely knew had bedeviled his thoughts for nearly six months.

Whenever he saw her, whether from a distance or in closer quarters at a friend's cabin on a Sunday afternoon, he watched her as vigilantly as if he were expecting some signal to pass between them and must be alert enough to catch it, but she was as reserved as if it were the first time they had met, and seemed to be warning him not to try to come any nearer.

Still, the clothes she wore, the way she moved and walked and the tones of her voice, a light, high voice with a strange minor music in it—even her perfume which saturated the air with a fragrance of violets—all were poignantly, if obscurely, significant to him. She wore a garnet ring on her right hand composed of a large stone surrounded by a cluster of smaller ones, and even this interested him, although it was certainly not an unusual ring. Her manner with her husband was gentle and almost maternal, in spite of the difference in their ages, and he tried to imagine why they had married and whether or not she loved him, but promised himself that if the opportunity came he would ask her no questions suggesting answers he might not like to hear. He was curious to know what her life had been and what it was now, and told himself that if he were not so incessantly occupied with his work there was some danger he would be hopelessly addled by his obsession.

For it seemed to him she was concealing mysteries he must expose, and he had even come to believe that to possess her was a matter of crucial importance between himself and his pride; but she was plainly not eager to make the experiment, and he expected they would spend their lives bowing and smiling from distances, and he would never know anything more about her than he did at that moment.

And so his interest in her began to seem absurd, an embarrassment, not an infidelity, and this gave him some consolation when, early in the spring, the first papers and mail arrived and there were several letters from Marietta.

The sight of her handwriting, and the tenderness and gaiety with which she wrote, addressing herself to him and Pete, recalled him to his love for her and their shared responsibilities, and he and Pete read the letters and reread them, discussed every piece of gossip and information many times, and grew as homesick and remorseful as young boys.

"Morgan wants to enlist, for God's sake." Pete smiled, shaking his head. "A fifteen-year-old kid."

"He won't do it. I told him when we left he was the head of the house now and it was up to him not to let us down."

Pete sat on a stool, his long legs stretched straight, his hands in his pockets, and stared at the fireplace where Matt squatted on his heels, taking his turn at cooking their breakfast and flipping the pan of flapjacks with deft skill, for the men considered it a disgrace if they were obliged to turn them as a woman did. He watched Matt thoughtfully, and seemed as concerned about his brother's family as if it were his own. "And Lisette says they've got a kitten to bring with them. But should they come out here?"

"If we stay, they should."

"Morgan starts college next year."

"Do you think he's likely to prefer college to this? Pete, let's see what happens. You're still thinking maybe we shouldn't be here, and for Christ's sake, we've made more this last year than we'd have made in five years in the States. And the life is great, isn't it?"

"Great for men and horses," Pete quoted. "But hell on oxen and women."

Pete glanced around as if to remind him what this great life— from which they both drew keen enjoyment and some mystical fulfillment—was made of, and how unlikely it was to picture Marietta or Lisette there. The cabin, which they had built themselves in a few hours, after sleeping out-of-doors in buffalo robes for several months, was a pole framework plastered with dirt which did not keep muddy water from seeping onto them during a rainstorm. Green cowhides which stank as they cured were pegged to the dirt floor; there was a flour sack for a windowpane and a wagon sheet for a door; and with their picks and equipment, their guns and cooking pans and Pete's fiddle, it was crowded when they were in it together. Rats scampered about their feet while they ate, were sometimes kicked but usually ignored; their diet consisted of flapjacks and beans and venison and coffee, but still it was their habit, as they raised their glasses before taking a quick gulp of mountain whisky, to propose each time the same toast: "Here is life."

"Let's wait," Matt said again. "Let's see what happens. A man doesn't leave a place where he's had luck, and our luck's been god-damn good."

They read the newspapers, passed them about until they were ragged, and discussed with Finney and Webb and Flint and other men the mess that America was in now, the battles lost by the North and the general despair that the War would ever end, the passing of the conscription act and the Emancipation Proclamation, the specu-lations in gold which caused the market operators to sing "Dixie" on the floor of the Exchange when there was a Union defeat, and all these calamities seemed to belong to another country and even to an-other time. And then, as Andrew Danforth had predicted, they began to be aware that they were in a different mess right here.

Throughout the winter, while the rough part of the town's popula-tion congregated in saloons and gambling halls and whorehouses, shot at one another often and sometimes aimed straight enough to wound a man or kill him—waiting, as Dr. Danforth had said, for the others to dig up enough gold to interest them—those others, who saw this place as an opportunity for work and exploitation on a bigger scale than anything they had found before, continued to dig shafts, experimented with building quartz mills, worked twelve or fifteen hours a day on a gravel bar; and by spring many of them had ac-cumulated several thousands of dollars, which was both a joy and a concern, for they had no place to hide the money and no way to get it out of the mountains but to carry it out themselves.

A few men, supposing they were rich, left for the States. But the first mail told them that several of those who had started home some months before had never arrived, and there spread a gradual reluctant awareness that the desperadoes had come to the mountains on business of their own and were not visiting in Bannack only for the sake of its diversions. The recognition of what was happening came slowly, was suggested and shrugged off, and no one was ready to admit that he was scared or even worried, but they began to take new precautions, slept with their pistols beside them, and were care-ful to speak quietly whenever there were strangers about, and many of them grew suspicious of their friends and even of their partners.

"I've got an idea," Matt announced one morning. They stood out-side the cabin, scrubbing their faces, and he mumbled through the towel as he worked it vigorously over his hair and beard. "Came to me in the middle of the night," he added, as if the brilliance of it still surprised him.

"What's that?" Pete returned to the cabin and Matt spoke to him through the flour-sack windowpane, a little glad Pete could not see him.

"We don't know what these buggers are up to exactly, or who they are for sure, or how much they know about us. But we do know they're not likely to bother a respectable woman."

Pete was rattling pans and lighting the fire. "They don't need to. What's your point?"

Matt appeared in the doorway now, ashamed to hide any longer be-hind the flour-sack pane, and spoke with simple eagerness, quite con-vinced his idea was both reasonable and honest. "Let's ask Mrs. Dan-forth to be our banker." He was combing his hair and peering into a scrap of mirror stuck on a shelf, his feet spread apart and his knees bent to bring him to its level. "What about it?"

"Good idea, if she'll do it. You think she won't tell Mrs. Finney?"

"If you think she might, we won't ask her."

"No. She won't, of course she won't. Go ahead."

"Will you come with me?"

"What for? She'd think we were a committee."

Pete smiled, and Matt, joyous and filled with an irresponsible hap-piness, wondering why he had not thought of it before, assured him seriously, "I'll go down in the middle of the morning. It'll be better if I can convince her not to mention it to the Doctor."

"That old boy is our best ally. He kills more men than he cures," and they laughed, for it was quite true that when Dr. Danforth was called to treat one of the hoodlums, his recovery was slow, and some of them had died.

They worked, with the three men they had recently hired, for sev-eral hours. Matt was determined to show no impatience, and it was almost noon before Pete remarked as he passed him, "Don't forget your conference," and Matt gave a snap of his fingers and set off, hop-ing he had not overplayed his part.

He walked along blithely, but was taken with another attack of dread and awkwardness as he knocked at the door and stood waiting. She opened it after a few moments and looked at him with a slight smile, which annoyed him, for he supposed it must mean she had been expecting to see him there sooner or later.

"Dr. Danforth isn't here, Mr. Devlin."

"I know, but may I come in? I want to talk to you."

She hesitated, but then bent her head with the same gesture of compliance which had so pleased him the first time, and stepped to one side. The small room, which he had not observed very well the day he had been there to dinner, was meticulously neat and seemed, after the reckless disorder of the one he and Pete lived in, almost lux-urious, and he glanced about it admiringly, noticing the curtains which concealed the two wall bunks, the bright cushions in chairs which were actual chairs, not contraptions nailed together from logs and boxes, the pewter mugs filled with spring wildflowers, and the sense of cleanly domesticity was as comforting as if it had belonged to him.

"No one's sick?" she asked. "There hasn't been another accident?"

"No one's sick. I've come to ask a favor of you."

His first impression had been that she looked quite different today, and now that the room had put him at ease and he was able to look at her, he found that she did. She was wearing a morning dress made of some pale yellow cotton stuff, printed with flowers, the sleeves were turned to her elbows and the neck unbuttoned, and she had the slightly distracted look of a woman interrupted in the midst of something important to her, sweeping her house or planting flowers or some similar activity which he had learned from Marietta could acquire deep and occult significance, as if rituals were involved which were incomprehensible to the masculine mind, and this made her less formidable to him.

"Then come out to the kitchen, won't you? The Doctor bought me four eggs this morning," she said confidingly and went ahead, took up two of them and held them between her fingers to show him, as if he might have forgotten what they looked like. "Salt Lake City eggs. The shipment just came, and they cost three dollars apiece." She set them down again, carefully placing them in the bowl with the others, and made a slight gesture, so appealing that he was ashamed of having gloated over her in his daydreams. "I'm making a yellow cake and, to tell you the truth, I'd meant to keep it a secret, save all of it for Andrew and me." She asked him to sit down, poured a cup of coffee from a pot on the little iron stove, one of the few so far brought into the mountains, and went back to her work, measuring sugar and flour and breaking the eggs with as much sober care as a chemist. He watched her for several moments, feeling a comfortable peace and no inclination to talk about what he had come there for but only to enjoy this intimacy, until she glanced at him. "You wanted to ask me something?"

"Yes. I hope this won't seem peculiar to you, Mrs. Danforth, but I've heard that other women do it—and so I thought perhaps you'd be willing to." This remark alarmed him as he heard it and he frowned, disgusted with himself, but could think of no way to correct it without making it worse, and since she had not glanced up he went on. "There've been an unusual number of robberies lately, and some men are getting killed who don't belong to the rougher element." Jenny nodded absently, lifted the bowl in one hand and poured the batter into a pan, turned in a quick sinuous motion and set it in the oven, then began to study the stove with a look of concern, as if now that it had received the treasure she did not trust it. "My brother and I have been lucky with our claims, and these fellows probably know it by now. What I want to ask, Mrs. Danforth, is whether you'd be willing to keep our dust for us."

She seemed amused, either by the request or by his expression of earnest humility, as if he might be pleading for a different favor altogether. "I'll be glad to, Mr. Devlin, and I'm flattered that you both trust me. We're all strangers here, after all, and there's no way of being sure who's honest." She raised her eyebrows. "How did you choose me?"

"Because I'm in love with you." That remark surprised him as much as the first one had. He had had no intention of saying it and was not sure whether it might be true or had only come from an impulse to reassure her, for he had thought she was looking at him suspiciously. She smiled again, and started toward the other room. As she passed him, Matt reached out quickly and his fingers grazed lightly across her arm, as if to inquire about the texture of her skin.

She walked to the door and Matt followed, rubbing his fingers together appreciatively and thinking of what he had been told recently about the Indian method of breaking a wild horse: stroking its head and legs and body, slowly and gently, with a tender patience, until at last it was seduced into meek submission, and could be ridden without danger or difficulty from that time on.

"You'd better leave now, Mr. Devlin. This place has all the disadvantages of civilization."

"You don't like living here, do you?"

"I hate it." She spoke quietly and was not looking at him but through the window and he had a moment to study her face which, in spite of its bitter and angry expression, seemed the most beautiful he had ever seen, and he was admiring her mouth when she glanced at him sharply. "This is a world that doesn't exist. A few hundred people who've come here from every part of the country, and every kind of life—and this is what we've made." She gestured. "This noisy filthy dangerous ugly little camp. What are we doing here? What are you doing here?"

Matt slid his hands into his pockets, rocked slowly on his heels, and was as much concerned to answer her truthfully as if the question had never before occurred to him. "That's the way it seems to a woman. To a man it's something a little different. We see what you hate, we know what it looks like and we know about the danger, but either we ignore it, or we like it. Dirt doesn't bother us much and danger is a tonic. I don't think the money we may or may not make has much to do with it, either—although that's what you talk about when you say good-bye, because it's the one goal no one questions. Maybe, more than anything else, it's the chance to find out who you are once and for all, without any of the refuges or disguises we all use at home, even when we don't mean to." He narrowed his eyes slightly. "I came here because I was lying there waiting for that hole in my gut to heal, when all of a sudden I knew I had no intention of ever drawing up another contract or arguing another case. And when I could finally get around again, it made me sick to see men who'd gotten rich selling shoddy to the troops strutting the streets with diamonds stuck in their teeth. I decided it was time for me to get out and, of course," he added, "it had been on my mind for years."

They said nothing for a few moments but looked at each other as if each might be wondering how much reason they had to trust this sense of old familiarity and yearning. But before they had spoken again there was a light rap at the door.

She opened the door and Erma Finney walked in, looking quite pleased, as if this was a meeting she had been expecting. Mrs. Finney was a small woman, whose face might be pretty or might be inconsequential, he could not tell, and whose only unusual feature were her round and bulging gray-blue eyes, the natural consequence, as he supposed, of keeping a perpetual watch on her neighbors.

With as much alacrity as a boy at dancing school, Matt smiled and expressed his pleasure at seeing her. Mrs. Finney appeared to be taking the room's moral temperature, as she had done at the ball, and Jenny excused herself to look at the cake, saying, "I'll send the Doctor to you, Mr. Devlin, as soon as he comes home."

"Oh? Someone hurt again, Mr. Devlin?"

Matt went backing out the door as if Erma was pushing him. "One of our men cut his foot with a pick."

"Not seriously?"

"I don't think so." He raised his voice. "Thank you, Mrs. Danforth, good-bye," and Jenny returned, standing in back of Erma, and gave him a little wave as he walked swiftly away, swearing under his breath and telling himself that these good women were the scourge of the earth.

He asked Pete to deliver their dust to Mrs. Danforth, partly because he did not want Pete to think he was eager to do it himself—for Pete would have begun to pity Marietta and he felt obliged to protect her from his brother's pity even if it seemed he was unlikely to protect her from his own restless cravings—and even more because he was convinced that Erma Finney, who lived near the Danforths, had leaped some steps ahead of them and believed they were lovers. She had looked at him, Matt thought, with accusation and reproach and he imagined he had also seen a gleam of rabid curiosity, and this made him so angry that for the next several days whenever he thought of Mrs. Finney he began to swear and was obliged to tell Pete he had blistered his heel.

He was resentful of the time Pete was away, delivering the dust, thought he was gone longer than was necessary, hailed him when he got back as if he had been on a long journey and looked at him carefully, thinking there was as much suspicion in his own soul as in Mrs. Finney's.

"Everything all right?"

"Everything's all right. Safe as a national bank. She sent you a present."

"A present?"

"A slice of yellow cake." Pete extended a package, neatly wrapped, and Matt took it, opened it carefully and smelled it eagerly, for after nearly a year of flapjacks and venison and beans the sight and smell of a piece of cake had acquired some wonderful powers. He started to bite into it, but paused.

"What about you?"

Pete had picked up his fiddle and was plucking at the strings, listening intently. "I had some." He laughed. "Go ahead. Before the rats get it." He began playing, a song he had played often at home, and the sound of it kept them quiet for a time as Matt sat in the doorway, ate the cake slowly and assured himself that it contained miraculous ingredients—while the slice she had given to Pete had been only a bit of ordinary yellow cake, possessed of no magical properties whatever.

He waited to hear what more Pete might have to tell him about Jenny Danforth, and was determined to say nothing himself and to ask no questions. But after a few minutes, when it had grown almost dark, Pete put the fiddle aside and they began to get ready for bed, discussing a claim which had been offered them by a man who wanted to go home, and Matt again assured himself that so far as Pete was concerned, Mrs. Danforth was a woman to admire but not to molest.

"I heard today about a guy who came into town for supplies not long ago and told some of his friends, I've got as good a thing as I could want—meaning his squaw—and the word got around so fast that when the poor bastard left half a hundred men followed him, and he was damn near killed before he could convince them it was a woman he was talking about and not a new placer." Pete laughed, striking his thigh and rattling the bunk over Matt's head, and they were quiet again. "We've come to a place," Pete said slowly, "where each man is his own law, according to his own nature."

Matt turned uneasily, thinking the subject was not one he was ready to debate and hoping Pete was not expecting him to, drew in a deep breath, mumbling as if he was too far gone to be coherent, and they both fell asleep.

But he was surprised to realize a few days later that it had been the truth when he had told Jenny Danforth he was in love with her, and this discovery, though it startled him, also put him on better terms with himself than he had been for some time, while he had supposed that what he wanted was only to win a contest.

He had come out of Finney's store, a little dark cabin with a false front, stacked with boxes and barrels, shovels and pickaxes and gammons of bacon hanging so low he had to creep under them, and stood talking to Lem, who was rubbing his hands together and mumbling his latest information that there had been a new strike, a real one this time and something spectacular from the reports that were beginning to circulate, though still very cautiously, for the men who had returned for supplies were even more secretive than miners ordinarily were. "The guy who told me about it, and I only got it out of him because he owes me about five thousand he can't pay, says it's the biggest thing yet."

Matt was staring absently up the street and was eager to be on his way. "You know prospectors, Lem. They go chasing around the mountains and every time they raise a little color they think it's a bonanza. Where is it?"

"Alder Gulch. About eighty miles from here. We could make it in a day."

Matt smiled, for of course Lem Finney was no more eager than anyone else was nowadays to travel alone. "Maybe, Lem. I'll talk to Pete."

"Talk to him right away. If it's a strike, we need to get there early."

Matt narrowed his eyes, peering far up the street where he saw a woman on horseback, riding quickly in the other direction, who looked like Jenny Danforth, and all at once he gave Lem a clap on the shoulder. "I'll talk to him right now." He started to run, calling, "So long. See you later," and set off at a gallop, as if she might be trying to escape from him.

It was Jenny, although he had sometimes been fooled and gone dashing after a woman in a black riding habit who had some trick of sitting very erect in the saddle or who turned her head in what seemed a familiar movement, only to find himself catching up with a stranger, and he would go hurrying on by, lifting his hat and looking sheepishly apologetic.

Presently she started up toward the hills, and was apparently riding for the pleasure of it, and he stayed a little distance behind her. But although she must have heard his horse's hoof beats following steadily along, taking the same turns she did and riding at almost the same speed, she did not glance back and might be supposing he would presently take another path and was not following her by intention.

He wondered, as they passed groups of men at work with rockers and sluices, and at last got beyond the scattered cabins and tents into the open country, if it was possible she knew who it was and was teasing him; and then she wheeled her horse around and started at a gallop down a trail which led back to the camp.

She must have become suspicious or frightened now that they were beyond the edges of settlement, and he began shouting her name as he started across a low, deeply grassed hill, waving his hat and bellowing, "Mrs. Danforth, it's Matt Devlin," until all at once this flight and pursuit seemed so absurd that he reined in his horse and sat watching her running from him, smiling and shaking his head. He supposed he had lost her and felt a sense of keen injustice that on this spring day of clear sky and fresh winds, surrounding him with fragrances he smelled with hungry appreciation, they must miss this meeting, and he had an impulse to start after her again, but did not move. And all at once she stopped, turned and raised her arm, and he heard her call his name in a questioning tone.

"I wasn't sure who it was," she said, when he had ridden up beside her. "I was a little alarmed." She did not look alarmed, but was composed and smiling, and raised her eyebrows as if to say he could believe her or not, as he liked. "Have you heard about the strike at Alder Gulch?"

"Just a few minutes ago—just before I saw you."

Her head was bare and her hair, as she always wore it, was parted down the center and twisted into a complex knot low on her neck; her skin was even whiter in the sunlight and, Matt thought, looked so thin and finely textured it seemed an unlikely covering for bone and muscle, while the tracery of blue veins at her temples gave him some uncanny impression of being able to perceive all those secrets he had spent so much time speculating upon.

The rolling country surrounded them in every direction, the grass billowing as the wind passed over it, and whether they had come here by accident or by some obscure mutual consent, they were alone and unlikely to be discovered even by Erma Finney, and Matt settled down in his saddle with the intention of assuring her his motives were innocent, took his feet from the stirrups and crossed one leg over the horn, folded his arms, and began discussing the new strike as if he had nothing else on his mind at all. But he continued to glance about now and then, to make sure there were no other riders in the neighborhood. "Lem Finney told me about it. What have you heard?"

"A man came to tell the Doctor this morning. He says it's the richest strike ever made—several men are getting ready to leave right now."

"Several men leave every time they hear any kind of rumor."

"My husband is going tomorrow morning with a party of men who are getting their equipment together very secretly. By tomorrow night the town will begin to look empty. You're skeptical. But I've seen these things happen so often. Almost overnight, in only a few days' time, one town disappears and another is there in its place, with some of the same people you've seen before and, if it's a real strike, thousands of others, too—God knows where they come from." She smiled as she talked, glancing at him occasionally to see if he was watching her and then looking away again, over the moving surface of the grass, and seemed to be telling him only the day's routine news, something she thought might interest him however little it meant to her. "Perhaps we'll all be rich." She looked back, alertly. "What would you do then? Go home?"

Matt laughed softly, for the question had had a challenging sound and he thought she was resentful that while he sat gazing at her with a look of longing he was aware of but could not control, he would cause her unhappiness if she would let him, thinking ahead, as women did, not to their pleasures, but to what they might pay for them sooner or later. And this, after all, was something he could no more change, whatever reassurances or lies he might offer her, than he could change his love for Marietta and his children, as real to him at that moment as at any other and perhaps, he considered with some ironic humor, even a little more real at that moment.

"What the hell," he had sometimes felt obliged to say to Pete on the nights when they set out to visit Milly Matches' house, "man is a tomcat." But he could not so easily have explained Jenny Danforth, and did not mean to try.

"No," he told her. "I'd have them come out here, whenever it seemed sure enough, and safe enough."

Her green eyes turned brightly malicious, and she must have spent some time thinking about what was to happen between them, for she was, he understood very well, almost his captive at that moment, waiting with an anticipation in which he could sense both eagerness and fear; but her reluctance came from distrust of the future, and not from coldness or hypocrisy. "You didn't come out here because you were escaping from them?"

Matt laughed. "No. Men can escape from their wives right at home, and do it all the time. This is where I mean to stay."

"And never go back?" She sounded incredulous.

"I don't think so. Not if our luck holds out."

She looked away from him again, and seemed thoughtful and serious, but then laughed softly. "I know the ages of your children and what their names are. I know that you and your brother went from Pennsylvania to New York to study law, and decided to stay there. I know that your wife's maiden name was Morgan and that she has two sisters, Susan and Ceda. I know that Ceda is an old maid, although she could have married, and Susan is married to a man who's getting rich, or hopes to very soon. I know that you lived in a house on East Fourteenth Street." She opened her hands. "You see how much I know about you? And it wasn't even necessary to ask."

"Erma Finney had spilled it all out before you could stop her."

"Yes, she had."

"But no one's been able to tell me very much about you. Where did you come from and why are you here?"

She gave him a clear, straight look, tipping her head to one side in the way which had sometimes made him mistake other women for her. "We came from Ohio, and I think you know why we're here."

Matt's face turned red. "I'm sorry." He leaned forward suddenly and covered her hand. "I'm in love with you, Jenny, do you believe me?"

She drew her hand away quickly, and her face was reproachful and almost angry. "But you've just told me you didn't come here escaping from your wife, don't you remember?"

"It's true, I didn't. And it's also true I'm in love with you." He smiled, though she was watching him distrustfully, as if she knew he would not be able to manufacture any reasonable reply. "Women are better at these mysteries—you explain it to me."

All at once he was convinced she had chosen the moment as well as he, and glanced about to be sure there was no one in sight, but she turned aside just as he would have touched her mouth, placing her fingertips between them. "No—I need a little longer."

"I was clumsy." He caressed her face. "I'm sorry."

"I'm still afraid of you," They started on and, quite inadvertently, he turned and looked back to the crest of the hill, with all the regretful nostalgia of a man leaving a place where he has known more happiness than he ever expects to find again, and as he glanced at her found her smiling almost sadly, as if she had made him a promise and broken it. "You think I'm lying, I know, but it's true."

She left him, holding out her hand as if she had been the hostess and he an uninvited guest to her outdoor parlor, and rode away without glancing back while he watched her, smiling with admiration for the way she held herself, and aware of a sense of pitying sorrow because her pride and vanity would finally protect her so little, no better than he would be able to do.

He watched until she had turned down another road, and then set off at a brisk pace, and now he was so busy putting together a plausible excuse that he had passed two or three groups of men on horseback and well laden with supplies before it occurred to him they must be leaving for Alder Gulch, and at this realization he gave his horse a sharp kick and went on at a gallop.

He found Pete and Lem Finney and Josiah Webb standing apart from the men they had hired, talking, and ran toward them, hoping his excuse would not be dissected by these three sharp and questioning minds, but before he could begin his explanation, Pete spoke. "We've been looking for you, Matt."

"Everything's set," Lem told him. "We start at four tomorrow morning."

"No use waiting," Josiah Webb agreed.

Matt looked at them, glad to know they had been too much preoccupied to think of where he might have been, and was all at once full of that excitement and fierce energy which overcame men at the news of gold, causing sensible men to rave like lunatics, to see visions and hear prophecies, befuddling their senses and sharpening their rivalries until it was no longer easy for them to recognize each other or themselves.

"More men are leaving every hour," Lem said. "My store is cleaned out. In another few days it will be a stampede, and it's up to us to get there while the pickings are still good. This may be it—what we all came out here for."

IV

Alder Gulch, as men quickly found, was indeed what they had come to the mountains for, and two weeks after the first news had been cautiously passed, Bannack was almost deserted. The trail between

the camps became a highway traveled continuously by men and
women on horseback and mule trains laden with furniture, the skeptical ones who had started late galloping along to make up for the
time they had lost, while those who had gone early and now returned
for their belongings paused to cook or rest their horses, and gathered
in groups about the camp fires, squatting on their heels as they
bragged over their good fortune and bargained with their claims.

At Alder Gulch they promptly set the willows afire, chopped down
the spruce and fir, dug up the earth, pitched tents and braided wickiups, threw haphazard cabins together, made homes of overhanging
rocks draped with blankets or established their temporary quarters in
shallow holes and, in less than a month, had contrived another unsightly little town which was growing day by day as hundreds of newcomers arrived, so swiftly it seemed they must have been lurking
about nearby unseen, only waiting for this opportunity. They came
up the Missouri on steamboats and barges, and by horseback from
California and Nevada and Salt Lake City, as if the news of a strike
flashed across the mountains of its own mysterious power, and four
weeks after the first discoverers had returned to Bannack for supplies,
swearing every man they met to secrecy, it was agreed that this was
the greatest gold strike of them all and that nothing like it had been
seen in the world before.

For almost fifteen miles there were strings of flumes propped up
on crutches, water wheels creaked and turned, at night the valley
glowed with campfires, and they congratulated themselves upon living in a metropolis of ten thousand, give or take a thousand or two
from one week to the next.

Muslin buildings were soon replaced by log structures, false fronts
began to appear, tents turned into cabins were pitched upon hillsides,
the streets were blocked with wagon teams waiting to unload, hotels
and grocery stores, saloons and hurdy-gurdy houses and brothels had
more trade at every hour than they could accommodate, and the sidewalks were crowded with men in buckskins and pilgrims wearing
smoked glasses which did not disguise their astonishment or dismay,
each of them moving along at the same swift sure gait, as if they
knew exactly what they had come there for and where to find it, although in fact most of them had no idea at all but would have been
ashamed to be suspected of qualms, much less the terror which attacked them in the midst of so much energetic enthusiasm; and the
small group which had lived in Bannack felt themselves to be an aristocracy, something better than and different from these newcomers.

The camp, it seemed, held a thousand millionaires, but Lem Finney was not disconcerted by their present reluctance to sell their
claims. "Most men," he assured Matt and Pete, "have only a small
store of enthusiasm, and when it's gone they can be persuaded to sell
anything. The best claims will be on the market in a few weeks' time,
and some of them sooner."

"And if we look in the other direction for a minute or less," Matt
told Pete, when Lem had gone on his way, "it'll be Lem Finney who
buys them."

But they grinned at each other and were not very much worried
about Lem Finney or anything else, for their luck had been so good it
was easy to believe they had come west under the protection of some
enveloping benevolence which would not desert them even briefly.

During the next weeks they worked their claims, traded them and
bought others, and made several trips to Bannack, although it had
immediately become clear that solitary travel over that trail, amid
canyons and mountains, was dangerous—for men arrived in Alder
Gulch or Bannack with tales of having been stopped and searched by
masked men on blanket-covered horses and advised to bring more
dust with them on the next trip, or be killed.

They established their own bank, separate from Finney's, in a muslin building on the main street in the midst of the busiest section,
and very soon Devlin Brothers was an institution, trusted and venera-
ble, for they had not failed once in nearly ten months of service in
Bannack and here in Virginia City. In the middle of July they con-
tracted to have the muslin building replaced by a log one, in an even
better location they had bought from a miner who had dug up ten
thousand dollars in two months and was ready to go home.

"A man must be insane," he told them, "who would spend his life
here, a thousand miles from everything that makes life worth living.
So long, boys, and good luck. I'm getting out while I can."

They shook his hand, smiling as if they knew secrets about this
life he would never guess, and watched as he walked away. "Poor
bastard, I hope he makes it. But I wouldn't lay any odds."

Matt agreed; but although he thought Joe Warfield's chances of
getting safely to his home in Wisconsin were probably not very good,
and got somewhat worse from one day to the next as the road agents
grew bolder and more numerous, he did not doubt his own ability to
travel to Wisconsin or Bannack or wherever he chose, through a forest of road agents.

For his accumulation of good fortunes, and his recent private triumph with Jenny Danforth, had given him the unexpected but entire
conviction that he was invulnerable, and for the first time in his life
he felt within himself some sense of perfect harmony and achievement, an exultation which seemed almost precarious, until he reminded himself no man might covet this joyful awareness of
limitless authority because no one suspected him of owning it. But
whoever Matt Devlin was, and whatever needs had concentrated to
form him, he believed himself complete at that moment, and could
now and then persuade himself this elation would remain with him
forever.

For the strike at Alder Gulch had served many purposes, and when
he had returned to Bannack a few days later to pack their belongings

and try to hire new men to work their properties there, Dr. Danforth was celebrating his own good luck and had given Matt a letter to take to his wife.

"Tell her," Andy suggested, "that my professional services are required here." Matt had smiled at him tenderly, and could not resist clasping his shoulder in an access of affectionate gratitude. "And as far as that goes," Andy added, "they are. There were two men shot this morning, and both of them are pretty low."

Pete, however, continued to raise objections. "I hate like hell to have you make this trip. Too damn many men dropping out of sight nowadays."

Matt laughed. "I've got no intention of following the road, and there isn't a horse in the mountains that could catch Rattler, is there?"

"I hope not," Pete said gloomily.

But, at this, Matt grew even more expansive and confident, grinning as if it had not entered his mind that he might be among those who had recently set out on a trip but never arrived, and he was, in fact, more worried that Pete might insist on going with him, against which he had prepared several convincing arguments, than he was of being stopped by one of the hooded riders on a well-blanketed horse. "You've got to have a little faith in luck," he told him confidingly.

"Sure." Pete observed him carefully for a moment, and Matt was stricken with a sudden fear that he might know quite well why he was so recklessly eager to make the trip.

"Look at it this way, Pete. So far there hasn't been a single Mason killed," and at this piece of logic, both of them laughed.

"Take care," Pete advised him, early the next morning.

"I'll be back in three days, four at the most."

The trip was uneventful, whether because they, whoever they were—and that was the essential mystery which made their predicament as eerie as it was dangerous—knew he was not carrying dust, whether it was because he did not follow the road but doubled back and forth across it at random; or whether, as he believed, he could encounter no disasters at this favored time of his life even if he had gone courting them, and he arrived in Bannack rather late, near midnight as he guessed, and rode through the camp with wonder and surprise, for it appeared to be almost deserted.

Several saloons were dark, Milly Matches' house was empty, for she had been among the first stampeders, and many cabins had been abandoned, their owners dashing away without even troubling to close the doors. He passed Jenny's house, which was dark, looked into their own cabin and found it no more disorderly than it had been the day they left, and circled once more about the camp, arguing with himself as he went but knowing quite well what he would presently do.

And before very much longer he set off rapidly on foot, walking through the uncannily quiet streets at a swift, steady pace, rapped softly at her door, speaking his name and repeating it urgently when there was no response; and it only occurred to him later that from the moment he entered the house until she whispered, as he drew away, "God help us," there had been none of the awkward embarrassment he had been dreading, and they might have had many such encounters.

He left before daylight, telling her he would come back near noon to bring the Doctor's letter, and confound Erma Finney by their demonstrable innocence, and she smiled a little sadly, as if she might have begun so soon to regret the soaring pleasures she would be no better able to relinquish than he. But then she brushed his face with the backs of her fingers, kissed him once more, and gave the same soft sigh which had told him earlier that she was chastened and consoled.

He had no wish to sleep, for sleep might somehow deprive him of these rewards he had so lately accomplished, and so he went to their cabin and ransacked it as thoroughly as a burglar, searching through the odds and ends they had left there—boots, tin cans, empty bottles, buffalo robes, blankets, Pete's fiddle, which he had promised to bring back—and all the while was aware of a sense of dazed disbelief, so that he felt rather light-headed, even a little separated from himself. He took a drink from the flask he had brought, in the hope of quelling this giddiness, and went back into town to find out if all the restaurant owners had stampeded or if there might be one left to serve him breakfast.

He spent the morning attending to various details of their business, remarking wherever he went that only a damned fool would carry any dust with him nowadays, and at noon he approached the house with an easy sense of proprietorship, for, it was true, he would never again be able to think of Jenny as married to Andrew Danforth.

It did not surprise him very much that Erma Finney was there, with another of her captives, Reba Church, and he greeted them cordially, delivered the letter to Jenny and sat drinking coffee as she read it aloud, reflecting as he watched her that they were a pair of born conspirators, cut out by nature to practice the tricks and deceptions by which they might hoodwink the world's Erma Finneys—not to mention those others who deserved a better treatment from them—and congratulated himself that he was a more finished rascal than he had supposed.

"It's very dangerous to travel alone, Mr. Devlin," Erma reminded him, when he had delivered his messages from Lem Finney and Silas Church and was ready to leave. "I'm surprised you would risk it."

"I had things that needed attending to, Mrs. Finney," Matt told her gravely. "There was really no choice."

Mrs. Finney, he thought, had a peculiarly inquisitive light in her eye, and he left them with several excuses, too many, as it seemed later, asking himself how in the name of God it had been possible to transport that prudery two thousand miles without a crack or a chip in it anywhere.

Late that same night, after once more reconnoitering the neighborhood to convince himself that everyone was asleep, he entered the house and, this time, was more sure than ever before that Jenny Danforth had some mystical magic meaning for him, something apart from the influence of beauty and beyond the reach of his own reason or will, and in the darkness and silence they lay deeply entangled, striving for unendurable excitements which, as it seemed, must leave them permanently impoverished and with nothing to give each other in the future. And yet, once again, the sense of irresistible peril resolved into quiet spreading relief, the danger, whatever its nature, passed over them harmlessly, and as they fell into drifting reverie Matt heard himself murmur in a slow, reflective voice, "It's true, after all, the present is more than the past—whatever the past has been."

And from that time on, he began to believe more profoundly than ever before that no harm could come to him, that his will was not to be frustrated, and that he had achieved a sudden drawing together of his powers and resources; and that, he thought, was all any man might expect of his life, and more than most of them got.

He was back in Virginia City on the fourth day, as he had promised Pete, so full of good humor and pride that he listened with a sense of incredulity to his description of the latest murders, one man found dead on the road to Bannack the day before and another shot in Troy's Casino last night, both of whom had been known to have made money from their claims. He heard what Pete had to tell him, staring down into the dirt and narrowing his eyes, trying to picture himself as that dead man on the road he had just traveled and, when he could not, glanced up quickly.

"Well? Here we are. What do we do? Run for cover? I'm a pretty good shot, so are you. If they come after us we could give them a little trouble."

"Oh, Matt, come off it. Some other guy will get it, not me. Is that what you think?"

"I think we can't let ourselves be scared pissless by a bunch of roughnecks."

"Let's sell the Bannack claims.",

Matt laughed. "I tried. Nobody wants them. They think all the gold has moved to Virginia City."

"The next trip, I'll go. But we won't go any oftener than necessary, either of us, and we won't travel alone. Talk to Finney, if you don't believe me, or Webb or Flint, or anyone else we know. Things are rough, worse than they were even four days ago. First thing you know, they'll have picked us off one by one and have the bloody place to themselves."

"No, they won't. They want somebody to do the digging for them."

Pete looked disgusted, but rather amused, too, as he had when they were children and Matt had bragged that he could beat up another boy or run faster or jump higher.

But he promised Pete they would make no trips they could avoid, and that they would be more cautious than ever about the men they trusted or even talked to. "Finney and Webb are all right, we know that. Jeremy Flint, probably. Silas Church and Floyd Hart. That's about it. And Andy Danforth," Pete added, smiling, which alarmed Matt, for now Pete asked, "Do you know what happened the day before yesterday?" Matt frowned, but declined to guess. "The Doctor was called in to treat one of those guys, and what did he do but saw off his leg. When he told me about it he said, 'Now that's one son of a bitch who'll never be a road agent again,' and I'm damned if he didn't look as pious as a deacon who's just laid the choir singer."

Jenny Danforth presently arrived with Erma Finney and Reba Church and several other women whose husbands had gone to escort them, but although he contrived excuses to visit her, during the first few weeks she was living in a tent pitched among the pine groves south of the main part of town where, once again, Erma Finney was only a hundred yards away, and they were obliged to speak in whispers and take care not to touch each other; but the memories had nourishment enough in them to last until there came some opportunity for replenishment and, until it did, he must occupy himself with other ambitions.

In August a stage line was established between Bannack and Virginia City, and almost immediately the coach robberies began. But still men climbed aboard and set out in a spirit of joviality and comradeship, as if they were embarking on a pleasant adventure, and no one seemed to doubt that this coach, because he was on it, would come through without molestation.

"This one is on me," Matt said, toward the end of August. "I'll wind it up, one way or another, and the hell with it. I'm sick of being a walking gold mine."

"Let's forget it," Pete suggested. "Three thousand dollars isn't worth that much to us any more."

"It never was. But neither of us is ready to lie down and play dead for those bastards, and my turn's come up. I'll try Finney's trick, hide most of it and keep enough in a poke to satisfy them if they ask for it."

Like many others, they had grown deeply ashamed of the fear which permeated the camp. Men propped their cabin doors shut and slept with pistols beside them, they were afraid to walk the streets at night, and some had become so abject and dispirited they were indifferent to the news of another murder, only shrugged and predicted the road agents were so numerous, so well-organized and so ruthless, that in time they would destroy them all. But Matt and Pete, with

Lem Finney and the few others they trusted, were scornful of this meek cowardice, and Finney insisted on making the trip with Matt because he owned a third of the claim.

They left Bannack before sunrise in seeming high spirits and evidently every man among them had decided to demonstrate once and for all, to himself and his fellows, that his was a cool head and dauntless heart, and it was true that while some men had been turned into cowards by the rule of the road agents, others found a fierce exhilaration in the danger and their gaiety and confidence were real.

They rode for several hours, with brief pauses to change horses every ten or twelve miles, and were rocking and swaying and teetering about, pitching forward and back, knocking heads together and offering apologies, passing a bottle from hand to hand and laughing at every joke and, presently, at every comment, not troubling to look at the countryside, when the coach began to slow down and then stopped.

"Aha!" cried Lem Finney.

Matt lowered the window and put out his head, to confront a double-barreled shotgun held by a man whose face and shoulders were covered by a hood. "Step out, folks," he called cheerfully, "and keep your hands up while you're doing it. We'll shoot every son of a bitch who puts his down."

One of the men started to draw his gun, but Matt grabbed his wrist. "They've got us here like hens in a coop. Use your head. I'll get out first." He glanced around quickly, with the implicit warning that if anyone began to shoot he would be the first to be killed, and climbed down, his hands raised high. He looked carefully at the man holding his shotgun poised, but he was well concealed by the hood and blankets, and his horse was draped to the hoofs. There were four other men similarly covered a little distance away, each holding a shotgun as Matt's companions emerged, hands raised and looking less confident than they had a moment before, although Lem Finney was as unperturbed as if this was a regular morning occurrence and no more alarming than being asked to make a donation in church.

"Shell out," one of the riders directed, and Matt thought the voice was familiar but could not be sure. He pointed at Matt. "You—search them. And see you do a good job."

Matt glared, hesitating, but the five shotguns swung toward him and he turned to Lem, saying shamefacedly, "I'm sorry. Where's your buckskin?"

"No apologies, Matt. It's in my coat pocket, you'll have to rip the seam."

Matt reached into the pocket, tore the seam and handed the pouch to the nearest man, who bounced it appreciatively in his hand and tossed it to the one whose voice Matt now thought he recognized, but the man seemed dissatisfied and spoke sharply to Lem.

"We expected something better of you."

"Sorry, gentlemen."

"Don't disappoint us next time or we'll let you have it. Get to work," he advised Matt who now proceeded methodically along, ripping coat seams, removing boots, tossing up one pouch after another while the five men weighed them suspiciously, peeked at the contents, and agreed among themselves that so far it was not a good day's work, very disappointing, in fact, and perhaps they had the wrong coach even though it had been plainly marked; and when Matt reached the last passenger, whose face was white and whose whole body trembled as he pleaded that he had brought nothing at all with him, the leader gave an angry yell.

"That's a lie, you son of a bitch. We know what you've got. Strip him." Matt turned and looked at him and he shouted, "Strip him, I said!"

"Go to hell."

The man raised his gun swiftly, sighted down it and, for a moment, Matt felt that he stood somewhere else, watching himself waiting to be shot. There was a brief silence before he lowered the gun, nodding to Matt. "We'll take care of you one of these days. You—" He pointed to another passenger. "Search him."

Matt felt that the hair of his head was wet and his scalp cold, but his heart was beating again, although for an instant he had doubted it would, and he watched with contemptuous detachment while the man's trousers were unbuttoned and dropped about his heels and he stood there looking comical and pathetic in red woolen underwear, shaking harder than before and weeping as he told them, "It's in my boots," and lifted one foot and then the other for them to be removed.

Matt's own wallet contained several hundred dollars' worth of dust, the amount he and Lem had agreed they would spare to buy themselves a safe passage, and they were ordered to return to the coach, although the man in his woolen underwear could not climb in without lowering his hands and, after he had made several attempts, the leader gave him permission to pick up his trousers and get aboard. "Skeedaddle," he told their driver, and raised his voice. "If anyone wants to try target practice we'll catch your nags pretty damn quick."

They sat glaring at guns pointed in their faces, so close that one blast of buckshot would wound every one of them, and then they were on their way, swaying and lurching more violently than before while they could hear the driver swearing at his horses and cracking his whip. Lem Finney gave Matt an approving smile, complimenting him for having refused to let them scare him, rubbed his hands together briskly and remarked, "Very businesslike, weren't they? Quite expert, in their own way."

But apparently there were no other philosophers among them, and they looked at Lem gloomily. The man who had been stripped was buttoning his trousers and putting on his boots, and Matt supposed that when he grew calm enough to realize how absurd he had seemed, he would leave the mountains forever. After awhile they passed the bottle around and talked in undertones, as if the road agents might still be with them.

"They cleaned me out. I'm done."

"I almost brought two thousand more, but something told me not to."

"I recognized one of those guys—he's the—"

"Why say it? We don't even know who's riding with us. No offense, gentlemen, but that's what it's come to." And the others nodded in agreement, told no more jokes, and looked at one another skeptically.

When they reached Virginia City and climbed out in front of the stage office, some of them beginning to describe the horrors of the trip almost before they touched the sidewalk, Lem beckoned Matt aside. "I recognized one of those fellows."

"Which one?"

"The one who poked his gun in the window. He's a barber in Kellogg's Saloon."

Matt said, "And the guy who seemed to be the leader is a faro dealer in Troy's Casino."

"You see? They are becoming known. And I've heard of others. I'll tell you about them."

On Sunday, Matt and Pete went into town, for Matt wanted to hear the faro dealer's voice while it was still clear in his mind, and found that the news of his presence in a robbed coach had spread and, with it, the story of his defiance of the road agents. Men stopped him and shook his hand, slapped him affectionately on the shoulder, and Matt looked at Pete, grinning and surprised, but warmly pleased. "Easiest way I know to become a hero."

Troy's Casino was a rectangular log building with a skeleton roof covered by canvas, a hard-packed dirt floor, twelve or fifteen gambling tables, and a bar where men were gathered four deep. It was lighted by whale-oil lamps hanging from overhead rafters almost to the level of Pete's and Matt's heads, and was so dark in midafternoon that men were squinting to see their cards. Three fiddlers on a platform sawed at their untuned instruments and stamped their feet, the bartenders flew about, and the smells and sounds seemed to compose a solid through which it would not be easy to pass.

Pete made his way to the bar while Matt, seeing his faro dealer at a table near the door, paused and watched the play for a few minutes, placed a bet, and listened as the man called out the numbers. The dealer did not look at Matt until he had been there for some time, and then he glanced at him uneasily but continued with the play. Matt joined Pete at the bar.

"That's the guy, all right."

They began to drink with other men, and were exchanging tales of the road agents, for it had become a kind of distinction to have been robbed by them and, no doubt soon, a man who had not been would be under suspicion, when Green Troy joined them, smiling.

"Congratulations, Mr. Devlin. I hear you showed sand."

Matt raised his eyebrows and grimaced, to indicate either that if he had it was not very remarkable, or that Green Troy's opinion might be prejudiced.

Green Troy, who had been in Bannack and, before that, in Florence and Oro Fino, owned the camp's most successful gambling hall and was one of its richest men, although he was not yet thirty. There were two legends about his past—one that he had been brought up in a whorehouse in St. Louis and had won forty-four thousand dollars at faro before he was twenty, and the other that he was the son of a planter whose property had been destroyed early in the War. Matt and Pete had agreed it was the second story Green Troy seemed to prefer, for he spoke in a soft voice, never gambled or drank, and wore well-tailored clothes which were seen in the mountains only on gamblers or English tourists; and his deeply folded eyelids gave him at all times a look of gentle sorrowfulness, as if he brooded over the wrongs he had seen done. But, of course, no one asked him what he had been doing running a gambling house in Elk City before any plantations had been destroyed.

He looked from Matt to Pete, with that same absent and wistful expression, and spoke to Matt again. "My faro dealer, Arch Bigelow, tells me you forgot to collect your winnings. He's holding them for you."

Matt returned to the table and stood for a minute or two as Arch Bigelow continued to call out the numbers and seemed unaware of him, but as Matt turned impatiently to go, Bigelow signaled another dealer to take his place and followed him. He put a pouch into Matt's hand, murmuring, "Here's your winnings, I told the boss you forgot them." Matt glanced down, found that he was holding the same pouch which had been taken from him a few days earlier, and stared at Bigelow with incredulous outrage. "Maybe you've been traveling with the wrong crowd?" Bigelow suggested. "We can use another good man."

"You stupid bastard. I'll see you hang one day."

Bigelow smiled again and shrugged. "You guys don't know what you're up against. Well, I suppose you know enough to keep your mouth shut?"

Matt returned to the bar, still looking astonished and angry and, in spite of himself, amused. "The son of a bitch tried to recruit me." He shook his head. "They've got the gall of a Kansas City pimp."

As they reached the door Green Troy once more emerged from the midst of the dim room, like a genie taking form from the smoke, and came toward them. "Bigelow gave you your winnings? You were satisfied? Good day, gentlemen. I run an honest house, as you see."

A few doors farther on they entered a grocery store where they stood looking at each other somberly and eating oysters out of tin cans. "Know what I just heard?" Pete threw back his head and dropped another oyster into his mouth. "They've got more than a hundred men. A hundred men, for Christ's sake. That's an organization."

"And here we stand, slobbering down oysters and talking about a hundred men set to rob and kill us and nobody doing a god-damn thing about it." Matt threw the empty can into a box. "And every day there's another man killed. A man for breakfast every morning, we tell one another, like it's a good joke. One of these days it'll be our turn."

They set out again, walking slowly among the eagerly treading, wide-eyed newcomers and the veterans of a dozen strikes with their expressions of fanatic zealousness, nodding now and then to men they knew or recognized.

"It might be," Pete said. "But the fear of getting killed isn't the worst thing that's happening. It's the suspicion—so thick you can reach out and grab it." He made a quick gesture, clenching his fist. "Arch Bigelow. Green Troy. The sheriff, some say. That fellow over there, maybe he's one—he looks rough enough. But then, look at you. Look at me. A fine pair of pirates we could be taken for. That kid who came asking for a job the other day, what's his name—Zack Fletcher? Anyone at all." He gave Matt a brief, fierce glance. "Shit. Men can't live together that way. We've got the right to find a way to protect ourselves, however we have to do it."

"However we have to do it, Pete. But only a few days ago I heard you arguing with Finney and Webb about a vigilance committee."

"I think we can accomplish the same thing in a different way. A vigilance committee is an ugly business. These men, whatever they've done, should be tried by the miners' court and a jury."

Matt gave him a skeptical smile, for while these discussions went on the road agents kept busily at work, serenely convinced the honest men would continue to talk about legal procedures but would not be able to agree on a means of stopping them. And as the weeks passed they became less concerned to conceal their identity, grew more reckless, and at last paralyzed the camp into a state of bewilderment and fear and universal suspicion which it seemed impossible to break, until the first natural death occurred and the funeral showed how many Masons there were among them.

"Now," said Lem Finney, "we see what we must do."

Matt and Pete were invited to a Sunday afternoon reception at Dr. Danforth's newly finished cabin, and Matt supposed he must endure sitting there with Erma Finney quickly attentive each time he spoke to Jenny, balancing a plate on his knee and drinking coffee, while the women talked together and the men muttered in embarrassed undertones—as if their wives must not know of such peccadilloes—that another man had been found dead not very far out of town, with a rope about his neck which had been used to drag him off the highway, his face and shoulders pecked at by magpies until he had looked like a rotten apple when he was discovered.

Matt went reluctantly. He had not been alone with Jenny for more than a few minutes at a time since his trip to Bannack nearly six months ago, and whenever he saw her at these Sunday afternoon gatherings was overcome by self-consciousness and guilt, and so he delayed for as long as he could, insisted upon finishing a letter to Marietta and polishing his boots, mended his shirt, and, when Pete finally grew impatient, set out with a long face and walked silently with his hands thrust deep in his pockets. The other guests had arrived, since they were more than half an hour late, and he stepped into the small room which startled him by looking exactly like the one in Bannack, to discover that Jenny was not there and neither was any other woman but only Lem Finney, Josiah Webb, Jeremy Flint and Silas Church and Floyd Hart, Dr. Danforth, and three others he knew only slightly, all of them sprawled in chairs, smoking cigars and drinking Valley Tan.

They shook hands quickly, as if they immediately understood that this was no reception but a serious meeting, took the glasses Dr. Danforth handed them and sat down, and after a few moments during which no one spoke, Lemuel Finney went to stand before the fireplace, and began to talk in a voice which was quiet but peculiarly sharp and penetrating, the same voice he used when he was persuading a man to sell his claim for less than it was worth.

"Gentlemen, we are all old friends, we know and trust one another, and that is why we're here. We've come a long way at great expense and hardship for one reason only—not for our health, not for our reputations, which served us very well at home, but for wealth, and we've found it in abundance. We have, each of us, hopes and plans and every expectation of achieving them—if we live." He paused, looking from one solemn face to the next and all around the group. "But unless we're willing to risk something now, any one of us may be the next corpse brought into town and put on display for men to cluck their tongues over. The road agents believe they have us cowed and every day men are being shot, not only for their money, but for sport or even for luck, and this must have a stop put to it." There was a low murmuring approval. "We aren't the only group meeting today, and when we act we will act as a unit, quickly, resourcefully, and finally. What we propose, gentlemen," and he bent forward, "is to form a committee to act upon this matter without any further delay. Living here without law, we must make our own laws or perish. If we agree, then we can proceed."

Matt went to shake Finney's hand and, as at a signal, the others stood and handshakes went around from one to another, and they returned to their seats.

"Good. Now, let us get down to cases. What this Territory needs is a great deal of rope and a great many men who know how to tie the proper kind of knot." Lem's small hands quickly described a gesture of tying the hangman's hondo. "And then—the ball will open."

The first trial took place a short time later before nearly two thousand miners and lasted four days, and although they finally hanged

two men, they let two others go and there was so much confusion, so
many threats and mutterings, that even those who had continued to
insist they must conduct each trial with due respect for the criminal's rights were ready to agree the system was not practical in these
circumstances.

"Juries are not suited to this work," Lem Finney told them. "There
are too many honest men who always sympathize with a criminal.
We'll have to handle this in our own way." He glanced at Pete, who
remained unconvinced that it was not possible to find a better solution than a vigilance committee which functioned secretly. "Now,
this is a matter of individual choice, please understand, but in a few
days a couple of dozen men are going hunting for these fellows
who've begun to hide out. No use dragging them all over the mountains just to give the boys here a necktie party."

"I'll go," Matt said.

"So will I," Pete agreed and, when Matt looked at him, shook his
head, saying, "It's wrong, but they seem to have left us no decent
choices."

V

Zack Fletcher had appeared at their claim one day, stood watching
them work with a slight smile of amiable but detached curiosity and,
when they paid no attention to him, greeted them with, "Hi, got any
use for an extra hand?"

He was taller than either Matt or Pete, and his chest was so broad
and his shoulders so large and heavy that the hard work of placer
mining should be only pleasant exercise for him, but they had not
seen him before and looked at him carefully for several moments,
trying to guess whether the blue eyes which gazed back at them
with guileless shrewdness might be concealing any secrets, and Matt
asked, "Where are you from?"

"The other side. I came across with a bull train. I'm broke," he
added, as if it made little difference to him but would, at least, explain why he was asking for work.

"You got here at a bad time," Pete told him.

"So I've heard."

"Done any mining?"

"Not yet. But I can learn it pretty quick."

They glanced at each other and Pete said, "Okay, you're on. Ten
dollars a day."

He had whistled, wrinkling his forehead, and for the past few weeks had been working fourteen hours a day with such enthusiastic industry and good humor that when the weather turned cold they invited him to share their cabin, where he slept in a buffalo robe on the floor. He had told them little more than that his parents had migrated from Kentucky to Missouri when he was five years old, that he was now twenty-two, and that he had seen some fighting in the border wars, and Matt concluded he was a Rebel. From time to time he mentioned various escapades, and although he referred to them so impersonally they might be things he had never seen or experienced but only heard about, they decided their employee was not so naïve as his age had suggested.

He had, Pete said, the step of a leopard and a frame fit for a gladiator, and he did the work of three men without ever tiring or even seeming to hurry. "I like the kid," Pete decided. "He's all right."

"He seems to be, but let's not give him any information he doesn't need."

Nevertheless he surprised them one night, as they sat cleaning their pistols, which nowadays took much of their leisure time, by casually remarking, "You know, I'd like to go along on that hunt. I can shoot," he added, and Matt and Pete glanced at each other, for the Vigilance Committee, as they now called themselves, had been painstakingly secretive, met only in small groups, and preferred to pass the word along casually in the street or over a drink in a saloon.

Zack Fletcher smiled, looked at them briefly, and went back to oiling his pistols. "Sure. Why not?"

"Where did you hear about it?"

"The word gets around." They worked silently for another few moments, and then Fletcher leaped to his feet. "What was that?"

Matt blew out the bacon-grease light and they listened intently, heard footsteps moving near the cabin, and threw themselves to the floor with that alacrity men soon learned in the mountains, as Matt shouted, "Who's there! Stop where you are!"

A boy's voice cried out pleadingly. "Don't shoot, Mr. Devlin. It's me, Billy Church." They burst into relieved laughter, Pete lighted the wick, and Matt opened the door to find Silas Church's ten-year-old son gazing at them with a worried and earnest expression. "Lucky thing you didn't shoot me."

Matt put one arm about his shoulders. "I'm sorry, old fellow, but you know these are nervous times."

Billy wiped his forehead, sighing. "I know it." He looked as if the troubles of the Vigilance Committee were his own. "Mr. Devlin, I've got a message for you," he said with severe importance, and gave Matt a direct man-to-man look. "Nobody else is supposed to hear it."

Matt glanced at Pete, indicating that they must have decided to send a party out tonight, and he and Billy left the cabin, walked several steps away, and Matt bent down as Billy cupped one hand to his mouth, whispering, "It's from Mrs. Danforth. She says you must see her right away. But she doesn't want anyone else to know about it."

Matt straightened quickly. "Has something happened to the Doctor?"

"I don't know. But she said to tell you to come as fast as you can. I think she was crying, anyway she was pretty upset."

He went to the cabin, lifted his greatcoat from a peg, muttering, "I'll be back before long, nothing to worry about," and shut the door before Pete could ask him a question.

They walked swiftly, with Billy giving a running skip now and then, and talking eagerly about the recent excitements. "When will they hang somebody else, Mr. Devlin? What are they taking so long for? I saw the first one, I was right there." He made a sound, apparently meant to imitate the noise of cracking vertebrae. "The dirty bastard, he should have gone up long ago. But he died game, cursing his executioner. I can't wait for the next one."

Matt breathed in the cold air, thinking that it smelled like snow which, if a posse did set out, would make their job easier. "I'm surprised your father let you go, Billy."

"He didn't know I was there. Somebody else got shot today, did you hear about it?"

"No, who was it?"

"Nobody we know," Billy said deprecatingly, as if the friends of nice boys did not get murdered. "Another gambler, I think. And a man came up and threatened Mr. Finney."

"When did that happen?"

"Couple of hours ago. Walked into his store and told him he should get his right there, and what do you think Mr. Finney did? Looked him square in the eye and said, 'You wouldn't dare and you damn well know it.' How's that for sand?"

"You seem to be pretty busy these days."

"I sure am."

"We're almost there, Billy. I think I can make it the rest of the way alone. Will you be all right? You're not afraid?"

"Afraid, Mr. Devlin? Not me. What of?"

"Nothing. They wouldn't hurt a kid. Thanks, Billy. And this is our secret?"

Billy raised his right hand, briskly nodding. "You bet. So long, Mr. Devlin," and he dashed away, disappearing while Matt watched him.

Jenny opened the door before he had knocked, and he walked into that room which might have been transported intact from Bannack, even to the letter box covered with seashells.

Jenny, as Billy had told him, had been crying, and at sight of him she covered her face with her hands and turned her back. Matt liked women's tears no better than other men, but perhaps because he had never suspected Jenny Danforth would cry whatever happened, he did not become angry and defiant as he did when even Lisette cried, supposing she was blaming him for something, but put his arms about her and held her, softly whispering, "Jenny, Jenny—what is it?"

She did not answer for several moments, but then drew a deep breath, and spoke in her usual voice, as if she talked of something which had happened to strangers. "Two men came here about an hour ago—I'd never seen them before—and said that a friend of theirs was at Dempsey's ranch with his legs frozen, and Andy must go out there with them to treat him. Andy said he would go in the morning, that it was late and no sensible man wanted to ride around the mountains with strangers nowadays. They took out their pistols, told him he had no choice—and he went." She threw herself into a chair, as abandoned to grief as a terrified child. "They'll kill him, Matt. You know how foolish he's been, bragging about the men who've died after he treated them."

"What else did they say? Nothing else?"

"They said, 'Don't worry about him, Mrs. Danforth, he'll be safe. But we have to take him. We have to take him,'" and Jenny bent forward, lay her head upon her knees, and her body shook with gasping sobs.

Aware of some small disgusting jealousy, Matt watched her in astonishment, for it was true he had been accustomed to tell himself that even Andy Danforth must know his wife needed a man who could give her better pleasures than he was likely to do, and with this reasoning he had succeeded in making of Andrew Danforth so perfect a nonentity in his own mind he had supposed he was the same to her.

"I'll go out there."

But Jenny ran to the door, as if to bar his way. "And let them kill you, too?"

"I won't go alone. Pete will go with me—maybe some other guys."

"Why not the whole Committee?" She began to pace the floor, and now and then cast him a menacing glare, full of bitter accusation. "If he dies, I'll spend the rest of my life alone, do you know that?" She passed near him and Matt looked into her face, marveling at this unknown woman who had leaped at him out of Jenny Danforth's body where she had been so well concealed, and was suddenly more eager to escape than he had ever been to approach her. But then he told himself a hysterical woman was at the mercy of some powers he could not judge and that she needed his help, if he had any to give. "I'm sorry, Matt, please forgive me. But you know he isn't at Dempsey's, if that's where they said they were taking him."

"No, I don't think he is, either, but they may have been telling the truth."

"They didn't look as if they were telling the truth."

He smiled. "Could you be so sure?"

"I'll agree, it isn't easy to know when a man is telling the truth." She gave him another pleading look, whispering, "I don't know what I'm saying. I feel as if I'll go out of my mind." She whirled around. "What are you doing?"

"I'm going to talk to Pete and Lem and tell them what's happened.
I'm going to try to find him."

"But that's absurd. Do you expect to go knocking on doors asking
if they've got Dr. Danforth hidden inside?"

"Jenny, what do you think we should do? What do you want me to
do?"

"I don't know. I asked you to come here not because I had an errand to send you on, but because I was terrified. When Andy went out
with those two men—I knew I'd never see him again."

"They won't hurt him. They may have needed his help, but they've
got murders enough to account for without committing a new one.
They're scared stiff and they're running. I understand why you're
frightened, but they won't hurt him, I'm sure of it."

She smiled. "You're sure of it." She crossed her arms, clasping her
shoulders as if to warm herself, then drew in a deep breath, touched
one hand to her hair, and finding a loosened strand went to the mirror and was for a time absorbed in smoothing her hair and studying
her face with critical disapproval, apparently surprised by her distraught and furious expression, for when she turned back she looked
quite different. "Do you know, Matt, the moment Andy was gone I began to blame you, because I'd be left alone if they killed him. I knew
you wouldn't protect me. Does that make you despise me?" She smiled
a little, but so sorrowfully that he approached her, longing to comfort
her and ashamed even to try, but then held her in his arms and neither moved nor spoke for some moments, until she murmured, "Oh,
I love you so much, Matt," and they retired to the curtained refuge,
forgetful of Andy Danforth and any dangers he might have met—
until all at once Matt awakened and sprang up, staring about the
room as if he had never seen it before, and had some deeply terrifying conviction that there had been a catastrophe of which he would
momentarily be accused.

He began to dress, pleading urgently with Jenny, who only gazed at
him with speculative thoughtfulness and seemed amused to watch
him dashing about the room, building up the fire and rattling the
damper, trying to peer through the frost-coated panes, breathing
upon them and scrubbing them with his warm fist, and finally lighting a lamp. "My good God, it's two-thirty! Jenny, please, get up, get
dressed, they'll be here any minute."

Jenny stretched and yawned and combed her hair with her fingers.
"Who'll be here any minute?"

"The men bringing Andy back. Someone else looking for him. Pete
looking for me. I don't know who the hell will be here," he barked,
throwing water on his face from a basin, "but you can't be found like
this. Please, Jenny," he begged her and she began to dress, slowly and
indolently, as if she only did it to humor him.

While she moved about, picking up one garment and then another,
Matt opened the door a crack and peered out, having no idea what he
expected to find but convinced he would find something, even taking

the precaution of poking his pistol through the opening, and discovered that it was snowing; a smooth white covering showed no tracks approaching the house and, in fact, their guilt was established, only waiting for the first caller to discover it.

He closed the door and locked it and stood gazing at the floor, rubbing his hand along his jaw and marveling at his own stupidity, while Jenny buttoned her dress and put on her shoes, giving him humorous glances from time to time, and then stood before the mirror brushing her hair.

"It's snowing," he told her, in the same heavy voice he might have announced that he had been sentenced to die and, at that, Jenny swung about and enraged him by laughing.

"Snowing? Oh, Matt. Sin does have its own set of problems, doesn't it?" He glared at her ominously, assuring himself that women were in some fundamental sense out of harmony with this world, that they became hysterical when there was no reason for it and turned frivolous when they should be despairing, and she added, "I suppose that's what the road agents are telling themselves just about now."

He sat down and stared at the floor, and began to sort rapidly through a variety of excuses which presented themselves almost immediately, but was forced to discard one and then another. Jenny, who had been winding her hair and losing hold of it and winding it again, until at last she had it arranged to satisfy her, came to sit opposite him, with her hands in her lap and her face obediently sober, though there were still occasional flashes of irrepressible amusement. "I'll leave now," he told her, "but first we must decide whose footsteps walked away in the snow without having walked here in the snow. Oh, hell, we don't even know when it began. I'll stay here," he decided, "and when Andy comes back we'll tell him the truth."

"The truth?"

Matt gave her another warning glare. "We'll tell him you were frightened and sent for me and I stayed to—comfort you." He smiled, in spite of himself, and they sat quiet and contemplative, although from time to time Matt leaped up and looked out the door again at the settling snow, banging it shut each time and swearing.

"Let's hope," suggested Jenny, "our first caller isn't Erma."

"Jenny, I beg of you, don't make fun of me. You told me I wouldn't protect you and, by God, I haven't."

He looked so desperate and filled with self-disgust that she became serious, walked over to stand beside him, and touched his hand. "Andy will believe us. He'll believe me. He trusts me, Matt," she added, with a naïve, wondering smile, and Matt glanced up at her, thinking that she might, in fact, be rather pleased that now there were two men obliged to protect her where a little while since she had complained of not having even one. She sighed from time to time, went to smooth the bed once more, and finally remarked, in a tone which might be taunting or might be serious, he could not be sure, "They say that a man or a woman becomes better or worse by a trip toward the Pacific. Which are you? Which am I?" She gave him an inquiring little smile, innocently curious.

He would not answer and sat watching her so sternly that she had nothing else to say until there was a soft knock, and at that they gave each other startled glances, for it had begun to seem they might sit there solemnly confronting each other for all the rest of their lives. Matt went to stand with his pistol pointed at the door, almost expecting that in another moment a horde of road agents would come tumbling in, and Jenny called, "Who is it?"

"It's Green Troy, Mrs. Danforth. I must see the Doctor."

"He isn't here. He's with a patient."

"This is an emergency, Mrs. Danforth. Please tell me where I can find him."

"I don't know. He's been gone for some time."

"May I talk to you, Mrs. Danforth?"

"You may not. Now please go away."

"Then may I talk to Mr. Devlin?"

Jenny gave an impulsive cry and Matt opened the door and put his pistol against Green Troy's handsome overcoat, a gesture which caused Troy to move back slightly, smiling. "You won't need that. I'm alone. May I come in?"

Troy stepped in, looking as languidly polite and bemused as he ordinarily did, blinking snowflakes from his thick blond eyelashes and holding his hat in his hand, and Jenny stared at him with the haughty air of a lady beset by unwelcome visitors. Matt thought of explaining that the Doctor had asked him to stay with Mrs. Danforth, thought next of the untracked snow, and decided to listen instead to Green Troy. "Your husband is quite safe, Mrs. Danforth, he hasn't been harmed, as I'm afraid you're thinking, but he isn't entirely sober. Through no fault of his own, of course. It's a cold night. He took a little something to keep him warm." He spoke as casually as if he had drawn no conclusions either from the untracked snow or the time of night, and now he turned to Matt. "If you'll come with me, Dr. Danforth will come back with you."

Matt told himself glumly that he had walked into the trap and let it snap shut behind him and was now nothing more nor less than Green Troy's prisoner, and had for the moment very little left of his recent convictions of raging omnipotence. He gave Jenny a sheepish glance, wondering if she found him as absurd as he found himself, and, hoping she understood that shooting Green Troy would help neither of them—nor the Doctor, for that matter—he got into his coat, which felt like a leaden tent, bowed ceremoniously to Jenny while she stood straight and still, as if in obedience to a warning he had somehow given her; Green Troy bowed, and they left the cabin.

They started toward where two horses stood, and Matt demanded, "How did you know where to find me?"

"I went to your cabin first, but it was empty. Your brother and that kid who works for you were both gone. They're with the Committee, I suppose, because a group of them set out several hours ago. They're all over the mountains tonight, I've been told, routing men out of their sleep and hanging them to corral gates and cottonwood trees. Then, at a friend's suggestion, I went to Mrs. Danforth's." He looked at Matt, smiling. "Of course you're curious about the friend." They started down the hillside, riding at a comfortable pace, and apparently Green Troy wanted to talk. "But before we get to that, I'd like to ask you a question. I understand your Committee has had my name under discussion. Is that true?"

"It is. But we haven't decided what to do with you yet."

"And I'm to expect that any morning now I'll have my door hammered in and be told I'm wanted for questioning? What am I accused of?"

"I'm not the god-damn Committee. I'm one guy out of hundreds. What the hell do you want, Troy?"

"I want you to convince them of what is true. I'm a gambler, not a road agent. I've got nothing to do with that bunch."

"You have one working for you."

"I have? Who?"

"Arch Bigelow."

They rode a little farther before Troy said, "Arch Bigelow is from one of the best families in the South."

"I know. Most of the road agents in the mountains are from the best Southern families, and all the whores are orphan aristocrats."

"Bigelow is a young boy, only nineteen, and perhaps he got into bad company. At that age——" he added, as if he and Matt, two old men, should understand that youth had temptations they had forgotten. They were riding along the main street, empty now of most traffic, though a few lights were burning as they got nearer the town's center. "But until the accident tonight, I had no idea how he was spending his spare time."

"Accident?"

Troy drew his forefinger across his neck. "A drunken customer cut his throat in an argument."

"Dead?"

"No, not by any means, it was a superficial cut. But he needed medical attention, and so we brought the Doctor."

Matt raised his eyebrows. "Hmm——"

"But we thought it might be wise to have you here, too. We've heard about the Doctor's habit when he thinks he has a suspicious patient. This boy doesn't deserve to die, and we want to be sure there aren't any mistakes." Troy reined in abruptly and they stopped before the two-story log building which was Milly Matches' new house. Smiling amiably, pleased with his little surprise, Troy swung down, fastened the reins over the tie-rail and waited for Matt to follow.

"He's in Milly's?"

"Bigelow's been living here with Gussie for the past few weeks."

They stood on the sidewalk in the thickly falling snow and looked
at each other. "We won't mention to Dr. Danforth that I found you at
his house, of course." He smiled, as charmingly as if he were standing for office, and as full of seeming good will. "That was Milly's
idea."

"I'm a son of a bitch."

"Only a hunch. That's why she's successful." He laughed, as if to
share the humor with him, and opened the door, Matt following
grimly along and feeling as if Troy led him by a halter.

He had not been in Milly Matches' house in Virginia City, but the
room looked very much like the one in Bannack. It was sparsely
furnished, and the windows were covered with yellow velvet draperies, too long for the low ceiling, so that their rusty gold fringe lay
upon the floor in tangled piles. A large mirror with golden cupids
frolicking around its frame covered most of one whitewashed wall,
and a picture of Milly covered most of another. The artist had shown
her lying naked on an unmade bed, casually fondling one heavy
breast, with the mass of hair which was sometimes pink and sometimes orange spread about her, and she seemed to be asleep, smiling
with such completed bliss her customers had called it a very good
advertisement. But then, for reasons which puzzled them, the artist
had added a yellow vase filled with some ugly flowers which appeared
to be made of iron, and around the stem of one had twined a snake,
reaching its muzzle eagerly toward her; its eyes shone greedily and
its tongue flickered near her lips. Some of the men thought the
snake's presence was humorous and some thought it did not belong
in that otherwise serene paradise, but the picture was famous all
over the mountains and added something to Milly's own legend.

Milly, it was said, was a clergyman's daughter, seduced very young
and abandoned when she was pregnant, but while this might or
might not be true, many of the miners had known her in Oro Fino
and Elk City and Florence, as she and her girls followed them de-
votedly from one strike to another, and remembered Milly helping to
plaster the chinks of her first cabin and Milly and her girls standing
in the rain to protect their dresses from the leaking mud roofs, and
they liked to tell one another that Milly Matches, even though she
was now thirty-three, not only had most of her luxurious attractions
left but was, furthermore, as shrewd a businessman as any one of
them.

Andy Danforth was alone in the parlor, sitting on the sofa beneath
Milly's picture, with his coat off and his sleeves rolled up, and there
were bloodstains on his shirt and arms. He held a glass and was gazing into it, and although he did not look up immediately or even seem
aware the door had opened, when at last he did, he turned to Matt
with an expression which was sad and confiding and humble, saying, "Well, Matt, here I am."

Matt went to him quickly and patted his shoulder reassuringly, no better able to believe he was Jenny's husband than he had ever been. His imagination refused to marry them, and Andy Danforth was now only a friend to see home on a cold night when a drunken man should not travel alone. "Okay, Andy?" he asked him solicitously. Andy nodded, and gave a sigh.

The door into the next room opened and Milly came sailing through it in a yellow dressing gown, with her hair, more orange than pink tonight, over her shoulders and down her back, crying his name with the exasperated relief of a hostess whose guest of honor is very late. "Matt! Well, you got here, after all." They shook hands, while Green Troy gravely explained it had taken him a little time to find the right cabin.

Milly asked if he would have a drink, and while Matt and Troy hung their coats on a rack she poured one and brought it to him, standing close and looking at him with sly, inquisitive amusement. Matt gazed down at her and smiled in reply, for though he should be angry with Milly for having put him in this predicament he was not, and he emptied the glass quickly, wondering what was expected of him next.

But Green Troy quite plainly intended this meeting as a preparation for the future and meant that they would bargain politely, Troy for his own safety and that of his faro dealer, and Matt for their silence, while Milly, he supposed, as a part owner of Troy's Casino had her own investment to protect and possibly Jeremy Flint's, as well. Troy offered Matt a cigar, held a light to it, poured the Doctor another drink when he was unable to do it himself, and seemed to have nothing on his mind but to make them all comfortable, until Arch Bigelow's voice yelped from the next room.

"Hey, Devlin! Welcome, old fellow. Come on in here, I want to talk to you."

Matt glanced sharply at Troy, who dashed out and shut the door. Presently he reappeared, smiling pleasantly and smoothing the sides of his blond hair with both hands, a frequent although useless gesture, for his hair never needed it. "He's been drinking—to deaden the pain—and he's not very clear-headed. But if you'll come in, Mr. Devlin, he wants to apologize. Will you excuse us, Doctor?"

Arch Bigelow was lying in Milly Matches' bed, which was so disorganized he must have been there for some time. His shirt was unfastened over his chest, he wore his trousers and boots, and his neck was wrapped in a bloody bandage. He was pale and seemed feeble, but was grinning foolishly and Matt thought he looked like an idiot on a spree, drunkenly unconcerned with his troubles.

Gussie lay beside him, propped against pillows and wearing only a muslin chemise, and she smiled and nodded to Matt. Gussie had been with Milly Matches in Bannack and, though one of her eyes was crossed, she was popular with the miners, for she had big breasts that bobbed against her ribs, and hips narrow as a scissors, details

Matt remembered quite well for he had once watched Gussie and another girl, both of them naked, playing leapfrog about the parlor with some of their customers.

Bigelow now raised one hand in a salute. "Mr. Devlin, I certainly meant no disrespect, sir, you know that."

"Go to hell."

Green Troy began talking to Matt, as if this confidential matter was equally important to both of them. "We've got to get him out of here before they come looking for him. We know he's on the list, you understand." Matt supposed it must have been Jeremy Flint who had told them this, but continued to listen, since there was nothing at all he could argue about. "He's too nice a boy to be hanged in public like a dog."

"I agree. He should be fried in his own grease. He's killed two men, maybe more."

"That's a lousy lie," Bigelow shouted and tried to get up, but Gussie held him down and Troy's quick scowl quieted him. Milly wandered about the room, and seemed casually bored, but patient. She hummed softly, moving objects around like a fastidious housewife, and pushed a basinful of bloody water under the bed with her foot.

"Now, we want him to leave as soon as the Doctor says he can travel, preferably before it's light, and we'd like you to tell us the best route for him to take, where he'll be least likely to meet any of the Committee."

"I don't know where they've gone. I knew they might go, I expected to go with them, but the last I heard they weren't sure where they'd head for first. Why don't you ask the guy who gave you the rest of your information?"

"After all, Matt," Milly explained reasonably, "you're on the Executive Committee." And Jeremy Flint was not. "He'd better keep off the roads altogether, don't you think so?"

At this, Matt began to laugh, Milly joined him, and Green Troy gave a small smile to show that he appreciated the humor. When they were done laughing, Matt shrugged, glancing at Bigelow. "I think he'd better, but I wouldn't lay odds he'll make it, whether he meets any of the Committee or not. Not in the shape he's in."

Bigelow had been lying with his mouth fallen open, his head against Gussie's breasts, and looked as if he had fainted or possibly died, but at this he began struggling to get up. "I'm all right, who says I'm not? I'm as tough as any man in the mountains, by God, I'm a man with the bark on. Get me a horse and I'll leave right now, right this—" He fell back, closing his eyes. Gussie put her head to his chest, stroking his face and whimpering, while Milly watched her with amused contempt.

"Always so sentimental, these little whores."

"Now, Mr. Devlin, just one thing more, and I think our work is done," Green Troy said. "Bigelow needs your horse."

"That's just one god-damn thing too many, Troy. I'll tell the Committee you're an honest gambler. I'll tell them Bigelow wasn't the guy I recognized that day, after all. But that's it."

Troy smiled sadly. "Still, his only chance is a good fast horse and, as you know, all the others are in service tonight. I'll give you five hundred dollars in dust or a half interest, with Milly, in a mine I have. We'll both be living in this community long after these trou-bles are over and forgotten, and I want your good will. You under-stand?"

Milly linked her arm through Matt's, leaning against him and giv-ing him her famous smile which opened her mouth wide and nearly closed her eyes, but she did it with a kind of professional coquetry, affectionately impersonal. "Take the mine, Matt. You can tell Pete you got drunk and made a trade for it." She indicated a table where there was paper and pen, and Matt scratched off the bill of sale as Milly, watching, stroked her fingers over one breast with the same in-different admiration she had just shown him.

"Thank you. And now, if you'll wait a moment, I want the Doctor to look at Arch once more."

"If the Doctor can still see," suggested Milly.

At that, Bigelow roused from his stupor, and proposed one more toast to the Confederacy. "Here's Jeff, fellows!"

Green Troy gravely and gently led the Doctor to the bedside and Matt stood waiting in the parlor, gazing at the floor and marveling that a sensible man, as he liked to believe himself to be, should have become the victim of those he had intended for his own.

"What do you care?" Milly asked him. "Let him go, that insignifi-cant ass in there."

Matt looked at her thoughtfully. "You women always take the criminal's side, don't you?" For it had been the women, in fact, who had interfered in the first trial, crying and pleading until the culprits were given horses and sent out of the mountains—back to their mothers, the women had recommended—and that had made it nec-essary to find another way of solving the problem.

"Maybe we sympathize with their mothers."

"Even when they kill other mothers' sons?"

"Don't be logical, Matt. Troy wants him out of here."

"And it's for Troy's sake he's going, not his mother's. What's it to Troy if he chokes?"

"Bad for his business, to have employed a road agent. You know what's going to happen, now that they've finally begun it—they'll hang every man they ever held a grudge against and, when they do, they'll be telling themselves he deserved it, whether he did or not."

"And, of course, if Bigelow disappears he's less likely to talk about Troy."

Milly shrugged. "Why worry about it? Oh, don't look at me that way. You can't tidy things up all by yourself. What we've asked of you tonight is very little, very little, I think you'll agree? And your lady is perfectly safe with us, you know that."

Milly's face was rather impudent, but still friendly, and finally Matt said, "Milly, tell me when you decided to look for me at the Doctor's cabin. Did you bring him down here with that in mind—or did you think of it later?"

"Oh, now, Matt," Milly protested. "These things are delicate." She pretended to take some embroidery stitches. "I can't be sure."

"Who told you I might be there?"

"No one. I'd seen you talking to each other on the street one day. It seemed a likely place for you to be, when we knew where the Doctor was."

Matt smiled with reluctant admiration, not quite convinced. "You'd heard nothing about us?"

"I didn't need to." From the bedroom there now came renewed wailing from Gussie and the Doctor reappeared with Troy. "How is he?"

"He's fine," Troy assured her. "And he's going to leave in a couple of hours."

They went out, Milly stood for a moment in the doorway but began to shiver and waved good-bye, and together Matt and Troy hoisted the Doctor into the saddle. Troy gave them a salute, and walked quickly away.

They rode silently, with Matt now and then reaching out to steady him, until Andy finally spoke. "Matt, we won't tell Jenny where we were, will we? We'll think of something, something—"

"We'll say we were taken to someone's cabin. I'll figure it out." And he told himself that in the meanwhile he had better get the rest of his lies in a row.

But the problem turned out a simple one.

Pete and Zack Fletcher did not come back for several days, and by then Matt had joined another group and was riding about the mountains chasing men who were running for their lives but who showed, after their earlier bravado, remarkably little inclination to save themselves. They were found hiding in cabins and most of them came out meekly, seemed eager to confess their crimes and those of their friends, and were left hanging on corral gates and cottonwood trees with the Vigilante emblem—3-7-77—pinned to their coats.

Arch Bigelow disappeared. The Committee agreed they did not have any real evidence against Green Troy, and there were other men who needed killing worse. Five men were hanged in a row and a madam came screeching up to the guard, begging for her lover's body. A Mexican was shot and thrown back into his burning cabin and two whores panned his ashes the next morning, but complained they had not found gold enough to pay them for their trouble. The sheriff was among the last to be hanged and, in less than three weeks, the Committee had killed at least twenty-four men, probably more, they admitted privately, and the community was thought to be, if not stabilized, at least chastened.

And when it was done they wanted to forget it, for most of them had been shocked and sickened by the discovery of how much pleasure they could find in killing, how little pity they were able to feel, and how uncanny a sense of hating rage had taken hold of them, in spite of the solemn and businesslike manner with which they went about it.

Matt finally mentioned this to Pete as they sat wrapped in buffalo robes, their boots almost in the fireplace and giving out a sharp cooked smell which caused Matt to think of the cremated Mexican, so that he laughed angrily, and Pete, smoking a cigar and watching the flames, gave him a glance.

"Pete, I wouldn't have believed it, the way I feel when we find one of those bastards and he first looks at us and knows we've come to kill him. I swear to God I feel as if it's the one thing I've been waiting for all my life. Now, what kind of an unusual fiend must I be?" He watched suspiciously, expecting that Pete might remind him of his own opposition to the Vigilance Committee, but Pete looked into the fire, scowling, said nothing for several moments, and finally sighed. "I know. I felt it, too. Everyone does."

"Jesus, I hope so. I'd begun to wonder if maybe they shouldn't hoist me up next." But Pete's reply had given him hope that perhaps they were all as bad as he, and Matt now quoted what Pete had said at the first meeting of the Vigilance Committee. "After all, they left us no decent choices." But they did not talk about it again.

Pete accepted his story of trading Rattler for a half-interest in a claim, though neither of them had done anything so foolish before, and when the deed was sent to him by a boy who carried messages for Milly, designating Matthew Devlin and Milly Matches as joint owners of a mine one hundred feet deep and twenty feet wide, running from the stream back to the first ledge of rocks, third from the discovery claim in Daylight Gulch, Pete seemed amused. "Milly's a woman of honor."

"Or a sense of humor." For, of course, there had not yet been a paying claim in Daylight Gulch, and sagacious miners were convinced there never would be.

The men returned to their winter occupations of sawing lumber and building and repairing sluices, and in February, Matt and Pete, with Lem Finney and Josiah Webb, organized a company for the purpose of testing the gulch by sinking to bedrock. Many men had sold their claims and started home before the Vigilance activities had begun, and at that time they had bought a number of new claims and were planning to install machinery. Matt saw Green Troy occasionally, now and then stopped to talk to Milly, Jeremy Flint had joined him in sponsoring Troy at the Committee meeting but had not mentioned it since, and before very long it would have been easy for him to believe the embarrassing episode had never happened or that, if it had, it was of no significance.

Jenny, however, thought she had suffered some contamination and would not be reassured, whatever he told her.

"It may matter a great deal to Erma Finney whether or not we're in love with each other, Jenny, but it doesn't mean a damn thing to Green Troy or Milly Matches or Jeremy Flint. They wanted my help, they found a way to get it, and that's all there is to it. God knows I'm sorry, but it's useless information to them now."

"But some day it may not be." Jenny raised her eyebrows, as if to tell him that episode had made her more nearly his responsibility than she had ever been before, and he believed it himself. For Jenny Danforth, as he had early suspected she might, seemed to have reached back into his life before he had known her and drawn parts of it to herself, and would no doubt in time acquire additional territories, whether or not he offered them.

In the spring, when the first mail came, he had Marietta's letter. They were going from New York by train to Chicago, then to the end of the railroad in Iowa, where they would take a coach to St. Louis and come up the Missouri to Fort Benton, the same route he and Pete had followed two years earlier. And if the prospect of traveling with five children and a great deal of furniture and baggage dismayed her, there was nothing in Marietta's letter to indicate it; nor did she give him any clues that the long separation might have made her doubt him.

Pete was exultant, played his fiddle with greater enthusiasm and drew more poignant music from it than he had in a long while, and seemed struck with joy. Matt watched him, smiling, pleased by Pete's delight and by the thought of seeing them, and troubled about Jenny.

He delayed telling her, explaining to himself that he must find the right time for it and detesting the cowardice which made him decide each opportunity was the wrong one, and when he came upon her unexpectedly one day, seated in the buggy which was a recent present from Dr. Danforth and watching the men at work on her new house, they talked for a few minutes while he told himself he must say it now and no better time would come.

Jenny eagerly discussed the plan of the house, said their furniture would arrive soon from San Francisco, and looked so happy and so unsuspecting that he thought he could not do it, after all. But then he said, "My family will be here some time in June."

She sat watching the workmen, her face intent and thoughtful, and finally looked at him and smiled. "Well? We knew they would come sooner or later. And you'll be going to Benton to meet them?"

"Yes."

Jenny gathered the reins quickly together, gave them a slap, and as the buggy started to move, she said, "Then I won't see you again," and drove off in that reckless style which made pedestrians hop for the sidewalk, while Matt gazed after her, more bewildered than if she had cried, and later decided she had meant it, for whenever they met she ignored him, if she could, or gave him her old remote and knowing smile, making a stranger of him once more.

He had done what he believed she wanted, made no attempt to see her either before he went to Benton or when he got back, until this afternoon when she had come to him with her tale of the girl from Milly Matches' house; and now he looked at her with that same sense of wondering recognition he had felt when he had seen her first.

"It's so hot, isn't it?" she asked him plaintively. "It makes me a little sick. And that girl—I can't stop seeing her kneeling there before Andy with that terrible wound in her scalp." She wiped her moist face and neck with the handkerchief, closing her eyes, but then looked at him again and smiled wistfully, as if she were ashamed of her spitefulness. "I'm sorry, Matt. Of course you're glad to have them here. Is that your son, working with Zack Fletcher?"

She indicated the distant hillside where several men, Pete and Fletcher among them, were working with furious energy, apparently unaware of the heat, breaking up the earth with pickaxes and wheeling it to the flumes, while across the road and wherever they looked, hundreds of others were at the same work, for the season was a short one and pilgrims and veterans alike dashed at it as if convinced that if a fortune was to be made at all it must be done that day.

Matt nodded. "That's Morgan. He and Fletcher have become great friends. Jonathan is working with Pete."

"Erma tells me you have twenty-four men now."

"Twenty-five, we hired another one yesterday. There are plenty of new men coming in, but most of them don't know a damn thing about placering. And it's not easy to make miners out of hog-raisers from Iowa and pumpkin-pilers from Missouri." They were talking, it seemed to him, with as much casual ease as two friendly neighbors, and were even able to exchange amused, understanding smiles. "And there, by God, is my daughter and her friend." Two young girls, in light summer dresses, had ridden over the crest of the hill, and their horses moved restlessly about as they paused to talk to Zack Fletcher and Morgan. "They ride every afternoon and they always pay us a visit. She's quite pretty, that little Allen girl, do you know her?"

"No. I always felt sorry for her and meant to talk to her some day, but I never did. I'm glad she's found a friend."

Matt laughed, a kind of tenderness and pride showing on his face. "She certainly has. Lisette has practically adopted her, and Lisette's friendships are not casual."

The horses started down the hillside and Jenny made a quick movement toward the buggy. "Oh, Matt, here they come—oh, my God, I can't see them—"

"I want you to meet Lisette."

"I can't, not this afternoon." She looked frightened. "Some other time."

"Of course you can. Erma talks about you, they're all expecting to meet you. Jenny," he added sharply, "be sensible. What can possibly happen?"

"I don't know, but I don't want to meet her just yet." But then she turned back, and watched as they came trotting forward.

The two girls, one very dark and the other so blond the sun turned her hair almost silver, drew up to them, and as Matt made the introductions, Lisette glanced from her father to Jenny, her eyes bright and questioning.

"Where have you been today?" Matt asked her.

"Oh, all over." Lisette swept out one arm in a gesture to take in vast spaces. "We're going to ride down this road, and then home. Good-bye, Mrs. Danforth. I'm very glad to have met you." Nella repeated the phrase, Jenny smiled from one to the other, nodding, and they were on their way again, galloping down the hillside and leaving them both a little bewildered by so much energy and joyousness.

Jenny watched them go and laughed softly. "How young they are. And how pretty your daughter is, quite a beauty, in fact. But didn't she look at me strangely?"

"Of course not," Matt assured her briskly, relieved by the unexpected meeting, something he had dreaded which had now taken place without disaster. "That's Lisette's way. She was admiring you."

The girls had disappeared and Jenny turned back to him slowly, seemed to study his face for a moment, finding whatever traces of love and pride Lisette's passage might have left there, and at last she said, "It's true—the present is more than the past. Whatever the past has been."

Matt scowled defensively, then took off his broad black hat and held it before him, humble as a beggar about to ask her for alms. "Jenny, I may as well tell you this now," and he looked serious and ashamed, as if he had to confess to her some dreadful crime he had lately committed. "My wife—" He paused, trying to think of another way to say it, and then, with a fierce and challenging expression, he blurted out, "Jenny, Marietta is pregnant."

VI

Lisette and Nella sat in the late afternoon sunlight, their heads close together as they talked, whispering and giving bursts of laughter, and then murmuring soberly and thoughtfully over the remarkable insights they were able to discover; an endless supply, it seemed, for during the past three months they had not been able to exhaust it. They were stitching hems in handkerchiefs, snipping them from a string of unfinished squares, and this work, like everything else which happened in the Devlin household, seemed important and interesting to Nella. The cat Shekel, swollen with kittens, lay sleeping on the edge of Lisette's skirt, and occasionally the tip of her tail moved, as if she crooked a beckoning finger. Inside the house, Marietta was serving tea to Erma Finney and Reba Church, and there was other activity in the neighborhood—women washing clothes, men returning from their work, and a little distance away a group of children were playing a game of Vigilante.

"I want a drink of whisky!" a sharp little voice cried, and Nella and Lisette glanced toward them, exchanged tolerant smiles at this infantile entertainment, and went on sewing. The child was standing on a box, with a rope twined about his neck and thrown over a tree limb, and he declared, "I want to see my woman!"

A tow-headed little girl, five or six years old, replied firmly, "That played out in 'sixty-three. We don't bring women to the place of execution."

"Then get me a pair of moccasins. I swore not to die with my boots on."

"Men!" called Robert Devlin. "Do your duty!"

There were shouts and threats and a great deal of swearing, and the box was dragged swiftly away as the road agent jumped stifflegged to the ground with his head twisted to one side, and there he remained, rolling his eyes, while the others confronted him in a silent satisfaction which lasted for several moments.

"His neck is broken," Douglas Devlin announced. "He is dead."

The road agent stood in the same rigid posture as slowly, with awesome curiosity, the others began to circle about him. They touched him from time to time, giving him light cautious shoves, but he stared steadily upward all the while they trudged around and around in quiet wonder.

"Mother thinks they shouldn't play Vigilante," Lisette said. "She's afraid it will give them nightmares. Oh, Nella!" she cried, and touched her hand. "How thoughtless I am."

For Nella, who often stayed with them overnight, sleeping in Lisette's bed, had once roused the household with groans and sobs and, when Lisette woke her, shaking and holding her at the same time, she had been dazed and helpless and could only say she had been dreaming about a dead man who came back to life. But she had admitted privately to Lisette that she had seen five men hanging in a row in an unfinished cabin, and two more lying in another building. "Their faces were blue," Nella had told her, for Lisette insisted upon details, "and their eyes looked as if they were still alive. The ropes were lying nearby and there were deep marks in their necks. I can't remember any more, Lisette. Please don't ask me to."

And now, as Lisette apologized, Nella gave a shy smile. "I don't have them very often now."

"That's because you're with us."

"I know," Nella agreed softly, and she concentrated on threading a needle, as if otherwise she might begin to tell Lisette how grateful she was, and that could make her start to cry.

"But it must have been an exciting time," Lisette said, for the hangings, although they had taken place only nine months before, seemed to have happened in the remote past. "Wasn't it?"

"It was exciting for the men, I guess. They never bothered the women. It was hard to know who they were, because some of them were quiet and well behaved, and the sheriff, they say, was a gentleman. But there were others who were violent and vicious. One man showed Rick a string of dried ears he said he'd cut off the men he killed."

"What? Oh, I don't believe it."

"Rick swears he saw them. Maybe he was just making it up," she added, for Lisette had covered her face with her hands.

The children were voting on the little girl's guilt, and now she was told, "We'll hang you damn quick."

"A string of ears," repeated Lisette, and returned to her sewing, clucking her tongue and shaking her head. "I'm going to ask Father if he ever saw it. But of course he'll tell me I mustn't know about such things." Lisette bit a thread between her straight white teeth. "The things they think it isn't fit for me to know, Nella." She sewed a little longer and seemed contemplative, given over to some deep problem. "Suppose I told you a secret—would you keep it a secret?" She glanced up quickly and captured Nella with her dark eyes.

"Of course I would, Lisette."

"Promise?" Lisette leaned closer, whispering. "I think my mother's going to have a baby." The two girls looked at each other for a moment, until Lisette gave a confirmatory nod. "She went to see Dr. Danforth the other day. I know, because I heard my father ask if she'd seen him—and she wasn't sick." Lisette moved back, spreading her hands. "That's the way it was before Douglas and Robert were born. I remember it very well. But why don't they tell us? Are they ashamed?"

Nella frowned, as if either the confidence, being such a solemn one, or Lisette's distrust had troubled her. "They will. When it's time."

"Do you want to get married?" Lisette demanded, so quickly that Nella gave a start.

"Of course. Don't you?"

"I don't know. I'd like to have a husband, but I'd like to know what to expect of him. Beaux are one thing and husbands are another, I told my mother not long ago. And she said, 'Indeed they are, Lisette, indeed they are.'" Lisette gave her another quick, searching glance. "What do you suppose she meant by that?"

Nella's face became virtuously aloof. "My mother used to say that if girls knew the truth about marriage they'd never get married at all."

"Oh, it can't be as bad as all that," protested Lisette, but without

conviction. "My mother and father love each other, I know that," Lisette remarked slowly, and her face grew tender as she held up a completed handkerchief and studied it for flaws, then laid it flat on her
lap and began tugging at the edges to straighten them. "And my
mother says that a woman's only happiness is to love a man and his
children." She sighed deeply. "I'm so selfish, and sometimes so in-
considerate, it makes me ashamed. But she says I'm still young and
wait until I'm older, then I'll know it's true. Of course, my mother is
thirty-four, and I suppose when you reach that age you've had time
to get used to a lot of things that seem strange to us now, don't you
think so?"

This subdued and wistful uncertainty of Lisette's, so unlike her
usual merry restlessness, gave Nella unexpected courage, and she
leaned toward her eagerly. "Lisette, you're the luckiest girl I've ever
known. You could never guess what I thought the day I saw all of
you riding in to town. Remember how you were holding onto Shekel
and you saw me standing there and smiled at me, just as if I was
someone you were glad to see?"

Lisette looked at her thoughtfully. "Yes, I remember. I was glad to
see you. I knew we'd be friends."

"But how did you know? Oh, I hoped so, but you knew it. I'd been
reading *Ivanhoe* again, it was all I had to do when Rick made me
stay home, and I thought you were the Norman conquerors and the
rest of us were the Saxons you had come to rule. I did, Lisette, that's
exactly what I thought."

"Nella, how sweet you are." Lisette's eyes were misty and she
blinked, sniffed a little, and went on with her sewing, and then, in an
instant, glanced up. "And who is your Ivanhoe?"

"I have no Ivanhoe." Nella's white skin had turned pink, even her
ears and neck, and Lisette laughed, clapping her hands.

"Oh, Nella, how I love to tease you. But I don't mean it." She
touched her arm. "You're the best friend I have or ever will have,
aren't you? And if you'd grown up with four brothers, you'd know
teasing is only a way of showing someone you love them. Doesn't
Rick ever tease you?"

"Not exactly," Nella said, after a little hesitation. "He's too busy."

The girls went on with their sewing, and presently Mrs. Finney
and Mrs. Church stood in the doorway, shaking hands with Marietta.
Lisette and Nella stood soberly watching, until Mrs. Finney smiled
and told them good-bye, whereupon they made quick curtsies, and
Erma Finney and Mrs. Church drove off. Lisette wrinkled her nose
and shrugged and turned to find her mother watching her and smiling.

"Why don't I like her?" Lisette asked. "But I don't. Do you, Nella?"

Nella shrugged but said nothing, for even after three months she
was reserved and uncertain and easily alarmed, still afraid that one
day she would be dismissed from her new home. She had gone to
their cabin early the morning after they had arrived, and although

she had stopped several times on the way and started to run home again, finally she had made the journey, rapped at the opened door, and now she was there almost every day and no doubt it would have seemed to anyone else that her acceptance was accomplished and complete.

And they appeared to believe it themselves, for if she went home they asked her why she must leave, and after Rick had gotten into a fight and summoned her to take care of him, they had welcomed her back with such enthusiasm she believed she might live there the rest of her life, as Lisette had more than once asked her to do. Even so, she felt unworthy of her privileges, most of all in Marietta's presence, for it was easy for Nella to believe that Marietta would one day look at her critically with her speckled hazel eyes, ordinarily so soft and glowing, and send her away. Yet Marietta seemed to love her and to pity her, too, not for the reasons Nella believed she deserved pity, but because she had only her brother and no other family at all; and Marietta's pity, gently disguised, was so comforting she enjoyed it as Shekel enjoyed having her belly scratched.

"What was Mrs. Finney finding fault with today?" Lisette asked.

Marietta smiled, and to Nella the smile seemed a wonderful mixture of whimsicality—the same look which appeared so often on Lisette's face—and a kind of reflective compassion, as if it might very well be true that Marietta had become used to many things which still seemed strange to two young girls. "Mrs. Finney says it would surprise me to know how much misbehavior goes on out here." Marietta seemed to consider this moment, gave a slight low laugh and came to sit with them, bringing a petticoat she was making for Lisette.

One of the great charms of living with the Devlins had been the discovery that it was possible not only to be continuously busy but that work could be enjoyed, for Marietta and Lisette went from one task to the next as easily as the children progressed through their various phases of the Vigilante game; and Nella joined them eagerly, convinced that each time she swept the floor or measured flour for a cake she had made a fundamental discovery about why they were exactly the people they were, and she liked to believe her participation in these rituals might in time make her come to resemble them.

Lisette had given her much sober advice on the lore and art of housewifery, but even their mastery of this knowledge—so much more extensive than Nella had suspected—seemed only another demonstration of their superiority. And the cabin itself, the old-fashioned furniture, heirlooms of Marietta's and each piece with its history—the center table where they all sat down to eat, the several dark paintings of fruits and animals and trees, the plates marked with blue willows which were used at every meal without any concern that they might be broken—gave her intimations of that other world they had come from, and reminded her constantly that whether they knew it or not she was unworthy of them.

"Mrs. Finney is a mean woman," Lisette said, and closed one eye as she threaded a needle. "There are a lot of mean women in the world—more mean women than men, if you ask me."

"But let's not talk about Mrs. Finney," Nella pleaded. "Tell us another story, Mrs. Devlin, won't you, please?"

Marietta smiled at her again, a different smile from her earlier one, this one as gay and direct as a glance from Lisette, and Nella marveled again at Mrs. Devlin's smooth skin, her hair which was almost red where the late sun shone through it, and indeed all her warm luminosity, so beautiful to Nella that she suffered constant forebodings of being someday deprived of it. "What do you want to hear, Nella? One I've told you before—or a new one?"

Nella considered this gift very seriously. "Which one," she murmured, as Lisette smiled. "The one about—no—the— Oh, Mrs. Devlin, I'd like to hear a new one. What would you like, Lisette?"

"I know them all. Tell Nella about great-great-grandmother Bannatyne. But it'll make you cry, Nella," she warned her. "It's the saddest story in the whole family, isn't it, Mother?"

"I suppose that depends upon how much of it you believe."

"But isn't it true?" asked Nella, surprised and disappointed. "I thought all these things had happened to your family."

"All of them are supposed to have happened, Nella, but you know family legends are susceptible to improvement from one generation to the next."

"I don't care whether it's true or not," declared Nella, with such combative loyalty that Lisette gave a burst of laughter. "I'll believe it anyway."

Whenever they sat, as they usually did for an hour or so late each afternoon, to sew and talk, Marietta told them stories of the two families, Morgans and Devlins, and other names Nella usually forgot, and they had become for her a bewitched troupe of ancestors, strong and vital ghosts who restlessly clung to the world they had loved with so much vehemence and very often with so little wisdom, and now Marietta began to talk to them, in her slow, soft voice.

"Her name was Rebecca Taggart and she was brought to America when she was seven or eight years old, in 1718, I think it was, after the English had made it impossible for them to live any longer in Ulster—"

"How I hate the English," muttered Lisette. She repeated the refrain from time to time whenever her mother told these stories, for the English were blamed for all their troubles, whether in Scotland, in Ireland, in Wales, or in America.

"They went to Boston first but, being Presbyterians, of course they weren't welcome to those Puritans, and they migrated to Pennsylvania. When Rebecca was about fifteen and had become a very pretty and lively young girl, an itinerant portrait painter came to the house one day, painted her miniature, the one you've seen in Lisette's bedroom, and they fell in love. They were married, and after several years he had become famous enough to want to try his fortune in New York, just as people do today. They had had three or four children by this time, but Rebecca was still beautiful, and a merchant saw her and tried to persuade her to leave her family. When she refused him, the merchant, who was rich and powerful, abducted her and took her to live with him somewhere outside the city. Her husband went mad with rage and jealousy, and after a few months he found where they lived, and he killed them both, stabbed the merchant first—and then his wife."

Nella gave a shriek and caught her hands to her throat, and then, as Marietta and Lisette stared at her, she turned red and lowered her head, mumbling, "I'm sorry I screamed like that, I don't know what made me do it."

Marietta, looking serious, pressed her hand. "I'm sorry, Nella, to have frightened you. We're all so used to these stories that we forget how they may sound to a stranger."

"But why didn't he kill only the merchant?"

"Well," said Marietta, "the other side of the story is that she ran away of her own free will."

"I don't believe it," Lisette declared. "She doesn't look like a woman who would run away from her family. The merchant stole her, and her husband should have been hanged, but the jury granted him clemency," she told Nella indignantly.

"After all, Lisette, you're as much his great-great-granddaughter as you are hers."

"He was a murderer, whichever way you look at it." Lisette shuddered. "A murderer right in our own family. We shouldn't have told you that story, Nella. What does Father think about it?"

"Your father thinks she ran away." Marietta smiled.

"Oh, he does? Then what about his great-grandmother—the Quakeress who went into church and took off her cloak and stood in front of the congregation without a stitch on?"

Nella now sat bolt upright, looking from Marietta to Lisette, and could not manage to conceal her astonishment. "What ever did she do that for?"

"She was expiating a sin, Nella," Marietta assured her gently.

"What sin?"

Lisette smiled. "What sin do you suppose, Nella?"

"Lisette, that was an unladylike remark. In any event, Nella, she was whipped for it. I think it's time now to finish getting supper," and Marietta gathered her sewing together and went into the house and the two girls followed quickly, bringing the stools and the cups and saucers and teapot, for they regarded their afternoon sewing as a picnic and made elaborate preparations for it. At the door, Lisette caught hold of Nella's arm and made her turn to look at her.

"You aren't shocked, Nella, are you?" she whispered urgently. "You won't think we're disreputable?"

"Of course not, Lisette. How could I ever think a thing like that about people I love so much?"

Lisette gave her an impudent and wicked grin. "But maybe we are a little, just the same. I could tell you other stories, about pirate ghosts and Indian tomahawks thrown through the dining-room window, and a girl who got locked in the attic one afternoon with her cousin and then had a baby—what do you think of that?" Lisette's black eyes were brilliant and challenging, and Nella, gazing into them helplessly, felt no better able to cope with their sins than with their virtues.

But whether Lisette teased her or asked her questions she could not answer, or however painfully she sometimes felt her own shyness and timidity, most particularly when Matt and Pete and the two oldest boys were there—when she often found it difficult to talk or even to look at them directly—Nella grew slowly more accustomed to being with them.

By Lisette's fourteenth birthday in early October, Nella had become so self-confident that she ordered Lisette out of the kitchen where she and Marietta were preparing special dishes, held whispered consultations about presents with Robert and Douglas, made an exhilarating speech at the table when she gave Lisette her own gift, a locket she had coaxed Rick into letting her buy, clapped her hands and sang with Pete's music, and later went spinning about in waltzes with Matt and Morgan and Jonathan and Zack Fletcher, and by the time they were ready for bed was so full of her evening's triumph she could not sleep at all. And, furthermore, she was dazzled and somewhat confused to have discovered that she had fallen in love with Lisette's oldest brother, Morgan, although of course she had known it the afternoon Lisette had asked, as mischievously as if she knew the answer, who her Ivanhoe was.

She might have fallen in love with him because she was in love with them all, and Morgan, the oldest son and one year older than she, was her logical choice; or perhaps she would have fallen in love with him even if she had met him without knowing his family, for he had an almost fierce intensity in his expression which she found pleasantly disturbing, and yet a tenderness, when he talked either to Marietta or Lisette, that she longed to share. But whatever it was, Morgan had so occupied her imagination that even though he paid her very little attention, and when he did seemed preoccupied and almost impatient, she nevertheless believed she knew him very well and understood him better than even Lisette, who never pretended that he was not her favorite.

Morgan had walked home with her the few times she had gone back to her cabin. Sometimes Lisette walked along with them, once both Lisette and Zack Fletcher had come, and two or three times she and Morgan had made the quarter-mile trip alone and in silence, with Nella now and then humming nervously but unable to make him talk, so that she hoped he might be tongue-tied out of his desperate infatuation.

One night, very much to her surprise, she turned at the door and asked if he would come in for a few minutes, but he gave her a look of suspicious disapproval, shook his head and told her curtly, "Good night, Nella," and went off, not pausing or seeming to hear when she called after him in a pleading tone.

"I meant for only a minute."

The next time she saw him, however, seated across from her at the dinner table, she glanced up from a discussion with Robert and found that Morgan, whose eyes were even darker than Lisette's and equally bright and shining, was watching her, and in another moment Lisette, who missed nothing at all, began talking to her brother in an undertone, a rudeness for which she was often corrected; she always apologized, but in another few moments did it again.

They had, Morgan and Lisette, their own private world within the family, and although their comradeship gave Nella no jealous or envious pangs, she longed to know if they were talking about her and, if they were, what they said. It was Lisette, however, who did most of the talking, while Morgan inclined his head toward her, listened seriously, sometimes smiled with a skeptical or incredulous expression, and now and then laughed out loud, which always made Lisette indignant.

It had occurred to Nella, somewhat vaguely and more as a hope than a scheme, that if Morgan were to fall in love with her, she would no longer be afraid of them and, what was far more important, would not be in danger of losing them, either. But to bring this about in the midst of his watchful family she concluded was something beyond her resources and, anyway, she had few practical theories on the art of fascination to help her.

And then one evening not long after Lisette's birthday, as she was helping Marietta wash the supper dishes, and Lisette had gone to sweep the living room for the fourth time that day, she heard them talking about her and another girl; and, glancing around to be sure Marietta was occupied, she lingered beside the door and listened. "Does she remind you of Suky?" she heard Lisette ask.

The two younger boys were studying, Matt and Pete were discussing a new business venture with Lemuel Finney, Jonathan and Zack were playing cribbage, and apparently Lisette and Morgan thought their conversation could not be overheard.

"Not at all." Morgan's voice sounded defensive. "How could she? She's not more than five feet tall and she's—in fact, she's nothing at all like Suky."

"She's blond, she's pretty, and she has that same weird stillness about her."

Morgan gave a sharp laugh. "But Suky isn't still because she's frightened. And, anyway, she doesn't have Suky's strong dignity."

"Suky's strong dignity! Oh, Morgan, you make me tired sometimes. I'll never get over the way she pretended to be sick when we left." Her voice became scornful. "Dying of love for you, that's what she wanted you to think. But Suky won't ever die of love for anyone, unless she gets sick of herself someday. Oh, don't look at me so ferociously, you know you can't scare me, and why do you always defend her?"

"Maybe to protect her from you, Lisette."

There was a pause while, Nella supposed, they studied each other as she had often seen them do, each apparently trying to guess whether the challenge had gone far enough, and then Lisette said, "Be careful with Nella, Morgan. Don't tease her, don't ever do anything to hurt her."

Morgan laughed again and Nella moved away from the door, dismayed to think of this other girl, whoever she was, and deeply ashamed to have learned she did not have her strong dignity. "What makes you think I'd ever hurt your friend?"

"I'm afraid she may want you to."

Nella gave a protesting little moan at this and covered her ears, then told Marietta that she had felt a sharp pain, nothing to speak of, only one of those convenient pains to which young girls were so continually subject.

It required great effort and constant self-control not to ask Lisette who Suky was, and after a few days the effort became too much for her.

"Suky?" Lisette repeated, as they were taking turns brushing each other's hair before they went to bed. Lisette was standing in back of Nella, drawing out her fine hair into long ribbons and polishing them with tender diligence. "You must have heard me talking to Morgan. I hope we didn't say anything you weren't meant to hear."

"I was just curious. You hadn't mentioned her before."

Lisette continued brushing and took a little time before she answered. "Suky is our cousin—Susan Ching—who always lived near us in New York. She and Morgan are just about the same age, and to tell the truth, Nella, Suky and I are bitter enemies and always have been. It's more or less a family joke, although there's nothing funny about it as far as I'm concerned. Of course, she pretends not to be even aware of it. I'm just her baby cousin, too young to count." Lisette gave Nella the hairbrush, sat down on the edge of the bed, her hands folded in her lap and almost hidden by the ruffles about the wrists of her long white nightgown, and as Nella began to ply the brush Lisette turned and gave her an upward glance, a smile of conspiratorial malice on her face. "Oh, if Morgan would only fall in love with you, Nella—how I'd love to write her that letter." She turned back and Nella looked sober and thoughtful as she continued to brush Lisette's hair, glad to have her blessing in this imaginary romance for any reason at all.

But Nella felt that it was some disadvantage to be observed by her friend and discussed as if she were their cat Shekel or the new baby

they now knew would be born in a few months, and occasionally
came near to asking Lisette what she thought of Zack Fletcher. But
each time she lost courage for fear Lisette would tell her it was none
of her business and might even drive her out of the house, for Lisette had a spoiled and protected girl's prerogatives and was candid
when she wanted to be, secretive when she preferred that, and
passed readily and inexplicably from one humor to another, being
by turns, but without warning, merciful and delicately cruel, arrogant and wheedling, and Nella had not learned to predict which way
she might jump next. Sometimes Lisette talked to Zack with mocking flirtatiousness, asking where he had come from and why he did
not tell them about himself, and other times she ignored him and
became petulant if Morgan suggested she had been rude to his
friend.

"I don't understand him," she said. "He's like a wild animal that
doesn't want to be petted. I don't trust him."

"Then don't rile him." Morgan grinned.

And Lisette took care not to rile him but, Nella had noticed, whenever Zack thought he could do so without being seen, he watched
Lisette as intently and persistently as if she were a new species of
creature he was studying, and his face showed tenderness and continuous surprise, and a kind of stealthy calculation; but then Zack
Fletcher was twenty-three and, no doubt, they all seemed like children to him.

One Sunday near the end of October, when the days were as brilliant as they had ever been but the air had begun to sharpen, reminding them that before very much longer they would be yearning for just such a day and convinced there would never be one, the
four of them set out to explore the country farther up the hillsides,
beyond the diggings, where the earth, not having been found profitable, had been left alone.

Lisette and Zack rode ahead and Nella and Morgan followed,
Nella on Morgan's horse Puzzle, which he had given her for her afternoon rides with Lisette. They trotted along quickly, and occasionally
waved or called out to someone they knew, gaily announcing that
they were going picnicking.

Very soon they had passed the edge of settlement and were riding
along the tops of the hills, and, at this liberation, they became merry
and frolicsome and let themselves be influenced by the wind and hot
sun and the motion of their horses traveling lightly and swiftly
along the paths. Zack and Lisette galloped ahead, with Lisette putting her horse through every maneuver he knew, which Zack pretended had him baffled until he set his own to bucking for a minute
or two, then made him squat on his haunches as he leaped off, and
went to help Lisette dismount.

Nella, with her long hair spreading and drifting about her back
and shoulders, glanced at Morgan and found him watching her, and

grew courageous enough to say, "The last time I was here, there were white violets growing down there, and this bank was covered with blooming wild roses. I kept wishing there was someone I could show it to."

"We'll see it," Morgan assured her, looking very grave, as if the promise bound them both, and Nella gave him a beseeching smile, so dazzled by happiness she longed for some way to humble herself.

Zack was showing Lisette, far out on the horizon, where an antelope moved, rising and falling in slow, continuous arcs, and as Morgan came to help her, Nella slipped down, into his arms and out again before he had quite caught hold of her, but then laughed at his own surprise, the same laugh Lisette often gave when something unexpected happened.

Zack and Morgan set quickly to work, spreading blankets over the deep, dry grass, gathering twigs and breaking branches for the fire, unpacking the basket of food, while Lisette and Nella wandered a little distance away with their arms about each other's waists, talking in low, confidential voices although they were discussing only the magpies, the color of the cottonwood leaves, and whether they should have brought two beefsteak and oyster pies instead of one.

Zack knelt and prepared to light the fire but Lisette sprang forward. "Oh, maybe we shouldn't do that. Suppose there are some Indians around?" Zack glanced up, grinning, and Lisette looked from Morgan to Nella, to find them watching her and smiling. "Oh, all right, go ahead and light it. But suppose we all get scalped?"

"Zack has lived with Indians," Morgan told her. "He'll talk them out of it."

Zack got the fire going and rested back on his heels, adding fuel when it began to smoke. "Have you?" Lisette asked.

"For awhile."

Lisette frowned, not sure but that they might all be making fun of her, for of course it was the style out here to create a background of exploit and variety to confound the pilgrims and more particularly the pilgrim women. "Is it true they mistreat all the women they capture?"

Zack looked at Morgan, who smiled and shrugged, telling him he was on his own. "They sure as hell mistreat all the ones they don't kill," Zack said slowly, "and they mistreat some of them, too." Lisette gave a screech and Zack frowned apologetically at Morgan. "I suppose that was the wrong thing to say, but she asked me." He addressed Lisette again, speaking very soberly. "To tell the truth, it's a good idea to keep out of their way—that's the best advice I can give you."

"I don't want to hear any more about it. I'll never be able to forget it, no matter how I try. Just like that dead man we saw last month." She turned appealingly to Nella. "Oh, Nella, see what I've done."

"What man?" Morgan demanded.

Nella touched his arm. "Oh, please don't tell your parents. We went to see him after the hanging, and we made a vow never to tell anyone."

"And I've broken it." Lisette was contrite and ashamed. "But Morgan, everyone else went. The teacher took Robert and Douglas and the whole class, just to teach them a lesson."

"I know. But she shouldn't have. And neither should you."

Lisette wandered away and pretended to become absorbed in studying the clouds. Zack was making the coffee and for a few minutes no one spoke; and when Lisette finally glanced around, Nella and Morgan were strolling toward the creek bank and Zack was watching her with a wry grin. She came back quickly. "When I heard about it I had to go—I couldn't keep away. I can't explain it, and I won't try."

"The women who come west," Zack told her slowly, "have got to learn a few things they managed to hide out from in the East. Not all men die in parlors wearing their Sunday suits." Morgan and Nella were moving farther away, and although she hesitated a little longer, at last she sat down, determined to show Zack Fletcher he did not intimidate her, however many Indians he might have known. "And so now you've seen a man hanging." He was serious and watched her so steadily that she became confused all over again. "What did it make you feel?"

"I don't know."

"Of course you do. What was it?"

Lisette considered the question, and then spoke clearly and decisively. "I felt that I hated him and that he had deserved to die. And yet I'd never seen him before. But Nella—"

"I didn't ask about Nella. I asked about you."

"I haven't been able to understand it, and sometimes I think there must be something evil in me I hadn't known about before. But he looked so grotesque and yet so pitiful, with his neck twisted and his boots worn and dusty, as if he could still walk off in them, that I either had to hate him, or hate all the others who had done it to him. And how could I hate them? My father was one and so was my uncle—maybe you, too."

"Yes, I was one of them. So were your father and uncle. So was Morgan."

"Morgan was there?"

"Of course, why wouldn't he be? Every man in the camp was there, and most of the little boys."

Lisette was looking off toward where her brother stood, far in the distance, talking to Nella, who leaned against a tree and gazed up at him with an expression Lisette could imagine very clearly. "And they told us they'd been out with Mr. Finney inspecting a new property—at night." Zack smiled, as if to remind her that men often made up lies because women insisted on it.

"Suppose we'd told you we'd been helping, along with several hundred other guys, to hang a man for stealing seven hundred dollars when he was drunk?" He smiled a little, watching her across the fire, and his expression and the soft sound of his voice seemed almost to have lulled her into imagining she might trust him. But that set up new doubts and apprehensions.

"How many men have you killed?"

"With my bare hands?" He spread his hands, big and square-fingered with the thumbs set almost at right angles from the palms and curving sharply backward.

"Morgan says you were with the Border Ruffians. Were you?"

"For a few months."

"You're a Rebel," she said accusingly and after a moment added, "But you don't seem to hate us Yankees."

"I don't believe in hate. I don't feel hate." He looked into the fire again and stirred it with a long stick, then sprinkled on a few twigs, rather reflectively, and took a pinch of needles and added those, as if he were following a recipe. The coffee was boiling and its fragrance spread richly.

"My father was in the War, you know that." Zack nodded and Lisette said gently, out of some impulse to comfort him, "And the South, they say, is almost defeated now. Do you believe it?"

"I suppose it is. And how easy it seemed, at the beginning. I remember when we used to say—if a Yankee points a gun at me I'll ask him how much he wants for it. And now, Atlanta's gone." He pushed the black hat from his forehead and squinted through the smoke at her, finally gesturing. "Well?"

"I'm sorry," Lisette said, with more tenderness than she had intended. "That is, I'm sorry you've lost, but I'm not sorry we won." She cocked her head sideways, pretending to listen to those words, and when he poured the coffee and brought a cup to her, she smiled at him and put it carefully to her lips.

He went back to the other side of the fire and began to poke it, wrinkling his forehead in the familiar grimace, and she supposed he was reflecting on the certain punishments which came to those who made bad choices, road agents or nations; at least, it was what she thought should be in his mind.

It had seemed to Lisette from the time she had first met him, that there was something unruly in Zack Fletcher which it was some woman's duty to subdue, not by complaints or correction, since men were impervious to such tactics, but nevertheless it needed doing, for he would otherwise escape civilization entirely, and as it was he seemed wary and suspicious of its simplest habits. She was convinced, and it troubled her, that he had no inclination to engage in, or even to share, those things which other men had agreed to find meaningful; and since there was no one about to tell her it was impolite to ask questions, she asked another.

"Haven't you any family? Haven't you any home?"

"Sure. I ran away."

"You ran away? When you were young? I mean, younger?"

Zack seemed to be trying not to smile and, in fact, she believed the struggle was a constant one, for apparently he found her more entertaining than she meant to be. "Nine tenths of the men on the frontier ran away from home. Suppose you grew up in a family where your mother had a new kid every year and your father had a farm that grew more weeds than anything else and half the time you had a pain in your belly and you hung around the wharves in St. Louis? You just might take a notion to run away yourself."

"Oh—I'm sorry." She reached toward him, but when he looked at her hand questioningly, she drew it back.

"I don't need anybody to be sorry for me. I've had things happen to me the last twelve or thirteen years I wouldn't trade for the best gold mine in the Territory. I like to travel alone, and then I like the crowds and racket and, as a girl would think, the sinfulness of the camps, too, the places where men go. There's no way I could tell you what I mean and I won't try, but you kept asking me questions and that's about all the answers I'm prepared to give. Satisfy you?" He looked at her sharply and Lisette sat up straight.

"Indeed it does."

Zack broke a few twigs, dropping them into a small, neat pile, studied them as if perhaps their design would show him an omen, and after awhile shook his head, saying thoughtfully, "I just hope it won't be too rough on you when you come to get educated yourself."

"As it happens," Lisette assured him haughtily, "I have been educated in a very good academy in Connecticut where I studied French, music, dancing, and drama. What are you smiling about now?"

"If I was smiling, it wasn't intentional. Men do a lot of smiling, you know, for no other reason than that what they're looking at makes them feel happy." This admission seemed to embarrass him, but it mollified Lisette and even gave her a sense of feminine triumph. "And so you've studied French and music and drama. But you don't really call that education, now, do you? Those are parlor tricks, and a good thing for a girl to have, I'm sure. Makes her prettier, and whatever makes her prettier improves her as far as men are concerned. But the only real education a girl gets, she gets from a man."

Lisette had been listening with such absorbed concentration that it was a moment before she reacted to the last sentence, and then she cried, "What makes you think you can talk to me like that?" She started to get up, but found him standing over her.

"If you do that your brother will ask you what the trouble is, and what will you tell him? That I was insulting you? Good God, but you young ladies are brought up to be suspicious." He dropped down beside her, and as she watched him from the corners of her eyes, he lay flat on his back, put his arms comfortably behind his head, and crossed one foot over the other. "I wasn't insulting you, and in your heart you know it." He turned and looked at her, then covered his eyes with his hat. "Nothing will happen to you while you're with me that your brother or your parents could ever take exception to. I respect your father as much as any man I've known. He's a man from the ground up. Your brother, too, even though he's still just a kid. But give him a couple of years out here and you'll be surprised. You won't know him."

"I hope that doesn't happen." Lisette watched Morgan and Nella walking along the bank, and now and then she could hear Nella's light, rippling laugh, which sounded as fragile as Nella herself. "I don't want him to change."

"But he will. Life in the mountains is like going to sea, it puts age and experience in a man. He seasons fast out here."

"I don't want anything at all to change. I want us always to be exactly the way we are now." She leaned forward, found he was not smiling, and asked, "Is that possible?"

"No, ma'am," he told her positively. "It is not." He pushed the hat down until it covered his nose.

Lisette sighed, watching Nella and Morgan. "I know it isn't." They were talking again, Nella with her hands clasped behind her and her head tipped back so that her hair fell straight almost to her hips, transparent as a veil, and Lisette thought it was remarkable they had discovered so much to say, those two who had only mumbled shyly at each other before. "I wonder," she said, as if to herself, "if Morgan is in love with Nella. Has he ever said anything about it to you?"

Zack sat up abruptly, but when she turned he shook his head and filled the coffee cups. "Not a word to me. Not one single word." He set a cup beside her and gave her a look of bland but interested curiosity. "Is that what girls think we spend our time talking about? Whether maybe we're in love with one of you or not?"

"They say men are always talking about women."

Zack gave his knee a slap and laughed with so much gusto that she stared at him reproachfully, frowning. But then he grew quiet again and seemed embarrassed by this outburst, glanced at her alertly and spoke in an apologetic tone which was not entirely, she thought, meant as mockery. "Men don't fall in love the way girls do, for the fun of it."

Lisette considered that, watching him carefully, and a little disturbed to find that he seemed very near, although he had not moved. "Then why do they fall in love?"

"Only when they can't help themselves, not before. They don't go around looking for it, I can tell you that."

Lisette did not like the sound of this remark, for it proved exactly what she had thought about him all along—that he was irresponsible and, in some fundamental sense, immoral, since a moral man would understand it was his duty to fall in love and to accept its consequences for the rest of his life; but she felt that even though a lecture might do him good, it was not in her power to deliver it at that moment. For he had, by some mysterious means, some concentration of physical strength and independence, made her feel young and uncertain, and that forced her to retire into dignified seclusion, refusing his challenge, if he had meant it to be one.

They had nothing to say for a time, as Lisette watched her brother and Nella with a wistful troubled expression, until Morgan, who had taken hold of Nella's hand, bent toward her with a quick, impulsive movement and kissed her briefly before she stepped away. Nella started running toward them, beckoning Morgan to follow, and as they came Lisette turned, pretending she had not seen the kiss. Zack got up and kicked the fire into activity, and when Lisette looked up furtively he was grinning at her again, and then he began to stretch unself-consciously until it seemed he had grown in all directions at once, expanding in some uncanny way which alarmed her.

"You're a little girl, Lisette. A very pretty little girl."

VII

Nella went into the cabin while Morgan and Zack and Lisette waited. In a moment she opened the door and stood before it, as if she might be guarding something. "Rick's here. I've got to fix his supper." She started back in, but then turned. "I enjoyed the picnic very much—thank you."

Rick had two visitors. She had met Abel Hawker, and did not like him. He was about Rick's age and thought of himself as one of the toughest men in the mountains, a man with the bark on, as they described themselves when they imagined they had reached that eminence where their presence in a whorehouse or saloon gave other customers queasy feelings of doubt and anxiety. "How." He gave her a salute but did not get up, only lay on the lower bunk, gazing fixedly overhead.

The other was Green Troy, who stood and bowed when Rick introduced him, and she remembered having seen him the afternoon the Devlins arrived in town. He sat down, crossing his arms, smoking a cigar and watching her thoughtfully, while Nella took a stool against the wall and Rick paced about until finally he turned, stamped his foot as he did when he wanted to scare her, and demanded: "What have they been saying about me—your friends?"

"Nothing, Rick. They haven't mentioned you."

"Tell the truth!"

Rick glared at her, Abel Hawker seemed skeptical, but Green Troy said, "Allen, stop bullying your sister."

"Something's the matter, isn't it?" Nella spoke very softly, and might have been making a statement about something which had happened a long time ago. "Rick's in trouble, is that it?" She turned to Green Troy. "Is he, Mr. Troy?"

"Well, now, Miss Nella, he may not exactly be in trouble, but he is in some embarrassment."

Nella sighed and looked at her hands, folded in her lap. "Oh, Rick. I knew this was going to happen. I've tried to tell you."

"The hell with what you've tried to tell me."

"Look here, Allen, I haven't the day to waste." Green Troy became businesslike. "There have been some rumors about your brother and Hawker, Miss Nella, none of them true, of course, but the community is still too unsettled to take any chances. Give him a fair trial, and then hang him—that's the motto nowadays. The Vigilantes like to say they've disbanded, but of course they haven't, as we saw only a little more than a month ago. Without discussing just why or how it happened, the fact is they've become suspicious of your brother and Hawker, and we've decided it would be advisable for them to take a little trip, until the atmosphere changes. You can stay with your friends while he's gone, can't you?"

Nella closed her eyes. "Of course not. If he's under suspicion, they won't want me."

"They may not know it. I heard all this in a roundabout way. You can tell them he's gone prospecting." Green Troy smiled. "And if they ask you any other questions, naturally you won't answer."

"You're god-damn right you won't."

"If they say anything unusual, you must tell me at once. It could mean your brother's life."

"That's right," Rick agreed, and Nella looked at him sorrowfully for Rick, unquestionably, was enjoying his predicament, whatever it was, and plainly believed it gave him a new and ominous importance as a man whom other men might at that moment be planning to kill.

Troy and Abel Hawker left, after the three men had muttered together outside for a few minutes, and Rick set to work industriously, cleaning his pistols and supervising while she packed the supplies Green Troy had recommended—crackers and sardines, so that it would not be necessary to build any fires, a blanket and ammunition —and all the while refused to answer her questions. When that was done Rick still paced about, peeked out the windows from time to time, stamped his foot and snapped his fingers, and Nella sat watching him and marveling at whatever had become of this Sunday afternoon, which now seemed to have happened so long ago. She thought of the man she and Lisette had seen hanging, who might one day be her brother, but was too stunned and defeated even to cry.

After several hours, when she had begun to grow sleepy and had to remind herself to stay awake, Rick announced that the time had come. He went to the door, carrying the bedroll and supplies she had packed, and apparently intended to go away without another word; but then he stopped. "I've left some dust in that buckskin, you can get along on it for awhile. If you need any help, go to Green Troy—it ain't all a one-way street between us, but don't tell him I said so. Well—" He glanced around. "That's all."

Nella caught hold of his arm. "Rick, please promise me you didn't do anything wrong."

Rick hesitated, but then went out and Nella leaned against the door, crying, though it still seemed these things had happened long ago, and not to her but to someone else.

During the next few days she pretended she had never known the Devlins, but it did not occur to her to go to them with some explanation of her brother's absence. She ate little and became even thinner. She did not light a fire, though the weather had become very cold, and most of the time lay in bed covered with a buffalo robe, waiting, but had no idea what she was waiting for. Sometimes it even seemed that she was grateful, curiously relieved, to have been so suddenly deprived of all her ambitions.

Then, one morning, she was startled by several sharp raps at the door, and Lisette's voice, calling to her as she rattled the latch. "Nella, Nella—answer me! Are you in there?" When Lisette continued to call she got up, wrapped in the buffalo robe, opened the door, and they stared at each other with as much surprise as at their first meeting. "Nella, what's the matter with you? Is Rick here?"

"No."

"Can I come in?" She slipped inside, turning back her hood and looking curiously and disapprovingly about the cabin with its litter of unwashed dishes, heaps of clothes, and dusty floor. "Not even a fire—and you aren't dressed. Have you been sick?" She took hold of Nella's shoulders, gazing at her with anxious accusation.

"No, I'm not sick."

"Why didn't you come back? We were afraid that if we came here Rick might not like it. But finally, this morning at breakfast, we had a family conference, and I was chosen to find out what was wrong. We thought Rick wouldn't do anything to me, but might take a shot at one of my brothers." She laughed merrily. "Where is he?"

"He went to try some prospecting." The lie seemed so logical she was almost convinced by it.

"And left you here alone? He's a fine one. Nella—get your things together. You're going to stay with us. Yes, you are," and she gave her a little shake. "Mother said to bring you back and she'll take care of you."

"She did?"

"Of course. Now hurry up. What shall we take?" Lisette began to snatch dresses from the wall hooks, picked up petticoats and night-gowns, Nella was dressed in a minute, and they ran out of the cabin and went dashing down the hill as if they were making an escape.

Marietta took her into her arms and kissed her, telling her she might stay with them for as long as she liked, and Nella reminded herself that this was only another interlude, until they found out

what an impostor she was; but even so her body felt warm and satisfactory to her again, when all during these past few days she had felt
dispossessed from it, as if she had no further need of it and never
would have.

Robert and Douglas greeted her with joyous shouts when they
came in from school, and as it got nearer the time for the others to
come home, the two girls went into Lisette's room to comb their hair
and tie fresh ribbons, washing their faces and chattering excitedly.
"Morgan's missed you, Nella," she whispered. "He's been gloomy, I
promise you he has."

Matt and Pete came into the house first, with Zack and Morgan
and Jonathan close behind. Lisette stood in the bedroom doorway,
Nella behind her and out of sight, and when they entered Lisette
made a sweeping gesture and stepped to one side as Nella appeared,
smiling. "Evening, Mr. Devlin. Evening, Uncle Pete. Hello, Zack.
Hello, Jonathan—Morgan."

Matt hugged her fast. "Welcome back, Nella." Pete kissed her, she
shook hands with Zack and Jonathan, and when she came to Morgan
she turned red and made him a curtsy, which confused her so much
that Lisette put her arm about her waist and drew her into the
kitchen, nodding significantly to her brother as they went.

After a few more days Nella was glad Rick had gone, and only
hoped that wherever he was he would not do anything reckless
enough to get himself hanged or otherwise die with his boots on, as
he had often gloomily predicted was bound to be his end. For now
it was Rick who seemed unreal, only an imaginary brother, while she
was where she wanted to be and, she thought, no longer an admiring
spectator but one of them herself.

The past two winters had been so unusually mild that no one was
prepared for the surprises of this one. It began to snow before Christmas, the roads were closed, the streams frozen, and the placering
work had to stop. The camp was isolated and the snow lay so deep
that men shoveled narrow paths to their cabins; in town they hung
about the stores and saloons and gambling houses, and many of
them would have nothing left by spring.

Zack and Morgan continued to work at the diggings, sawing lumber and repairing flumes, and from time to time talked of what they
would do when spring came. "I must be fiddle-footed," Zack said. "It
begins to hamper me if I stay put too long. But you decide for yourself. Your old man's made a pile, and maybe you're better off here
than anywhere else."

Devlin Brothers, in fact, had a capital stock of one hundred thousand dollars, of which Matt and Pete kept the controlling shares, and
the others had been sold to Lemuel Finney, Jeremy Flint, Josiah Webb
and Silas Church, and other men they had known in Bannack. Most
of their time was spent at the office in town, or they went dashing
about the streets, bundled up with their hats pulled low, full of resolution and more schemes than they could count.

And quite often they congratulated each other on their industry and good luck, giving as much credit for their success to one as to the other, for in spite of Lem Finney's conviction that a man owed his good fortune only to himself, neither Matt nor Pete was able to believe that in a camp which had dug up nearly ten million dollars in its first year, and where the Chinese laundrymen became prosperous panning the water from the miner's shirts, it was only their natural superiority which had singled them out.

"By God, but I'm glad we came here. Where in the hell would we be now?"

"In New York, for Christ's sake."

"And we'd have missed all this."

Pete gave a wave of his hand, taking in the town, the wooden sidewalks where men slid along their icy surfaces, the piles of trash burning in the streets, the half-finished buildings with their false fronts and overhanging signs: Cigars. Newspapers. Turkish Baths. Gold Bought Here; and at the unsettling thought that they might never have seen it, they stopped for a drink, clicking the rims of their glasses smartly together.

"Hell on women and oxen."

"But great for men and horses."

They had heard at a meeting of the Executive Committee that Rick Allen and Abel Hawker had arrived in Helena, and there was some discussion of sending a few men to teach them that passing bogus gold dust was no more acceptable than robbing stagecoaches had been; but the members thought it was time to let the People's Court function as it was meant to do, and Matt argued that they had no proof but only suspicions. "This isn't the same situation we were up against a few months ago. Anyway, Allen's sister is living in my house and I don't want it on my conscience. Go ahead, if you think you must, but Pete and I will resign."

The others puffed at their cigars and Silas Church suggested that neither Allen nor Hawker was worth their trouble. "I've had a bellyful of killing men."

"So have we all," Lem Finney agreed. "And anyway, we don't have to. When these young fellows begin trying to live up to their reputations as dangerous men to have around, they don't last long."

"One of his own kind will take care of him," Josiah Webb predicted, and they agreed to let it go at that.

They found a proprietary pleasure in seeing Nella Allen—who seemed quickened into responsiveness by whatever attentions any of them paid her—become more happy and contented with every day. She played games with the two younger boys, had a collection of her favorite songs when Pete took up his fiddle, and at times, Matt thought, she showed a remarkable intuition for the gestures and expressions which would please a man, but these did not appear often and never when Marietta or Lisette was in the room, a coincidence which surprised him and caused him to berate himself for his suspiciousness.

Then one night, when Rick had been gone for several weeks and Nella was in the kitchen with Marietta and Lisette, Matt was startled to hear an outburst of tears, and walked quickly to the door to find Marietta with her arms about Nella while Lisette hovered anxiously about, stroking Nella's hair and murmuring her name in a pleading voice.

Lisette drew him back into the other room. "It's my fault," she whispered distractedly. "We were all being very deep and philosophical and I showed her the motto on the clock. I thought she knew it was there, but she'd never read it before. She stood and stared at it for awhile—and then this happened."

Matt went back to where the others sat, grimacing when they asked what the trouble was. "The motto on the clock, apparently." He looked around from Pete to Morgan to Jonathan, all of them gravely concerned, and Robert and Douglas were frowning with sympathy and bewilderment.

"*'Every hour wounds,'*" Robert quoted slowly, "*'the last one kills.'*" He thought about it, and then turned to Douglas. "It doesn't make me sad—does it you?"

Nella Allen, apparently, was a girl with vague but real troubles, possibly not all of them concerned with her brother and none of them, Matt hoped, with his oldest son. But, Matt told himself, a man could expect to juggle only so many problems at one time, and he had others more immediate.

As the winter got colder, flour became so scarce it was selling for twenty-seven dollars a sack and Lem Finney, who had predicted early in September that the supplies were not adequate if the winter proved a severe one, had brought in a large shipment from Salt Lake City and hidden it in his warehouse, a piece of forethought which made him rub his hands together with satisfaction at every new storm. "What did I tell you?" he asked Matt and Pete. "You've only got to know what the cities are long on and what the camps are short on. If this weather holds until April, it will go to five hundred a sack."

"And yet," Pete said, with a slight wry smile, as they walked out of Lem's store, "he'd be ready to shoot the first guy who suggested he was a species of road agent himself. Of course, he says he'll always take care of his friends."

"For a price."

"Thank God we can pay it. Those kids can't spend a winter living on beef straight. Nor can Marietta."

And it was Marietta whom Matt worried about incessantly, finding himself as concerned and scared as if she had never had another child. Dr. Danforth, who saw her from time to time, assured him she was healthy and, what was more important, confident and serene, promised to give her a whiff of chloroform if she needed it, and jovially asked if Matt was not yet used to his wife having babies. Matt intended, whenever he saw him, to tell Andy he expected him to be sober when the time came, and once astonished himself by setting out for the Doctor's house with some plan of discussing it with Jenny. But this seemed the more ridiculous the nearer he got until he could imagine Jenny, whom he had not seen alone since the day she had come to tell him about Milly Matches' girl, looking at him with incredulous contempt, and demolishing him with a laugh. Finally, he stopped Dr. Danforth on the street one day.

"Andy, you know, you're a damn good doctor," he told him slowly.

Andy began to deprecate his skills, but then understood what Matt was trying to say. "Don't worry about it, Matt. I won't let you down. We've been through too much together."

Still, he obliged Andy to make the same promise almost every time he saw him, for he continued to feel that there was some unusual danger involved for Marietta in this birth, and because he could imagine no reasonable explanation for these morbid fears, he at last decided that in some monstrous fashion he was expecting her to atone for his own transgressions with Jenny Danforth.

He had become so wary of Jenny nowadays, and so distrustful of himself, that he turned into the nearest building whenever he caught sight of her, skulking away before she had seen him, or so he hoped; but whether she had or not, he was obliged to get out of her way, grimly assuring himself he had become a most accomplished coward and hypocrite and that if Jenny despised him, as he believed she must, he deserved it.

By February the telegraph lines were down to Salt Lake City, and the camp was as isolated as Bannack had been during its first winter. It was too cold to work out-of-doors many hours at a time, and Morgan and Zack occupied themselves with target practice, or played poker with friends of Zack's in the old cabin, which they had kept as a bunk house for the boys, and one day Pete inquired, "Are you so sure it's a good idea to let Morgan and Jonathan stay out here?"

"You think they should go back to the States to school? They don't want to. We've talked about it."

"Are they old enough to make their own decisions?"

"I don't know how old a boy should be to make his own decisions, do you? I don't believe Morgan, for instance, thinks of himself as a boy nowadays."

"I don't believe he does, either."

They looked at each other, and were somewhat guiltily aware that these surroundings, so agreeable to them, had a way of turning very young men into ruffians like Rick Allen, or convincing them that work was an occupation suitable only to old men of thirty or more. "You mean, the little Allen girl? There's nothing we can do about that. She's got the two best guardians I can provide her with. If they can't protect her from my sixteen-year-old son, no one could." Matt frowned at the end of his cigar. "I'll admit, he seems to have grown up a little quicker than I was expecting."

"He needs something new to think about. Morgan's never liked to be idle."

"I've been wondering if I should offer him my share of the Daylight Gulch claim." Matt felt uneasy whenever the claim was mentioned and expected each time that Pete would tell him he knew what had happened and there was no use pretending he had ever been drunk enough to trade in Rattler for a claim in Daylight Gulch. But Pete seemed no more suspicious of the claim than he had ever been, and Matt now leaned eagerly forward. "I'll make him a proposition." He slapped the desk top enthusiastically. "By God, I'll do it tomorrow. If he wants to make decisions, I'll give him one to make. It's time I take him up on the mountain top and show him the broad valley below."

And this notion of tempting his son with a choice of possible riches or possible loss, possible success or possible failure, pleased him so much that he was eager to get about it, studied the claim again, chuckling reminiscently, and the next morning after breakfast asked Morgan to take a walk with him.

They started out, their faces muffled in woolen scarves so that only two pairs of bright black eyes still showed, and went tramping along between frozen walls of snow, which lay so deep over the hillsides that even the summer's accumulation of heaped rock and earth had been buried beneath it. Their noses turned red and their eyes began to smart, they walked very fast, and as they went Matt asked Morgan what he wanted to do when spring came, reflecting with some rueful humor that the greatest enigma in a man's life was his first-born son, and that compared with this mystery the mysteries supposed to be represented by women were childishly simple.

"Zack and I have been talking about trying some prospecting on our own, sir. Maybe in Helena or Silver Bow City. They say there've been some good strikes there."

"Nothing like this."

"But the good claims are gone here—and if one comes on the market it's taken up by a company that can afford a higher price for an option than we could."

"I know. It's grabbed by Devlin Brothers or Lem Finney or Josiah Webb, or some other guy who got here early with money to spend." They glanced at each other, smiling, and Matt felt a little sheepish that he should have this advantage over his son. "If you and Zack decide you want to go, I won't try to talk you out of it. But before you make up your mind, I'm going to offer you my half interest in a claim. My partner and I've put in only enough work to hold it, and it may not be worth a damn, but there's no way to be sure until someone works it for a few months. I've been offered two thousand dollars down for my share and another two thousand in six months, with a one third interest in the profits."

Matt glanced at him and found he had become almost defiant about forcing Morgan to make his decision not as his son but as another businessman, a discovery which surprised him a little but made him no less determined that this young man, if he had serious cravings for independence, be required to earn it. "Of course, the offer may be too high, I think it is, but I can get it because other men think I'm lucky. And, by God, I have been," he added truculently. "I'll sell it to you, or to you and Zack, for eighteen hundred down and another eighteen hundred in six months, with the same one third interest." Matt stopped, and after some difficulty got a cigar lighted. "Remember, I've never pretended I think a man should treat his son like a child, once he no longer is a child."

"Thank you, sir," Morgan told him, and Matt thought there was a slight smile buried in the muffling scarf. "If you'd offered it as a gift, I wouldn't have taken it, and neither would Zack." Matt told himself that his speech had been made, Morgan had been shown a view of the broad valley, and now he must decide what was to happen. "I've saved most of what you paid us this summer—I've got about twelve hundred dollars. But Zack hasn't twelve cents left. In other words, if we took it we'd have to borrow several hundred dollars."

"We'll loan it to you at two percent a month. We usually get five." Matt turned apologetic again. "This won't make you a capitalist overnight, Morgan."

Morgan looked at him, his eyes shining with amusement. "I didn't expect it would, but I appreciate it anyway, sir. I'll talk it over with Zack and we'll let you know."

A few days later Morgan told him, with the air of one giving a valuable confidence, "Zack and I think, sir, that between working our ass off on a half interest and working it off on one we'd have full title to, we'd prefer to try locating one of our own, when the roads open up."

"Good. But I'd suggest you keep it to yourself for awhile. No use upsetting your mother just now. Or Lisette, either, for that matter."

"I agree, sir," and they smiled at each other with masculine understanding, for Lisette was less likely than Marietta to think the time had come for Morgan to leave them; and, of course, if Lisette did not know he was going, neither would Nella Allen.

For Nella had begun to infest his thoughts during the day, and he was tormented by thinking of her when he went to bed at night. He watched her whenever he thought Lisette would not catch him, listened for that unexpected laughter, soft and secretive, and whenever she prepared a dish for dinner ate his portion greedily, and he had begun to be afraid these symptoms might mean he was in love with her.

This notion alarmed him, made him sullen and remote, for the thought of love led him to the thought of marriage, and he had it as his ambition never to get married at all. Once, it was true, he had intended to marry his cousin Suky, but now he was ashamed of that weakness and trusted Suky to forget they had ever talked about it. And each time he refused to go with Zack Fletcher to visit Milly Matches' house—for he could not get rid of the conviction that his family would find it out—he became that much more ashamed of his innocence, supposed Zack must despise him for it, and Nella Allen preoccupied him more than ever. Still, he was convinced he would never see her alone, and the perils of family life all at once struck him as formidable and, no doubt, insurmountable.

Then late one afternoon he entered the house and found Nella in the kitchen, gazing absently out the window as he had often seen her do, and when he caught hold of her and turned her quickly about, she surprised him by her responsive eagerness. Her lips separated, her arms folded closely about him, and when at last he let her go she looked up at him with questioning excitement, touched his mouth with her fingertips, and gave her little laugh, so much like Suky's, even though in every other way she was as different from Suky as a girl could be. "I was just that moment thinking about you, Morgan."

He interpreted this as a sign of her womanly intuition and wisdom, qualities he yearned for her to have as compensation for his own ignorance and the agonizing confusion it caused him, but as he started to kiss her again, Douglas and Robert arrived and Morgan left very quickly, convinced they must have looked guilty even to two small boys. But Nella, he remembered later, had become instantly gay and playful, began to ask them about school and what they wanted to eat, and he marveled at how early women became resourceful in love, and how instinctively they protected themselves.

He thought of her body, as slight and unresisting as if he had held a plant against him, and was ashamed to realize that what made her most appealing to him was her vulnerability, as if he expected this submissive, pliable young girl to give him the confidence he only had when he was away from her.

His longing presently gave way to defiance, and while he was playing poker with Zack and their friends he imagined himself several years older than he was, hardened by experience and remorse for his many crimes against amorous young girls, but the next time he saw Nella, smiling at him from across the table, he stared at her gloomily and thought she must be taking pleasure in his misery. Girls, he had heard often enough, delighted in torturing men and had devised more schemes than he could imagine for their frustration, the only advantage, as they seemed to believe, which nature had given them.

These reflections made him so surly that one day Lisette whispered, "What ails you lately, Morgan? You've made Nella think you don't like her. Why don't you ask her to go for a walk with you? Talk to her a little, pay some attention to her. She adores you." Morgan glanced at his sister furtively, so astonished by this advice he supposed she must be joking, but Lisette looked very serious, and gave his hand a tap with her fingers. "Don't tell her I suggested it."

He waited until Lisette reminded him again, scowled as if he was

a busy man and his time too valuable to spend that way, but finally
shrugged and said that if she insisted, then he would do it to please
her. But once they were away from the house, neither of them could
find anything to say and they scuffled along in the snow peeking sideways at each other every so often, until all at once Nella began to
laugh, then stopped still and covered her face with her mittened
hands while Morgan watched her resentfully.

"What's the matter, Nella?"

She lowered her hands. "Don't you think we're funny?"

Morgan started on, and after a moment she came skipping along
beside him, took hold of his arm, and said nothing more until he
looked at her again and surprised himself by smiling. "You think
I'm funny, do you?" he asked her. "Well, I guess I am. To tell you the
truth, I'm no expert where girls are concerned."

"I was afraid you were mad at me."

"I'm mad at myself."

"At me, too, just a little?"

"At you, too, just a little. But that's not your fault."

He had expected she would retreat into that apprehensive watch-
fulness with which innocent girls were said to regard all men, but
Nella, apparently, was either too innocent to guess how he felt about
her, or trusted him too much to be suspicious, and so he turned her
around and marched her back to Lisette and Marietta. As she left him
to go into the house, she looked back at him pleadingly. "I love you,
Morgan."

It was Nella who first suggested they go to her cabin, explaining
that she had promised Rick to keep it clean and ready for him whenever he came back, and Morgan decided she had had warning enough
and it was no responsibility of his to remind her that neither Rick
Allen nor anyone else was traveling around the mountains in this
weather. And, since she had made up the lie, she must know as well
as he did what to expect when they got there.

Once he had lighted a fire and thrown off his overcoat, he found
Nella smiling at him with a curious mixture of humility and invitation, and when he began to talk, for he had come prepared with
some extravagant compliments, she put one finger against his mouth,
took hold of his arm and drew him toward the bunk and sank down
upon it, opening her legs and guiding him with her hand. But later
on, as they lay quietly, Morgan stroking her back and thighs and full
of a triumphant exultation and pride and such gratitude and relief
he was convinced he had fallen in love with her in spite of his resolutions, he all at once raised up on his elbow and gazed at her with distrustful curiosity.

At that she sighed, and turned her head away. "I know what you're
thinking."

He began to kiss her imploringly. "I wasn't, Nella, I swear to God
—I was thinking that I love you." Nella lay motionless, taking the
kisses like so many presents she did not deserve, and he began talk-

ing to her again, more than ever determined to make her believe him because of his own uneasy sense of loss.

Finally she sat up, raising her arms and twining her hair about her head, and then slipped away from him, moving deftly sideways when he reached out to her. "Someday I'll tell you why Rick and I came here." He took her into his arms again, finding her so slight that it seemed if he pressed her close enough she might disappear into his body, but although he tried to make her smile, coaxing her to say that she was happy, she looked as wistful and uncertain as she ever had when she had first come asking Lisette for her friendship.

The discovery that she was not a virgin had surprised him, but he was even more surprised that no one guessed what had happened, for he had been sure their guilt, and pleasure, must have lit up both their faces, and even imagined that his skin had a different smell, and his body's new knowledge a way of announcing itself. But none of this was apparent even to Lisette, his most constant and keenest observer, and he finally became convinced they did not suspect him of making love to Nella for the same reason they would not have suspected him of committing any other large or small crime—and at the recognition of his freedom he grew more and more importunate and, it seemed, was in danger of coming to think of nothing else.

As Nella had promised, and in spite of everything he could say to stop her, she began to tell him about her family. She told him of her father's death in a guerrilla raid, she described their poverty and the efforts of her three older brothers to support them, one brother running away and then another, until there was left only their mother, and herself, and Rick. And from time to time, she gave a baffled little laugh, just as Suky did whenever she was very much disturbed, and this kept him listening with a reluctant attention, even though she seemed scarcely to know he was there.

"My mother died two years ago. That left us all alone—and that's when Rick began to hate me."

Morgan sat at the edge of the bunk, staring at the floor, bewildered and angry because Nella Allen had had so little to be happy about, and blaming himself because sooner or later he would add his own share to her troubles. "Rick doesn't hate you, Nella. What a thing to say." He tried to pretend they were talking of something inconsequential, and Nella laughed again, as if perhaps they were. "Oh, yes, he does. Our name isn't Allen, either, it's Malachy. And my name isn't Nella, it's Nola. I made up Nella Allen myself."

"It's very pretty."

"Oh, but Morgan, I didn't make it up because it was pretty. It was just the first thing I could think of." Morgan smiled, nodding. "I won't ask you not to tell anyone, even Lisette, because I know you won't."

"Certainly I won't," Morgan agreed, rather offended at what he took to be a reflection on his honor which, no doubt, she thought he lacked. For of course girls imagined that a man's honor began and stopped with his treatment of them.

The next time they were alone she told him that Rick had killed a man and that was why they had come to the mountains. Morgan had decided that whatever she said, he would show no surprise and no disapproval, for she seemed to be slowly approaching some confession she expected would enrage him, and so now he nodded and remarked that the Territories were full of men who had gotten into fatal fights at home. "But that was my fault, too," she said.

"Nella, for God's sake, don't blame yourself for everything that's ever gone wrong."

"I only blame myself when I caused it to go wrong." She walked about the cabin, wrapped in the buffalo robe because she had taken off most of her clothes, and then came back to stand before him. "Don't you?"

Morgan looked resentful. "There are so many different ideas about what's wrong."

"But this was wrong." She was not looking at him but examining the cabin, gazing abstractedly at the lopsided table and stools, the cowhides pegged to the floor, and he supposed must be asking herself how soon she might come back here to stay. "Rick killed him because he found him with me one day a few months after our mother died. You know what I mean by that. He came in and there we were, in bed. Rick thought he had attacked me, and he killed him, stabbed him to death." Morgan was staring at her now with incredulous horror, and felt as he supposed he might if he had been knocked unconscious and begun slowly to return to awareness, not quite sure of where he was or what had happened. "Don't you believe me?"

"I believe you. But why did you tell me? My God, Nella, I hope you haven't told this to anyone else?"

"Of course I haven't. Do you think I'm bragging about it? I told you because I love you." She wandered away from him. "His name was Jim Holley and he was a friend of Rick's—and I thought I loved him." She laughed softly. "Now I can't even remember what he looked like, and I've tried so often." Morgan was watching her with his eyes partly closed, squinting, as if he studied some phenomenon he could not recognize, and Nella said, "I know what you're thinking —that we got here a year and a half ago, and so I wasn't even fourteen when it happened. Well, maybe that's why Rick killed him. If I'd been any older, he might have killed me, instead."

After a few days, Morgan realized that the picture she had shown him of a girl and her brother and his friend was an indelible one, for he could scarcely look at her without seeing it, and when he was away from her it stayed with him as persistently as if he was intended to draw some moral from it which applied to himself, and perhaps to the rest of his life as well.

But the precise mystical meaning of it he could not locate, for though she frightened him a little now, this childlike girl who had caused a man's death, he was as eager as he had ever been, and, so it seemed, was she. He debated with himself from one day to the next, asking what he owed her, supposed that like other girls she would take the rest of his life in payment if she could get it, but had not even found courage enough to tell her he and Zack would leave as soon as the roads opened, when the household was thrown into commotion by the birth of the new baby.

Matt went dashing out of the house early one morning, Robert and Douglas were quickly given breakfast by Lisette and sent to school; and while the others ate, glancing uneasily at one another, Lisette ran back and forth, carrying dishes to the kitchen, whispered at them to finish eating and leave, and tried to make her mother go to bed. Every few minutes she put her arm about Marietta or snatched a dish from her hands, as if the weight of it might injure her, stroked her head, and asked how she was feeling.

Marietta smiled. "Lisette, stop fussing over me. Your father wanted to bring the Doctor here to keep him sober. As soon as your father comes back with Dr. Danforth, you and Nella are to leave. Go to Nella's cabin and stay there until we send for you."

Late in the afternoon Jonathan came to tell them they could come home now and that Lisette had her wish, a sister, and Lisette went galloping down the hillside, slipping and sliding through the snow, and burst into the cabin to find her father and uncle and Dr. Danforth having a drink, her brothers and Zack standing about, and all of them smiling as if at the accomplishment of a great project in which they had, somehow, participated.

"Can I see her?" Lisette whispered to Matt.

"Go ahead, but be quiet."

Lisette tiptoed to the bedroom, beckoning Nella to follow her. "Mother?"

"Come in, darling. Here she is, not very pretty just yet."

The two girls hovered over Marietta and the baby, and as they stood there, speechless with awe, the baby began to squall. They jumped back guiltily, as if they might have brought it on, and Matt appeared.

"Come along. That's enough. Your mother is supposed to sleep."

Lisette bent down and kissed Marietta, approaching her with solemn caution, spilled a tear which she tenderly wiped from the baby's head, and they went out softly, to find that everyone had become peculiarly silent and embarrassed. The boys went wandering about with their hands in their pockets, Matt was helping Dr. Danforth into his coat, and Morgan stood looking at Nella, studying her, it seemed, with an intense and suspicious curiosity.

For several days they discussed the baby's name, holding long, amiable arguments, until finally they had selected four they liked best. Lisette was blindfolded by Jonathan and drew a slip from Morgan's hand, read it, and gave a triumphant little jump. "Annabel! My favorite!" They smiled and exchanged significant nods, for Pete had marked each slip with the same name.

The snows were still deep and the roads remained closed, but somehow news arrived that Richmond had been captured. Most of the camp was, however, more interested in the fact that flour had now gone to one hundred dollars a sack, for many of them had eaten nothing but unsalted beef or venison for several months. A man was reported to have sold his wife for one hundred dollars in gold and two sacks of flour, a transaction which made the women indignant and set some of the men to wondering. Lem Finney, who observed the market and the weather with care, had sold his supply at a very good profit, and when five hundred men went marching through the camp, searching warehouses and stores and some private homes, confiscated what they found and sold it at more reasonable prices, Lem met them cordially and showed them that he had only two sacks left. But there was not enough to go around, and the excitement did not fill their stomachs for very long.

At the end of the month news was brought that the President had been assassinated almost two weeks before, and Robert and Douglas came home with black eyes to describe their fights with the Rebel children who had cheered and danced jigs. The town was draped in black, although there were thought to be more Southerners than Yankees in the population, and men felt for a time that they had not gone so far from their earlier homes as it had seemed.

And then the bull trains were reported to be near the city, carrying the first supplies to arrive in five months. The streets filled with people, laughing and crying and shouting, and men rode out to meet the trains, returning with flour sacks across their saddles. The big wagons came in to town groaning and creaking and rattling their cable-chains, with the drivers, who looked ugly as baboons and fierce as wolves, grinning amid their beards as children ran along beside them and women held out their clasped hands in thanksgiving. The roads were opened and prospectors went swarming away, water began to run in the streams, and the winter which they had been ready to believe would never end, was over.

Morgan and Zack were making their preparations to leave secretly; Matt told Morgan that he had talked to Marietta and she preferred not to discuss it. "She wants you to go, if you think you must, but she isn't very sure she could talk about it calmly. It's up to you to tell your sister, and the others."

Morgan spent some time trying to decide whether he should tell Nella first and then Lisette, talk to Lisette alone or to them both, and finally, when the date they had set was only three days away, blurted it out at the dinner table and turned red when his brothers gaped in astonishment, Nella sat bolt upright, and Lisette stared at him disbelievingly. Zack looked embarrassed, apparently expecting to be blamed for it, and there was a brief silence until Lisette cried, "Morgan, you can't leave just when the weather is getting nice!"

That made even Lisette laugh, and the three younger boys began to question them eagerly, for it seemed the finest adventure any of them had ever had. But Lisette refused to talk to Morgan or Zack until the morning they left, when Morgan found her in the kitchen, crying, and put his arms about her, as Nella quickly left the room, ignoring the pleading look he gave her over Lisette's head.

"I don't want to go away and remember you crying, Lisette. I'll be back in a little while, I promise you—please—"

"A little while, you say, Morgan. But a little while may turn into a long while and, anyway, you know this is the end of everything. We'll never never never again be the same." But she let him hold her and stroke her hair until Zack Fletcher appeared in the doorway, scowling self-consciously and gesturing to Morgan.

"Lisette," he said humbly.

Lisette whirled around. "It's your fault, Zack Fletcher! Why couldn't you go away by yourself and leave him here with us?"

"You handle her, Zack," and Morgan went looking for Nella.

He found her outdoors, where the younger boys were running about excitedly, examining the horses and equipment. The afternoon before, at her cabin, she had seemed so well resigned that he had been a little offended, and now he asked her softly, "You won't be unhappy?"

"Of course I will."

"It won't be more than two or three months."

"That's not very long, is it?" She smiled and gave a light shrug.

The others had gathered and he began to say good-bye, playful with his envious brothers, sober and respectful with Matt and Pete, apologetic with his mother, who whispered, "I know, Morgan. Don't say anything more." And then Lisette appeared, still arguing with Zack.

"When there's so much gold around here, why must you go looking for it somewhere else?"

"Because the gold around here don't happen to be ours," Zack told her seriously. He made three formal bows and backed away, then turned and leaped onto his horse with a bound. Morgan kissed Lisette, stepped quickly past Nella, and as they started down the hillside Lisette was wildly waving her handkerchief. But when they had turned the corner, still followed by Douglas and Robert and Jonathan, trotting gaily beside them, she ran into her bedroom and cried almost all the morning, refusing consolation from either Marietta or Nella.

Late in the day, when she had been wandering about the house, sighing and trailing her fingers over the furniture, she became unexpectedly bright. "Maybe they'll come back tonight and surprise us. They might only have been joking."

Nella, seated beside the baby's cradle, gave her a skeptical smile but said nothing, and Marietta looked at her tenderly, shaking her head. "They won't, darling. They weren't joking."

"I just don't understand it."

"That's because you can only think of Morgan as your brother. You don't think of him as a man."

"He isn't really a man yet."

"What we want, as women," said Marietta reflectively, "is to keep things together, keep them as they are, at almost any cost. But what they want—is something very different." Both girls were watching her with questioning intensity. "What they want is to test themselves."

"Is that all?" asked Lisette scornfully.

"That's a great deal, and it takes up their whole lives, more than we would like to think."

Nella went out of the room and Lisette watched her go, then whispered to Marietta, "He just walked off with only a kind of a funny bow —and I was so sure he wanted to marry her."

Lisette was still unreconciled to Morgan's absence when, a few days later, Rick Allen arrived and claimed his sister, took her back to keep house for him. He rapped at the door and Lisette opened it, to find a bearded young man she did not recognize, standing with his hands on his hips. "Beg pardon, miss. I'm Rick Allen, Nella's brother. I was told she's been here while I was off prospecting. Where is she?" Nella appeared behind Lisette. "Oh, there you are."

"Why, Rick," she murmured. "You're back."

"That's right. Get your duds, you're coming home." Marietta moved between them and they looked uncertainly at one another for a moment. "Much obliged, Mrs. Devlin, for looking after her. I'll be glad to settle her board bill with you—"

"Oh, please don't say that. We all love Nella. We had her with us because we wanted her."

"You left her alone all winter," Lisette told him accusingly. "Why must you have her back now? She's become a member of our family."

"She's my sister and I'm her legal guardian and I need somebody to keep house for me. She's it. Come on, Nella."

"She'll come later," Lisette said, trying to frighten him with her dignity. "She has to pack."

"She'll come right now, miss."

"Please don't argue with him." And, just as quickly as Nella had come to live with them, she had packed her clothes, climbed up behind her brother and ridden away, waving to Lisette and Marietta.

"Come back early in the morning," Lisette called.

"I will, I promise."

Rick had no explanations to make about where he had been or why he had returned, but he was full of tales of his exploits and he rattled them off glibly. "I'm tough," he assured her. "Any guy that fools with me has a big surprise waiting for him. When I shoot I aim at the head, and I can fire five loads in three seconds." He snapped his fingers, one, two, three. "Hell won't be no treat to me."

Nella watched him with despairing amusement. "Oh, Rick. Stop bragging."

"There've been plenty of changes since you saw me last, you can bet on that. I'm a man with the bark on, a man from the ground up—and there's no son of a bitch in this camp who don't know it when I get on the prowl. I'm not afraid of any man alive—and they know it." Nella began to laugh, and at that Rick stamped his foot. "Shut up, Nella, show some respect when I'm talking to you."

"But it sounds so funny, Rick. It doesn't sound like you at all."

"There's some fellows lying around the mountains ate up by mountain lions with their eyes pecked out by crows who thought Rick Allen was somebody they could take a chance on, and that's the God's truth."

Nella cringed and folded her arms, bending down to put her head in her lap. "Rick, don't say such things. I can't stand it."

"Maybe I used to be a scared kid once, but no more. I'm not scared of anything, not one bloody thing, man or beast, in all these mountains." He made a wide, swinging gesture.

"You're going to get into trouble if you go around talking this way. You know it only causes fights."

"Fights are what I live for. Fights are my meat, and the bloodier the better," and Rick was out the door while Nella sat, her eyes closed, murmuring to herself and rocking back and forth. For this, she knew, was where Rick had been heading ever since they had come to the mountains, growing tougher and meaner and louder until finally, once too often, he would challenge the wrong man. And it happened before very long.

She was asleep late one night when there was a commotion outside, the door was thrown open, and Abel Hawker shouted at her. "Get a light there, for Christ's sake. Your brother's been hurt."

Nella fumbled about to light the lamp, and found Rick being supported between Abel Hawker and another young man. Both of them were drunk, and Rick was either drunk or unconscious. They laid him on the bunk and Rick moaned, turning his head from side to side, while Nella knelt beside him, opening his coat to find a spreading red stain on his shirt.

"What are you waiting for?" she asked Hawker. "He needs a doctor."

"There's one on the way." But Hawker shook his head warningly.

"How did it happen? Was he fighting?"

Abel Hawker was unsteady on his feet and supported himself by leaning against the bunk, but his face was serious. "Self-defense. Rick and another guy got to quarreling over a poker hand. Troy didn't want him there so we brought him up here—and by God, it wasn't easy."

"A poker hand," Nella repeated, as if there must be a better reason for her brother to die.

"He's got it," the other man mumbled. "Take off his boots."

Hawker knelt down, but Nella pushed him away. "Don't you dare touch him," she whispered fiercely. "Suppose he can hear you." She took Rick's hand and held it to her face, stroking it, while he moved uneasily and began to mumble. "You're not going to die, Rick, the doctor will be here soon."

"Go ahead," Rick told them. "Man can't die with his boots on. That you, Nella?" Nella bent down and put her forehead against his, helplessly sobbing. "They've scooped me." He drew in a long, slow breath. "I'm played out."

Nella remained for several minutes with her head pressed against his, crying, until at last Abel Hawker laid his hand upon Rick's chest. "He's gone up."

She drew back slowly, stroking Rick's hair. "He's dead?"

"He's dead," Abel Hawker said, and his voice had become almost tender. "And he died nice."

VIII

It was Joshua Ching's habit to waken at six o'clock and review the plans he had made the night before, sorting through them in orderly precision, reconsidering each in turn and, when the day's program satisfied him, to dress very quickly and leave without having spoken to his wife, Susan, who was either asleep or pretending to be, or seeing his son or daughter or Susan's sister, Ceda. The ritual was so well established that any of them would have been as surprised as Joshua if one morning Susan had opened her eyes and spoken to him or Suky had encountered her father dashing out the door; but the possibility seemed so extraordinary that it never happened.

Once he had left the apartment, Joshua knew, there would be brisk activity, for he had made arrangements to prevent them, now that they were living in a hotel without the distractions of housekeeping to occupy the women, from loitering through the day. Steven, who was fourteen, would leave for school almost as energetically as his father set out. Suky had graduated the year before, but she had responsibilities to a variety of private tutors who would arrive in scheduled relays, so that after elocution lessons and French lessons, piano practice and ballroom dancing, she would have less time than most young girls for gossiping with her friends and worrying about her health.

Suky made no objection, and never had, to her father's supervision, and from the time she had been a very little girl had seemed instinctively to perceive that these accomplishments would last her a lifetime and she could not do them too well. He found much satisfaction in her docility and obedience—although her mother had remarked that for all Suky's willingness to please, she was in reality not so flexible as an iron fence—but he approved even more Suky's composure and serenity, which made all her achievements seem so natural and inevitable a part of her beauty.

He had not been equally successful in providing his wife and sister-in-law with duties to replace those they had lost when they had moved into the hotel two years earlier, and their days were passed in activities about which he knew, it sometimes seemed, both nothing at all and a great deal too much.

They called upon the wives of his business associates, set aside one day a week to receive calls, had their dresses fitted and refitted, and engaged each other in endless conversation, which puzzled him all the more since Ceda had lived with them during most of the nineteen years of their marriage. Recently they had been able to add two new subjects to their repertoire—the ball which was being given in December in the hope that Suky's future husband, whoever he was to be, would make his appearance, and from the ball they proceeded inevitably to the wedding itself, planned, apparently, in every detail but that of the groom. And they always talked as if Suky had only to be put on display and then, at her leisure, choose among a variety of suitors, all of them young, handsome, rich, educated, and passionately in love with Suky—and perhaps Suky believed it herself.

"What you will not remember, Susan," he had told her more than once, "is that such men, if they exist at all in this town, are either married, or looking for the best bargain they can make."

"Are you saying, Joshua, that Suky may have some difficulties in getting married?" Susan turned upon him with her look of cool reproach, for Suky and Steven, Joshua knew, were regarded by his wife very much as master strokes dealt by one diplomat to another.

"I'm saying what you know well enough yourself, that the kind of husband we want for Suky is not easy to find and, if he is found, his price won't be low. I only hope to be able to meet it."

"You underestimate Suky."

Ceda objected more loyally to these remarks than Susan did, for Suky had been her favorite niece almost from the day she was born, and Suky's triumphs were equally Ceda's. When Suky was three years old, strangers had stopped them on the street to look at her more closely, and Ceda's pride battened on the attention. As Suky began to grow up, she did not grow too fast, or become awkward, or suffer fits of self-consciousness which made her shy, and, by the time she was ten, she had looked like a miniature woman, and had behaved like one, too.

Ceda had dreamed, some years ago, that she saw Suky as a great lady, hung about with pearls and diamonds, wearing the most magnificent gown there had ever been, and with a small crown on her head. Neither Suky nor anyone else had been very much surprised by the dream, for she had carried that air almost from the moment

she began to walk; and it was a family tradition, which had become
entrenched after she had predicted the crash of 1857, that Ceda's
dreams came true.

Evidently it had not occurred to Ceda or Susan, or even to Suky,
that if Joshua had not worked with such perseverance as to have acquired at last nearly half a million dollars—although he had not let
Susan suspect it might be so much—Suky, beautiful as she was,
would have fallen in love with a young man who had nothing to offer
her but the kind of hopes Joshua had once had himself, and none of
them would now be expecting a brilliant marriage as her natural
right. But Joshua's ambitions kept nimbly ahead of his accomplishments, the success he had had so far he was beginning to despise as
unworthy of him, and he was very much concerned about the name
his grandchildren would bear.

During the past two or three years Joshua had spent much time
considering how he might solve this problem, and had his private list
of suitable husbands, though he had made no mention of this to Susan or Ceda, and Suky of course knew nothing about it. For it was
the quality of Joshua's mind, as Susan had tactlessly observed, that
once he set upon a given problem he worried and twisted and mauled
it, but never laid it aside or let it cool or turned his back on it until it
was solved. Ever since Suky's seventeenth birthday, in fact, two
months ago, it was Suky's debut and Suky's marriage which preoccupied him more hours a day than his own work did.

He had consulted the same private detective agency which advised him about men he did business with, and was now in possession of reports upon the character, habits, associations, mistakes in
judgment, financial condition, secrets, and vices of his list which
would have astonished any one of them. It had also served the useful, though disheartening, purpose of eliminating several prospects.
By August, when the ball was only four months away and seemed to
be advancing upon them at an alarming pace, Joshua had sifted the
list and resifted it, becoming steadily more critical and more cautious, until he was satisfied with no one but Philip Van Zandt, whom
he did not know.

Joshua had followed the practice, ever since he had arrived in
New York with his brothers Aaron and Samuel, twenty-two years ago,
of learning what he could of the weaknesses of any man he meant to
cultivate, and it was Philip Van Zandt's weakness to speculate recklessly in the market, with almost no capital. The Van Zandt family
was an old and honorable one, exactly to Joshua's taste, but it was
also very large and had little enough left but its name and seclusive-
ness. Philip, apparently, was the only one among them who had
strayed outside the conservative Dutch environment and begun to
participate in the city's fashionable life, and Joshua supposed he
must be looking for just such a marriage as he himself had in mind.

Not long ago Van Zandt had acquired a seat on the Stock Exchange
and made himself noticed by his dashing way of doing business, as

if a mystery which had not been unraveled by older and more experienced men would give way readily enough to his urgent tactics; but then Philip was only twenty-one years old, too young for a husband, perhaps, but Joshua thought a very good age for a son-in-law.

For Joshua had no wish to marry Suky to a man who would control her, whether through love or some other power, nor did he want a son-in-law who would be troublesome to him, and Philip Van Zandt, a member of the nation's aristocracy, if it had one, seemed all the more desirable because he was inexperienced, he had no money, and he was young enough to be overawed by Suky's beauty.

"You must never," Joshua had told Suky several times these past few years, "forget what your appearance means to other people, because if you do there will be someone at hand to take advantage of you. Your life won't be easier for you, looking the way you do, but it can be much better, if you make no mistakes in how you use it."

"You're talking to the poor child as if she has a weapon, not a gift," Susan had objected.

"She has both. A gift that is a weapon. And she will be much more successful if she uses it as a weapon and doesn't dissipate it, which is what most people do with their gifts. You understand me, Suky?"

"Yes, Papa. Of course."

He had other advice to give her, and had laid down for Suky and Steven—but more particularly for Suky—a system of commandments, repeating them so often they must by now have been incorporated into her blood and bones.

He did not urge her to look for what most women did, happiness and love, but taught her that these were petty ambitions, and the actual needs and ends of a dignified life were something quite different. "Let other women concern themselves with whether or not they are happy. So long as they wonder about it, they never will be. The great thing in life, Suky, in small affairs and large ones, is to be infallible. Make no mistakes, and when you do, never admit them. Let other people admit their errors if they like, and be charitable when they do, but never admit your own, and you'll discover that by not admitting it—it has ceased to be a mistake."

Whenever he talked to her in this way, Suky looked at him with her face rapt and contemplative, and only murmured from time to time, "Yes, Papa." She had always pronounced Papa and Mama with the accent on the last syllable, a ruse which had forced Susan to accept it, even though she would have preferred to be called something else.

And Joshua had sometimes thought Suky might have understood him if he had never discussed these principles, for she seemed to know them as well as he did. Indeed, all during her childhood he had had the impression that Suky was observing the world about her to discover where she was and what were the best means of imposing her terms upon it. "Plan whatever you intend to do," he told her, "and never begin a course of action without knowing where it will

end." But then, she never had, and when the other children had run
about excitedly, playing games and climbing trees, sometimes
breaking bones, Suky had only contemplated their folly with aloof
amusement, but had nevertheless contrived to establish herself as
their sovereign.

And now she was quiet and graceful, a little taller than most
women, with a slender, flowing figure and the small waist which
came of wearing a corset to bed every night for the past several
years. Her hands were long and her fingers finely shaped, very much
like his own, Joshua thought. Her voice was soft, she spoke rather
slowly, and there was a tenderness of tone which was more alluring
than she seemed to suspect. But it was by her face and blond hair
that Suky created her greatest effects, and people fell to studying her
as abstractedly as if she were a picture of a woman, while her blue
eyes gazed back at them imperturbably and she smiled very slightly,
accepting the compliment of their interest without humility.

Suky loved not only her own beauty, but whatever might contribute to it, and Joshua had often heard her mother and aunt asking
Suky's advice about clothes and furniture, hair styles and jewelry,
for her taste seemed to be finished and perfected, as if she had been
studying herself seriously for years to know what belonged to her
and what did not, as surely as a woman much older might know it.

Joshua's favorite theory, the cornerstone of his own life and, he
hoped, of Suky's, was his theory of the natural aristocracy, to which
all the Chings belonged, and he had, of necessity, been obliged to in-
clude the Devlins, as well.

This natural aristocracy was composed of those who were handsome to look at, whose minds were quick to perceive their advantages, and whose consciences were supple enough to make the most
of all such advantages, and it was these natural aristocrats who entered into the older, fixed institution and served to keep it a fresh
and growing plant. If Suky believed this as devoutly as he did, and
she seemed to, then neither Philip Van Zandt nor any other accred-
ited aristocrat would be able to intimidate her, and once Joshua had
discharged his responsibility of finding a husband who would take
her into that world, he confidently expected to enjoy her great triumphs as Ceda had enjoyed her small, early victories.

He therefore went hurrying out of their apartment early each
morning, his plans for the day well fixed in his mind and with flexibility enough to accommodate the surprises and opportunities of
Wall Street. His first stop was the barber shop, where he lay luxuri-
ously back and put some finishing touches to his schemes, for he
preferred them to be complex and was convinced that a simple plan
was, by definition, an unworkable one. A few minutes later, his
carefully shaped blond beard now fragrant and brushed, his skin
healthily glowing, he walked briskly into the dining room, nodding
to men he knew but did not at that moment wish to speak to, and

while he ate a large breakfast and drank several cups of coffee, read the three morning papers.

He left the dining room at seven-thirty and found his carriage at the door, gave directions to the driver, Huggens, and set out for the other end of town, once again making good use of the hour it took to reach his office and, for the most part, quite unaware of the city's racket and confusion. Now and then he glanced out but paid no attention to what he saw, and found it difficult to remember that twenty-five years ago it had seemed to him monstrous and threatening.

But that Joshua Ching, whom he now thought of more as a young nephew than his own earlier self, had been seventeen years old and, with his brothers, paying the city a visit during a college holiday. All three of them had returned—Samuel, who was one year older than Joshua, and Aaron, who was younger—after graduation; and the city had long since come to seem as familiar as the small town in northern New York where they had grown up in a family which was comfortably prosperous, owning farms and newspapers, and where Joshua had spent his summers at work on one of those farms, a circumstance to which he attributed his robust health and the physical strength he believed made him better suited to the alarms and excitements of a broker's life than most other men he knew.

In those first years after their arrival in New York he, and Samuel and Aaron, had worked twelve or fourteen hours a day as office boys for a brokerage firm, and when he was twenty-two Joshua had borrowed three thousand dollars and bought a seat on the Exchange, convinced that the stock market was not only congenial to his temperament but the right sort of business for a natural aristocrat.

There were a few difficulties associated with those years which Joshua, as he advised Suky, preferred not to admit, and since he never had, they troubled him no longer but were accepted as a part of his necessary education. Samuel had drawn upon some funds available to him as a commission merchant, and Joshua, in an operation to depress a group of stocks, had made nearly one hundred thousand dollars so easily that he went directly into another pool to depress a railroad and there lost his own profit, and his brother's, as well. After that, Joshua had decided that one of them should be a lawyer if they were to work efficiently together, and the choice had fallen upon Aaron.

For some time Joshua had attempted no more speculations but applied himself to learning the peculiarities of the market. At his next venture he had succeeded modestly, and just before his thirtieth birthday, which he had set as a crucial date in his life, Joshua and Samuel had established the firm of Ching and Ching.

He was still, however, trying to locate the one infallible clue to impressive wealth; but he believed himself to be nearer to it than ever before, and expected that momentarily his eye would catch sight of it, wherever it lay hidden. He knew the city well and had a large acquaintance, for he never lost a man who might one day be useful to him, and he had acquired the distinction of being known by his friends and enemies as a smart trader, with a small loyal following of men who believed in him because his advice had helped them to make money. He had another following of those who detested him and said that Joshua Ching was not so honorable as the devil himself, and that if any man was fool enough to listen to his blandishments, his persuasive logic and mesmerizing invocations, he could expect to be stripped bare and picked clean.

Whatever his enemies said about him, however, made very little difference when Joshua began to outline his plans, drawing them carefully and patiently and leading his listener from incredulity to skepticism and finally to admiration and acquiescence. This was an art, as Joshua saw it, which few men understood so well as he, and he was aware that his appearance was a part of his authority, for he was straight-backed and lean, immaculately shining, and his manner had more of austerity and condescension than charm, which was a quality he thought suitable only to actors or women, or whoever else must rely upon the pleasure of others.

For the past ten or twelve years, Joshua had been cultivating the favor of a man named Brooks, who could give him no points on the market and had nothing to invest, but who had used his position as sexton of one of the city's fashionable churches to make himself an arbiter of balls, receptions, and funerals, none of which could hope to succeed without him. If a man, grown suddenly rich, became ambitious to give a great ball and was either ignorant of Brooks or could not persuade him to manage it, he must expect a shattering fiasco. But Joshua Ching and his family had attended his church regularly from the day Joshua had heard of Brooks, and now when he went to him with a sealed envelope and a proposal for the ball, Brooks began to discuss it with serious enthusiasm.

"How many do you plan to entertain, sir?"

"What do you suggest?"

"Between four and five hundred, I would think. People love a crush, and would rather have their clothes torn to ribbons than stand about a half-empty ballroom." Brooks looked, with his red face and squat body, like the kind of man he kept out of the houses where he stood guard, but he was the only man in New York who could make people accept invitations they might otherwise refuse, he knew where to find numbers of young men who could be dressed in black coats and white cravats and passed off as the sons of good families, and he had an assortment of foreigners with titles. "And now," said Brooks, "we must decide where it's to be held. People have begun to like innovations—I suggest Delmonico's."

Joshua, who felt at a disadvantage because he had no ballroom of his own, made a deprecatory grimace. "Shoddy?"

"Not at all, sir, only a little unusual. These entertainments have been getting bigger and bigger ever since the beginning of the War, and they will get still bigger. No private house in the city can hold such crowds. There will always be a few carpers, diehards, but those people are passing out of fashion, you may take my word for it. And the decorations?"

"The city is full of peculiar effects nowadays. Hostesses wearing lighted gas chandeliers on their heads, footmen in gold and silver livery. We don't want anything like that."

"Certainly not, and it would not be permitted at any entertainment of mine." Brooks remained outside during the entertainment, took the invitations and scrutinized them carefully and, when it was over, saw the guests into their carriages or into one of his own fleet, but the entertainment was his, nevertheless.

"My daughter suggests white lattices and white roses, candles, and a great deal of greenery."

"Very pretty, yes, I like that."

Joshua took a folded paper from his pocket and passed it to Brooks with the sealed envelope. Brooks put the envelope into a drawer and glanced at the list, studying it and drumming his knuckles as he whispered a few of the names to himself.

"You may think of others I've overlooked."

"Leave everything to me, Mr. Ching. Don't trouble yourself any further."

They shook hands and Joshua left in high spirits, for once Brooks had agreed to do the job everything essential had been attended to, and the bills to be paid—even the ball itself—might be considered secondary.

The carriage continued on toward the lower end of the city, bumping along over the paving blocks with Joshua hanging to the tug-strap and reading articles he had not finished at breakfast. They passed along Broadway—a street of five- or six-story brownstone buildings, their windows filled with displays of silver and jewelry, bolts of satins and brocades—where a few hours later elaborately dressed women would be parading their dogs. Flags whipped out in the windy, sunless morning, signaling from every building, and the sky showed a tangle of telegraph wires. Farther downtown the traffic increased, and they were caught from time to time in the moiling jams where carriages and street-trams drawn by bony horses, hand carts and pedestrians, found themselves stuck together amid shouts of rage and shrill cries, threats and occasional fist fights, until all at once it opened again and the traffic surged forward at that pace which bewildered and terrified newcomers. Those who lived there long enough became as indifferent to it as Joshua, or grew to enjoy it as a necessary condition of the city itself, and when they went to other towns, less noisy and confused, less crowded and hurried, less angry, they felt a sense of loss at being cheated of their palliative excitements.

Far down Broadway Joshua got out again and made a dash into a narrow building, very dark inside and with a musty smell he had come to associate with the firm of Spinnage and Achroyd itself, so that he had sometimes amused himself by wondering if it was perhaps the very smell of secrecy and furtiveness. He hurried up to the second floor, imagining as usual that the veiled woman he passed had seemed to recognize him, and walked into a large room where several men and two women, also heavily veiled, sat on benches against the wall.

A door opened and a head appeared briefly; then it closed again. Bells could be heard in distant rooms and a voice whispered hoarsely through a speaking-tube into the ear of a man who sat at the desk. On one wall a blackboard was marked with twenty numbers, one for each detective, and opposite several of these numbers was chalked the word *Out.* Whether or not this atmosphere of desperate suspicion was a necessary part of managing a detective agency Joshua did not know, but during all the years he had gone there it had never changed and, he sometimes thought, even the clients might be exactly the same: jealous husbands; jealous wives; businessmen like himself.

The door opened again, Spinnage peered at him and crooked his finger, and Joshua entered his private office. Here, in a small room, stiflingly hot and dimly lighted, Spinnage greeted him sourly and they sat down to face each other across a desk where an ugly cat lay like a paperweight upon the firm's documents, moving them about with its restless tail. The cat had been there for as long as Joshua had been a client, but neither Joshua nor the cat had ever recognized the other's existence. Spinnage, pursing his lips, ruffled through a sheaf of papers, squinted at one page and another, and passed them to Joshua.

"Lord Giles Haldane, as you see, is no lord at all but an ordinary Englishman."

Spinnage waved one hand, as if these discoveries were no worse than he had expected and Joshua, reading carefully and quickly, nodded and tossed the papers down. "So much the better." Spinnage raised his eyebrows, disappointed that the news had not been disturbing, and sorted through another file. Joshua sat back, smiling and considering what a good joke it was on his friend Amos Cottrell that his daughter was being courted by a bogus nobleman. "And Mr. Van Zandt?"

"Mr. Van Zandt is very difficult. Of course, sir, your instructions were to shadow him only on Thursdays and Sundays, between five P.M. and three A.M." Spinnage grimaced, handing Joshua a few pages which described Philip Van Zandt's recent travels about the city. Joshua was interested in the habits of his future son-in-law, if he should become that, and more interested yet in how much money he had, how he spent it, and whether or not he was likely to get engaged. But Spinnage and Achroyd charged ten dollars a day for one of their detectives, as well as his expenses, and it seemed they must eat well, drink often, and take hacks in pursuit of their quarry; and the appetite for private information, Joshua had found, had a tendency to increase as the information increased, until a man might find himself spending large sums for it.

"Miss Stuart?"

Spinnage pointed to one of the pages. "As you see, sir, they meet quite often." He nodded sagely. "Three months now, a very good record for Mr. Van Zandt. The lady must be charming."

"Charming," Joshua agreed. "But impertinent."

Two or three weeks earlier Joshua had sent Miss Stuart, who danced in the opera ballet, a large basket of white camellias with a note telling her how much he admired her and asked if he might call. He had signed his name Marvin S. Bradshaw and Miss Stuart had replied: "Dear Mr. Bradshaw: How nice of you. But I am not what you think. Sorry. Allegra Stuart. P.S. Some of the girls are, but not I."

Spinnage had pondered this note, squinting his eyes as he searched for inspiration. "Try some French candied fruit. Ballet dancers are mad for it. Some of our clients have had great success with it." But Miss Stuart had not even thanked him for that present.

"Perhaps you'd like to know a little more of her background, sir?" Spinnage asked now.

"What background can a ballet dancer have? Do you imagine I'm interested in knowing when she goes from her boarding house to rehearsal? Remember the other girl—whatever her name was." Joshua had made the acquaintance of another dancer Philip had been interested in, but after he had paid her five hundred dollars for whatever she could tell him, Philip had lost interest. "No, I'll wait a little with Allegra Stuart, or Mademoiselle Alexandrine, as she calls herself on the program."

Spinnage shrugged again, philosophical about the loss of an assignment, for he had known Mr. Ching for many years and had no doubt of a new opportunity soon. Joshua gave him another name to investigate, a city politician, and stood up. He had never offered to shake hands with Spinnage and treated him with no more ceremony than he did a shopkeeper, but Spinnage followed him to the door and, as he opened it, said, "If you really want to see the girl, why not try a more impressive present?"

Joshua looked amused. "What is an impressive present in the opinion of a ballet dancer?"

Spinnage considered this, frowning at the cat. "A chinchilla muff?" He described one approximately a foot square. "Just large enough to show her you mean business."

Joshua smiled, and walked out quickly, down the stairs and into his carriage, relieved to have that interview over for the week with no awkward encounters. But he did not expect to make any new efforts to meet Miss Stuart unless she proved more durable than Van Zandt's other recent infatuations.

Presently the carriage approached the area surrounding Wall Street and Joshua now put aside the newspapers, sat up alertly and leaned forward, looking out the windows with intent interest and feeling himself grow as keen and eager as if he were about to engage another man in a physical test of strength where great prizes were at stake. It was not quite ten o'clock and the narrow streets, with their close-set buildings, many of them mansions of the city's earlier years remodeled into offices, were crowded with brokers, dressed, like Joshua, in high silk hats and frock coats and striped trousers, or very young men wearing derby hats and docky coats with gold chains across their vests who strutted pugnaciously, for they were the clerks with powers of attorney, and visitors to the Street were surprised to discover it was these twenty-year-old ruffians who attended to the buying and selling, while more substantial men remained out of sight in the offices.

Now, just before the Trinity chimes struck ten, that familiar music which acted on them as a gong to a prize fighter, there were groups gathered on the sidewalks, men shouting and gesticulating, other cabals of two or three talking quietly and earnestly, and Joshua studied each acquaintance he passed, observing what expression he wore today, and took note of who his companions were. He had discovered long ago that in Wall Street there was no such thing as an unimportant observation, and he had the faculty, trained now to concert pitch, of taking in more details with a glance than other men usually got from a careful survey. By the time he entered his office, later than usual this morning, he was ready to tell Samuel that they would buy one stock and sell another, ask one client to cover his losses and urge another to increase his, and although he had never been able to explain how he reached these conclusions, they were, more often than not, accurate.

Ching and Ching was in the building on New Street where they had first opened for business, and like most successful brokerage houses their rooms were small and bare, with a few battered chairs but no armchair, and nothing which might indicate prosperity but the presence of six busy clerks on high stools and a procession of callers which sometimes became numerous enough to be backed down three flights of stairs and into the street. Joshua was suspicious of the few ornate offices which had appeared in the city, and he enjoyed this atmosphere of sober attention to business with nothing so sybaritic as curtains or a carpet to distract him.

They had four rooms, with the six clerks perched in a row behind a railing in the first, a room to one side where their clients were taken to be consoled or congratulated, and separate offices for Joshua and Samuel with windows looking into the next building where there were offices so much like their own it sometimes created the uncanny sense that they were observing themselves in a distant mirror.

It had never occurred to Joshua to move to large offices or improve the furnishings of these and, in fact, he found it reassuring to sit every day at the same red-felt-covered desk and know he had sat there on bad days and good days, despondent and jubilant, and that Ching and Ching was twelve years old, in a town where a firm of brokers was thought lucky to endure for five years.

The city was unstable nowadays, filled with millionaires who appeared and then disappeared, rose to the top and sank to the bottom with such suddenness that almost before they had been seen they were gone from view again. But Ching and Ching had survived the crash of 1857 and the losses of the first year of the War. When stocks had risen forty percent in the second year, Joshua had made three hundred thousand dollars in one day of trading, and during the last two years he had acquired such a variety of interests and investments that not even Samuel knew all of them, for Joshua expected his brothers to prosper with himself, but not to the same degree.

These conditions, so new and astounding, filled moralists with chagrin. How did it happen that a man was a bootblack one day and riding in his own barouche the next, with a diamond stickpin the size of a robin's egg in his shirt front? And yet that same man, after a year or two, vanished, barouche, stickpin, and Fifth Avenue mansion, as if he had been no more than an apparition from the beginning.

Joshua had observed these casualties of the nation's growth with more interest than dismay, and from them had discovered a law of economics congenial to his temperament which, under favorable circumstances, would one day make his fortune: Many men supposed the way to get rich was to construct a business, but in fact the greater profit came from knocking apart a business another man had built, reorganizing it, copiously watering its stock, and selling it at a profit. Joshua had used this technique successfully on one small railroad and one small factory, but he had not yet been able to catch hold of a company large enough to satisfy him, and only within the past several months had he begun to believe the opportunity was marching toward him in the person of Milton De Groot.

Many years ago, when Joshua was new to the city and to Wall Street, he had been accustomed to eat his lunch of crackers and cheese in De Groot's liquor shop on Exchange Street, and while the two young men discussed ways and means of making money, De Groot was adulterating the bottles and whimsically confiding to Joshua, "They don't give a damn what it tastes like, what people want is fuddle." For a long while Joshua had had no hopes of De Groot at all, had thought him stupid and inept, a man who would be selling bad liquor to young clerks and serving them crackers and cheese long after he himself had moved on to more exclusive surroundings.

But De Groot had chanced to learn that the federal tax on spirits was about to be increased, had bought every barrel of whisky he could find and sold it at so great a profit he now owned De Groot

Distilleries, and Joshua was glad to have him as a client, even though De Groot had four or five other brokers and shuttled from office to office throughout the day. De Groot was now forty-six years old, a tall man with a ponderous body who wore a piratical black beard, plastered his hair so tight to his head it looked like a coat of paint, and smelt so rank that Joshua threw open the windows whenever they had a conference. Joshua's keen and fastidious nose had caused him much uneasiness, but never more than when he was with De Groot.

Several times a week, and more frequently during the past few months, Joshua and De Groot sat in Joshua's private office, side by side on the dilapidated sofa, smoking cigars, while De Groot sipped absinthe, and they discussed the alarms and scandals of the street, for there was a new peculation or swindle every day of the year, and Joshua patiently listened to all that De Groot had to say, convinced that one day he would hear a phrase of talismanic significance. Or they had lunch together at the downtown Delmonico's, near the Stock Exchange, and amused themselves by reminiscing while they ate cold pickled oysters, filet of beef with mushrooms, and half a grouse each, drank carefully selected wines and observed the other brokers in the room, an assembly of well-dressed and prosperous men.

De Groot picked up much gossip and Joshua heard it all with interest. "Learn everything you can about everyone you know," he had advised Suky. "No information is ever useless. But always remember, people are willing to talk to someone who seems sympathetic, but not curious." De Groot, apparently, found Joshua Ching to be more sympathetic than curious, and had been slowly drawn into telling him most of what he knew. That fellow in the corner, the one with the mutton-chop whiskers, was badly overextended. You could expect to hear of his collapse any day now.

"But what the hell, aren't we all overextended?" De Groot asked. "There's no such thing as a cautious businessman nowadays. That went out with beaver hats."

"Take care, Milton. I don't like to hear you talk that way about a company I'm interested in."

But, as Joshua knew, De Groot had begun to believe as other men did that there were better ways of making money than the careful management of his business, and it was Joshua's hope that in time, and with some help from himself, De Groot would have his company in such condition that a judge could be found to appoint a receiver and, since Joshua owned several thousand shares, what better receiver might there be? He was still, however, looking for a judge who could be bought at a reasonable price, even though he had begun to suspect there were no longer any bargains in judges.

De Groot would not hear these warnings, grinned confidently and nodded, giving Joshua the same whimsical leer he had long ago, and assured him there was no sounder company in America than De

Groot Distilleries, sound as his own belly, and he gave it a powerful thump. "The one business you can count on winter and summer, in good times and bad. The one business that will grow with the country, no matter what happens."

Joshua thought this might be true, although he would have been as interested in any other company whose owner showed tendencies to dip into its funds for his own use, to pay no dividends, and to sell short whenever he believed he could turn a quick profit. Other men were treating their companies with the same contemptuous familiarity, but De Groot was under the disadvantage of letting a friend who owned a large share of it make the discovery, although not all of Joshua's information had come from De Groot. Most of it he had learned by paying De Groot's messenger to let him read his instructions before he delivered them, and the boy often came into Joshua's office, sidled up to him, and held out his palm suggestively. Joshua expected to own De Groot Distilleries one day, but perhaps not quite soon enough.

For Suky and Susan and Ceda were planning their ball gowns one day and, it seemed, having them fitted the next. Brooks reported that he expected a success, one of the winter's spectacular entertainments, and late in October Joshua decided to try once more to see Allegra Stuart.

He left Spinnage and Achroyd's one morning and started on downtown, decided this girl must by now have heard something he needed to know—for he was sure Philip Van Zandt was not old enough to have learned his own firm principle of never confiding in a mistress —and told Huggens to drive him to Stewart's. He found such a chinchilla muff as Spinnage had described and set out for Bleecker Street, not very well pleased with himself, but remembering that his first and most important business was to see his daughter suitably married.

Twenty years ago Bleecker Street had been a fashionable neighborhood of large houses for families of means, but it had become a curiously anomalous district which few who were not New Yorkers ever saw. The families had moved away and their brownstones been turned into boarding houses for ballet girls and minor actresses, and women who waited for the occasional visits of their husbands.

The carriage stopped in front of a four-story brownstone which had a wistaria vine trained over its doorway, and Joshua peered upward with disapproval and suspicion before he stepped out, carrying the package and his cane, went up the steps with the quick tread he used when he approached a situation he did not like, and pulled the bell. In a few moments it was answered by a woman who looked at him with even more suspicion than his own face showed.

The woman stared at him until Joshua thought of turning on his heel and walking off with Miss Stuart's chinchilla muff, but then she opened the door and he entered an old-fashioned parlor, its draperies drawn to keep the light from fading the upholstery and, perhaps, to make the worn surfaces of carpets and sofas less noticeable, and was instantly offended by odors of badly cooked food and seeping gas and faulty plumbing.

"I'm Mrs. Gosnell, the landlady, and I hope you understand, Mr. Bradshaw, that my girls are respectable. Some of you gentlemen seem to imagine—"

"I imagine nothing of the kind, Mrs. Gosnell," Joshua told her sharply, but reminded himself that whoever travels into unfamiliar territory will inevitably be subjected to the vagaries of the natives. "May I see Miss Stuart now, if you please?"

Mrs. Gosnell sniffed, as if to tell him no gentleman in a silk hat could intimidate her, but swept out of the room and left him to contemplate the horrid possibility of being one day forced to live in a boarding house himself. He was not, apparently, so well convinced of his destiny as he believed, and the dark house, with its suggestion of miscellaneous and unrelated lives, made him think of a saying he had heard: New York is the best place in the world to take the conceit out of a man.

Mrs. Gosnell reappeared. "She'll see you. She says you're the ballet manager. Are you?"

Joshua nodded brusquely, wishing that Miss Stuart had thought of some better reason for his visit, and followed Mrs. Gosnell into a hallway darker than the parlor and up a flight of stairs which creaked at every step and where he could feel that the rises had begun to slant unevenly. At the first landing they passed an open doorway and Joshua, hearing a giggle, turned his head to see a pretty girl in a purple dress and hat gazing at him with a knowing smile, while two other girls, both wearing white wrappers and with their hair undone, looked at him over the tops of magazines held before their faces. He and Mrs. Gosnell continued their slow progress to the second floor and then on to the third.

"Those were three of my girls. I have thirteen of them here this fall, all beautiful dancers and all decent girls, Mr. Bradshaw."

"I hope so, Mrs. Gosnell," Joshua assured her solemnly, "inasmuch as I am the ballet manager."

On the third floor she led him down a hallway toward the front of the house and knocked lightly at the last door, putting her head to it with an inadvertent gesture which served to warn Joshua that Mrs. Gosnell was in the habit of listening to her boarders' conversation. "Here we are, dear, shall we come in?"

After a moment a voice called, "Open the door, Mrs. Gosnell, I can't move and you know it!"

The quality of the voice surprised him, for it was low-pitched and compelling, a skillfully used woman's voice, when he had been expecting to hear a juvenile squeak. He had very little idea what Allegra Stuart—or Mlle. Alexandrine—looked like, for although he had once asked an usher to point her out, on that vast stage behind the calcium lights he had gotten only an impression of someone not very tall with smoothly shaped arms and legs which contrasted pleasantly with the knotted ones of the other dancers, shining blond hair, and round breasts, all the information he had needed at the moment.

Mrs. Gosnell opened the door into a large room holding an inconvenient amount of furniture, and a black poodle met him, barking, a parrot squawked warningly, and across the room stood Allegra Stuart with her back to them, wearing a white wrapper like those of the other girls, her bare feet spread wide, and her head in a washbowl.

"Come in, Mr. Bradshaw, I'm dyeing my hair but I'll be with you in a moment. You can close the door, Mrs. Gosnell, he'll only be fifteen minutes." Mrs. Gosnell hesitated and Joshua turned, put a bill in her hand, and Mrs. Gosnell left reluctantly. As the door closed Miss Stuart, now pouring water over her head from a pitcher and working a lather into her hair, muttered savagely, "The old bat. Starves us and expects us to eat our morals. Sit down, Mr. Bradshaw."

Joshua, who had begun to resent being called Mr. Bradshaw, moved across the room with the dog at his heels and sat on the edge of the chair, the muff on one knee with his hat over it, and glanced around with amused curiosity. The windows which extended across the front of the house were open even though the day was brisk, the shades were raised high and the draperies drawn aside, and after the murk of the rest of the house, the room seemed filled with unusual light.

There was an old-fashioned square piano, many photographs of famous actors and actresses, and a full-length mirror before which, he supposed, she practiced her ballet stances. Two dresses hung on hooks, along with a crinoline and several petticoats. An imitation Paisley shawl covered the sofa, where apparently she slept since there was no bed; an opened trunk overflowed with pink ballet tights and other costumes; library books were piled on the floor, and the dressing table was littered with bottles and jars and boxes enough to supply make-up for the entire company. The dog sat at Joshua's feet, gazing at him with alert interest, but the parrot moved back and forth along his perch, hung his head and kept a wary eye on the bottom of his cage, and seemed concentrated upon his grievances.

Miss Stuart was rinsing her hair and now asked, in her rich, commanding voice, "What brought you here, Mr. Bradshaw?"

"Bad company, by God!" screeched the parrot, and fell to grumbling again.

Allegra Stuart burst into laughter, a rush of sound which astonished him, beautiful to hear and, he thought, a little disconcerting, for it seemed to belong not so much to that girl energetically scrubbing her hair and wringing it out and scrubbing it again, as to certain merry and malicious deities he had overheard from time to time, laughing at his folly when he was least inclined to laugh himself. The next moment she got soap in her eye and began to swear, very softly, lapsing into an Irish brogue, and, as Joshua reflected that Miss Stuart was not at all what he had been expecting, she snatched up a towel, swept it around her head and twisted it tight, and turned to face him.

"All right, Mr. Bradshaw, now tell me what you want."

Joshua was in the habit of taking at least one close, sharp look at everyone he met, even though he might afterward scarcely glance at them, and now he studied Miss Stuart with frank interest. She was small, but held herself straight and her head haughtily erect. Her eyes were light brown and remarkably lustrous, her eyebrows slightly arched, and her mouth showed an expression which so curiously mingled joy and melancholy, giving her a look at once sadly pensive and so humorsome that no man, having seen it once, was likely ever to forget it; and Joshua had not.

"I know you," he told her. "You're the girl who jumped naked out of the papier-mâché pie at that petroleum banquet last spring." She had seemed saucy, and Joshua expected this might subdue her.

"Oh, not naked at all! Didn't I have on a black velvet G-string?" She smiled with impudent malice, and Joshua perceived it would not be easy to confuse this self-possessed young woman. The dog put his paws on the chinchilla muff and she gave him a nudge with her toe, settling him onto his haunches again. "That's Selah," she explained, and threw Joshua a capricious little smile, by which he understood her to say: You're a fool if you think you can do business with me that way. Better try something else.

"How old are you?"

"Seventeen, last month."

"My God, you're no older than my daughter. Do you make such appearances often?"

"Only when I can't pay the rent, or my teacher. After all, Mr. Bradshaw, the Academy is closed half the year, and doesn't run most of the time when it's opened."

"And have you other ways of supplementing your income, Miss Stuart?" Joshua asked her severely, for whatever he had known before he arrived about her meetings with Philip Van Zandt, it now seemed to him a criminal indecency that this young girl should be dancing at banquets with her clothes off and meeting a man in the afternoons, even if it was his hoped-for son-in-law. He felt, in fact, that she should be lectured and set back on the right path before it was too late.

But at this she gave an impatient sigh and walked away, crossing the room toward the mirror and watching her bare feet as she went. She stood before the mirror, and as she unwound the towel and began to comb her hair she told him, "If you're hoping I'll have an affair with you, I won't. I don't have time for such frivolity. It's only the little dancers, *les canailles,* who can afford to be dissipated." The parrot gave a protesting squawk, ill-timed, Joshua thought, and she said, "That's Consuelo, he hates strangers. My consolation, I expected him to be." She went to Consuelo and shook the comb at him.

"That was before I knew what kind of disposition the damn bird had."

Allegra Stuart, Joshua decided, did not belong in any category of fallen women he had previously known, but still, he thought there must be some way to put her at a disadvantage before they began to discuss business. "You've refused me, Miss Stuart, before I've asked you."

She swirled around. "Then what is that?" She pointed the comb at the package on his knee.

"I've brought you a gift, but not because I want you to sleep with me." She came forward, Joshua stood up and presented it to her ceremoniously, and as she tore the package open, Selah pranced excitedly and the parrot repeated his greeting.

"A muskrat muff!" She put it to her face, then brushed the fur across her lips, and held out one hand to him forgivingly. "I know it's chinchilla. Thank you, Mr. Bradshaw. And there really are no strings attached?" She turned it over, looking at it from all sides to discover the strings, and Joshua sat down again, pleased he had brought it whether she proved useful to him or not. "You can smoke if you want to. Selah hates it, but it doesn't bother me." She tossed the muff into the trunk and went on untangling her hair.

Joshua lighted a cigar, frowning at the dog, who barked at him once and went to the other side of the room. "You're a very clever young lady. You dance, you dye your own hair, you play the piano, apparently, and I suppose you sing. You're ambitious."

She turned from the mirror and looked at him seriously. "No, I don't sing. Singing would spoil my voice, and when I come to play Juliet I would never be able to do what I want to." She came forward again. "Remember what happened to Charlotte Cushman," she said warningly.

"When you come to play Juliet, Miss Stuart?" Joshua inquired, and was expecting her to pounce at him now from another direction, but her face was curiously tender and rueful, and she might have been asking him not to laugh at her.

"I'm going to be an actress, Mr. Bradshaw, a great Shakespearean actress. Oh, yes," she added. "I don't expect you to believe me, but it's true."

"Miss Stuart, please tell me—what were you doing jumping out of that pie? Was it you?"

"Yes, it was." She sighed. "To tell you the truth, I didn't think there'd be anyone there I knew. I make thirty dollars a week, when I'm working, and I pay my elocution teacher ten dollars for every lesson. There he is, this one right here." She pointed to a photograph, and then walked over and stood gazing at it with reverential intentness. "He was a very great Shylock," she said softly, more to herself than to Joshua. "Of course, I never saw him, that was a long time ago and he's an old man now, but he's shown me, when we're working together."

Joshua considered this new Allegra Stuart, asking himself how much of this passion was youth and how much belonged to her in the sense that his own ambitions belonged to him. "And so you expect to escape out of this ugliness into dignity?"

"Well, Mr. Bradshaw, must you hate me for that?" She spoke so wistfully that Joshua was ashamed.

"I admire you for it very much, but I must say you've surprised me."

She swept her hand about to survey the room. "This looks ugly to you, but it's the biggest room in the house and the most expensive, and I don't think it's ugly at all. There's everything here I need." She tipped her head to one side, smiling in a way which puzzled Joshua and made him rather uneasy. "You don't know much about the city, Mr. Bradshaw, do you? Have you ever seen Five Points?"

Joshua gave a deprecating wave, meant to tell her he had been too busy to go sightseeing in the slums.

"Can you imagine what it might be like to live in a cellar no bigger than this room, with twenty other people—not to mention the rats—with no furniture but cots, and no walls but some rags strung up here and there? Or a tenement that's so dark a man can be murdered or a little girl raped in the middle of the day and no one could ever guess who did it? Nearly half a million people live down there, more than half the city's population." Her voice was low and as she talked she watched him steadily, until Joshua, convinced she accused him of these crimes against the people of Five Points, felt his face burn and his flesh crawl. "The outhouses don't have doors, because who the hell cares? Poor people can't afford modesty. The pigs are the street-cleaners, but even so the garbage piles up in hills, and in the spring, when the snow melts, the streets turn into rivers of filth."

"I assure you, Miss Stuart, I pity the poor as much as anyone."

She threw back her head, giving once more that disconcerting laugh, put her forefinger to her lips as if they had a secret, and slyly inquired, "Made you cringe a little, didn't I?" She turned, crossing the room, and murmuring, "But it's all true, it's all true. That's the way it is down there."

Joshua was telling himself that even if he could no longer expect to make her feel at a disadvantage for her appearance at the petroleum banquet, a small sum would surely seem large to her, when she turned again, showing him a smile so ironic that he warned himself he must take care with her, for she seemed preternaturally able and self-contained, with that wisdom the slum children acquired which seemed to make them keepers of secrets the rest of the world had never guessed. "We haven't much more time, Mr. Bradshaw. Any minute now, Mrs. Gosnell will be rapping at the door. Why did you come here? I mean, for what reason besides delivering my chinchilla muff?"

"I came here to talk to you about something I think will interest you very much."

"And what is that? Money?" As she held forth one hand with the fingers suggestively curled, her expression assumed the mixture of guile and servility he had seen on the faces of child beggars who crept up out of Five Points to accost ladies and gentlemen in the politer parts of town, and Joshua decided that whether or not she was an actress, she was certainly an uncanny mimic. The expression disappeared, as if it had been only a trick she was showing him, and she knelt in a chair, sitting on her heels with her body held straight and her hands on her knees, enveloped by the wrapper as if she wore a tent. "Well, then, if that's what you're here for, how much money are you talking about, Mr. Ching?"

IX

Joshua had become so accustomed to hearing himself called Mr. Bradshaw that it was an instant before he realized she had used his name and, when he did, he sat up alertly. "I beg your pardon?"

"I wouldn't have let you come here if I hadn't known who you were."

"You know who I am?"

"You're Joshua Ching. Aren't you?"

Joshua drew in a deep breath and smiled, glad to be rid of that nonentity, Marvin S. Bradshaw, for whom he had not even troubled to provide a vocation and who could be taken for a ballet manager or any other kind of flunkey. "I am," he admitted, and felt all at once that Joshua Ching was a man of significance and renown, more, even, than he had guessed, since he could be recognized by ballet dancers and, very likely, by many others who were too discreet to let him know it. But that gave him a new suspicion. "You say you knew who I was before you let me come here? How did you find out?"

"I asked the boy who brought the flowers and candied fruit what you looked like, and he told me." But Joshua did not ask how his messenger had described him, for he had never believed a sensible man would want to know what he looked like to his inferiors. "I gave the description to a friend and the friend said, 'Why, that's nobody but Joshua Ching himself; what's the son of a bitch want with you?'" She laughed merrily. "Of course, it was wise for a man of your quality paying a call to Bleecker Street to take some precautions. We're quite desperate down here, you've seen that." His surprise must have pleased her, for now she told him in a confiding voice, "My name's not Allegra Stuart, either."

Joshua settled back, puffed at his cigar, and watched her with amusement. "I didn't think it was."

"Shall I tell you my real name? Betty Mulligan." She pinched her nose between her thumb and forefinger. "Sure, and it's Betty Mulligan's me name. Can you imagine that for a Shakespearean actress? But Allegra Stuart—that's another matter, isn't it?"

She seemed so pleased with Allegra Stuart, after Betty Mulligan, that Joshua felt obliged to ask, "Where did it come from?"

"I made it up. They have all kinds of books at the Mission School, you know," she said, quite as if he must have visited the Mission School to see for himself how the charitable ladies were educating the slum children. "I thought of Deirdre for awhile, but she brought misfortune, and so I chose Allegra instead because it means happiness and gaiety, a much better omen, don't you agree?"

"I hope it proves a true one," said Joshua, gravely gallant, not only because it was his habit to approach all business dealings with soft deference toward his opponent, but also because he found this child, as she seemed to him, both entertaining and touching. "And where did you find Stuart?"

"Mrs. Stuart was the lady who took me out of the Mission School to live with her. I lived in her house from the time I was nine until I was thirteen. I ran away then, but that wasn't her fault. She was kind to me and wanted me to learn a useful occupation so I could support myself honorably." She gave him a droll smile. "But in the meanwhile, she'd taken me to the opera, and to some plays, and I had no taste for an honorable occupation, after that. Of course, if she'd left me in Five Points, I guess by this time I'd be a ragpicker or a whore, or maybe a waitress in a concert-saloon." Her face acquired a look of subtle bitterness, neither hard nor accusatory, but disquietinᵍ, all the same. "There isn't much choice for us immigrants in your big country—all the equal opportunities seem to have been passed out sometime before we got here. How do you suppose that happened?" She put out her hand to scratch Selah's head as he presented it in her lap. "I was three when we landed in New York, my brother and sister were a little older. Before very long my father disappeared—I can't say I blame him—and then, in another year or two, my mother died. She threw herself out of a window, and when they carried her up from the street she was dead." She had been talking with the same air of indifference and detachment she had shown when she described the slums, and she gave a light sigh. "My brother ran away from the Mission School. My sister died of smallpox." She glanced away, frowning a little.

"I'm sorry," Joshua said, for he hated to hear of misfortunes, and had a superstition that there was something contagious in them.

"So was I, for a long time. In fact, I was just god-damn mad. But I know something most people never learn." She looked at him again and her face became fiercely intent. "I know that it's a sin to waste yourself, no matter what you are. Oh, you may think it was a waste, jumping out of that pie, but that was only a little detour, not important." She gave a gesture, somewhat magical, apparently, for it made the papier-mâché pie equally unimportant to Joshua. "I've learned to find a meaning in everything that happens to me. Do you think that's because I have my own private fate, my own daemon, or is it only that I can find meaning where other people find nothing but confusion? Well, Mr. Ching—there you are."

"Miss Stuart," Joshua said seriously, "I congratulate you."

She went on scratching the dog's head, and watching him with her earlier whimsical smile. "That's my history. Of course, there's a great deal more of it to come." There was a rap and she sprang up, startling the dog, who followed her, barking, as she ran to open the door and went outside, where he heard her arguing in low tones with Mrs. Gosnell. She came back, softly laughing and shaking her head. "Five more minutes, Mr. Ching. I told her it was my fault, telling you my life story, and she understood that, because she loves to tell her own."

Joshua was less inclined than he had been when he had arrived—prepared to offer her one hundred dollars today and more whenever she managed to discover anything which interested him—to talk to her bluntly about Philip Van Zandt. Still, he was known among his friends and enemies for his tact, his circumlocutions which said what he meant but left his hearer baffled as to how it had been done, and no doubt he could find a way to state his business without offending her quite immoderate pride.

"I'm a businessman, Miss Stuart," Joshua said, modestly deprecating. "I'm a stockbroker, and I have other interests, as well—and a businessman sometimes needs information he can't come by, as you might say, directly. I need to know, for example, when a man plans to buy a stock or sell it, go long or short of the market, sometimes even when or if he intends to marry, since marriages nowadays, at least where money is involved, are also business arrangements." While he talked she strolled to the windows and stood with her back to him, concealing a scornful little smile he had seen begin, and as she stood buffing her nails the strong light showed how skillfully she had used whatever stuff she had been putting on her hair when he came in. "As it happens," Joshua continued, though not so confidently as he had expected, "I know that you're acquainted with a man I'm interested in just now."

"Philip Van Zandt," she said, but did not turn or glance around.

"You're very quick." Her tone had not been encouraging and he hoped to flatter her.

She glanced over her shoulder. "Who else could it be? I don't know any other gentlemen."

"Have I offended you?"

"Oh, by no means, Mr. Ching. Did Mr. Van Zandt tell you that he knows me?"

"Certainly not. I found it out by accident. Please don't ask me how. As it happens, I've never met him."

"Well, then, why does he interest you so much, and why do you come here to my home talking to me about money? Tell me quickly, before I decide I don't want to hear it."

"I think you'll want to hear it, whatever I have to say. I respect your ambitions and admire your determination but, after all, that can't help you very much if you go on indefinitely working in the ballet and jumping out of pies at men's banquets. What you need, if you expect to become an actress, is time to study and a little independence while you're doing it. How much does Van Zandt pay you?"

She threw the buffer across the room so violently that the dog leaped as if she had aimed it at him, stamped her bare foot and glared at Joshua, shouting, "He doesn't pay me a bloody dime! What do you take me for?"

Joshua, pleased that she was not so much in command of herself now, watched her with polite interest, and as she glowered, he soothingly inquired, "Are you in love with him? All right, then, is he in love with you?" She looked at him sullenly, but refused to answer, and finally Joshua said, "Would you be angry if I asked how long you've known him?"

At that she smiled rather slyly. "Since the Petroleum Banquet. Oh, I was a great success that night, let me tell you."

"Five months and a half. Then you know him quite well, don't you?"

"Well enough."

"Miss Stuart, please sit down and let me talk to you. I need a little information about this man, as I expect to do business with him before long, and I'll pay you very well for whatever you tell me."

She refused to sit down and continued to look petulant and resentful, which convinced Joshua that even though she needed the money she was brooding over this discovery of her great romance and hating him for having suggested that she turn a profit on it. Still, he thought, if she could not learn to be practical, her ambitions would be only absurd. Joshua did not believe in paying more than he had to, whether for a suit of clothes or a piece of information, but considered himself adept at judging the price he must pay eventually, whether he haggled over it or not. And Miss Stuart, who looked now like a hurt and sullen child as she stood beside the windows, glancing out from time to time and back again at him, taking up handfuls of fringe from the draperies and running them through her fingers, evidently believed it was more honorable to jump naked out of a pie than to sell him her knowledge of a man she probably thought she loved distractedly.

"I'm not asking you for anything which could be harmful to him, if that's what's troubling you. On the contrary, I'm interested in his welfare. It's not dishonest, Miss Stuart, and I don't think you need be ashamed of it, if you decide to do it."

"I don't agree that spying isn't dishonest, but it's true I might do it and not be ashamed. Anyway, how I feel about it doesn't concern

you, and why should it?" She came sauntering back, sat down opposite him, and clasped her hands around one knee. "How much will
you give me today?" Joshua reached into his pocket, as if to see what
small change he was carrying, and brought out several bills. She
shook her head. "No greenbacks, Mr. Ching. I'm not that simple."

"Will you take my check?"

"I'll take your check, but I won't talk to you until I've cashed it."

Joshua smiled, complimenting her on this feminine sagacity, and
went to a small table, covered with books and papers where, he noticed, she was writing advice to herself on the character of Juliet,
and made out a check for five hundred dollars which she examined,
blew upon, and waved back and forth a few times, and kept in her
hand as she walked with him to the door. "What kind of man is he?"

"The kind of man he seems to a woman can't have much to do
with how he would seem to a man, now can it, Mr. Ching?"

"I'm also interested in how he seems to a woman."

"Oh? Well, I'll tell you, Next time." She waved the check. "Day
after tomorrow."

Joshua held out his hand and, for a moment, thought she might
refuse to take it, for she looked at it as if wondering what it was
there for, and then shook it perfunctorily. "Someday," she told him
ominously, "it will no longer be necessary for me to live by my wits,
but only by my talents—and that is why I shake your hand. I need
your help as much as you need mine. Or I need it more, because I
have a better use for the future."

Joshua smiled tolerantly, gave her a bow, and walked out, slightly
puzzled and not at all sure Allegra Stuart would prove a valuable
agent to have. He hurried down the staircase, eager to be out of the
house which seemed to close about him again, and as he got into the
carriage, glanced up at her windows, expecting she might be watching, but she was not and he drove away, amused to find her impudence had not made him angry, though if she had been any older
and not so pretty, it might have. Still, any information was better
than none, and once she had drawn him a picture of Philip Van
Zandt it was his responsibility to find a use for it.

Two days later she met him wearing the same white wrapper, explaining that she must save the one good dress she owned, but now
she seemed reconciled to her bargain and as cheerful as if they were
two old maids gossiping over the tea table about a mutual friend. She
knelt beside him on the couch, sitting back on her heels with her
body very straight, as she had the first time, folded her arms, and
as she talked watched him steadily and smiled, so that he wondered
if she thought the joke was on him, after all.

"To begin with, he's very vain."

"All handsome young men are vain."

"He's arrogant—and he's snobbish."

Joshua smiled. "Surely that's natural enough in a Van Zandt."

"He's weak."

"Perhaps you're misjudging him."

"He's vindictive. And he's cruel."

"And yet you're in love with him?" Joshua smiled skeptically.

"What you're buying from me, Mr. Ching, is information about Philip Van Zandt, not about Allegra Stuart. But in spite of everything, he's so charming that every woman and a great many men are glad to forgive him. And he knows quite well what his name means to all the eager parents who want their daughters to glitter with something more than diamonds when they enter a ballroom." She nodded with mock solemnity. "And that's what you're really concerned about, isn't it? You said you had a daughter just my age."

"That doesn't make any difference to you, does it?"

She spread her hands in wonderment, got up quickly and went to the long mirror where she stood for a moment, trying on various expressions like so many hats, observing one thoughtfully and frowning at another as if to dismiss it from her future repertoire. All at once she turned to him with a look of such gentle wistfulness and trust that he was slightly alarmed. "That's my Juliet face, first act, third scene." She looked at herself again. "No. I haven't found it yet." She came strolling back, idle as a child kicking at rocks and concentrated on a private world. "He isn't going to marry me, after all, so what difference does it make who he marries? He hasn't any money, you know that." She raised one eyebrow and might have been wondering why this list of deficiencies was no discouragement. "But then, a son-in-law without money can't afford much independence, can he?"

"Why be rude, Miss Stuart?"

"I suppose I'm jealous. You take such good care of your daughter. Is she pretty?"

"She's an extraordinary beauty."

"Oh." She thought that over a moment, and then became briskly businesslike and again began talking about Philip. When he left she agreed she had not earned her fee, and said that when she made a discovery she thought might interest him she would send him a note.

Joshua felt they had become good friends, cronies who knew how to measure each other and the world without being too much dismayed by its absurdities, and asked, "You still refuse to tell me how you found out my name?"

"I still do, Mr. Ching."

The night of December the twenty-first was advancing upon them with what seemed to Joshua a remorseless speed. Ceda had been filled with apprehensions and prophetic dreams for several weeks, and she came into Susan's room on the morning of the ball while Susan was having her gown fitted once more, her maid Maxine arranging the skirt at the dressmaker's instructions while the dressmaker's two assistants knelt around the edge of its vast surface, pinning and draping and gathering. "Susan! My dream, oh, my dream!"

Ceda looked haggard, as if she had not slept at all, certainly not long enough to dream.

"What dream this time, Ceda?"

"I dreamed that the musicians' balcony collapsed and buried the most important guest there."

"Who was the guest?" demanded Susan, who had begun to show the strain and was sometimes sharp with her sister.

"That's what was so terrible about it. I don't know. But Susan, we mustn't tell Suky, nothing at all must be allowed to upset her."

"We won't, Ceda." Susan sounded more kindly now, a little ashamed of her bad temper. "Perhaps this dream will be the exception. After all, musicians' balconies don't collapse very often."

"Neither do nations," Ceda said gloomily. "But I dreamed it once and it happened."

The dream was hidden from Suky and from Joshua, too, and late on the day of the ball, while her mother and aunt were having their hair dressed, Suky slept soundly for more than two hours and woke up serene and refreshed, as if she had nothing more trying in store for her than their usual dinner in the hotel dining room. "The girl has nerves of iron," Susan said.

"She's sensible," Joshua corrected.

"Alarmingly sensible."

But he seemed no more disturbed than Suky, got dressed while the hairdresser was at work in Suky's room, and left with Steven. The women would come later, in the separate carriages he had hired because of their skirts, and Maxine would accompany them to make last-minute rearrangements.

Brooks was waiting with an air of firm confidence, assured him there were no failures where he was in charge, and Joshua went to inspect the ballroom which had been disguised in green foliage wired with hundreds of white roses, globe lights rather than the chandeliers which threw unflattering shadows onto the prettiest faces, softly wavering candles, and tall mirrors which were to reflect all that happened and give them an ephemeral portrait of this first great venture for the Ching family, and Joshua found himself so well pleased he was neither resentful nor concerned over the money, nearly twelve thousand dollars, which would be spent tonight.

In the supper room there were epergnes filled with hothouse fruits, more candles, bottles of champagne ready to be chilled in relays as the guests grew thirstier; and when Joshua appeared, the waiters stood alertly at attention. At midnight they would bear out platters of hot oysters, cold boned turkeys and game pâtés, bonbons and trifles and, at Suky's suggestion, cups of hot soup after the French fashion, all of this destined for some of the city's most distinguished stomachs.

As he surveyed all he had provided, Joshua was taken with a keen sense of his benevolence and power, his miraculous ability to wave into existence men and women, food and flowers and music, for a

few hours and then out again, and in spite of a tightness in his chest
and throat and a tendency to flex his hands which he found it difficult to control, he was eager to have it begin; and even more eager
for it to end. He was, in fact, more interested in knowing what had
happened, how much success they had achieved, than he was in the
ball itself, a somewhat painful experience they must all endure so
that they might enjoy it later. All of them, at least, but Suky, who
plainly believed that tonight, for the first time, she would be where
she belonged.

Susan and Ceda arrived and greeted each other almost as if they
had expected never to meet again, and Joshua studied them carefully, finding they looked quite different from the way they did at
home, where they were taken as much for granted as the furniture,
the background before which he performed his role of husband and
father.

Susan was thirty-six years old, not a woman's best age in Joshua's
opinion, and she had the further disadvantage of being his wife,
someone he knew too well and who knew him too well and was not
always tactful about her knowledge; but tonight she might have
been a stranger, a handsome blond woman he would have been glad
to meet for the first time. Her hair was artfully arranged and so
much thicker that the hairdresser must have resorted to whatever
mysterious means they did for achieving such effects. Her dress,
which had cost him fifteen hundred dollars, was made of a light
green silk which drifted as she moved, and it had been designed for
the discreet display of Susan's best features, her smooth shoulders
and full breasts, the family characteristics she shared with Ceda
and Marietta, though not with Suky. Joshua gave her a kiss of approval and Susan smiled, as if to say she had meant to surprise him
and was glad to know she had, and Joshua, thinking that this woman
would never learn the power of flattery, turned to compliment Ceda.

Ceda's gown was neither so expensive nor so impressive as Susan's, nor was it meant to be, for it was Ceda's role in life and chosen
by herself to experience her most important satisfactions through
others, although she had been a lovely young girl, as Joshua could
remember, and might have seemed a convincing beauty even now
but for her habit of looking uncertainly into every face, as if she was
eternally asking some question no one had ever answered. But he had
accepted her long ago as his responsibility, for the Devlin house had
early been monopolized by children, and now he praised her with his
most solemn and reassuring manner and Ceda smiled at him gratefully, as Susan would never have done. But then, Susan was not dependent on his good will and expected him to know it.

The musicians, hidden behind ferns and trellises on their balcony,
were tuning their instruments, Steven walked about with a grim
face, and Joshua, seeing that it was nearly eleven, began to inquire
for Suky.

"She's in the dressing room with Maxine."

"Did anything go wrong?"

"Not a thing," Susan assured him.

"Shall I see if she's all right?" Ceda asked, and was starting away when Joshua stopped her.

"Never mind, Ceda. She'll be here. We don't want to make her nervous."

There was a flurry at the door, the three of them gave slight starts, and then laughed with relief to see his brothers with their wives, and Samuel's two grown children. The women fell to examining one another's dresses and hair, and Susan, Joshua noticed, assumed her manner of supercilious politeness with her sisters-in-law, Harriet and Amelia, both of whom she had always believed pitied her because her husband was such a busy man, out early in the morning and back late at night and in his office every Sunday, so that she must be enjoying this chance to show them at last what had kept him so well occupied all these years.

Almost immediately there came bearing down upon them another small army of men in black coats and white cravats and women in teetering skirts, tossing clusters of curls, festoons of diamonds, pearls, green and blue and yellow gems of all shapes and sizes, and Joshua recognized four brokers he knew only slightly— not the first arrivals he would have chosen, but nevertheless he was glad to have them there, for he had been wondering if the ballroom would remain empty all night long, the musicians play only for them, and the boned turkeys be fed to the waiters. Caught up by a terror he had not anticipated, Joshua now heard himself talking, saw the men bowing, the women inclining their heads and smiling, and then the avalanche passed on into the room and he was himself again.

"Well," he said to Susan. "It's begun." He had been left rather weak and shaken, though, as if he had just gotten up from a bad sickness.

Suky was there—she must have followed the first guests into the room, passing him while he was in a fit of remorse at having subjected them to this merciless ceremony where, at great cost, a man could expose himself and his family to worse indignities and crueler judgments than they might suffer any other way. Fashionable society, he had warned them, was composed nowadays of people who had money and were willing to spend it, something quite new, since no one had been rich enough for such elaborate entertainments before the War, and even a natural aristocrat was not recognized at first glimpse but must cultivate patience and humility. But the sight of Suky reassured him.

She was talking to her cousins, both reliable servitors, disciplined gently by her these many past years, and she seemed better prepared than any of them to perform her role for the evening: the charming young daughter who would see that her friends had partners before she danced herself, and who would show as much consideration for girls she had never seen as for those she knew, most of them rela-

tives or former schoolmates. She had prepared herself for this evening, in fact, as well as he ever prepared to depress a stock, and with
the same serious dedication he saw Allegra Stuart giving to her own
ambitions, and it was Suky's reputation in the family that she never
miscalculated. Joshua had often paid her the compliment of saying
that she was like him, but whether one imitated the other or not it
would have been impossible for either to say.

He observed her with critical admiration as she stood a little distance away, smiling slightly as she talked. Suky never grimaced as
many young girls did when they meant to be fascinating, but knew
how to control her eyes and mouth and the muscles of her face so
that she gave an invariable impression of sweetness and tranquillity.
Joshua suspected this meant that her nature was cold, her emotions
as well regulated as her face, and he hoped that it did, for she would
then be in no danger from a woman's greatest enemy—her own impulsiveness.

She stood very straight, but easily, her neck seeming to rise out of
her shoulders to an unnatural length which gave her head the appearance of having been placed with precision by a great sculptor.
Her white tulle gown showed her shoulders, and her hair was done
up for the first time, drawn high off her neck with two twining curls
which fell to her waist, another subterfuge of the hairdresser's, he
supposed, but found it very becoming. Maxine had made a wreath of
white roses which circled the crown of her head, and she wore no
jewelry but the bracelet of small pearls he had given her for her seventeenth birthday. And for a moment Joshua, though he detested
sentimentality, grew a little nostalgic, thinking of that early beauty
of Susan's, which had been perfected and refined in her daughter.

As if she sensed that he was looking at her, Suky turned, opening
her eyes wide to ask what he thought of her, and when he smiled,
nodding, she gave him back a quick, tender smile, meant to thank
him for this night in which she saw no hazards at all; and after that
there was such a parade of black-and-white men and brilliant
women, many of whom he had never seen before, that he presently
discovered the room had become crowded and his worst fears were
over.

And when the dancing began and Joshua began to sniff success in
their eagerness and gaiety, just as he could sniff the premonition of
good days and evil ones in Wall Street, he told himself that Brooks
deserved no credit, for they would have been there tonight—with
Brooks or without him. He remained near the door with Susan and
Ceda and Steven, who stood like a boy at military school, bowing
with a smart, bobbing movement and saying sir and madame in
tones which sounded as if he might be reproving them for being present at such a frivolous function. Steven looked like his father and
even had many of his characteristics, for he was never ingratiating
and seemed to have decided long ago that he would go through life
with seriousness of purpose and strict attention to business.

The waltzes began, that German dance of death against which young girls were warned as dangerous to their health and sanity, and all at once the floor was crowded with skirts spinning across it like so many escaped balloons, whirling around and around as if the girls made no efforts of their own but were propelled by their partners' advancing force, keeping them in steady retreat. Along the walls the older women, in heavy silk dresses, sat fanning themselves and talking. The procession moved on by Joshua, more brightly dressed women, their coiffures shooting forth plumes and twined with flowers, their husbands giving him glances of slight surprise and congratulation, and, catching the general intoxication, they hurried to join the dancers.

Suky caught Joshua's eye, imploring him to let her dance, and he spoke to Steven. "Dance with your sister, Steven."

Steven had been told to expect this summons and stalked over to her promptly, made her a bow and led her off with surprising authority, sweeping her around in wide loops and driving her forward with steady determination while Suky sped away in swift, sure steps, gazing over his shoulder with such yearning wistfulness that heads turned to follow their passage. She looked into their faces as she went by, but not, as they might have supposed, because they interested her, rather because she wanted to know what they thought of her. And in this, Joshua believed, she was entirely right, for she could make no more important discovery tonight than to measure her beauty's effectiveness; and luckily she knew it without having been told.

The supper room opened at twelve o'clock and Joshua, relieved of his duties at the door, danced once with Susan, once with Ceda, and began to reconnoiter, pausing here and there to talk to men he knew and watching warily for Philip Van Zandt.

"Your daughter is charming," several women told him, and it pleased Joshua that the younger ones said it too eagerly, and the older women with something of Ceda's own admiration for her niece.

"The most beautiful face I have seen in America," Lord Giles Haldane pronounced, and Joshua observed him carefully, for he intended to talk to him a little later, when his lordship had drunk a few glasses of champagne.

"Isn't that what I've told you?" Amos Cottrell's daughter asked him triumphantly. Jemima, who was Suky's age, had been her best friend for several years, adored her as Suky intended her to, and trusted her with idolatrous faith, perhaps because she guessed Suky would not want to steal Giles Haldane from her, and now Jemima took him to meet Suky and left Joshua and Amos Cottrell together.

"Everyone says it's brilliant. I congratulate you, old fellow."

Amos Cottrell was a little man, quite round, with a bald, round head and plump cheeks which seemed always to have just been scraped clean by a razor. He had come to New York at about the same time Joshua had, with neither money nor very much education, had borrowed a newspaper, found an advertisement for light porter to a stockbroker, and had risen very quickly to clerk and head clerk and partner. By the time the War began he was, like Joshua, comfortably established and alert to other opportunities, and his firm had been given an Army contract for pork. Two years later he was worth three million dollars, but he soon lost two million by bulling gold against the Union victories, and Joshua had often promised Amos that one day they would find the very opportunity they were both looking for.

They talked casually, watching the dancers, and Joshua listened with thoughtful seriousness while Amos described his latest coups, and at last he inquired, "Amos, would you like to join a small group I'm forming to take over a company that's letting itself drift into bad condition?"

"Of course I would, Joshua. But how much will it cost—and what is the company?"

"Now, Amos, that's a little too much to ask all at once, isn't it? Suppose we talk about it later?" He started away and Amos grew alarmed he might have lost the chance.

"When can we talk? I'm a little short of cash just now."

"We don't need any yet. This isn't one of those quick operations, Amos. It will take time and patience, but I think you'll be glad to have a share in it."

"Much obliged, Joshua, I want to hear about it."

"You will, Amos, when it's a little riper. The fruit's still green, by no means palatable yet."

He raised his eyebrows, Amos smiled understandingly, and Joshua circled about the floor, found Suky in the supper room with Lord Haldane and invited her to dance with him, murmuring as he followed her, "Discourage that young man before your friend gets upset. I don't want any difficulties between you and Jemina Cottrell."

They joined a quadrille, more to Joshua's taste than a galloping waltz which obliged a man to treat any woman as if he were chasing her in some desperate rout, and as they advanced toward each other and retreated, they talked in undertones.

"It's beautiful, Papa, I'm so happy. I've never been so happy before."

"Don't make yourself too agreeable, you don't need to."

"Papa?"

"And don't dance too often, you know it's bad taste."

"But, Papa, I haven't."

At that moment Joshua caught sight of Philip Van Zandt, who had just come in, late enough, Joshua thought, since it was almost two o'clock, with a man he recognized but had met only twice, William Talbot, and Talbot's wife. Joshua kept an eye on Philip as the three made their way about the room, stopping now and then as they met friends and, he thought, looking condescendingly amused, as if they had come in some spirit of idle mischief, and this infuriated him so that he had trouble managing his face. Suky made another remark or two, realized he was not listening, and they finished the dance without speaking again, whereupon Joshua took firm hold of her arm and led her to where Ceda was talking to Mrs. Cottrell.

"Sit here, Suky, and rest."

He looked at her significantly, and before she could ask how long she must rest he was off in pursuit of Philip Van Zandt, but lost him again when Philip began to dance with a girl Joshua had never seen before and who looked as if she must have slipped through Brooks' cordon. Her dress was too low, her smile was too wide, and as Philip took hold of her she briefly closed her eyes. Joshua hovered about uneasily, hoping Van Zandt would not take a notion to leave with the girl before he had been intoduced to Suky and, when he encountered Giles Haldane, was in a bad humor.

"Beautiful party, sir, beautiful women, fine music—"

As he watched Philip, Joshua asked, "What was your name before you changed it to Haldane?"

Lord Haldane sucked in his breath and Joshua stared down at him severely, as if his lordship might be a boy he was reprimanding for having played naughty jokes on his elders. "I beg your pardon, sir?"

"Never mind, I have friends in England, some of them here tonight." Giles Haldane looked around the room with stricken eyes. "You're in no danger from me, young man. If you can get away with it, I'm willing to let you. You'll soon be engaged to Jemima Cottrell?"

"Why, sir, I haven't—"

"Her father and I are friends and, sometimes, business partners, did you know that? Keep your ears open, you may hear something interesting."

"But Mr. Cottrell doesn't discuss his business with me, sir."

"Aren't you a businessman? Don't you make investments on behalf of your family—and don't you ask Amos Cottrell for advice?"

"Not exactly, sir. The truth is, I haven't any money to invest."

"Of course you have," Joshua assured him. "I'm in my office every morning by nine." Joshua nodded and walked away, thinking that was one more small piece of business accomplished tonight, and the greatest schemes in the Street, after all, were put together out of very little pieces, one fitted neatly into another.

The dance was over and Joshua followed as Philip Van Zandt took the girl to some older woman, talked to them for a few moments, and, as he turned, nearly collided with Joshua. Both men stepped back, and introduced themselves.

"I'm sorry we're a little late, Mr. Ching. I came with the Talbots and they had to stop somewhere else first." Joshua did not like to hear there was a competitive entertainment in the city that night, although Brooks had mentioned it and he knew quite well that nowadays people liked to shuffle about, meeting one another perhaps two or three times in one evening, but he made a deprecating gesture and smiled with more intentional charm than was his habit.

"It's very kind of you to have come, I'm sure."

He looked carefully at Philip, and found it easy to attribute to him all the qualities Allegra Stuart had described. Philip did not look as young as he was, but to Joshua he nevertheless looked almost indecently youthful. He was not quite six feet tall and, although he was slender, had wide shoulders which, so Allegra said, he cultivated tediously with dumbbells and exercise bars. His face was handsome, lean and lightly tanned, and he wore a mustache, no doubt with the intention of making himself more impressive. His blue eyes sparkled with humor and health, he seemed pleased with himself in a naïve but certainly not innocent way, and Joshua could have found much fault with him if he had not been Philip Van Zandt.

"Have you met my daughter, Susan?"

"I haven't, sir, but I would like to."

Joshua led him to where he had left Suky with Ceda and Mrs. Cottrell and, as he made the introductions, was pleased to see that Philip seemed somewhat taken aback, as any man should be at first sight of Suky.

Philip apologized, very gallantly, for his late appearance, and asked Suky to dance with him. Joshua watched them approach the dance floor, telling himself at least that much had been accomplished, and when Suky's hand touched Philip's shoulder and they moved into the crowd, Joshua lost sight of them and made his way to where William Talbot and his wife stood talking to another couple.

William Talbot was one of the men whose friendship Joshua coveted, but he was not an easy man to woo and, indeed, had an arrogance which seemed more authentic than Joshua's own, for Talbot had inherited a good business and made it a better one, and his City Exchange Bank prospered through times of calamity and national success alike. He was about fifty years old, very tall and somewhat stooped, and with his large head and sharp blue eyes gave a picture of such strength and austerity that Joshua could imagine him transfigured in some future incarnation into a fierce and menacing bird, or perhaps a huge insect. As they talked, he looked at Joshua shrewdly but indifferently, a signal that nothing Joshua Ching had accomplished so far had made him yearn for his good will.

"Such a charming party, Mr. Ching," Mrs. Talbot told him, and Joshua noticed that as she studied the guests and the decorations she was looking for indications that these Chings—whoever they were— had given themselves away by one gaucherie or another, and Joshua instantly disliked her.

She was much younger than her husband and, Joshua knew, had married him several years after his first wife's death. Coral Talbot was called a beauty, one of those married belles who had lately become the fashion, and if Joshua had not been put on guard by her amused curiosity, he would have admired her himself, though she was unquestionably a difficult woman, pleased with herself and her position in the world and not at all prepared to tolerate rivals. She wore a gown of magenta silk, and there were diamonds fastened in her black hair and on her arms and around her neck and in her ears, worth, Joshua quickly calculated, about one hundred and fifty thousand dollars of William Talbot's money. "Are you new to New York, Mr. Ching?"

"Not by any means, Mrs. Talbot. My brothers and I came here almost twenty-five years ago from Troy, and my wife's family has lived in the city since 1814."

"Oh?" She glanced at her husband, as if to ask how it happened she had never heard of them.

"We've always lived very quietly."

"I see." She smiled a little. "But still, this is a very nice party."

Joshua looked at her soberly and was promising himself that one day he would find a way to be even with her, though not at the expense of his own interests. "Thank you, Mrs. Talbot."

The music ended and Suky approached them with Philip. Joshua took her hand, introduced her, and was gratified by Mrs. Talbot's expression as she examined Suky, who stood straight and still, gazing back at her with thoughtful interest.

"Your daughter," Mrs. Talbot repeated, raising her eyebrows. "How pretty you are, my dear—and so shy." She glanced from her husband to Philip. "I think we must go, isn't it terribly late?" They went off, leaving Suky and Joshua standing side by side and watching as they moved quickly through the room.

"She didn't like me, did she?"

"Perhaps not," Joshua said soothingly. "But you must be very agreeable if you ever see her again. You know who they are."

By three-thirty, although the dancing was still going on, the room was less crowded and Joshua found Milton De Groot hanging about the edge of the supper room and staring at the dancers as they whirled by. De Groot was a passionate admirer of beautiful women, or even moderately pretty ones, but he was intimidated by his own ungainliness, had never married, and was comfortable only with whores, for he imagined they would not dare laugh at him. Otherwise, Joshua had sometimes the uneasy suspicion De Groot might have asked to marry Suky, and to refuse him would have spoiled his own plans.

They stood looking into the ballroom without speaking until at last De Groot, who had been drinking most of the night, gave Joshua an aggrieved and challenging glance. "Some son of a bitch is out to get me, Joshua."

"What did you say, Milton?" Joshua leaned his head to one side, listening attentively.

"I said, some son of a bitch is out to get me. Somebody's after me, that's what I said."

"What makes you think so?"

"Think so, my ass, I know it. Petty stockholders going into court, five of the bastards by now, trying to start action against me."

"But what for?" Joshua asked indignantly.

"Inefficient management, so they say. No dividends. Challenging my god-damn charter, by Christ."

"These things happen all the time. Ignore them. They haven't upset you, Milton?"

De Groot rocked on his heels, looked into his empty glass, and glowered. "De Groot Distilleries," he mumbled. "By Christ, but they'll get a surprise." He turned to Joshua. "But who is it? Who's the crud who thinks he can get hold of De Groot Distilleries, now tell me that, will you, Joshua?"

"I wish I could, Milton. If I hear anything, I'll let you know, but I wouldn't worry about it, if I were you. Are you enjoying yourself?"

"Very much, Joshua, very very much."

By four-thirty the last guests were on their way out, the musicians were packing their instruments, the roses had wilted and the greenery shriveled, and the carpenters arrived to begin knocking apart the trellises and the musicians' balcony. And Susan and Ceda, with Joshua and Steven and Suky, stood clustered together in the middle of the empty floor and looked at one another, as if to ask where they were now, and what had happened.

"It was a great success," Ceda wailed, and began to cry.

"Oh, Ceda," protested Susan. "For heaven's sake, don't do that. Oh, if only they'd wait a little," she moaned, as the carpenters went on hammering, dragging down the roses and tossing them into heaps on the floor and over the chairs.

Suky whispered, "Papa, I'm a belle, am I not?"

Joshua smiled. "It's much too easy to be a belle."

But Suky seemed not to hear him and all at once, as Steven sat down and folded his arms and Ceda cried more and more loudly, Suky went waltzing alone over the floor, circling about the carpenters and the roses, moving down its entire length and sweeping back toward them with the same bewitched smile she had had all night long, until Susan pleaded, "Oh, Joshua, call her, I beg of you. I've never been so tired. Oh, please, can't we go home?"

X

The room Philip had taken on West Twenty-fourth Street was crowded with furniture and Allegra found that comforting, for the bareness of the tenements troubled her still, and each time she entered it she strolled about with a proprietary little smile, examining the carved grapes on the chair backs and touching them with her fingers, sat down in the settee which looked like two seashells placed back to back, and marveled over the carpet's pattern of tangled red roses.

Philip, however, had said to her, "Sooner or later, you know, you'll develop good taste in spite of yourself."

And since it was Philip Van Zandt who disparaged her taste, she believed him, for she accepted whatever he told her and never doubted that she loved him unreasonably. Indeed, for a few months she had been so awe-struck that Philip Van Zandt sent her notes and flowers and candies, and an imitation Paisley shawl—which looked real to her until one of the girls at Mrs. Gosnell's made fun of it, saying she hoped it had not cost her anything—that she was more concerned with pleasing him than with all her plans to become a Shakespearean actress. And these plans, when she confided them to him, not with the same confident bravado she had announced them to Joshua Ching, but almost timidly, he prophesied would come to nothing.

"You simply don't know what it means, Allegra. How many young girls do you think have the same idea?"

"But what do I care about them?" She was dismayed that he would not take her ambitions seriously, but ready to defend them.

He smiled at her tenderly and somewhat pityingly, and touched her chin. "I wish you well. I can give you only one bit of advice, if you're serious. Go to England."

"How in the name of God can I go to England? It's all I can do to get to the Academy, or here."

Philip laughed and kissed her and forgot what they were talking about, until several weeks later, when she came late from her elocution lesson to find him walking up and down, scowling and snapping his fingers, and when she told him what had delayed her, he said, "Americans only respect foreign actors. If you can't get this notion out of your head, then become a foreigner."

She thought about that until she was superstitiously convinced he had given her the clue she needed, for she absorbed whatever happened between them with devoted greed, and liked to pretend that she packed all those treasures into the catchall bag she carried back and forth to the Academy, so that when she returned to her room at Mrs. Gosnell's she could take them out and study them at the leisure they required. For surely whatever came to her from Philip Van Zandt, his advice or criticism, his smiles and caresses, his quick and forceful love-making, and the ready return of his appetite for it, held some magical properties for Betty Mulligan.

"Go to England," she told herself, next time she faced the mirror in her room. "Become a foreigner." She reflected on that for a moment. "What the hell, I am a foreigner! Well, let me think about it."

But how she would get there, or support herself when she did, even Philip had never explained, and she could not find the courage to ask him, for fear he would think she wanted money. "I'll take care of you," he had assured her at their first meeting, but never mentioned it again, and she was not quite sure what he had meant, anyway.

She supposed that any one named Van Zandt was too rich even to imagine that everyone else was not, and thought that one day he intended to surprise her with a very grand gift, perhaps a diamond necklace, like those she saw when she and the other ballet girls joined the street crowds after the performance, to watch the audience coming out. They murmured excitedly in one another's ears as the parade passed, selecting this necklace and that pair of earrings, this gown and that wrap, for their own use.

"That dress belongs on you, Allegra. You'd do a hell of a lot more for it than that old bitch does." And Allegra would generously give her friend the chinchilla cape worn by the woman whose face was too red and body too fat to do it justice.

They would look at one another and sigh, shrug their shoulders at the world's injustice, and run to get onto a horsecar which would take them back to Mrs. Gosnell's. Her friends knew nothing about Philip or her occasional appearances at men's banquets, and she explained Joshua Ching's calls by telling them he was a friend of her brother's, a story they smiled at tolerantly, saying she had no reason to be ashamed of being kept by such a fine-looking gentleman, and asked when she intended to leave them and move into her own house.

"You'll forget all about us then, won't you, Allegra? And when you pass us in your carriage, will you wave at us and smile, or just pretend not to see us, like that girl who left last year—what was her name?"

"I told you the truth, God damn it. He's a friend of my brother's, and he comes here to bring me money from my brother. My brother's an important man."

They laughed merrily at this, asking why her brother did not bring the money himself, and Allegra would dash upstairs to her room, lock the door and tell herself she had no time to waste with these little ballet dancers who could see nothing beyond their own sad and dismal lives. She refused to participate in their feuds, took no sides when they quarreled, and while they gossiped and sewed Allegra reminded herself that one day was as precious as another, remained alone with Selah and the irascible parrot, and occupied herself according to the advice of her elocution teacher, who had outlined a program of study which would have kept her busy even if there had been no rehearsals, no performances, and no meetings with Philip Van Zandt.

She had observed the life about her with attentive interest, and took it as a solemn warning. The other girls liked to imagine they would be rescued by one happy accident or another, saved at the very moment they were ready to perish of the city's multiple vexations, just when it seemed they could not endure another nine o'clock rehearsal in the dark theater while the leader of the ballet yelled and swore at them until they cried, could never again rush out at midnight to scramble home on an omnibus crowded with drunken and abusive men, and could not possibly eat another meal at Mrs. Gosnell's. But Allegra noticed that most of them, nevertheless, continued to do these things for as long as they were able.

And those who did escape fared no better. Some married poor young men and had to return to the Academy to help support their children. Others imagined they had a bright future as the mistress of a rich man, and made the adventure, but it never lasted long and the rich man had turned out to be stingy, after all. While a few considered that several rich men were better than one and gave up their jobs, only to reappear in a year or two or three, full of their troubles and cynicism.

Good luck, it seemed, was what they were waiting for with so much innocent faith that she pitied them, but not enough to give them her own discovery that good luck was not so prevalent as bad luck, and that it was at best a treacherous ally, with destructive possibilities of its own.

Her meeting with Mrs. Stuart at the Mission School was, she thought, the only good luck she had had so far, and even that, she suspected, had not been luck so much as a nine-year-old child's guileful recognition that this lady would help her if she could be persuaded that Betty Mulligan deserved help. It was Mrs. Stuart who had shown her it was comfortable to be clean, that her hair was prettier when she washed it, had taught her to eat at the table, a challenge so formidable she had fits of terror even now remembering the first Sunday dinner with Mrs. Stuart's grown children and visiting relatives, and had encouraged her to her to lose her brogue, a much easier achievement than the polite manners she had also been obliged to learn.

Allegra believed, in fact, that the happiest part of her life was over and that it had been spent at Mrs. Stuart's where, for five years, she had had a small, low-ceilinged room entirely her own which no one ever entered except Mrs. Stuart for her periodic inspections. There she had mimicked everything she saw on her excursions into the servants' quarters, or out into the streets where she watched the women passing in their carriages and studied the smiles they cultivated, finding in those smiles something more wonderful than she saw in their silk gowns and flowered hats, for in the tenements the women seldom smiled, though they sometimes grinned, but most often only stood in the doorways with a sullen glare, seeming to see nothing at all. She observed the way these cherished women walked, how they handled their skirts and draped their shawls, listened to their voices, and when she had gathered all she felt able to hold onto for that day, she returned to her room to perform to her mirror.

She might have remained with Mrs. Stuart much longer, for her only responsibility was to learn and she was given much praise for her cleverness, but one of the footmen, who was not much older than she, visited her, cajoled her into bed, and for fear of being caught by Mrs. Stuart she had run away. The footman had no doubt been discharged, betrayed by some other servant, and she occasionally remembered him with tender amusement, that awkward and anxious young seducer who had been so frightened he had saturated her bed with his sweat, and liked to imagine that one day he would be hanging about the stage entrance when she came sweeping out after one of her most triumphant performances. She would have liked even better to imagine Philip Van Zandt loitering there, humbly trying to catch her eye, but could not convince herself that Philip knew how to look humble.

For Philip seemed to have a natural imperviousness to all the more disquieting emotions, knew nothing of compassion or embarrassment, and enjoyed a gay conviction that what he wanted he would have. "I'm a poor man, Allegra," he told her one day, and she supposed he intended it as an excuse for having given her nothing but bonbons and an imitation Paisley shawl. She smiled skeptically. "Don't you believe me? But it's true."

"You don't mean poor the way I mean poor," she told him, and looked rather petulant, for his complaints seemed childish to her.

"Maybe not. But I'm poor compared to the people I know and that's even worse. You grew up expecting nothing, and I grew up expecting a hell of a lot." He wandered about the room as he talked and Allegra, getting dressed and wondering if she had time to walk to the Academy or must take an omnibus, made a face of mock pity. "We each have our fortunes to find, don't we?" he asked.

"You were born with yours—think of the fathers who are looking for you."

"But so many of them are the wrong kind. After all, a Van Zandt, nowadays, is a rare commodity." He turned down his mouth reflectively and watched as she stood at the mirror, setting her black velvet hat a little forward and then a little back, until it pleased her. She was wearing, as she always did when she met him, the prettiest dress she owned although, it was true, she owned just two.

Still, this one pleased her very well, and each time she wore it she enjoyed the glances she attracted, imagining they had even more to do with the dress than with her shining blond hair and lively face and her way of walking as if she skimmed the pavement on invisible skates, a buoyant young girl going somewhere in a hurry, elated by the conviction of her own power. It was very often not the way she felt, but she could make them believe it, and that sometimes suited her almost as well. The dress which accomplished these wonders was of taffeta patterned with small black and white checks, fitted tight to the top of her body, with its skirt held out by a crinoline. There was a wide white linen collar tied with a black taffeta bow, and white linen cuffs finished the long tight sleeves. Mrs. Stuart, she had often thought, would approve of such a dress, but Philip Van Zandt had never mentioned it, and this had given her some doubts about the magic garment, which might be quite ordinary after all.

She turned away from the mirror, swung her black wool cloak about her shoulders, grabbed the catchall bag and rushed to the door, for she had been taken with a sudden terror of arriving too late, finding the performance had begun without her, and was so intent on saving herself she might have left him without another word. But when he spoke she stopped and glanced at him with a look of guilty apprehension. He walked toward her slowly, smiling, and was, she thought, enjoying her fears and his own leisure.

"What time is it?" she asked.

"Not quite seven."

"Not quite—oh, my God, I'll be late, I'll be fired, don't keep me, Philip."

He took hold of her, kissed her, and as she tried to free herself, he said, "If you ever buy another dress, try lilac—you'd be surprised what an effect you'd get with that hair."

"Lilac, lilac," she muttered distractedly. "Good-bye, Philip." She started down the stairs, then hurried back up again, now almost more afraid she might have offended him than that she would be late. "I have to hurry, don't be angry, I love you, Philip." He came to stand in the doorway, laughing with such good humor and indifference that she was sure he thought it ridiculous to take seriously anything so inconsequential as her job at the Academy.

She was longing to be away, for the fear had started her heart pounding and her stomach seemed churned by paddles, but never-helpless." She had nothing to say to that, the remark seemed to make his palms, she looked at him with the same beseeching humility she liked to imagine on the face of the young footman. She knew what her expression showed him as well as if she had been looking into a mirror, but could not change it, for she seemed to have been captured by her own conviction of loving him and the greater conviction that she did not deserve to be loved by him.

"You're a strange little girl, aren't you? So independent, and so helpless." She had nothing to say to that, the remark seemed to make her dwindle even further, and then he let her go. "Don't be late."

"I won't, I won't," she promised him, persuaded now that if she was it would be her own fault, and went scampering down the staircase and into the street, finding to her relief that she was free of him, even though each time they met she was sure he had taken possession of some vital part of herself and forgotten to return it. But this, she believed, was the essence of love, and she had an eagerness for whatever experiences came to her from it, a determination to be happy and unhappy and no inclination at all to defend herself even though she knew that sooner or later, and quite by accident, she would suffer some disastrous loss she might never repair.

She went dashing toward Broadway, trying to hold the cloak about her with one hand and to keep her hat from blowing away with the other. The streets were crowded with men and women hurrying along at her own desperate pace, darting this way and that to make a path for themselves, colliding with one another and then tearing ahead once more upon whatever frantic errand had sent them into the streets.

Allegra grew more distraught, infected as she always was by the general noise and excitement, and at last squeezed herself into one of the Broadway cars and stood quite rigid as it went careening along. She clutched her catchall bag against her ribs as she glared warningly at her fellow passengers, threatening the first pickpocket among them with a fine display of Irish invective, and she watched them suspiciously, for she never rode a car without imagining she could see fleas, in the act of hopping from her nearest neighbor onto her. Surreptitiously she began to scratch her arm, then the back of her neck, then her head, and all at once brought her heel down smartly upon the foot of a man who hovered too near, exploring her skirt with his hands.

She tried to peer out to see how near they were to the Academy and, as it flashed by, began to fight her way out, thrusting with her elbows until at last she burst through the door, feeling as if she had crawled from a collapsed building, and went hurtling toward the Academy where she astonished the other girls, most of them in costume, by her wildly demented face.

"Am I late?"

"You're not early."

As she began to undress, she vigorously scratched her scalp and reached between her shoulder blades, remembering that when she had first been taken into the Mission School they had thrown away her clothes and poured kerosene over her head and body to kill the lice, a humiliation which enraged her still. "Oh, Allegra Stuart," she told herself, "you'll wind up yet like Betty Mulligan if you don't do something to help yourself."

She spoke peremptorily to one of the girls who lived at Mrs. Gosnell's. "Give me a hand, for Christ's sake, or I'll never lend you my Paisley shawl again." The girl began to help her but not, as they both knew, because of the shawl—only because they regarded each other as common victims, workers at a puzzle neither had begun to solve.

It had seemed, when Joshua Ching had given her five hundred dollars, that her life would change radically. But she had been in debt to her elocution teacher, to Mrs. Gosnell, to several of the ballet girls, to the dressmaker for her checkered taffeta dress, and after she had settled these bills, going grandly to her various creditors, most of it was gone. And as the money disappeared, so did her fund of information about Philip Van Zandt whom she had, by now, described so minutely to Joshua Ching she had very little hope left of another payment. He still came occasionally, early in the morning on his way downtown, and she tried to make him believe she had a new secret to sell, but was disappointed herself by how inconsequential it sounded.

"He's called on my daughter twice," Joshua Ching told her, one January morning. "Has he mentioned that to you?"

Allegra had been doing her laundry, and wet petticoats and drawers and chemises were hung across the room on a rope tied to the gas jets. She sat in her white wrapper mending a stocking and grimly reminding herself that in the opinion of this solemn gentleman a ballet girl had no tender feelings he need consider. "No, he hasn't," she said, but continued weaving the needle back and forth and did not look at him. "If you think he'll ask to marry her you're wrong, Mr. Ching."

"Perhaps he will."

"He's poor, or thinks he is."

"Can't you find out how much he has?"

She stuck the needle into a cushion, dropped the thimble and stretched her arms above her head, sliding her bare feet forward on the carpet. "I know how much he has. His house. That's all." She spread her fingers. "He's going to take me to see it one day, are you interested to know what it looks like?"

"I certainly am."

"Then don't you owe me something more?"

Joshua Ching laughed. "Miss Stuart, five hundred dollars is a great deal of money, and I think it entitles me to know what his house looks like. After all, you haven't done much to earn it, now have you?"

"I've told you everything there is to know about him, I've turned him inside out and upside down for you, what the hell more do you expect?" She gestured quickly, describing a child tearing a rag doll to pieces, and shook her finger at the parrot as he began to squawk.

"You haven't mentioned that he went to Harry Hill's last week."

"I didn't know it. Who told you that?"

"Now, Miss Stuart, I rely on your advice, but not only on your advice. Does it displease you that he went to Harry Hill's? After all, it's one of the sights of the town."

"I know Harry Hill myself."

Joshua leaned forward, and she grinned. "You do? How well?"

"Not well at all, if that's what you mean. He's a friend of my brother's."

"You really have a brother, Miss Stuart?"

"I have a brother who is a politician."

"Politician is a broad word. What kind of politician?"

"That's all I'll tell you, Mr. Ching. Your five hundred dollars has nothing to do with my brother, remember."

Joshua stood up and, as he had done on his first call, reached into his pocket and brought out several bills while she watched him warily from the corners of her eyes; he looked them over, started to return them to his pocket as if he had remembered her earlier scorn of greenbacks, and then she bounded toward him eagerly, holding forth one hand in which he placed two fifty-dollar bills. "If you can find out anything about a distiller named Milton De Groot, I'll be glad to know it. The tenements, as you've probably heard, are full of illegally operated stills, and your brother may be able to learn something about De Groot's. What's his name—Mulligan?"

"It was Brian Mulligan to begin with. Now it's Hoke O'Neil. He changed it when he ran away from the Mission School, for fear they'd catch him and bring him back."

Hoke O'Neil seemed not to be a name Mr. Ching had heard before, but after he had gone she peeked out and found him making a note on a pad he quickly thrust into his pocket; he tipped his hat to her and went on downstairs, not at all disconcerted by their mutual suspiciousness.

She saw Hoke seldom, but they had contrived not to lose each other entirely. Hoke had run away from the Mission School, an eleven-year-old boy who began to live as thousands of other homeless children in the city did, shining shoes and selling newspapers, stealing what he could on the wharves or from storekeepers, and when he was thirteen he had achieved his first local fame by getting a corner on dead rats which he sold, for ten cents each, to less enterprising boys who liked to hurl them at their schoolmates. This venture succeeded so well he had become the head of an organization and able to rule his gang not only by his fists but also by his largesse, providing them with beer dregs and cigars.

His rule had at last been challenged and he had met his challenge in a battle from which he came forth considerably damaged but a hero nevertheless, for he had beaten the other boy into a state so terrifying he was not soon troubled again, and so had established himself as a prize fighter. Hoke gloried in the destruction he could do; broken teeth and broken bones, bloody noses and black eyes, kicked groins and crushed toes gave him ecstatic pleasure, and he swaggered about his neighborhood, relishing the fears and toadying he inspired.

And, because he could not only hit like a mule's kick, but neither drank nor talked too much, he had come to the attention of the leaders of the Bloody Sixth ward and was made a precinct worker, adept at bringing Democrats to the polls and slugging anti-Tammany voters senseless. Lately, he had been bragging that Oliver Foss was his friend, Oliver Foss trusted him, Oliver Foss gave him confidential work to do, and at night Hoke was usually to be found at Harry Hill's on Houston Street, the city's most famous concert-saloon and a gathering place for politicians and stockbrokers, judges and doctors, as well as pickpockets, prize fighters, pimps, sailors, thieves and burglars, and the prettiest whores in town.

Allegra had gone there a few times, once when she wanted Hoke to find out who the Marvin S. Bradshaw was who wrote her letters and sent her presents, and now and then when she needed to borrow money; but these excursions had not been profitable, for Hoke was as poor as she was.

After Joshua Ching had left, she occupied the day as she always did when there were no rehearsals, no lessons, and no meeting with Philip—copying the parts her teacher had assigned, reading aloud for two or three hours, playing whole scenes before her mirror, and late in the afternoon she stood staring down at the street, telling herself she would never act for anyone but Selah and Consuelo, and became so despondent she convinced herself there was no one else in the world so unfortunate as Allegra Stuart. But then, when one of the girls knocked to tell her they were ready to leave for the Academy, she flew about the room, calling out for them to wait for her, was dressed in a few minutes and, giving Selah the saucer of tea and milk he expected every night, set off with the other girls in what seemed her usual confident high spirits.

When the performance was over she left the theater alone, hurrying out before they could ask where she was going, tied a veil over her face to cover the heavy make-up, and got into a hack. As she rode along, clinging to the tug-strap, she gazed out the window, hating everything she saw, but when they got to Harry Hill's she jumped out eagerly, told the driver she would be back in an hour or less, and entered the building with a restored conviction in herself which sent her sweeping past the bar and up to the second floor, where she directed a waiter to bring Hoke O'Neil to her with an air of such authority he went to do it.

The walls of the big room were covered with mottoes warning the patrons there was to be no vulgarity, obscenity, profanity, indecency, or blasphemy on these premises, for Harry Hill insisted upon the respectability of his concert-saloon. There were no rooms to hire, no men might be robbed there, and if one of the well-dressed young whores drank too much she was told not to come back, a worse punishment than being sent to jail, for they could get out of jail soon enough, especially if they happened upon a sympathetic examiner, but they could never again get back into Harry Hill's.

Men in frock coats and silk hats stood at the bar and the girls were resting between dances, gossiping as they sat on benches along the walls, or smoking cigars and drinking at small tables. It was another inflexible rule of Harry Hill's that everyone must either be drinking or dancing at all times and he set them a lively pace, never allowing more than a few minutes of rest before they must be up and whirling about while he charged among them, snapping his fingers at girls who sat too long or did not look as ecstatically gay as he liked to see them, bellowing, "Order! Order! Less noise there! Attention! On your feet, girls, find a partner or get out!" The music began and Allegra told herself this was what paradise would be if a reformed prize fighter had invented it—loud music, merry whores, and drunken men spending money.

A man asked her to dance and when she refused him he grabbed her arm, she slapped his face, and Harry Hill arrived. "Order! Order! Why, is that you, Miss Stuart?" Harry Hill led her around the edge of the room, barking as he went and sending lazy girls skittering out of his path and onto the floor. "Your brother's here, I saw him only a few minutes ago. You!" He snapped his fingers. "Go find Hoke O'Neil! Sit down here, Miss Stuart, what will you drink?"

"Champagne."

"Ah." He clapped his hands. "A bottle of Cliquot. How are you, Miss Stuart?" He sat beside her but never stopped watching the floor or calling his orders, and Allegra smiled and drummed her fingers on the table, telling herself the night was a good one, the omens favorable, and she had had no reason to sink into her earlier morbid spell. "Here's your brother." Harry Hill jumped up and was off again, shouting as he went.

Hoke kissed her and sat across the table, then quickly scowled and peered at her, as if he could not believe his eyes. "What's on your face?"

"Grease paint. I was in a hurry to get here. Anyway, it's no thicker than anyone else's." She gestured at the girls on the floor.

"That's different."

She shook her head, smiling at him. "Hoke, you're a real Irishman."

Hoke was five feet nine or ten inches tall, stocky and muscular, with an agility which dismayed every man who had ever fought him. He had brown hair, the color her own had been before she had read a recipe for dyeing it blond, and his eyes were blue, very bright but with a peculiar glaze, as if they might be marbles stuck into his head. His nose had been broken and twisted, to Allegra's sorrow, one ear was puffed, a deep scar slanted across his forehead and another ran the length of his jaw from ear to chin, while his fingers had been broken so often that each now had its individual form. He looked belligerent and good-humored, arrogant and friendly, tough and strong and brutal, but there was nothing about him to suggest petty meanness and he had no subtle cruelties.

Allegra looked at him for a moment, sitting there in the black frock coat and silk hat he had lately adopted as his official uniform, sadly thinking that this scarred and hard-fisted man who looked much older than twenty-three, her brother, was a flagrant compound of the Irish virtues and vices and that when you judged him he forced you to judge Ireland herself. He had made no effort to lose his brogue and was resentful that she had, regarding it as a treachery to their common heritage, just as he had never liked her choice of Allegra Stuart as a name when she had been born to honest Betty Mulligan.

"That's a pretty dress. You got it the way you should, I hope."

"Of course I did, Hoke."

"What the hell's this?" he demanded, as the waiter opened a bottle of champagne. "Take that stuff away, I can't afford it."

"I'm going to pay for it, Hoke, we're celebrating. Oh, don't worry, I got it honestly." She picked up the glass, carelessly spilling some, and took a sip, smiling at him across the rim. "Wealthy water."

"You got it honestly?" He plainly did not believe it was possible for people like himself or his sister to get money honestly. When a Mulligan had money you could count on it that it was stolen, counterfeit, or otherwise tainted.

"I did someone a favor."

"I hope you wouldn't be ashamed to tell me what it was."

"Drink it, Hoke. I'll tell you later. Here, pour me another glass."

"Not so fast there, Betty, you'll be tight."

"No, I won't. Anyway, I have a hack to take me home."

"A hack?" He jumped, jarring the table, and she grabbed the bottle only in time to keep him from knocking it over. "For Christ's sake, now, you better tell me what's going on. Don't sit there smiling like that—what the hell have you been up to?"

"Remember the man I asked you to find out about?"

"Joshua Ching."

"Well, I did him a favor, and he gave me some money. Not what you're thinking, Hoke—I just told him some things he wanted to know about one of the girls at Mrs. Gosnell's. He gave me fifty dollars." She waved the bill at him. "Now, will you drink with me? Here's to us Mulligans, God bless us. We're both still alive, and that's something." Hoke grinned and touched his glass to hers, and when she had watched the dancers for a few moments, she said, very softly, "Remember, Hoke, the night the Mission ladies took the kids up on the roof to see the Fourth of July fireworks? All those red and green and blue streamers. It wasn't very long after our mother died, and you know, I was afraid to say so, but I thought it was heaven they were showing us." She gave him a quick, shy glance, afraid he might laugh at her, but his face was grim and angry. "And remember the time they took us on an excursion way up to where the Park is now? I'll never forget it, trees and streams and flowers—you ran away not long after that."

Hoke was staring at his glass. "Sure. I found out there was more to the world than Five Points." They glanced at each other, nodding with secret understanding. "Well, the hell with it. What're you doing down here, Betty? I don't like you in this place."

"Allegra, God damn it. What if I called you Brian?"

"Okay, okay. But why did you have to pick such a fancy one?"

"Never mind, it's my name and I like it. Hoke, I think I've got a chance to make some money, if you'll help me. Maybe quite a bit, enough to get to England on and study until I can get a part."

"How much?" He lighted a cigar, puffed at it eagerly, and surrounded himself with a cloud of smoke.

"Maybe a thousand dollars."

Hoke turned sideways, throwing one arm over the chair back and crossing his legs, and as they talked he glanced cautiously about to be sure no one was listening. "A thousand dollars ain't enough."

"It would get me over there."

"What about my half?"

"Your half? I didn't say I'd give you half, Brian Mulligan!"

"Then why should I put myself out?" he asked her blandly. "I'm a busy man nowadays, got more damn irons in the fire than I can handle as it is." He folded his arms on the table, and lowered his voice so that she had to lean forward to hear him. "Let me tell you a couple of things, Betty—Allegra—for your own good." He began to trace a plan on the table top, moving his forefinger in and out of the puddle of champagne. "It's easy to make money nowadays if you've got two things: some money to start with, and some guys you can trust because you've got something on them. That's all there is to it, simple as a mousetrap. Now," he continued imperturbably. "I'm your man, because right now there's not another guy in the whole Bloody Sixth that Foss likes any better than he does me. What's the proposition?"

Allegra looked out at the floor and thought she might begin to cry, as she sometimes did when she was very angry or believed that her last illusion was gone. "I thought you'd do a favor for me."

Hoke smiled ingratiatingly and leaned back with the cigar between his teeth, his hands in his pockets and his knees spread wide. "Now, wait a minute." He lifted one hand and assumed a look of solemn reproval. "You came to me, remember. I didn't ask you for anything, and I don't recall I ever did. If you think there's a thousand in this I can tell you there's at least five, maybe more." He banged the chair down, leaned forward again and began to wheedle. "Jesus, Betty, don't you think I need money myself? This may be what I've been looking for."

"What you've been looking for? Damn you, anyway, it's what I've been looking for! What would you do with money if you had it?"

Hoke gestured vaguely. "A politician don't need money to spend, he needs it to give away. Be sensible, Allegra. There's something in this for both of us, but there's nothing for either one without me. And you know it. Consider yourself lucky to have me for a partner, why don't you look at it that way?"

She sighed. "Tell me about Oliver Foss."

Hoke moved his chair so that he sat beside her. "There he is over there—don't look right now—the little guy Harry's talking to. That's Oliver Foss, and he runs the Bloody Sixth. Know what he was doing five years ago? Five years ago he made a name for himself at the rat pits. Oliver could kill more damn rats with his teeth than any fox terrier you ever saw." Allegra gave a protesting moan, and Hoke assured her, "That's all over with now—he gave it up after he got to be so important. Foss likes me because I brought in more repeaters at the last election than any other guy in the ward. I worked my tail off, and he appreciates it."

"Would Foss know somebody named Milton De Groot?"

"Sure. I know Milton De Groot myself. Anyway, I've met him. He was here the other night with Foss. Distiller. You see, Allegra? I'm your man. What's De Groot got to do with our five thousand?"

"I don't know. Find out as much as you can about him and then we'll see."

"Who's interested?"

"You don't think I'd tell you that?"

Hoke looked at her shrewdly. "I can figure it out for myself."

"Go over and ask him about De Groot now. I'll wait."

"Betty, you got no head at all for politics. That just ain't the way it's done. I've got to ease up on him, wait until the time's right. It's something you feel in your guts—not here." He tapped his temple smartly, and shook his head. "It'll take me a few days, maybe two or three weeks." Hoke escorted her down to the hack, and as she got in he gave her a tight wink, nodding. "I'm taking charge, Allegra, just leave everything to me. Us Mulligans stick together, and you can count on that."

She had heard nothing from him, however, by the time Joshua Ching next appeared, although she had spent many hours adding and subtracting figures, knew just how she meant to spend her share of their profits, and was so convinced she would presently escape from Mrs. Gosnell's, from the Academy, from the horsecars and rehearsals and this city she despised, from Joshua Ching and even from Philip, that she was whimsical and mocking when she described her visit to Philip's house.

"If your daughter ever marries him, you'll have to rebuild that house from top to bottom. There's no bathroom, the carpets are wearing out, the furnaces don't work, and there's not a stick of furniture in it that's less than forty years old." She ran one hand up the back of her neck and into her hair, tipping her head forward and smiling at him as if the situation delighted her for reasons which had nothing to do with any money she might have gotten for this information, but only because something sardonic in her nature was pleased by it.

Joshua Ching regarded her thoughtfully and finally asked, "You're enjoying this, aren't you?"

"Truthfully, yes."

"And you imagine that if he had his choice he'd prefer to marry you."

"I think he might."

"Well, Miss Stuart, would you be quite so saucy if I told you he meets another woman from time to time in the same room where he meets you? A Mrs. Talbot," he added, thinking that if this urchin should decide to blackmail her, why, so much the better.

Allegra's mouth fell open and she closed it quickly, took in a deep breath and stood up. "I don't believe you."

Joshua Ching walked to the door, gave her his customary curt bow, and left, while she stood staring dazedly at the floor and, in another moment, threw herself onto it and sobbed with rage and humiliation, hating Joshua Ching as much as Philip Van Zandt, and herself more than either of them. For the real fault, of course, lay with Betty Mulligan, who had been giving herself airs and goading Allegra Stuart into believing a gentleman might fall in love with her.

She went to their next meeting with a fierce but somewhat vague notion of ridding herself of both these tormenters, Betty Mulligan and Philip Van Zandt, in one grand declamatory scene which, if it accomplished nothing else, would at least give her a permanent place in his memory. She arrived early, let herself into the room and walked about looking it over scornfully, though her knees seemed stiff and she felt very much as she had the first night she appeared at the Academy, convinced that everything depended upon her own performance, and equally convinced she would not be able to move. When his key turned in the lock she gave a frightened jump, but then smiled as he shut the door. He started toward her, paused, looked at her curiously, and laid his hat and cane on the center table.

"Is something wrong?"

She walked toward him, imagining herself as very menacing. "You said you were in love with me, Philip."

"I am."

"And are you in love with someone else, too, that Mrs. Talbot, whoever she is?"

He frowned, pretending to be puzzled, and then laughed. "How did you hear about that?"

The speech she had prepared disappeared and she shouted, "You took me for a whore, didn't you? You knew I needed money, but since I never asked for it you thought you could save a few dollars. I've never taken a dime from you, not a single thing but that lousy Paisley shawl and you can have that back—I wouldn't wear it again if it was real!" She swept it from her shoulders and flung it at him, dashed past him as he caught it, and started down the stairs, trembling, but filled with a sense of power and joy as she pictured his face, for he had looked quite astonished and had not managed to speak. "Betty Mulligan, again," she muttered, as she hurried down, eager to get out of the house before someone opened a door and asked if it had been she making unseemly noises in this quiet retreat for genteel persons, as the advertisement described it.

She reached the first landing, and was part way to the next when she heard his voice. "Just a minute there!" She looked up and he was leaning on the bannister, smiling at her, and that outraged her more than if he had brandished a gun. "Is this what you wanted?"

She went on, but then glanced up to see several greenbacks fluttering toward her. She ran down several more steps, determined to show him how he had misjudged her, but then quite against her will, full of a horrid embarrassment and feeling small and corrupt and unworthy, she began to snatch them up and stuff them into her catchall bag. A few more drifted to the landing and as she scrambled back to get them he started to laugh, a stage laugh if she had ever heard one, but she picked up each bill before she made him a contemptuous signal, a gamine's gesture for which she had been punished at the Mission School, and was out the door and into the street.

She looked up the street and down it, frantically searching for a place to hide, for she expected that in another moment he would come demanding that she give the money back: she saw Philip seizing hold of her and shouting that she had picked his pocket, and then, while bystanders gathered and a policeman came sprinting toward them, eager to assist a gentleman, he would grab the catchall bag and display it to the crowd, and she would be taken off to jail —for who would not believe him, after he told them his name, and who would believe her, a ballet girl?

It was the middle of the afternoon and there were not many people about, a few children who observed her with interested surprise as she darted a few steps in one direction, then spun about and started off in the opposite direction, and she ran steadily, glancing back from time to time, reached the end of the block and turned south, hoping that this canny maneuver would outwit him, and as she ran she looked into each face she passed with an anxious and pleading expression, as if begging them to stand by her when the time came. But, finally, she could run no farther and she stopped, leaning against a wall and panting, and realized all at once that she was running away from her own imagination, for the one thing Philip Van Zandt would certainly not do was follow her and make himself conspicuous on the street.

And, at the recognition of that truth, she continued on her way, walking now, and her face acquired a sly smile, as she promised herself, "Oh, I'll be wiser the next time."

XI

Throughout the summer prospectors moved about the mountains, staking claims and digging holes, each man expecting to find a golden mountain all his own where he could work without the shovels and pickaxes of other men at his elbows. By now, there were hundreds of camps strewn along the gulches, some of them abandoned after only a few months, while others grew into flourishing towns

like Virginia City and Last Chance, whose citizens had renamed it
Helena, more appropriate, they thought, to their ambitions for its
future.

Morgan Devlin and Zack Fletcher followed the alluring gossip
from camp to camp, until late in the fall they found themselves in
Butte, and there, with two or three hundred men and a few women
and children, they were snowed in for the winter. The summertime
picnic, as it had seemed to Morgan, ended suddenly.

He and Zack sat in their cabin wearing buffalo coats, crowded so
near the fireplace they occasionally scorched the toes of their boots;
the snow fell steadily, often for several days without stopping, the
wind swept off the mountains and through the valley, and wolves
skulked in the streets and sometimes boldly approached to drum
with their paws at the cabin doors. Much of the time the two men
stared into the fire and had little to say, for as the weeks went on and
their supplies disappeared, they became increasingly preoccupied
by hunger.

The camp was isolated and had entered the winter without adequate supplies if it should prove as severe as the last had been, and
Morgan and Zack, like the others, had decided to take a chance on a
mild winter. For several weeks, even after it had turned cold, they
were filled with mountain optimism, but then it became difficult to
buy flour or salt or coffee or even beans from the one grocery store,
owned by a man scarcely five feet tall, Bruno Favorite, who also sold
whisky and ran a faro game and poker table.

There were no hoarded supplies, either, as there had been the
previous winter in Virginia City, and as the supplies disappeared
from Bruno Favorite's, the unmarried men who still had small
amounts of flour and beans made gifts of it to the men whose wives
and children were with them. When that was gone they ate unsalted
venison or beef three times a day, then twice a day, and finally only
once a day. It became a matter of pride not to discuss it, to pretend
unawareness of the aching and cramping of the belly, and no one
ever mentioned the delirious daydreams in which there appeared before them steady processions of steaming and bloody roasts, salted
and sprinkled with herbs, veal pies crammed with peas and glazed
with egg yolk, tureens of hot oyster soup, piles of fresh strawberries
sprinkled with coarse brown sugar, and pitchers of cream too thick
to pour. They lavished upon themselves the best food they could remember and imagined feasts they had never enjoyed, but which they
now promised themselves if it took the last pinch of dust they had
dug out.

"Why the hell didn't he go to Helena for supplies?" Morgan had demanded, the first time Bruno Favorite told them he had nothing left
to sell.

"Why the hell didn't we?"

Morgan was ashamed of having asked the question, and took

Zack's answer to mean that if he had been looking for chances to test himself, here one was; for he was still embarrassed by Zack's greater size and strength and his superior knowledge of the country, and it rankled that he was not yet eighteen while Zack was twenty-four.

It was difficult to remember that Helena was only seventy miles away, a lively town of three or four thousand which they had passed through during the summer, where mining locations sold for ten thousand dollars, a cabin rented for two hundred dollars a month, and the surrounding countryside had been crowded with freight wagons coming in from Fort Benton; and Virginia City was so unimaginably remote that Morgan had had no letters from his family since the day he and Zack had left. While here, there were perhaps a hundred cabins, with low ceilings and dirt floors, scattered along a very wide main street, but no hurdy-gurdy houses, no saloon like Green Troy's, and no elegant whorehouse with yellow velvet draperies, like Milly Matches'. In fact, the only prostitute in town that winter was a washwoman who was persuaded to augment her income on behalf of the unmarried miners.

Her name was Queen Victoria Butler and she had appeared in camp late in the fall, riding in with a party of three prospectors which included one other woman, and had established herself in a small cabin where she began to wash the miners' shirts and underwear. She was about forty years old, or so the men guessed when they called to take her their laundry, and looked the way they thought a washwoman should, strong and red-faced. Three or four teeth were missing and her hair was cropped short, her big breasts shifted about without any support from a corset, and she smelled as if she washed nothing but her customers' clothes, but they were indifferent to these deficiencies until, one day, they realized that the camp whore had departed for Helena.

The men began to make jokes about their predicament when they stopped to talk in the streets, for they spent much time drifting aimlessly about, visiting one another's cabins, playing poker or faro at Favorite's, and exchanging news and gossip with everyone they met.

"A hell of a camp this is. Nothing to eat and nothing to screw."

"I heard pioneering was rough, but damned if I ever expected to spend a winter without any tail."

"I don't see any future for this camp. No enterprise to the place. No grub. No women. The hell with it."

"There's a woman," Bruno Favorite said, and grinned significantly.

"Who's that?" one man asked, and the others looked at him pityingly, for there was always someone who would ask the foolish question when more seasoned men kept still.

"Queen Victoria Butler," said Favorite, and contorted his face into a caricature which brought a quick response of laughter.

"Woman? That sow? No thanks, not for me."

"I'll never get that hungry."

"I'll catch me a mountain sheep first."

"This is a lousy way to talk about a respectable lady who's washing our shirts for us."

And yet, in spite of the general surprise and shock at Bruno Favorite's suggestion, before another two weeks had passed it began to be noticed and remarked upon that Queen Victoria Butler had more customers than ever before, that men went to her cabin carrying absurdly small bundles of laundry, and that a few who had not been known to change a shirt since they had arrived were now taking shirts to her.

Bruno Favorite presently made another suggestion. "Gentlemen, I think it's only fair to Mrs. Butler that we preserve her reputation with the other ladies. She is not, after all, a sporting woman by nature."

"She sure ain't," one of them agreed glumly.

"And it behooves us as gentlemen to make sure she doesn't lose her social standing in the community. The respectable women would be mighty severe on her if the news got around."

The men agreed that it was a matter of simple justice to protect her, and Mrs. Butler continued to appear at the parties, escorted by one or two miners, and called upon the married women to gossip whenever she could find time, telling them that her laundry business was so profitable she intended to go to California in the spring and retire.

The next time Morgan and Zack took her their laundry they were astounded to see that she had become coquettish. She stood at a rough table which served as an ironing board, her face streaming sweat as she pushed a heavy iron carelessly about, smiled furtively at them and made a switching movement which set her breasts into quivering action.

"You're two nice-looking young fellows," she said, then turned and bent to pick up another flatiron from the fireplace, presenting to them a wide expanse of skirt at which they gazed with wonderment and horror before she raised herself once more and slammed the iron onto the table. "Ever get lonesome?"

"No, ma'am," said Zack.

"Can't say we do, ma'am," Morgan agreed, and they left hastily, casting each other surprised looks as they closed the door.

Zack shook his head. "Nope," he said, as if talking to himself. "Not a chance. Not a chance in the world."

Morgan was relieved, for if Zack had suggested that desperate men must find desperate remedies, he might have been obliged to meet the challenge, just as he had thought he must meet it in Helena when they had visited a whorehouse, although he had felt uncomfortably guilty about Nella, whom he had left only a few days before. But he had gone, determined to convince himself he was independent, not of Nella only but of his mother and Lisette, too, wanting to think it had taken no longer than this for him to change so greatly he would never again have a boy's need for his family, but only a man's affectionate tolerance.

But, by now, he was disappointed to find he had not leaped at a single bound into manhood. He missed the chatter of his younger brothers and the gaiety of his mother and Lisette, and whenever he remembered Lisette's look of grieving accusation the morning they left his throat ached and he felt a despair which seemed childish, but which he could not control.

Nella appeared in his dreams, awake or asleep, and as the cold and hunger began to weaken him it seemed that he turned to her more and more often, for comfort and reassurance. He sat with his arms pressed to his belly, trying to push against the hunger, and stared into the fire, thinking of her. Now and then they threw on some wood to keep it blazing, and when it was time for dinner they stuck a piece of beef or venison on a stick and roasted it, ate it with revulsion and greed, and drank melted snow, for the whisky supply was short, too.

In the cold, bare cabin, so low-roofed he and Zack could not stand straight, in the perpetual dusk, for candles were scarce and the sky often gray, she became an idealization of Nella Allen, and he promised himself that when spring came—if it ever did and if he was still alive—he would go back to her.

For as the winter went on and the cold and hunger seemed to grow worse, one in proportion to the other, he had begun to wonder, as many of them did, if the camp could survive, or if they would all be discovered by some party of prospectors who would come upon an apparently empty town one hot summer day, and enter the cabins to find dead men and women, rotting in their buffalo coats, beset by rats and wolves and mountain lions. They made no mention of these fears, either, but liked to pretend they enjoyed these tests of their courage and resilience, and that when it was over each man would have been measured once and for all, and that measurement would become his permanent stature.

Then, in early December, a six-year-old girl died and they looked at one another with shocked and guilty faces. They had been afraid to think about the women and children, and had pretended they would survive as well as any of them. But the child had developed pneumonia, which was usually fatal in the mountains, and died three days later.

The funeral was held in her parents' cabin, and since there was no minister, one of the miners read the services, while outside in the thickly falling snow every man in camp stood silent and stunned. They could not dig into the frozen ground and so built a platform as the Indians did and placed the coffin on it; but for the first time they felt that either they had blundered into disaster through their own stupidity in having not prepared for what they must have foreseen, or that fate or God had determined to destroy them all, and the most helpless and blameless among them first. They looked gloomy and sullen, and the child's death seemed to have abolished whatever was left of their determination to pretend this was no worse than any other mountain winter.

Morgan left the funeral and went back to their cabin, but Zack, throwing him a look of accusation and anger, walked off, saying that he was going down to Favorite's. Morgan felt a quick rage at the expression on Zack's face and started after him to ask what he had meant by it and how it happened he dared show him so much contempt, but then shrugged and went to the cabin where he collapsed upon the lower bunk with his coat and boots on and lay staring at the ceiling.

He was still there when Zack returned in the late afternoon, throwing the door open with violent force, and entered like a rampaging giant, his eyes glittering and his face red. He slammed the door and stood staring at Morgan who sat up suddenly, jerked out of his stupor, and glared back at him.

"What the hell's eating you, Fletcher?"

"I know what's on your mind!" Zack shouted. He moved unsteadily, weaving from side to side and forward and back.

Morgan stood and they confronted each other, hunched over with their heads thrust forward. "You're drunk," Morgan accused him, and Zack lunged toward him with his hands held as if to seize him by the throat.

"I'm not too drunk to handle you." Zack's lips were drawn back and his face twisted into a look of such crazy anger that Morgan, full of responding rage, moved cautiously forward and they stood close together, watching each other suspiciously and each convinced that he confronted at last his long-sought-for mortal enemy.

Morgan watched him alertly, waiting, and when Zack gave another slight lurch, he reached for his gun and fired as he drew it. Before he could fire again, Zack struck him a blow across the side of the head with his pistol and Morgan collapsed, knocking over the table and smashing two stools as he fell, and lay sprawled on his belly. Zack gazed at him, surprised and disbelieving, and shook his head, sighing deeply. He moved unsteadily to the water bucket, dashed it carelessly over Morgan, and when that had no effect he turned him over and knelt to look at him. There was a cut on his forehead, a streak of blood and a broad blue bruise, and Zack knelt beside him for some time, examining the damage and scowling over it, as if he ought to be able to find a way to undo it.

At last he dragged Morgan to the lower bunk and got him into it. He lurched about the cabin setting the table upright and then, as if on an impulse, hurried outside and brought back several armloads of wood, threw some sticks onto the fire and seemed puzzled the room was still cold until he noticed the door standing open. From time to time he went to observe Morgan, who continued to lie as he had arranged him, flat on his back and motionless. Zack shook his head sorrowfully and went to fill the bucket with snow, set it beside the fireplace to melt, and made a compress to cover his forehead.

When Morgan opened his eyes nearly half an hour later, Zack was sitting beside him, still wearing his coat and hat, with his hands clasped and a look of anxious tenderness on his face, almost sober again. Morgan's eyelids began to flicker and Zack leaned closer, as if trying to help him, and when at last he opened them, Zack smiled and drew another deep sigh.

Morgan looked surprised, but frowned with pain and told him, "I thought you'd be dead." Zack threw back his head and laughed loudly, slapping his knee, then grabbed Morgan's shoulder and leaned closer.

"You're all right? I didn't hurt you much?"

"By God, if you didn't, then I've got a cast-iron skull." He touched the knob on his head and explored it gently. "What the hell was that all about?"

Zack began to move nervously about the room, kicked at the fire, and finally swung around with a broad, pleading gesture. "That kid, I guess. I began to think you hated me for having brought you here. We're all going crazy. Down at Favorite's just now, Carter took a shot at McGuirk, almost hit him, too. The whole damn camp's on the prod."

They patched the hole made by Morgan's wild shot and said nothing more about it, and when Morgan's head stopped beating like a huge, swollen artery he was humiliated to realize that Zack, even drunk, had shown more presence of mind than he, for he would have killed him, and this terrifying knowledge made Zack seem not only noble and benevolent, but more indispensable to him than ever before. For no man could expect to survive very long in the mountains without an ally, and Zack was a formidable friend to have. His strength and agility, his skills with guns and horses and his knowledge of the mountain lore of keeping alive and reasonably comfortable, were invaluable. The other men respected Zack and, Morgan knew, respected him for being Zack Fletcher's friend, when they might otherwise have felt obliged to test this young greenhorn with only a year and a half in the West to his credit.

There were no road agents in the camp, for it was not rich enough to attract them, but every man wore a brace of pistols and a bowie knife in his boot, and contests among them went on continually. Men shot at one another as a kind of daily joke, although they usually did no damage, and yet Zack had established his reputation so quickly and effectively that neither he nor Morgan had been challenged.

Throughout the summer, Zack had trained him relentlessly in target practice, showing him how to hone the catch to give the trigger an easy action, how to draw and shoot with just enough deliberation to make the shot effective, never from the hip as some foolish ones did, but with the pistol balanced across his forearm, or from a kneeling position. "The frontier's no place for amateurs," Zack assured him, and had trained him with tact and patience until Morgan began to believe he was skillful enough to protect himself without any help from Zack Fletcher, but he had that illusion no longer.

When it became clear there would be no more supplies until spring, they had to stop squandering their bullets and began to spend more time at Favorite's, playing poker. The stakes were low, but no one took the games less seriously for that. They sat with their hats pushed back and cigars between their teeth, drinking bad whisky and improving their knowledge of human nature which, Zack insisted, could be done better at a poker table than anywhere else.

And presently Morgan became aware that he no longer felt he had abandoned his family or that he must return to them when the roads opened, and when he thought of Nella Allen it was not with guilt but only the same frank lust which had troubled him in the beginning, and before much longer he was willing to believe that if there had been another pretty girl nearby, he might have all but forgotten her.

These changes, running deep and wide in his character, as he imagined, Morgan attributed to a happy access of masculinity, a farewell to the confining hypocrisies of the East, and he smiled to think that here he sat playing poker with men who looked as if they would cut a throat for pleasure and yet did not venture to cut his; and he did not doubt that with his hair grown long and his black beard combed with his fingers, in his greasy buckskin shirt and patched black trousers, he looked as ferocious, as cruel, and as dangerous as any one of them—these accidental comrades of the winter who peered at the cards they held in a room so dimly lit it was not even easy to see who was in the game.

By late February even the beef supply was low, and when Buckshot Carter announced one day that he had shot a young fawn and invited some friends to the feast, there was rejoicing and toasts were raised to Buckshot as tumultuous as if he had discovered another bonanza. They gathered in his cabin late in the afternoon, Zack and Morgan, Bruno Favorite and Henry Halloway, who had been sent west for his health, Carter's squaw, Dancing Rabbit, Mrs. Butler, and a man who called himself Dog McGuirk and who posed as the wickedest man in camp.

McGuirk claimed to have gotten his nickname when he had eaten a dog to save himself from starving, and whenever he thought it was time to intimidate a man, he nudged him and whispered, "Go on, I know it's on your mind, ask me if I'm a son of a bitch." His victim usually cowered away, mumbling that no such notion had entered his head, until one day he said it to Zack.

"Why should I ask you that, McGuirk?" Zack blandly inquired. "When I know god-damn well you are." He had a pistol at McGuirk's belly and McGuirk, nonplussed, shrugged and turned his back but soon became his obsequious friend, boasting that Zack Fletcher and he were a pair of hard-cases, tough enough to tear up the town if the whim came over them some day.

Carter's cabin was so small there was not room for the guests to move about but only to sit, some on the lower bunk, others on boxes they had been asked to bring, along with knives and plates, forks if they used them, and a tin mug. At first there was a nervous stiffness among them, as if this occasion might require some formal niceties of which they had never been capable or had forgotten, and they sat gingerly, perched on the boxes and looking at Queen Victoria Butler, who grinned patronizingly at them, or shyly glancing at Dancing Rabbit as she bustled about in her soiled pink satin gown which Carter had given her early in the summer and which she had worn ever since, after ripping the armholes to make it more comfortable and splitting the train so it could be tied around her waist.

Buckshot Carter passed from one to the other, filling their mugs with whisky, asking if the fawn smelled good, apologizing because he had not been able to find salt for it, and presently they were laughing heartily, taking off their coats as the room grew hotter, and had begun to believe this was one of the most convivial groups they had ever joined, that Queen Victoria Butler was in her way a good old soul, and that Dancing Rabbit was quite a pretty squaw, once you got used to the gamy reek.

The fawn was carved and they passed their plates and then fell suddenly silent, eating hungrily, and eagerly accepted more when Buckshot offered it. Within ten minutes the fawn had been devoured and they were lighting cigars and thumping their satisfied bellies, complimenting their hostess on her cooking, and telling Buckshot he was a friend they would remember when the time came.

Buckshot stood beside the fireplace, cleared his throat and held up one hand. He was a young man with a cheerful and stupid face who described himself as the black sheep of an illustrious family, sent west to save them the disgrace of his various escapades. "Gentlemen," he said solemnly, "and ladies," he added, bowing to Mrs. Butler and the squaw. "Fellow sufferers in this land of eternal cold and unsalted beef. It is my pleasure to inform you that that delicious young fawn we have just eaten with so much relish was only yesterday prowling about the camp in a wolf skin." They stared at him distrustfully, thinking he must be drunk, and Carter beamed from one to another. "You're skeptical, gentlemen? You don't rely on a friend's veracity? But the skin is now hanging outside my door, as you may see for yourselves, and the contents of the skin you have just eaten for supper."

"What?" yelped McGuirk. "You fed us a lousy rotten stinking—"

"McGuirk!" called Zack. "Where's your sense of humor? You liked it while you ate it, didn't you?"

"I liked it because I thought it was—"

Buckshot gave a shout of laughter and the squaw dragged in the frozen hide and trailed it across the floor as the men laughed and stamped their feet and clapped and only Mrs. Butler sat looking queasy and pale until she dashed out the door, followed by Henry Halloway, who solicitously took her coat to her.

By the next morning everyone in camp had heard about Buckshot Carter's feast, which soon became so famous that half a hundred men at least were believed to have been present. The ladies were disgusted by Carter's exploitation of his friends' hunger, but the men were grateful to him for giving them something to talk about and a joke they could all enjoy.

A few days later Henry Halloway, whose health had not improved and who looked white-faced and thin, his eyes peering anxiously about as if to find someone else who looked no better, came to Zack to show him his frostbitten feet and ask what he could do to cure them. Zack was believed to know more than anyone else about the art of living in the mountains, and the men stopped him on the street or approached him in Favorite's or came to the cabin to ask his advice about frozen noses and ears, snow-blindness, stomach cramps, flesh wounds, or any of the other accidental ailments which were prevalent.

Henry took off his shoes and his feet were swollen and puffed and splotched with purple. Morgan instantly looked away and turned to study Zack's face. But Zack was gazing at Henry's feet with an expression of thoughtful concern, as if it were only one more case of ordinary frostbite for which he would suggest a salve of gunpowder and hog's lard.

"How long ago did this happen?"

"Eight days. At first I thought it was getting better, but now it seems worse. I didn't want to croak about it, but the pain never stops. I don't know how I can get my shoes back on."

"You'd better not." Zack's voice was tender but casual. "Lie down and rest for awhile, Henry. I'll try to think of something."

He went outdoors and Morgan followed him. They stood and stared at each other for some moments, until finally Zack shook his head.

"What can you do for him?"

"Nothing. Not a damn thing. And for Christ's sake, there isn't even a doctor in camp."

Henry Halloway stayed with them that night, and Morgan rolled up in a buffalo robe on the floor. But the gangrenous smell kept him awake and whenever Henry moved or asked for water he leaped up to get it and hovered over him in a passion of horror and repugnance, for it might, after all, have happened to any of them.

Throughout the next day men came to the cabin. They studied his feet, tried to conceal their abhorrence, and talked to him encouragingly, assuring him the gangrene would presently heal, he would be as good as new, and cited friends they had known and others they had heard of whose condition had been much worse. Each man saw that it was himself lying there, helpless and silent, gazing up at the faces which surrounded him, suffering and lonely and expecting to die in this distant place, among strangers. Most of them brought the one thing they could give which might help him—some of the last of their whisky supply, for there was neither chloroform nor ether in the camp.

But he was not eager to drink it, and seemed to believe he must be as alert as possible, discuss the condition with them and ask for their suggestions. As the day passed his suffering grew worse, he began to drink, and at last lay staring at the bunk above him, his feet propped on a box Zack had placed there, the only thing anyone had been able to do for his comfort.

Late in the day a woman came, knocked lightly, and when the door opened, looked in at the gathering of men who stared at her with angry, condemning faces, resentful of what they took to be the officious curiosity which had sent her here. They found it harder to accept this pain which had been caused by accident than they would if one man had shot another and killed him, for that, they would have said, was a contest between equals or, if they were not equals as individuals, at least they were equal because they were men; while this seemed only the haphazard effect of some mysterious malice against humanity they felt to be a part of nature here in the West. They were filled with superstitious dread, wondering if this was a sign, a warning that they had come to where they were not welcome, for purposes of looting the earth, and that this punishment or some other would finally overtake each of them.

The woman entered hesitantly, looking from one to another as if for their permission. They nodded brusquely, two or three removed their hats, and they made it plain that she was not wanted, that there was nothing she could do, and that she should not have come.

"Can I help?" No one answered and she moved to the bunk where she stood looking at Henry Halloway with concern and sorrow, until finally she turned to Zack, who stood beside her brooding over Henry as he had ever since he had first come to them. "What are you going to do?"

Henry Halloway opened his eyes and looked up at her, his face pleading and, even now, hopeful. "Oh, Mrs. Nichols, you're here. Thank you for coming. What do you think we should do?" From the beginning he had spoken as if it were a problem which belonged not only to him but to everyone in the camp, and now they felt that in truth it did. For while he must endure the pain and, probably, death, they deeply and individually shared it with him.

She knelt, pressed her hand to his forehead and face, and asked him softly, "Could you stand it if they operated on you?"

"Mrs. Nichols!" Zack spoke sharply and took hold of her shoulders to draw her away, but she made a quick, impatient gesture and shook her head. The men glared at one another, for they had talked about it but thought he would die anyway and that it was better to wait than to amputate his feet.

Henry gazed at her helplessly, tried to answer and finally said, "I don't know. Should they do it?" He watched her anxiously, as he did with each person who spoke to him, always expecting that something miraculous would occur, some brilliant and saving thought would come.

Mrs. Nichols stood up, and since it was Zack who had spoken she turned to him. "It's the only chance he has."

"We don't think it's a good one, ma'am. We took a vote on it this afternoon."

"He'll die before morning." Her mouth only formed the words and she nodded, placing the blame if it happened on each of them.

The men began to talk, nervously and quickly, watching Henry who, once more, lay with his eyes closed, as if he were unconscious or, at least, too absorbed in his suffering to pay them any attention.

"He's worse than he was yesterday. A hell of a lot worse."

"It can't do any good. He's too far gone."

"Shut up, you god-damn fool. Do you think he's deaf?"

"If it was me, I'd shoot the son of a bitch who started for me with a saw."

"Let him die with his feet on," said McGuirk, who had sat there all afternoon drinking, and Zack gave him a backhand slap that sent him staggering, caught him before he fell and, opening the door, flung him out, all before anyone else could move or McGuirk could protest.

They went on talking until Mrs. Nichols said, "Good-bye, gentlemen. Let me know if I can help." She opened the door and Buckshot Carter, glancing out, saw McGuirk still sprawled in the snow and went to pick him up.

"Maybe we'd better try it."

"Go ahead, if you want to, but it's murder," one man said, and left them.

Zack bent over the bunk. "It's up to you, Henry. We don't know."

Henry stared at him for some time, his face began to work grotesquely, and, to their horror, he began to sob, choking and covering his mouth with his hands. They glanced at one another and then stared at the floor, and some watched in a helpless fascination as he writhed, drawing up his knees to touch his feet. Then he lay still again and looked at them with his face sheepish and ashamed. "I guess there's not much sand in my craw," he murmured apologetically. "But if you think there's a chance—then—why, then, all right. Zack, will it help?"

"I don't know, Henry. It might. I hope so."

He turned his head to the wall. "Go ahead. Get it over with."

Another man turned and left the cabin. Zack spun around. "What's going on here? We need help. What's the matter with you guys? Want to come and gawk but not help out when help's needed? Come on. If we're going to do this let's get on with it. If we wait, it'll be too late." He looked challengingly from one to the other and, all at once, they began to prepare the cabin.

Henry was given more whisky and now drank it eagerly, while they urged him to take as much as he could. McGuirk, who had been outside yelling threats, came back meekly and asked what he could do. They decided to lay him on the floor, and, when no one else offered or seemed willing, Zack said that he would perform the amputation.

"Maybe he wants to write a letter," one of them suggested.

Halloway shook his head. "No, thanks. No letter. They wouldn't want to know about it."

The men carried him to the floor and knelt. Morgan clamped one knee upon his chest and held one arm, while they bore down upon him as if he would leap away. As he saw Zack approach, very slowly, Morgan shut his eyes and clenched his teeth and felt the sweat pouring off his face and soaking his clothes. He sensed the movement which indicated that Zack had begun to cut but did not open his eyes, only bore more heavily upon Henry's chest and began to pray as he heard the saw working into the bone. He heard grunts from the other men and Henry gave a feeble whine, and while Morgan's ears sang furiously he steadily prayed, repeating over and over again beneath his breath the beginning of the Lord's Prayer, until at last Henry sighed deeply, grew rigid, as if he were struggling to rise, and fell inert.

XII

Coral Talbot believed herself to be the luckiest woman she knew, and whenever she took a few moments, as she did quite often, to count her blessings, she was invariably pleased by their number and variety. Her friends envied her, for which she did not blame them; her enemies feared her, with good enough reason; and there was nothing she wanted she had not been able to have. She sailed about her world with the ease of a skater, dazzling and confounding all beholders with the magical way in which she performed tricks none of them could account for.

She had been born Coral Hallam, the only girl in a large family grown rich in the China trade and, at seventeen, she had married into a family richer than her own. William Talbot had been thirty-eight years old at that time, and it had been five years since his first wife had died. The two children he had had by that wife were also dead, and so Coral had inherited no competitors. Within a year she had given birth to a daughter and, two years later, a son, and would have considered her obligations to her husband discharged—but the little boy, who was named for his father, had died at the age of six, just three years ago.

His death had been the one disaster of her life, for she had loved him extravagantly and had believed he would grow up to be like her, with a man's prerogatives to command his needs. The little girl, Felice, did not please her so well and never had—although William adored her enough to compensate for any indifference the child might sense in her mother—for she had felt, even on the day of Felice's birth, that her competitor had arrived, this little, witless creature squalling in its cradle amid ribbons and satin coverlets and velvet quiltings, who would one day replace her.

The infant had seemed to predict the eventual disappearance of her own beauty which, Coral superstitiously believed, would slowly be conveyed from the mother to the daughter: someday she would be old and Felice would still be young, at least as the world saw it, even though there were only eighteen years between them.

And so, all during Felice's babyhood and early childhood she had contrived to overwhelm her with her own beauty and strength, and Felice was now a docile and obedient child of eleven, who seemed to Coral the unlikely product of two willful and determined people like herself and William. But why it was that the gods which had been so kind to her in every other way, should have chosen the son to die, if one of them must, was the insoluble mystery in her otherwise brilliant life.

It might have been that some kind of malevolent celestial bookkeeping had demanded this sacrifice of her; or perhaps it was a sign that she was expected to produce another child for, after all, it had been her intention not to. Whatever cryptic explanation might be hidden behind the catastrophe, she had developed a craving for maternity, a powerful longing she had not felt before the birth of either Felice or the little William, and soon convinced herself this was why she had taken a number of lovers, although it did not explain why she had begun to take them even before the little boy's death. She met these men, so she supposed, to assuage her own unruly sensuality, and as a secret revenge against William.

The trouble between them was a simple one and had begun soon after their marriage—they struggled together like two wrestlers for dominance. But all the same she took great pride in him, and would not have wanted to be married to another man, for he was not only her favorite antagonist, the one from whom she drew her strength, he was also a demonstration made by her to the world that Coral Talbot, being the wife of such a man and under his protection, was a woman they must defer to, and they did.

Whenever she saw him enter a room where there were other men, she had an instant appreciation for the way he looked, and for what he represented. He was not, at fifty, any more handsome than he had ever been, and perhaps less so now that the bones in his clean-shaven face had become increasingly prominent and the dark, thin hair had receded from his forehead. But he had in his very tall and spare and stoop-shouldered body a look of power and ruthlessness, while his manner of ironic scorn for everyone beneath him, as he supposed everyone to be, the elegance of his behavior and clothing, the narrow and shrewdly investigating blue eyes which fixed upon each face with persistent inquiry and skepticism, looking for a weakness and expecting to find it quickly, made her relationships with other men more meaningful than they would have been if she had had only a mediocre husband to outwit.

Coral Talbot had, as it seemed to her, much to be grateful for, and she took it all for granted. And although she had begun on her twenty-fifth birthday to worry about growing old, foreseeing that there would be no adequate compensations for the homage she now enjoyed, she was nearly thirty and still had not been able to discover, either in her mirror or in the eyes of men who saw her for the first time in a drawing room in full regalia, or later in a bedroom with nothing on but her jewelry, that these years had done her any harm.

Her body was as supple as it had ever been, her muscles taut and her flesh firm, and with her heavy breasts and compressed waist and round hips, she seemed to be in the process of a remorseless blossoming, growing steadily more luxuriant, more polished, and more aggressively desirable, as if embellished by her own need to capture and fascinate.

Perhaps she thought it a pity to save all this for only one man. Whatever it was, she found the satisfaction in her exploits a collector might find in paintings or snuffboxes, and her lovers, selected from among the husbands of her friends, or William's business associates, usually emerged from a few sessions with Coral Talbot more dissatisfied than ever with their reticent and unimaginative wives. Though some of her lovers, it was true, were relieved when the romance was over, and dismayed to find they had less confidence in themselves than they had had before.

And, like a collector of paintings or snuffboxes, she was continually snooping about in search of a new item, more rare, more choice —some galloping passion, pitiless and harrowing, for she valued a heightened emotion, and was convinced that something, though it was indefinable, had so far eluded her.

When they first met, she had not thought of Philip Van Zandt as a potential lover. He was seven years younger than she, and it occurred to her that he might one day be a suitable husband for Felice, and she mentioned this to William. "After all, it's not too early to begin thinking of her future."

"It's much too early," William told her, and it seemed the notion of Felice's eventual marriage made him angry, for William had appropriated her and was apparently determined to bring her up as if she had no mother. "How can you think of marriage in connection with a little girl who's still rolling hoops?"

"Naturally, I wasn't thinking of it in connection with a little girl rolling hoops. She won't always—"

"Never mind," William told her. "Anyway, he'll be married long before she's grown up."

By now, however, Coral imagined herself to be in love with Philip, and had grown jealous of her ambitions to have him marry Felice, just as she was jealous of any girl he might marry. They had been meeting, for the past two or three months, at a house on West Twenty-fourth Street, in a bedroom full of old-fashioned black walnut furniture, and there, in the black walnut bed with its carving of grapes and roses, he had been able to satisfy her most exacting demands, found her fretful and eager and soon had her in a transport of delight which, at last, reduced her to victorious sobs; and after that he enraged her by lighting a cigar and strolling about the room in a dressing gown, talking of other things.

"I've lost money in the market lately," he remarked, and stood with his back to her, looking out the window. "And I had bad luck at faro the other night."

"Money, money." Coral frowned, resentful that anything else should interest him, and she began to dress. "You're always talking about it."

"That's because I don't have any."

She stood before a mirror, pinning a loose strand of hair, and gave herself an insolent smile, meant for him. "I hope you're not expecting me to make you a loan."

Philip laughed, a peculiar sound which convinced her that was what he had been expecting, and assured her, "You know such a thing would never occur to me, Coral. And why laugh at me? I don't enjoy being a poor man."

Coral got into a gown of lemon yellow velvet, and while she was fastening it Philip came nearer, looking thoughtful and concerned as she fiddled with the buttons, and at last he said in a rueful voice, "One good point in the market—that's all I need."

Coral turned brusquely away and went to the mirror again to adjust the little sable hat, setting it exactly where it belonged the first time, picked up a sable muff, and walked past him, saying, "Talbot never discusses the market with me, Philip, I've told you that before. Good-bye," and was on her way out the door when he caught hold of her arm.

"You're not angry?"

"Of course I am."

"When will I see you again?"

She shrugged, and ran down the stairs, smiling to remember the last glimpse of his face, so humbly beseeching, and the carriage set off toward the other side of town while Coral sighed impatiently now and then, swung her foot, and tapped absently at the windowpane, noticing when they turned down Fifth Avenue that the old woman she had seen earlier that afternoon was standing there still, her arms full of wilted lilacs, plucking at the sleeves of passers-by.

There was less traffic here, and she began to imagine that a hack was following them, and as she turned to look through the back window she realized that it was the same hack which had been standing a few doors away when she had gotten into the carriage, and it had been behind them ever since.

She told the driver to draw over to the curb, and was thinking of her various enemies, men, or women, and reflecting that the city was lately filled with blackmailers who had, by their habit of sending anonymous letters requesting money in return for keeping a secret, usually not clearly specified, made a guilty conscience more inconvenient than ever before.

After a moment she peered through the window again, and the hack stood some distance behind them, waiting. She rapped at the driver to go on and the carriage started off and, presently, so did the hack. It occurred to her to jump out and confront him, whoever he was, but although she had no fear of violent excitements or irremediable harangues, Coral reminded herself that she might, after all, be mistaken.

Her carriage turned at Fourteenth Street, circled around, and drove up beside their house, a four-story brownstone with a low stoop and small plot of grass behind a black iron fence. The house was lighted, the shades were drawn, and when they approached the stables, in back of the house on an adjoining lot, she jumped out before the footman could help her, snatched a carriage whip from the rack, and went running down the driveway toward the street.

In the darkness she saw a man standing beside the hack paying the driver, and she ran toward him, drawn irresistibly forward at surprising speed by rage and exultant power, and even before she knew clearly what she meant to do or had admitted to herself that the man was William, she had drawn back the whip and sent it singing toward him. It snapped forcibly across his shoulders and, as he turned, she sent it after him again, striking him this time upon the chest with a blow which made him stagger.

She drew back her arm once more, but before she could strike, the footman had seized the whip and there was an outcry of voices, her own among them, windows were raised, footsteps came running from many directions, and only William stood staring at her in silence.

"Someone's followed me!" she cried. "Don't let him get away!"

"Madame, for God's sake, it's the master!"

"Can't you recognize him, madame? You've struck the master."

"Oh, Hail Mary, Mother of God, the master's been hurt!"

Windows slammed, and Felice came running out, crying, "Is Father hurt?"

Coral went toward him, moving very slowly, and all at once the ecstatic rage was gone, she was tired and sickened, and whispered, "William, my God, my God, what did I do?"

William put one arm about Felice's shoulders, for she was crying, and he spoke to her tenderly. "Only a little accident, Felice."

"Did the horse bite you? Oh, I've been afraid of that mean horse—"

"Go indoors, Felice," William told her and, reluctantly, she left them.

William started toward the house and Coral followed, pleading with him, begging him to speak to her, to assure her he knew it had been an accident, that she had been terrified and had not been able to recognize him in the darkness, and as they reached the doorway he paused and looked at her carefully, as if his eyes could penetrate flesh and examine her to the bone.

"You believe me, William?"

"Why would you lie to me?"

They went in, to find the butler skulking through the hallway, looking embarrassed, not knowing whether he was to seem solicitous of the master's hurts or to ignore them, since they had been denied. He came forward and took William's hat. Felice was hanging over the bannister, her face anxious and frightened and wet with tears, but she quickly disappeared, showing only the flounces of her skirt and petticoats, and her footsteps could be heard running down the hallway to her room. There was an atmosphere of the others, maids and cook and governess and footmen, having hidden quickly, as at the entrance of a dangerous animal into the forest, getting out of the way until it had declared its intentions, whether to devour them at once or pass peaceably by.

Coral appealed to William again, but he turned and went toward the library and she started up the stairs, feeling that she was being watched from whatever hiding places servants were able to discover, holding her head high and fixing a remote and dignified stare upon her face as she told herself that she had been finally betrayed by her stubborn refusal ever to alter an impulse.

The house, like others along Fifth Avenue and on the cross streets, was furnished with old French chairs and sofas and tables, thick carpets, large dark paintings, and many mirrors. There were gilded walls, frescoed ceilings, green velvet draperies, and silver vases filled with roses and lilies, and the house stated quite clearly that the people who lived here took what they owned for granted and did not expect anyone else to be impressed by it, either.

Coral went down the second-floor hallway to her own suite. Her maid was there, and her face, too, was apprehensive and sheepish, as if they had all participated in something shameful which they must pretend had never happened but which, nevertheless, had aroused a nervous, obscene curiosity. She told the girl what she would wear and went into the bathroom, pressed her hands against her cheeks and was not surprised to find that she felt feverish. She looked at herself in the mirror, trying to imagine what her face would have shown him if it was William who looked back at her, and began to explain to him quite plausibly that he could not blame her for having tried to protect herself, for she might very well have been in danger: "You know what the city is like nowadays, William. Murders and robberies and women being attacked every day. Why, I read only recently about a girl who was being followed by a man, and she ran into a livery stable to hide from him, but he followed her there and she took a whip and beat him. An actress, I think she was, or a dancer—something of the kind."

Still puzzling over how he had known where to find her, she went back to the dressing room and the sight of her own face in the mirror produced an unexpected shock.

"Van Zandt—of course. The damned idiot must have been bragging." But after a moment she shook her head, frowning, and fastened the necklace. "No, no, that's impossible. Even Philip's not that big a fool, and he's afraid of William himself. Someone else, someone else," she murmured, and as there was a light tap at the door she gave a jump, then laughed angrily at her cowardice. That was not William's way of knocking, it was Felice's. "Come in." The door opened slowly and not very wide, and Felice peeked in uncertainly. "Come in, darling, what do you want?"

Felice shut the door and stood with her back against it, breathing quickly, her head lowered so that she gazed at Coral from beneath her straight black eyebrows. There was nothing accusatory in her expression but, rather, a look of tragic despair which amused Coral a little, and annoyed her, too. She turned to the dressing table, dipped a stick in rose water and kohl and drew a line around her eyes, slanting it at the outside corners. Her hand was quite steady and for a few moments she concentrated upon her work, then took up a mirror to examine the back of her head and, finally, glanced across at Felice who had not moved.

"What's the trouble, Felice?"

Coral had been scrupulously gentle with Felice all of her life, had seldom punished her or spoken to her sharply and, in fact, had left her training to her father, and the tutors and nurses and governesses he provided. She was being instructed in a variety of subjects which seemed absurd to Coral, who occasionally suggested to her husband that if he did not moderate this educational program he would turn her into a bluestocking or, worse yet, a strong-minded woman, that terror of men. William, however, having only this one child left to him, was determined upon her perfection, and Felice studied Latin and geometry and Greek and French, which she spoke as well as she did English, for her governess was not permitted to talk to her in any other language. She was given lessons in painting and sketching. She must practice the piano for three hours each day, playing the scales with two pennies balanced on the backs of her hands, and her teacher rapped her knuckles when one of them fell off. She took elocution lessons and read the books her father selected—Shakespeare and Thackeray and Emerson—and was obliged to memorize long passages upon which he regularly catechized her. He also had a plan for making Felice healthier than most young girls, and she rode horseback and skated, practiced archery, and had been promised a pair of trotters which she might drive herself on her fourteenth birthday.

Whether or not Felice was made happy by this scheduling of her life Coral did not know, although she thought it unlikely; but that was a problem between Felice and her father, for William had forbidden Coral to discuss it with either of them.

Felice came forward quickly now. "Oh, Mother, the servants are saying the most terrible things, the most terrible things I've ever heard in my life!"

"I've told you, Felice, to keep away from the servants' quarters." Coral sprayed her hair and shoulders with that dense, musky perfume which enveloped anyone who came near her, and which now caused Felice's nostrils to flare.

"I wasn't there, Mother. I heard them talking in the hall when I came downstairs. They're saying that you knew it was Father, and that you did it intentionally." She began to cry again, wringing her hands in some mockery of a woman's grief which Coral found astonishing. "I know it isn't true, but they mustn't say it. I'm so afraid Father might hear them. Oh, can't you make them stop?"

"I'm surprised at you, Felice. What difference does it make what servants say?"

"But when they say—"

"Don't repeat it," Coral told her crisply, and, as Felice seemed more bewildered and frightened than before, Coral put her fingers beneath her chin so that she could look into her face.

Felice was rather tall for her age and quite thin—straight as a stalk of asparagus, Coral thought—but she held herself with purposeful erectness, as her father had commanded her to do, and often walked about the house with both hands clasped behind her back to make sure she would not forget. Her eyes, like Coral's, were very large and black, and her dark brown hair, tied at the nape of her neck with a velvet ribbon, fell to her waist. She was a dainty child, fastidious and graceful, and Coral took pride in her, even though Felice was something of a puzzle, for she had an air of aloof dignity and seriousness which seemed extraordinary in a girl only eleven years old. Felice gazed back at her intently, and presently Coral kissed her cheek, slipped one arm about her shoulders, and smiled.

"Your father must be waiting. Come along, Felice, and promise me you won't think of it again."

They walked down the hall, with Coral keeping her arm about Felice and smiling at her encouragingly, but Felice did not return her smile and moved along beside her with that same look of anguished concern. It somewhat spoiled the picture Coral had intended that when they entered the drawing room Felice was frowning and biting her lower lip. William stood there, dressed in evening clothes, with a whisky glass in his hand, and greeted them as if this were any ordinary night. Coral smiled at him quickly, but she hoped not beseechingly, for William would despise her more for that than for what she had done to him, and she turned to Felice, touching her forehead.

"You mustn't frown, darling. It isn't becoming and it will make lines when you're older. No matter what happens, you must always remember to look pleasant. Mustn't she, William?"

He nodded, acknowledging the soundness of this advice, and Felice smoothed her forehead, stood with her feet fast together, her hands folded, and watched them intently. Dinner was announced, but William filled his glass again and Coral began to stroll about, looking at the paintings as if they were new, moving a vase, ruffling her fan, and rearranging a few roses. She felt sure there was no hope for her, that William had invented his punishment and was enjoying its prospect, and she felt curiously indifferent and resigned, as if to show him that whatever he might do, he could not intimidate her.

No one spoke for several minutes until William abruptly finished his drink, offered Coral his arm, and they went into the dining room, with Felice trailing after them. They sat down solemnly, as was their habit, and certainly no waiter or butler could be surprised if they had little to say to each other tonight, for they had little to say on any night, unless there were guests, and then William discussed politics and the stock market, while Coral talked animatedly of plays and operas, music and books and new fashions, and Felice ate with her governess in the nursery dining room.

The waiter began to bring in the courses, and as Coral told herself she must eat although the sight of food disgusted her, William asked Felice about her lessons and she answered him readily, but was obviously having to struggle with herself not to cry again, so that William's voice grew exceedingly tender, trying to reassure her, and he praised her for several responses, although it was his usual policy that more than one compliment a day would spoil the most sensible young girl.

Coral liked to drink three or four glasses of wine with dinner, but now refused it, for William did not want her to drink in Felice's presence and had recommended that if it was necessary to her, she drink in her own room. The dinner was long and seemed longer than usual, so that she began to wonder if the servants were taking advantage of their trouble to stir up quarrels of their own, and as it progressed she was stricken with increasing amazement at what she had done, and her sense of disbelief grew until she began to feel estranged from herself, repudiated Coral Talbot, and despised her intensely. After almost two hours they returned to the drawing room, and there Coral quickly seized upon Felice, sat beside her at the piano, and humbly asked for a Chopin etude.

Felice looked inquiringly at her father, and when he nodded she played one briskly and efficiently, striking the notes clearly, making no mistakes and doing credit to her music teacher, who drilled her with many threats and no reward. When it ended Coral hugged her close, praising her effusively and stroking her hair while Felice sat very stiff, plainly bewildered by this unusual demonstration, and stared ahead as if she did not dare look at her mother.

"Didn't she play it beautifully?" asked Coral, relinquishing her at last and turning to William.

"Felice, it's time for you to go to bed."

Felice got up promptly and with obvious relief, kissed her mother first and then her father and walked out with her chin held high and her neck stretched long, her feet pacing swiftly one straight before the other, and her face had the careful expressionlessness of a sleep-walker in a play.

"She isn't a very gay child, is she?" Coral asked, when she had gone.

"I'm glad she isn't. Gaiety is an affectation I hope she never acquires."

Coral smiled, for of course it was thought to be one of her charms that whenever she chose she could give forth a flashing radiance which made other women seem stolid and flat, lacking vitality and zest and even most of their femininity.

William lighted a cigar and Coral remained in the chair near the piano and, after a few minutes, began to feel a peculiar dread which crept across her shoulders and down her back, as if in anticipation of being beaten herself. Finally she got up. "I think I'll go to bed, William." Since any excuse she gave would sound as foolish as any other, she added, "I have a headache." She smiled at him vaguely and started toward the door, but stopped when he spoke to her.

"I'll see you in half an hour."

The maid was arranging her bed, and as Coral walked in the girl gave her once again her earlier look of shamed embarrassment. Coral stood and let herself be undressed, slipped the long white nightgown over her head before she relinquished the last of her undergarments, and sat at the dressing table while the girl dismantled her elaborate coiffure, removing braids and puffs and extra curls, then industriously brushed Coral's hair and braided it in one long pigtail, straight down her back. She seemed unusually solicitous, asked eagerly if there was anything more she could do for madame, and left only when she was told to. Coral sat there awhile longer, looking at herself, and was not so well pleased as usual by what she saw. She had no speech to give him when he came and had decided it would be useless to prepare one, and could not understand why she had not had the presence of mind to have stepped out of the carriage and looked pleasantly surprised to see him.

"But I didn't," she muttered, and poured herself a half tumblerful of brandy, added some water, and drank it slowly, keeping an eye on the clock, and grimly reflecting that those who had been condemned usually liked to ease their penalty with some such opiate. She went to fill the glass again, but set it down slowly when she heard the door to the sitting room open.

The key turned in the lock and Coral faced the door with her heart beating fast. He came walking toward her and she watched him doubtfully, trying to make herself look haughty and forbidding, and opened her mouth to say something, she had no idea what, but then, before she knew he intended to do it, he had struck her a hard, ringing blow across the side of her face and head. She gave a protesting cry and he struck her once again. She tried to back away from him but felt two more heavy blows, on one side of her face and then the other. She could no longer see clearly and as she tried to cry out his hand closed over her mouth, clamping her teeth together, and he struck her once more, sending her floundering away so that she would have fallen, but he seized her arm and spun her onto the bed, and she lay with her hands covering her face and her knees drawn up to protect her belly. It seemed as if some terrible and unexpected accident had occurred in the streets before crowds of idle watchers, depriving her of dignity and pride and even her individuality, and, at that moment, she had very little awareness that it was William who had attacked her with the quick and quiet and authoritative skill of a professional bully who punishes his victim without calling attention to his crime.

He took hold of her hands, dragging them away from her head while she struggled to keep them there, and she saw his face above her, showing no more expression than it had during dinner, or while he sat listening to Felice play the etude.

"Keep still," he told her evenly. "Stop that whining or you'll be heard. Listen to me, and don't pretend I've hurt you, you'll recover from this soon enough. I was waiting today when he went in, and I saw you go in a little later. You spent two hours and a half with him. The landlady told me he comes there often, usually with someone else. Don't deny it and don't deny you knew who was in that hack. I only want you to remember that if you ever see him alone again, I'll kill you both. Do you believe me?"

She stared up at him, and her body had begun an uncontrollable trembling. "I believe you."

He straightened, and turned to leave. She watched him, and as she became convinced he had finished with her, sprang off the bed and ran toward him. "I hate you." But she remembered not to scream it, for she had a sense of listeners all about, and when he paused she backed away again, like a child whose courage has failed at the crisis.

"That makes no difference." He went out and closed the door softly.

Coral rushed to the door and locked it and then turned with her back against it, staring crazily about as if she had forgotten something of great importance. All at once she ran into the bedroom and put her face to the mirror, ashamed of the ugliness of her expression, though she could not change it. She turned her head from one side to the other, opened her mouth and examined her teeth, explored her hair line and raised her chin, expecting to discover some irreparable damage, but although her flesh was bruised and her lips swollen, there were no marks which would not disappear in a day or two.

XIII

Joshua now came and went in Mrs. Gosnell's boarding house with perfect ease and freedom, no longer sneaking by opened doors or fearful that low-pitched voices were discussing him and his imagined courtship of the little ballet dancer. He smiled coldly at the landlady and pressed a bill into her palm. He passed anyone he chanced to meet as if he did not see them; and he stepped briskly in and out of his carriage, giving his driver Huggens instructions in a curt, clear tone. It seemed to him, in fact, that his fortunes were ascending at an astonishing rate, and although it kept him dashing from here to there on more errands and expeditions than ever before, he believed each of them essential to his several designs.

Sitting in his carriage, on his way from one appointment to the next, Joshua pulled his plans apart as ruthlessly as if they had been designed by someone else, examining them for flaws which might yet appear; but more often now he glanced out to observe this city which was his personal realm, and found the streets full of interest. There were oddments of humanity he had overlooked before—old women smoking pipes and opening oysters at corner stands, pinched little girls selling flowers, men who seemed about to be carried aloft by the clusters of balloons they held; there were buildings going up and buildings coming down, streets torn apart and littered with lumber and gravel piles, and this entire disrepair and filth of the city gave him encouragement, for the national inability to take satisfaction in any achievement was a part of himself, and he knew there were advantages to be found in such ceaseless restlessness and change.

There were unexpected aggravations from time to time, it was true, but Joshua assured himself there was no man or woman capable of devising an obstruction which Joshua Ching could not find a way to pierce or move aside.

Susan and Ceda, and perhaps Suky, too, although she did not say so, had been disappointed in the effect of their great ball, and this irritated him more than his own disappointment, for he would have preferred they be unaware of any slights they must all expect as they advanced into this new world. Susan received many cards and letters, and several young men came to call on Suky, bringing bouquets and boxes of bonbons, but these young men were of no consequence in Joshua's opinion and he soon discouraged them.

"You'll make an old maid of her," Susan told him reproachfully.

"Nonsense. I would never permit my daughter to be an old maid."

Ceda, who took no offense at his remarks about old maids, said, "Joshua's right, of course. We mustn't be too quick about making new acquaintances."

"We haven't made any new acquaintances at all, have we?" demanded Susan, and frowned at her sister to let her know she was not to take Joshua's side in every argument simply because he clothed and fed her. "We know the same people we've known all along."

"Wait," said Joshua.

Philip Van Zandt appeared one Sunday afternoon and sat for half an hour with his hat on his knee and his cane beside him and talked to Susan and Ceda and Joshua, while Suky, who had been advised by her father to show no eagerness over any caller, seemed to be thinking of other things.

"Mr. Van Zandt is thought to be very charming," Joshua remarked, a few days later, for Suky had not mentioned him.

"Oh, he is, I'm sure."

"He doesn't interest you?"

"How can I be interested in a man who isn't interested in me, Papa?"

No doubt she was right, thought Joshua, for the first thing any woman, and more particularly a beautiful woman, noticed about a man was not the man himself but his response to her and, afterward, she would decide how much he pleased her.

Ceda put her arms about Suky. "Remember my dream—and I know it in my heart. It's your destiny, Suky, to marry beyond any of our expectations. You believe that, don't you, darling?"

Suky inclined her head and gave Ceda a smile which seemed to Joshua subtle and rather surprising, for there was wisdom and mockery in it, too delicate for Ceda to detect. "Of course I do, Aunt Ceda. You know your dreams always come true."

"If it isn't Mr. Van Zandt, it will be some other young man you'll like even better."

Joshua found this naïveté annoying, but had no intention of telling them the world was not so simple. For his own part, he was concerned only about how much he might have to pay to provide this marriage beyond their expectations.

If he was to believe Allegra Stuart, Philip had run deeply into debt, had borrowed from everyone who would still trust him and, in spite of all this, continued to speculate recklessly; and he supposed that Philip might by now be grateful for any offer of rescue. They met one January night in a private dining room at Delmonico's, and began the dinner with a discussion of politics—the general dissatisfaction with the President, the growing impudence of Tammany Hall—

and this carried them through oysters and turtle soup and into a leg
of mutton with caper sauce.

Joshua waited for him to mention Suky and, at last, he did. But he
only asked if she was well and then immediately inquired for her
mother and aunt, as if one of the three meant no more to him than
any other, and Joshua decided to waste no more time. "Someone," he
said reflectively, "I can't remember who, told me that you were soon
to be married. Congratulations."

Philip laughed, and made a deprecatory gesture. "Whoever told
you that, Mr. Ching, was wrong." He smiled, one man assuring another that only women hurried to get married. "Of course, it's true
that my sisters would like to see me married—they even have a little
second cousin in mind." Philip smiled again, and Joshua supposed
he might be thinking of better entertainments to be found with little
ballet dancers.

"But sooner or later, of course, you'll marry her." Philip glanced
up alertly, and this time Joshua smiled. "The little second cousin."

Philip looked serious, or, Joshua supposed, he meant to look serious, for in his own opinion there was an incurable frivolity in the
handsome face of Philip Van Zandt, which he thought neither bad
luck nor trouble could subdue, and which perhaps even old age
would leave intact. "No, I'm afraid I'll have to disappoint them,
much as I love them all—my sisters, I mean. Whoever I marry, it's
not likely they'll be pleased."

Joshua raised his eyebrows. "You wouldn't marry against their objections?"

Philip laughed at this old-fashioned notion. "Of course I will. I'll
have to. They've paid very little attention to what's been happening
the past ten years, and imagine things are still exactly as they remember them."

"And they're not?" Joshua seemed surprised to hear there had
been changes.

"They're not," Philip assured him. "There are new people, and new
standards, and the truth of it is that families like mine must marry
money or disappear. My sisters won't believe it."

"Well, then," said Joshua, and rang for the check, explaining that
he had a meeting to attend, "I can only wish you luck."

"Thank you, sir," Philip told him, although, Joshua thought, as
they shook hands and bade each other good night, Philip seemed
rather surprised, and disappointed, that the conversation had gone
no further. But just as Philip might never cure his frivolity, neither
could Joshua easily cure his passion for a bargain, and he hoped that
in a few days or a few weeks Philip would come asking for Suky, willing to marry her only for the sake of her beauty and the hope of
participating in her father's future. And, since Philip had said he was
not eager to marry, Joshua thought it best to give him time to make
a few more misjudgements in the market.

But then Spinnage and Achroyd reported that Philip was meeting another woman at that same house on West Twenty-fourth Street, and Joshua was surprised to find the woman was Mrs. William Talbot—although he imagined he had guessed it the night he had seen them come into the ballroom together. Pleased by this opportunity for combining revenge with advantage, Joshua dashed off an unsigned note to William Talbot, gave it to a bootblack to deliver, and from time to time smiled to himself, wondering what kind of scene that news had caused in the Talbot household.

And before very much longer there was consternation in his own house when Jemima Cottrell's engagement to Lord Giles Haldane was announced. Ceda had a crying fit, Susan obviously blamed him for the disgrace of having Jemima married before Suky, and even Suky, who was to be one of the bridesmaids, looked listless and sad. For here was Jemima, only an ordinary girl, without any of the vivacity which might have rescued her from plainness, about to become an English nobleman's wife, and Joshua could not console them with the news that Giles Haldane was as much a lord as he was himself.

These annoyances, however, for which the women had no philosophy to sustain them, seemed to Joshua very small when he measured them beside his plan for Milton De Groot, a plan which, as with all Joshua's best schemes, required caution and daring in equal amounts, demanded accurate judgement and explicit timing.

Joshua had taken Amos Cottrell, and another broker, Lorenzo Flagg, into the pool, which was to be under his direction. Flagg was a tall man, remarkably gaunt, his chin whiskers dyed jet black and no tuft of hair left on his high-domed head, who had outfitted a ship in 1849 and arrived in California early enough to sell his cargo at many times what it had cost him and his partner. He had contrived to cheat his partner of the profits, and sometimes bragged of his sagacity even now, and that had been the beginning of his fortune, although it was not until he had been on the short side during the Panic of 1857 that he became rich enough for Joshua to follow his career with interest.

In the cautious way of Wall Street pools, they had agreed each to contribute one million dollars in cash, to lock it up in a bank vault, and leave it there until the pool disbanded, and for several weeks Joshua was so preoccupied with the difficulties of getting that much cash, selling his stocks and borrowing from his brothers, that he slept little and conceived a fierce hatred of Milton De Groot.

De Groot complained that he was surrounded by enemies nowadays, and he described the machinations of these enemies who had brought so many petty lawsuits against him, spreading rumors of his company's unstable condition and his own habit of selling its stock short, that at last the stock had begun to fall off. "You know the Street, Joshua," he told him, and while De Groot sat on the couch sipping absinthe, Joshua paced up and down, slipping his fingers occasionally into a vest pocket where he rubbed them delicately together, as if testing by this superstitious device the present stage of the negotiations. "Why can't you find out who's after me?" He cast Joshua a resentful and petulant look.

"I've tried to, Milton. But whoever's in this is very careful."

"I've got an idea who the son of a bitch is, Joshua." De Groot glared at the floor, turned with a look of such fury that Joshua expected him to accuse him, and ran one hand over his black hair, carefully wiping the grease upon his trousers. "And I know what he's after. He thinks I'll negotiate a settlement so he'll let me alone." De Groot winked. "If it's the guy I think it is, he's played this game before."

"Cheer up, Milton. We'll find out what's going on one of these days. I'm surprised they can rattle you so easily. Your company's in good shape, I hope?"

"As good as can be expected, under the circumstances."

It was April before Joshua had his first conference with Hoke O'Neil, who had sent word through his sister that he was ready to talk to him, and as Joshua drove up to Mrs. Gosnell's he noticed six or eight young men in black coats and trousers and stovepipe hats standing across the street, watching as he got out and entered the house. He mounted the stairs more slowly than usual, thinking that no doubt it had been a mistake ever to make Allegra Stuart's acquaintance, and paused for a moment outside her door, hoping to hear some conversation. But they were either silent or whispering, and Joshua rapped sharply. The dog gave a loud bark, the parrot squawked his greeting, and a young man opened the door and stood grinning at him.

"Hoke O'Neil. Glad to see you."

Allegra, who was fully dressed for the first time, crossed the room swiftly and introduced them, but she looked defiant, and Joshua guessed he might have interrupted a quarrel. "Come in, Mr. Ching," she cried, with mocking hospitality. "You wanted to meet my brother and here he is."

Joshua looked at him for a moment, then walked to the window. The young men were leaning against a wall, staring up and down the street as if this neighborhood was new and interesting to them. "Are those your friends?" Allegra and Hoke laughed, glanced at each other, and Hoke came to the opened window where he gave a long, piercing whistle, and, when the heads turned upward, made them a signal which convinced Joshua he had blundered into a worse predicament than De Groot's.

"That's my Bible class," Hoke told him. "A man in my position can't afford to leave his own ward without protection."

"I see," said Joshua thoughtfully, and noticed with disapproval the scars on O'Neil's jaw and forehead, the creases in his black trousers, the shining but expressionless eyes, and wondered if this man was actually Allegra Stuart's brother, or if they were playing a trick on him. He glanced at Allegra, who stood behind a chair sorting the fringe which ran across its back, untangling it and laying it flat, but she would not look at him and went on unsnarling the fringe with concentrated industry.

"I can be of some help to you, Mr. Ching," Hoke said. "And, just the other way around, I can do you some harm. Suppose we sit down and talk it over."

Joshua sat on the couch and Hoke took a chair which he pulled so close that their knees almost touched. "I'm a friend of Oliver Foss," he told him, with the air of one who gives a valuable confidence.

"So I've heard."

"But have you heard what good friends we are?"

Joshua had thought for many years that the Irish immigration was being overdone, and now he felt a rising hatred of every Irishman who had come to this country to prey on the native Americans. "Whatever that means."

Hoke began to explore his teeth with a toothpick, leaning back in the chair until Joshua expected him to topple it over, and craned his neck to make a grimace at Allegra. She scowled, but then went to the door, opened it and looked out and closed it again, and stood leaning against it, watching them with sullen disapproval. "Betty's mad," Hoke explained.

"Allegra!" she shouted.

"Allegra," agreed Hoke. "Anyway, she's damn mad. She don't think it's nice to screw one guy out of his company so some other guy gets it."

"But that is business, my dear. Why should it concern you?"

"That's what I tried to tell her, but she's got her own ideas. Anyway, Allegra and me, we're tired of being poor. We need money."

Allegra came to stand beside them and looked down at her brother with an expression of such remorseful sorrow that Joshua was surprised to feel a guilty chill along his back. "Oh, but Hoke, this money is so dirty."

"Don't worry about that," Hoke advised her. "We'll fumigate it." She looked from Hoke to Joshua, condemning them both, then abruptly went to a table where she began to arrange a vaseful of lilacs, and for some minutes pretended to have forgotten them. Hoke shrugged. "Don't worry, she'll take her share, all right. Anyway, I'm in charge from now on. Now let's begin at the beginnning, Mr. Ching. De Groot, you think, has put his head in a noose and handed you the other end of the rope. He sells his own stock short. He takes money out of the corporation and gives it to himself. He prints some extra bonds whenever he feels like it and converts them into stocks, and he dumps those on the market and then wonders where the hell they've gone to, so he prints some more. He buys rotgut from the tenement stills and peddles it under his own label. He speculates on his account and forgets that if a man lets himself get caught holding more than he can carry, his friends will gang up and leave him too dead to skin. His brokers give him bad advice, but he takes it anyway, and tells himself the next point he gets will set everything straight again." Hoke stretched his legs and slid down until he had achieved some precarious balance, and observed Joshua with a look of wicked satisfaction.

"I know all that." Joshua had decided that whatever this professional Irishman said to him, he would show no surprise.

"You know that De Groot's found out who's in this pool?"

"I doubt it."

"Doubt it? You and two other guys—Cottrell and Flagg."

"Well, suppose he has? There's nothing he can do about it."

Hoke snapped himself upright again and gave his knee a crashing blow. "Oh, yes, he can. And that's why I'm here. You can take your choice. Talk turkey with me and Foss, or try to guess what De Groot will do and when."

"Why should I trust either of you?"

"What choice have you got by now?" Hoke looked cruelly pleased at this advantage, enjoyed it for a moment, and then leaned forward again, serious and businesslike, and jabbed his bent forefinger at Joshua. "I'll tell you why. De Groot, who's a left-footed son of a bitch, as you know well enough, made the mistake of supporting the wrong candidate a couple of elections back, sold out to him hoofs, horns, and hide, and Foss's been waiting for something like this ever since. And then, Oliver wants the money. So do I." He nodded. "And Allegra."

"How much do you want?"

Hoke gestured and made a face, deprecating the amount, so small a sum for so large a service. "Foss wants ten. The judge will get twenty. And I get five." Allegra swung around, and he added, "Half of it goes to my sister."

"Who's the judge?"

"Don't worry. He'll be there when you need him. We'll take half in advance and the other half when the receivership's been awarded."

Joshua looked at him for a moment. "Where do you want it and when?"

"I'll come to your office tomorrow morning. With my Bible class."

Joshua went to the door and Hoke followed him, they shook hands and Joshua glanced at Allegra, still watching them from across the room, silent and stubbornly reproachful, and as he went out, Joshua heard Hoke say to his sister, "Now that, by God, is the way to do business. What's the matter, cat got your tongue?"

Hoke's Bible class, to Joshua's relief, paid him no attention as he got into his carriage, and when Hoke arrived the next morning he left them standing on the sidewalk. In Joshua's office Hoke sat counting the bills, licking his forefinger and mumbling. When he had counted through each envelope twice he put them into his coat pocket, lighted a cigar from a box on Joshua's desk, and began talking in a voice so low that Joshua leaned forward to hear him. "De Groot figures you intend to try to put him into a receivership, and he's ready for you. He's got a syndicate of his own set up and, whenever he gets the notion, or somebody tells him you're ready to move, he'll back off and claim his banker's got the warehouse receipts, he's out of it, and you can fight among yourselves."

"Who's in his syndicate and who's the banker?"

"Not so fast, we'll take this one step at a time. His warehouses are in my ward and when he decides to clear out, we'll know it. Matter of fact, he's counting on my boys to move the stuff for him." Hoke stood up. "Well, Mr. Ching, if it hadn't been for me and Foss, De Groot would have left you with nothing for your trouble but four walls to look at, wouldn't he?"

"He'd have made it a little harder for us, perhaps."

Hoke smiled. "He'd have rammed that receivership right up your ass. So long. You'll hear from me."

Samuel came to Joshua as Hoke shouldered his way through the men who had gathered for the morning session, his face puzzled and amused. "A new client?"

Joshua nodded. "He owns a vigorous bone-boiling establishment." He threw Samuel a look of mysterious significance and returned to his office where he sat at his desk, placed the tips of his long fingers carefully together, and gave himself up to a moment's contemplation of the manifold wonders of his own destiny.

As Hoke O'Neil had promised, Joshua heard from him from time to time or, rather, Hoke came to his office, perhaps because he did not trust messengers, who were notoriously liable to be abducted, and during the next few weeks Hoke kept him advised about Milton De Groot. Both Cottrell and Flagg were full of admiration for their controller's management of the pool, assuring him that of all the pools they had joined this one seemed least likely to fail.

And on the day Jemima Cottrell was to be married to Lord Giles Haldane a note was delivered signed with Hoke's name, although the handwriting was Allegra's, advising Joshua to wait until Hoke got there; and when he had not arrived by four o'clock, Joshua sent his carriage to bring their dress suits.

It was nearly six-thirty when Hoke appeared, to find Joshua in evening clothes, pacing nervously about and envisioning empty warehouses and locked receipts and De Groot's piratical face obscenely grinning, and at sight of Hoke he went toward him with a swift menacing gait, demanding, "What's gone wrong, O'Neil?"

"Not a god-damn thing. Everything's on schedule, just like I said it would be. De Groot wants the warehouses cleaned out tonight."

"Tonight?" Joshua approached nearer, softly asking, "And where is your judge?"

"I brought him along."

"We're late, Joshua," Samuel reminded him. "Amos won't like it."

Hoke returned, proudly ushering his judge before him. "This is his honor, Judge Azariah Gill."

The judge, dressed in black, even to his gloves, looked at Joshua with solemn suspiciousness, removed his hat and carefully rearranged the curled lock on his forehead, acknowledged the introductions to Samuel and Aaron, and declared the court to be in session.

Hoke sat with his arms folded and his eyes squinted almost shut, Joshua paced restlessly back and forth, twining his watch chain about his finger, and Azariah Gill listened soberly as Aaron presented his reasons for asking that his client, Joshua Ching, be given the receivership of De Groot Distilleries, and, as he listened, Judge Gill whittled at a stick he drew from his pocket and brushed the shavings into a neat pile on Joshua's desk. From time to time Gill asked a question, pondered the answer, and then signaled Aaron to continue. All at once he put the knife and stick back into his pocket.

"The court finds that Mr. Joshua Ching has good and sufficient evidence of the incompetence of Mr. Milton De Groot to manage the company known as De Groot Distilleries, and therefore appoints Mr. Joshua Ching receiver. Mr. Aaron Ching, counsel, will submit an order."

"I have the order prepared, your honor."

The judge began to study the order, frowned as he read it and then read it again, while Hoke yawned and Joshua reminded himself that these Tammany judges insisted upon their dignity, and at last Azariah Gill signed the order, gave the papers a heavy slap as if to place his seal upon them, made them a curt, general bow, and walked out. Hoke lingered behind.

"The other half," Joshua told him, "is due tomorrow morning. After we've inspected the books."

During the drive uptown, Joshua said nothing more about De Groot Distilleries, and Aaron and Samuel, accustomed to his superstition that talk was the certain destruction of any plan, sat silent, and left Joshua immersed in a joyous arrogance, a hatred of Milton De Groot, which occasionally gave way to the dismayed certainty that Foss and Hoke O'Neil would betray him, that De Groot's warehouses were being emptied at that moment, and that by morning there would be nothing left of their grand scheme but receipts assigned to a dummy corporation they could never touch. He was alternately gloomy and elated, and became more and more impatient to reach the reception, since it was now too late for them to go to the church, and imagined that once he came face to face with De Groot he would perceive at that instant which of them was to win this contest, as if its conclusion was even now predicted on their faces.

They passed the church, where a few men and women were still waiting for their carriages, and continued on to Amos Cottrell's house on Twenty-ninth Street, and here there was a concentration of carriages and a crowd had gathered behind ropes strung by Brooks to keep them at bay. Policemen pushed against them as they surged forward and back, loudly asserting their right to pass judgment, and there were catcalls and critical blasts blown by a tongue fanning a mouth when they were displeased.

"Hey, look at her with a bird on her head, is it a live one do you think?"

"Gold on her shoulders, I tell you I seen it. Not to mention the tits."

"Careful there, watch your talk, you're as good as in church, re-member."

"What did I say wrong, officer, tell me, eh?"

These celebrations of what the newspapers called the upper ten thousand had begun to have some magic significance for the city's poor, who attended their weddings and funerals and receptions and balls with faithful devotion, so that the guests were forced to run their gauntlet and could only hope to stricken with miraculous deafness, or to win their approval.

Joshua at last forced his way to Brooks' side, muttering, "This is a disgrace, why don't they lock them up? Have you seen Mrs. Ching or Miss Morgan?"

"They've gone in, sir. Miss Ching and the other bridesmaids, too." The night was hot and Brooks' face was dripping. "I'm sorry, sir. You know what it's like nowadays, no respect for anyone."

Joshua set his mouth grimly and joined the procession filing into the house. Every floor was lighted, the windows had been thrown open, and as the music began there was a burst of applause from the watchers. The house, when at last he entered it, had been emptied of furniture and seemed now to contain nothing but flowers and people. Women were screeching and chattering on the staircase, their skirts making it nearly impassable, and again Joshua was obliged to sum-mon his patience while he smiled at men he knew going down as he went up, and heard a woman ahead of him saying, "And she's just as happy as if he were a real lord, isn't she?"

Joshua thought he saw Milton De Groot pass the head of the stairs and, all at once, was unwilling to see him, to make that conclusive test of his future; but by the time he arrived at the top the man, who-ever he had been, was gone. Joshua glanced about, searching for Susan or Ceda, but could not find them, and he joined another line marching slowly to where Amos Cottrell stood, looking tonight like a benevolent imp and repeating over and over, as if to enjoy the savor of it, "My daughter, Lady Haldane. My son-in-law, Lord Hal-dane. My son and daughter, Lord and Lady Haldane. Lord and Lady Haldane."

Jemima's face gleamed with her triumph, and Lord Haldane, thought Joshua, looked tired but relieved. Joshua kissed Jemima and she gave him a shy smile, whispering, "Look at Suky, she's more beautiful than ever tonight."

"Not as beautiful as you are, my dear."

"Shall I curtsy to you?" a girl asked Jemima, and was unable to re-sist doing so.

"I'll never dare call you Jemima again," another girl said, and laughed exultantly to think she knew someone who had become a Lady.

Joshua gave Amos a significant look, but Amos had temporarily forgotten their pool, their contract which had locked up three million dollars, and would have stared at him blankly if he had spoken of injunctions or receiverships.

Suky, dressed like the other bridesmaids in a gown of white gauze, seemed as rapturous as if this were her own wedding, and as Jemima was about to begin the dancing, the two girls suddenly looked at each other with tears in their eyes.

"Oh, Jemima, darling," Suky told her with soft and graceful admiration, "even if you are Lady Haldane, you will always be my dearest friend."

They kissed, taking care not to ruffle each other's hair or disarrange Jemima's veil, and Joshua, congratulating himself on having a daughter whose tact never failed, heard Lord Haldane whisper, "Tell me, sir, for God's sake, have you heard any talk?"

"Not much," said Joshua, and left him to search for Susan.

He found her with Ceda, on the floor below where the presents were displayed, circling about the tables with other guests, examining the gold and silver plate. Some had ventured out into the garden, but soon retreated from the watchers who peered at them through the iron fence.

The police patrolled their edges and now and then took a pickpocket or an outspoken whore away to the station house. There had been numerous fights and drunken quarrels, and from time to time the crowd burst into spontaneous singing, which the police stopped. But they agreed it was one of the biggest weddings of the year and several inquired whose house it was and who was so important as to cause this furor. One declared it was Boss Tweed's daughter, and another insisted it was a shoddyite, grown rich on cheating the government. When a policeman announced that an English nobleman had married an American girl, the catcalls and jeers swelled to a howling chorus which lasted for several seconds before uniformed elbows began to jab into faces and necks, backhand slaps froze Irish brogues, and random knockings with clubs produced mutters and temporary silence.

Susan looked skeptical at hearing he had been kept at his office, but Ceda began to describe the ceremony, assuring him it was Suky who had attracted all the attention. "If only you could have seen her, Joshua, walking up that aisle. What a bride she will be."

At that moment, Joshua saw Milton De Groot enter the room. De Groot gave it a quick, searching glance, his face drawn into so tight a scowl that his eyebrows and whiskers seemed almost to merge, leaving his black eyes peering between; then he went out again. And Joshua, thinking De Groot had meant to throw him a challenge, though he had not looked at him directly, left them without a word and started after him, suddenly as filled with the urge for combat as the crowd outside, and when he reached the hall and saw the back of De Groot's head a few feet away, he called out to him peremptorily.

De Groot turned, and watched from the corners of his eyes as Joshua approached, then gave a lurch which brought him around so that they stood face to face. And De Groot, he noticed instantly, whether because of the hot night, the general excitement, or his own apprehensions, was sweating copiously and stank somewhat worse than usual. He smelled, in fact, Joshua told himself, like nothing so much as a heap of rotten onions, and this might signify De Groot's premonition of defeat.

They shook hands, observing each other warily, and began to talk about the wedding, the presents, the crowd, and Joshua felt himself begin to expand with the conviction of limitless power which accompanied all his victories, a feeling of such mighty invincibility that he was left with only a pitying contempt for any man rash enough to have imagined he might outwit Joshua Ching.

Next morning he set out for the office before six, and was going over the ledgers when the clerks arrived at eight. But then he retreated into his office, saying he was not to be disturbed, that he was not there if Milton De Groot came, and would see no one but Mr. O'Neil. For the next three hours he paced about, growing angrier and more convinced that Hoke O'Neil and Azariah Gill and Oliver Foss had been paid better by De Groot than by himself, and when Hoke appeared at eleven Joshua stood behind his desk with his hands clenched in his pockets and glared at him, unable even to wish him a good morning.

"The job's done," said Hoke, snapped his fingers sharply, and two members of his Bible class came marching in, carrying between them a basket filled with ledgers and receipts of De Groot Distilleries, followed by two more bearing another basket. They set them down and went marching out again, and Hoke selected one of Joshua's cigars and lighted it. "The notice is up, the bailiff's there, and so is De Groot. He's more puzzled right now than mad, but when he finds out his books are gone it's likely to be the other way around. He went to see Foss to find out how it happened, and Foss told him the only way he can figure it is that you must've spent more to keep the stuff in the warehouse than he did to get it out." Joshua had begun to poke among the books, and now selected three at random and opened them. "When I left, De Groot was saying he'd take his case to court, if it cost him his last nickel, and no son of a bitch was going to run his company for him." Hoke counted the bills, mumbling to himself while Joshua continued to examine the ledgers, and when Joshua looked up, he was gone.

But for several days Joshua continued to experience the same uncanny sense that it was not Milton De Groot but Joshua Ching who had lost control of De Groot Distilleries, and even when De Groot came to talk to him, assuring him he would pay off his creditors and repossess the company, Joshua found himself wondering if it might, after all, actually happen that way.

"I hope you do, Milton," he told him soothingly. "This receivership is a hell of a burden for me, you know that. I wouldn't have taken it on for anyone else. We'll work this out together."

"I overextended myself, Joshua. Spread myself too thin. Money's a little tight just now, but I'll get it. Now, for Christ's sake, all I ask of you for old time's sake is don't impound my bank account."

"I hope it won't be necessary, Milton."

The news passed about the Street quickly, and men Joshua had known for years greeted him deferentially and nudged one another as he walked by, striding purposefully along and taking no notice of the attention he attracted. Scarcely a week had passed when Philip Van Zandt appeared in his office, to open an account, so he said, and astonished Joshua by complaining that he had called twice in the past few days and been told that Suky was not at home.

XIV

Late in April the valley turned a hazy green, and the sky which for six months had been a low covering of clouds receded to vast blue heights and displayed to them once more the tops of the surrounding mountains. The wind carried the smell of earth and early wildflowers and, very quickly, the streams were overflowing and they went back to work.

New men appeared in camp, some with their wives and families, and two prostitutes established themselves in cabins which had been abandoned during the winter. Queen Victoria Butler lost her patronage, and was further disconcerted when a Chinese arrived from Utah to wash the miners' clothes more efficiently and economically than she had done. She grumbled about these changes and would not understand that it was a part of what the West called progress, in which her own misfortunes were only one more small but necessary sacrifice to the country's development.

The miners, who had shown Mrs. Butler so much gallantry during the winter, were too busy now to hear her complaints. For the valley sprang into a turmoil of activity before daylight, and for seven miles along the creek men were pounding rocks and building sluices, teams of ox trains hauled gravel from more distant diggings, and when the sun went down they retired to their cabins, smoke spread away in thin streams from chimneys and campfires, and by nightfall the camp was silent.

Zack asked Morgan one day if he thought they should go back to Virginia City. "The ore here isn't worth much. Low-grade to start with, and too damn much silver mixed up in it. Maybe we'd be better off working for your old man."

They sat at their lopsided table, eating beans with slabs of fat bacon cooked in it, and greedily sopping up juices with chunks of bread, for after the past several months of nourishing themselves on unsalted beef and, as an occasional treat and scurvy preventive, a dish of raw potatoes and vinegar, they now approached each meal with ravening hunger, half expecting it to turn into a mirage before they could gobble it up. As they ate they could feel a glowing warmth spreading throughout their bodies, and when they could eat no more they sat in stupefied contentment, enjoying a profound exaltation which seemed almost mystical. Zack went to get a cigar from his coat pocket, tossed one to Morgan, and threw himself onto the lower bunk, closing his eyes and sending forth luxurious clouds of smoke. Whisky and tobacco were back in the camp, too, and no one now thought of objecting because they were so expensive, but rather seemed to marvel that they had ever been cheap.

But, although going home was what Morgan had promised himself he would do, he now began to give Zack several reasons why they should stay where they were. "How much have we made? Less than a thousand between us. We got a late start, remember,."

"We might make more there."

"Wouldn't it look as if we don't have much enterprise—gone for less than a year and back again because the winter was rough?"

Zack said nothing for a few moments, then gave a sleepy grunt and rolled over, kicking off his boots and throwing his trousers across the room. "Okay, if that's what you want. This suits me fine."

For it was quite true, as they had lately heard Bruno Favorite telling a pilgrim, that life in the mountains was a young man's sport. "Not one of those guys," said Bruno, gesturing to where Morgan and Zack sat playing poker on a Sunday morning with Carter and Mc-Guirk, "is over twenty-five, and two of them are barely eighteen. If you're young enough, it seems better out here than it is."

But not all the young men were able to think the life was better than it was, and when they heard that Harry York had cut his throat, early one morning while he was getting breakfast, they reacted with cautious disapproval, as if this deed had been done to spite them.

"What the hell was he thinking about?"

Even his partner had no idea why he had done it. "He seemed all right when I went to get some water, and when I came back, there he was." He slid his forefinger from one ear to the other.

"What could make a guy do a thing like that?" they were still asking, as they left the graveyard.

"The Indians don't often commit suicide," Zack told Morgan. "But when they do, it's big medicine, a high religious act." He shrugged. "Maybe they're right."

Nevertheless, they avoided talking about Harry York, his partner found another man to work with and, very soon, he might never have been among them at all.

And a few weeks later, near the end of June, Lily Jones arrived on a Sunday morning, when no newcomer could have gone unnoticed and certainly not a girl who rode astride a black pony, between two fierce-looking men laden with firearms. Men were buying groceries and listening to the auctioneers, passing in and out of Favorite's, exchanging gossip and leaning against the buildings, expecting no more of this day than any other—when the three of them came ambling slowly down the middle of the street, apparently indifferent to the commotion they caused, and only the girl glanced occasionally into the faces which gawked from doorways and windows.

A man stuck his head into Favorite's. "Hey, don't miss this. Parade going by." The players seemed not to hear, and he added, "Real live female—new one."

The men who stood at the bar crowded to the door and McGuirk got up, offering to reconnoitre. He peered out, giving his head a peremptory jerk, and the others arrived as the three rode by, walking their horses at a slow, deliberate pace, and the girl let her moccasined feet drum against her horse's sides with every step, Indian fashion.

She wore buckskin trousers and a red flannel shirt and this interested them profoundly, for it showed that her body was slender, flat-bellied and narrow-hipped, and her small breasts bounced with the pony's leisurely gait. They were so absorbed in taking this inventory they might not have noticed her face, but Carter nudged the man who stood on either side of him.

"She's pretty, too."

"So she is."

She appeared to be about twenty years old and looked briskly healthy, full of confidence and self-esteem, and no doubt this made her seem prettier than if they had wanted to judge her by any strict standards. Her face had a fresh impudence and her eyes, either blue or green, they could not be sure, glanced at her audience with the honest appeal of a child who wants to be admired. Her face and neck and forearms were tanned, and whenever she turned her head her light brown hair, cut off straight an inch or two above her shoulders, swung from side to side like a heavy silk tassel. They watched her with rapt, serious faces, for it seemed there was something wonderful in her appearance in this isolated camp, and when she glanced down into the crowd gathered outside Favorite's and gave them a quick, impersonal grin, there was a general nervous start and the men in front stepped inadvertently backward, whispering, "Who was that for?"

Carter groaned softly. "I know one of those guys, the one on the far side. If he hasn't changed his name, he's Gaius Jenkins and he was in Kansas in 'fifty-eight. He's bad medicine." He seemed stricken with pleasurable terror at this appearance of an authentic bad man in a camp where few men had yet been killed. "Never shoots twice at the same man," he assured them, and scowled defensively at Zack's smile. "Well, look at him, for Christ's sake, a traveling arsenal."

The three riders went on, and after studying the girl's straight back and small waist and buttocks, they glanced at each other, shrugging, and returned to their game. Sometime later a young boy brought back the news that they had pitched camp four miles or more from the edge of town and were now cooking dinner. One of the men, he said, had thrown a rock at him, and when he paid no attention to that, had drawn a pistol and leveled it.

"That's Jenkins," said Carter triumphantly.

After a few days the girl and the two men began to appear in town, and they swaggered around the empty streets as if they had been intended for their private use. They bought provisions, paying for everything in gold dust, and inquired about the camp, its prosperity and future hopes, asking how much a paying claim was held to be worth, and, when they left, leaped at their horses and galloped away, yelling joyously at one another and racing out of town. They had a very small weekday audience for these activities, but their indifference and camaraderie made them more fascinating than if they had shown any inclination to be friendly, and they became the subject of many rumors.

Before the week was out their names were known. She was Lily Jones, and the men were Gaius Jenkins and Charles Hamilton. Jenkins, it was said, wore a pair of ears in his vest and his gun was notched, and this finally convinced them Carter had been telling the truth. Hamilton was younger, and though he looked less haggard and sullen than Jenkins, he had his own manner of purposeful desperation, so that if it had not been for the girl, who gave to their activities the air of a bravely performed comedy, they would have been taken for a pair of road agents. Even so, there was some discussion about how they were to be handled when the robberies began.

The young boy who had followed them the first day sneaked out again, and reported that their tents were made of potato sacks and old shirts, with empty whisky barrels for chimneys, and there was no indication that they intended to do any mining, for he had found no picks or pans among their equipment.

"What are they up to?" the men wondered.

"Just prospecting the place."

"Trying to decide if we're worth fleecing."

"Or maybe resting up for their health."

Morgan wondered about her from time to time, where she had come from and what her real name might be, since Lily Jones sounded manufactured, what she was doing with Jenkins and Hamilton, and which man had her for his property. He tried to imagine what the advantages might be to a man who had a girl like that, one who seemed to be splendidly enjoying her freedom and adventurousness, and finally asked Zack, "What's a girl like that doing in a place like this?"

"Girl?"

"Lily Jones. Had you forgotten her?"

"Not by a damn sight. She doesn't mean for anyone to forget her. As for what she's doing, she can do it here as well as anywhere else, can't she?"

Morgan had appropriated Lily Jones, and Zack's careless way of calling her a whore without any better evidence than they had, offended him. For his own part he had taken a broad-minded attitude, telling himself that even if she was one man's girl today she could be another's tomorrow, and assured himself she had the same right to change her mind about men that they did about women. For after all she was no ordinary girl, staying at home in the protection of her family, lacing herself into a tight corset that made her faint and vomit, and waiting for some unsuspecting man to cross the threshold where she could catch him with her wiles and secure him with her skittish virginity. This girl was living the life they did, taking the chances they did, and he thought she deserved the same degree of respect they gave one another and for the same reasons.

"A girl who looks like that and dresses like that," Zack said, "isn't looking for a nice, peaceful life."

Morgan laughed. "I hope not."

"But she'll pick your pocket just as quick and maybe quicker. There are plenty of women who come west and put on men's clothes and try to act like men. What's special about her?"

Zack, he supposed, might have known such a girl and let her take some advantage of him, for it was Zack's contention that girls had no other real interests, but Morgan complimented himself that by now he was too experienced to worry about what Lily Jones might do to him. "Any guy," he told Zack, "who lets himself be made a fool of by a woman must be a fool to begin with." He was somewhat surprised by the smug sound of this statement, and grateful that Zack only smiled and began to talk about the Frenchman and the half-breed who had recently been put into the camp jail, a ramshackle log cabin, for selling whisky to the Indians.

Lily Jones and the two men did not come in to town the following Sunday, although they were expected and there were more men about than usual, for those who had not yet seen her felt they had been cheated, and there was an atmosphere of gaiety and excitement which, as the day passed and they did not appear, changed to disappointed indignation.

During the next few days they appeared less often and remained at their own camp, practicing target shooting. The girl, it was said, could shoot as well as the men, and those who had gone out and watched from a safe distance brought back alarming tales of their skill. All at once they seemed sinister, a menace to lives and property, and before very much longer it had become a matter of pride on the part of the earlier settlers to make contact with these seclusive interlopers.

They began to talk about it as soon as they had gathered at Favorite's at noon on Sunday, and would not discuss anything else.

"What the hell right have they got to come to our camp and act like we're not even here?"

"Hey, Bruno, what's the last thing they said to you?"

"The last thing? Well, I guess the last thing was that Jenkins says he's got the best horse in the mountains."

At that the men set up outraged howls. There had been several drinks poured by each since morning and they were filled with the exuberance which came to them only in summer and even then, as Bruno Favorite had said, only to those who were young, eager to fight each other and race their horses or in other ways prove their endurance and hardihood.

"Let's challenge the son of a bitch!" shouted Carter. "I've got a good horse. So have you, Devlin. So have you, Fletcher. By Christ, we've all got good horses." They glanced at him with calm superior smiles and, as he began to rant and bellow, continued to place their bets. "Come on, let's go." And all at once he dashed out, jumped onto his horse and set off in the direction of their camp.

"There goes Carter," McGuirk observed philosophically. "He'll come back like a sieve."

"Maybe his squaw knows a tasty way to cook a man."

From time to time a comment was made about Buckshot Carter, whether or not he was dead yet, whether they owed it to Dancing Rabbit to get his mangled remains and deliver them to her, who should read his funeral services and what story they would write to his parents. When an hour had gone by and still Carter did not limp in without his horse and bleeding, McGuirk spoke up.

"You know, it just came to me that maybe we haven't been so very neighborly with our neighbors. They're likely as not setting out there expecting us to pay a call and here we are, wrapped up in ourselves and not even concerned that they might be lonesome and bored with each other and craving our company."

"We've hurt their feelings, sure enough."

They divided their gains and losses in approximate fashion, bought four bottles of whisky and one of champagne, taken out of the ice shed as a present for Lily Jones, and set off at a gallop for the encampment.

The afternoon was hot and windy, blowing the grass and wildflowers flat, and the broad valley, with its surrounding hills and the great butte which rose out of the plains to the north, could not be imagined today as it had looked during the winter.

"Nobody's there!"

"They've taken Carter out to bury him. We'll be in time for his services."

They rode nearer, shouting and waving the bottles to announce their peaceful intentions, and all at once the girl and the three men appeared. Jenkins and Hamilton leveled their rifles and Carter stood between them as hostage. The group arrived, keeping at a slight distance, and called out that they were not Vigilantes but had come on an errand of mercy, and at last Jenkins and Hamilton lowered the rifles, gesturing them on, but glared suspiciously and seemed to think they were under siege.

Lily Jones stood grinning at them, looking from one face to the other with quick, shrewd scrutiny, and turned to Jenkins, muttering, "Put away the artillery, for Christ's sake, can't you see they've brought a peace offering?" She gave them a gay little salute, touching the brim of her hat. "Hi."

"How," Zack replied solemnly, and they walked their horses a little nearer, while Carter pleaded with Jenkins not to start any wars with a lady present.

"Roll off," Lily Jones told them. "My friends here aren't civilized."

"Thank you, ma'am."

"That's very kind of you, ma'am."

She threw back her head, laughing as if she had never heard the word before and could not imagine what it meant. "Her name's Lily Jones," Jenkins said, and cast them a menacing scowl. "I'm her cousin, and Hamilton here is her stepbrother."

They mumbled politely that Bruno Favorite had told them as much. Zack swung down, watching them warily, and the others followed. He walked forward, gave them his name with dour formality, and presented his friends, who seemed nervous and self-conscious as they approached this girl who smiled up into each man's face as she shook his hand and repeated his name, nodding briskly. They were quite sober now and mumbled cautiously to one another, asking why they had come out here. One of the men wanted to go back, but they hung about, furtively observing Lily, who seemed as much at ease as a lady receiving her friends in a parlor—for this girl had somehow contrived to supply herself with enough poise and impudence to baffle them—and each man assured himself he felt no more foolish than his friends.

Morgan approached her only after she had met the others, imagining this would give him some particular significance, but as he stepped toward her an attack of shyness made his heart beat heavily and motes danced before his eyes, the penalty, as he supposed, for what he had been thinking about her.

She smiled broadly, showing square straight teeth which he thought the smile almost indecently exposed, looked at him with an expression that was frankly inquiring, and as he took hold of her hand he found it to be warm and small, with calluses he could feel. There were freckles on her nose and cheeks, her eyes were more green than blue, and fine lines fanned out around their edges, proving that whatever might be her history she had, at least, spent much of it out-of-doors. Her brown hair was streaked unevenly by the sun, and she seemed a curiously poignant and almost comical little braggart, at once touching and provocative. He moved aside quickly to join the others, and as he passed Zack he gave him a glance of sheepish defiance, for he believed by now that Zack Fletcher, bastioned behind his cynicism, was able to read his thoughts before he had become aware of them himself.

Carter, as a reward for having scouted their expedition, was chosen to make the presentation speech, and she accepted the champagne with a joyous cry, saying she would drink it before it got warm. She went to one of the tents, returning with a tin cup, popped off the cork and raised the cup toward where they still stood huddled together, and emptied it.

Jenkins at last gestured that they were to sit down, and they squatted on the beaten grass and handed one of the bottles about the circle, while Lily sat cross-legged and lighted a cigar, studied the clouds, and now and then frowned thoughtfully as she listened, or pretended to listen, to what they were saying. She seemed very well aware that they watched her, covertly but persistently, and refused to look at any one of them directly, although now and then she smiled at some secret amusement and tipped back her head, giving her hair a vigorous shake.

Jenkins said nothing for several minutes but stared into one face and then another, as carefully as if he had been sorting the pictures in a rogue's gallery and was looking for a particular man.

"We hear all the good claims are taken," he said at last. "Is that right?"

"The creek's staked out from Silver Bow to Butte."

"Nobody's getting rich," Zack told them. "Just making wages."

"Too much silver, and some copper. Gold assays between eleven and fourteen dollars an ounce."

Jenkins turned down his mouth, and McGuirk advised him, "Don't buy any real estate. There's no future in this camp. It'll be dead in another year."

"We didn't plan to," Jenkins said ungraciously. "Did you take us for pilgrims?"

Zack, who was beginning to look annoyed, said, "We hear you claim you've got a fast horse."

"I have."

"Want to try him out?"

Jenkins shrugged. "It wouldn't be fair."

The others jumped up, talking excitedly and beginning to make bets, while Lily poured the rest of the champagne and drank it, tossed away her cigar, and squinted at the sun. Jenkins and Hamilton went with them to examine the horses and left her there, hunched over with her arms clasped about her ankles, watching them with a charitable and pitying smile.

"Which of you runs against me?" Jenkins asked.

"Take your choice," said Zack. "Any one of us can beat you."

Hamilton gave a derisive laugh. "What a crock!"

"Let's draw straws."

"Wait a minute, now," Jenkins put up one hand. "Let my jockey decide."

"You got a midget around here?"

"Lily's my jockey."

"Lily!" they shouted, horrified. "Miss Jones!" some of them corrected as she came sauntering up with her hands in her pockets and her charitable smile turned mocking and contemptuous, as if she dared them to back out now. They scowled, gestured, and protested all at once.

"I won't race a girl."

"We can't beat her and we can't let her beat us. How can we race?"

"Don't race, then, if you're such god-damn gentlemen. But she's as good a man as any of you."

They looked at her surreptitiously, standing beside Jenkins and rocking on the heels of her boots. "What's the matter with you fellows?" she asked them reasonably. "Haven't you heard about women's rights?"

"All right," Zack agreed. "We'll race you, ma'am—Miss Jones, that is." But they looked morose, peevish and sullen, while Jenkins and Hamilton were grinning, and Hamilton gave Jenkins a nudge with his elbow.

She glanced from Zack to Morgan, then to Carter and McGuirk and the others, surveying each one from head to foot and making them feel foolishly betrayed, inept and clumsy, and walked away, saying, "I'll race Devlin."

Zack was appointed banker and set up his office on a barrel head, writing their bets around the edges of a letter McGuirk found in his pocket. They agreed to throw their weapons into a common pile, where no man could reach for his without being seen by the others, flung their hats and boots and shirts over them, and had presently scheduled a program which promised to take not only the rest of the afternoon but perhaps the entire week to complete. Carter and Hamilton went to mark off the course, while Lily prepared herself for this contest with as much ritualistic superstition as an Indian about to take the warpath.

She pulled off her boots, threw her hat aside, and tied a blue handkerchief around her head. She ran a few yards one way and then back again, flexed her fingers and suddenly doubled her fist, raising it toward the sun, and when she found Morgan watching her, she looked angry and suspicious, as if he might have broken the medicine. But then she walked toward him, announcing, "I'm going to beat you."

He smiled. "Is that why you picked me?"

She looked at him intently, but when he expected some other mockery, she gave a light sigh. "Do you want to know why I picked you?" She glanced around, as if to make sure she would not be overheard. "So you'd remember me."

He threw back his head, laughing with real amusement. "I would have anyway."

"Of course, I wanted to beat you, too."

Zack had insisted that they race bareback, some small compensation for the eighty-pound difference in the weight of the two riders, and after Lily had shaken hands with Jenkins and Hamilton, she grabbed her horse's mane and sprang onto his back with the alacrity of a circus performer. The men glanced at one another, exchanging meaningful nods, and as they jostled the horses into place, Lily looked as grimly concentrated as if she expected Jenkins would thrash her if she lost.

McGuirk fired the starting shot and Morgan's horse gained several yards before she drew up to him, lying almost flat, with her bare feet steadily pounding her horse's flanks. She began to gain, and, as she went by, glanced at him sideways, startling him with her look of rapturous frenzy. While he gazed in surprise at that distraught face, she edged into his path, his horse stumbled, nearly pitching him over his head, and before he had recovered she was several yards away.

He came abreast of her again and they rode side by side, watching each other distrustfully, for Jenkins' jockey had proved uncommonly resourceful, but then quite inadvertently he grinned, and it seemed she took this as capitulation. They swept around the halfway mark and once more she tried to throw his horse off stride, forcing him so far out that as they started back she was two lengths ahead, and when he drew near she cast him a menacing glare, as if she would be ready to kill him for it if he won. Then all at once she gave a hard triumphant slap at her horse's shoulder and began to swear, as if she were reciting an incantation, and in another few seconds had crossed the line two lengths ahead. She rode on a short distance, swung the horse around and trotted back, flinging up one hand in a salute as Jenkins and Hamilton ran to congratulate her, but she did not dismount, saying she would walk the horse and cool him.

Morgan looked apologetically at his friends, who stood observing him with curiosity, as if to ask how a man felt who had let a girl defeat him. "I'm sorry, she beat me," he explained, afraid they were thinking he had let her win from gallantry or infatuation. "I swear to God she did."

"Surprised you, didn't I?" she demanded, and was smiling with such delighted vanity that they began to congratulate her, and she leaned down to shake their hands while they assured her they were honored to have lost money to her cousin and step-brother. "You can ride, Miss Jones, you sure can ride." She nodded immodestly, giving Morgan a quick, sly smile.

The others were noisily preparing for the next race, Carter against Hamilton, and seemed to have forgotten Morgan's humiliation and their own losses. Morgan and Lily walked their sweating horses and, when they passed, exchanged brusque nods, until finally he smiled, hoping he looked tolerantly amused, and she raised her eyebrows.

The next time they passed she was sitting sideways, with one knee drawn up, as much at ease as if she sprawled in a chair. She had taken off the scarf and her hair was lifted by the wind, slapping across her cheeks and forehead, and she was singing in a light childish voice the obscene verses of "Joe Bowers." All at once she reined her horse about and came trotting up to him. "You're curious about me, aren't you?"

"We're closing the books, Devlin," Zack shouted. "Are you on this race or not?"

"Want me to bet for you?" Morgan asked her.

"Half an ounce on Carter. Hamilton's horse has a bad right leg. Oh, it's true," and she added, as he went to place the bets, "Come back, I want to talk to you."

Zack, seated at his barrel-head desk, shook dust into two tin cups, and as he returned the pouches to Morgan he screwed up his face in a mimicry of condolence. "I'd be just as happy if somebody gave me a mountain lion for a present."

Jenkins glanced around, but then turned his attention to the race and Morgan rode to where she was trotting her horse about in small circles. As he approached she gave him a smile of such engaging frankness that she seemed once more only a young tomboy playing with her cousin's friends. "I think your cousin Jenkins takes a dim view of our conversation." Morgan said. "He didn't look very friendly just now."

"My cousin Jenkins, the hypocritical bastard. One time he's my cousin and next he's my brother and then all of a sudden he's my husband." She took out a cigar and chewed it, scowling. "He knows I don't give a damn what people think." She tilted her head. "Do you think I'm bad?"

Morgan laughed, but quickly composed his face. "It's none of my business."

"That isn't what I asked you. I asked you if you think I'm bad." She sat with one leg drawn up, comfortably holding her ankle, staring at him and plainly wanting him to tell her she was bad indeed, the wickedest girl he had met.

"No, I don't. But I do think you're making things pretty hard for yourself."

"What do you mean by that?"

"Dressing up like a man. Traveling with men. Living a man's life."

She gave a derisive hoot. "It's a hell of a lot easier life than a woman's, I can tell you that."

"Easier for a man. Not for a girl."

"Easier for anybody."

"You can't get away with it."

"Can't I?" She swelled her chest, thrusting her breasts against the shirt. "I do. I am."

The men were yelling as the horses came pounding along, and as Lily had predicted, Carter was several lengths ahead, while Hamilton's mount was throwing his leg sideways in a clumsy and careless fashion. "You're young, that's why." Morgan said. "How old are you?"

"Nineteen, next month."

"Seven months older than I am."

She smiled condescendingly. "That's in years."

"You've seen the elephant," he suggested, and hoped he looked as if he had seen it, too.

"And heard the owl." She grinned maliciously, chewed at her unlighted cigar, and spat out the shreds.

"You like living this way?"

"Of course," she agreed briskly. "Don't you?"

He smiled. "Yes, I like it. If you think it's really the same life we're living."

"It's more the same than you'd be willing to admit." She crossed one leg over the other and leaned her elbows on her knees, prepared to become serious and confidential. "Don't you men think a woman ever wants to do anything but change her clothes and fix her hair and clean the god-damn house and have babies? I've been married, I know what I'm talking about." Morgan glanced toward Jenkins and she scowled. "Hell, no, not that baboon. My husband was a gentleman, or I thought he was. I went out to Frisco to meet him three years ago, but he was having such a good time he couldn't be bothered with me. But one of his friends could. So off we went to Sacramento and, what with one thing and another, here I am. Traveling with Jenkins and Hamilton."

"Planning to do some prospecting?"

"I could use a little of the yellow medicine." She made the Indian sign for money, holding her right hand before her right breast, her thumb and forefinger curved to form an incomplete circle. "They say it's good for whatever ails you."

She gave her horse a kick and it bolted away so sharply he expected her to lose her balance, but she clung to its mane and in another moment hauled it up and leaped off, strolled over to Hamilton and stood with one bare foot crossed over the other, leaning against his shoulder. After that, she paid no more attention to Morgan but talked to the others, drank whenever the bottle was passed her way, and before the afternoon was over had beaten McGuirk in another race. But by this time she had them captivated, and McGuirk would have been disgraced if he had won.

All at once, they decided it was time to go. They buckled on their guns, hauled on their boots and buttoned their shirts, and, in the faint twilight, waved and shouted and rode away, back to Bruno Favorite's, where they rushed to the table and took their seats, dealt the cards and began to concentrate with bland faces and aloof disdain for the curiosity they knew surrounded them, until at last one of the men approached McGuirk.

"What's she like?"

"What's who like?"

"You been out there the whole god-damn day. What the hell kind of a woman is she?"

"Miss Jones," Zack gravely assured him, "is one hell of a good jockey, and don't let anybody tell you otherwise."

Morgan avoided any discussion of the races, and was glad that Zack did not ask what Lily Jones had talked to him about; and then, as they entered their cabin a few nights later, a voice whispered, "Don't be scared—it's Lily."

Morgan lighted a candle and they found her crouched in a corner. She stood up, smiling. "It's only me."

"Where's Jenkins and Hamilton?"

She spread her hands. "Gone."

Zack looked angry. "Don't tell us that. What kind of a trick are you up to?" He peered about and kicked at the lower bunk, running his hand swiftly across the upper one. "You trying to make trouble?"

"Of course I'm not. Don't you believe me?" She appealed to Morgan. "Don't you?"

"Why'd you come here?"

"I came here for help. They've gone, cleared out, that's all, and left me strapped. Even took my dust—everything I won on the races. Can you believe it?"

"I can't," said Zack. "I don't trust those two birds and I don't trust you, either."

"But it's true. They've left me. I'm all alone."

"What do you expect us to do, take up a collection?"

"Let me stay here with you—just for a little while, until I can get my bearings."

"How are you going to do that, Miss Jones?" Zack asked her.

She smiled at him humbly. "Please don't call me Miss Jones. Please call me Lily. Miss Jones means you don't like me—you want to be formal. I thought you would be my friends." She turned to Morgan. "Won't you?"

But Zack answered. "Friends aren't what you need. What you need is a husband. Somebody who'll take care of you so you don't go ricocheting about like a stray bullet, bouncing off one mountainside and then another."

"I had a husband," she told him, and looked as grimly accusatory as if the fault were Zack's. "And he left me, too."

"Luck runs against you where men are concerned, is that it?"

Lily and Zack stared at each other defiantly, but Morgan said, "Maybe you're right, Zack, and what she needs is a husband. But she doesn't have one right now—why can't she cabin with us for awhile?"

Zack smiled wryly. "No reason I can think of, no god-damn reason at all."

She waited a moment, as if expecting him to change his mind, and then held up both hands and bowed her head in the sign for thanks. "I knew you were gentlemen. What can I do to help?"

"What can you do to help?" Zack asked. "You can get supper, that's what you can do. And tomorrow you can set to and clean this cabin up. It sure needs it because Morgan and me haven't been very good housekeepers." He stuck his thumbs into the top of his trousers and twiddled his fingers against his hips. "You know, this might not be such a bad arrangement, after all."

She gave him a frown, warning him not to make fun of her in her distress, but promptly began to prepare their supper. Zack and Morgan went outside to wash and as they stood there, splashing until their beards and hair and shirts were soaked, Zack muttered, "I don't believe a word the little bitch says."

Morgan had decided that she was his property, just as he had known the first day she rode into town, and considered it his responsibility not only to defend and protect her but to justify her, as well. "You think they sent her here as a decoy? They know they could never get away with that."

"They may be gone but they'll be back, and when they come they'll be loaded for bear."

"Zack, what the hell's the matter with you? You've made up your mind without knowing anything about her."

They turned and Morgan was angrily surprised to see in Zack's expression a kind of pitying scorn. They stared at each other, alert and careful, almost as they had the day of the little girl's funeral, but then suddenly Zack threw back his head, slapping hard at his thigh, and burst into laughter, and the moment when a quarrel might have begun was over. They stood looking across the valley where smoke was coming from the shacks and the big butte stood in shadow, almost black, and felt a surprising sense of well-being to know that in their cabin was a girl, doing the work they had done and preparing to make them comfortable. They stood silent for a few minutes, smelling the smoke from their own fire, and when she appeared in the doorway, calling "Let's grub!" went in eagerly.

She looked at them questioningly and then, sensing that they had decided to be grateful for the comforts and companionship she brought them, she gave them a wide, happy smile and they sat down to the beans and bacon and coffee like three old friends who had traveled much together, seen many things and shared many experiences.

Thinking, perhaps, that she was expected to entertain them, Lily began to brag about her venturesome life and they listened with serious interest, never once smiling or glancing at each other. "That was just before I was captured by the Indians," she said casually, swiping at her plate with a bread crust and stuffing it into her mouth. They glanced up, as if this was one too many, and she added, "Of course it was lucky for me I was only four. They're very good to children, you know."

"How did you get away?"

"I was ransomed. It was after a big battle—oh, my God, when they go on the warpath an Indian camp is a madhouse. I can remember it as if it was yesterday—"

She described her experiences with the Indians, and at last told them she had run away from home when she was fourteen, disguised herself as a boy, and gotten a job riding for the Pony Express. But at that Zack belched loudly, sucked on his teeth, and leaned back against the wall, inquiring, "Maybe your real name's Johnny Frey?"

"You think I'm lying. Well, maybe I am sometimes, but you can bet I haven't spent my time working embroidery and painting water colors." She drew herself up, still sitting spraddle-legged on the stool, and whacked hard at her ribs. "I'm tough as hickory and hard as bull quartz," she informed them, quickly bent her right arm and leaned toward Morgan. "Feel that." He smiled and she leaned closer, with urgent seriousness. "Go ahead. Feel it." Morgan reached out and gingerly poked at her muscle. "Not like that!" she cried. "Feel it." He grabbed her arm and clenched it and, as she had said, she was tough as hickory. But when she made the same offer to Zack he shook his head.

"I pass." He stood up. "Well—now that you've given us fair warning, how shall we sleep?"

"Take my bunk," Morgan said. "I'll sleep on the floor."

"No," Lily told them. "I will. I don't want any favors from either one of you. I invited myself here and I'll earn my keep."

There was a brief embarrassment as they wondered what concessions were to be made first. But Morgan and Zack went outside and returned to find her wrapped in a blanket spread over one of their buffalo robes; they blew out the light, and when they awakened she was dressed and squatting before the fireplace, frying bacon and boiling coffee. She gave them a merry salute, and when they had gone outdoors to wash and returned, their breakfast was ready. She stood in the doorway when they left, waving and smiling, and Morgan looked back to see her sweeping the packed dirt before their cabin with all the frantic determination she had displayed in winning a race.

"You take her out for a ride tonight, if she's still there when we get back," Zack said, "and I'll dig up our dust and bury it somewhere else."

"Where else? She's got all day long to look for it, if that's what she's after."

"I'll move it every so often—if she stays."

"She'll stay. She likes us better than she liked them. Zack, don't worry about it. She's my responsibility. I like her and, what's more, I feel sorry for her."

"How in the hell can you feel sorry for a girl like that? You know how she'll wind up."

"Maybe. But that's not what she is right now."

She was there when they returned, the cabin was cleaned and dinner was ready, and Zack could find no evidence she had been searching for their cache. "It's too early. She knows we don't trust her yet." Morgan did not argue, and assured himself that Zack might know all the secrets of mountaineering, but he had discovered very few about women.

The news of her presence in their cabin spread quickly through the camp and before long Mrs. Nichols—just as she had come to offer her help the day Henry Halloway died—came to plead for Lily Jones. She rode up at midday and they stopped their work, removed their hats, and greeted her politely, with faces so guilelessly solemn she was forced to spend a few minutes discussing their mining methods and the unusual plague of flies. But at last she came to her subject.

"Miss Jones, I understand, has been abandoned by her cousin and stepbrother?"

"Yes, ma'am."

"And that's why you've taken her into your quarters, of course."

"Yes, ma'am."

Zack slid his hands into his pockets and seemed ready to listen to a long and entertaining harangue, but Morgan stared at her gloomily and his eyes glittered with a resentment she seemed to find disconcerting, but only for a moment. "We don't question your motives, but we decided that even in a camp like this one a young girl must be protected, and so we want to offer her our homes. She may stay with Mr. Nichols and me for as long as she likes, and if she wants to leave she can go to Mrs. Collins, or one of the other married ladies. She can help us with the cooking and housework and, in return, we'll give her board and lodging. We think she'll be much happier."

Morgan and Zack glanced at each other, and Zack, after frowning in careful consideration, said, "It's a nice offer, Mrs. Nichols, and we'll tell her about it tonight."

"Why don't you call on her, Mrs. Nichols?" Morgan asked, as Zack turned away and began, with unusual clatter, to shovel rocks into the sluice box. "Explain how you feel, and ask her what she wants to do."

"Very well, I will." She turned, and then paused. "It makes me sad when I think of what you might have been, if you hadn't come west. The West has spoiled more young men than it ever improved. The West, if we told the truth about it, is our national disgrace."

"But one thing's sure, Mrs. Nichols," Zack told her, "whether we came west or didn't, we'd still be men."

"But you might also have been gentlemen."

She rode away, and Zack gave Morgan a hearty blow across the shoulders. "You might have been a gentleman, you son of a bitch, but I'm god-damned if I would have!"

They found Lily seated cross-legged in the doorway and so absorbed in examining herself in the three-cornered mirror which, with a harmonica, were the only possessions she had salvaged from Jenkins and Hamilton, that she did not see them until they got quite near, and then she leaped up with a joyous whoop and came running toward them. "The missionaries were here today! Mrs. Nichols and Mrs. Collins and a couple of others. They want me to put on skirts and let my hair grow and stop smoking cigars and riding astride and swearing and playing poker and racing. They want me to be like them," she added, with enthusiastic incredulity.

"What did you tell them?"

"I told them I was glad to have only two men to worry about because I'd just escaped from a whorehouse in Frisco. Here's a letter for you." She took an envelope from her pocket and gave it to Morgan, explaining that the first mail had come in today and she had gone to get it. "I was going to read it, but I was afraid you'd be mad and throw me out."

He tore it open and Lily stood leaning against him with casual familiarity, while Zack went quickly into the cabin, looking as apprehensive as if he expected to hear the Vigilantes wanted him, and when he came out Morgan handed the letter to him. "Here—read it, if you want to. Lisette asks to be remembered to you. The baby's walking and talking. My father and Pete and Lem Finney are building a silver mill. Nella Allen's brother got killed not long after we left—and no one's seen Nella for more than a year."

X V

Zack was willing to admit that Lily had made their lives more comfortable, and certainly they were the two cleanest men in the mountains. There was hot water waiting for them each night, the cabin and its contents were swept and scrubbed, and she promised to make them a great delicacy she knew, a dish called China Chilo, as soon as she could get the ingredients for it. And she had adopted them and all their concerns, as Zack did not fail to remind Morgan she had so recently adopted Gaius Jenkins and Charles Hamilton.

The news of Morgan's family and their friends continued to interest her, and apparently she studied the letter during the day, so that when they sat down to dinner she was ready to catechize him on unclear passages and to advise him on their problems. "Devlin, I think your family should make that move to Helena," she told him one night, more than a week after the letter had come. "I hear Virginia's about played out." She was sopping up the molasses from her plate, for she ate it with every meal, and seemed to find some exquisite delight in its flavor which Morgan and Zack envied, wondering why it was not so delicious to them. "Just think, Virginia's got French classes and a theater and dancing classes and churches and sleigh rides and oyster suppers and it sounds so god-damn refined it makes me want to puke. But Lisette likes all that, doesn't she?"

"I suppose she does. Do you think she shouldn't?"

"What the hell do I care? Only it worries me sometimes to see the country closing up so fast. You know, it won't be much longer before all this will be over." She gave a wide, sweeping gesture to indicate the cabin and its haphazard furnishings and, beyond it, the valley, wide and somber in the twilight, which she loved for its isolation and dangers as much as for its hot summer days which were deceiving them once more about the winter. "Someday," she said solemnly, "the missionaries will take over the whole shebang." They smiled as they watched her, leaned comfortably back in their chairs with their feet propped on the table, and she shook her finger warningly. "Mrs. Nichols and Mrs. Collins and the others, the respectable women, damn their pure, pinched souls, will creep across the Territories like an eclipse. And we'll all look at each other and say how in the hell did it happen. But it happens." For the first time she seemed sorrowful, deserted by that vital gaiety they had supposed was inexhaustible and dauntless. "It happens—and nobody in the world can stop it."

Morgan stood and bowed to her. "You're making a damn good try. My compliments."

"You're laughing at me again."

"I'm not, I promise you. This life is hard enough on a man. I don't see how you get by and I don't know how much longer you can keep it up, but I admire your guts."

"I can tell you how much longer I'll keep it up. For the rest of my life. I'll never become a Mrs. Nichols or a Mrs. Collins or even a nicer kind of respectable lady like I'm sure your mother is, and your sister, and Miss Nella Allen. I'll never walk the white man's road, so help me God." She banged her fist on the table.

Zack, who had been smiling tolerantly, stretched his arms over his head and opened his mouth in a noisy yawn. She turned to him, ready for battle, and at that moment he threw back his head and gave a Rebel yell, an eerie, wild cry, tremulous and terrifying, which filled the cabin with sudden horror, and then as they both stared at him, the cry stopped short and he began to laugh. Quickly, he stood up and left the cabin.

"What a sound," she whispered, running her hands over her arms and huddling down, as if to protect herself. "I never heard it like that before." She gave him an embarrassed glance. "He was making fun of me, wasn't he? Of course he was. Sometimes I guess I do crow pretty loud. I tell myself I'll never do it again, but then something happens and I can't help myself. I rare back on my haunches and start in." She laughed softly, and they looked at each other questioningly, surprised to be alone. All at once Morgan took hold of her shoulders, bringing her to her feet.

"Hey, what if he comes back?"

"He won't be back soon."

She pulled away. "How do you know? You been drawing straws?"

He began to kiss her, and although at first she pushed against his chest and shoulders, her mouth was responsive, and she gave herself to him with an eager impatience that matched his own, and proved to be as selfish and companionable in this as in everything else, moving beneath him with quick, nimble agility, so lively and vigorous and intent upon securing her own pleasure that when it was over he wasted little time wondering if now he must say that he loved her, but told himself that what she wanted was what they had had. And this happy conviction filled him with a warm and grateful tenderness, and made him marvel more than ever that Zack could be suspicious of any girl with so much simple honesty in her body; but then, Zack must have wanted her for himself, and envy had made him distrustful.

But if Zack was jealous he showed them no evidences of it, either when he came back to find them playing cribbage, or the next day when he and Morgan were at work; and after dinner he announced that he had left an unfinished poker game at Favorite's. Lily stood in the doorway, watching him walk away and smiling. "Fletcher's got more charity in him than I gave him credit for." She turned to Morgan. "I hope he isn't mad. After all, this was his cabin before I came and now he thinks it isn't." She parted her lips greedily. "Oh, I was so afraid he wouldn't go."

Even so, he was concerned about her during the day, and when they returned and found her squatting before the fireplace preparing their dinner, he entered almost warily, expecting she might have begun to brood over her martyrdom, as he believed women liked to do, but she greeted them with such enthusiasm she might have been afraid they would not come back. She never once fell sullen or looked at him with hurt quizzicalness, waiting for some pretty compliments he had not invented, but met him joyously, and, when she lay beside him in sleepy satisfaction, stroking his shoulders and chest, she murmured no sentimentalities but only random musings about the heat, the ride she had taken that afternoon, or a visit from Dancing Rabbit, the only woman who would speak to her.

And they sometimes found Lily and Dancing Rabbit sitting crosslegged outside the cabin talking to each other in sign language, with a few extemporaneous grunts and a great deal of laughter, for the little Indian was a humorist in her fashion and filled with goodnatured contempt for Buckshot Carter and every other white man in camp, while the women, but for Lily, roused her mordant scorn.

"She says we're all bad cooks," Lily told them. "And we smell bad, too." Lily laughed delightedly, clapping her hands. "She can't wait until her lease runs out and she can go back to her people."

Morgan, she advised Zack seriously, must learn more sign language, for to be in Indian country without it was to be deaf and dumb, and so they sat at dinner and signaled for mercy, for thanksgiving, announced the approach of friends or enemies, swapped horses and bartered whisky, for two or three hours at a time; and one afternoon as they approached the cabin, Morgan asked Zack, "You like her better now, don't you?"

"She's an unusual female, I'll agree to that."

The first time Lily went with them to Favorite's, she was invited to play poker with them, and after that she took part in their activities as she had the day they visited Jenkins' camp, while even Zack stopped teasing her and listened soberly to the stories she told, and if now and then he pointed out some small or great discrepancy, she denied having ever told them any different version and insisted they must have heard it from someone else.

"I'm quite well known, after all," she assured them. "Why, I'm the best-known woman in Kansas and Missouri. Ask anyone there—they've all heard of Lily Jones." She tapped her finger meaningfully on the table. "But not as well known as I will be. I'll be famous one of these days, you wait."

"Famous for what?" asked McGuirk.

"Famous for being myself."

The others concealed their smiles and went on playing, and by now were quite ready to believe it might be true and that Lily Jones, if she could survive the life, would be more famous than any of them.

She might never get rich and she would certainly never be respectable, the dry air and hot sun and biting winds would make her look years older than any man her age, her light voice might turn hoarse and no doubt she would smell of too many cigars and too much bad whisky, but even though she might become a woman they would look at no longer with secret covetousness, she would nevertheless be the Lily Jones of her own legend and, in time, would become a legend to men and women who would never be able to imagine the merry and impudent girl who now sat there among them.

"I'll be famous," she said, "because I've got guts. The rest of you won't amount to a good god-damn." They smiled patiently and studied their cards, for Lily insulted them with such bland equanimity that a man could only make a fool of himself by taking offense at this honest and impartial appraisal. "There's one exception here." She glanced about. "One of you will be rich, and that's Devlin. If Fletcher gets money it'll be by accident, and you other guys won't ever see thirty."

"Who the hell wants to?" asked Carter.

"If I ever get money," said Zack, "it'll be no accident, it'll be a bloody miracle. Devlin? Maybe that's another story. I'm not sure."

"Neither am I," Morgan agreed, and thought it was at least as true as Carter's statement that he did not want to live another ten years.

In fact, none of them thought very much about money and only Lily Jones seemed to have a clear ambition for her future: to live the

rest of her life as she lived now. For the camp was as various as a
city to them, the dark little cabins housed them as well as mansions,
and the valley with its surrounding hills and distant mountains
pleased them better than any garden.

Morgan glanced about the table at his bearded and dirty friends
and the slight girl who sat across from him, peering at her cards
with concentration, and felt a surprising and intense conviction that
this was the happiness men talked about and that for the rest of his
life he would never experience it in any more acute and definite
form. The others, he believed, felt it as he did, and this companionship seemed to have taken its origin the afternoon Henry Halloway
had died, leaving each of them with the sense that it was he and no
other who had failed to keep him alive; and so his death had formed
a bond between them which might not, finally, be a permanent one
but which was for the time strong and reliable.

But although he pretended to be as indifferent to the future as any
of them, Morgan nevertheless spent much time roaming the camp
and talking to other miners. Several of them were experienced prospectors who had not come here to wash out only enough gold to buy
their groceries and pay their gambling debts, but were preoccupied
with mining and had little interest in improving their skills with
cards and guns and the art of looking dangerous.

They talked to him willingly, took him down into the shafts to
show him what they had found, and declared it was Butte and not
Virginia City or Helena or any of the other hundreds of camps now in
the Territory which would one day astonish the world. There were
some who had built experimental smelters, and Amos Muspratt had
filed on several properties and expected to ship some ore to Baltimore, since there were no refineries in the West which could process
it.

Morgan visited Amos often and listened while he described the
troubles he was having and his conviction that one day, when a railroad came into the Territory, he would be a rich man. He gave Morgan samples of the ore, which Morgan showed to Zack as surreptitiously as if the railroad would arrive next year. But Zack shook his
head and seemed to suspect him of developing prospector's delu-
sions, and he quoted the Mexican proverb: "Only three classes of
men work silver mines; those who have other people's money to
spend, those who have more money than they know what to do
with—and fools."

The summer seemed quickly gone. The nights were cold again,
the aspens turned yellow and the cottonwood orange, and the wild
geese began their southward migrations. Most of the camp had decided to stay through the winter, hoping it would be easier than the
last, and, if it was not, they were at least better prepared for it.

Morgan and Zack made the decision, without asking Lily what she
wanted to do, and Morgan congratulated himself he had contrived to
dominate her so well she was ready to stay if they did. She had been

living with them now for nearly three months, and although he occasionally wondered what she would do when he returned, as sooner
or later he would, to Virginia City, he preferred not to think about it;
for this seemed, in many ways, as pleasant an arrangement as he was
ever likely to make.

"There's something I think you should know about," Zack told him
one day, when they had taken refuge from a rainstorm and stood in
a small grove near their diggings. "You may not like it much." He
glanced curiously at Morgan.

"Go ahead."

"I been moving our dust from time to time, just to be on the safe
side. Guess what I came across." Zack seemed sorry he had begun
this, and finished quickly: "I came across a fresh burial spot, down
there at the southeast corner, just inside the wall, and what did I find
but a can with three pokes in it. Must be about a thousand dollars or
a little more, I reckon."

Morgan's face had turned dark red. "Where is it now?"

"I put it back, but next time I looked, it was gone."

"How long ago was this?"

"Last Monday, as I recall."

"Why the hell didn't you tell me then?"

"You should be able to figure that out, Morgan. You like the girl
and she came to us telling us she was strapped, threw herself on our
mercy, remember. Well, she ain't strapped at all, she's an heiress."
Zack grinned, as if to placate his friend for having brought him this
news. "Maybe we should've been charging her board."

"I'll be a son of a bitch, she lied to us. Let me talk to her."

When dinner was over and they sat smoking, Morgan, looking
quite gloomy, for he had become unexpectedly sentimental about
her, told Lily the cache had been found. She stared at Zack for a moment with cold hostility, gave Morgan a glance which seemed to
measure the degree of his anger and distrust, and then eased back on
the stool with her thumbs hooked into her pockets, spread out her
knees and asked him blandly, "What of it? Are you sorry I'm not
broke?"

"You told us you were, but that's not the point. Where did you get
it? Zack says there were three pokes."

She nodded and became as matter-of-fact as if she were a banker
and they had come asking for a loan. "That's right. Three. Mine.
Jenkins'. And Hamilton's." She looked truculently from one to the
other. "What're you going to do about it? Take me back to Helena
and turn me over to the Vigilantes?" She smiled scornfully and
bounced her knees up and down, quickly raising and lowering her
heels.

"How did you get it?" Morgan asked.

"None of your damn business. I took it, that's all."

"Held them up, maybe?" Morgan smiled ironically.

She stared at him suspiciously and then at Zack, her eyes glitter ing, and suddenly leaped up and went pacing about the room, glowering as she moved back and forth, and at last turned swiftly and accusingly to Zack. "It's mine! You can't have it. I knew you were looking for it and that's why I moved it. I won't give you an ounce, not a pinch, not a—" She gestured beneath Zack's nose, measuring with her fingers the infinitesimal amount she would not give him.

Morgan began to laugh. "For Christ's sake, Lily, we don't want your dust. All we want to know is whether or not your friends will be back after it."

"Suppose those two bastards kill all of us in our sleep one fine night?" Zack suggested.

"Oh, is that what's worrying you?" She gave them a sly smile. "They won't be back. I thought of everything."

"Good for you," said Zack. "But suppose you tell us what you thought of."

She hesitated, apparently not sure she should trust them with her secrets, but all at once threw her arms wide in a gesture of triumph. "I wrote 3-7-77 on a piece of paper and pinned it to their blankets." She gave a cry of delighted laughter and went dancing about the room, leaping onto the lower bunk and off again, twirling around Morgan and Zack, clapping her hands and stamping her feet in a wild and, they thought, rather uncanny celebration of her victory. "You should have seen them!" she howled joyously and then, as they only looked at her solemnly, stopped still. "What's the matter? Don't you think it's funny? I didn't owe those two bastards anything. They were just waiting for a chance to leave me in the lurch, I heard them talking about it once. I had to protect myself, didn't I?" Her face was red and she yelled at them, slashing the air with her hands, then rushed out the door and slammed it hard enough to make the walls shake.

Morgan and Zack looked at each other, and Zack quietly observed, "All the refinements of a Sioux Indian."

Morgan looked angry and cynical, thinking that Zack had understood the character of their household pet much better than he, and now crossed his arms over his chest and stared at Zack, as if asking what else he had to say. Zack, however, said nothing and no doubt thought the lesson was plain enough without exposition. He leaned against the wall, pushed his hat down over his forehead and shut his eyes, while Morgan fixed his gaze upon a nail in the opposite wall, and they remained without moving or speaking until, from the corners of his eyes, Morgan saw her peek into the window and duck out of sight again.

"Come in here," he shouted.

The door opened slowly and she poked her head in, then entered briskly and sat down facing them, her knees and feet together and her hands demurely folded.

"When your friends come back," said Zack, "looking for their dust, what do you figure to do about it? Meet them in a nice friendly way and hand it over, with five percent interest?"

She pursed her lips, as if she meant to answer him insolently, then turned to Morgan and seemed to expect him to defend her. But he looked even angrier than Zack, and she addressed them both with an air of perfect simplicity and candor. "I did it because I hated them, especially Jenkins. He beat me up when he got drunk and did terrible things to me, I can't tell you what they were." She glanced covertly at Zack, to find a look on his face which indicated that he did not believe a word of it, and turned to Morgan. "I did it to get rid of them—so I could be with you."

Morgan gave Zack a quick look, warning him not to laugh, and Zack rubbed his chin thoughtfully and examined his cigar, frowning.

"They won't come back," she whispered, and had become remarkably ingratiating.

"What makes you so sure?"

"The Committee is down on Jenkins. They gave him warning to get out of Virginia City and he got. He was with a party that robbed a coach and he killed the driver. Used to brag about it when he got drunk. That's not the only man he killed, either. There was another one in Helena—"

"Never mind the list," said Zack. "We don't give a damn who he's killed in the past, we're only interested in who he might kill in the future." He tapped his chest and glanced significantly at Morgan.

She made a spitting sound. "You're better shots than either one of them. Jenkins is full of tricks, fans his gun and shoots from the hip and likes to impress people with the border shift." She threw an imaginary pistol from one hand to the other, then stuck both hands in her pockets, half closed her eyes and gazed at them with mocking incredulity. "If I didn't know both of you so well, I swear to God I'd think you were scared of Jenkins and Hamilton. But of course that can't be true."

Zack went to the door. "I wish it was only Jenkins and Hamilton we had to worry about."

"Zack Fletcher, are you suggesting that I—"

"I wouldn't trust you as far as I could swing a cat by the tail."

Zack went out and she turned to Morgan. "Are you going to let him say such a thing about me?"

Morgan stood up, and as he passed her she caught hold of his arm, but let him go and he started after Zack, now some distance down the road and softly whistling, "Bring Your Families West."

"Zack." Zack stopped, and waited for Morgan to reach him. "Shall we get rid of her?"

"She's your friend, not mine."

"You think she's in cahoots with Jenkins and Hamilton?"

"I think she's in cahoots with herself. But if Jenkins comes back looking for his dust, I wouldn't want to lay any odds we could count on her."

"Neither would I," Morgan agreed gloomily. They walked on, and the farther they walked, the angrier and more embarrassed he became, until he had decided to go back and tell her to leave that night and never trouble them again. But all at once Zack gave him a tap on the shoulder.

"Look here, Devlin, are we going to let a nineteen-year-old girl scare us pissless? What the hell are we, men or pilgrims?"

They returned to the cabin, with Morgan assuring himself he would not be fooled by her again and that, furthermore, the discovery was a lucky one because now he could stop worrying about what he owed her in the future. He banged at the door with his fist, and they discovered her seated at the table picking food from a frying pan with her fingers. She gave them a nervous, questioning glance, but at sight of their amused faces she smiled, bowed her head and continued eating, and none of them mentioned it again.

Before very much longer Morgan was able to convince himself she had been sensible to take the dust, for certainly a girl who had no husband and no relatives could not be so scrupulous as someone like Lisette; and it became easy for him to imagine that Lily Jones, for all her droll bravado, was in reality as helpless as Nella Allen. He looked at her as she sat staring at a hand of cards or mending their shirts, as she now began to do, and felt as much tenderness and desire as he ever had.

"After all," he told Zack, "we're good to her and they weren't. I think that's all there is to it."

"Maybe," said Zack. "But we'll take no chances."

Morgan remembered rather uneasily Zack's remark about the two prostitutes, Froglip Sadie and Rowdy Jane: "When a man wants a piece of tail bad enough—it's remarkable how his judgment fails him." But that, surely, did not apply to his own charitable feelings for Lily Jones.

Zack began to move their cache every few days and considered asking Bruno Favorite or one of their friends to keep it for them, but decided he did not trust them, either. They had almost four thousand dollars, most of it washed out during the summer, and although they had told Lily often enough that their luck was bad and claims all around them were paying very well while their own was practically worthless, he thought she no more believed that than he believed Morgan's theory that she would never do to them what she had done to Jenkins and Hamilton because they were kind to her.

The dirt floor was honeycombed with his tunnels, and lumps protruded where he had filled in the holes and shored up his vaults. Occasionally he buried the pokes out-of-doors, but never left them long, for a pack rat might carry them away. It seemed incredible to him that he could have become so concerned about money which, ordinarily, meant little to him, and he began to resent Lily Jones for obliging him to play this absurd and futile game while, he was sure, she waited with amused condescension, knowing she could find it whenever she wanted to.

Zack told himself she had come to them, not because she was in love with Morgan, but because she was the kind of woman who found satisfaction in reducing men who were otherwise securely fixed in their self-esteem to a condition of distrust and apprehension, making them doubt that they were as stable as they had believed, or even as manly. He looked at her across the table at dinner, wondering in what deceitful way she had spent her time during the day, and it seemed to him that no trickery was beyond her, that she was the embodiment of treachery and cunning, and that before she was done with them she would have not only stolen their money, but destroyed their friendship and possibly contrived to get them killed. Lily, however, seemed not to guess that he had such thoughts and behaved just as she had, showing him only a little less affectionate familiarity than she showed Morgan. This, Zack thought, was all the proof he needed that she was deep in schemes and plots, for otherwise, certainly, she would be abashed by the glares he gave her.

They were scarcely aware that it was almost Christmas, when Mrs. Nichols stopped Morgan one day as he and Lily and Zack were riding toward their cabin. Zack and Lily rode on, but Lily turned to watch them disapprovingly.

"I didn't want to seem rude to your friends," Mrs. Nichols told him pleasantly. "But Mr. Nichols and I, and some of the nicer people in the camp, are giving a little party on Christmas day, and we would like to have you and Mr. Fletcher join us."

Morgan answered her deferentially. "Thank you, Mrs. Nichols, but we plan to spend that day with our own guests." He bowed again, and Mrs. Nichols went on her way, frowning.

"What did she want?" Lily called. "After you to become a Christian again? Might as well sing psalms to a dead horse."

"She wanted us to come to prayer meeting on Christmas day." Zack screwed up his face in a look of agonized incredulity. "I told her we were holding one of our own."

And with great enthusiasm they began to plan their Christmas party, drawing up the guest list, discussing the menu and decorations, allotting funds for brandy and champagne, and considering the possibilities for music or other entertainment. Before they had reached the cabin the plans were complete, and they agreed that Mrs. Nichols had provoked them into the greatest spirit of the Christmas season any of them had felt for several years.

Lily announced the next night that she had delivered the invitations and all but one had been accepted. Queen Victoria Butler refused to join them. "The old toad looked at me like I had smallpox and she said—so help me God—'I could never spend Christmas in the company of sinners.'"

Froglip Sadie and Rowdy Jane, however, invited her into their

cabins, offered her coffee and smoked a cigar with her, and assured
her they would appear in their finest gowns. Dancing Rabbit was the
only other woman, and the men included Bruno Favorite and Carter
and McGuirk and those others with whom, for the past year and a
half, they had been playing poker and drinking, racing and fishing
and hunting. The older and more serious miners, like Amos Muspratt, were not invited, for they might dampen the gaiety.

The excitement increased as the days went on, until finally Zack
conceded that a girl who took such delight in a Christmas party
might not be quite so bad as he had suspected. He watched her tasting the bean soup, reflecting upon its flavor and adding salt and more
molasses, then tasting it again and licking her fingers, murmuring
ecstatically to herself, and thought that he had misjudged her—or
perhaps the spirit of Christmas had possessed him, too.

On Christmas Eve, Morgan and Zack went to the City Bathroom
where, for the first time in months, they had their hair cut and their
beards trimmed, and there they found Carter and McGuirk and the
others, clean or about to become so, and all of them filled with vast
conviviality, passing a bottle from hand to hand. They had left Lily
heating water for her bath and she had told them, proudly, that she
had borrowed a dress from Froglip Sadie. But they could not imagine her in skirts and a crinoline, and objected so vehemently she
promised to give them no such unpleasant surprise.

"At least I'll wear a ribbon in my hair. Get me some green and red
ribbon, all the ribbon there is, I need it for the decorations."

Lily and Dancing Rabbit had nailed pine branches to the cabin
walls, and when they returned with the ribbon she snipped it up and
decorated the branches with bows, moving about from time to time
to study her work, as if she had in her mind's eye some exact and
perfect spot for each bowknot. When that was done to her satisfaction, she tied one more green bow and one red bow and fastened
them in her hair, asking what they thought of her now.

"But where will they all sit?" She wrung her hands distractedly.
"Oh, I wish we had more room." Morgan gave Zack a triumphant
glance, meant to tell him that perhaps she was, after all, more domesticated than any of them had guessed, even Lily herself.

The guests arrived at four o'clock on Christmas afternoon and
staked their horses about the cabin, bringing stools and forks and tin
cups, and several had taken the precaution of getting drunk before
they came.

Only Dancing Rabbit had not celebrated the occasion with a bath
and she sent forth a rank and fetid odor, stronger than the venison
or whisky or coffee, which for a time was disconcerting; but the
room was crowded, the fire was hot, the prostitutes were heavily
doused with eau de cologne and soon, as when Carter had fed them
wolf meat, they forgot that she made them queasy and uncertain
about doing their share of eating and drinking.

Three men crouched in the lower bunk and two climbed into the upper one where they sat swinging their booted feet precariously about the heads of those below, and passing down their plates and tin cups to have them refilled. Zack and Morgan sat cross-legged on the floor. Froglip Sadie and Rowdy Jane perched on stools, both in low-cut gowns with velvet ribbons about their necks, steadily smiling and behaving with a kind of finicking elegance they found increasingly difficult to maintain, occasionally gave raucous hoots of laughter, but stifled them quickly and looked brightly about, studying one man's face and then another's, and seemed to be thinking thoughts none of them could have guessed.

Dancing Rabbit helped Lily serve the dinner, but then opened a champagne bottle with such reckless gusto, shooting out the cork with a sound which made them jump nervously, that Morgan or Zack opened the other bottles. The food, everyone agreed, was the best they had eaten and could be compared favorably with anything which had ever been served on a Mississippi River steamboat. There was the hot bean soup, venison and dried apple pie and coffee, and as much champagne and brandy as they could drink, for once Zack and Morgan had decided to have this Christmas party they were determined to make it the most lavish, the most brilliant, and the gayest celebration ever held in Butte City.

There was immediate and violent objection when one of the men took up a fiddle and began to play a hymn. "Lay off, for Christ's sake," he was advised. "Religion's played out, old fellow." And so he gave them, instead, "Joe Bowers" and "The Dying Californian," but most of this was lost in a welter of talk and laughter which soon became a babble of shrieks and singing, muttered threats which caused no trouble because it was not possible to tell who they were meant for, and sudden shouts of joy and defiance.

Lily, for a time, seemed in better control of herself than most of them, but after two hours or more she lay down on the floor, put her head on Morgan's leg, and closed her eyes. McGuirk fell asleep; Froglip Sadie danced a jig and began offering to take off her clothes; Dancing Rabbit collapsed into a corner and sat staring with sullen rage at Carter and now and then crawled over to shake her fist in his face, but then retired again to her corner, mumbling.

Other men who had not been invited began to arrive, and presently there were demands for hymns, which the fiddler played with doleful screeches, causing Buckshot Carter and the two whores to burst into tears. Lily shook her head in disgust, grimly set her mouth and sat up, lighting a cigar.

Morgan drank steadily and, at last, had no better picture of what was happening than the others did, but only a vague impression of a murky room growing continuously darker as the candles burned out. He heard a fiddle squeaking on interminably, saw one of the whores lying across the lower bunk being kissed by two men, realized dimly that a little later there was trouble between the women, who were quieted by sharp slaps from Carter, and finally permitted himself to sink slowly and gratefully and, he imagined, gracefully, into a softly floating detachment where he seemed to have achieved perfect peace and happiness, awesome even for a Christmas night.

The Christmas party passed off without fatalities or serious wounds and they never stopped talking about it, but referred to it throughout the winter, over and over again, as if it had brought to them unimaginable pleasures and the conviction that life could be good, that despair and death were illusions, that man was meant to love his fellows and could do so more easily than they had ever known before. They talked about it in large groups and small, for by the end of the night there had been an uncounted number of guests, and by early spring it seemed to have happened a very long time ago, when they had all been young and happy; for the winter soon reduced them to sorrow and anxiety, made them despondent with its length, and tired and listless from the deprivations.

"That was what I call living," they told one another. "Best goddamn time I ever had."

And Lily and Morgan and Zack were hailed wherever they appeared, with a welcome fit for heroes, and complimented upon their generosity in having given to this forsaken camp a Christmas which, according to Bruno Favorite, had combined the best features of a bacchanalian festival with a Christian obeisance to brotherly love. The decorations were exaggerated with each description, the supply of fine wines and liquors multiplied by gallons, the food increased in quantity and quality until Delmonico's would have been pleased to serve it, and the company's own wit, camaraderie, the beauty of the ladies, the hilarity of the jokes, had leaped beyond any possibility to imagine for those who had not been present. The guests became a brotherhood and, finally, a cult.

Part

II

XVI

IT HAD not been easy for Lisette to endure the insult of having her best friend chosen to represent Columbia in the Fourth of July parade, even though Georgina had assured her the ladies of the committee had made no invidious comparisons, but reached their decisions in sober impartiality: the cherished role had been given Georgina Hart because she was tall, and had blond hair which could be let down below her waist where it made an impressive and rippling display.

"Let's stop talking about it," Lisette said crossly. "I don't want to be Columbia, you couldn't force me to be Columbia, and as far as that goes, I'm glad I'm not tall enough to be Columbia."

Georgina sighed. "I know. How I envy you, being so little, and having all that beautiful red hair."

Lisette turned on her so suddenly that Georgina stepped back, alarmed. "I've told you my hair is not red, Georgina Hart, it's brown! Look at it—do you call that red?"

Georgina bent to examine the top of Lisette's head and Rachel joined her in an attentive study. They glanced at each other, widened their eyes and shrugged, and walked on as Georgina said, "Of course it's brown. Don't be mad at me, honey. I'm always saying the wrong thing, I just don't know what's the matter with me."

Lisette gave her a quick smile, hoping that neither Rachel nor Georgina had been able to recognize her surliness for what it was, painful pangs of jealousy because in less than five weeks Georgina Hart would ride in the Fourth of July parade, wearing a white robe on which her mother was even now at work, with silver cords bound about her long narrow waist, and her blond hair falling loose for everyone to see and admire as she passed through the streets in this most spectacular opportunity to reap general admiration which a nice girl might ever hope to enjoy.

But painful as she found this first defeat, and shocked as she was to have learned the world could be as unjust to Lisette Devlin as to anyone else, Lisette had reminded herself it was not the mere accident of height and coloring which made a monarch, and she expected them to know it.

Rachel Finney, with her brother Jacob, had arrived a year and a half ago and had immediately become Lisette's admirer and inseparable companion, a substitute, as Lisette had at first supposed, sent her by the Lord to comfort her for the loss of Nella Allen. But Rachel Finney, she had discovered, was no more capable of offering solace than Erma Finney was, and Lisette soon learned never to mention Nella Allen to Rachel.

It was Lisette's belief that Nella Allen's disappearance had caused her to grow up all at once, so that although she was not yet sixteen while Rachel and Georgina had each the advantage of being one year older, they seemed to her young and simple, without awareness or understanding of the riddles which lay beneath even their own lives; naïve little girls, she often thought them, who believed the world was only what it seemed—for they had never been forced, as she had, to find those answers others refused to give and, once found, never to let anyone guess she understood more than she had been told.

Nella had come back to them after Rick's death, but then, only a few days later, she had left the house early one morning, saying that she had promised her brother to take a message to a friend of his, and they had never seen her again.

Lisette had gone to their cabin late in the afternoon, expecting to find Nella there, but her clothes were gone and the cabin looked as it must have the night Rick had died, so that she had run from it in as much horror as if she had happened upon a murder.

"She'll be back," Matt had confidently predicted.

"But where is she now? Why did she leave us?"

At the dinner table Lisette sat silent and forlorn, wondering if Nella had gone away because she had found a friend she liked better, someone perhaps who never teased her, and often at night she began to cry and cried so violently that Marietta came in and sat beside her, but could make no promises about when Nella would return to them.

"She must be sick," Lisette told her father. "She wasn't feeling well, but I thought it was the shock of seeing Rick die. She was sick and she was afraid it might be catching, and so she went away to protect us—and now she may be dead." By the time she had spoken this prediction it seemed to have come true—Nella was dead at that moment, or dying and praying for them to come to her—and she threw herself into Matt's arms, sobbing so hard that she began to retch and was put to bed by her mother as if she was once again a little girl, sick as the consequence of her eager appetite.

She lay there, when the door was closed and the lights were out, and all at once, as if Nella's voice had spoken, she knew what the sickness was. For what else could explain the expression on her father's face when she had told him of Nella's sickness—and for what other reason would Nella have left them?

Those long walks, when Nella and Morgan had disappeared for an hour or two or three; Morgan's frequent look of sullen impatience and Nella's shy, pleading glances—all those signals which had seemed so romantic to her as she pretended not even to notice them, and which had made her almost resentful of their uneasy absorption in each other, she now understood, and the sorrow she felt at this knowledge, the righteous rage, possessed her all the next day, until Dr. Danforth was sent for to find out what ailed Lisette. She was grieving, he told them, over her little friend, something quite natural at her age, and he prescribed several cups of hot sage tea.

She questioned her father every day during the next months, and looked at him with her eyes brightly shining and a small, accusatory smile on her lips. "Perhaps she became a hurdy-gurdy?"

"No, Lisette. She hasn't."

"Maybe she was drugged. Spirited away by some old woman and put into one of those places."

Matt laughed at this, somewhat self-consciously, she thought, but probably that was because she was not expected to have such information. "Whatever gave you an idea like that?"

"I've read about it in the papers."

"Well, it doesn't happen often and it doesn't happen out here. She's gone back, as I've told you, to live with her aunt. You'll get a letter from her one of these days."

"But she would have told us first."

"Lisette, I know she was your friend, but she was an irresponsible young girl, and when her aunt sent for her, she left without thinking about any one else."

"That isn't like Nella."

"But it's what she did, darling. Her brother's friend told me about it. You're making a mystery where there is none."

"Oh, but there is," said Lisette wisely, and when her father gave her a sharp, inquiring glance she felt her face grow hot and quickly retreated, and after that she had nothing more to say about Nella Allen. For either there was a conspiracy and she was expected to join it, or she had come into unlawful possession of a knowledge she must guard very carefully, so that no one else might be harmed by it.

She had made a grim ceremony of tearing in two the photograph of herself and Nella, and had wrapped it carefully in a handkerchief and placed it in the bottom of a bureau drawer, with the locket Nella had given her for her fourteenth birthday and the gold-clasped bracelet made of Nella's blond hair. These keepsakes she had handled gingerly, as if contamination might spread from them, and intended never to look at them again. But at last she retrieved them, sometimes wore the locket or bracelet, and carefully pasted the picture together, and now she imagined that because of this painful experience she looked wise and contemplative, and she supposed this was apparent to everyone who saw her, even though they could never guess what had produced this ripeness of understanding in a girl not quite sixteen.

The day was warm, for summer had begun at last. Wild pink roses covered the bushes which only recently had seemed a snarl of wire, unlikely ever to break into this massive blossoming, and there was a wind which kept them brushing the hair from their faces. The subject of Columbia had lost its interest, as if the Fourth of July had come and gone and had meant nothing to them after all, and they began to discuss whether or not they would invite one of their friends to the party Rachel's parents were to give for her seventeenth birthday.

"My mother," said Rachel, "says that Anna Grace Burgess is not a nice girl. She likes the boys."

"How did your mother find that out?" asked Lisette, and put on a look of sly innocence.

"My mother is very observant. She's been watching Anna Grace ever since the night of the oyster supper, when Anna Grace went outside with Homer Grimes and didn't come back for almost ten minutes."

Lisette clucked her tongue. "What does your mother think they were doing all that time?"

"My mother has no idea what they were doing, but you'll have to admit it was very foolish of Anna Grace."

Lisette snipped at the grass, then drew out a stalk and chewed its juicy end to shreds. "It was certainly foolish of Anna Grace to let your mother see her go outside with your beau." Lisette and Georgina burst into merry, artificial laughter, exchanging delighted and taunting glances of purest cruelty.

"He is not my beau, Lisette Devlin, how can you say such an awful thing to me?"

"Awful?" Lisette and Georgina glanced at each other.

"Are you ashamed of him, Rachel, honey?" Georgina leaned solicitously toward Rachel, touching her fingers, but Rachel withdrew them. "I don't think she should be, do you, Lisette?"

"Just because he's got spaces between all his teeth? After all, he's Mr. Mercer's editor, isn't he?"

"Mr. Mercer, Lisette?" Georgina inquired.

"Of course—Mr. Mercer. What do you think I call him?"

"Is it true he's proposed to you?"

Lisette seized Georgina's wrist, and spoke to her in a savage undertone. "Who told you that? Tell me, Georgina Hart. Tell me who's been talking about me!"

Georgina gazed at her imploringly, but finally admitted: "Rachel told me."

Rachel stood up and Lisette leaped to her feet. "My brother told me that Mr. Mercer either has proposed to you, or he will, as soon as he can get up his courage. It's no secret he's mad for you, Lisette, everyone knows it."

Lisette began to laugh. "Ralph Mercer mad for me? But I scarcely know him. Anyway, I wouldn't get married now no matter who proposed to me. Would you, Georgina?"

Georgina blushed, for Georgina, as Lisette knew quite well, had some such expectations from her own brother, Jonathan. "Not right away, I guess. Not until I graduate."

"Oh, marriage," whispered Lisette, and gave a mock shudder. "How many babies are you going to have, Georgina?"

They were starting back toward town and Rachel turned, confronting her. "I'm surprised at you, Lisette, a girl brought up as carefully as you've been, asking such an indecent question."

"But we all think about it, don't we?"

"I do," Georgina admitted.

Rachel shook her head. "I don't."

"Never, Rachel?"

"Never. I think it's disgusting to think about babies when you're not married."

Lisette's face grew yearning and tender. "But imagine what it must be like to be a married woman and have a baby to take care of. I'm going to have lots of babies, one right after the other." She gave Rachel a wicked, sideways glance, found her red-faced and solemn, and threw one arm about her shoulders, hugging her close. "Rachel, what do you think we were made the way we are for?"

"Oh, Lisette, I wish you'd find something else to talk about. Beaux and babies and babies and beaux, that's all you two ever seem to think about nowadays."

Lisette looked at Georgina, they shrugged and smiled, pitying Rachel, and began to talk instead about the new dancing teacher but, before long, they had disturbed Rachel again by insisting that he was dangerous and fascinating, while Georgina gave it as her further opinion that he was divine.

"Georgina, that's blasphemy."

"Oh, Rachel," Lisette cried, "how can you stand to be so good? Are you really—or are you just pretending?"

"I think you're the one who's pretending, Lisette. I've noticed lately that you seem to want to shock me, and I can't imagine why."

"You have?" asked Lisette, surprised and doubtful. "Maybe it's be-

cause I've been wondering if we're all shocked by the same things."
She gave Rachel another sly glance. "I'm testing you, Rachel. That's
what it is, but I only realized it just now." All at once Lisette took
pity on Rachel, begged her pardon, and linked her arm through hers,
reflectively murmuring, "It's so hard to know when we're right and
when we're wrong. Isn't it?"

"It isn't hard at all, Lisette, and I'm surprised you should think it
is."

"But have you ever had someone you love very much do something you'd always been told was wrong—and still loved them anyway?"

Rachel paused, and when Lisette turned she found Rachel looking
at her with such suspicion that she waited, holding her breath, expecting Rachel to tell her that her mother also knew about Morgan
and Nella Allen, and why Nella had run away. But then Rachel shook
her head. "No, and if that ever happened, I wouldn't love them any
more. Not if I knew it, and not if I knew it was wrong."

And, thought Lisette, she was telling the truth, for Rachel Finney
would never doubt that she knew what was right and what was
wrong, and she had no tendencies toward forgiveness, perhaps because she never expected to need it herself. Rachel would spend her
life, as Mrs. Finney did, observing the weaknesses and mistakes of
her friends, and admiring her own virtue as other women admired
their own beauty.

For although she and Georgina found their entertainment in flirtation and gossip, and the conquests they made, Rachel made no effort to attract the young men they knew and even Homer Grimes,
who had arrived several months ago with Ralph Mercer, had drifted
to Rachel only after Lisette and Georgina and two or three other girls
had rejected him. Rachel refused to be jealous of their popularity,
was not impressed when one of them gleefully reported having received another proposal, and had once coolly remarked that her
mother said it was vulgar to be too much admired, for men usually
admired girls for the wrong reasons.

And Rachel, of course, was never troubled by any of the thoughts
which so often took Lisette by surprise, suffered from none of those
obscure yearnings and curiosities Lisette scarcely dared admit
even to herself, and had no experience of the delightful and terrifying sense of confusion which now and then came over her in the
midst of a waltz, or when a young man looked at her with unusual
concentration; and Rachel, no doubt, would make an admirable wife,
while Lisette sometimes wondered if the man who married her
would not regret it sooner or later.

"One day," she confided to Marietta, "I think I can't wait to be married. And the next day, I think it would be intolerable to have a husband. I wonder if Suky likes being married?"

Nearly a year ago there had been a letter which told them that her
cousin Susan Ching had been married to Philip Van Zandt and gone

on a long honeymoon tour of Europe. "It was love at first sight for them both," Susan had written. "Unfortunately, they were not willing to wait, and were married informally in our apartment—a great disappointment to Ceda and me."

"It must have been," Lisette had said. "Suky had her wedding gown planned by the time she was twelve. White moire antique with a Brussels veil seven yards long and two pageboys in dark blue velvet to carry it. And she gave all that up because she couldn't wait?" Lisette tapped the letter against her teeth, pondering once more the nature of the great mystery to which, even yet, she lacked some significant clues. Marietta, however, had assured her that she knew all any girl needed to know before she married, and suggested that too much theoretical knowledge might only confuse her more. "Susan Van Zandt," murmured Lisette. "Well—and now Suky's a wife." Her smile was derisive and whimsical. "She'll have to think about someone else now and then for a change, won't she?"

"Don't cultivate jealousy, Lisette," Marietta told her. "It's an ugly quality in a woman. Suky has never done anything to harm you."

"She's so vain."

"And so are you, darling."

Lisette gave a guilty little start, and ran to look at herself in the mirror. "I am?"

"Don't be ashamed of it. A woman without vanity is a woman without charm."

"Like Rachel," said Lisette softly and sat down, took the baby Annabel onto her lap and began to brush her hair, thinking of her cousin Suky who was now a married woman and who could, at least, never marry Morgan.

Sometimes she envied Suky for being married and no longer condemned to innocence, and other times she marveled that Suky, who had seemed to her cold and reticent, should be obliged to lock herself up every night with a man and humor his whims, whatever they might be. For that was one thing, at least, which even Rachel admitted to be true about marriage: husbands bore little resemblance to the gallant young men they met at picnics and sleigh rides and dancing classes. Some vague and ominous change, it seemed, came over the best of them once the ceremony had been read—but try as she would Lisette could not discover the exact nature of that change and, whenever she asked her, Marietta smiled at the question.

"Where do girls pick up such notions? Oh, I remember, I had them myself."

"But is it true?"

"Of course it isn't true. How can a man be a monster if you love him?"

"You mean," Lisette said gloomily, "he is one but since you love him you don't care."

Marietta laughed softly. "No, Lisette, that isn't what I mean."

"I have it all figured out," Lisette confided to Georgina. "Men have two different characters and, until you're married, you have no idea which one he's been hiding."

Georgina giggled at this and Lisette gave her a moody stare, thinking that this silly girl had no idea what surprises were in store for her.

"Haven't you ever been frightened?"

"Frightened of what, Lisette?"

"Of a man. Of the way he looks at you."

Georgina smiled. "Oh, maybe just a little."

"Well, then, what do you think it would be like if it wasn't just a game? Where's your imagination, Georgina?"

Lisette's imagination sometimes startled her by its vigor and immodesty, and her responses to situations which must have looked ordinary enough to anyone else were so vehement she was later ashamed, for once the seeming danger had passed she realized there had been no danger at all but only her apprehension of it.

It embarrassed her still to remember the first night she had met Ralph Mercer, an event quite awful to her, and yet to everyone else it had only been one more weekly hop of Professor Bundidge's dancing-class; and so, no doubt, it would have been to her, had she not entered the room with a sense of great excitement and a keen hatred of Georgina, convinced that this contest for Ralph Mercer—whom neither of them had met—was the culmination of all their rivalry.

Jacob Finney had introduced them, and Lisette had looked up at Ralph Mercer with a smile into which it seemed she had concentrated her whole self, and the intensity of her determination to conquer him was so great that she grew momentarily dizzy and could not even see him clearly. But the smile had exerted its charm so effectively upon Ralph Mercer that he promptly asked her to dance with him, and she waved in a gesture of triumph and farewell to Georgina as he took her sailing across the room.

Almost immediately, however, she became aware of having lost the initiative of her magic smile. Ralph Mercer, it seemed, must have made his own interpretation of it, for he was guiding and controlling her with a precision which was delicate and insistent, as if he had no misgivings about his authority, or her willingness to submit to it. The music seemed to grow louder and faster, sending Lisette fleeing about the room, stricken with panic and terrified by his close following, so that no matter how fast her feet went he was there and she must keep going at the same furious pace or be overtaken and, she imagined, knocked down before she could cry out a warning. Other faces, as they passed, she thought looked at them with alarmed concern, and perhaps this rout was as dangerous as it seemed to her; but then it ended, and he thanked her and walked away before she had found the courage to stop smiling.

She was able to look at him by now, of course, though she was still rather mistrustful of that powerful smile; for if she used it too recklessly he might, as her friends believed, propose to her, and, if he did, neither she nor her parents would take it as a kind of complimentary joke, which had been their reaction to the three proposals she had had so far.

Ralph Mercer was twenty-four years old, and his family lived in Albany, New York, where they owned newspapers and banks and real estate. He had graduated from Princeton and spent a year in Europe, and then set out to investigate the West, only because it was something he must see before he settled down to participate in his family's businesses, and Alder Gulch had pleased him so well that he had established the *Virginia City Journal*. He had not been there three months before he was acknowledged the town's most eligible bachelor by the parents of all Lisette's friends, while the girls themselves agreed that Ralph Mercer, with his serious, handsome face, his good manners and confident bearing, would have been the town's most eligible bachelor even if he had no money.

But after that hop at Professor Bundidge's, both the girls and their parents seemed resigned to having him captured by Lisette Devlin, and Lisette was more frightened at this possibility than she liked to admit.

She felt, in fact, something of the same sense of subdued alarm, vague but real, in Ralph Mercer's presence which she had felt whenever Zack Fletcher looked at her, and this seemed all the more curious because, when she was truthful, she admired them both. And it made her angry still to remember Zack Fletcher saying, "You're a little girl, Lisette. A very pretty little girl," as if her youth was something he held against her.

She was not, perhaps, so grown up even now, and yet when she looked at her naked body in her bedroom mirror she was surprised, sometimes by admiration, and sometimes by embarrassment, to see the full curves of her breasts and hips, her round buttocks and belly, and the black mask, tapering between her legs, and she would put her hands on her waist, squeezing it hard and lifting her breasts, and then be all at once overcome with shame so that she hurried to get dressed, wondering what fatal flaws there must be in Lisette Devlin, to have made her so vain and so wanton.

But it was, she found, just when she was most aware of herself, that she became most resentful of Ralph Mercer's interest, and most inclined to perplex him with new caprices, even though she defended him from her friends—whenever their jealousy made them critical.

"Mr. Mercer is divine," said Georgina, and by now they had picked handfuls of wildflowers as they made their way down Daylight Gulch, and were adding to them as they went along. "Only he does look a little bit severe."

"He does not. He looks dignified."

"That's what it is, honey, dignified. Anyway, I'd be afraid he'd always have some fault to find with me."

Lisette laughed scornfully. "Maybe he would, Georgina."

"I," said Rachel, "admire Mr. Mercer's moral dignity," and at that Georgina and Lisette exchanged glances and winked, for Rachel had never yet admired a man for his dancing, his curly hair, or the ardent expression in his eyes, as other girls did.

Then all at once Lisette was eager to be away from this ominous talk and she began to run, calling, "Let's go visit Mrs. Danforth."

Dr. Danforth had died almost a year ago, and Lisette and Rachel and Georgina stopped two or three times a week after school to spend a few minutes with her. Their mothers had asked them not to forget Mrs. Danforth, and supposed they went to see her as they might have gone to a sick friend, never imagining they regarded Mrs. Danforth with such awe and curiosity that the sight of her driving her buggy, at that same reckless speed, dressed in black crape which flowed over her from her widow's cap to her shoes, gave them a sharp and delicious sorrow and made them yearn for widowhood more intensely than they yearned for husbands, convinced that to be a young and beautiful widow, driving about muffled in black crape and visiting a husband's grave, must be life's most glorious experience.

They felt cold chills as she passed them, too preoccupied by her sorrow to see them or anyone else, and each time Georgina gave a long sigh, enviously whispering, "Poor Mrs. Danforth. Poor, poor lady. Her life is over." Other widows, they thought, were pathetic and tiresome, but Jenny Danforth, condemned to public sorrow, unbecoming black draperies, retirement and solitude, seemed to them more strange and baffling than ever before, and they always expected that on their next visit she would astonish them by revealing some fearful secret, or by telling some extraordinary tale of her past life.

All she ever told them, however, was the name of the book she was reading, and the only secrets she shared were her paintings, which she brought out and set on the small easel, asking them shyly and with her sad smile which ones they liked best, and she had given each her choice.

But she always looked pleased to see them standing at the door and staring at her silently, as if they expected she might refuse to let them into the little darkened house, holding tight to their offering of wildflowers, and at her invitation they stepped in almost stealthily and went to the chairs each had selected for her own, and there they sat, straight-backed and alert, as if expecting at any moment to be called upon to recite or to spring up and defend themselves, perhaps from the Doctor's ghost.

And whether they could not forget that a man had died in the next room, or because Jenny Danforth's own stateliness and reserve intimidated them, they could think of nothing to say, answered her questions self-consciously, and were as eager to escape as they had been to come there. They watched her carefully and steadily, kept their voices very low, so that she often had to ask them to repeat whatever they had said, and when she left the room to get some of the yellow cake she usually gave them, as if it might be a bribe, they began to whisper, accusatory and excited, but were once again sitting stiff and silent as she returned carrying a tray and smiling as if, so they thought, she knew exactly what they had been doing.

It was Rachel who most often caused the disturbance during Mrs. Danforth's absence, for the moment she disappeared Rachel leaped up and tiptoed about the room, peering here and there as if she knew quite well there was a valuable clue lying about, while Lisette and Georgina wagged their fingers protestingly.

"Sit down, Rachel, you've got no business snooping around like that."

"Keep quiet," Rachel told them. "I have a right to look at my hostess's belongings."

"But you have no right to open anything," Lisette whispered fiercely, as Rachel lifted the top of a box covered with seashells, peered inside, replaced the cover and, with a smug smile, sat down only just in time, for Mrs. Danforth was back more quickly than usual.

Lisette jumped up. "Let me help you, Mrs. Danforth." She carried a plate to Georgina and presented it ceremoniously, but when she gave another plate to Rachel she stood between her and Mrs. Danforth and formed a word with her lips: "Spy."

Rachel lifted her eyebrows and smiled and spoke to Mrs. Danforth in the voice she kept for her elders, precise and artificial, it sounded to Lisette, with a suggestion in it of obsequiousness. "My mother says you used to make this cake in Bannack, in the old days."

Jenny Danforth smiled at Rachel. "Yes, I did. In the old days, five years ago."

"Only five years, Mrs. Danforth?" asked Georgina, and seemed dismayed.

"Five years ago you were all just children. Now, tell me about your newest beaux. Lisette, your mother says you have another admirer."

Rachel and Georgina looked instantly at Lisette, fixing her with the same intent and amused and skeptical stares they would have shown if she had been called on in class to demonstrate a geometrical problem she had not prepared, and Lisette looked into her teacup, blushing. "Oh, no, Mrs. Danforth. That's my mother's imagination." Rachel sniffed and Georgina shook her head, and Lisette made a vow to take her revenge on them both as soon as they were outside.

But when, after what seemed a very long time, they retreated from Mrs. Danforth's house, giving her many excuses for where they must go next, what errands and duties they must perform, and backed off toward the sidewalk still waving as she closed the door, Lisette turned and seized Rachel's wrist, demanding, "What was in it?"

Rachel winced and tried to draw away, while Georgina urged them out the low gate, pleading, "She may be watching. She may be listening. Oh, don't talk about it here. Come on, come on."

They went through the gate but Lisette did not let Rachel go and confronted her again with her eyes dark and angry. "Tell me!"

"There was nothing in it. It was empty. That's the truth, Lisette," she added haughtily, as Lisette continued to look suspicious.

"The curtain just moved," whispered Georgina. "She's watching us. Oh, sometimes she scares me, I think she must be a witch."

"She is not a witch, how can you say such a thing?" Lisette demanded.

"Her husband died so suddenly."

"Pneumonia," said Lisette. "It carries them off like that in the mountains."

"Don't talk about the dead," Georgina begged them. "He'll come back to haunt you. But the box was empty—nothing in it at all?"

"Not a single thing," said Rachel, and her exclusive information made her even more authoritative than usual.

"And yet it was a letter casket, I mean a letter box," Georgina corrected, and gave another backward glance at the green-shuttered house. "She has nothing left, her life is over. Poor poor lady."

"My mother says that if the truth is ever known about Mrs. Danforth there will be a lot of pretty surprised people around here."

Lisette turned to Rachel grimly. "What do you mean by that, Rachel Finney? That's slander."

Lisette had never yet found a satisfactory explanation for the impression made upon her the first day she had met Jenny Danforth, standing beside her father as she and Nella rode up, for it had seemed to her that their faces were secretive and defiant, and her father had looked for the moment ready to protect Mrs. Danforth, or even to defend her if necessary, so that she had felt herself a temporary stranger to him and her presence unwelcome. But, though she had looked carefully, she had never again found that expression on his face in Mrs. Danforth's presence, and preferred to think she had imagined it.

"It is not slander," said Rachel.

"You were implying that Mrs. Danforth—"

"Oh, please, please, please," cried Georgina, and urged them along a little farther. "Every time we visit Mrs. Danforth we fight about something. Last time it was her new carpet."

"It was my mother who implied it, Lisette."

Lisette leaned closer. "And did she make you promise never to repeat it to anyone—ever?"

"Of course she made me promise."

"And you've broken the promise. What would your mother think of that?" Lisette gave her skirts a twirl and walked on, while Rachel followed, begging her not to tell her mother she had broken the promise. "Don't ever say it again, Rachel, I warn you—or I will tell your mother." Lisette shook her finger in Rachel's face. "I thought you had more conscience, I'm surprised at you."

XVII

Their new office, built a year ago to replace the first sod-roofed cabin, was two stories high and made solidly of brick. A sign extended across its front with Devlin Brothers painted in large black letters, and a gilded clock hung over the board sidewalk, its hands pointing perpetually to twelve, and the inscription Gold Bought Here was written on its face. The clock, Matt assured Morgan, as he snapped open the padlock, had become one of the Territorial landmarks, a point of orientation and a convenience to citizens and strangers alike.

He lit the hanging kerosene lamp and made a welcoming gesture to Morgan, who stood just inside the doorway, looking about with an air of distrustful curiosity, as if he might decide not to enter this eerie place, after all.

The office was dark even with the lamp burning, for it had only one window. Two flat-topped desks, scratched with mottoes and dates and initials, stood side by side in the middle of the room; there were several chairs, a ceiling-high safe against one wall, three filing cabinets, a black iron stove and two spittoons, brimful. And, as if he would like to know what Morgan thought of it, Matt stood with his hands in his pockets, smiling and looking at his son.

Since Morgan and Zack Fletcher had arrived four days ago, they had had no time alone, and it seemed to Matt that he and Morgan had been made strangers by this separation of two years, an estrangement he was now afraid might prove to be permanent, beyond the ability of either to repair. And Morgan, perhaps, preferred that it not be. For he had said nothing of his plans, whether he intended to stay or where they were bound for, had given no explanation for their return—not even the polite excuse of homesickness—and both he and Zack had been reluctant to talk about what had happened to them in Butte.

Lisette had wept as bitterly as when he had left, and Marietta had greeted him in silence, closing her eyes as he held her, and the expression on her face had unexpectedly reminded Matt of the way she had looked on the day of his birth. Robert and Douglas were shy in the presence of two such formidable conquerors, eager for tales of their exploits with Indians and bears, but when Morgan soberly assured them they had fought no Indians and killed no bears they had jeered at this false modesty. Jonathan had shaken hands with them, looking rather skeptical, and Matt thought he might have been glad enough if his older brother had not come back. Still, they poked at each other with self-conscious affection and exchanged compliments on their advancing manhood, until Lisette said, "Just wait until my friend Georgina Hart sees you!" And at that Jonathan gave him a glare, fair warning that he was not to return bearing the aura of his travels and use it in competition with him, for their childhood fights would have more serious consequences nowadays.

"Have any luck?" Matt had finally asked, and Morgan had glanced alertly at Zack, who stared at him with an impassive face.

"Not much. A few of the guys were luckier than we."

Matt asked him no more questions, for it seemed he was no longer entitled to his son's secrets, and was so convinced that one day soon he would lose sight of him forever, that when Morgan had spoken to him the night before, saying, "I wonder if we could have a private talk, sir? Can I come to your office early in the morning?" Matt had looked at him with pleased surprise.

"Of course. We'll go down together and you can see your sister ride by in the parade. Martha Washington is her cross to bear, but she's determined to bear it with style."

"I could have dyed my hair and been Columbia," cried Lisette, looking sulky, for her disappointment grew keener as the day came nearer, and had been much intensified since they had tried on their costumes and Georgina had looked more like one of the Greek pedestals in Lisette's picture album than the stiff and severe goddess of her nation.

They arrived at the office a little before nine o'clock for, although Matt and Pete were usually there by seven, the day was not propitious for business. Even then the streets were crowded, the sidewalks had become almost impassable, horses galloped by with howling, drunken riders, the saloons and hurdy-gurdy houses were open and busy, and hacks rattled up and down bearing noisy men and whores dressed as if for a ballroom. All during the night bonfires had burned upon the hillsides and men had ridden through the main streets giving the Rebel yell and firing their pistols, and when the flag was raised this morning there were some mutterings in the crowd, elbow nudges and sneers, but no one had tried to keep it from going up and no one had tried to shoot it down.

"There'll be some men killed today," Matt said, as Morgan slowly shut the door. "The War's over—but sometimes I think it isn't, and maybe it never will be. There are more Southerners in the Territory right now than there ever were in all the Confederate states put together, if you listen to them talk."

Morgan smiled, and Matt was pleased to see that however he might have changed, he had kept his characteristic smile—that sudden change of expression from something near defiance to a charming, though unconscious, deference, a gift he might hope never to lose, for it was pleasing to men and women alike, and perhaps saved him from looking too proudly intolerant.

At Lisette's insistence, they had dressed in black trousers and black frock coats with white shirts and silk cravats, correct formal dress for any occasion in the mountains, and had looked rather odd to each other when they had met at the breakfast table. But they also wore cavalry boots, broad black hats, and pistols stuck in their belts, and these familiar accoutrements made them feel less as if they were in disguise.

While Morgan began to stroll about, Matt lighted the stove, dumped some ground coffee into a pot, added a dipperful of water from a barrel, and watched him covertly, as if he no longer had the right to study this young man who seemed so intent on preserving his separateness. Morgan examined the gold scales on the desk, then moved over to the map which covered one wall, indicating every claim in the Territory, marking the streams, the timber stands, the towns and banks and newspapers and warehouses, each ranch, and the site of every mill and proposed smelter. There were the stuffed and impressively antlered head of a stag nailed to the back wall, several law books and ledgers on a crowded shelf, and a dish filled with nuggets which Morgan bent over quickly, as Matt remarked, "Fool's gold. We keep it to remind ourselves, and our clients, that the hardest way in the world to get gold is to dig it."

Morgan nodded again, made no reply, and continued around the room, looking at the head of a mountain goat with its curling horns and one glass eye, the pile of marked newspapers on a chair, the buffalo boots thrown into a corner, the rattlesnake skin, almost three feet long, which hung from a nail, and all the while he had the soberly interested, conscientious manner of a man passing slowly and methodically through a museum of natural curiosities. The room seemed to have become densely quiet, while outside there was a continuous din of celebration, and Matt felt a growing irritation as Morgan pursued his scrutiny of the office, for he had begun to imagine that he was being supercilious. But then he reminded himself that Morgan was at a peculiar disadvantage with him now, for he was too young to have Matt's authority and too old to accept a boy's position of subservience to his father.

Matt poured coffee into two tin cups and set them on the desk, taking his accustomed chair and sliding down in it, and very promptly Morgan took the chair opposite him, facing the window, where they seated their clients, the better to watch their expressions while partly concealing their own.

They looked at each other for a moment, Matt offered him a cigar and lighted one, and was again surprised to find how distrustful they had become. "All right, Morgan. You wanted to talk to me."

Morgan straightened, and looked as guilty as if it had been an accusation. "Yes, sir," he agreed, but frowned, and they kept silent.

Matt, suddenly annoyed and almost angry, demanded, "What about?"

"I want to ask you, sir, if you know where Nella Allen is."

"Oh." Matt nodded slowly. "That's what's been bothering you."

Morgan looked remote and gloomy, but again he agreed politely. "Yes, sir, it has."

"I do know, and I'll tell you. But neither your mother nor Lisette knows anything about it, and I don't want them to." Morgan was watching him with his eyes shining and intense, his face straining as if from some violent impulse to yell or leap from the chair, but he remained motionless, waiting. "She's all right, Morgan," and he spoke gently now, for Matt was continuously and keenly aware that his own relationship with Jenny Danforth gave him small reason to be critical of anyone else.

"Thank God," Morgan whispered, and his face was moist. He drank the coffee quickly, then resumed his careful attitude of watching Matt and waiting for what he would say.

"She's living with Green Troy."

Morgan looked puzzled. "Green Troy?"

"Troy's Casino." Matt smiled slightly. "Great public philanthropist. He's got a habit of tossing gold nuggets into the streets for the kids. I think he could be elected mayor."

But Morgan continued to look strained and unhappy. "What's she doing with him?"

Matt stood up abruptly and walked to the stove, filled the cups, and then leaned across the desk, demanding, "Where the hell did you expect to find her? Attending the Literary Association meetings?"

Morgan opened his mouth, but thought better of the reply and glanced away, saying softly, "I guess so."

"You may get god-damn mad at me for saying this to you, Morgan, but here it is anyway. You can do whatever you want to in this world —but, for Christ's sake, if you make up your mind to behave like a bastard, then don't be virtuously surprised to discover that the people you didn't bother to consider have been hurt. You've got to live with the pain you cause others—whether it troubles you a lot, or only a little—or give up the pleasures you may get by causing it. Now, isn't that simple enough?" Matt, hearing himself, was taken aback by these moral preachments, sounding as if they must come from a man who would unhesitatingly give up his own pleasures, rather than cause another person the smallest sorrow.

"Yes, sir," agreed Morgan, and they stared at each other with such ferocity and eager rage that Matt had a momentary impulse to shoot out his fist and strike his son in the face. But then, ashamed, contrite and aware that his self-contempt had unexpectedly turned against Morgan, he gripped his shoulder reassuringly and sat down.

"I'm sorry. I swore I wasn't going to play the stern parent and I've done it. Nella went to Troy, who had been a friend—or an employer, might be more accurate—of her brother, when she found out she was pregnant." Morgan gave a slow sigh but said nothing, and Matt went on. "He sent her to Dr. Danforth and—" He paused, wondering whether or not to tell him Jenny had come to him, asking what should be done, and said, "The Doctor talked to me. I told him I thought he'd better go ahead, and he did. She's been with Troy ever since. He treats her well, so far as I can tell. He has money—it's the gamblers and whores who get rich out here, you know that. He buys her clothes and jewelry, nothing she could pawn for a fortune, but enough to make other girls envious. They live in their own world. It's unlikely your mother or sister or any of their friends would see or hear about her, and they haven't."

"Have you seen her?"

"A few times. She doesn't look very different, a little older, of course, in those clothes and with her hair done up. But now let me tell you one thing more and this, by God, is important. Keep away from her. I've had some dealings with Troy in the past and I want you to understand that you can cause not only yourself, but other people, some serious trouble if you go looking for her. He's possessive, and let's hope he stays that way. Leave her alone."

"I will." Morgan leaned quickly forward. "You don't think much of me, sir, and maybe you're right. I'm sorry for what happened, but I suppose that even if I'd known it was going to I'd have done the same thing—because at that time it seemed to be the most important thing that would ever happen to me. Now, of course, it doesn't seem that way at all." He opened his hands. "So I guess I deserve whatever you think of me."

This earnest humility, after his earlier remoteness, surprised Matt into wondering how it was possible that they two, who had always before seemed affectionate and tolerant, should have come this distance toward a quarrel. He shook his head and gazed at Morgan thoughtfully, and rather sadly.

"No, Morgan. That's not true. I sounded more like a prig than I meant to. I feel guilty about Nella myself, I suppose, because I knew what you were doing, and didn't try to stop it. Maybe I should have, I don't know. According to the rules and regulations we're supposed to live by, I should have. But then, according to the rules and regulations—" Matt gestured, and as the door opened and Lem Finney appeared, he jumped up, greatly relieved. "Come in, Lem. Come in, Jake. Do you remember my son Morgan? This is Jacob Finney."

They shook hands, and as Morgan inadvertently glanced at Matt, to find him watching him with a slight, pleased smile, Matt gave a nod and they understood that the interruption had been a lucky one, and felt a bursting flow of renewed affection and trust, as if now that the danger had passed they had been reconciled by its potential violence.

Lem Finney looked brightly and shrewdly at Morgan, estimating the changes since he had seen him last. And Jacob, Morgan noticed, did not at all resemble Lisette's description of him as a clumsy buffoon, but was deft and confident, with his father's sharp blue eyes and his mother's supercilious smile. "You've just come from Butte?" Lem asked, and watched him as carefully as if his face would show important clues to the camp's worth.

"Yes, sir. Zack Fletcher and I left early in June. The placers were about played out, and the camp was emptying fast. I don't think there'll be two dozen people there by the end of the year."

Lem Finney looked as disappointed as if he had some placer locations in Butte himself. Each time there was a strike which proved less profitable than its discoverers had expected, each time a hundred miners stampeded to another Territory, each time a man collected his dust from one of the banks, called in an auctioneer, bought a pepper-and-salt suit from a street vendor and left for the States, Lem Finney felt that he had been betrayed, and argued with such persuasiveness that men intending to leave avoided him. "I've been told the gold there is low-grade, but that there's some copper that averages as high as seventy percent. Is that right?"

"There is. But no one's been able to make a smelter work, and once they ship it to Baltimore or Wales, the profit's gone. One guy who sold his ore to a freighter got twenty-eight cents a pound."

Lem Finney clucked his tongue disapprovingly and glanced at Matt. "We could put a better mill in there."

"You could," Morgan said, "but a land company located every mill and water right."

"Bastards. That's the kind of thing that's holding this country back. Did you lease your claims there, or sell them?"

"Leased them."

"Want to sell them?"

"No, sir."

"Why not? You say they're no good."

"They're no good now. The railway could make a difference, if it gets out here as soon as everyone hopes."

Lem Finney gave Matt a wink. "Chip off the old block. If you change your mind, come talk to me. Plan to stay around here?"

"I don't know, sir," Morgan told him, in a tone so decisive that Finney asked him no more questions, and Matt now poured whisky into four tin cups, passed them around, and raised his own. "The Union."

"The Union," Lem agreed. "But we'll have a quorum of Rebels with us this afternoon. Well, much obliged for the drink, Matt. Got a few errands to run before parade time." He nodded, gave his tight smile, and they went out.

As the door opened, Matt and Morgan became aware that the noise, which they had scarcely noticed a few minutes ago, was increasing. There were continuous Rebel yells and pistol shots, horses neighed and mules laughed, and someone set off a gunpowder explosion that was followed by terrified screams. They sat down again, and although Matt was sure there was something more that Morgan wanted to say to him, he had decided that Morgan must convince himself to say it without any other help than he might get from the whisky.

"Pete and I are in a new company with Finney and Webb and Hart and three or four other guys, and we've been gathering up all the claims we can get hold of. The worst mistake that's been made out here is to put in machinery without knowing if you've got the ore to supply it, and we know by now that we have. This may surprise you, but our company, the Meridian Gold and Silver Mining Company, is capitalized for one million dollars." Matt smiled, pleased at the progress they had made, and eager for Morgan to be impressed by it. "Jake's got a share in it." He paused and Morgan leaned forward, spreading his knees wide and bending his head as if to study the floor. "Maybe you'd like to join us."

"Thanks. I wish I could. But I can't."

"Why not?"

"I haven't any money."

Matt took care to sound only mildly surprised. "You haven't any money?"

"No, sir."

Morgan did not glance up, kept his head low so that his face was hidden, and Matt looked at him in astonishment. For Morgan had gone off with Zack Fletcher two years ago to make the beginning, as they had supposed, of his fortune; and now he sat staring in embarrassment at his hands and announcing that he had no money. And, it seemed, he had no wish to tell him what had happened, whether he had been robbed by a road agent or cheated by a black-leg gambler, or perhaps had done no mining at all but spent his time as many young men did, drinking in the saloons, dancing with the hurdy-gurdies, and entertaining the girls in the whorehouses.

"Well, Morgan," he said finally, and it seemed Morgan's embarrassment had now taken possession of him, as well, "if you want to talk about it, go ahead. And if you don't want to, for God's sake, don't. It's up to you."

Morgan raised his head quickly, looked at him for a moment, then sat up straight and put his hands in his pockets. "What I came here for, sir, was not to get your sympathy, but to ask for the money I left with you."

"You can have it. Twelve hundred dollars, at five percent a month. Do you want it today?" Matt's voice had become sarcastic again, and he changed its tone. "I think you'd be well repaid to invest it in our company. Unless you've got a better use for it."

"I have to pay a debt."

Matt looked thoughtfully at the end of his cigar, then put it back in his mouth and blew rings, watching them form and rise with intent interest and telling himself that if Morgan wanted to keep his secret he could, for certainly he would not try to wheedle it out of him.

Morgan jumped up, crossed the room swiftly and came back again, and now he began to talk with a passionate urgency, as if to get it said before he changed his mind.

"I owe it to Zack Fletcher. We didn't make much but we worked god-damn hard all the same—we had about four thousand between us, or maybe a little more. We didn't have it weighed often, nobody did, they didn't want the other guys to know what they had. But we kept it hidden around the cabin and got along all right that way until just before we left, when someone stole it." He continued to pace about and, from time to time, stopped and glowered at Matt, as if to warn him not to laugh. But Matt was watching him seriously, and gave no sign of amusement or incredulity. "Now, you're thinking that if our dust got stolen there's no reason why I owe it to Zack, any more than he owes it to me." Morgan was so plainly humiliated that Matt guarded his face carefully and reminded himself it would be very easy to lose his son's confidence forever at that moment. "But there is a reason—because it was stolen by a girl who was living in our cabin with me. She was there with both of us, but she was my girl, and just a few days before we were ready to leave she disappeared with a guy we all knew and his squaw, and our dust. She had been saying she was going to Helena with us—and one day we came home and she was gone." Morgan threw his hands wide in a furious gesture. "That's why I need the money." He stopped and stood across the room, as if studying Matt to find if he pitied him now.

Matt slowly shook his head, looking solemn and impressed as if at the end of a sermon, then carefully tapped a long ash from the end of his cigar. For a time neither of them moved or spoke, but then, as shouts rose louder in the streets, Matt went to the door and remained there several moments, as if he had found something of unusual interest. He shrugged and closed it again. "Mule race. Well, Morgan, I'll get it for you tomorrow. We don't keep much cash on hand. I'm sorry you had bad luck, I guess that's about all there is to say, isn't it?"

"Thank you, sir."

"And what are you going to do next?"

"I haven't decided yet, sir."

"The placers are washing thin here. Companies like our own are taking all the property they can get hold of. The claims in Helena are higher than they were two years ago. You need a grubstake, Morgan." Morgan nodded, still unhappy and chagrined, but no longer belligerent, and Matt thought the confession had done him good and had perhaps not been so agonizing as he had expected, after all. "Pete and I are going to open a branch in Helena, and Pete's going to manage it. Jonathan will stay here with me. We're spreading out and we're making money, we're doing as well as any one in the Territory, and we expect to do better. I'd like to have you in it with us—but that's your choice. If you want to go to Helena with Pete, let me know, and we'll talk about it." He went to the door. "It must be about time for the parade to begin. Suppose we take a look."

They had been closed in for long enough, he thought, with Morgan's confusion and dismay, for there was no possibility of making him believe that even though he never again expected to feel confidence in himself or pride, he nevertheless would. For now, at least, the girl's theft had convinced him he was not so strong as he had been imagining himself to be, not clever enough to have prevented her from doing it, and he supposed that whoever knew of it would despise him as he despised himself.

The sidewalk was so crowded that they did not notice Milly Matches coming toward them in a black and yellow dress, making deft use of a black lace parasol to pry her way along and smiling her famous smile as the men stepped out of her way, until she stood beside them. "I must talk to you," she told Matt. "It won't take long."

They sat at the desk, and Matt watched with bemused interest as she talked. Her eyes closed briefly and the next moment opened wide, her lips smiled and pouted, her head tipped back and her neck arched, her fingers gestured as if beckoning him, until he began to wonder if these grimaces might have become so habitual they continued even in her sleep, like the movements of a dog's legs as he dreams of chasing rabbits.

"Matt, you probably won't believe me, but I'm going to get married. Oh, don't look so god-damn polite, I know you're horrified. But we aren't going to get married here, we're going away, and we aren't even going away together, because one of these days we may come back. And if we ever do, I promise you you'll never be able to recognize me—I'll look like any other respectable middle-aged woman." She leaned forward confidingly. "I'm not naturally red-haired, you know, and I'll be bloody well glad to stop dyeing it." She laughed, throwing her head back and closing her eyes, while Matt marveled at what she could possibly do with these mannerisms once she was a respectable middle-aged woman. Or, perhaps, she was looking forward to abandoning them along with the red hair. "How much do I have with you now?"

"Fourteen thousand five hundred. You're not leaving today, I hope? Ten thousand would just about clean us out."

Milly wrote a check and spun it across at him, then leaned back with both arms folded behind her head. "Not today, but soon. Next week."

"The one thing this Territory needs most, next to a railroad, is capital." Matt smiled. "And here you are, one of our leading capitalists, getting ready to leave us. I'm sorry, Milly."

Milly sighed, the relentless vivacity came temporarily to rest, and she looked rather sad. "Just think, Matt, what a hell of a lot we've all been through together since the old days in Bannack. Time is different on the frontier, have you noticed that? The day before yesterday is hard enough to remember, and what happened five years ago can only be something you imagined or heard about." She shook her head. "And now, the respectable element's taking over." Milly, it seemed, intended it as a compliment that she had never counted him among the respectable element, or, at least, not among her enemies on that side. "Matt, what shall we do with our claim? We've never gotten much out of it. Of course, we never expected to."

"It's no Confederate Bar, but we may as well hang onto it, someone may make us an offer for it. Who's going to take over your house, Milly?"

"Green Troy. I sold him my interest, and my contracts with the girls, for whatever they're worth. Oh, how glad I'll be to be done with those stupid little whores. I was never a whore myself, Matt—or only for a little while—I was always a businesswoman, and a pretty god-damn good one, too." Milly stood up, holding out her hand. "Well—I wanted to tell you I'm leaving, and I wanted to say good-bye."

Matt took her hand, and was surprised to find that it seemed he was losing an old friend, one he had known long and loved well, and even though he suspected this must be only one more of those deceptions of the frontier, nevertheless it seemed that some significant phase of his own life was ending, too. "You don't want to tell me who you're going to marry?"

"You don't know?"

"I think I can guess, I'm not sure."

"It may be better if you aren't." Matt leaned down and kissed her, lightly and tenderly, and Milly gave an embarrassed little laugh, turned and went to the door, but when he opened it, she backed hastily inside. "Here comes the parade. My God, what would your daughter say?"

Matt dashed out, horrified that he might have missed Lisette, for he had quite forgotten the parade while he sat there moping over the past. But Lisette's part of the procession had not reached that corner, and a wagon drawn by white mules was going by, crowded with little girls dressed in white, all smiling and waving whenever they recognized someone. Among them was Flora Pim, the only girl Robert and Douglas and their friends had ever admitted to their gang, and at the sight of Matt's black eyes and bearded face conspicuously showing above the heads of shorter men, she waved both arms and screeched, "I'm coming to the picnic, Mr. Devlin!"

The wagon was followed by a troupe of men on horseback, and most of them seemed self-conscious and sheepish as they nodded to real or imaginary friends. Jeremy Flint was among them, and Floyd Hart and Josiah Webb, but Lem Finney and Matt and Pete had refused to join the parade, explaining that there must be a few left to cheer when they rode by.

And now, behind the Masonic contingent, which some men were muttering was nothing less than the Vigilance Committee itself, came the wagon which carried Columbia, Uncle Sam, and Martha and George Washington, followed by the band playing "Hail, Columbia" with trombones and drums and clashing cymbals, and as they approached a wild cheer went up and hats were thrown into the air and sent skimming across the street. The Car of State was covered with evergreen boughs, and the six horses which drew it bore plumes of dyed red and white and blue gamma grasses. Georgina

Hart, in her white robe bound with silver cords, her blond hair blowing from beneath a crown set low on her forehead, stood erect, holding in one hand a pair of gold scales, and passing her benediction across her worshippers with the other. She moved her gaze over the crowd with unseeing impartiality, and appeared to be deeply persuaded that for this moment she was the spirit of her country, while Uncle Sam, who was several years younger than Georgina, skulked forlornly behind her and cast forth meek and apologetic smiles, as if to his parents, who might be disapproving of the inconsequential figure he cut.

Lisette, standing in the back of the wagon, plainly had no such commitment to her own role of Martha Washington, and at sight of her Matt tried not to smile, for there was no doubt the part did not suit her and the costume seemed an unnatural structure, more like a suit of armor than a dress. She wore a white cotton wig, with two curls of horsehair dangling across one shoulder, and she was smiling, a slight but mischievous smile, as if to ask what they thought of this silly charade anyway, and when she discovered Matt she gave an open laugh, throwing her head to one side with a toss which toppled the wig into the crowd.

Georgina looked haughtily about, searching for the source of this laughter, and several men and boys went scrambling into the street while Lisette leaned out of the wagon, crying, "Throw it!" A man pitched the wig to her, she caught it and set it on her head again, a little askew this time, and as the wagon passed on by she turned once more to smile at Matt.

Milly Matches disappeared into the crowd as Morgan entered the office, laughing. "Lisette told me she wouldn't let Georgina Hart have everything her way. Mother's at the Plantation House with Mrs. Finney and some other women. Suppose we should go over there now?"

"You go, Morgan, I'll be along soon. I have to see someone for a few minutes—I'll join you as soon as I can."

Morgan left, and Matt, suddenly nervous and alert, his heart beating as it had when he first arrived in the mountains, told himself there had not been one actual lie in that statement. He stood looking about the room as if he had lost something and was trying to remember what it was, but he made no move to search for it, and after a few moments he set off up a street which led away from the main part of town, back to where it was quiet and there were few people to be seen.

Every house he passed seemed empty today, even the dogs had deserted their usual patrols, and as he slowly mounted the terraced hillsides he could hear the band music, the shouts, the occasional firing of a pistol, as if it were happening in some place he scarcely knew.

There were many newly begun stone and brick houses, and he saw this evidence of Territorial prosperity with satisfaction. The camp's most reckless citizens had disappeared by now, and although a few miners were still panning for gold, most of them, like his own company, were washing out the banks by hydraulic pressure and building stamp mills, and the gulch could scarcely be imagined as it had looked four years ago, full of alders and willows following the stream bed. That it was ugly enough today he did not doubt, but he had never looked at it as a landscape—only as a business opportunity, and this gave it some charms the women could not discover as they searched for familiar beauties, worrying over the trees and flowers they planted as if they had been sick children.

He began to ride more quickly, and at the crest of the hill he dismounted, opened the low iron gate at the entrance to the cemetery, and approached the bench where Jenny sat, her back to him and her head slightly bowed, as if she might be reading. She turned slowly, as at the approach of some unwelcome stranger, silently watching until he stood beside her.

The black veil covered her face, and just as it had happened several times before, Matt had the impression, uncanny and disagreeable, that he stood in bright sunlight while where she sat, only a few feet away, night had fallen. But then she turned the veil aside, and to his relief the disconcerting illusion was gone, although now her face looked startlingly white.

"I was sure you'd come," she said, and her voice sounded curiously poignant, so that he began to expect some news he would not like to hear.

"You didn't think I'd get a note from you and not come, now surely, Jenny?"

"I thought you might not get it. The town's so confused today, isn't it?" She gestured vaguely, as if she might be referring to the progress of some distant battle which did not concern her.

Matt sat on a bench nearby, and as they looked at each other he was thinking that the two who had seen them together and known they were lovers had been Milly Matches and Erma Finney, and this made him smile. Dr. Danforth, he liked to believe, had never suspected them, as he thought Marietta did not, and so they had been left to make their decisions without accusation or interference to keep them virtuous. The conspiracy, if there was one, seemed a general agreement that Jenny Danforth and Matt Devlin be given as much freedom as they could tolerate.

His resolutions had disappeared not long after Annabel's birth, although they had not been alone often and only then, it seemed, by accident. Sometimes he stopped to see her and, perhaps, she had no guests, and was expecting none. Or she appeared at their office to discuss her investments—for the Doctor had been less improvident than his friends had supposed and Jenny had inherited nearly twenty thousand dollars—and a few times it had happened that no one else was there.

"Why is it," she had asked him not long ago, "that we never feel guilty in time?"

"Thank God we don't." For he was reconciled by now to loving Jenny Danforth for the rest of his life, and his earlier need to explain to himself why this should be true was gone.

If such a thing had happened to Pete, Matt supposed he might have fallen back on one of those mystical theories he had suspected Pete of harboring ever since Lorena's death—perhaps blamed it on the continuity of souls from one age to the next—but as for himself, Matt was satisfied that his continuous awareness of her, and that surprised sense of old familiarity he experienced whenever he encountered her unexpectedly, was all the explanation he needed or would ever find. He did not think that even her beauty was an essential part of it, though he was willing to believe her pride and its vulnerability might be more significant than everything else, and indeed he understood the real reasons why he loved her no better now than he had at that first meeting in Bannack.

They sat quietly, until Jenny said, "There's a picnic today, isn't there?"

"Are you coming?"

She smiled mockingly. "What would Erma Finney say?"

"What the hell do you care?"

"No, I'm not going. I can't be gay, and even children are depressed by a woman in mourning clothes, have you noticed that?" She held her hands before her, as if to study her wedding ring and the cluster of garnets she had worn in Bannack. "Matt, do you know it's been almost a year since Andy died?"

"I know."

"I'll soon be more or less free again, won't I? A year of mourning is long enough, isn't it?"

Matt scowled, pretending the sun hurt his eyes, for he thought she meant to remind him how little real significance her mourning for Andrew Danforth had had. "I don't know, Jenny. Some women mourn all their lives, and some never mourn at all." It had occurred to him that if it had been his death she was mourning she might now be asking that same question of another man, and this attack of jealousy made him stare at her with his face grim and accusatory, although she seemed not to notice it. He had sometimes thought that Jenny found a morbid pleasure in mourning, and in the interest and pity she aroused by appearing in the frightening weeds, and that she might even have discovered in these dramas a compensation for loneliness.

She folded her hands and turned, looking at him directly. "I'm going to get married, Matt."

He sat back, watching her distrustfully. "I don't believe you."

She smiled. "You didn't think I would live this way for the rest of my life, did you? I know other women do, but I can't. Matt, I'd have killed myself sooner or later."

"You're going to get married?" he repeated doubtfully, and was still expecting to be told she had said it only to test him, but never-

theless he felt that his body had become heavy and almost immova-
ble, and this seemed a warning.

"Yes. I'm going to marry Pete."

XVIII

By noon many campfires were burning, and smoke drifted through
the pine grove in dense clouds. Several families had arrived at the
picnic grounds in carts or buggies, others had come on horseback,
and the animals had been turned loose to feed where deep grass had
grown among felled trees. The women were unpacking baskets and
spreading tablecloths, or they sat in small groups, gossiping and
watching the children. Most of the men were in deep discussion of
the Indian problem and, as they talked, bottles were raised regularly
and passed from hand to hand.

The Reverend Obadiah Bream had earlier led them in prayers,
while the women stood with their eyes closed, the children stopped
their game of Civil War, and the men removed their hats. The flag
had been raised up a stripped pine trunk, while some of the men
kept a suspicious watch on their Southern friends, and Lemuel Finney had read the Declaration of Independence in a voice which gave
many of them patriotic chills. After these interruptions, patiently endured, the men were glad to return to drinking and the Indian problem, the women to their gossip, and the children to their games; and
the smells of roasting pig and venison, turning slowly over deep
pits, and brewing coffee, made them alertly hungry.

Marietta sat with Erma Finney and Reba Church, Cornelia Bream
and Blanch Hart, who had been accepting compliments on her daughter's portrayal of Columbia, while Martha Washington, they assured
Marietta, had been an original interpretation, no question whatever
about that.

Georgina had changed her costume reluctantly, after suggesting
that it might be more in keeping with the spirit of the day if she wore
it to the picnic. But when Lisette jeered, throwing her white wig
across the schoolroom, "Then don't blame any of us if the boys all
laugh!" Georgina gave her a look of hurt dignity and put on a pale
blue muslin dress with a blue satin sash.

Lisette had pretended to have lost a gold ring set with a small diamond, which Matt had given her on her tenth birthday, and had
spent so long looking for it that the other girls left, and when she
finally came galloping up the hillside between Ralph Mercer and
Jacob Finney she was dressed in a black alpaca riding coat and long-
trained skirt, with a white silk cravat and a white veil streaming

from her high black hat. The girls glanced at one another, frowning questioningly, for Lisette had assured them she would wear a green muslin dress no different from any of theirs.

She came sauntering toward them, looking very happy to be the center of attention again, and although Rachel had nothing to say about the treachery of the riding habit, Georgina, after trying to ignore it for several minutes, plucked at Lisette's sleeve. "What happened to your new dress, honey?"

"New dress? Why, I forgot all about it." She smiled impudently and turned to Morgan, whispering, "Where's Zack Fletcher? He told me he would come to the schoolhouse after the parade and ride here with me."

"I haven't seen him since early this morning."

"But he will come, won't he?"

"You've got at least two admirers here I can count offhand—won't that last you for the afternoon?"

Lisette frowned, and murmured, "What do you think of him?"

"Fletcher?"

"Of course not, Morgan. Don't tease me. And don't look at him now, for heaven's sake," she added, and pretended to brush lint from his coat. Standing side by side, dressed in black with white cravats, their dark eyes shining and the same conspiratorial amusement on their faces, Morgan and Lisette looked for the moment remarkably alike, and proudly conscious of each other and the effect they made together.

Lisette, of course, was asking him what he thought of Ralph Mercer, and that probably meant she was thinking of marrying him, an idea which seemed so absurd when she was not yet sixteen that Morgan solemnly replied, "I've heard he's all but engaged to Rachel Finney."

Lisette gave a little yelp, clapped her hands over her mouth, and as she and Morgan began to laugh, glancing at each other with delighted malice, they seemed finally to have retrieved whatever had been lost by his absence, for even with Lisette he had been cautiously aloof, afraid to admit her back into his confidence, lest she accuse him on behalf of Nella Allen or pry loose his secret about Lily Jones.

Georgina, as Lisette had predicted, had been much impressed by her oldest brother, although it was Lisette's belief—and she had accused her of it—that what Georgina really wanted was to realize that perpetual dream of all Southern belles and get two men to fight over her. Morgan was angry enough at himself that he would have been glad to fight his brother, or anyone else, and he and Jonathan had exchanged some menacing glares, but Lisette had so far been able to keep peace between them by whispering to Jonathan that Georgina bored Morgan.

And indeed it was true that Morgan had come to the conclusion that boredom with women was his best and possibly his only defense against them. Between Nella Allen and Lily Jones, he thought that he knew enough about women to last him a long while, and that what he had not discovered from either of them he was unlikely to learn from Georgina Hart.

Zack, he believed, despised him and would for the rest of their lives, and this loss seemed to him far worse than the loss of the money, which he could earn again, or even the loss of his pride, which he supposed must be permanently gone.

And if Zack was not here now, it was very likely his way of letting him know that he was glad to be done with him. Lisette, however, must have been eager to display her popularity, for she seemed distracted as she glanced about, looking down the hillside and off through the trees, but when Morgan caught her eye she murmured, "I'm not looking for him! I'm looking for Father, why isn't he here?"

A few minutes later, when Morgan passed Marietta, seated with several other women, she looked up with a quick but uncertain smile, which troubled him, and as he went by to join the men he noticed that they were discussing Jenny Danforth.

"Of course, I thought we had to ask her to come today," Erma Finney was saying. "But I'm glad she didn't. After all, the Doctor's only been dead for eleven months."

"She's mourned for him very faithfully, though," Cornelia Bream said, and the other women glanced at her questioningly.

"Why shouldn't she?" Erma smiled. "She's mourned faithfully, and ostentatiously. But then, Jenny is ostentatious in whatever she does."

"I don't think that's fair, Erma," Marietta told her. "Jenny doesn't mean to be ostentatious. It's her bad luck, in a sense, to arouse so much curiosity. She doesn't seek it, and she doesn't enjoy it."

Erma looked at Marietta, so intently that the other women, too, turned their attention to her, and then Erma asked, as gently as if she inquired about some sickness, "You like Jenny Danforth, don't you, Marietta?"

"Of course I do," Marietta answered quickly, and she laughed, though the laugh seemed to her not quite successful.

Still, she thought she had answered the question truthfully, and would not even have been disconcerted by it, but for Erma Finney's look of one bent on inquest. There had been a time when she was convinced that Jenny and Matt were in love with each other, but now she was less sure of this, and thought it might never have occurred to her if Erma Finney had not kept such careful watch over them. Perhaps it had been as a defense against Erma, or perhaps there was some natural liking between her and Jenny Danforth, but whatever it was they had become friends, and the friendship in itself seemed to Marietta a protection against her own suspicions.

"Jenny Danforth is my oldest friend here," Erma said. "And I think I know her better than any of you—but that doesn't mean I know her very well. Jenny," she told them with a meaningful nod, "is a riddle." She looked at Marietta again. "After all, there must be some reason why she's so secretive."

At those words, it seemed to Marietta her heart had been caught hold of and fiercely squeezed. She could not look at Erma, but jumped up and ran after Annabel, who had wandered too near the older children's game, and carried her back, and as she stood holding the little girl, ashamed she needed this shield against Erma Finney, Marietta said, "The reason may be only her sense of privacy. Must we all know everything about each other?"

But a few minutes later, when Matt stood beside her saying, "I'm sorry to be late, but one of our depositors wanted a large amount of cash today, and I had some trouble getting it together," Marietta felt a relief almost as great as if he had left her for Jenny, and come back.

Matt made his way among the children who were now flourishing scalps of horsehair dyed with berry juice as they trudged about in a circle, shuffling their feet in a slow rhythm while they fluttered their palms over their mouths and sent up ululating shrieks in celebration of their latest massacre.

He went to stand between Jeremy Flint and the Reverend Bream, and Flint was swearing ferociously at the recent Indian depredations, while the Reverend watched him blandly and seemed to hear neither profanity nor obscenity. Pete stood across from them, but even though Matt had taken that position so that he might look at him, he found himself not only disinclined to see Pete's face but it even seemed a physical impossibility to focus his eyes upon him.

And so he drank when the bottle reached him, and heard himself discussing the general belief that the Indians had two hundred thousand fighting men ready to take the field and were convinced they would extinguish the white race before the end of summer. The Territory's merchants and bankers had contributed money and supplies to send a volunteer force to supplement the Army reserves, and prospectors had been warned to keep to well-traveled roads. Some of the ranches had been desolated, men had been killed and women and children captured, detachments of soldiers ambushed, and stagecoaches and wagon trains were being attacked all across the plains.

"And here we are," said Silas Church, "in the middle of bloody nowhere, with painted savages burning and killing in all directions, and a toy army to defend us."

The talk went on, and all the while Matt felt a compelling need to look at Pete, study his face, and to discover whether or not Pete would look different to him now, as it seemed he must. For, at the moment Jenny had told him she was going to marry Pete, he had had a conviction that Pete had proposed to her because of some malice toward himself—perhaps from some quixotic notion of protecting Marietta. Pete's face had come sharply into his mind and he had been alarmed to find it a stranger's face, someone he did not know who had had the capacity to make this plan in secrecy, to carry it out secretly, and who seemed therefore capable of someday performing other secret acts, perhaps with some design against himself.

"Pete's never talked about you to me," he had told Jenny. "When did this happen?"

"Yesterday afternoon. Matt, I know you're surprised, and I know you're angry. You think that somehow we've cheated you."

"No, no, that isn't what I was thinking, Jenny," he protested, so quickly and earnestly that she smiled. "I want you to be happy," he said piously.

"But not with Pete?"

"I have no right to say that, or think it."

But he felt a raging jealousy and a resentment greater than he could have imagined. And, against his will, he demanded, "Are you in love with him?"

"Yes, Matt, I am. Or perhaps you don't believe it's possible to love two people at the same time?"

"You've been wanting to say that to me for a long time, haven't you?"

He was eager to ask her other questions, how often they had seen each other, when Pete had first fallen in love with her and she with him, but found himself an outsider, and thought Jenny must be enjoying her triumph.

But she leaned forward, perhaps taking pity on him because of the way he looked, and touched his hand. "I know what you're wondering, Matt." He glanced up sharply. "No, we haven't, and he hasn't asked me to."

"Why not?"

Jenny laughed. "Pete, I should think you would know better than I, is idealistic."

"He isn't that god-damn idealistic."

"He is about me."

"What does he know about us?"

"Nothing. I'm sure of it, Matt. If he did, he wouldn't be able to hide it."

"He managed to hide the fact that he was in love with you for quite awhile."

"That was because he thought he should. After all, I was married, and then, after the Doctor died, he didn't want to court a woman who had just become a widow, and so he waited."

"God-damn scrupulous." But instantly he said, "I'm sorry for that, please forgive me."

At last, as if he were making a significant decision, Matt looked across at his brother. Pete was listening to Lem Finney, who was describing his newest theory of Indian extermination, and Matt fell into fascinated contemplation of this man he had imagined he knew so well.

Pete, too, was dressed for Lisette's benefit in a black frock coat with a white silk cravat, and Matt assured himself grimly that the whole damned family looked as if they had come here expecting a wedding or a funeral. Matt stared at him for some time, feeling almost stupefied by hatred of this man who would soon, in no more than six months, marry Jenny Danforth and take her into his bed and deprive him of her for the rest of their lives. And as he looked at him it seemed that it was Pete who had been treacherous, hiding his plans, never letting him guess what he meant to do, until at last Matt believed he could kill him at that moment with no smallest expectation of remorse, and he turned and walked away, as if there was a real danger he might do it.

He began to stroll about, and stood watching the children at their Indian game, carefully fixing upon his face a smile which felt taut and artificial, but which he hoped indicated a tender and reflective interest in their innocent bloodthirstiness.

"Let Pete tell you about it," Jenny had said. "He wants to, but he wants to wait until the year of mourning is over. And we won't be married until he's built a house in Helena."

"And then I'm supposed to look surprised and grin like a jumping jack and shake his hand and tell him he's a lucky son of a bitch." He gave her a look which must have been more ominous than he intended, for she leaned toward him again and her face had a surprising sorrow and tenderness. Jenny, he thought, was perhaps the kind of woman whose nature would never let her live quietly or at ease in the world, who feared tranquillity far more than pain or despair, and who unknowingly but inevitably made those choices which kept her at all times both defensive and defenseless.

"Love doesn't change, Matt. I've loved you ever since that day you came to me in Bannack looking for the Doctor, and I'll love you as much on the last day of my life. But I can't live alone. I can't endure life unless I have a man to build my days around, and I can't live any longer on jealousy and waiting—how can you want me to?"

"I don't, Jenny, of course I don't."

"I'll make Pete happy, I promise you I will. I know what a man expects of his wife, and I won't disappoint him. Pete needs to be loved more than you've ever guessed."

And with that, of course, she had stepped away from him toward Pete, so that when he had left her on that bare hillside with the grave markers to remind him she could not continue to live surrounded by death, he had felt what seemed the deepest shame and self-condemnation of his life, wondering how it was he had never guessed that during those eleven years since the death of Lorena and his young son, Pete had been engrossed in an intolerable loneliness. There was a legend among the women of the family that Pete's love for Lorena and their son had been so deep his sorrow could never be cured, and they had told one another they could hear that sorrow speak plainly whenever he played his fiddle, a romantic fancy Matt had thought very much exaggerated, and yet now it seemed they had been right. For Pete had folded his grief in upon himself, as if to protect it from examination by alien hands or eyes, and had been willing to trust it to no one but Jenny.

This recognition seemed all at once to cleanse him of envy and hatred, so that he turned abruptly and walked to where Pete stood and gave him a warm and confiding smile, feeling a puzzling new affinity for his brother which made him so eager for his happiness that he was forced to control an impulse to make him a speech in which he grandly presented Jenny Danforth to Pete with his compliments, and then backed out of their lives once and for all. This reformation gave him some small amusement, and from time to time as they talked he glanced at Pete with curiosity, discovered new qualities in his face, and found that he admired him more than ever before. The pity was, he could not tell him so.

The Reverend Bream now raised both arms, and announced that the moment was here, the time when the children had been promised they might shoot off their firecrackers, launch their rockets, ignite their sparklers, and use up their fireworks in one vast holocaust. With howls of delight they thrust the scalps into their pockets and rushed upon their supplies, cached in a community arsenal under the trees, grabbed burning twigs from the bonfires and started to touch them off, shrieking in ecstatic terror as the explosions began. But then Lemuel Finney called out in a voice so authoritative they turned to stare at him suspiciously.

"Children, just one moment, please. No more noise for a moment, I have something important to tell you."

"Mr. Finney!" they protested.

Lem Finney smiled benevolently, but shook his head. "This day is a solemn one for our nation, a day when we celebrate not only our independence from British tyranny, but the preservation of our union. Ladies and gentlemen—the North and the South! May the only future strife between them be which shall perform the greatest services for our common country."

The children, grouped before him, yelled and cheered, while the men waved their hats and the women got to their feet, applauding and wiping their eyes. Lisette sighed and closed her eyes and rested her chin on one hand, and as the speech continued she sometimes glanced about, searching through the thick haze of drifting smoke, seemed not to find what she was looking for, and closed her eyes again.

Lem Finney was reminding them of Plymouth Rock and bloody feet at Valley Forge, effete monarchies and prostrate lions, and as he shouted "Great Meadows!" they cheered. "Monongahela!" he cried, and they responded. "The Plains of Abraham!" They shouted the words back to him. "The Battle of Saratoga!" They yelled so loudly and for so long that he pleaded for silence and got it only reluctantly, and then he spoke with unexpected gentleness. "There were our beginnings, not one hundred years ago, ladies and gentlemen." He de-

scribed to them other triumphs, over Indians and French and Mexi-
rans and Spaniards. He reminded them of their trading ships on all
the world's waters, of cities built in the wilderness, of railways reaching across the continent and soon to meet. And as he described American sagacity and bravery, nobility and sacrifice, victory against
odds, he seemed to gather them up and take them with him, swooping over the country like eagles borne on the wind, passing the ridges
of its mountains and circling its plains and deserts with intoxicating
swiftness and power. He dropped them to earth again and made
them creep with him beside covered wagons, thirsty and despairing
and exhausted, and by the ringing tones of his voice and his own un-
abashed pride, precipitated them for a sudden, glorified instant into
a flooding sense of love for one another and for their nation.

They were listening, silent and engrossed, as Zack Fletcher appeared, emerging from the surrounding trees and thickening smoke,
and moved carefully forward until at last he stood beside Morgan.
Lisette, who had succumbed to Lem Finney's spell and her own ardent patriotism, gave a start and cried out in alarm. Zack glared at
her, and others glanced about, frowning at the disturbance.

Zack put his mouth close to Morgan's ear, whispering, "I just ran
into Jenkins and Hamilton." He smelled as if he had ridden hard for
some distance and had had a quantity of unusually bad whisky to
drink.

Morgan's head turned swiftly. The look of surly distrust and resentment which had been on his face for the past three weeks was
gone and his eyes shone with surprise and hate. "Where?"

"Troy's Casino."

Morgan and Zack moved slowly and quietly away, while Georgina
and Lisette watched them and exchanged questioning glances. At
the edge of the crowd they stopped and confronted each other.

"The son of a bitch damn near took a shot at me. I think he would
have if Hamilton hadn't stopped him. He said you're the guy they're
after."

"For what?"

Zack's unexpected appearance, with its implication of trouble and
haste, had brought Morgan sharply out of the state of stupidity and
doubt, self-pity and fear he had been in, and this announcement of
danger tightened his muscles, sent the blood moving and his heart
beating faster, and filled him with keen anticipation that now, finally, something violent must happen.

Lem Finney's speech had ended, and amid the shouts and applause,
while Lem pleaded with the children to wait until after "The Star-
Spangled Banner" had been sung, Zack said, "For stealing their
dust."

Morgan's face twisted into an expression of demented fury. "Stealing their dust?" He spoke as if the words were so fantastic he did
not know what they meant.

"Easy, now, hear the rest of it. They met Lily in Helena and she said it was your idea to chase them off with the Vigilante sign, and that you lost the dust playing faro. Jenkins says he didn't trust you from the minute he laid eyes on you and, in other words, the first time you two meet—the ball will open."

Morgan looked crazy with rage, so ugly and malign that Zack gave him a nudge in the ribs to indicate that Lisette was watching them, and began to sing. Morgan placed his hat over his chest and sang with the others, but after a few lines he muttered, "Where are they?"

"Not far, over beyond the trees. I had a hell of a time talking them out of following me here."

"Let's go."

"Wait a minute. Don't worry, they'll be there." Zack grinned. "Be a patriot."

The anthem ended after what seemed to Morgan an interminable number of verses, they stood with their heads bowed as the Reverend Bream began to ask grace, and then moved swiftly and quietly away. Lisette, peeking up, waved one hand to stop them, but before the prayer was done they had gone deeper into the grove and were obscured by the smoke.

As the Reverend finished his prayer, firecrackers began to go off and Lisette cried, "Morgan, Zack, it's time for dinner—oh, don't go away now!" Men were firing their pistols and the children gleefully shouting as Morgan followed Zack toward the clearing, where horses wandered grazing in the deep grass.

"Jenkins says he'll fight you at fifteen yards, though he wanted to make it ten, and you empty your weapons. If one of you isn't dead by then, he'll consider his honor's been satisfied. But make no mistake about it, he means to kill you." Morgan nodded, as they trotted along, as if Zack was explaining to him the rules of a game; and he had, in fact, no clear conviction that it was any more dangerous, for he felt no fear, but only an unreasonable and eager joy. "Morgan, remember what I've told you. Take your time, don't shoot too fast, and aim for his head. Wait here. Keep out of sight." Zack stepped into the open, shouting, "All right, you guys, I brought him with me. Where are you?"

Jenkins rose up slowly, some distance away, and Hamilton appeared beside him. "Come on out, Devlin. We're gentlemen, you son of a bitch. We don't bushwhack a man, we kill him in a fair fight."

Jenkins walked swiftly forward, followed by Hamilton who was smirking self-consciously, and Morgan stepped out to stand with Zack. They could still hear, though dimly, the pistol shots and firecrackers and the band had begun to play "Yankee Doodle," which sounded in Morgan's ears with the unusual clarity of a meaningful but obscure signal.

Zack spoke brusquely. "No use fooling around with this. You two guys don't like each other and who's right or wrong makes no goddamn difference." He glanced from Morgan to Jenkins. "Ready?" Neither answered and Zack indicated where they were to stand, smiling slightly as he remarked, "We might add a few frills to this, but when one man wants to kill another, I've noticed the formalities don't count for much." Morgan and Jenkins, standing back to back and so rigid it seemed unlikely they would be able to move when they were told to, continued to glare straight ahead and might not have heard him, and Zack shouted, "Now, march!"

Morgan and Jenkins moved off at a steady pace, their faces solemn and bewitched, and stopped, to stand once again straight and rigid, waiting.

"Present!" Zack shouted, and they wheeled. "Fire!" Jenkins fired first, and Morgan the fraction of a second later.

Jenkins looked astonished, staggered one step forward and fired again. Morgan vaguely heard Zack yell at him and believed he was telling him to fire, but he felt as if a horse's hoof had struck him in the chest and his right hand hung at his side, not to be lifted by any exercise of will. He heard another shot and supposed he had fired without his own knowledge, as Jenkins, who had twisted slowly around, dropped to one knee where he poised uncertainly for a moment and pitched forward, then flopped over onto his back.

Morgan began to stagger uncertainly toward him, determined to see, before he fell himself, whether or not he had killed him, and what he looked like now that he was dead. He walked slowly, his shoulders hunched, trying to be dignified and disdainful, but feeling that he was drunk and absolutely helpless. His eyes had blurred, but he had a fierce greed for the sight of Jenkins' face, and he brushed one hand impatiently before his eyes, trying to clear his vision. After a journey that seemed to cover many miles, he arrived at where Jenkins lay on his back, one leg doubled under him, the blood bursting from his throat in little fountains. His eyes were rolled back and his face was loosened and expressionless; his breathing was hard and uneven, and he would be dead soon.

Morgan knelt slowly and carefully, and was still hoping to pretend to Zack, wherever he was, that he only wanted to look at Jenkins more closely, but then, irresistibly, he slipped lower and lower, and when presently he saw Zack bending over him, realized that now he lay on his back beside Jenkins, though it surprised him he should be there and he gave Zack an apolegetic frown, mumbling, "Get right up."

He tried to move, but Zack put both hands on his shoulders, firmly, but gently, and there was a curiously tender and reflective look on his face as he opened Morgan's shirt. Morgan's eyes closed, he forgot Zack and Jenkins in a powerful yearning for sleep, but then, convinced there was something more he had to say, whispered, "Tell my father I died like a—"

"Shut up," said Zack, but his face was still tender. "You won't die from this. Lay still, I'll bring a doctor."

"Where's the other guy?" He could not remember his name, and hoped Zack would know who he was talking about.

"He won't bother you, don't worry about him. And don't try to move." Zack disappeared and Morgan once again let his eyes close, aware of some incomprehensible feeling of gratitude, and a perfect indifference which he took to be peace and possibly the beginning of his own death.

XIX

On Sunday morning an unusual quiet settled over the island and visitors were awed, wondering by what magic its citizens had disappeared into seemingly empty houses and drawn in after them streetcars and hacks, horses and carriages and milk trucks, as if some catastrophe had obliterated the city's life and left only the city itself.

Along Fifth Avenue, where the brownstones made a steady procession which was now reaching beyond Thirty-fifth Street, it was possible to walk for some distance past these nearly identical houses, each with draperies drawn behind heavy curtains, without hearing any sound or encountering any movement. Above Fifty-ninth Street, the squatters in their village of shacks built amid the rocks overlooking the Park were invisible, and only a few goats and dogs went wandering and sniffing among the garbage dumps, where the squatters ordinarily found their best ammunition against invasion. The wharves along the North and East rivers were lined with ships from every port in the world and here, too, there was silence. The fashionable gambling houses and brothels on East Fourteenth Street and West Twenty-third were shuttered and locked. In the Battery drunken men and women slept beneath the trees. The slum children were the earliest risers, and began to emerge from the cellars and tenements still half asleep, but with their faces washed and their hair combed, and stood solemnly amid the heaped refuse, waiting.

Even the newsboys were subdued and seemed reluctant to disturb this universal peace, and a bootblack, when at last he came upon his quarry, obsequiously inquired, "Black your boots, sir?"

By the middle of the morning girls were hurrying into saloons in the poor wards, a few carriages appeared uptown, and fashionably dressed men and women had read the newspapers and were on their way to church, preferring to walk if the weather was fine. Young men dashed by in yellow kid gloves, whores with demure faces walked two by two to church, and presently the city rang with bells, hymns were sung, and men and women and children settled back to give an hour's contemplation to whatever interested them most at that moment.

Later, when these ladies and gentlemen had once again strolled slowly home, bowing and lifting their hats to friends, and retired into their brownstones, most of them not to reappear until morning —though some had funerals to attend and some drove in the Park, and the men usually took a brief evening walk—the rest of the city sprang to life, as if beckoned out of hiding by the disappearance of those decorous ones, and by late afternoon the beer gardens and concert-saloons, the whorehouses and gambling halls were once again as noisy and crowded as if the day of idleness had built a strange and violent energy; there were more fights than usual, and the policeman's club, calling for help, beat steadily upon the pavements.

But now, on a Sunday morning in late September, the wilder part of the community was still invisible and the congregations of the fashionable churches emerged, blinking as they confronted the sharp sunlight, and preserving the expressions they had worn throughout the services, which made them look concerned and doubtful but nevertheless improved. They stood outside the churches, exchanging gossip, an occasional laugh was heard, and the spell of imminent perdition slowly dissolved.

The Chings stood together, Joshua and Susan and Ceda, surrounded by his brothers and their wives and children, and Joshua, wearing striped trousers and a frock coat, with his silk hat in his hand, was bowing and smiling graciously, accepting all compliments on the birth of his grandson as if they belonged to himself rather than to Philip. It even seemed they were spoken directly to Joshua, while Philip stood looking amused and unconcerned and made no effort to claim the child as his own.

"And what is the baby's name?" he was asked.

"Joshua," said Joshua.

"Joshua Van Zandt—how nice." The woman inclined her head to Philip and Philip gave her a prompt, smart bow, then fell to looking abstracted again.

The strollers set out, up and down the Avenue, admonishing little beggar girls to go home and not loiter about the streets on the Sabbath, and the Chings took their places in the parade, the four children walking ahead, followed by Harriet and Melissa who were followed in turn by Susan and Ceda, and after them walked the men, engrossed in serious conversation, and all three, Joshua noticed—his brothers and his son-in-law—were careful in their deference.

"He's a smart man," was a frequent saying nowadays about Joshua Ching, and he was pleased to know that many men, including these three, believed that during the past year and a half, since he had taken over De Groot Distilleries, he had made three million dollars by trading in and out of the market, and this was in some respects almost as satisfying as if it had been true.

He knew his present reputation very well, for it was his own invention: Men said that Joshua Ching was a veritable manufactory of schemes and plans, that he owned judges and politicians, that he maintained his private secret service system, that he hired other

men's confidential employees and sent his own to work in the offices
of his enemies.

So far, it was further said, he had never made a serious mistake
or, if he had, it was not known and the corpse had disappeared—a
fair enough warning. It was thought to be just as well to fear Joshua
Ching a little, and no sensible man should deliver him an open
challenge. And Joshua, as he knew, looked sleeker than ever before,
as if flattery fed the glands of his skin. His step was ponderous, decisive, almost threatening in its implication, while his clear blue
eyes, when once they fixed upon a man's face, never flickered until
he had satisfied himself that the other was either his captive or of no
consequence.

Still, Joshua had lost hold of too many opportunities he had believed to be firmly grasped and had experienced too many narrow
disappointments, while others had been most miraculously avoided,
not to have more humility than he was willing to show. Once, very
long ago as it seemed, he had believed that other men who were successful were only luckier than he, but now that men had begun to
envy him he despised them for imagining his success had been accomplished by simple accident, when at any moment, by even the
smallest inattention or most minute miscalculation, he could have
lost it all, and still might.

"You've been lucky, Joshua," Susan had said to him recently, and
to his surprise Joshua had felt an instantaneous rage which flooded
his head and reddened his face, and had only with much difficulty
controlled himself from advancing on her in a shouting fury. He had
made no reply, but he entered the insult in his ledger where, if Susan
only knew it, the balance was beginning to run heavily against her.

"The more money I make, Susan," he told her some time later,
when the danger had passed, "the more arrogant you become."

"Perhaps it only seems that way to you, Joshua. You may be expecting that eventually I'll be as meek as Ceda, but it's not likely."

Somehow or other, as they both understood, they had not only
fallen out of love but had begun to distrust each other, and Joshua
thought this small disaster, for it did not seem a large one, was irreparable. And he found it to be in many ways quite a convenience,
for he was obliged to tell few lies, and Susan seemed satisfied with
only the pretense of hypocrisy.

Since Suky's marriage, just a year and three months ago, he had
moved into her bedroom, politely explaining to Susan that he would
not wake her when he got up early or came home late, and now took
it for granted he would never again get into bed with her. Susan, he
thought, was as much relieved as he, and Joshua had begun to consider finding some girl who pleased him well enough that he would
establish her in a house, but so far he continued to patronize the
more expensive brothels in the neighborhood of the Fifth Avenue
Hotel.

If Susan had been as clever as she liked to believe, he assured himself, she would show him some small deferences which, after all, would cost her nothing, but Susan preferred to let him understand that whatever he had contrived to represent in the outside world she, at least, saw him as he was. Still, he did not dislike her, although he foresaw that one day he might, and supposed he and Susan liked each other neither better nor worse than any other couple who had endured more than twenty years of marriage, and, at least, she had given him Suky, though he had no similar enthusiasm for Steven.

Joshua had sent Steven away to school, with the intention of emancipating him from his mother and aunt, and Steven, having had several beatings at the hands of his schoolmates, returned for the summer vacation a hardened and cynical young man, which caused Ceda to weep over him while his mother approached him uncertainly, as if he might be sick.

But the change had only confirmed Joshua's suspicions, whatever they were, and he remarked to Susan, "He's done even better than I hoped for. I expected it would take them four years to make an insufferable prig of him and he's practically achieved it in six months. I'll send him to Germany next year, and that will finish the job." But Susan looked at him, rocking on his heels and beaming malevolently, and shook her head in sad wonderment, for the humor was his usual kind, sharp and sinister, with his real meaning vaguely disguised by flippancy.

It had been Susan's antagonism toward him, Joshua was convinced, which had been responsible for most of the difficulties before Suky's marriage, and he did not doubt that if he had been any less resourceful Suky would not now be Mrs. Philip Van Zandt, there would be no firm of Van Zandt and Ching, and the ten-day-old Joshua Van Zandt would never have existed at all.

Certainly he did not expect ever to forgive Susan for the look she had given him when he emerged from Suky's bedroom to announce that she would marry Philip the following week. For even though it grieved Joshua to deprive Suky of the great wedding she had planned, it would be no public triumph if the Van Zandts refused to attend it, and Philip had gravely assured him they would not. "And after all, Joshua, she could have done so much better without your help, couldn't she?"

"Don't make me angry, Susan," he warned her, for, it was true, his long discussion with Suky had cost him the last of his patience. "You've done enough mischief."

The trouble had begun a few days before that, when Joshua had met Ceda tiptoeing down the hall on her way to Suky's room, just as he was ready to leave, and since this unprecedented encounter must have an explanation, and because Ceda looked guilty and embarrassed, he had gone into Suky's room and found that she was sick, too sick to go driving that afternoon with Philip Van Zandt, as Joshua had told her to do.

He had very little faith in Suky's illnesses, for it seemed they at-

tacked her whenever she was angry, although she would never admit
it, or frightened, and she would not admit that, either, or when she
was suffering from some disappointment. Then, invariably, she
grew pale, developed wandering pains and symptoms which puzzled
the doctor, and went to bed, insisting that she was too weak to move.
And there, he thought, she lay with her eyes closed and waged her
contest with that anger or fear or disappointment, until one morning she awoke miraculously restored, threw away the pills and po-
tions, and once again gave the impression that however fragile she
looked she was made of some indestructible material. But each time,
when he heard that Suky was sick, there was a moment of nauseating terror, when he told himself that this was the time she really
might be.

He sat beside her, holding her hand and putting his palm to her
forehead and face, questioning her about her symptoms, when they
had begun and what course they had taken, and was soon convinced
that Suky was not any sicker than he was. "Send for the doctor," he
told Susan, "and see that she takes whatever he prescribes."

Susan followed him into the living room. "We hadn't seen Mr. Van
Zandt for five months, and now he's called three times in the last
week. Where has he been all this time?"

"Where has he been, Susan?" Joshua's tone was crisply scornful.
"I suppose he may have been investigating other possibilities, don't
you?"

"And he's decided that Susan Ching is the best he can do?"

"Susan, are you trying to interfere with my plans?"

"Oh? Then you do have plans. Well, Joshua, suppose they aren't
agreeable to Suky?"

"They will be."

Susan had given him a mocking smile, but he supposed it only
meant the three women were indignant that Philip Van Zandt had
not proposed to Suky while having his first waltz with her, and certainly he did not intend to tell them Philip was back only because
he had given him a check for one hundred thousand dollars, deeded
to him three lots on Forty-fourth Street and Fifth Avenue, and agreed
to make him a full partner in a new brokerage office.

But a few days later Philip appeared in his office late in the afternoon, looking more baffled than resentful, to report, "Mr. Ching,
your daughter doesn't want to marry me."

"But that's impossible."

"I saw her this afternoon." He smiled. "It was quite a surprise."

Joshua stood up. "There's been some mistake," he informed him,
as brusquely as if he were a client who had miscalculated his market
winnings. "Are you sure she understood you?"

Philip smiled again. "I'm sure."

"What did she say?"

"She said that she wasn't ready to get married. Her aunt, who was
with us, cried more tears in less time than any woman I've ever seen.

I wasn't quite sure if it was chagrin or relief. I asked Susan whether or not she might change her mind and she looked at me—you know," said Philip, as if Joshua would know which look he meant, "and she said that she didn't think so."

Joshua stood for a few moments with his arms folded, gazing out the window and into the next office where clerks sat on high stools before ledgers, impatient clients walked about snapping their fingers, and errand boys darted back and forth. Philip was smoking a cigar and plainly thought this was not a problem for him to solve.

At last Joshua turned. "I'll talk to her. She may think you'll love her more than ever now. I don't pretend to understand them."

Joshua had always supposed that Susan's observation that Suky, in spite of her seeming submissiveness, was in reality less flexible than an iron fence, had been only the comment of a woman who was jealous of her daughter's greater beauty. But when he began to discuss with Suky her refusal of Philip, he became quickly aware that it was no exaggeration.

He had arrived to find the apartment growing dark, no lights burning, and Susan and Ceda in Suky's bedroom, for Suky's sicknesses were authentic enough at least to her, while they lasted. He sat down, asked Suky with an unusual tenderness how she was feeling, took her hand and found it surprisingly cold though the day was hot and the bedroom stifling, and said, "Mr. Van Zandt was in my office at four o'clock." Susan sat straighter, and Ceda gave a start, but Suky's hand lay motionless in his, and it was too dark to see her expression. "He was almost distraught, Suky."

Suky withdrew her hand, and gave that familiar soft little laugh, known to him ever since her early childhood, as if she was at once baffled and skeptical. "Somehow, I can't picture it."

All at once Joshua was convinced they were not telling him the truth, and that the three women had a secret. He moved his chair a little nearer and spoke to her confidentially. "Have you ever lied to me, Susan?"

"No, Papa."

"Then tell me what it is you're concealing."

Ceda, at that, gave such a gasp that Susan walked out of the room, as if now she had spoiled everything, but Suky raised her arms and clasped them behind her head, and slid a little farther down in the bed. "How did you guess, Papa?"

Joshua smiled, and gave a suggestive sniff. "It was in the air. Tell me about it." And, in fact, the cloying smell of the tuberoses in a vase beside her bed, had reminded him that there had been several such bouquets about the apartment recently.

"I want to marry someone else," she said, in a voice so low he leaned close to hear her, and then drew back again.

"But you don't know anyone else." He raised his voice. "Susan! Come in here." Susan appeared in the doorway. "What is she talking about?"

"Must I tell him, Suky? Well, then, Joshua, she's fallen in love with another man."

"What's his name?" Joshua was now as infuriated as if he had been told that she had eloped and he had lost the three lots, the one hundred thousand dollars, and his new firm of Van Zandt and Ching.

"Frederic Hallam."

"Where did she meet him?"

"At Jemima Cottrell's wedding."

"But my God, that wasn't two weeks ago."

"He's in love with her," said Ceda rapturously, and Joshua gave her a glare, as if to ask what experiences had equipped Ceda for such a judgment.

"How many times have you seen him?"

"Twice."

"I see," said Joshua, and leaned forward with his elbows on his knees and fell to gazing at the floor, until at last the women grew restive, and then he lighted the lamp beside Suky's bed, taking care before he did so to fix upon his face an expression of tender concern which, he hoped, concealed the ferocious determination he felt. "Has he proposed to you?"

Suky gave again her soft, baffled laugh. "After all, Papa." She smiled at him from the corners of her eyes, as if to say they both knew proposals took a little more time than that, and she began to pleat the lace edging on one of the pillows between her fingers.

"What do you intend to do, Suky?"

"I hadn't intended to do anything. I was going to wait."

And, with the same intensity of concentration he had given to Milton De Groot in the days when De Groot still signified something to him, Joshua set about convincing Suky that she must do what he asked of her. "You imagine that Frederic Hallam loves you, although you've see him only twice—"

"What difference does that make, Joshua?"

"Be quiet, Susan, or leave the room. The Hallam family is rich, they have no need of money and, if they did, I haven't enough to interest them. When Frederic Hallam marries, it will be some girl whose family offers them a favorable business alliance. That, whether you like it or not, is the way these things are handled nowadays."

"Joshua, I don't agree with you at all." Joshua turned quickly and stared at Susan, but she went on talking. "Mrs. Talbot was here yesterday afternoon, with her daughter, and they took Suky for a drive. On the way, they happened to pass Frederic Hallam and he joined them. She was extremely friendly, wasn't she, Suky?"

Joshua turned back. "If you let a woman like Coral Talbot begin to suspect that you're in love with her cousin, you'll be making a mistake you may never be able to undo."

Suky looked surprised, stopped pleating the pillow edging, and sat up again, folding her hands in her lap. "What harm could Mrs. Talbot do me?"

"She can make you ridiculous—is there anything worse than that?"

"Are you trying to frighten the poor child?"

"There's a good deal to be frightened about in this world, as it happens. Now, let's not confuse the real issue we're discussing, which is a suitable marriage. It may be true enough, as you think, Suky, that Frederic Hallam is infatuated with you, or in love with you, if you like that word better. Young men fall in love very easily with beautiful young women, it happens quite automatically, and quite automatically they fall out of love with them again, if they encounter too many difficulties. The Hallams imagine that they are among the city's original aristocrats and, like all those people, they have no liking for men like me, newcomers. Roger Hallam would never permit his son to marry Joshua Ching's daughter."

Suky looked at him steadily for some moments, and though there was a slight smile on her mouth, it was more knowing than complaisant, and her eyes seemed to slant a little at the corners, as they did whenever she perceived some unexpected advantage to herself. "Then why does Philip Van Zandt want to marry me?"

"He has no reason to consider his family's wishes, because he has nothing to gain from them. Frederic Hallam, on the other hand, does —and if he defied them, what would he have left? Nothing you would want, my dear," he assured her kindly.

"I don't agree with you, Joshua," Susan began, but Joshua glanced at her across his shoulder.

"Susan, leave the room, if you please." Susan raised her eyebrows, hesitating, but then following Ceda, who had left the moment he spoke to Susan. And then he turned back to Suky with the same air of patient persistence which she could certainly recognize and interpret for what it meant, that however long they might discuss this, in the end she would do what he asked.

But when he began to talk to her, showing first one reason and then another why she must stop imagining that Frederic Hallam would marry her, and parading forth the advantages of being Mrs. Philip Van Zandt, Suky fiddled with the ends of her hair, sighed from time to time, looking ironically amused and indifferent, and Joshua was disconcerted to recognize a habit of his own which had baffled every man who had ever entered a business negotiation with him. And, at last, he was horrified to see tears in her eyes. "I won't be happy if I marry Mr. Van Zandt."

"But how do you know, my dear?"

"I know. And I know I will be happy if I marry Frederic Hallam."

Joshua took her hand again, finding it still cold and motionless. "There's very little happiness to be had in this world, Suky, and you must believe me that of all the places where you might hope to find it, love is the one with the best reputation but the smallest return."

Suky thought about this, glanced at him, and sat up quickly, shaking back her hair. "I'm never going to get married at all."

"That's too absurd to discuss. You've seen what kind of life an unmarried woman can expect. Is your Aunt Ceda an ideal you'd like to achieve?" He lowered his voice, for Susan might be hanging about the hallway. "You imagine there's nothing in the world so important as to marry a man you think you're in love with. My dear child, why hasn't it occurred to you that if he loves you now, there's no reason he should love you any less because you're married?"

Suky looked surprised at this, considered it a moment and gave an embarrassed little laugh, shaking one finger at him chidingly, as she had done when she was a child. "I'm sure you don't mean that the way it sounds, Papa."

"I'm sure I do," said Joshua gravely. And, in another year, when she knew more about the world than she did today, she would agree with him. "Whatever you do in the present, Suky, you must think of its relationship to the future. If you marry Philip Van Zandt, you'll be able to take advantage of whatever success I may have. If you wait, and lose him, and Frederic Hallam marries someone else, you won't make another marriage that will do as much for you. If you want to be admired by men and envied by women, and you do, then you must live in such a way that men will admire you and women envy you. Beauty is nothing of itself, without the proper setting."

Suky folded her hands, placing her forefingers together and touching them to her lips while she thought about this, keeping her eyes lowered, until all at once she looked at him again, inquiring, "And what will you give me, Papa, if I do this for you?"

"Do this for me, Suky? Wherever did you get such an idea as that? You aren't doing it for me, you're doing it for yourself."

"But all the same, it's something I don't want to do."

For a moment Joshua was tempted to announce that she would do as she was told, but then reminded himself that Suky was the best ally he had, and her marriage would make her a better one, and so he offered her a long European wedding trip. She took that, but she wanted more, she must have Maxine with her, and so Joshua gave away Susan's maid. Women, he had decided long ago, were blackmailers by instinct, it was their natural way of negotiating their emotional business, and she extracted from him one thing at a time, until at last he told her he had nothing more to give.

"I can at least refurnish his house, can't I?" she asked him wistfully.

"Wait until after your first child has been born."

"What has that to do with the house?"

"We'll see," he told her.

The wedding ceremony had scarcely been read when Joshua's mind began to rove over possible means of recapturing the money he had given to Philip, and the lots—upon which he meant to build his own house one day—and by the time they arrived at the boat he had fixed a general scheme by which, one day, Philip would return it all, not by coercion, but only as the result of his fatal business habits of recklessness and optimism.

"Learn all you can about art," was Joshua's parting and confidential advice to Suky. "When I build a picture gallery I don't want it filled with those lost masterpieces they sell to Americans." He bent to kiss her, murmuring, "Be happy." It was contrary, of course, to his theory that happiness was not a goal for a natural aristocrat, but he had said it inadvertently.

Suky and Philip were away for nearly six months, and by the time they returned Joshua thought it would have been impossible for any one to guess they had married for any other reason than a spontaneous enthusiasm for each other. And when it was discovered that she was pregnant, Joshua was not reticent in letting her know that if the baby was a boy he must be named for his Grandfather Ching. Philip showed all the pleased smugness of a vain man married to a startling beauty, and Joshua thought it a stroke of good luck she had not married Frederic Hallam, whose wealth would not likely have made him so agreeable a son-in-law. He might, for instance, have preferred to have his first son bear his own name.

Joshua had sprung upon his grandchild with eager joy, had observed him proudly and critically, held him and walked about with him and stopped to see him every day, bringing him presents and marveling at his slanted eyes, his minute nose, his damp, fuzzy head and his nails, which looked like tissue paper. While Philip, though he seemed pleased with the baby, grew quickly bored and, thought Joshua, seemed to recognize his own minor role in its birth. For as they came out of the church on that Sunday morning it was Joshua, not Philip, who, as they paraded slowly in the direction of Philip's house, accepted most of the compliments and answered most of the questions about Suky, saying each time that she was very well, quite recovered, even though this was not true.

As they approached the house the two youngest cousins, Seth and Evelyn, ran ahead and went dashing up the stairs in a race to reach her first. They crept softly down the hall and peeked through the opened doorway to see Suky lying on a sofa in the sitting room, while Maxine brushed her hair.

"May we come in?" whispered Evelyn.

Suky smiled and they ran forward, stopped a few feet away, and stood gazing at her in rapturous admiration. "The sermon was so edifying," Evelyn told her.

"What was it about?"

"Other sheep have I yet in the fold," Seth proclaimed.

"Everyone was asking about you."

Suky went on smiling as they talked, and stroked the poodle Romola, one of Joshua's gifts to his grandson, but these two healthy children made her feel that she was not nineteen but a very old woman, her life used up and its most significant experiences forgotten, or only remembered in self-pitying sorrow.

For the baby's birth had taken her as much by surprise as if she had set out on a pleasant journey and found herself in a train wreck. The smell of chloroform, the pain she had refused to believe would be as severe for her as it was for other women, the hours of effort and despair, when again and again she had longed to give up, let herself die and the child die with her, the doctor's probing hands which were sometimes smeared with blood, the cries she heard without recognizing that they were her own, she believed she would never be able to forget, even though Susan assured her it would all fade from her memory so completely that no effort of will could bring it back. And when, after almost twenty hours, the baby was born and presented to her, the doctor proudly displaying the small, crushed creature as if he had only now invented it for her, she had turned away and put up her hand to fend it off, feeling it to be not her child but an alien and hostile object, and when it began to cry she covered her ears and begged him to take it where she could not hear it.

Joshua and Philip were not told any of this as they waited downstairs, smoking cigars and drinking port and discussing their plans for Van Zandt and Ching, and Susan and Ceda were sent out of Suky's sitting room and wandered about the halls and up and down the stairs, listening in awe and fear when her voice carried through the walls. All of them, it seemed, had come to believe the family myths about Suky, and this evidence of her common humanity shocked them.

Even when she had slept and recovered enough to smile modestly and humbly at her father and husband, Suky was filled with deep shame to know she felt no interest in the child and no sense of having accomplished its birth but only a profound emptiness, as if she had been forcibly deprived of something which had belonged to her but now did not, and she became very much concerned to hide what she felt, for it had been her confident expectation that the baby would flow painlessly from her body and that her tender madonna's smile would be a real one.

She blamed each of them in turn—Joshua and Philip and Frederic Hallam, who had not asked her to elope with him once he knew she was engaged to Philip—and whenever she began to blame them, separately or together, she had such a longing to cry that she could prevent it only by reminding herself of her father's remark about Ceda: that tears were an old maid's solace.

Susan and Ceda came in next, with Harriet and Melissa, and the little cousins stepped obediently to one side. They kissed her, touching her hair and twitching a fold of her skirt, asking in whispers if she was better, if the doctor had been there, and Suky smiled at them and contrived to make her face so luminous it almost seemed that she liked this role, after all.

Joshua came forward, their skirts swayed and parted for him and he stood looking down at her, studying her critically before he kissed her forehead and took hold of her hand. "I've brought you a surprise."

Susan and Ceda glanced at each other, for they had not heard of it, Philip kissed Suky's cheek and she seemed scarcely to notice it, being so intent on the surprise, and as Joshua's brothers and the two older cousins entered the room and heard that a surprise was coming, the excitement became so keen that even the poodle awoke and began to whine expectantly, wriggling on its fringed green velvet cushion and fluttering its short tufted tail.

Joshua reached into the breast pocket of his frock coat, brought forth a flat white satin box and held it out to her, and the room became extraordinarily still, though the two little cousins whispered and Philip coughed.

Suky opened it with precise movements of her long fingers, and displayed a strand of diamonds from which hung a dark, pear-shaped sapphire, the size of a robin's egg. The women caught their breath, the brothers raised their eyebrows, Philip took a forward step as if to assess its value, and Suky sat gazing at it with a dazzled expression, seeing it fastened about her throat as she entered a ballroom in a white tulle gown.

Joshua bent down, fastening the catch, and Suky murmured a few words to him the others could not hear, and, as they crowded forward to examine it, Joshua threw Philip a meaningful and possibly challenging glance.

Lord and Lady Haldane arrived, and Jemima, whose first child would be born soon, joined the women inspecting the necklace, while Lord Haldane talked to the men. Amos Cottrell either had not discovered or was too stubborn to admit that his daughter had not married a real nobleman, and continued to speak of his son-in-law as Lord Haldane, so that every man who did any business with him or hoped to was obliged to follow his example.

"Why, Suky," Jemima cried, "it's as if the necklace were a part of you. That's what you look like. Diamonds and sapphires."

"I wish she'd thought of another comparison," murmured Susan.

"I don't," said Ceda. "It's a perfect description."

"But I must see the baby. Where is he?"

Susan pulled a bell cord and told the maid to have the nurse bring him in.

"But, madame, he is just this minute—"

"Never mind," said Joshua. "Bring him in."

However, the baby's appearance was not prompt and Joshua asked Giles Haldane what he thought of the American way of doing business, for Amos Cottrell had put him to work in his office.

"Very original, sir," Lord Haldane assured him blandly, and seemed to believe that his acceptance as a nobleman had made him one. He stood with his teeth bared and tapped the ivory head of his cane against them, a dandy's habit which made Joshua yearn to crack him with it, and rolled his blue eyes. "Very original. You Americans, if I may say so, seem to have discovered several ways of making money that have never occurred to my dull-witted countrymen."

Joshua began to reply to that, but then turned, as if at the entrance of a great statesman or a beautiful woman, when the murmurs rose to indicate that the baby had appeared and, at the next moment, it began to cry.

The nurse carried an embroidered cushion upon which the baby lay, squirming and howling, clenching his fists and gasping for breath between each howl, looking furious and violently frustrated. He wore a white mull dress, trimmed with Valenciennes lace, which fell halfway to the floor, and his head was covered with a lace cap tied with blue ribbons, but even in this finery Suky thought he was remarkably ugly and had some doubts he would ever improve.

The women went swooping toward him, and as he continued to scream and brandish his fists, Joshua took the baby and his cushion and began to walk about, clucking and reasoning with him and, to the women's surprise, the baby presently lay still and gazed up at him as if mesmerized. At that moment they discovered Coral Talbot, standing in the doorway and smiling slightly, as if to ask whether or not she might come in.

She wore a brown taffeta gown embroidered with black braid and a small black hat and she looked, as she always did, discreetly but aggressively fashionable. Her black eyes swept from one face to another, as if recognizing them all but actually seeing no one, and then, with a slight inclination of her head by way of greeting, she walked to Suky, took her hand, and asked how she was feeling.

"I'm much better, thank you," Suky said, as meekly as a little girl, for she was still afraid of Coral Talbot, and more than ever now, when Coral's look of vital health and patronizing concern seemed to diminish even further her own depleted energies.

Coral studied the necklace. "An excellent sapphire, I must say."

She turned and went to look at the baby, still being carried back and forth by Joshua, and Felice, who had followed her mother into the room, now approached Suky, smiling deferentially as she passed and dropping a curtsy to Susan.

Felice kissed Suky and then stood very straight, with her hands folded and her big dark eyes gazing down at her with a kind of anxious adoration. For, ever since the day Felice had accompanied her mother and Suky on the drive where Frederic Hallam had unexpectedly appeared, Felice had been Suky's greatest admirer, surpassing in her worshipfulness all previous votaries. She seemed to have discovered in Suky, who was seven years older, some combination of friend and mother and sister and heroine which had aroused her eager devotion, and it amused Susan to see them together, talking as earnestly as two school friends, for Felice was at once the twelve-year-old girl aware of her age, and a confidante of older years and superior wisdom.

"Whatever can Suky and that child find to talk about?" Susan asked.

"Never mind," said Joshua, "what they talk about. Her father is William Talbot, remember that." And Suky had smiled with that peculiar smile which was enigmatical to Susan but which Joshua supposed he read easily enough.

What they found to talk about, in fact, was Felice's cousin, Frederic Hallam, although Suky had not seen him since the day Felice had been sent as his emissary, after Susan had refused to let him see Suky and had not found the courage to tell him that she was engaged. Felice, who came with her governess, had asked Suky to drive with her, and once again there had been an unexpected encounter with her cousin, who sent the governess ahead in his own carriage and drove with Suky and Felice. This meeting, never mentioned by Suky to any one else, only three days before her marriage, had furnished the material for all their subsequent conversations, and it seemed there was still so much left in it which fascinated and absorbed them they might go on talking about it for some years to come.

Felice had sat between them, bolt upright and motionless, staring straight ahead, and Frederic had taken hold of Suky's gloved hand, confirming with his fingers her engagement ring. They had exchanged glances across Felice, who remained quite rigid, scarcely daring to breathe, and Felice had later told her, "Suky, he was heartbroken." But by then, of course, Suky had been married, gone on a honeymoon trip, and would soon have her baby. None of these events, however, had affected Felice's loyalty to that first best love, spoiled forever in her mind by Philip Van Zandt who had, in some roundabout fashion, contrived to cheat her cousin.

"Oh, Suky," Felice had told her, "to see the look on his face when you left us that day was the saddest thing that's ever happened to me—or ever will."

And Suky had kissed her, saying, "I hope it is, darling." She longed to ask Felice why it was, if her cousin loved her so much, he had not asked her to marry him then and there, but she was not at all sure Felice knew the answer or that she wanted to hear it if she did.

"How are you feeling, Suky?" Felice spoke in a tense undertone, as if she had met a fellow spy in a dark place to exchange secrets.

"I'm better, darling."

"Are you sure?"

"Of course I am." The others were watching them and seemed to be waiting to hear what they had to say to each other, these two who could talk in lowered voices for an hour or more without seeming aware of anything but their own engrossing conversation. And Suky suggested, "Tell me about the sermon."

"It was inspiring." Felice clasped her hands and announced in her carefully trained voice: "*Oh, my wasted life! Oh, the bitter past! Oh, the graves over which I have stumbled! God help me! God pity me!*" She glanced about in surprise as there was a low murmur of laughter from the others, and Suky smiled, knowing that Felice had found in the sermon one more clue that even in heaven there was consternation over the thwarting of her cousin's love.

Presently the women gathered in one group, the men formed another, the cousins fell into some minor dispute, Coral Talbot and Philip stood at the window, and Felice sat beside Suky, taking the puppy onto her lap and stroking him as they talked. "He was there," Felice whispered, and her black eyes kept alert watch over the room.

"He was?" Suky's eyes deepened and shone brightly, an effect she could achieve at the mention of his name, only because Felice would have been disappointed not to see it—that soft glow, at once ardent and pathetic and so deeply moving to Felice. "Did you talk to him?"

"Yes."

"Alone?"

"Of course."

"What did he say?"

"He asked how you were feeling."

"How did he look?"

"He had on a black coat and gray trousers and white gloves, and a gardenia. He looked wonderful—but sad."

"Is that all he said?"

"He said—Suky, he looked at me as if he wanted me to tell you— he stared at me until it almost made me dizzy, and he said, 'I'll never feel any different, Felice, do you believe me?'"

"Of course I believe you."

"No, no! He said, 'Do you believe me?' And I said that I did."

They gazed at each other for a long, serious moment and finally both of them sighed and shook their heads and then, at a new thought, Suky asked, "Did you tell him that I never would, either?"

"Yes, that's what I said. 'Frédéric, neither will she.' Oh, Suky, what a tragedy."

"Shh," cautioned Suky, for Felice's lower lip had begun to tremble and her black brows drew together in a frown. "I'm so grateful to you, Felice. Without you, I'd have lost him completely."

"I'd do anything for you, Suky."

"I know you would. But now, you must talk to the others. Your mother is looking at us." Mrs. Talbot, Felice had reported, was curious about their long conversations, and Felice had told her they discussed the books they read.

Quickly and gracefully, taking care not to look at her mother, Felice rose to her feet, returned the puppy to its cushion and crossed the room with her gliding walk, to intercept the nurse as she started to carry the baby from the room. "Mr. Ching," she said, peering first at the baby and then up into Joshua's blond-bearded face, "he looks more like you every day." Joshua smiled and kissed her on the forehead and Felice clucked over the baby, grew silent and pensive, and at last gave Suky a slow, uncertain glance. But Suky, surrounded by her aunts, did not see it.

Other voices were heard in the hallway and Amos Cottrell and his wife came in. All at once the room seemed crowded and noisy, and Coral Talbot took her departure, passing expertly among them, and, with a glance at her daughter, left the room.

Felice rushed back to Suky. "I must go," she whispered, and looked quite desperate. "But I'll see him this afternoon—family dinner. I'll tell him I saw you."

Suky touched Felice's sleeve. "But tell him I'm looking well."

"I'll tell him you're more beautiful than ever," Felice declared, and went skimming out of the room, dropping another curtsy to Susan from the doorway.

X X

As Zack Fletcher predicted, Morgan did not die, but the bullet had grazed his chest and entered his right shoulder, and by the time they had carried him back down the hillside on an improvised stretcher he had lost so much blood that his skin looked gray beneath its tan. Matt and Pete and Zack remained with him while Dr. Raymond Chaffinch, Andy Danforth's successor, probed for the bullet and at last—more or less by accident, Zack thought—found it; and by that time the Doctor admitted privately to Matt and Pete that he had no great hope of his recovery.

"But then, he's healthy and you say he hasn't been sick much. He may make it. Keep him absolutely quiet, if you have to tie him down, and for God's sake don't let Lisette have hysterics over him again. I'll be here early tomorrow, but send for me if there's any change, especially if he starts to sweat and turns cold."

After a few days, however, although Morgan had been in coma most of the time, only regaining consciousness long enough to drink quantities of water, Dr. Chaffinch was ready to agree with Zack.

There was no suggestion of bringing either Morgan or Zack to trial, for every man present at the Fourth of July picnic had been a member of the Vigilance Committee and swore to having witnessed the ambushing of Morgan Devlin and Zack Fletcher, who had been lured to meet Jenkins and Hamilton on the pretext of being paid a gambling debt. And other men were found who had heard Jenkins bragging that he intended to make a sieve of Morgan Devlin and his friend Zack Fletcher before the day was out.

As the story was reported in the *Virginia City Journal*, Morgan and

Zack were heroes who had imperiled their lives to save the town
from infestation by two desperadoes, former members of Quantrill's
Raiders, road agents who had been warned out of Helena, and
crooked gamblers who traveled about the mountains taking advantage of gullible miners with their three-card monte game and their
horse races, abetted in all this by a notorious young woman named
Lily Jones who wore men's clothes and had for several years roamed
about the West, leaving a characteristic trail of destruction wherever she went.

Zack showed the article to Morgan one day when they were alone
in the parlor, where his bed had been set up. Morgan read it slowly
and, at last, handed it to Zack, who slid it beneath Lisette's albums,
as if he thought they were not supposed to have seen it.

"Who the hell wrote it?"

"Lisette's beau, that guy Mercer."

"Where'd he hear about Lily?"

"That's what I asked him. He says that when he talked to the fellows around town they all told him about Lily Jones. You didn't know
it, old boy, but that was a famous woman you were keeping company with."

"You mean," said Morgan, who still looked to Zack more dead
than alive, "that was a famous woman who made a horse's ass of
me." He tried to smile, but it became a ghastly and almost furtive
grimace, embarrassing for Zack to see.

Zack sat beside him, leaning forward and staring at him thoughtfully. It was the first time either of them had mentioned Lily since
they had returned to their cabin and found her gone; and at last Zack
softly inquired, "Which of us are you blaming?"

"Myself. Who the hell else?"

"Me, for one. I should have done a better job hiding the damn
stuff. Or Lily—when in doubt, most guys blame the girl, don't they?"

"What difference does it make now who's to blame? You warned
me she'd be hard to curry and she damn well was."

He smiled again, this time a little more naturally, but then closed
his teeth and held them fast, trying not to wince while Zack watched
him with that same intense, suspicious interest, as if he was still
waiting for him to betray some weakness or cowardice and thereby
capitulate himself back into childhood, losing all at once whatever
dignities of manhood this wound might have earned him. In a
sense, Zack thought, the contest between them, his own patient waiting and Morgan's awareness of his presence, which he seemed to
have sensed even before he was quite conscious, had been a goad to
his recovery.

, For the women—not only Marietta and Lisette, but Jenny Danforth
and Erma Finney, Rachel and Georgina and others Zack could not
recognize—had surrounded him during those first several days,
whispering and crying, while Zack watched them with angry resent-

ment, longed to drive them away, and wondered how it was they could not understand that this primitive grief might kill him.

Zack was there almost constantly for the first several days, and although occasionally he wandered outside or went down into town, he was soon back again and seated beside him, for it seemed a matter of deep if obscure importance that this vigil be maintained, and he even had some superstitions that his presence might help to protect Morgan from the malign influences exerted upon him by the troop of whispering, sighing, weeping women.

He watched Lisette continually for they sometimes sat near the bed for many hours, without speaking. At other times she was in the room but a little distance away, sewing or reading, and she seemed to have a belief similar to his own, that it was her presence which kept her brother alive. At night, when Zack dozed in a chair or fell asleep on the floor, she came out in her nightgown and stood beside Morgan and, as Zack lay spying on her, he saw that sometimes she prayed, clasping her hands and closing her eyes, moving her lips like a child. Then she would bend to kiss him, and go back to her room, without ever having seemed to notice that Zack was there.

He grew bitterly envious, thinking that this family had no need of outsiders, and found a vindictive satisfaction in reflecting that Lily Jones had known that as well as he did, and had invented her own revenge.

But then he was ashamed of this mean jealousy and even more ashamed because it meant he felt himself of little significance. It was his speculations about Lisette, however, which troubled him most, for he could not get it out of his mind that there were some more meaningful pleasures than any he had enjoyed so far, contrary as this might be to his devoutly held conviction that one woman was like another and that individuality was lost in the intensity of excitement.

The only cure, he decided, was to go away. For Matt, he knew, by one of those infallible signals which might pass between two men, would never let her marry him, and this knowledge enraged him—until he thought of the damages a domestic woman could do a man who cherished his freedom, and at that he laughed to himself, causing Lisette to glance at him with alert reproval.

By the time Morgan was well enough to read the newspaper account of his fight with Jenkins, Zack's decision had been made and he was as nervously discontent as if someone was trying to prevent him from leaving.

"Did my father give you the money?" Morgan asked him one day.

"He did, but I'm not sure I should take it."

"Don't be a god-damn fool—it's yours."

"Why is it? I let the girl stay there, too."

"You let her stay, but she was staying with me. It's yours, all right, take it." Zack gestured, to indicate that maybe he would and maybe he wouldn't, and Morgan went on. "You know, these last two or three weeks, or however long I've been lying here trying to hang onto the room to keep it from turning around, I've been thinking— and I think my father's right when he says the hardest way to get gold is to dig it. And the big strikes, around here, anyway, are over. If you want to make money now, you've got to do something else."

Zack smiled. "I've been thinking, too, and I'm not so damn sure I want to make money." Matt had suggested that he invest it in merchandise, for it made no difference what a man imported to the mountains, if only he had made a good bargain in the beginning he could not avoid taking out a handsome profit a few months later. But Zack had said he was no more fitted to be a merchant than a miner; and, in fact, he felt a kind of repugnance for quantities of money and some scorn for the men who spent their lives accumulating it, as if it was the one justification they could discover for being alive. "My trouble is that so far I've only found out what I don't want."

Morgan nodded, seemed to think about that for a moment, then looked at him with the first direct concentration Zack had seen on his face since the injury, and he grew wary, anticipating some question he would not be able to answer. "Zack, there's something that's been bothering me. That article says Hamilton was dead, too, and so you must have shot him." Zack stared at him as impassively as if Morgan had him on the witness stand and the answer he gave might lead to his conviction. "After the first few seconds, I couldn't tell what was going on. But now tell me this, and for Christ's sake, tell me the truth. Did I kill Jenkins, or did you?"

Zack gave a loud laugh, slapped at his knee and stood up. "You did, you son of a bitch, does your conscience hurt you?" He bent down, and said with grim earnestness, "Your first shot got him, I swear to God." And Morgan looked so relieved that he walked out, wondering if he had told the truth, for he had shot at Jenkins a moment after Morgan's first shot; but whether it was true or not, Morgan plainly needed to believe he had killed him, and Jenkins seemed unlikely to rise up and settle the mystery.

Zack set the day for his departure but then postponed it. A week later he made himself another promise and this time, instead of leaving, he spent the night with Gussie, who was still working at Milly Matches' house, as it continued to be called, although Milly had left the Territory and it was owned by Green Troy.

Gussie's pendulous breasts and narrow hips, her smooth skin and one slightly crossed eye, her skillful carnality which persuaded each customer that he was her favorite, seemed to him a satisfactory substitute for Lisette, and, anyway, he was afraid of a girl brought up as Lisette had been, for he had heard many dark rumors of the humiliations a man must suffer before he might spread one of those capricious virgins beneath him, and the scant reward he could expect for his trouble once he did.

He came out at ten o'clock the next morning and started down the street, telling himself the day had come, the moment when he was so entirely freed of desire, so gratified in nerve and muscle, at once depleted and restored, that neither Lisette Devlin nor any other woman seemed likely to disturb this equanimity for some time.

He continued along the street, inquiring as he went for the whereabouts of his horse, and was beginning to swear beneath his breath, convinced the animal had been stolen, when he heard a familiar laugh and glanced up to see Lisette on Morgan's horse, Puzzle. And, of course, she was not alone; Georgina Hart was with her. "What are you looking for, Zack?"

He gazed at her submissively, feeling that he was too big, too awkward, that his hands hung at the ends of his arms like the paws of a gorilla, that he needed a bath and stank of whisky and sweat. And she was laughing at him, for there, he did not doubt, stamped upon his forehead in sharp black print, was the news of his conduct with Gussie the night before. He frowned, removed his hat, ran his hand over his snarled blond hair, for he had not thought to comb it, then hastily scratched through his beard, sighed unhappily and banged the hat back onto his head and crushed it down hard.

Both girls, in black riding habits and hard-topped hats, looked fresh and energetic and, as girls always seemed to when they discovered a man either afoot or embarrassed, highly charged with triumphant excitement.

"Good heavens, Zack, what's the trouble with you this morning? And what happened to you last night? Did you forget we were all going to Georgina's to play charades?"

It had been the first time that she had left the house at night, and she had begun only recently to leave for an hour or two during the day. The party had seemed to have some unusual significance to her, perhaps because of her long deprivation, and although Zack had promised to go it had, in fact, been the absurdity of trying to imagine himself playing charades which had inspired him to visit Gussie.

"I forgot," he told her sullenly.

Lisette and Georgina exchanged smiles, which caused him to wonder if all the town knew where he had been and what he had been doing. He could think of no other possible explanation for their persistent amusement, until it occurred to him that sixteen-year-old girls were habitually delighted without any reason which would have seemed adequate to someone a little older; and all at once his ten more years in the world seemed a heavy burden.

"We were afraid you'd left us," Lisette said, and though her smile was still teasing and condescending, her eyes were serious. "Morgan says that's just how you'll do it—disappear someday, without saying good-bye to anyone." She leaned forward, mockingly earnest. "You must promise me you won't, Zack. Do you promise?"

He felt more than ever as if he had been trapped, backed into a corner, and was now being poked and tormented for the fun of seeing him squirm, and he gave Lisette a steady stare of warning which it seemed she instantly understood. For she sat straight once more, glanced at Georgina as if to give her notice of something, and spoke to him with a pretense of casual kindness. "Zack, I know what you're looking for, and I know where he is, too. We just passed him. He's standing outside Green Troy's place." Zack grinned, sourly amused, for like most respectable girls she would not say the word saloon and yet, she knew who owned it. "You must have left him there last night."

She seemed to be waiting, expecting him to tell her where he had been, perhaps confess that he had gone into Green Troy's place and had a drink or two, and he stubbornly refused to make up a story, or even to acknowledge that she had any right to her curiosity. "Thanks." He lifted his hat and started on, but after taking a few steps he turned to find them looking over their shoulders at him, and he came back. "Is there anything I can do? Can I carry something home for you?"

She gazed at him thoughtfully, as if she was sorry for her impudence, even though she would not apologize. "I wish you would, Zack. Mother gave me such a long list."

"Where shall I meet you?" All at once he was filled with an irrational eagerness, which did not disappear even when he reminded himself she had contrived once more to put him in the position of one who must supplicate small favors.

"The Ladies Emporium."

"The Ladies Emporium," he repeated, as if he must make sure not to forget this precious code word, and he started at a lope up the street, found his horse and set off for the Ladies Emporium, galloped up to it at full speed, swung down and tied up next to Puzzle, then ducked beneath the low doorway and stood peering about the dark and musty little store, one of Lemuel Finney's several projects, finding himself surrounded on all sides by boots which hung from the rafters so that he was forced almost into a crouch to make his way around. Bolts of cloth were piled upon the counters and the floor, shelves were stacked with ready-made suits and women's skirts and shawls, and, to his horrified dismay, an unhooked corset, somewhat soiled, hung in full view on a nail just over the head of the clerk, a young boy who was busily putting together Lisette's order, so that it was almost impossible for him and Lisette to look at each other or even to recognize each other's presence without also tacitly admitting that they knew the corset was there.

Lisette smiled at him and continued to read from a long list while Georgina sauntered back and forth, idly turning things over, examining a shawl which she twirled about and momentarily cast over her shoulders, then wrinkled her nose in a sign to Lisette and tossed it aside. Zack prowled through the store, trying to avoid coming near Lisette in the corset's neighborhood—for he was unable to glance at it without a resurgence of the same uneasiness which had sent him to Gussie the night before—and that so ridiculous an object should have acquired such ominous significance and power suggested to him that he had even now lost the moment when he had been meant to leave.

He broke into a sweat, wiped his forehead with the back of his hand, tried to stay away from both Georgina and Lisette and fidgeted unhappily, longing to run out of there and escape from her once and for all, never see her again and never subject himself to the frustrations and embarrassments which had been his lot whenever he was in her presence and which, he now foresaw, would afflict him when she was nearby for the rest of his life; he had a sense of unworthiness and guilt which made him feel that he was ugly and cruel, a kind of mythical monster wooing a mythical princess and experiencing all the ancient horrors of the beast who must love beauty.

When, at last, she called to him that she had finished and even added an apology for having been so long, he rushed toward her anxiously, swept up the bundles and hastened from the store as if he expected to be arrested for shoplifting.

He loaded his own horse, leaving theirs free, helped them to mount and then, exactly as he had anticipated, they set off gaily, riding ahead, glancing back from time to time and laughing, whispering to each other, while he followed sullenly along, feeling that every man on the street must think he was making a monkey of himself.

They let their horses saunter easily but kept just far enough ahead that they could talk without being overheard, and occasionally they waved to someone they recognized. When they passed Devlin Brothers, Matt was standing on the sidewalk talking to Jeremy Flint, and Matt gave him a grin which affected Zack as if he had shouted at him and called him something he could not at the moment identify, but which he would never forgive. He smiled at Matt sheepishly, though he felt sick with humiliation and rage, and plodded along in their wake. At Jenny Danforth's house they paused and held a consultation, apparently discussing whether or not they would call on her, but at last went on, and when they reached the road which led up to the Devlin cabin they stopped.

"I want to ride a little longer," Lisette announced as he came abreast of them. She gave him a direct, cool look which roused the uncomfortable suspicion that she was being critical, that he had inadvertently been tactless or foolish, and he made no reply. Now her glance became even colder, defiant and accusatory. "Will you ride with me?"

Zack gave her a smile of such gratitude that Lisette and Georgina exchanged humorous glances, and he reflected that a man was never in worse company than when he is with two women, for they had, even when little more than children, an uncanny knack for stripping off his manhood, his dignity, his masculine contempt for them, and turning it instead upon himself.

"Georgina will take the packages home for us." Zack nodded, thinking that now, for the first time, he was to be alone with her—in broad daylight, it was true, and with her family's knowledge, since Georgina would report where they had gone—and yet they would be together without anyone to watch them and hear what they said. The prospect terrified him and he wanted to say that he had to meet someone, but instead he sat there, until Lisette asked him, "Will you arrange the packages for her, Zack?"

"Of course!" he cried and began quickly and efficiently to transfer the load, packing Georgina's horse as if he were preparing her to set out on a prospecting expedition, and in a moment Georgina waved good-bye, gave Lisette a last conspiratorial smile, and took the road which led to the Devlin cabin while Lisette and Zack turned their horses and started along the path they had ridden when they had gone picnicking with Nella Allen, and down which Morgan had been carried on a stretcher five weeks before.

Zack had decided that he would talk as little as possible, say nothing he did not need to say and, he hoped, protect himself from the possibility of a supercilious smile. They rode past new shacks and abandoned ones, for Virginia City was losing population to Helena, following the wandering humps of stone and gravel, and continued on toward the grove at the hill's crest.

"I asked Georgina to come with us," said Lisette, when several minutes had gone by, with Zack still as silent as he had planned to be. "But she didn't want to."

"Oh," agreed Zack, and continued his resolute scrutiny of the houses, the children at play, and the women hanging clothes to dry or spreading them over the stiff grass. "She didn't want to come," he repeated thoughtfully.

"No. And can you imagine why?"

"No, ma'am, I can't."

"Because she wanted to see Morgan!" cried Lisette, and gave a laugh of such joyous savagery that Zack looked at her in startled disapproval, thinking that just when a girl seemed to be entirely civilized, gentle and well-mannered, bred by her parents to a life of Christian charity, she suddenly revealed herself as having neither scruples nor compassion nor any kind of humility. "She's mad about him, you know," Lisette continued confidentially, and her eyes were glittering with what looked to him like hatred, though her mouth had a small and subtle smile. She watched him as she talked, as if to discover what he would think of this scandalous news, and was obviously deeply concerned in her friend's infatuation for her brother.

"I thought Jonathan was Georgina's beau," offered Zack helplessly, for it was clear to him that he must participate in this discussion and he only hoped there would not be much of it, for it seemed peculiarly disloyal to Morgan to talk about him while he was still lying helpless.

"He was, until she saw Morgan. I think Morgan and Jonathan

would have had a fight over it long ago, if Morgan hadn't been hurt. They used to fight all the time when they were little—anything would set them off. But I don't think Morgan cares about her, do you?" She watched him carefully, apparently expecting to derive his opinion from his expression rather than from what he said.

"I don't know, Lisette," he told her seriously. "He hasn't said anything about it. I don't think he does, if you want me to guess."

"I'd die if he ever married Georgina Hart." She was not looking at him but staring gloomily ahead, her eyes half closed, her chin set and stubborn.

"What do you care who he marries, for Christ's sweet sake?"

"I don't care. It's his business. But it isn't, really, it's mine too, and Mother's and Father's and Pete's and everyone's in the whole family. If any of us ever marries the wrong person, we'll all lose something by it. Oh, you think that's nonsense, but how would you know, after all? You don't have any family." She turned with her gloved hand to her lips, and then shut her eyes and shook her head. "Forgive me, I didn't mean to say that."

"It's true, I don't have. Oh, I had some brothers and sisters—two of them are dead, and the others have forgotten me by now, I suppose. No, you're right. I don't know anything about it."

Obviously not very repentant for her rudeness, she was still engrossed with the subject of Morgan and Georgina Hart. "I want her to marry Jonathan. He adores her and they'd be right for each other. And then she can't ever have Morgan."

Zack grinned, irresistibly pleased by her selfishness and frank determination to have her own way without any concern for the others involved, for she was sure that she was right, that she knew what was best for all of them, and seemed quite convinced that marriage put an end to all vagrant yearnings.

When they reached the grove, Lisette said that she wanted to walk a little, commune with the spirit of the place, he supposed, and think of the day of their first picnic with Nella and that disastrous recent one. It occurred to Zack to tell her that they would keep riding, start back immediately, in fact, and he looked at her solemnly, hoping she would understand it. But she smiled and made an impatient gesture and Zack, shrugging as if to let her know she had chosen her own peril and was not to blame him later, helped her to dismount and let her go very quickly. But her face was close to his for a moment and this continued to trouble him, so that even as she began to stroll about, giving little switches of her riding crop at the grass, he stood staring resolutely in the opposite direction, and tried to fill his mind with details of the country which surrounded them, duly noting clouds and trees, magpies and sage, and the remnants of a recent campfire.

After a few moments he turned slowly and stood watching her. She was some distance away, and might have come here alone or with someone so unimportant she had forgotten his presence. And, to his dismayed astonishment, a sense of excitement began in him and quickened, and had soon become as vigorous and as demanding as if he had never spent the night with Gussie, purifying himself against this temptation.

He started toward her, running, and moved so fast and so quietly she did not turn until he called, "Lisette!" Even to him his voice sounded strange, hoarse and beseeching, and she whirled about with a look of alarm, probably thinking he was warning her of some danger.

He caught hold of her, expecting a struggle to begin, one of those desperate defenses he had heard about, but Lisette's arms closed around him and her mouth accepted his, and as his hands began to move over her back she sighed and her lips parted. Even then he continued to give himself cautionary reminders, and still imagined that in another moment he would let her go. But as the kiss was prolonged a leaping eagerness engrossed him, and when his fingers separated the buttons of her coat, feeling her nipples rise at the grazing of his hand, he was no longer surprised by her responsive excitement but bent over her and, the next moment, felt a stunning blow at the back of his head, another across the side of his face, and Lisette was running away from him, holding her skirt with both hands and running so fast that she stumbled, but scrambled to her feet again and ran on.

He started after her in a raging stupor, bent on some punishing revenge, and then stopped, laughing softly, and called out, "Come back here, you damn little fool, I won't do anything to you. I promise," he added chidingly, as she stopped and turned to look at him. She began to fasten her coat, not very quickly, and perhaps was not so eager to escape from him, after all; and Zack shook his head in wonderment, assuring himself that nice girls were a greater responsibility than he was ready to undertake.

She approached cautiously, still fastening the coat. "Did I hurt you, Zack? I'm sorry. You frightened me."

"I know. Well, don't go riding around alone with men who are in love with you."

"In love with me?" She came a little nearer, and Zack smiled inadvertently, reflecting that it was a pity any girl with so natural a wanton appetite should be obliged to go hungry for the very sweetmeats she craved most. He stooped and linked his fingers, indicating with a nod that she was to get into the saddle, but she still hesitated.

"Climb aboard, Lisette," he advised her. "It won't do to drag this out too much, I'm not long on good resolutions. Anyway, that's a job for your husband, whoever he is."

He gave another nod, this one peremptory, and after a moment she placed her foot in the cradle of his hands and he lifted her into the saddle, then dashed after his own horse with some notion that any delay about this retreat was certain disaster, and set off at a gallop, signaling her to catch up with him, and when she called to him in a pleading voice, "Wait for me, Zack," he laughed aloud, angry and bitterly pleased to think she would take the safe pleasures and miss all the better ones for fear of some unknown dangers, but then reminded himself that a little more patience on his own part might have brought them both to an easy deliverance.

XXI

"I'll be in Troy's Casino this afternoon. Come see me or I'll come see you. Lily Jones."

A young boy brought the message to Morgan and Morgan sent him to find Zack Fletcher. Zack gave the boy a vague resentful glance, for he had been absorbed in trying to explain to himself what course his life must now take, and though he had occupied the better part of five days in this way, still he had reached no conclusions.

Troy's Casino, he told himself—the most famous saloon and gambling house in the mountains—was the obvious setting for Lily to choose. It was open twenty-four hours a day, and during most of that time was crowded with prospectors and assorted adventurers, those men who moved nervously about the frontier and who, in each new town, could always discover their own kind where they might hear the news that interested them, make whatever contacts they needed, and spend a few pleasant hours in the company of others who lived on excitement and danger and unlikely ventures. And there, of course, Lily would have an audience best able to appreciate her.

It was midafternoon when Zack entered the building and found it filled with familiar and comforting noise, dense with smoke and crowded with men who hung about the gambling tables, kicking their booted feet in the sawdust and shuffling it about. Most of them looked more or less as he did, bearded and well-armed, dressed in buckskin turned black from grease and long wear, or red shirts and black trousers, while the few gamblers in frock coats and diamond stickpins seemed incongruously elegant. A man sat on a high stool in one corner with a double-barreled shotgun across his knees, a symbol that order had come to the mountains, and mirrors had recently been installed behind the bar. At the far end of the room, three musicians twanged ceaselessly at violins and a banjo, but the sound could scarcely be heard a dozen feet away. There was a continuous clatter from the bowling alley next door, and the rhythmic call rang out: "Make your game, gentlemen, make your game." Now and then a girl led her client through a side door to where, Zack knew, there was a string of rooms of about the size and luxuriousness of a pack-

ing case, and taken all in all it seemed that Green Troy, in constantly
expanding his enterprise, had made of it a world so entire that a
man, once entered, need not leave again for any purpose whatever
until he was either penniless or dead.

Zack paused and drew in a deep breath and all at once his eyes
were glittering and his face wore a wise, superior smile, for he was
at home here, not an interloper as he had always seemed in the presence of respectable people, and more so than ever these past few
days. For the aftermath of his impulsive caressing of Lisette had
been a profound contempt for himself, as if he had finally been
shown for what he was, a savage and conscienceless ruffian. Sunk in
a misery of guilt and self-condemnation he had stood about for hours
on the street corners with his hat pulled low, as if no one could recognize him in that disguise, hating himself for his crudities, his ungov-
ernable yearnings, and because he had acted all of his life—and did
still—only upon his present needs. For none of those needs had been
admirable ones, he told himself, as he looked back over the course of
his life and found it stretched out very long and creeping after him
like a pet snake, reminding him of his ugliness, his brutality, and the
pleasures he had always found in those activities which decent people abhorred.

He had returned only once to the Devlin cabin, recalled there irresistibly by his guilt, and had quite expected to find that Lisette
showed the effects of his rapacity, might have lost her freshness and
begun to wither and grow old, hateful to other men, all because of
him. His imagination proved so riotous that he entered the house
cautiously, sneaking in, as if he might be able to observe her secretly and learn whether or not his work had been as disastrous as he
believed. For her look of alarm and the flight she had made had persuaded him that he was a monster with a monster's rare capacities
for damage, a basilisk whose eye or breath was fatal, whose saliva
was acid and whose hands left permanent marks, infamous and brutal.

He found Morgan alone, dressed and reading, as he did constantly
these days, in fact memorizing a book Matt had given him: Hitch-
cock's *Elements of Geology*. And Morgan, at least, had apparently
been unable to see the effects of his ravages, for he saluted him with
a broad grin and tossed the book aside, running one hand through
his hair in a gesture of relief at the prospect of companionship, and
asked what was happening downtown.

Zack was somewhat relieved, but by no means convinced, and
he perched on the edge of a chair, behaving not as if this were a
house where he had lived for long periods of time but as if he had
come there either to sell or to steal something. He found it difficult
to look straight at Morgan, after giving him a quick and shrewdly
questioning glance, and stared with a thoughtful frown at the floor.

"There was a cockfight Sunday in back of Troy's. Big crowd."

Morgan smiled. "How much did you lose?"

"Not much. About a hundred dollars, I guess. Most of the dust is still in your father's office. I don't trust myself with it."

As he heard his own voice admitting that he did not trust himself he gave Morgan a defiant look, as if daring him to suggest there was some other meaning to that remark, and then Lisette appeared in the doorway, whereupon he leaped up, removing his hat, and bowed stiffly.

"Why, it's Zack—you've been away so long." She came forward, lifting her hands to touch the sides of her hair, and he noticed that she had dressed it in a new style, something which looked remarkably complicated, for it was drawn to the crown of her head and gathered there in a mass of curls, decorated with a black velvet bow; and she looked as fresh, as dainty, as vital and whole as she ever had, while her eyes glowed with a warmth which puzzled him hopelessly.

"I've been busy," he muttered, and turned away.

"You're not going, Zack?"

"I've got to meet somebody and talk over a deal." He was still muttering, unable to speak in a normal voice, and unable to look at her. "I might go out as a guide for an Englishman who wants to hunt." It was true he had heard of such a position and had discussed it with the Englishman, but finally refused to go. Now, as Morgan smiled knowingly at this tableau between his sister and his friend, Zack backed across the room, but was scarcely outside the door when he found Lisette beside him.

"Zack—I have something to tell you."

He turned warily and felt the yearning begin to crawl through him, a treacherously spreading warmth which took its course through his loins and belly, giving him fair warning that no amount of remorse was likely to change him. "I'm sorry, Lisette," he told her. "I'm more god-damn sorry than you can imagine."

"Sorry?" She smiled, parting her lips and showing him the inside of her mouth, a new smile of hers so far as he knew and one of which he did not approve, for surely it was improper for a nice girl to use the tricks of a whore. She was looking up at him with an expression at once so provocative and so submissive he was reminded of one of those flowers he had seen in desert country which unfolded overnight, as if spread wide by a touch. And this, perhaps, was the harm he had done her.

"I shouldn't have kissed you and I shouldn't have put my hand on you, and I hope you'll forgive me." He spoke in a monotone, determined to make this speech and then disappear forever.

She came a little nearer and, inadvertently, he backed away. "You said you love me, Zack. Did you mean it?"

"No, I didn't mean it," he told her sharply, and was dismayed to realize she was expecting him to propose to her. "That is to say," he began, wondering how he might correct this latest blunder, "I meant it, but I don't want to marry you." He sighed unhappily, for she looked as if she would begin to cry, and, deciding there was no more to be said, he left her, broke into a run as he got farther away, and did not once look back. He should, he supposed, have explained that he had too much arrogance to let himself become the subject of a family debate, and could not tolerate being picked apart and inspected by her father and uncle and mother and brothers; but even this admission would have seemed shameful.

But he was relieved of his florid imaginings of the harm he had done her and now, instead of his earlier humility and self-disgust, he felt justified and cleansed and buoyant, eager to move on, to leave the country, to roam freely without direction or intent as he had always done, responsible to no one but himself. Even so, he had continued to hang about the town for a few days longer and that was when Morgan had sent the note from Lily Jones.

He started through the room, peering over the heads of the crowd as he went and glancing from side to side to see who was there, which men he knew or had seen before, who was his friend and who was—or might now be—his enemy. For since the killing of Jenkins and Hamilton, he and Morgan had begun to acquire reputations of men who were dangerous with guns, not so much because they had killed two men as because those men had had similar reputations.

As he made his way along he found the path easier than usual. Fewer men had to be tapped on the shoulder and asked to let him by, several turned their backs and pretended not to have seen him, even though he had known them by sight or by name, either here or in Helena or Butte, and had seen one or two in the river towns before the War.

Zack smiled, thinking that he had become something of a celebrity in the frontier underworld, and felt an ironic amusement at the swelling and brutal power it gave him, for now he flashed about him with threatening looks only for the pleasure of bringing fear into a man's eyes or, just as satisfying to him, challenge and hatred. It completed his conviction of the absurdity of trying to tame himself sufficiently to make Lisette a good husband, or any husband at all, and divested him of what had remained of his ambitions to be a part of civilized society. For there was no such simple way of acquiring renown in that peculiar and complicated world so far as he had been able to discover and, even if there was, where then would he have found the sense of excitement and danger to which he had become addicted and which it was the persistent task of that world to abolish, striving at all times for the tidy order which had been so rudely knocked apart by Jenkins and Hamilton on the Fourth of July.

Men stood three or four deep at the bar, most of them talking in loud voices but some murmuring earnestly, whispering and glancing warily about, as if describing their latest strike, richer than Virginia and Helena and Confederate Gulch combined. At one end, surrounded by six or eight men, he found Lily Jones, standing with her back to the bar and her elbows against it, her black hat turned up on one side, holding court as she had done in Butte, tapping the ash from her cigar and laughing with that semblance of joyous abandon which he still suspected might not be real.

There was no question about it, thought Zack, as he watched her, Lily Jones seemed to be a bargain. She might run off with your dust or your friend, or both, but she had the faculty of making respectable women seem tiresome and even sinister, since what she would steal was quite easy to replace and they could be content with nothing less than a man's life.

At that moment she saw him, blinked her eyes disbelievingly and, giving an Indian whoop she must have learned from Dancing Rabbit, started toward him with an expression of such delighted recognition that no one could doubt he was her dearest friend, her lost lover, or some tardily recovered relative.

"Zack Fletcher!" She held forth both arms but then, just as she seemed ready to embrace him, she pulled a solemn face, extended her right hand, and they shook hands like two prospecting partners settling a deal. "How."

"How," replied Zack, with the same solemn look.

Lily reached scarcely to his chin and now she stood with her moccasined feet apart, her fingers spread across her buttocks, and tipped back her head to look at him, pondering deeply while she waited for the men to grow quiet. When she was satisfied, she inquired very softly, "How is he?"

Zack smiled, but obediently straightened his face. "Okay. Still rather white about the gills, and for awhile there he was pretty close to the cash-in. But he'll make it now."

Lily frowned, bit her lips, and at last shook her head and sighed. "Boys," she said, and turned to them with an air of simple confession, "if it wasn't for Zack Fletcher here, there would have been another good man killed in a fight over me. His friend Morgan Devlin would have gone up when Jenkins bushwhacked him."

"Now look here, Lily," Zack began, but she gave him a quick warning glance and shook her head, then turned again to the others.

"Thank God Zack Fletcher was there because Gaius Jenkins swore he'd kill the man who took his girl if he followed him for twenty years." She nodded and the men, either believing her or not wanting to seem skeptical of a lady's story, nodded in reply. Lily clapped her hands smartly. "That calls for champagne, fellows, doesn't it?"

And presently the bartender was popping corks and filling the glasses with a flourish, while Lily raised her own and cried, "Here's to Zack Fletcher and Morgan Devlin, and may God bless them both!" She leaned closer to Zack, and the others, now that Lily was concentrating her attention on the man who had killed Charles Hamilton in a feud over her, shifted about, wandered away, or began talking among themselves. "Tell me the truth," she whispered. "How is he?"

"I told you. He's okay. What's the matter? Wish they'd got him?"

"My God, Fletcher, how can you say that? I know you think I'm a bitch, running off with your dust, but will you tell me what else I was to do? I knew when he came back here he wasn't planning to take me along. Besides," she added and scowled, scuffled her foot in the sawdust and dragged at her cigar, "I was god-damn mad."

"You still in love with him, Lily?"

Lily bowed her head and stared at her feet so that all he could see was the top of her hat, and then quickly looked up at him again. "I guess so," she admitted, and sounded like a forlorn child, lost and unhappy. "I wish I could see him. Can I?"

"Hardly. He's just out of bed. He couldn't make it down here if there was a diamond strike."

She gave him a malicious smile. "Let's go pay him a visit. Wouldn't that be a nice surprise for a sick man? All right, Fletcher, don't say it—but I do wish I could see him."

"What for?"

"What for?"

"That's right. What for? He's going to live in Helena, when he gets back on his feet, and he's going to work in his father's business. His father's a big frog in this puddle—banker and miner and real-estate owner and I don't know what the hell else. You've got a good assortment here—pick out one of them and forget about Devlin."

She considered this advice, then gave him a mysterious smile. "How do you think I got from Butte to here? Made it over the mountains by myself?"

"You left with Carter and his squaw. What's happened to them?"

Lily gestured, showing him the palms of her hands, with nothing concealed in them. "We woke up one morning and Dancing Rabbit was gone. She told me she was going to find her people the first chance she got, and she lit out. Carter and I went on to Helena to have a look and, no doubt about it, that's the next town, not this one. You can't even find a place to sleep—we hired a billiard table one night. Anyway, in Helena we ran first off into Jenkins and Hamilton. We went into Murphy's Exchange and there they were right inside the door playing faro. We tried to edge back out, taking a kind of sidewinder motion, but Jenkins, who was always the smart one of the two, was on us quick and the first thing you know they were marching us down the street doing a pretty lively step to keep a jump ahead of their bowie knives. They took us out in back of a livery stable, jammed their guns into our bellies and asked for their pokes. Just like that." She shrugged. "Naturally I gave them to him—yours and Devlin's, and what I had taken from them in the first place. You don't blame me?"

Zack had listened impassively but now he leaned back, lounging on one hip. "Lily, that's what I call a geometrical lie. It's got length and breadth and height and thickness." With both hands he quickly described the lie's measurements. "When I ran into Jenkins and Hamilton here on the Fourth of July they said they were after Devlin because you told them he was the one who got you to pin the Vigilante sign on their bedrolls, that he took the money for himself and, what's more, lost it all at Bruno Favorite's."

"Is that what they said! And you believe them and not me, Zack Fletcher! And you dare to stand there, as well as we know each other, as long as we cabined together and I mended your damn shirts and cooked your grub and tell me to my face that I'm a liar." She rolled her eyes and threw out her hands in despairing resignation.

"Not so loud. Why let everyone else know I called you a liar? But you are and we both know it because I just heard you tell a whopper here this afternoon."

"What's that?"

"Think hard."

"So help me God, every word I've said here is true."

"Now look here, Lily, you know as well as I do that fight we had with Jenkins and Hamilton wasn't over you."

"But it was over me. What else was it over?"

"It was over their dust, and since you stole it and put the blame on Morgan I suppose you could stretch things and say it was over you, but it had nothing to do with Jenkins being mad because Morgan stole his girl. In fact, Jenkins told me he was damn glad to get rid of you, that you were more trouble than you were worth, and that he'd be looking for Morgan to shake his hand if it wasn't for the loss of his dust."

Lily listened to his recital and, when he had done, sighed and frowned. "I never heard of such a thing. Everybody's against me." She turned away, patiently despondent, and hung her head.

"If they are it's your own fault, Lily," Zack told her philosophically. "You're a natural-born troublemaker. I knew it the minute I set eyes on you, rambling through town on that horse, throwing out your challenge to every guy who saw you."

At the assurance that she was a natural-born troublemaker Lily's despondency vanished. She looked up at him with her eyes bright and penetrating and a smile came irresistibly to her mouth. "I can't help it if men are always fighting over me. It's happened wherever I've been, but I don't do anything to cause it."

"You won't cause me any trouble, I can guarantee you that. I'm no Jenkins or Hamilton or Carter, or even Devlin. I'm the same kind of no-account rascal you are, in fact. Where's Carter?"

"Dead."

"How'd that happen?"

"This is one thing you can't blame me for, Fletcher. After Jenkins and Hamilton took our dust, we pawned one pistol each and started to play faro trying to get us back some little stake. We played for a few days, being pretty cautious and just about keeping even, when we won enough to buy a good dinner and went out to get it. And that's when it happened. Carter was walking along talking about all the grub he was going to eat, fairly drooling over the peach pie and venison steak and brown gravy, when just like that a gun went off. I looked around to see where it came from and the next thing Carter grabbed me and all but brought me down with him. The guy came running toward us and I tried to get loose, scared stiff he'd hit me next time, but Carter hung on and kept begging the guy not to shoot him when he was down. 'Get up then,' he told him, and when Carter had crawled to his knees and tried to reach for his gun, he shot him again, and this time right through the forehead. And with that he turned to me and said, 'Sorry, miss, but there was an old grudge between us.' What do you think of that? And he walked off."

"Nothing else to it? Just walked off?"

"He was arrested, but after an hour or two they let him go because he swore that when he and Carter last met in Salt Lake City they promised to kill each other at sight, and he'd seen Carter go for his gun. Maybe you don't believe that one, either?"

"I believe you, because this one does you no credit. Who brought you here?"

He thought that Lily, who believed she roamed the West as safely as if she were in a New England village, unintimidated by winter snows, vast distances or the various mountain ailments, impervious to wild animals, Indians and gunfire, was nevertheless not likely to be traveling alone.

"A friend. Right there in back of you." She raised her voice. "Powell, I want you to meet one of the jolly lads I told you about, the man who killed Hamilton in the Fourth of July fight over me—Zack Fletcher."

Zack turned to find a man about thirty years old, with a sparse beard and a grin which showed that several upper teeth were missing, who seemed eager to shake his hand. "John Powell. Glad to meet you, Mr. Fletcher. I've heard about you, not only from Lily."

Zack narrowed his eyes suspiciously, for he had become as distrustful nowadays of other men as it seemed they were of him. "Heard what about me?"

"Man with the bark on."

Zack accepted that and he and Powell fell to studying each other, while Zack wondered if possibly Lily had contrived another of those situations at which she seemed so adept, wherein men who had nothing against each other and who cared little about her found themselves forced into enmity. Then he ordered drinks. They raised the glasses, mumbled "How" in chorus, and emptied them.

"Powell's with one of the biggest papers there is," said Lily, and signaled Zack with her eyebrows, indicating that here was an opportunity for both of them to become famous. "Which one is it again, Powell?"

"*Tribune. New York Tribune.* They sent me out to write a series of articles about life in the West, and I've been traveling for the better part of six months. But I'm not so much a tenderfoot as you may be thinking, Mr. Fletcher, because I was in Kansas and Missouri during the border troubles, and that's when I heard about you."

They finished another drink, each speaking again the ceremonious word and, as John Powell now began to discuss his favorite subjects, the mountain whisky, the murders in Helena which had averaged one a day for the past several weeks, and the steady migration across the plains, Lily fell silent, sometimes nodded or shook her head, frowned or smiled, and finally lapsed into a reverie where Zack supposed she was moping over Morgan Devlin, the man she had apparently decided to cherish as her great lost love—without which, he was convinced, no woman ever felt her life complete.

Still, her infatuation and whatever embellishments she might have given it, had not prevented her from running off with Carter or finding a substitute for him in Powell and, Zack believed, neither would it make her squeamish about deserting Powell for him, once he thought of a tactful way to dispose of Powell.

A few more drinks should solve that problem; and in the meantime Powell seemed full of vast friendship and an admiration which was almost embarrassing, for he plucked at Zack's sleeve and clapped him affectionately on the shoulder, laughed at his every remark, and had the ecstatic air of one who basks in the exhilarating presence of his hero.

Powell, even after several drinks, remained alert and intent and watched Zack as he talked, quickly eager for his impressions, and was plainly pleased to have chanced upon two such authentic specimens as Lily Jones and Zack Fletcher. While Lily seemed keenly aware that behind John Powell's every remark and question, each shrewd, observant look he cast at her, or Zack, there was imminent an article to fill with awe and fascination unadventurous thousands who sat quietly at home reading about the wilder parts of their country and its strange inhabitants. Zack, unallured by the prospect of appearing in some newspaper article he would never see as a reckless frontiersman, listened patiently and urged Powell to drink again, wondering if his tolerance for this bad whisky was greater than he had anticipated.

"Shall I tell you what I've discovered, Fletcher? This is the last frontier. Right here." He pointed to his boots. "When this Territory is civilized, our country will no longer have a real frontier, and that part of our history will come to an end."

"Let me tell you something, Powell." Zack gave him a slow, solemn wink. "In just one more year Helena will be given over to the lyceums and ladies' clubs—and your frontier will be all gone." He snapped his fingers and he and Lily nodded gloomily.

"It's true, Powell," Lily agreed. "I've lived in the West, one place or another, ever since I was fifteen years old, and they keep you on the run, those missionaries, to stay only a jump ahead of them. The respectable women and their daughters, who are never satisfied to be good themselves but want everybody else to join their study clubs and benevolent societies. Fletcher knows what I mean." She grinned. "Don't you?"

Zack stared at her warningly, but Powell threw back his head and laughed, slapped his thigh and said this called for another drink. "To the typical western woman, Lily Jones!"

Zack, however, refused to drink the toast and Lily looked at him antagonistically, but asked no questions. "She's not typical, Powell. And that's something we can all be grateful for."

"But she's so charming. A child of nature. A free spirit. Yes, I envy you both. You're two of a kind, you know. In fact, I would venture to say that in all my travels in the West you are the most perfect examples of what life on the frontier means to those who give themselves over to it. Neither of you, I imagine, intends to go back home once you've made your fortunes?"

Zack and Lily burst into loud laughter and looked at each other, then Lily clapped both hands to her belly and laughed again.

Zack decided it was now time to nudge Powell out of Troy's Casino and he started out, ushering Lily ahead, while Powell followed along, plaintively inquiring where they were going and why they were leaving this congenial place. Zack mumbled a few unintelligible words and presently they were outside where they were surprised to find that, although many hours seemed to have passed, it was still bright daylight. A few doors up the street Zack found what he was looking for, a likely place to abandon Powell, and pushed Lily into a hurdy-gurdy house, summoning Powell with a jerk of his head.

There was music in the back of the room, a fiddler and trombone player and a drummer, and girls in bright-colored dresses danced with men who chewed cigars and swung them off the floor in their exuberance, giving occasional joyous or defiant shouts. Powell was now earnestly interested in his new surrroundings and Zack gazed at him with reflective tolerance and pity, for Powell's conscientious curiosity made him seem to Zack the most perfect tenderfoot he had yet encountered.

Zack went to where the girls, resting between dances, sat in a row on benches, wiping their faces and necks and armpits, and blowing out their cheeks in protest against the heat. He stopped at the railing which momentarily guarded the girls from their customers and gave a sharp whistle between his teeth. They glanced around alertly and one ran toward him. He whispered to her; she considered his message, nodded, and Zack returned to Powell.

"I've just done you a big favor. See that girl over there? The one with the blond hair and yellow and green dress? Her name's Nellie Sullivan, an old friend of mine, and the best dancer in the mountains. What's more, she's a decent girl, out here with her mother, and her mother's usually here as chaperone, but she's home tonight with the summer complaint and so if you'll just come along with me,

Powell, I'm going to arrange for you to have this next dance with her."

And, though Powell glanced back at Lily to assure her these events were beyond his control, he was propelled hastily across the room by Zack, paid his fee of one dollar in dust to the cashier, and when he was introduced to Nellie Sullivan, bowed and asked as formally as if he were attending a private ball if she would favor him with the next dance.

The fiddler began to stamp his foot, shouting, "Take your partners!" and as Powell and Nellie Sullivan launched upon a frantically whirling waltz, Zack and Lily started out and Zack turned to see Powell spinning at a rate it did not seem likely he could long continue. As he gave one last backward glance he saw Powell stumble, and Nellie Sullivan was trying to help him to his feet.

"She'll take him home," Zack said. "We can pick him up there in the morning. If we want to."

Lily nodded, hooked her thumbs in the belt of her trousers, and they strolled along, both of them now unexpectedly quiet and thoughtful. They walked for some distance, observing with grave disinterest the life around them, and at last went into a grocery store where they bought cans of oysters and stood in a corner picking them out with their fingers and eating them hungrily. Zack now kept a covert watch on Lily, not sure whether she had acquiesced or might raise some sentimental objections when he took her to a hotel, and Lily looked idly at the women in big-skirted dresses and shawls pulled tight across their chests and shoulders, most of them with the sorrowful faces of women who had lived long in the West. They continued on their way, inspecting the town in silence, and when at last they entered another saloon and stood facing each other, Zack spoke to her in the tone of a severe parent lecturing an errant child.

"Those weren't the only lies you told, either."

"Most likely," Lily agreed.

She smiled with that moody and enigmatic look which he remembered appeared each time she had drunk more than she was accustomed to, as if she had a streak of maudlin self-pity ready and waiting to attack her whenever the mountain whisky had weakened her resistance, and it had sometimes led to long harangues on the tragedies of her past life in which he and Morgan had agreed they recognized parts of many legends and frontier songs.

"You're no twenty years old, now are you?"

"What the hell do you care how old I am, Fletcher?"

"You're closer to thirty."

She gave an outraged cry. "I am not. I'm twenty-six."

"Why'd you say twenty? Twenty-six is no disgrace. I'm that old myself."

"I said it because he was eighteen."

"He? Oh—Devlin."

"Zack, will you make me a promise? A solemn honest-to-God promise?"

"I know that look. This is just before you start singing the thirty-first verse of 'Joe Bowers.' What is it?"

"Bury me next to Devlin, will you?"

She spoke so softly and wistfully that for a moment he seemed scarcely to have heard her, but then he asked, in the voice of one who has been deeply offended, "Next to Devlin? What the hell are you talking about, Lily? He ain't even dead himself yet."

"I know," she whispered. "But when he is. When we both are."

"For Christ's sake! Come on!" He hurried her out to the street, and though she continued to beg him for the promise he gave her a smart slap on the buttocks and told her it was bad luck to talk about dying. "You women have got no morals of any kind, now have you?" They stopped and faced each other and the crowds passed around them, glancing with curious amusement at the slight girl in buckskin trousers and red shirt gazing up at the tall, blond-bearded man, talking together as earnestly and intensely as if they were alone, and drunk enough not only to be oblivious to everything but themselves but to be taking each other with a desperate seriousness. "You tried your damnedest to get him killed with that story of yours to Jenkins and Hamilton, and you know it. There was no other reason for you to tell that story except to get him killed, now why don't you admit it?"

"I did not. I told it to save myself." Her voice grew louder, her hands began to wave, and passers-by were grinning. "They were going to kill me for having stolen it and to save myself I told them he made me do it." She lowered her voice. "The first story I told you was a lie, I admit, but this one's true."

Zack rocked slowly backward and forward, glowering at her and shaking his head. He felt some obscure but strong need to accuse her and to defend Morgan, to have some justice in this matter at this very moment, though he was unable to decide what form it should take—possibly only her confession of guilt. "You wanted him killed," he stubbornly repeated. "You wanted them to kill him, you damn well know you did."

Lily's face acquired the same look of demented exaltation she had shown when she was racing, or the night they had told her about finding her cache. "Yes, I did!" she cried triumphantly. "I wanted him to die." The admission seemed to surprise her and she hung her head, looked away and drew a long sigh. "But now I don't. I don't hate him any longer."

Zack had a conviction of having found some profound and significant truth and it seemed quite clearly his duty to bring her to justice, if only by a reprimand, but he made the regretful discovery that the mountain whisky had affected not only Powell, and though the words he meant to speak were plain to him at one moment they had dis-

appeared the next. He had intended to tell her she was an evil
woman who should be made to suffer for the wrongs she had done,
the harm she had intended, and the two men who lay dead because of
her lies, but finally, with a look of gentle bewilderment, he asked,
"Why did you ever hate him?"

"Because he didn't love me."

They started walking again and after a moment Lily linked her
arm through his. He continued to tell himself that it was his responsibility, as Morgan's friend, to do something about this barbarous admission, but he had no idea what to do and walked along
with a growing sense of bland indifference until at last he shrugged,
turned down the corners of his mouth, and decided it was not up to
him to unravel all the mysteries and redress all the wrongs.

When it seemed they had walked so far they must have left the
town behind, even though he was vaguely aware that they passed a
steady procession of buildings, and men and women came dashing
toward them at dangerous speed, he heard her say, "Let's have our
picture taken. Have you ever seen a photograph of yourself?" They
stood before a cabin, bearing the sign: Will Remain In This Place
Only One Week.

The photographer was asleep on a cot but sprang up eagerly,
beckoning to them. "Of course, of course, how would you like to be
taken?"

Lily and Zack consulted each other. "How are most people taken?"

"That all depends. Now, if it's husband and wife—"

"We're not husband and wife."

Lily had been strolling about, examining his specimen photographs, and now she pointed to one. "Take us like that."

He asked them to sit at a table and placed before them an empty
bottle and two empty glasses. He now went frantically to work, retreating under the black cloth and asking them to shift their stools
one way or another, and at last fastened their heads in clamps and
warned them not to move. They gazed fixedly at the camera, each
holding a lighted cigar, their hats pulled low and, with ferocious
stares which would have delighted Powell, began to discuss the future.

"Powell and I were talking about Texas."

"Don't be a damn fool. Indians have closed the roads to Texas.
Want to keep your hair, or not?"

"Or maybe the Sweetwater River strike."

"Not me. I've had enough of twelve or fifteen hours a day on a
gravel bar. I've been thinking about the Union Pacific."

"What the hell would I do on a railroad?" demanded Lily, hurt
by the implication that they might, after all, not travel together.

The photographer implored them not to move, then ducked beneath the black cloth and cried out encouragingly, "Smile. Look
happy." Their expressions set in grim stolidity and their eyes glared

with the fervor of concentration; there was a faint click and Lily leaped up, brushing at her hair and clothes as if she expected to find herself in flames, or shot in some vital organ.

"Where shall I send it, sir?"

"When will it be ready?"

"I can have it tomorrow afternoon."

Lily was strolling about, whistling "Joe Bowers," and seemed to have no interest in the picture now that it had been taken. "Tomorrow afternoon we'll be gone," Zack said, and she gave him a quick approving glance.

"I can send it to you."

"We got no address."

She nodded briskly, but refused to tell him she wanted it sent to Morgan. Zack spoke to the photographer in an undertone: "Send it to Devlin Brothers. Wrap it up and mark it for Morgan Devlin."

Lily smiled, as if to congratulate him for this perspicacity, and went skipping out the door, and, as Zack emerged, she again caught hold of his arm.

XXII

Joshua had once heard Amos Cottrell remark that a successful man was one who, on many crucial occasions in his life, had the good luck to encounter a stupid opponent, and although Joshua now privately agreed that this might be true, for the sake of his own reputation he praised De Groot's astuteness, and magnified the difficulties De Groot had created before Joshua had at last owned De Groot Distilleries outright.

During the months while Joshua dawdled over investigating the books, and he and Cottrell and Flagg traded in and out of the speculative market taking whatever profit was left in the company, De Groot spent most of his days in Joshua's inner office, sipping absinthe and complaining about his plight, and demanded petulantly that Joshua help him put his company in order again, as the court had appointed him to do. "Don't be impatient, Milton. It took you a long time to get into this predicament and it's going to take us awhile to get you out again." Joshua never referred to De Groot's predicament as having been brought on by any other agent than De Groot himself and, as time went by, De Groot seemed willing to believe it.

But Joshua, though he passed in and out of the room briefly nowadays and held his conferences in Samuel's office, kept a careful watch over De Groot, for it seemed he would never observe a better lesson in defeat. Many men he had known or heard about had succeeded for a time, and then in some irremediable catastrophe lost everything, and either disappeared or, perhaps some years later, returned and stood about the streets where they had formerly gone striding like gods, predicting general ruin and croaking their story to anyone who would hear even a part of it.

And Joshua perceived, looking at De Groot pouting and winding his watch chain about his forefinger, that such men had first been overwhelmed by the fear of failure. They despaired of being able to maintain the combination of schemes and plots required to keep a man rich in Wall Street, could not endure the repetitive panics and rumors of panics and, losing confidence, they turned unlucky, made small mistakes which multiplied and grew larger, until all at once they found themselves defeated, but, at least, having now the actuality of failure they needed no longer to fear it. And, indeed, De Groot began to give the impression that his failure had some strange allure about it, almost as death might have allure for a man hopelessly sick.

Perhaps, thought Joshua, as he glanced sideways at De Groot, there was a peace in failure he had never before recognized; but that notion seemed a subtle assault upon his will and nerve and energy, and because De Groot's appearance had put it into his mind he began to despise him even more than before.

By late fall, when De Groot had been occupying the couch in his office for nearly six months, and Joshua and Cottrell and Flagg had agreed the speculative market had yielded its maximum profits, Joshua advised De Groot that his findings showed De Groot Distilleries to be bankrupt. De Groot took this in silence, glowered ominously, and declared he would permit no liquidation.

And then one day Judge Azariah Gill approved a sale to Samuel Ching for ten percent of the company's original value. "I'm sorry, old fellow," said Joshua, and spoke to De Groot quite tenderly, "but someone had to take it over, after all."

"And so you've done me the favor."

Joshua made a deprecating gesture. "If you like to think of it that way, Milton."

They stood face to face, and though Joshua reminded himself that pity and generosity are the weaknesses of gamblers and other small men, in fact he felt no pity for De Groot but the most intense and painful loathing. For during the past few months he had come to despise everything about De Groot—his huge, awkward body, his black beard and the way his hair seemed stuck to his head, his clothes which were always wrinkled and usually soiled; and he had begun to feel that De Groot had some contagious sickness so that he kept at a distance from him, avoided shaking his hand, and would not sit beside him. And whenever De Groot left, Joshua threw the windows wide, for the pervasive and familiar smell of De Groot seemed to have become thicker and even more nauseating. In a little longer, he told himself, if De Groot did not stop paying him these interminable visits, he would become as obsessed by his detestation of everything that was Milton De Groot as some men were by a woman's flesh or hair or breasts.

Still, he spoke to him softly. "You'll pull yourself up, Milton. These things happen to everyone."

"I'm disgraced, Joshua. Who will ever trust me again?"

In spite of his repugnance, Joshua advanced and gripped his shoulder. "No man is disgraced by failure, Milton—unless he's permitted himself to fail for a trifle. And De Groot Distilleries, even in its present condition, is no trifle." Hearing himself speaking these words, Joshua was inclined to smile but corrected the impulse.

And during the next few days he often explained De Groot's troubles to men he met in the street or in a restaurant, saying, "After all, a great many brilliant and daring operators have gone down because they tried to carry too much."

Three or four months later the new president, Samuel Ching, announced that his examination of the books showed the earnings to have been underestimated, whereupon he declared a large dividend payment, the stock became active, grew lively and popular, and once again drayloads of whisky began to move out of the tenement warehouses. The stock, in fact, attracted the attention of conservative investors who had recently shunned it, and although Joshua had had to bolster it with more money than he was presently worth, it began to repay him generously.

De Groot disappeared from the Street, and from Joshua's offices, but Hoke O'Neil, when Joshua made one of his periodic inspections of the warehouses, told him De Groot had been in Harry Hill's the night before, talking to Oliver Foss.

With his share of the profits, Hoke had bought the Red Onion— securing it at a reasonable price by scaring its owner out of the ward with a series of midnight raids and small fires—and as a rising power he now had his private office, a neighborhood saloon where he sat splendidly at his ease, giving audience to patronage seekers and listening to the troubles of his constituents, planning future strategy and taking credit for past successes.

Hoke's sister had left the country without telling Joshua she intended to go, and he heard it from Hoke just a few days after Judge Gill awarded the receivership. "Betty's gone," Hoke announced. "Poodle, parrot and carpet-sack. Left her trunk in Mrs. Gosnell's cellar, sold the piano, and left." He snapped his fingers. "Just the way she said she would."

"Gone where?"

"England." Hoke grinned wickedly. "What do you think of that?"

"I think she was very foolish. She hasn't any money."

"She thinks she has. We've been poorer than skim piss all our lives, and it seemed to Betty she'd fallen into an inheritance. Well, anyway she's gone. She says she don't like the natives here worth a damn and she's going back to where they make no pretense of being kindly toward the Irish." Hoke began to pick his teeth with the ivory toothpick which had been his other present to himself. "Well, that's Betty for you."

Joshua had forgotten Allegra Stuart long before Hoke told him about De Groot's visit to Harry Hill's. "You should have seen the pair of them. Foss sits there and scowls like it's the dirtiest trick he ever saw and tells De Groot he always warned him the brokers were a worse lot of thieves than the politicians." Hoke laughed loudly and gave his knee one of the frequent slaps which enraged Joshua, but he smiled grimly, for he had hopes of finding more uses for Hoke O'Neil and had suggested there might be some money for Hoke and his friends in awarding Joshua Ching one of those city contracts they were nowadays distributing like handbills. The opportunity was there, though Joshua thought it might not last long, for even the indifferent citizens of New York must notice sooner or later that their city was the dirtiest in the world, heaped with refuse and subject to outbreaks of cholera, that the wharves and docks were rotten and there were no bridges and no adequate sewer system, that it thronged with pickpockets and thieves, and gangs of hoodlums patrolled its streets.

"I'll be thinking about it," Hoke agreed. "But, after all, every businessman in town wants to do business with the city today."

De Groot's talk with Foss seemed to have revived his yearning for his distilleries and the significance the company had given him, and a few days later Joshua came into his office to find De Groot pacing about and bellowing that he would have justice, that his company belonged to him no matter who Judge Gill had sold it to, and that he was the victim of some gigantic conspiracy in which enemies became friends and friends became enemies by methods so mysterious and awful it must be the devil's own handiwork. Joshua paused, watching him curiously and thinking it was undoubtedly true that defeat in Wall Street came nearer to loosening a man's reason than any other indignity life could put upon him.

De Groot strode up and down, shouting, "I'll find the bastards and I'll ruin them, I'll ruin them, by Christ, if it takes the rest of my life!" He whirled, his massive body shaking the unstable floor, found Joshua there, and advanced toward him with a slow, lumbering walk. His eyes were red, his beard streaked with saliva and he looked as if, at any moment, he might go insane, cut his throat, leap from the window, or attack Joshua. But Joshua stared at him steadily and coldly and De Groot hesitated, his face so contorted he seemed ready to burst into blubbering tears, and at last cried out piteously, "How did it happen, Joshua? For God's sake, tell me who did this to me?"

And when Joshua passed him without answering, De Groot looked sheepishly away and seemed now entirely humiliated by the realization that he had been outwitted by some unknown adversary who had imagined and developed this plan against him. Joshua spoke quietly to one of the clerks who, as De Groot whined and clutched at his hair, opened the safe and brought him a neat pile of newly printed De Groot Distilleries bonds. Joshua took them to De Groot who, at first, backed away as if they might be dangerous, but then snatched hold of them and began to count them.

"Five hundred, Milton," Joshua told him.

De Groot nodded, counted a few more, apparently wanting to make sure he was not being cheated, then glanced guiltily at Joshua, who continued to watch him with the same warning stare, and after awhile he left, carrying the neatly stacked bonds close to his chest. They listened as he walked down the steps, pausing from time to time, and Joshua at last smiled faintly at Samuel.

"Five hundred, Joshua. Wasn't that a little generous?"

Joshua went to open the window. "The shroud without the corpse, Samuel. What difference does it make?"

Joshua found some ironic pleasure in knowing that there were incidental effects and repercussions echoing about the city where his influence would never be suspected, and it gave him a sense of majestic and sinister power which was very much to his taste, heightening his conviction that inscrutable forces operated in his behalf. This mystical sense of his potency and influence filled him with pride and a kind of menacing dignity, of which he expected to take full advantage the first night he went to meet Rose Michel.

For it was expected of Joshua Ching, so he reasoned, that he capture a public beauty and incarcerate her. He could afford to keep a mistress now, provided she was not the most expensive kind, and it seemed he should have one not only for his pleasure but to give tone to his life, as he would later acquire valuable paintings and fine horses, build houses and give extravagant entertainments.

He had taken Susan and Ceda to *The Black Crook,* although there were men who would not permit their wives or daughters to see one hundred blondes in pink tights and ruffled skirts, and during the performance he had sorted carefully among them until he found the one who pleased him best.

Whether or not Susan became suspicious of his alert attentiveness, she seemed bored and, when they left, said irritably, "I don't understand why women go to such a thing."

Joshua beamed, pleased with his discovery and imagining the treats in store. "Comparison, Susan, comparison. A woman spends most of her life comparing herself to other women. Well, *The Black Crook* gives her one hundred different comparisons to make—quite a bargain, you must agree."

Spinnage and Achroyd soon had the girl's name and, before much longer, the few other details which composed her history. She was eighteen years old and she lived in a boarding house on Bleecker Street, not very far from Mrs. Gosnell's. Her father, according to the publicity furnished the newspapers, was a prosperous shipbuilder who had disowned her for going on the stage; but in fact, she came from a family of factory workers in Hartford, had arrived alone in

New York three years ago, spent a few months in one of the more expensive whorehouses, and left there to live with a man who had soon grown tired of her, and a year ago she had found a job with *The Black Crook*, replacing one of the girls who had grown homesick for France.

This background suited Joshua very well for it meant that she was moderately worried—since even *The Black Crook* could not run forever—that she was not clever enough to be troublesome but was worldly wise in the ways which interested him, and, finally, that she would not be difficult to approach or very expensive to maintain, and would be easy to get rid of in a year or two.

Joshua then began a floral bombardment, sending her each day the same bouquet, a great collection of pink roses set off by a paper frill and blue satin rosette with streamers four feet long. After a time he began to enclose a card, signing it "An Admirer," since there was no reason yet for her to have his name and he knew men who had been blackmailed with less evidence.

Spinnage and Achroyd, meanwhile, kept a chart of her daily activities which Joshua studied. She seemed to know few men, returned to her boarding house after the evening performance, sometimes shopped in the afternoons with other girls from the chorus, though they bought little, and went to the theater carrying his bouquet, which she flourished and told her friends came from an oil man in Pennsylvania who had offered her a house and phaeton if she would leave the stage and come to him. Then, somewhat to Joshua's annoyance, she would toss the bouquet aside, thumb her nose at it, and dress for the performance. The cleaning woman took it to her quarters in Mulberry Street and was becoming a celebrity in the neighborhood through her miraculous way of bringing beauty and fragrance back with her every morning.

Joshua decided he would have nothing more to do with such a silly girl, and one so unappreciative, but after a few days he no longer cared what she did with his bouquet, and he sent a message inviting her to have supper with him in a private dining room at a fashionable restaurant on Fourteenth Street, the Maison Doré.

As he anticipated, she was shrewd enough to reply that she was engaged for the night he suggested and, when he named another, she was engaged for that one, and at the third suggestion she agreed to meet him.

Joshua arrived half an hour before he expected her, discussed the food and wine, ordered whisky and water and lighted a cigar and sat with his back to the door, thinking not of Rose Michel but of the railroad charter Lorenzo Flagg had uncovered, and its future possibilities.

As it was now, the charter was of little use even to its Ohio proprietors, but if they could buy it and persuade William Talbot, with his knowledge of railroads and their financing, to organize a construction company, Joshua foresaw that they might accumulate wealth as he had now begun to conceive of it. For he thought no longer of hundreds of thousands, nor of a million or two, not even ten millions by now held awe for him, but had begun to think of twenty or thirty as the least that could satisfy him. He sat with one elbow on the table, sipped only occasionally at the whisky and water, and became so lost in his project that even the reason he was in the room left his mind and he drifted about in a nebulous world of securities and commissions, bribes and certificates, corporations and charters and bonds and, best of all, public loans.

There was a light knock and, surprised to remember that he was expecting a visitor, Joshua turned to see Rose Michel standing there, his bouquet in her hand, and a tentative expression on her face, as if she might have called at the wrong address or on the wrong night.

"Miss Michel," said Joshua gravely, and gave her a ceremonious bow.

She walked in and glanced suspiciously around the small room. But it held no indecent suggestions of intimacy, only a well-set table, a gas chandelier, and four small chairs; that seemed to satisfy her and she looked at him over her shoulder, slightly lowering her head and giving him a smile which was almost timid.

Joshua, delighted that she was even prettier than she had seemed on the stage, suddenly found her enchanting and adorable. He took her cloak, gray wool and edged with some doubtful fur which looked as if it had been worn by someone else before her. But her dress pleased him better for it was made of pink silk and, though it displayed her smooth shoulders, not even Ceda would have called it immodest. It looked quite expensive and was probably the best she had, carefully preserved and kept fresh for important occasions.

As he stood looking at her she faced him simply, letting herself be examined without resentment or self-consciousness, and Joshua sensed that she had come to him tonight with very much the attitude of a clerk he might employ, needing a better job and hoping to get it, ready to please him if she could, but, because she presently had work, neither desperate nor ashamed; and Joshua, who believed he could tell when he met someone who possessed peculiar or unusual qualities, saw immediately that Rose Michel was only a pretty girl who must take what advantage she could of her looks before she began to lose them, that her life would probably be sad, ending perhaps in sickness or poverty while she was still young, or she might marry a poor man and have the troubles of her parents from which she had hoped to escape. Seeing all that, he knew that she was very well suited to his present needs and so he gallantly drew out a chair for her, poured champagne, and sat down across from her and continued to study her, smiling slightly but taking care not to betray as much interest as he felt.

He did not want her to be too much at ease and even preferred that she be somewhat frightened, for she was not to imagine he would humor her, put up with her tricks and foibles, plead for her

favors, or be grateful to her once he had them. She was to understand that if she became his mistress she must forget her own
wishes and think only of his, she must know that he would offer her
nothing of himself, whisper to her none of his business secrets and,
in fact, would give her from every point of view the worst of the
bargain. And, if she chose to make it with him anyway, she was no
more to complain than a man should complain who buys a piece of
property and finds most of it under water and the rest in quicksand.

She gazed at him uncertainly but, Joshua thought, with admiration for his handsome, blond-bearded face, his well-cut clothes and
appearance of somber dignity, attributes of which he was aware
and which he valued for the added power they brought him. And all
at once Joshua found himself enjoying the interview, though it had
scarcely begun, glad to know he now had the money to command situations which poorer men found trying and often embarrassing, as
he had himself in the past when, for the mere sake of a brief pleasure he had been obliged to humble himself, to invent or try to remember phrases, and to beg for what a dog could easily come by in
any street.

"I see that you have brought the bouquet I sent you," he remarked
pleasantly. Her face looked so fresh and almost unformed, showing so much more of youth than of character, that he had a sudden
disconcerting vision of himself as an old man—though forty-four ordinarily seemed to him a very good age—and for a moment was
inclined to tell her to run along and leave him to his business
musings.

"Oh, I always do!" She had laid the bouquet on the table and now,
as she touched it, he noticed that her hands were small and the
fingernails square, the undeveloped hands of a child, and this gave
him a morose recollection of gray-haired men he had seen entering
one of the panel-houses along the side streets off Broadway, holding
a twelve-year-old girl by the hand.

The waiter served the terrapin soup, ladling it out while she
watched greedily and Joshua saw her nostrils flare at its steaming
fragrance, so that once again he was reminded that although he had
no great appetite at this hour she was young enough to be hungry all
the time. She looked at the soup with so much the same rapt and
pleased and meekly obedient smile she had given him, eager for the
waiter to leave so that she could eat, that Joshua was annoyed. As
the waiter went out she picked up a spoon but then, as if belatedly
remembering a lesson, paused and looked at him for a signal that
she might begin. Resigned, he nodded and they sipped the soup,
Rose watching the plate steadily as the soup disappeared, while
Joshua sourly told himself that in another ten years this little trollop
would be the size of a barn.

Nevertheless, the eagerness she showed in satisfying her hunger,
the expression of bliss when she had swallowed several spoonfuls,
and the quick upward glances she gave him from time to time, as if

to make sure he did not disapprove of what she was doing, seemed charming, and he began to forgive her for having had another interest than himself.

The waiter returned, this time with a filet of beef surrounded by mushrooms, and she gazed at it with yearning and admiration and, once more, fell upon it as if she had not eaten for several days, but still continued to glance at him between every few bites. She said nothing and apparently thought she should wait for him to talk to her, and he decided that in itself was a virtue in a woman he might spend considerable time with. He therefore decided to say no more until the succession of dishes had satisfied her, and began to enjoy her presence as much for what she did not do as for the way she looked. He ate little but watched tolerantly as she disposed of three slices of beef, a large salad of cold string beans and truffles, and a dish of almond custard.

She was quiet, she seemed docile, her perfume was faint but delightful, her brown eyelashes curled, and, now that she had eaten, she looked contented and happy and sat back, smiling at him as if to thank him for it. "How I love terrapin soup." Her voice was soft, spoken somewhat below its natural tone, and she breathed as she spoke so that every remark seemed to be made under some emotional stress. She sipped the champagne carefully, for she had not drunk more than one glassful, and he approved of that, too. "Everything was perfect."

"Thank you, Miss Michel, I'm glad you enjoyed it."

"The theater is exhausting work, it makes me hungry."

"How do you happen to be on the stage?"

She glanced down, pouting slightly. "Oh, I got so bored at home. Father was so stern—a manufacturer, you know, very rich."

"I read that your father was a shipbuilder."

"Oh, of course, a shipbuilder, too. That's what I meant. He manufactures ships. And there was nothing but music lessons and dancing lessons and balls and cotillions, and I wanted to see something of the world, and so—" She looked at him steadily and intently for a moment, and then smiled, parting her pink lips and showing him her straight, white teeth, an asset which she displayed with confidence. "I came to New York."

"Miss Michel, please don't be disturbed by what I say, but you may as well not trouble yourself with the rest of your story." Her eyes opened wide and her face and neck flushed. "I know your background, I've taken the trouble to inquire about you."

"Why!" She threw her napkin onto the table and started to get up, but the next moment she hung her head, asking plaintively, "You do?"

Joshua smiled, thinking that her defeat was charming and absurd, and glad he had brought it about in this way, for if he had told her this at the beginning, he would never have seen her lively account of her family or her quick collapse into futile embarrassment.

"Yes, of course. I was very much interested in you, and naturally I inquired about your background."

"You inquired? Who from?"

"That's not important."

"But no one knows. I've been very careful. I've never told anyone." She covered her face with her hands. "Oh, how terrible. Why did you do it! You'll tell everyone, won't you?"

"I won't tell anyone at all. As I've said, Miss Michel, I'm very much interested in you."

And, in fact, he realized it was quite true. For she was, despite her pretenses, soft and tender, and the texture of her skin, the pale yellow color of her hair, even the small, inept movements of her hands which could not sustain the airs she tried to convey by lifting her chin and twisting one shoulder slightly forward—all these attributes and mannerisms had begun to give him a quick and increasingly urgent sense of future pleasures. For he found that although he had watched her on the stage with admiration and feelings of vague longing, there was now a warm, impatient desire, stirred into being by all the qualities she had of sensuality and provocation, but even more by her unawareness that he wanted her not for those qualities she tried to emphasize but for those over which she had no control, her defenselessness and the eager simplicity of her appetite, her clumsy romanticizing of her earlier life, and her automatic reaction of defeat.

She raised her head and looked at him again. "You are?" She picked up the bouquet, put it to her face, and delicately reassured herself with the roses.

"I am."

The waiter returned, bringing ices and small cakes and another bottle of champagne, though they had not finished the first, but she ate nothing more, only continued to watch Joshua with a serious and questioning look. And still he had not told her his name and she had not asked. The girl plainly had not had very good luck so far in her life and did not expect to have. But then, he was not looking for spirit and fiery independence, troublesome enough in a wife, and intolerable in a mistress. "My name," he said slowly, "is Joshua Ching."

"Oh, yes," she whispered. "I've heard of you—everyone has."

Joshua bristled at this and stared at her suspiciously, but then decided that perhaps it was true and he might be more famous than he had realized and, anyway, if she was trying to flatter him, so much the better.

"I'm married, of course." She nodded. "I have grown children." She nodded once more, watching him carefully, her head lowered as if she were listening for some expected sound, a little girl listening for her father to open the door, perhaps, or a teacher to announce the recess. "And, without beating any further about the bush, I want to find a place for you to live, hire a servant or two and a cook, buy you some clothes, provide you with a carriage, and visit you when I have time." He nodded, having stated his terms clearly and succinctly, for it was getting late and he must be up early in the morning.

"Would I stay on the stage?"

"Certainly not. Also, let me tell you, I expect fidelity and will be sure to get it. I have no intention of spending money in order to be made a fool of."

"Oh, of course not. I wouldn't think of it."

Joshua smiled. "Of course you would. But think twice, when you do. Now, Miss Michel, I'm going to send you to your boarding house and leave you there—don't worry, a boarding house is not my idea of a rendezvous—and we'll meet again in a week or so. I'll have to send you a message, because I have some evening engagements during the next few nights."

He stood up, held her cloak but made no effort to kiss her, squeeze her about the shoulders or essay any other quick caresses, though she looked at him doubtfully as if she thought there must be something more to be said and done, and they went out. He sent her off in his carriage and then walked to the Fifth Avenue Hotel and went to bed, well pleased and full of happy anticipation. How lucky, he thought, that she was as she was, so mobile, unthinking, smooth-skinned and, of course, eager for luxuries she did not possess.

A week or more later he was about to send a note to tell Rose Michel that his carriage would call for her after the performance, when late in the afternoon Hoke O'Neil's messenger brought him word of a meeting that night at eleven o'clock to discuss the city contract Joshua had first mentioned nearly a year ago.

Hoke had recently come to his office with the news that he thought a franchise for supplying the city with sand and gravel might be put through the Common Council. "It's taken me a little time," Hoke admitted. "A lot of guys have to be brought to agree, but as soon as I can get them all together, we'll meet at The Marquis Club."

Joshua shook his head. "I never play for high stakes, don't believe in it."

"You think I'm a roper-in for McDuff?" Hoke grinned, and Joshua thought he looked like an evil and only partly grown urchin, as if his face were a mask assumed very young. "Gambling's not my natural trade. I'm a fighter and a politician by instinct and that's the way I'll stay; it gets a man nowhere to go outside his instincts. McDuff, you see, is like this with Foss, and also he's a friend of mine." Hoke shrugged, as if to qualify the word. "He's got some private quarters upstairs where he lets his friends gather for a quiet talk—no playing, just talk."

"Very well. I'll be there."

"Don't start out with bargain prices—these boys ain't monkeys fond of peanuts."

The message, like others Joshua had received from Hoke, was brought by a ten-year-old boy named Mud Foley who had recently attached himself to Hoke, followed him about, ran errands and delivered messages—never in writing, Joshua noticed—and slept in Hoke's saloon, where he had settled as a permanent tenant. He wore few clothes and no shoes, though it was mid-November, his skin looked hard as leather, his hair was a gray, gumlike mass, and his face so coated with grime the few clean patches about his mouth and fingertips seemed suspicious and obscene. And, to Joshua, Mud Foley smelled like a wet dog. He came darting into Joshua's office, whipped a rag from his pocket and knelt to polish Joshua's shoes, mumbling his message in a street jargon so unintelligible that Joshua had to ask him to repeat it several times.

As he drove up to The Marquis Club, a four-story brownstone on West Twenty-fifth Street, not far from Fifth Avenue, Joshua thought of what Hoke had told him about Marquis McDuff, who was seldom seen by the men who came there to play, but directed the establishment from his apartment on the top floor. "You wouldn't think it from the layout he's got today, but six years ago McDuff was running a pool hall with a couple of card tables in the lousiest little trap in the whole god-damn Sixth. What's the secret of his success? Well, that's a long story and it's none too clear in spots, but he got part of it fighting, part of it he picked off a drunk he says he found murdered on the docks, and part he got from a rich sucker who lost ten thousand to him in one night. Marquis wasn't his name to start with, either, just Mike, but somebody told him Marquis would be good for his business."

A butler took Joshua's coat but let him keep his hat and cane, and led him past closed doors and up a staircase carpeted in green velvet, dimly lighted by gas brackets, where the walls were hung with dark paintings and many mirrors. Behind those closed doors there would be ten or twenty men going soberly and quietly about their play, while others sat in the library reading, or talking over some device for making money.

On the fourth floor the butler tapped at the door, and after a brief pause it was opened by Marquis McDuff, who gave Joshua a fierce smile and shook his hand. "Good evening, Mr. Ching, please come in. What will you have to drink?"

McDuff was a large man with muscular shoulders which strained against his evening coat, and when he bowed slightly it was as if his body functioned on oiled hinges, perpetually set to spring. He had straight black hair with thick brows overhanging black eyes which glared at Joshua as if even now in his grandeur McDuff had not forgotten the streets and their menace; but then, the next moment, he relented and smiled once again.

This room was even more elaborately furnished than those downstairs, with rosewood panels, ceiling-high gilt-framed mirrors, and gilt furniture covered with dark green and red brocade. It looked, thought Joshua, like an Irishman's dream, complete with six or eight politicians wearing tall silk hats and smoking cigars, and a pretty girl, smiling at Joshua with faint curiosity as she sipped a drink.

Hoke came swaggering forward, grinning and plying his ivory toothpick with casual dexterity, for it was seldom out of his mouth and Joshua confidently expected to see him swallow it one day. "Gentlemen," said Hoke, "Mr. Joshua Ching." As Hoke spoke their names, proceeding about the circle, each nodded brusquely, and they continued to study him with as much thoughtful concern, Joshua told himself, as a medical student might give to his first cadaver. "You know Oliver Foss."

Joshua shook hands with Foss, whose narrow head and body seemed to have been pressed together by some large piece of machinery, and Joshua could never meet him without remembering Hoke's description of Foss' early career in the dog pits, which gave him disconcerting visions of Foss snapping at rats' necks with his long teeth.

"Judge Gill." Joshua and Judge Gill shook hands as peremptorily as if they had never met before, and the Judge returned to whittling at a stick which must have some magical properties about it for, though he whittled continuously, each time Joshua saw him the stick was exactly the same size. Not very long ago Joshua had contributed twenty-five thousand dollars to the Judge's assessment fee, although it grieved him to do it, but he had arrived at that peak of success where a judge was more necessary to him than a clerk, and Azariah Gill was the judge who had happened along at that moment.

"Leon Pumphrey."

Pumphrey was a private detective, and another constant companion of Oliver Foss, and Joshua had sometimes wondered if Pumphrey exchanged information with Spinnage and Achroyd. If he did, however, there was no way he could stop them; and he could not guess, from Pumphrey's broad, stolid face, whether he knew his secrets or not.

"Senator Amasa Stirt." Joshua had not previously met Stirt, a state senator, and Hoke presented him proudly, for not long ago Joshua had asked what acquaintance he had in the state legislature and Hoke had been evasive, so that Amasa Stirt must be a recent acquisition.

"Alderman Kell and Alderman Greaves."

Hoke introduced them together, as if either they were a team or not important enough to be presented as individuals. Kell sat up very straight, with his cane between his widespread legs, puffing at a cigar and frowning. Greaves had a slight smile which looked to Joshua as if he might be pleased by the recollection of some small, mean trick by which he had lately surprised a friend.

"And that," said Hoke, "is our company." He glanced at Oliver Foss for his orders and Foss, with a lift of one eyebrow, apparently signaled him to sit down and keep quiet, for Hoke promptly took a chair, crossed his legs, and seriously studied Foss' face as if determined to learn from it every lesson which might appear there.

"What about me?" the girl demanded. "I'm Minnie Conway, Mr.

Ching." Joshua bowed to her as if she might be an important official, and McDuff muttered a few words which, it seemed, hurt her feelings. "I don't have to leave the room, do I, Mr. Foss? I won't know what you're talking about anyway and I get tired of being by myself all the time."

"Let her stay, poor child, what harm can she do?"

"Of course, Oliver, if you say so. Only she's a damn nuisance."

"But such a pretty nuisance," protested Judge Gill, and she smiled and lowered her eyes, glanced admiringly down into her dress, and began to sip the drink once more.

"Very pretty," agreed Foss, but even before he spoke he had turned his attention to Joshua and, when he did, every other man instantly resumed his sharp and critical and untrusting surveillance. "Mr. Ching, O'Neil tells me you are interested in organizing a company which will supply the Department of Public Works with sand and gravel. Is that right?"

"It is."

"There are several such companies in existence right now, of course. I suppose you've noticed the streets are piled high with sand gravel, as it is."

"So they are," Joshua agreed. "It's my intention to organize two companies, one to supply the city with sand and gravel for its building projects, and the other to contract for some of those buildings."

Foss nodded at Gill and Stirt and, in reply, received their nods. "How are you capitalized?"

"I can get any amount that's needed, once I have the franchise. After that, we can begin to survey and submit plans almost immediately."

"Of course you know these franchises are in great demand. As popular, I would say, as a pretty girl like Miss Conway." He smiled gallantly and she giggled, crushed her breasts together with both arms, then cast a nervous glance at McDuff as he lifted the back of his hand toward her. "Alderman Kell, how many sand and gravel companies have franchise applications before the Council?"

"Twenty-three," barked Alderman Kell self-consciously. Apparently he was not accustomed to being asked his opinion before others, even when it was only the number of franchise applications, and he turned red and clenched his fists, anxiously watching Foss to learn if he had made the expected reply.

"Twenty-three, Mr. Ching. Naturally, we can't grant them all."

Oliver Foss, after some brief remarks to Stirt and Gill, suggested that forty thousand dollars would be a likely sum for a city franchise.

"My partners and I," said Joshua, "are only interested, you understand, in a perpetual franchise."

Oliver Foss sucked on his teeth at this, not so much with astonishment, it seemed, as with pleasure. "A perpetual franchise. Ah?"

"Anything else would not be worth the trouble of organizing and managing two new companies."

"But a perpetual franchise, Mr. Ching—"

At the end of another hour Joshua had agreed that he and his partners, Amos Cottrell and Lorenzo Flagg, would each put one quarter of
a million dollars in cash in a bank where it could be drawn out on
the day the franchise was voted. It was understood that his two companies existed only on paper, that he would neither deliver sand and
gravel nor construct public buildings, but would be awarded a three-
million-dollar contract for certain work to be stipulated by the city,
and that he would let those contracts to other men who would, at the
lowest price he could arrange, do the work, while one third of those
three millions would return to the men participating in this meeting,
the Common Council, the Board of Aldermen, the Boss, and other
men Joshua would never meet.

Joshua went away quite elated at having found a way to participate in the profits of city government, and yet, as the days passed and
he heard nothing from Hoke O'Neil, he began to wonder if, like De
Groot, he had now fatally overextended himself and was about to fall
prey to an unknown enemy who had been waiting for this moment as
patiently as he had waited for De Groot. As he considered, with
greedy and nervous apprehension, his possible gains and losses, it
came to seem more and more absurd that he should go into partnership with the city politicians, men who were swindling the public on
a scale never even attempted before, and he fell to imagining that he
was sick, that he would soon be a pauper, and so completely lost interest in Rose Michel that he forgot to send her his daily bouquet.

At the end of a week Hoke notified him that the franchise had been
voted and Oliver Foss wanted to talk to him again. That Oliver Foss
should want to talk to him seemed to Joshua a portent so ominous
he took no joy in the franchise and did not even tell Cottrell or Flagg
it had been voted. At this meeting, also held in McDuff's apartment
at eleven o'clock, there was only Hoke, Foss, and McDuff, whose
lowering face and appearance of villainous, uncontrolled strength
made Joshua uneasy, as if Foss had kept a gorilla about on a light
chain.

The meeting began in a spirit of congratulation and conviviality.
McDuff poured champagne and they toasted the Metropolitan Sand
and Gravel Company, the perpetual franchise, Tammany Hall and
one another, and at last Foss announced, "Now, to the second part of
our project." Joshua leaned alertly forward and watched Foss with a
bland and politely inquiring expression. "Next week, the Common
Council is going to vote a perpetual franchise to another sand and
gravel company—absent-mindedness, you understand, so many
things to keep straight nowadays."

"Mr. Foss, what the hell are you talking about?" Joshua threw a
vicious glance at Hoke, and had a brief, clear picture of himself
throttling Hoke O'Neil to death while Hoke hung helplessly from his
hands, begging for mercy.

"Don't tell me you've never met this plan before, Mr. Ching?"

"If I have, I didn't know it."

"You're a suspicious man, Mr. Ching. You think you've happened into a den of thieves, but please remember that you're one of us, and although there may not be honor among thieves, there is self-interest. Now—this is the way it works. Once there are two franchises voted for the same company, the only way to settle it is to go to court."

"So it would seem," said Joshua gloomily, and was predicting that before another month had passed these malefactors would have picked him clean and thrown his bones out to bleach.

"Judge Gill will try the case, of course. But it won't be called for two or three months and in the meantime we—O'Neil and McDuff and you and me—will contract for delivery in three months' time of all the stock we can print at something less than the market price. The second franchise will be repealed, due to some defects in its clauses which were overlooked, the stock will drop, we will deliver and—" Foss spread his hands and smiled benignly as Joshua sighed and leaned back, feeling a wave of coldness pass over his sweating face and body. "The last time, we all made fifty-nine dollars on each and every share."

Joshua awoke the next morning with a powerfully revived interest in Rose Michel and, as he bathed and dressed, examined himself in the mirror, looking for indications of age or debility he might not have noticed but which would be plain to a girl one year younger than Suky, and the sight of his muscular chest and arms, his flat belly, and his neat buttocks, was so reassuring he sent a message telling Rose Michel where to meet him that night.

He left the theater before the play was done, asking Philip to see the women home, and took a hack to a bed-house on West Twelfth Street where he had rented a room. He had chosen a bed-house, though he did not like them, because he would meet her here only this one time and, after that, either never see her again, or he would rent a house for her to live in.

There were several carriages standing along the block, but his own was not among them, and although he started up the steps, thinking to dodge inside before someone he knew came by, it immediately struck him as ridiculous to sit there alone in a small, hostile bedroom, and he had an image of himself as a small boy dressed in his best clothes, seated on a chair too high for him, waiting to be taken for an outing. He began to walk swiftly along the street, watching for his carriage, and as he walked he rehearsed the speech he would make to her, but interrupted it to improve, instead, on a speech he would make tomorrow morning to Amos Cottrell and Lorenzo Flagg, when they met to discuss the combination of five small trunk lines in the northern part of the state.

A carriage passed and he heard a woman's merry laughter, ringing out and startling him. And when it had gone by Joshua was surprised to realize it was no longer possible for him readily to understand why a woman's voice should sound so recklessly light-hearted. The world had never been a jolly place so far as he was concerned, and though he was not aware of thinking of it as gloomy, either, nevertheless the surprise he had felt at the laughter, passing close to him but unconcerned with him or with anything he knew about, was disconcerting. And he began to wonder if Rose Michel, who had seemed an affectionate and simple girl, might be able to remind him that laughter was as persistent as his own ambitions.

After a few minutes he saw his carriage coming from the direction of Broadway, and as it stopped before the bed-house he went toward it quickly, eager to see her again and wondering how she would look and what would happen between them; perhaps some mild disappointment or, as he hoped, the intimation of pleasures which, carefully cultivated, might grow in intensity.

He opened the door and she looked at him with an expression of serious wistfulness but then smiled, and he helped her out. They ran up the steps and he rapped at the door. It was opened immediately by a woman they could scarcely see in the dark vestibule, and as they entered Joshua's nose flared with fastidious disapproval of the musty smells, the scent of escaping gas and stale cigar smoke, and some peculiar perfume he could not identify.

"George Smith," Joshua mumbled, and wished he had never come there.

"Yes, sir. The ten-dollar room." She held out her hand, Joshua paid her, and she led them up a narrow stairway, set the lamp on a table and shut the door so quietly he did not immediately realize she had left them.

They stood for a moment, looking at the room, but neither of them yet ready to look at the other. For a bed-house, it was better than he had expected, but nevertheless it made him melancholy, for as Joshua's nose disliked strong and evil smells he also disliked squalid surroundings and shared with Suky a need for luxury, meticulously maintained.

The room was paneled with dark wood and had little furniture but the bed, freshly made, a basin and pitcher of water on a table, with several towels, and a worn carpet. On one wall hung a picture of a dog carrying a bird in its mouth, and on the opposite wall was the familiar lithograph, "The Stages of Life," in which young and old and middle-aged were packed together in one small boat, rowing upon Life's seas, and that picture disgusted him more than anything else, as if it might have been put there by the bed-house proprietor to remind him of his foolishness in coming here with this young girl.

He stared at it for a moment, and then realized that she was watching him with eager wistfulness, almost, he thought, like the bird-carrying dog in the picture. The expression caught at him unexpectedly, and he was surprised to feel a pitying tenderness and the conviction that he owed her an apology.

"I'm sorry."

"Sorry? But why?"

"This place. It's ugly."

She glanced at the door, reminding him to lock it and, when he did, found she had thrown the cloak aside and stood with her hands folded, dressed in the same pink silk gown, and smiling as if she thought he might need encouragement. "Shall I put out the light?" she asked.

"No, I want to look at you."

He removed his coat and hung it over the chair, across her cloak. That struck him as an immodest thing to have done, but it would have been absurd to change it and so he lay over it, as well, his cane and gloves and silk hat. To his relief the girl stood still, made no flirtatious overtures, and waited for him to approach her.

It was his intention to deliver the speech he had composed and come to a financial agreement first of all, but instead he began to kiss her and, in another few moments, she was throwing her clothes aside, scattering them about the floor, and she lay down, watching as he undressed, and lifting her arms as he bent over her. Her legs clasped about his back and he had a last glimpse of her face, become suddenly serious and intent, waiting, and as he slipped into her body she gave a sharp little gasp and then sighed deeply, and at that moment it seemed he fell as much in love with her as he had ever been with anyone, and felt a secret gratitude for the gift of her responsive excitement.

But, nevertheless, he later told her what he would do for her and what he would not do, and again she listened as she had the first night, as if to be sure she understood the lesson and would remember it. "I'll rent a small house for you, not pretentious, I assure you. I'll hire a cook and a maid and a coachman, no footman." She nodded. "I'll buy you some clothes, but not a great many, and no jewelry to speak of. I'm not a rich man, and I can't afford to squander money. I'll visit you when I have time and I don't suppose it will be more than once or twice a week, because I'm busy. When I'm not there you can do what you like, provided of course that you see no other men and, I may as well warn you, to save us both embarrassment, I'll take care that you don't. If you do, then of course you must move out of the house. I won't be seen with you in public and I won't travel with you. However, from time to time, I will entertain business acquaintances, and will expect you to act as hostess. You're able to do that, I hope?"

"I can learn. I don't think it's very hard."

"Nothing will be expected of you except to be charming, whether you feel like it or not." In spite of himself, Joshua smiled faintly as he heard that, and found some irresistible amusement in her solemn and devoted expression. "Now—what have you to say? Do you want to live with me under those circumstances?"

"Yes. I want to. I will."

"Good." That sounded as if he had just concluded a conference with Hoke O'Neil or Oliver Foss, and he thought it required some softening, but then he added, "I probably won't love you, and I may not make you very happy."

"I don't expect someone else to make me happy." She stroked her fingers across his hair, and this gesture, done gently and unself-consciously, recalled to him the woman's laughter in the passing carriage, and at the reminder of this sound, so mysterious, and so peculiarly nostalgic, he put his mouth to her throat and breasts and, presently, lowered himself upon her again.

XXIII

The marriage of Jenny Danforth and Peter Devlin was at first intended to be performed more or less secretly at the Devlin house, but the plans grew increasingly elaborate until the wedding at last became one of the major social enterprises of the winter.

Pete had made the announcement one night after dinner, casually remarking, "I'm going to marry Mrs. Danforth on the twenty-third of December."

Matt barked out, "What?" and glanced at Marietta, wondering if he had sounded shocked, happy, horrified, angry, or, as he believed, as if he had rehearsed this response so often it had lost any possible spontaneity. But Marietta had her arms around Pete and was kissing him, while Lisette swung about the room, humming the "Wedding March" from *Lohengrin* and kissing each of her brothers in turn as she passed him.

Matt advanced to shake his hand, and was followed so quickly by Morgan and Jonathan and the two younger boys that Pete could not have examined his face if he had wanted to. "I'm so glad, so glad," Pete was mumbling. "I wasn't sure—but she's been in mourning over a year. Other people won't disapprove, will they? She's very shy, you know." He said this to Marietta, as if only a woman would understand this description of Jenny Danforth. "She hates to be talked about." And then, when they assured him that a year was long enough and it was no one's business but theirs, Pete declared he must go to her immediately and tell her how delighted her new relatives were. "She was worried, I may as well admit it. She kept saying we're all so close that if we didn't like it—if all of you didn't like it, I mean—it would be terrible. You know what Lisette says: If any one of us married the wrong person it would do some harm to all of us."

"Oh, but Uncle Pete, Jenny Danforth isn't the wrong person." Lisette turned, looking happily amazed, while for the past several days she had been quiet and thoughtful. "Just think—Jenny Danforth is going to be a part of our family."

Pete made a dash for the door, then stopped. "Matt, come with me. She'll say I'm exaggerating."

Matt felt his face turn hot and, as he replied, his voice sounded both falsely jovial and harsh. "My God, Pete, no. A woman doesn't want a third person hanging around when her fiancé tells her that his family approves." He laughed, and was again critical of the strange sounds he seemed to be making. "Tell her we give you both our blessing and—" He stopped, for whatever the speech was that he had prepared, and which as he silently delivered it had sounded warmly pleased at the prospect of his brother's happiness, even including some jocular comments on the bride's celebrity as a beauty, that speech had quite disappeared.

Pete went out and Matt glanced furtively at Marietta, but she and Lisette were even then beginning to plan the great celebration it would be.

"Oh, I could have bawled when he told us," Lisette said. "He looked so mystified and so helpless—how lonely he must have been all this time. And now, he'll be happy again." At that, however, she began to cry and ran out of the room.

"Fletcher," Morgan said. "That's what's ailing her."

Matt nodded, sat down and picked up the paper, having noticed against his will what time it was when Pete went out. "Has he left the Territory?"

"He must have. I haven't seen him for almost two weeks."

"Good."

"You don't like him?"

Matt scowled at the paper. "As a man, all right. Not as a husband for Lisette."

"Why not, sir?"

Matt slapped the paper onto the table, as if Morgan's question had challenged him. But he warned himself that this fact of Jenny's marriage to Pete was something which he must, from this moment, contrive to assimilate and contain, and he smiled, though rather sourly. "Because he's ignorant, fundamentally lazy, has no moral principles to speak of, can't see any further ahead than his next meal or drink, would never be able to provide any regular way of life for her—and sooner or later he'll either be shot or hanged. Is that reason enough?"

A few days later Pete and Morgan left for Helena to establish the new branch of Devlin Brothers and to oversee the building of Pete's house. It was still almost four months before the wedding, but the women began to hold meetings and to write long lists, planning the food and the music and even the dresses they would wear, and Marietta told Matt she was glad that Lisette had the excitement of the wedding to think about.

"She mopes every minute she thinks I'm not watching her, and she holds Annabel and rocks back and forth with her and cries until the poor child's hair is wet with her tears. And when I ask what's troubling her she shakes her head and runs out of the room. I think she really wanted to marry him, Matt."

"Did she? I'll fix that."

When dinner was over he called Lisette to him and gave her a photograph which had been delivered to his office by the traveling photographer. Lisette examined it, then frowned and narrowed her eyes, for the two figures were blurred and dark. "Who is this?"

"Zack Fletcher. Don't you recognize him?"

"No, no, the other one—the woman. Is that a woman?"

"I have no idea."

"When was it taken?"

"About three weeks ago."

"Just before he left, then." She studied it a little longer. "And he must have left with her." She held the picture between her thumb and forefinger and extended it to him. "Let's save it for Morgan."

A few days later Marietta told him that Lisette had stopped weeping but had become, instead, so gay and saucy, so impudent and provocative with Ralph Mercer and Jacob Finney and her other beaux that she would soon wear out their patience, and so filled with energy and a restless craving for work of any kind that even Jenny Danforth had remarked that Lisette must have been disappointed in love.

"I'm glad she has," Matt said. "The best thing he could have done is to disappoint her. Just once is much better than a thousand times."

"But it hurts me to see her unhappy, and maybe you're wrong, Matt. Maybe he would have been different if he had married her."

"Like hell he would. Marriage changes no man." That remark surprised him, as did many others he heard himself making inadvertently these days, for it sounded ominous, almost as if there had been a signal given. But it seemed best, as it had before, to ignore whatever meanings might be there, and hope they would not be as plain to Marietta as they were to him.

Pete and Morgan did not return from Helena until the day before the wedding, and Lisette beckoned her brother aside when the cabin emptied out after breakfast, led him to the window and breathed upon it, rubbing the frosty pane with her warm hand to let in more light, and, with a look both sly and condemnatory, held the photograph before his face. Morgan smiled.

"It looks like him, all right."

"Morgan," she protested, and gave an aggrieved sigh. "Don't tease me. You know that I was—well, maybe I wasn't in love with him, exactly, but he was in love with me. He told me so. Who is that woman?"

"Her name's Lily Jones."

"But what kind of woman would wear men's clothes and smoke cigars and sit there drinking whisky as if she just came through with a bull train?" Morgan laughed, and she went on angrily. "Where does she live and how does she earn her living? I've seen women on the streets who look like that, but you know what everyone says they are."

"What difference does it make? He's gone."

At four-thirty the living room had been swept and scrubbed and Lisette and Georgina and Rachel Finney had decorated it with branches of fir and juniper, wreaths of pine cones, each with a candle set in the center, and fir garlands looped across the walls, so that it smelled like a forest and was similarly dark and shadowed, lighted only by the candles and the wood fire.

The men and the two younger boys were in black suits and white silk cravats, and stood talking with the Reverend Bream about a lumber company in which they had recently invested, for even Pete seemed to think it necessary to act as if this might be the beginning of any ordinary evening party. Marietta and Erma Finney and Cornelia Bream, largely swollen with her first child, sat together in their glistening silk dresses and talked softly, while now and then one of the men gave a self-conscious laugh.

"I'm very happy about this wedding," Erma Finney said. "It's what they've both needed."

Cornelia Bream said, "But Mrs. Danforth was afraid you might not approve."

Marietta glanced away to conceal a smile, Mrs. Bream looked as if the remark had not had the sound intended, and Erma lifted her shoulders in her habitual nervous movement. "I can't imagine why. She might have waited longer, of course, but then, knowing Jenny as I do, I think she may have waited long enough." She glanced at Marietta, but Marietta was watching Matt, though he stood with his back to them, and seemed not to have heard her. "What Jenny Danforth needs are children to care for."

"She knows that, Erma," Marietta said quickly, and they exchanged glances across Cornelia Bream, who began to fidget uneasily, picking at the folds of her skirt.

Robert had stationed himself at the door and had been peeking out every few moments, and all at once he announced, "Here they come!"

There was a low murmur, then a hush, the door opened again, and Jenny Danforth stood there smiling uncertainly, with Lemuel Finney at her side.

Marietta went to take her coat and the two women smiled shyly at each other, as if they were strangers meeting on an occasion of great but different significance to each of them, while Lem Finney stamped his feet and told them it was the coldest day of the year and would be colder still before the night was over.

Jenny now turned slowly, and, though she was smiling, she looked mistrustful and almost frightened, as if she thought there might be some who wished her ill or resented her presence among them, and for a few moments the silence continued, for she seemed to have taken them by surprise and they might never have seen her before.

It was, in fact, the first time she had been seen out of mourning in nearly a year and a half and this alone made her look almost shockingly different, quite indecently exposed, even though her gown was sober enough, made of purple silk which fastened at the base of her throat, with long sleeves and a wide skirt drawn toward the back. Her face was whiter than usual and her lips so pale they seemed to have no more color than her cheeks, and her black hair was brushed smoothly from its center part and folded into a low chignon, where she had fastened a spray of cedar at one side; and Matt, remembering she had worn it that way on the night of the ball in Bannack, believed she was reminding him to think of her no more, and his loss seemed complete.

She had appeared at his office a few days ago, late in the afternoon, explaining that she had come to discuss a prospective buyer for her house, and she had stayed, pretending to read over papers left her by the Doctor until everyone else had gone, and he turned out the lights to indicate they were closed for the day. But later, as she was leaving, she asked him, "How many people are we going to hurt?"

"We won't see each other again, Jenny, you know that."

"We think so today."

And now here she stood, her purple dress shining in the light from the candles and fire, looking doubtfully and questioningly from one face to another, until all at once Lisette sprang forward, threw her arms about her and kissed her.

"Don't be frightened, dear Mrs. Danforth. Why, you look as if you don't trust us." She turned gaily to the others. "Isn't she marvelous in this dress? Oh, Mrs. Danforth, how happy I am today." And Jenny smiled at her and touched her cheek gently, her look of uncertainty vanished, and all at once the room seemed to have overcome its awe and resistance to her presence.

The Reverend Bream stepped forward briskly, with the same rigorous smile which he used in the pulpit, took his position before the fireplace, and opened very slowly the Book of Common Prayer, frowning over what he saw there. Pete and Jenny stood before him with their backs to the others, and Lem Finney stood at Jenny's side. The women sat in a row across the room, with Marietta holding Annabel on her lap, and Matt and the four boys stood in back of them, and as the Reverend Bream began to speak their faces took on expressions of solemn wonder and sorrow, while even the baby watched in silence, looking thoughtful and concerned.

" 'Dearly beloved, we are gathered here today in the sight of God—' "

At these words, spoken in his powerful and resonant voice, Lisette found herself touched and affected as it seemed she had never been before, and her breath caught in an uncontrollable sob. But some-

one's hand—her father's, or Morgan's—reached down and gently
took hold of her shoulder, she straightened, wiped the tears away,
and the service continued.

" 'You take this woman, whom you hold by the hand, to be your
lawful and married wife—' "

"Yes, I do."

" '—and you promise, and covenant in the presence of God and
these witnesses, that you will be unto him a loving, faithful, and
obedient wife until you shall be separated by death.' "

"Yes, I do."

Pete slipped the ring onto Jenny's finger and the Reverend's voice
rose. " 'I pronounce you husband and wife, according to the ordi-
nance of God; whom therefore God hath joined together let no man
put asunder.' "

Lisette started instantly to her feet, ready to participate in the first
congratulations and wishes for happiness, but again a hand reached
out to restrain her and this time she turned and saw that it was Morgan, shaking his head to signify there was something more to be
done and, inadvertently, she glanced at her father to find him staring
straight ahead, not looking at Pete or Jenny, with an expression as if
he had just seen something which had terrified or enraged him. She
turned away, resentful that she had been made, against her will, to
discover what must be Jenny Danforth's meaning to him. But she
was Jenny Danforth no longer, and whatever it might have been, it
was over.

There was a moment after Pete had put the ring on her finger during which, but for Lisette's outcry, no one moved or made any
sound, while Jenny and Pete stood perfectly still and watched the
Reverend Bream, as if waiting for him to set them free of his spell.
He smiled, nodding at Pete to encourage him, and Pete turned with a
resolute motion to confront his bride, but found that there were
tears on her face and she had once again that frightened and unsure
smile. As they looked at each other Pete appeared for a moment to be
helplessly baffled, but then as he reached his hand rather clumsily
to her face Jenny laughed, tipped back her head and moved a step
toward him, and Pete swept her into his arms and kissed her with an
ardent and, it seemed, defiant enthusiasm.

Lisette gave a deep sigh at this happy outcome of the difficult moment and sprang forward, crying gaily, "Uncle Pete, save something for your honeymoon."

There were three or four minutes of general confusion, kisses and
hand clasps and embarrassed laughter, some further commotion as
coats were brought and hats searched out, and then very quickly, as
if by mutual agreement, they were ready to leave for Folger Hall,
where their friends were waiting. Matt dashed urgently about, packing the women into one carriage, Jenny and Pete set out first in another, and the men followed along on horseback; and by the time
they were trotting down the hillside there had been such expeditious

haste, almost as if they were escaping from the darkened and fragrant cabin, that not even Marietta could recall whether Matt had looked reconciled or unhappy, and only Lisette remembered with dismay the expression she had seen on his face.

Jenny turned and waved, giving them a brilliant impartial smile, and moved closer to Pete, who drove smartly away.

"Oh, isn't she beautiful," murmured Lisette. "Just think, from now on I can call her Aunt Jenny, can't I, Mother?"

Marietta laughed. "Of course you can. That's what she is."

"Jenny," said Erma Finney, and it seemed she looked more than ever concerned and baffled, "has been a mystery ever since she arrived out here and, do you know, I think the mystery is less in her past than in her character."

"To have a mysterious aunt," Lisette said quickly, "oh, what an exciting idea, Mrs. Finney," and she began to point out the bonfires burning all along the main street, saying that it looked as if the whole town had set itself afire for this festival, though it was, of course, only the weekly burning of accumulated trash and offal.

Folger Hall was a two-story building, put up within the past year, which served for community and private balls and receptions, dancing classes and Masonic meetings and performances by traveling theatrical companies, and by the time they arrived it was crowded with guests who greeted the appearance of Jenny and Pete with joyous welcoming shouts. The room was decorated as the cabin had been, with boughs of fir and cedar and many candles stuck into tin wall sconces, and at the far end three musicians played the "Wedding March" from a balcony scarcely big enough to hold them.

The men attacked Pete with aggressive cordiality, and Pete, his black eyes shining even more brightly than usual, stood at his full height and looked aloof and dignified, as if to warn them away from taking too much advantage of his good humor. But Jenny was kissing the women and accepting the kisses of the men, and had surprised them by seeming to have softened and turned warmer since they had seen her last, and when finally she began the dancing with Lem Finney, she gave Pete a tender smile across Lem's shoulder which those who saw it remembered for some time to come.

Others soon joined them on the dance floor, bottles began to appear, women traveled up and down the back stairs to attend to the littlest children put to sleep there, and wives admonished their husbands not to drink too much.

"Remember what happened when Margaret Pim got married," was the most frequent warning, for only a few months ago when Flora Pim's mother had married Josiah Webb the celebration had at last grown so unruly the bridegroom had taken a shot at the best man and, in retaliation, had been carried away before the consummation of his marriage and kept out in the Gum Patch all night. In a week or two it had seemed a good joke, or so Josiah Webb pretended, but Mrs. Webb was still bitter about the wedding customs of the mountains and declared that nothing of the kind would have happened in New Hampshire.

Matt danced first with Marietta and then with the wives of his various partners, trying all the while not to look at either Pete or Jenny, and when one of them got accidentally into his field of vision he veered off sharply in another direction, carrying his startled partner before him with relentless haste.

It had occurred to Matt at almost the same moment he entered the room that these men, his old friends of Bannack and the early days here in Virginia City, were enjoying a vicarious pleasure as they contemplated that very soon now Jenny and Pete Devlin would be in bed together, and this notion had quickly become an obsession, smiles looked to him like leers and every glance he intercepted was furtive and guilty, so that he began to prowl about the room, coming upon one group and then another and hoping to catch some old friend at his obscene jesting, though what he might do to him when he did, he had no idea. But the remarks he overheard had nothing to do with Jenny or Pete, the jokes were about something else, and after an hour or more had passed he wondered if it was his own imagination which troubled him. Yet he felt a steadily rising rage, which increased until it included at last every man in the room, and he found then to his horror that it included, as well, his brother.

For though it had seemed, even on the day she had told him about it, that the marriage was an impossibly long time in the future, as distant as death or any final disaster, it had come as he had refused to believe it could, and had found him unprepared.

"A woman's life isn't made up of big events or important occasions," Jenny had said, "but only of the things that happen every day, and that's the part of you Marietta has. That's why she can stand this, and why I can't. There's nothing for us to anticipate—every time we meet it's a catastrophe."

He had assured her he knew she must marry and wanted her to, and this had made him feel magnanimous for awhile, but he was unable to summon this feeling now and seemed to have been invaded by every shameful and mean and small, envious quality his nature possessed, forcing him to discover faults more humiliating to his pride than any he had previously acknowledged. For all his resolutions, she continued to seem an inseparable part of himself, and that he must now recognize a final separation was a worse injustice than he had been able to imagine.

But nevertheless Matt reminded himself that it was his responsibility to endure this night without destroying what they had so far preserved, and though eventually he must dance with her or risk the kind of intuitive conclusion by their friends which revealed men's secrets more surely than all their confessions, he found one reason or another for delay as he moved stealthily about the room, his face mutinous and sullen, though he optimistically believed it showed nothing, and when at last someone approached him quietly and placed a hand on his shoulder he wheeled about, wildly glaring. Finding Pete there, he gave a burst of laughter, and shrugged to excuse his peculiar behavior.

"For Christ's sake, Matt, who were you expecting?"

"I'm sorry, Pete. I was thinking about the old days in Bannack, about how far away it is now—and how I almost miss it."

Pete, he realized, had had little or nothing to drink, and while the few drinks Matt had had were ordinarily no more than he could accommodate, he felt that tonight they had hopelessly befuddled him, and, in another moment, was convinced that Pete's sobriety made it possible for Pete to read his face, guess at his thoughts and feelings, as he could never have done if they had met on terms of equal intoxication.

As they stood looking at each other, Matt was caught by a terrified certainty that Pete was about to accuse or denounce him, shout that this man, Matthew Devlin, had been in love with his bride and was still; and, as he waited for it to happen, he was aware that the dancers continued to spin about, while the music seemed to grow steadily louder and less rhythmical, cutting off into jagged, snarling lines from time to time before the weaving and muddled musicians hauled it back to a semblance of its original structure, and the activity of the room grew more confused and bewildering while the laughter had begun to sound to him quite demented.

"Yes, Bannack," Pete agreed, after what seemed to Matt an inconceivably long and dangerous interval of silence. He looked thoughtful and remote, tenderly speculative, and Matt wondered if he was remembering—as he had been himself—the night of the first public ball at Bannack, when Pete had stood about, unable to dance because of his injured ankle, and he had taken advantage of the commotion over Milly Matches to ask Jenny to see him. But, after all, Pete could not remember what he had not overheard, and yet he was convinced that Pete knew everything there was to know about him and Jenny, and that he had come there to tell him so.

While his mind was busy with these lurid preparations, Matt chewed his cigar and rocked slowly backward and forward, keeping his fists deep in his pockets, and was surprised that Pete now turned from him to watch Jenny dancing with Silas Hart. "I've never told this to anyone else, Matt," he said at last, and Matt gave him a sharply challenging glance, thinking that now it was to begin. "Not even Jenny. But I want to tell someone, and you're the one I want to tell. I've been in love with her all this time. Think of it, Matt—more than five years." He smiled confidingly. "But of course I never expected we'd be married. You know what you've always said—that I'm the one in the family who thinks it over, while the rest of you go ahead and do it. Well, this is one time I went ahead and did it, wouldn't you say?"

Pete turned and showed him a broad grin, so startling that Matt stepped backward, as if to avoid it, for though his eyes had become cloudy and unable to focus, the smile was dazzling and almost painful. Pete nodded, as if to say that was the message he had come to deliver, and walked away while Matt asked himself if it had been only the boast of a happy man who was his brother, or the threat of a possessive and jealous husband, still, his brother.

Across the room there was a scuffle, a protesting screech in a girl's artificially hysterical voice, and Matt glanced up to see Jonathan lunge toward Morgan as Morgan, apparently determined to play the dignified older brother, raised one arm to ward him off. Georgina Hart stood with her hands covering her mouth and Lisette ran toward them, crying, "Morgan, I told you!"

Matt moved swiftly, without any clear intention of what he intended to do, but as Jonathan again drew back his fist, Matt grabbed his arm, swinging it violently aside, and shouted, "What's the matter with you two? This is your uncle's wedding reception!"

As if at a military command on the field of battle, both Jonathan and Morgan straightened, bowed with embarrassed apology in the direction of the other guests, and deferentially replied, "Yes, sir."

Matt gave them a meaningful nod, smiled suddenly at the others, and as the musicians resumed their thumping and scratching he turned, feeling once again alert and filled with responsibility, discovered Jenny nearby, and went quickly toward her. "Mrs. Devlin, will you dance with me?"

Jenny smiled, inclined her head, and they went onto the floor while Lisette whispered to Jonathan and Morgan, "What's the matter with you?" They grinned shamefacedly, and she shook her finger at them. "Do your fighting at home. I'm surprised at you." She whirled about and went to dance with Ralph Mercer for the fourth time that night, a declaration which had been noticed by everyone but Matt.

Lem Finney proposed a toast to the bride and groom just as dinner was announced, halting them in their dash toward the tables, for it was his invariable strategy to wait until his audience was eagerly intent upon its next sensation and then to interrupt them and hold them captive for as long as he could. But tonight when he had talked only four or five minutes, Josiah Webb called out, "I'll vote for you any time you want to run for office, Lem, but suppose you do your electioneering some other time. I move we eat."

They rushed at the long table which stood laden with an assortment of all the delicacies the mountains could provide at that time of year, and Jenny went from one woman to another, kissing each one and thanking her with such a show of affectionate gratitude that when she had gone by they exchanged glances of surprise, and whispered that obviously Jenny Danforth had needed to get married again.

Matt had left her the moment the dance ended and now was determined not to look at her again tonight, to think of her no more, and to take charge of himself while he still had time, and this made him almost grateful to Jonathan and Morgan for the flurry they had created which had dragged him so abruptly out of his wallowing self-pity. Aware of a raging hunger, he began to eat with concentrated attention, and, while he did, listened to Count Manzoni describe his newest invention, a machine to destroy grasshoppers, though he would not commit himself to any large investment in it, and was surprised to realize he still had so much prudence and such clear awareness of that world outside himself.

A year ago Count Manzoni had been a barber, and his wife a laundress, but he had shown an aptitude for land speculation which put him nowadays in the company of the town's most respectable citizens, and even though they might not believe he was a nobleman escaped from the revolutionary activities of 1848, they concealed their doubts for the sake of his wife, a little dark woman with a face as clever and sly as a monkey's, and a kind of eager charm which might, they thought, be damaged by their skepticism.

"It's what the Territory needs," Matt told him seriously. "More than anything I can think of."

"Let me show it to you."

"I will, I will. Tomorrow morning—or the next day."

Convinced that food was his salvation, Matt emptied the plate and started back, but partway across the room he became aware that Jenny and Pete were no longer there and, at almost the same moment, heard a whisper: "They've gone." By the time he was packing his plate at random, the news had swept the room, there was a rush of laughter, soft, knowing, and a sudden relaxation, as if this was the moment they had been waiting for.

Matt stared at the food but could scarcely see it, for his eyes had begun to ache as if the blood in his head would burst through them, and it seemed a long while before he was able to clear his vision enough to know what he was doing. He moved slowly down the table, thoughtfully placing a slab of venison beside a slice of dried peach pie, recognizing it as Lisette's from the style of her latticework, as carefully woven as a wicker basket, and he found this so engrossing that he was again taken by surprise to hear a voice speak almost in his ear.

"Sir."

He spun around and, as he saw Morgan beside him, looking puzzled but carefully polite, he smiled and gestured, mumbling that he had been preoccupied, thinking about a deal that had come into the office that morning, and hoped Morgan would not ask which one he meant.

"That's what I wanted to talk to you about, sir. A deal I've got in mind." They stood side by side, each holding a plate piled with food and eating slowly, while Matt looked into every face which passed with a careful and intently searching gaze. His eyes shone brightly and his expression seemed, though he did not know it, to combine fear and rage and sorrow with a profound bewilderment, and it was this which caused every person who glanced at him to look once again, wondering what he might be thinking of and, because he was talking to his oldest son, they supposed there was some business difficulty being discussed between them. "Are you still willing to sell me that mine in Daylight Gulch?"

Matt smiled and found himself unexpectedly pleased to have this transaction to discuss, quite as if Morgan might have sensed his despair and come to rescue him by talking of claims and leases and interest rates and such matters as must drive less rational thoughts from a man's mind. "What's your offer?" He took care to blend in his face and voice the same nice mixture of indifference and interest he would have shown to any prospective buyer who walked into Devlin Brothers without an introduction.

"What do you want for it, sir? As much as you did then?"

"What did I want then?" Matt gave him a sharp, sideways glance, meant to warn him not to imagine his memory was confused, although in fact it was, and he remembered only that the original offer had been intended to demonstrate there was no easy way to make money, even in the midst of a gold strike.

"You wanted eighteen hundred down for your share and eighteen hundred more in six months, and one third of the profits."

Matt whistled with admiration at this hard bargain. "But it doesn't look promising, Morgan, that's why we haven't bothered with it. I don't recommend it, to be truthful."

"I can make it pay, sir. At least, I think I can."

Matt glanced at him again, amused and skeptical, but Morgan looked so intently sober that Matt reprimanded himself for his frivolity, and scowled as he pondered the complexities of this proposition. "You'll never take five thousand out of it, and you'll have to spend more than that to get at whatever is there—but maybe you see something I don't."

"I see something I'm looking for. But I want to own it outright."

"I'm not authorized to sell my partner's share. I'll sell you mine for two thousand, and no interest in the profits."

"I'll give it to you tomorrow."

"Where the hell did you get it?" demanded Matt, surprised. And then he added, almost humbly, "If you want to tell me."

"I located a supply of tobacco for one dollar a pound and sold it for three-fifty. Friend of mine from Butte had it and was in a hurry to sell. He was on his way out of the Territory, and wanted to travel light."

"Oh?" Matt looked at him curiously, pleased and a little sorrowful at one more sign that Morgan was moving surely and steadily away from him. "I'll have to explain about your partner—it happens to be a woman. But that can wait."

Morgan started away as Lisette came running toward them. "I want to tell you something!" She seized each by the wrist, standing very close and looking distractedly from one to the other, seemed almost to lose courage, but then whispered, "Ralph Mercer has proposed to me." She nodded, very earnest now, and as they stared at her as if she had brought some dreadful news, she held them tighter. "Don't tell anyone—until I make up my mind." She smiled, but when they did not, she laughed a little. "Just think," she said, and was gone, back to where Ralph Mercer waited.

"I'll be damned," said Matt, and all at once felt as if he had been stricken with some sickness.

But then, close on the sense of momentary shock and helplessness, he became aware of a deep relief, for Ralph Mercer was a thorough Yankee, not only serious but solemn, and as much addicted to hard work as if he did not know that his family was rich, a grim and stubborn man for his twenty-four years, and these attributes Matt thought he would need if he married Lisette who had—though no one else seemed to suspect it—some of his own lawless inclinations. And, at least, she would not fall into the hands of Zack Fletcher who, Matt thought, might have passed very well for a half-breed if nature had not made him blond, and under whose lenient discipline she would no doubt revert to a natural condition of feminine savagery, quite as a tame mare joined a wild herd and soon became as wild as the others.

"They're getting ready," Morgan said. "We'd better join them."

All about the room men were dragging black hoods over their heads, tipping up bottles to holes in their masks, some were smearing their faces with soot, and there was an increasing commotion, children shrieking in pretended horror and men stalking up and down with their overcoats on backward, waving their arms and laughing ominously as they prepared to charivari the bride and groom. Morgan's head was covered with a loose black hood and Matt now drew his own from his pocket, slid it over his head and shoulders and, as he did, was all at once convinced that he had become entirely invisible.

Very quickly, as if they had waited eagerly for this moment, they took their clattering leave down both stairways, bearing with them their paraphernalia of horns and tin pans and spoons, drums and fiddles and heavy sticks snatched out of the woodbox, and when they assembled in the street they looked like a horde of road agents about to embark on some project more desperate than any which had been undertaken during the early days. The women were crowded at the second-story windows, calling to them to remember that they were gentlemen and the bride was a lady, and they set off at a gallop, hooting and howling, banging upon the pans and firing pistols into the air, scaring the few quiet citizens who were still about, and yelling at the others who ran from the saloons to see them go by. They dashed in a body through the main part of town, past the house where Dr. and Mrs. Danforth had lived, yowling as they went and bringing frightened men and women from their cabins in terror of an Indian attack, but reassured them as they swept on by, yelling: "*Shivaree!*"

Those who arrived first leaped off their horses and banged on the door, and in another few moments the others had dismounted and gathered, some forty or fifty, before the unlighted cabin, and were hammering at the walls, beating pans and blowing horns and threatening to tear the house down if they were not given something to drink.

The noise continued for several minutes without the door opening or a light appearing, for the newlyweds must permit the serenaders to reach their highest pitch and not satisfy them too early. Morgan stood beside Matt and both were yelling crazily, since this was expected of the groom's family, when Jonathan approached so quickly he had struck Morgan a hard blow before either had seen him.

In an instant they were swearing and weaving and darting about, striking and retreating, until Matt sprang between them and forced them apart with a strength which sent them staggering. "God damn you both," he yelled, and struck first at Jonathan and then at Morgan. The hood seemed miraculously to have freed him and he bellowed, "This is your uncle's wedding night!" in a voice which sounded to him like a stranger's, though the words came out with an almost intolerable relief.

At the next moment, seeming to Matt a reply to his shout, though it had been drowned by other voices, the cabin was lighted, there was a sudden stillness among the men, and Pete opened the door and stood smiling at them pleasantly, as if at the most seemly visit from his pastor. He was, to their disappointment, dressed as he had been earlier, his cravat knotted neatly and his hair smoothly brushed, and he gave them a brisk, formal bow.

"Gentlemen, please come in and have a drink." He gestured, as if the cabin could accommodate them easily.

And then, still wearing the purple dress and with a cloak over her shoulders, Jenny appeared beside him. She smiled, but her green eyes were mocking, telling them plainly they were a pack of fools to have come here like this, even if it was the custom of the country. "Please do come in."

The men stood silent and perplexed, and presently some of them began to pull off their hoods.

"Oh, hell, Pete, we're sorry."

"Excuse us, Mrs. Devlin, we just wanted to drink your health."

"Oh, but please do," protested Jenny.

They began to mutter among themselves and a few mounted their horses and started back down the hill, while others debated whether or not they should enter the cabin, and as they mumbled and argued Matt spoke in a sharp undertone to Jonathan.

"What was that all about?"

"He can't have her," whispered Jonathan, and was breathing so hard that he sucked the hood against his face and looked like some weird piece of leaden sculpture. "She's going to marry me. I asked her tonight."

"Holy Christ, next it'll be Annabel."

Morgan and Jonathan shook hands and Morgan was offering his congratulations, but Matt, vaguely aware that these contracts for marriage in his family concerned him, was nevertheless unable to feel that any vital reality existed at that moment apart from his own raging sorrow, directed toward the man and woman still standing side by side in the lighted doorway. Lem Finney and Floyd Hart and four or five men now entered the cabin, passing Jenny as deferentially as if they had not come there in a howling mob only ten minutes before, while the others were saying it was a damn-fool thing to have done and they were sick of it and would go back to Folger Hall and do their drinking there.

Morgan and Jonathan waited for Matt, but as he stood there watching the closed cabin, they started away and Matt was soon alone, staring at the figures which passed before the small window, and when the door opened and Lem Finney came out he moved to where he could not be seen.

He felt an inclination to stay, to watch the others leave until he knew that Jenny and Pete were alone, but the idea disgusted him, and he set out instead at such a pace that he soon overtook Finney and Floyd Hart, and the party arrived at Folger Hall, subdued and embarrassed, to rejoin the women, feeling that they had gone upon an unworthy adventure.

He pulled off the hood and walked quickly to where Marietta was waiting, her face anxious and sad, and bent to kiss her. "Lisette and Jonathan," she whispered, and shook her head, as if she wanted to cry but hoped she would not. "It seems so soon, doesn't it?"

XXIV

Suky consulted no oracles but her face in the mirror and there, several times each day, she searched for signs and portents both good and evil. She was unable to remember her earliest recognition of herself as an ally, but it must have happened a long time ago, for by now these consultations had acquired the significance and even the solemnity of a religious ritual in which she was at once divinity and high priestess, while her only acolyte was Maxine.

Even when Maxine had first been found by Susan among the immigrants at Castle Garden, a girl no more than sixteen or seventeen, able to speak only a little English and terrified of her new country, she had had a knack for arranging hair which had been so improved over the years that with the help of rouleaux and chignons and Japanese bark she could reproduce the most complicated style Suky might describe. Maxine could take a few fresh roses and some bits of wire and twine them into a wreath for Suky to wear with a ball gown; she had taught Suky to draw a line along her eyelashes with kohl, to paint the insides of her nostrils pink, to identify the veins of her breasts with a faint sketching of blue pencil when she wore a low-cut gown, and to use too much perfume, not too little.

At least twice a day, and sometimes more often, Suky and Maxine met to observe the rituals, and they understood each other so well they might spend an hour or more at that dressing table, with Suky gazing intently into her present and past and future across all the carefully arranged paraphernalia of crystal bottles and china jars, tortoise-shell combs, gold-backed brushes and hand mirrors, jewelry and lighted candles and vases of white roses and tuberoses, and neither of them ever speak a word. If Maxine had one quality which made her more valuable than any other it was her intuitive understanding of when to talk and when to keep quiet, for it was during the time she spent making up her face and having her hair dressed that Suky consulted the oracle, reviewed the past, and planned all future strategy.

"You must learn to take advantage of the way you look," her father had told her several years ago, "or other people will use it to hurt you. Real beauty frightens men as well as women."

She had not been pleased by this advice, wondering why he should want to make her distrustful of a gift in which she expected others to rejoice as she did, but before very much longer she had understood that he told her the truth. And, because it had always been easy for Suky to perceive herself as the victim in any situation, she began to plan what she must accomplish for her own protection, until by now it seemed she could never have allies enough.

In ten years she would be thirty, and although Jemima Haldane and other young women she knew were quite sure they could never be that old, however long they lived, Suky had settled upon that year as the crucial one in her life and had made of it a secret goal toward which she worked with as much well-concealed desperation as her father had ever given to any project of his own.

She was glad to be Mrs. Philip Van Zandt, and not very much troubled by his family's objection to the marriage. For these quiet and clannish and conservative relatives of her husband did not seem important to Suky, who thought it would be as futile to revolve only among the retired old families like the Van Zandts—who had retreated in voluntary abdication to small islands which were never visited by those who inhabited other islands in the surrounding rich texture of the city's geography—as it would to be thrown among the shoddyites.

Philip had taken her to visit his three older sisters soon after they had returned from Europe, whimsically explaining that they could never be persuaded to journey so far north as Eighteenth Street, and, after a long conference with Susan and Ceda, it had been decided that she would go, waiving her right to a first visit from them with such casual disdain they would be chagrined by their own rudeness.

After a few days, Philip went to see them again and repeated the conversation to Suky, for Philip liked to tease her, as he called it, though in Suky's opinion it was only a streak of petty cruelty, no more sinister than his other vices. "They all agreed you're very pretty," he assured her. "And Thelma said, 'She's an excellent mimic, too, and that may serve her well enough as things are nowadays.' Ottilie insists that the modern young woman is an entire new species, brought into being by the new money." He looked at her, trying to guess how she had reacted to that, and finally shrugged, admitting, "My sisters have always thought they were their own best company."

"Perhaps they are, Philip."

Suky added these remarks to her list of the faults she found with Philip, but assured herself that if this was his notion of revenge for the absurd figure he cut as Joshua Ching's son-in-law, sent scurrying about like an errand boy from the Exchange to the Gold Room—for Joshua expected him to pretend, at least, to work for his livelihood— then her first premonition, perceived, as it now seemed, only a moment before Joshua had suggested it himself, was a true one, and her marriage to a man who was dependent upon her father left her almost as much freedom as if she were not married at all.

And, if Philip had only known it, the smiles she practiced on him were meant for someone else, and the pleasures they shared were not exclusively theirs, either; for now that the fear of love was gone, her imagination went wandering after new conquests or, as it seemed to her, new ways of assuring her future safety.

She saw Frederic Hallam now and then, usually because Felice had told Frederic the Van Zandts would be at the Academy of Music, or a wedding, or a reception, and at sight of him she became so remarkably, and almost painfully, aware of herself, of the way her hair was dressed, the clothes she wore, the movements of her body and the expressions of her face, that it seemed this magical awareness must cause something startling and decisive to occur between them; but it never did. Frederic watched her with longing, but had spoken to her only briefly, and formally, and Suky concluded that Frederic Hallam was one of those men who accepted his disappointments and made his peace with them.

For Frederic, she had learned after several sessions of gently persuading Felice to tell her something she was concealing, had been intended for some years to marry a second cousin, Alvita Van Alstine. Suky knew who the Van Alstines were, and this convinced her at last that her father had been right when he had told her Roger Hallam would not have allowed Frederic to marry Joshua Ching's daughter.

"It was one of those family understandings," Felice had assured her, when she finally made the confession. "Frederic was away for seven years, you must remember. When he went to Europe she was only eleven, and he hadn't been back more than a few weeks when he met you." Felice spoke of Alvita having been eleven as if she had been only a little girl while she, who was now thirteen, had acquired a lore of mature wisdom which made such children inconsequential. "But after all, Suky, he needed a little time. How could any of us have guessed you would elope?"

"But how could I know—"

"That's the tragedy, Suky. He didn't know, and you didn't know— and now you must always love each other hopelessly." Felice sighed, for it was, Suky knew, what Felice believed to be the hopeless nature of this love between her two idols which gave it its great significance. "I know Frederic. He loves you still, and he will love you always." Felice looked serious, frowned a little but remembered her mother's warning, and touched the tips of her fingers between her eyebrows. "You'll see each other this summer at Long Branch— something will bring you together, I can feel it."

"I'm not at all sure we should see each other. What good can it do?"

Felice's dark eyes grew unusually large, and her small, proud face turned reproachful. "What good can it do? You'll give him a little happiness, just to look at you. Isn't that enough?"

The Talbots had been going to Long Branch ever since Felice had been a baby, for it was part of her father's program that Felice spend the summers riding and swimming and walking—even though he complained that Long Branch had become too gay and too crowded, and there was little hope it would ever again be what it had been once—a retreat for quiet Philadelphians—and Suky thought this might be why Joshua had decided to transport his own family to the seashore this summer.

They had a series of rooms on the second floor of the Stetson House, Joshua and Steven in one, Susan and Ceda in another, Suky and Philip in a third, and one more for the baby and his nurse, and had scarcely arrived when Suky began to plan what she would say to Frederic Hallam—for two years had passed since that first meeting at Jemima Cottrell's wedding to Giles Haldane, and he seemed more a stranger to her than he had that night.

Joshua was in town for several days each week, as were Philip and William Talbot, but there were numbers of young men not much older than Steven who lived in boarding houses and made it their responsibility to see that every girl was a belle; and it was these young men in lavender gloves against whom William Talbot warned Felice.

"It would take at least five hundred of them stewed down to make a teaspoonful of calf's foot jelly," he had told her, and forbade her to dance with them or she would not be allowed to attend the hops. Felice had laughed joyously when she repeated that to Suky, and confided that when she was old enough to fall in love it would not be with any young man in lavender gloves, but with someone so vehement and so forceful she would fall in love with him against her will.

"That's the only real way, isn't it? Not to be able to help yourself. Oh, what a glorious feeling it must be!"

But although Felice became rapturous at the prospect, she was now so busily occupied with the summertime schedule her father had arranged—riding and swimming every morning, and following a program of reading—that when she saw Suky it was as they met in the crowded lobby, or when she paid her a brief visit, played with the baby for a few minutes, and gave her the latest news of Frederic. "He's coming down," she told Suky one day, "to spend the last three weeks of August with friends," and Suky looked so alarmed that Felice slipped her arm comfortingly about Suky's waist, saying, "I know just how you feel."

Felice counted the weeks until Frederic would arrive, and gave Suky from time to time her report of the arithmetical progress made so far, as if these abstruse calculations could not be performed by anyone else. And Suky—who believed that a man's dependence upon a woman was the sum of the pleasures he had enjoyed with her, multiplied by whatever guilt he felt for any harm he might have done her —was at work inventing an ingenious formula to please him with, composed of gaiety and seriousness, for Frederic was not the man to like one without the other, humility and pride, and these two must be even more judiciously mixed, and reticence with passion, the exact recipe for which she sometimes despaired of ever obtaining.

But she had a sustaining conviction that Susan Van Zandt had a particular destiny to enact which would astonish others with its clear and striking pattern, and was, like Joshua, continuously alert for clues and indications of which direction she was meant to travel and so could discover signs posted in the most unlikely places, marking a trail made plain to her but which would have been obscure enough to anyone else. And so one afternoon, when she overheard a quarrel between her parents, she listened carefully, and found one more warning that a woman who neglected to provide for her future while she was still young had made a mistake she could never hope to repair.

The day had been hot and Suky lay, dozing, the shades drawn, thinking of what she would wear that night, and when she heard Susan and Joshua talking on the verandah outside her room, where they had apparently met by accident, she sighed and kicked at her petticoats, wishing they would go somewhere else.

"Look where we are, Joshua," Susan said, and, after some moments, asked, "But how did we get here?"

This remark might have had several meanings, but Joshua seemed to know the one she intended, and Suky woke up all at once, turned onto her side, leaned her chin on her palm and listened with a scornful little smile.

"We're god-damn well off, Susan, as a matter of fact, and since you've had the bad judgment to raise the subject I'd like to remind you we were no more congenial before I made money than we are now. In fact, I think we'd both have some difficulty if we tried to remember just why we got married in the first place."

Suky clucked her tongue, but Susan said slowly, "I remember, Joshua, why I married you."

"You do?" He sounded skeptical.

"I was in love with you." Suky raised her eyebrows and shook her head, marveling that these two people who had brought her into the world might have missed marrying each other and never produced herself. "That didn't last very long, did it?"

"I have no idea," replied Joshua imperturbably, "how long it lasted. You were more tactful then than you are now." Suky nodded approvingly at this direct hit. "We've lived this way for years, Susan, and it's been as much your preference as mine. Now why in the name of God do you choose this moment to maul it over?" Suky could imagine the stern and majestic gaze he was directing on her, which had never been so effectively persuasive with Susan as it was with other people. "In fact," he asked Susan, "what the hell ails you?"

"Joshua, do you know how old I am?"

Thirty-nine, replied Suky silently, but Joshua suggested, "Thirty-eight?"

"Thirty-nine. I'm thirty-nine years old."

"At least that's one thing you can't blame me for." Suky smiled again, shaking her head, for her father had learned to hold his own in these domestic contests, and was not scrupulous as to how he did it, either.

Susan's voice answered sadly. "I have a grandchild. Everything's over—and I can't make myself accept it."

"That's absurd, Susan. Why, you're still a very beautiful woman. You always will be."

"Men never admire women after they're through being really young."

"Men seem to admire Coral Talbot," said Joshua, and Suky sat up at this, even more alert.

"But not because she's young, you know that."

And then, to Suky's keen disappointment, Ceda interrupted them, their voices disappeared back into their rooms and Suky lay down again, flat on her back with her arms behind her head, and stared at the ceiling, narrowing her eyes as she considered these warnings:

that love was brief and time passed at a treacherous speed; and all at once she caught her breath, opened her eyes wide as if at recognition of some command, and fell to pondering over this prophecy —that she would have Frederic Hallam's child. Why it should have occurred to her at just this moment, in some bright aftermath of that quarrel, she could not guess, but in only a little longer she was convinced that it was inevitable, beyond any power of her own or Frederic's to prevent, and it even seemed she had known it for a long while, perhaps since their first meeting. And, after that, she found new portents and signals strewn all along her path.

Near midnight, in the ballroom, Joshua appeared and asked her to dance. And when they had circled the room three or four times, she asked him, a little humorously, what it could possibly be which kept him occupied at all hours nowadays with Amos Cottrell and Lorenzo Flagg and, sometimes, William Talbot. "Everyone's curious."

"They are?" He smiled.

"But what are you talking about, Papa?"

"Railroads."

She leaned back so that she could look up at him, tilting her head sideways, and murmuring, "Oh—railroads," and she sighed.

The dance ended and he guided her to the verandah, where all day long men sat with their feet on the railing, smoking cigars and reading newspapers, but which was hung now with colored lanterns and decorated with rows of palms, and they joined the slow procession. "Next month," Joshua said, "is young Joshua's first birthday, isn't it?"

"Time flies," she conceded.

"Exactly. He must have a little brother or sister. You're happily married, aren't you?"

"Well, Papa!" she retorted.

"Six or eight children should be the average product of a well-assorted marriage, wouldn't you say?"

"Six or eight? Papa, where did you get such an idea?"

"You well-brought up young girls," said Joshua chidingly. "How does it happen you all turn out to be hypocrites?"

"You want us to be genteel—and then you accuse us of being hypocrites."

Joshua laughed. "Well, then, three or four."

"Three, perhaps."

"This modern fad for small families is pernicious. Your mother would be less discontented today if she had had more children."

"Papa, do you remember that you promised me to refurnish the house after young Joshua was born?"

Joshua glanced at her suspiciously. "What has that to do with what we're discussing?"

"But you do remember, don't you?"

"I can't afford it just now. I have too many commitments."

"It's old-fashioned and it's hideous. I hate it." They had returned to the ballroom and Suky left him, smiling and giving a little wave over her shoulder, while Joshua looked vaguely perplexed, but replied to her smile with that reluctant admiration he felt each time she made him realize, to his own discomfiture, that although their ways were different, they were very much alike.

And she had, like Joshua, no inclination to make a decision and then hurry into it, but preferred to come to it slowly, after various advances and retreats, a prolonged reconnoitering, until at last she gave herself up to what had come to seem irresistible; and so she set out each morning at eleven o'clock to walk with Susan and Ceda to where they met Felice having her morning swim, with some vague apprehension that this might be the day when Felice would tell her Frederic had arrived. And, much too soon, as it seemed, that was what Felice told her.

A grassy plateau ran along the bluff above the ocean, and across the avenue stood the hotels with their tall pillars and multiple verandahs, embellished with fretwork and painted in dull yellows, reds, and browns. Flags and banners blew from the rooftops, as if a victorious army had encamped there, and the striped awnings at every window, the gilded domes and spinning weather vanes of the gambling houses, gave it more than ever the air of belonging to some barbaric chieftain. Every hotel was surrounded by beds of bright flowers, and on their lawns brass bands sent up a competitive din. Women, dressed as elaborately at ten in the morning as they had been the night before, drove in open carriages, and some of the footmen looked as if they had stolen their livery from the wardrobe of the Academy of Music. Riders went galloping by, and on the boardwalks women clung to their skirts and hats, for the strong winds might turn a woman's costume inside out, and had sometimes loosened entire coiffures and sent them wafting away.

Nearly perpendicular flights of stairs descended to the beach, and Susan and Ceda and Suky approached them each day with misgivings, wrapped their skirts about their legs and, when at last they stepped onto the sand, glanced at one another with relief, then settled their skirts and adjusted their hats and raised their parasols again. The beach was crowded for two or three miles in either direction, although few were in bathing clothes, and fewer still went into the ocean.

They looked about for Felice, saw her in the distance with a group of girls, all of them in ankle-length Zouave trousers covered by short skirts, jackets and small straw hats, and as she caught sight of them Felice came bounding across the sand, buoyant and unself-conscious as a young animal, and showing her usual eager delight at the comparative freedom of her bathing dress and the excitement of the wind and sun and the sound of the ocean slamming upon the beach.

Felice had grown much taller during the past two years and, it seemed, was not destined for her mother's rich figure but had inherited the spare and elegant frame of her father; and her eyes still overpowered her face with their intensity and radiance, as if she were

more concerned with observing the world around her than in reflecting upon that other one within herself.

"Oh, Suky, I wish you'd come, too!"

Felice had often begged Suky to go into the water, assuring her
she would be astonished at the sensation, not only for the way it
would make her feel while she was there and perhaps somewhat unpleasantly surprised by the coldness and heavy force of the surf, but
for the invigoration she would feel later. But although to look at Suky
and listen to her laugh, it might have seemed that water was her
natural element, she had no intention of subjecting herself to the
freezing waters, only to emerge looking like nothing so much as a
scarecrow on a rainy day. That was all very well for Felice, who was
only a child, but for Suky it would be an experience as disastrous as
if she had been dumped down a coal chute on her way into the ballroom.

Suky smiled, but shook her head. "No, darling, not this morning."

"But it makes you feel so splendid." And she gazed at Suky wistfully, before she dashed away, calling, "Well, good-bye, here I go!"

Felice went prancing about in the waves, was knocked down and
sprang up again, and soon came scampering toward them with that
frightening energy and enthusiasm which possessed the bathers at
the moment they left the water, making them seem all at once in
opposition to those who stood in their blowing skirts and sack coats,
struggling with parasols or leaning a cane into the sand, enduring
but still combating the elements and dreading the return climb up
the steep side of the cliff, and as Felice ran to one of the little dressing rooms which lined the bluff, Suky became aware of a curious
apprehension, for Felice seemed eager to tell her something.

Felice was back in a few minutes, wearing a white blouse with a
blue pleated skirt and straw hat, her hair hanging in a long, wet
pigtail down her back, and her skin looking as if it had been polished
by the salt water. And as she started up the steep stairs, for Susan
always insisted that Felice lead the way, she gave Suky a brief significant glance and whispered, "He's here." And then she went
tripping nimbly up the steps and stood watching as they toiled toward
the top, taking each in turn by the hand as they stepped back onto
the plateau.

Suky had reacted to the news with a kind of dizzy shock which
made her expect even more than she usually did to lose her footing
and go tumbling back, head over heels, into the throng of men and
women who stood below, and even thought it might be a relief if
she did. But when she and Felice had walked ahead, Suky asked,
"Have you seen him?"

"This morning. He came to the hotel and we had breakfast together. Oh, I was praying you would come in—Suky, aren't you
happy? You look a little strange," she added doubtfully.

"Do I, darling? I'm sorry. But these things are serious, perhaps
more serious than you realize, Felice."

"It's because it's serious that it's important. If it were only a flirtation, well, of course you would never demean yourself with such a thing."

Suky looked into Felice's intense and candid little face, trying to remember when she had been as young as that, seven years ago, and felt that perhaps she never had been. "No, Felice, I wouldn't." And that, at least, was the truth.

"You'll see him on Saturday, at the picnic. Frederic and I have everything arranged. We'll ride—and that won't make anyone suspicious because Father knows I'm mad for riding on the beach—and he'll be waiting at a place we know, where Frederic and I used to ride when I was young. And he told me that I must stay with you every minute. 'You know how cruel people can be to a beautiful woman, Felice,' he said to me." Felice looked extraordinarily proud as she repeated these words. "You see how much he loves you?"

"Yes," Suky agreed, and fell thoughtfully silent, for she was busy changing the dress she had intended to wear for this first meeting with Frederic Hallam. She had been imagining that she and Felice would go driving one afternoon and would meet him accidentally on Ocean Avenue, where everyone in the resort appeared at four o'clock, but this pleased her even better, for if there was one costume she thought more becoming than a ball gown, it was a riding habit of strict tailoring with a long chiffon veil and her pale hair twisted tight beneath a black silk hat. "I see."

XXV

Suky and Felice, on shining and lively horses, led the procession which strung along Ocean Avenue for almost half a mile, attracting curious glances as it passed. Suky's four cousins and Steven followed, also on horseback, after them came two carriages with the women and two more with the men, who were looking sober and reserved—perhaps to indicate that even on this frivolous occasion there was no frivolity among them, for they had the world's work to do. And in their wake rode two hacks sent by the hotel bearing blankets and dishes and baskets of food, bathing clothes for the children and servants to wait on them, for this was no ordinary picnic but a kind of grand outing to celebrate the founding of the Corporate Engineers.

The Corporate Engineers had been in the process of being created ever since Lorenzo Flagg had discovered the charter of the Ohio Fiscal Agency a year and a half ago, but it might never have come into existence if he had not at last despaired of finding a way to profit by his discovery without letting anyone else share those profits, for Flagg's early experience of cheating his partner of his share of the California venture had made him suspicious of ever having a partner again; but then at last he realized it was an impossible dream, and began to wonder what he must do next.

He had known Joshua Ching and Amos Cottrell for most of the years they had been in Wall Street, and they had been in pools together, had shared some minor successes and failures; but it was not until Joshua Ching had put together his syndicate for acquiring control of De Groot Distilleries and, in spite of his reputation, had played none of the tricks which pool managers often did, that Flagg had begun to consider taking him into his confidence. When Joshua had organized the Metropolitan Sand and Gravel Company, asking him to participate in that also, Flagg decided that it must be true, as men were saying, and Joshua Ching was a man worth courting. Amos Cottrell, in spite of the fiasco of his son-in-law, continued to prosper, and when Lorenzo Flagg at last persuaded his banker William Talbot to join them, it seemed they had as flexible and functional a group as any of them could hope for.

Even so, several months passed while they dickered with the Ohio Fiscal Agency for its charter and small railroad, and when they agreed to buy it for five hundred thousand dollars, Joshua was still protesting. "That's a hell of a lot of money for a few miles of buckled iron in northern Ohio."

"We're not paying for their buckled iron, or the rust on the nails, either," William Talbot told him, and there was a look on his face which made Joshua wonder if he suspected him of not being able to provide his share. "We're paying for their charter and nothing else, and if the company officers hadn't let themselves be scared by an investigation, we wouldn't get it for that. What do you say, gentlemen? We've spent time enough on this, in my opinion."

Joshua's heart had begun beating at a hard, uncomfortable speed, his throat and mouth were so dry that he sucked on his cigar, and his head felt as if it were expanding against his hat, all the sensations he had come to expect whenever he made one more move in the direction of acquiring his fortune. Flagg and Cottrell agreed, Flagg gloomily and Cottrell with his usual amiable smile, as if money had no desperate significance for him, Joshua nodded his assent curtly, and now it was done.

But De Groot's example remained clear in his mind—though he saw De Groot infrequently—and every now and then it seemed he got a pungent whiff of the smell of De Groot but could not account for where it had come from, quite as if some wandering, swamplike odor recalled from a childhood summer outing had invaded his nostrils while he strolled down Fifth Avenue. De Groot had begun several law suits, intended to recover his company, but this was a minor nuisance, for he had not enough money left to persuade a judge; and it puzzled Joshua that he should continue to be, in this curious way, haunted by him, for it almost seemed De Groot was warning him to take care the same disaster did not happen to him.

On this morning, however, as he rode with Flagg and Cottrell and Talbot, discussing the Corporate Engineers, Joshua felt joyously convinced that this was the beginning and not the end of his progress.

"We won't bother with Washington until after the elections, don't you agree?" Cottrell asked William Talbot. "Why waste money on men who may disappear this fall?"

"Do you know Grant?" Talbot asked him.

"No, but I know some of his friends. Do you know him?"

"Certainly not," Talbot said, and the suggestion seemed offensive to him. "Nevertheless, I can handle the matter when the times comes. And you, Joshua, can manage for us in Albany?"

Joshua nodded gravely, as if he could do that and much more, whenever it was required of him. "I can." What he was to manage in Albany, in fact, was to have their Ohio charter metamorphosed into a New York state charter with perpetual privileges, so that they could use it for other enterprises, too. "But I don't think it will be cheap." He was rather pleased to make demands of his own upon their money.

"Who's your man there?"

"Amasa Stirt."

"Stirt," Talbot repeated, and stared off at the ocean. "Amasa Stirt would rather do a thing badly than permit someone else to do it well."

"It takes a hundred thousand nowadays," Flagg said dolorously, "to accomplish what used to be done with one thousand."

"The War destroyed the country's moral fiber," Joshua assured them, but Talbot contradicted them again.

"Nonsense. We're no more corrupt than our parents. We simply have more money. The nation is richer, there's nothing more sinister to it than that."

"All the same, William," Amos Cottrell reminded him, "it's made a hell of a difference in the way we do business."

"It's also made all of us a hell of a lot richer than we would have been otherwise."

This comfortable talk of riches in the presence of rich men made Joshua scornful of his earlier misgivings and, indeed, he was beginning to regard those nervous reactions to each new enterprise with philosophic detachment, very much as if he had suffered from some ailment which recurred from time to time, under peculiar circumstances, but which otherwise left him free to move about as normal men did and even to feel quite healthy. And, it was true, these attacks did not occur so often as they once had when the prospect of making any sum of money at all had set him spinning and weaving to distraction.

For Joshua had by now surrounded himself with such numerous

evidences of his developing power that whenever he began to fear
that he had, like De Groot, overextended himself, would presently
collapse entire and, when they investigated his corpse, be found to
have contained nothing but schemes and fears, he could count these
evidences over one by one, and so reassure himself.

There was De Groot Distilleries, the Metropolitan Sand and Gravel
Company, and now the Corporate Engineers, not to mention his network of investments which varied each day by hundreds of thousands of dollars and often by a million or more. There was his new
firm of Van Zandt and Ching, and there was his grandson Joshua
Van Zandt. Susan was sometimes troublesome but Ceda was docile,
Suky was just at the beginning of her own achievements, and only
Steven gave him some qualms, for Steven, after all, was his destined
heir.

Still, the boy's stiff and sullen dignity was envied by other fathers,
and Joshua had very early undertaken to train Steven so that he
need never suffer the humiliation of men whose sons waited only until they had their full growth to mount the dunghill and begin to
challenge their parents' supremacy. For if Steven was capable of being hard with others but obedient with him, ambitious to grow but
not to usurp, dominant abroad and prudent at home, then they might
work together as time went by, but if he had not that much common
sense, Joshua was prepared to set him loose to make his own way,
and Steven knew this.

With all these assets presently to his credit, it seemed to Joshua
he had become a patriarch of ancient mold and stamp, a man who
ruled his family with sternness and justice, who dispensed his favors
and sometimes withheld them; who, indeed, dominated his private
world as a man should do.

And, of course, there was Rose Michel, of whom he had not yet become sated even though nearly a year had passed since the night he
had outlined the conditions under which he would support her, and
she had agreed to live with him.

He had rented a small brownstone for her on West Twenty-first
Street, not far from Fifth Avenue and a walk of only three or four
minutes from the hotel, so that he often stopped there early in the
morning on his way downtown and had stayed there whenever he
was overnight in the city this summer. The house, which he had
rented furnished, was filled with black horsehair chairs and sofas,
worn carpets and faded draperies and lithographs, and the beds and
wardrobes were, in his opinion, hideously ornate, like miniature
Gothic cathedrals, but even so he had not offered to buy new furniture and kept to his resolution not to begin too soon to live like a
rich man, for he had seen the expense of it bankrupt many of them.

He forbade Rose to visit the old friends of her days at Annie
Wood's or *The Black Crook,* but did not ask himself what else she
found to amuse her, for Rose Michel, after all, had renounced her

rights in order to live irresponsibly and lazily, although precariously, upon her youth and good looks and talents as a voluptuary. He had warned her that whenever he came there—and his visits were erratic, dictated not only by whimsical desire but also by jealousy— she was to be fresh and dainty and as well dressed as the money he gave her would permit, and this responsibility alone he believed would prevent her from getting bored, if she had sense enough to be bored.

But her breath always smelled as if she had been eating apples, she was clean as a prize cat, her round little face, childish and pathetic, was very appealing to him, and whenever he did not see her for a few days he began to wonder if she had yet found a way to be unfaithful to him, though this would have taken more ingenuity than he thought she had, for he had appointed Spinnage and Achroyd as her guardians.

Whenever he had business nowadays with Hoke O'Neil or Oliver Foss they met there rather than in the private dining room of a restaurant, where he had always felt that someone in the next room had his ear to the wall, for Joshua's natural inclination toward suspicion was aggravated by his increasing wealth. And when the time came to draw Senator Stirt into the Corporate Engineers, Joshua would begin by inviting him to dinner at Rose Michel's house.

They were still talking of the Corporate Engineers when they arrived at the picnic site, and in a very few moments the footmen were spreading blankets and rugs upon the sand and strewing cushions over them, the children ran about shrieking, baskets of food were unpacked on trestle tables, champagne was opened for the women and whisky for the men, and soon there was a big bonfire a hundred yards down the beach, for the day had become chill and the ocean was cold and dark and violent.

Joshua, with the other men, drank off a tumblerful of whisky and went to inspect the food, finding a scallop of chicken and mushrooms, cold potted fowl and tongue ornamented with jelly, a veal pie in a fancifully cut crust, molded puddings, and baskets of fresh fruit. The children danced about distractedly, begging to be permitted to eat, but it was proposed that everyone walk on the beach, collect shells, study the grasses and small flowers which grew in crevices on the bank, and attempt seriously and conscientiously to become a part of sand and ocean, wind and shells, and the women as they walked ahead did discuss these things, though the men continued to discuss business.

They strode along with their sack coats blowing, gloved hands clasped behind their backs, gravely discussing the recent news of Wall Street, who had failed and who had gained, who had gone down and why he had, quickly passed the women who went dawdling along picking up shells and examining bird tracks, and were so deeply engrossed in rumors of stocks about to be split and reissued

that they saw neither the sand, the sky, the small flowers growing
on the bank, nor anything else the picnic had been designed to show
them.

Far down the beach Suky and Felice were galloping and splashing
along the edge of the water, and all at once they went flying off and
had soon disappeared.

They rode very fast, with Felice looking back now and then to be
sure they were not being followed, and it seemed to Suky her fear of
him had gone, been blown away in the salt air and drowned in the
noise of the surf, and she asked Felice, "What if he didn't wait?"

"Suky, how can you think of such a thing? He'd wait all day long
and all night, too." And a few minutes later she cried, "There he is!"
Felice lifted one arm and waved, calling his name, but the sound of
the ocean took it away.

Frederic came riding toward them and Felice gave her horse a
sharp flick with her crop, sending him into a headlong gallop, and as
she and Frederic passed each other their fingers touched and Felice
continued on up the beach, but Suky reined in her horse and sat
waiting, and found herself once again uncertain and mistrustful.

They were silent, looking intently at each other, as if at each new
meeting they must discover whatever it was that had confounded
them during those waltzes at Jemima Cottrell's wedding. Finally,
with an extraordinary seriousness, he said, "Thank you for coming,
Susan," and she smiled, but the smile was diffident, only trembled
briefly on her lips and was gone, and she was surprised to feel some
impulsive yearning to cry.

"I wanted to see you." Her voice was so low, scarcely audible, that
he perhaps supposed it to be an accusation, and looked even more
serious than before.

She held out one hand, and when he had helped her dismount they
began to walk and, for some time, had nothing to say. Frederic
glanced at her every now and then, but Suky, moving along beside
him with gliding steps, pretended to be absorbed in the place itself,
the strong wind which whipped at her skirts and had loosened a
strand of hair, the little hopping birds at the water's edge and the
gulls wheeling and calling overhead, while far away Felice was
capering her horse, maneuvering him through one pattern after another, and when she made him prance on his hind legs Suky laughed
aloud and Frederic smiled, perhaps taking this laughter to be her
forgiveness.

They stopped and turned to each other, as if each waited to hear
the answer to some unspoken question, and Frederic reached out and
caught the strand of blowing hair, tucking it beneath her hat with a
deliberate and tender concern, and at last said, "I wanted to marry
you, Susan—didn't you know that?"

Suky looked down the beach, watching Felice. "My father had his
plans made," she said slowly, for she was no more eager than Joshua
would have been to admit there might have been some family objec-

tions to their marriage. She glanced at him, finding that same expression of profound and guilty seriousness, telling her Frederic Hallam lived with an uneasy conscience, a ready fear of having committed some inadvertent injury, and so she added, "What could I have told him, Frederic?"

He frowned, accepting the blame. "It was my fault—I should have talked to him."

"But you didn't know, and I didn't know—as Felice says." She smiled, a little more confident now, though she still looked troubled and sad.

"I'm a cautious man, I suppose, conservative by nature and by training, but it was my plan that in another year or two we would be married—"

They heard Felice's warning cry and Felice came galloping toward them, pointing down the beach, where another rider had appeared from the direction of the picnic site. In another moment Felice was beside Suky and they were on their way, with Felice saying consolingly, "You'll see him again soon, I promise you. Look—it's your cousin Ada. Can you look calm? Leave everything to me."

"Where have you been?" Ada called. "Your mother sent me to find you," she told Felice. "Everyone was beginning to worry."

"We met one of the natives," Felice said coolly. "He wanted us to buy his shell collection, but we didn't have any money."

And as they rode, with Ada and Felice arguing about whether or not it was safe for two young females alone to stop and palaver over sea shells, Suky was thinking of Frederic's face, the expression in his eyes, the gesture of his hand as he replaced that strand of hair, and from all these signs and intimations it seemed she could infallibly perceive that once he had made love to her he would take her as his responsibility as surely as if he had married her.

They reached the picnic site to find the others eating, and Felice went quickly to her mother, delivered a terse, respectful explanation and then, like a royal courier, marched soberly to her father and recited the same message to him, but she avoided looking at Suky again until they met some time later at the table where they were selecting fruits for their dessert, and Suky was amused to see that her dark eyes sparkled all the more with the challenge of outwitting these hostile troops. "In a few days," she whispered, "we'll ride over and call on the Laceys. He'll be there."

"But you mustn't leave us alone again, Felice."

"I won't, I promise. But even if you saw him alone you can trust him, Suky, you must believe that."

"It isn't Frederic I don't trust, it's other people."

"Oh, I know, I know exactly what you mean."

They met, with Felice as chaperone, three times more, and then he came to the Stetson House for the season's last Grand Hop. There, as they strolled on the verandah, they encountered Joshua passing with Cottrell and Flagg, and although Joshua seemed scarcely to notice them, being so deep in the Corporate Engineers, Suky was aware that her father never failed to notice anything of possible interest to his present or future plans, and would be most unlikely to overlook Frederic Hallam wherever he met him. And so it had been this time, for Joshua said nothing about Frederic for several days and then, when she no longer expected it, met her early one morning in the lobby and took her by surprise as he liked to do.

The activities of early summer were now being enacted in reverse, lines of men stood before the desk checking out, porters bearing trunks on their backs were dashing down the staircases to throw them into vans and busses, and in another few days the summer holiday would end. They talked for a moment as Suky indifferently watched the busy men and women, who had recently begun to whirl about the hotel as if they had suffered some belated attack of conscience for the idle weeks, and Joshua seemed to be thinking of other things until all at once he said, "Are you blaming me, Susan?"

Suky, standing very straight and motionless, her gloved hands lightly clasped, seemed more puzzled by this question than surprised. "Blaming you, Papa?"

"Yes, you do, but you're mistaken. He's mistaken, too, for I've no doubt he believes what he tells you." This was Joshua's usual tactic, to pretend he had overheard private conversations, and Suky continued to watch the activity all about her, as if these frantic men and women belonged to some curious separate species. "William Talbot told me the other day he is going to marry his cousin, one of the Van Alstine girls. Suky, are you listening to me?"

"Yes, Papa, I am."

"You're angry, but even if you are, don't forget what I've told you, a woman must never extemporize with her life."

"I haven't. I won't."

"You've thought very carefully about what you're doing?"

Suky smiled, but only briefly, and went back to her contemplation of harassed men and fretful children and impatient women. "I have thought about it carefully, Papa."

It occurred to Joshua that this would be a good moment to offer to refurnish Philip's house, but though he was on the edge of it, prudent voices spoke in his ear, reminding him that the Corporate Engineers had taken another fifty thousand dollars last week, that the bills for this summer excursion were unpaid, and there was still to be arranged the qualification of the New York charter, which Hoke O'Neil had assured him could be done if he and his friends were willing to meet the going price on perpetual state charters.

And Hoke's own price had risen steadily since that first meeting at Mrs. Gosnell's boarding house two years and a half ago, so that Joshua sometimes looked at him resentfully, wondering how it was these Irish politicians had captured him and other respectable men in their toils; for the city belonged to them, the state itself was under siege, and Hoke had once confided their designs were larger still. But nevertheless Hoke continued to live in two rooms above the Red Onion and spent his days hurrying about the ward which, when Joshua was occasionally forced to visit it to inspect the warehouses, made his skin crawl with apprehension of strange diseases, and he was as eager to escape as if he might be chained there and forced to spend the rest of his life in the midst of this stinking filth.

"Where does the money go, Hoke?" he asked him one morning, when Hoke accompanied him through the warehouses, followed by four members of his Bible class and two clerks Joshua had brought. "I see the diamonds get bigger and your clothes are more expensive, but where's the carriage and horses and the brownstone and yacht?"

"A guy like me don't need all that crap—what's more, I don't want it. But I do need money because that's the way you buy their loyalty, not with kind words and promises to think the situation over but with this, right here." He reached into his pocket and jingled some coins. "Take a walk with me someday. I'll show you families living in cellars where in a bad rain the kids can row a boat. Hogs in the same room with people. Rooms so dark you can't see your hand in front of your face in the middle of the day, where two or three families live together and a man's never too sure whose wife or kid it was he just screwed. Old whores so sick and ugly they only come out late at night to catch the drunks. Women lying dog-drunk on a July afternoon in the manure piles they call a back yard." Hoke jingled the coins again. "What do I do with it, you say?"

"You can't help them."

"They think I can and they think I do."

"It's your money, do what you like with it." It was true, however, that even after he had given it to Hoke, Joshua continued to regard it as his own, and Hoke's careless use of it offended him. "But I would think you'd like to move uptown."

Hoke gave a sharp laugh. "A likely figure I'd cut uptown, now wouldn't I? Another wild Irishman with my nose busted to show I didn't have a proper upbringing." Joshua glanced at him as they walked among the whisky barrels, stepping through puddles and treading lightly over the rotten flooring, and Hoke's face had a bitter shrewdness. "Too many guys have moved uptown lately who should have known better. They think the public's dumb and it is but it ain't completely blind, at least not when the Boss rides by in a coach with four matched horses. Well, that's their worry, only sometimes I wish they didn't have to show everything they've got. Nobody loves a rich man, and everybody suspects him." Hoke shrugged. "Well, anyway, it's a feast of bones while it lasts."

"Shall we talk to Stirt before the state elections, or wait?"

"Wait for what?" Hoke inquired practically. "We know how they're coming out. Let's get on with it."

But Amasa Stirt, Hoke warned him, was a stickler for keeping his dignity and would undertake to arrange no bribes at all unless it was done upon the most genteel basis. "A good dinner," Hoke prescribed.

"Champagne and a little game of draw, and a couple of pretty girls to rest his eyes." And, with an air of modest generosity, Hoke suggested, "I'll bring my girl, you'd be surprised what she looks like when she's dressed up and has her hair combed."

Joshua had seen Hoke's girl several months before when he was leaving the Red Onion and a shrill young voice had called, "Hi, Mr. Ching! Say hello to Rose for me, will you?" Joshua had straightened abruptly, enraged that he had been called by name in this part of town, and discovered her leaning her elbows on the second-story window sill and smiling down at him with gay familiarity. Her blond hair was caught up in a tangle into which she had stuck a few hairpins, as if a child were trying to learn to arrange its hair as grownups did, her eyelids were smudged with kohl, and the shawl which was wrapped about her shoulders seemed to be all she had on. "Rose is a friend of mine," she explained, and spread her hands, making a grimace at Hoke, as if to say she had not meant to start any trouble with so innocent a remark.

Joshua glared at Hoke, and Hoke picked his teeth. "My girl, Tessie Spooner."

"Does she know Rose?"

"They used to work in the same cat house, it seems."

Joshua, who preferred to forget how Rose had acquired some of her most valuable arts, spoke coldly and severely to Tessie Spooner. "Have you seen each other recently?"

At this Tessie fluttered her hands protestingly, for now Hoke was glowering at her. "No, Mr. Ching, I haven't seen Rose since she left Annie—I haven't seen her for a hell of a long time. She met some of the other girls in Stewart's one day and they told her about Hoke and Rose asked Hoke about me when he was there last and so help me God that's all there is to it!" She slammed the window down and disappeared and Joshua, after giving Hoke one more reproving scowl, entered his carriage and drove away.

Rose, when he had accosted her with this information, had first declared she did not know Tessie Spooner and had retreated, steadily pursued by him, through one lie after another, until at last she admitted she had met two girls from Annie Wood's on a shopping expedition and, as they stood gossiping over ribbons and laces and artificial flowers, Hoke O'Neil had been mentioned. By the time she had made this confession, Rose was crying such piteous sobs that Joshua forbade her to discuss the subject any longer.

"Don't become friendly with those girls again."

"I won't, oh, I wouldn't dream of it." She closed her eyes, feebly gasping. "I want to forget all about it, just pretend those terrible things never happened to me."

Still, if it was Hoke's opinion that a pretty girl would make Amasa Stirt more comfortable, Joshua thought it more preferable to have a girl Hoke could control than one who might talk about the meeting. "She wouldn't dare open her trap, I can promise you that."

"Bring her along, then."

Joshua had some misgivings about the way Tessie Spooner would look, even with her hair combed, and was relieved when she arrived with Hoke to find that either she or someone had learned to arrange her hair, she had adopted a shy, demure manner and reduced her voice almost to a whisper, and she wore a modestly cut and fashionable gown which Joshua guessed had cost Hoke O'Neil about one thousand dollars of Joshua Ching's money.

Senator Stirt presently arrived and Tessie was introduced as Miss Michel's cousin, visiting her from Buffalo, and while the men drank whisky and water, Rose and Tessie withdrew to the far side of the room, sat primly on a sofa and talked in low voices, looking all the while like two schoolgirls who must be discussing beaux and parties.

Amasa Stirt, whom Joshua had seen only twice at McDuff's, seemed suspicious and hostile, and Joshua imagined that he was criticizing the old-fashioned furniture and thin carpets and had possibly been influenced by them to take an unfavorable attitude toward the Corporate Engineers, so that Joshua longed to sweep away horsehair sofas and lithographs in one gesture and cursed himself for not having replaced them long ago, thinking that the fault was more Rose's than his own, for it had been her responsibility to show him how they might look to someone else. And all the while, he and Hoke O'Neil and the senator stood slowly drinking, studying one another's faces, and talking about the national elections.

The senator was several inches shorter than Joshua and his body was thin but for a taut, round belly which tempted Joshua to thump it. His head was large and he emphasized its size by combing his whiskers and hair into a flaring halo so that his eyes seemed to peer from the midst of a great, round brush, and this effect must have been the one he wanted, for now and then he took out a comb and, to Joshua's deep disgust, swiftly ruffled his whiskers. But the gesture reminded Joshua of a preening male grouse and made him glad of Tessie Spooner's presence, though the senator had taken care not to glance at her after his first surprised and thoughtful scrutiny.

The senator became more congenial when he sat down to dinner, found Tessie beside him and terrapin soup steaming in his nostrils, and by the time he was pulling apart a pheasant stuffed with walnuts and drinking a third glass of champagne, he and Joshua had begun to discuss the recently opened road for trotting horses in Harlem Lane, and Tessie, Joshua guessed, had brushed his leg a time or two as she retrieved the napkin from her slippery silk lap. Hoke seemed bored with this preliminary discussion, in spite of his earlier warning that they must proceed carefully with Stirt, for the senator might try to play honest, and at last interrupted them.

"Horses are fine for the rich but the poor need other ways to get about, which brings us to the Corporate Engineers." Joshua and Senator Stirt exchanged glances to indicate that this irrepressible fellow was amusing in his own way, but continued to discuss horses until Hoke announced sharply, "Bugger the horses. Let's get on with the railroad."

Joshua glanced at Rose and she and Tessie left the room, though not before Tessie had dropped her napkin again and given the senator such a smile when he picked it up that Joshua had some misgivings Amasa Stirt would be able to keep his mind on the Corporate Engineers. The senator turned to Joshua, frowning. "I've heard about your company, Mr. Ching. Very good men in it, solid men." He nodded approvingly. "But what is your problem again? It's slipped my mind."

"We have no great problem, Senator," Joshua assured him, and, as he began to describe the Corporate Engineers, felt that reliable renewal of himself, his coercive powers which he always doubted until he became aware they had once more appeared at his summons. The senator interrupted him with questions Joshua thought frivolous, and Joshua continued imperturbably to build a pyramid before the senator's eyes and to pile upon it trunk lines and main lines, all passing through fertile farms, surmounting it with fifty million dollars in capitalization, deftly balancing charters and land grants and mortgage bonds upon his structure, until the senator gazed at him in mesmerized rapture. "There," said Joshua softly, "is our plan." He made a slow, spreading motion of his long, straight-fingered hands, and laid them flat upon the table top.

The senator mused for a time in silence, as if he might be making an effort to retrieve his wits, scattered broadcast by this alluring recital, while Hoke leaned his elbows on the table and cracked walnuts between his fingers. "And all of this," asked Senator Stirt at last, "depends upon having your charter qualified in New York state?" His face grew shrewder, as if he had only begun to perceive the possible advantages to himself, and he murmured, "But that, Mr. Ching, is almost impossible nowadays. A perpetual charter with the state of New York's qualifications?"

Joshua poured the wine, gently explaining to Amasa Stirt the trouble it had cost him to get this 'forty-eight Madeira. "Of course, Senator, if we don't have the New York qualification, we will have another state qualify it."

"I wouldn't think of that just yet, Mr. Ching. You plan to increase your board of directors, I suppose?"

"Of course. Other men are interested in serving on it." Joshua gestured vaguely. "Frederic Hallam, for example."

"Of the Commercial Trust?"

"Yes, and other men of the same caliber. We actually intend to build railroads, Senator, you must understand that." Joshua smiled. "We have no intention of fooling the public."

"Certainly not," the senator agreed. "One of these days it's going to become noticeable there are too many railroads being built from nowhere to nowhere. No, it's a national disgrace, I would never participate in any such thing."

Hoke was tossing nutmeats greedily into his mouth and his eyes shifted from Joshua's face to Senator Stirt's, as if he expected some sleight of hand to take place between them which he must apprehend. "How much will your friend want?"

Stirt looked thoughtful. "Two hundred thousand, at the least."

Hoke whistled and Joshua, who had an immediate picture of himself writing another check for fifty thousand dollars, smiled deprecatingly and began to explain why his partners would never agree to spend two hundred thousand dollars for something they did not actually need, but when the senator got up to leave he was still repeating the same figure and, it seemed, it had stuck in his head and could not be dislodged. "Even at that, Mr. Ching," he said sadly, "I cannot guarantee to persuade him that this would be in the national interest."

Rose appeared in the doorway. "You're leaving, Senator? I'm sorry." And in another moment Tessie was shaking the senator's hand and gazing wistfully at him.

Senator Stirt thanked Joshua for the dinner, bowed to Rose, and remarked as he went out, "Let me sleep on it."

Joshua stood staring gloomily at the floor and contemplating these demands for money which came at him from all directions and, it seemed, at an ever-increasing speed, and was so engrossed that only when the door slammed did he realize Tessie Spooner had followed the senator. He glanced at Hoke, to find him lighting a cigar with no more apparent concern than he would have shown to see his bartender setting out drinks, and, when he found Joshua looking curiously at him, Hoke grinned. "Well? The old boy said he wanted to sleep on it, didn't he? He may as well sleep in comfort," and Hoke laughed and sharply slapped his thigh, enjoying the joke on Tessie Spooner.

XXVI

"This country needs two things, Pete, and if we could get those taken care of we'd have everything corraled. Somebody's got to kill off the Indians and somebody's got to lend us more money."

Pete smiled. "The same guy, Lem?"

They sat opposite each other across the desk, their feet hoisted onto ledgers and contracts, and the day had turned so cold that the stove's belly was glowing red. "The same guy, all right. Uncle Sam. If we could wake up some morning and find the Indians dead and a loan of a few millions at a reasonable interest, say about two percent—"

"A year?"

"That would be about right. This country would change over-night."

"I have the impression it has changed overnight. Look what's happened in less than seven years. And we'd still need a railroad—we're the hell and gone from anywhere."

"The railroads would come with the money."

"Or the money with the roads? Look at it this way, Lem. Seven years ago this Territory was empty—a few prospectors passing through, some Indian tribes, wild game. Now there are seventy steamers in one summer, and some twenty thousand mules and oxen hauling in three thousand tons of freight a year, or better. Jesus, that impresses me—it doesn't you?"

"But it could be more, it should be more." Lem complained often about the national inefficiency and seemed to believe there was a conspiracy of laziness against which he must continuously remonstrate.

"Sixty millions taken out of these gulches." Pete whistled softly. "Thirty millions in Alder alone, the first three years. What the hell do you want, Lem?"

"And where is it now? Who's made any good use of it—except for you and Matt and Webb and a few of the rest of us? Most of these guys have no sense and less imagination. Suppose they do make a strike—what do they do? Sluice it away because they're too damn lazy or too stupid to learn how to work it. And once they get a pokeful of dust they give it to the first faro dealer or madam they meet, or sew it inside their cheap-johns and light out for home. And if all this isn't bad enough, the government's turned the Indians loose with weapons and ammunition enough to wipe us out!" Lem leaped up and went marching back and forth, shouting. "When we first came here there was no one to bother us but those lousy Sheep-eaters, but now the Blackfeet and Piegans have decided it's their war and I tell you, Pete Devlin, if something isn't god-damn well done about it soon our houses will be burnt and our women butchered and while the crows peck our eyes out some bare-assed Blackfoot will be flaunting our scalps on his coup stick!" He hovered over Pete and when Pete sighed, nodding, Lem went pacing along the far side of the room again. "They give guns to the red bastards to coax them into signing a treaty and two weeks later they're killing settlers—which occasions a great deal of official surprise in Washington, for our representatives know only as much about Indians as they read in James Fenimore Cooper."

"I'm no better satisfied with our predicament than you are, Lem. But you know why we're in it."

"We're in it because the government leaves us in it! We're supplying bloody well near half the nation's gold right now, but they won't protect our families! They send their tax collectors, though—treat us like orphans and expect us to pay for the privileges of citizenship."

"Do you pay them?"

"Hell, no. Do you?"

"We pay what we can't lie out of, like everybody else. The truth of it, Lem, is that the government's poor—it can't afford to support a big peacetime army."

"If a party of Piegans picked you off some day or attacked this town, would you tell yourself the government couldn't afford to protect us? We're contributing, taxes or not, to the country's development, and they owe us protection even if they can't afford it."

"I know, I know. But still, Lem, we're damn well off. Do you know anyone who's done any better than Finney and Son or Devlin Brothers?"

"Maybe not in the Territory, Pete, but for Christ's sake, what does that mean compared with the East? Back there, while we're thinking about ten thousand, there are men thinking about a million. Where we say a million they say a hundred million. While we're working our tails off, guys are sitting around overheated eastern offices hatching schemes to make millions without lifting a finger." Lem raised the little finger of his right hand and wiggled it feebly, then paused and gazed at the floor, reflecting, Pete supposed, on this unjust division of the nation's work. All at once Lem rushed forward, holding out his hand. "Got to be on my way. Any message for Matt?"

"Just the usual one—I need more currency. But then, so does he." Lem had the door opened when Pete said, "Lem, come home with me to dinner. Jenny will be disappointed if you don't."

Lem paused, studied Pete's encouraging smile, and shook his head. "Thanks, Pete, but I've got a long trip ahead. Some other time. Oh, and Pete, you know how much both Erma and I think of Jenny. Someone—I can't remember who—told Erma they'd heard that Jenny was sick a few months ago. She's well now, of course?"

Pete's face turned dark red. "Whoever told you that lied. Jenny hasn't been sick at all."

"Good. Erma will be glad to hear it."

Lem gave him another brisk salute, and as Pete stood in the doorway he set off through the dense traffic as if now he must recover those minutes he had lost berating Indians and the government and eastern financiers, and when he had disappeared Pete smiled again, a little ruefully, telling himself that of course Lem had wanted to have dinner with them, and his proprietary jealousy had condemned his friend to dine in a restaurant off fat, rusty bacon and underdone game, eggs fried solid in rancid grease and doughnuts green and bitter with saleratus, if indeed he could choke it down.

All at once Pete locked the door and started for home with that same disquieting eagerness he felt whenever he was about to see Jenny after an absence of even a few hours, for he was ashamed to realize fourteen months of marriage had not yet persuaded him that his old habit of unhappiness—begun with the death of Lorena and their son—had been a long sickness, of which this marriage to Jenny Danforth should have cured him by now.

He held many hot arguments with himself, but even though he thought any impartial eavesdropper would find these discussions marvels of ingenious philosophy, it disgusted him to find the world as full as ever of portents and mysteries; and wherever he looked he found traces of those creatures of the supernatural who had decided long ago that Peter Devlin had no right to simple happiness, though what might be the nature of their grudge against him he could not imagine.

But then how did it happen that his greatest hopes, at exactly the moment when he had agreed to believe in their fulfillment, were spoiled—and why should that first loss, so long ago, seem no accident but an omen?

And who was it who had told Erma Finney that Jenny had been sick?

Pete stopped to talk to a man who hailed him, and all the while he gravely discussed a claim the man wanted to sell, Pete never once relinquished his hold on these problems, so that when presently he rode on he was able to resume his mulling exactly where he had left off, taking up the question with Dr. Chaffinch and demanding to know why he had not kept their secret as he had promised he would. The Doctor, however, insisted that he had told no one and suggested that perhaps the neighbor woman, Mrs. Hatch, had found the secret too interesting to keep. By the time he had begun to interrogate Mrs. Hatch, Pete was shaking his head in wonderment and disbelief at his own suspicious nature, and reminded himself that other women had miscarriages and their friends heard of it, and he must give up these apprehensions and forebodings before some real disaster was provoked by his fears.

By now, his memory of himself galloping about the town, yelling and swearing in his pursuit of the Doctor, seemed comical enough, but the sight of that bright, staining stream, spreading slowly between Jenny's feet as she pressed her hands against her belly, must have sent him into a momentary insanity and still woke him at night with his heart pounding and his flesh wet and cold.

While he had searched for the Doctor, he had been sure the blood was still flowing and that she would die before he got back, and when he found her in bed being tended by Mrs. Hatch, who briskly informed the Doctor he was no longer needed, he had been so overwhelmed by gratitude and grief that he had attacked Dr. Chaffinch with savage fury for having been so hard to find, so long in coming, and so useless when he got there, until Jenny covered her ears, the Doctor declared he would defend his honor with his fists or pistol, and Mrs. Hatch had thrown her arms about his waist and forced him to drag her after him as he stalked the Doctor.

Of course, after that performance it was not surprising if Jenny told him whatever she thought he might want to hear, and so he interpreted her assurances that they would have a child, for he did not believe it and was by now willing to agree it might be the penalty he must pay for the gift she had given him, this conviction of owning his private world, into which envious outsiders were sometimes allowed to peek, but where they were never encouraged to loiter.

He stopped presently to talk to another man, and was all the while aware that hidden inside this treeless conglomeration of cabins and false-fronted buildings, set between distant mountains and low hills which surrounded it like a cup, was his own house toward which he made a leisurely progress; and as he thought of the house and the dinner they would eat together, he had some warm intimations of those pleasures which might follow and which, he could almost fancy, the man was able to read in the restless glancing of his eyes. But then, just as he was jealous of every man nowadays, for he took them all to be her secret lovers, so he supposed they must be jealous of him.

His house was on the camp's west side, in an area which was still almost empty, and although Jenny declared that this town was even more ugly than Virginia City, Pete and the other men looked around at their handiwork complacently, and reflected that for a new and busy camp it served their needs very well: there was a tree, of unusual size and strength, which had saved them the trouble of improvising a gallows when they needed one. The meandering stream carried away a perpetual burden of offal, flung into it from the butcher shops, and deposited it in an open sewer far enough from the center of town that they did not smell it unless the wind was blowing that way. True, they agreed, the back yards and vacant lots were littered with heaps of tin cans and discarded hoop skirts, but there was no more convenient way to dispose of them. And there was a continuous reassuring clatter of hammering and sawing and pounding nails, singing and fiddling and excited shouting, so that no man need ever hear a sudden, disconcerting silence and wonder if his fellows had gone sneaking away to a better camp.

But while this general dishevelment of human life in the mountains kept the women in a frenzy of protest and activity, it seemed to the men these were meaningless details in a broad atmosphere of rattling optimism and high excitement, where even the men who failed continued to believe in success, and only a madman could honestly lose his faith. Pete took the town for granted and even admired it for what it represented of his own efforts, but Jenny lived here as she had in Bannack and Virginia City, with a scorn for everything outside her own house, and a disdainful intolerance of all those who were not her friends or his.

The house stood on a corner, near the crest of a hill which rose in a long slope from the end of the main street. Mrs. Hatch's house was farther down the hillside, and there was a one-room cabin some distance above, but they were otherwise isolated in the midst of projects not yet begun, and the vacant lots were covered with sagebrush and cactus and dense matted grasses.

There were five rooms in the house, three of them quite large, and it was built in two stories, rough stone for the lower half and white painted clapboard above, with a pitched green roof. There was a stone chimney at either end, several windows, and a white picket fence about four feet tall, for Jenny insisted a fence was necessary to her sense of well-being. On the adjoining lot was a barn for their riding horses, and the new buggy Pete had given her for a wedding present, glistening black with bright red wheels, which Jenny drove as if its elegant lines exerted some peculiar challenge on her driving skills.

A small entrance hall opened to the left into the living room, and to the right into the dining room and kitchen, and a narrow flight of stairs led from it to the bedrooms, the one they shared and the other, which was usually closed, for Jenny had furnished it as a nursery.

There was nothing of her house in Virginia City but the carpet with its pattern of water lilies in a deep blue lake, and the piano, and yet it reminded Pete and everyone else who saw it of that house, and even of the earlier cabin in Bannack. There was the same dim light in the living room which she kept shadowed on the brightest days, the same easel for her water colors, the stacks of sheet music and shelves of books, a portfolio of drawings she had made, most of them sketches of single blossoming plants, intricately detailed, which lay on the marble table in the center of the room, and many plants clustered near the windows, for no one had yet been very lucky with flowers, and a few dandelion seeds which had arrived the year before had caused as much excitement among the women as a French dress.

It was partly to assuage this mystical yearning for flowers that Pete had surprised her by ordering a bouquet of wax flowers from New York, roses and fuchsia and lilac and mock orange, encased in a glass globe, and at its arrival the women had gathered to examine these specious blossoms, hovering over them and discussing in reverent voices the several varieties and where they had last seen them growing naturally. Jenny's wax flowers, in fact, which stood on the dining-room sideboard, were coveted by her friends more than her house or her clothes or her new buggy, and envied more than her beauty, which they could not hope to have, while any of them might have a bouquet of wax flowers if only they had a husband generous enough to pay the cost of transporting them there whole and uncrushed, with a glass dome to keep them that way.

The house, Pete thought, was a felicitous blending of that civilized world they had left half a continent away, with some few indications that they had come to a wilderness to live. The head of a buck he had shot on a hunting trip received hats and coats on its antlers in the vestibule, and beside it hung a gilt-framed mirror, ornately carved.

The windows, which would have shown Jenny that bare hillside which depressed her, were hung with starched white muslin curtains and dark-blue damask draperies, looped in some baffling fashion and trailing upon the floor. The furniture was rosewood, upholstered in the same deep red damask which covered the walls, and steel engravings of distant cities they might never see but liked to contemplate hung with several of Jenny's water colors of flowers and bowls of fruit which he had framed, for usually she gave them away to anyone who admired them.

The dining-room table could be extended to seat a numerous party and the walls were covered with crimson flock paper, very gay by contrast with the sober and contemplative atmosphere of the living room, and there was a black bearskin rug on the floor, another testimonial to Pete's hunting skills. And it was in this combination of the treasures, trivial and significant, of their previous lives and of this new one, that Pete found certain obscure but reassuring signs that he was meant to accept his present good fortune, and traffic no more in past disappointments.

But however often he made this resolution, circumstances fashioned small peculiar shocks and disturbances, and now he saw with alert apprehension that Jenny stood on the porch talking to the peddler woman Mrs. Honeybone, and apparently they were arguing, for as Jenny reached toward her opened valise, Mrs. Honeybone clapped it together and backed away.

The valise, Pete knew, contained garters and hairpins, soaps and combs and pencils and china buttons on cards, bean shooters and mouth organs and green glass beads, all the miscellaneous rubbish by which Mrs. Honeybone made her living, for she was to be seen in every mountain camp, in the stagecoaches and traveling the highways on muleback like a prospector, and was thought to be so old she was now expected to live forever.

Pete had often seen her going along the streets, staring with obscene curiosity into every face she passed, as if she knew each man's most cherished secret, and often she grinned, meaninglessly, but nevertheless he and others tried to avoid that grin and glanced guiltily away at sight of her. The children taunted her, called her names and threw rocks and chunks of manure at her, screaming with nervous hatred until she would turn on them, swearing and making gestures they interpreted as curses so that they would fall away from her and gather solemnly together, vying for her disfavor, and at last one among them would be chosen to have received the curse and must expect any day now a new set of warts, a withered hand, his brother's sudden death, or the loss of his favorite marbles. Jenny had bought trinkets from her before, though she said the woman frightened her and she would never let her in the house.

Their gate stood open and Mrs. Honeybone's usual retinue of four or five children stood watching the two women in rapturous silence, no doubt waiting for some extravagant gesture to happen between them which would repay their patient dogging of Mrs. Honeybone's steps.

Neither Jenny nor Mrs. Honeybone nor any of the children noticed Pete, and as he approached the gate Mrs. Honeybone shook her fist at Jenny, who smiled at her, a vague but oddly menacing smile. "It's worth a dollar, Mrs. Devlin, and so help me God, you'll pay me a dollar or you won't have it!"

"I don't want it, go away." Jenny turned her back and opened the door.

Mrs. Honeybone began to scream, and Pete started forward at a run. "I'll predict your future, Mrs. Devlin, shall I? And it won't cost you a cent!" Jenny turned, still with that strange and rather ominous smile, challenging Mrs. Honeybone to read her future. "You'll die a sudden and violent death—" Pete grabbed Mrs. Honeybone's shoulders, shaking her hard, and while the children capered joyously Pete pushed her down the steps, even though Mrs. Honeybone dug in her heels, and shoved her toward the gate, thrust her outside, and slammed it shut.

"Don't ever come back here again, you filthy old bitch!" Mrs. Honeybone spat at the fence, the children were clapping their hands, and all at once Pete heard Jenny laugh and turned in astonishment to find her leaning against the door, her head thrown back and her eyes shut, laughing as he had never seen her do before. "Don't come near us again," he told Mrs. Honeybone, muttering so that Jenny could not hear him, and all at once, to his surprise, he picked up the valise and hurled it at her. As he followed Jenny into the house, Mrs. Honeybone was standing in a shower of buttons and combs and hairpins, shrieking and brandishing her fists.

Jenny stood in the vestibule, gazing intently at herself in the mirror, and he stood in back of her, watching her with such anxiety that when at last she gave him an upward questioning glance he was horrified to discover in his own expression such dread and shock she could only think he must believe the prophecy would come true. Jenny smiled, though the smile had the same quality of vagueness and menace she had shown Mrs. Honeybone, and he followed her into the living room, unable to think of what he should say to comfort her. She twirled slowly around, laughing softly, and gave a flourishing movement which sent the shawl winding across the sofa where she let it drop. "The poor old woman's crazy, isn't she?"

"Of course she is. She shouldn't be allowed in the streets, she's dangerous as a mad dog."

"Dangerous?" Jenny shrugged. "Only if you believe her."

"What were you arguing about?"

"She wanted too much money, she always does."

"A dollar, Jenny. Why didn't you give it to her?" He was thinking, in spite of himself, that the powers of the universe never took anyone by surprise but always announced their intentions well in advance of their deeds, and they might have chosen Mrs. Honeybone as well as any other agent to deliver this warning.

But Jenny seemed amused and unconcerned, and was stirring her fingers through a heap of shells in a blue glass bowl on the table. "It wasn't worth a dollar. Of course, if she weren't so disgusting, I might have given it to her anyway." She glanced at him and her eyes were clear green and filled with light, as they always looked when she was excited. She moved quickly to the windows, deftly separated the muslin curtains and peeked between them, frowning.

Mrs. Honeybone was picking up her belongings, squatting and bobbing up again as she retrieved each pencil and garter and mouth organ. A dog had joined the gathering and was barking continuously, while the children went prancing about her and now and then one of them grew bold enough to snatch up a button and make her chase him for it. Pete and Jenny watched them silently for several moments.

"Maybe I should help her," Pete suggested, thinking he might condition his help on her withdrawal of the curse.

"No, she'd only think she frightened us."

"What were you buying?"

Jenny laughed. "I'm ashamed to tell you." But he smiled at her tenderly, and after a moment she said, "I was going to buy a dream book. Can you imagine?" She went to the piano and sat down. "Let's play something, while we wait for Morgan. He's coming to dinner— he got back from Virginia City this morning." She was sorting through sheets of music and Pete took his fiddle from the case, she glanced at him, and they began to play a song of the southern frontier, a plaintive melody which appealed to them for its poignance; but although Jenny played with her usual rapt attention and did not glance up as Morgan entered the house, Pete played absently, for he was still wondering how he might find a way to reason Mrs. Honeybone out of the curse.

As they finished the song Jenny went to Morgan, paused as he kissed her, and left the room, saying she would have dinner on the table in a few minutes, and all at once Pete pretended to discover him, for it embarrassed him to see another man kiss Jenny, and embarrassed him even more that he was capable of being jealous of his nephew.

"What happened out there?" Morgan asked.

Pete went to the window, and Mrs. Honeybone, beset by the barking dog and her circle of prancing tormenters, now fastened the valise and began to spin with it, holding it at arm's length and turning at a speed which would knock down anyone who got within her range, and as she spun she set up a steady keening which, before long, made the children back off to stare in silence and awe at the wheeling black figure, its cloak flapping and undulating in a vast circle.

Morgan and Pete watched for several moments, as silent as the children, and all at once Pete rushed out the door, drawing his pistol as he went and yelling, "Get the hell away from here, you damned old witch, and don't come near this house again!"

Mrs. Honeybone gave a yelp and went scampering down the hillside, and the children, released from their spell, broke once again into howls of laughter and dashed off in her wake.

Taken aback by this success, Pete grew sheepish to think he had brandished a pistol as recklessly as any tenderfoot, and at an old woman, and he returned the weapon to his belt. He started toward the house and found Jenny and Morgan in the doorway, standing side by side and watching him, their faces as carefully inscrutable as if they had decided it was he, rather than Mrs. Honeybone, who was insane.

"Well," said Pete apologetically, "she's gone."

Jenny ran toward the kitchen, calling, "Don't talk about anything important until we're at the table," and Pete was grateful she had not taken advantage of his foolishness.

Still, he felt obliged to give Morgan some reason for his peculiar behavior and, as he poured whisky, told him with a pretense of casual indifference, "The old woman cursed Jenny, and I guess I lost my head."

"Cursed her?"

"Predicted she would die by violence."

"But you know she's crazy, Pete."

"I know. But all the same—oh, the hell with it. How was the trip?"

But he did not hear what Morgan said, and when they sat at the table and Pete asked grace he included a silent request for the curse to be nullified, slyly smiling to think an agnostic like himself should take these superstitious precautions.

Jenny looked tranquil, as if she had forgotten the curse or gave it no more significance than a mad old woman's ravings deserved, and as Pete carved the roast and they began to eat he found that the warmth of the whisky and food, the feeling of the room and house surrounding him, with Jenny talking eagerly to Morgan and asking, as she always did, about each member of the family, even to the cat Shekel, had convinced him the episode would never have happened if he had not somehow provoked it.

It even began to seem quite absurd as he listened to Jenny laughing over some family gossip he had failed to hear, that he should not have laughed at Mrs. Honeybone. But all the same he decided to seek Mrs. Honeybone out and give her some small present, not a bribe, only an indication of his pity and good will, and that gesture in itself would eliminate the memory of what she had said and the grimace she had made when she spat at the fence.

They were talking about Lisette, he realized, for Lisette had married Ralph Mercer the summer before and would have her first child in three or four months, but Pete found himself disturbed by this talk of pregnancy, which he fancied might make Jenny feel she had failed in what other women accomplished easily.

"It's so strange to think of Lisette married," Jenny said, and it seemed to Pete that now Jenny was brooding, blaming herself, and he stopped eating to gaze at her pleadingly, but Jenny did not notice this. "She still seems to me only a little girl."

Morgan smiled. "She doesn't think so. She thinks she's as old and wise as anyone ever gets to be."

Pete now began to question Morgan about various properties he had been out inspecting, finding questions enough to prevent Jenny from asking any others, and although this selfishness gave him guilty pangs he could not listen to her any longer, showing so much interest in the everyday lives of other people.

By the time Jenny had cleared the table, with Pete keeping a furtive watch over her, for he could not convince himself she was no more disturbed than she seemed, he was waiting impatiently for Morgan to leave, and was suddenly so eager for her, so fretful and anticipatory, that it seemed there was some danger he might send Morgan away with little more ceremony than he had shown Mrs. Honeybone. But Morgan, perhaps, read his impatience in those glances he gave Jenny, and was presently shaking his hand; and as he went dashing out, Pete lighted another cigar and now that they were alone was willing to spend some leisurely moments in the contemplation of his pleasures before he enjoyed them.

Morgan climbed onto Puzzle's back with difficulty, which reminded him that his coat pockets were laden with ore specimens he had forgotten to discharge, and he set off at a lively canter, intending to go first to Devlin Brothers to unload these samples before he forgot which hole in the ground had produced each one, and as he rode along, grinning to himself and thinking of how eager Pete had been to get rid of him, a woman's voice called his name, and he saw Nella Allen sitting in a buggy some distance away and smiling at him.

That it was Nella Allen, he did not doubt, but, because he had been dreading this encounter for almost four years, he dismounted and approached the buggy slowly, squinting as he asked, "Nella?"

She did not answer, and when he stood looking up at her and shaking his head in wondering surprise, she continued gazing at him, almost as distrustfully as if a stranger had come up to her in a lonely place where, if he chose, he might do her some injury.

The long blond hair, which had fallen straight to below her waist and engrossed his imagination by its shifting movements when she walked, was curled now and dressed in some complicated style. She wore a brown sealskin coat, its collar turned up to her chin on this windy, cold day, and there were diamond earrings fluttering beside her face, so that it seemed Green Troy was as generous as gamblers were believed to be. Her lips had the same childlike submissiveness, the same suggestion of compliant sensuality which had been so accurate a prediction, and, in fact, she had grown into a very pretty young woman, with all her fragility and wistfulness still there, and some elusive new quality he could not at first define.

"Don't you recognize me, Morgan?"

He nodded, thinking that her distrustful expression was a sign that she hated him, and he almost hoped that she did, for he deserved that and worse punishments—which, according to the world's whimsical justice, he would escape. He searched about for some magical words in which he did not himself believe, and failing to find them was disappointed to hear himself say, "You've changed."

"You've changed, too, Morgan." She laughed, and he recognized the sound, that soft, baffled laughter which had often reminded him of Suky.

He stepped a little nearer, and spoke to her in a voice so low she leaned forward to hear him, and when she did he inadvertently backed away. "Did you know it had happened when Zack and I left?" This careful, prudish avoidance of the word pregnancy embarrassed him even more, but it seemed to amuse Nella, or perhaps she was only pleased to see him so meek, so subdued and discomfited.

"I wasn't sure."

"Why didn't you tell me?"

"But what difference would that have made?" She looked even more amused, mocking and derisive, so that apparently there had been more changes in Nella Allen than the style of her hair and the clothes she wore.

"I should have guessed it," he mumbled. "I should have waited." And it seemed that if only some obedient devil would appear at that moment he would be glad to exchange the rest of his life to be married to her and have the child they might have had—or never to have seen her at all, and that, of course, would have been his first choice.

"But the longer you waited, Morgan, the more likely it was to happen. Don't you remember? It was impossible for us to let each other alone, after that first time." She tilted her head, as if to ask what memories he still had left of those afternoons. "Of course, that's the way it always seems at the beginning, isn't it? But neither of us knew that. We thought we'd made a great discovery, all our own—didn't we?"

"Of course we did," he told her sharply, but then had a sense of tenderness and regret, so painful that it seemed he might momentarily ask her to leave Green Troy and come with him. "We had," he added gently.

"And now, sometimes, I can't be sure it ever really happened."

"You can't?" he asked, honestly shocked, for although those meetings were often so vague to him they seemed quite imaginary, he would not have supposed they could be the same to her.

"Except for that afternoon in Dr. Danforth's office. I remember that well enough. Oh, don't look that way, Morgan, I'm not blaming you."

"Of course you are, and of course you should. But Nella, believe me, I know it sounds like a lie, but I never thought it would happen."

"No, I know you didn't. I didn't, either, until it did. Your father thought of it, though, he told me so when Dr. Danforth sent me to see him. 'I've been afraid of this, Nella,' he said." Nella shrugged, still curiously smiling. "But I don't blame him, either, I suppose—he simply didn't care what happened to me, any more than he cared what happened to Zack Fletcher. He was only interested in protecting his family."

"That's not true, Nella. I've talked to him about it. He was very much concerned about you."

"I know, he was concerned that I might want to wait, and marry you—he thought the baby was a trick of mine to interfere with his own plans. Oh, he was very kind, I'm not saying he wasn't, Morgan. He even offered to give me money, so I could go back to my family. But when I asked him what family he meant, he said there must be someone." Nella leaned her head against the side of the buggy, gazing down at him with the familiar look in her long blue eyes, as if she might just have finished crying or was about to begin, and he remembered that this expression had been the first thing to attract his attention, making him wonder what mysterious sorrows must be troubling this uncertain young girl. "How angry you look, Morgan, and so much like your father when something happens he doesn't like." She laughed, very softly, and then sighed. "You can't imagine how I've missed all of you."

"You have?" But he looked at her warily, thinking this was only another way to catch his guilt. "They've missed you, too. Lisette talks about you all the time, no other friend has ever meant so much to her—and even Annabel imagines she can remember Nella Allen."

"And Lisette didn't marry Zack Fletcher, after all, even though she wanted to. Your father wouldn't—"

"My father had nothing to do with it, Nella," he told her brusquely. "Lisette made her own decision."

Nella blinked in mock dismay at that reprimand, and she laughed again, shaking her head. "You always defend one another, don't you? Oh, I'm not being critical, I admire you for it, I always did. I suppose it was what I wanted more than anything else when I first went to live with you, to mean enough to all of you that you would defend me, too, if I ever needed it. But it didn't happen, I wasn't made a blood member of the tribe, after all, and neither was Zack. Only Jenny Danforth—Jenny Devlin, I should say now. She's the one I hate."

"You hate Jenny? But that's not fair, Nella, Jenny's done nothing to you, you scarcely knew her."

"I scarcely knew her, but she was the one who talked to your fa-

ther after I'd seen the Doctor, and it was her idea that he should operate. She decided what was going to happen to me."

"I don't believe that."

"They're in love with each other still, your father and Jenny, and
they still see each other, I suppose you don't believe that, either?"

"Of course I don't."

"But they do. Fong Chong told me about it—he works for me, too."

"Fong Chong doesn't speak any English."

"He doesn't?"

"Hi-hi-lo." Morgan mimicked Fong Chong's perpetual chant, smiling to let her know she could not fool him. "I've never heard him say
anything else."

She turned her head to one side, as if to ask was it possible he
had been taken in by that old trick. "Just tell me one thing more, and
then I'll let you go. Do you still have that clock in the kitchen?"

"We still do."

Every hour wounds, the last one kills. She shivered, a light delicate movement of her shoulders, and smiled wisely. "I like the one
outside Devlin Brothers better: Gold Bought Here." She picked up
the reins, slapping them lightly, but then leaned over once again. "Is
it true Jenny had a miscarriage not long ago? Is it true she almost
died? She deserves to be unhappy, any woman who's so willing to
make other people unhappy." And, as if they were two old friends
who had stopped for a few minutes to discuss the weather and exchange the newest gossip, she raised one hand in a little wave, rather
indefinite, like all Nella's gestures. "Good-bye, Morgan."

XXVII

No sooner had Joshua told Rose to modernize the place, improve it
somehow or other and without spending too much money, than he
began to resent the changes he saw, for they convinced him that he
was destined to be surrounded by women who lived on him, and from
time to time he had a picture of himself as a vast banqueting table
upon which they dined, merrily spearing up morsels with their
forks while he writhed in anguished protest—Susan and Ceda, Rose
and his sisters-in-law, and, if he did not take care, perhaps other
more distant female relatives and acquaintances as well.

Pink roses appeared everywhere. They bloomed on the wallpaper
and on the carpet, on draperies and upholstery, and he was not surprised to find them on a china spittoon. She peopled the house with
many little statues—dogs and shepherdesses and marble heads upon
pedestals—and seemed to know them as well as she knew Tessie

Spooner or himself, and when finally she had a parlor which pleased her so well she began to call it a drawing room, Joshua gave her permission to refurnish the dining room but warned her to stop right there, before her extravagance ruined him.

And it was quite true that premonitions of financial disaster continued to trouble him, with good enough reason.

William Talbot had recently departed for Washington carrying two hundred and seventy-five thousand dollars in a satchel and come back with the satchel empty, though he brought in its stead a large grant of land, and an assurance that the provision in their charter against issuing mortgage bonds would be removed.

Suky continued to ask him for new furniture, and only smiled skeptically when he told her, "It's impossible just now, I've been living up to the very selvage of my income." He liked this phrase and used it often, but it seemed to make no impression on Suky.

"The very selvage, Papa?" and she measured between her thumb and forefinger a minute distance, then gave such a conspiratorial laugh, at once gay and enigmatic, that he smiled, reflecting that she was indeed the most artful blackmailer he had met, beside whom the little flower girls who entered men's offices and threatened to scream for the police if they were not given money, were novices.

"It will be done, Suky," he assured her, "as soon as I can see my way clear. I promise you."

For in fact he felt rather sheepish whenever he considered the possibility that Suky, or even Susan or Ceda, might somehow find out about Rose Michel whom they would, of course, take to be no simple, affectionate young girl but a scheming woman, who, through the peculiar techniques of her trade, had learned to drain money from him in a steady stream, almost without his knowledge, while the honest members of his family were forced to beg him for necessities.

But, apart from these occasional qualms, Susan and Ceda circled the periphery of his life, two idle women who lived upon his work and of whom he had never wondered or inquired how they spent their overflowing leisure, and he asked of them only that they not insist he pay attention to their plans and projects and the petty annoyances which seemed to riddle their lives.

From early morning until late at night Joshua traced an intricate path in his carriage, a new one with a shining black body and dark red leather upholstery drawn by two handsome black horses, their manes and tails braided, their silver bridles polished; and with Huggens seated before him in the rain or snow or heat and Stokes equally exposed in the rear but glaring forcefully ahead while he kept his arms folded almost on a level with his chin, they traveled smartly from the Fifth Avenue Hotel to Suky's house, from Spinnage and Achroyd's to Van Zandt and Ching, and from the Academy of Music to Rose Michel's, where quite often he spent whatever was left of the night. All day long he shuttled about among the offices of his several partners, stopping at the downtown Delmonico's where, in the company of other successful brokers, he ate for lunch a dainty bird bathed in some rich sauce; but however fast he went, his next destination was always some distance ahead, and he found invariably that even before he had arrived he should have left and gone on to the next place.

With all these activities, Rose must wait her turn, and he never let her know when it was coming, either, for other men he knew had found a girl and set her up in a rented house, given her a rigid schedule for their visits, and been very much humiliated in return for their trustful carelessness.

Joshua, therefore, arrived at seven o'clock in the morning or at midnight, came for two consecutive days and ignored her for the next week, sent a message that she was to expect him at nine that night and did not go and, he thought, by this time Rose Michel was not likely to imagine she could fool him. Even so, he arrived there one night at about ten-thirty, paused before applying his key to the lock, for most of the lights were out, giving the windows a blue and eerie glow, and all at once was convinced he would find another man in the house. His heart began to beat with rage and he opened the door and entered so quietly he congratulated himself with bitter humor that he would, if all else failed, surely make an excellent footpad.

The parlor was dim, for he often cautioned her not to burn gas needlessly, and only one wall jet flickered above the piano. There was no immediate indication, as he peered around, of anyone else's presence, and he stood for a minute or two in the vestibule, waiting and listening, for the house was small enough that voices carried from upstairs to downstairs and from one room to another.

And then, from the floor above, where she had her bedroom and sitting room, he heard Rose's voice, hilariously laughing, and without removing his coat or hat or even his gloves, and taking a firm hold on his cane, should he need it for a weapon, Joshua began to steal softly across the floor, pausing whenever a board gave way, and stopping at the foot of the stairs when he heard her laugh again.

He began slowly to mount the stairs, preparing himself for a dramatic moment of denunciation, and then realized it was not only Rose's voice he had heard laughing and chattering but that of another girl, as well. He was wondering if he should sneak back down, go out of the house and return with a slam of the door which would bring her flying to meet him, and was infuriated to think his jealousy had put him into this absurd predicament, when he heard Rose say, "A year and a half on May seventeenth. That's pretty good."

"Good enough," Tessie agreed. "If he wasn't so bloody stingy."

This enraged him even more than the expectation of finding a man there, and he moved slowly up the staircase and stood to one side of the partly opened sitting-room door, through which he could see Rose in the lighted bedroom beyond, wearing a lilac silk corset and a thin white chemise which just reached her knees. Her feet were bare and her hair was tumbled about and hung in strands over her exposed breasts and down her back and, in fact, she looked more like a trollop than she ever had in his presence, for then she was careful to seem, as he had warned her she must, well-bred and genteel.

She stood before the dressing table, staring at herself in the mirror, and presently she raised her arms and pinned up some loose tendrils, examining the blond ends, for he had insisted she let her hair grow out to its natural brown color, and remarked to Tessie, "Shh—don't talk so loud."

"What the hell. Everybody's in bed."

"What if he came in?"

"What if he did? Aren't you allowed to have even one friend?" Tessie strolled up behind Rose and the two girls looked intently at each other. Tessie was wearing a dress of bright green plaid, drawn back to show the lines of her body, and there was a purple velvet hat set sideways on her head with a feather curling along her cheek. Joshua examined more carefully than he ever had before her little crushed face, sensual and stupid, her wide forehead and round chin which she now set stubbornly as she confronted Rose, and told himself that she looked like a wicked urchin who had trafficked in vice before she had her second teeth. She picked a piece of candy from the box on the dressing table, and walked out of his sight again. "He's got the shit scared out of you, hasn't he?"

Rose watched her, twitched up one side of her mouth in a mocking smirk, and went back to playing with her hair. "Who's got the shit scared out of them, Tessie Spooner? Hoke O'Neil beats you up whenever he feels like it, he sends you around to get screwed by any old fart he's doing business with, and he'd throw you out in a minute if you lost your looks or caught something—and you damn well know it." She snapped her fingers and smiled cruelly into the mirror while Joshua marveled, nonplussed, at where Rose had hidden this fishwife, for this was the first glimpse he had had of her. She took up a perfume bottle, removed the stopper and passed it beneath Tessie's nose, and dabbed at her armpits. "This is imported French perfume," she told Tessie, speaking very grandly. "He won't let me wear anything else."

"Perfume and chocolate candy, but he locks up the liquor closet and takes the key with him. If you're so damn smart you should be able to figure that one out."

"No use," Rose told her. "He counts the bottles. He can count them without even looking at them. Just gives a glance, like that, and has the whole works added and subtracted and divided. Same thing when he goes in the kitchen." She nodded soberly. "That's why he's so rich."

"Balls. He's so rich because he's as big a crud as Hoke O'Neil is any day." Tessie was not in sight but he heard her laugh, a loud and prolonged laugh during which, from time to time, she gasped and shrieked.

"Shut up, Tessie. Laugh at Hoke, if you want, but lay off Mr. Ching."

"Mr. Ching? Mr. Ching? Oh, my God!" And, once again, Tessie began screeching with laughter until, abruptly, Rose slapped her face and told her to behave herself or leave the house.

"What's the matter with you?" Rose whispered. "The servants are all paid to spy on me. Suppose Mr. Ching heard about you talking like that? Where would I be? Remember your manners, or get the hell out of here. I'm god-damned if I'll lose everything I've worked myself up to because you haven't got sense enough to keep your mouth shut when you're in a gentleman's house."

Tessie's voice sounded hurt and sulky, although apparently she did not want to leave. "You worked yourself up, and take it from me, you'll work yourself right back down again."

"What do you mean by that, Tessie Spooner? Tell me if you dare."

Tessie sat down, crossed her legs and seized one knee in both hands, so that her striped black and green stockings were displayed almost to her thighs, and he found that not only were her legs remarkably graceful but she had a kind of petulant and whimsical recklessness which must be what Hoke O'Neil liked her for. "You know where we'll both wind up, don't you? Maybe not next year and maybe not the year after that, but sure as hell in five years, we will."

"Speak for yourself."

"We'll get one of those little houses off Washington Place or Twenty-fourth Street—you know, the kind where they pretend they took such a fancy to the fellow they let him come home with them and next took such a fancy they let him screw them. But that won't last long—and then it's a parlor house in Greene or Wooster where they expect you to put on a circus and bore holes in the walls to give everybody a good laugh on the rustics—"

"It won't happen to me," Rose shrieked. "One of these days I'll surprise the pants off you by the clothes I'll wear and the house I'll live in—"

With a crowing laugh Tessie flung her arms into the air and banged them against her sides and then, as Joshua stepped into the doorway, Rose screamed and covered her mouth with both hands, and Tessie gave a mournful wail.

"Get out of here," Joshua told Tessie, and without even a glance at Rose, who looked as terrorstruck as if it were not Joshua but his ghost which had materialized, Tessie snatched up her skirts and ran by him, ducking as if she expected to be hit and squeezing close to the opposite side of the doorway, and went clattering down the stairs.

"Don't tell Hoke, oh, I beg of you, Mr. Ching, don't tell Hoke.

He'll kill me. He'll kill me." She stood at the bottom of the stairs, her hands clasped and lifted toward him prayerfully.

"Be still, and get out of here." He loomed across the railing, tall and shadowed in his black coat and silk hat, and with a last despairing cry, she backed away, then ran out and the door slammed.

As Joshua turned, Rose's mouth opened as if she was about to speak, but before he could reach her, she slipped to the floor and lay there, giving such piteous moans that astonishment intruded on his anger. "How long have you been there?" She was cringing, like an animal which has often been beaten, and her hands covered her head as if for protection.

"Get up, Rose," he said at last, whereupon she raised her head suspiciously, rolling her eyes to peck at him, as if to discover if he meant to kick her or give her a stroke with his cane.

"Get up?"

"Certainly. I don't like to see you groveling as if you take me for another Hoke O'Neil." She sat up, shaking her head and giving deep sighs, as if there was no more hope for her now. "I came to pay you a visit. I wanted to surprise you." At that she gave a bursting sob and threw herself upon the floor again. "Rose, I insist that you stop that. I detest lack of pride." It was true enough, or at least he thought it was, and yet her collapse had made him feel a warmer affection for her than he had at any time since the night he had informed her that he knew she was lying about her rich family and had seen her abruptly and unprotestingly sink into humiliated despair. "Come in here. I want to talk to you."

He walked briskly into the bedroom, put aside his gloves and cane, removed his hat, took off his overcoat and laid it on a chair and, as he turned, found her scuffling slowly into the room, disheveled and tear-stained, subservient and still frightened, and though he wanted to laugh at the sight of this exaggerated woe he decided that for the sake of future discipline he would lecture her gravely, warn her kindly but severely, and at last allow her to persuade him, by means of the tricks and wiles she had learned at Annie Wood's, to forgive her only this once, and it would never be necessary again.

But then one day, only a few weeks later, she told him, in the shamefaced manner of a schoolgirl admitting she has a stomach ache because she has eaten too much candy, that she was pregnant.

"What?" Joshua shouted, and gave a kick at a footstool which sent it hurtling against a table upon which stood several small china dogs and shepherdesses, and toppled it with a crash. He glared at Rose vindictively as she stood over her broken treasures, her eyes full of tears but not daring to cry, and he felt a mean satisfaction at the destruction, for neither the dogs nor the shepherdesses nor the small paperweights with their flowers and whirling snowstorms had ever pleased him. She knelt down, set the table upright, and as she began to retrieve the bits of glass and china, Joshua found that this damage he had done had had a calming effect, and he spoke to her qui-

etly. "I told you not to let this happen, Rose. There's only one thing
for you to do. Go to Mrs. Grindle or Madame Restelle. And go tomorrow."

"I will," she whispered, but did not look at him. "I don't know how
it happened."

Joshua gazed steadily at her, and when she glanced up he gave her
a smile which surprised her even more than the broken bits of china,
for it was sardonic and accusatory. "I think you know. Go there tomorrow and don't agree to pay her more than five hundred dollars."

He left in a raging anger to think she would play such a trick on
him when she had known so well how to avoid it, but nevertheless
was annoyed to find that he worried about her the next day until his
concern began to interfere with his efficiency, and when he went to
her house in the middle of the afternoon he found her sitting in the
parlor with the curtains drawn and the gas lighted in one wall
bracket, dressed in street clothes. Her face was wet when he kissed
her, and she held a wadded wet handkerchief in her fist.

"What did you do today?" he inquired briskly, and told himself
this girl had never been intended as a serious or permanent part of
his life, and that was what he would make clear to her now.

She took his coat, keeping her head bent so that he could not look
directly at her, but Joshua impatiently thrust aside the draperies to
let in the sunlight, seizing hold of her chin to force her to lift her
head and, even to him, she looked pathetic. "I went to see Mrs.
Grindle."

"How much does she want?"

"One thousand dollars."

Joshua stepped back. "One thousand dollars? That's ridiculous."

"She won't do it for less."

"I'll talk to her. What name did you give?"

"Mine."

"She asked the man's name, I'm sure."

"I didn't tell her your name, Joshua. I didn't think you'd want me
to."

But Joshua did not find it possible to bargain with Mrs. Grindle,
a plump small woman with black hair dyed copper on top, wearing
many diamonds and sitting in the drawing room of her well-
furnished house which had, he thought, a surprising and somewhat
ghastly silence, for he must have been expecting to hear moans and
shrieks and protesting cries. He stared at her suspiciously, wondering if the tales he had heard about the town's two best-known abor-
tionists were true and they got rid of the bodies of their victims by
packing them in charcoal and shipping them off to be buried in distant cities. As he thought of these tales, Joshua glared at her with
hatred, horrified to think of her putting her hands on Rose, causing
her to suffer and possibly to die, and all at once he stood up.

"Good day, Mrs. Grindle, I'm sorry I came here."

She smiled at him indifferently, as if she had too much to do to concern herself about one customer more or less. "If you value the girl at all, don't send her to anyone else. The town is full of butchers and I, if I may say so, am an expert in my own field. But if you wait more than a week or two it will be too late and you'll be condemning her to death." She smiled again and shrugged, spreading her jeweled hands. "Of course, many gentlemen prefer that."

Joshua rushed out and stood at the bottom of the steps, staring up and down the street, dismayed to find it was after all a bright spring afternoon, women strolled by with parasols and poodles, nurses were wheeling baby carriages, children played battledore and shuttlecock, and delivery men passed with their carts, for he had dashed away from Mrs. Grindle with a dizzy conviction that the world had somehow turned over while he was in that quiet house, listening so intently for sounds which never came, and he must have expected to discover astonishing changes; but now he found that everything was as it had been when he had gone in, and perhaps only he had changed.

He did not see Rose for a few days and left her to brood over this wrong she had done him, dosing herself with Portuguese Female Pills and Infallible French Pills, which she insisted had proved their efficacy to many of Annie Wood's boarders, though Joshua had told her they were only sugar-coated bread pellets.

But then he awoke early one morning, restless and unable to put her out of his mind, left the hotel at a little after six and walked to her house. Once again he entered it softly, and found her asleep with her arms clasped about the pillow and, as he watched her, was surprised to find that the thought of having a child pleased him and gave him an unexpected conviction of his youth and vigor which he had not been aware of needing, just as he had not realized until the night he was pacing the sidewalk in front of the bed-house and had heard a woman's laugh in a passing carriage, that he needed someone who could remind him a woman might contribute to a man's life more than her endless requirements. And Rose, after all, gave him comfort and intense pleasures, she was not clever enough to be troublesome and she would, if he treated her kindly, be as pretty as she was now for many years to come.

And as he sat on the bed and bent to kiss her, she woke and smiled, not startled but reaching out her arms to him, confiding as a child, as if she had known all along he would not let her be harmed. Even so, he gave instructions that the nursery must be on the third floor, where the baby's crying would not disturb his sleep and the nurse's presence make him feel as imprisoned by domesticity as if they were married.

Now, however, Philip's house began to look as shabby as Suky said it was, and he observed the worn carpets and horsehair furniture with disapproval, seeing it for the first time just as Allegra Stuart had described it. He had not thought of Allegra for some time, and Hoke O'Neil had had no letters since she had left for England

three years ago, but whenever he gave the house another of his increasingly critical inspections he could see her sitting back on her
heels as she described with malicious humor the condition it was in,
the conservatory with its cracked tiles and broken fountain, where
no flowers had grown for years, and the sound of her voice echoed
mockingly in his ears, though he told himself it was only because of
the peculiar powers of Allegra Stuart's voice which lingered on long
after it had been thought forgotten.

He decided to tell Suky to do whatever she liked, but then reconsid-
ered that reckless generosity, and, after a few more weeks he
stopped one morning to speak his piece, reminding himself not to
mention the selvage of his income.

Suky kissed him and smiled, as if she might have a secret of her
own, and began to describe the house as it would look in another few
months. "I've had everything planned for years." First of all, she explained, there would be central heating and marble-paneled bathrooms. The drawing room would be white damask with the furniture
upholstered in pearl-gray velvet, and the dining room white damask
and sapphire-blue velvet. He grew increasingly distrustful as he
heard of a bedroom all white satin and maize velvet upholstery and
pearl-gray tufted brocade walls, while this very sitting room where
he now perched uneasily would be sapphire and maize, and when she
said that the furniture would be Louis XV, he raised one hand to
stop her right there.

"Louis Fifteenth, Suky, is very expensive furniture."

"But I know where to buy it at a reasonable price, Papa. There's a
man who went bankrupt not long ago who has a houseful of it, and
it's going to be put up at auction."

"Who went bankrupt?" Joshua demanded, and almost expected to
hear his own name; but to his relief she mentioned the victim of a
recent market catastrophe, one of those men who was described
as having come to grief through living in a brownstone house with a
marble façade, keeping fast trotters, and giving champagne suppers
to the girls of *The Black Crook* chorus.

"I'm going to have blue glass windows in the conservatory, and
tuberoses and blue orchids and hundreds of ferns, and white wicker
furniture, upholstered in a pale, pale blue. And there'll be a peacock
to walk about on the front lawn in fine weather. Oh, Papa, wait until
you see it."

"I'm glad you're pleased, darling," he told her, and in fact he preferred to think his decision had nothing to do with Rose Michel but
was meant to distract her from Frederic Hallam's marriage, which
they had attended not long ago, invited, he supposed, through some
familial machinations by Felice Talbot, and where he had seen Suky
and Frederic dancing together with expressions so noncommittal he
was convinced in a flash they were two distraught lovers, putting on
this charade for the benefit of Coral Talbot or any other hostile observers. And at sight of Frederic and Suky dancing together, Joshua

reminded himself of the old saying that it was impossible for a man and woman to have a platonic friendship unless they were married, and congratulated himself that Suky's patience and resourcefulness, her innocent face and guileful nature, would one day make Frederic Hallam his valuable business ally.

Frederic and Alvita Hallam were now in Europe and would be gone for several months, and, Joshua hoped, the house would modify her disappointment, although it was impossible to guess she might be disappointed until he went there one morning and found her in bed, looking pale and sad, and she began to cry when she saw him, saying that this time she knew she would die.

Her symptoms were as elusive as usual, she would not let the doctor examine anything but her tongue; and yet she lay there, crying much of the time, so Susan and Ceda reported, lost interest in the house, and said she would never live to see it finished. Joshua, who spent half an hour with her each morning and again in the late afternoon, watched her anxiously, although he had not failed to notice that this was the way she had looked, and this was what she had said, when her cousin Morgan had set out on his journey to the Territories, and so it would seem to be Suky's automatic response whenever she felt that a man she loved had deserted her.

This might have all been true enough, as it turned out, for after nearly two weeks of fending the doctor off she let him examine her and was found to be four months pregnant, and yet she looked not very much happier when Joshua called the next morning. "Are you pleased, Papa? It was what you wanted, wasn't it?" She nibbled a piece of toast and then set it aside, glancing skeptically at the tray and finally pulling off a cluster of grapes, for apparently she was making the conquest of her appetite a challenge to the cook who had provided, also, a cold roast squab, a boiled egg she had not broken into, biscuits and fried ham and bacon, honey and marmalade and strawberry jam.

"Of course I'm pleased. But for your sake, not for mine. Every woman needs children to complete her life." These pious words made Joshua wonder if he was making a covert apology for Rose Michel, whose swollen belly now reminded him each time he saw her of past indulgences and future obligations.

"If the baby's a girl," Suky told him, "I'm going to name her for Grandmother Ching."

Joshua kissed her and left, warning her to rest, to think of her health, but a few days later she was directing the workmen and seemed to have quite forgotten her prediction that she would not live to see the house finished; and Joshua was glad to be relieved of this worry, for the summer promised to be a difficult one and might, for some men, prove disastrous.

Everyone knew and had known for months that the gold market, most sorely tried of all the nation's markets, was being subjected to greater torments than usual, and by mid-August there was begin-

ning to be noticeable that form of incipient hysteria which attacked
brokers not long before a general decline in stock values, so that
when William Talbot returned from a few days in Washington,
Joshua and Lorenzo Flagg and Amos Cottrell sat about their whist
table in the reading room of the Fifth Avenue Hotel and questioned
him anxiously.

"This is something that could ruin all of us. No one knows what's
going to happen, I've heard a hundred different rumors," Lorenzo
Flagg said. "Will the government sell, or won't it?"

Talbot made a grimace. "Some say yes, and some say no. We all
know, of course, that Gould and his buffoon believe they have things
arranged to their liking—I'm not so sure."

"My son-in-law," Joshua said, "tells me he's been given good advice the President is in the clique or, if he isn't, is at least agreeable
to what it's doing and willing to leave them alone."

Talbot smiled austerely. "The President is a man of low instincts,
to be sure, and either doesn't know exactly what they are doing or
doesn't care—but when the time comes, I think he's not likely to
let them have their way."

Early in September, Talbot made another trip, and returned this
time to tell them it was his conviction gold might go to one hundred
and sixty but never to two hundred, and that only a fool would continue to gamble in the market now.

Joshua thought he was not likely to get any better advice and instructed Samuel to begin to sell quietly what gold they had, although when Philip announced that he would soon make his fortune, Joshua placed one hand upon his shoulder. "Philip, I hope so. If
you need to borrow money, let me know, I may be able to help you."

"I would certainly like to borrow money, Mr. Ching, a great deal
of money."

"How much?"

"As much as I can get."

"And your collateral?"

"Well, sir, after all, I haven't much. The house, the three lots."
The money, apparently, was gone.

"We'll talk this over, Philip."

"I've had very good advice on this, sir, although I can't give you
its source. The government will not sell, it absolutely—will—not—
sell. Gold will go to two hundred, and maybe higher."

Philip, Joshua thought, had that look of fanatic glee which charac-
terized those speculators who were convinced gold would reach
such heights they would all be made millionaires in a few hours.
"That's what I've heard, Philip. And, of course, other men are saying
just the opposite."

"But I know, I know."

Joshua had believed, for as long as he could remember, that the
greatest energies of the human race went into the devising and working out of schemes for exploiting one another, and, as the gold mar-

ket daily grew more frantic, he became convinced he would soon witness a dramatic demonstration of this cornerstone of his philosophy.

Philip presently applied to him for money, assigning as collateral everything Joshua had given him in the marriage agreement, all with a blithe unconcern which astounded Joshua, who had begun to feel that a catastrophe might destroy him at any moment, and it seemed small comfort that thousands of other men would be buried in the same heap of rubble.

He had strong desires to get out of the market entirely, take no more risks in this crazy carnival, but when William Talbot confided he was betting gold would go to one hundred and sixty, Joshua decided to take the same risk. By now men were predicting that the end of the week would see the riddle solved, one way or another, and Joshua looked so haggard that Susan said, "I'm worried about you, Joshua. Remember, anxiety is dangerous to the health. It can cause softening of the brain, or even premature death."

Joshua felt an involuntary chill run down his back and prickle his neck, and he glared at her. "Don't depend on it, Susan."

Thursday night, after gold had closed at one hundred and forty-four, the lobby of the Fifth Avenue Hotel was crowded with brokers and merchants, shouting their favorite theories. Joshua milled about with them for an hour or two, but went to his room before midnight and lay for some hours thinking of Talbot's assured prediction that the government would begin to sell before noon. He fell asleep some time near morning and, it seemed almost immediately, woke again to find himself sitting on the edge of the bed, staring into the darkness, and for some moments could not be sure if the day had come and gone, passing over him harmlessly, or if the general disaster had been so great he had been destroyed in it, for all his precautions.

At six o'clock he went down to the lobby and found it crowded with men who had, perhaps, remained there all night long, and several tried to stop him as he passed, plucked at his sleeve and addressed him pleadingly.

"What will happen, Mr. Ching?"

"Are you long or short, Mr. Ching?"

"Is the government for us or against us?"

Joshua considered their questions with an air of grave thoughtfulness, as if reluctant to assume his mantle of oracle, until all at once he realized that every man was an oracle today, and he answered no more questions but got into his carriage and drew the shades, placed together the fingertips of his long, thin and flexible hands, which Susan had once told him must mean he had been intended for a musician or a strangler, and went once again carefully and methodically over every possible chance the day might bring.

At Canal Street he told Huggens to continue on down to the Red Onion, and it was a little after seven when Joshua raised the curtains, though the foul smells seeping into the carriage had told him

several minutes earlier they had reached the Bloody Sixth. He stared
gloomily at the listless, haggard women, the men standing sullenly
in doorways, the children with their depraved and stricken faces, until all at once a small, dirty hand waved before him and, peering
down, he found Mud Foley jogging along beside the carriage, grinning at him. Joshua nodded and Mud Foley shrieked a few unintelligible words, for each time Joshua came into the ward Mud Foley
appeared and escorted him the last several blocks, and Joshua had
decided there must be a secret code by which slum people notified
one another of the arrival of strangers from the world outside.

The ritual was the same each time, even to the stained and ragged
crew of children gathered before the Red Onion and into the midst
of which Mud Foley now leaped, flailing about with arms and legs
and bare feet, so toughened as to be useful to him as weapons, keeping the children at bay until Stokes opened the door and then, as
they always did, they fell into startled silence, gazing at the tall,
blond-bearded man who emerged and walked swiftly between them
and into the Red Onion.

But at the instant he disappeared, they began crawling under the
carriage and beneath the horses and trying to open the doors. Huggens and Stokes remained on their seats, ignoring the children as
their master had done, while Mud Foley cursed them shrilly and
raced from one to another, dragging them away, slamming them
down, until there was a piercing whistle and Hoke O'Neil stood in the
doorway. At the sound, the children stopped their capering and
screaming to face him dutifully.

"Knock off," Hoke advised them and, all at once, brought one hand
out of his pocket, gave a swift upward motion and let a shower of
coins fall among them. Hoke left the children scrambling to pick
them up and returned to where Joshua sat at the saloon's only table.
"Know what they'll do now? Get drunk on swipes. You know, swipes
—dregs at the bottom of the beer barrel." He made a face. "Turns my
stomach to think of it. But then I was always particular about what
I ate and drank. Me and Betty, both. Neither one of us would ever
eat rotten food out of the streets the way the other kids did. Well—
what's up? I hear the bulls and bears are at it again."

"They are. That's why I'm here."

The saloon had not yet opened for business although Hoke, Joshua
was convinced, must sleep fully dressed on the bar if he ever slept at
all, for whenever he had felt obliged to travel into the Bloody Sixth,
Hoke was there whether he arrived early or late and, it seemed,
took as much pride in this dark, narrow building with its sawdust-
covered floor, its white painted stove standing in the middle of the
room and the big mirror behind the bar, as any successful broker
might take in his brownstone house. To Joshua it was always unpleasantly warm and moist, and smelt of stale whisky and unemp-
tied spittoons, but it was Hoke's domain: his court, where he had in

constant attendance his small lackey Mud Foley, who hung about
with the air of an alert dog who might momentarily be sent on an errand or thrown a bit of food, his feudal army of fighters, his serfs,
and his consort, Tessie Spooner; and with all that it was the neighborhood social center, too.

"This is one of the most desperate days in the nation's history,"
said Joshua solemnly. "If the gold maniacs succeed, God knows what
will happen. Hoke, I need four men I can trust."

"Trust for what?" Joshua smiled slightly but Hoke was staring at
him with those blue eyes which, though they looked flat and dead,
lightless and apparently without depth or any reflections from his
emotions, were nevertheless so intense, so sharply penetrating and
watchful, that Joshua never looked into them without a sense of having been warned.

"I want them in my office. No broker whose clients lose money today can feel safe and, if there's trouble, I want to be ready for it.
When a man loses money, as a great many men will, he no longer
knows what he's doing."

"That's if he ever thought much of it in the first place." Joshua
made a gesture, dismissing such a frivolous remark, and Hoke spoke
to Mud Foley, rattling off four names which sent him at a run out
the door.

"How much do you want for these men, Hoke?"

Hoke studied his shining black boots, picked his teeth with the
ivory toothpick, and suggested, "Five thousand."

"My God, Hoke, I've told you the nation's desperate today."

"Maybe the nation's desperate, but I ain't. You can count on those
four guys, they're all smart. If I gave you some dumb ones you'd wind
up with your safe cracked, your head split open, and your office
burned down. Anyway, you need them, you say."

"The richer you get, Hoke, the greedier you get."

"The richer you get," corrected Hoke, and stabbed a bent forefinger at Joshua, "the greedier I get. You know the old Tammany
rule: Take what you may—keep what you can."

There was a scuffling and knocking of heavy shoes and four men
came through the slatted doors. None of them was very tall but each
bore various marks of his trade—malformed ears and noses and
scarred chins and cheekbones; and all were dressed like Hoke, in
black frock coats and high black hats, though their diamond stickpins were smaller. Hoke introduced them, clapping each in turn on
the shoulder, but neither Joshua nor any of the men spoke a word in
greeting. "Patsey Higgins. Mickey Shannon. Tom Geigan. And this
one's called The Doctor. I forget why and so does he. Gentlemen, this
is Mr. Ching, and I want you to remember how much the Boss thinks
of him."

Joshua stood up slowly, reaching to his full height and looking
down at them for a moment before he began to talk. He told them

what he wanted done and, when he had finished, demanded, "Is that clear?" They went on staring at him in silence, and he turned to Hoke. "Did they hear me?"

"They heard you. Okay, beat it. And get down there before Mr. Ching does."

They marched out and Joshua and Hoke strolled after them, Joshua inquiring, with a slight ironic smile, "How did you happen to start studying politics, Hoke?"

"You know every Irishman studies politics from the cradle."

They found the children gathered once more, but they were silent now and looked quite stupefied, perhaps from their breakfast of swipes, though at sight of Hoke a few of them raised a small cheer which he acknowledged, but threw them no more coins. Joshua, seated in his carriage again, drew the curtains and fell into communion with himself, not emerging from this profound study until they approached the financial district, where he once more looked out, instantly alert, and studied the faces he saw for portents of the day.

It was still more than an hour and a half before the Exchange would open, but the streets were crowded with men who went dashing purposefully by, only to pause, looking puzzled, and start just as purposefully in the opposite direction. Most men walked alone, sometimes looking around as if they were pursued, and others stood in slowly milling groups, talking loudly and gesticulating, while any man who shouted above the others seemed able to gather an audience that listened in hypnotized fascination, and on each of these faces Joshua saw that look of inspired fury which foretold panic.

There were, he noticed, not only the usual frock-coated brokers and messenger boys, but men from other businesses and professions, and these members of the speculating public who appeared in the Street in large numbers only on days of disaster, seemed to him the worst omen of all. A peddler passed among them, selling toy bulls and bears, and some bought them to pin on their lapels but others pushed him aside, angrily demanding how he dared make fun of the nation's predicament. Many policemen patroled the streets, and whether gold rose or fell, a general riot was now being freely predicted, for whichever way it went thousands of men must be thrown into bankruptcy.

At last, when his carriage had stood motionless for two or three minutes, Joshua got out and walked the remaining blocks to his office, took the stairs two and three at a time and came to a bounding halt at the top, adjusted his collar and cravat and walked in calmly, to find Hoke's men seated on benches reading newspapers, and one of the clerks approached to say they had been waiting outside when he had arrived and he had let them in. He looked, however, quite anxious, and plainly thought Joshua might tell him to put them out again if he could.

"They're all right. They buy for some of the City Hall people."

Joshua went into his office, paused in the doorway to make a discreet signal to The Doctor, who was beside him with disconcerting speed, and Joshua put the desk between them while he explained that Geigan was to stay with Mr. Van Zandt, wherever he went, Shannon was to stay with him, and The Doctor and Higgins were to remain in the office to keep order and prevent the safe from being opened. Joshua thought of making some explanation for his unusual suspiciousness, which included not only his clerks but his son-in-law and his brothers, but this seemed unnecessary as he looked at The Doctor's face, intent and watchful as Hoke O'Neil's, and so he sent him out and locked the door and stood at the window, gazing into offices in the next building where men were even now dashing about, yelling and waving their arms.

As ten o'clock approached Joshua paced back and forth and once or twice opened the door when fists pounded at it, confronting demented faces and backing away from hands which tried to clutch at him.

The bidding began at one hundred and forty-five; there were no sales, and it continued to rise. Joshua stood before the tape, and was vaguely aware that the men in the outer offices and even in the street had fallen still, so still that at last he walked to the door, opened it a crack and found them staring at the blackboard where a clerk was recording the figures. But one man saw him, and before he could close the door they came charging forward, begging him to tell them what the government would do, and though he tried for a few moments to hold the door against them, at last he threw it wide, bellowing, "Come in, for Christ's sake," and, as they came tumbling in, rushed down the stairs before anyone could catch him, with Shannon close at his heels.

Shannon went ahead to clear the path, for the streets and sidewalks had become impassable, and Joshua set out for the Gold Exchange. Wherever he looked there were men gathered at opened windows, perched on rooftops, clinging to pillars and porticoes, and at each new bid the news swept over them in an instant, raising shouts and groans, joyous hoots and sickened grunts, and while he was still some distance from the Exchange there fell another silence, more ominous than the first, while men glanced about with dazed expressions, as if there had been the announcement of a mass death sentence which they had not quite understood or believed, repeating in awed whispers, "One hundred and sixty."

The bid was taken and went to one hundred and sixty-two. At that there were roars of "Settle up!" and the answer came back, "Never! Do your worst!"

Men began to scream piteously, as if under some unendurable physical torture, tearing at their collars, throwing off coats and hats, and as fights began policemen belabored heads and shoulders with their clubs. Joshua, close behind Mickey Shannon, who had his own way with a crowd, struggled with his neighbors and had become

as lunatic as any one of them. And then, in the midst of another waiting silence, a man appeared on the Treasury steps, shouting, "Fellow citizens, God reigns and the government at Washington still
lives! I am instructed to inform you that the Secretary of the Treasury has placed ten millions in gold upon the market!"

There was a break in the crowd, a surging back and forth, and
when they started to run, yelling, "Hang Fisk and Gould!" Joshua
stopped Mickey Shannon in the act of joining them, with a demand
that he take him back to his office.

Philip came to him late that same day, moaning, "But what went
wrong? Why did they change their minds?" He clutched at his head,
swaying his shoulders from side to side, and Joshua wondered if perhaps his son-in-law would follow the example of other bulls and
shoot himself, though he doubted that Philip had that much firm purpose.

"Ah, Philip," Joshua admonished him. "These questions, they
can't be answered, you know."

For more than a week the district was lighted every night and
Joshua, like other brokers, stayed in his office, trying to untangle
credits and losses, what he would be able to collect and what he
would not, and when at last he thought of Rose Michel it was with
a sense of wondering surprise, as if she were someone he had known
many years ago, and he felt an uneasy premonition that his child had
been born on one of these days when he would not have troubled to
read a note from her, if she had dared send it.

He found her in bed later that same day, smiling and reaching one
hand toward him as he appeared in the doorway, just as she might
have done if the child had been legitimate, and he approached her
with some caution, telling himself that apparently a woman was able
to turn herself into a wife when the need came to her own satisfaction, if not to the world's.

He kissed her carefully, marveling that this should be the same
girl for whom he had felt only an impatient sensuality, and she sent
Mrs. Stump to bring the baby—a boy, Rose told him, and asked
rather anxiously if he was pleased, for he did not look pleased and, in
fact, was still too much preoccupied to be eager to see the baby or
even fully aware that this child was his own.

But, at her question, he grew embarrassed, thrust his hands into
his pockets, and walked about as he had been doing for the past several days. "Of course," he assured her, and frowned. "What story did
you tell her?"

"I told her my husband was killed in a trotting race accident six
months ago and that you're his second cousin. Was that all right?"

"Of course," he assured her again, and turned as Mrs. Stump entered with the squalling baby. Joshua put his hands behind his back
and advanced toward him, looking grave and concerned, but even
after he had studied him for several moments he was unable to con-

vince himself that he had any other concern with it than to call upon its mother and offer his congratulations.

"What do you think of him?" she asked at last, and her eager smile had become doubtful.

"Fine, very fine," Joshua replied promptly and, as if to prove his interest and good will, inserted one forefinger into the baby's hand and let him seize it in a seeming fury of energy.

"You don't like him?" she asked sadly. "You don't think he's pretty?" She turned her head aside and closed her eyes, and when Joshua glanced at her he saw that tears rolled steadily across her nose and cheeks, dampening the pillow case.

"Of course I like him, Rose," he told her, but when he left she was still crying and he did not return for several days, hoping that when he did she would have stopped.

XXVIII

Once he was able to leave the bed where he had spent most of two months recuperating from his fight with Gaius Jenkins, Morgan had sprung at his work with as much determined agility as a man leaping to mount a galloping horse. Convinced he had wasted his time until then, he began a program of chasing about the mountains, from camp to camp, wherever Devlin Brothers owned property or heard of a likely investment, inspecting their placer and quartz mines, buying ore and riding the treasure coach to Corrine or Fort Benton when they had bullion to ship east, and went knocking at the doors of their creditors when they least expected to see him.

He was twice shot at from ambush, but he and Matt and Pete agreed this was an occupational hazard of any bank doing business in the mountains, and they thought there was no reason to make the women nervous by telling them it had happened.

"It's comforting to know," Matt remarked, "that if they pick you off, there's nothing personal in it. They don't hate your guts, they just love their money."

As he traveled he made constant comparisons between one camp and another, watching the streets as carefully as if he were looking for a lost sweetheart, was able to read the Territory's prosperity or troubles in a miner's eagerness or reluctance to sell, a woman's gown, the pace of footsteps along the boardwalks, and he rejoiced to see a well-dressed new whore, for the men assured one another that one was like the first robin, while a flock of them could only mean a prosperous summer was coming.

Helena was called a metropolis nowadays. A larger theater was to open soon. Carpenters and masons were knocking buildings together and tearing others down to replace them with more substantial structures. Coaches departed every day and in all weather for Corrine and Salt Lake City. All the places of amusement were crowded, and even though it was agreed the placers were washing thin, Helena had become the Territory's freighting center and could not die while the hundreds of camps scattered along the gulches, and the increasing numbers of farms and ranches, continued to support it.

From time to time, as Morgan came riding into town in the early morning, winding down the terraced hillside where his cabin perched, he paused and spent a few moments thoughtfully considering a body hanging from the city gallows, the great bare pine tree in Dry Gulch. The Vigilance Committee was quieter now than it had been in the early days and usually gave no warning that they were at work, and so it often seemed their victim had sprouted there overnight, a man dangling from a limb with his head awry and his vest and trousers so disheveled he must have fought his judges, his boots stiff and wrinkled, with a label pinned to him announcing the crime for which he had died. He hung there sometimes for two or three days, slowly turning and twisting, and his presence roused much curiosity and uneasy, guilty excitement.

"Who is he?"

"Never saw him before."

"Must have just come to town."

"Suppose he got here a little too soon?"

Still, the stores were beginning to close on Sundays and some of the citizens were proud of this sign of their developing civilization, though others predicted the Territory's prosperity would now dwindle away and vanish.

Morgan had, as even Lem Finney agreed, a good nose for ore, and they were willing to trust his recommendations that they buy a property or sell it, collect on a loan or renew it. But even with these honors to his credit, Morgan found that when two years had passed he had only a few hundred dollars more than he had had the day Lily Jones went off with Carter and Dancing Rabbit, and this sometimes disturbed him, although at other times he told himself the life was a good one, just to his taste, and perhaps he was not intended by nature for a rich man, or even for a successful one.

He had given Matt two thousand for his share of the mine in Daylight Gulch and, reminding himself that however truthful a man might have been, self-interest made him a systematic liar as soon as he became interested in gold mines, he went out one night with a shotgun loaded with gold dust and pellets and fired it into several crevices, raked the dirt with the heel of his boot, and began to look for a buyer. It was some time before he could persuade a tenderfoot to pay him three thousand dollars for this promising claim, but after a few months of working the property the tenderfoot came to him in a mood of puzzled reproach—for it was the habit of the tenderfoot to believe that someone should have given him timely warning—and offered to sell it back to him for one thousand. Morgan bought it, resisting the temptation to remind the tenderfoot of that motto of the mining camps, that honesty is the root of all evil, and money the best policy, and visualized a series of such transactions, carefully spaced.

He invested most of the money in leasing new claims in Butte, and each time he went there, paid a ceremonial call on Amos Muspratt, descended his shaft in a bucket made of half a whisky keg, and listened with sober interest to everything Amos had to tell him.

Muspratt, however, would not lease his claim or sell it, and although men tapped their heads suggestively whenever Muspratt's name was mentioned, Amos remained, as he had always been, serenely aloof. "Boys," he assured them, "say what you will, but Butte will someday be a Christer." And he told Morgan, with the air of an old magician imparting his secrets to a young novice, "This is the richest three miles square on God's green earth, you mark my words."

"I believe you, sir," Morgan respectfully agreed, although by now there were scarcely one hundred prospectors left in the camp.

The shacks were mouldering and overrun by rats, their doors hanging open or fallen off and the window frames carried away to be used somewhere else. And of the men Morgan had known well only Bruno Favorite was still there, though he had few customers now and none who sat playing poker on a Sunday afternoon, drinking mountain whisky and telling one another competitive lies about their past and present and future. And no one, they agreed, who had not been there in the early days could ever hope to understand what it had been like—for even if they had now been cast out of paradise, once, at least, they had known a mystic camaraderie and that sense of living vast, perilous experiences which had changed them all, replacing innocence with wisdom and apprehension with confidence.

"McGuirk and Carter and Lily Jones," Bruno would begin to chant, almost at sight of Morgan, and his green eyes were more doleful than ever. "Dancing Rabbit and Queen Victoria Butler. Zack Fletcher. Henry Halloway. Rowdy Jane and Froglip Sadie. Where the hell are they now?"

On Morgan's first trip he had told Bruno about Dancing Rabbit, run away to find her people, and Buckshot Carter, shot dead as he was walking to a restaurant with Lily Jones, and they had drunk several toasts in his honor, recalling the feast of young fawn which had turned out to be wolf meat. And Zack Fletcher, Morgan told him, had left most of his money invested with Devlin Brothers and gone away, though he did not mention that Lily Jones had gone with him. "He'll be back some day," Morgan predicted.

"They'll all be back some day, the ones who are still alive. They'll be back and when they come, I'll be here. By God, but that will be a reunion, won't it?"

"I hope so, Bruno."

He was not able to persuade either Matt or Pete to make any Butte investments, and they regarded the ore specimens he showed them with skeptical disinterest and spoke to him each time the one word: "Transportation?" And, of course, he had no better answer to that riddle than anyone else.

He traveled when the roads were closed by snow, and when it was so dark he could not see his horse's ears, was in Helena eating dinner with Jenny and Pete one day and, the next, brought Lisette a string of partridges he had shot on his way to Virginia City, sat down at her kitchen table to drink coffee and eat some of the ratafia cakes she made for him, and played with her baby girl, although at first the baby had made him feel rather strange. And one day Lisette looked at him intently, and asked, "When are you going to get married, Morgan?"

At that he felt his face grow hot and, with a constrained and sheepish laugh, announced that it was time to be on his way, he must get to the Reynolds ranch before dark or he would be caught there and invited to spend the night. "I don't know," he told her, and frowned defensively. "Maybe never."

She followed him to the door, and as he waved good-bye she called, "Everyone's getting married, Morgan—you don't know what you're missing," and laughed so merrily he was even more embarrassed, for even the word marriage had lately acquired for him sinister connotations, until it almost seemed there was a general conspiracy to speak it in his presence, and his ears grew sharper in anticipation of hearing it. He even found himself nowadays at many weddings, and sometimes had the further bad luck to be chosen best man, a responsibility he could not always escape by being in Fort Benton or Diamond City on that day.

When Lisette had married Ralph Mercer, he was Ralph's best man, an office he had thought he might one day perform for Zack Fletcher. When Rachel Finney had recently married Homer Grimes, he was Homer's best man, and in another few weeks he would be Jonathan's best man at his wedding to Georgina Hart. And, of course, he was made aware that as Matt Devlin's oldest son he had become the object of various schemes and plots against his freedom.

The town, it seemed, was full of rather pretty young girls who were not to be seen about the streets, but who appeared in alarming numbers whenever he made the mistake of accepting an invitation to one of their dances or skating parties. And it was enough to look at any one of them, to have a vision of himself five years from then, married to that same girl, who was no longer fresh and eagerly determined to enchant him, but beginning even then to betray that tiredness and inclination to remorse he had observed in so many young wives; for most girls, he thought, had only energy enough to last them until they were married, and afterward there was nothing left of the lures by which they had surprised and won a husband, so that they deteriorated rapidly before his eyes until, in time, he must defend himself by paying them no more attention.

These girls did not seem to him to be individually very clever, but apparently they shared some primitive intuition which guided them in this one great adventure of their lives; or it might be they pooled their information and resources as did other secret organizations. Whatever it was, he was wary of them all, and when one night after he had taken Anna Grace Burgess to a sleighing party, she unexpectedly gave him a moist, open-mouthed kiss, he developed an abject terror of them all and vowed never to go to a respectable party again.

For even if he should find some such extraordinary girl as Jenny had predicted he was looking for, he could think of nothing needful a wife might contribute to his present sense of exuberant well-being.

His cabin, the first thing a wife would change, was furnished with two bunks, two chairs and a table, carelessly carpentered by the previous owner, and might have been carted down there intact from Butte. Shelves were stacked with tin cups and plates, bottles and rocks and books on geology and chemistry stood here and there, and picks and gold pans were thrown into a corner. His front yard was the hillside itself and his garden, composed of sagebrush and cactus, required no tending. Lisette had given him a red-coated hound she had named Music, and although the animal was reported to mope during his absences, it forgave him the moment he reappeared and held no grudges for the neglect it had suffered, as a wife would be sure to do.

He ate in restaurants or hotels or camped along the road, or, when he was in Virginia City, with his parents or Lisette and Ralph; but it satisfied him as well to cook a steak in the fireplace, cut from the forequarter of beef which hung outside his cabin during cold weather.

For his amusement he preferred to go to the theater with men, for he did not have to take them to an oyster supper afterward at the St. Louis Hotel. There were horse races and prizefights on Sunday afternoons, and now and then he played a game of poker, remembering Zack Fletcher's advice that there was no better way to study men's characters. The whorehouses were well-stocked, and if he wanted to dance the hurdy-gurdy houses were lively places, noisy and crowded, where the girls were much better dancers than any girl trained by Professor Bundidge; and in one of them, the Bella Union, he had recently met a girl named Ula Malloy.

He had seen her first on the streets of Fort Benton, coming out of a hotel with another girl, and in order to get a better look at her bright red hair and lively face, had stepped deliberately into her path, dodging back and forth as she tried to pass around him, and, when she glared at him, gave her that sudden smile which had proved its magic too well with other girls. But not with her, apparently, for she told him to get out of her way and went on, and he watched until she and her friend entered a restaurant and then forgot about her until, a week or two later, he went into the Bella Union and saw her again.

He stood studying her for some time but did not dance with her, for it seemed that Ula Malloy was the camp's new pet, and he decided that she was not beautiful, perhaps she was not even pretty, but nevertheless she piqued his curiosity as no other girl had since the day he had first seen Lily Jones, and he began to wonder what her secrets were.

She had blue eyes which shut tight when she laughed, and a nose not much bigger than a baby's, and her freckled white skin glistened with sweat as she went whirling about the room with one partner and another. She was constructed for her work, he thought, like an Indian pony, with a compact body and short, muscular legs; and once he had danced with her and put his hand on that firmly muscled back, and noticed that her hair curled even more as it was dampened by exercise, he acquired a determination to test his luck with this buoyant young girl which only became more insistent each time he failed.

Popularity and success—for he heard a rumor that she earned thirty dollars or more a night—had made her tyrannical, and it was two weeks before she would let him see her home.

"You can't stay." She wagged her finger. "You must promise me you won't try to."

"Of course I won't," he agreed, and humbly added, "if you don't want me to."

She smiled wisely at this lie and he entered the cabin, finding it furnished in luxurious mountain style, with braided rag rugs and black walnut chairs and sofa, white muslin curtains and red flock wallpaper. The air was permeated by the fragrance of dry grasses which had been used to stuff the mattress, and as he glanced inadvertently in the direction of the bedroom she bounced across the room and shut the door.

They sat facing each other, looking solemn and formal, but had nothing to say, until at last she leaned forward and whispered, "You won't believe me—but I'm a virgin." He looked, perhaps, more startled by this news than she had expected, for she threw back her head and laughed until he began to wonder what kind of joke she had meant it to be, and then she spread her short-fingered hands upon her breasts, asking, "What's the matter? Haven't you ever met one before?"

For a week or two he was scrupulously respectful, seeming scarcely to notice that she flirted with him as if she had no idea what such gestures and smiles might provoke. But at last he tried to kiss her and, when he did, she slapped him smartly and ran across the room, as if to defend herself with some piece of furniture, and only ventured out when he turned to go, looking so angry she must have been afraid she would never see him again. And then she slipped one hand about the back of his neck and caught hold of his coat with the other, telling him he could kiss her but not do anything more, and he was by now so determined to expose this little fraud that he was prepared to endure far worse torments than she had made him suffer so far.

As he left Lisette and rode toward the Reynolds ranch, he fell to brooding again about Ula Malloy, her white freckled skin and red hair, her eagerness to be caressed and stroked, for she approached him like their cat Shekel, brushing against his hands and body, and though he had sometimes left there so confused and exasperated it seemed he would gladly strangle her, he had assured himself he was more stubborn than she was.

The nearer he got to the Reynolds ranch, however, the less real she seemed, for his feelings were invaded by ominous dread and a cowardly reluctance to confront Mrs. Reynolds with bad news.

There were many small farms and ranches in the mountain valleys and their owners were in constant need of money. One farm or ranch looked like another, and even the ranchmen's wives, pallid, thin women, worn and stringy, apparently both old and young at the same time, looked so much alike it would have been easy to imagine the same family of tow-headed children popped up out of the ground the moment a stranger appeared. These small farms and ranches seemed to have none of that reckless enthusiasm which infected the rest of the mining country, but were as dismal and lonely, as preyed upon by discomfort and disease as those farms he had seen in Missouri along the river bottom lands, as if there was a penalty exacted from men who tried to make the earth productive, rather than attacking it forcefully and blasting and crumbling it into releasing its riches.

But it was the women who troubled him most, for they gazed at him in sullen silence, and he felt that each of them accused him and their husbands of having condemned them to this life which made them grow old early and die young, and drove many of them into insanity.

He had a hope, of which he was somewhat ashamed, to avoid Mrs. Reynolds on this trip, and argued with himself, as he approached the ranch-house in the late afternoon, riding toward it over a trail from which she would not be likely to see him from the house, that he had no personal responsibility for any of their sorrows; neither Indians nor grasshoppers nor drought could reasonably be laid to his door—and yet she would do it by a glance.

Reynolds pretended to be glad to see him and would probably have been glad to see any one, and Morgan edged him into the barn while they talked of recent disasters. But the children had discovered him and came to hang about the doorway, staring at him as they always did in apparent wonderment at his height and dark skin.

"We had a good crop last year, the best so far, and then they came

—a cloud that settled down overnight, and we could hear them while we lay in bed. It sounded like a pouring rain. In the morning everything was gone, chewed down to the ground."

Morgan frowned and, inadvertently, sighed. "I know, Reynolds."

"Some of the ranches weren't touched. We lost everything." He shrugged. "Next year we may be luckier, if we're still alive." He lowered his voice and gestured at the children but, though they backed away, they soon began to creep nearer again. "What's going to happen? They give us no protection, let the buggers run loose in all directions, armed better than the soldiers. Four Blackfeet showed up not long ago begging for food and we gave them everything we had, but after they'd left she was so streaked she went to bed for two days, couldn't even talk or feed the kids. Why don't they do something?" he inquired, watching Morgan as carefully as if he would be sure to find the answer if he stared deep enough into his eyes.

"I don't know any more than you do what's going to happen, Reynolds. Wherever I go everyone's scared. Maybe you could send your wife and kids into town?"

"On what? We've all got to stay here and hope to Christ they don't get us. And what about the mines? Fellow came through here the other day saying it was the last season they'd be worth anything, that everyone would clear out in the spring and I'd better sell if I had a chance."

"I don't think so," Morgan told him, in a low apologetic voice, but then he began to discuss the possibilities of a sale, not because he believed Reynolds could sell his farm profitably, but because he did not want to ask him for money. And, at last, he had delayed too long and was urged into the house to have supper with them, and entered the low-ceilinged room with his hat in his hand, ducking his head slightly, and with a beseeching smile for Mrs. Reynolds.

There was an oppressive sense of unluckiness about the man, his wife, his children and his house. The room was chill, in spite of the warm day, and had a peculiar rank odor which seemed the smell of poverty or, perhaps, misfortune itself, something he could not identify or describe, though he had encountered it often in these isolated farmhouses. He and Reynolds sat on stools, the children on boxes, and the woman waited on them, saying she was not hungry and would eat later when her appetite returned.

Morgan ate quickly, taking care not to taste the food, for she was a cook who could remove all flavor from meat, make the coffee taste as if there was lye in it, and produce bread which was a hard, pasty ball, and though he tried to avoid looking at her he found himself compelled again and again to meet that reproachful gaze while he discussed the Territorial politics with Reynolds.

At last he lighted a cigar, after deferentially asking Mrs. Reynolds if he might, gave one to Reynolds, and took a small notebook from his hip pocket, flipped it open and scowled, pretending to study it, while Reynolds and his wife and children watched him silently, as if scarcely daring to breathe. At last, with as much casualness as he could contrive, he turned to him. "Reynolds, I don't like to tell you this but if we loan you anything more, we've got to have a first mortgage not only on your land but on all your traps, including the cattle."

Reynolds nodded, as if this generous offer was a better one than he had hoped for, but the woman moved away. He got up quickly and went to the door, bowing toward her back. "Thank you for supper, Mrs. Reynolds. I've got to be on my way now." He started out, then paused. "I'm sorry, but we have investors to protect."

She looked at him slyly. "I only wish you'd take it all at once."

"We don't expect to take it, Mrs. Reynolds," he protested. "Your husband has a good farm here." Reynolds again nodded briskly and seemed glad to have an ally against his wife. "But it takes a little time to get it going."

"And if he does get it going? What have we then?"

Reynolds coughed, and he and Morgan and the children left the house. The children, who had sat in silence during the meal, occasionally whimpering or pinching one another, now began to run about, yelling gleefully, as if at the release from their mother's presence, and Morgan was as urgently eager as they to escape, for all at once it seemed there was nothing in nature so oppressive as an unhappy woman. He wished Reynolds luck, though it seemed to avoid him, waved at the screaming children and set off at a gallop, less concerned at the thought of traveling alone at night than of having to confront Mrs. Reynolds again.

Now, just as he had used the cigar to get rid of the taste of Mrs. Reynolds' cooking, he summoned up Ula Malloy, speeding about the Bella Union in her low-cut, short-skirted dress, and running ahead of him to her cabin, breathlessly laughing as if she could not wait for them to get inside, and assured himself that only such women, spoiled and demanding, were worth a man's trouble.

He knew her contours by now as well as he knew the mountain roads and passes, for she was the most artful temptress he had met, willing to allow him anything but what he wanted most, and sent him away just when he was least expecting it, a tactic which no doubt brought him back much sooner than he would otherwise have come. And it also kept him thinking of her while he traveled, her gasps and shudders, the easy tears and laughter of this ruthless young virgin, and even while he prowled about the Butte hillsides it seemed he must hurry back before some other man got the benefit of the volatile excitability he had cultivated with such care.

But one day he heard from Bruno Favorite some news which put even Ula Malloy out of his mind for the moment.

For Bruno reported the third visit in eight months by a man who had bought three claims outright, hiring their former owners to work them for him, and taken leases on two others. And this man, Morgan decided as he watched Bruno's mimicry, must be Lem Finney.

The glitter of his eyes as he rubbed his hands crisply together, the quiet tone in which he asked questions, his way of deprecating the property, shrugging and gazing into space, mounting his horse and setting off and then, as at some afterthought, returning to ask another question although he seemed not to hear the reply, was certainly no one but Lemuel Finney.

"He's a prospector," Bruno told him. "That's his story, anyway. But he looks too smart for a prospector. I don't predict he wastes any time moping along on his pony staring at rim-rocks and imagining each one lays at the door of his private treasure house. Not this one, he's a different sort altogether. Rides up at a nice clip, hops off his horse like he's all business, and asks who hasn't been doing so well lately. He leaves most of his drink but pays for two or three to keep you talking and then, just as if someone had pointed a finger and said to him, there's the road straight to El Dorado, he sets out with as much confidence as if he knew better than anybody else where to find what he's looking for."

Morgan felt as angry and as jealous as if he had heard that Lem Finney had been calling on Ula Malloy. For Lem, he thought, had gotten rich enough from his several enterprises in Bannack and Virginia City and Helena and Fort Benton, while he had nothing for the labor of the year and a half he and Zack had spent in Butte but his knowledge of the ground and his clues to some of its mysteries.

But he was not able to surprise Lem Finney into admitting he had ever been in Butte, although Lem showed a lively interest in hearing that someone had been buying claims and taking leases. "You say the fellow sounded like me?" Lem smiled. "I won't ask you what the description was, Morgan. It could be a bad jolt, hearing what we look like to someone else. But maybe, if that's what's happening, I should buy up a few claims—what do you think?"

"Don't bother unless you're ready to spend a hell of a lot of money, because there's no other way to get it out."

"Money, of course," said Lem. "That's always our problem out here, isn't it?" He gave Morgan his characteristic smile, at once pert and crafty. "Still, I wouldn't like to find out someday when it's too late that I'd overlooked anything, now would I?"

XXIX

For those who were rich enough to afford it, it was the gayest holiday of the year. Every woman who was not sick or in mourning opened her house from noon until midnight, and men in frock coats and silk hats sped about the city in their carriages or hired hacks, or, if they could make no better arrangements, on foot. Early in the day they were to be seen stepping smartly out of carriages, strutting up the steps of brownstones and, after five or ten minutes, dashing back down. As the day wore on their progress slowed. They staggered up and lurched down, until finally many of them were carried off by friends still sober enough to help those no longer able to help themselves, and at midnight the streets grew quieter, carriages disappeared and the ladies, often as befuddled as their guests, were undressed by their maids and put to bed, relieved to have that New Year's Day over.

Joshua had promised Suky she might have her first reception in the newly furnished house, though the workmen had been there all through the summer and fall months and he thought they might have become permanent residents. Then, to his surprise, the house was finished and looked exactly as Suky had first described it seven months ago. The workmen disappeared, and only in time, for the baby was born not a week later on the eighth of December; a girl, as Suky had predicted, and she named her Sarah, after her Grandmother Ching.

By nine o'clock on New Year's Eve Suky was fast asleep, and when she woke at eight the next morning the preparations had begun and Susan and Ceda were there to oversee them, while Suky drank coffee in bed and waited for Mr. Ducarcel, who described himself as an artist in hair and whose services had been demanded by so many women she was apprehensive he might be stolen from her.

The traveling punch-maker was busy in the kitchen with bottles of brandy and champagne, rum and chartreuse and green tea and some special syrup, artfully combining a potion which was intended to take immediate and lasting effect and was said to be so delicious that a man who got drunk on it did not disgrace himself. The secret was guarded by him as carefully as Mr. Ducarcel guarded his supply of Japanese bark and hairpins and switches. For he was known to make the best punch in the city and was extremely irascible as he worked, suspicious of bystanders, gesturing them back and threatening to leave without completing his job if they did not stop spying on him, until Susan heard the commotion and rushed in to scatter them away, declaring she would stand guard until he had completed the mixture.

A long trestle table stood against the rear wall of the drawing room, closing off the doors into the library and conservatory. It was covered with white damask and set with silver candelabra and epergnes, borrowed from Philip's sisters, but the only other changes which had been made in concession to the hordes expected to go trampling through today had been to take up the light gray velvet carpet.

The florist presently arrived to begin his constructions of white roses, and he set pots of lilies of the valley on all the windowsills and over the fireplace. Portraits of Philip's Dutch ancestors hung on

the white silk walls, overlooking this new environment of gilded
French furniture, but Suky was talking nowadays about Corot and
Gérôme and Meissonier, and no doubt those Van Zandts would soon
retire to the library.

The caterer's wagon drove up to the kitchen door, and under
Ceda's eager inspection he bore in boned turkeys and roast chickens,
hothouse fruits, barrels of oysters, game pâtés, cakes decorated as
elaborately as a lady's skirt—food enough to feed one thousand men,
he assured them. The butler was given the keys by Joshua, and two
footmen came trampling up from the cellar with cases of whisky
from De Groot Distilleries, and down from the attic with a Madeira
he had bought at auction, sold by a broker who had not managed to
survive the gold manipulations of Black Friday.

Mr. Ducarcel was let in at exactly nine o'clock and sped nimbly up
the stairs to Suky's room, and Ceda, who had seen him go by, ran to
tell Susan he had come.

He was still there when they went to dress at nine-thirty and they
peeked in to see Suky seated erect and motionless at the dressing
table, with that look of remote unconcern she was able to assume
when she was most intently concentrated, while Mr. Ducarcel
frowned and sighed, darted to one side and then the other, retreated
across the room and came dashing forward again with an attitude of
impetuousness and despair, as if he were at once determined to create his masterpiece and yet not hopeful it could be done.

He rolled a curl about a mass of fuzz and, when she glanced at
him in the mirror he unrolled it again, throwing his arms out wide.
"Oh, madame, I do my best—but nothing, nothing satisfies."

"Of course it does, Mr. Ducarcel," she told him kindly. "But I
know what a perfectionist you are." She gave him an appealing smile
and he flew at his work once again in a flurry of enthusiastic frustration. Susan and Ceda closed the door very softly, but neither Suky nor
Mr. Ducarcel had noticed them.

He had drawn her hair back from her face and off her neck, leaving only a curling wisp which might have accidentally escaped
the brush, and was now arranging the cluster of curls which was to
fall down the back of her head. He had tried, earlier, to pin on a frizzle
of bangs, but after Suky had observed it for a moment with her impartial gaze he had, with a sigh, removed the fringe and flung it into
the satchel, petulant and disappointed, but then had told her in an
outburst of confidence that she had been right, she had been quite
right, as she always was, and it would be a pity to confuse that forehead with a mess of tangled hair.

"Most women, madame, have no idea what they look like. They
look at themselves and they don't see what's there, only what they
wish were there." He shrugged, turning his mouth down in a philosophical grimace. "That's why they look the way they do."

He took a length of velvet ribbon from Maxine, made several deft
maneuvers, and then began to work it into the coiffure so that it ap-

peared in the midst of a cluster of curls, formed a careless-seeming loop, and disappeared again, and all the while he scowled and drew deep breaths. At last, Maxine presented him with the garland of white roses she had just completed, and as all three of them watched the mirror with anxious, doubtful faces, he let it hover about her head for a moment, seeking its proper place, and at last brought it slowly to rest. They sighed, and Suky gave him a bright, forgiving smile.

He now hastily threw his tools into the satchel, made her a short little bow and would have dashed away, but she held forth one hand and as he took it he discovered she had given him a gold watch, engraved with his name and the date, and he kissed both her hands in gratitude, telling her he would come to her at any hour of the day or night, without any notice at all, and wherever she might chance to be.

Suky went into the bathroom and Ceda and Susan, in their dressing gowns, came to confer with Maxine, asking if Mrs. Van Zandt had suffered too much from the hairdresser, if he had tormented her with his tantrums for which he was known and dreaded, or if he had used her gently, and if his final result had been a happy one.

"I've never seen such a beautiful head," Maxine assured them.

They left again and Maxine began to lay out the clothes, going about her task with an unusual reverence. Some commotion could be heard in the streets, though it was not yet ten-thirty, and even the poodle Romola had caught the excitement and followed her about, prancing on his hind legs and barking, snatching at the edge of the petticoat where it lay across the chaise, and when he caught up one of the white satin slippers and carried it behind the draperies, Maxine spanked him sharply and put him into the hall, where he went scooting away with his ears flat and his tail held tight.

Suky returned, and once again they fell silent as she began to make up her face. Many women, and she had heard that Coral Talbot was one of them, had their faces done for them on important occasions by another artist who, like Mr. Ducarcel, hurried from house to house along Fifth Avenue from Washington Square to Thirty-fifth Street, with occasional excursions toward Madison Avenue; but Suky was convinced no one knew a woman's face but herself—if, indeed, she did. Someone else, not knowing what the face was intended to show, would be sure to impose some mistaken illusion upon the original, and however alluring it might look to outside spectators, its owner could never feel at peace with it.

She was still at work when Susan and Ceda tapped at the door, and she called out to let her see them. Susan swept forward with a somewhat challenging air, but Ceda seemed only to hope there was nothing actually wrong with the way she looked. For Suky had by now completely taken over the role of arbiter. It was she who decided where they went, what they talked about and read, what painters and composers they admired or disliked, how they dressed and arranged

their hair, what their attitudes were toward friends and enemies
and strangers, and though Susan was still sometimes stubbornly defiant enough to enjoy a play which Suky found tiresome, none of them
doubted her infallibility. Susan had once inquired where Suky managed to learn all this, and Ceda had replied that she knew it by instinct; while Joshua declared it to be one more evidence of his theory
of a natural aristocracy.

"She's clever, and she's sensitive. Doesn't that explain it?"

"Suky could advise the Van Zandts," Ceda said. "If they had the
slightest ambition of being anything but frowsy."

Still, their clothes for this day had required an unusual number of
long conferences. Susan had proposed to wear a gown of rose-colored
satin, which they knew was more becoming to her than any other
color, but Suky had gently persuaded her that under the circumstances—and of course they knew she meant the circumstance of
Susan's fortieth birthday—nothing could be more elegant than black
velvet, heavily beaded.

Some women committed serious mistakes at their New Year's Day
receptions. They appeared in gowns with low necks or short sleeves,
wore too much jewelry or not enough, took off their gloves or wore
white ones when they should have worn beige; and no amount of
food or punch could cancel out such blunders, for the men carried
the news from house to house, and even though respectable women
were advised to keep off the streets on that day they knew in precise detail the triumphs and disasters of all their friends.

"Everything," Suky had warned them long ago, "must be exactly
right."

Now she approached them, murmuring, "Oh, Mama, how beautiful you are." She carefully touched her cheek against Susan's, and
Susan, who had been at the edge of either a slight martyrdom or outright hostility, smiled and turned slowly about, while Suky stood
with her hands clasped, shaking her head in wondering admiration.
"And Aunt Ceda—oh, how proud I am of you both."

Their dresses, and Suky's, had narrow skirts, puffed out in back
just below the waist, a curiosity which had first begun to appear a
few months ago, and although in the beginning it was not taken seriously, dismissed as an aberration no one would accept, it had swollen
steadily and at last been recognized for what it was—a bustle.

No one knew what the style signified or why it had come into being, nor could it be explained away like the hoop skirt—a device to
conceal an empress' pregnancy. But the bustle was formidable as the
hoop had not been, for though the hoop had many detractors who
insisted that a woman wearing it looked like a creature inhabiting
a bowl which tipped and careened perilously about her, it had been
an inoffensive garment, protesting the presence of virtue hidden
safely inside it; while this new grotesquery was not to be so simply
understood, nor could anyone predict its future, for it had no recognizable past.

Neither Susan nor Ceda had been eager to have their new dresses bustled but Suky had convinced them, by means of sketches sent to her from France, and now, as she questioned them gently and humorously, they admitted there was something satisfying in this distortion, so mysterious as to acquire almost magical significance, filling beholders with awe and producing uneasy sensations in those who lacked it.

The poodle Romola returned, squeezing through the crack in the opened door, and made a bound to land on Suky's petticoat, but Maxine put him outside again and Susan and Ceda followed, for Suky liked to dress in private. Neither Suky nor Maxine spoke until she was ready for the dress, and then Maxine came toward her carrying it tenderly, a gown of heavy white silk with pearl embroidery. "Oh, this one, madame, is my favorite of them all. This is the most beautiful gown ever made." Maxine looked as if she might cry over its beauty, but did not for fear of staining it before it had ever been worn.

And when she had it on, Suky stood observing herself, and was once again a little surprised to find the young girl she had seen earlier that morning, looking rather wistful and subdued, transformed into this assured and stately woman who now approached the mirror, giving herself a more ruthless examination than she ever gave to any other woman—for she could tell with one quick glance whether or not the other was her competitor and, if she was not, Suky had no interest in what she was wearing or how she wore it, the style of her hair or the sound of her voice. She turned slowly one way and then another, while Maxine was whispering her compliments in French, and the gown's long train twined itself about her legs and untwined; other women often kicked at their trains as if an offending dog had sat on them and would not move, but Suky had learned to manipulate hers with easy unconcern.

She tilted her head to put belladonna drops in her eyes and, at the sound of Philip's voice, opened them to see only a swimming haze, through which Philip moved toward her. She blinked to settle the drops, touched the corners of her eyes with a handkerchief, and noticed that Maxine had left the room. Philip, whose troubles on Black Friday had made him sarcastic and short-tempered, as if he blamed someone else for his losses and had not quite decided where the blame lay but, meanwhile, was taking the precaution of distrusting everyone, now paced around her, nodding and humming as he went.

"How remarkably well you're looking today, Mrs. Van Zandt." He smiled wryly at this phrase each caller addressed to his hostess during the four or five minutes between his arrival, his gulping of bouillon or punch or champagne, slipping a few oysters into his mouth, gobbling a pheasant leg, and dashing away again.

Suky looked at him and smiled, though his face was only a blur she might not have recognized if they had met unexpectedly in some public place, and all at once he was peering into her eyes, taking hold of her chin and pinching it slightly to keep her from turning away. "The doctor's told you not to use that stuff. You'll ruin your eyesight for the sake of being fashionable."

It was rather easy for Suky to imagine that if Philip had been a few years older she might have despised him, but because he was so nearly her own age she thought of him as a naughty and mischievous playmate, charming and exasperating, who remained convinced it was his duty to raise the Van Zandt banner from time to time here in the enemy camp of the Chings. Whenever the notion took him, as it had more often since Black Friday, he began to taunt her about her fashionable pretenses and snobbish foibles, as if he himself lived in the modest style of the old Knickerbockers or, at least, would have preferred to if the choice had been given him.

"Are you in a bad humor today, Philip?" She moved away, slipping around him with one of those characteristic sinuous movements, for Suky moved with a boneless grace, confounding all observers, and now she began to spray her hair and arms and neck with tuberose perfume.

"You're expecting a great success, I suppose?" Suky was buffing her nails, but did not answer. "Will Frederic Hallam be here?"

"Perhaps. I don't know."

"You don't know?" He stood before her, bent his knees to bring his face on a level with hers, and although Suky still refused to look at him he smiled wisely, and it occurred to her to give him a sharp rap on the temple with the ivory side of the buffer, but she tossed it to the dressing table and began pulling on her gloves. "Have you seen Hallam since he got back?"

"Of course not, Philip, you know that." And she had not, for Frederic had returned from Europe only a few days before Sarah was born.

"Did you know his wife is pregnant?" He watched her, and then grinned, as if he had caught her in some self-betrayal, some frown or catch of breath, and he walked away again.

Suky began to sort among the bottles and jars on the dressing table, pretending to look for something, and finally turned her head and smiled ever so slightly, looking at him from the corners of her eyes. "Who told you that? Mrs. Talbot?" Philip gave a theatrical laugh, but would not answer, and now he began to talk about Alvita, whom he knew much better than Suky did, for Suky had seen her only twice, once when she and Felice had met her on a shopping expedition in Stewart's, and on the night of her wedding.

"She would be a valuable friend for you to have, wouldn't she, Susan?" Philip had never called her Suky, perhaps because that was Joshua's name for her.

"Would she?"

"The Van Alstines. The Hallams. All their connections—Delafields and Laceys and Talbots—quite a help to you if you could manage it."

Suky had been thinking the same thing, ever since Frederic's engagement had been announced, and this suggestion by Philip struck her as a little uncanny, almost as if she might have been talking in her sleep, murmuring of Delafields and Laceys and Van Alstines. And there seemed no reason why it should not happen, if Philip or Coral Talbot or some other enemy did not spoil it, for she had observed Alvita carefully during that afternoon when Felice insisted they leave Stewart's and go to her house to have tea, and had discovered that Alvita was one of those girls to whom it would never occur to make a man very unhappy, or to make him very happy, either; and furthermore she would not think it would occur to any other woman.

"I like her. She's very kind, very agreeable," murmured Suky.

"Very easy to deceive."

All at once Suky raised her right hand and, as she had foreseen, rapped Philip sharply across the temple with the buffer, he gave her a light, quick slap on the cheek, they stepped swiftly apart, as if to decide what was to happen next, and there was a loud knock before Joshua opened the door. They turned, to find Joshua looking at them with a grim, skeptical face, as if he might have surprised two children playing erotic pranks. "A very happy New Year to you, sir," Philip said, most solemnly, and was gone.

"Come in, Papa." Suky was busy now, collecting her gold scent box, her ermine wrap, if the house should become cold from doors opening and closing, and asked herself angrily how it was that Philip had all the jealous possessiveness to which he thought a husband entitled when he was, in fact, his father-in-law's absolute captive.

"Was he being troublesome?"

"Philip?" She raised her eyebrows, unable to guess what he might mean, then gave a laugh that sounded like spilling water, and took Joshua's arm, explaining she could not see because of the belladonna, and that was what they had been quarreling about.

"He behaves as a husband should?"

"Of course, Papa."

"He's kind to you?"

"Of course he is."

"He's in no position to be troublesome, remember that."

They went down the staircase where, at their appearance, a maid ran to draw the draperies and began to light the candles. Suky gave a backward motion of her arms to throw her skirt into its proper lines, and as she walked into the drawing room she was met by Susan and Ceda, while the waiters retreated to a flanked position across the room.

Joshua left them to set out on his own rounds, saying he would come back in two or three hours, and as the women stood together there was a clattering of wheels upon the pavement, a band began to play, and a score or more of young men tumbled out of a wagon with Corporate Engineers painted across it, and came jogging up the

steps. But they grew shy as they entered the house, until Suky gave
them a tolerant encouraging smile, and while the serenade continued they fell eagerly upon the food and drink and mumbled their
greetings to Suky.

"Fine day."

"How extraordinarily well you're looking, Mrs. Van Zandt."

"Can't stay but a moment," and in less than five minutes they were
gone again, leaving the room empty and strange.

Suky strolled about, rearranged a few flowers, passed the gold
scentbox beneath her nose and glanced into the mirror, and then her
uncles Aaron and Samuel arrived with their sons and, presently, as if
not only the door but the entire front of the house had been thrown
open, the room was crowded with men—some they knew, some they
could recognize, and others who had heard that Mrs. Van Zandt was
beautiful, the house was newly furnished, the table would be bounti-
fully set and the punch generously served. It was their habit to exchange names as they passed in the streets, shouting from carriage
to carriage, adding new names to their lists and checking off those
they had visited, though sometimes they forgot and came back
again; but after the first few hours neither they nor their hostesses
noticed this mistake, and late in the day most of them stuffed the list
into a pocket and went barging confidently into any house they
chose.

They passed rapidly by Suky and Susan and Ceda and, still wearing their coats and hats and gloves, went to raid the table and drink
the punch, and by two o'clock Ceda was whispering that the reception had been too successful, these marauders would wipe them out
before sundown.

"How many calls?" they asked one another.

"Beautiful afternoon."

"Another glass of punch?"

"Don't care if I do."

Men continued to arrive and the room became a confusion of
voices, a rattling of glasses and cups and plates, the servants dashed
about to keep the platters filled and carried out baskets piled with
used plates, while men in black coats swirled through the room, a
changing army of admiring strangers whose presence in her house
was no more disconcerting to Suky than if an experienced actress
had found unknown faces in her audience. She moved slowly among
them, sometimes throwing the little ermine cape over her shoulders
and sometimes trailing it at her side, and they watched her, observing the gentle sway of her hips and pliable turns of her body, never
supposing she heard nothing they said and did not even look at them
when she smiled, that tender impartial smile which seemed a kind
of benediction.

"Are you all right?" There was Joshua again, standing beside her
and looking concerned. "This isn't too exhausting?"

"I'm not tired, Papa."

"It's almost five o'clock."

"So late?"

The noise in the streets was increasing. Carriages and coaches went by with their passengers loudly singing. Voices shouted continuously and they heard more often the sound of a policeman's club striking the pavement in his call for help, and once they were startled by a pistol shot, which brought momentary silence to the room, but then, as if in agreement no harm had been done by it, there was a general outburst of laughter and they plunged again into the oysters and pâté.

Several young men had collapsed by now and been carried out by their friends who mumbled apologies as they passed Suky, marching away as solemnly as pallbearers, but she smiled compassionately, and when someone lurched into a vase full of white roses and smashed it to bits she took that, too, as only a part of this massive and unrestrained tribute being paid her by the men of the city. But the triumph would not be one if Frederic missed it, and by now it had grown dark, the callers were in retreat, and she was beginning to pity Susan Van Zandt when she saw him standing in the vestibule doorway, wearing a black overcoat with a sealskin collar, and watching her with the same grave and thoughtful expression she had seen last, as they were dancing together, nearly seven months ago.

He crossed the room, and she touched his hand. "I was afraid you weren't going to come, Frederic."

"I wasn't."

Suky glanced about, casting random smiles, sniffed at the scent-box, and felt sure she would begin to cry. "Have you seen Felice today?" She looked up at him. "Please help me."

"I've just come from there. It was the first New Year's Day her mother's let her stay downstairs."

"Did her mother make her wear another blue dress?"

"Another blue dress, but a very pretty one. She sent you her love." He looked more serious still. "She made me promise to come here."

"You weren't coming, Frederic?" she repeated incredulously. "But why?" Suky felt the room begin to dip and turn and the floor slid beneath her feet, threatening to throw her off balance, while her ears had set up a gentle humming.

"I didn't think I had the right to. But then Felice said, 'Who has a better right than you, Frederic?'" He smiled sadly. "Is she as beautiful as Felice says she is?"

"She may not be as beautiful as Felice thinks just now—but she will be, when she's a little older. She's such a dainty baby, and she's quick and alert, tiny as she is."

"Sarah," Frederic said. He nodded slowly. "Sarita." And, at that, Suky laid one hand against his shoulder as if to support herself, he caught hold of it, watching her with a look of alarm, and she shook her head, frowning and smiling at the same time.

During the first few minutes after Frederic had gone the noise in the room seemed deafening and the young men looked drunken and stupid, certainly no guests of hers, and when, after some indefinite time had passed, she heard Joshua's voice again, she gave a start. "It's nearly eleven, your mother's worried about you. And so am I. Midnight is late enough, I've given instructions to put the last of them out by then." He left, saying to Susan, "I still have a few calls to make."

"More calls at this hour, Joshua? That's absurd."

"Not at all," he assured her, and went to his carriage, directing Huggens to Rose's house, for he had saved that call for the end of the day after his other duties had been fulfilled. The streets were less crowded now, but the men who were still driving or staggering about were in conditions of advanced drunkenness, and it seemed unlikely to Joshua there was another sober man in the city but himself—and Frederic Hallam.

As he rode Joshua gave himself up to enjoying the day's triumphs, and reflected a moment on Suky, whose house matched her so well as if one might be imitating the other, for the colors were clear and soft, and the furniture, with its carved, foaming waves and sprays of flowers, had her same light, supple grace. He thought of Philip, whom he had met in various houses during the day, looking nearly as sullen as Milton De Groot, for not only had Philip lost the three lots, but Philip was now so deep in his debt he had agreed to waive his share in Van Zandt and Ching until he somehow contrived to repay him. And, finally, Joshua thought of Frederic Hallam as they had talked together this afternoon, for he had seen in Frederic's face, plain as a newspaper advertisement, that Frederic had some guilty intimations of being the father of Sarah Van Zandt, and, of course, if he was, or if he thought he might be, the future advantages to Joshua Ching were beyond all present calculation.

Joshua touched the red pearl stickpin in his cravat, and its smooth surface against his fingertips caused him to smile, for when Suky had given it to him this last Christmas it had seemed vaguely familiar, but it was not until today when he stood talking to Frederic Hallam that he had realized Suky must have admired Frederic's stickpin so much she had wanted him to have one like it.

He found Rose's house brightly lighted, though the draperies were drawn, and as he walked up the steps he heard voices singing and the piano being played in Rose's unmistakable style. A basket hung on the door, after the tradition of those ladies who would not receive callers, but it held no cards. He paused, a little angry, as he was each time she surprised him, and then realized there were only three voices—Rose's, Tessie Spooner's and Hoke O'Neil's—though they were singing loudly and with great fervor a favorite song of Rose's with which she sometimes entertained him.

> "I have not loved lightly, I'll think on thee yet,
> I'll pray for thee nightly, till life's sun has set."

Joshua knocked and there was immediate silence, but the door did not open and he waited with grim amusement, able to imagine Rose and Tessie gaping in dismay and Hoke O'Neil, making merry in his house during his absence, taken aback for the first time in their acquaintance. For every man alive, Joshua was convinced, could recognize his superior when he met him, and though Hoke O'Neil had often caused him to wonder if there might be exceptions to this rule, in a moment, he did not doubt, Hoke would demonstrate his essential fear and awe of Joshua Ching.

But Hoke disappointed him again, for he threw the door wide open and stood there as confidently as a man guarding his own house against unwelcome guests, holding a champagne glass in one hand and a cigar in the other, and, while Joshua noticed that the cigar was one of his own—though Hoke must have provided the champagne, unless he had brought one of his men to pick the cellar lock—Hoke grinned and gave a hospitable wave. "Come in, come in, you're just in time."

Joshua smiled sardonically, but Hoke was rather drunk, as he was not very often, and the rebuke was lost. Rose sat at the piano, apparently stricken into immobility, and stared at him in guilty confusion. She was wearing her favorite dress, a long-trained pink taffeta gown with garlands of pink taffeta roses circling the skirt, which she wore on every occasion she could pretend was a formal one, and Tessie Spooner was dressed almost as elaborately, though her hair was pinned in a haphazard snarl.

Joshua bowed, intending to frighten them with his reproachful dignity, but Rose took it for a signal of forgiveness, and ran toward him. "Oh, I'm so glad you've come, I was afraid you'd forgotten me."

Joshua let her take his coat and hat as she questioned him eagerly, asking how many calls he had made, if the streets had been as noisy as usual today, if there had been many accidents, and all at once Tessie approached him with a wheedling smile, and stood on tiptoe to kiss his cheek. "Happy New Year, Mr. Ching. We were just singing 'The Last Link Is Broken.' "

"Yes," agreed Joshua. "I know."

"Would you like to hear it again?"

"Oh, no!" Rose cried. "Of course he wouldn't!"

Hoke stood before the fireplace, smoking and having another glass of champagne, grinning as if it was Joshua who had been caught at a disadvantage this time, and all at once Joshua gave them a gracious smile. "Of course I would, please sing it." He poured champagne, noticing that the label was not from his cellar, and felt an unexpected benevolence for these three homeless waifs, gathered here in his house for mutual warmth and comfort, and while they sang he smiled at them pleasantly and again reflected on Suky's triumph, imagining others to come, and these agreeable thoughts made him nod his head and tap his foot in time to the music, although he remained aloof from their singing.

Their voices rose, began to throb and shake, and Joshua noticed with some surprise that Hoke O'Neil had an unusually good baritone, some part of that legacy given his sister, and then suddenly Hoke announced, "Tessie, time to go. I'm drunk as a boiled owl. So long, Rose. So long, Ching. Let's hope the public stays dumb for one more year."

X X X

Fong Chong passed among them, treading deftly in his thick-soled shoes, and as Marietta poured coffee he carried the cups about, stepping among the heaped skirts and mistaking no hidden toes, offered fruit cake and little sandwiches, and when they had been served he disappeared.

Cornelia Bream whispered, "Sometimes I think he knows more English than he pretends." She looked at the others, the twenty-two members of the French Class, gathered for the first time in Marietta Devlin's new house—for there had been an exodus from Virginia City the year before as complete as that earlier one from Bannack —and she nodded, adding, "Suppose he listens to what we say?"

There was a vexed and thoughtful silence before Mrs. Jeremy Flint, who had arrived recently and had met none of them until today, asked, "But why should he?" And at this crisp inquiry, making their conversation too inconsequential to interest Fong Chong, the women's heads turned and they gazed steadily and intently at Irene Flint, just as they had been longing to do.

Jeremy Flint, of course, many of them remembered from the early days in Bannack, but his wife was new to them, a widow, so he said, whom he had met in San Francisco and married almost three years ago. And not only had Jeremy returned with a wife, but he had discarded his black bearskin overcoat in favor of a frock coat and white cravat, had not once been seen publicly drunk, and had taken offices where he was prepared to litigate the Territory's mining disputes. And, so their husbands told them, he talked of trips to New York and Europe and showed an awesome familiarity with expensive hotels in distant cities, the best food and wines, trotting horses and steamers, which had made the women somewhat antagonistic to Irene Flint even before they had met her, for, surely, if that was the life she was used to and liked, she had no right to come here and give them qualms of provincialism.

Mrs. Flint had been variously estimated by those who had seen her driving her buggy to be thirty-eight or forty or, in Erma Finney's opinion, her own age, forty-two, but what concerned them most just now was the elaborate style of her hair, put together with more dangling curls and intricately twined braids than they had ever seen, and she was, furthermore, the only one among them wearing a bustle.

Lisette had observed her clothes with alert interest, for she yearned to manufacture a similar deformity for herself, and was thinking that any woman whose blue eyes looked into the faces of all these curious doubting strangers with such confident composure, must have something in her history more interesting than Erma Finney or, for that matter, most of the others could claim, rigorously dedicated as they were to the cult of ladyhood. For Lisette sometimes studied them nowadays and skeptically asked herself if Erma Finney or Cornelia Bream or Reba Church or her friend Rachel Grimes, knew anything of the warm and strenuous pleasures made possible to them by marriage. And then, as Polly began to cry in one of the upstairs bedrooms, Lisette rose in a whirling motion which sent her skirts spinning and disappeared from her seat by the door.

Erma Finney had set her lips, as if to answer Mrs. Flint, when Marietta asked, "Have you decided on your costume for the masquerade ball, Mrs. Flint?"

Mrs. Flint smiled—and perhaps she held some reservations about their masquerade ball, too. "I thought I might wear a black wig and dress as a squaw."

"A squaw?" repeated Erma, and turned to look at her, as at some curiosity never seen before.

There was general consternation, an exchange of frowns and sighs, and Cornelia Bream put her hands to her cheeks, for Mrs. Bream suffered as much from another woman's mistakes as from her own. "An Indian!"

Erma Finney spoke with an air of firm but kindly patience. "Mrs. Flint, you're new here, but I think you should know that to those who live in the mountains any Indian, even a squaw, is not a whimsical matter. And a squaw, I'm sorry to tell you, is known to be even more cruel to captives and wounded men left on the battlefields than the braves."

"I don't think Mrs. Flint was serious, Erma," Jenny said, and raised her eyebrows slightly in warning that their guest was not to be mauled. "Countess Manzoni, what are you going to wear?"

But before Countess Manzoni could speak, Lisette came rushing back. "Don't tell us, Countess Manzoni, keep it a secret!" She turned. "Oh, please, let's have a real masquerade."

"Darling, you know that isn't possible," Marietta told her. "We all know one another too well."

"But let's try. Or why should we go to all the bother of making costumes and wigs? And we have only three more days to wait."

They agreed that it should be possible to keep their secrets for another three days, and presently they were complimenting Marietta again on her new house and its handsome furnishings, the finest

mansion in the mountains today, and as they began to leave, letting
in gusts of cold air, Lisette shivered and drew Mrs. Flint aside,
murmuring, "Please don't go yet, stay a little longer and talk to
Mother and Aunt Jenny and me. Won't you?"

Mrs. Flint looked surprised, and must have thought none of them
would forgive her jest about the squaw. "Do you want me to?"

"Of course. Let's sit down over here." She led Mrs. Flint to a sofa
before a tall, gold-framed mirror, where she might study Mrs.
Flint's coiffure from every angle, though it looked even more complex than she had thought.

"Mrs. Finney begins by suspecting everyone," whispered Lisette,
with the air of giving a precious confidence, and as she talked she
gazed into Irene Flint's face with concentrated interest, thinking
that however old Mrs. Flint might be she had a look of completeness and decision which few women achieved at any age. "She was
the same way with us, when we first arrived. And the others let her
intimidate them, I don't know why."

"Perhaps because she seems to have opinions, and they don't."

"Of course, that's just what it is. I've never liked her, but I didn't
quite know why, and it upsets Mother when I say it. And yet her
daughter, Rachel, is one of my best friends—my very best friend, she
thinks." Lisette gave her a conspiratorial smile. "As best friends go,
that is, among women. You know."

"Yes," Mrs. Flint agreed, and returned Lisette's smile. "I do
know. I suppose the women here spend a great deal of time together?"

"We have to, after all. The men are so busy. At least the husbands
of the women who were here are busy. We're thankful for that.
Things haven't gone well the past year or so. The last mining season
was practically a failure, and there was that terrible fire that burned
down all the middle part of town. And the Indians, of course—and
the placers are playing out." Lisette sighed, as if her recital of their
woes had made her sad. "How did Mr. Flint decide to come back? So
many others are leaving. We've lost half our population these last
two years."

"He had several investments here, some of them with your father,
as it happens. And he believes the Territory has a rich future, richer
than its past."

"But not until the railroad comes, everyone agrees to that."

Marietta and Jenny came back, laughing as they went to stand before the fireplace. But then, as if afraid that Mrs. Flint might have
misunderstood the laughter, Marietta said, "Erma Finney insists
she's met you before, and is frantic because she can't remember
where it was. Erma, you'll find, never likes to be at a loss. In a few
weeks she'll be calling on you every other day, and dropping in so unexpectedly that you'll be longing for this afternoon again."

Jenny laughed, nodding, and Lisette said, "That's when she's decided you have some secret, something very wicked she must pry out

of you. For your own good. Though no one's ever been quite sure what Mrs. Finney means by wicked."

"Oh, yes, we are," said Jenny, with unexpected emphasis. "She means life." But then Jenny looked as if she wished she had not spoken so impulsively. "Perhaps I'm wrong."

"But you're not wrong at all, Aunt Jenny. That's exactly what she means—and it's what Rachel means, too." She nodded. "Now I see everything so clearly."

Marietta smiled. "You do?"

All at once their condemnation of Erma Finney had created among them an admiring affection, and Mrs. Flint held out her hand to Marietta, saying, "I want to thank you. You're all so generous—you surprise me."

Jenny and Marietta gazed at her seriously, but Lisette had a humorous smile. "Generous? Are we so generous as all that?"

"Of course we aren't," Jenny replied quickly, "but how nice of Mrs. Flint to think we are."

In the vestibule they fell silent, as if their new friendship had deserted them, and while Fong Chong helped Mrs. Flint into her sealskin coat they stood looking at one another in helpless embarrassment. It was almost dark and the houses glowed with yellow lights, and as Mrs. Flint was about to get into her carriage, Marietta said eagerly, "Here comes my husband, Mrs. Flint, I want you to meet him," as if she was relieved to have this one more friendly gesture to make.

"I'll introduce myself, Mrs. Devlin. Please don't wait, it's so cold." As Matt rode abreast of the buggy she leaned out. "Mr. Devlin, I've been at the French Class this afternoon and your wife wants us to meet. I'm Irene Flint."

Matt dismounted and came toward her. "I know your husband well, Mrs. Flint, he's an old friend. We spent the afternoon together, looking over some properties he has an interest in." He smiled, and inquired with the ironic solicitude of a Westerner in the presence of a tenderfoot, "And what do you think of our flourishing city, Mrs. Flint?" She said nothing, and so he asked, more banteringly, "Aren't you impressed by our gem of the mountains?" He gave an expansive gesture, taking in the surrounding terraced hillsides and the business section below, and then unexpectedly she laughed, with a sound he remembered quite well. He put one foot on the step and leaned into the buggy, seizing her hand to draw her closer. "Milly?"

"Irene." She threw her head back, arching her neck and closing her eyes as she smiled. In a moment she straightened, repeating, "How do I like it? This bloody little town?"

"I'll be a son of a bitch, I swear I didn't guess it."

"I told you I was going to get married. Didn't you believe me? I suppose it never occurred to you that Jeremy Flint might actually marry Milly Matches."

"Has anyone recognized you?"

"How can they? Would you? My hair isn't red, or orange, or whatever the hell color it used to be. My clothes are made in France, and I'm a perfectly good imitation of a respectable woman—I even fooled Erma Finney."

Matt laughed. "But whatever made you decide to come back?"

"Jeremy thinks the Territory's best prospects are in the future—and he's a stubborn bastard, you know that. He never got over being mad about the night they threw us out of that stupid Christmas ball." They looked at each other, reminiscently smiling, and at last she said, "They all seem to be very happy."

"If they do, the credit isn't mine."

"Of course it is. They love you, and women won't see what they're afraid to see, don't you know that?" Matt gave an embarrassed laugh, glancing uneasily toward the house, as if someone might have come out and now stood nearby, hidden by the darkness, listening. "Go on in, Matt. They'll wonder how you could spend so long talking to a woman you just met. But first tell me—how do you like me without red hair? Do I look ordinary?"

"Of course you don't. Were you depending on that red hair?"

"I suppose I was. And the yellow satin. I never wear that any more, either. I'm afraid it might turn me back into Milly Matches." She laughed, but this time there was only a trace of her earlier laugh, so celebrated in Bannack and Virginia City that some lonely miners had insisted it sounded better to them than a Christmas carol. "By the way, what did your son do with our claim?"

"He's traded it a few times, you've made about four thousand. Do you want to sell it?"

"I think I'll keep it, for sentiment's sake. Good night, Matt." She leaned toward him, smiling a little sadly, or so he imagined, and all at once he kissed her and the buggy began to move.

He watched it start down the slippery roadway, and then walked toward the house, aware of the quickening excitement he felt each time he was about to see Jenny, as if his own body warned him, creating this mild sickness of apprehension, an unpleasant but stimulating combination of eagerness and reluctance he had expected would have disappeared long ago.

For although they had not been able to keep all their resolutions, he could now congratulate himself it had been more than six months since he had seen her alone, and so he supposed the danger must finally have passed. And yet it dismayed him to know he could not look at her, or be in her presence, without re-experiencing all those early sensations of fearful and exhilarating curiosity, and this was all the more strange because in everything else he seemed to have a more perfect command of himself than ever before, had never been so energetic, so alert, so ready for challenges in whatever form they came to him, or so lucky in everything he undertook. Nevertheless, he had, each time he expected to see her in the presence of other people, a conviction that something unprecedented would happen, destroying once and for all this careful balance of love and distrust which existed among them.

He went up the steps, treading more heavily than usual to announce his arrival, and threw the door open with a bravado which made him frown disapprovingly at this evident lack of composure.

Marietta approached him and Matt seemed surprised to see her, quite taken aback by his wife's presence here in his house, then kissed her quickly and, when he could delay it no longer, he looked at Jenny, standing beside the fireplace with her hands behind her back and her head slightly lowered, smiling with an expression she often showed him nowadays and which he interpreted as both mockery and defiance.

Marietta went to stand beside Jenny and he turned his back on them both, making quite a disturbance as he moved bottles about on the small corner table, searching for some special decanter, and by the time he had poured a drink the two women were discussing Irene Flint and Erma Finney and sounded so scornfully amused by the meeting of the French Class that he was able to face them with a polite smile, which lapsed from time to time into an abstracted frown as he seemed to contemplate some thorny problems of contracts or loans.

Nevertheless he observed them carefully and critically as they stood there, talking with easy affection, quite as if one had nothing to conceal, and the other nothing to fear. Marietta, he had sometimes suspected, was indulging in the peculiar feminine pleasure of forgiving those who had injured her without exacting tortures from them in payment for that forgiveness; but, he told himself now, more likely Irene Flint had been right in saying that women would not see what they were afraid to see, for, surely, there was no other explanation for their friendship.

And it came to him as a curious surprise that when he compared these two women it was Marietta who was the more appealing to him, and he found himself smiling at her with tender longing and admiration, and marveling once again over her thick, shining brown hair and hazel eyes and, most of all, her ardent and to him very touching assurance, in which her need to please those she loved was never corrupted by any misgivings about her independence.

Jenny, he thought, suffered by this comparison, and he began to find fault with her skin for being too white, and her hair too black, her face too startling, and indeed anyone might see that she betrayed in all her gestures the restlessness and pride which made her as challenging as he knew her to be. These reflections, so charitable to Marietta, and to himself, caused Matt to conclude that he was a reasonable man again, the same one he had been before he had met Jenny Danforth—and he went on to remind himself that, after all, none of them was young any more, and so could scarcely expect to have kept those illusions of fidelity and honor which might have troubled them once.

Matt lighted a cigar and poured another drink, and fell to examining his new house—seven rooms and two stories, built all of stone and with four big stone chimneys. Their furniture had been sent out from the East and they lived once again among familiar possessions —Brussels carpets and gold-stamped muslin curtains, black walnut furniture upholstered in crimson damask, his books and the many dark paintings, seldom examined but nevertheless vaguely reassuring because they had seen them always, and he asked himself as he had before what imp had prompted him to build for Marietta a bigger and more luxurious house than Pete had built for Jenny.

By the time he had finished the second drink he was warmly assuring himself that selfishness was too natural an impulse to be wrong, and it had even begun to seem there was some saving humor in the situation, after all. For this was the usual course his feelings took each time he saw Jenny—the giddy presentiments of disaster, and then a sliding away of tension, resolving into a return of his confidence with a heightened sense of power and decision, swelling to such proportions he could not even imagine what it was that had disturbed him.

"I told Pete I'd stop to drive him home," Jenny said. "What time is it?"

Matt looked at his watch. "Six-fifteen."

"I'm late, I must hurry, or he won't be there." She laughed softly and the laugh seemed to him mysterious and disturbing, for he took it to mean that she and Pete were accomplices now, sharing secrets which must always baffle him.

Marietta held her coat—a new one of brown sealskin, for these coats, too, were epidemic among them—Lisette tried on the sealskin hat while Jenny pulled on her boots, they kissed one another hastily and Jenny was out the door, having quite forgotten to tell him goodbye.

He followed her, saying, "I'll ride with you. The roads are bad tonight."

"Oh, no, please, there's no reason to."

She started down the stairs but Matt seized firm hold of her arm and slowed her retreat. Neither of them spoke as he handed her into the buggy and they set off down the hillside with Jenny ahead, driving cautiously for once. They passed snow-banked cabins with smoke weaving from every chimney, and though they were greeted here only by barking dogs, as they came nearer the center of town they found it crowded with men dashing as purposefully along the sidewalks as if the day was just beginning.

At Devlin Brothers, which had been rebuilt since the fire last spring, he found Morgan still at his desk. "Pete?" Matt asked.

"Went home half an hour ago. He's going with me tomorrow to look at that quartz property near Deer Lodge."

Matt repeated this to Jenny with a quick, impersonal urgency, as if he did not know her very well and was in a hurry to discharge this

obligation and be rid of her. She leaned out, and her voice was pleading.

"Don't come with me, Matt. I drive when the streets are much
worse than this."

He remounted, made her a gesture, and they continued on their
way across town, for Jenny, as it seemed she inevitably would, lived
isolated from their friends, some of whom blamed her for this even
though it had been Pete who had selected the property and built the
house before Jenny ever saw it. As they rode, Matt was scowling and
had grown quite angry with Morgan, who had had no reason, he
thought, to have mentioned that Pete was going with him tomorrow.

The buggy turned into the driveway, and almost instantly Pete appeared and came running toward them. Matt watched as she stepped
down into his arms, but once again Jenny forgot to speak to him and
Pete remembered only as they entered the house, shouting his thanks
when Matt was a hundred yards away. By the time he got home, Matt
had organized a program for the next day which would leave him no
moment during which he would not be with another man, or with
several others, either at his office or theirs, at a warehouse or their
assay office or the quartz mill, frozen again and in need of his attention.

During the night the chinook began to blow, and from midnight
until it grew light the wind rushed off the hillsides and through the
gulch, rattling doors and windows and rooftops, scattering woodpiles
and upsetting outhouses, making the dogs howl and cats scream and
causing men and women and children to turn restlessly in their beds
or go to the windows to see what damage had been done. By morning the ice had melted and the streets were so deep in mud that
horses' hoofs splattered and carriage wheels spun, spewing forth
streams as they went; and there was the premature hope that this
might be the beginning of spring.

Matt left home a little before six, convinced he must lose no time
today, that there was more to be done than he could hope to accomplish, and as his horse ambled down the slick hillside, his hoofs making loud sucking sounds in the mud while Matt swayed comfortably
and lazily in the saddle, apparently as relaxed as an Indian, he
chewed his cigar instead of lighting it and spat out the shreds, while
once again he considered the many things he must attend to: so
many, in fact, that he had gotten up an hour earlier than usual, insisting to Marietta he wanted nothing but coffee and would make it
himself.

And then, in spite of his earlier lack of appetite, he stopped at the
St. Louis Hotel, took a seat beside the window and ordered oatmeal,
fried potatoes and ham, and pancakes with syrup, all of which he
ate methodically and with relish while he stared in apparent absent-
minded contemplation across the square and farther up the street
toward his office, where Morgan's horse waited at the tie-rail and
there was smoke coming from the chimney. Full of a nervous excite-

ment, he watched the building as he ate, pouring syrup and cutting the ham without looking at it, concentrating upon all that was going on in the street. He finished quickly, sooner than he had intended, glanced at the plate after spearing the fork aimlessly and, finding nothing, signaled for more coffee.

Men passed whom he knew but he stared at them blankly, as if he was foundered so deep in thought as not to recognize them, for he did not want them to come in and talk to him and distract his attention from his steady surveillance of the office.

Lem Finney went by but he, as usual, was too much engrossed in his own concerns to glance toward the hotel windows, and Matt added to his list a call on Lem Finney to discuss the purchase of a stand of timber they would presently need to feed their quartz mill.

As he sat, frowning and from time to time giving his fist a swift wipe across the pane as it clouded over again, ducking his head nearer and peering intently, as if the steam might have obscured from him something of importance, Matt found himself growing angrier and more suspicious of Pete, and this anger and suspicion had begun the night before, almost at the moment Morgan had glanced up and told him that Pete would go with him to Deer Lodge.

It was unusual for Pete to travel at all nowadays, for although he might offer to inspect a ranch or mining property, Morgan seemed to understand the offer was not to be taken seriously, and this trip, arranged behind his back by Pete and Morgan, as it were, had given Matt some qualms that it was perhaps Pete's intention to test him. But Pete, after all, would not arrange tests of his faith when he believed him faithful.

As he drank coffee and chewed on another cigar, he was trying to persuade himself that although he had been sitting there for half an hour or more—an absurd time for a busy man to spend at breakfast when others came and went in five or ten minutes—he was in reality as busy as any of them, for while they sped aimlessly about he was employing his time economically, planning in exquisite detail just how he would pass the day.

This was no usual procedure, for he, like the others, rushed down to his office and tore into whatever work first appeared at hand, and continued at that same rate until six or seven at night when he went home, still seething with plans and arguments. But he now assured himself this calm moment early in the day, only a brief period of sorting and examining his plans, would prove itself so valuable when he later compared his achievement with what he accomplished on an ordinary day, that not only would he adopt the practice as a constant one, but would recommend it to Pete and Morgan and even to Lem Finney and Josiah Webb.

At this, he gave a sharp laugh, slammed his hand upon the table and got up, reaching for his coat on the hook beside him, while he still peered through the windows. They clouded again as a man rode up and dismounted before Devlin Brothers, he wiped a clean patch and saw, as he expected, that Pete was hurrying in as if he were late and apologetic. Matt could very plainly imagine himself running over there to listen with amiable skepticism while Pete made his explanations, letting him understand that he knew as well as anyone what could delay a man in the early morning; and then he hung the coat back on the hook, ordered another cup of coffee, and continued watching.

For a moment he seemed to feel a great relief and a spreading ease moved throughout his chest, even seeping down into his legs and arms and affecting him with a benevolent paralysis, so that he believed he could not have moved if he had tried to, and remained there as if he had become his own prisoner, helpless and inert, but unprotesting.

Morgan and Pete reappeared and Morgan mounted quickly, eager to be on his way, as he always was. Pete put one foot into the stirrup, reluctantly, Matt thought, and a man stopped, began to talk, and Pete turned to him. Matt sank slowly back into the chair and by now his face showed such anxiety and rage that other customers thought he was watching for a man he intended to kill, and a few began to talk about leaving, to be out of the way when trouble began.

Pete and the other man, whom Matt did not recognize, were talking in pleasant and confidential fashion and Morgan had joined their discussion. They might, it seemed to Matt, talk in that way for an hour or two or the entire day, and at this prospect his rage grew so intense he told himself in disgust that he had become something worse than he had ever expected or would have believed. He longed to rush at them, yelling that it was time for them to be on their way, to stop dawdling and hanging about the streets, and that picture brought forth an irresistible although unpleasant laugh which caused several more doubtful glances in his direction.

Then, with sudden haste and decision, Pete mounted his horse, they slapped at their saddle reins and set off at a gallop. Matt bolted from the dining room and stood there until they had disappeared, when he returned, seeming miraculously restored, paid the bill and went strolling to the office which he entered with a feeling of conquest, swaggering about and examining carefully every evidence of their recent occupation as if he would discover some faint but valuable clues.

There were two coffee cups on Pete's desk, the ledger in which Morgan had been entering his latest transactions, a newspaper folded at a description of the property they were going to look at and which Matt read with intensive interest, as if to convince himself the mine was a real one, and as he noticed a pistol lying on the desk he reared back with as much horror and astonishment as at the appearance of a rattlesnake. But then it seemed far more astonishing he should have reacted so violently, for none of them ordinarily took more notice of weapons than of buffalo overshoes. He was standing staring at it, still rather suspicious that it should be there, when

Douglas and Robert came in, and he glanced up as if at the entrance of unwelcome intruders, but grinned quickly and gave a gesture which might have indicated both welcome and surrender.

"Morning," he said, and went back to studying with earnest attention the article on the mine.

They were carrying school books and Robert explained, "I left my sled here last night, and I thought it might snow again."

Matt glanced sideways, first at Douglas, then at Robert. "How's your mother?"

Both boys seemed puzzled by the question, but Douglas replied, "She's fine, sir."

Matt scowled, as if he was too absorbed in the article to have noticed what he was saying, and then solicitously inquired, "Was she still asleep when you left?"

"Oh, no, sir. She cooked our breakfast."

"You know Mother," Robert added.

"Of course," Matt briskly agreed, and gave them another foolish grin. "What were her plans for the day? Was she going visiting? Any club meetings or lunches?" He smiled, an amused benevolent comment on the nature of women's daily occupations, but they shook their heads, declaring she had not mentioned her plans, and left him.

He promptly threw off his overcoat and lighted a cigar, drawing upon it deeply, and grew aware of a conviction of comfortable righteousness, as if he had banished the evil and vengeful and dangerous portions of his nature which had so alarmed him only a few minutes earlier, sat at his desk and began to consider thoughtfully and with intense concentration the various contracts and letters, making notations of details he would discuss with Pete or Morgan. He sat there for an hour or longer, so concerned with these problems he thought no more about the fact that Jenny would be alone today and, very likely, tomorrow, too; and when he was convinced he had settled back into his familiar self and need fear no new aberrations he got up, gave the two clerks some instructions, and went outside.

The streets were crowded by now and a cold wind had begun to blow so that men bent into it as they walked, blinking their eyes and gasping out frosty clouds. He joined the northbound traffic and walked swiftly, eager and intent, and so pleased with himself he believed it had become impossible ever again to disappoint his expectations of Matt Devlin.

Two blocks farther on he went into Finney and Son, and there he sat opposite Lem and discussed a small herd of cattle they had been offered at what Morgan had said was a good price.

"Let's go out there right now," said Lem, "and take a look." He stood up, while Matt gaped at him as if he had suggested they set out for the States. "The price seems too low, doesn't it to you?" He had his coat on now. "Come along, Matt."

Matt shook his head. "Not today, Lem. Pete and Morgan are both away. Make it tomorrow." He left quickly. "Seven tomorrow morning?" He slammed the door and hurried on in the same direction, annoyed to find that once again he felt pursued and angry, as if a new tormenter sprang into his path each time he had dealt with the last one.

He approached the small white-painted clapboard building which housed the *Helena Post* and went in to talk to his son-in-law, though he could think of no significant news he must tell him, and once again he stood near the window, making a peephole in the glass with his warm fist and glancing continuously into the street. All at once he snapped his fingers. "There he goes," and with no other explanation, he dashed out again, strode several yards and stopped, looked up the street in one direction and then surveyed it as carefully in the other.

He saw Reba Church approaching and ceremoniously removed his hat and bowed, gravely inquiring about their youngest daughter's illness while he reflected that it was Billy Church, now sixteen years old and one of Douglas' best friends, who had been the original messenger between himself and Jenny, and as he talked he stared steadily and intently into her face, trying to decide whether or not she knew it. But in a moment he told himself it was like staring at a pudding and trying to guess the number of raisins it might contain, and he removed his hat once again, bowed, and they went in opposite directions.

He walked swiftly and purposefully for three or four blocks, nodding to acquaintances, noticing that there were the usual numbers of strangers passing through town, and although he refused to ask himself where he was going, who it was who was next on his list of important conferences to be held, he realized that he was no longer so clear about his objectives as he had been while he sat eating breakfast and planning projects enough to fill not only that one day but all the rest of the week.

In spite of the cold, he was not eager to go back indoors but told himself he was more clear-headed out here, better able to plan and to make decisions which, in the end, would save all of them time; and, furthermore, if Morgan and Pete should decide to come back, he would see them immediately and they could take up the important subjects he had outlined.

This piece of dishonesty offended him by its blatancy and sent him into the next saloon where he stood at the bar for several minutes, staring about him with the same wary and threatening expression which had made his breakfast companions uneasy.

Two drinks seemed to restore him and he emerged with energetic determination, only to hear a childish feminine laugh he took to be directed at him and he spun about, searching for the culprit, to find Flora Pim, her school books clutched to her chest, gazing up at him with the look of a whimsical conspirator. Flora was eleven now, and though she sometimes went coasting with the gang of boys, she had become too ladylike to permit them to hang her for a road agent or shoot her as a Southern spy. The sight of her pleased him, quite as if this chance meeting was plain evidence that somewhere fate had been busy with him.

"Don't worry, Mr. Devlin," she told him confidingly. "I'll say I saw you coming out of the Gem on my way home from school—not on my way there." She laughed again, wrinkling her nose with the delight of teasing him, and looking up at him humorously, a very old man, as he supposed she thought him to be, crotchety and droll and perhaps even pathetic.

"Maybe we'd better protect each other, Flora," he suggested. "This isn't the way to your school, either." He smiled at her warmly and was well pleased to be having this playful conversation with Flora Pim, another reminder that he and his family could go nowhere about this town without encountering friends and acquaintances and being recognized by others they did not know.

She smiled and tilted her head to one side, then gave a little sigh. "I know it isn't. But do you want to know why I come this way? I'll tell you if you'll promise to keep it a secret."

"I promise."

"I come this way so I can see him."

"Oh?"

"Morgan," she whispered.

Matt laughed, but then grew instantly sober. "Morgan's gone away today, Flora, that's why I laughed."

"I know it. Douglas and Robert just told me. Mr. Devlin—don't let him get married until I grow up, will you? Promise me?"

"I'll do what I can, Flora. But Morgan's old, you know. He's almost twenty-two."

"I don't care how old he is. Promise."

Matt bent and kissed her cheek. "I'll try," he said, telling himself that however oppressive his own troubles might sometimes seem, they certainly caused him no greater pain than did Flora Pim's secret love for Morgan. And then, thinking that he was able to moralize about everything he saw or heard this morning, finding more lessons in his brief walk than in the entire *McGuffey Reader* Flora was carrying, they shook hands to bind their vow.

He walked several blocks, then turned and started back again. In the distance he saw Fong Chong with a basket over his arm going into a meat market with Margaret Webb. He paused now and then to talk to men he knew, and at last told himself severely it was time he stop this idle rambling about town.

But nevertheless he continued until he had admitted that what he was waiting for was not Pete's return but Jenny, driving up to their office or, perhaps, going on by because she dreaded to meet him as much as he feared her. At this recognition that he had once again made promises to himself which had not been honest ones, he started in desperate search of some means of saving them both and, as he went dashing along, caught sight of an overhanging sign with a mortar and pestle outlined in black and the words City Drugstore printed beneath, and went into the little brick building as if this was where he would, at last, find his salvation; for here the Reverend Obadiah Bream could be found six days of the week, ministering to sick bodies.

Matt had no intention of discussing his predicament with the Reverend Bream and had only some vague notion, more ironic than serious, that a few moments in Obadiah Bream's sanctimonious presence might send him back out into the street cleansed and purified, at least for the day. And one day at a time, he thought, was as much as any man could hope to contain.

Reverend Bream stood at the counter, taking pinches of herbs from various apothecary jars and measuring them judiciously upon a scale, while a woman Matt had never seen before waited impatiently, glaring at him as if he should not have intruded at this sensitive moment. Matt and the Reverend exchanged nods, and Matt thrust back his coat, for the small room was stiflingly hot, jammed his fists into his pockets and sauntered about, peering at labels and examining bottles with as much interest as if he had never seen another drugstore.

"Will this help me?" the customer asked in a querulous whine, and Matt guessed she was one more of those women who had migrated from Missouri, thin and sick with chills and fevers, who suffered for a time, dosing themselves with various medicines, and presently died.

"I assure you it will, madame. It's the best thing in the world for—"

"Shh!"

"For your complaint, madame."

Irresistibly, Matt gave a loud laugh, glanced apologetically at Bream, and continued studying the labels, frowning and whistling between his teeth. There was a jar of Roback's pills, recommended for ladies of sedentary habits, many bottles of Swiss Stomach Bitters, reputed to cure anything no other cure could be found for, long, thick bars of pink soap, jars of camphor, a great deal of candy for the children, and roots and herbs he supposed might be as healing as tearing up so many weeds in the street and stewing them into a potion. The Reverend's pharmacopoeia, in fact, seemed to him as unrelated to physical ills as his theology was to the soul's morbid ailments.

As Matt pursued his steady scrutiny of the labels, and the woman behind him wheezed and sighed, he reflected with a kind of savage delight on the Reverend's simple notions of sin and virtue, and of what consternation he might cause his pastor by stepping to the counter when the woman had gone to tell him the symptoms for which he was seeking an easy, reliable cure: His deep jealousy of his brother, and his inability to believe that any other man could possess a woman he had chosen for himself; but, also, his sense of repugnance and rage whenever he thought of them together, curious enough since he refused to believe in the reality. All this, of course, would so overwhelm Obadiah Bream with horror and disgust at the existence within his congregation, and even his private circle of friends, of so great a rascal, that very likely nothing would ever again persuade him human nature deserved salvation.

The door slammed as the woman left and Matt spun around in mock surprise, exchanging smiles and shrugs with the Reverend, whose face looked as bland and pious as if he had never encountered or even imagined there was a devil who plagued men, but who, nevertheless, could deliver sermons which so graphically described the torments awaiting sinners that Matt would shake his head admiringly and, beside him, Marietta would give a light, sad sigh.

Matt now went stalking toward him, his hands still in his pockets and his eyes glowing. "And what have you got for my complaint?" he demanded, and was pleased to see that the Reverend Bream looked somewhat alarmed, as if he suspected that this fierce, truculent man, whom he had never seen other than good-tempered and gentle, might be raging with some pain which made him temporarily dangerous.

The Reverend folded his hands as he did on Sundays while he patiently waited for the choir to get done, and inquired solicitously, "And what is it, Matt? What is your complaint?"

Matt stared at him, finding nothing of solace or comfort in the Reverend Bream's face, and was instead filled with scorn and disgust, not only for himself but for Obadiah Bream whose mild and vapid temperament must indeed be a great help in the maintenance of his virtue.

"Look at me," Matt told him loudly, and both his appearance and voice seemed oddly balanced between humor and potential violence. "I've come to you—what do you think it is?" He thrust his head forward, glaring, and to his satisfaction the Reverend backed away, and upset two large jars which he turned to catch, but one of them crashed to the floor.

The Reverend Bream glanced at the door, as if hoping to see someone come in. "I don't know, Matt. You and your family always seem to be in good health, I can't imagine, I'm sure, but I'll agree you don't look as you should today." And, as if at a happy thought, he asked, "What are your symptoms?"

Matt laughed again at that and swung about intending to leave, for he had decided that this particular stratagem had failed him, but then turned and said, with the sly solemnity of one propounding an impossible riddle, "I see spots in front of my eyes. My heart's going like a triphammer. I get hot and cold sweats, I'm sick at my stomach and have lost my appetite. When I take a drink it tastes like there's a dishrag in it and, by God, I feel like the top of my head might blow off any minute now." By the end of this triumphant recital he was shouting and he gave a sweeping outward motion of both arms, then grabbed his hat and pulled it down tighter, as if to hold his head in place, while the Reverend Bream clucked in wondering sympathy. "Very bad, very bad. I only hope it isn't smallpox."

"I've been vaccinated."

"Or typhoid."

"Oh, yes," added Matt, "and lately I've been having nightmares." At that, the Reverend's face grew brighter. "Ah. Dyspepsia. I have just the thing for it. Plantation Bitters—calms agitated nerves, as well." He began to rummage among the bottles while, out in the streets, Matt became aware of a sudden tumult, many feet running, pounding along the sidewalks, horses dashing by, and he threw open the door, shouting to ask what had happened.

"Bull-whackers' duel—in back of Troy's Casino!"

Filled with sudden excitement and pleased to have been so opportunely provided with a distraction, Matt set off at a galloping run. Men were coming from saloons and stores and offices, shouting their questions, for the town was still skittish about fire, and many of them joined those who went jogging along toward Green Troy's, their faces avid with joyous expectation.

Behind Troy's Casino the yard was closed with a high board fence, and there, from time to time, cockfights were held, and boxing matches, and during the winter months or in early spring when enforced idleness had turned them ugly and restless, two bull-whackers might agree to lash at each other with their twenty-foot whips until one of them lost his nerve.

When Matt arrived, pushing through the crowded alley, piled with tin cans and bottles and boxes filled with refuse, ashes and bones and fresh bloody offal over which cats crawled and snuffed, the contest had begun, and men stood along the fence, watching the two bull-whackers with an intense and greedy concentration. Next door, Nola Malachy's girls were gathered at the second-floor windows, wearing wrappers, some of them staring listlessly as if they were not yet wide awake, while others gazed down with such seeming rapture it occurred to Matt these little whores must find some profound satisfaction in the sight of two men preparing to slash each other to ribbons.

Nola Malachy's had opened several months ago, but Matt had not mentioned it to Morgan nor Morgan to him, and only he and Pete had shaken their heads over Nella Allen's new identity, but they did not discuss it, either. Matt had told himself long ago, after Jenny had come to him with the news that Nella had consulted Dr. Danforth, that Nella Allen was one of those girls who drifted steadily toward some negative unknown goal, and after that he had refused to think about her.

The bull-whackers had stripped off their coats and stood in black trousers and red woolen shirts, the sleeves rolled above their elbows. Neither looked more than twenty-five and both were bearded and dark-skinned, and they smiled slightly as they faced each other across the field, trampled by now into ankle-deep mud. On one man's

throat was a thick welt from which the blood oozed, and the other's
shirt had been torn at the shoulder, leaving a gash in the skin. The
driver standing nearest Matt now writhed the whip over his head,
making it circle and spin, then shot it out straight and, before they
could see the metal popper touch him, a streak of blood appeared
high on the other's cheekbone. He gave a spasmodic muscular twitch
of which he seemed instantly ashamed and grinned in reply, swept
his whip about his head, and with a report like a pistol shot caught
the other on the jaw. He staggered a few steps, but when several men
sprang forward to support him he shook them off with a look of contemptuous pride and studied his opponent, as if to determine where
he must bleed next.

The alternate strokes continued, one swiftly following another, the
whips cracking each time with a sound that could be heard a mile
away and which, Matt thought, was no doubt causing great consternation among the women, who must be gathering on the streets
and gabbling together in angry, excited groups, for of all the violent,
dangerous sports which mountain life seemed to make agreeable to
the men, the women detested most of all these contests of the bull-
whackers.

Their foreheads and faces were smeared with blood, their mouths
were swollen and cut, blood seeped from their long hair and
streamed through their beards, and some men were beginning to
mumble uneasily while others grew quite still and only stared with
shining eyes, as at something which fascinated them to the verge of
insanity.

Presently Matt gave an inadvertent glance toward Nola Malachy's
windows and saw that Nella Allen now stood alone at one, gazing
down at him with a rapt and contemplative expression. Her face was
pale and still, her blond hair fell straight as when he had known her
first, and at sight of her he felt a quick and uneasy surprise, as if he
knew she had been waiting a long while for this opportunity to study
him at her leisure and now had him trapped, unable to escape, for
the whips went flashing in all directions. He smiled and removed his
hat. But she gave no recognition of the smile, seemed not to notice it,
and continued to gaze at him with that same intent and thoughtful
expression, so that he began to wonder what it was she knew about
him.

But then he returned his attention to the bull-whackers, assuring
himself she had not been looking at him at all but only staring idly,
as he had often seen her do when she was living with them—apparently forget them all and fall into some private reverie which might
last for several minutes.

The whips popped almost as fast as a man could have fired a pistol, ripping at their faces and arms and throat, tearing apart the red
shirts and exposing bloody chests, and several men had begun to
mutter that it was time to stop them before they killed each other or
did some permanent injury, tore out an eye or laid a cheek open to

the bone. Several who stood near the alley were leaving and others moved about, bellowing in protest and sucking their feet from the deep mud.

Matt glanced up again, swiftly and surreptitiously, and Nella Allen was still staring at him with that same steady absorption. Once again he smiled, more broadly this time, grinning in what he thought must seem an absurdly obsequious fashion if anyone were to notice him, trying to curry the favor of this young madam, and he raised his hat so high off his head and held it there so long, nodding, she could not possibly mistake that this greeting was intended for her. At other windows her girls were gesturing excitedly and squealing like school-girls at a mouse, covering their faces and peeking between their fingers at the two panting, bloody men.

But once again she neither smiled nor in any other way acknowledged his greeting, and Matt stared at her sternly for a few moments, hoping to bully her into smiling at him, until with a sense of outraged surprise he realized that she hated him, and with that there came an eerie and disturbing warning.

She turned her back and disappeared and her place was taken by three girls, screeching and gesticulating, pointing their fingers as one of the men staggered helplessly and others ran forward, seizing the whips and bundling the men into their coats, and, with them both protesting, they were pushed, sliding and scuffling, through the muddy yard and back into the saloon to be revived with whisky and hailed as heroes.

Matt left quickly, shoving his way through the alley with the others, all of them now muttering and dissatisfied, and at last reached the sidewalk, tired and bewildered and ashamed to have seen it, for he could scarcely plead as he once had that it was a novelty and he must miss nothing of this strange new life. Then, as it seemed quite automatically, he started walking toward the west side of town, taking one foot path and another up the hillsides and striding purposefully along, neither rushing with wild haste nor stopping to reconsider, and in fifteen minutes found himself before Pete's house.

The buggy stood ready, the horse harnessed and in its shafts, and the little neighborhood boy who was their ostler was hanging idly about. But there was no indication that any caller had come to postpone her ride and he walked through the gate and up the steps, knocked sharply and stepped back to wait for the door to be opened, and his heart had begun to beat so heavily that he felt a curious sickness and a feeling of weakness and languor passed through his body. The door opened after a moment, slowly and cautiously, and then she gave a slight gesture to indicate that he might enter and lowered her head as he passed her. She closed the door softly and stood with her back to him, her hands pressed against the door, as if to make certain it did not spring open again.

XXXI

The parlor looked exactly as it did each time he had seen it, apparently just cleaned, and with the fanatic attention he had always paid to the smallest details of Jenny's appearance and surroundings, he saw a coffee cup on the center table, two or three opened magazines, and in a chair beside it a heap of ruffled red silk, so that she must have been at work on her costume for the masquerade ball.

She turned slowly, and still had not looked at him, though she extended one hand. "Let me take your overshoes, Matt."

He glanced down, as chagrined as if this trampling of mud from Green Troy's Casino and the streets into Jenny's tidy house was an inexcusable offense, and apologized in a mumbling undertone, offering to leave them on the porch.

"No, give them to me." He handed them to her with a kind of shy reluctance, and she smiled, although she still had not looked at him, told him to go into the parlor, and disappeared through the diningroom.

He began to stroll about, started to light a cigar but blew out the match, for he could scarcely avoid one of her woman friends if they found the room full of smoke, and a minute or two passed while he assured himself the visit was quite usual, he had come in Pete's absence to be sure she was not worried at being alone, and that in exactly ten minutes, neither more nor less, he would take his leave, thereby astonishing them both but most particularly, of course, himself. And with this firm resolve he began to feel that he was, after all, something of a hero.

He glanced at the magazines she had left opened on the table, seeing that one was a catalogue of flowers and seeds, for the women were determined to make flowers grow about their homes if they grew nowhere else, and the other a dream book. He leaned down, curious and resentful at these evidences of the life she lived quite unrelated to him, and had begun to read it when her hand covered the page, she snatched it up and backed away, smiling and defiant.

"You don't want me to read it?"

She shook her head quickly, but kept it behind her back, as if he might try to take it by force. "I don't believe in it. It's just something I amuse myself with sometimes. Morgan gave it to me," she added, as if that would explain why she had it at all.

Matt smiled. "Jenny, it doesn't matter to me if you believe in dreams. Did you think it would?"

She tossed the book onto the table, but looked as if the discovery of this secret had put her at a disadvantage. "I shouldn't do it even for amusement. It's wrong and I know it." She circled the table, glancing at the dream book with a wary and suspicious expression. "It fills my mind with silly ideas. These books are crammed with evil predictions and sorrow, you know. I'm going to throw it away." She approached the table, reached forth one hand as if to carry out the threat, but instead retreated and circled the table in the opposite direction, keeping some distance from him.

He was sorry his discovery had upset her, and amused by this childishness she usually concealed so well, not from him only but from others too, and all at once Jenny left the room, saying she would bring coffee and something to eat.

Matt wandered about, examining the room and its contents more carefully than he ever did his own house. He looked at the music on the piano, to learn what they had been playing, and noticed that she had given Pete the new fiddle about which she had consulted him several months ago. There was a water color on the easel near the window, a bouquet of spring flowers she might be hoping to grow this year. He looked at two books to find out what they were reading, and tried to guess which of them had selected each one. He opened a humidor, as if it made some difference to him how many cigars it might contain, and then, quickly, afraid she would walk in and find him snooping, sat down and assumed a stiff, straight posture for a moment before that displeased him and he shifted slightly, crossed one leg over the other, leaned his elbow on the table's edge and began turning through the flower catalogue, for it seemed unlikely she could object to that.

She came in carrying a tray with cups and saucers, a coffee pot and slices of yellow cake, and they sat across the table from each other, sipping hot coffee and eating the cake, exactly, he told himself, like two children who have decided to have a grown-up tea party and then run out of inspiration, can no longer play their roles authentically and so fall into embarrassed silence, correctly copying their elders' gestures but unable to reproduce the accompanying conversation. He emptied the cup and watched with profound interest as she filled it again, until all at once she laughed and he glanced up, supposing she was laughing at him.

"Oh, Matt, aren't we funny, though?" She sat very straight, folded her hands in her lap and raised her eyebrows, and then glanced whimsically sideways. "I wish someone could see us, don't you?"

"Pete, for instance?"

"Why not?" She cut the slice of cake in two and picked it up between her fingers, long and flexible, with polished nails, and he looked guiltily away. "You don't think he'd object to finding you here, do you? I supposed he had asked you to come."

Matt smiled, shaking his head in wonderment. "You thought he asked me to come here?"

"Didn't he?"

"Jenny—for Christ's sake!"

She frowned and lowered her eyes, sipping the coffee, and he reminded himself the ten minutes were gone and it was time for him to leave, rise up from the chair promptly and decisively, like a man who knows exactly what he means to do and who will not be kept from doing it; and yet he continued to sit there and began to drink, more slowly, another cup of coffee. After a few moments Jenny gave a light sigh, and he looked at her again.

"How did he happen to go?" he demanded, so abruptly that she smiled, contemptuously, as it seemed.

"Why shouldn't he have gone? The property's valuable, you've seen it, and it was a decision for all of you to make. I heard you tell him the other day you thought he should go."

"But I didn't think he'd do it," he said slowly, as if Pete's decision still baffled him, and he sat staring across the room toward the door, almost expecting that Pete would now open it and walk in. "I saw him leave this morning. They didn't see me because I was eating breakfast in the hotel," he explained, for he had no intention of admitting even to Jenny that they had not seen him because he had been spying. "I thought he'd changed his mind when he came so late, about an hour later than they'd agreed on." He looked at her swiftly and his black eyes gleamed with accusatory malice.

Jenny, however, bowed her head and began to trace with her fingertip a pattern in the shawl which covered the table. "I know he was late, it was my fault." She looked humble, quite unnaturally submissive he thought, but she had also a slight and secretive smile. "It wasn't what you're thinking, as it happens."

"What the hell do you think I'm—"

"Oh, Matt, of course I know what you're thinking." She looked down again, retracing the pattern. "Shall I tell you why he was late?"

"Of course I want to know, but of course I've got no right to. No, don't tell me. The less we know about each other nowadays the better off we are."

"You say that, Matt, but you don't mean it. And, anyway, even if you did, there's no way we can avoid knowing everything about each other sooner or later. Is there?"

He stared across the room, looking grim and stoical. "Why was he late?"

But he had guessed the answer, and as if in reply to the expression on his face, she said, "I was afraid to tell him about it any sooner, because of what happened the last time. But it's nearly three months now, and Dr. Chaffinch is sure—and so am I."

Against his will he turned, glaring at Jenny, examining her breasts and belly, and felt a horrified disgust to think that soon she would lose that graceful symmetry he admired, grow big and misshapen and, at last, expel from her body Pete's child, and these images as they passed before him were so cruel, vindictive and bloody, that his spontaneous hate brought a rush of pity and forgiveness, and he reached out to touch her hand. "I'm glad, Jenny."

"You are?" She smiled skeptically. "But at least, Matt, we don't have to blame ourselves for this." She laughed, then put her hands to her face. "Oh, what a dreadful thing to say. Why can't I get over finding some kind of perverse humor in everything that happens to me?" She was serious again, as if she hoped to make him share their feelings about the child. "You can't imagine how relieved I am, Matt. It's been almost a year and a half since I had that miscarriage, and I was terrified I'd never become pregnant again. Sometimes I even thought it might be my punishment for what we've done—"

He got up, hoping to prevent her from telling him anything more, and walked to the door. "Has Pete ever given any indication of suspicion about us?" He was disgusted to hear himself ask the question, and she stared at him angrily.

"Of course not. Has Marietta?"

"We can't talk today, Jenny. I'm going."

She came quickly toward him. "Marietta knows it, Matt."

"She does not. Why do you say such a thing?"

"Because one day she told me that the only real sin is hate—and that the ability to love gives a human being whatever dignity he has. Why else would she have made such a remark?"

"Because she believes it."

"But did she always believe it? Or has she been made to learn it?"

"She's always believed it."

"She has? Even when she was young? I doubt it. Young people don't believe such things, no one does who hasn't had to learn to protect themselves against some awful danger." She smiled, looking so ironic and aloof that he longed to shake her. "What about you? Do you love Pete as much now as you ever did?"

"It's Marietta's notion that love is the universal panacea, not mine."

"Not mine, either. Not any more, at least."

Matt knew he had stayed too long, the talk had turned treacherous, and he went dashing to the kitchen and there began a search for the overshoes which had him peering behind the stove and under the sink, beneath the table, and he still had not found them when he saw Jenny in the doorway, smiling. "Where the hell did you put the goddamn things?" he demanded loudly, and Jenny laughed, sat down at the kitchen table, and beckoned him to come sit opposite her, suggesting that he have another cup of hot coffee before he confronted that cold cold day, for the wind blew hard now, and the house creaked with its force.

"You never expected me to say such a thing, did you, Matt?"

"I've tried not to expect anything of you, Jenny, since you've been married to Pete." He did not sit at the table but went rambling about the kitchen, glancing warily into corners and once he twitched back the curtains and peeked out, finding the day had turned darker, and the sun quite disappeared.

"Sit down, Matt, please." Her voice was coaxing, she still smiled at him, and she gestured toward the coffee cup, but although he picked it up he would not accept her invitation to sit opposite her, and he looked at her as she raised her arms, smoothing her hair, with as much hostile suspicion as if he had been brought there by force and, by force, was being kept there. She clasped her hands on the table and watched him, following his restless movements, and she still continued to smile, though it seemed to him rather a curious smile, wanton and stealthy, compelling his attention, for he took it to be a warning. "You know me, Matt, don't you?" she asked, and he grew more uneasy, set down the coffee cup and stood against the door, studying her with his eyes slightly narrowed, as if this was some phenomenon never met before, a woman preparing to tell the truth, as he guessed she meant to do whether he was willing to hear it or not. "You know how selfish I am and how deceitful I can be, and how little I deserve to be loved." She fell into silent contemplation, perhaps comparing her supposed virtues with her known vices, and at last laughed softly at some private whimsy. "You won't talk to me, you're angry. Well—I didn't send for you, you can leave."

He started out, ready to make a dash for his freedom, but as he went by she caught at his arm and he stopped, looked questioningly at her, and at last grinned reluctantly and, when she gestured at the chair, sat down. "I'm not angry, Jenny, I'm ashamed," he told her, and lowered his head, giving her a sheepish glance, for it was true enough, and he could remember no other humiliation to match what he felt at that moment.

But Jenny spread her hands in a graceful gesture, widely separating her fingers, as if to show him the wedding ring on her left hand, the large garnet with its circle of small stones on her right hand, and drew in a slow breath. "Don't be ashamed," she whispered. "You have no reason to be. I don't love you any more." He gave her a glance of such fury and accusation that she held up one finger in a cautioning gesture. "At least, that's what I try to pretend sometimes. And they say if you pretend anything convincingly enough, it all comes true." She looked up quickly. "Have you ever tried it?"

Matt gave her a wry smile. "I've tried pretending that I'm glad you're married to Pete."

"And now you are?"

He slapped his hand onto the table, making the cups bounce and the coffee spill, and Jenny gave an angry outcry and leaped up, then ran to the sink to wipe imaginary stains from her dress. He was partway through the dining room when he heard her begin to cry, and although he went on to the vestibule and got into his overcoat, at last he returned to the kitchen, put his arms about her and held her head against his chest, an old familiar posture into which it seemed they fell by some instinct, and was presently stroking her hair and her back, her shoulders and arms, and murmuring whatever words he used to soothe her, just as he had done many, many times, while Andy Danforth was still alive.

They stood there for what seemed a long time, and it was with a sense of honest surprise that Matt found he had begun to caress her breasts, opening the dress and exploring their contours with his hands and mouth, as if to discover recent changes, and then they were running through the dining room, Jenny glancing back at him once with a look of imploring anxiety, and they hurried up the staircase.

But once they had entered the bedroom and she turned to him, he went clattering back down the stairs, snatched his hat from the rack of antlers, dashed part way back up and, once more, ran down to turn the lock in the door, and this time he entered the bedroom like a man finishing a foot race, his face pitiless and quite demented. He knelt before her as she laid her hands upon the sides of his face and, at the familiar shock, closed her eyes and drew in a long, slow breath.

Now, to delay a little longer that final quest, he began to contemplate the room and its furnishings, and took careful notice of each separate detail, fixing his eyes first upon the flowered wallpaper where her drawing and water colors hung in narrow gilt frames, then studying with minute care all the rest of this indoor garden, for there were flowers on the carpet, luxurious fantastic blossoms, and flowers on the drawn muslin curtains, which kept this room as coolly shaded in daylight as the living room habitually was.

He watched the movement of her head as she let it fall to one side, the opening of her hands in supplication or despair, and still continued his careful inventory: observing the two long mirrors on opposite walls, the silver-backed brushes and combs laid in careful design upon a dressing table, and all the while was aware of some slight surprise that this did not seem a room which any other man had ever entered, they might be in some stranger's bedroom; and yet the room was of an extraordinary interest to him and he seemed to miss no slight detail, for it could prove useful to him later, when he began to reconstruct these moments.

All at once the room disappeared, the reality of flesh returned, and at a relentless pace, with increasing tyrannical impatience, he carried her at last beyond the edges of delirium and they clung fast, as if to save themselves and each other from the world's overturning, that brief suspension of both their lives from which there had never seemed any certain return. But then Jenny's fingers caught hold of his shoulders and he heard a sound which kept him there immobilized, condemned to be caught, if he must be, kneeling there before her, with his face, as the mirror showed him, the face of a lunatic, as stupefied and malevolent as if the interruption had taken his senses.

He had heard only the sounds of their breathing and nothing else, for some unknown period of time, but now footsteps crossed the vestibule, went swiftly through the dining room and back again, paused once more at the bottom of the stairs, and came running up. They watched each other, transfixed with terror, and Matt was vaguely aware of his heart beating as if it knocked about in a large, empty box, causing his body to shake, and noticed, with some surprise, that sweat ran steadily from his face, dropping upon his shirt. For several moments there was silence, and then the footsteps returned down the staircase, crossed the vestibule, and as the front door slammed they started violently.

"Don't move," he whispered. "He may still be in the house."

They listened for what seemed many minutes longer, until Matt found his body wet, his muscles intolerably aching, and although it seemed he would not be able to move, he sprang up and went to the window, to see a man galloping off down the hillside and by then too far away to be recognizable. He watched, squinting and drawing back the curtain, and when at last he turned he showed her a smile which made him look so peculiar, almost evilly triumphant, and as sinister as if this unknown invader had entered his own home, that Jenny frowned and came toward him with a look of yearning and pity, whispering, "Matt?"

"I couldn't see who it was."

"But it was Pete—the door was locked, it couldn't have been anyone else."

"It could have been anyone else," he told her sharply, and snatched up his coat and got into it rather clumsily, finding it had grown much heavier since he had removed it. "He didn't come up and he didn't see us—whoever he was. And when Pete comes back, if he should ask where you were this morning, you were at Mrs. Hatch's and, for Christ's sake, get on over there." He dashed down the staircase, as fast as the other had gone, and, like the other, he paused midway. "Whatever he says," he called, "you weren't here. You weren't here!"

He went into the kitchen, found the overshoes readily this time, and went out the back door, glancing warily about as he pulled them on, but saw no one in the street on this cold day. He walked swiftly toward town, cutting through alleys and in back of houses where dogs came barking, looking over his shoulder from time to time and feeling that he was any criminal escaping from his scene of crime.

He thought of going back to the office, but if Pete was there he must take it as a declaration of Jenny's guilt with his own, and decided that he must wait until they met by chance, for the initiative was no longer his own. And so he set out to look at the cattle he had promised to investigate tomorrow with Lem Finney, after first stopping a young boy on the street and sending him to tell Mr. Finney that Mr. Devlin had left at ten o'clock.

"Don't forget to say ten," he warned him. "You'll be a businessman yourself some day, and then you'll understand that we can't always tell the truth if we want to make money."

The boy grinned and winked and promised to remember that he had gone at ten, and Matt returned near midnight, approaching his house with dread and the conviction that Pete was there with Marietta, waiting to accuse him; but he found Marietta asleep.

"Have you seen Morgan?" he asked, when she awoke to find him standing beside the bed, curiously watching her.

She smiled, very much to his surprise, and he realized that nothing at all had happened today to disturb her. "Of course not, Matt. They were going to be gone until late tomorrow, don't you remember? Jenny came here and we had dinner together."

But even so he was unconvinced, for he had continued to hear the footsteps mounting quickly, pausing, then running back down, the door slamming hard, and each time these sounds were repeated he listened with horror and disbelief, and a vague sense of resignation as if he might, after all, be glad enough to have some violent end to this heavy and wearing guilt, for the illusion of having achieved absolution had not lasted beyond the sound of that first step in the lower hall. Now, Matt told himself, quite reasonably, that he did not deserve to escape and should not escape, and then remembered that unless he did neither would Jenny—and, of course, neither would Pete.

He heard nothing from Jenny, that day or the next, and set out for Folger Hall at eight o'clock in a carriage with Marietta and Lisette and Ralph Mercer, feeling as he rode along the same stoical despair a man might feel, he told himself sourly, who has just heard the doctor whispering that he cannot last out the night.

For he had by now had time to invent so many morbid scenes of what would happen when next he and Pete saw each other, that he had vivid expectations of being shot at sight and was convinced that whether or not he would be dead before morning, he would at least have seen the annihilation of everything which composed the essentials of his life—his reputation, the happiness of Marietta and his children, he would have been forced to witness Jenny's disgrace and, it almost seemed, he was anticipating that this night would finally set him free of his long practice of hypocrisy and deceit, even though it must be at the cost of widespread destruction to those about him.

Lisette was a gypsy, dressed in a torn skirt striped with many bright colors, a white blouse cut low on her shoulders; her hair fell to her waist, and her head was bound in a green silk scarf. She had big gold loops in her ears, wore all the gold bracelets she had been able to borrow, her skin was stained brown with berry juice, and she carried a package of cards in her reticule with which she confidently predicted she would earn the Library Association one hundred dollars by telling fortunes.

"I'm psychic, I know I am. At least for tonight. But Father, what a shame you're not in costume." Matt had refused, like many other men, to wear a costume, and would only agree to put on a mask when they got there. "Everyone will recognize you the minute you walk in, mask or not."

"I suppose so," he agreed glumly. "But it wouldn't have done any good to go in disguise."

Lisette laughed delightedly. "In costume, not in disguise. It isn't quite the same thing."

Marietta was dressed as Queen Berengaria, a character which Lisette had proposed to her because, in a sense, they had come to the mountains on a crusade, to find honor and adventure as well as riches, and she wore a gown of purple velvet with sleeves which swept the floor and a train decorated with white rabbit fur spotted with ink. There were long chains and strands of beads about her waist, a tall gilt crown on her braided hair, and in the darkness of the carriage she looked to Matt so regal that he felt himself even further reduced, an unworthy vassal of this proud and beautiful lady.

"Oh, there's nothing more revealing than a masquerade, is there?" Lisette asked. "There we'll all be, so sure we can't be recognized in our costumes and masks, and then—all at once—at twelve o'clock!" She slapped her hands smartly together and Matt gave a nervous start. "Off come the masks and we all see one another as we'd like to be. What a wonderful idea, and why haven't we had one before? Whoever thought of it? Did I, Mother? Did you? Oh, look how crowded the streets are. We're almost there."

She leaned forward, her face glowing with joyous anticipation, and Matt looked at her sorrowfully, reflecting that she might very soon see her father killed or, what seemed to him much worse, shown as a man so unprincipled he would make love to another man's wife, and that man his brother, for he had resigned himself to submitting without any gesture of self-defense to whatever punishment Pete thought fitting for him.

Folger Hall was brightly lighted, the walls and ceiling hung with flags and garlands of fir and cedar, and Matt stood with Ralph Mercer while they waited for Marietta and Lisette to join them, observing with superior disapproval the masked and costumed men and women who were strolling about arm in arm, gathering into groups and laughing, as it seemed to him, like so many lunatics; about what, he could not imagine.

But he had discovered upon fastening the mask over his face that it was so great a relief to be able to retreat behind it, to look out without being looked at and to see without being seen, that he was struck with wonder to think they were not worn habitually, for surely it was more natural than being obliged to strain muscles and set teeth rigidly in an often futile effort to show the world some appropriate expression. And, he thought grimly, if he had not been able to cover his face he would have left immediately, for the screams of delight as they examined one another's costumes and wigs, the shrieks as they guessed who was dressed as what, the rac-

ing from one end of the room to the other, filled him with a helpless
and bitter rage and he was unable to resist seeing these neighbors
and friends and business partners as a pack of fools, dressed up like
so many scarecrows in specious finery which must not be seen any
nearer than five yards lest the slight illusion disappear, all pretending they could not recognize one another but were perfectly baffled
and taken in by the cleverness and completeness of the costume. On
any other night, of course, he would have been as amused by the entertainment as they were, but now he felt a keen resentment and disapproval at the sight of so many queens and peasants and pilgrims
and pirates and clowns, as if they should, like himself, be thinking of
more serious matters.

Pete and Jenny had not arrived and he thought they would not for
awhile, for Jenny refused ever to enter in the midst of a crowd. But
nevertheless he was preoccupied with inventing some terrible scene
which might be taking place at that moment between them and at
which he should be present, to defend Jenny, if not himself, instead
of standing here glowering at what was certainly an innocent and pathetic amusement.

Lisette now approached and looked eagerly into his eyes and her
own were sparkling so brightly that the gypsy fortune-teller would
be recognized the instant she walked onto the floor. "Isn't it wonderful? What a success."

"A success that isn't even begun," he reminded her, and was
ashamed of his inability to share her pleasure.

"Oh, but it is a success. Can't you feel it? I can," and, taking
Ralph's arm, they went swiftly into the crowd where she was presently laughing and shrieking like the others, examining ruffles and
gold braid and feathers, turning about with a quick twirl, clapping
her hands and dangling her reticule over her head as she announced
that it contained the precious cards by which she would later tell the
fortune of anyone willing to contribute a dollar to the Library Association fund.

After a few moments Matt turned to Marietta when she approached
him, with a longing to undo the harm he had done her, to take back
his crimes and mend his life so that he could once again present it
to her whole and not, as it seemed to him tonight, a ragged and
shabby affair which might presently end with no sorrow to anyone.
She was looking at him with what he thought was a sad dismay, as if
she had guessed his preoccupation, but she smiled quickly, and
when she suggested that they join the gathering he gave her his arm
and marched into the midst of the floor as resolutely and with as
great terror as if he marched before a firing squad, condemned to be
shot in the back without warning.

As it approached nine he could only nod more or less steadily, letting others talk, but unable to speak or to judge any more costumes.
Yet the fear was even now tempered with resignation, for he had
never conceded that a man's destiny might be foreseen or warded

off but only recognized for what it was, perhaps too late. Whatever stratagems he might have tried, hoping to avoid this moment—and he believed he had exhausted them all before he had gone to Pete's house the day before yesterday—he could have changed nothing, everything would have happened as it had, only perhaps on some different day, and from these reflections he drew bitter satisfaction.

And then, to the accompaniment of gasps of astonished admiration, Irene and Jeremy Flint entered wearing the only costumes which were at all impressive or convincing, for she was dressed as a Chinese lady, with a headdress which rose a foot and a half, dripping crystal beads and many small mirrors, her hair was covered with a black wig, and thin black eyebrows were painted diagonally above her domino mask, while Jeremy, in a yellow brocade robe and pigtail, tottered along beside her, mincing and fluttering a fan. As a shout of congratulation went up, Matt wryly reminded himself that life must have its obscure justice, for here at last was Milly Matches being welcomed to the ball with greater enthusiasm than anyone who had yet arrived.

All at once the musicians, who had been idly picking at their instruments, tuning and winding them and blowing small unpleasant sounds, began with a flourish which caught the dancers off guard, the leader announced the Grand March, and there was a rushing about which made it impossible for Matt to take his place in the line with Countess Manzoni—Mary of Scots tonight, with a sinister red ribbon about her neck in token of her destiny—and to watch at the same time for the entrance of Jenny and Pete.

Presently he was being carried forward by the music and the swift pace of the others, as if he had become an automaton, an individual no longer but only a part of this frenzy which had captured them all, sending them into mad laughter and excitement. When the march was almost done, he saw Jenny and Pete swinging arm in arm about the room, Jenny prancing with a blithe and surprisingly bold walk, as spirited and decisive as a horse being shown, and she was smiling, a bewitching smile he had never before seen her display in public but which was, perhaps, a signal to him that the crisis had passed, flown over their heads after all and spared them, at least for the present.

But in spite of Jenny's smile and prance and the peculiarly defiant rhythm of her walk, meant to complement her character as a Spanish dancer in a flounced red skirt with a black shawl drawn tight across her breasts and secured at her waist, the high comb in her hair and the tambourine to which she now gave a rattling smack, Matt looked covertly at Pete, whose face, like his own, was concealed by a full black mask, pacing beside her with the pride and sullen stateliness of a don; but Pete was concentrated upon the march and did not see him.

The march ended, leaving them at opposite ends of the room, and

Matt stood where the music had stranded him, smiling dutifully at Countess Manzoni and trying to decide whether he must seek them out immediately to congratulate Jenny on her costume and ask Pete about his trip, and at this prospect he felt a prickling at the back of his neck and his heart started nervously. Or it might be more plausible to wait until there had been a few dances and then walk up to Pete and throw one arm about his shoulders as he often did when they had not seen each other for a few days, and inquire what he had found at Deer Lodge. Then again it might be best to let one of them come to him, Jenny with whatever news she had, or Pete with his challenge, if he meant to deliver it.

And while he was damning himself for his cowardice and vacillation, more than for his recklessness which had precipitated them into this dilemma, he remembered that there were few opportunities in this world for a man to make attractive and cautious bargains, whereby he might both risk and protect himself at the same time.

There was a swirling activity of searching and taking partners for the next dance, and he heard a high-pitched chant in his ear which caused him to swing about, stiff-armed and with his feet spread to brace himself for whatever he would find. Irene Flint stood there in her embroidered yellow satin robe, giving him her imitation of the inscrutable smile of the Orient. "Don't you remember asking me for this dance?"

Matt scowled, baffled and unhappy, for it seemed his worries had cost him his wits tonight, and as the music began, a lively and demanding waltz, he seized hold of her and began to circle swiftly about, taking no notice of those they passed but determined to rush around this hall with one partner after another at as great a rate as he could go, until Pete either demanded to talk to him or denounced him publicly.

And so, grimly and doggedly he took upon himself a series of ladies—Pocahontas and Queen Rose and a Shepherdess, Cinderella and Mary of Scots and Mrs. Bloomer, and each of them he sent speeding about so fast they could neither talk to him nor call out to their friends but must concentrate upon their footing. And in that way he was able, for what seemed to him several hours, plausibly to take no notice of Jenny or Pete, for by his own contrivance they were one place when he was another and there seemed no way they could catch him if, indeed, either of them was trying to.

He discovered at last that Lisette had become his partner, and heard her describing the success she had had with her fortune telling, declaring she had made almost twenty dollars, and that after midnight, when they went to supper, was when she would have her real opportunity. "Before the night's over I'll tell the fortune of everyone here."

Matt laughed heartily, momentarily dragged loose from the sense of surrounding sorrow and danger and the repetition in his head, like a song he could not get rid of, of the steps mounting and descending and the slamming door. "I never knew you had this accomplishment. Where did you pick it up?"

"I bought a deck of fortune-telling cards and a book from that crazy old peddler, you know, the one who cursed Jenny. Mrs. Honeybone."

She leaned back and looked up at him, smiling so impudently that Matt had the sense of being able to see better what she was thinking because of the mask, which she imagined was protecting her, than if she had not been wearing it, and it seemed to him that she knew about him and Jenny and had known it for a long time. And this meant, of course, that Morgan knew it and Marietta, the younger boys and certainly Pete, and then he was convinced that everyone in the room knew their secrets and that all of them, behind their masks, were watching him and watching Pete and waiting for what would happen between them.

As his conviction increased that they no longer had a secret and he would presently be stripped naked and displayed to all of them, as wretched and prideless a sight as the road agents he had seen hang, Lisette continued talking with a gay and random unconcern which made him believe that in some obscure way she was mocking him, taking advantage of his helplessness to revenge herself for what he had done to all of them, but most of all, no doubt, to Marietta and herself.

"I told Jenny's fortune a little while ago. I told her that I saw fine things for her, because I don't believe it's right to predict trouble or disaster, but the card that turned up most often was the ace of spades, and that means something dreadful will happen—either to you or to someone you love." Her face was serious now and she still watched him. "Of course I don't believe it, but it gave me chills, all the same. Well, here's Morgan, at last. I thought he wasn't coming." She waved and then left Matt standing alone as she ran toward him, crying, "Oh, he's spoiling everything, he's got to wear a mask, at least!"

Morgan produced a mask from his pocket, covered his face, and they stood talking with Lisette looking steadily at Matt, while, from time to time, Morgan glanced his way. Matt tried not to look at them but to watch the dancers rushing by, but now was sure that Lisette hoped something spectacularly terrible would happen to him and Jenny, for he had often observed that the gentlest women became vindictive and bloodthirsty upon discovering that what they believed to be their natural rights had been flouted or ignored. And Lisette very likely thought herself as much entitled to his fidelity as Marietta was.

The music stopped and Matt turned, positive the moment had now come so close it would overwhelm him in an instant, and found himself confronting Pete who had just approached and reached out to put a hand on his shoulder.

"Pete, for Christ's sake," he cried sharply, and then began to stare into Pete's eyes, as dark and shining as his own, trying to imagine what was to take place between them, what Pete knew, and what he had guessed. "Did you just get back?"

But now it seemed that Pete was someone he knew only slightly, a man who would interfere with his own needs and desires, and with his cherished conviction that it was essential to his integrity to follow his impulses whenever they were fundamental to his nature, and follow them through to completion.

"I got back this afternoon late."

Pete's voice sounded neither unnaturally hearty, which would have seemed treacherous, nor strained and intense, as it was likely to be when he was trying to conceal anger. Nevertheless he continued to stare at him with such steady eyes that Matt felt he was being tested and watched, as if he had believed himself to be alone in a room but sensed that someone was there with him, although hidden and silent.

"What did you think about the Deer Lodge property?"

All at once Matt found his fears gone, the antagonism vanished, and was again alert and in command of himself, for whether Pete had returned yesterday out of suspicion and whether he had confirmed that suspicion or not, he was nevertheless a man with whom he had spent his life and who would not, as Matt now thought he must have known all along, do anything which would be hurtful to Marietta or Lisette.

"I didn't see it." The music had begun again, the dancers passed them swiftly, but they continued to watch each other. "I didn't get there, after all."

Matt hesitated and then quietly asked, "Why not? Didn't Morgan go, either?"

"I think he did. But I came back to get the power of attorney Lem had given me for his share, in case we decided to buy it." Pete smiled, though not, as it seemed, from any particular amusement. "Something happened that morning before I left home and—like a damn fool—I forgot to get Lem's signature."

"What did you do then?" Matt found with some disbelieving surprise that it was he who had become the inquisitor, and Pete who must explain the moves he had made, but, however humorous this turn might be, he stared at Pete as he waited for his answer as if Pete owed him not merely a convincing explanation, but an apology.

"I decided I'd never be able to catch up with him, and so I went on to Boulder to look at the mill. Lucky I did, too, because that bastard of a supervisor had disappeared with a month's salaries for the men."

And though this news would ordinarily have made him angry, it seemed so plausible that Matt was now perfectly convinced of what he had told Jenny without having believed it himself, that Pete had come into the house, heard nothing, when he would have expected

her to call out if she was there, and had left in the hope of over-
taking Morgan.

The band leader was shouting that when they played the next
notes it would be midnight, and directed everyone to remain in
readiness so they could unmask all at the same time. The music
blared, and throughout the hall men and women were removing
their masks and turning to look at one another, laughing with a curious self-consciousness, as if the few hours of having hidden their
faces had made them ashamed to be seen again. Matt slipped the
mask off and turned quickly, meaning to catch Pete's expression, but
Pete had left him and was making his way through the crowd toward Jenny, and after watching him for a moment with a suspicious
glare, Matt went to find Marietta to take her to supper.

Part

III

XXXII

THE Charles Baxter Dramatic Company had been advertised for several weeks by a swarm of posters which appeared magically one morning, plastered upon fences and store fronts, as if by some supernatural agent who had arrived in their sleep and departed before they awoke, but who was later discovered to have been a twelve-year-old boy, employed by mail to do the job for them.

They rode into town on an early June morning, near noon, preceded by a coach carrying their baggage and scenery, and that same young boy now rode beside the driver, loudly ringing a bell to announce that the extraordinary event had come to pass. As the news traveled, men appeared at windows and doorways, for the entrance of a new troupe of actors was anticipated with as keen a delight as the blossoming of wild roses, the first hot sunshine, or the fresh fruits and vegetables sent in from the neighboring valley farms.

The Baxter troupe followed the first coach at a little distance, and, perched on top, wearing a blue and red plaid dress with a parasol to match it, sat Fan Moffat who, the posters had promised, would perform the part of Mazeppa for them. The men looked at her with approving interest, trying to guess how well she would please them once she had been stripped down to tights and a short

tunic and bound to a horse's back, and agreed that she was the prettiest actress who had so far come to the mountains. They liked her
dark red hair and the way she held herself, as if she admired her
body and expected them to, and she smiled at them gaily, waving
to one side and the other, and seemed to have no doubt that every
man on the street that day had come out only to see her, so that none
of them might have guessed she had complained from the moment
they left St. Louis about the bad food on the steamboat, the hideous-
ness of Fort Benton, the heavy rainfall, the discomfort of being
crammed into a coach with eleven people who quarreled incessantly,
and had told them again and again it was a horrible mistake to have
accepted an engagment in this howling wilderness. For now she
looked merry and light-hearted and, furthermore, she was new,
someone they could speculate about—the beginning of summer,
she seemed, for many of them were tired and despondent after
the long winter.

Homer Grimes appeared at the St. Louis Hotel to request an interview with her even before the champagne baskets which carried
her dresses and costumes had been sent up, and she stepped onto
the balcony with him to observe the town, since he had begun by
asking her what she thought of it. "What do I think of it? It's a pigpen." She tapped her foot and gave him a scowl, as if the fault might
be his own. "Don't tell me people live here?"

"Yes, ma'am," said Homer meekly. "We thought it had improved
lately. Look at the brick buildings." He pointed them out, Devlin
Brothers, Finney and Son, the Ladies Emporium, a new three-story
office building just constructed by another leading pioneer, Jeremy
Flint, but she had no admiration for these, either.

She narrowed her eyes as she peered off at the green hillsides,
long since deprived of their trees, spotted with cabins and laced
with winding paths, and her nostrils flared as she told him that
furthermore the town smelled like a cesspool. "I heard this was a
gold camp," she said, and cast him a look of frowning censorious-
ness. "That the people here walked around with nuggets as big as
plums on their watch chains. It doesn't look rich to me. It's nothing
like Frisco or St. Louis. Those are towns," and she shook her finger
at him. "Maybe we won't play here, after all."

At this Homer protested with honest dismay, for he had been looking forward to seeing her tied to the Wild Horse of Tartary and carried up the ramp and into the mountains while the ballet girls
screamed with terror. "You wouldn't do that to us, Miss Moffat, now
surely you wouldn't. Why, the town's been covered with posters for
weeks. Everyone's been talking about it, and Miss Moffat, please
believe me when I say you're the greatest star who's ever appeared
in the Territory." He had been studying her carefully while she
looked at the town, observing that her eyes were blue and she drew
a wide blue band around them, her skin was white and not rouged,
while her lips were rather thin but mobile, and these attractions

Homer dutifully noted, even though he knew he would not be allowed to describe them for the readers of the *Helena Post*. "And the most beautiful," he added, making her a gallant bow.

"Am I?" She turned, smiling again, but then stared at him skeptically until at last, apparently convinced by his look of simple earnestness as well as the note pad he held in his hand, she went back into the hotel and gave him some last advice with her hand on the doorknob to her room. "Don't forget to say that I'm constantly studying to improve whatever part I play. And if you'll leave me alone now that's what I mean to do, though God knows I've played this lousy Mazeppa until I could choke—but that's an American audience for you."

"You're not an American?" he asked, and prepared to set her answer in his notebook.

"Of course I'm an American, you idiot. Whatever gave you that idea?" She closed the door sharply and Homer Grimes, after making a few more notes, returned to the *Helena Post* and found that his notes were of no use to him, for it was Ralph Mercer's policy that all ladies were beautiful and amiable, all oyster suppers and balls brilliantly successful, and all visitors to the mountains nonplussed to find so advanced a civilization set here on the crest of the Rocky Mountains—for that, Ralph Mercer often assured him, was the way to preserve their circulation.

However, as he sat at his desk frowning and trying to imagine what Fan Moffat should have said, scratching his ribs and shuffling his feet, the small building was suddenly invaded by Lisette and Rachel and Georgina Hart who had been, for a year and a half, Georgina Devlin.

He jumped up and pretended to welcome them, though these excursions ordinarily meant some kind of mischief, and, as he kissed Rachel's cheek, Lisette went by him with what he took to be a provocative smile and began to prowl about the room just as she always did, glancing at the tear sheets, observing the bed press and questioning the compositor who was setting the type, and he watched her warily as she roamed back and forth in her bustled red silk dress, for he was sure she had learned his secret from her husband, though she had not yet been so unscrupulous as to tell it to Rachel.

For Homer was not, as his wife supposed, Ralph Mercer's best friend, but had come west only because Ralph's parents had insisted that if their son would go exploring he must have a companion to help him where he was not very much accustomed to helping himself, and so they had sent along the butler's son. But this was regarded as a disgrace by Ralph Mercer, and before they had been traveling for two days he had sworn Homer never to admit to being anything but his friend. And indeed as they had gone beyond the edges of civilization, it was discovered that although Homer Grimes had been sent along to protect his master it was, after all, his master who was obliged to protect him. He carried him across streams on his back when Homer could not negotiate them himself, repaired Homer's shoes when they came apart, and gave Homer his coat to wear when Homer stood too near a campfire and burned the skirts of his own, and these several mishaps, with many others, Homer was more concerned to hide than his position in Ralph Mercer's family. And each time he saw his master's wife, this young girl who threw him enigmatic glances, it filled Homer with terror for fear she would one day, out of some whimsical impulse, tell the truth to Rachel.

Now Lisette paused beside the desk, and while he sighed unhappily she began to read aloud his account of Miss Moffat's tributes to the city's size, its impressive buildings, its busy and happy population, and then, to the accompaniment of gasps from Rachel and Georgina, she read Fan Moffat's remarks as he had jotted them down in the notebook. " 'It's a pigpen, don't tell me people live here?' " She looked inquiringly from Rachel to Georgina, while Homer walked to the windows and peered out, hoping to catch sight of Ralph Mercer, though there was little chance of finding him, for like other men who came to the mountains with capital, Mercer had involved himself in a dozen projects at once, and among them the *Helena Post* and *Virginia City Journal* were not of the greatest interest to him. " 'I haven't seen a well-dressed woman or a man who looked fit to be anything but an usher in a minstrel show.' " Lisette began to laugh, but Rachel and Georgina were chattering with outrage.

"Why, this dress was made in New York."

"So was mine—and most of Mrs. Flint's come from Paris."

" 'What kind of audience can a place like this provide for an artist?' " Lisette inquired, and as Georgina and Rachel began to argue about whether they should boycott *Mazeppa* and tell everyone else what Miss Moffat thought of their town, Lisette pulled off her gloves, brought a fresh note pad before her, selected the sharpest pencil and told Homer Grimes to sharpen another, and quickly began to write. Homer edged nearer the desk, trying to see what she had written, and when he found that she was describing the interview as it had taken place, he groaned aloud. "Oh, Mrs. Mercer, please don't make me print it that way. She'll be in here with a buggy whip if you do."

"Are you afraid?" She glanced up, gave him that familiar conspirator's smile, and returned to her work.

"But it's not what a gentleman would do, Mrs. Mercer. What can she think of a man who would use a lady that way in public?"

"What do you care what she thinks? Have that set exactly as it is, don't change a word. And if she comes in here, you can tell her your publisher's wife wrote it. Send her to me," she advised him imperiously.

"But you know I wouldn't do such a thing, Mrs. Mercer," he protested, though he was never sure when she meant what she said and when she only meant to tease him, and as Morgan walked in he rushed toward him, extending the note pad. "Oh, thank God you're here. She—Mrs. Mercer, I mean—just wrote it and says it's got to go in this way."

Morgan read the article through, and returned it to Homer, telling him soberly, "After all, Grimes, your publisher's wife—I can't help you out."

Georgina and Rachel were reading the interview, with Georgina demanding why Homer had let her say such things, and Lisette led Morgan to the back of the room. "Morgan, I'm going to ask you a question, something very important, and you must promise to tell me the truth. Will you?"

He was smiling and seemed not to believe there was anything so serious as she tried to pretend. "What can it be?"

"Is Nella Allen known as Nola Malachy?"

He looked at her with a shrewd distrustful face. "Who told you that?"

"No one told me. I found it out myself. It's true, isn't it?"

"This isn't anything you need to know about." He turned aside, scowling, and Lisette put herself before him again.

"Yes, I do. She was my friend, Morgan, and when she went away I was more unhappy than you can ever imagine. I've always loved her, and no one ever explained to me what happened to her after she left us. Then, a few months ago, I passed a girl in a carriage who looked so much like her that it was almost as if I'd seen someone dead begin to move and talk again. She didn't seem to see me, but after that I always watched for her whenever I was walking or driving, and then not long ago I saw her again, the same girl—and I know it's Nella, even though she looks older and rather strange, with her hair done up and wearing jewelry and silk dresses. I asked a boy on the street to run after her and then come and tell me where she went." She was breathing quickly and her eyes glistened as if she was about to cry. "He said she drove into the carriage entrance of Nola Malachy's Tivoli, and got out there. That's who she is, isn't she? Nella Allen. It can't be anyone else."

Morgan did not answer for a moment, but then admitted, "Yes—it was Nella."

She shook her head and flicked the tears away with childish impatience, brushing her fist across her cheeks. "She came to us for help. She was lonely and frightened—don't you remember her that first night, carrying Shekel in her arms because she hoped to make friends with us? Is this the way we helped her?" She put her hand to the side of his face, trying to make him look at her. "She was in love with you, Morgan. Did you know that?"

"I suppose I did."

"Why won't you look at me? Do you imagine I'm still your little sister? I've been married for three years, after all. I've had one baby and I'm going to have another. I know what must have happened to make Nella leave us so suddenly, and I think I guessed it then, except that then I couldn't understand it and I was ashamed, not only for you and Nella, but for all of us. You know how frightening those things are to a young girl, when she knows nothing about them, but now, of course, I can see so well how it happened—so easily."

"And you blame me."

"I blame all of us."

"Everyone but Nella."

"Nella was the only one of us who hadn't strength enough, or selfishness enough, to know when to protect herself." She was looking at him with a kind of sad bitterness. "I told you she might want you to hurt her."

As Homer had predicted, Fan Moffat came into the office the next day only a few minutes after the first copies had been distributed, threw the door wide open and stood staring at Homer Grimes, then suddenly raised one arm, pointed straight at him and shouted, "You!"

She came rushing forward with, he was sure, a glare in her eyes of intended murder, and as she advanced he looked to see if she had either a buggy whip or a pistol about her, wondering how he could combat a lady if she chose to use either one, and before he had moved she flung back her arm and lashed at him with her reticule which caught him heavily on one side of the head and felt, as he later explained, as if she had filled it with nuggets. She flailed at him again and again while he pranced about, cringing to avoid the blows, and the men came from behind the composing machines to watch with detached amusement as she pursued him around the room, screeching.

But all at once he dashed outside and took refuge in a saloon two doors down, made his way to the far end, and there remained until evening, when he crept forth, cautiously approached the *Post* building and discovered no one inside but Ralph Mercer, smoking a cigar and reading the day's copy. "Well, Grimes. Any good stories today?"

There was no account written, however, of Fan Moffat's attack on the editor for, Ralph Mercer told him solemnly, one such story would breed other episodes as surely as ponds bred mosquitoes and rotten meat bred maggots.

"I'm sorry, sir. I guess I should have stayed and let her hit me, but my God Almighty, she'd have cracked my skull. She's touchy as gunpowder."

"You showed good judgment, Grimes. Damn good judgment. But Mrs. Mercer, you know, won't like having missed it."

"There was no time to send for her, sir. She took me by surprise."

The story of Fan Moffat's attack on the editor of the *Helena Post* spread through the town on shouts of laughter, and by seven o'clock every seat had been sold and the streets about the theater were thick with curious onlookers, hopeful that the star of *Mazeppa* would arrive with a pistol and pick her tormenter out of the audience.

Homer Grimes, surrounded by his wife and her parents and brother, slunk into the theater with his hat pulled low, and in spite of the great interest felt in him tonight, he was not recognized. But in the lobby Rachel caught sight of Lisette, wearing a fashionable black silk dress, her hair drawn high in a massive arrangement of curls, and a black feather hat perched over her forehead, all no doubt in defiance of Fan Moffat's scorn for western elegance, and she looked so wickedly pleased with her own part in the excitement that Rachel caught hold of her arm, just as she had done when they were in school and quarreling, fiercely whispering, "Lisette Devlin, you've ruined my life."

Lisette turned slowly, seemed surprised by Rachel's distraught appearance, and gently inquired, "Whatever are you talking about, Rachel?"

"You're cruel, Lisette, and you're willful. You don't care what happens to someone else, even to someone as devoted to you as I've always been. Now, for the rest of his life, my husband will be reminded that he ran away from an angry actress with a reticule." Rachel's face was white and so vindictive that Lisette drew back a little, in mock fear, but then Ralph spoke soothingly.

"Rachel, you know it was only a prank, a good joke at Miss Moffat's expense. The town's been afforded a little unexpected amusement, that's all."

"At my husband's expense, not Miss Moffat's," Rachel corrected him, and turned back to Lisette, who had been watching her with a tolerant skepticism. "I've never believed you had any real feeling for anyone outside your family, and now I know it. I'll never trust you again. When you want to do something, you do it—and whoever gets hurt shouldn't have been in your way."

As Lisette took her place she turned to speak to Marietta and Jenny, seated behind her with Matt on one side and Pete on the other. "Rachel's furious with me. It seems I've started a feud; this will probably go on for years."

"It's gone on for years, as it is."

"But now it's in the open. What a relief. I won't have to pretend to like them any more."

"Yes, you will," Matt told her quickly. "It's not that kind of feud."

Lisette glanced at Jenny and, to her surprise, found that she was watching her with a serious and troubled expression, and Jenny said, very softly, "No, it isn't that kind."

The orchestra was preparing to play, twisting at the strings of their fiddles, thumping at the piano, scratching and rattling lightly at the drum and giving out slight piercing sounds of the flute, while children and dogs went screeching and barking along the aisles and the men in the audience talked in loud voices, and, from time to time, began a concerted stamping as they shouted for the performance to begin. But Lisette sat gazing at the curtain and silently arguing with Rachel Grimes, demanding that she tell her exactly what she had meant by saying they all did whatever they wanted to do, and how she had come by this false knowledge in the first place —for if Rachel had said that when she was too angry to be careful, she must have been thinking about it for a long time.

Inadvertently she glanced around and caught Jenny's eye. Jenny looked at her for a moment, as if to ask what she wanted to say, but when Lisette smiled, a tentative and rather pleading smile, she leaned forward and kissed her cheek. "Don't worry about it, darling. They can't hurt us."

"I hope not," Lisette said softly.

But Jenny's warm smile had seemed reassuring, and Lisette assured herself that if Jenny ever had loved Matt she would not have begged Marietta to be with her when her child was born.

"I'm terrified," Jenny had told them both. "You've got to promise not to leave me alone, Marietta."

Lisette had watched in awed silence as Jenny paced back and forth, wondering if this was some premonition of death, a foreboding that the old peddler's prediction would come true and she would die in childbirth, but Marietta had told her soothingly, "Every woman's afraid, Jenny, and the miscarriage has made you superstitious. If that hadn't happened, you wouldn't feel this way."

"Yes, I would. I'm a coward—you can despise me for it if you must, but it's true. I'm terrified of pain and I know I'm going to make a fool of myself. You've got to promise me, Marietta, that when it starts you'll make Pete leave the house—and not come back until it's over."

"I promise, Jenny. I'll stay with you."

And Lisette wondered on the day of the baby's birth how Jenny had so clearly foreseen what would happen, for the labor was long and difficult, she had screamed hysterically as she predicted she would, and had scared Dr. Chaffinch so that he had begun to drink in the hope of calming himself, and, when at last the baby was delivered he had declared that if ever she had another child some other doctor must attend her, for she had even refused his suggestions of chloroform with a cry of such incredulous horror that he had backed away from her in alarm.

"Are you mad? Don't let him near me, Marietta—don't let him give me that poison! My God, can't you see I'm bad enough when I know what I'm saying?"

And she began to cry despairingly when they told her that the baby was a girl, for Pete had wanted a son. "What's wrong with me? I can't bring happiness to anyone, and I've tried, I've tried. But I knew I'd fail."

Pete had looked disappointed when Marietta met him at the door, warning him first, but by the time the baby was two weeks old, it seemed he had forgotten that he had wished for a son and was as obsessed with his daughter as if no other man had ever had one.

Matt had been out of town on that day and for three days longer, and when Lisette saw him enter the bedroom she thought he had looked as awkward and bashful as a young boy. He had presented the tiny creature with a gift, a silver-mounted pistol with a mother-of-pearl handle, bending over the cradle as he held it on the palms of his hands, and speaking to her in a tone of tender supplication. "I had intended this as a gift for your brother, Leila, but even a girl might find a use for it here in the mountains." He gave it to Pete, and his face was darkly flushed. "I was so sure she'd be a boy."

"If she has a brother, I'll give it to him. And if she doesn't—I'll give it to her."

The little girl was nearly a year old now, with hair as black as Pete's and eyes as green as her mother's and now Jenny could seldom be brought to leave the house, while Pete was so full of pride and anxiety that other husbands were criticized for being indifferent fathers.

The curtains had parted but the audience continued to talk, the children and dogs ran about the aisles, and as a black-cloaked figure came sneaking onto the dark stage, loudly whispering, "Olinska!" there was a stamping of feet which shook the walls and made the kerosene lamps swing to and fro, and the figure ran off again. They began to hiss and boo, tongues clattered derisively against teeth, and after several minutes Charles Baxter, in the robes of the Castellan, clutched at the green curtain and hid behind it, as if for protection from a hazard of rotten eggs and vegetables, gazing at them with such reproachful melancholy that for a moment they grew silent, thinking there might have been a mishap backstage and he had come to tell them about it.

"Ladies and gentlemen, you have us at your mercy." Even the children now paused in their gallops to gaze at him curiously, and their playmates, the dogs, whined and patted their feet and caught at their coattails to remind them of interrupted games. "We have come here—"

"To this pigpen," called a funereal voice.

"To your fine city," corrected Charles Baxter, and once again feet stamped and hands clapped in unison.

But when the Castellan did not reappear, another voice shouted: "You've got our dust, old fellow. Now let's see your show."

Charles Baxter once more faced them, wrapping the curtain about himself like a shroud or toga. "I am afraid, ladies and gentlemen," he told them, so sorrowfully that again they expected to hear the report of a fatal accident in that small world beyond the tallow footlights, "that we have lost your favor and can never hope to please you—"

"Send her out, Baxter," called a voice, as commanding as if he addressed the Vigilance Committee while road agents stood before them. "We'd like to make the lady's acquaintance."

"Tell her we're gentlemen. We won't toss her in a blanket just because she deserves it."

"Miss Moffat, ladies and gentlemen, is indisposed, and begs your kind indulgence."

"Too late."

A young man climbed onto a bench and wove back and forth unsteadily, until all at once he toppled over and was caught by his friends who, with an air of hastily covering over some gross indecency, picked him up by the legs and arms and carried him out of the hall, and this had the effect of calming the audience, as if it proved that perhaps Miss Moffat had not been entirely wrong about their mountain civilization. The men sat up straight, looked solemn and penitent, gestured the children onto benches and quieted the dogs, and all at once presented to Charles Baxter a hallful of faces as sober and docile and apprehensive as any minister might have wished to see from the pulpit.

"Shall we continue?" he asked them politely.

"Continue what you haven't begun," someone advised him.

Mr. Baxter considered his predicament a moment longer and then, with a flourish by which he slung aside the green curtain, he gave them a deep bow and left the stage with a sideways lurch which instantly set them to clapping and cheering, as if he had delivered a long and difficult part.

The black-cloaked figure came sneaking back, and with many pauses and furtive glances toward the audience, at last arrived beneath the balcony, loudly whispering, " 'Olinska! Dear Olinska'!" A peculiar and ominous silence had fallen over the audience and the figure turned toward them, unable to concentrate upon Olinska while that condemnatory silence continued, and then there were sounds throughout the theater as of a snuffling pig, others took it up, and in a moment the auditorium was filled with hogs, rooting and wallowing and snorting. Fan Moffat began to speak, gestured at them to be still, and then burst into loud sobs and ran from the stage.

But two pairs of hands reached from the wings and thrust her back, and although she tried once more to escape and was once more pushed roughly onto the stage, finally she bowed her head so submissively, seeming to present herself as ready for any punishment they chose, that all at once they took pity on her and the snorting stopped.

"Don't be afraid of us, Miss Moffat. We ain't wild hogs, we're domesticated porkers."

She smiled slightly, and Fan Moffat and her audience examined one another carefully for several moments. "Ladies and gentlemen," she cried imploringly, and came to the edge of the stage. "Please believe me when I tell you that I was misquoted."

There was a mumbling and muttering and heads turned, searching out the churlish editor of the *Helena Post,* but Homer Grimes did not venture to defend himself, and all at once it seemed they were overwhelmed by a rush of tolerant affection.

"Leave her alone, you guys. This is no way to treat a lady, no matter what she called us."

"We forgive you your opinions of us, Miss Moffat. Let's see if we can forgive your acting."

She laughed impudently, Olinska reappeared and the play was resumed while the audience sat contrite and skeptical and seemed determined to prove to her how she had misjudged them.

She strode vigorously about the stage in her guise of noble young page, crying out her lines in a clear high voice which was monotonous but insistently feminine, and at the end of the act they clapped with such polite restraint that the actors disappeared like guilty servants, and the men filed out to discuss her over a drink while the women wandered up and down the aisles and talked to friends.

As the play continued, the audience fell into its old habits of participating in the dialogue, advising the performers and prompting the prompter, and these indignities the actors bore with resigned patience. When the time came, Mazeppa heard the Castellan pronounce the death sentence with as little horror as she might have shown to hear an announcement of the stagecoach's departure for Virginia City, the steed came clattering onto the stage and was instantly recognized as an old and docile hack-horse which belonged to one of the town's livery stables.

His ovation caused him to pause and look wisely at them, before he flipped both ears and leaned down to place his muzzle upon the drummer's bald head with an air of benevolent curiosity. The Castellan's men seized Mazeppa and pushed her back and forth with what seemed unnecessary energy, and when they retired carrying her cloak with them she was found to be wearing only pink tights and a tunic which scarcely reached her thighs, while her dark red hair fell abundantly loose.

The men began to stamp and howl and Fan Moffat was hoisted to the horse's back, tied fast, and the Castellan, bellowing, " 'Let scorching suns and piercing blasts, devouring hunger and parching thirst, rend the vile Tartar piecemeal,' " gave a mighty kick at the animal's flank which started him slowly and reluctantly plodding up the ramp.

But then he stopped, apparently surprised by the unusual posture of his burden and confused by her shrieks and the shrieks of the three little ballet girls, and stood gazing down at the floor ten feet below. At this Fan Moffat screamed more loudly still while Charles Baxter ran distractedly back and forth. The horse continued on his way, pausing at the first platform to receive a lump of sugar, and Charles Baxter dashed up the ramp, kicked him once again, and came skidding down as the curtains were drawn together. In a moment they parted to show Mazeppa lying far out on the steppes, and as the horse put his nose to the back of her neck, the men rose with a shout and she came toward them, smiling and throwing her arms wide, and at last bowed so low that her hair fell forward to touch the stage.

XXXIII

After that, the troupe was required to perform nothing but *Mazeppa* and all the rest of their repertoire must wait until the miners had sated themselves on the sight of Fan Moffat in tights and a tunic, tied to the back of the hack-horse, who never properly learned his role and each night showed too much familiarity with the audience and too little willingness to mount the incline.

Men sent her gold nuggets of various sizes, and pouches of dust were delivered at the end of every performance when she stood before them with her hair undone, bowing and smiling humbly, and it seemed she delighted them even more because she had first insulted them and they had quarreled, like lovers who had begun with hostility and discovered it to be only a camouflage for their violent attraction.

She often appeared in the afternoon, walking alone, nodding and smiling on all sides as she had done the day they arrived, and stopped to talk to small children who backed away or grew tongue-tied, giving one little girl a book, which was immediately determined to be a copy of Emerson's *Essays*, and another a package of hard candies upon which the excited child almost choked.

Most of the men agreed that though her face was not beautiful, she gave an immediate impression of attractiveness and charm, and she paraded forth a series of plaid taffeta dresses, striped silk gowns, and hats piled with ribbons and feathers and flowers, while small diamond earrings dangled at her ears even when she played Mazeppa.

But after she had been there for two weeks, they still knew only as much about her as they could see—that her breasts were big enough to please them, her waist small enough, and her legs delicately formed. And though there were men who had established themselves as authorities on the subject of Fan Moffat, discoursing at length on whether or not her costume was padded and her hair dyed, and could persuasively argue that she was chaste, wanton, a virgin or an experienced voluptuary, it was only speculation, for Charles Baxter had warned her that if she caused them any scandal in this town it would be the end of her contract. The western camps, he said, were no longer what they had been ten years ago, but were inhabited by numbers of New England ladies who thought of actresses very much as their ancestors had thought of witches.

"No more ambiguous episodes," he said meaningfully.

"No more distraught admirers who must be hit over the head with bottles," his wife would add.

A few days after the first performance she came to the office of the *Helena Post* and, once again, threw the door wide and stood surveying the room. The two men at the composing machine showed ready interest, and Homer Grimes stood up and faced her defiantly. But all at once she smiled, closed the door softly and walked toward him with a movement of her hips which exaggerated the sway and teeter of her bustle, setting one foot before the other with a kind of gliding motion, as if she were feeling her way along the floor, smiling as she came, although he glanced warily at her reticule. "I want to thank you."

"Thank me?" Homer peered at her suspiciously.

"For the interview. It's been responsible for most of our success. Mr. Baxter says without it they'd have been tired of *Mazeppa* after three shows, but now he says we'll be here all summer."

Homer became dignified and condescending. "I'm glad if I've been able to help, Miss Moffat."

She laughed. "You didn't mean to help, remember. You must have taken a great dislike to me that day, and I suppose I was a bitch—but you have no idea what we'd been through getting here." Her eyes grew bright and her face predatory. "Why don't we sit down and I'll tell you about it? It would make a wonderful story."

She sat sideways, her bustle billowing in a mass of puffed taffeta and her parasol planted like the tip of a sword on the floor, while she confided that her parents had been captured by Turkish pirates and herself put in a harem at the age of six, from which she had escaped at nine to live for a year or two among the gypsies. "For Christ's sake, write it down as I go along. You'll never get it straight otherwise." Homer recorded that she had married a rich Englishman in Tripoli who was on his way to shoot elephants but was killed on the expedition, and after that she had met Mr. Baxter and his family on a ship going from Majorca to New York and had agreed to join their troupe, though not without misgivings.

She was gone before Ralph Mercer came in and he read it with a smile which ended in laughter. "She's a gifted liar, though she doesn't bother to keep her chronology straight. But the town's taken a fancy to her and if we don't publish her yarn the *Herald* will."

The story was a fabrication upon which Fan embroidered from time to time, for she thought it would disappoint them to know she was the daughter of a doctor in a small Illinois town, who had decided by the time she was fifteen that she had a brilliant destiny and had left with the first man who asked her to, only to find herself three months later alone in Chicago with no money. She had lived for a year or two on a precarious combination of acting and prostitution, and her employment with the Baxters was the most respectable she had known, though it might not last much longer, because not only Ermina Baxter but every other member of the troupe disliked her and could not understand why the public should be so easily duped into finding her an amusing minx, and so naïvely ready to take her as she wanted them to for an artful but refreshingly candid and provocative scamp.

They told one another sourly that there was no way to explain why it was that however often she betrayed the disposition of a bad-tempered alley-cat and the tongue of a shrew, she had some mysterious and probably sinister knack for making a theater filled with people like her, forgive her, and finally fall in love with her, and they were aggrieved to know that their present success depended upon Fan Moffat's faculty for seeming more charming than she was, more clever that she was, and even prettier than she was.

"The tunic's too short," Ermina told her one morning, as they sat in the hotel dining room. Ermina was in the seventh month of pregnancy, and laced herself so tight that her flesh was usually mottled and her face looked as if it had been pummeled. "I've heard the comments, and although I won't repeat them before the children, that tunic must be longer by tonight."

Fan Moffat turned on her as fiercely as if she had threatened to take the part away and play it herself, while the children giggled and the others smiled and passed knowing winks about the table. "Too short! It's too long, if anything. I've seen pictures of Adah Menken wearing one at least two inches shorter."

"Adah Menken is beside the point. We're a decent family company and you must lengthen that tunic by tonight, Miss Moffat, or I refuse to play with you."

"Who do they come to see? You? Mr. Baxter, you've got to make her leave me alone. She's pestered me until I'm so nervous I'm ready to collapse—and then where would you all be?"

Charles Baxter did not rescue her from his wife but only continued to look melancholy and depressed, an habitual expression Fan attributed to his dyspepsia, but which gave him the air of romantic sorrow spinsters and young girls admired. And after Ermina had spent several minutes stuffing pancakes into her mouth, during which she acquired a benign and contemplative look and seemed to have forgotten their quarrel, she abruptly emerged from the trance and pointed at Fan. "I know you, I know your tricks. I'll tell you what you're plotting, shall I?"

"By all means tell me—or how will I know what I'm plotting?"

"You're biding your time, you're waiting, until one day it won't be possible for me to appear—and when that happens you intend to play Lady Macbeth." She shook her finger so near Fan's nose that Fan was forced to move back or run the risk of having it briskly tapped. "Can you imagine, my dears, what kind of Lady Macbeth she would make?"

And, a few days later, Fan announced to Homer Grimes, "I'm going to play Lady Macbeth night after tomorrow." She twirled her parasol and smiled at it, as at an old confiding friend.

"Lady Macbeth?"

"Why not?" she demanded, and jabbed the tip of her parasol at the floor with a gleeful malice which made Homer quickly place his feet beneath the desk.

"I thought that part belonged to Mrs. Baxter. She's been announced in it."

"She's been announced but she knew god-damn well—don't say I said god-damn, now, will you?—that she'd never be able to play it by the time we got here. She's so big she can't get into the costume for the sleepwalking scene and, besides, the audience would have fits at a women about to give birth playing Lady Macbeth. They wouldn't swallow that even here. Don't say I said even here—I like the bloody place, you understand." She sighed and rolled her eyes, passing one hand distractedly across her face. "Oh, hell."

"Do you want to discuss your interpretation of the part?"

"Of course, that's why I'm here. Now, please pay careful attention, because I want to be sure they understand what I'm doing. First of all, the part of Lady Macbeth is the most demanding role in the theater because she's on the stage only intermittently, but she must show cumulative excitement—did you get that?" She glanced about, annoyed, as the door opened and a man she had seen on the streets and in the hotel dining room paused there, and walked in.

She had wondered who he was and, perhaps because she had a natural admiration for black-haired men, who gave her delicious qualms of being subjected to their violent impulsiveness, she had thought of him sometimes as she lay alone at night, fretful and languishing over her enforced chastity and listening to the sounds which carried through the hotel's thin partitions, of voices muttering, swearing and arguing, furniture being shoved about and bed slats creaking, all creating an intimacy which caused those who were closed up in the hotel overnight to observe one another the next morning in the dining room with heightened interest, resentment, or suspicion.

"Miss Moffat," said Homer, and she started slightly. "Miss Moffat," he repeated, "may I present Mr. Devlin—whose sister is married to Mr. Mercer—who owns this paper?"

"Oh?" she asked, and rose from the chair as if drawn slowly upward by a string, turning partway to show him her breasts and the provocative bulge of her bustle; her skirt swirled about her legs and the train laying before her feet in such confusion she could not move without kicking it aside. "I'm very glad to meet any relative of Mr. Mercer's, he's been so kind to me." She smiled, and the smile seemed to possess a magical power, giving her command over them both.

He bowed slightly, looking quite solemn, so that she supposed he

was stricken dumb with embarrassment, and all at once she fell in
love with him, for she believed profoundly in sudden love and not in
any other kind at all. "I want to apologize for my sister, Miss Moffat."

"Not at all," Fan assured him graciously, but then wondered why
she had said it.

"It was my sister who wrote that first story, not Grimes."

"Your sister wrote it?" She looked at him carefully, for his smile
was ironic, and he was observing her with a kind of confident anticipation which, in company with that ironic smile, had her ready to
defend herself, or quarrel with him. "What did she do such a thing
for?"

"I suppose she was a little annoyed to see what you thought of us.
It isn't that we're pigs by nature—only that it's more than a few
thousand men can do overnight to fight one another for the gold we
found here and build a neat and sanitary city."

"But I didn't mean it, I only meant—I don't know what I meant."

She glared at Homer, who said, "Miss Moffat has promised us her
Lady Macbeth night after tomorrow."

Morgan smiled. "I'll look forward to it." He opened the door.
"Good luck."

The next morning at breakfast Charles Baxter looked more than
usually gloomy. "You know your lines, I hope?"

She gave him a mean, darting smile. "I've known them for years."

"Babbled them in the cradle," suggested Ermina, who had predicted they would all be made ridiculous by Fan Moffat's tawdry
performance.

The rehearsal gave no indication of what they might expect, for
she insisted that no actress of sensitivity would perform at a rehearsal, and agreed only to read the lines in her shrill, high voice.
But they watched her suspiciously and mumbled among themselves
until she turned with a shriek so uncanny that the two little daughters clasped each other in alarm and the second old man nodded to
the ingenue. "Maybe she can do it. Maybe she can."

The dressing room opened into a narrow hall, where the ceilings
were so low that Charles Baxter kept his knees slightly flexed as he
moved about, peeking in anxiously from time to time to ask, "Are
you ready yet, Miss Moffat? I want to see you."

The small rooms were crowded, and in a perpetual state of such
confusion that before each performance some wig or cloak was lost
and only recovered after a frantic search. They accused one another
of hiding these accoutrements, and since Fan had herself hidden a
rival's costume on some few occasions, she now took the precaution of bringing hers from the hotel and hung it beside her corner of
the make-up shelf, and there she sat to make up her face with very
white grease paint, kohl-blackened eyelids, and brows which
slanted to her temples.

Ermina sat sprawled in the opposite corner with her hands clasped

on her uncorseted belly, and kept a jealous watch over Fan's preparations. The witches, who were the two young daughters and a
fourteen-year-old boy, were dressed in their ragged wigs and flapping
robes and sent to peek through the curtains. And as Fan began to
brush her hair, so long and thick that more than once it had been
clutched and tugged by one of her fellow performers who hoped to
prove it was not her own, Ermina sniffed and Fan gave her a swift
fierce glance.

At last she took the dress from the hook, struggled into it without
help and fastened it, and swung around to ask slyly, "Well, Mr.
Baxter, will I do?"

"Very well, Miss Moffat, very well indeed."

He seemed relieved, for the dark red velvet gown with dangling
sleeves and a train six feet long might be effective enough to distract
them from her performance, and he left them to count the house.

"Miss Moffat," said Ermina. "That neck is too low. Lady Macbeth
is not a trollop."

"Don't be ridiculous."

"Miss Moffat, put in a handkerchief. Put it in, I say, or by God,
I'll play the part myself."

Fan whirled, her fists clenched. "Are you trying to spoil my performance?" But as Ermina glared at her steadily, she whisked out a
handkerchief and tucked it into the neckline. "There! Does that
satisfy you, you bloody old sow?" and she ran down the hallway to
where Charles Baxter stood peeking through a hole in the curtain,
caught his arm and leaned against him whispering desperately,
"Your wife is driving me mad, you've got to make her leave me alone."

"Remember her condition," he advised her sadly. "Come, now, look
out there. That will cheer you. They're here to see you, remember
that."

She put her eye to the curtain, squinting, and beyond the smoking
candles the big, dim hall was crowded—more than one thousand
men and one or two hundred women, most of them talking, some
staring at the curtains; but not one seemed to know she was there,
waiting to give them her interpretation of Lady Macbeth, or guessed
that their lives would presently be all but shattered by the strength
and viciousness of her performance.

And as she stood thinking of the power she must bring to bear
upon them she grew so weak and so despondent that she felt the
floor begin to weave beneath her, and Mr. Baxter had to hurry her into
the dressing room. She sat in a chair, leaning against the wall with
her eyes shut, letting them wave handkerchiefs in her face and mas-
sage her wrists and pass smelling salts beneath her nose, and knew
that she would not be able to walk upon the stage or, if she did,
would not be able to speak.

At last, she opened her eyes and found Charles Baxter's face,
shining wet, hovering above her. Tears rolled down her cheeks and
her head fell to one side. "I'm sick. I'm—maybe I'm dying."

"Remember," he told her fiercely, "you must trust to luck, because ten o'clock is sure to come."

And at these words, the magic incantation by which hundreds of actors throughout the nation might at that same moment be trying to encourage one another, they heard the orchestra moving eerily among a series of chords and partial melodies, the curtain rose on the three witches, and there was no more hope of escape.

Feeling as if she might be recovering from some long illness, Fan sat up slowly, to find them watching her with awed concern, and while she sipped water, waiting with a dismal resignation for the moment when she must go out there, she could hear the voices from the stage, but nothing she heard seemed related to any play she knew. In another moment the prompter was calling her name, and with as much surprise as if she had been absent and returned only at that moment, she found that Ermina was pulling her to her feet and pushing her toward the stage.

"What do I say?"

" 'They met me on the day of success,' " Ermina whispered, thrust a paper into her hands and gave her a shove which sent her stumbling forward. But then, hearing a roar of applause, she faced them, smiling and bowing, with some furtive hope that they might applaud all night.

But at last they grew quiet, and with a sudden rush at the lines, afraid that if she did not plunge into them and ride upon them they would abandon her and she would drop into space, she began to speak, smacking the letter with her hand, and was swept by a sense of infallibility. The messenger entered and she talked casually to him, and then Charles Baxter, looking more puzzled than ambitious, more discouraged than determined, clanked toward her in his armor across which was slung a cape of buffalo hide.

She turned to him with an air of frantic relief, as if he had come late to a party which was important to her, crying, " 'Great Glamis, worthy Cawdor!' " and as he took her into his arms she whispered, "I've forgotten the rest."

He tightened his hold. "You can't, God damn it. Remember your lines, remember them, I say," and he clutched her until she winced, and the audience burst into appreciative applause. "Wing it, then," he told her, and signaled the prompter.

As she left the stage she grabbed the prompt book from Ermina, who met her with a face as dour and accusing as if she had committed a far worse crime than any Lady Macbeth had intended.

She studied the next lines, mumbling them until she rushed back onto the stage and recited those she could remember, waited for the prompter, and as she realized that she had lost all contact with the play and with the other players, she glanced at the audience, for she felt an irresistible need to see the expressions on the faces of those who sat nearest the stage.

Morgan Devlin emerged as sharply as if he were alone in the hall, and it shocked her to see that his expression was serious and concerned. He was leaning forward and he stared at her with such intensity, his eyes brilliant and compelling, that it seemed he was willing her to speak, to take up her part and perform it, and she turned back with a determination that, since he wanted it, she would do it for him.

The prompter was giving her the lines and Charles Baxter whispered, "Damn you, you bitch, read these lines. Read them, I say."

She spoke the next lines in a voice which trembled and brought her some brief applause, but she did not look at the audience again, for if he was displeased with her still then she would be hopelessly tongue-tied, perhaps faint, and have to be removed as ignominiously as a dog sick of poison. And when she came to the sleepwalking scene, she found it such a relief to wring her hands and wail that they shouted and stamped, and after that she stood beside Ermina in the wings, both of them watching the stage with as keen interest as if they had never before seen the play's conclusion.

Malcolm had not completed his final speech when the applause began, yells and cheers as wild as were ever heard at a Sunday afternoon cockfight. Charles Baxter held out one hand and she came forth, made him a low curtsy, and when she turned to the audience she saw that Morgan Devlin was smiling as proudly as if he were the parent of a small child who had contrived to avoid disaster in a school performance, and she gave him in reply a hesitant smile, shy and humble, which seemed to please him, for he nodded and made her a signal with his thumb and forefinger.

The others came tramping on with sullen faces, bowed one after another and tramped off again, but she still stood there, unable to get enough of this homage, for it seemed they had become inseparable friends, she and the audience. At last she stood in the wings, watching wistfully as they began to leave, until she realized that even the stragglers were not coming back, and then she approached the dressing room hesitantly, for though there had been noisy approval from the audience, there had been none at all from her fellow performers. And the theater had fallen into such an ominous silence she wondered if it might be she had lingered there much longer than she had realized and they had gone back to the hotel.

They had not. They crowded the two dressing rooms, partly undressed, wigs and armor tossed aside, and though they glanced at her surreptitiously, no one spoke as she stood in the doorway, gazing at Ermina who sprawled on a stool while her husband held one hand and her younger daughter the other, and the elder applied a compress to her forehead. "What a disgrace," Ermina cried at sight of her. "What a horrible, horrible disgrace."

"Disgrace?" Fan turned to Charles Baxter. "Did I disgrace you?"

"Don't ask him. He thinks he's got to be a gentleman. The applause, oh, my God, when I think of the applause." Ermina covered her ears. "They pitied you because you're young. Oh, how I wish you

were ten years older and played that way. You're no actress and you'll
never be an actress. You're a vain, vulgar slut—"

"Ermina, no, no," her husband begged, and as Fan pushed her way
through the room, he herded the men and boys back to their own
quarters.

Fan paid no attention to Ermina's groans and whimpering, the
excited chattering of the girls, but dressed and left without a word,
ran back to the hotel and pitched herself onto the bed, sobbing in an
enthusiastic rage until at last she fell asleep. She woke some time
later to undress and crawl into bed and lay until daylight staring at
the ceiling, thinking it was quite true she was not an actress, and
was filled with abject terror as she considered what, indeed, would
happen when she stepped onto a stage in ten years and created such
a fiasco.

But at noon she got dressed, and as she drew the blue line along
her eyelids, she examined her face carefully and decided that ten
years was a long time away. She went downstairs to drink coffee,
and when the clerk told her the whole town was singing her praises
she smiled in happy surprise, but then gave him a quick, shrewd
glance to discover if he was teasing her.

"Your mail, Miss Moffat, delivered by hand early this morning."

The clerk presented to her, ceremoniously, the first letter she had
received, and she retreated across the lobby to read it. It was an
invitation to ride that afternoon, signed by Morgan Devlin, who apparently had no doubt she would accept him, for when she read it
again it was not so much an invitation as a statement that he
would call for her at two o'clock.

For a moment it seemed she ought to be insulted, but she had
decided long ago that girls lost many pleasures by protecting their
pride, and so she drank three cups of coffee and went upstairs to
unpack her riding habit, and all at once was as pleased with herself,
with the sunny, hot day, and even with this little mountain town, as
if her performance had been all she had expected it would be.

And when she looked at herself in the brown riding habit with its
red velvet waistcoat, set the black silk hat straight across her forehead and stamped the floor a time or two with the heels of her
shining black boots, she was convinced he was hopelessly in love
with her and meant to propose marriage that afternoon, if only her
charm did not make him timid. And, after that, it would never again
concern her whether she forgot Lady Macbeth's lines, or the hack-
horse stepped off the ramp with Mazeppa tied fast to his back.

She went onto the balcony and stood at the railing, looking up
and down the street with alert eager interest, for the town did not
seem so squalid as it had the day she arrived and, in fact, the brick
buildings which Homer Grimes had pointed out had begun to grow
larger, the cabins and shacks on the hillsides were amusingly picturesque, the Sunday procession of ox carts and buggies and galloping horses made an impressive pageant, and all at once the East

seemed alien and diabolic, a challenge she would gladly forsake.

"Are you looking for someone, Miss Moffat?" Charles Baxter stood beside her, morosely examining the riding costume.

"Yes, I am."

"I hope your success—which you understand was the result of both ignorance and chivalry on the part of the audience—hasn't made you reckless?"

"What an idea. Can't I ride in the middle of the day with a gentleman?"

"Are you sure he is a gentleman?" He studied her face, as if to discover whether she was, as he suspected, wanton and foolish, or whether it might be his wife's envy which made him misinterpret the natural vanity of a young girl whose skin was smooth, whose hair shone, and whose body was resilient and graceful. "You know how it is when a girl once gets herself talked about—it's all up with her. The world won't ever let her alone after that."

"Won't it?" she asked him. In another moment she saw Morgan, riding one horse and leading another. "There he is. Does he look like a gentleman to you?"

"He does not," Charles Baxter told her positively.

"But his family," she whispered, "own half the gold mines in the Territory." She raised her eyebrows, as if to ask whether or not he looked like a gentleman now, and hurried along the hallway, followed by Charles Baxter, who was muttering in her ear.

"Be back before dark, Miss Moffat, I warn you, I know your tricks, now mind what I say."

She ran down the staircase, almost afraid he would not be there, and found him standing in the lobby. She crossed it quickly, smiling at him as they walked out, and without either of them having spoken he helped her mount and they set off through the crowded streets, where she was kept busy acknowledging the compliments of men who saluted her from the sidewalks.

She took this deference as no more than she deserved and grew quite intoxicated on it until, all at once, she was caught by a treacherous conviction that Ermina and Charles Baxter had been right, she had made a fool of herself and their obeisance was not only chivalrous but mocking. She gave him a doubtful glance and found him watching her and smiling. "What are you looking at me like that for?"

"I was admiring you."

"You were?" But the question had too much intensity in it, and she took care to sit straighter, not to lean toward him as if she longed to touch him, although, it was true, she did. "Was I terrible last night?"

"You heard the applause." He was still smiling, a rather curious smile, she thought, tender and amused, suggesting to her more abundant satisfactions than any she had had for a long time, not, in fact, since Ermina Baxter had become her guardian.

"But they said it was only because you felt sorry for me. Please tell me the truth, was I awful?"

"You didn't know the part, after all. Why did they put you in it?"

"I knew it. I knew every line. I could recite it backward for you today. But then when I tried to do it the way I thought I could—well, it happened, that's all, the worst feeling I've ever had in my life. Now I know what they mean when they talk about stage fright, and before I always thought it was something actors pretended to have to make themselves seem temperamental. They told me I'm not an actress, and never will be." She sighed, rather disappointed that he did not contradict them. "I guess it's true."

They had been slowly mounting the hillsides, winding along those paths she had seen from the hotel balcony but never explored or wished to, passing cabins and houses, where children at play stopped to gape as they filed by, and now emerged on the crest of a hill above the scattered little town she had described as a pigpen not three weeks ago, and while he observed it with intent interest, as if it was something quite new, Fan studied the shape of his head and neck, his shoulders and chest and his hands resting upon hard-muscled legs, and found him so vital and authoritative, with stores of savage energy he would not hesitate to spend, that she grew quite dazed at the prospect and finally sighed.

After awhile he started on, without so much as a glance to make sure she was following him, to that evidently he had read her dumfounded admiration better than she had meant him to, and she made a vow to concentrate on trees and clouds and distant mountain tops. He began to ask her questions, about the Baxters, about the towns she had visited in her travels, and she answered not only those questions but others he did not ask, until presently she had admitted that her story to Homer Grimes was a lie and, furthermore, that the Baxters were not a family troupe, but only a miscellaneous crew picked up whenever they found someone willing to work for almost nothing. "Do you think it's wrong for me to tell those lies? I have to."

"Of course you do."

"You agree?" she cried, delighted by this understanding between them, growing momentarily deeper and more tantalizing until, if she did not take care, she would next blurt out that she had fallen in love with him. She frowned, remembering that men were not always so flattered by those declarations as she had expected they would be and that, in fact, they sometimes took them as a warning. "I don't suppose I really like to act," she continued, for the desire to talk to him was almost as keen as the desire to submit herself to him and she seemed no better able to control it than if she had been drinking, begun to talk, and found herself powerless to stop. "But I do like to be looked at by all those people." She glanced at him, to see what he thought of that. "There's a peculiar sort of pleasure in it, I can't describe it, and the only time I've never felt it was last night." All at once she touched his arm, and then withdrew her hand as quickly as a scolded child, wistfully asking, "Were you angry with me last night?"

"I was afraid you might not be able to finish the part."

"Suppose I hadn't?"

"No man wants to see a woman humiliated before other men, you know that."

"Oh?" She thought about that, and decided he had meant it for a declaration of love, for men could not always be counted upon to make those declarations explicit, and yet it seemed plain enough his concern meant that he loved her.

They had been riding for an hour or more when he stopped before a cabin strewn about with a litter of barrels and boxes and tin cans, with a pair of antlers nailed over the door and a stiff line of marigolds planted across the front. He dismounted and stood looking up at her, slightly smiling as her face grew wary and suspicious.

"Where are we now? What's this?"

"This is where I live."

"You live here?"

He smiled. "In New York, I'll agree, it would be an indifferent stable. But here it's a mansion."

She looked at him doubtfully as he waited for her to slip down, and although he must know it was his duty to give her some excuse for having brought her here, he only waited, as if he knew she would go in whether he asked her to or not.

She thought of several arguments. Mr. Baxter had forbidden her to enter a man's house, but that might seem she had done it before and been caught. The neighbors would see them go in, but there were no neighbors very near, and furthermore it would intimate that if she went in she might be there for some time. She must be back before dark, but that was ambiguous, too; and at last she shrugged and slipped into his arms, turned deftly out of them, and entered the cabin. He followed her, ducking his head beneath the low doorjamb, and pushed the door shut, for the wood had warped and it hung slightly askew.

She began to saunter about and felt she must not pause or he would take it for submission, and as she walked she picked up bits of rock from the shelves and asked him what they were. He replied with some mysterious words and she shrugged again, but smiled, to indicate she was not scornful of this interest. Trousers and coats hung from wallpegs, the bunk was spread with a single blanket, books and magazines were piled on a table, and as she wandered about, touching the gold scales with her fingertip, turning over the buffalo robe with the toe of her boot, she was thinking that it was exactly this air of dazed bewilderment, as if she had been led against her will into a situation she did not understand, which she should have shown for the sleepwalking scene.

He was watching her and smiling curiously. "Looks like hell, doesn't it?"

She stopped before a shelf and read, in a voice full of wondering admiration, "Church's *Analytical Geometry.* Dana's *Mineralogy.* Mitchell's *Manual of Practical Assaying.*"

She avoided looking at him and felt that the room grew constantly smaller, shutting them in with some ruthless force of its own. She stood turning the pages of a magazine and frowning at the words as they danced about, and at last, as if now was the time to make her escape, she whirled and confronted him, and slipped her arms about him eagerly, parting her lips and closing her eyes and sighing with relief.

When he released her, they smiled at each other with confident anticipation, she dropped her coat to the floor, stepped out of the skirt and stood on one foot, pulling off her boot, and at the sound of a shriek from the kitchen she tried to cover her naked breasts with her hands as a red-haired girl came raging in at them, yelling, "You dirty son of a bitch!"

The girl seized rocks from the shelves and began to hurl them, and Fan turned her back and bent over to protect herself, but when she did the girl grabbed her hair and yanked it and Fan straightened, screaming. He was trying to catch the girl and was pleading with her softly, murmuring some weird western chant, "Ula, Ula, Ula—" but all the while she continued to yell and the rocks bounced from the walls and through the windows, and, as suddenly as she had appeared, the girl swept up Fan's coat and skirt and boot and ran out the door.

"My clothes, oh, good Jesus Christ, she's stolen my clothes!" Fan clasped her hands and moaned.

He dashed after her, but Ula Malloy was partway down the hillside and too far away for him to catch her by running barefoot across the rocks and cactus. She made him a vulgar gesture, turned into the next alley, and disappeared. He pulled on his boots and went after her, surprising a group of children as he sped by them, and found her backed into the corner of a fence gesturing away a big dog which barked threateningly at her. She did not have the clothes and she faced him stubbornly, refused to answer his questions, and at last sauntered away, pointing to a nearby outhouse and daintily pinching her nose between her thumb and forefinger, so that he was obliged to tell Fan, with as guilty a look as if he had disposed of them himself, that he had not recovered her clothes and would not be able to.

"But what will I do?" she wailed. "I can't go back like this." She indicated her ripped chemise, her one bare foot and undone hair, and he turned away and stared out the window, rubbing his hand over his chin as if he were studying the situation carefully.

For several moments he gazed out the window where his dog Music had now appeared and lay close by the door, ready to scare off the next intruder, while Fan whimpered distractedly, sighing and running her hands through her hair, as stunned as if she had been attacked by robbers on a dark street and left lying there, naked and beaten.

"I guess we can consider ourselves lucky it wasn't a road agent," she said finally. "I heard the country was wild, but my God—" She stalked over to him, her hands on her hips. "Who was that bitch?"

Morgan stretched his mouth in a comically rueful grimace. "I'm sorry to say she's a girl I know."

"A girl you know?" she repeated slowly, with such menace that she was once again arrested by admiration for her own effects and tried to place it in *Mazeppa,* for it seemed unlikely she would ever need it for Lady Macbeth.

Morgan nodded, and they studied each other doubtfully, until it occurred to them both that although it was true her clothes were gone and there was no very good way to get her into the hotel without them, nevertheless it was not four o'clock and they had time enough later to worry about that. For now the heat of the cabin, the hot sun coming in upon them, the smell of the dust scuffled up by Ula Malloy, the excitement and absurdity of her attack, combined all at once with their earlier need and they retired to the bunk, after Morgan had locked the door, pushed the table against it and pulled the curtains together, so filled with eagerness and haste that it was not until later that Fan, now laughing and content, pulled off her chemise and turned back to him with the suppleness of a young animal, burrowing against his chest and enclosing him with her arms and legs.

Some time after dark he lighted a candle, went into the kitchen to look for something to eat, and returned with a bottle of bourbon and some cold baked potatoes he had found in the fireplace, buried in ashes. The night had grown chill and they sat at the table, Fan wrapped in the buffalo robe, smiling at each other as they ate the potatoes and drank from the bottle, though she had some uneasy premonition that by now he had learned all there was to know about her: that she had forgotten her lines and might have given up altogether if it had not been for him, that she was a liar, that she was frantically greedy for the pleasures he gave her and that she would, furthermore, drink this treacherous whisky with scarcely a shudder. But whatever he might be thinking, his smile was so reassuring that she was unconcerned about how she would get back to the hotel, and even had some sly hopes that Charles Baxter would discharge her and she would become Morgan's responsibility. And soon they returned to the bunk, warmed by the whisky if not very much nourished by the potatoes, and remained there until, when it began to get light, he woke her.

"You've got to go back, Fan, my God, it's late."

For awhile she was too drowsy to understand what he was saying, but presently he lighted a candle and she found that he was getting dressed. She stared at him with bewildered resentment, yawn-

ing, and he brought what was left of her clothes to the bed, though
she pushed them away, looking sullen and hurt. "I can't go back like
that."

"You've got to. There's no one on the streets now, and I'll pay the
clerk to let us in through the back."

"What will I wear over them?"

"My buffalo overcoat."

"I can't wear a buffalo overcoat in July." She held her legs out
straight and wriggled her toes.

"Come, Fan, please—it gets light early."

She was trying to find some other objection, but he was so insistent and, it seemed, so efficient, that presently she stood before
him with her hair hanging loose and wearing the overcoat which
she laughed to see dragged on the floor. He went after the horses
while she stood in the doorway, yawning and stretching, and the air
was so clear and fresh that she was soon wide awake and gleefully
smiling to think that in spite of Ermina Baxter she was now in safe
possession of all those recent joys, so exhausting and invigorating,
which she would no doubt need to recall in some bleak future they
would arrange for her.

She had refused to put on the one boot Ula Malloy had left, and
so he carried her across the rocky patch of ground and she crawled
onto the horse's back, sitting astride with her chemise about her
thighs, and shaking her head firmly as he tried to persuade her to
ride as a woman should.

They set off down the hill and, when they had gone a little distance, she pulled off the coat and flung it at him. His horse shied,
and as he began fighting to keep it from bolting, she gave a triumphant whoop and went galloping down the hillside, her hair writhing
and floating about her. She looked around, calling to ask if he was
having trouble, and as he came on at a faster rate she kicked at her
horse's flanks with her bare heels, laughing delightedly as she heard
him coaxing in a soft urgent voice, "Fan, for God's sake, Fan—don't
ride into town like that. Fan, I beg of you, don't be a damn fool—"

XXXIV

"The old man wants twenty thousand from you, twenty from Talbot,
twenty from Cottrell, and twenty from Flagg." Hoke O'Neil nodded
briskly and, as he spoke each name, showed Joshua one more extended finger of his right hand. "And he wants it now. I'm going up to
Albany with it tomorrow."

Joshua looked at him grimly, for he had thought for some time now that the Irish politicians had lost all sense of proportion and could no longer tell one dollar from one hundred thousand dollars. "We all know bribery is a form of blackmail," he reminded him. "The price goes up continuously."

Hoke shrugged and slid a little lower, until he had so precariously balanced the end of his spine against the edge of the chair that it seemed the next slightest movement would send him sprawling to the floor of Joshua's office. Still, although Hoke usually looked as if he had taken some stance or position he could not hope to maintain, and though Joshua had confidently expected for years to see him topple headlong down a staircase, fall out of a window or off a chair, it seemed he had some catlike sense of balance, and his body held for long periods whatever taut posture he set it in until, abruptly, he changed that position for another, equally precarious. "Maybe so," he agreed. "But so does your take."

This, of course, was true. For since the Metropolitan Sand and Gravel Company had been chartered three years ago, the city politicians had passed their Act for Adjusting Claims Against the City which had made it possible for such companies to be reimbursed at a constantly increasing rate until, by now, the claims were more valuable than any rights conveyed in the original charter. And, no doubt, Hoke thought they should be grateful for what they were allowed to keep, for the Ring was so strong it seemed likely to rule forever. Hoke had recently begun to wear on the lapel of his frock coat a gold tiger's head with ruby eyes and three diamonds stuck in its forehead, and this emblem pleased him unreasonably.

He would come, he said, with The Doctor and Geigan and Higgins and Shannon tomorrow morning, for Joshua had never yet admitted to having so much as one thousand dollars in available cash, and Hoke remarked, as he stood at the door picking his teeth with the ivory toothpick, "Oh, yes, and I'll be needing a little something myself for contingent expenses."

Joshua returned to his desk to consider where he would take twenty thousand dollars from and how he would adjust it in his Home Office Annex Account, a set of books he kept according to a system he had invented, and in which he entered every expense required of him by the city, the state, or the federal government. This Home Office Annex Account was at once his pride and despair, for the sums it showed him as having disbursed to these claimants were great; but it pleased him, too, for the bookkeeping was esoteric and could have been understood by no one else, and he worked on it at odd moments or sometimes late at night, when he was restless or troubled and returned to his office to spend a few hours amid these reassuring surroundings.

Occasionally, part way through a performance at the Academy of Music, or at a ball or reception, Joshua discovered with a sense of vague surprise that he had not heard the music for some time and

had no idea what was being played; or he saw his partner gazing at
him with that look of anxious and doubtful gaiety which meant she
knew he was not aware of her, but merely went twirling about the
floor remorselessly as a top because the music had spun him into
action. And he would realize that he must get into his carriage and
return to the dark, quiet streets for which he was yearning.

Once he stood in his office, smiling slightly as he drew off his
gloves and laid aside his evening coat, the torpor left him and he
was again aware of that marvelous keenness and some deep and
joyful harmony. Then, very often, he worked through the night at
his private bookkeeping or sat with his elbows on the desk and his
fingertips pressed together, reconsidering each plan, and changed
his clothes only before the clerks came in the morning. Nor did
these sessions leave him tired, but restored and refreshed him as
surely as his shrine's refuge might restore any other communicant.

He had few doubts nowadays about his methods, whatever they
might be, for those deities which presided over American businessmen had decided at last to reward Joshua Ching for his years of faithful and diligent devotion, and although Black Friday had eliminated
many men from the Street, through some happy combination of
luck and acumen it had passed over Joshua Ching harmlessly, leaving him money enough that he began to think of himself, though
still with due caution, as a rich man; and before many more months
had gone by he was able to make himself a present of two handsome
trotting horses.

Some of the city's businessmen had recently turned Harlem Lane
into a course for trotting horses, and there they raced in the late
afternoons, careening along behind two gawky trotters, cutting
perilously in and out and sometimes tipping over, amid a din of
screaming excitement from the crowds gathered in the open fields to
one side, and applause from their wives and daughters standing
on hotel porches on the other. Joshua had several times watched his
son-in-law participate in this pageant, for Philip, it seemed, had
spent most of the marriage settlement on his horses and their upkeep,
and it had caused Joshua pangs of envy to observe Philip's skill
and bravado, the cheers he provoked as he executed some daring
maneuver, and the swagger with which he entered the taproom
later.

Little by little this jealousy became an obsession, until finally
Joshua had convinced himself that he was harming his prestige in
Wall Street, where a man was judged by his trotters as well as by his
followers, and so he decided to spend thirty or forty or, if he must,
fifty thousand dollars to make himself conspicuous in Harlem Lane.

With Marquis McDuff, who was said to know as much about
trotting horses as he knew about faro or poker, Joshua began to visit
the horse markets on Twenty-fourth Street, assuring McDuff he was
in no hurry, a pair of trotters was a major investment not only of a

man's money but of his reputation, and now that he had made this decision he must have the best trotters in the city, whatever they cost him. For at his first appearance, Joshua was determined to enter the traffic in Harlem Lane with dash and fervor, handling his animals with such cool skill and hot recklessness that his enemies—and he counted Philip among them—would be more than ever convinced that Joshua Ching was their master.

"There are as many bogus horses on the road as there are bogus stocks," he warned McDuff, who stalked beside him in a silk hat and black suit so conservatively cut he might have been taken for a minister if it had not been for the size of his shoulders, the diamond stickpin in his tie, and the slope of his forehead with the shining black hair sprouting above it. However, Joshua had become accustomed to McDuff and concluded that even he had his misshapen conscience, sufficient at least for the purpose of advising him on a pair of trotters.

They strolled about amid the crowds for an hour or more every few days for several weeks until these two men, one dark and fierce, the other blond and imperial, became quite familiar to the dealers, who knew, without having been told, just what it was they were looking for, but it was a long while before Joshua or McDuff showed any interest in the animals they watched being groomed and curried, stamping in their stalls and whinnying querulously.

At last Joshua bought Tamarack and Asia, a pair of two-year-olds, lean nervous geldings with sleek black coats and white forelegs, for forty-eight thousand dollars, and had them sent to the stables in back of Philip's house which he had recently been refitting, although Philip had not guessed why until one day he discovered there those preternaturally keen and excitable creatures.

The stalls had been padded and lined with leather for their comfort, and Joshua hired three men to attend them. Four times each day they were fed oats mixed with bran according to careful calculation, and steamed with boiling water to make a mash which Joshua watched them eat with a kind of envious sympathy. The stables smelled of leather and beeswax and oil, and this fragrance gave Joshua such peculiar satisfaction that it became, for a time, even more agreeable to him than Rose Michel's soaps and perfume.

Philip, quite as Joshua had expected, was as jealous of Tamarack and Asia as any demented lover, and often appeared in the stables when Joshua was there. Asia, Philip reluctantly agreed, had a blazing eye and a buoyant step, he was an animal of truly heroic proportions, ardent and domineering and as handsome as Ethan Allen. "And," said Joshua darkly, for even Philip's compliments were not pleasing to him, "he runs like a swallow." But Philip did not similarly praise Tamarack who looked, or so he said, more like a narrow escape from beauty, than beauty itself.

At this, Joshua longed to strangle him into a respectful silence, but said nothing, for he thought Philip did not deserve to be reminded of the principle, so ever present in his own thoughts, of letting them laugh who win.

During the summer Joshua was oftener in town than at Long Branch, and he now made a study of Tamarack and Asia as intensive as his earlier study of Milton De Groot. Under McDuff's tutelage he became familiar with their habits and eccentricities, refurbished his forgotten skills, and perfected some maneuvers he had never seen before, and doubted if Philip had, either. By August he set the date for his first appearance in Harlem Lane and he chose a Friday in September, almost one year to the day after Black Friday, for by this superstitious choice he meant to cast the shape of his future.

"We might lay a wager," Philip suggested, as he had before, and Joshua smiled indfferently.

"I suppose we might."

McDuff had also, while Philip was away, tried the pace of Philip's horses, and had some advice to give Joshua. "They're fast, but they can't last two miles. He'll want to make it one, but insist on two, and if you can get away quick enough you can wilt them. If not—" and McDuff made a motion suggestive of a man ramming his elbow into his rival's eye.

And by the first of September Joshua had become as intent and eager, as honed to a sense of murderous rivalry, as he customarily was when he reached the most minutely detailed and crucial phase of a market manipulation; and so the day approached.

Between four and five each afternoon a parade of every kind of wheeled contraption moved up Fifth Avenue and through the Park, to debouch in a noisy confusion of buggies and butcher carts and cutters into the narrow dirt road of Harlem Lane, and there a man might expect to enter local immortality if only his horses behaved spectacularly and he showed himself a courageous and ruthless driver. While the others, the butchers' boys and draymen, might enjoy their own minor participation in the excitement, no large bets were placed on their races, no ostlers rushed to blanket their horses, no well-dressed women waved to them from the hotel porches, no men looked at them with envious approval as they entered the taproom, and they were left, in fact, with nothing but the pleasure and danger of the venture itself.

Susan and Suky and Ceda were on the verandah of Bertholp's Hotel that afternoon, and Joshua rode through the Park at a negligent pace, exchanging remarks with men he knew but refusing their offers to race with a meaningful smile and shake of his head.

As he crossed the narrow isthmus into Harlem Lane, Joshua found himself in the midst of a yelling crowd, traps went racing in every direction, two or three abreast, and he paused, for he saw nothing at all of his own adversary. But then, after a moment, Philip came trotting toward him with a wide smile, as confident as if the race were over and he had won it, and Joshua gave him a brusque nod but

had nothing to say as they brought themselves into position, exchanged glances, and set off, with Joshua, as McDuff had advised
him to be, well in the lead.

Joshua leaned forward, yelling at Tamarack and Asia and flailing
their backs, no more concerned about his dignity or the expression
upon his face—which suggested that here was a maddened fanatic
on the loose—than he was when he got into bed with Rose Michel.
He drove them at the top of their speed and urged them to go faster,
and they strained at the reins until it seemed his arms would be
drawn from the shoulder sockets and the muscles of his legs dissolve, but he did not once look back for that, he thought, might bring
on bad luck.

And yet, when they had passed the first mile and Tamarack and
Asia were running along as if the pure exultation of the race had
freshened their energies, Joshua's eyes opened wide in a shock of horrified disbelief to see Philip draw up beside him, as blinded by rage as
he was himself and looking at least as distraught. At that glance
Philip began to draw ahead, or would have but for Joshua's wheels
cutting deftly close, swerving almost into his trap, and Philip's
horses lost stride as Joshua rushed by, grinning cruelly and glad of
the dust clouds which surrounded him as obligingly as any smoke
screen a magician might send up to conceal his legerdemain. But
Philip was closing in behind him again and now, enraged beyond
being clearly aware of what he was doing, Joshua raised his elbow
in McDuff's same gesture and flicked his whip so sharply before
Philip's eyes that Philip clutched at the reins, his horses broke their
stride, and the last Joshua saw of Philip he was yelling at his two
animals as if they, and not Joshua, had played this prank on him.

A little distance up the road Joshua swung his trap about and
trotted slowly back, gratified to hear the shouts of congratulation,
and sprang down as a boy came running to lead Tamarack and Asia
into the tying-up sheds. As gracious as a king on the day of his
coronation, or a triumphant actor, Joshua sought out the three
women and, without approaching the verandah, casually waved to
them and walked into the taproom, where there were friends and
acquaintances and strangers to shake his hand and ask him to have a
drink.

Philip came in a few minutes later and Joshua gravely inquired
if he would like to have another brush on the way back, but Philip
explained that one of his horses was a little lame and must have
thrown his leg when he stumbled in a rut. Joshua took this explanation with a solemn face, nodding sympathetically, and was pleased
that Philip understood Joshua Ching was as willing to risk his own
neck as another man's if his courage or skill was on public display;
and it seemed Philip must have learned the lesson well, for it was
never again necessary for Joshua to endanger their horses or their
lives for the sake of beating him.

Joshua drove Tamarack and Asia almost every day after that, and though he never allowed himself to be beaten by men he thought of no financial consequence, he occasionally let Frederic Hallam draw ahead of him—or some other man for whom he had made a place in his future plans—and Bertholp's taproom became another office, where he sat discussing horses and pools and cliques for an hour or two in the late afternoon.

He had some time ago suggested to William Talbot the possibility of coaxing Frederic Hallam onto their Corporate Engineers board, but Talbot had not been optimistic. "It isn't the kind of thing his family likes."

This offended Joshua quite as much as Talbot's earlier intimation that Roger Hallam would not agree to Frederic marrying Joshua Ching's daughter. For they had a government loan of five hundred thousand dollars, contingent upon the miles of track they built in the next five years; they had handsome offices with plate glass windows and walnut furniture, where they served lunches of lobster salad and champagne encased in blocks of ice to likely stock purchasers; and they had spent more than one hundred thousand dollars a year in Washington and Albany for the past three years to bring all this about.

They had called the series of lines they were building, and the others they had bought to tie into it, the Baltimore-Missouri. Various sections in the Ohio and Mississippi Valleys were presently under construction, though their engineers were not enthusiastic about the quality of the work, for the board of directors whittled constantly at their expenses, dourly reminding them that stockholders would pull away if they were deprived of their dividends, and their maps showed that although the Baltimore-Missouri was projected as a mighty line, it was still only a collection of short trunks and spurs, connected to inconsequential villages.

Even so, Joshua had asked William Talbot, "Why wouldn't the Hallams like it?"

"Too many accidents, slipshod maintenance," Talbot had reminded him, listing their mutual sins as if they concerned Joshua but not himself. "Most of the roads are only scraped and graded, whatever our prospectus says about them, and the Hallams make a practice of sending their experts to look things over."

"It's a young company. In a year or two it should look much more attractive to them."

But even though the Baltimore-Missouri had made no great progress a year later, only adding a few more spurs and scraping and grading still other roadbeds, nevertheless the general public enthusiasm for railroads, their own persuasiveness with investors, and the generosity of the government in granting them new loans, combined with Joshua's observation that Suky and Alvita Hallam were now together almost as often as Suky and Felice Talbot had once been, to convince him that Frederic Hallam might presently be had for the asking.

Felice had been sent to Europe with a chaperone to spend a year and, her father said, make sure she did not become a clever dunce and premature woman of the world at fifteen, and ever since she had gone Joshua had observed that Suky and Alvita Hallam went shopping together, had lunch at one house or another and, when Alvita began to give receptions and dinners the winter after her first child was born, Suky and Philip were usually asked. How Suky might have accomplished this, he could not imagine, and he admired her achievement all the more because this subtle relationship between two rivalrous women was quite as mysterious to him as his own accomplishments might be to any outsider.

The invitation was extended to Frederic by Joshua—who said nothing of it to his partners, though he did take the precaution of mentioning it to Suky—and after that he was willing to let this problem resolve itself with no further help from him.

And so, one cold bright day in January, Joshua drove his sleigh in Harlem Lane, slipping along over the frozen snow with miraculous ease, and went stamping into the taproom in heavy boots and a sealskin coat and cap, nodding to men he knew who sat around the glowing iron stove, and, as he ordered a hot toddy, noticed that Frederic Hallam was in the room, for the first time in several weeks. Frederic had not seen him, so far as Joshua could tell, and yet he was so entirely persuaded that Frederic had come there to tell him he would join their board that he made no effort to bring himself to Frederic's attention, but began to talk to a man he had recently met who wanted to buy Tamarack and Asia.

Each time they met, Abijah Everest asked Joshua if he would sell them, and Joshua had fallen into a habit of discussing them with him, pretending that he was vacillating, sometimes mentioned defects they had, other times extolled their fine qualities—unmatched throughout the city, he would declare on such occasions —and allowed himself for five or ten minutes this careless luxury of tormenting the man's lust for Tamarack and Asia, for in the end he would tell him regretfully he did not think he would sell them after all, that they were as dear to him as his grandchildren, and afforded him more pride than any company he owned.

He would not have sought out Abijah Everest, for there was nothing Abijah Everest owned which he coveted, only a few small railroads in upper New York state, a factory or two, some real estate in Troy and Albany, and although this provincial empire seemed a matter of pride to Abijah Everest, Joshua was now inclined to be contemptuous of any man who had reached the age of fifty with no more than a million dollars to justify his existence.

Abijah Everest had lately sold most of these assets, constructed by him with so much devoted care, and appeared in Wall Street with the intention of multiplying his fortune several times, but, Joshua thought, he had come too late, for the complexities which other men took twenty years to learn, Abijah Everest supposed he would unravel in a year or two, and several brokers had made bets that someone would have picked him clean in less than six months' time.

Abijah Everest, however, seemed to have no natural inclination for the stock market. He distrusted pieces of paper which had no reliable value and was remarkably stubborn, for a newcomer, about staying out of pools and ignoring points. What he really wanted, though he did not know it, Joshua had decided, was another railroad or factory, for even Tamarack and Asia seemed to him a better investment than stock in a company he could not control. Everest was, he had told Joshua several times, a builder of things, a man who yearned to construct with his own hands, as it were, a railroad or a factory, and though Joshua had no doubt there were many such men, all convinced they were building a nation out of an empty continent, it seemed to him they were quixotic and romantic, conducting an adventure rather than a business. And so he had begun to hint to Abijah Everest, during their discussions of Tamarack and Asia, that he owned a pretty little railroad in the western part of the state, and described its charms so vividly that Abijah Everest asked about it each time they met.

"Go and look at it," Joshua told him. "You'll be surprised at the changes I've made. Two years ago those four lines weren't worth fifty thousand dollars."

"I remember."

"And now their capital stock is doubled, the New York legislature has passed an act which makes it impossible for the new bond issue to be questioned, and public confidence has been restored."

Abijah Everest heard of these miracles with a look of rapturous envy, for he had nothing similar of his own to describe, and the money he had acquired from the sale of his properties gave him no such pleasures. Joshua went on talking of the improvements he had made, and then, as Frederic Hallam joind them, Joshua turned his back on Abijah Everest to let him know that he had, as things stood now, no very good claim to the attention of a busy and successful man.

Frederic smiled, the first such smile Frederic had given him, for whenever they had talked he had been serious and formal, reticent and aloof and, in Joshua's opinion, had behaved exactly as such a man as Frederic Hallam might be expected to behave with the father of a girl he loved against his good judgment. "Mr. Ching, I'll be glad to join your board, if the place is still open."

"It is, indeed," Joshua assured him, and reflected that there was surely something remarkable in the effect a woman could have on a man, for who would have guessed to look at Frederic Hallam that he would allow himself to become besotted over any woman, even Suky.

"There are some conditions to be met," Joshua told William Talbot, "but I think we'll agree to them. More building, better construction—and of course I said that we planned to make substantial improvements in the line itself."

Pleased as he was, however, Joshua spoke somewhat ruefully, for he was as little inclined to improve a roadbed or the rolling stock as he was to buy Susan the diamond necklace she wanted or Rose Michel a new carriage, and it seemed to him that a railroad, once constructed, should run indefinitely without repairs. Still, if it was necessary for the accomplishment of some integral part of his design, Joshua was ready to spend money, after first making sure that the money he spent was not his own.

It did not surprise him very much that one of the first benefits of the announcement that Frederic Hallam had joined their board was Abijah Everest's decision to buy the railroad in western New York, and he sold it to him for three hundred thousand dollars in cash, with the promise that if Everest had trouble with it he would be glad to buy it back again. Abijah Everest laughed at this notion, assuring him nothing of the kind would happen, for he knew railroads, and most particularly small railroads, as well as any man alive. "I hope you can handle it, Abijah, but if you can't, I'll be glad to help you out. So many things can go wrong with a road, you know."

Joshua did not, he thought, have any hankering to destroy Abijah Everest financially, just as he had had no such predatory impulses toward Milton De Groot, but nevertheless the plans he made as he sat in his office late at night or rode in his carriage which pleased him best and gave him the keenest appreciation of his creative faculties, were those plans by which another man must lose whatever he had built. And, of course, there was more money to be made by wrecking companies than by managing them with prudent care; so that Joshua regretted only that this aptitude of his, embedded in his nature, had never yet been put to use in the demolishment of some very large structure which could be expected to send ripples over the ground in all directions when it fell.

In a few months, Senator Stirt had promised, the state attorney general would sue for revocation of Abijah Everest's charter, and the road's stock would drop so low Everest would no doubt be glad enough to have Joshua Ching come to his rescue. And Joshua thereupon turned his attention to the Metropolitan Sand and Gravel Company, for newspaper editorials and articles had begun to accuse the Irish politicians of thievery, and William Talbot thought they should dispose of it while there was still time to sell at a profit.

"What can they do to us?" Hoke demanded. "The Boss got a big laugh out of it."

A few days before the elections, forty thousand men wearing oilcloth caps and capes and carrying kerosene torches marched in a heavy rain to converge upon Tammany Hall in the greatest celebration of the city's history; and when the votes had been counted, Hoke confidently announced the scare was over and Tweed would rule forever. "The poor like us, the rich need us, and nobody else gives a damn. We're in and, by God, we'll stay in."

When the *Times* began to publish transcripts of the controller's accounts, Hoke and Oliver Foss showed indignant surprise, for the accounts had been copied by a man in the controller's office who had not been suspected until the damage was done. O'Brien, it seemed, was the culprit, for it was O'Brien who had seduced his friend into making the copies, and for no better reason, Hoke said bitterly, than that he had demanded more money than the Boss thought he deserved.

"This is the kind of thing," Hoke told Joshua, "that sends me to bed tired in the middle of the day."

Still, they remained hopeful that the summer's heat, the town's comparative emptiness, and Tammany's own tight and intricate organization would distract attention from the articles. But in the middle of July there was another of those street battles which erupted out of the city's tensions and, without warning, filled the streets with screaming men and women and children, running for safety while rocks were hurled from rooftops, doors and windows were barricaded, muskets sent rattling shots against walls and into the regiment of parading Orangemen, and looters broke open stores and ransacked houses. By nightfall the city was remarkably still and one hundred men, more or less, were thought to have died in this skirmish for the right of a Protestant Irishman to parade the city streets.

"This will finish them," Talbot predicted. "It's time to get rid of that damned Sand and Gravel, if we have to give it away."

"That won't be necessary, William, I have other ideas." But, Joshua did not doubt, Talbot would hold him responsible if their own participation in city politics should one day appear on the front page of the *Times*, although Hoke O'Neil insisted it could not, for the reason that the Metropolitan Sand and Gravel Company had never been entered on the controller's books by that name.

"Don't worry about it," Hoke told him. "I know what I'm talking about."

Joshua had arrived that afternoon from Long Branch, and he and Hoke sat in the garden behind Rose Michel's house, waiting for the other men to join them. "They can't publish what they can't find, now can they?" Hoke had thrown off his coat, rolled his shirtsleeves to his elbows, and as he scooped a chunk of ice out of his glass and wiped it over his forehead, Joshua, in his frock coat, watched him disapprovingly and willed himself not to sweat.

"You're sure of that?"

"Sure I'm sure. I've seen the books, and I tell you the Sand and Gravel's not on them. Rose, honey, why don't you bring me another drink?" Rose frowned at him, but took the glass and returned to the house.

The garden was surrounded by a six-foot fence and had neither

grass nor flowers, but was strewn with white pebbles. A great ailan-
thus grew in one corner, and an arbor covered with a mesh of pink
and red roses stood opposite it. Near the house were several black-
painted iron chairs, twisted to imitate broken branches, and Rose
had recently installed a fountain, the stone figure of a young girl
pouring a pitcher of water into a basin at her feet.

Rose spent the hot summer days there in her wrapper—although
Joshua had forbidden her to go into it unless she was fully dressed
—reading in the arbor or playing with the baby, drinking iced lem-
nade, and sometimes gossiping with Tessie Spooner, happy and
content and thinking that if only she had a few more dresses there
would be nothing else she might long for.

After the baby's birth—and he was now almost two years old
—Rose had stopped worrying about where she would be or how
she would eat in ten or fifteen years, though she was sometimes horrified to think she had bragged to Tessie Spooner that she had had
the baby for her own protection. For she had seen too often, in the
days when she was a boarder at Annie Wood's, the old whores who
went picking through refuse heaps, cuffed about by the policemen,
who took a special pleasure in tormenting them, beset by small boys
and even, it had seemed to Rose, hated by the dogs, and whenever
she and Tessie had passed one of them they had held fast to each
other's arms, as if to defend themselves against these predictions
of their future.

But Rose now felt that she, at least, had escaped that future,
even if Tessie was likely to accost her one day as she stepped from
her carriage with her handsome young son in his velvet suit, and
beg of her only enough to buy herself a mug of swipes.

The picture seemed clear to Rose as she and Tessie sat rocking
in the garden on an afternoon when Joshua was known to be in Long
Branch, eating candy and discussing the various callers they had
had at Annie Wood's, laughing merrily as they talked and enjoying
that prolonged delirium the summer gave to those who remained
in the city, lifting them into some realm of dazed irresponsibility
and depriving them of any need to worry about their usual troubles,
or even to think their usual thoughts.

They often ended by quarreling, or sometimes began by quarreling and ended peacefully rocking together, and quite often Tessie
ran out of the house screeching that she would never come back,
for good fortune had made Rose smug, while Tessie was still
critical of Mr. Ching and told Rose that in spite of the baby he would
get rid of her one day as all gentlemen did, and had ways to do it
so quick and clever it would be over before she suspected it had even
begun. They taunted each other with visions of what would happen
to them in their old age, hissing with such vindictiveness and cruelty
that often they pulled each other's hair and tore each other's
clothes.

But neither had another woman companion and so, as soon as the

scratches had healed, the gown been mended, the barked shin
stopped aching, they began to long again for a woman to talk to,
someone with whom they need not be charming, attentive, humble,
submissive, tightly laced and softly spoken, pretending that nothing
in their past or present lives had affected them and they were still
as credulous and filled with stunned admiration for masculine powers as they had ever been in the early years of their girlhood.

"It's better to be an old man's darling than a young man's slave,"
Rose quoted to Tessie when they began to compare their respective
positions in life. When she said it, it seemed to her clever and apt,
but when later she contemplated that one day Hoke O'Neil might
mimic her in Joshua's presence, she marveled that she had not better
sense, and hurried to bring Hoke a drink or to light his cigar as he
held it cocked meaningfully in her direction.

"When he throws you out," Tessie had said, "you can blame yourself. You're the stupidest god-damn whore I've ever known."

"I'm not as stupid as you think, you bitch," Rose told her serenely.
"It's my garden you're sitting in and it's my lemonade you're drinking."

"When the lemonade turns to champagne, maybe I'll believe you."

But when she acted as Joshua's hostess it seemed to Rose then
that she became a different person and she was convinced it was
her real self she became at such times, the self she would have been
if she had not instead become Rose Michel. For that seemed to have
happened by some series of accidents so involved she could no longer
unravel them and did not try, for it filled her with angry frustration
that she could not even find the first mistaken choice, the first
decision which had determined that for the rest of her life she must
hope for a man's indulgence and might never expect to make a
wife's confident demands.

During the first few months after the birth of little Eugene Michel,
Joshua had avoided any open recognition that the child was his own.
But then he began gradually to enjoy him and, by now, Rose was
convinced that for once in her life, at least, she had invented a
scheme and carried it through to her own benefit, and so she no
longer worried when Joshua did not come to the house for a week or
two, when he seemed not to hear the small gossip she had to relate,
or left as abruptly as if he did not know she was there.

She might whimper a little, but presently she would be singing
with her collection of yellow canaries, twenty or thirty of them in a
cage in the small conservatory which overlooked the garden, each
named for a man Joshua had brought to the house and one named
for Joshua himself, though he did not know it, or she played with
the gray poodle, Frou Frou, which Joshua had given her recently.

Hoke dipped promptly into the glass she brought him and rubbed
the ice under his chin and behind his ears, swearing with relief. He
hooked his thumbs into the tops of his trousers and chewed ferociously on his cigar, as if to relieve himself of the pangs which heat

gave him. "You guys want to sell, is that the idea?" Hoke glanced at him and Joshua saw that look of concentration, almost alarming in its suddenness and intensity, which appeared quite often on Hoke's face.

"We're not sure. What do you think will happen?"

"I'm an alderman, you got to remember, and naturally I don't think the city government can go down by flood or famine or earthquake." Hoke shook his head, smiling reflectively. "The Boss says it don't mean a god-damn thing what the papers print, the people are with him, he's a popular hero, and the party machine's so well oiled there aren't enough monkey wrenches in the country to put it out of commission."

The others began to arrive, Leon Pumphrey glancing swiftly and eagerly about, peering into the dim corners as if to find a counter-spy or a client, Judge Azariah Gill, Oliver Foss, Kell and Greaves and Marquis McDuff. They talked idly and amiably while the butler passed whisky and water, and no one was eager to proceed to business, partly because of the heat, and even more because the business was disagreeable, and so they rambled about the garden, crunching the stones noisily, complimented Rose on her pink muslin gown, and were pleased when Tessie Spooner came bursting through the door as gaily as if it were a cool fall morning.

But after two or three drinks they went into the house and sat down to a nine-course dinner in a dining room made even hotter by gas lights and candles, where the pots of fern which hung by chains in the windows had wilted, and there they let Rose and Tessie entertain them while they continued to avoid the dismal subject they had gathered to discuss and had no more to say about politics than if they had been a party of shoemakers, until at last the footman passed a basin of perfumed water and they dipped their napkins into it, scrubbed their mustaches and beards and wiped their dripping faces, and were left alone with port and cigars and the Metropolitan Sand and Gravel Company.

Even then they sat paring cigars, loosening their collars, complaining about the weather, and yet avoiding the issue. They were waiting for whatever Joshua had to say, and when it seemed he had tormented them long enough, he pleasantly remarked, "My partners and I have been wondering if this might not be an appropriate time to arrange several new city contracts for widening and grading streets?" He glanced from one face to another, amused to see their reactions of carefully concealed surprise, the downward twitch of Foss' mouth, as if he might have just bitten the neck of some imaginary rat, McDuff's raised right eyebrow, Kell's and Greaves' bewildered faces, Hoke's abrupt emergence from the listless trance he had fallen into part way through dinner, and which had caused Joshua to suspect he was not so optimistic as he pretended. "We think the city should take a larger share in our stock than it presently has."

"New contracts, Mr. Ching?"

"A larger share of stock, Mr. Ching?"

"But that would require another charter, wouldn't it?" they asked one another.

"Not at all, gentlemen," Joshua assured them brusquely, and at that they turned obediently meek, agreeing that such a contract might, under very special conditions, be awarded without a separate charter. They discussed for several minutes the means by which this might be done and Joshua, watching their faces, realized they had come here expecting that he and his partners had been about to sneak away from Tammany and that they were perhaps not flattered by this request for greater participation, but were at least relieved at the prospect of unanticipated profits, however they might assure one another they were a permanent fixture and no more likely to be dislodged than Trinity Church or the Park. "We'd like to sign the contracts by the end of this week."

"The end of this week, Mr. Ching?" Oliver Foss stared thoughtfully at Hoke. "No, that's out of the question, I'm afraid." But then he turned to Joshua with a bright smile. "At the beginning of next week, perhaps?" He went on to explain the complexities involved in negotiating these new contracts, but when Joshua said that unless the contracts were signed by the following Monday he did not think his partners would want them, they agreed it could probably be done if they all worked at it with single-minded dedication.

The table had been cleared, the butler brought cards and brandy, their coats were slipped off and, almost before they were aware of it, it seemed, they had begun to play poker, and after that they talked very little, but at two-thirty, when they decided to stop playing, had conceded that not only could the contracts be produced by the end of the week but they would not be as expensive as earlier contracts had been; for it was quite possible, of course, that unless some way could be found to curb this mania for reform, they might not be able to give new contracts to Joshua Ching or any other businessman.

Rose and Tessie came back, looking as if they had been asleep, and stood about dazedly until Judge Gill suggested they divide the night's winnings between them, and at that they pounced at the table, and, while the men put on their coats, fell to squabbling over the division, until Joshua sharply reminded Rose that their guests were leaving.

Hoke was still there when the others had gone. "You took us by surprise, all right," he admitted. "We're glad to get the money, but I don't think the boys were expecting you to cough up any more just now." He looked at him curiously, but Joshua would not tell him what use he might have for new city contracts at a time when most men were beginning to regret having any.

When Talbot and Cottrell and Flagg gave Joshua the checks for their share of the new contracts, Talbot remarked that this was the last money Tammany could expect from him, and even when Joshua reminded him the Sand and Gravel Company had made nearly two million dollars, after Tammany reimbursements, Talbot still looked grim. "They're inconvenient tools for other men to use. I'm glad to be done with them."

"We're not done with them yet," Flagg said gloomily, and Joshua once more took note that Lorenzo Flagg's great weakness was his unfailing pessimism, a characteristic which had often tempted Flagg into the market sin of becoming involved in many bear operations at once, and which, in Joshua's confident belief, would one day give control of the Corporate Engineers to William Talbot, Amos Cottrell, and Joshua Ching. Indeed, Lorenzo Flagg's constant expectation of disaster was beginning to give Joshua as keen a dislike for Flagg as he had once felt for Milton De Groot.

He had been rather disappointed by De Groot's recent successes in the market, for he had supposed a dead man would not rise again, but once it occurred to him that De Groot might be persuaded to buy their Sand and Gravel Company with its attractive new contracts, he began to use De Groot with the same tender concern of several years before, while De Groot was plainly impressed by the financial company Joshua Ching kept nowadays and glad to think he was back in his confidence again.

The sale, when it was made in October, was arranged by Talbot's City Exchange Bank, and De Groot was surprised to learn the next day that the company was mortgaged to them for almost half a million dollars, which Talbot insisted he pay at once or let the company go into a receivership. "Something, De Groot," he told him, "I should hate to see happen, just as you were beginning to get back on your feet."

For it often happened to a man in Wall Street that once he had failed disastrously it became easier for him to fail again, as if with each successive failure he grew more inclined to overlook the signals of warning, examined all sides of every transaction and yet somehow did not see that dark side he should have inspected most closely; and as De Groot faced Talbot he was sweating and twisting his great body like a tortured porpoise, grunting with the effort to discover his salvation.

"But that would make my company worthless."

"It isn't your company yet, De Groot."

De Groot began to plead with him, and though William Talbot listened sympathetically, at last he sent him away to get the money within twenty-four hours or see the stock sold for whatever it would bring.

"You know all the fools never die," Hoke remarked, when he heard the news, for Hoke was preoccupied by then with problems of his own.

The Committee had met to examine the city's books, only to find the controller's office had been broken into and the vouchers stolen from a glass case, and the charred scraps were presently discovered in the City Hall attic. It was Hoke's opinion this should satisfy the reformers but, instead, stocks slipped about nervously and a rumor streaked through the city that the mayor had gone mad and had to be held down by four men who took him home in a carriage. And, before very much longer, the Boss was arrested for fraud.

He was released on one million dollars bail, but even though Tweed still insisted nothing would come of these maneuvers, some of his aides began to leave for Canada or Europe. Joshua's suggestion that it might be prudent for Hoke to do the same, however, only made him angry. "Like hell I will. I'm in no more of a hurry to go to Canada than I was to move uptown."

Joshua took care not to smile, even though he thought that Hoke O'Neil, city alderman and sole proprietor of the Red Onion, must soon be stripped of his honors. "Loyalty, Hoke?"

"You're god-damn right—and I'll stay loyal, too, until I can figure out which way to jump."

Tammany Hall was dark and silent on that election night, and its doors were closed, but even after two boards of aldermen had met, and the old one was finally forced to dissolve, Hoke continued to wear the gold tiger's head on the lapel of his frock coat and declared to Joshua that in a few weeks, more or less, Tammany would have recaptured its power even if it was forced to take a temporary position of respectability. "If it's reform they want," Hoke assured him, "they'll get reform, all the bloody reform they can stand."

X X X V

Morgan woke to find himself sitting upright, wondering what had brought him out of deep sleep. But then the door was violently shaken, and Music began to bark in his deep voice which drew nearer the cabin as he returned from one of his nocturnal ramblings.

"Come on, Devlin, open up here, for Christ's sake. What's the barricade for?"

He flung the door open and peered out for a moment before he asked uncertainly, "Fletcher?" for he had so often dreamed Zack Fletcher had come back that now he was sure some other man stood there in the darkness. He struck a match and applied it to the candle, and as the light flared Zack walked into the cabin, slightly smiling and glancing around with amused curiosity.

Zack circled the cabin once, then wheeled and came straight toward him, stared at him seriously and searchingly, and solemnly remarked, "How."

"How."

They shook hands, firmly but casually, taking care to pretend they had seen each other only the day before yesterday and not nearly five years ago. Morgan emptied a box of wood into the fireplace, set out a whisky bottle and glasses, and took a stool across the table from Zack, who pretended to be so engrossed in lighting his cigar that it was several moments before he gave Morgan a sharp, almost accusatory glance. But then he shrugged, asking, "What's new?" and they raised their glasses and hastily emptied them. "Same old rotgut."

Zack's body was as lean as it had been and he moved with that familiar, uncanny grace, while his face, which was clean-shaven now, might, Morgan thought, have looked quite vicious but for the shrewd, whimsical expression in his blue eyes. He could not guess how different he might look to Zack but hoped, as Zack seemed to be studying him, that he was glad to find him no longer a nineteen-year-old boy, as perhaps he had been expecting.

"Where the hell have you been?"

Zack grimaced. "Here and there. Where've you been?"

"Here." They raised the glasses again.

"Here?" Zack repeated doubtfully, in the manner of one who has returned from such distant and varied lands, such circuitous voyages, he cannot believe that everyone else had not been upon those same journeys.

"Around the Territory. I've been back to Butte several times."

"Anyone left?"

"Bruno Favorite. Amos Muspratt. Maybe forty or fifty guys altogether. But the placers have played out and nobody's happy any more but the owls and magpies."

"It wasn't much of a camp in its best days."

"Its best days are coming up. Zack, you should go down there and take some leases, you can get a handful for a few dollars. They'll sell to anyone who offers cash or dust."

Zack shook his head. "I'm not a miner. I'm not exactly sure what I am, but I'm dead sure I'm no miner. It just don't happen to be my style."

"There's a fortune there in silver—and sooner or later somebody's going to get at it. I've hung onto what we had, and traded some of our claims for others that looked better."

"You can have my shares." Zack made a spreading gesture. "They're yours."

Morgan watched him affectionately, smiling and thinking that nothing could have been more absurd than to imagine this impatient and mutinous man married to Lisette and submitting himself to her passionate domesticity, and, if Zack had once had any such ambitions, a better acquaintance with his own lawless nature must have cured it by now. Still, he felt a kind of responsibility for Zack, for it seemed likely that one day his improvidence would make him glad to have those shares. "Hang onto them—with transportation and some capital, that camp could change overnight."

"Capital." Zack turned down the corners of his mouth, for discussion of money had never pleased him. "Capital is ten cents or a million dollars, depending on what you mean to develop. How much are you talking about?"

"Fifty or seventy-five thousand to begin with. A hell of a lot more later on, if the big butte has what we think it has."

"Why don't Matt and Pete go into it?" Zack smiled and Morgan thought the smile showed traces of resentment, for however indifferent Zack might seem to those around him, he was nevertheless continuously and sharply perceptive, with an intuitive knowledge of what other men were thinking; and, for that matter, of what women were thinking, as he had demonstrated by his suspicions of Lily Jones.

"They've got their own investments, and they think they're better and surer than Butte. You have to have been there like we were and poked around in that ground enough to be convinced it's waiting for you. Otherwise, you know what it is, Zack. There are a hundred strikes every year, but nobody's picking up any fortunes in a creek bed nowadays. The top's been skimmed and from now on you can only get it out with heavy machinery." He leaned forward. "And that means the kind of capital you can't get from a grubstake or win in a poker game."

Zack had been watching him carefully, as if he were not only measuring with precision Morgan's evaluation of the Butte properties but, even more, his character, his standards, and his judgments. "How much do you need to get under way?"

"At least another thirty thousand."

Zack grimaced, lifted his big shoulders and leaned back with his arms folded over his chest, his legs straight out so that the toes of his boots were at the edge of the fireplace, and he stared into the fire. After a few moments, as if he had thoroughly considered the difficulties of finding or earning thirty thousand dollars, he said very slowly, "You know, Devlin, I've got with me right now the answer to your problem. A guy with money. Only trouble is, mines don't interest him. He's partial to cows." Zack smiled, looking sage and humorous, and filled his glass again. "Fellow I've been traveling with the past few months."

He glanced sharply at Morgan, as if to ask if he wanted or expected to discuss Lily Jones now that the subject of his travels had been broached, but Morgan stared back at him with the same impassivity Zack himself might have shown, and Zack sucked on his cigar and scowled. Then all at once he grinned, as if relenting in some small but perpetual enmity which had nagged at him until that moment, and leaned across the table with the first indication of complete good will since he had entered the cabin. "I know what you're thinking: If you want to make me your friend, don't puzzle me. Well, there's no puzzle to it. The guy I'm traveling with is an Englishman, for Christ's sake, and I'm his bodyguard and guide." Zack looked defiant, as if he now expected Morgan to laugh outright or smile sympathetically and, if he did, was ready to leap across the table and throttle him into respectful solemnity. "He's paid me in advance, that was just to make sure I got mine even if he shot himself instead of a buffalo, and we're headed for the Yellowstone so he can see for himself if all those stories he read are true or not." Zack smiled sourly. "Now ain't that a lousy job for a self-respecting man, if I am one?"

"How long does your contract run?"

"It's about run out. I met him in Abilene last November. He walked into a saloon in an overcoat down to his heels with a monocle in one eye and a cigar in his mouth, holding a revolver in his right hand ready to shoot the first son of a bitch who laughed." Zack slapped his knee in delight. "You know what happened? Not a goddamn thing. Nobody laughed. I went over and shook his hand and next thing you know I was hired." He snapped his fingers. "Ten thousand. For six month's work, if you can call it work." All at once he looked gloomy, hunched his shoulders and rested his elbows on his knees, gazing at Music, who had come to lie between his feet, whining as if to court his favor and glancing up at him from beneath his wrinkled brows. "I'm shot with luck, Devlin. Shot with luck. How do you figure it out?" Remembering Zack's peculiar sensitivity, which, it seemed, had intensified, Morgan took care to let him see no signs of surprise at such employment or, as he might have expected, eager cupidity at the news of ten thousand dollars, but continued to smoke and watch the clouds he blew, and assured himself that eventually whatever was troubling Zack would disappear, or he would tell him about it.

They sat in silence, Zack scratched the whining dog, and at last he began to talk. "Three years ago I sold some cattle I was trailing up north for about five hundred percent more than they cost me. Since then, would you believe it, I haven't been able to do a thing wrong—it all goes my way whether I help it along or not." Morgan nodded and continued to show serious appreciation of this confidence, for it seemed that Zack had spent half an hour in desultory conversation, reconnoitering their relationship, as it were, and was finally ready to tell him where he had been and what he had been doing since they had seen each other last. "You know what they cost me? Not much. I drifted down toward Texas after—" He paused and, once again, gave Morgan a questioning look, but when Morgan said nothing, he went on. "Anyway, I drifted down to Texas and pretty soon got into what they call a cow hunt. There's cows all over the place, been running wild since the War, and they belong to anybody who can catch a herd long enough to get it branded. Now, that sounds easier than it is, because there's quite a few guys out catching herds for themselves, and the bloody critters got a way of hiding in the mesquite so you can only get at them by tearing yourself to ribbons, while once you rope a herd you've got as good a chance of getting them to a market somewhere as you've got, for instance, of getting that silver out of Butte. The trail north is meaner than anything here in the mountains, because if you make it across the Staked Plains you'll run into the Indians, and if you buy your way past them, you'll turn right around and find yourself face to face with a bunch of ex-soldiers who'll cut out half your herd and sell it back to you again, at their own price or, if you show fight, tie you to a tree and beat you to rags. But if you're shot with luck, like I said, and make it far enough north, you might run into somebody who'll pay you thirty dollars a head. That's what happened to me, by God, and I turned the herd over to him one night and rode off as free as if I'd been keeping charge of an orphan asylum."

The room had grown light and they guessed it was about five-thirty. Morgan went to the lean-to kitchen to make coffee and Zack stood yawning and stretching, then leaned against the doorjamb looking out over the town and, presently, he began to sing, softly and slowly, as he had done in Butte, seldom because he was happy but most often, Morgan thought, because he was worried or angry about something he would not discuss.

> "Nut-brown maids and bread that's white,
>   These shall be our lot tonight;
> Maids of white and bread of brown,
>   Shall greet us in tomorrow's town."

Morgan brought the coffee pot in, set it on the table and filled two tin cups. Zack stood a moment longer in the doorway, then turned swiftly and gave Morgan a diabolic glare. "You want to know, but I guess you won't ask, so I'll tell you. She left me in Santa Fe and was headed for California." He nodded decisively. "That's the last I heard of her and that was—let's see—just about four and a half years ago."

They sat across the table and Morgan began to grease his boots with hot tallow, kneading and working them into flexibility. "Okay. I didn't expect you to keep track of her."

"Keep track of her?" Zack yelled. "I'd quicker keep track of a garter snake." Now Zack seemed to grow expansive and confidential, as if relieved to find he had mentioned her and neither of them was going to make an issue of Lily Jones or where she went or whom she went with. "When she came through here she was traveling with a guy named John Powell, a newspaperman who was sent out here to write about the gaudy doings on the frontier, and damned if she didn't bullshit him into writing a story about Lily Jones, the terror of the mountains, the girl desperado who wears men's clothes and rides and shoots like Plummer wished he could, and when I saw her last she had that article in her pocket and would show it to anybody she met who could read and if he couldn't, she'd read it to him. She got more damn pleasure out of that article than all the dust she ever stole." Zack slapped his thigh and gave a shouting laugh, but when Morgan said nothing, did not look at him but continued to work the boots, he scowled and scratched the dog, drank the coffee and poured another cup and fidgeted uneasily until at last he protested: "That was a lousy thing to say. I didn't come here after all this time to make a jackass out of myself."

"The hell with it, Zack. It happened and I let it happen, that's all."

"Even so, I should have had better sense than to say it. And for whatever it's worth, she was still talking about you when she left." He closed one eye significantly. "Wants to be buried next to you, would you believe it?" Zack slid down, again straightening his legs in the tight, greasy buckskin trousers and folding his arms. "She admitted she wanted to get you killed and told Jenkins and Hamilton you put her up to stealing their dust. You couldn't exactly call her a nice girl, now could you?" He made a gesture of drawing his right forefinger across his throat in the sign for a Sioux. "But then, she's older now and maybe age has quieted her down some. She's thirty-one, my same age." Morgan looked surprised and Zack added seriously, "She never was as young as she pretended—that was only for your benefit."

Morgan started to dress and Zack brought a basin of hot water from the kitchen, bent to a partly crouching position before the mirror and scraped away the whiskers, scrubbed his face in the soapy water, brought a toothbrush from his pocket and cleaned his teeth at the front door, and although they had nothing to say during these ceremonies, by the time Morgan was dressed in black trousers and boots and a blue shirt and black tie, these simple formalities so often performed together seemed to have re-established the old ease and affection, so that Zack was able to inquire with casual politeness, "How's your family? Matt and Pete and your mother and—" He gestured vaguely, as if the list was so long he could not remember the rest of it.

Morgan had his back to him and was shaving, and, thinking Zack would be more comfortable if he answered without looking at him, continued to clean his face. "They're all fine. Pete married Jenny Danforth and they have a little girl almost two years old."

"I'll be damned," murmured Zack, and sounded so honestly surprised that Morgan wondered again if what Nella Allen had told him might have been true. "Married Jenny Danforth. Well, that's good. And—"

Morgan threw the soapy water onto the cactus in his front yard. "Lisette married Ralph Mercer." For the first time since he had known him, Morgan felt a sense of pity for Zack who looked, at that moment, as helpless as if he had experienced some acute physical pain or sense of sudden isolation. "Not long after you left," he added, for whatever comfort it might give.

"She's happy," Zack said finally, in a tone which neither stated a fact nor asked a question but left it to Morgan to do that for him.

"Of course—that's Lisette. They have two children, a little girl named Polly who's almost three, and a boy, Frank, born last December."

"I'm glad. I'd like to see her, like to see all of them, while I'm here."

"You will. Jonathan's married too, to Georgina Hart. They named their baby after Father."

Morgan gave Music a basin of water and a cut from a side of beef, and he and Zack started down toward the town.

As they rode Morgan pointed to where their mill was, indicated various lots they owned, showed him the office buildings of the *Helena Post,* and Devlin Brothers with its iron shutters to protect it against the next fire, whenever it might come, pointed out their assay office, and told him they presently had on deposit three hundred and twenty-five thousand dollars, a sum which caused Zack to whistle between his teeth. He showed him a warehouse they owned in partnership with Lemuel Finney, filled with mining machinery and equipment, various houses and office buildings, and indicated where small ranches lay on which they held mortgages, until by the time they walked into the St. Louis Hotel Zack seemed nearly as impressed as Morgan had hoped he would be.

They sat near the window in the small dining room which provided fresh Baltimore oysters before anyone else had them, clean linen, though it was often damp, and French wines, but which nevertheless could not keep flies from buzzing about the faces of its customers or eliminate those smells of grease and lye soap which hung in every western restaurant. They ordered broiled antelope steaks garnished with kidneys, potatoes and onions, fried trout, and, should that not be enough to satisfy them, hot cakes and syrup, and while they ate Morgan described their various projects, for he was eager to have Zack know what they had done while he was off hunting cows and acting as chaperone to English sportsmen.

"You say your Englishman's interested in cows. There are about seventy-five thousand stock cattle in the Territory now—a lot of them around here. A Frenchman was through here not long ago looking for grazing land, who said they've decided in Europe the American West may be a good investment, after all. They didn't expect us to make it through the War with a shirt left to our backs, and to see us come out better off than we went in has convinced them we may be worth taking a chance on. Want to show him one of our ranches?"

Zack grinned and seemed to have gradually but steadily shed his caution and resentment, peeling out of it layer by layer, as if he had been afraid to expose himself all at once, expecting to find himself tender and vulnerable, but was at last persuaded he was in no danger from his friend. And yet, Morgan thought, there was no other way in which he had ever seen Zack show fear or caution, and so it must be that he had suffered from his longing for Lisette, and whatever cruelties she had inflicted galled him still.

"I'll show him your cows, but I won't guarantee he won't shoot them. I've never seen anyone like an Englishman for killing. They're all over the southern range right now, and I'd be willing to bet there won't be a buffalo left in another five years." He shrugged. "Not many Englishmen, to tell the truth, but you can't miss them. Wait until you see mine. James Gordon—Sir James Gordon, so help me, but he says never mind the title while he's in the West, he wants to be democratic." Zack shook his head. "You show me this and you show me that. Looks like you own half the town, but you still can't get hold of any capital."

Morgan laughed. "We don't keep it in sacks in the fireproof so we can take it out and look at it. You know that."

"I don't know a god-damn thing about money or its habits, which are peculiar, it seems to me. But I can tell you how to make some. That's what I came here for, not just to hash over old times. I've got a chance to make a pile, don't ask me just how much because that depends on a lot of things, and I need someone I can trust who'll go into it with me. That's you," and he made a quick jab with his forefinger. The waiter rattled the plates, stacking one upon another, poured more coffee, and they settled back to smoke. "If you're interested."

"What is it?"

"This is between us."

"Sure."

"Whether you go into it or whether you don't, nobody else hears anything about it."

Morgan smiled. "Train robbery?"

"Nothing so simple. When Gordon and I came through St. Louis, I met a guy I knew in Missouri before the War—said he'd sell me sixteen thousand gallons of reservation whisky for eight thousand dollars if I'd get it out of his warehouse right away. I took it and it's coming up the river early in June, every gallon laced with enough strychnine and laudanum to make a man puke or go blind or cut off his wife's head." Zack nodded with reflective appreciation. "Just what they're crying for on the reservations. I think after you take out what it costs to bring it here and peddle it, there'd be a clear fifty thousand, maybe a little better."

"Why did your friend sell it?"

"He's a businessman. Buys whatever he can get cheap enough and sells it quick whenever he finds somebody who'll give him a good profit. But he's too dainty a fellow to go out on the range among those stinking Blackfeet and take his chances getting caught." Zack spread his hands wide, palms down, as if placing a benediction upon the table cloth. "Well, that's it."

They looked at each other for several moments, Morgan filled with eagerness at the prospect of making so much money but troubled for reasons Zack seemed to have guessed, for he watched him as carefully as if this was his final test of Morgan's character and the culmination of their friendship, during which each had studied the other and the friendship had continued only because neither had yet been convinced the other was not worth his respect.

"What's my part in it?"

"To put up four thousand for half the whisky, plus half of whatever it takes to cover the cost of shipment, and one third of the total profit to pay me for going out on the range with those bastards. They get drunk pretty quick, you know, and when they do, they've got no more fondness for you than for anybody else they happen to look at. What's left over, we split."

They were silent for a few moments, until Morgan said, "I can't do it, Zack."

Zack's hand slammed the table. "By Christ, that's what I expected." He leaned forward. "Why not?" Morgan looked at him, but had no ready answer, and was surprised to discover that, in fact, he felt it was he who was in the wrong. "If you don't want to tell me, I'll tell you: Your old man wouldn't like it."

"Neither would Pete. Nor anyone else in my family."

Zack hung one arm across the back of the chair and turned sideways to stare into a corner of the room, rubbing his hand along his jaw. At last, apparently having decided what he thought about this to his own satisfaction, he turned back. "Okay. That's that. Whisky peddling to the Indians wouldn't set well with your family." He smiled. "Because it's a federal offense?"

"I'm not sure I'd want this on my conscience, whatever they might think about it."

"Your conscience," Zack repeated slowly. "I don't know what the hell you're talking about. Do you?"

Zack looked bitterly angry, not simply challenging him as he had in the past, asking questions Morgan might find difficult to answer because the answers would be meaningless to Zack Fletcher, but angry as if at the recognition of an old antagonism, a justified grievance, so that he must have come back with the hope of making this discovery and, by making it, lay some unsatisfied yearnings of his own finally to rest. For if it had been Zack's lonely jealousy which had sent him away with Lily Jones, now it had brought him back again, still hoping to prove they had been wrong to exclude strangers like himself and Nella Allen, even while they admitted Jenny Danforth and Ralph Mercer.

Presently Zack began to talk, his voice low and his face thoughtful, and as he talked he stared across the room and might have forgotten Morgan was there. "I had a friend once who made the mistake of letting himself be taken prisoner by a party of Blackfeet—forgetting, it seems, that Indians don't take male prisoners. Anyway, this guy was buried up to his neck, his scalp taken, his nose and lips and ears cut off, and left to die as best he could." Zack nodded, confirming this tale. "The buck who thought that one up was quite a hero around his village—and he's still bragging about it."

"I know. It isn't eastern sentimentality, don't get that idea. I'd be glad enough to see them all dead. It's something else."

"Something else," Zack whispered, and turned down the corners of his mouth, marveling over what the nature of this something else might possibly be. But then Zack sat silent, tipped back his head and closed his eyes, and went on smoking.

And, in fact, as Zack left him to commune with his conscience, Morgan found that he actually had no very good reason but the one he had given: his family would not like to have him caught peddling whisky to the Indians. Yet he had spent the past five years careening about the countryside, had grubstaked so many prospectors it sometimes seemed he had his own army inspecting every rock ledge in the mountains, had traded claims in various camps and owned a five percent partnership in Devlin Brothers, and after all this he had accumulated only eighteen thousand dollars, so that without some unusual piece of luck such as Zack was offering him there seemed no reason to expect he would ever acquire the working capital to develop a silver mine. For a silver mine, as Matt reminded him, was an expensive hobby.

Bruno Favorite had offered to invest five thousand dollars, when he began the work, and Irene Flint had promised him ten thousand, but they were his only potential investors.

Irene had been living there now for more than two years, but although she occasionally attended the French Class or a lyceum lecture, she did little calling and did not encourage others to call upon her, and so she was still regarded with suspicion and resentment; for Erma Finney had taught the other women to believe that each newcomer must make an industrious and humiliating effort to be accepted, and must endure a period of probation before being admitted to their full companionship.

But when she and Morgan talked she was tolerantly affectionate, and recently had said to him, "I'm superstitious, you know, and it's my superstition that you're lucky. Don't smile, that's not deprecating—luck isn't only what happens to you by accident, it's also what you arrange to have happen."

He was still in need of that stroke of luck, whether accidental or arranged; and yet it seemed he was, like the businessman in St. Louis, too dainty a fellow to accept it now that it had come seeking him out.

But he had no wish to begin a discussion of his conscience, and so he said, "Tell me this, Zack. Your Englishman's paid you ten thousand, you sold your cattle for eight, and you've got almost four on our books, counting the interest. Why do you need a partner?"

Zack was staring at him with an expression which would have seemed menacing if he had found it on another man's face and, though he continued to remind himself that Zack Fletcher was his best friend, it was quite true the past five years seemed to have finished him into a tough and angry, resentful and quick-tempered species of western man, the kind every tenderfoot dreaded and yearned to meet. "You shouldn't need to ask me that, Devlin—we're both of us capitalists with our capital tied up, which is what I've noticed seems to happen to money once you get it. You got to put it where nobody else can get at it, and so you change it into something else. You've changed yours into machinery and buildings and some holes in the ground. Well, I've changed mine, too, but I've changed it into something I can grab hold of if I want to and eat, if I have to. Cows—that's where mine is."

Morgan laughed and, apparently, the laugh brought Zack out of his lowering resentments. "If you don't look out, Zack, you'll get rich in spite of yourself."

"That's just what I've got in mind."

"Well. You've changed."

"God-damn right I've changed," Zack agreed, and seemed calm and amiable once again. "When I left here I thought I was pretty damn old and knew a pretty damn lot about the world. But five years of knocking around from here to there can season a man more than he expects, until all of a sudden he wakes up and finds himself with a whole new set of notions he can't quite account for. When I was a kid, down in Missouri, nobody had money and I guess nobody thought about it. I didn't. My folks didn't, I know that. All we thought about was keeping ourselves alive, and that wasn't so easy to do in those days, either. But now, since the War, everything's changed—and by God you might not believe it, but even in Missouri they want to be rich." He laughed, but became quickly serious again. "To tell you the truth, I still don't give a damn about money, but I do care what other men think of me, and there's just two kinds of guys who get respect these days. Rich men—and outlaws." He smiled. "I'm too old to become an outlaw, so I've got no choice, I'll have to be rich. I wouldn't say I'd have picked cows if someone had asked me what I wanted, but I fell into them, in a manner of speaking, and they suit me as well as anything for what I want."

"Zack, I'll go into that deal with you."

Zack pretended to recoil with the shock. "What happened?"

"I've been sitting here trying to figure out another way I could make twenty thousand by putting in five, and I haven't been able to do it." He stood up. "Come on. I've got to see how we're getting along at the mill—ride out there with me, I'd like to show it to you."

They found, with some surprise, that it was bright daylight, and the streets, deserted when they had gone into the hotel, were active and crowded.

"Come have a look at my Englishman first, got to make sure he's still alive."

They found him in Troy's Casino, smoking a meerschaum pipe, wearing a tweed suit with two pistols strapped about his waist, the eyeglass fixed into his left eye, and before him stood a stack of twenty-dollar gold pieces which Morgan guessed must be worth about one thousand dollars. He was of medium height, blond-haired and blond-bearded, with a fresh pink complexion and, though he had not slept, glistening and merry blue eyes. He looked about thirty years old and had a guileless, innocent face, although this, Zack had assured Morgan, was only camouflage, for Sir James was in reality no more innocent than Green Troy and less guileless than he was himself.

The hand was played out and, apparently, Sir James had surprised them by showing better judgment at poker than an Englishman or any other greenhorn was supposed to have, and now he reached forth to add another stack of coins to his winnings, remarking, "I say, upon my word." He seemed as much at ease as if he were in his London club, and had plainly determined that nothing about this wilderness of western America should take him by surprise.

"There he is," said Zack, as if he were displaying his prize nugget, a walking horse he had bought or was trying to sell, or some other natural phenomenon in which he did not entirely believe in spite of the evidence of his eyes.

"What time is it, old boy?"

"Morning," Zack told him. "Must be eight o'clock."

"Oh, I say. As late as that?" He glanced inquiringly at the other players, and, presently, the game had broken up.

Zack introduced Morgan to Sir James and asked if he wanted to see some mines and a stamp mill, explaining that his friend was a partner in one of the Territory's most successful enterprises and that this was his opportunity to observe exactly what these nervous Americans were about, for Sir James had remarked that the country was in a state of agitation he had not believed even though he had heard it described, brimful of a restlessness and discontent so extreme it could only lead either to a rapid and unprecedented conquest of a great land, or a fatal national collapse. The haste, the hurry, the impatience, the optimism, puzzled him—and his comments puzzled those who heard them, for few men thought they were so anxious or so mobile as he portrayed them to themselves as being.

"Right, right," he agreed, shaking Morgan's hand. "A gold mine, is it? What a good thing to have."

Before they had reached the door, Green Troy appeared. "I want to thank you, Sir James, for having rescued Mrs. Malachy's lap dog. Your kindness has been appreciated."

"Quite all right," Sir James assured him. "Hate to see an animal mistreated. Small one, that is," he added, for his prowess at buffalo shooting had been discussed during the night and Zack Fletcher had estimated that at a conservative guess Sir James had personally discharged at least five thousand buffalo, not to mention several hundreds of gazelle, deer, cougars, and rattlesnakes enough to stretch from one coast to the other. Troy bowed, and they emerged onto the street. "My kindness was appreciated," murmured Sir James. "Do you suppose that's why I won so easily? I thought it was the mountain air."

"What happened to Mrs. Malachy's dog?"

"He made the mistake of coming into the room alone and before he could get out again one of your ruffians had seized him and cut off his tail and was, I think, about to skin him alive, when I warned him off."

"You warned him off," observed Zack.

"With my pistol, you know. And gave the dog to one of the guards." He smiled. "It caused quite a furor at the time and I was threatened with having my throat cut, myself made into a sieve, and my balls into a lady's reticule. But when I asked the fellow if he would like to have it out, he was no more eager than if I'd been a member of your Vigilance Committee." He nodded, still smiling. "The ass knows in whose face he brays. Now—shall we look at the mine?"

XXXVI

Zack Fletcher's Englishman soon became as celebrated as Fan Moffat had been the year before. He granted interviews to Homer Grimes and to the rival paper, describing his winter on the southern range, and Zack Fletcher vouched for the truth of Sir James' claim to have killed one hundred and eighteen buffalo in two hours, while seated on a campstool. He spoke with familiar affection of the Wild West, to which he had become addicted during an earlier hunting trip in Alaska, and assured them he was having a frolic now but intended to return one day and spend a year or two helping to develop the country before taking up his ancestral responsibilities. And he accepted Erma Finney's invitation to lecture to the Ladies' Study Group, although Zack refused to go, declaring there was nothing in his contract which stated that a Ladies' Study Group was dangerous territory.

"He's a real westerner," the men told one another as Gordon walked by, usually accompanied by Zack, although he was no

longer in need of him as bodyguard or guide and Zack had asked
that he be allowed to retire.

"Not at all," Gordon assured him. "I enjoy you too much, and it's
only a little longer. Be patient, old boy, although I suppose like all
your compatriots you're full of schemes you can't wait to get under
way."

And he would smile with his bland, knowing smile which, according to all mountain standards of behavior, should have enraged
every man who saw him but which, somehow, did not. For it seemed
they had become infatuated with James Gordon, found him an original and entertaining tenderfoot, phlegmatic as a reservation Indian
and merry as a child, and so they forgave him his eyeglass and
meerschaum pipe, his accent and his tweed suit, and pleaded with
him to remain among them.

"I'll be back," he promised. "I'm on the make myself by now." He
liked to use these Americanisms and was often complimented on
his mastery of the language.

But first, he said, he must return to England. Morgan was leaving
for New York, where he meant to spend two or three years at Columbia University studying those peculiar metals, silver and copper,
and Sir James announced he would accompany him.

During the few weeks between their arrival at the beginning of
May and the time when Zack expected to keep his rendezvous with
the whisky consignment, they traveled from camp to camp, inspected
ranches and mines, and everything he saw Sir James admired, for it
seemed the sight of so much that was young and new and, it might
be said, raw, never depressed him as it did other visitors.

Morgan showed him the stamp mill, which aroused his wonder,
not so much for its size as for the fact that it had been hauled so
great a distance before being set up where it was now, washing and
grinding the earth and forcing it to produce bars of gold. He was interested to find that a gold mine looked only like a collection of lopsided shacks, with a shaft poked down fifty or sixty feet into which
they could descend in an ore bucket, and one day he bought a mine
from a man who had fallen down the shaft and injured himself too
seriously ever to work again.

"Very primitive, very primitive," he regularly mumbled, then
added with an apologetic glance at Morgan and Zack, "Of course,
that's half the charm."

They went to Butte, trailing a string of mules laden with supplies
for Bruno Favorite, and Morgan filled eight large sacks with ore
samples to be assayed in Baltimore. And while Zack and Bruno
remininisced and Sir James listened to tales of racing horses with
Lily Jones, the feast of young fawn which turned out to be wolf
meat, the Christmas party, and the tragedy of Henry Halloway's
amputated legs, Morgan squatted on the slag heap of Amos Muspratt's mine and talked to him with a more serious and beguiling

intensity than he had ever shown Ula Malloy in the days when he was courting her. But Muspratt refused to sell his mine, was not at all concerned that his friends wound their forefingers and pointed to their temples whenever his name was mentioned, and could at last be persuaded to give him only a six month's lease for four thousand dollars and one fourth the profit, which Muspratt would work during Morgan's absence, and when they left Morgan was still disappointed and rather angry not to have been able to buy it outright.

"Have you ever thought," Sir James inquired, with the air of one who hopes to distract a fanatic, "that perhaps these minerals are too costly? A cow, after all, increases in value at the rate of about eight dollars a year for only one dollar in maintenance. In Nebraska," he added, as Morgan looked at him skeptically. By the time they had returned to Helena, Sir James had also bought four small ranches and about two thousand head of cattle, and was planning to send Hereford and Angus bulls in to improve the stock.

And as they roamed the countryside through which they had first passed seven years ago, Morgan was relieved to find this repetition of their earlier experiences had either dissipated Zack's animosity or he had wrestled it into submission, and once again there grew between them the sense of peaceful and satisfying companionship he had remembered. But Zack had not mentioned Lisette again and Lisette, when she heard Zack Fletcher was in town, demanded, "Is that bull-whacker with him?" Morgan smiled and Lisette walked away, and he decided that those two, his sister and his friend, were not after all so free of each other.

The night before Morgan and Zack and Sir James were to leave for Fort Benton, Jenny gave a farewell party in Morgan's honor, a celebration intended not only to insure him a safe journey and an early return, but to create an unbreakable continuity during his absence, and to this festival she invited James Gordon and Zack Fletcher.

Zack showed Morgan his invitation, and the honor of having been included made him shy and uncertain, as if he expected Morgan to say it was only a formality and he was meant to decline. But Sir James had no such qualms about his own welcome and was eager to be entertained in a house where he might discover if it was true that all western Americans lived in bare cabins littered with mining tools and ore specimens, ate jerked beef and green biscuits, and shared one tin plate and one tin cup between every two people.

Those guests who would attend the dinner and those who would come later had been divided with judicious concern. Fong Chong was put through a rigorous training by Jenny, and for many days there was such a pounding of almonds and mincing of meat, squeezing of jelly bags and peeling of chestnuts, that their houses were fragrant of cinnamon and cloves and burning sugar, and they neglected their ordinary tasks to gather in one another's kitchens, tasting and advising, and, when the day finally came, the children were sent to scour the gulches and hilltops for all the wildflowers they could find.

Morgan's cabin had been rented, the sacks of ore had been sent ahead to Fort Benton, and because he dreaded it unreasonably, he found an hour before he was due at Jenny's that he had not yet said good-bye to Ula Malloy.

She had long ago become as troublesome to him as a wife, and more than once he had hoped their latest quarrel was their last one. After Ula had stuffed Fan Moffat's clothes down the seat-hole of an outhouse, he had had some hopes of being delivered from her relentless love; but then one day he found his cabin decorated with branches of spruce and cedar and dried sweet grasses and had known, with some premonitory dread, that Ula had forgiven him again, and so he had shut the door, knowing well enough what he was going to do when she came running out of the kitchen this time.

"It's only because I love you so god-damn much," she explained, whenever she had thrown a shoe or a plate at him, yelling that she never wanted to see him again.

He knocked at the door of her cabin, and when she did not answer he found her sitting at a table piled with copies of eastern magazines from which she tore sketches for her dressmaker. Her hair was uncombed, she wore a blue silk wrapper, and she leaned on the table with both elbows, staring at him as if she had been expecting him for hours or perhaps for days. Her cat was prowling restlessly and giving out sounds of distress, as if she had made it nervous, and it whisked by him and rushed away. The room, which was usually neat, was in a state of such disorder it seemed that from time to time she must have picked up something and hurled it at random.

She did not move but lowered her head, gazed at him a little longer, and said sullenly, "Take me with you."

He looked at her warily, trying to decide whether she had thrown everything she intended or was keeping something, perhaps the coffee pot, in reserve for him, and at last he gave her a tentative smile. "I've brought you a surprise."

He reached into his pocket and took out a diamond of three carats and held it toward her. He had hoped that a present, an expensive one, might distract her long enough for him to leave, for she had often described the diamonds her friends had and told him they advised her to find another beau, someone more generous even if he might not be quite so handsome.

"What the hell is that for?" She snatched it and slid it onto the fourth finger of her left hand, glancing up at him uncertainly, and he found that he had made another mistake.

"I'm sorry, it's just a present. That's all," he added apologetically.

"Not an engagement ring?"

He looked regretful. "No."

"You son of a bitch. You think that's what I want—a present?"

"I thought it might be," he admitted.

She held out her hand and studied it, skeptical and greedy as a prospector with a bit of ore and, at last, folded her arms and put the diamond out of sight, as if he might ask her to give it back if she would not reward him with a few suitable words of thanks. Thinking that he was fortunate if there was to be no more than this to their farewell, he decided it was the right moment to leave.

"Ula," he said in a low, propitiatory voice, "my family is—"

"I know all about it." She gestured contemptuously toward the newspaper on the table. "A farewell dinner party is being given tonight for Mr. Morgan Devlin, that energetic and capable and determined young man, blah blah blah, known to all of you, blah blah blah."

She thrust her tongue between her lips and blew loudly and Morgan gave an involuntary burst of laughter. As if that had been a signal she sprang up, drew back her hand and lashed out so swiftly that she caught him across the cheek and he felt the stinging impact of the diamond. He grabbed her arm, and she kicked him sharply on the shinbone. He spun about, telling her, "Good-bye, Ula," and started for the door as she picked up the coffee pot and threw it, the lukewarm coffee spraying over his clothes and the furniture. As he bolted out the door she followed him with a small flatiron and pitched that at him, although it was too heavy to sail very far and, when he mounted his horse, she tore off the ring and threw it with a wild swing.

"Don't you ever come back here, Morgan Devlin," she shrieked. "I never want to see you again." But by the time he glanced around she was searching for it amid the prickly pears of her front yard, too absorbed even to look at him.

At the hotel he discovered that the ring had left a gash across his right cheekbone, and while he shaved and got into black trousers and a frock coat and white silk cravat, he invented a story of being stumbled over in the middle of the night by the stranger who shared his room and came in drunk.

Jenny's house had recently been repainted and she had at last achieved a lawn which, though it would not remain green after July, now looked thick and fresh; low bushes grew along the fence, cottonwood trees stood on either side, and a border of red geraniums bloomed near the house.

The dining-room table was set with fourteen places, and another in the living room with nine. Vases of wildflowers and branches of cedar stood on tables and on the floor, candles in silver sticks were ready to be lighted, and Fong Chong, in a new coat, was carrying chairs and buckets of ice.

Morgan found the women in the kitchen, Marietta and Jenny and Erma Finney, Georgina and Cornelia Bream and Margaret Webb, Annabel in a new dress, and then Lisette and Ralph arrived, carrying between them a basket where the baby Frank lay sleeping, with Polly holding fast to her father's hand. Lisette ran up the stairs, followed by Ralph carrying the basket, and in a moment came flying back down again, to twirl about before him and ask what he thought of her new dress and the way she had done her hair, and as she glanced at the door her eyes were unusually dark and brilliant.

The dress was bright yellow taffeta, the color he thought became her best, and was decorated with scrolls of black braid, while a row of jet buttons ran straight down the front to the hem. She wore jet earrings, long and swinging, and her hair, however she might have accomplished it, looked to him a marvel of ingenuity. He complimented her, smiling, and the smile seemed to make her self-conscious and rather defiant, so that she became preoccupied with refolding napkins, moving bouquets, inspecting the kitchen, and brought in the two almond cakes she had made to show them to him.

When Rachel Grimes arrived, with Homer and her infant son Lemuel, Lisette greeted her with such affection that Rachel seemed baffled, but pleased, for they had been a little distant ever since the day Fan Moffat had chased Homer with her reticule. Matt and Pete came with Lem Finney and Josiah Webb, and Jonathan with Jacob Finney. Douglas had gone to bring Flora Pim, who was now thirteen and had surprised them by turning into a precocious beauty, with her hair as white as ever and her earlier tomboyishness transformed to provocation. The Reverend Bream came next, Robert bounded in, and when all the dinner guests had arrived but Sir James and Zack Fletcher, Morgan noticed that Lisette had disappeared.

The men gathered near the windows and began to drink, and presently the women came in, rustling their gowns and arranging their skirts, and Annabel took the oldest children to eat in the kitchen. But now they had fallen surprisingly quiet and were perhaps a little suspicious of this Englishman who was about to appear among them.

And then Pete was ushering them in, Sir James in full evening dress, smiling with his look of guileless modesty, while Zack skulked along with his head down, looking as if he hoped not to be noticed. To Morgan's disbelieving astonishment, Zack was dressed like the others, in black trousers and frock coat with a white shirt and white silk cravat, and he glanced at Morgan with a resentful and almost anguished expression and seemed to be blaming him for the clothes he wore which made him awkward and ashamed, as if he expected momentarily to make a fool of himself.

Sir James had met the women on the day of his lecture and now demonstrated that he had also memorized their names; but Zack glanced about sheepishly and fell to studying the floor again until, as Lisette appeared with a dazzling if rather artificial smile, he started slightly, narrowed his eyes and peered at her as she came toward them, but would not look at her when they shook hands. He seized the glass Pete offered him and seemed about to drink it at a gulp, then took instead a deep swallow, stared gloomily at what was left and, once again, flashed Morgan a menacing glare. The men had now begun to question Sir James about his travels in America, and Zack moved until he was standing with his back to Lisette.

They perhaps intended to trap Sir James into some unflattering remarks: the crude and ugly western cities, each with its small population of boosters; the national habits of bragging and chewing tobacco, spitting on floors and sidewalks and whittling everything in sight, wearing hats indoors and taking coats off, putting feet on desks and chairs and railings; the hypocritical morality which was said to have culminated at last in pantaloons for piano legs; the railroad and steamboat wrecks, so numerous that a man setting out on a journey was given a hero's farewell; the hideous architecture which had been borrowed from every country in Europe and not improved but degraded; the ramshackle national capital with its unpaved streets and look of impermanence which shocked even native tourists; the western methods of vigilante justice and claim-jumping and their attempts to rid themselves of the Indians by starving them and killing them; their women who were judged by Europeans to be thin and unhealthy and, particularly in the West, tolerated more than was good for them; their corrupt federal and city governments and the entire collapse of what had once been a stern system of ethics—all those topics upon which visiting foreigners became so quickly expert. But James Gordon was nimble and adroit, stepped into no concealed holes and stumbled against no camouflaged barriers and, when Lem Finney said, "In the East it is believed that we are a half-civilized and immoral community," Sir James only lifted his eyebrows in a sign of polite incredulity.

"And, by God, we are," said Matt. They laughed heartily at this. "But so are they."

Now they turned with relief from a wary inclination to defend themselves and began to talk about what interested them, the troubles they had as part of a generation which was trying to make a nation of a continent, and were soon discussing their problems with America as if they were themselves a foreign power.

"Why don't you join the Union?" Sir James suggested.

"We haven't been asked."

"We prefer to be autonomous, for the time being."

"But they owe us something for our contributions, and they don't give us a damn thing. The Indians, for instance."

At this they began to talk as excitedly as if Sir James had praised the government Indian policy.

"Do you know what it costs the United States to kill an Indian? One hundred and fifteen thousand dollars for one lousy Indian."

"I say, upon my word."

"And the government troops fight under the rules of civilized warfare. They even take prisoners, for Christ's sake."

"They blow the bugle at night to let the Indians know they're going to sleep, and they blow it again in the morning to let them know they're getting up."

"I say," Sir James agreed. "Upon my word."

As they continued to talk Zack stood silent, staring into the glass, and found that slowly he was losing his painful conviction of looking like an organ grinder's monkey in his new clothes, as well as the curious fear and reluctance he had felt at being once again with this family he had lived with for nearly a year, so that he was finally able to look at Pete, and saw that Pete was now clean-shaven and looked if anything more somber and thoughtful than before, while his black eyes seemed to gleam with an even brighter intensity. Pete glanced at him, as if he had become aware of what he was thinking, and Zack turned his attention to Lem Finney who, by shaving his beard, had revealed himself as a man whose blue eyes were no sharper and no more calculating than the rest of his face. And, at last, he looked at Matt.

Like the others, Matt was clean-shaven, but for a mustache, and Zack found a kind of mean satisfaction in seeing that Matt's face had a look of almost ferocious intensity, nothing at all of his brother's sensitive vulnerability, but a challenging and defiant expression which was not concealed even when he smiled, and which a laugh only made more surprising. And this had the effect of increasing Zack's resentment, as if by the very act of shaving his beard and exposing himself, Matt Devlin had committed himself to whatever ruthlessness and violence was natural to him, and which he might before have tried to conceal, or divert.

And yet Zack remembered that once he had felt for Matt a kind of awestruck admiration, while Pete had seemed a complex and essentially unhappy man of a kind he could never understand and, no doubt, if it were not for Lisette, he would admire Matt still. It disgusted him that his emotions toward these people were neither generous nor justifiable, for he preferred clear and uncomplicated responses—love or hate or rage or pity—but these peculiar mixtures seemed to him as dangerous and unwholesome as the practice some young girls had of secretly eating chalk to make themselves thin.

Pete filled the glasses again and Zack began to talk, showing as much indignation about the Indians as anyone else, until all at once he met Matt's glance and seemed to hear, with an uncanny clarity, the words he imagined Matt had shouted at him the day he rode past Devlin Brothers, trailing after Georgina and Lisette and carrying their packages from the Ladies Emporium: "Go ahead and make a horse's ass out of yourself if you want to, but if you think I'd ever let her marry you you're a god-damn fool." These words, although they had never been spoken, Zack now seemed to hear ringing across the room, above all the talk of Indians and railroads and unjust taxation, and they filled him with such raging self-righteousness that if Matt had demanded at that moment to know what he was thinking, he would not only have told him but would have disrupted the farewell dinner party with a scene which would show everyone there that he was as uncivilized as Matt Devlin thought he was.

But then, as he looked into the empty glass, he smiled slightly, thinking how surprised Matt would be, for no doubt he thought he admired him as he once had or, of course, he probably never thought of him at all. The talk, Zack found, had now turned to buffalo hunting.

And at the mention of hunting, James Gordon, who until then had been blandly agreeable to everything his hosts said, smiling when they did and frowning when that seemed expected, flashed into glittering excitement and began to describe the winter he had spent with Zack, living in a tent, often hungry, sometimes nearly frozen, but filled with an exaltation of killing which astounded them.

"How long will it take to get rid of them?" Pete asked.

"On the southern plains?" Gordon glanced at Zack. "Four or five years?"

Zack looked sullen. "Maybe, can't tell."

"The plains are a putrid, stinking desert," Gordon told them enthusiastically. "And the stupid beasts, of course, haven't the foggiest notion of protecting themselves, but if one of their number goes down come stand around him and talk things over while you pop them off one after the other." He laughed. "I sometimes think there is a peculiar pleasure to be found in killing a creature that does nothing to defend itself, which is absent when you kill one who resists you and hates to be killed but would rather kill you instead." He looked about, his eyes sharp and inquisitive. "What do you think?"

Zack sucked in a deep breath which made them all glance at him as if he were about to deliver an official pronouncement and said, in a surprisingly loud voice, "That all depends, Gordon, on whether it's men or animals you're talking about killing."

James Gordon laughed, as if the concept pleased him and gave a new and subtle flavor to his theory, and Lisette came toward them with a protesting cry. "Whatever are you talking about? Depends on whether it's men or animals, indeed." She looked up at Zack, smiled slightly and shook her head, as if she had found him once again strewing his seeds of anarchy and confusion.

Zack's face began to burn and he gave her a stiff bow. "All the same, Mrs. Mercer, it makes a whale of a difference."

"I should think so," said Lisette. "It's time for dinner." She glanced around. "All this ferocious talk must have made you ravenous."

James Gordon had turned instantly to Lisette, his face shining with another kind of enthusiasm, and Lisette gave him a provocative smile, as if to ask his lordship what he thought of her now that he had studied her so carefully. Zack turned away and wandered across the room as if he might leave the party in disgust, but he had noticed Ralph Mercer watching his wife, and felt sourly pleased she should be causing another man these pangs of jealousy, not himself.

They were taking their places at the tables, but still Zack hung about, tossed down what was left in his glass and paused sharply, taken aback, as he watched Lisette sauntering arm in arm with James Gordon toward the dining room. The row of buttons down the front of her dress had disconcerted him, and now the bustle, which wavered invitingly as she walked, caused him to frown, shaking his head, and he felt some inclination to approach Ralph Mercer and tell him that he had his sympathy—for whatever it might be worth —but went instead to find where he must sit.

Jenny, whether from compassion or impudence, had seated him opposite Lisette, who had Morgan on her right and James Gordon on her left, and as the Reverend Bream now rose and began to cough his request for their silence, Zack was vaguely aware that Matt and Jenny were at the table in the living room, with Ralph Mercer, while Pete was in here and, perhaps as chaperone, so was Erma Finney, who sat beside him where she might keep Lisette under surveillance. And he paid no attention to where the others sat, for his head felt swollen with blood which seemed likely to burst through his eardrums if he could find no way to settle this unexplained terror and rage.

As the Reverend Bream began to pray, asking for the safe journey of Morgan and politely including a request for James Gordon's welfare, Zack tried to compose himself by studying the table. Oysters embedded in ice had been set before him in a silver scallop shell, several knives and forks and four goblets stood at each place, there were crystal bowls of flowers and silver bowls of fruit, and white candles burned in silver sticks, but all these refinements only made him more melancholy. The wax flowers which stood in a glass dome on the sideboard and which he had at first mistaken for real ones, seemed to him particularly displeasing, and everything about the house, its cleanness and comfort, made him feel that it was hard to breathe; for if he had married Lisette, she would of course have tried to force something like it on him.

He gave her a sudden look of accusation, but she was gazing dreamily down at her lap, a reflective smile on her mouth, and probably heard no more of what the Reverend Bream was saying than he did.

He had been surprised and perhaps somewhat disappointed that the past five years, her marriage and the two children she had borne, had not changed her so much as he had expected or, at least, she had not changed in the way he had expected. Nothing about her had been spoiled, there was no diminishment of vitality and, indeed, new attractions had developed. She had the same daintiness and vivacity which he had first admired, but now he could discover, or imagined he could, traces of an aware sensuality in the expression of her mouth and even in the lowering of her eyelids as she pretended to listen to the Reverend Bream. She had, he remembered, a little mole on her right breast, but why this should seem so extraordinary a charm he could not imagine, and surely he was lucky to have escaped this girl who would have dominated him unmercifully if she had been given the chance.

He had often recited to himself all the harms she would have done him, and he recited them over again now. First, of course, she would have made him stop swearing, and next she would have corrected his grammar; she would insist that he wear underclothes and not go about like an Indian, naked beneath his shirt and trousers, and, in no time, she would have deprived him of his medicine bundle. And once she had succeeded in this feminine vindictiveness, he might have expected the instant visitation of his doom.

Nevertheless he was unable to get out of his mind, for it ran there steadily as a nagging song, his memory of that one kiss and the feel of her breast in his hand, and these memories quickly became disquieting sensations, beckoning him on to the vision of better satisfactions and stronger excitements. But, no doubt, she would have convinced him he was a lewd rascal trying to use up the limited supply she had of freshness and youth and beauty in the service of his lechery, and so he might have—for he could think of no better use to make of freshness and youth and beauty.

He gave a philosophical sigh, noticing that she still wore on the little finger of her right hand the ring Matt had given her on her tenth birthday, and assured himself again it was better for them both that she had married Ralph Mercer, a gentleman and devoted to her, though a little grim in his Yankee way, and if her husband perhaps unwittingly deprived her of some of a woman's best pleasures, no doubt he intended his reserve as a compliment.

Lisette, who had promptly decided that this was to be one of the most important days of her life, sat in dazed confusion and heard nothing of the Reverend Bream's prayer. Five years ago she had imagined that Zack Fletcher had destroyed her confidence and, for several months, had been determined to exact her tribute from numerous unsuspecting admirers for the humiliation and sorrow he had caused her; and yet she had soon married Ralph Mercer, and she was happy with him.

Those months when Nella Allen had lived with them and when, as it seemed to Lisette, she had been longing for something from Zack but had never guessed what it was until after he had gone away or, more likely, until after she married, all that which was safely past had assumed some of the attractions of an enigma to be solved. But she had not solved it, and he remained as perplexing, as unruly and dangerous as he had ever been.

The Reverend Bream sat down and the rooms filled with talk and laughter. Lisette gazed intently at James Gordon across the rim of her wine glass as she asked him, "And what brought you all this distance, Mr. Gordon?" Zack scowled, whether at the question or the tender tone of her voice, and glared at her vindictively when she gave him a humorsome glance, as if to inquire if perhaps he found the room too warm or the chair too small.

"Well, you know, Mrs. Mercer, it's quite the thing nowadays—your West."

"It is?" Lisette smiled at him mockingly. "And what do you think of it?"

"Oh, come now, Mrs. Mercer, you know there isn't any right answer an Englishman can give to that question. But I wish you would tell me about something which interests me very much. How do your western women change so quickly—only by crossing the Missouri River?"

"Do we change?" Lisette looked at Erma Finney, asking her to answer this knotty question.

"I have not changed by crossing the Missouri River," Erma Finney assured them.

"Maybe we don't change," Lisette said softly. "Maybe it's only that out here we become what we were all along—but never dared to be."

"Bravo!" declared Sir James.

"What Mrs. Mercer means," said Zack, "is that they didn't dare in the East because there were too many of them and they couldn't get away with it. We're a little short on females out here, and it's remarkable how quick they are to see an advantage and take it."

She looked at Zack, as if she would like to quarrel with him, but Zack had begun to discuss, with Pete and Morgan and Josiah Webb, the Territory's prospects for a railroad. Fong Chong was carrying out the oyster plates and replacing them with cups of clear soup, and presently he was filling their glasses with sherry, to James Gordon's evident astonishment, for he must have expected the eternal bitter biscuits, molasses and fried steak which was the lot of travelers from the Missouri River to the Pacific Coast.

Lisette fell silent as she began to eat, scarcely aware that her face had become wistful and sad, for she was thinking that now was the time to ask Zack Fletcher why he had let her run away the day they had gone riding alone, when surely he had known much better what it was she wanted than she did. This impulse quickly acquired an uncanny power which threatened momentarily to overcome her judgment, and in a terror of hearing her own voice, Lisette drank her third glass of champagne.

Zack Fletcher was grinning at her now, and although she gave him a warning frown, the next moment she was caught by a sharp sorrow, the keenest and most anguishing she had ever felt, though whether the sorrow was for Zack, and whatever might now be lost to them, or for Morgan's leaving she could not tell.

All at once she pushed back her chair and stood up, saying distractedly, "The baby's crying, I must see what's wrong."

She ran from the room and up the stairs and paused at the top as she marveled at the treachery of those three glasses of champagne which had shown her not the truth, as superstitious folk believed, but only lies about herself, and went into the darkened room.

"Shh," Annabel warned her. "I have them all sleeping. Don't wake them up. Is the party over?"

"No, darling." Lisette covered her face with her hands and stood still, and in the darkness it seemed she felt more irresponsible than before, until she heard Annabel's voice, curious and accusatory.

"Lisette, are you tipsy?"

"Of course not," Lisette whispered, and now she could see Annabel, seated on a chair near the window, her hands folded in her lap as she watched her. She went to where her young son lay sleeping and picked him up, holding him close, as if she might have been in some danger of losing him, and then sat down and opened her dress, tenderly holding his head and closing her eyes. She continued to sit in the dark, surrounded by the sleeping children, for several minutes, a period of time she could not guess, until Jenny came in.

"Lisette, is anything wrong?"

"Frank was crying."

"He was not crying, Lisette," Annabel objected. "I had him fast asleep."

"Fong Chong is serving the dessert. Can't you leave him now?"

Jenny was standing beside her, and Lisette, her mouth against the baby's head, smoothing with her fingertips the fine hair about his temples, had a frightening premonition that Jenny knew why she had run away. And yet she felt so entirely safe here, surrounded by the children, in the dark quiet room, that it seemed to make no difference if Jenny did know, for the moment had been an aberration, something she had not wished for and could not help, and now it was gone.

Jenny moved about the room, looking at one sleeping child after another, kissed Leila and hung over her with that wondering expression Lisette had often seen when Jenny looked at the little girl, and softly left the room, glancing back as she closed the door, and giving Lisette a smile which made her throat ache with pity. For, at this moment when she had so much reason to mistrust herself, Lisette understood that Jenny had made her own dismaying discoveries of the difference between what she was and what she wanted to be, and she had come there to console her.

At last, Lisette lay the baby in the basket and started to leave, but as she passed the mirror she paused and stood looking at herself in the dim light, forgetting Annabel, who sat silent and motionless, watching her with a perplexed and troubled face. Lisette moved closer to the mirror, searching for some inadvertent betrayal there of what she had recognized at last, this legacy left to her by Zack Fletcher of unexperienced pleasures, her own longing for a voluptuous liberation, and it all seemed to be there, lighting her eyes and changing the expression of her mouth. She took a backward step, observing the yellow dress with its long row of jet buttons, and thought of the Quakeress in the family legend, throwing off her cloak and standing naked before the congregation, and she laughed softly.

"Something's wrong with you, Lisette," Annabel said. "You're not yourself today."

"Hush. You don't know what you're talking about." But then she turned, swooped at Annabel and caught her in her arms, holding her fast. "I didn't mean that, darling, I'm sorry I said it."

"Lisette, be careful, please, you're mussing my hair." Annabel was reaching up to protect herself.

Lisette kissed her, asking in a whisper, "Well, what if I am? I fixed it for you, didn't I?"

Annabel shook her head, smoothing her hair and shaking out the curls. "Sometimes you don't seem like my big sister at all."

Lisette sighed. "I know."

She closed the door and stood at the top of the staircase, listening. The dinner was over, there was a smell of cigar smoke, and she heard James Gordon saying that this in itself made it worth a man's while to live in the mountains, for no eastern gentleman dared smoke without retiring to his funk hole. Fong Chong passed swiftly through the vestibule, carrying a coffee tray, and she could hear the voices of later arrivals, Irene and Jeremy Flint, Count and Countess Manzoni, Dr. and Mrs. Chaffinch.

She started slowly down the stairs, quite sober again and much chastened by her experience, as if she had gone off on a dangerous and foolish errand, met with a serious accident which was in part her own fault and, during her convalescence, acquired both philosophy and humility. Her face no longer glowed with audacity, but was contemplative and vaguely smiling, and when Ralph appeared in the vestibule, glanced up and saw her and stopped, she seemed as much surprised to find him there as if they had met by chance in a strange city.

He was smoking and stood with one hand in his trouser pocket, staring at her with a grim and angry look. "What is it?" she asked, very softly, and to her bewilderment it seemed she could not have spoken more loudly if she tried. "Is something wrong?" She reached the bottom of the stairs and faced him, puzzled that he should be glowering at her, and even more puzzled that it seemed she had not seen him for a long, long time. He continued to stare at her, so searchingly that her face became extraordinarily innocent, for what could he find there, after all? Surely no clues to her secrets, since she scarcely knew herself what they were, and she whimsically reflected that if all husbands and wives were mind readers the world would be even less orderly than it was.

This notion made her smile, a rather remote and ironic little smile which appeared without her being quite aware of it, though she could see its effect a moment later in Ralph's somberly threatening expression, and heard it in the tone of his voice as he pointed his finger at her, saying, "You're my wife, Lisette."

"Of course I am, darling." She reached out to touch him, but he moved quickly, avoiding her.

"Don't forget it."

He walked into the living room, leaving her as astonished as if he had slapped her, and as her cheeks began to burn she pressed both palms to her face, murmuring, "Why, Ralph."

She peeked around the corner and saw that Ralph now stood with his back to her, talking to Jonathan and James Gordon. She gave a shrug and a little sigh and went into the living room, and was soon laughing and vivacious and no longer afraid of herself, though she took care not to flirt with Sir James, and whenever Zack Fletcher approached a group where she stood she moved warily away, refusing to look at him.

After a time she began to imagine that Zack was following her, that however often she ran away she encountered him soon again, watching her with a steady, absorbed concentration she could not discourage, either by pretending to ignore him or by giving him back a cold and haughty stare, certain to disconcert any sensitive man, though it only seemed to amuse him.

Her heart was beating quickly and she began to feel as breathless as if she were in reality running from him. At last she fled to the kitchen where Fong Chong was washing dishes, and there she spent some time, tasting the Bavarian cream and the iced chocolate pudding, but, as she came into the dining room, as crowded now as the living room, he was waiting for her in the vestibule, hanging about near the door and pretending to be interested in the stag's head, a western curiosity he seemed never to have seen before.

She hesitated, but then walked toward him rapidly, pausing as he reached out to catch her arm, and raising her eyebrows as if to say that whatever tricks he might have up the sleeve of his unlikely frock coat, they would do him no good. But he smiled, and it surprised her that he could still become, in an instant, as soft-spoken and tender-eyed as a woman. "Are you happy, Lisette?"

"Am I happy? Certainly I'm happy." She tipped her head to one side. "Don't I look happy? Don't I act happy? I have all any woman could want—youth and hope and health and occupation and amusement. Meat and clothes and fire." She laughed. "And what more has England's queen?"

He did not seem impressed by this list of her assets, produced with such businesslike confidence, but looked at her seriously, questioningly, and a little sadly. She started to pass him and, this time, he touched her arm, keeping here there. "You're still afraid of me, aren't you?"

"Still afraid of you? What an idea. I was never afraid of you."

"Or is it me? Maybe it's yourself. You might find out you're not the genteel young lady you're supposed to be, after all." Her face turned pink and, at that, he smiled more widely and seemed pleased to have got this admission from her. "Could that be it?"

She picked up her skirts, as if to protect them from touching him, stepped a little to one side and passed him with a warning look, though she was smiling again as she entered the living room and met Ralph's glance, still watchful and accusatory.

Looking for some convenient place where she might hide from them both, she joined Morgan and Matt standing near the window before Jenny's conservatory of potted plants, which by now hung in green strands to the floor. They were talking, as men interminably did nowadays, about the troubles the Territory was having, and Lisette slipped her arm through Morgan's, leaned her head against his shoulder, and closed her eyes.

"This may be about finished," Matt was saying. "Something in the East may suit you just as well, or better."

"I'll be back—I still believe it's all ahead of us. In Butte."

"I wouldn't expect very much of your Uncle Joshua."

"I don't expect anything of him, I remember him too well."

They laughed reminiscently at that, and Lisette glanced from one to the other, shaking her head in agreement about their Uncle Joshua. "You know the old saying," Matt reminded him. "Money is the most timid thing in the world, and dislikes pioneering. And it seems Pete and I have begun to dislike it, too, or I suppose we'd be more eager to put some of it in Butte. But we've seen too many banks fold because they loaned money to friends and partners and relatives. When you get back, though, Morgan, if you've been able to raise some capital, we'll lend you an equal amount—"

Jenny sat at the piano, and as Pete began to twist the strings of his fiddle, the room grew quieter, and at the first strains a subdued hush came over them, as if this music would have some unusual significance for all of them. Lisette held tighter to Morgan's arm, and as Jenny's clear minor voice rose, uncertain at first, but then grew stronger, with a troubling piercing sweetness, Lisette drew in a slow deep breath, and her tears fell steadily, for she could no longer hope to control them.

"Come all ye fair and tender ladies,
Be careful how you court young men—"

Lisette looked up at Morgan with a quick distrustful glance, as if she suspected him of meaning never to come back here, and as she began to cry he shielded her in his arms, for Ralph was watching her angrily and Zack Fletcher looked as guilty as if those tears were not for her brother, but for him.

"They're like the star of a summer's morning,
They'll first appear and then they're gone—"

XXXVII

The trip to Fort Benton took only two days, for Morgan and James Gordon had sent their baggage ahead and Zack traveled with nothing but the clothes he wore and a bed roll behind his saddle.

The plains were scattered with bluebells and purple anemone, wild pink roses bloomed along the stream banks, and the soft, gray-green haze of early summer lay over the land. It rained hard throughout both nights, when they camped near a bull train and slept comfortably in the shelter of a wagon, but the days were fair and cool until the hot noon sun appeared, and Sir James only regretted the absence of animals big enough to shoot. Still, he found other amusement in listening to the curses of the bull-whackers, loitering whenever he heard one shouting at his animals with unusual originality, and then came galloping along to catch up with them, vowing, "I say, I'll never swear again. It's futile, you know, like trying to play the fiddle after you've heard Paganini."

They had set out less than four hours after they had left Jenny's dinner party, and it seemed that Zack's disposition improved as he got farther away from Lisette, so that he listened with an indifferent smile when Sir James told Morgan, "Your sister, if you will permit me to say so, old boy, is a young woman of more charms than any I've met in a long, long while. What a pity the American girls marry so young."

"Fallen like a propped mine," observed Zack, as serene as if Sir James might be talking about some girl he had never seen.

But Morgan was now continuously troubled at the thought of Zack going out among the tribes—where he would set up camp as a wood chopper—and his dreams at night and during the day were haunted by tales he had heard of prolonged torture as the Blackfeet practiced it, until at last, when they could see the dust clouds which hung over Fort Benton in the summer, he turned to him while Sir James was occupied with an inspired bull-whacker. "Let's sell the god-damn stuff in Benton."

Zack glanced alertly sideways. "Your conscience fretting you still?"

"Not my conscience, for God's sake. I'm worried about you—it's a fool thing to do."

"Maybe. But it would be a hell of a lot more foolish not to do it. You can have your share back, but I'll find someone else. I don't plan to give this chance away."

As they approached the town they heard the booming of cannon, announcing the arrival of a steamboat, and they passed an increasingly heavy concentration of mule and bull trains, whose drivers yelled and cracked their whips with a sound which echoed across the plains as if a platoon of infantry was in action somewhere nearby. For the last few miles they were obliged to ride slowly, for the town was surrounded by thousands of mules and oxen and horses, and the wagons and tents had created a second city to envelop the first, dense as a slum. Hundreds of campfires sent streaks of smoke into the windy sky and suffocating clouds blew across the prairie, carrying swarms of mosquitoes and stinging flies which drew blood and left welts.

The town itself was a single street of warehouses and hotels, brothels and gambling halls and restaurants, facing upon the broad, shallow river and looking toward the bluffs across it where an Indian village was pitched. During the winter months Fort Benton was empty, and the few men and women who remained there confined to this narrow edge of the plains swept by snow and gales that howled across it for weeks at a time, but during the spring and summer it became the largest trading center on the northern plains and through it passed supplies for the mining camps to the west, the towns on both sides of the Canadian border, the forts from which the frontier was patrolled, and the reservations.

There was not a tree to be seen, the streets were garbage dumps and the river a flowing sewer, and when at last they left their horses in a corral and set out to find a hotel, they were in some danger of losing one another in the crowds which trampled up and down the boardwalk and levee twenty-four hours a day, arranging passage back to the States, inspecting merchandise, bargaining with bull drivers, selling horses and cattle and lumber, dancing with the hurdy-gurdies and patronizing the whorehouses, in a perpetual state of excitement and blazing energy which caused Sir James to pause in wonderment every now and then, forgetful of his destination. For here, at last, he might observe the entire frontier population— French-Canadian trappers, half-breeds, traders and soldiers—all of them going at a lope, quite as if they had been picked up at random over a thousand miles and dumped out of a bag into the streets of Benton, there to scramble to their feet and dash pell-mell in all directions.

Morgan and Zack had been there many times and agreed it must be true, as the bull-whackers had said, that in spite of all gloomy predictions this summer would be the most prosperous in the history of the upper Missouri. Five boats had arrived and were tied at the river bank, and they were told that two more had reached Cow Island; the river was swarming all the way to St. Louis, and at least eighty boats would arrive before summer was gone.

They went from one hotel to another, most of them log buildings with cloth partitions, and at last were shown a room with two roped bedsteads, two stools, and a mirror. They could hear, as if there was no wall, the sounds from the adjoining saloon, the scraping fiddles and click and clatter of roulette wheels, the faro dealer's monotonous voice and the shouts of the players.

"When does that establishment close?" Sir James asked the clerk, who gave him a pitying smile, and Sir James turned to Zack and Morgan. "I'll sleep on the floor tonight."

"We'll figure that out later," Zack told him. "When you're in Benton there's seldom much time for sleeping."

In the hallway they washed from a pail of water, shaved and combed their hair, and in ten minutes were out again in search of a boat, for Morgan and Zack had agreed that once they had booked passage, Sir James would be much too occupied getting his bears' heads and buffalo skulls aboard to notice their absence when they met with Zack's Indian friends, for during his travels Sir James had accumulated a great treasure of bones and hides, horns and stuffed animals, and it waited for him now at various way stations across the country.

The river bank was crowded for a distance of more than two miles with lumber, stacks of robes and pelts, and crates and barrels piled eight or ten feet high. Deck hands in red flannel shirts ran nimbly across the loading planks, carrying upon their backs and shoulders burdens which bent them double but did not prevent them from scampering along as if they were carrying only bales of feathers, for the season was a short one, even the most skillful pilot could make no more than two trips a year, and so it seemed that whoever worked on a steamboat or rode on one had been jabbed into a condition of desperate haste.

The first two boats where they inquired were leaving the next day, and they were directed to one farther down the levee, walked aboard it up a narrow plank thrust into the mud and rambled about, looking it over with the condescending curiosity of buyers who must be coaxed.

The boats in use on the upper Missouri were not the elaborate creations of the Mississippi which had so dazzled the nation with their democratic grandeur that they had been taken for models to copy in their houses. These were small craft, sturdy and plain, with nothing more decorative than a fretwork edging about the roof of the texas, like a bit of tatting added to a coarse towel by an industrious housewife. On the lower deck much of the upstream cargo was still standing—mining equipment, supplies for the reservations, crates of cats for the army posts, furniture and bolts of silks and velvets—and the deck hands were hurrying it off. They went up the narrow flight of stairs and glanced into the Ladies Saloon, where the paper streamers which had festooned the ceiling hung in strips to the floor, ripped down by some drunken celebrator of their safe arrival. On either side of the long narrow saloon was a row of staterooms, each with two doors, one opening into the saloon and the other onto the deck.

"Damned ingenious, I must say," Sir James observed. "All the proprieties, none of the inconveniences. You Americans are without doubt the world's most practical people." The interior of the staterooms, however, struck him as less marvelous than the arrangements for entering and leaving them inconspicuously. They were uniformly small, six or eight feet square, and contained two bunks, a mirror, and a closet, and they had not been cleaned since the boat's arrival.

There was nothing about this boat, Morgan and Sir James agreed, to recommend it to them, but they also agreed that it would do as well as any other, for they were equally uncomfortable, equally liable to be sunk by running into a hidden snag or raft of interlaced trunks and branches, one no more immune than another to the hazards of river travel—exploding boilers, sudden sinkings in the middle of the night, bad food, and troublesome fellow passengers; while the river itself was generally agreed to be equally unsuited to every kind of craft, the meanest and most refractory river in the world. It was capable of changing its course as one looked at it, its bluffs falling away with thunderous roars, taking the cabins and cattle of incautious settlers, sucking up horses or men who were not alert enough, building sand bars and putting them where not even the most experienced pilot would expect them, manufacturing with malicious dexterity intricate nests of roots and branches captured from fallen trees—a capricious expanse of flowing mud swept by violent storms at every season of the year, and covered for days at a time with clouds of whirling sand which were often mistaken for smoke by inexperienced travelers. Navigating it at low water was said to be like putting a steamer on dry land and sending a boy ahead with a sprinkling pot; while during the weeks of high water, a boat went booming along downstream, more than ever at the river's mercy, but must still crawl north, fighting for every mile it made.

They asked for the pilot and were sent to look for him in the texas, where he stood talking to a pretty girl and, it seemed, impressing her unreasonably with his checkered suit and brocaded vest, high silk hat and patent leather shoes, leaning upon his gold-handled cane and telling her tales of running at night through a storm, followed along the shore by a pack of howling Blackfeet on horseback, and as they listened Morgan and Sir James glanced at each other and grimaced, for it very well might be true.

"What do you want?" the pilot demanded curtly, and was plainly displeased to see them. But when he was told they had come to book passage, he bowed to the girl and excused himself. "Cabin or deck?" he inquired quickly, for although Sir James looked unquestionably a cabin passenger, Morgan, in his red flannel shirt and dusty black hat and boots, seemed a likely deck passenger and, as such, a species of freight which had not even the merit of being inanimate. But he smiled broadly and offered to shake hands when they told him they wanted two cabins, saying that his name was William Johnson, the captain was Richard Lennox, and they would cast off on Sunday at two o'clock. He showed them the cabins which were still available, assured them the boat would be immaculate by Sunday and the saloons elegantly furnished, that their chef was the finest anywhere, and described the pigeon pies, the beaver tails and wild honey which would be their fare and, when they had each paid him three hundred dollars, grew so expansive he invited them to make their home aboard. "It's the best hotel in the West," he said proudly, but now that the arrangements had been made he was eager to return to the girl and they went ashore, where they were soon rushing about with the others.

They lost one another and went their separate ways, learned of one another's exploits from strangers and left messages with bartenders and clerks when they wanted to meet, and it seemed they would never accomplish everything which must be done in only four nights and three days. For the life of the town was so insistent, grabbing each newcomer and carrying him about in confused haste from one place to another and upon such various businesses and pleasures, that it soon became impossible to perform or even to remember the habits and routines of other towns.

"Don't miss the girl they call Silverheels at Ford's Exchange," Zack advised Morgan. But before he had explained why he was to look for Silverheels, Zack was gone, and Morgan forgot her in the midst of his other activities until he encountered Sir James, overseeing the loading of his hides and antlers, locked together in great bundles which would cost him dearly to ship, though the captain had not been able to persuade him to part with even one.

"Have you seen that girl at Ford's Exchange who dances the can-can? She takes them off. Private exhibition, you know."

"That's all?" Morgan asked him, dubious of such tame pleasures.

"Why not see how persuasive you are?"

She was, Morgan found, quite a pretty girl, smiling and gay as she went whirling about the room and, from time to time, disappeared into one of the curtained cubicles along the wall. He hung about playing faro for two or three hours, but her popularity was even greater than Ula Malloy's had been when she first arrived, though it was true Ula had given her customers no such inducements as the can-can danced without drawers, and Zack found him there.

"It's all set. The guy's been paid. I've counted the merchandise, and we'll meet Left Hand tomorrow. Be ready to leave about four."

Morgan waited another hour, and then decided he was too drunk for it to be worth his while to wait any longer and, of course, though he was ashamed to admit it, the prospect of riding with Zack to that lonely rendezvous had vanquished most of his interest in Silverheels.

They set out a little after four and once, inadvertently, Morgan glanced back to see the flag striking out sharply above the remains of the old adobe fort. He caught himself too late, giving that nostalgic farewell to civilization, but refused to find out if Zack was smiling and sat very straight, his face grim and stern, while he continued to be visited by pictures, brightly gory, of his own black scalp and

Zack's blond one waving from the coup stick of some Blackfoot brave.

"We'll be back before sundown," Zack said. "Okay?" Morgan nodded and they rode for some distance without speaking, galloping along at a steady pace and Zack, at least, seemed to take his usual keen interest in everything about him, smelling the morning air, watching a distant gazelle's swiftly flowing movement, listening intently to singing birds hidden among thickets of blooming roses, until at last he glanced at Morgan. "You know, Devlin, maybe you riled me a little that day, after all—talking about your conscience like it was something you'd gone and bought and put up out of reach where guys like me couldn't get at it." He seemed, for Zack, to be unusually philosophical and perhaps, though Morgan could not be sure, he meant this to be something in the nature of an apology. "I only hope you didn't go into this thinking you had to do me a favor because of the old days."

Morgan glanced around, found Zack watching him with a canny and suspicious expression, and laughed. "You know why I went into it."

"There's no god-damn reason to pay any attention to what the federal government says about Indians; we live with the bastards, they don't. The federal government didn't encourage us to hang the road agents, either, but there wasn't any other way to get rid of them that anyone could figure out and, naturally, a few guys got it who shouldn't have. If the government would leave us alone, let us peddle this rotgut they're so thirsty for, our Indian troubles would soon be over. In two years we would make women of them. I may not ever brag about this, any more than Pete or your old man or Lem Finney are bragging about what they did with the Vigilance Committee, but don't get the idea I'm ashamed of it. I'll keep my mouth shut for my own good, and yours, and if I've got any regrets it's only because whisky is slower than rifles—but, you can bet, it's just as sure."

"Just be careful, Zack—if there is any way to be careful when you get out there alone with them."

"Don't get caught?"

"Don't get killed."

"I haven't got a worry in the world, Devlin, not a worry in the world. A man spends his life getting ready for whatever he's doing on whichever day you happen to run into him, and when those Indians run into me, that's what I've been getting ready for—as much as for anything." He was silent a moment, gazing ahead. "I know this country. I know Indians and, believe me, the risks don't look very big to me. Just so I don't lose my medicine-bundle," he added and smiled, somewhat wryly, then reached out, pretended to catch something invisible, grasped it hard in his fist and slipped it into his pocket, where he gave it an affectionate pat.

A little before noon Zack said they were in the neighborhood which

had been agreed upon for the rendezvous, and instantly Morgan felt
the skin on the back of his neck begin to prickle. Zack assured him
again that they were quite safe, for even an Indian's imagination acquired the power of prophecy when whisky was involved, but he
continued to expect that momentarily arrows would begin to whistle,
war whoops would fill the air, and his only hope was to be dead before a squaw got her hands on him.

All at once a party of eight or ten young men sprang up from a
stream bed some distance ahead, appearing with that uncanny surprise and swiftness and silence which created terror and superstition
in white men, and signaled them to stop. They wore breech clouts
and leggings, blankets were wrapped about their bare chests, and as
Morgan and Zack approached they stared enviously at their big
horses. One of them, Morgan noticed with morbid amusement, had
strips of the American flag and strands of long blond hair plaited
with his own.

Zack talked to them in Blackfoot, using some signs when his
vocabulary required it, and looked as composed as if he had, actually,
spent his life getting ready for this moment. They argued for a few
minutes about whether or not Left Hand would meet them both,
saying they had been expecting only one white man, and at last Zack
wheeled his horse and shouted that unless Left Hand appeared immediately he and his partner would return to Benton and they could
go thirsty this summer.

At that, three of the braves rode off and the others remained with
Morgan and Zack, chattering with that animation which surprised
white men who had seen Indians only in the mining camps or forts,
and they presently returned with a man who wore a single feather,
the chief himself, as Zack indicated with a nod.

He and Zack exchanged solemn greetings and, after a moment,
dismounted to shake hands. He was tall and thin and hard-bodied,
with the look of pride and arrogance for which his people were
known and, as he waited for whatever Zack would do next, he watched
him steadily, without fear or admiration but only a kind of distrustful
curiosity.

But, at least, he was not painted for war and neither were any of
his young men, and this made Morgan more hopeful of getting back
to Benton eventually, if not by sundown as Zack had promised—for
the Indian had a liking for long and ceremonial conferences, and
when the discussion was to concern something so important as
whisky they might expect to palaver indefinitely while Zack tried to
find out how rich they were in pelts and horses, how many more
they were prepared to steal, what assurances of protection they
would give him, and how much whisky he might trust them with at
one time.

Zack now became so grave and so haughty that Morgan observed
him with wondering fascination, for these were accomplishments he
had never imagined, and Left Hand himself was no more formal

than Zack as he stalked over to where his horse grazed, brought forth a pouch and, as the chief's eyes began to glitter with anticipation, made him so long a speech Left Hand seemed to despair of ever receiving the gift, ten pounds of tobacco. Still, he did not move, faced Zack with that same remorseless stare, and when at last Zack extended it, he held up both hands and bowed his head in the sign for thanks Lilly Jones had given the first night she came to their cabin.

They sat cross-legged in the grass to smoke, and, as the pipe with its garland of braided cloth was passed to Zack, he took it with the same fine stateliness and a disdain for his health which Morgan observed with amusement and some concern and which, when his own turn came, he tried to imitate.

Zack then brought forth a sample of his wares, a flask he gave to Left Hand, and Morgan noticed the flashing gleam which lighted the eyes of the young men who watched, as if in profound agony, while their chief raised it to his mouth, drained it, greedily smacked his lips, and asked if there was more. Zack shook his head, the conference began and, for more than two hours, while Left Hand rested on his haunches and whittled, Zack talked to him, sometimes fell silent and seemed so resentful of the chief's arbitrariness he was about to leave, and it was midafternoon when they again shook hands and started for Benton, with Zack muttering that they must not look back but ride as if they were neither scared nor distrustful.

They had gone several miles before Zack reined in his horse, turned and studied the countryside in all directions, and suddenly laughed, clasped Morgan on the shoulder as he had sometimes done in Butte, so that it seemed their friendship was at last repaired and had, after all, survived whatever damage either Lisette or Matt might have done it. "Couldn't have been simpler, could it? I'll take a small supply with me, and if they don't give me any trouble I'll go in with the whole shipment later."

James Gordon, they found, had met one of their fellow passengers in a poker game and concluded that he was a professional gambler. Three new boats had arrived and their own was by now so laden with hides and crates that it had sunk deep into the water and looked as if it might not keep afloat. But still the deck hands continued to run across the planks, carrying aboard trunks and carpet-sacks belonging to the cabin passengers, who wandered about inspecting their quarters; and they were, Morgan noticed, when he locked the samples of ore in his cabin, the same conglomerate assortment he remembered on his trip up the river eight years before. There was a sound of fiddles from the deck below and the pilot strutted about, idle and pompous, while the captain was obliged to help the deck hands. The saloon had once again been hung with colored tissue paper, and every now and then the furnaces were fired, bells rang and steam puffed from the funnels, warning them to be aboard at two o'clock the next day.

Morgan had bought an embroidered buffalo robe as a gift for Suky, and it had caused him much concern to have it smell no more like a wild animal than necessary. He had asked the squaw who sold it to him to hang it in the open air for a day or two, but when he returned from the conference with Left Hand and went to smell it again he told her she must smoke it or somehow make it stink less, asked her to embroider it with more porcupine quills, and at last carried it aboard and threw it on the floor, thinking that if it did not improve during the voyage he would engulf it in perfume when they reached St. Louis. With this, the last of his errands accomplished, he set out for Ford's Exchange, intending to treat himself to a dance with Silverheels, and whatever more one hundred dollars might persuade her to, by way of celebrating his safe return; and he sought out the proprietor to open negotiations for him.

She leaned back upon his arm as they danced, smiling confidingly, and when they went into the curtained cubicle she seated herself astride his legs, unbuttoning her dress to expose taut breasts, and as his hands closed over them she put her mouth against his, sighing deeply as he thrust into her body and sliding her hands about his head and into his hair. In a few minutes she had refastened her dress, and he walked down to swim in the river near the end of the levee, wondering if the peculiar intensity of delight had been because of the girl or if, more likely, it was a response of simple relief at finding himself alive and still able to enjoy such pleasures.

The next afternoon Morgan and Zack and James Gordon hung at the railing and watched the other passengers come aboard, speculating on who they were and what kind of companions they would make for the next two or three weeks. At last the whistles began to shriek, the paddle wheels turned and stopped and began to turn again, and they were surprised to see one last passenger mincing daintily up the plank, a young woman in a black alpaca traveling dress and black pork-pie hat, who looked at no one but kept her eyes cast down, and Sir James murmured that this prudent female was no one but Silverheels. They turned to watch her but could see no silver on her black shoes, there was no silver ribbon in her hair, and even her breasts, compressed by the stiff black gown, looked smaller. They shrugged and agreed that it might be Silverheels, for they could not remember her very well, or again it might be someone else.

The wheels were churning more strenuously, the boat shuddered as with a sudden uncontrollable chill, and as the officers shouted and bells rang, it moved slowly out into the river, creaking and shaking, and they noticed that it was riding with the water at its deck level. Sir James and Morgan glanced at each other and smiled with the condescension of seasoned and cynical travelers, resigned to whatever was in store for them. The cannon at the fort sent echoing shots of farewell into the clear, bright air, and before they had gone one hundred yards downstream it seemed they had been forgotten by those who stood on the levee. The three of them turned, abandoning this mountain city, walked into the saloon and sat down to drink.

Zack slept in Morgan's cabin that night, and when the boat drew up to Cow Island the next afternoon they were observing a studious and deliberate silence and bade one another good-bye with such grimness that bystanders might have imagined they were three men parting only in time to avoid a fatal quarrel. Gordon and Morgan stood on the cargo deck, watching as the two crates were put ashore, and Morgan saw three of the young Indians they had met with Left Hand, staring at the crates with the avidity of long-deprived men unexpectedly shown into the presence of a naked woman. Zack walked down the plank, raised one hand in a brief salute, the boat began to move, and Morgan and Sir James returned to the bar. "I say, I hope he's not doing anything reckless."

"So do I," Morgan agreed. But then he told himself that if he was going to spend the next several months worrying about Zack, he should not have agreed to his own share in the venture, and so settled himself to endure as well as possible the twenty-five-hundred mile journey down the river which only the children and James Gordon expected to enjoy.

The boat jiggled insistently and was quiet only at night when they tied up at a bank; but all day long it shook and quivered and seemed so much alive that they discussed it as if it were either a human being or an animal. The hull's vibrations and the noise of the engines made it difficult to read and almost impossible to write letters or, as Sir James tried to do, keep a journal; for he believed that if he did not take immediate note of his impressions they would be gone forever and, with them, this moment in time when an entire continent seemed to be moving, shifting ceaselessly from place to place, and convinced that any move whatever must be an improvement. It was his belief that travel was now a part of the nation's religion, and change itself was perceived as a form of progress, undertaken not for a whim but in obedience to some command upon the people to move to another farm or town, and rest there for a time, content at having progressed that much farther.

"Progress, old boy," he said to Morgan, "is a matter of space with you. Space and activity."

Even Silverheels, they presently discovered, was deeply involved in the national mania for progress.

They did not see her the first night, and it was not until after Zack had gone ashore at Cow Island that she found them in the pilot house with several other passengers, watching the pilot outwit the river. He had been frightening the children by pointing to the graves along the shore, for the Missouri, he said, was a graveyard that stretched from St. Louis to Fort Benton, and a lesser pilot would have capsized them on that raft of sunken trees they had passed only two minutes ago. Morgan had asked all the questions he could imagine on their trip up the river and he had no more to ask now, but James Gordon was greedy for information and as well pleased with a lie as the truth, and so was engrossed in conversation with the pilot when she peeked in, still wearing the constricting black dress and pork-pie hat.

Morgan stood smoking and watching the river banks as they glided along. They were surrounded by vast grassy plains, almost treeless, with a few cottonwood groves here and there along the high banks, and in the daylight the river appeared to be only a wide and crooked streak of boiling mud, impossible to penetrate, upon which it seemed they merely skated.

She had come close before he noticed her, and when she whispered, "Hello," he turned with surprise.

As he looked at her he had no conviction that here was a girl whose body was familiar to him, but rather that he was meeting a stranger, and she seemed so timid and uncertain that he smiled encouragingly. "Hello."

In the sunlight her hair was nearly blond and her skin smooth and unpowdered so that the freckles on her nose and cheeks showed plainly, and she looked not at all like a girl who would be suspected by other women of leading a frivolous life but would, no doubt, be mistaken for the daughter of an Army officer or Fort Benton merchant, being sent east to a girl's seminary.

"Where's the other one?"

"Gone ashore. Why?"

"No reason, I thought you were traveling together. Where are you going?"

"I'm going to New York. My friend is going home to England."

"England," she whispered, and looked carefully at Sir James, as if the place might be imaginary. "I'm going to Chicago. Have you ever been there?" As she asked the question she looked at him with the same careful inquiring expression she had turned upon Sir James, and he thought that certainly in her high-necked dress and small hat, twirling her parasol and whispering, too demure even to speak in an ordinary voice, it did not seem likely she could be a girl who went into small booths to dance the can-can and sit astride her customers like a squaw on a pony. "My name is Ruby Howard," she told him confidingly and waited a moment, apparently to let him accuse her of also being called Silverheels if he meant to.

"Mine is Morgan Devlin."

She whispered behind her hand: "I've retired." He showed no surprise at this news, and she added, "I'm going to Chicago to open a house with a friend of mine. I spent one year at Ford's Exchange and I made almost twelve thousand dollars. I don't have it with me," she added quickly. "I sent it by Wells Fargo." But then she seemed to suspect that for all his sober and respectful face, he might be working some quick arithmetic, and she opened her eyes wide, sighing. "I don't know how it happened. It just seemed that I got to be a rage, everyone wanted to dance with me. Maybe it was the silver shoes and silver ribbon—I can't account for it any other way." She gazed up at him. "Can you?"

Sir James joined them, and she told them she was lonely and
frightened and asked them to take care of her, which they promised
to do, for in fact she seemed, now that she had retired, to have become suspicious of men and had a constant expectation of being
molested, visited in the night by some thief or murderer, and she
pointed out to them several dubious characters who infested the boat,
nudging them as they sat with her in the Ladies Saloon or walked
about the deck. The preacher, she said, was a road agent in disguise,
the woman gambler was really a man, and the Indian who had come
aboard the day before was leading them into an ambush farther
downstream where they would all be scalped and left to rot with their
bellies ripped open and their entrails wrapped about their necks.

When she was not entertaining them with her suspicions and the
identities she gave each passenger, never accepting them for what
they said they were but seeing through their disguises to the truth
which was, each time, an ugly one, she talked about how she would
furnish her house in Chicago and asked their advice, shot at birds
and animals under Sir James' instruction and, at night, when the
dining tables had been pushed aside and the waiters removed their
aprons to take up fiddles and banjos, she showed great pride in
being the boat's most popular dancer with men who expected of her
only that she dance the polka waltz, and she would smile at Sir
James and Morgan as she whirled by, asking them to share this
triumph, naïvely pleased that she should be sought after even with
her drawers on and no silver ribbon in her hair.

Presently they left the wide grassy plains to enter the Bad Lands
and now the passengers lined the railing all day long and half the
night, pointing and marveling to one another about this country they
lived in which, they agreed, must have more of curiosity and strangeness and incredibility about it than any other on earth.

They passed for several days through gorges where there rose
above them great red and yellow and black castles two or three
hundred feet high, glittering white walls marked by arches and windows and grottoes, moving slowly by a procession of ancient ruined
cities of weird design and perfect reasonableness. For they agreed
that there was nothing impossible in the terraces and shrines and
domes, pipe organs and forests of pilasters and parapets, garden
walls and ramparts and enormous petrified animals of some breed
never before seen and yet instantly recognizable, as were the massive forms of frozen vegetables. For once it was accepted that this
was the work of a whimsical architect who had been able to realize
his fancies on a tremendous scale, as the days passed and they saw
nothing else it came to seem that here was a creation more rational
than they were themselves in their peculiar clothes, while even the
boat which upon embarkation had been taken for granted became,
by contrast with such eerie splendor, a kind of excrescence upon the
river's surface, out of context with its surroundings, until finally it
had turned into a fairy vessel passing silently and briefly through

this giants' land, where some of them began to feel they were being watched from the castles and cities by those who had been here eternally and who were scornful and impatient of their intrusion. When at last they left the place behind, they were relieved, and sighed as they looked at one another, convinced for the first time in many days that, after all, they and their fellow passengers were fully human and the product of some weird but actual logic.

By the time they had been on the river three days the cabin passengers knew one another's names and faces and the occupations they professed, where they had come from and where they were going. No one, it seemed, had recognized Silverheels, but she asked them to pretend they were related to her lest the women passengers— many of them as suspicious as Ruby herself—begin to gossip, and Sir James volunteered to introduce her as his American cousin. She surprised Morgan by coming to his cabin two or three times late at night, and he supposed she visited Sir James on other nights, her way of paying for their protection.

When it was cold, as it often was, the passengers huddled about the stoves, wearing heavy overcoats and gloves and, whether pacing the deck or playing cards, eating or drinking or dancing, they all wore hats and looked as if they had come aboard only for a brief visit. The boat stopped wherever it was hailed, passengers were brought out in a yawl or climbed up a plank run in to shore, and every day there were new arrivals and departures, new faces to cause speculation among those who had embarked at Benton and, as the *Shiloh*'s oldest residents, now believed the boat belonged to them.

At Fort Charles a man had come aboard who gave his name as Rory Sims, but Ruby whispered that he was a professional gambler, although she could not explain how she had recognized him. For the first few days Mr. Sims either refused to play at all, merely standing by and watching the others, or wandered about talking to the passengers. But then he let himself be persuaded to play and, presently, was winning so consistently that other passengers were soon muttering about him and going to Captain Lennox with the complaint that there was a blackleg on the boat, and a gentleman could not have a friendly game without being fleeced. The captain assured them Mr. Sims was no professional gambler but a successful St. Louis merchant, and that if he seemed to be winning more often than he lost it was because he was an expert player, and either they should not test their skill against him or be willing to suffer the consequences.

But still the passengers grumbled and began to discuss methods of handling the situation themselves, since the captain was obviously an accomplice and they must either stop playing and while away the hours in boredom, talking to the women and staring at the scenery, or somehow rid themselves of Mr. Sims who did not, it was true, look as river gamblers were supposed to, sleek and well-dressed with diamonds and a thick gold watch chain, but was a slouching, sallow man with an apologetic manner whenever he won, as if he were truly sorry it had happened again.

Morgan and Sir James refused to play with him after two or three games, but others came to them with their angry complaints, and by the time Mr. Sims had been aboard for a week men were gathering in small groups and muttering to one another as they passed on the deck, arranging Mr. Sims' punishment while he sat, unaware, playing for stakes never so large as he suggested, but large enough that he was steadily accumulating other men's money.

Ruby soon guessed the men were plotting against Mr. Sims and asked so many questions that Morgan and Sir James agreed to tell her nothing at all, lest she take a feminine pity on him and warn him, for by now the men were as eager to punish Mr. Sims as they had been to hang the road agents.

Late one night, as the boat lay tied at the bank and pine-knot torches lighted the cottonwood trees, Mr. Sims was visited by seven men, Morgan and Sir James among them, who demanded that he open the door and kicked it open when he refused, seized him in his nightshirt, and, covering his mouth as he started to cry out, hurried him along the deck and down the stairs where the deck hands stood curiously staring, and sped him off the boat and back into the forest. There he fell to his knees, pleading with them not to kill him and promising to leave the boat at the next stop, and looked so piteous that Morgan and Sir James suggested they let him go, but a court was convened and the other five voted to have him flogged. At this, he began to scream and they bound his mouth, stripped him of his nightshirt and tied his hands to a tree, and had given him twenty lashes when a woman's voice began to shriek, and so, hastily, like a group of boys caught torturing a schoolmate, they untied him and left Rory Sims there, snatching up his nightshirt and searching for his wig and whiskers which had come off during the flogging. Someone brought his clothes and carpet-sack and threw them to him, and a guard was set to keep him from sneaking aboard again.

The next morning at breakfast everyone knew, as if there had been a bulletin board posted, that Mr. Sims had been beaten and left alone in the forest, still begging to be taken aboard as they had cast off in the early daylight, and though the women declared it a shocking and disgusting procedure, the men were as boastful as if it had been done by all of them and not by only seven, for at the last moment most of the others had refused to participate.

Ruby Howard scolded them and said it was a heathenish thing to have done, for he would die of exposure or be captured by the Indians. "Men are terrible," she declared, exasperated by their patient but unremorseful expressions.

"But, my dear," Sir James gently reminded her, "you know it's the custom of the country."

"But he looked so harmless."

Mr. Rory Sims was soon forgotten, and almost immediately they were swept by an epidemic of fishing, so that during the next several days from early in the morning until late at night, men and women and children lined the deck, dangling their improvised fishing poles, and some became so fanatic they refused to go to bed.

They had now entered a more luxuriant countryside of thick woodlands and many wildflowers, and occasionally they passed a settler's cabin where a barefoot woman sat rocking on the porch staring at them with such indifference she might have been living on a crowded city street and tired of the sight of her fellow men, for it was not often these women either smiled or waved, but only watched the boat's passage without wonder or curiosity and seemed to find nothing about its presence there—or her own—which was at all surprising or unexpected.

They had not yet begun to tire of their fad for fishing when, during the midday dinner, the boat scraped against a sand bar, sending a shudder over its frame, upsetting glasses and spilling plates into their laps, and as they glanced at one another in questioning alarm there came a jolt which made them leap up, crying out protestingly as the women snatched at their children, and the boat sank slowly onto the bar while the paddlewheels churned and the boilers sent forth clouds of steam in an effort to force it across. They came rushing out of the saloon, hung at the railings and chattered, and when the captain dashed by in a raging fury, he refused to answer their questions. The children ran about in eager excitement, and now that they knew they were safe, everyone prepared to go ashore as if it were, after all, a diversion which had been arranged to break the monotony of what, but for Mr. Sims' flogging, had been an unusually quiet and uneventful journey.

Ruby Howard ran to her cabin to get her shawl, other women went for sketchbooks, men brought rifles and fiddles and banjos, and while the crew were making preparations to grasshopper the boat over the bar they went trouping off, laughing as if it were an excursion into the park, and seemed to have forgotten they were still in a wilderness infested by wild animals and Indians.

The crew, with much commotion, began to set up the spars. Ruby and Sir James went prowling about the low hills, for Ruby was determined to have a stag's head to decorate her mantelpiece. The children were playing a new game, Flogging the Blackleg. Men gathered wood to start a bonfire at the river's edge and a group clustered near it, singing, while the crew bellowed and swore and had long since frightened away any game which might have been in the neighborhood. Nevertheless there were other hunters, too, and from time to time a shot cracked out but nothing was hit, only a meadowlark which one of the men shot by mistake and hid before it was discovered by the women. Presently the bartender began to bring them mint juleps and the party grew very gay, even though several dead buffalo had floated onto the bar and the stench of their swollen bodies filled the air like a palpable substance.

Morgan wandered from one group to another, watched the children at their game and talked to an artist, Alfred Hughes, who had set up his easel on the river bank to record "The Grasshoppering of the *Shiloh*," as he meant to title it. He had been traveling through the West for a year or more, painting and sketching, and though he admitted he had sold none of his work, Morgan now told him that if he would paint Ruby Howard into the picture with her foot on the head of a large stag, he would buy it.

It was late afternoon when, after several unsuccessful attempts, the boat began to lift slowly, easing across the sand bar upon spars which like crutches raised it into the air. The children had abandoned their games to watch, Ruby and Sir James returned with no trophy but a rabbit, and amidst a clanking and grinding of machinery, shrieking whistles and shouted commands, the *Shiloh* rose unsteadily, hovered, lurched, and then rose again; but before they had begun to cheer its successful ride across the sand bar, there was a trembling scream and one of the deck hands sank into the river.

They tried with every means they could invent to rescue him. Several crew members and two or three passengers went in and swam about beneath the boat and far out into the river's currents. Guns were shot off and, while the cook protested, loaves of bread were cast onto the water to make the body rise. But although they hovered about until sundown he was not seen again, and when at last they went aboard they were gloomy, each one thinking it might have happened to him, for even the fatalistic felt the river had some special malice in its heart for those who traveled upon it.

After supper, in memory of the drowned deck hand, the women decorated the saloon with bouquets of wildflowers they had picked during the afternoon and the preacher, the same whom Ruby had thought a road agent in disguise, delivered a eulogy upon the man whose first name had not been known so that he was obliged to refer to him as Mr. Brown as he described his good fellowship and willingness to undertake daring tasks, his self-sacrificing nature and fine musical voice, his courtesy to women passengers in whose hearing he never used rough language, and whatever other virtue occurred to him as becoming a man who had died a deck hand on a Missouri River steamboat, his family and friends unknown to any of them, for he had come aboard at St. Louis, been surly and uncommunicative, and it was the opinion of his fellow workers he had been either an Army deserter or an escaped convict. The women knelt on the floor, hands clasped and heads bowed, and the men stood holding their hats against their breasts, grimly staring.

"If only it hadn't happened," Ruby told them after the services. "I know that was a five-point buck I saw and I'm sure I could have hit him, too."

Sir James turned to her. "My dear, if you will accept it, I would be happy to make you a present of my finest specimen, and only ask that you promise never to forget this voyage we three have taken together, jolly comrades making their small contribution to a people's great migration." He looked solemn and bowed, so that Ruby blushed and seemed to think he was making fun of her, but gratefully accepted the stag's head with its impressive spread of mossy horns.

Presently they slipped into Kansas where, it was said, the West began—somewhere between its borders—and passed through swampy bottoms and rich valleys thickly populated with groves of walnut and oak and hickory. There were now many settlers' cabins, and these women often smiled or called a greeting, as if their more frequent contact with other human beings had preserved in them a livelier sense of community than was left to the isolated inhabitants of the upper river. Violent storms rocked the boat and churned the river to foam, sending clouds of whirling sand which drove them indoors while it dashed against the glass panes hour after hour and made the boat's invalid, a girl of fifteen traveling with her mother, fall into fits of coughing so terrible that several passengers predicted she would not last until they reached St. Louis.

The girl, whose name was Maud Mowbrey, had spent much time in her cabin, and until she was believed to be dying the other passengers had scarcely been aware of her, preoccupied as they were with the thousand details of the journey. Then, as the news ran over the boat that she was sinking rapidly, she began to have many visitors, most of them women who crowded her cabin day and night, made the air stifling with the smells of their clothes and bodies, and kept her from resting while they questioned her about how she felt and whether or not she was prepared to die.

Ruby Howard went often to see her and brought back bulletins on the girl's downward progress, though Morgan and Sir James suggested that Maud Mowbrey might benefit more from quiet and rest than from the babble of avid women. She described the girl's symptoms with the same morbid fascination she had shown each time they passed one of the platforms where a dead Indian lay amid fluttering rags and the usual companionship of magpies and crows, though her superstitious alarms had not prevented her from signing her name on a skull they had found one day in a deserted village and left there as a record of their passing.

"She's a strange girl," Ruby said, as they stood at the railing enjoying the evening appearance of the river and watching Alfred Hughes at work, for only then or in the early morning did the artist find it a subject fit for his brush. "Do you know," she whispered, "she refuses to discuss her death?"

Morgan scowled, and grew as angry with her as it seemed he could remember having been with the women who had gathered at his own bedside, expecting they might catch him in the act of abandoning life. "So would I."

"I say, why should she, poor thing?"

Ruby looked at them with her eyes wide and reproachful. "In order to prepare herself. Does she expect to meet God without any preparation?"

Morgan and Sir James stared somberly at her and at last Sir James asked, with an air of gentle solicitude, "My dear, do you?"

"Heavens, no, but then I'm not likely to, just yet."

"Why don't you leave her alone?" Morgan asked. "If she must die, at least don't make her listen to all that hypocritical crap about her immortal soul."

"That's a wicked thing to say." She glanced meaningfully at the sky, nodding. "I'd be careful, if I were you."

Morgan and Sir James agreed in her absence that not only Ruby Howard but the others, too, were disappointed as the days passed and Maud Mowbrey remained alive and still refused to admit she might die, only smiling at them gratefully for their visits and trying to make them discuss more cheerful subjects.

The patient's condition, however, did not occupy all their time, and one night they tied up at an Army post and several officers came on board to join in the dancing while, on the deck below, two of the hands fought a bare-knuckled fight and so many of the men crowded down there that the women sent word for their husbands to come back to the ballroom.

They had reached that part of the river where there were no more snags or rafts to be encountered and, after that, they traveled at night and woke in the morning to a different countryside. They paused briefly at many new young towns and several of the passengers complained they were tired of new buildings and would be glad to see again old houses and old streets, but most of them argued that newness in itself was a virtue and a sign of progress.

And then, quite surprisingly, for they had become reconciled to traveling forever on this boat, moving continuously down the river but never to arrive at any final destination, they came to St. Louis and went scrambling off, forgetting in their haste and excitement even to say good-bye to the friends and enemies who, only the night before, had seemed more important than any they had ever had, went dashing about the crowded levee where boats much bigger than the *Shiloh* were berthed side by side for a distance of two miles or more and where, in the confusion, porters snatched at their baggage and hastened away with it, carrying helpless travelers after them to hotels they had no wish to visit; and within a few minutes they had parted company with their recent companions and no longer cared whether or not Maud Mowbrey had made a proper peace with her soul.

Morgan and Sir James had to remain for a few days in the city,

Morgan to transact various commissions for Devlin Brothers, and Sir James to trace if he could the remainder of his horns and hides. Ruby stayed with them so that she might have their company on the train journey to Chicago, and they went directly to the Planter's Hotel where they sat down to stuff themselves with fried chicken and waffles, and grew more and more expansive and merry as they felt the effects of their escape from the bondage of the little boat.

Ruby left them in Chicago, and after they had seen her trunk loaded onto a hack and had arranged the stag's head and "The Grasshoppering of the *Shiloh*" on the seat beside her, they hurried to get back on the train while she hung out the window, waving and calling to them not to forget to visit her next time they came through Chicago, and as the train moved out they stood on the steps, waving back, and found they were rather relieved to be rid of her, too.

XXXVIII

Morgan sat on the Stetson House verandah, watching the traffic in and out of the hotel and inspecting every pretty woman who passed with keen interest, supposing that each one, as she came nearer, would prove to be Suky; but although he had sat there for nearly an hour while James Gordon had gone off on a ramble of his own, he had seen no one he knew, had begun to look gloomy and sullen as he brooded over the absurdity of wasting his time on a hotel verandah in Long Branch, and could not understand how he came to be here.

They had arrived in New York several days before, and almost immediately he had been displeased and irritable. The Chings, as he had known, were away for the summer and he had instructions to telegraph so they could reserve a room for him but, instead, he had found one reason and then another to stay in the city, and when he finally announced to Sir James that they would go to Long Branch the next day, they left without sending a telegram and, of course, he should not have been surprised when no one met them at the station, or when the clerk said the Chings and Van Zandts had gone to Shrewsbury Bay early in the morning.

The city had annoyed him unreasonably and he liked it no better than most pilgrims like the frontier towns. Indeed, whatever he liked there, he disliked here. The crowds and the fast pace at which they moved seemed pointless to him, for he could understand neither why so many people should congregate on one island nor why they should rush about so distractedly once they had. The unceasing noise, grinding of iron wheels upon paving blocks and cries of street vendors, strolling singers and whining beggars, made him long to add to the din his own protesting shout. It enraged him when he must leap out of the path of careening grocers' carts and public hacks and omnibuses. The extremes of wealth and poverty disgusted him as if he had never seen it before, nor would he admit that the Park was now quite pretty with its shaded walks and cages filled with singing birds, its bandstands and carousels and little ornate bridges; he would not even agree that it was a great city, but condescendingly assured his lordship it was only a collection of villages.

The intensity of his dissatisfaction and uneasiness mystified him for a day or two, until he was forced to admit, though not to Sir James, that he had returned after eight years to this place where he had been born, a species of greenhorn, clammy-handed and dry-mouthed at the prospect of once again confronting eastern ways and eastern manners. He remembered the old saying, so often quoted by Joshua Ching: "New York is the best place in the world to take the conceit out of a man," and though he smiled grimly to recall it, neither would he share that small joke with Sir James.

For it had shocked him to realize he had become envious of James Gordon, and he began to watch him surreptitiously, to see if he might discover just what had caused this new suspiciousness and disapproval—something, perhaps, which had been in his lordship's character all along, but which he had somehow overlooked. Or was it something Sir James might have concealed while they were in the West and only brought out now, like a new suit saved for this occasion?

Morgan had, as it happened, bought a new suit himself and he found it to be hot and uncomfortable, for it was made of stiff black broadcloth, inflexible as armor. The vest encased him unmercifully, the starched white shirt and high cravat seemed a further indignity, and to show his scorn for these foppish garments he had refused to let the tailor fit them properly, but had informed him with a menacing glare that he had other matters to attend to and his appearance was the least of his concerns. And indeed, he had always supposed that it was.

Sir James' appearance, on the other hand, had lately become of extraordinary interest to him, and although he had previously thought him a pleasant-looking Englishman, now he began to notice how fresh and rosy his lordship's skin was above his blond beard, how sleekly his hair was combed, how often girls and women looked at him with wistful admiration, and how quickly they responded to his smile and, it seemed, even to his accent, which was apparently more attractive to them than Morgan would have expected an English accent to be to an American woman. Then, too, he noticed Gordon's manner of slight self-deprecation, not at all humble, but a kind of compliment paid his hosts, as he took the entire nation to be, quite as if he might be visiting royalty, graciously prepared to spare them the discomfort of inferiority feelings. With all these charms, as well as his continuous comments about America for which, Morgan sourly observed, his countrymen had an insatiable appetite, he now foresaw that Sir James would be so interesting to his aunts and uncles and cousins they would scarcely notice that he had returned after all these years.

And once he had made this admission, he decided he might as well also admit that what he really feared was to see Sir James capture Suky's attention away from him, walk up and cup it into his hand as easily as if a languid bird had remained too long in his path. But the admission made him no more eager to see it happen and, in fact, he only grew increasingly critical of Sir James, and more angry at his own anger.

And now he sat waiting for Suky, convinced that if only he could catch sight of her unexpectedly, see her first from a distance, there would be no danger of making himself ridiculous by greeting her in confusion and dismay.

He had not sent a telegram because he did not want her to meet them at the Long Branch station, but even so he peered anxiously through the windows when he and Sir James arrived, just as a hard rain storm was ending, expecting she would be there anyway, and was surprised at the relief he felt when she was not. Nevertheless, he sat alert and erect as they drove along Ocean Avenue, searching the carriages that passed, trying to catch some identifying glimpse, and craned his neck after girls cantering by on horseback, so that he supposed Sir James must be amused to find an American more astonished by the sights of his native land than he was himself.

The unpaved streets were muddy sloughs and the salty air thick and oppressive, without a breeze from the ocean, so that the golden weather vanes stood motionless and flags hung limp and idle. On the lawns of the vast hotels, structures which looked almost as improbable, as turreted and spiraled as anything they had seen in the gorges of the upper Missouri, surrounded by beds of purple and orange and scarlet flowers which might have been mistaken for Oriental carpets thrown onto the grass, brass bands were playing the afternoon concert. At shooting galleries children aimed at Indian chiefs and elephants, while upon the steep and uncertain stairways which led down to the sea men and women were slowly toiling; but he did not find her among them either, and he felt a momentary pang when the clerk told him they had gone to Shrewsbury Bay.

"Mrs. Van Zandt expected you some time ago, sir. They left instructions that if you arrived in their absence, there is to be a Grand Hop tonight, and they want you to attend with them."

"I say, upon my word, this is a jolly good welcome—a Grand Hop," Sir James added quickly, as if Morgan might otherwise think he meant to be sarcastic about his neglectful relatives. "What a treat."

Morgan asked himself bitterly, as they followed the scampering porters up the outside staircase, if Sir James had the same enthusiasm for the customs and habits and accidents of his own country, but then was ashamed of this petty meanness, too.

He was disappointed to find that their rooms did not overlook the front of the hotel, for then he might have been able to watch her come in without any danger of being seen himself. And so, once Sir James had gone off to reconnoiter, Morgan nodding curtly as he stood on the upstairs verandah smoking a cigar and raging at the clerk for having put him there, he threw the cigar away and, as stealthily as if he were setting out to spy on an enemy, he slipped back down the staircase and went roaming along the hotel corridors.

He passed through the lobby and walked the length of the dining room, set with long narrow tables and what he guessed to be several acres of white linen, hundreds of glasses and thousands of knives and forks, where moss-covered baskets of billowing fern hung in every window. He went stalking along the verandah, glancing surreptitiously at chattering women who sipped drinks from pink and green straws, and he disapproved of their voices as being too insistent and of their expressions as too animated, for it could not be possible that life in Long Branch was so much more joyous than it was anywhere else, and although artificial gaiety had always offended him, now he took it as a personal affront. Suky, of course, had none of these hysterical mannerisms but knew how to be quiet, and this in itself seemed an extraordinarily graceful and soothing talent.

At last, having walked with pretended great purpose from one end of the hotel to the other and along the verandahs on every side, he sat down not far from where carriages were drawing up and a procession of men and women were entering the hotel, and all at once it seemed some incredible folly that he had permitted himself to be caught in this way with nothing to do but wait.

He watched various children, most of them accompanied by nursemaids in dark dresses and white aprons and caps, and tried to guess if any of them might belong to Suky. He observed with a scornful smile the young men and women playing croquet on the wet lawn and asked himself what else they did with their time, for it seemed he had now become as suspicious of all easterners and their activities as he had heard men usually did after a few years in the West. Several girls were shooting with bows and arrows, and when they missed the target their companions ran to pick up the arrows and gave them back with as much ceremony as Zack had shown in presenting the tobacco pouch to Left Hand; and this unexpected memory brought a powerful surge of homesickness, keener and more painful than he had felt when they had left for the Territories.

He thought of Zack, going ashore at Cow Island with only a glance over his shoulder, as if they might meet tomorrow or never again, perhaps at that moment dickering with Left Hand in some lonely place so far removed from this tableau of contrived gaiety that it seemed there could be no whisky peddlers and no Indians ready to tear off a man's scalp in a piece as neat and round as a silver dollar, in any world which also contained these girls and young men absorbed in their flirtations and croquet games. He thought of Lisette and Marietta, of Matt and Pete and his younger brothers and Jenny and, to his surprise, of Irene Flint sitting in her parlor wearing a wrapper in the late afternoon and drinking champagne. And then, it seemed, these memories restored him, and he sat with stoical patience, assuring himself that only the first moment would be awkward, for he had not yet been able to decide whether he would shake Suky's hand or kiss her and whether or not, if he kissed her, he might kiss her mouth or only brush lightly across the side of her face, and after that they would be, once again, friends and conspirators with nothing at all to fear from each other.

He set himself the task of thinking of other things, for the more he brooded about the meeting the more he dreaded it and, of course, the more likely he would be to betray himself to whoever was there to watch them—her husband, or Joshua Ching, or even Sir James Gordon, benignly beaming.

He began to pick out the prettiest girls, but even as he chose one for her stately walk and another for the quick, ardent smile she gave the young man who was with her, it occurred to him that these girls, too, were searching out husbands and determined to capture one before their short season of brilliance was gone, for it seemed they were yearning to please whoever looked at them, and must believe that future husband was even now hovering about and must not miss seeing them at their lively best.

And then, most surprising in the midst of this agitated femininity, a girl approached—accompanied, as he vaguely realized, by some young man—whose face was grave even though she was slightly smiling, and he watched with interest as she came nearer, noticing that her dark eyes, so large they seemed the most important part of her face, did not dart or glance about, searching for admirers, but gazed with a contemplative and rather baffling expression directly before her, while she listened to whatever her escort was saying.

She was tall and slender and her neck was so long and thin that her head seemed poised upon it with the uncertainty of a flower too heavy for its stalk. She was, he guessed, sixteen or seventeen years old, and because she was still so young he was all the more impressed by her air of composure and had again a sense of surprised delight when, at something her escort had said, she turned to him and her face became instantly warm and alert. He glanced enviously at the young man, recognized his cousin Steven Ching, and sprang out of the chair and went toward them, holding out his hand.

"Steven—it is you, isn't it?"

They shook hands, looking at each other with interest, and Morgan found that his cousin was now a young man of twenty-one, more supercilious than ever, and quite conscious of having fulfilled all predictions to become a striking replica of his father. And, even though Steven had never been his favorite relative, Morgan was now so pleased to find some member of the family that he greeted him as if he had made the journey only for the satisfaction of seeing him again.

"Miss Talbot," he heard Steven saying, "may I present my cousin, Morgan Devlin."

Morgan turned, eager to look at her again, close enough this time to find whether she was as unusual as he had thought, or whether it had been only one more of those mirages of feminine attractiveness which disappeared upon near inspection. She smiled at him, not that determined grimace which had troubled him on so many faces this afternoon, but a slow and somewhat reluctant smile, and lowered her eyes, creating the impression of having bowed in acknowledgment of the introduction, even though she had not moved.

Her eyes were as large and glowing as they had seemed from a distance, and looked back at him with candid interest, neither flirtatious nor self-conscious, and he found this oasis of her dignity a blessing and relief, making her seem a rare and marvelous creature because she, or someone, had had the judgment not to allow her to become another flirtatious and greedy belle, sucking hungrily at every compliment and nosing about for more.

"Suky's best friend," Steven said, and quickly, wondering if he had been staring at her with too keen interest, Morgan smiled in appreciation of this news, nodded as if to congratulate her on such good fortune, and then heard his name called in Ceda's tremulous voice.

He spun about, expecting to find Suky there but she was not, only Susan and Ceda, who had just driven up, and he ran forward, kissing them as they gathered together skirts and parasols, gloves and shawls, and stepped down into his arms.

"We were beginning to worry about you, Morgan."

"Have you seen Suky? She came back early, to get some rest."

As they started toward the hotel he found that Steven and Miss Talbot had disappeared, and they paused near the steps with the traffic streaming about them, while Susan and Ceda questioned him about their life in the mountains, for plainly they had believed nothing of what Marietta had written.

"Is Marietta very unhappy? Of course, she pretends to like it, but how can she?"

"You must persuade them to come back here, before it's too late. I've had the most terrible dreams, and you know, Morgan, my dreams are predictions."

"You have terrible dreams about us, too, Ceda," Susan reminded her, and Morgan gave an exultant laugh, caught hold of their hands and kissed them both again.

"I don't think I've ever been away," he declared in an outburst of affectionate enthusiasm, and was all the more surprised that it seemed to be true. For now that he was with them he could not imagine how he had let himself flounder into those deep fears of meeting Suky again, and felt that he loved them much more than he had known, for in truth he had almost forgotten them.

They began to discuss him, turning to consult each other from time to time, and he stood watching them and tenderly smiling.

"He looks more like Matt than I thought he would."

"Not at all, Susan, he looks much more like Pete. Around the eyes, especially."

"Whoever he looks like, he's become wonderfully handsome. Of course, Morgan, you always were. And your brothers?"

"We all look alike, Aunt Susan, you know that."

"Morgan, we simply can't believe that Pete got married again."

"But he's been married for four years and a half and their little girl will soon be two."

"I know, but somehow it isn't real to us. We knew Lorena so well, and he was so grief-stricken when she and little Matthew died. A new wife and another child—how strange."

"But then, we've all changed, haven't we?" Susan smiled, and her face had a kind of ironic humor, although she looked even more impressive than he had remembered, but that, of course, might be the effect of expensive clothes and jewelry.

A carriage stopped and Joshua, with two other men, approached them, shook Morgan's hand and looked at him with a shrewd and appraising curiosity, and seemed not altogether pleased that he had come back. For, as Morgan remembered, Joshua Ching did not like and had never liked the intrusion into his life of people or events for which he had not himself arranged, and had responded even to unexpected guests with a stiff resistance which had made them feel they must have intruded at some moment of family crisis. And, of course, Morgan always imagined that Joshua had been on guard to keep him and Suky apart.

"Mr. Talbot, and my son-in-law, Mr. Van Zandt."

Mr. Talbot and Mr. Van Zandt were looking at him as carefully as Joshua had, and it occurred to Morgan that in the East men were even more suspicious of strangers than they were in the Territories. For here was Suky's husband, a handsome blond man only three or four years older than he, scrutinizing him as if he might be a pickpocket, while the father of the pretty girl was staring at him coldly and no doubt asking himself if there was any possibility that his daughter would find him attractive. And here, Morgan understood, in the person of her father, was the reason why Felice Talbot had not become a gay and flirtatious belle, for this man would have been horrified to have such a daughter and must have forbidden her long ago to be frivolous, making sure she understood very early that life was a serious matter even for the daughters of rich men and, perhaps, more serious for them than for anyone else.

"I'm going to tell Suky you're here," murmured Susan, and touched his arm as if she were giving a confidence.

As they walked away he heard Ceda say, "Oh, wait until Suky sees him." But Susan pressed her hand in warning and they nodded in agreement not to speak again until they were inside the hotel. "Did you see Joshua's face?" Susan asked then. "He always thought they were in love."

Ceda frowned. "They were only children."

"They were almost sixteen when he left."

"Even so, Susan. Sixteen."

"Yes, Ceda, sixteen. A very good age for lovers."

Ceda paused. "Lovers?"

"For being in love, then." Susan started on and Ceda followed her. "Don't you remember the morning he left? Suky had been sick in bed for days, and the doctor came and she wouldn't take any of the medicine he prescribed? What do you think that meant, Ceda?"

"Only that she wanted to suffer and that was the first good opportunity she'd had."

"Ceda, you haven't learned very much about love through your observations, have you?" Susan rapped at the door. "But then, maybe that's no way to learn. May we come in?"

At Suky's reply, spoken in what seemed an unusually faint, high voice, even for her, they opened the door and were disappointed to find that Felice had arrived before them, for now they could not see what would happen to Suky's face when she heard the news, and the little messenger was, it seemed, rather guilty at having spoiled their surprise, for she stood at stiff attention against the wall, feet together and arms behind her back, and smiled apologetically as she greeted them and made two quick curtsies.

Suky had on a dressing gown and her hair was loose, so that Felice had perhaps come in while she was asleep, for it was Suky's habit to sleep an hour or two in the late afternoon in the belief that she was replenishing herself, and Susan had sometimes thought that Suky was so kind to herself, so generous and considerate, there seemed no reason she should ever grow old and she might even live forever. "Felice was telling me she just met Morgan." Suky smiled, but so vaguely that although Susan wondered what she was concealing she had no hope of finding out, and it seemed that she and Felice were waiting to resume their interrupted conversation. Ceda sat down, ready for a long and comfortable description of their guest, but Susan drew her away.

"Come along, Ceda, it's time to dress."

"I may not be down for supper, Mama. The boat made me rather queasy, I don't think I'll be hungry."

Susan smiled knowingly, Ceda urged her to take a thimbleful of Plantation Syrup, and Suky closed the door as Felice came swiftly forward and stood gazing at her, looking so joyous, and so troubled, that Suky put her hands to Felice's face. At that, Felice laughed softly, but then looked away. "Isn't it absurd, but you'd told me so much about him, I couldn't believe I was meeting a stranger." She looked at Suky again, and now her face was quite anxious. "Do you think that's ridiculous?"

"Of course I don't, Felice. There isn't any other way to fall in love, is there? It always seems as if you've known him all along—whoever he may be."

But, at that, Felice looked so ashamed that Suky walked to the dressing table, where she sat and looked at herself, finding a rather curious smile on her face and one she had apparently not been prepared for, for she studied it for several moments while Felice stood pondering her own perplexities. But then, as Suky began to sort among the china jars and the bottles with their gold and silver stoppers, sniffing at almond pastes and cucumber cold creams, Felice was beside her again. "Oh, but I didn't mean love. I only meant—" She was standing in back of Suky, and now she bent and stared across her shoulder into the mirror. "Is that what I meant?"

"Suppose you did, Felice?" Suky moved the boxes and bottles about, joining patterns with them, and seemed indolent and unconcerned, as if she was thinking about something quite remote from Felice's excitement. But then, as Felice continued to watch her in the mirror, Suky turned, catching hold of her hand. "Are you my friend again, Felice?"

"Again, Suky? I've always been your friend."

Suky looked at her seriously and accusingly. "Are you sure? Sometimes I've thought you didn't trust me."

Felice grew more confused and tried to draw away, but Suky held her, and finally Felice knelt, looking up at her with a pleading and humble expression. "You know you're dearer to me than anyone in the world, Suky, anyone at all in the world. You've been my friend ever since I was a little girl and I've always worshipped you—you know that." Felice's voice sounded tragic as she pleaded her case, but Suky only continued watching her with that same rueful and ironic smile. "Why should you say such a thing?"

"Because I thought you didn't."

Felice began to protest again and grew so distraught she put her forehead against Suky's knee and Suky stroked her hair, to calm her, for it was true that Felice distrusted her, and true that ever since Felice had come back from Europe a year ago she had been strange in her presence, wary and doubtful, as if she had made some discovery she dared not mention, and perhaps had not quite dared admit even to herself. What she had discovered, of course, was that her friend and her cousin were lovers, but whether Felice had overheard some conversation between them, or some gossip among the servants, whether Coral might have given her a hint which Felice had been ingenious enough to solve, or whether it was only Felice's sensitivity to faces and voices and the feelings which were thought to be well concealed, neither Suky nor Frederic had been able to learn; and yet Suky saw it in Felice's manner, as if they had betrayed her by having for each other a different kind of love from the one she had believed they should have.

Felice still seemed at times to be as feverishly idealistic as she had been four years ago, when she had carried messages back and forth between them, but she had also developed an inclination to fall silent and to seem preoccupied with thoughts she would not discuss and, at such times, Suky would be alarmed to find Felice watching her with a look of brooding skepticism, for it almost seemed Felice might be asking how she had the heart to deceive those who trusted her, and to look so innocent while she was doing it.

But Frederic did not agree that Felice was suspicious of them. "She's a young girl, after all, and young girls think deep thoughts, but I doubt if any of them are about us. She has her own feelings to consider nowadays, and they must be very interesting to her."

Nevertheless, Suky was eager, for her own sake, to have Felice fall in love, and that was the first question she asked when Felice came home from Europe, but Felice had laughed and seemed to think the question was not meant seriously. "I was forbidden to fall in love before I left. Father says I'm not to marry a foreigner, no matter who he is."

"No beaux?" She had looked at Felice with a meaningful smile, and asked her coaxingly, "Not even one?"

"Not even one."

"But what did you do all that time?"

"Oh, there was enough to do—operas and ruins and churches and concerts and museums and fittings. I wasn't bored, and of course I never get lonely. I've been alone too much for that." Felice had shrugged a little and, Suky thought, given her that distrustful and mysterious smile which made her feel that the young girl who had gone away, mourning that she would not see her for one whole year, had never come back, but had sent someone else she called Felice Talbot instead.

And now here she was, kneeling with her head bowed against Suky's knee, and Suky whispered, "Wouldn't it be strange if it should be my cousin you fell in love with?"

Felice looked up quickly and her face showed as much rapturous devotion as it ever had before she had begun to divide her sympathies between her idol and her idol's victims. "But Suky, if I should fall in love with him that would be partly why, because I love you so much. The first time I saw you, I wanted more than anything in the world to be your friend—and you let me be your friend. And you know, I could almost have fallen in love with him without ever seeing him, you'd told me so much about him."

"I had?" asked Suky doubtfully, and saw that Felice was now yearning to be overcome by love, very much as she let herself be overcome by the waves beating upon the beaches, and must go plunging into them again and again, until at last she came staggering out looking as if this rapture of combat and submission was more than she could endure.

All at once, Felice threw her arms about Suky, held her fast for a moment, and sprang up. "Suky, if I ask you a question, will you promise to tell me the truth?"

"Of course I will, Felice. I've never lied to you, have I?"

"No, you haven't, I know you haven't." She spoke so urgently she might even have begun to mistrust her own suspicions. "What if I should fall in love with him? I don't mean that I will, but if I should —would you be pleased, or not?"

"I'd be pleased, darling, you know that." Suky smiled. "But don't you think you might wait until you've danced with him a time or two?"

Felice laughed with such bright gaiety that it was plain enough she had no need to dance with him or even to speak to him, for she was letting it happen, moment by moment, until no doubt the process would be complete by the time she went downstairs to the ballroom. "I must dress." She ran across the room, then dashed back and kissed Suky. "Which one shall I wear?" But before Suky had answered, the door opened, Philip came in, and she ran off to make that first decision for herself.

Philip, it seemed, was in a petulant humor. He glanced at her with a sharp and disapproving suspiciousness, but said nothing, and thrusting his hands into his pockets began to roam about the room and presently went out to the verandah.

Suky saw him standing there, surveying this summer domain of his into which the intruder had just entered and, no doubt, wondering what accusation to make first. She brushed her hair, buffed her nails and tried a variety of smiles to find the one she wanted to show Morgan, and when she heard Philip's laugh, pleased to have caught her, she raised her eyebrows and shrugged, not at all disconcerted.

"I met your cousin just now."

"So did Felice. Did you notice how distracted she was?"

He stared at her and might have been trying to find out how distracted she was, but she had lied to him so often Suky thought he was not likely to be able to guess any longer when she was telling the truth. "What brought him back here?" Philip asked her crossly.

"I've told you. He's come to study."

Philip smiled. "And to persuade your father to finance his gold mine?"

"I don't think he expects that."

She approached Philip and brushed her fingertips across his mouth, teasing him to smile at her, but Philip pretended to be sternly indifferent, an aggrieved husband who wanted to discuss his grievances, though presently he followed her into the bed, where he always imagined he would teach her this time that his will was indomitable and, each time, she somehow eluded him. For in spite of the sighs she gave and the soft, moaning cries, pleading and remorseful, as if the intensity of feeling was nearly unendurable, once he left her she would fall asleep like a comforted child and wake an hour later or the next morning, surprised if she found him there.

He was gone when she awoke this time and she got up quickly, thinking she might have slept too long, missed the Grand Hop and her meeting with Morgan, and was relieved to find it was not quite nine o'clock. She bent to the mirror, for it was Suky's conviction that a woman's looks were improved by voluptuous pleasure; it made her eyes shine, she thought, polished her skin and softened her mouth, and gave her expression something at once inviting and enigmatic.

She was still hovering there, trying to imagine how different she would look to Morgan after these years that had passed, when the hotel maid arrived with hot water, and by the time Maxine came she was manipulating stick pomatums and camel's hair brushes and had fallen into a reverie Maxine did not venture to disturb.

From time to time she laughed a little, remembering how they had met to make their plots—whatever they were—in the latticed summer house, where the roses, though they were soon gone, seemed in her memory to have lasted the whole summer long. And whether he had fallen in love with other girls, or whether he might presently fall in love with Felice, she believed he was still sworn to her, she might ask whatever she chose, and, what was more, she might trust him. For she trusted no one else and indeed had so many reasons for distrusting not only Philip and Coral Talbot, but Joshua and Susan, even Frederic—everyone she knew, in fact— that she sometimes thought her life was approximately as precarious as a street beggar's.

"Madame," said Maxine at last, "looks so *spirituelle* tonight."

"Oh?" asked Suky, for even Maxine knew her too well by now, and she had Joshua's preference for keeping those who loved her at a convenient distance just when they imagined themselves on terms of perfect confidence.

The white gauze gown was hooked. Suky gave the skirt a sweep up and down the room, and as she sprayed her hair and shoulders with tuberose perfume, Maxine remarked in her soft, sad voice, "Sometimes, so I've heard, there's a special kind of love between cousins."

Suky had nothing to say to that, only gave Maxine one of her warning glances, plucked a white rose from the vase on the dressing table, and set off down the empty hallway, walking swiftly, until at last, with a keener sense of excitement than she had anticipated, she began to run. She had sent a note asking him to meet her on the far side of the south verandah at ten-thirty, in a place quite remote from the dancers and promenaders, and as she paused to catch her breath, she saw that he stood there, his back to her, and moved toward him with light stealthy steps, intent on taking him by surprise, according to their old habit. The night had become warm and the wind was down, though a brominic smell of stranded weeds came from the ocean, and the night itself might have been a part of all their reminiscences.

When she was quite near, she paused. "Morgan?"

He turned, slowly, as if he thought she would not be there, after all, and they advanced toward each other, solemn as children playing some sacred game, walking almost hesitantly, until Suky extended her right hand, fingers straight, palm upward, and, after a moment, he covered it with his right hand, palm downward. She brought forth their ancient symbol of silence, the white rose she held behind her back, and extended it, and at that he caught hold of her and kissed her mouth with such fervor that when he let her go she stared at him in bewilderment, as if she had shut her eyes and collided with a wall, been knocked down and must be helped to her feet again.

"Why, Morgan, you aren't the same any more."

He laughed, and it seemed that her surprise pleased him. "Neither are you." His hands were spread across her back and he drew her toward him, then released her abruptly. "I've brought you two presents. A buffalo robe and an English knight—which do you want first?"

XXXIX

"The glutton sits down to the feast with a very good appetite." Matt spoke in a low reflective voice, humorous and bitter, but Jenny lay motionless and, presently, she began to cry, though the sounds were muffled, as if she had covered her mouth and hoped he would not hear her or, at least, not try to comfort her. He got into his clothes, groping in the darkness, and the smothered sobs continued for, he supposed, she must be regretting at this late moment whatever impulse had sent her into his office that morning, murmuring as she passed him, "Come tonight, Matt—I've got to talk to you. Please?"

She did not wait for an answer, but went out, giving him a glance over her shoulder which had abolished in a moment all his recent carefully wrought pretense of being able to find as much happiness in the contemplation of another man's good fortune as if it were his own.

For until that moment he had honestly believed that he had not been alone with her for nearly a year only because he had made a conquest of himself at last. The raw, restless cravings of the past, galling him into new indulgences and penalties, he was sure would never stir in him again. And if it should happen that some chance smile or tone or gesture of hers might begin the old invasion working, then he found mockery the best medicine for his ailment, and he had made a lavish use of it, dosing himself liberally whenever it seemed there was no other help for him.

But there he was, wandering about the neighborhood at eleven o'clock on that same night, impatiently waiting for Erma Finney and Margaret Webb to leave, enraged they should have chosen this night to pay one of their unexpected calls, and attributing the coincidence to Erma Finney's intuitive talent for interfering between him and Jenny. He thought of interpreting their presence as an omen that this meeting was not meant to take place, and he might have left if they had not come out when they did; though it was more likely, of course, he would only have walked to the bottom of the hill and come tramping back up again, determined to defy Erma Finney and everything she represented.

Jenny let him in and touched her finger to his mouth to caution him, whispering that Leila was wakeful. She ran up the stairs, giving him once again that urgent and imploring look which had brought him there, and he heard the door to Leila's bedroom close.

For half an hour or more he was left to sit rigidly on the sofa, afraid to move for fear Leila would hear him and demand an investigation, and while he waited he stared at one part of the room and then another, taking as careful an inventory, he wryly reflected, as if he expected to inherit it and live there himself one day. Jenny seemed to think that changes in her house were likely to disturb the memories she was preserving there, as carefully as she preserved the wax flowers under their glass dome, and so it looked almost as it had the first day he saw it; indeed, the only changes seemed to have been made by Leila or for her.

The books they read to her were on the table, two dolls sat side by side in the chair which Pete usually occupied, and she had left a tiny gold locket on the couch where he found it with surprise, started to pick it up, but then withdrew his hand as guiltily as if he had meant to steal it. For it was Leila who had made it so difficult for him to think of Jenny as his own possession and it was, he guessed, because of Leila that his resolutions were more often kept nowadays. It even seemed he admired Jenny most whenever he saw her with Leila, who was her miniature, a beautiful and merry child with black hair which Jenny wound into a single loose coil that hung down her back, her eyes as green as her mother's, and her black eyelashes so long that every glance seemed to have a calculated coquetry in it.

At last, unable to control the impulse any longer, he picked the locket up and examined it on all sides, dangling it by its chain and smiling, and then opened it to find Leila's picture on one side and Pete's on the other, and he snapped it together and put it back on the sofa. This, he told himself, was the second omen, and it was time for him to go.

He stood up and found himself hovering there, his heart beating hard, and as he tried to find some reasonable explanation why this should be so, shrewdly smiling at his own dishonest naïveté and assuring himself he was the same unprincipled rascal he had always been and his resolutions good for nothing but temporary disguise, the bedroom door opened and he gave a start, expecting to find Pete there. He ran into the vestibule and Jenny stood at the top of the stairs, looking down at him and smiling.

She had no secret to tell him, as she had suggested, and had almost nothing to say until he bent to kiss her good-bye, when she touched his face, murmuring, "Matt, it was never fair for me to marry him."

"Don't say that!" He gave her shoulder a rough shake. "You're happy together." He felt himself grinning viciously in the dark, as if at some adversary, and he scowled and put on a solemn look.

"He knows about us," she said. "Sometimes I find him watching me—and I know exactly what he's thinking. I almost denied it once."

"Guilty people have lively imaginations," he told her, and wondered at how it was he should be so little concerned at her concern.

But then, to his dismay, Jenny began to laugh, and when he shook her again, afraid that Leila would come in to learn what was wrong with her mother, Jenny only laughed more uncontrollably, so that he crossed the room, eager to escape before that laughter brought on some real disaster.

"Good night, Jenny." He closed the bedroom door and stood for a moment, listening intently, then started down the stairs and, when he reached the bottom, drew a deep breath, and was suddenly eager to be out of the house. He moved cautiously into the vestibule, groping over the rack of antlers for his hat and coat—and became aware that someone else was there.

He peered into the dark mirror, assuring himself he was mistaken, that he was alone, and in another moment would have found the coat and would be out of the house and free of it once and for all. The coat had been left hanging there, he was sure of that, but he could not find it and was so reluctant to go into the living room that he assured himself it would be more sensible to leave without it and think of some plausible lie for traveling about on a cold April night with no overcoat.

Guilty people, he reminded himself, have lively imaginations, and he groped about rather noisily, knocking against one prong after another in search of his rightful belongings, and swearing beneath his breath. Then all at once he stood rigid and stopped breathing, thinking he might catch the other, if he was there, moving nearer to him, preparing to attack, but still he hesitated to draw his pistol for, of course, he was convinced that the man who stood behind him, just inside the living room door, was Pete.

He dropped both hands to his sides, waiting and listening and still staring into the mirror, and felt a sense of resignation as uncanny and profound as he had heard overcame the road agents at the moment they confronted their captors and knew they would soon be dead. And in this dazed condition of numb peacefulness he could not tell if he stood there for a few seconds, a minute or two, or perhaps a very long time, as each tested the will and courage and patience of the other.

At last, convinced he might be alone, after all, Matt felt a kind of sliding ease move throughout his chest, into his arms and legs, a lifting and exquisite triumph which turned him, for the moment, benevolent and self-righteous. He walked the two or three steps to the door, took hold of the knob, and was caught by a blow across the side of his head of such force that he grunted with protesting surprise, his knees gave way, and as he slipped toward the floor, still convinced this was happening only in his imagination, a man's body leaped upon him, fingers clasped his throat, and they fell, locked fast together, heaving and thrusting as they struggled in a perfect silence.

The man lay upon him heavily and Matt tore at the fingers until he had pulled them free, drew in a deep gasping breath, and they closed about his throat again, pressing deeper, until the blood swelled into his head and seemed ready to burst through his mouth and ears. He had a thought that presently he would be dead, and, though it seemed momentarily beguiling, he began struggling to push him off, but the other clung fast, embracing him with his legs and smothering him beneath his chest, holding him with such tenacity and power it seemed he must die to be free of him.

At last he lay still, and felt himself to be swimming effortlessly in a warm stream, half-drowned, and was willing to stay there forever, never breathe in air again or fight against gravity, and when he opened his eyes was astonished to see Jenny standing above him, wearing a long white nightgown, with a candlestick in one hand and Leila's silver-plated pistol in the other, and at sight of this apparition he slowly sat up as she closed the door.

"I saw him," she said, though he could not imagine what she might be talking about.

He got to his feet and leaned against the wall, his head hanging as he stared in stupefaction at his booted feet. Jenny set the candle down, locked the door, and folded her arms about him, holding him until he longed to thrust her away,too.

"It was Pete," she murmured. "He looked up just as I started down the stairs."

He shook his head, put his hands against her shoulders and moved her aside, pleadingly, for it seemed he might be smothered by her closeness and die there, after all. "Are you afraid to stay here alone if I leave now?"

"Of course I'm not—but you can't go, Matt. He's waiting for you."

He smiled, with an incredulous and pitying look. "Whoever it was, Jenny, it wasn't Pete, he isn't waiting for me and, if he is—" His muscles quivered and his legs were unsteady as he walked, but he went back to the living room, found his hat and overcoat, and paused as he slid the coat on. "Lock the door. Go back upstairs."

"You can't go out there, Matt!" She seized his arm and he drew angrily away but then, ashamed, turned and spoke to her gently.

"Go to bed, Jenny, it was some sneak thief, I recognized him. He's been hanging around town the last few days," he added positively. "I'll report him tomorrow." It seemed to Matt that he was so remarkably calm, so reasonable and self-possessed, and so well convinced he was telling the truth, that he could only pity her, for in fact he thought she looked quite demented. "It's almost daylight, he won't be back. He didn't hurt me—just a little scuffle. No harm's been done."

He smiled, meaning to encourage her, and although she tried again to keep him there he pulled himself free and went out, waited until he heard the key turn, and set off toward town, walking slowly, listening carefully, and it seemed his senses revived in the cold air until all at once he paused, stricken with wonderment that when Pete had decided to kill him he should have gone about it in that way, when he might have killed him very easily with a gun or a knife; but, perhaps, he had dreaded to spill his blood. He shook his head, marveling over this as if it were some natural curiosity he had discovered while he was searching for something else. At last he walked on, reflecting with even greater wonderment on how little terror he had felt and how little determination there had been to save himself, only surprise and disbelief and some physical resentment at the pressure of the man's body, weighting him to the floor.

On the main streets several buildings were still lighted, a few men were wandering about, and he heard music which seemed to grow more discordant as the night wore on and the musicians got drunker. He walked to the Devlin Brothers building, unlocked it, and, without glancing about, went in and sat down at a desk near the door, once again keen and alert, for he supposed this was where he and Pete had agreed to meet and that presently Pete would come walking in. But then, after he had sat there awhile, this began to seem as improbable as that it was Pete who had attacked him, and once again he began to believe his own lie about the sneak thief.

Finally he decided he had waited as long as he must to prove either to Pete or to himself that he was not hiding, and realized that he was eager now to see Marietta, as he had been only a little while ago to see Pete. He did not intend to sleep but found that he was very hungry and had a picture of the breakfast he would soon eat—a small rare steak, an omelet with oysters, perhaps some pancakes, many cups of coffee, and this ravenous interest in what he would put into his stomach seemed proof that the fight had, indeed, been only a scuffle, one brother's warning to another, for Pete had had all his life an occasional temper but a fierce one, and that he should have attacked him no longer seemed even slightly surprising.

And he was pleased to find as he rode along, winding up the hillside, that his habit of putting events into their most rational perspective had not deserted him now, for he was smiling to remember something that had happened the summer of his twelfth birthday and Pete's thirteenth, which they had spent at a farm visiting school friends. He had ridden off early one morning on Pete's pony, or the one given him for his own during that summer, and Pete was waiting in the barn when he came riding gaily back, having taken it for the entire day, although he had meant to keep it only a little while.

Pete had come rushing at him and they had fought for what had seemed most of an hour, rolling and tumbling about, never speaking but fighting so hard that at last they got up with eyes blackened and noses bloody, scratched and bruised and marked on every part of their bodies, and their clothes torn almost off. And yet that night they had slept together in the same bed, very quiet and peaceful—although Pete had not failed to remind him once again that he was not to take his pony without his permission, for he had lost all of a summer's day by it.

And how could it be possible that same boy should have tried only a few hours ago to kill him, Matt now asked himself in a spirit of disinterested philosophical inquiry, and replied in the same spirit that no man of Pete's judgment would kill another only because he had made him suffer, for they both knew well enough that one man might suffer unbearably at what would only cause another to shrug, or smile. But none of this—apart from the humorous episode of the pony—seemed to pertain to him or to his life, but only to certain abstract issues of violence and courage, loyalty and deceit, will and submission, for there could never again be anything so clear or so simple to be decided between them as that question of the pony, nor any such conviction that one had used the other unfairly.

He explained to Marietta that the man he had gone to see had been away, and he had decided not to wait for him but to ride back during the night, and when she made no objection to this story he went to shave and change his clothes and came out to eat breakfast, feeling refreshed and vigorous, as ready for this day as any other he could remember, for now that the night was past it seemed as weird, as unreal and vaporous, as some bad dream which had terrified him at the time but which he could now scarcely recall.

The usualness of everything that happened for the next half hour reassured him even more. Robert and Douglas were at the table when he came in, Annabel presently appeared, and he talked to them while they ate breakfast together, found a number of things for them all to laugh about, and when they left he still sat there, reading some newspapers which had arrived from New York, smoking a cigar and drinking coffee. Nothing, it seemed to him, could have gone very wrong in a world so reliably ordered, and so unsuspecting, and he began to enjoy a sense of luxurious well-being, for it no longer seemed possible that a few hours ago he had been ready to surrender his life without resistance.

Marietta carried the dishes to the kitchen, brushed crumbs from the tablecloth, and at last sat down and poured a cup of coffee, sipped it as it cooled, and all at once he glanced up and found her watching him. His eyes narrowed slightly, his face becoming keen and contemplative, and he was aware that he must look like a man who has put himself on the defensive. He raised the newspaper, intending to hide behind it, and Marietta said softly, "Pete was here last night."

He was silent for a few moments, staring across the table at the carved sideboard with its ironstone tureens and silver candlesticks and, above it, the big gilt-framed picture which had been in their dining room in New York for so long he could not remember when they first got it, a dark painting of a bleeding rabbit hanging by its feet, cleaned fish on a platter, a few onions lying upon a crumpled white cloth, and though the picture had always seemed to him quite ugly he liked it for having kept them company all these years.

As he looked at it he was wondering what she knew and, therefore, what lie he could reasonably tell, and finally he said, "Pete went to Deer Lodge yesterday morning. I talked to him just before he left— and from there he was going to two or three other camps. He couldn't possibly have made it in a day." She smiled and he had the feeling, which had not happened often, that Marietta was pitying him. "What time was he here?" He spoke sharply, as if she might otherwise try to hide something from him, some important or necessary part of this testimony he meant to extract.

Marietta leaned her arms on the table, cupped her chin in one hand, and spent some moments examining the picture, and he found himself as intensely alert as if he lay waiting for the first sounds of a battle to begin. "He came a little after eleven o'clock. Douglas was out, Robert and Annabel were asleep, and I was reading."

"How long did he stay?" He frowned again, displeased with the harsh abrupt sound of his voice, and watched Marietta as if this were some woman he did not know who brought him evil tidings.

"I think about an hour." She looked at him quickly, and though he tried to return the look with bland innocence, at last he glanced away. What Marietta might know about his deep and possibly morbid involvement with Jenny Danforth, or what she might have guessed, seemed to him a mystery so terrifying, and so carefully guarded, that he had never dared explore it, and had chosen instead to convince himself they had taken such care to protect her that she had no suspicions and had therefore lost nothing by it. Even so, he knew it could not be true.

"Eleven o'clock, or later," he said, and drew on the cigar, giving this piece of information his careful consideration. He narrowed his eyes, then turned to her with a suspicious questioning look. "That seems a strange time for him to come here—after saying he was going to Deer Lodge."

He congratulated himself on this canny logic, putting Pete in the wrong for having lied, and Marietta, too, for having made Pete welcome in spite of the lie. But she was not disconcerted, and he experienced a heavy and sorrowful conviction that Marietta must have by now her own vengeful feelings.

All at once this struck him as an outrageous injustice—Marietta's disloyal sympathy for Pete, and her secret critical hostility toward him—and he found himself with a sense of powerful and determined antagonism against them both, as if they were the aggressors and he their blameless victim. For, after all, he had not gone searching for the sorrows he had caused, he had been taken as much by surprise as anyone else, and he had at least the judgment to understand what it seemed neither Marietta nor Pete was willing to acknowledge: that men were not reasonable beings but were, in fact, governed in all which was most meaningful to them by impulses they could neither understand nor control, and that these impulses were often not benevolent ones. Such notions, depending as they did upon elements of capricious or malign supernatural tampering, he found more congenial than Pete's rigorous demand that men were entitled to justice, or Marietta's belief in her universal medicine of love, when she must know as well as he did that love was as dangerous, as deceptive, as destructive as hate—or possibly more so, because of the beguiling camouflage it wore.

He leaned forward, demanding sharply, "How does it happen he came here? Why didn't he go home?" He looked so vindictively accusatory he might have been suggesting that Pete had come here for the same reason he had gone to Jenny. And, though he was instantly ashamed, he continued to watch her with a condemning and challenging stare.

"He came here because he wanted to talk to me."

"Talk to you?" Matt smiled. "At that hour? What about? Something very important, it must have been."

"Matt," she said warningly, and he grew more alertly combative but then turned sheepish and apologetic, for it now seemed quite remarkable that during all this time he had believed Marietta had let them fool her. "I opened the door and he was standing there looking so tired and haggard that he frightened me. You know how Pete looks when he's troubled—like you do, and the boys do—furiously angry." Matt nodded, recognizing the description. "At first I thought he might have been drinking. He stood there after I'd asked him to come in and stared at me with the wildest expression I think I've ever seen on his face. It made me think of the day Lorena and little Matthew died."

Matt gave a deep, inadvertent sigh, shaking his head and yearning over Pete's sorrow, as if he himself were in no way the cause of it. "I remember." He stared at the tablecloth and Marietta went on, speaking so softly and tenderly that he listened as if to a catalogue of all his crimes.

"Finally he said that he wanted to talk to me, and he came in. He didn't ask if you were here."

"That's because he knew I was going to Marysville," Matt said quickly, for it seemed he must answer each accusation with some defense or, if he could contrive it, some accusation of his own.

Marietta went on, as if he had not interrupted. "I was afraid he might be sick, but he insisted he wasn't, only tired and distracted. He asked me if I thought Jenny was happy, and if I thought she loved him."

Matt winced involuntarily and narrowed his eyes. "He asked you if she loved him? Pete wouldn't do a thing like that."

"Do you think I've invented it?"

"No, of course not. But it's such a curious thing for Pete to say, even to you. He has too much pride to ask another person if his wife loves him, or if she's happy." He sounded, now, as if he thought Pete had had no right to slough off his dignity long enough to have asked that question.

"Of course it was curious. But I've been trying to tell you, Matt, that he was distracted and confused—he might have been drunk or sick or grieving—I had the feeling that he wanted to cry but didn't dare, only because he never has."

"That's ridiculous." Matt now grew elaborately scornful, prepared to wipe away his brother's fanatical doubts with a few quick swipes of reasonableness. "What can he possibly be worried about? Where would he get such an absurd notion? Why would he think Jenny didn't love him? Why would he imagine she might not be happy?" He glared at her. "What the hell's come over him? A man with all his good fortune, prowling around in the middle of the night, calling on people and scaring them out of their wits with his threats and violence. I want to talk to him about this, by God, the minute he gets back." His black eyes glittered, he felt strong indignation against Pete, and he faced Marietta with a menacing truculence.

Marietta looked at him thoughtfully. "Are you sure you want to talk to him, Matt?"

He leaped up. "Of course I want to talk to him. I will talk to him, and by Christ I'll put an end to this nonsense. What did you mean by that? Do you imagine I'm afraid to talk to him? I know him better than you do—or than Jenny does." He heard himself shouting, but went on. "This doesn't concern you, Marietta. Don't interfere between us, don't do anything you'll be sorry to have done when it's too late, don't—"

"Matt!" She ran out of the room and he stood, dazzled and confused, then followed her into the kitchen, and as he came in she asked, "What are you trying to do?"

"Pete is troubled, I want to help him." He smiled ironically. "Do you mean to say you don't think I should?" He waited for a moment, then shrugged, as any sensible man might do in the face of one of these obscure demonstrations of feminine illogic, and left the house.

Still, he was somewhat surprised to have found her such an able antagonist, and all the more so because he could not be sure if she knew what it was he meant to hide. As he rode, he found himself chastened to realize that perhaps there were values more meaningful to Marietta than her love for him, and to protect them she had been able to endure humiliations she might have otherwise refused to accept. He grew ashamed of his self-righteous and indignant behavior but obstinately refused to turn back, assuring himself that though he might not have been a courteous gentleman, at least he had prevented any words from being spoken which neither of them should hear.

But he found himself more puzzled than ever before to understand why it was that after long intervals he was once again compelled to offer Pete one more challenge, as if each successful test of wills and chance made him doubt himself that much more, and made yet another test become necessary and inevitable.

He walked briskly into the office, passed the two cashiers and three clerks as if his mind was occupied with the day's business, and glanced into Pete's office, where he was surprised to see not Pete but Jonathan, talking to a man he did not recognize. "Where's Pete?"

"He's not back yet. He expected to be gone until Saturday."

"I'd forgotten."

He nodded at the stranger and left them, for Jonathan had developed as many schemes as Morgan had had before he left, and this gave Matt a moment's salutary reflection. Jonathan and Morgan, after all, had fought as children over every smallest slight either of them could imagine or invent, and had even fought over Georgina Hart on the night of Pete's wedding to Jenny; but that rivalry had disappeared, they had their different ambitions now and one did not interfere with the other. And so it must be, he thought, between himself and Pete; for as he strolled about the office during the morning, writing letters, examining contracts, discussing loans, considering new projects, it was very easy to see that such an attack as Pete had made on him was possible only late at night when a man might have been tired or drunk or distracted by his fears, still pursued at such a time by the hobgoblins of his childhood, but certainly no man would destroy what they had built together for so trivial a reason as some imagined harm to his manhood.

If he could have been asked at that moment to give Jenny up once and for all, he was ready to agree with as little resentment as if he had been asked to contribute a few dollars to the Christmas tree fund or to lend the second floor of their office building for a Masonic ball. The simplicity, in fact, with which he now viewed their relationship had about it an uncanny tranquillity which he found slightly surprising, for it seemed only that he had lost some not very significant game and was quite willing to concede the prize.

He was elated by these discoveries and eager for Pete's return, convinced that no discussion between them would be necessary, for they would understand each other, as they had so often, with only an exchange of glances.

And, as he judiciously weighed, as if upon their gold scales, all the minute and larger grains of the situation, he became quite well satisfied that things were not so much out of balance as they might have seemed and, indeed, that there was no reason why they should not be able to restore the past—though it was not so clear which part of it they should restore, and indeed it seemed they might have to go back far enough to reach a new beginning, before either of them had ever seen Jenny Danforth.

But it was quite obvious to him now, as it had not been before, that Jenny Danforth—as he usually called her in these conversations with himself—was a kind of natural accident in their lives, for there was no other cause for rivalry between them, and there never had been.

This discovery, though he could not explain why he should not have made it long ago, showed him at last what he must do to put their lives in proper order once again, and now that he understood it so well he was magnanimously prepared to undertake the responsibility for all of them, whether or not they ever recognized the debt they owed him. And to this rather simple task, as he had convinced himself it would be, he need bring only the love and good will he bore them both, and his present eagerness to submerge his own wishes in their common happiness. It seemed, as the morning wore on, more and more remarkable that his character should have been so regenerated overnight—all his past and future sins absolved in an attack which even these few hours later seemed never to have happened at all.

At twelve o'clock he went to the St. Louis Hotel and there he took the table by the window he had taken on the morning more than three years ago when he had waited with as much impatience for Pete to leave as he now felt in waiting for him to return. He expected, as he had all morning long, to see him at any moment, for he supposed Pete must have recognized as he did that he had at last stepped free of those humiliating years when he had been in love with Jenny Danforth and unable or unwilling not to be.

The streets were crowded, he saw many men he knew passing by on horseback or hurrying along the sidewalks, but not anywhere among them did Pete appear, and he grew more and more anxious, but could not think where he might go to look for him. He was so engrossed in searching for Pete that when Jenny drove up and stopped before their office he did not instantly recognize her. And then, as if someone had struck him from behind, he was out of his chair with a bound and tore down the street, rudely pushed aside a young boy who had stepped forward to help her and gave her his hand, bowing slightly as she passed him, but neither of them spoke.

He followed her inside and now was convinced she had brought him bad news, that Pete had gone out of his mind, threatening scandal and disaster to all of them, or had tried to kill himself—and this seemed such a logical punishment for Pete to have inflicted on himself that during the few moments it took them to cross the floor to his private office he had seen Pete lying dead of his own hand and all their sins exploded before the town's face. He closed the door carefully and quietly as she turned to him, sure that at last their long career of crime against the people they loved was to destroy them all, the guilty and innocent ones together; and the conviction was so strong that when she said, very softly, "I haven't seen him," the shock turned him weak with a profound disappointment that nothing had been finally resolved after all.

"Sit down, Jenny." He drew back a chair, then walked around and sat across from her, leaning on the desk and looking at her insistently, as if to force her to tell him the truth.

She was wearing a new dress, made of red and black plaid taffeta, its broad white linen collar tied with a black velvet bow, and her hair was arranged in some complicated new style he did not like so well as the simple way she had worn it when he had seen her first, though he dared not ask her to change it because, after all, this might be Pete's preference. Her eyelids were darkened with kohl, she smelled of violet perfume, and yet for all this carefully wrought elegance her skin had the dull opacity by which he could always recognize that she was tired or sick, and as he studied her carefully it seemed she was someone he did not know very well—perhaps one of their clients, come to discuss what they were doing about investing her money.

This reminded him that it would be a good idea to seem, if anyone should walk in, that this actually was what they were discussing, and he stepped quickly to the door, calling, "Bring me Mrs. Devlin's portfolio." He sat down again and they waited, without speaking, for the papers to be brought, though Jenny smiled slightly and seemed amused he should think they could still pretend to have some legitimate business together.

The twenty thousand dollars Dr. Danforth had left her seven years ago had been invested in mining claims and small farms and ranches, timber stands and town lots and two or three office buildings, until by now it had acquired a value of nearly sixty thousand and, from time to time, Jenny liked to pretend she was overseeing these investments, though actually she took little interest in what was done and left all decisions to them.

When the folders were placed before him, Matt spread out the papers and frowned at them studiously for a few moments, until he heard her laugh and glanced up. He gestured defensively at the papers, started to tell her it was his opinion she might sell her share in the Marysville claim and put it into a better one, but then he leaned back, hooked his thumbs over his belt, and spoke in a voice which might be overheard by anyone passing the door. "He isn't expected back until late tomorrow or the next day."

"Whatever are you talking about?"

His face became hard and sly and as filled with determination as if it were a man who sat across from him arguing about some business problems they shared. "There's no reason why he should have come back any earlier than he expected to," and he leaned toward her, demanding sharply, "Is there?"

"What good will it do to pretend, Matt? He tried to kill you."

His hand slapped hard on the desk top, and it now seemed to be Jenny he distrusted and Jenny who was his enemy, to be watched for the harm she meant to do, not only to him but to Pete, if he did not stop her. "If he had meant to kill me, he could have."

"You're as strong as he is."

"He could have shot me."

She smiled, looking still more ironic, and he found himself infuriated, longing to seize her and physically force her to admit she had neither heard nor seen anyone else in her house last night. "Not with Leila there," she reminded him. But then her face grew serious and she leaned toward him. "Matt, you mustn't let yourself believe this was only a small dispute between you, something inconsequential you'll both forget in a few days. He came into the house that day when we were upstairs, though he's never admitted it. And he attacked you last night. He means to kill you—and he will. I think he's gone mad."

He laughed and turned partly away, for now he found it difficult even to look at her. "That's ridiculous. He's saner than either of us."

She said nothing for a few moments and then asked, in a light reasonable tone, "Well? Suppose he is? Does that make him trustworthy?"

Finally he leaned toward her, thinking that with their tense faces, their taut muscles and muttering conversation, they might be taken by any observer for a fine pair of conspirators. And it occurred to him that neither of them would ever know how much of their captivity was love and how much the fascination of being fellow criminals, turning each crime into an act of faith. Yet it seemed to him very clear that Jenny was no longer involved in whatever had happened between him and Pete, or in whatever was yet to happen, and that he must convince her of this.

After a moment she frowned, and finally sighed, as if he was defeating her against her will. "When I opened the bedroom door you were lying unconscious and he was kneeling on your chest, with his hands around your throat. He tried to shield his face as he jumped up, but I saw him."

"You imagined you did," he told her stolidly. "You expected to see him, and so you thought you had. That happens to all of us sometimes."

"His dog was quiet. If it had been anyone else, he wouldn't have let him come near the house, you know that."

"What is it you want, Jenny? What are you trying to do?"

"I'm trying to make you recognize what happened. How else can you protect yourself?"

"Protect myself?" He raised his voice angrily, but lowered it again and bent toward her, his hands in his pockets. "You can't imagine I'd try to protect myself against Pete, can you?" He peered into her face, searching it ruthlessly, and his own was distorted and cruel. "This doesn't concern you, Jenny. Remember that."

After a few moments she pulled the cloak about her shoulders and stood up. He stepped quickly toward the door, brisk and confident and hoping they would come out looking as if they had decided that, after all, the Marysville claim was worth keeping a little longer. But then she stopped, and seemed so helplessly bewildered he was ashamed of having bullied her.

"Everything scares me now," she murmured. "That old peddler woman came by this morning, Mrs. Honeybone—the one who cursed me the day Pete threw her valise into the street. She never comes to the door any more, I suppose she's afraid of Pete, but I was looking out the window and as she went by she shook her fist at the house. I was so terrified I began to cry and couldn't stop for a long time."

He looked at her yearningly, but though now he longed to offer some consolation he did not dare begin to comfort her, and tried to tease her out of it instead. "You've always had these premonitions, Jenny—dreams and ghosts and malicious old women. Dogs howling at night and crowing hens." He smiled, coaxing her to pretend that all premonitions of disaster were as trivial as those. "You collect superstitions the way other women collect china mugs."

"I'm not troubled for myself, Matt."

"I know." He drew his fingers along the side of her face with gentle affection. "Maybe it's time we admit we're two fairly reasonable human beings—if it hadn't happened that we met each other?"

X L

Morgan and Sir James took rooms at the Hoffman House on the corner of Twenty-fifth Street and Broadway, and while Sir James applied himself to investigating the city, Morgan enrolled at the Columbia School of Mines and spent several days in Baltimore having the ore samples assayed. They ran higher in both silver and copper than he had expected, or than assays made in Utah had shown, and he asked Joshua Ching for an appointment to show him the reports, although once he put them before him Joshua ruffled them idly, remarking that he was not eager to buy a hole in the ground.

"There are innumerable corporations all over the country, Morgan, as you know, organized to sell gold and silver and oil stocks to unsuspecting investors."

Joshua, seated at his desk and smoking a cigar as he blandly questioned his nephew's honest intentions, looked to Morgan enviably successful—indeed, so successful he could afford to maintain the same shabby quarters three floors up which he had had many years before.

Joshua had inquired about their life in the West and listened with smiling incredulity to Morgan's enthusiastic predictions of the Territory's future. Matt Devlin, as Morgan interpreted his uncle's smiles and nods and silences, might have done very well in the West but, after all, it was still in the West, a place for adventurers to run off to and undesirable aliens to be encouraged to go to, but certainly not a place to be taken seriously. And he thought it likely that Joshua Ching preferred to occupy his eminence in as much solitude as possible, and would be as disappointed to have him get rich as Suky would be to meet some comparable beauty.

"What good is mining? Why is it necessary?" Joshua asked, and, as it seemed, looked at him with infinite suspicion and distrust. "We have all the gold we need. We have little use for more silver. What we need, Morgan," and he stared at him with thoughtful sternness, "are railroads."

"God knows we need them in the West. Everything we try to do is slowed up or stopped because we haven't transportation. But that's another story, sir, I think. I came to talk to you because you're an investor and I need money." He gestured at the sheaf of papers he had laid before Joshua. "The silver's there, you don't doubt that, do you?"

Joshua, who seemed to have scanned the pages too quickly to notice any figures, now moved them about with the air of a man not too well pleased with what has been served him for dinner but who will nibble at something out of mere politeness, and drew forth three pages clipped together. "Very well, you need money. I'll buy this property for thirty thousand dollars. I will spend fifty thousand more to develop it with you as manager at a salary of five thousand a year. If at the end of the first year it proves satisfactory, I will then consider whether or not I want to invest any more and, if it doesn't, I'll sell it—to you, if you like. Unless someone offers me a better price, of course."

Morgan smiled, shaking his head. "That's what usually happens to discoverers, but I don't intend to have it happen to me."

"That's the best I can do. To be truthful, it's a better offer than I'd have made to anyone else. You understand?"

"Yes, sir." He gathered the papers and started out.

Joshua shrugged. "I don't like mines," he admitted. "Morgan, let me tell you one thing, and I hope you'll remember it. Since the beginning of the year, the country's merchandise imports have been rising steadily. It began, in fact, last year. This is a sign of trouble ahead, probably a panic, and probably not very far in the future, and any man who ignores these warnings is likely to lose everything he has."

"Thank you, sir, although I haven't anything to lose just now."

"I don't think this is a suitable time to begin reckless new enterprises." Joshua tilted his head sideways and raised his eyebrows in sympathetic understanding of a young man's plight, fortunately no longer his own. "You'll be meeting various friends of ours, and in your search for capital let me suggest that you do not listen to points, no matter where you hear them, nor trust advice, no matter who gives it. And always remember—you're more likely to be struck by lightning going home than you are to be struck by luck in the stock market." Morgan nodded, thinking that Joshua Ching had now performed his duty to his nephew. "Talk to Talbot—he may like silver mines, though I doubt it. You might as well try Amos Cottrell and Lorenzo Flagg while you're about it, but I think they're more likely to offer you shares in the Corporate Engineers. Are you quite sure neither Matt nor Pete would like a few hundred shares?"

James Gordon, Morgan knew, had bought three thousand shares of Corporate Engineers in spite of the flurry of rumors carly in September that the Crédit Mobilier was about to be subjected to Congressional investigation, a catastrophe so near their own interests that Talbot and Joshua and his two brothers had immediately disappeared from Long Branch, leaving Morgan and Sir James to bring back the women and children with their retinue of maids and nursemaids, dogs and birds and dozens of trunks, as well as the summer's accumulation of seashells, pressed flowers, feathers and beetles and curious rocks the children refused to give up.

Their combined efforts had apparently been sufficient to buy their company a temporary peace, and Joshua confidently predicted two or three weeks later that there would be no Congressional investigation of the Crédit Mobilier or anything else until after the Presidential election.

"A great many men," Joshua observed one night at the dinner table, "have been caught with their hands in other men's pockets. And this," he added, smiling with a look of reflective and bitter amusement, "is only a beginning. The scandals will accumulate. Unfortunately, what these lawmakers don't understand is that the exposition of bribery and theft among the large companies does the nation more harm than good. It undermines public confidence and prepares a receptive atmosphere for economic catastrophe." However, this prospect seemed so agreeable to him that Morgan assumed neither Joshua Ching nor any of his partners would be caught with their hands in other men's pockets, and might even have found a way to make good use of a national catastrophe.

And, once they had become aware that in Sir James Gordon they had a real English nobleman, both titled and rich, and not another Lord Giles Haldane, whose success had made them wary of all visiting foreigners, they began to invite him to their homes, to balls and banquets, to the opera and the theater, until at last Sir James confessed, rather sheepishly, that he had given Joshua a check. "I don't quite see what they've done, except on paper, but your uncle's devilish persuasive, all the same."

The reason they had not tried to be devilish persuasive with him, Morgan was chagrined to realize, was that he had nothing to invest, and this financial nudity caused him to feel he had dwindled in stature and strength, and convinced him that whatever significance he might once have seemed to have, out there in the Territories, had been only some gilding with his father's luster.

He was reluctant to ask Joshua Ching's friends for money, but there was no chance of borrowing it from strangers and so he approached them humbly, and was refused, as he had expected to be. Amos Cottrell tried to persuade him to forget this nonsense about silver mines and put whatever money he had into the Corporate Engineers, and Lorenzo Flagg drew him a gloomy picture of the future of silver mining in the United States, expressing surprise that a young man who looked so purposeful should delude himself with such an unlikely project.

He had saved William Talbot for the last, and would have been glad to invent some plausible excuse not to approach him at all. For Talbot, he believed, had distrusted him at sight, and whenever they met, at dinner at Suky's or at the theater or one of the balls, to which he trailed along with Suky and Philip and James Gordon, it was Talbot, even more than the others, who seemed to believe that here was another example of that special breed, a western man, whose character had been changed by his transportation to the West, and changed permanently.

A western man, they thought, was proud without reason and arrogant because he was unsure of himself, and his temper had been honed to a fine edge, causing him to imagine that his pistol could solve problems better than any logic could do. He was impulsive, intolerant, reckless and extravagant, whether with money he owned or money he borrowed; he was filled with dreams and plans which would bear no examination by himself or anyone else, but which he would nevertheless chase about trying to execute, changing his mind from day to day and moment to moment as he imagined that a better plan offered itself. And, of course, he was not a good risk for the City Exchange Bank.

But nevertheless Morgan went there one morning. The City Exchange Bank in Broad Street was a six-story marble-fronted building where clerks were at work behind glass walls, riffling through bills and piling up coins with the speed and dexterity of professional gamblers and something of their same air of casual unconcern, as if they did not quite believe in the reality of what they were doing. Messenger boys went dodging and darting about, and black-coated men in silk hats waited in line. Morgan sat for some time after he had sent his name in, watching the crowds, regarding the money with a covetous eye, and grew more and more uneasy the longer he waited.

The night after Talbot and Joshua Ching had left Long Branch, he had danced twice with Coral Talbot, a woman he found so imposing and splendid and, indeed, so terrifying, he scarcely dared speak to her as he sped her about the room, and yet when he thanked her she had murmured some few words which had sent him some hours later sneaking along the hotel corridors in search of her room, and, afterward, sneaking back to his own room, rejoicing over his good luck in having discovered, so unexpectedly, this woman of knowledgeable sensuality. Once they returned to the city she came to the Hoffman House, and it took his best efforts to mollify her, for she expected each time to be deprived of her senses, carried to the limits of her own endurance and his, and he complimented himself he was able to do it, for her husband was not very likely to be still capable of such heroic feats. But she never talked about love, as he had supposed all women did, and he was grateful to her for that, for it might have spoiled their pleasure, dimmed its fury and softened its ruthlessness.

His success with Coral Talbot had made him more reluctant than ever to ask a loan of the City Exchange Bank, so that when he was at last led in to see him, Morgan entered with a determined stride, stood very erect as they shook hands, and expected to be accused of misbehavior with Coral Talbot, who never seemed, while he made love to her, to be Talbot's wife or any other man's.

As Talbot began to discuss current business conditions in the same gloomy fashion Joshua Ching had done, he watched Morgan with a steady, gleaming stare, until Morgan felt that the office was overheated, his tie was knotted too tight, he could not find a comfortable position, and he was almost abjectly grateful when Talbot asked, quite politely, "And what progress have you made in persuading capital into your mining venture?"

"None at all, sir," Morgan told him meekly.

"It's very difficult for a young man just beginning life." He gave him a slight, inquiring smile, to which Morgan replied with a frown, rested his elbows on the chair arms and clenched his hands together. "A young man, after all, is expected to be skilled only at weapons, cards, and women. Isn't that your western code?"

"No, sir."

"I had understood that it was." Talbot smiled again, not encouragingly. "And what will you do, if you can't raise the thirty thousand dollars you say you need? Give it up?"

Morgan grinned and, for the moment, forgot that it was Coral Talbot's husband sitting across from him. "Of course I won't. I didn't come here with any great expectations of raising money. I know well enough how eastern businessmen distrust the West, although I might say, sir, that in some respects I think you're more reckless than we are. These railroads, for example, built without any reference to the needs of the population, only because one company can scare another into selling by building in the neighborhood. The assumption that panics are good for the economic system, like a dose of physic given on principle every so often." He smiled again and, to his relief, so did William Talbot.

"Nevertheless, the country needs railroads and must expect to pay some price for them. It does not, however, need silver. How long do you intend to remain in the East?"

"Until I've learned what I need to know—engineering, metallurgy, geology, chemistry."

"But suppose you could raise the capital you say you need for a beginning? You'd be eager to get to work?"

"I'd be eager to get to work, of course, but I'd still have to finish what I'm doing here." This sounded ambiguous to him and he was afraid it might sound equally so to William Talbot. "My first mistake might be my last one." He scowled at the floor, reminding himself to speak more slowly, for the conversation seemed to be getting slippery. "I hope you understand, sir, that silver mining is a serious business, like any other?"

"I understand you believe it to be. In my opinion it's only another form of gambling, somewhat less reliable than poker. But I have some followers who are avid for any investment at all—if only I will recommend it to them."

"I appreciate your offer, sir. I wish you might make it again two years from now."

"But you can't leave now?"

"I can't, I'm sorry," he added, so apologetically that Talbot looked surprised.

"Then I'm afraid there's nothing I can do for you."

Morgan dashed out, amazed at his freedom, and stood for a moment outside the City Exchange Bank, profoundly baffled as to why, if William Talbot had no suspicions, he should be so eager to send him back to the West. And then, with a flash of insight, he saw that it was not his wife Talbot was concerned about but his daughter—that grave and lovely young girl he had seen first with Steven and a few times since with Suky, but had thought about scarcely at all. And, indeed, it embarrassed him to think of her now, for just as Coral Talbot seemed to have no husband, so she also seemed to have no child.

He shook his head in disbelief, then slowly smiled to think a man like William Talbot should be afraid he might take his daughter, and at last set out to walk back uptown, smiling from time to time in incredulous wonderment. It almost seemed that Talbot, for whom he now felt a patronizing pity, deserved to have him go back and explain that he had not come all this way to fall in love, for he had important things to do at this stage of his life, and love was a luxury he could not afford and did not wish to acquire even if he could.

He stopped almost every morning to see Suky before he went to his first class, and sometimes he met Philip just leaving. Philip looked faintly surprised at each encounter and perhaps he, as well as Talbot, hoped he would soon be gone, but nevertheless Philip would smile and spend a few minutes discussing the national elections and the various symptoms of financial trouble, and all the while they watched each other with bristling suspicion, though why it was he felt such instinctive dislike for Philip Van Zandt, he could not say.

Suky might be in the nursery on the third floor or, if he came a little later, she would be in her sitting room talking to the housekeeper— for Suky's life was so carefully planned that his own seemed haphazard and unkempt, like the clothes he wore. And it was not only her daily life which was planned in every detail, he soon discovered, but she knew what was to happen to her from one year to the next and perceived quite clearly events taking place on horizons so distant he had not even begun to contemplate them; yet he remembered that even when they were children she had preferred long schemes, intricate and subtle, to those he proposed, which only required that they attack the enemy without delay and put him to rout.

The Van Zandts, she said, did not like her and they never would, and though this made him angry, for he had the same combative impulses toward anyone who might not appreciate Suky that he had always had, Suky smiled in her mystifying way and explained that the Van Zandts served their purpose in her life, whether they accepted her or not. "They've never found out that there's no longer just one circle in New York, but many many different circles, each one complete in itself. Thirty years from now, Joshua Van Zandt will be the head of the Van Zandt family." She laughed, a clear, lyrical and rather mocking laugh he remembered very well.

"Thirty years," he repeated softly, and shook his head.

They were in the conservatory, her favorite room, it seemed, for she led him there each time they were alone. Hundreds of ferns were banked against the walls and clustered about white wicker chairs or sofas, and the air was scented with a mixture of sweet and pungent flowers and rotting leaves, agreeable as the smell of a forest in deep summer. The fountain kept up its continuous, gentle play, and the light from the panes of blue glass, unchanged by whatever happened in the skies outside, made it seem moonlight all day long.

"Thirty years, Morgan," she reminded him gently, "goes by whether we plan for it, or not." She smiled, tipping her head sideways as she looked at him, and he experienced once again that unsettling fear that somehow he had disappointed her, though of course it might be only his eagerness for her approval which caused such ideas to occur to him. "And Sarita, I promise you, will be something extraordinary."

"I'm sure she will." Sarita he had thought a provocative little minx, quite well aware of her destiny even at three and by no means dismayed by the prospect of it, for she was at once bold and shy, demure and gaily vivacious, and he suspected she would grow up to treat her admirers cruelly.

"Her best friend will be Cindy Hallam. And, of course, your daughter."

Morgan gave a start. "My daughter?"

"Well? Surely you mean to have children, don't you?"

"I don't know. I don't think so. I don't even expect to get married."

After these sessions, he found the library and the laboratories and lecture rooms a haven, and was grateful for a place to hide where he might immerse himself in the study of analytical geometry and calculus, inorganic chemistry and mining German, give himself up to the contemplation of cabinets filled with mineral specimens, models of furnaces and drawings of Root blowers, the real business of his future life.

Now and then he accompanied Sir James on his tour of the city, and wherever they went their escort went along, four sturdy and battered young Irishmen in frock coats and stovepipe hats, drawn by Joshua Ching from some capacious grab bag into which it seemed he might dip at will and bring forth various devices to astonish a prospective investor like James Gordon. Sir James had at first objected that he had never once required the protection of his western bodyguard, but Joshua had assured him there was no town in the West so wild as the Seventh Ward of New York City, where a man was liable to be robbed and killed and his body stuffed into a furnace for twenty dollars, more or less.

They visited Harry Hill's and The Marquis Club, where no money was to be seen but only ivory checks, discreetly clicking as they passed from hand to hand. At John Allen's the dancing girls were no more than eleven or twelve years old, but drunk and quarrelsome and so lazy they must be driven to their work by the proprietor's fists. They saw celebrated fox terriers able to kill one hundred rats in half an hour. They wandered through the slums and were taken into Mulberry Hall, a vast tenement housing hundreds of families, and they inspected cellars where ragpickers sat amid piles of stinking rags and bones, sorting them as carefully as a lady going through her jewel box. Waitresses in pink tights sat at tables with them in the concert saloons on Mercer Street and Greene Street, but their bodyguard refused them permission to go upstairs, a territory they could not keep under surveillance, where hands reached through sliding wall panels and into the pockets of unthinking customers as they lay in bed. At a livery stable they watched dog fights and cock fights and that special attraction which crowded the house—two women wearing silk trunks, naked above the waist, fighting with boxing gloves.

From Five Points to Harlem Lane and from the Gold Exchange to the village of squatters in the midst of Central Park, Sir James covered the city's sights with scrupulous attention, and when, after three months, he told Morgan he had taken passage and would leave in a week or ten days, he gave it as his opinion that the American man went about his sinning with the same grim determination and relentless persistence he gave to his business.

"It isn't an art with you, you know. It's only a necessity."

"I suppose we aren't a very light-hearted people. We've got too god-
damn much to do."

"But need you do it all at once? You'll presently have the country
latticed with railways and bedeviled with cities, and what will all of
you do with your time when that day comes, old boy?"

Morgan laughed, for all his suspicions of Sir James had disappeared the moment he met Suky on the south verandah of the Stetson
House, and he found him once again an amiable Englishman,
smoking his meerschaum pipe in the Seven Sisters' parlor and the
rowdiest concert-saloons, fascinated by this new breed of men
sprung out of the American earth which might have been harboring their seeds for millennia, a race of people never seen before or
imagined; though what they might make with all their energetic
activity, he refused to prophesy. "It will bloody well astonish the
world, but just what the nature of that astonishment will be I can't
predict. Can you?"

Although Morgan did not admit it, he was more eager now than
ever before to make himself master of a great silver mine, for he was
sure it was the least Suky expected of him, and sometimes he grew
so expansive, telling her all he meant to do and describing what he
would bring into being on the nether side of Butte Hill, that he
would pause, taken aback by his own confidence, and wonder if she
was secretly laughing at what she must interpret as one more example of the western man's propensity for myth-making, seeing his
land in the same enlarged perspective that travelers on the plains
saw distant mirages.

"Does all this sound impossible?" he asked her one day.

"Not in the least. Morgan—what kind of women do you admire?"

He sat up straight, laughing self-consciously, and marveling at
how she had got from that subject to this one, which he was not at all
eager to discuss with her. "What kind?"

"Blondes, brunettes? Slender ones, round ones? You know what I
mean."

"I admire beautiful women."

"All of them?"

"Of course."

Suky smiled. "Men think there are more beautiful women than
there really are." She would ask him about Coral Talbot in another
moment, he was sure of it, and he got up and began to wander about,
sighing in perplexity. "But one of these days you'll have to make a
choice and marry her." He laughed at this preposterous notion, and
all at once she stood before him, too close, with her fingertip against
her mouth. "Which one?" She tipped back her head, and her eyes
were nearly closed. "Felice?"

"Of course not! What gave you an idea like that?" It seemed so
preposterous that she should suggest he might marry a girl he did not
know, a girl he scarcely noticed when he saw her, a girl he was em-

barrassed even to look at, that all at once he contrived, with surprising agility, to slip past her and out the door, calling as he went that he was late, very late; and he refused to go back for several days, while he brooded over Suky's treachery, the deceitfulness he had always known was in her character but never expected to have turned against him.

For Felice Talbot was the worst possible choice Suky could have made. He had seen Felice several times, and each time it shocked him to be reminded that this young girl he admired for her dignity and look of elegant austerity, was the daughter of Coral Talbot who, in fact, had never once mentioned her to him. Of course, he agreed, there was no reason why she should, for a woman having an affair with a man eleven years younger than she was not likely to remind him of her seventeen-year-old daughter.

And all three of them—Suky and Coral Talbot and Felice—troubled his thoughts so frequently that at last he remarked bitterly to James Gordon, "These damned women are idle."

They sat in the Hoffman House bar, toasting Sir James' voyage and his early return to America. The room was crowded with well-dressed men, several of them in evening clothes, wearing silk hats and smoking cigars, and from time to time giving their considered attention to the bar's two celebrated paintings, "The Vision of Faust" and "Nymphs and Satyr," vast canvases swarming with naked women, swirling about in an indiscriminate mass of breasts and buttocks, arms and legs and fat thighs which, Sir James had remarked, was enough to make a vegetarian of any man. And, as Morgan spoke, Sir James glanced questioningly at the canvas, for the women sometimes seemed about to fall upon them, dropping into their drinks and onto their laps like so many locusts upon a wheat field.

"Eastern women," Morgan told him. "The wives and daughters of well-to-do men. In the West, even a rich man's wife has to do most of her own housework and take care of her children. But here they surround themselves with maids and cooks and nursemaids, and haven't a god-damn thing left to do but think about men."

His trouble, as he saw it, came from this social accident and nothing else, for these women, pampered by themselves and by everyone they knew, endlessly concerned with their hair, their clothes, their voices and mannerisms, which only heightened their native sense of conquering femininity, seemed to him strange, incomprehensible creatures, living out their lives in moist, artificial gardens, where the moonlight lasted all day long.

Sir James regarded him thoughtfully. "My boy, let me warn you of something. You must be falling in love."

Morgan, who had been moping over the drink, snapped his head up, almost snarling in his indignant outrage. "What did you say?"

"That's the way it happens, I've seen it a hundred times. A chap begins to find fault with the whole sex or even, as in your case, just with the eastern half of it, and although he imagines he's safe because he sees so plainly what's wrong with them and knows exactly why they offer him no threat, it's only one of the earlier symptoms of a fever that often turns out to be fatal. Think it over, Devlin. Which one is it?"

"Gordon, you've got a hell of a sense of humor."

"You'll see."

He gave him a grim, defiant smile, but changed the subject. "When will you come back?"

"Can't tell, you know, but I'll be back. And mind, now, don't forget to send me three hundred shares of your company, as soon as it's organized. And get me word of old Fletcher, when you can." He raised his glass. "How."

"How," Morgan agreed, and his thoughts began sneaking about, from Suky to Felice to Coral Talbot, wondering if there could be any truth in what Sir James had told him.

Sir James had not been gone quite a month when Morgan went one night with Suky and Philip to hear *Don Giovanni*, and there he sat between his two aunts, listening with a solemn face to the music, and felt as ashamed in his new suit of evening clothes as he ever had when he had been dressed up as a child and sent off to Sunday school.

He had begun some time ago to suspect it grieved Suky to see him at balls and the opera in an oversized frock coat, and so he had arrived that night in a handsomely tailored and expensive black swallow-tailed coat, neatly fitted black trousers, white silk cravat and patent leather boots and white kid gloves, smelling of Hungary water, and though he had promised himself that the moment he crossed the Missouri River he would put these dandy's garments away and never wear them again, he had been surprised by his own appearance in them and surprised even more by Suky's knowing smile.

Still, he felt that he had assumed a disguise, that anyone who saw him would know instantly that he was an impostor, and he kept his neck rigid and glared fixedly at the stage, wondering how much of his life must pass before he would sit in such a place as the Academy of Music and feel that he belonged there and had not crept in surreptitiously to occupy the seat which was rightfully Joshua Ching's.

The Talbots owned one of the twelve proscenium boxes, while Joshua Ching's family occupied one of that semicircle of boxes toward the back, and he had noticed instantly that Felice was there, Coral Talbot was there, they had guests, and William Talbot was not there. This seemed some extraordinary coincidence, he could not imagine why, and he took care to avoid looking at them, although Felice turned once and smiled in their direction and this caused him to glance inadvertently at Suky. After that he refused even to shift his eyes about for fear of seeming to be watching that young daughter of William Talbot's, whose charms grew inexplicably greater and more compelling, as if each time he met her in one of those occasional and accidental encounters, he had somehow contrived since their last meeting to learn much more about her. But since he never thought about her, and talked of something else whenever Suky mentioned her, that could not be true and she was, in reality, as much a stranger as the first day he had seen her, five months ago.

Nevertheless, he waited impatiently for the end of the first act, and had decided that only if Steven went to visit the Talbot box would he take it as a challenge and either get there ahead of him or squeeze in later and force his cousin out. For Steven, he thought, paid too much attention to Felice Talbot, and perhaps his father had suggested that a marriage between their two families would be a great advantage to Joshua Ching. A girl like Felice, Morgan was convinced, could never be happy with a husband like Steven Ching, and it annoyed him to see them talking together at the dinner table or playing a game of backgammon afterward.

He sat gazing resolutely at the stage, over the bare shoulders and backs of the women, and the entire vast auditorium seemed crowded with women's heads, intricately coiffed, flickering diamonds, furs thrown over chair backs, and solemn gentlemen in black and white evening dress with beards pomaded and clipped as if by the hand of a topiary expert. From time to time, for all his efforts, Morgan caught himself looking toward the Talbot box and, each time, he instantly returned his attention to the stage. At the moment the curtain came down he sprang to his feet with as much alacrity as if he had been told an Indian raid was about to begin, looking almost as fiercely resolute as if it had, and forgetting he had meant to take his clue from Steven, he escaped from the box before Suky could ask where he was going.

The audience was shouting and while the singers bowed again and again, ushers came trampling down the aisles bearing enormous baskets of flowers. The noise increased, and amidst the distraction Morgan approached the foyer of the Talbot box, paused a moment, and then entered it as stealthily as if he were tracking an animal and everything depended upon the element of surprise. As the applause and shouting continued he stood in the partial darkness, staring down at Felice's back, his eyes glowing with a fervent concentration of which he was not at all aware, until suddenly he found that the singers had disappeared, the gas jets brightened the auditorium, and Coral Talbot turned and caught him there. She smiled and asked him to sit down, though every seat was taken, and turned again to her other guests. Morgan hung in the doorway, wondering angrily if he had been dismissed, for Felice had only glanced around as her mother spoke, nodded slightly, and immediately began talking to a woman who sat beside her, speaking in a very low voice and seeming engrossed in the conversation.

He imagined that Suky and Susan and Ceda were watching him through opera glasses and must be amused to see him in this dilemma, or perhaps Suky was pitying him for the grotesque figure he cut, ignored by both Felice and Mrs. Talbot, and he backed slowly out of the little red-velvet-lined foyer, feeling abjectly ashamed and dishonored by this expedition which had failed at its beginning. Two of the men got up and passed him, without a glance, and at that moment Felice turned and held out her hand.

"Please sit down." She smiled. "You weren't leaving us?" He moved forward, slowly and reluctantly, watching her distrustfully and afraid Mrs. Talbot would turn and send him away, and finally edged himself into a chair and sat facing her, overcome by an anguish so peculiar he longed to rid himself of it by some violent action. But he only confronted her seriously, watching her very carefully and with the determination to find out once and for all exactly what she looked like and what was the substance of her personality. "I want to know what you think of the performance. Do you think it's very bad, as we do?"

"I've enjoyed it," he admitted, and leaned a little nearer, slowly, so that she would not move back, for it seemed this examination must be a minutely detailed one and nothing at all must escape him. She smiled, and he found himself gazing at her in a helpless trance, contemplating the shape of her mouth and its soft pink flesh, the straight black eyebrows, the quality of her skin and the planes of her face, and marveled as he examined her that she combined in both her appearance and manner something of Nella Allen's pathos and vulnerability with Suky's strong dignity, a mixture he found as poignantly appealing as if he had been searching for it all along.

And he found a further attraction in the ardent and concentrated rapture she brought to everything he had ever seen her do, whether she sat listening to music or galloped along the beach, and a time or two he had been treacherously surprised into wondering if she might one day, when she had escaped her father's surveillance, bring those same qualities to a man she loved. For her look of restraint and uncertainty he had decided was only a camouflage for her eagerness and the fears that eagerness vaguely roused; and now, as she submitted herself to his searching, and continued to discuss the performance, she began to talk more quickly, sighed once or twice, and at last, with her eyes shining she said, "Perhaps the reason I find so much fault with the performance is that I've never liked this opera, even though I love the music. Why does Elvira still love him? I don't think she would. Do you?" She gazed at him intently.

"If she loved him at all, I think she would," he told her, and it seemed some profound secret he had only that moment discovered and which he must not only share with her, but persuade her to believe.

She gave his opinion some moments of careful thought, idly flicking her fan open and closing it again, and then looked up at him so quickly he found he had leaned even nearer and, obediently, drew back. "You think she would? I don't agree at all. Love doesn't last forever, not if it's misused."

"Sometimes it does," he muttered distractedly. "Sometimes it does.

No matter what people do to each other." He looked at her more critically now. "I thought that women, at least young women, preferred to be made unhappy. Isn't that what they want?" He was astonished to hear himself ask the question and even more astonished that it seemed whatever she said next must have some crucial significance for them both.

She looked away, down into the mass of restless heads and shoulders beneath them, and her face was rather sad, so that apparently the subject was as meaningful to her as it was to him. "I don't know. Perhaps it's true, I only have theories." She turned back, looked at him questioningly, and then spoke in the manner of one who gives a precious and profoundly serious confidence. "All the most important events of my life have happened to other people."

This, it seemed, must have been what he had been waiting to hear, for the next moment he was horrified by the thought that he was in love with her, though it no sooner entered his mind than he was on his feet again, bowing to her and to Mrs. Talbot's back, and left so abruptly he knocked over a chair and must pause to set it upright, but did not look at her again.

"Tell me about Felice," Suky whispered. "Her hair is different tonight."

He scowled, shaking his head to indicate he knew nothing about Felice or how she had done her hair, and Suky smiled as if that admission had told her all she wanted to know. After that, he was more than ever afraid of some chance encounter at Suky's house, avoided going there for several days, and lived in terror of Coral Talbot's next visit.

Coral Talbot arrived one night a week or so later, while he sat writing another of the letters he sent every few days to Bruno Favorite, warning him not to let any of his claims go unworked under the new Act of Representation. For Lemuel Finney, he sometimes imagined, was busy at that same moment, finding loopholes and flaws in his representation and preparing to slip his most valuable claims away from him.

Talbot, she explained, was in Washington and she was on her way home from a reception, and as if to prove it she dropped her sealskin coat to the floor and showed him her white satin gown, covered with black lace, the diamonds in her ears, and the long white gloves which she next pulled off. He looked at her distrustfully, but she sat in a corner of the sofa and crossed one leg over the other, extended her foot and contemplated the toe of her satin slipper, and talked about the reception and the people she had seen there, as if he would know them all, and quite unexpectedly she asked, "Are you in love with my daughter, Felice?"

To his disgusted surprise, he laughed. "To be truthful, Mrs. Talbot," he mumbled, and fancied he must have turned bright red, "I'm not sure." All at once he was ashamed of this cowardice, and added, "I think I am."

"Well, then, you must fall out of love with her."

He sat down, rested his elbows on his knees, and leaned forward, smiling at her as if they were two accomplices met only for the purpose of deciding how he might escape from this predicament. "I expect to."

She threw back her head and gave a peal of ringing laughter, which was not at all convincing. "You expect to," she said chidingly. "But you must. That's what I came here to tell you." She looked at him intently for a moment, as if she had met him for the first time and was trying to decide what there was about him which might appeal to a young girl like Felice. "She's never been in love before, her father's refused to let her have beaux, and so she's taking this much more seriously than another girl would."

He stared at her with a look of horror. "She's taking what seriously?"

"She's fallen in love with you. She told me so a day or two ago."

"But she doesn't know me!"

"What difference does that make? It isn't necessary to know someone to love them. Knowing them is only likely to spoil it."

"But I couldn't get married if I wanted to, and I don't want to—please believe me."

"Married," she whispered, as if the word was unfit to say aloud, and now she frowned, touching the back of her hair. "What an idea. We would never permit it. Never at all, under any circumstances, would Talbot and I permit Felice to marry you, or anyone like you." He glanced at her, warning her not to trifle with his Scotch-Irish pride, and she added, "It has nothing to do with you as a man, of course."

"I wouldn't have expected that it would." They looked at each other for several moments, and Morgan became aware that he was now remarkably critical of Coral Talbot, who seemed to him a bold and somewhat spurious beauty, guileful and selfish and extravagantly vain.

"I'm sure you know quite well that Felice is the daughter of a rich and, in fact, a rather important man who is determined to have her marry into a position as much like his own as possible." She removed the earrings and tossed them onto a table, and as he began to pace about, she also kicked off the white satin slippers. "And, let me tell you, Talbot has never accustomed himself to mishaps. You can't have her, that's all there is to it—and I'm glad you don't seem to want her." He was at the other end of the room now, frantically distracted to find that as she went on taking off her clothes, peeling off stockings, stepping out of her dress, unhooking the front of her corset, nothing about that conversation had diminished his alert desire for her, and when she asked, "Will you promise me not to see her any more?" he turned, warmly eager to assure her he would not, and found her standing there naked, smiling at him. "Let's pretend we never mentioned it."

XLI

They had all been obliged to become skilled mechanics, and spent
much time tinkering and building small scale models of mills and
assaying furnaces in the hope that one day they would find the invention which would cure these stubborn and unreliable machines
once and for all. But, so far, it had not happened. The mills became
frozen in good weather and bad and the interminable clatter came to
a sudden startling halt.

The quartz mill owned by the Meridian Gold and Silver Mining
Company had been built near the end of the gulch where the town's
main street disappeared into what had once been a thickly timbered
area, long since hacked and burned over, and in this isolated place
the mill looked like a big, rambling cabin, surrounded by immense
piles of rocks being broken into fragments by men wielding sledge-
hammers, while others tossed the fragments into wheelbarrows to
be trundled inside and crushed beneath the eight-hundred-pound
stamps which rose and fell, once every second, all day long and
often through the night, shaking the building with their thunderous
clatter and filling the air with a heavy choking powder. The crushed
rock was dumped into containers and passed through a series of
settling tanks, amalgamating pans, agitators and separators until at
last the precious metal was collected into the fire retort, to be freed
of its quicksilver and emerge in bricks of pure silver or gold. The
machines performed all these complex actions with a miraculous
fidelity when they were on display in St. Louis, but once they arrived
in the mountains the trouble began, and it was not often twenty-four
hours passed without one failure or another.

In spite of his impatience with these problems, Matt had been
forced to learn the whims and caprices of the machinery, even
though he could never minister to it without an angry face, frequent
curses, and now and then a random kick.

And if it should happen that Pete and Jonathan and Lem Finney
and Josiah Webb were away at the same time, and he was left to cure
it without help, he grew more and more exasperated as one remedy
and another failed until, after a few hours, he was too infuriated to
be dexterous and there was little hope the machinery would run
until someone less excited by these frustrations appeared to put it
right. And so, by the time Pete had been away for two days and a half,
the quartz mill had stood silent for most of that time, and Matt had
become so frantically eager for Pete to come back and get it to working
again that he quite forgot there might be any reason he should dread
to see his brother.

Then, late in the afternoon of the third day, Matt glanced up to see Pete standing in the doorway, and beckoned eagerly to him. "Thank God, you're back. Let's see what you can do with this bloody thing." He sounded, even as he listened to his own voice, so honestly relieved, and so guiltless, that he had no slightest doubt of what Pete would do.

Pete came forward quickly, knelt down after giving him only a brief glance, and they became absorbed in their common struggle with the machinery. And as they worked Matt assured himself that, just as when they had been very much younger, the fight had cleansed them both, for they could remember, if they chose to, other times when Pete had been forced to defend himself by attacking him.

At last the stamps began to rumble and clatter, trampling the ore, they gave instructions to the men, and started back toward town.

As they rode, Matt began to ask about the trip, showing a lively interest in the properties he had gone to inspect. Pete described what he had found, in Deer Lodge and in the other camps, and his report was so complete that by the time they arrived in town Matt was assuring himself the man who had attacked him had not been Pete at all, but either the sneak thief he had described to Jenny or, more likely, some apparition which had appeared to each of them. He found no explanation for Pete's visit to Marietta, and because he preferred not to think about it, had determined that Marietta must forget it had ever happened, just as he had ordered Jenny to believe the man she had seen was not Pete.

In fact, when he now asked Pete to have a drink with him and Pete agreed without any slight hesitation, Matt was convinced that if the women did not disturb this equanimity they might all be restored to a kind of original purity in their feelings for one another; and it seemed a remarkable and wonderful thing to have happened for it had been achieved, after all, without blood. He faced Pete as they stood at the bar, raised his glass to him, looked at him with a keen and steady interest, and found that he loved him better than ever before.

A few days later Matt set off with Jonathan to inspect other properties and to collect overdue debts, and found so many compelling reasons why he must interview various ranchers and small farmers and owners of isolated claims, that they were gone for more than a week and he returned with the serene conviction that by now even Jenny would be ready to admit the man had not been Pete, but a stranger.

He was not eager to see her, however, and invented excuses to avoid the places where they might meet. Irene Flint had one of her rare evening receptions, and at the last moment something kept him from going. Jenny gave a dinner party, and he was not able to be there, either. There was a dance at the Masonic Hall, but he was away on an overnight trip. When he had finally begun to wonder why he should be so unwilling to meet her, and what possible danger there might be in it for either of them, she passed him on the street, flying by in the red-wheeled buggy, and leaned out, giving him a signal to come to her.

He approached quickly, glancing about to see if there was anyone who would recognize him, and then confronted Jenny, who looked down at him as he stood waiting with an air of solemn obedience for what she might have to say to him. She invited him to sit beside her but he refused, saying he must be on his way, he had only a moment, Lem Finney, in fact, was waiting for him. He continued to gaze up at her with that same sober and, he hoped, inscrutable face, being careful to take no particular notice of how she looked, for it seemed clear enough that the less he was aware of her the safer and more comfortable all of them would be. Jenny watched him with a kind of ironic amusement, and when she smiled he was sorry to see she had understood his thoughts.

"What have you been doing, Matt?"

He stared at her impassively. "Working."

She laughed at this and gave a little gesture, telling him there was no use trying to fool her, for she knew him too well. "Every now and then, you and Pete surprise me by being so much alike." He made a slight grimace, but did not answer. "He described his trip to Deer Lodge just as if he'd been there."

"He was there, Jenny. He brought back signed contracts, promissory notes, several leases. He was there."

She gazed at him with a thoughtful and pitying expression, letting him know that he and Pete might delude themselves if they must, but she could not. "He kissed me when he came in, just as he always does, and asked me what I'd done while he was away." She paused, watching him. "And he seemed even gladder than usual to see Leila. He kissed her over and over again, and wouldn't let her go even when she started to squirm." She lowered her voice. "As if he knew he'd almost lost her."

"That's absurd," Matt told her curtly. "Stop imagining these things."

"He did try to kill you, Matt."

Matt stared at her angrily for a moment and started away, but when he had gone a few steps he ran back, caught hold of the buggy just as it was starting to move, and covered her hand and held it fast. "You've got to believe me. It wasn't Pete."

Jenny looked at him and at last shook her head slowly. "He's ashamed he tried to kill you—but he wishes you were dead." He stepped back, glaring at her with a menacing fury, and Jenny flicked the reins over the horse's back. "Take care, Matt," she advised him, and drove away.

After that he was so angry he began to ask himself if he had ever loved Jenny Danforth at all, for his loyalty to Pete had now become so intense and his devotion to him so warm that Jenny seemed some alien influence, beckoning him and Pete into fatal disharmonies which, without her, would never have occurred. To convince himself of this, Matt presently suggested to Pete that they go on a hunting trip, over near the Missouri River, telling him, "Marietta thinks she needs a black-tailed buck for the foyer."

Pete agreed more readily than he had expected, and they made plans to leave at the end of the week. And this seeming eagerness of Pete's caused Matt to wonder, before shame overtook him, if perhaps he should find some excuse not to go. But then he remembered that the suspicions were Jenny's, not his, and became more than ever determined to make this test, challenge himself to prove he was not a coward, and Pete to forgive him once and for all, or if he could not, then to kill him as Jenny said he meant to do.

Again he tried to avoid seeing her, but she came into the office one morning just after Pete had gone out, and found him there alone. He confronted her across his desk with that expression of distrustful waiting which nowadays came onto his face at sight of her. But this time she talked to him with such urgent intensity she might be trying to save the life of a man determined to kill himself and impervious to reason.

"Don't go with him, Matt, I beg of you."

"What a thing to say, Jenny," he told her, shaking his head wonderingly.

"But this is what he's been waiting for."

He gave her a long and gravely mocking look. "Well, then, if it's what he's been waiting for, I've given it to him. If he wants to kill me, he can do it—and no one will ever have to know how it was done." He smiled again as the door opened and Count Manzoni came in. Jenny left, and Matt and Pete set out at four o'clock on Friday morning.

Several days later they returned with the black-tailed buck slung across Matt's saddle, and humorously explained to men who saw them riding in to town that they had got the buck they went after but could not be sure which of them it belonged to, for they had crossed the trail of a stag which took them by surprise as it trampled threateningly toward them, and had fired at almost the same instant. The animal was a handsome one and roused much admiring attention as it lay across the saddle and later at the taxidermist's, where men stopped to examine it and comment on its points, and when it was ready they tossed a coin for it. Matt won the toss and sent it home to decorate the foyer, and found its presence there a talisman guaranteeing there would never again be trouble between them.

Jenny, however, saw something different in it the first night she and Pete came to dinner, and Matt noticed the skeptical look she gave it as she entered the house, quite as if the stag's head might belong to some impostor, a guest she did not expect to like and whose true identity she would presently disclose.

Three or four hours later, when the guests were leaving, Jenny came downstairs holding Leila in her arms. The little girl was asleep and as Matt took her and carried her toward the vestibule, Jenny walked beside him, murmuring, "I suppose in time we'll become such perfect hypocrites we'll all believe our own lies."

"Are you sorry he didn't kill me?"

"I'm sorry we're all so dishonest."

"We aren't any more."

"What difference does that make?" And, as if to prove her point, Jenny began to talk with unusual animation to Erma Finney and Marietta about the plans for the Fourth of July picnic, still several weeks away.

Jenny had no trust in the human capacity to forgive those who disappoint cherished beliefs, and so she had never told Pete, or Matt, that Leila was not her first child; because she had not told them early, she was afraid to tell them late. For her repudiation of that child when she had been only a few weeks old seemed to Jenny the unforgivable deed of her life, and the sorrows she might have caused Marietta or Pete were inconsequential beside it.

On the day she and Dr. Danforth had set out for the gold camps, Jenny had warned herself that now it was too late, the injury she had done she must live with the rest of her life, and, because it had seemed irrevocable, she had not written once to Andy Danforth's sister. After Leila's birth, Jenny began to imagine that this new child might be a sign of forgiveness, or, perhaps, she was meant to be another test, one more trial of her integrity, and her love for Leila was so beset with apprehensions that when she went upstairs late one afternoon to wake Leila from her nap and found her irritable and shivering beneath the blanket, though the day was warm, complaining that her head ached, it seemed only the fulfillment of an old prophecy.

She stood in the doorway, listening to the little girl's voice and the petulant sound it had with what seemed an extraordinary keenness of attention, and all at once ran to the bed and gathered her into her arms, smoothing her hair and holding her fast, rocking back and forth and patting her, and began to cry in an ecstasy of terror. Leila lay inert and unprotesting for several moments, but at last tried to free herself and, very gently, Jenny laid her down and bent over her, wiping the tears from her own face and smiling. Leila gazed up at her, but though she had an expression of vague unhappiness, there was no fear, and she plainly believed the discomfort would be gone with the confession that she felt it.

Jenny spoke to her urgently, whispering, as if to tell her a secret. "You mustn't be frightened, darling. It's nothing, I know it's nothing and you believe me, don't you?" Jenny shut her eyes, covered her face, and sobbed until her body shook the bed. But all at once she stopped, sat rigidly still, and then took Leila's face between her hands, softly asking, "You felt well when you went to bed?"

"Yes, Mother, I think so. I didn't feel so well. But I didn't feel sick."

Jenny kissed her cheeks and found them surprisingly cool and moist, then took her hands and held them tight between her own, as if to warm them. "But you should have told me, Leila, you should have told me the minute you began to feel bad."

"I was afraid you'd make me stay in bed."

Jenny stood up, drew the blanket to Leila's chin, and spoke to her seriously and confidingly. "I must go for the Doctor, darling. If Mrs. Hatch is home, I'll ask her to go for me, and if she isn't then I must go myself. But you must promise me that you won't get out of bed, that you will lie here and rest, and you must not be frightened. You'll be well again very soon, perhaps by tomorrow, but you can't play any more today. Will you promise?"

Leila nodded, and smiled. "I won't be frightened—and neither will you."

Jenny kissed her, then ran down the stairs, through the kitchen door and across the rows of her vegetable garden, and burst into Mrs. Hatch's house without knocking, screaming her name as she ran through one room after another and ran back out, leaving the front door standing open. She dashed toward a group of children playing a little distance down the hillside, crying imploringly, "Leila's sick!" They turned in astonishment, for she looked nothing like Mrs. Devlin, nothing like Leila's mother, and her appearance of fanatic desperation alarmed them. "Which of you will go for the Doctor?" She looked around, searching one small face and another, and longed to seize them and shake them into a recognition of what she had said, for they still gazed at her with stupid uncomprehending expressions. "Which of you? Bobby—" She seized a little boy's arm and turned him about, shoving him sharply as he hesitated. "You go. Hurry, hurry, for God's sake, you little fool. Oh, Bobby, forgive me, I'm sorry, I didn't mean that— but run! Can't you!" She clapped her hands and he dashed away, but after a few steps he stopped and turned and looked at her uncertainly. She made a wild, sweeping gesture. "Run, run, I told you! And when you've found the Doctor, find Mr. Devlin and tell him to come home." She waited a moment as the boy pelted on down the hillside, and then ran back to the house.

Dr. Chaffinch arrived in less than half an hour, and Jenny met him at the top of the stairs with a look of such venomous hatred that he paused. "I came as quickly as I could, Mrs. Devlin."

Jenny watched as he passed her, her face so condemnatory he paused once again to look at her, then went into the room, took Leila's wrist and began to count her pulse. Jenny stood just inside the doorway and had begun to shiver uncontrollably, folding her arms as the trembling became more violent, and at last her teeth began to chatter. She watched as he looked at the child's tongue, put his ear to her chest, asking Leila to tell him how she felt, and her eyes were hard and unforgiving, as if she knew the fault was his if her daughter was sick.

At last he straightened, frowning, and looked down at Leila, who lay very still, gazing up at him and expecting to hear some magical words which would make her well again. "What is it?" Jenny demanded. He did not answer and she seized his arm. "It's nothing to be concerned about, is it? Is it?" she cried, then stopped, for Leila was gazing at her reproachfully. Instantly Jenny became quiet, her body stopped quivering and she stood erect, speaking to the Doctor in a quiet reasonable voice. "What do you think it is, Dr. Chaffinch?"

Dr. Chaffinch looked at her soberly. "I don't know, Mrs. Devlin. It's too early to be sure. Perhaps she has measles." He touched Leila's cheek caressingly. "If you have, my dear, you must be very quiet for several days, but your mother will read to you, and I promise the time will pass quickly. Will you do exactly as I tell you?"

"Yes, I will, Dr. Chaffinch. I don't like to be sick."

Jenny bowed her head and covered her face with her hands and for several moments scarcely dared to breathe for, if she did, it seemed she would begin to rave and scream, dash herself against the walls of the room and destroy herself before them both, the serious and troubled doctor and the bewildered sick child. At last she let her arms fall to her sides. "What can I do for her?"

They walked out, after asking Leila's permission as if she were their hostess, and at the foot of the stairs Jenny turned and waited for him. "Do you really think it's measles?" She looked at him skeptically, as if to say it was neither fair nor necessary to fool her.

"Mrs. Devlin, I truthfully don't know what it is."

"Pneumonia?"

"I don't think so. We won't know for a day or two. You were a doctor's wife—you know how ignorant we are. But she's always been a healthy child and, though she looks delicate, she's strong, and she's happy. That makes a difference. But one thing you must remember, Mrs. Devlin—"

"I know," Jenny interrupted. "I mustn't frighten her. I won't."

"And you must not let her father frighten her, either."

Jenny gave him an unpleasant smile, warning him not to try to enter their lives at this crisis but to stand aside, leave them to their fear and sorrow, and it seemed he understood her, for he quickly began to discuss the treatment, most of which sounded to Jenny as absurd and impotent as Dr. Danforth's pharmacopoeia.

"Hot elderberry tea will make her a little more comfortable. At least, it can do no harm. I think a mustard plaster on her chest and onion poultices to the soles of her feet, changed every three hours, and a tablespoonful of castor oil—"

"I won't give it to her. She hates it. And I don't believe it will help."

"She must have it, Mrs. Devlin."

They stood staring at each other, Dr. Chaffinch gazing at her guiltily and sadly for it was clear that she blamed him, not only for Leila's sickness but because he could not tell her what it was and because he had only these remedies which, as they both realized, could cure nothing.

There was a clatter upon the stairs, and Pete came dashing up.

He flung the door open and stood holding it wide, and in back of him beyond their white fence Jenny could see the children gathered, gazing toward them with spellbound faces, for a sudden sickness in the mountains had often meant they never again saw their small friend alive, and she felt that their expressions and the manner in which they stood there, six or eight of them together at the gate, was another omen and somehow more sinister than her own fears, for theirs seemed something in the nature of an animal's forewarning of approaching death. Pete looked as distraught as if he had been sent word of a fatal accident. He stared at Dr. Chaffinch and then at Jenny, and without having spoken a word to them, went leaping up the stairs, taking them in no more than three or four reaches of his long legs, while Jenny continued to watch the Doctor with her look of implicit warning, until he left her, saying, "I'll be back in two or three hours."

She walked into the living room and stood watching the children through the curtained glass, marveling at how still they were able to be, these youngsters who were usually running and shouting together. Then she went to the kitchen and began to prepare the elderberry tea and the mustard plasters, but she moved listlessly, and when she heard Pete come in, turned to him with a look of such despairing resignation that he seized her hands, and then took her into his arms. "What does he think it is? She told me she's feeling better."

"Of course she did. She knows we're terrified and that's frightened her. Pete, whatever happens, don't ever let her see you looking as if you believe she may not live."

He moved back, releasing her as if he had hold of something dangerous. "My good God, Jenny—"

"Never do, Pete. She must believe we expect her to be well in a day or two."

"But she will," he cried imploringly. "Jesus Christ, do you think she won't?"

"I don't know. Go back to her. I'll be up in a few minutes."

"Shall I send for Marietta?"

She turned quickly. "Why?"

Pete looked embarrassed and sad, as if she had accused him of something shameful. "Because she's a very good nurse. And she loves Leila."

"I'll take care of her. I don't want help."

He started out, then paused and came back to her. "Jenny, I know you're scared, so am I, but we have nothing to be afraid of yet."

"Please go to her, Pete. We mustn't leave her alone. Read something. *Aesop's Fables*. She likes that."

After a few minutes she came upstairs with Dr. Chaffinch's prescribed remedies, including the castor oil. Leila lay on her side, gazing thoughtfully at Pete as he read, and when Jenny came in she glanced at her and smiled with such sweet confidence that Jenny's fears vanished and she gave a soft laugh, wondering at how quick she was to imagine catastrophe. She sat beside her and began to coax her to take the castor oil just as she might have coaxed her to take a spring tonic, playing with her, though Leila was wary and not inclined to agree it would make her feel better, and as they discussed it, arguing at some length over the castor oil's immediate faults and presumed future benefits, Pete watched them with a relieved and adoring smile.

But she did not improve during the night and Dr. Chaffinch continued at a loss to understand the nature of her illness. Matt came in the early evening, stayed a few minutes, and left. In the morning, Marietta appeared before seven o'clock, and after that the living room was occupied all day long and until late at night with neighbors and friends who stood about anxiously and fearfully, for the young children died very easily there in the mountains, it seemed, and were not so much invigorated by the climate and altitude as they were made more susceptible by it.

Jenny did not come downstairs, but stayed with Leila as she grew more apathetic, the chill changed to fever, and she began to complain of pains in her legs and back and neck. She threw herself restlessly about, begged them to keep the shades down and covered her eyes protestingly with her hands, and cried in despair when they could do nothing to stop the headache. She sometimes lay silent and stupefied, her eyes closed, or she watched them distrustfully, for they had not been able to help her and she grew skeptical of their promises. After three days she looked at Jenny and Pete and Dr. Chaffinch, watching her so gravely. "Will I die?" Pete gave a moaning outcry and rushed from the house.

Lisette was not permitted to enter the house because of her own children, but Marietta was there all day and sometimes remained through the night, cooking the meals, serving coffee to the vigilant women who sat about the fireplace—for although it was early June the mornings and evenings were very cold, a strange year, they agreed—and talking to the children when they came to the door, as they did several times each day. The women stopped Dr. Chaffinch as he came downstairs and questioned him about the symptoms, the changes since his last visit, and both Erma Finney and Irene Flint had diagnosed the sickness before Dr. Chaffinch was willing to give his opinion. At first they had thought it must be measles but, after five days, they came to another conclusion.

"I know what it is," Erma Finney said, when Marietta left the room.

"So do I," Irene Flint agreed. "But none of us should say what we think. We may be wrong."

"I hope we are, but the symptoms are those of spotted fever." The women murmured, shaking their heads, and agreed that this was their own diagnosis.

On his next visit Dr. Chaffinch found her pulse weaker and the rash, which momentarily disappeared as he lightly pressed the skin, was spreading over her body and had begun to turn into livid spots, like the marks of dark bruises, and so he had to agree.

Pete rushed in and out of the house like a man escaping each time from a terror which was growing too great for him to confront, dashing away when he could tolerate it no longer and then, because he could no better tolerate being away, imagining she might die in his absence, he would rush back again, entering the darkened room stealthily to stand watching the sick, restless child who often lay in a silent stupor which lasted several hours, then emerged from it, babbling and whimpering in confused sentences which only Jenny seemed to understand.

As one day passed and another, Jenny slept very little and even then she would not leave the room or lie down, but dozed beside the bed and woke with a start, looking ashamed and guilty and, if anyone else was in the room, demanding in an angry whisper why they had not wakened her. When Pete spoke to her she seemed not to hear him, and if he tried to make her listen she stared at him with a cold and condemnatory look, then turned away.

At last he approached Marietta. "Jenny doesn't need me. She doesn't want me to help her. She looks at me as if I'm a stranger—or her mortal enemy. What shall I do?"

"She doesn't know what she's doing, Pete—can't you see that when you look at her? What she does or says to you can't matter to you now, can it? Leave her alone with the child. Don't ask anything for yourself." Pete then grew as silent as Jenny, avoided passing through the living room where two or three friends were always gathered, crept timidly about the house, and when he entered Leila's room had nothing to say, only hovered over the little girl and from time to time smoothed her hair, sighing deeply as his fingers touched her.

Jenny no longer spoke to Pete or Marietta, asked no questions of Dr. Chaffinch, and never left the room. She sent them on errands with a glance or gesture, to bring water and clean towels and sheets, to empty the basins when Leila began to vomit, to carry away the bandages which were used to cover the massive areas spreading from the first pustules and which soon sloughed, destroying the surface of her skin with bloody sores. When she began to have convulsions the Doctor wanted to tie her to the bed, warning them she might injure herself, and Jenny turned on him with a gesture which drove him away, protesting to Marietta that she was demented and no one was safe in her presence. But he soon came back, though he gave no more advice, only hovered about as Pete did, silent and watching.

As the sickness grew worse, Jenny left the trays Marietta prepared for her untouched, and no longer fell asleep even briefly but sat through the night, alert and ready, seeming as resigned to each change as if she knew what to expect at every moment and had prepared herself to endure it with stoical patience. At last, when Leila had been in deep coma for most of a day and night, Dr. Chaffinch laid his hand on her chest, passed his fingers across her closed eyes, and pronounced her dead.

Jenny sat motionless for several moments, looking at the child, but at last turned to Marietta and shook her head slowly. "She's dead? So soon?" She gazed at Marietta with a look of wonderment. "It's almost as if she slipped away from life. Almost as if she had never been here at all." She seemed unaware that Pete had fallen to his knees beside the bed, sobbing, or that Matt stood nearby.

Finally she sent them away, saying that she and no other would prepare her child for burial, wash her and dress her, and asked them to leave her alone. When she came out, some time later, still with the same uncanny look of having no actual awareness of what had happened, she passed Pete without noticing or speaking to him, went downstairs for the first time in almost two weeks, smiling vaguely at Marietta as they met on the staircase, and when Matt approached her in the dining room, she paused and looked at him. After a moment, she went into the kitchen where she stood looking out the window, slowly drinking a cup of coffee, and had nothing to say to anyone.

Throughout the day the living room was crowded, but Jenny seemed not to know they were in the house. Erma Finney came two or three times and, each time, had a look of baffled surprise she could not seem to lose. Whenever she spoke to anyone it was to tell them, "It was God's will."

Most of them nodded, but Irene Flint murmured angrily, "Don't ever say that to her parents."

"It might comfort them."

Marietta caught her arm. "Nothing will comfort them, Erma, and don't say it again. You can't honestly believe it, and it's a cruel thing to say." Late in the afternoon Marietta sent them all away. "They don't want us here now, it's best to leave them alone."

Pete stood at the door as the last caller left the house, and when he went back to Leila's room he found Jenny seated beside the bed where the little girl lay in a white cambric robe, with her hair brushed smooth and twined into a single long coil which lay across her shoulder. Jenny was looking at her with a curious, faint smile, as if she might have just said something to amuse her, and she held open on her lap the copy of *Aesop's Fables.* She was dressed in the black weeds she had worn after Andrew Danforth's death, and had gone almost immediately to the trunk where they were stored, as if she would not believe in the reality of the child's death until she had put them on.

He sat beside her until the room grew quite dark, and then asked, "Can't you rest now?"

"Of course I can't rest." He could not see her, but she sounded aloof and as reproachful as if she wanted no participation from him in this experience which was to be only hers.

Matt and Marietta returned early in the morning, for the funeral was to be at ten o'clock, and when Matt came to help him carry the coffin downstairs Jenny rose instantly and without speaking to either of them, avoiding looking at them, went into their bedroom and closed the door.

Children and neighbors came continuously with flowers collected from their own gardens and from the hillsides, and Marietta strewed the coffin with the wild roses and violets brought by Leila's friends. Jonathan and Douglas and Robert moved the living-room furniture, setting up rows of borrowed chairs and benches there and in the dining room. Jenny had left the funeral arrangements to Marietta, and she had decided that since their friends and neighbors wanted to be present, even the children coming to ask if they could see Leila once more, that all who wished might come, and intended to seat Jenny and Pete and the other members of the family in the dining room where they could not be seen. By nine-thirty they had begun to arrive, Erma and Lem Finney first, and presently the room was crowded, but even the young children sat so still the house might have been empty.

When the Reverend Bream arrived, Pete went upstairs and found Jenny in their bedroom, her back to him as she looked out the window where, he supposed, she had been watching their friends, or possibly she had not seen them at all, for she was as dazedly un-believing as she had been at the moment of Leila's death. She wore the bonnet with its veils streaming over her shoulders and down her back and he looked at her in sorrowing dismay, for she seemed once more to have retreated into that sheltering solitude of the mourning clothes in which he had found her after Dr. Danforth's death; though then, as she had told him, she was longing to be rescued, and now she refused to let him approach her and would not have his comfort or share his pain.

He waited silently until, after several moments, she turned and was holding on the palms of her hands the silver-mounted pistol Matt had given to Leila. Pete's face twisted in an involuntary gri-mace and he came quickly forward to take it from her, but she held it to one side, away from him. "I want this to be buried with her. Will you lay it in the coffin?"

Pete approached a little nearer. "Jenny, I don't want anything to happen between us today. I only hope to God we can endure it. But I beg of you, don't ask me to do such a thing. You know it's impossible."

She smiled slowly and still held the gun carefully pointed away from them both, but it nevertheless seemed to him there was some-thing ominous in the expression of her face and the poise of her hand as she held it, delicately, as if it were only a toy. "Why is it impossible? It was the first gift she received. Don't you remember Matt said he'd intended it for her brother—but even a little girl might learn to use it if she lived here?"

He moved forward with a sudden determination to take it from her, but she backed away. "Pete, don't come near me." Then all at once she held it toward him, presenting the ornamented butt end, as if she were offering him a choice of dueling pistols. After a moment he took it, slipped it into his coat pocket, and stepped to one side. As she passed him she gave a sideways glance, curious and mocking, or so it seemed, for her face could not be clearly seen through the dense thicknesses of the veil. She paused at the door. "Will you do it?"

Pete hesitated and, at last, said, "I can't, Jenny. Bury a little girl, my child, with a pistol. And if I did, you would blame me for it later, when you've—" He had begun to say she would blame him when she was sane again, but he paused and then said, "When you've had time to think."

She held out one hand. "Give it to me."

"I'll keep it."

"I want to put it there myself. I'll go into the living room, in front of them all, if you won't." She had seemed to feel, from the moment she had known Leila was sick, that their friends, the Doctor, perhaps all of them but Marietta, had become her enemies, and that they were in some sense triumphant over her sorrow.

He shook his head. "No. We must go downstairs, Jenny, it's time for the services to begin."

"If you won't give it to me," she said slowly, "and if you won't do what I ask, then I'll ask nothing more of you—ever."

"Jenny, Jenny, dearest, you don't know what you're saying." He held out his arms. "You're hysterical."

She went slowly down the stairs and he followed her into the dining room where he took his place at her side and, presently, could hear the Reverend Obadiah Bream begin the prayers. He bowed his head and did not look at her again until the services were completed, had no awareness of what had been said, and heard only vaguely the sounds of crying which seemed to surround him; and all the while Jenny sat straight and motionless, staring at the wall.

When they were asked to pass by the coffin, she continued to sit there until he came back into the dining room and found her alone, and when he held out one hand, she turned slightly away, saying, "I want to see her last."

He walked into the living room, which was empty again, paused beside the coffin but could not look into it, and went to stand on the porch, staring down at the floor, feeling naked and helpless before his friends who were gathered on the lawn, trying not to look at him. After several minutes there was a slight murmur, and as he searched for its cause he found them gazing at him with sympathetic shame, for Jenny was quickly crossing the yard and now climbed into Marietta's buggy, leaving him to make the trip alone.

Matt and Jonathan, with Lem Finney and Josiah Webb, came out of the house, bearing the small coffin on their shoulders, and the procession set out, passing through the streets which wove about the

hilltops, avoiding the town's busy center. The Reverend Obadiah
Bream walked first, Pete followed him, and forty or fifty men and
women walked behind them, while the children fell into a group to
the rear and, finally, there came six or eight carriages, the last with
Marietta and Jenny. The sound of the mourning bell, rung by the
Reverend Bream, brought women and children to the doors and windows, and some ran to the street's edge where they stood watching
the procession file silently by.

The day was cold and very windy, the sun came intermittently,
and the sky was filling with clouds. There was prophecy of a summer
storm, and by the time they reached the cemetery it had grown quite
dark. Jenny remained in the carriage as the coffin was lowered into the
grave, the final prayer was spoken, and they started to move slowly
down the hillside. When they had gone a discreet distance, they
walked more quickly and some began to run, to reach shelter before
the storm broke. Pete remained kneeling beside the grave, Matt stood
near him, and Lisette was crying in Ralph's arms and could not stop.

At last Marietta turned to Jenny. "Shall we go back?"

Jenny nodded and Marietta maneuvered the buggy around. The
wind had begun to whip at the curtains, the darkness increased, and
all at once there were sharp spatters of rain against the buggy top,
then a pelting of hail, and Jenny gave a protesting cry and began
climbing out of the buggy as Marietta tried to bring it to a stop. Matt
and Pete whirled around, shouting a warning as she tumbled forward
and pitched onto her knees, bracing herself with both hands. She
remained there for a moment, her head hanging, as if she had been
hurt, and they ran toward her. But as they approached, Jenny scrambled to her feet and started to run, taking another direction, back up
the hillside.

They followed her until, as if at a command, Matt stopped still,
and all of them watched with disbelieving, stricken faces as Pete
caught hold of her, for she began to fight him, screaming, "Let me
go, I can't leave her here alone!" She struggled with him frantically
and then, as he held her, she struck him a hard blow across the face.
"Let go of me, God damn you!" She sprang away, picking up her
skirts, and ran on.

XLII

Morgan was married one early May morning to Felice Talbot in the
parsonage of a Presbyterian church on lower Broadway, a little un-
fashionable church they had chosen for that reason, and Felice had
impulsively confided to the Reverend Hodge's wife that they were
eloping. At this the Reverend, perhaps thinking a girl so well dressed

might have a troublesome father, objected to reading the services, so that Morgan undertook to convince him with such passionate arguments he momentarily convinced himself he was as eager to be married as he seemed.

But even as he stood beside Felice in the dismal little parlor, hearing the maid snuffling in back of them and Mrs. Hodges sighing from time to time, he was thinking with regret of the stratagems which had failed him, and wondering how it happened that scarcely eight months after he had seen her first, he should be getting married to a girl he knew little better today than he had then.

This seemed all the more strange because, for several weeks after Mrs. Talbot's warning, he had supposed himself out of danger. He had spent more time in the library and laboratories, had gone twice to Baltimore to observe the assay furnaces, and was soon congratulating himself the scare was over, had passed by and left him unharmed, after all. But then, through some connivance between Suky and Felice, he saw her again.

Suky asked him to ride with her in the Park one winter afternoon, just as there was a staining glow of sunset over the black branched trees, and without any slight suspicion he climbed into the sleigh, wrapped the embroidered buffalo robe cozily about them both, taking hold of her hand in the folds of its concealing warmth, and talking to her happily of the session just begun, confiding his enthusiasm for geometry and chemistry and Egleston's *Metallurgical Tables.*

The weather had been cold for some time, the streets frozen hard, and as they went sliding up Fifth Avenue they passed other sleighs, gaily painted and decorated with floating red horsehair plumes, their bells chiming, carrying men and women in fur coats and hats. They coursed through the Park, with Suky teasing him for having neglected her, and at last drew up beside a pond which lay off Fifth Avenue, between Forty-sixth and Forty-seventh Streets.

Here a brass band was playing, bonfires burned, vendors were selling hot coffee and doughnuts and, as if he had known exactly where to look, he saw Felice skating alone, absorbed and seemingly unaware that anyone she knew might be there as she went circling and spinning through one figure after another, while the chaperone who had accompanied her to Europe sat on a bench not far away.

Morgan turned to Suky, ready to accuse her for this treachery, but instead surprised himself by climbing out of the sleigh, waving to Felice, and she came gliding up to them, stopped herself with a downward thrust of her skate into the ice, kissed Suky, and gave him such an appealing smile he knew she had expected him to be angry.

But now that he confronted her again, this girl he felt obliged to run away from, he looked at her carefully, with the intention of finding out once and for all just what it might be that made her seem so extraordinary. He contemplated her with a thoughtful seriousness, skeptically watching the changing expressions of her face as she talked to Suky and pretended not to know he was looking at her, one moment intensely concerned as they discussed a ball she had been given permission to attend, only to have the permission summarily withdrawn by her father, and the next laughing merrily over Suky's description of Sarita's morning prank. She was reserved and aloof, next she gave way to a fervent enthusiasm, and in a few moments he was taken aback to find himself yearning over her with a lover's anxious curiosity.

She glanced at him, found him watching her, and fell into a confusion which charmed him hopelessly. But she recovered from it and asked him to skate with her as artlessly as a child might ask a respected adult to join it at play, and as he went to rent a pair of skates he was reminding himself that several young girls had wanted to marry him—and their fathers had wanted them to marry Matt Devlin's son—but Felice Talbot was the only girl he had known who had nothing to gain by marrying him, and indeed she had much to lose. And this, perhaps, was the explanation he had been so carefully seeking and so diligently avoiding, the reason why this girl of promise and accomplishment who seemed to insist upon nothing at all but was ready to let herself be guided by whoever gained her confidence, struck such terror into him.

There were not many skaters left on the pond and they were free to spin and whirl, growing more exultant as they danced together, smiling into each other's faces while the illusion grew that they had acquired this capacity for effortless movement, skimming about the earth's surface in triumphant freedom, disentangled from other lives and so absorbed in each other that Morgan was surprised to see another sleigh drawn near Suky's and Frederic Hallam standing talking to her. He turned to look at them as he and Felice went sailing by, for he had lately begun to be as suspicious of Frederic Hallam as he was of Philip Van Zandt, but the jealous pang was soon gone, he smiled once again at Felice, and promised himself that if Zack Fletcher was not scalped by the Indians and sent him even ten thousand dollars, he would marry this girl.

Less than a month later he received a letter from a St. Louis bank, informing him that twenty-three thousand dollars had been deposited to his account, but still he hesitated and, once again, tried to avoid meeting her while he scribbled figures over many pages to convince himself that marriage was beyond his financial capacity. Then one day, with an air of theatrical unconcern, he asked Suky if Steven was possibly expecting to marry Felice Talbot. Suky laughed, tipping her head back and gazing at the blue-glass ceiling of the conservatory, then turned to him, murmuring, "I imagine Papa would like that, don't you?"

Now, as he stood beside Felice in the Reverend Hodge's parlor, it was not easy to believe he was there, and even though he could scarcely blame Felice for it, since he had proposed to her only three days ago, demanding that she marry him immediately and without telling even Suky about it, nevertheless he stared grimly at the Reverend and was still expecting some timely interference to save him.

He had warned Felice, during those few minutes they had spent alone in Suky's conservatory, when he had astonished himself, though apparently not Felice, by asking her to marry him, of all the hardships and disappointments he had time to describe. But whatever he said only made her eyes shine more brightly, and at last he despairingly concluded that romantic young girls like Felice relished difficulties put in the way of their marriages even better than they relished elaborate wedding gowns and crowds of gaping friends at the church. Another kind of girl might not have been so eager to sacrifice herself, or to defy her parents for the sake of having him, but he found as he stood beside her, hearing only vaguely the words spoken by the Reverend Hodges, that he was not so much grateful to Felice as he was stunned and bewildered at knowing she was now his wife and he need no longer admire her from a distance, but might soon find it necessary to keep her at a certain distance, lest she envelop him.

She leaned toward him, he reached out with a quick, mechanical gesture to take her into his arms, then bent his head and carefully kissed her. As he drew back, feeling wretchedly embarrassed before the Reverend and his wife and the crying maid, he saw that her eyes were opened wide and she was gazing up at him with a pleading and rather frightened expression, and at this he forgave her for having married him and felt a painful tenderness and a longing to comfort and reassure her, take back the threats of loneliness and unhappiness and give her, instead, a great many promises he would never keep.

Abruptly, Morgan shook hands with the Reverend and left a twenty-dollar bill in his palm, and ushered Felice out with Mrs. Hodges following along and begging Felice to come to see her as soon as she returned from her honeymoon. "Are you going to have a honeymoon?"

Felice stood on the porch and Morgan raised an umbrella over her head. She turned back pleadingly to Mrs. Hodges, as if to ask her forgiveness for this unceremonious departure. "I don't know, Mrs. Hodges. Are we?"

Morgan gave Mrs. Hodges a slight stiff bow. "Yes, ma'am, we are," and hurried Felice down the steps and into the hired hack he had left waiting, telling the driver to take them to the Hoffman House.

He jumped in, slamming the door, sat as far to one side as he could get, and stared out the window. The sky was peculiarly green and the rain fell hard and steadily so that the traffic proceeded at a very slow pace and occasionally they came to a halt, but it seemed neither could think of anything to say and they sat trapped together in an impenetrable silence; the beginning, he now sadly remembered, of endless hours they would spend alone. And all at once it struck him with renewed terror that this girl was a virgin, for what had seemed to him before some advantage, seemed now a baneful responsibility to thrust upon a man, a kind of unfair trick contrived by her parents to test him on the one occasion he might be least likely to meet any kind of test with authority.

He glanced sideways at her, glowering suspiciously, and she was looking out the window in the other direction. He could see only the back of her head and the side of her face, but something in the posture of her body, held alertly erect, and the way she had folded her hands in her lap, gave him once again that sense of painful tenderness which had made him want to marry her and, for the moment, his fears of her vanished.

All at once, however, he was surprised to hear himself declare, in a harsh loud voice, "I may not make a very good husband. I'm not even sure I've got any business being a husband at all."

She turned, looked at him thoughtfully, and at last smiled, and the smile made him more uneasy than ever, for it convinced him she knew what he was thinking about and always would. She made no answer and they rode on a little farther while he marveled that he should feel this bristling resentment against her when, in fact, if either of them had reason for resentment, Felice did.

The heavy rain beating upon the roof of the cab, the black slippery streets, the women clutching their wet skirts and holding umbrellas, the men hunched into their coat collars with water streaming from the brims of their hats, all served to convince him that he and Felice were somehow isolated from the rest of the world which was going about its business with a grim determination to ignore them at this moment of crisis, leave them alone to solve the riddle before they would once again be permitted to emerge into the world. And as he gazed through the steaming windows, envying those who were out upon the streets, a mournful self-pity overtook him which he despised, though it seemed an inevitable reaction to the fact of having been married only half-an-hour before. For no man was ever happy on his wedding day, as he had heard often enough, and could not expect to be, considering that he had given most of his life away only a few minutes ago and would never again be able to act without some reference in his mind and heart to this young girl, now more strange to him than she had been at their first meeting.

Still, if he was to get married at all, he was glad it had been necessary to elope and so have none of the artificial hilarity of weddings, but to do the deed in a sober and somewhat penurious atmosphere, such as the Reverend Hodge's parlor and, furthermore, to have done it in secrecy.

All at once Felice held out her closed right hand, saying, "Suky gave me this yesterday."

He took from her a small gold watch, snapped it open and found it engraved in Suky's ornate handwriting: *To Felice Talbot Devlin*

from Susan Van Zandt. With my love and devotion. May 2, 1873."
He sat looking at it, wondering and bewildered, and was ashamed
that he felt an inclination to cry.

At last he said, in a soft reproachful voice, "But you promised me
not to tell anyone."

"I had to tell Suky, Morgan. She would never have forgiven me."

But he did not ask what Suky had said, or if she had seemed
pleased, and when the cab stopped before the Hoffman House he
sprang out. "We're not going in. Wait here, I have a suitcase."

She leaned forward. "You'll come back?"

And at that he gave a shout of joyous laughter, took her face between his hands and kissed her mouth, not timidly, as he had before, and went dashing into the lobby, eager to be on his way, for he
had been told by Sir James Gordon of a secluded hotel not far out of
town, and meant to take her there.

Earlier that morning he had assured himself that one bed was the
same as another for such a duty as he had to perform, but now he was
contemptuous of his cynicism, and even as he threw his clothes into
a suitcase he sniffed the air for traces of that musky perfume Coral
Talbot seemed to distill from her own skin, and hurried out again.

The fact that she had now become his mother-in-law seemed a
freakish accident, at once horrifying and grimly humorous, an ironic
whimsy he should have foreseen, and possibly had.

But once he got into the hack, sitting midway on the seat this
time and rather surprised at his own boldness as he smiled at Felice,
once or twice stroked her hair, and began to lose his apprehensions
in an increasing desire, he forgot Coral Talbot and Suky, and was
even grateful for the privacy given them by the rain; and by the time
he awakened beside her the next morning he was amazed to remember those first bitter thoughts, for it seemed he should have
known all along that this marriage to Felice Talbot was his announcement to the world that he intended to walk with large steps, and that
whatever he wanted was not only what he would contrive to have but
was, furthermore, only just good enough for him.

There was, he had been relieved to discover, no great difficulty
about a virgin, but then Felice confessed that it was Suky who had
advised her. " 'Let him do whatever he wants. Things may seem a
little strange to you at first—but you'll soon get used to being married.' And she was right," Felice added, smiling until he felt his face
grow hot at the thought of Suky's hidden participation. "Wasn't she?"

Between arrogance and humility, confidence and doubt, he tried
to grow accustomed to the fact that not only did he have a wife, that
awesome creature who might bring into a man's life so much of
either good or ill, but that he had more significantly a wife who was
an omen of the future.

He had been dreading the honeymoon even more than he dreaded
the marriage itself, and had wished it might have happened in the
mountains where he could have taken prompt flight into one or an-

other of his activities, his sacred work, his private chapel and own temple—the inviolable refuge where a man might retreat when he felt in danger of being surrounded and defeated by femininity—for the thought of ten or fourteen days with none of his usual occupations had given him premonitions of boredom and eternity. In fact, he had brought along copies of Peck's *Differential Calculus* and Kerl's *Metallurgy*, thinking he might retreat into them with pleas of preparing for the June examinations, should the privacy prove overpowering.

She would expect, he was sure, to hear endless compliments and declarations, and it was a few days before he realized he had much reason to be grateful to William Talbot for his strict and merciless supervision, which had taught her she must please the man she was dependent upon. But this made him jealous of Talbot, who might try to take her back again, and his original resentment gave way to a fear that when her father demanded she return to him, she would go, only bidding him good-bye with that expression of soft, gentle regret which sometimes appeared on her face; and he began to occupy himself with schemes for holding onto her when she was tempted, as sooner or later she would be, to leave him.

They had been gone a week when she told him she had written a note to her father and mailed it the day before, and he felt the same sense of panic and shame he might have had she admitted to having sent out a call for help. "You wrote him a note?" He stared at her somberly, as if this first infidelity was the one he had been waiting for. "Why did you do that, Felice?"

They had set out early in the morning on horseback, passing the pretty farmhouses and grazing cattle and earnestly barking dogs which made this countryside seem to him as unlikely as if he had stepped accidentally onto a stock stage and into the midst of one of those rural plays New York audiences admired, where hills and rivers and farmhouses had been slid out from the wings and rolled down on a painted curtain, and there he was expected to perform an extemporaneous version of the victorious bridegroom, confident he would depart forthwith to the West and stumble immediately upon a vein of silver several yards wide. That was the least Felice, or William Talbot, would expect of him, and now that he had married her it was the least he expected of himself, so that he had been somewhat ashamed to catch only three small fish for their lunch and blamed it on his own clumsiness, rather than the river's parsimony.

Felice sat with her back against a willow's trunk, idly braiding the long fronds which fell before her like a curtain, and as she told him of the letter he pushed the curtain away with an angry gesture, for it seemed she was using it as a screen. He knelt beside her and took hold of her shoulders, demanding to know why she had written the letter, and Felice looked up at him in such surprise he let her go, but still hovered there. "What made you do that, Felice?"

She smiled and touched his face, and he caught her fingers, hold-

ing them until he had made her wince. "I wanted him to know we
were married."

He leaned closer, and his voice was accusatory. "But you know
he's found it out by now. Suky's told her father—and he's told your
father." He narrowed his eyes. "What else did you say?"

"Nothing."

"Yes, you did." He shook her lightly. "Don't lie to me, Felice."

At that, she gave such a laugh that he moved back, hurt and full
of suspicion. "I told him I was happy and in love and that I hoped
he would be glad for my sake—but of course he won't be." She closed
her eyes and he grew alarmed that she might be going to cry, but
then she put her lips to the palm of his hand, as she sometimes did.
"But what must surprise both of them most is that I never argued
with them once." She glanced up, and her smile became quite mischievous. "Of course, I was never permitted to."

He was suddenly determined to force her to make all the admis-
sions he had been longing to hear, and so he spoke to her with a
stern almost threatening gravity. "Did you tell him the truth, Felice?
Are you happy?"

"I told him the truth. I'm happy."

He moved nearer, and took hold of her shoulders. "You love me?"

"I adore you."

He kissed her face and her eyelids, asking, "What if he won't see
you?"

"He never will," Felice murmured, and drew in a long sigh as he
began again to kiss her. "He never will."

"Of course he will, he loves you, too." His hands moved over her
body, and soon he thrust her back and lay upon her; for it had often
happened that what began with only a simple longing to kiss her, assuring her of his love and asking for hers, quickly changed, flared
into a disquieting need, and he would begin to make love to her. But
now she was protesting—someone would come by, someone would
spy on them—and it seemed the objections only made him angrier
and more than ever determined to vanquish William Talbot and his
influence. "If they never see you, will you blame me, Felice?"

"No, no, no, Morgan—"

He laughed softly. "Will you hate me when you're lonely, when I
leave you in Helena and go off to Butte?" She might not have heard
him and held him clasped tight until he finally paused, lay quiet, and
asked, "When the winter begins and you think it will never end—
will you hate me then?"

"I'll love you all the rest of my life."

"Whatever happens?"

Felice gave a long sigh, her head fell to one side and her fingers
opened. "Whatever happens."

"You've got to." He began to move again, saying, "But it won't always be easy," and then gave her no chance to answer that.

On the morning they returned to the city, he went to William Talbot's office, determined to be as humble as necessary and to keep his temper for Felice's sake, and this time he waited only a minute or two before the secretary was back with what Morgan took to be a warning look. "You may go in, Mr. Devlin."

Morgan walked in quickly. "Good morning, sir."

Talbot stared at him silently, then gave a curt nod. "Sit down. If you please." He was silent again, and finally asked, "Felice is with you?"

"Yes, sir. We have a suite at the Fifth Avenue Hotel."

"She's happy?"

"I think she is, sir." Then, rather defiantly, he said, "She's very happy."

Talbot frowned and Morgan expected the lecture to begin, but instead he began to talk in a quiet, though nervously intense, voice. "It would be ridiculous for me to pretend that I'm not still incredulously angry. I had no idea she was interested in you, and even if I had known she was, I would never have expected her to do anything she knew would cause me so much pain. I see that you're a very personable young man, and it may be Felice is more receptive to handsome faces and imposing physiques than I suspected. Perhaps I should never have permitted her to read Byron." He smiled sourly and studied Morgan with a contemplative skepticism. "That you have no money was one disappointment. That I know nothing about your family other than what Joshua Ching has told me, was another. But the greatest of all was that you should have married a girl who has been trained from the moment of her birth to occupy a position in the society of this town with grace and dignity, and that you now propose to take her to live in a mining camp. That is your intention still?"

"Yes, sir." Morgan smiled slightly, but then became solemnly attentive again.

"My daughter, as you've discovered, is an impractical young girl who is yearning for an opportunity to sacrifice herself for love. Now that she's done it, I'm enraged to think I could have failed to see it would happen. I'd have found a way to prevent it, you may be sure. However." He made a gesture. "I think I should tell you, if you haven't guessed, that I have no intention of refusing to see her or cutting off her inheritance. I love her, for one thing, and for another I would never permit outsiders to enjoy my misfortunes." He fell silent again, and for some moments they looked at each other. "You've had some training in banking, I understand." He seemed now to be talking not to his unwelcome son-in-law but to a prospective employee, a young man who sat before him waiting anxiously for his approval. "I would like to explore with you the possibility of what you might be able to contribute—I'm offering you no sinecure, of course, I recognize that you have your full share of youthful ferocity about your ideals—but there are various positions you might fill

here." He made a vague gesture to take in the entire institution, a
modest and seemly indication of everything that belonged to him—
banking house and brokerage firm, railroad enterprises and cash
supply locked securely away against threatening troubles, seats upon
boards of directors and controlling quantities of bonds and stocks in
a variety of enterprises. "There's no real reason for you to take Felice
to live in the Territories."

"I thank you for the offer, Mr. Talbot, and I understand why you
don't want Felice to live in a mining camp. But I'm afraid she must,
at least for awhile. Mining is what I know best, it's what I came East
to study, and it's where I've invested what money I have. I can't
give it up, and Felice doesn't expect me to."

Talbot stared at him thoughtfully, as if to decide whether or not
he was amenable to some form of bribery, and went pacing across
the floor several times, until he stopped directly in front of Morgan.
"I want you to understand that if she ever suffers in any way by
reason of having made this choice I will, by Christ, give you no
peace until I have your balls right here." He showed him his
doubled fist.

Morgan glared at him. "I want her happiness as much as you do—
and furthermore, I'm the one who's responsible for it now."

He left the office, congratulating himself he had not only held
his temper but, what was more, dumfounded William Talbot by it.
But even so he felt a pang of guilty sorrow when he saw Felice's
first meeting with her father, for although she seemed pleased and
surprised to be told he was coming, she was so gaily talkative as they
sat having dinner in their small suite that Morgan assured himself
she was as heartlessly selfish as any other young girl.

But then, when they heard Talbot's knock, she sat up very straight,
looking at him questioningly as if to ask what she must do now. And
the next moment she jumped up, ran across the room and threw the
door open, stepping back as Talbot came in and bowing her head in a
posture so graceful and contrite that Morgan was taken aback, almost
offended with jealousy. Talbot looked at her for a few moments, perhaps to see if any noticeable damage had been done, then touched
her chin and she quickly raised her head, stepped forward and kissed
him, and Morgan was left feeling that he might, after all, have taken
too much advantage of his appearance and his romantic western history, those qualities for which he knew she had married him.

Now that that reconciliation was made, he went the next morning to make his own peace with Suky, for he had been troubled by inexplicable forebodings, and found her in the conservatory, though it
took him a moment to discover her standing there at the far end,
gazing out the windows at something which must interest her profoundly, for even as he quietly approached, she did not move or
seem to know he was there.

She was smiling, and what had her so absorbed was the peacock, now in his full spring plumage, pacing up and down before the stalls of Tamarack and Asia, who watched him in bemused wonderment, flickering their ears and cocking their heads sideways. The peacock had never been given a name, and though its raucous cries often disturbed the neighborhood, it paraded in front of the house on sunny days, attracting many admirers, and made its home in the stable with Tamarack and Asia and the carriage horses. During the summer it moped about, its tail as sparse as if mischievous boys had caught hold of it, but then its hauteur returned with its feathers and it paced before Tamarack and Asia, swirling the tail like a court gown, and shook itself with the increasing excitement of its dance, while the horses began to shift distrustfully in their stalls, as if the bird's ecstasy was an embarrassment to them.

They had watched him together as he shivered and hopped about, then recovered his dignity and went stalking up and down until the frenzy took hold of him again, and now as they stood side by side, Suky put one hand on his arm, though she did not look away from the capering bird, and asked softly, "May I be godmother to your first child?" This took him so much by surprise he began to kiss her hands with all the humble fervor of a supplicant, and went back to the university with the greatest sense of imminent victory he had ever enjoyed.

For even Coral Talbot had only said, "But Felice, you promised me you would forget all about him."

"I know I did, Mother," Felice agreed meekly enough. "But then I couldn't, after all."

Felice had numerous relatives—Hallams and Talbots, Van Alstines and Laceys and Delafields—and presently they were being entertained by one after another, and, because he came from the Territories, Morgan enjoyed all the notoriety among them of a handsome foreigner whose title might or might not be a real one.

But the weather soon turned hot and in only two or three weeks there was a general exodus to Long Branch and Saratoga, he went back to the library and the laboratories, and Felice was occupied with sorting presents, deciding what would go into storage and what they would send west, and spent much time fitting the wardrobe her father had given her. By the end of June it had occurred to Morgan she might soon be unable to wear it, and this prospect filled him with dread and awe and made him watch her so carefully, studying each new symptom, that it was not easy to pretend to be surprised when she finally took him into her confidence.

Even so, the child acquired reality only when he began to wonder whether or not this boon to his pride might bankrupt him, and he became unusually attentive to everything he heard about the nation's financial condition which, as Joshua Ching and William Talbot had been saying for more than a year, was bad and getting steadily worse and, in fact, they were both so convinced a disaster was coming that they sent their families to Long Branch and remained in their offices during the summer, when small brokers and other optimists had gone to where the climate was more agreeable.

Early in September, when those optimists returned to the Street, the market was lively and seemed resilient and men talked about it in terms of slightly contemptuous affection, as if they were discussing a lady of easy virtue well known in her habits to all of them.

But very soon the atmosphere began to change and there was a vague sense of impending calamity, a superstitious anxiety which caused them to speak softly in offices and on street corners; and before very long the lady of easy virtue had turned into a sick giant, suffering from an abnormal and unhealthy absorption of circulating capital and a variety of other ailments, no one of them mortal in itself but, taken all together, liable at any time to lay him out in a raving delirium.

Joshua Ching and William Talbot began to look gloomy and excited, and talked throughout dinner the night of the first failure of what was to happen and who might be blamed for it. "As long as that soldier is in office," Talbot told them, "there will never be a sound currency, for he has no notion of what a sound currency is."

"Jay Cooke will be next," said Joshua, and soberly studied the small bird upon his plate, observing it as if it were, indeed, Jay Cooke's very corpse lying there as a reminder of what all men might come to if their financial policies were unsound. "And then the catastrophe will follow. The public will never believe Jay Cooke could be sacrificed without dragging thousands more along with him."

A few days later, Morgan encountered Joshua early in the morning, tearing through the hotel lobby, his eyes blazing as fiercely as if he went in pursuit of his most dangerous enemy, and though Joshua passed him by without seeming to recognize him, he turned and came back, seizing Morgan by the arm. "If you're in, for Christ's sake, get out. If you're out—stay out!" Joshua went charging through the door, leaving Morgan with a sense of envious relief that this crisis had nothing to do with him, and as a bellhop approached to give him a letter addressed in Suky's handwriting, he tore it open to discover what news she had to send him on this day.

XLIII

By the time Morgan arrived in the vicinity of the Exchange, the streets were crowded with hacks and carriages, and the sidewalks packed with excited men, stamping their feet and snapping their fingers in the way of Wall Street brokers in distress, drinking from flasks and swearing in loud voices, damning the government, the President, the Secretary of the Treasury, the machinations of the bulls and bears alike, the big operators and the small ones, the speculators, the railroads, the gold policy and the monopolies—all their usual goblins, swollen now to immense and unseemly size and running amuck, threatening total disaster.

Men in frock coats and silk hats plunged through the crowd with faces rapt and intense, jaws set and fists clenched upon their walking sticks, headed for the Exchange. "What do you think?" they were asking, and several caught at Morgan's arm, for one man's opinion seemed as good as another's.

"Don't hold a share," he was advised. "The party are getting out of it as fast as they can." What it was, exactly, that they were getting out of, he could not learn.

He heard of breaks and blocks and cliques and dead ducks, and many doleful predictions of the greatest financial disaster in the nation's history, but still he stood before the Commercial Trust Bank, skeptically examining its carved stone garlands and maliciously grinning gargoyles, holding fast to the envelope in his pocket, but could not persuade himself to go inside and ask Frederic Hallam for whatever advice he had to give today, as Suky wanted him to do.

Her note was in his pocket, the thick paper smelling of tuberose perfume, and he knew the meaning of that by now, too, for Felice had described her cousin's love for Suky, beginning with the night of Jemima Cottrell's wedding when Suky and the other bridesmaids carried bouquets of tuberoses.

But Suky had proved again how well she knew him, for the note only said that Frederic would be glad to advise him for Felice's sake, and now, taking advantage of a sudden impulse, he tore the paper into bits, flung it upward and ducked out of the shower and into the building. On his way up the staircase, he passed briskly by several portraits of ancestral Hallams, reminding himself of Suky's tales of the Red Sea trade and ships laden with ginseng, bound for China, and felt more than ever like a beggar come to plead for a species of alms he did not deserve.

He gave his name to a clerk as if he were delivering a challenge, and, when he had waited a minute or two, turned to leave, but the clerk ran after him. "Please go in, sir. Mr. Hallam has been expecting you."

He dashed in, scowling threateningly, only to confront Frederic Hallam, smiling, his hand extended. Morgan hesitated and then, since he could scarcely apologize for such an entrance, shook Frederic's hand, giving a nod toward the street. "They've all gone crazy," he said, and hoped this might explain his own wild appearance.

Hallam nodded. "Wait."

They stood at the window, looking down at men shouting and pushing and struggling together like a gang of well-dressed wrestlers, and when at last they sat down, Frederic Hallam watched the tape be-

side his desk, and like Joshua Ching and William Talbot he discussed
the market as if it were alive. "These past few failures have excited
the market, which was tremulous to begin with. This morning's opening was feverish," and he went on to describe other symptoms of the
patient's malady, so baffling to the best physicians. "No demand at all
for railroad stocks, but gold advancing steadily." He lighted a cigar,
offered one to Morgan, and continued to study the tape with his
eyes narrowed slightly, as if he might catch it in a misdemeanor, and
he added softly, "One decisive failure will send it all to the bottom."

While Frederic talked, Morgan watched his face with the same
careful and suspicious attention Frederic was giving to the tape, and
was dismayed to find he had never envied another man as he envied
Frederic Hallam. Frederic, so Felice had said, was thirty-three years
old, and he envied him those additional eight years. He envied him
his ancestors and their foresight to engage in the Red Sea trade, his
look of elegance and austerity, his reticent manner, so peculiarly appealing to women; and most of all, of course, he envied him his
knowledge of Suky, for there he sat, in full possession of all her
secrets, and Morgan was yearning to throttle him for it.

His face, Morgan did not doubt, showed some of this guilty ferocity, and he scowled and shifted about in his chair, blew rings of cigar
smoke, and assured himself no honorable man would take the advice
of someone he resented as he sat there resenting Frederic Hallam,
whether or not he might try to pretend it was only for Felice's sake he
had come. And yet, it was all the more surprising that he did not hate
Frederic and, indeed, in another few moments it even seemed the
envy was becoming corrupted with admiration, until there was some
danger he might come to like this usurper.

"I've happened to learn that Lorenzo Flagg is in trouble," Hallam
presently told him, and Morgan raised his eyebrows appreciatively.
"He was in here this morning and, in fact, he's pledged a substantial
block of Corporate Engineers. Of course, he hopes to redeem them before his partners find out what he's been doing, but he's in so deep
that kind of maneuver is a desperate one and not likely to work out
so happily." Frederic smiled slightly. "Would you like to buy it?"

Aware of a sudden buoyancy, Morgan leaned forward. "I'd like to
buy some of it."

"I'll give you a letter to my broker, Silas Holmes. He's agreed to
hold it a little longer, while Flagg tries to raise some more money,
but, after today, I think that's unlikely. Holmes will sell it to you by
tomorrow or the next day at about one-half, I think. It may go lower
during the next few weeks, of course, that's the risk you'll have to
take. But if you can hold it for six or eight months, I think you
should make rather a substantial profit. Your uncle and Talbot and
Cottrell will be looking for it by then." All at once his face grew intensely alert, with a look of surprise and conviction, and he slapped
one hand upon the desk. "There it is." He went to the windows. "Jay
Cooke's gone." Almost as he spoke there was a monstrous yell from

the men in the streets, and down below the heads and shoulders began to move in a swirling tide, while among them were fought small separate encounters, as if nothing could relieve their feelings now but to strike out and be struck in return.

Stocks fell steadily throughout the day, dropping a few points and then a few points more, but as Morgan passed through the hotel lobby at seven o'clock that night, it seemed that men had begun to make optimistic interpretations of the day's catastrophes. "This is the end of it," he heard them saying.

"The worst is over."

During the night it began to rain and he stood at the window for some time, deciding at one moment to invest everything he had in Corporate Engineers, and the next told himself he would conserve his resources and be glad he was not dependent upon this crazy device, the stock market, for surely Zack Fletcher's whisky-trading venture had been a safer and more honorable expedient. At last he went back to bed and did not awaken until seven, and he leaped up as if Lozenzo Flagg's stocks would be gone before he could get to Silas Holmes' office.

The hotel lobby was crowded with men who looked haggard and distraught, many of them in wrinkled clothes they must have worn all night; but even at that hour they were alert and filled with energetic excitement, and they shouted at one another across the dining-room tables, offering shares and buying them on the spot. He got into a horsecar and stood in the steaming box as it swayed and lurched along, having his feet stepped on and stepping upon others, filled with hatred for his fellow man, who seemed in such close quarters an animal of no appealing qualities whatever, foul-smelling, rude in behavior and speech, a damp and uncouth creature he heartily despised.

At last he got out, and joined the swift moving horde of men who converged upon Broad Street and Wall Street, and were packed in a dense mass from Broadway to Hanover, huddled beneath big black umbrellas which some of them used as weapons. The rain poured down steadily, umbrellas were pierced or crushed, and streams of water from roof tops descended upon top hats and frock coats. But they paid no attention to these casual discomforts, and it seemed obvious to Morgan that by now they had all gone entirely mad and by the day's end there would not be a sane man left in the city.

He let himself be carried along until he found himself at last outside the Exchange, and was borne forward upon a wave which swept him into the high-vaulted chamber, filled with men roaring and yelling, stamping and swaying and striking out from side to side in a light so dim it was almost impossible to read the figures on the board. The next moment, there came a sudden premonition that the president had closed the Exchange, men turned to one another incredulously, some of them began to sob, and an echoing shout arose as, following some single impulse, they rushed for the doors, fighting and yelling as they went, and tumbled once again into the streets, where the confusion had grown worse.

It took him twenty minutes to struggle the two blocks to Silas Holmes' office, and ten minutes longer to reach Holmes' reception room on the second floor, where he at last contrived to shout his name into the ear of a clerk. The clerk, however, seemed as distraught as the clients and several times lost his way, and, when Morgan approached him again, looked dazed at the sight of this dark, furious face which hovered over him, swearing. Finally, he left the room and Morgan stood looking about him with a grim curiosity.

A man stood nearby, sobbing and rolling his head from side to side and, now and then, giving it a crack against the wall, which did not stop the convulsive weeping. Others went pacing about, hands clasped behind their backs, scowling and grimacing, muttering to themselves, knocking into one another, stepping aside and continuing on their way. A few sat upon benches, glumly staring. Some prowled up and down, snapping their fingers and slapping their hands together as if at the recognition of a sudden brilliant idea, and not one of them seemed aware there were other men in the room.

After a few minutes the clerk signaled, and Morgan followed him into another large room where he found several men, not raving or pacing about but seated in chairs, looking thoughtful and absorbed and occasionally speaking quietly to a neighbor. The clerk rapped at a door, waited with his ear cocked against it, and presently opened it. Here three men were seated in what appeared to be a small parlor, and one of them came forward to shake his hand, a spare man whose beard seemed to have been clenched and combed by his fingers.

Silas Holmes greeted Morgan as if he were an old friend and led him into yet another room, and Morgan smiled to think what magic Frederic Hallam's introduction had wrought. "How much do you want? It was thirty-five when the market closed. I'd guess it can't be more than thirty now." Unlike the others, Mr. Holmes neither rolled his eyes, heaved deep sighs, nor announced that the nation was ruined, and seemed so well experienced in surviving these disasters it might have been any ordinarily sluggish day in the market. "I don't expect to see it go below twenty-eight. There are solid men in the company, solid men on the board."

Morgan gave him a check on the Commerical Trust for thirty thousand dollars, Silas Holmes agreed to put the stock in the name of Zack Fletcher, where Joshua Ching and William Talbot would not think of looking for it, and Morgan was on his way again, reflecting that a man might dispose of everything he had in one and one half minutes, more or less.

He struggled down the staircase and out again into the drenching rain, where he found the crowds grown much quieter, as if they had received a collective blow which had left them helpless and unprotesting, and after walking a block or two he went into a bar and stood staring as absently as any of them while he sloshed oysters in a glass of whisky, and tossed off that glass and another in his solitary feast of celebration or calamity.

During the next several days, while the Stock Exchange remained closed, it was realized that this was the greatest panic of them all, far worse than those of 'thirty-seven or 'fifty-seven, of which men had previously spoken with pride and awe, as if there was something heroic in a nation's being able to survive such disasters, quite as a man might take pride in his muscles and courage if he had fought a powerful adversary and committed himself bravely, even though beaten to a pulp.

It was impossible to borrow money, which was being held for three hundred and forty percent interest, and there began a nation-wide run on the savings banks. Almost immediately factories began to close, the streets became crowded with children who roamed in packs, begging at kitchen doors and crawling through windows to steal what they could, the bread lines grew longer, and the station houses could not accommodate all who applied to them for lodging. The stock market had reopened after ten days, with all stocks quoted far below their previous prices, and men remained in their offices for days at a time, not knowing what to do, but not daring to leave.

Railroad securities had dropped so low it seemed the roads would rust away, sink back into the prairies, and Morgan watched the Corporate Engineers anxiously, for it had been found after the market reopened to have fallen from eighty-three to twenty-nine, and Joshua Ching and William Talbot were more than ever given to piously bitter exchanges over the nation's financial and political morality. For the numerous scandals, they said, the investigations into the Crédit Mobilier which had shown fifty million dollars to be unaccounted for and unaccountable, and the findings of the Tweed trial that the city debt had risen in three years from thirty-six million to one hundred and twenty million, none of which could be found, had shaken the confidence of European investors.

"Tweed should never have been allowed to go to California," said Joshua. "The man belongs in jail, and his board of aldermen and state senators with him. Who has ever before thought of swindling the public on such a scale?"

They were not, however, searching for Lorenzo Flagg's stock, and possibly Flagg had assured them he had placed it in escrow until he might make a few adjustments.

Joshua seemed surprised and, Morgan thought, disappointed, when a letter came in December, to learn that the Territorial banks had been affected very little by the American panic, as Matt called it. And other letters must have been lost, for there were cryptic references to Pete and Jenny and to Leila which Morgan could not interpret, although Susan and Ceda told him it could only mean the little girl had died.

"It can't mean anything else, Morgan," Susan said, when she and Ceda had studied the letter, and Ceda had begun to cry. "But why should a man like Pete, who is so little able to endure these tragedies, have to suffer so many of them?" Susan gazed thoughtfully at Joshua, playing whist, and Morgan supposed she must be thinking that Joshua could very well suffer any tragedy at all so long as it did not involve his money.

As the winter grew colder, even the more polite parts of the city were invaded by homeless children, many of whom had drifted in from nearby towns and counties, haggard and blasphemous little barefoot beggars, petulantly whining as they held forth their hands, and they were often found at night by men and women returning from some entertainment, huddled together in the doorways and beneath the stoops, or were discovered in the early morning by milkmen and bakers' boys, dead and frozen. Numbers of twelve- or thirteen-year-old girls, and some even younger, appeared on the streets with their faces crudely painted, often still in childish dress, and accosted men with unprofessional insistence, sometimes seizing their hands and hanging onto them until they were driven away by an approaching policeman. Girls discharged from the New England factories sauntered about in pairs, looking frightened and aggressive, and their prices were so low, for they did not expect to compete with the whores sequestered in houses but only to survive, that there began to be a great deal of criticism about the state of public morality. Babies were found dead in ash barrels, disquieting tales were heard of tramps who roamed the countryside—men who refused to wait to die of starvation but set out to take their living from the countryside like any other marauding army—and the gloom and despair increased, spreading over the land in what seemed to some sanctimonious ones to be in a reasonable proportion to earlier convictions of national power and invincibility.

In the middle of January, Frederic Hallam told Morgan that Joshua Ching and Talbot and Cottrell were casting about for the remainder of Lorenzo Flagg's stock and that Flagg had, the day before, been forced to retire from the Corporate Engineers.

"They've found most of it," Frederic Hallam said, "but they want the rest, and they're offering thirty-five."

"I think I'll wait a little. Why shouldn't they be willing to pay forty?"

A week or two later Lorenzo Flagg, whose appearance had changed so remarkably he now looked like an unskilled actor's version of himself, came to Suky's house one Sunday afternoon and Joshua loaned him one hundred dollars, but did not invite him to have dinner with them. And, when Lorenzo Flagg had thanked him, though not effusively, and left, Joshua wrote the sum in a notebook, remarking, "There's no poverty so bad as Wall Street poverty. It's the very worst form of poverty there is." Lorenzo Flagg's visit and his dilapidated appearance seemed to have impressed or possibly offended Joshua, and later in the afternoon he spoke to Morgan with the air of giving him a piece of confidential and significant information. "There's no great surprise about Flagg, you know. If this panic hadn't done it, something else would have, because Lorenzo Flagg is unlucky by nature." His blue eyes peered shrewdly into Morgan's. "If a man is unlucky I don't want anything to do with him, for bad luck will stick to a man closer than a newspaper solicitor."

Morgan did not know what moral he was meant to draw from that, but he soon determined the time had come to sell the stock, for he had a kind of superstitious distrust of having Joshua Ching for a business partner, even when Joshua knew nothing about it.

If it had not been for the small street beggars and the little girls who pleaded with him to follow them for a minute—as if it might be time he was concerned with saving rather than the small price they asked—he might have been willing to risk holding Lorenzo Flagg's stock another few months. But the pervasive aura of disaster and its representation in these questing faces and eager hands and whining voices which were to be heard now on every street and at all hours, became in some mysterious way associated with the approaching birth of his own child, giving him an obscure but haunting conviction that it was necessary for him to welcome this baby into the world with a secure bank account, as if the infant would somehow sense that its arrival had been properly provided for and that it was safe from the hazards which, this winter, more than any other, threatened newborn children.

But even after all that had been done, he was plagued by premonitions and, when the day came, in mid-February, was seized by a terror so great that when Susan opened the door of their apartment to tell him that Dr. Montgomery was with Felice, he felt his body must disintegrate from this uncontainable force of feeling.

He stood in the doorway, afraid to go in, and finally asked, in a strange, hoarse voice, "How is she?"

"She's getting along very well, Morgan."

"Why didn't you let me know?" he demanded angrily. "She told me she'd send me word when it began."

"But what good would that have done?"

"What good would it have done?" he demanded. "For Christ's sake, she's my wife, isn't she?" He dashed through the living room as if he was bent on rescuing her from some extraordinary danger and burst into the bedroom, where he found Felice propped against pillows, the Doctor beside her, and as she smiled at him he paused, staring at her in distrustful astonishment. He walked toward her slowly and cautiously, as if his footsteps might cause some untoward happening, not even aware of the Doctor, whose office he had visited to ask if he thought Felice was strong enough for this ordeal. The Doctor had smiled and assured him she was but he had left unconvinced, for he supposed it was the habit of doctors who charged large fees to declare with confidence whatever a patient's husband might want to hear.

He paused, not daring to go nearer, and held his hat between his hands, but could only gaze at her pleadingly, full of a conviction that his love for her was limitless, expanding to the edges of his life. She looked at him, still smiling, and seemed puzzled and somewhat amused, but then she held out one hand, whispering, "Come here, darling."

Morgan slung away his hat at this signal of forgiveness, as he took it to be, and dropped to one knee beside the bed, pressing her hand against his mouth as he stroked her hair, distractedly mumbling. "Oh, Felice, my God, my God, what can I do? Please tell me, for God's sake tell me what to do!"

"But I'm feeling fine—I didn't want to go to bed, but Dr. Montgomery insisted."

He whispered in a passion of guilt and terror, "Forgive me, forgive me, I'm scared to death. Are you in pain? Are you afraid? Will you hate me?" He turned and stared furiously at the Doctor, who now touched his shoulder.

"Your wife is behaving very nicely, and I don't want you hanging about here any longer acting as if there's a tragedy at hand."

"What shall I do?" Morgan asked him helplessly and was, in fact, eager to be told he must leave. All at once he found Susan beside him, and turned to her as gratefully as if he were once again a very young child.

"Go to Suky's house, Morgan. She's waiting for you."

"I can't," he protested, feeling dazed and stupefied. "But how will I know—" He turned from Dr. Montgomery to Susan, and as Ceda entered the room he asked her imploringly, "How will I know how she is? How will I know when—" He stopped, feeling his neck and face burn, and seemed to have grown several feet all at once, with enormous hands and feet, and felt so awkward and deprived of muscular control that he had no hope of being able to get out of the room by himself.

Dr. Montgomery took his arm firmly. "We'll send you news, but I would not," he added, and lowered his voice, "expect to hear from us for several hours—perhaps not before morning. Why not try a little stimulant?" Morgan felt himself lulled into a sense of stupid acquiescence by Dr. Montgomery's persuasive gentleness, and was about to be propelled from the room when all at once he jerked his arm free and returned to the bed, bent over Felice and, studying her face carefully and intently, as if he might never see her again and must be able to remember for the rest of his life with perfect clarity how she looked at this moment, he bent down and reverently kissed her mouth, stroked her hair once more, and after whispering that he loved her, went out. The Doctor followed him. "I understand your feelings, Mr. Devlin, all young fathers are the same with a first child. But I'm confident she'll have no particular trouble. She's strong, and what is more she isn't afraid." He raised one hand to bid him goodbye, and Morgan left the apartment.

In the hall he paused, wondering if he dared return for his hat, and

saw Coral Talbot walking swiftly toward him, her face alert and serious. "How is she?"

"The Doctor says she's fine. I don't know. I wish to God this had
never happened."

"Of course you do. But you won't tomorrow. Now run along. Leave
us alone for awhile."

She entered the apartment and Morgan still hung at the door,
feeling that he was of no consequence and that those women inside,
Susan and Ceda and Coral, had had more to do with the baby than
he had. He was swept by a sense of angry self-pity in which he felt
utterly useless, as though those others, three women and an old man,
had been forced to take up where he left off and to rescue his wife
after he had abandoned her. All at once he ran down the staircase,
through the lobby, and out into the sharply cold night.

He went tearing along Fifth Avenue, where there were few people
on the street, and dashed up the steps of Suky's house and banged
upon the door, determined that here, at least, he would assert himself. The footman opened it and Morgan rushed by him, flinging his
coat aside, kicking off his galoshes and running the palms of his
hands swiftly over his hair to smooth it before he strode into the
drawing room and confronted Suky, looking up from her book in surprise at this furious entrance.

"Why, there's nothing to having a baby, Morgan," she assured him,
and gestured slowly, opening both hands and holding them toward
him in the shape of a cup. "Why don't you have a drink? The children
are in bed and Philip has gone out—we'll eat alone."

Still unable to believe there would not soon be a terrible castas-
trophe from which they would try to protect him, possibly not even
tell him it had happened—that the baby was dead, Felice was dead,
that he had brought disaster and death—feeling himself so great a
criminal, he finally took Suky's advice and poured half a glassful of
whisky, added ice and water, stared at it suspiciously for a moment,
wondering if this might not be one more evidence of his unworthiness at this crucial moment, and then drank it down and gave Suky a
swift, defiant look. But she was smiling as tenderly as before, and
he quickly crossed the room to sit beside her.

For a moment he resented her composure, but presently he felt
himself respond with an easing of his muscles, whether to Suky's faculty for lulling him into a blissful unconcern and detached ecstasy, or
whether from a similar faculty of the whisky he did not know or
care.

"I can't seem to make myself believe this has ever happened before."

Suky stroked her fingertip across his eyebrows. "It never has. Not
to you and Felice."

And, at that, words which seemed to him full of wisdom and compassion, the wisest kindest words he had ever heard, he felt a pre-

posterous gratitude which made him long to kiss her, but did not dare for fear of going about it with too much enthusiasm, and was relieved that dinner was announced and they went down to the dining room, where he was glad to find he could scarcely see her over the white roses and between the flickering candle flames which loomed between them.

Suky still talked gaily on, but he ate little and what he ate had a tendency to stick in his throat, so that he continued to wash it down with wine which the waiter poured again and again, until Morgan began to suspect Suky must have given orders to get him drunk, and refused to take any more. After some long period of time they returned to the drawing room and there she made him smoke, for the sake of his nerves, while she began to play, and he felt himself grow slowly enchanted by the music, the food and wine and the cigar, all these palliatives she had provided for the relief of his guilty conscience, until it seemed he became indifferent to everything but this room and was in some danger of forgetting why he was there.

At last she stopped playing, drawing him up from the profound reverie into which he had sunk, took a chair a little distance away, and lifting both arms was for a few moments rearranging pins in the back of her hair, while he watched her suspiciously, for the posture looked too inviting, and the movements of her arms, changing slowly from one pattern to another, at last caused him to lean forward; but then he sat back, angrily laughing as she inquired, "Have you ever killed a man, Morgan?" She lowered her head, gazing at him with a whimsical curiosity.

Suky, it seemed, believed as everyone else did that in the Territories he was lawless and barbaric, the original animal crawling out of his polite eastern skin as soon as he got beyond the railroads. "Yes," he told her finally, and was unaccountably embarrassed. "I have."

"How many?"

"How many? For God's sake, what do you imagine we're like out there? Just one," he admitted, and was a little sorry he had not a better record to brag of, perhaps a notched gun to display or a string of dried ears, since that seemed to be what she was expecting.

Suky was smiling and she still continued to fiddle with the back of her hair until he longed to tell her to sit up straight and put her hands in her lap, for he was not his most reliable self tonight. "Was it over a woman?"

He laughed sharply. "Men don't kill each other over women."

"I thought they did."

"Don't you believe it. There was—a financial misunderstanding between us." He leaned forward, determined to explain to her his fight with Gaius Jenkins. "Everyone wears a gun and everyone drinks, and that mountain whisky would turn a prairie dog into a grizzly bear."

She smiled, rather mysteriously. "Felice and I were talking about it the other day. I was sure you had—and Felice was sure you hadn't. I was curious to see which of us knows you best."

"You do, of course."

But no sooner had he said that, than he wished to take it back. He crossed the room, where he spent some time moving bottles and glasses about as he pretended to search for some particular label, and was by now almost frantically eager for Philip to come back. At last he turned and took a chair across the room from her, and Suky smiled again, saying, "Tell me about the Indians." He leaned back, drank slowly, and began to describe a quaint and noble savage dressed as splendidly as a wild bird, and so they sat for what seemed an interminable time, until Philip came in and Morgan sprang up to shake his hand.

At last they left him to sit there alone and wait until he was sent for, and when they had gone upstairs he became very resolute at preventing his imagination from following them. To anchor it in place he lighted another cigar, poured another drink, and took up the book Suky had been reading when he came in, Emerson's *Essays*, in which she had steeped herself for many years, but could find nothing there to reassure him on this occasion. He raked up the fire and began to read and presently fell sound asleep, sitting upright with the book opened on his knees, and awakened with a start to find Suky leaning above him, wearing a dressing gown and smiling tenderly but rather sadly. He stared up at her for a moment, still dazed with sleep, wondering what had happened and why she should be there.

"The baby's been born," she whispered. "A little girl. You can see her now—"

He dashed out into the cold air, ran back to seize his coat from Suky, then plunged into her carriage which waited there for him and started off at a lively trot, guessing, from the pale edges of the sky above the buildings, that it was sometime in the early morning. He rode along fretful and joyous, smacking his fist into his hand with a triumphant slam, recalling that she had said the baby was a girl and, to his surprise, not at all disappointed that it should be so but enraptured by visions of her beauty, went bounding up the staircase, and as he opened the door to hear the baby's voice, loudly crying, his face relaxed helplessly into a broad smile of relief and pleasure, as if this sound was one he had never heard before.

The Doctor opened the bedroom door and at last welcomed him in, and he was glad to find the women had left. He crossed the room softly and stood beside the bed, watching Felice, who lay with her eyes closed, seemingly asleep, and felt a bursting anguish and joy as he looked at this young girl he scarcely knew who believed she knew him so well, and who had now given him this small, crying creature which lay in an elaborately carved cradle, relic of Felice's own infancy, so muffled and bundled he could see only a pink mouth, opened wide. He bent down to look at her, filled with an even

greater sense of wonder than had overwhelmed him each time he had
been led into the presence of a new little brother or sister, for he
had never been able to believe it could happen, that the swelling of
a woman's belly would one day produce this fruit, and now, telling
himself this little squirming object was his own, it seemed a greater
happiness and a greater disaster than he could tolerate.

There was a faint smile on Felice's mouth, her hair was smoothly
brushed and tied back with a ribbon, and she wore a fresh white muslin nightgown, with an embroidered ruffle about the neck and ruffles
which extended over the backs of her hands as they lay upon the quilt,
and he gazed searchingly at her, trying to determine if she had suffered too much, if this experience might have changed her feeling for
him. "I love you, Felice," he whispered, and touched the ring on her
left hand, admiring her hands with their long fingers, and, when he
looked at her face again, found her watching him, her eyes grave and
questioning. "I thought you were sleeping," he murmured reproachfully, and drew back, afraid he might have disturbed her.

"I was waiting to hear what you would say."

"What I would say," he cried, astonished and delighted, and
stroked her face and hair, but then withdrew his hands, thinking they
looked too big, the fingers impatient and hard, feeling that he must
take great care with her now for he imagined her to be tender and vulnerable throughout, needing time to heal, to resolve once again into
what she had been earlier. "But there's nothing I can say."

She was still smiling. "You have."

"That I love you," he repeated, dazzled by the force of feeling.
"Oh, my God, but I do." He reached toward her, but again drew back.
"Felice, please tell me—"

"Don't ask me questions, darling. You're not disappointed—and I
didn't disappoint myself. I'm thankful for that."

The Doctor came into the room, telling him that Felice must sleep
and he must go into the living room. "Yes, sir," he agreed, but then
turned back the baby's blanket and gazed at it in marveling dismay,
for it looked so red and crumpled, although no longer crying, that
his confident predictions of its beauty and even the fact that it was a
tiny female, seemed somewhat absurd.

By the time he awoke, on the living-room sofa, cramped and stiff
after sleeping three or four hours, he no longer felt the curious sense
of disbelief which had occurred to him earlier as he looked at the
baby, quite as if it must belong to someone else, but was as confident
about his own possession of it as if the brief period of sleep had ef-
fected a reconciliation between two different parts of himself. He
got up, alert and filled with eagerness to see her again, and went
quickly into the bedroom, determined to have—before the Doctor's return and before the invasion of relatives and friends began, before
someone went to fetch the Irish nursemaid—a few moments during
which he might consider the baby to be his own, but he had scarcely
taken her up, had only begun to examine the minute and incredible

wonders she presented, when there was a rap at the door and he was forced to lay her once again in the cradle.

The waiter had arrived with breakfast but before he could drink a cup of coffee, Susan and Ceda came in, smiling at his uncombed hair and look of harassment, his bare legs and feet and the robe which strained at his shoulders and did not cover his chest, and he retreated in chagrin to the bathroom, where he made a conscientious effort to bathe and dress without making any sounds which might offend his aunts. At last he reappeared, looking sheepish, an actor caught on stage without costume or make-up, for surely it was unseemly for him to arrive through a bathroom door, and he felt a sense of keen shame that he had not provided doors enough and rooms enough to spare all of them this indignity.

But Susan and Ceda were glad to have him out of the bathroom, for they were preparing to bathe the baby, and at a glance from Ceda he went into the living room and stood drinking coffee and eating toast, staring out the window at passers-by wrapped in long coats which flapped and clung in the wind, and listened to the voices of the women, remarking on the baby's arms and legs and toes and fingers with as much admiring surprise as if any new baby might be expected to present an unusual set of features none of them had ever seen before.

Ceda came to the door. "You may come in now, Morgan."

He smiled, amused by this capacity of Ceda's to find even the nudity of a newborn baby as shameful as any other nudity, but he was filled with high spirits and a feeling of the greatest happiness and achievement, and he kissed Ceda and carried her along with him across the room, his arm about her waist.

"What are you going to name her?" Susan asked.

"Felice wants to name her Susette—after Suky and Lisette."

"Susette," they cried.

"Susette," repeated Ceda, and began to cry.

At that moment Morgan decided the atmosphere of femininity was beginning to stifle him and took his leave, kissing the baby and Felice and his two aunts, and went quickly downstairs, relieved to have escaped before the next comers should arrive who would be, he knew, Suky first, and then Coral Talbot.

He went into the bar and found it, at a little after eleven, quite crowded, and put a bill before the bartender, telling him to serve wine to the house. Bottles were opened and glasses filled, several men glanced in his direction, nodding in acknowledgment of whatever it might be he asked them to celebrate with him, and he returned their salute and drained the glass and left, superstitiously convinced that this communion taken with strangers had hidden within it some profound meaning for the fortunes and future well-being of the baby Susette Devlin.

Part

IV

XLIV

WHEN at last Jenny asked for comfort, it was Marietta she turned to, not Pete; and she seemed as little aware of the others as if she had never known them. Whenever someone else entered the room to find them softly talking, sewing or embroidering as they had often done on past afternoons, they fell silent, or Marietta greeted the newcomer with such bright, official cordiality that it was plain they were all interlopers, until at last Pete begged Marietta to tell him what they were talking about, hour after hour and day after day, and seemed concerned they might be talking about him.

"If I tell you, Pete, you may not believe me," she said, looking at him sadly.

"Please tell me."

"We talk about God."

Pete frowned, refusing such an answer. "Jenny isn't religious. She's superstitious, nothing more than that."

"She is now, Pete. Yes, she is."

"Why doesn't she talk to me?" He looked jealous and resentful.

"She will, she will. Some day. I don't know when."

But Marietta did not believe it, either, for Jenny seemed more like a terrified child begging for some charm against her fears than a woman searching for a way back to her former life. What she was searching for, Marietta thought, was a passage into some limbo where she could wait, separated from Pete, until the time for her own death should come.

"The presence of God has become a reality for me," Jenny told her one day. She smiled at Marietta with shy pride. "I've become a mystic, Marietta—like you." She bent her head again, carefully stitching, and now seemed rather embarrassed. "I wonder why it took so long? But at last I have some peace, for the first time in my life. Isn't that strange?"

"No, Jenny, it isn't strange. You had no need of peace before." Jenny raised her head quickly, but, when she found Marietta watching her, began to concentrate again on the sewing. But even though Jenny insisted she was now at peace, Marietta and the others had noticed that she spent her time on the intricate embroidery of a tablecloth, and had worked at nothing which could be used by Pete since Leila's death. "You and Pete must have another child."

"No," she said decisively. "That will never happen."

"You don't want it to happen?"

Jenny sat for some moments, staring at the cloth. "I want it to happen, but I'm afraid. How could I bear it if something happened to that child, too?"

"But, Jenny, you don't think of that. How can you?"

"How can I think of anything else?"

"Oh, no, Jenny, you mustn't." She reached out to touch Jenny's hand, but Jenny refused to look at her. "Love Pete, be kind to him. Have another child. Everything will change then. You've lost Leila, but you can have another child—and although he can't be the same to you, you'll love him just as much as you loved Leila."

"No," said Jenny, as if Marietta was trying to persuade her of something against which she had set herself with positive determination. "No," she repeated, but then added with an unusual tenderness, "I loved Leila too much. That's why I lost her. Too much love, no matter whether it's for a child or a husband or—" She stopped, putting her finger to her mouth as if in a private sign of warning, and concluded, "—for anyone at all is a sin, isn't it? God grows jealous when too much love is given to human beings, don't you believe that?"

Marietta looked at her carefully. "No, Jenny, I don't believe it." They sat in silence, both deftly stitching, and after several minutes Marietta looked at her again. "Don't you know, Jenny, that sorrow prepares us for death? If life were truly happy, it would be intolerable to know we will die." She gestured. "Even so, we must live."

"I know that," Jenny replied sharply, but then said, very humbly, "I'm sorry, Marietta, be patient with me, please. For just a little longer."

Marietta's patience lasted and was, Matt imagined, a greater comfort to Marietta than it could be to Jenny, for it had placed her finally, as if in ironic reward for her own years of unhappiness, in the role of confidante and teacher, superior in her wisdom and in her resilience to the harshness of living and, of course, he thought Marietta must also know she had at last no more cause for fears or suspicions about them, and would not ever have again.

Leila had been dead for nearly six months when he saw Jenny alone for the first time, and he had only been surprised to find how perfectly he had lost all desire for her, so that it was not this present indifference but the years of fanatic ardor which seemed unreal to him now.

She came late in the afternoon while he sat talking to Jeremy Flint, and as he heard her asking Jonathan if he was there, he sat up straight and gave Jeremy Flint an uneasy glance. But he went out quickly and watched rather warily as she came toward him, for it seemed once again, as it had after Andy Danforth's death, that there was something sinister and eerie in her mourning dress, as if these were the garments not of mourning but of penance.

"Pete hasn't come back yet?" Her voice sounded so light, muffled by the thick veiling, that he felt she might not be there at all, secreted among those voluminous draperies, but only her spirit, of which she talked so much nowadays, inhabited them in her stead.

Jeremy Flint bowed to her solemnly as he passed, for everyone continued to behave in her presence as if the child had died only the day before. Another man came to talk to Jonathan; someone inquired for Pete and, being told he was still away, went out again; and Matt stood watching Jenny, thinking that in some sense she welcomed this retreat from the world, this disguise which protected her from the interest other people had shown in her and which she had often seemed to resent, as if she was willing to be seen and examined only by those she loved. And Jenny had loved only a few, perhaps no one but himself and the little girl, for he was not convinced she had ever loved Pete and, if she had, she did no longer.

"I thought I might take the pearl necklace," she said. "I may want to wear it." Jenny had put her few pieces of jewelry in their safe, as if they were a frivolous temptation she did not want to confront, or a reminder too painful to contemplate.

Matt nodded. "I'll get it."

"Let me come with you," she said, moving quickly around the counter. "I may want something else. I've almost forgotten what's there."

They walked to the back of the building and she went ahead of him up the narrow staircase to the second floor, their board room, furnished with several safes and filing cabinets, and a long table with twelve or fifteen chairs around it. He unlocked one of the safes, brought out a small iron box and placed it on the table, and as she bent to unlock it he crossed the room and stood looking down at the crowded streets where, though it was not yet five o'clock, men and women were hurrying toward home in the cold darkness. He waited several minutes, hoping she would soon be done and would leave without talking to him, for he had some misgivings of his patience if she should begin to discuss her faith in God, or her mystical encounters with resignation.

But she said nothing and he heard her sorting among the rings and necklaces and brooches, moving them about with light clicking sounds, as if she were playing a game and they were pieces she must place accurately in the tray if she hoped to win, until finally she slipped onto her finger the garnet ring she had always worn.

"Come here, Matt," she said, so softly her voice scarcely carried to him and he crossed the room slowly, frowning and hoping she would understand that he wanted her to make her selection and leave. She had turned the veil back from her face, and as she held out her hand with the fingers separated, admiring the ring, he looked at her with intent curiosity, as if now that he had again, after so many months, this opportunity to study her, he would be able to learn what she was thinking and what she was concealing from him and what she intended, not only to Pete but to himself, and to Marietta—to all of them who participated with her in her adventures. For that even her child's death had been in the nature of an adventure to Jenny, he was aware, although he supposed she was not. All at once she removed the ring and tossed it into the box, and looked up at him, and her face seemed to reflect his look of calculation and suspicion. "Isn't it strange that I should have been the one who was chosen?"

"Chosen?" he asked her distrustfully.

"Yes, wasn't I? Nothing's happened to you, after all."

"I don't know what you mean," he said, angry and surprised by the sly smile and her air of propounding riddles.

"You're as guilty as I am. I've done no harm to anyone that you haven't participated in. And yet I'm the one God chose to punish, now why is that?"

He narrowed his eyes slightly. "Is that the interpretation you've made of your recent interest in religion?"

"It's one of them," she said, and once more began to move the bits of jewelry about, lifting one piece and another and then dropping them gently again. "I've made others."

"Jenny, I think you should go. I don't want us to do anything at all that can be misinterpreted. I don't believe in what you're saying, and I don't think you do, either."

She slapped the lid down sharply. "You think I'm lying?"

"I don't think you're lying. I think you're pretending. Jenny, I hope you'll understand why I ask, but I want to know why you don't have another child? If you don't, neither you nor Pete will ever get over this, don't you know that? It was a terrible thing to lose that little girl, but you'll make it even more terrible if you refuse to accept life again and, until now, you haven't."

"Has Pete told you that?"

"Pete has told me nothing, and you damn well know it. I know what you're doing to him, and I know why you're doing it, too."

"You know nothing about it, Matt, nothing at all." She was smiling, and the smile made him still more uneasy. "You ask me why I don't have another child—and the truth is that I can't."

He made an involuntary grimace and she gazed at him virtuously, as if she had come out of that encounter better than he. "I didn't know that, Jenny." But then, distrusting her viruous and defiant expression, he added, "You can't be sure. Wait a little."

"Yes, wait a little. But it will never happen. And do you know why? I'll tell you, Matt. It's because I don't deserve to, and so I never will." She hesitated, as if there was something more she had to say, seemingly decided not to say it, and walked to the staircase. He followed her, keeping some distance behind to avoid stepping on the trailing draperies, and partway down she spoke to him from over her shoulder. "There may be more kinds of justice than we ever counted on, Matt."

At the bottom of the stairs she shook his hand, nodded to Jonathan and the others as she went out, and did not speak or look at him again as he handed her into the buggy, but gave the reins a light snap and the hooded black buggy set out, wobbling slowly along the rutted street, for since Leila's death she had also given up her habit of driving along as if intent on dashing under her chariot wheels anyone not nimble enough to skip out of her way.

Matt watched until the buggy turned a corner, and at last shrugged and shook his head and darted back indoors, suddenly aware of the wind and acute cold. And there he stood at the counter, pretending to check over their transactions for the day, and smiled wryly to think Marietta imagined she had made a mystical Christian of this superstitious heathen, who had become as eager to experience the mortifications of her flesh as she had ever been for its delights, and, like a true convert, now despised those who had sinned with her and would not accept their fair share of sorrow. And so, of course, she was as estranged from him as she was from Pete.

But although this estrangement seemed to Matt quite natural and inevitable, Pete was unwilling or unable to accept it for himself, and did what he could to woo her with unusual attentions and various gifts, none of which pleased her. Then one afternoon, when they sat in Matt's office, their feet propped on the desk between them, drinking whisky and water, two men comfortably taking their ease at the end of the day as they smoked and talked of business matters, Pete gave a heavy sigh, saying, "I hate to admit it but, my God, I dread Christmas."

"I know."

From time to time, however he might try to convince himself that whoever had attacked him that night it could not have been Pete, Matt had a sharp picture of Jenny standing above him in her long white nightgown, her black hair coiling upon her chest, holding a lamp in one hand and Leila's silver-plated pistol in the other—the frontier woman, he had sometimes thought, with incredulous laughter at this ironic and unlikely picture, ready to defend her home against intruders, just as she had been told she must expect to do in this wild country of Indians and road agents and assorted desperadoes, only to discover that the intruders were men she knew very well. But the mockery of this vision did not console him nor the humor honestly amuse him, and he often wondered as he stood face to face with Pete, if Pete could see the picture as plainly as he could, for he had now and then an uncanny conviction that they were thinking of it at the same moment.

"She says," Pete continued, gazing thoughtfully at his booted feet, "that we will take no notice of Christmas, not even recognize that it's come, put up no decorations and attend no parties, even among the family." He nodded slowly. "And then she says it would be better, after all, if we pretend that nothing has changed and make it a Christmas like any other, as much as possible like the one the year we were married." He glanced at Matt and smiled slightly, questioningly, then slammed his feet upon the floor, finished the drink and left with a violent crashing of the door which surprised no one, for he had often been inclined to burst from quiet contemplation and seeming resignation into furious activity.

But Lisette, who had lately begun to be critical of Jenny, declared that no matter what Jenny said, she and Pete must not be allowed to spend the holidays alone. "We must stop worrying so much about Jenny. Our responsibility is to Pete." They were at dinner and, as she spoke, casually dismissing all such outsiders, Ralph glanced up quickly and Matt irresistibly smiled, then assumed a thoughtful conscientious frown. "I can't endure Pete's face these days. She's killing him."

"That's unfair, Lisette," Marietta objected, for each time it was Marietta who defended Jenny. "She has no intention of hurting him, she doesn't know she's doing it."

"Jenny has never recognized that she has any obligations to other people. She sees life and experiences it only from her own point of view. No one else really exists for her."

"She isn't like us. She feels things differently from the way we do."

"Why should she?" Lisette demanded. "And it's spoiling her looks, too. If someone told her that, she might change."

"I don't think she'd care at all," Marietta said, in a soft reflective voice, as if the truth of this surprised her a little.

Ralph had recently come back from a trip to Albany, for his father was beginning to urge him to give up this western experiment, and while he discussed with Matt the signs of economic catastrophe he had seen all across the country, Lisette and Marietta talked of their Christmas plans, until at last Ralph said, "Zack Fletcher came in to see me today," and at that, Lisette looked around alertly.

"What's he doing here?"

"He's been buying cattle."

"But where did he get the money?" asked Lisette, as if the notion of Zack Fletcher with money to spend was a phenomenon in which she could not easily believe.

"He didn't tell me, and I didn't ask him."

"I'm not sure it would ever be tactful to ask Zack Fletcher where he got his money," Matt said.

"He's Morgan's best friend, after all," Lisette objected. "And he lived with us for almost a year."

Matt smiled at this logic. "So he did, and stole nothing that I know of. I don't think Fletcher's a thief, but neither do I take him for a man with any more scruples than he needs to keep out of jail."

"You surprise me, Father," Lisette told him stiffly, but then her face became wistful, and she looked around the table. "Let's invite him to spend Christmas with us. He has no family, and he'll be lonely."

"We'll do nothing of the kind," Ralph told her sharply, and Lisette's eyes opened wide, but then she caught Matt watching her with a warning frown and fell silent, gazing at her plate.

They saw Zack Fletcher on Christmas Eve, standing outside the church, and there was a scornful look on his face, as if he pitied them. He nodded as they went by but did not smile or speak, and Lisette was carried quickly past him by the excited crowd, for the children were eager for their presents.

But then, while the choir sang "Silent Night, Holy Night," there began a commotion in the audience, a whispering and turning from one side to the other, hands cupped to mouths, heads shaking, questions asked and answered, men jumping up from their seats and being pulled down again by wives tugging at their coats, Santa Claus circling about the tree, replying to whispers from the front rows in pantomime, shrugging his shoulders and flinging his arms upward while the choir grew more puzzled and resentful of this interruption and some stopped singing, and, all at once, Santa Claus shouted, "Ladies and gentlemen, there has been what I can only call a disaster. Some of the presents have disappeared. They were here—and now they're gone."

The audience began to babble, women turned to one another, men muttered about the inconceivable blackguardism which would incite the theft of children's presents on Christmas Eve, there was some talk of lynching and beating, someone laughed and was indignantly reprimanded, chairs were pushed about and children began to cry, and several men and women, hauling their children along, started for the door and refused to heed the frantic pleas of Santa Claus that they return to their seats, remain calm, and bear with him until the presents could be found or new ones brought.

All at once, as if someone had shouted that the building was on fire, there was a general rush for the door, and they found themselves once again on the sidewalk, some of them gathering to discuss the incredible and bizarre prank—for it could have been nothing else, certainly not the work of a serious thief or confirmed criminal to have stolen a dozen dolls in bustles and hoop skirts and horsehair wigs, a few polished apples and gilded walnuts and candy barber poles—while others were so enraged at this travesty upon the Christmas spirit breaking into the midst of their own ceremonious good will that they rushed off up the street or dashed for their buggies and set out for home, declaring they were among barbarians and it was time to go back to where they had come from.

Pete tried to persuade Jenny to stay with the others and go with them wherever they decided to celebrate their private Christmas Eve, but Jenny seemed not to hear him, gathered her draperies to keep them from dragging in the icy mud and frozen refuse of the street, and started across it as if there was no other traffic in view, and Pete dashed after her, hurrying her out of the way of exhilarated horsemen and splattering wheels. She climbed into the buggy and it had started to move before he was able to get in, giving her a questioning look as if to ask if she had meant to run away from him. He took the reins, and after several minutes of maneuvering in the conglomeration of wagons and buggies, horses and dogs and bonfires lighted to celebrate the night, turned to her. "Where do you want to go?"

"I want to go home. I'm sorry I let myself be persuaded to leave."

"I'm sorry, too, Jenny. But we had no reason to expect a thing like that to happen." They rode the distance in silence, with Jenny sitting stiff and straight, conveying to him her resentment and some suggestion that he should not have let it happen and might have prevented it if he would.

When they reached the house she ran ahead, and he came in to find her seated in the chair she had taken the day they returned from Leila's funeral, the veil still covering her face and her gloved hands clasped in her lap.

They had not intended to decorate the house, for Jenny had said she could endure no reminder of what this season would have been if Leila were alive, but a few days earlier she had come back in the late afternoon to find that Lisette and Georgina and Rachel had hung the walls with evergreen festoons which must have cost them some hours of work to tangle together, and a tree stood before the window, looped with tinsel and popcorn strings, all the cheerful, gaudy litter which had lately become necessary to the day; and Pete had come home to find Jenny lying on the floor beside it in the dark, sobbing and half delirious. But she had neither removed the decorations nor asked him to and he had hoped that it was, perhaps, some comfort to her, after all.

Pete lighted a lamp on the center table where she had spent so much time with Leila—turning through books of pictures, discussing them and reading to her—but which she nowadays avoided, as if the memory of the little girl seated beside her with her chin cupped in her hand, eagerly asking questions, was too clear and too painful to risk. She would not talk to him about Leila, but kept her room as it had always been, her clothes were fresh, and her toys and dolls occupied the favorite places Leila had found for them, though it seemed to him neither of them could endure much longer this ambiguous treasuring of her memory, and denial the child had ever existed.

As Pete looked at her, Jenny stripped off the gloves and slowly removed the bonnet, setting it aside almost reluctantly, it seemed to him. He started the fire and warmed his hands, asking if she would like to have coffee or something to eat, if they might play some music, a favorite song or two, and at each question she shook her head, smiling faintly, as if his trivial efforts to distract her on this night did not deserve a serious answer.

He sat down, began to read but grew restless, crossed his legs one way and then the other, glanced at her obliquely every few moments and each time found her looking at him with that same slight smile, and all at once slammed the book aside and sprang to his feet to begin pacing about, staring at the carpet with its pond of water lilies as if somewhere in its depths he might find a clue to save them both. For several minutes he continued striding from one end of the room to the other, retracing his path and then abruptly taking a new one, as if convinced the clue was not in the portion he had so far surveyed but might yet be found a little distance away, and then Jenny spoke, in a light ironical voice, "What an absurdity."

He stopped and swung about, loudly demanding, "What did you say?"

"What an absurd performance that was tonight." She seemed pleased he had mistaken her meaning. "But of course it's easy to guess who did it."

"Who did what?" he cried frantically.

"Pete, you're behaving very strangely. It's easy to guess who took the Christmas presents."

He had forgotten the episode in his distraction and now, relieved to hear she had not been making fun of him, he nodded as if in agreement and went to stand before the fireplace, then realized that what she had said was puzzling and, he thought, incomprehensible, for he had not guessed and was sure she had not, either. "You think you know?"

"It must have been Zack Fletcher. I saw him outside as we were going in, with a smile on his face as if he knew something the rest of us didn't."

"Fletcher would never do such a shabby thing as that, play a lousy trick on kids on Christmas Eve. What kind of man do you take him for?"

"You're too much inclined to trust people, Pete, even when they don't deserve it. You really aren't very much like Matt, are you?"

"No," he said, and stared at her somberly. "I'm not very much like Matt."

"Zack Fletcher's in love with Lisette." She tipped her head sideways. "I suppose that's never occurred to you, either?"

"Yes, it has."

"And Lisette is in love with him."

"I don't think so."

"Oh, but you're wrong. Shall I tell you why she loves him?" Jenny went on talking, in a light, high tone, as if she might be talking to herself, and he listened as incredulously as if he had hidden in a room where people thought they were alone and was discovering secrets he had no wish to learn. "She loves him because she knows he can give her the one thing she wants most—to be carried to the limit of her endurance. Not all women need that, but some of them do, some of them do—and Lisette's one of those women. If a man can do that for her, she'll forgive him anything else." She shrugged. "Almost anything else."

"Don't talk this way, Jenny. It isn't true, and it isn't fair."

Jenny laughed. "It isn't true—and it isn't fair." She shook her head wonderingly. "Pete, you've never told me why you wouldn't let me bury the pistol Matt gave to Leila with her, have you? Was it because you knew I'm in love with him?"

"Jenny!" he shouted, and then, terrified of what she would say, he rushed out, and heard her voice calling to him when he was part way down the hillside, and now she sounded pleading and frightened, as if she had only become aware at that moment of what she had said. He walked on, and several hours later, when there were only the midnight sounds of music from the hurdy-gurdy houses, drunken men singing Christmas carols and horsemen galloping through the streets, joyously hooting, Jenny entered the office building and he heard her slowly crossing the floor in the darkness, repeating his name over and over again, until he could see her standing in silhouette at the doorway of his private office.

"You're here, Pete?" she asked him sadly.

He sat silent for a few moments but finally replied, "I'm here, yes."

She came to kneel beside him and placed her hand on his knee. "You must forgive me, Pete, I'm not even sure of what I said. But whatever it was, you must believe that I love you, that I don't love anyone else—and that I never did. Do you?"

"I believe that you don't know what you were saying."

"I promise you I don't, and now I'm afraid to know. That bedlam at the church, those crying children and swearing men and chattering women, all at once seemed like an omen of something dreadful that was about to happen, and I felt as if there was no more sense in anything but destruction. I made something up because I needed to hurt you. You must believe me, Pete—I'm telling you the truth."

He stood up, drawing her to her feet. "Come, let's go home."

"You do believe me?"

"Don't ever talk to me about it again."

"I won't, Pete. Never, for the rest of my life. Neither will you?"

"I hope not."

Her repentance was honest, but it was not true she had not known what she was saying, for it had seemed quite natural that she should talk to him about Lisette's love for Zack Fletcher, and of her own for Matt, unbelievable as the words sounded when she heard their echo. Still, it occurred to her that now she must owe Matt some kind of warning, but she could not decide a way to give it, and at last told herself he would not listen if she tried, for Matt nowadays preferred to believe in his own original innocence.

Then, early in January, Georgina gave birth to her second child, and there was such excitement over that, such a commotion about the baby's name, until at last Cecilia was agreed on, that Jenny was able to convince herself nothing could separate them, and felt that she was in some danger of becoming a victim of their strength and interdependence, for even her grief interested them less now that they had the new baby to contemplate.

As she studied them for clues, approached Matt and retreated without having spoken, it seemed she had no sooner made a decision than something happened to prevent her from carrying it out; first Georgina's baby was born and then, not ten days later, the town was again taken by fire—the alarm bells began to ring one morning, and all at once the streets were filled with men yelling and swearing and looking up at the sky from which a hard wind came, sure sign of another disaster.

A troop of angry, excited men converged upon the Chinese quarter, yelling that the damned Chinamen had set them afire again and that with this wind every man had better save his own property first. They found that it had begun, like the fire of five years ago, in a Chinese gambling house, and by the time they got there volunteer firemen were clambering over the shacks, dousing them with water and hacking them apart with axes, while the Chinese in stoic silence bore forth their furnishings and ran with them, ignoring the curses of the white men and, when they were knocked down, getting up and continuing on their way, seeming to take little notice of the fire, the shouted threats of lynching, or the kicks and blows.

Matt and Pete did not pause but only looked at the size the fire had assumed and the direction it was taking, for the smoke was rolling far into the sky and being swept across the city, carrying with it blazing shingles and showers of hot cinders, and with a swift glance of mutual agreement they ran back to find Jonathan and Douglas and Robert carrying the ledgers and strongboxes into the streets. One clerk had disappeared in spite of Jonathan's offer to shoot him if he abandoned them, and the two others were protesting they must save their own houses, until Matt yelled at them to get to work and, to his surprise, they did.

The fire moved swiftly, traveling in sheets of flame which lay for a moment against a stone building and then streamed through the roof, and presently there came the sound of buildings being blown up in its path. People ran before it, saving whatever they thought valuable, and as the fire marched toward the main business area, several men were carried away unconscious, while the streets had become so clogged with buggies and wagons and horses being driven from the livery stables that it seemed this time the fire must engulf them all.

Douglas went to hire a wagon and commandeered it at pistol-point, and they pitched strongboxes and ledgers into it, and sent it off with Douglas and Robert to Pete's house, as being remotest from the fire's path, while the others remained to work with the firemen, though by that time the flames were streaming up all sides of the Devlin Brothers building and licking about the edges of the roof. Sheets of flaming wallpaper were carried high over the city, and falling bits of fiery material burned their clothing. Exploding glass came down in finely splintered showers, and they moved before the fire as it advanced upon them, sweeping steadily down one street, or leaping over the city in haphazard fashion, until the air grew so hot it seemed they drew the flames into their lungs and, at last, they gave up the main part of town and retreated to watch as the black smoke swarmed across the valley and lay upon the surrounding hills, while the flames still rose through it, reaching upward twenty feet or more.

By noon the main section was a charred wilderness of collapsing walls and chimneys, and when after three hours the wind fell and the fire was brought under control, the town seemed to have disappeared, leaving a smoking waste. The post office and several hotels and livery stables were gone. Green Troy's Casino had burned to the ground and Nola Malachy's Tivoli, next to it. Barber shops and breweries and the *Helena Post* building, the Ladies Emporium and Lem Finney's office, the Reverend Bream's City Drugstore, Josiah Webb's and Floyd Hart's buildings, Count Manzoni's real-estate office, Folger Hall and the theater where Fan Moffat had entertained them with *Mazeppa*—all were gone; more than one hundred and fifty buildings had been destroyed, and the telegraph wires were down so that they could not even ask for help but were trapped in their ruined city, smelling rankly of wet ashes and the burned flesh of some animals that had not escaped, with nothing to be grateful for but that it had stopped when it did, before it had climbed the hillsides and taken their houses.

They meandered about in forlorn bewilderment, confused and despairing, though some were still aggressive enough to go about declaring it was time to wipe out the Chinamen, who had done this to them three times before.

Men sought out Matt and Pete as they went wandering around, talking of how soon they could begin rebuilding, and when they were told their money was safe and might be had by applying to their temporary offices in Elm Street at Pete Devlin's house, they looked relieved and a few were able to grin and, by the next morning, most men were beginning to seem cheerful again and had begun to talk, as they invariably did, of building a better city upon this one, declaring that Chicago's recovery would be put to shame by the speed of their own. Before the heat was gone, they were picking among the black and sodden remnants of their business community, and carpenters and bricklayers were joyously contemplating their profits.

"The next one," Matt said, "will by God be damn well fireproof."

And he and Pete squatted on their heels in the wet street, surrounded by the restlessly wandering men, and began to draw in the black damp earth the plans for their new building and then went in search of the contractor who had put up the last one, pausing along the way to have a drink at a saloon which had been set up in a small tent at the edge of the burnt-out section and to which the citizens were repairing again and again for the purpose, as they told one another with wry smiles, of jacking up their courage and screwing fast their determination.

"We'll be ready to open next Monday," Pete assured whoever asked them. "Things may be a little rough for awhile, but your greenbacks are safe and we didn't lose an account book."

"We've got our own fire drill and, by Christ, we'll empty a burning building with any man in the Territory," said Matt. "Just a little natural knack and some practice, and you've got it."

The town rang once again with the sounds of its earlier years as the carpenters and bricklayers set to work hammering and sawing and pounding with such zest and eagerness it seemed they would have the town back together again, fresh with the pungent smell of new wood and paint, the false fronts higher than before, the porches and sidewalks straight again, no longer rippling and hazardous even to a sober man, in only a little longer than it had taken to burn down.

By the following Monday Devlin Brothers was opened for business in a framework shell covered with canvas, while a crew of carpenters and stonecutters swarmed about, and they greeted their clients wearing buffalo coats and invited them to be seated on wooden boxes beside the red-hot stove. Homer Grimes scurried around town inquiring after everyone's progress, and the *Helena Post* was being printed in a similar canvas and frame building on as much machinery as they had been able to rescue, while Ralph Mercer had gone to Virginia City to oversee the freighting of additional equipment from that office. Throughout the camp there was an atmosphere of gaiety and ebullience, for no man dared seem less courageous, less adaptable to disaster than his friends and enemies, and even those who had lost everything and been uninsured took a humorously nonchalant attitude about their troubles and tried to pretend they were men with the bark on, not to be defeated by caprices of weather or fire or national panic.

For a few weeks the streets looked like the first camps, hopelessly disheveled by day, while at night the lighted canvas buildings glowed and, from a little distance, seemed to be made of radiant marble. This caused some of the earliest settlers to grow nostalgic as they reminded one another that nearly twelve years had passed since Bannack had had just that appearance of miraculous promise, a string of glowing boxes expected to contain a treasure for each of them; and so the fire soon acquired a mystical significance, convincing them although they did not say so that the flames had washed them clean and they would now advance into a new and splendid existence which might have begun, before that providential fire, to show signs of wear and strain and disillusion they had not been willing to admit or even to recognize; for all these flaws had now been burned away, leaving them whole and purified and in possession of new strength.

Matt was convinced that the fire and his and Pete's labors together during it had at last eradicated their sorrows and that they now met each other as they once had been, long ago, without jealousy or distrust. This seemed to him so true and he found so much satisfaction in it, feeling himself to have been forgiven any misdeeds he had committed, that he was astonished and offended when one day, late in February, Jenny came into the office saying she wanted to see what progress they were making and, as she passed him, murmured, "Take care," and went on, without having glanced at him.

He stopped still, scowling and staring at the floor, turned quickly to glare at her and then, shaking his head in wonderment at the vagaries of women, went to the counter to discuss a loan a ranch owner wanted to make, and thought no more about it. After all, he and Jenny had not been lovers for nearly a year and there seemed no reason she should choose to remind him of their ancient and dishonorable history when even Pete seemed glad to forget it, if indeed he had ever known it.

But although Matt imagined he had forgotten hearing her say that, put it out of his mind as a piece of unwelcome news he would not be persuaded to accept, and although she did not repeat it or try to explain what she had meant, it occurred to him a few days later when he was returning from a trip to assess the value of that same ranch property, the words flashing into his mind with ominous speed and ease, as if they had been waiting only at the edge of his consciousness, and for a moment he was puzzled and concerned, wondering why he should think of them now, until suddenly he became aware that there was someone traveling behind him, a lone man on horseback, like himself.

The ranch was not more than eighteen or twenty miles out of town and although he had intended to return late in the afternoon, the discussions continued longer than he had expected and the ranchman, once he agreed to recommend the loan, grew joyous and expansive and insisted he have dinner with them and, afterward, he had decided that since it was dark and there was some threat of snow he would sleep for a few hours and ride back in the early morning if the weather had cleared. And finding that it had when he woke near four o'clock, he had left the house quietly and set out in the cold, sharp air which no longer smelled of possible snow, riding swiftly and taking a vast delight in the journey, for it seemed that the world was silent and unmindful of itself while he, alone, was alert and filled with a keen intensity of pleasure. The sky was black and moonless, though full of stars, and he trusted to his horse's footing as they cantered quickly along the frozen road. He had been riding for what he judged to be nearly an hour when the words, "Take care" occurred to him and, in another moment, the realization that he was being followed.

But then he was ashamed and surprised to have thought the other rider must be following him and wondered what should have made him reach that conclusion rather than the more natural and likely one that another man was also riding into town in the early morning and happened to be some distance behind him, coming along at a steady gallop but still so far away the hoofbeats were dim and difficult to distinguish among the other mountain sounds—the rasping of dead leaves, the occasional booming and cracking of branches in the cold air, the coyote's cry which rose in the distance—and accordingly he slowed his pace, thinking that he would let him come near enough to call out and ask who it was. There was little danger of a solitary Indian, but the mountains still sheltered road agents and thieves who preyed upon incautious travelers.

As he slowed his pace, now listening intently, he discovered with a quick catching of his heartbeat that the other rider immediately came to a halt. He sat for a moment, wondering, astonished and still puzzled, determined not to become alarmed at so small a circumstance, for it was logical to believe that the other man was also concerned about his identity and did not want to approach any nearer without knowing whom he would encounter.

He waited for three or four minutes, but his horse was quivering so that he was afraid to let him stand, heated from the brisk run, and he started on, and was relieved to find that the other horseman remained where he was. He assured himself there was no danger, that these imaginings were absurd and, indeed, embarrassing, for why should he now begin to feel and to think like a greenhorn, a pilgrim, after all these years when he had considered himself a confirmed westerner, a man who knew how to handle himself in whatever situation the frontier might present, no longer skittish and apprehensive of both real and imaginary dangers as men were when they first arrived in the mountains, but perfectly confident that experience had given him full possession of himself, one who had been tested by this pitiless country, disciplined by it, seasoned and sharpened until now he could depend upon himself with infallible reliability. Why, then, should he be suddenly filled with confusion and dread?

Of course he was not. He rode on, angry that his heart should be pounding and that he was urging his horse to run at a pace which was not safe on that slippery road in the darkness, and gave a sudden laugh of surprise and indignation as he heard the other horseman once again start forward.

Deciding to put him to a test, he rode at a fast gallop for some distance and, although it seemed impossible, the other drew steadily nearer. They were still, he guessed, some six or eight miles from town and there was a faint beginning of light in the sky, as he noticed with a pang of relief which shamed him, for it seemed he should have no need of daylight for protection; and so he abruptly reined in the horse and, hearing the other coming on at a steady pace, shouted in a loud, furious voice, "Who are you? Are you following me?"

He waited, and the man continued to ride forward but made no answer. Thinking he might have been too far away to hear him, Matt shouted again, repeating the question, and added, "Come up here, whoever the hell you are! Show yourself!"

The man reined in his horse and stopped, but made no answer. In a sudden passion of rage, feeling that whoever this was had the deliberate intention of making a fool of him, Matt drew his pistol and started toward him at a gallop, yelling and swearing. The other horseman hesitated, then wheeled his horse, rode several hundred yards back along the road they were traveling, and turned off. Matt heard him clattering down the stream bed, with a sound, he realized for the first time, as if his horses' hoofs were muffled by gunny sacks, and at this he gave another angry laugh, for surely he must have encountered some timorous road agent and scared him away.

He resumed his ride toward town, watching carefully on all sides, though it was still too dark to see, starting at unusual sounds and expecting that at any moment the other rider would reappear, come dashing up out of the willows which bordered the stream, and he fired one bullet to make sure the pistol was in good working order, then stuck it into his belt.

But he heard nothing more, and at last saw the vague shapes of the first scattered houses with a relief greater than he would have believed possible, for his heart still beat with a hard and steady rhythm, and its clamoring excitability angered him, making it seem that his confidence and courage were less reliable than he had supposed. He had been followed before on trips he had made alone and, more than once, had been fired at, but never with so much alarm as he felt now, and he must have come to a nervous and cautious condition which filled him with intense self-disgust or he was, perhaps, better aware of the identity of the other man than he would let himself admit.

At that moment, as he was telling himself he had been frightened of nothing, scared out of his wits by a man who was even more afraid of him, and that it would be a good joke by the time he was drinking a cup of morning coffee—or perhaps he would make no joke of it but keep it to himself, since it would not be pleasant to admit he had grown nervous and almost sick with the intensity of his fright— there was a commotion nearby and a horseman sprang up from the stream bed, coming to a full stop not thirty yards away, and ran toward him, shouting, "Dismount!" Matt slid to the ground as the other

approached at a quick, loping pace, moving with a recognizable
rhythm, and as his hand took hold of the pistol slowly and reluctantly, the other shouted again. "Draw, will you?"

"Pete?" He peered at him, unable to see clearly.

"Draw, I said!" he yelled, and had now stopped no more than ten
feet away, holding the pistol balanced across his raised left arm.

Matt lifted his pistol but did not point it, only stood waiting, disbelieving and yet profoundly quiet, his fears vanished, feeling himself poised and ready but without the will or inclination to defend
himself. At last he asked, in a voice which sounded curiously tender,
"Do you mean to kill me, Pete?"

"Fire!" After a moment the other fired once, aiming high, and as
Matt still stood motionless, hovering there with the pistol hanging
at his side, he yelled, "Fire, God damn you!" His pistol fired again
and, after a moment, fired once more.

Matt's body spun partly sideways as the bullets struck, he began
to sway, took two or three uncertain steps, asking incredulously,
"Pete?" and pitched forward, sprawling on his belly.

X L V

He had been waiting for several hours, possibly three or four as he
judged by the sun, patrolling the neighborhood on horseback.

The house stood at the crest of a small knoll and was one of those
described as a mansion, not only by Ralph Mercer's editor, Homer
Grimes, who might be forgiven his sycophancy, but by grocery boys
and milkmen of whom Zack Fletcher had inquired its location,
and, as he circled the hillsides, keeping it constantly in view, he had
taken its inventory, duly noting that it was two stories high, that it
was made of brick, with no wood in sight but the white jigsaw trim-
ming at the windows and over the porch, that it had three chimneys
and a mansard roof surrounded by a little iron fence, and that a row
of cottonwood trees was planted at the foot of the knoll to separate
it from the wooden sidewalk. Not one of the houses nearby was its
equal and most of them were not much better than shacks, for the
surrounding property was being held for higher profits. It looked a
very suitable place for the town's leading newspaper owner to live in
and, if it had been any other day, Zack would have allowed himself
some sourly humorous reflections on how unlikely it was that he
would have provided her with this mansion, and certainly not seven
years ago, although he might of course have such a house now if
houses of that kind had been to his taste.

But with Matt Devlin dead, he had little enough inclination to think of anything else, and even his jealous resentments had disappeared in the shock and grief which had caught hold of the town early yesterday morning, when Matt had been found by a man who lived in a cabin not three hundred yards from where he lay, flat on his belly, with another dead man nearby, a stranger they could not recognize. The news had spread with an eerie speed. Zack had heard it as he was eating breakfast in the St. Louis Hotel, and, from then on, he had heard of nothing else but that Matt Devlin was dead, apparently killed in self-defense, for there had been one bullet fired by him but three by the stranger.

Zack had gone immediately to the cabin where they had been taken and had recognized that stranger, a man he had known only by sight and by reputation several years ago and, after some troubles with his conscience about what he must do with this information, had at last brought it to Lisette. But although the doors and windows had been hung with crape, she had not answered his knock; various delivery men had come and gone, and there was no smoke from the chimneys even though the day was piercingly cold, with a keen wind.

He had, however, met an admirer as he rode slowly along the paths which wound above the house, for Morgan's dog Music had greeted him with fawning ecstasy, whining and shaking his haunches, until Zack wondered if this sagacious beast had remembered him for two entire years, or if he would have been just as hospitable to any other predator, however he might come disguised as an old friend, full of innocent good will. Nevertheless, his sorrow was honest, and by that token he justified his presence here, for now that Matt Devlin was dead he loved him as well as he had once, long ago.

Zack rode easily, lounging in the saddle, smiling and nodding and tipping his hat whenever he encountered children or housewives, some of whom peered curiously and distrustfully at him, for the news of Matt Devlin's death had carried in its wake a general apprehension such as no one had felt for several years. The dog had at last grown weary of trotting beside him and had gone to lie on the porch, and Zack interpreted this to mean she would soon be back and that the dog, by some method he shared with Indians and children and other clairvoyants, knew it and was waiting for her. And, before very long, a closed buggy drove up to the house and from his vantage point Zack saw Lisette jump out, run up the sidewalk and steps and into the house, shutting the door as the dog sought to follow her.

He started down the hillside, debating as he went whether or not it was seemly to leave his horse Skewball standing there to advertise his presence inside, and laughed rather scornfully at such punctiliousness, but, of course, he was never able to forget in how many ways she was protected.

He gave a peremptory knock, waited a moment and repeated it, more loudly, and then stepped back in alarm as she opened the door and looked at him, but seemed not to recognize him. Stricken by her expression, he took off his hat, crumpling it in his anxiety and embarrassment, gazing at her beseechingly although he found it impossible to speak, and at last she stepped back, murmuring, "Come in."

The house was silent and the children had apparently been sent somewhere else, and as he followed her into the darkened living room where no fire burned, no lamp had been lighted and the shades were drawn to the windowsills, he glanced furtively about, feeling that he had no right to be here alone with her and that it was his duty to tell her quickly what he meant to say, and leave. Still, he was curious to see where she lived, and had often tried to imagine the place where she was not Lisette Devlin but Mrs. Ralph Mercer.

The room seemed very large and filled with an extraordinary amount of furniture and perilously arranged gewgaws, bronze statues and white marble heads, tubs of ivy to be stepped around as well as potted ferns and palms to be avoided. Several dark paintings nearly obscured the wallpaper with its pattern of red roses, and where they did not hang there were shelves of books. Carved tables, crowded with more books and miscellaneous objects, stood in his way, and there were tufted and fringed chairs and two sofas covered with green velvet. The windows were draped with green velvet, tortuously swathed, and these in turn were draped with white lace which trailed upon the floor. A marble clock on the mantelpiece ticked loudly and, Zack thought, disconcertingly, interrupting the silence.

All of it, he decided, looked as if it had been furnished to Ralph Mercer's sober taste rather than Lisette's, though what her own might be he had no idea, and indeed it had the appearance of something which, once established, might never be changed but must remain as it was for as long as they lived. Like Jenny's house, it gave him an immediate conviction of his unworthiness, made the flesh crawl along his shoulders, and he was eager to be away, for it seemed that not only Ralph Mercer must be able to sense his presence there but that Matt Devlin, too, was warning him that this property was not to be trespassed upon.

She stood near the piano, staring at the floor as if she had forgotten he was there, and she looked not at all as he had ever seen her before. Her hair had been tied back with a narrow ribbon, she wore a dark blue dress with the sleeves turned up to her elbows and the collar unbuttoned, and she looked so listless and dazed, it would have been easy to imagine this was someone he did not know. He went toward her, yearning to comfort her but afraid to try, for it seemed he was sure to be clumsy, destroy what he had meant to repair, and plunder where he had hoped to nourish.

"It's cold," she said, in an unfamiliar, plaintive voice, and shivered a little. She picked up the sealskin coat from where she had thrown it across a chair and hung it about her shoulders, clasping her arms, and all at once Zack became frantically busy, went dashing through the dining room and kitchen to bring wood, laying the fire and lighting it and then, as he squatted on his heels before the blaze, he looked up questioningly, as if he expected to be complimented for having known so quickly what she wanted him to do. "I've been home all night," she said, in that same unfamiliar voice. "But finally I had to leave."

He stood and looked down at her, thinking with a grim anger that even now when she had been married for almost six years, when there was trouble her home was Matt Devlin's house, and this made him at once sympathetic with Ralph Mercer, and rather scornful of him.

"I couldn't stay any longer. I couldn't stand the people—crying and shaking their heads and wringing their hands, and talking about him. And I couldn't stand having him there with us, not able to talk to us or move, ever again." She drew a deep, slow breath, pressed the palms of her hands together and touched the forefingers to her lips, like a child who prays or speculates on riddles beyond understanding. Zack stepped toward her, meaning to tell her what he had come there to say, and instead caught hold of her shoulders, trying to make her look at him. She stood quite still, then twisted slightly and moved away, whispering, "To die like that, as if he had been some kind of criminal." She glanced sideways at him, with a cruel, vindictive look, and, it seemed, was ready to blame him or anyone else for her father's death. But the glance was momentary and she crossed the room and sat on a sofa before the shaded windows, and again began to talk in that faint, monotonous voice, as if she only recited her thoughts aloud and did not intend them to be overheard. As she talked, she looked up at him from time to time, and each time that vindictive expression briefly returned. "I saw him before they had changed his clothes or washed off the blood, when they first brought him into that cabin. He hadn't been dead an hour then. Robert came here, a little before seven, and told us, and I went out there." She smiled. "They told me I mustn't go in and that I mustn't see him while he looked like that. I suppose they thought that if I didn't see him until later I'd be able to pretend he'd died in some more decent way, not shot down by a stranger and left lying there, bleeding to death on his belly in the mud. There were two wounds, here, and here, and his hands were covered with frozen blood where he'd been clutching them." She narrowed her eyes, gazing across the room. "Do you know it when you're dying—or do you only think you'll sleep for awhile, rest because you're tired, and then wake up again?" She waited, as if expecting he might answer her question, and went on. "What was he thinking about, lying there with that man not twenty feet away? Did they have anything to say to each other? Did he forgive him? I hope not." Zack knelt beside her, but she stared past him as if mesmerized by what she had seen. "He looks quite different now. Lying on his back, straight and dignified, in a black broadcloth suit—while they walk around and around staring at him."

She began to cry, and seemed not even aware that he took her into his arms, stroking her hair and kissing her forehead and face, but lay against him, sobbing as she must not have done until that moment.

And presently, as if in plain demonstration of all his worst suspicions about himself, Zack recognized the rising of those inclinations toward violence and sensuality he had always felt for her. He paced the room, walking back and forth while she cried, glanced into a mirror and was dismayed by the sight of his face, with its savage expression, and while he went on pacing looked at Lisette from time to time but made no more attempts to comfort her and was determined, when it seemed she could listen, to give her the information he had brought and leave.

All at once he spoke sharply. "Lisette, listen to me." But his voice sounded not at all as he had intended, and he corrected it to a gentler tone. "Lisette, I know that guy—the one who was found with Matt."

"You know him?" She sounded incredulous, and angry.

"I didn't know him, but I know who he is. His name's Gabe Foster. He was with the Border Ruffians in Missouri before the War. You've heard what it was like in those days, men killing each other and raiding around the country, burning houses and farms and whole towns. Well, one day Foster came back from a raid, and he was no gentleman himself when he went calling, and found his wife had been raped and beaten, she died later, and his house and crops set afire. He found out who did it, a guy named Jim Lowry, and he swore if it took him the rest of his life he'd find Lowry one day and kill him. I saw Foster three or four years ago, when I was south, still on the lookout for Lowry and still with blood in his eye. And I also heard that Lowry, like a lot of us Pukes, lit out for the Territories during the War. Lowry was a big guy, six feet three or so, just about Matt's size. From a little distance, and that early in the morning, it would be an easy mistake to make, and Gabe Foster was always pretty quick on the trigger."

As she listened, Lisette stared at him steadily, her face growing more more more distrustful and, finally, contemptuous, as if he had brought her some obscene lie and she despised him for it. "Are you trying to make me believe my father is dead because he was mistaken for another man? You're saying that that man was no enemy, there was no fight between them, and he's dead by some crazy accident?"

"That must be what happened. I went out to the cabin yesterday morning and I recognized him, that stranger they all stood gawking at, scratching their heads about how this could have happened in such a law-abiding community. He was here looking for Lowry and thought he'd found him."

"I don't believe you."

"There's no other way to explain it." He looked down at her with sorrowful yearning. "You wouldn't want to think he was killed by an enemy?"

"Every man has enemies, that's no disgrace!" All at once she looked so fiercely accusatory that he was startled. "I heard them talking yesterday morning. One of the horses had had his hoofs tied in gunny sacks so he'd leave no recognizable tracks." Her voice rose to a shrill, unnatural pitch. "Does that sound like an accident? My father had been wounded twice, and so had Foster, but there was only one bullet fired from my father's gun. Can you explain how that could happen?"

"Lisette, for the love of Christ, do you think I'm lying?"

"I don't know whether you're lying or not. But I do know that whatever happened yesterday morning was not so simple as you want me to think. Either it was no accident at all, or Gabe Foster wasn't the only man my father met there."

For a moment he was ready to retreat, beg her pardon and go away, but then her anger, and what he took to be her accusation, created a responsive rage and he went toward her, shouting, "What the hell do you mean, Lisette? Do you think I know any more than I've told you?" He seized her hands, and as she tried to free herself he held her fast. "What do you think happened?" He caught hold of her hair and gave her head a quick, hard shake.

"Let go of me, Zack Fletcher," she whispered, and, at that, he stepped away with a gesture of abject humility, muttering apologies as he backed across the room. "I don't know what I think. I don't know what happened. Don't try to make me say something I don't mean!"

"Do you think he was bushwhacked—maybe by someone he knew?" He spoke very quietly, as if he might trap her into making some admission which would justify all the resentment he had ever felt toward any of them. "Is that what you mean, Lisette? Is that why you think I'm lying?"

He started toward her again and, once again, Lisette moved away, watching him suspiciously. "I don't trust you, Zack Fletcher! Don't try to help us, we don't need you, we don't want your help!" She swung the back of her hand toward him. "Leave us alone!" She began to cry, covering her face with her hands. "You had no right to come here, God damn you!"

At that, his anger swelled with sudden energy and he took hold of her with as clear an intention as if this was what he had come here for in the first place. She began trying to free herself, struggling frantically, and when he gave her a light slap across the face, as he might have slapped at a troublesome child who sought to interrupt him at some moment of anguished concentration, she moaned softly, closing her eyes as if the slap had been a blow heavy enough to have knocked her down. His hands covered her breasts and he whispered, with an unexpected tenderness, "Hush, Lisette, be still—don't make me hurt you."

In another moment a table had fallen, and he noticed with wry satisfaction that a vase lay broken and water had spread over the carpet. The juniper branches it had held were scattered, two or three small china boxes lay almost beneath his feet, ready to be crushed if he chose to, and this minor destruction was so pleasing that he grinned, forced her onto the couch and lay upon her, separating her thighs with his knee.

He took care not to look into her face but had her crushed beneath him, clasping her head between his hands and entering the yielding flesh with what seemed a marvelous ease. She lay motionless, and he was dimly aware that she sighed deeply as he began to move, intending to take all the enjoyment he might and to guide her so skillfully, with such a slow, remorseless power that she would have to share with him, whether she willed it or not, this long delayed exaltation. For some time he was aware that she went on crying, but his pleasure soared steadily until, in a kind of drowning exhilaration, he turned pitiless, no longer cared whether she shared these wrathful joys or despised him, and, at last, sweating and shaking, he drew away, and finally stood up. Her hands still covered her face, and he lowered the dress and was for a few moments fussily occupied with arranging it, as if he must make sure that anyone seeing her lying there might never guess what had happened. Then all at once he was eager to be away.

"Forgive me," he whispered, "I had to do it," and left the house so quickly that he blundered upon the tail of the dog Music, asleep at the door, and stopped a moment to make his peace with him before he set out toward town. He glanced around once, frowned, as if at the consideration of some mystery, and shook his head, telling himself it would never again be any use to try to imagine he was anything better than the rascal Matt Devlin had taken him for; but, at least, now that he had satisfied those morbid and guilty curiosities which had tormented him for so many years, he was entitled to the lingering comfort and relief which, after all, had cost him only some small remnant of his own good opinion of himself.

And, thinking of it in this way, he grinned with truculent pride and complimented himself on his brutality, for without it he would be at this moment as confused and exasperated, as anxious for her approval as he had ever been, and would have nothing of his present profound calm, however likely it was that before many more minutes had passed this bodily appeasement might begin to suffer from servile feelings of remorse. But, since he anticipated the penalty, he was all the more intent on savoring the solace of blood and flesh and bone which made a little self-contempt seem to him quite a fair bargain—one he would gladly have made if she had given him the choice.

His first decision was to keep on going, out of the town and out of the Territory and, as he traveled, lose in the distance between them whatever shame he would feel when he was forced to admit that he had taken her today not only because he had found her alone, but that it had been, in fact, an act of revenge against Matt Devlin;

and when he had agreed to this much, he confronted a criminal and a coward he heartily despised.

He saw once again, with sharp clarity, the water spread upon the carpet, the smashed vase and scattered juniper branches, and what had seemed at the time only a trifling and agreeable piece of destruction, now seemed the wanton deed of a fanatic, the same one whose presence in his skin he had suspected for some time but never before had met at such close quarters.

Muttering beneath his breath, he shook his head incredulously, remembering what he had seen of her body and then, quickly chiding himself, sighed unhappily to think how he had stood above her apologizing as if he had done her no worse harm than to have trod accidentally upon her foot during a waltz.

He rode at a faster pace, trotted up briskly to the half-finished building of the *Helena Post,* and went dashing up the steps as if he charged a protected rampart.

Toward the back the presses were chattering and crashing and three men worked there, drawing forth the sheets with their columns of smeared black ink and stacking them in piles upon a long table. Homer Grimes sat at a desk, looking surprised and apprehensive at this melodramatic entrance, apparently convinced there was violence to follow, for a man could not be expected to enter any building with Zack Fletcher's look of impulsive rage, only to sit down and talk quietly.

Nevertheless, Zack now approached him and inquired, quite softly and agreeably, if Ralph Mercer was there and if he could see him. "I have something to tell him about the man they found with Matt Devlin," he added, and at this Homer Grimes leaped out of his chair and went scampering up the stairs.

Ralph met him at the top of the staircase, and as they shook hands Zack was surprised to find that not only had he no conviction that this man was Lisette's husband, but he felt toward him no ill will, no malice or jealousy, and in fact he felt no guiltiness, either. And even as he told him what he had told Lisette about Gabe Foster and Jim Lowry, he continued to be aware of a deep, sensual surfeit, for it seemed he had plundered gratifications enough to last him a long while. As he talked, reasonably and seriously, he even began to grow solicitous of this man who had been damaged by him and did not know it and never would, for he could infallibly perceive that he would not learn it from Lisette, who would keep the secret for both their sakes.

"I knew Matt Devlin well," he said, "and I respected him as much as any man I've ever known." He paused, recognizing that this was the truth, neither hypocrisy nor atonement, and went on. "And I wanted to tell you before the rumors get too big a start—and you know as well as I do how quick that happens out here—that he was killed because one guy mistook him for another. He wasn't killed by an enemy, and there's no use to let them start asking each other who it was that hated Matt Devlin enough to kill him, and trying to figure out what reason somebody might have had to do it."

"I agree. Because it's begun to happen even now."

Zack sat leaning forward, his elbows resting on his knees, staring at Ralph Mercer with more careful attention than he had given to any other man's face in his life before, but could find no suspicion there, only that he was tired and that he was stunned and sorrowing. "It may be a little harder just now for all of them, his family, I mean, to think it was an accident, because people tend to think accidents could have been avoided, but of course that's not always true. But after awhile they'll prefer to think of it that way, it will give them a little more peace." He spread his hands. "That's all."

Ralph Mercer thanked him and stood up. "You'll come to the house tomorrow morning? Ten o'clock."

For an instant it seemed incredible to Zack that he should go there, stand among them on that day and look into Matt Devlin's face again, and then it seemed even more incredible that he should not. "I'll be there," he agreed, and he left, marveling between humor and ironic disparagement that the most furtive and dishonorable acts might be so easily accomplished.

Now he began an aimless and idle ramble, having no plan and no purpose but to occupy himself until the next day and, when the memory came naturally and without being summoned, to experience once again those joys taken forcibly in the midst of sorrow and, perhaps, all the keener for that reason.

As he walked, he heard men talking about the crime. Some shouted and gesticulated and others stood staring gravely and silently, as if asking themselves why it should have been Matt Devlin who, less than forty-eight hours ago, had seemed a man in full possession of himself, which few enough of them would have claimed; and some of them had begun to reminisce, with a tender nostalgia, of the old days, ten or twelve years ago, when they were beset by the road agents and had banded together in a vigilante organization, many of whose original members would officiate the next day as pallbearers.

The town was too concerned and disturbed to go about its usual business, and carpenters and masons and bricklayers at work on the new buildings, storekeepers and their customers, bartenders and waiters, interrupted each transaction and each encounter, to talk of the murder, for so they were calling it.

And the crowded noisy streets, being rebuilt after the fire scarcely seven weeks before, gave it so much the look of a new western town that Zack was reminded of that Sunday afternoon, almost ten years ago, when he had stood on the sidewalk in Virginia City and seen Pete and Matt Devlin ride by, followed by Matt's sons, and a wagon in which sat Marietta and Lisette and the valuable cat Shekel.

There were the same clamorous sounds of sawing and hammering, the same shouts of carpenters and workmen, but there was not the same benign and dusty summer day, for now in early March the streets were muddy, the sky was dim and treacherous, and men dashed along in buffalo coats, wrapped to the ears with their hats pulled low.

He remembered, as he walked, what he had thought of often, both here and while in other places, strange bivouacs, that first glimpse he had of Lisette seated beside Marietta, with the cat in her lap, holding it tight and stroking it steadily as if to soothe any apprehensions it might have about this wild new home to which it had been brought. She had looked straight at him, her face merry and provocative, and the smile had stayed in his mind, ready to be recalled whenever he wished for it.

Zack had come at last to the place he had started for an hour or more ago, though he had postponed his arrival by his conversations with various men, and now he stood before the new Devlin Brothers building.

It was intended to be, as Homer Grimes had reported, three stories high, built entirely of stone, with plate-glass windows facing the street, and there would be no more splendid office building in the Territory. But today it was only a framework of wood which looked insubstantial as a stiffened web, with partial walls of roughly carved stone. The door was closed and locked, there were no workmen about, and black crape covered the window frames and hung from the rafters, and as Zack stood gazing upward he was taken with a sense of ominous dread, as if he might be in the presence of some vast unknown figure which would, at any moment, speak to him.

He gave his head a shake, telling himself the day was the wrong one for him to be up and about and that he had let himself be so overcome by Matt Devlin's death that in another minute or two he would begin to see ghosts and hear voices; and when he heard his name spoken he whirled about, to find Lem Finney standing in back of him and gazing up at the building, a thoughtful and sorrowful expression on his hard little face, as if somewhere in the building's fluttering black shroud he might discover the answer to a riddle which troubled him deeply.

They stood in silence for several moments until all at once Finney turned to Zack. "Have you seen Pete?"

"No."

"He got in from Deer Lodge this morning. Looks like hell. Matt looks peaceful enough, now that he's had the blood washed off and the holes in his gut covered with his frock coat, but Pete, by Jesus Christ, looks like they got him at the same time." He chewed his cigar. "It takes a long while to let yourself believe it—even when you see him lying there. There was too much life in Matt Devlin to have it go out like that. For no god-damn reason at all. Or maybe there was a reason," he added, and paused, reflecting upon whatever the nature of that reason might be. "I've been by here four times today. I keep thinking he's going to come walking along and start talking to me about that stand of lumber he thinks we should buy for the Confederate Gulch claim." And, apparently reminding himself it would not happen, he shook his head again and sighed.

Zack had been watching him as he talked and now stepped a little nearer and lowered his voice. "Finney, let me tell you something. You said a minute ago maybe there was a reason. I hope you don't go around town saying that to other people, because I knew Gabe Foster and I knew Lowry, and I god-damn well want you to understand there was no reason why Matt Devlin was shot except that early in the morning Foster couldn't tell one man from another, and didn't much care if he killed the wrong guy anyway."

"I know, I know, that's what I've heard."

"That's the truth," Zack said slowly, and had an impulse to grab Lem Finney and hold him by the throat until he forced him to swear he believed it. "So help me God, it's the truth. That's all there was to it."

"I hope so."

Zack bent down. "I warn you, Finney, don't ever let me hear you've been saying it could have happened any other way." He glowered at him a moment longer while Lem gazed back with a look of surprised bewilderment, and Zack walked swiftly away, thinking it was certainly a curious thing for him to have gotten so angry with Lem Finney who, after all, had said nothing he had not been thinking. Still, it seemed a matter of desperate urgency that there be no questions left in their minds after Matt Devlin's funeral tomorrow morning.

He walked along, paying no attention to the men he passed, ignoring greetings, going swiftly and with apparent purpose although he had none, and had walked some distance when a woman's voice called his name and he glanced around to see Milly Matches beckoning to him from a closed buggy, so transformed by her disguise as Irene Flint that it was no wonder the women had not recognized her.

"Zack, get in here for a minute. I've been following you ever since you left Finney." He climbed in, she slapped the reins lightly and they moved up the street, turning away from the main part of town. "I've driven by you twice before today. You must feel like I do, restless and baffled. I can't stay in one place, but I don't know where the hell to go or what to do once I get there. I've been to the house, they're all quiet, except for the visitors—Christ, those visitors." They continued to drive along slowly and, after awhile, she said, "You know, I loved Matt Devlin. The West, so they say, sets men free. You've heard that a thousand times, and you know as well as I do it's a bloody lie. I've lived on the border all my life, and the only men who get freedom out of coming here are the ones who know why they came and what they want out of it, the other poor bastards only get more confused.

Matt Devlin was one of the guys who knew himself and knew what he wanted to do, and did it." She glanced at him. "Maybe that's why he's dead?"

Zack smacked his fist into his palm. "What the hell do you mean saying a thing like that?"

"I don't know, I'm not sure what I mean. I've heard about Foster and Lowry, maybe that's all there was to it."

"That's all there was to it."

They rode for several minutes without speaking and, once again, Zack saw Lisette lying as he had left her, motionless and silent, her hands covering her face. At last Irene said softly, "But Marietta knows, at least, that she can never lose him again."

Zack made a forward leap, opening the door and landing upon the icy mud of the road while the buggy was still moving, and went dashing down the hill toward the camp's main streets, as if he needed the noise and confusion of busy people sprinting up and down on their errands.

He went into Troy's Casino, not completely rebuilt but crowded as it always was with men playing poker and faro, and the big room with its canvas top and dense smoke, the brass band setting up an agonizing din which went unnoticed, the smells of whisky and cigars and wet sawdust, again reminded him of the days in Virginia City when just such a half-finished building had seemed luxurious. He stood at the bar, tossing the first drink off quickly and contemplating its progress down his insides, then poured another and found that Green Troy was standing beside him, looking at him seriously.

"Will you go around and see Nella? You lived there at the same time she did, maybe it will help her to talk to you. I thought she'd forgotten all about them, but when this happened she went to pieces, like that." To Zack's surprise he gave him a friendly pat on the shoulder, the first such companionable gesture he had ever known Green Troy to bestow on him or any other man. "It hit everybody, I think."

Zack finished the second drink and, filled with dread and cowardice at the thought of trying to comfort a hysterical woman, he went through the door Troy had indicated, down a narrow, dark hallway and up a flight of stairs which led into the building next door, Nola Malachy's Tivoli. This was not completed, either. The walls were smeared with damp plaster, and random pieces of furniture, mirrors and paintings, were strewn along the hallway. With the air of a skulking culprit, as if he had not spent many nights in the previous building, he crept along, glancing sheepishly through opened doors in the hope of seeing someone who would tell him where to find Mrs. Malachy.

In one room he found a girl sleeping, and as he hesitated, afraid to speak to her, she awakened and he recognized a girl he knew and had often come to visit. But now she scowled as if to warn him it was too early, her working hours had not begun, and when he asked directions she raised one bare arm and pointed toward the end of the hall, yawned widely and pulled the blankets over her head.

He knocked, and when there was no answer, opened the door. No one but Green Troy ever entered Nella's apartment, where they lived, and she presided in the parlor with an air of reserved indifference, as if she hoped to give the impression of being headmistress of a girl's finishing school, and took no notice of any behavior which would not have been seemly if she were.

She was standing beside the window, wearing a light green wrapper, and her hair hung down her back, reminding him again of that Sunday afternoon, more distant now than ever before. As he came in she turned slowly and gazed at him from the corners of her eyes, and she looked, he thought, like a hurt little girl, her face seeming to have been kneaded like putty, scrubbed by her fists until her eyes and even her lips were swollen. The tears began to fall at sight of him, though she did not seem aware of them, and after several moments she spoke in a voice so low he moved nearer. "Jenny Danforth's to blame for what happened to him."

"You have no right to say a thing like that, Nella."

"Oh, yes I have. That terrible woman, why wasn't she killed instead? She's the one who deserved to die." She spoke very softly but with such hatred that he said nothing, only watched her with a sense of helpless sorrow. "Do you know what I keep thinking about?" She closed her arms about herself, shuddering. "That clock, that goddamned clock." She looked up swiftly and accusingly. "Do they still have it?"

He looked for the clock as soon as he entered the house the next morning, going through the parlor so swiftly he allowed himself only an indistinct glimpse of the coffin, covered with black cloth and decorated with handsome silver handles as, he thought with a twinge of guilty mockery, no doubt befitted a man of Matt Devlin's standing in the community.

Zack was dressed—as he had not been since the night of Jenny's and Pete's farewell party for Morgan—in the black broadcloth frock coat which made him feel conspicuously clumsy, as if he were bulging grotesquely around the edges of this civilized uniform, and he removed his hat as he entered, bowing to Mrs. Finney and noticing that although the living room was crowded with women in black bombazine and men in black broadcloth, no members of the family were to be seen, and he supposed they must be upstairs.

Branches of evergreen stood in jars, there were crosses and wreaths of ivy tied with black crape, and in a vase over the fireplace was a bouquet of flowers—lilacs and roses and mock orange—which seemed a remarkable thing to find blooming at that time of year, until he realized they were only the wax flowers he had seen in Jenny's dining room.

And as he walked about, avoiding the vicinity of the coffin and now and then exchanging murmured comments with someone he knew, Zack continued his furtive and anxious search for the clock and felt it had become necessary that he see it again, confront it and face it down, as it were, and possibly break the spell for Nella by the exercise of his own will.

At last he came upon it in the kitchen, on a shelf above the sink amid copper pans and cookbooks, and stood repeating its motto over to himself, *Every hour wounds, the last one kills,* until he had at last fallen into so rapt a contemplation of this hypnotic legend as to forget why he was in the house. All at once he turned and walked back to the living room and found that the escort of Masons had arrived, the pallbearers had gathered, and he was trapped here where he did not belong, with no one left in the house but Matt Devlin's oldest friends and the members of his family.

Pete and Jonathan stood beside the coffin with their backs to him, and the two younger boys, Robert and Douglas, looked dazed and forlorn, as if their father's death was not yet a reality to them. Zack started to move softly and quickly through the room, intending to escape without being noticed and without having looked at Matt, and then Ralph Mercer saw him and he stopped midway in his flight, feeling foolish and apprehensive, expecting that the least Mercer would accuse him of was trying to sneak away without performing his duty of looking at the dead man. He watched distrustfully as Lisette's husband approached.

"Fletcher, I want to thank you again. Mrs. Devlin asked me to say that we're all grateful to you."

Zack's face turned cold and wet, as if from some disagreeable sickness. He nodded brusquely and again began trying to edge away but then, ashamed to let Mercer know how afraid he was of Matt Devlin, he made a resolute approach to the group of men who stood gathered about the coffin, waited until someone noticed him and made way for him, and gazed down for a moment at the figure which lay there with a severe and somber expression upon the familiar face, become now so unfamiliar he could not believe this was all that remained of the man he had dreaded to encounter this last time. He turned away, drawing a deep breath, and saw Georgina, engulfed in black crape and veils, come into the room holding Annabel by the hand, and lead the little girl toward the coffin.

At the door he turned once more as Marietta and Jenny and Lisette entered the room and approached the coffin, but their faces and bodies were so concealed by black crape he could recognize them only by the differences in their heights, and he lingered there, helplessly fascinated by the sight of them and wondering at their silence, until at last Marietta took the artificial flowers from the vase and laid them in the coffin and, at this, Zack dashed out and retreated far to the back of the crowd where neither Lisette nor anyone else would be able to discover him and, as a further precaution, flexed his knees so that no one might catch sight of the top of his head.

Overnight the weather had turned warm, though the sky was cloudy, and it seemed a premature spring morning. The mourners, three hundred or more as he guessed, stood quietly, watching while the coffin was borne down the steps and slipped into the hearse, and the procession started down the hillside, the Masons marching slowly ahead, followed by the hearse drawn by horses draped in black, with black plumes blowing on their heads. A line of closed buggies fell in behind it, and strung out for a distance of almost a quarter of a mile were men on horseback, and Zack rode among them. The drums beat softly and the dirge music rose and fell, could sometimes be heard distinctly, but then faded before a gust of wind and left for some moments an unexpected disturbing silence, through which the drumbeats still sounded.

By the time the end of the procession had arrived at the church there was a large crowd gathered in the streets, and Zack hung at the back debating whether or not he had the courage to escape, when Ralph Mercer again beckoned to him and he reluctantly made his way through the crowd, casting apologetic embarrassed glances on all sides and meeting curious faces, some of them resentful, as if questioning why he should be given this attention by Matt Devlin's son-in-law. "Sorry, Fletcher, I thought you knew you'd been asked to attend the services." Zack nodded as if in recognition of a great favor having been conferred upon him, and followed him into the church where he was relieved to be shown a seat at the back, for if it had been necessary to walk down the aisle where Lisette might see him he was sure his legs would not have carried him there.

The room was crowded and very hot, and as the choir began to sing "There Is a Green Hill Far Away" Zack felt a sudden overpowering panic, began to sweat, and was only able to sit motionless by a desperate act of will. He heard women crying, a child's voice hysterically sobbing, and he turned once and looked wildly about, determined to dash through the door and save himself while there was yet time, for it seemed the danger was to him who would, by some quirk of ghastly humor, be buried alive while Matt Devlin would stand up, give them all a sardonic grin, apologize for the trouble he had put them to, and walk off, well pleased with having had his little joke at their expense.

He was, for a moment, so convinced it would happen that he sat bolt upright, staring with such intense concentration at the coffin that when the Reverend Obadiah Bream's powerful voice called out, "Matthew Devlin is dead," he gave an inadvertent start, and bowed his head, gazing at his hands spread upon his knees. "Before the shock of this news has passed away, it cannot be improper to recall that here was a man to honor and respect—"

Zack looked up suddenly, narrowing his eyes and staring accusingly at the Reverend Bream as he began to describe Matt Devlin's virtues, and grew so helplessly enraged at what he took to be this insult to a dead man that he willed himself not to listen and began quite deliberately, as if in defiance of these pathetic efforts to refashion men and their purposes into some more orderly pattern, less cryptic and less terrifying, to think of Lisette, lying silent and motionless beneath him, and became so lost in contemplation of his gluttony and the reward it had brought him that once again the Reverend Bream took him by surprise.

"To him we say—peace and farewell."

The organ music poured through the room and Zack rose with the others, to join once again that slowly moving file but, this time, shut his eyes as he passed the coffin. He did not glance around, for fear of seeing Lisette, but kept his head lowered, until at last he was in the churchyard and took his place near the end of the procession as it set out for the cemetery.

As they approached the main part of the town he noticed that many stores and offices were closed, doors and windows were draped in black, and men on the sidewalks watched them pass with rapt, serious faces, holding their hats against their chests. A woman began to cry, eerily wailing, and children stopped still, frowning as they had at sight of the dead road agents. During the time it took them to pass, the town fell quiet and absorbed. Zack noticed the old peddler woman, Mrs. Honeybone, wearing her rusty black cape and gazing at them solemnly, and at sight of her he felt a superstitious chill, as if the omen had appeared too late.

At the cemetery, he dismounted and approached the edge of the crowd to find that the Masonic ceremonies had begun, and, as the coffin was lowered, the Masons stepped forward, each to toss a spray of evergreen upon the box which had, it seemed to him, been slipped into the grave with a stealthy haste. Marietta stood with Lisette and Annabel and the three sons, and as she collapsed, falling forward without a sound, Pete caught her in his arms and the Reverend Bream's voice carried across the cemetery: *"Dust to dust, ashes to ashes, and the spirit to Him who gave it."*

XLVI

For almost a week after the panic of September the eighteenth, Joshua did not leave his office, but sat working over the figures of his mystical bookkeeping system, the accounts which revealed their content and meaning to no one but him. He ate little, slept only a few hours each night and then slept fitfully, and woke often to look out the windows where he could see other men at work in adjoining buildings or pacing back and forth; or, more and more often as the days went by, doing nothing at all, only waiting. Newspapers accumulated on his desk, for he read again and again the reports of banks failed and closed, factories shut down, businesses which had been thought sound gone into bankruptcy, friends and enemies and acquaintances destroyed.

But although the sufferings of other men sometimes frightened Joshua, they did not move him. Rather they served to remind him as forcibly as the thrust of a nail that these fates had been set aside for careless or gullible or unlucky men, and he held all three in the same contempt.

When he thought of all he had lost in this panic, and the two houses he had meant to build on those lots he had retrieved from Philip, it did him little good to remember that less than ten years ago he, like most speculators, had set himself the goal of making half a million dollars and never speculating in stocks again. Indeed, Joshua no longer regarded himself as a speculator, but as one who had evolved into that higher being, an investor. Nevertheless, speculation remained in his blood as a sordid reminder of what he had once been and, as he had often heard men say, was a passion which grew until it became at last fiercer than anger and more absorbing than love.

Love, in fact, was the first luxury he decided to eliminate as he sat scratching out columns of figures, sometimes sighing with rage, leaping up to pace back and forth, and then once again falling to his task; until by the sixth day after the Exchange had closed he left his office at ten o'clock at night, exhausted and indignantly angry with Rose Michel, and set out to travel back up the island to what had come to seem a remote and almost imaginary country, and tell her that his money must be spent on more important things from now on. The figures, he was convinced, justified his decision; for the rent of the house, the salaries of the servants and Mrs. Stump, Rose's clothes and carriage and furniture, had cost him more than ten thousand dollars a year for nearly seven years, and he was horrified to think he had squandered this sum on a girl he had not intended to support for more than a year or two.

The streets of the financial district were almost as deserted as they usually were at this hour, but many windows were lighted and behind several he could see men pacing distractedly, or standing in silhouette before them staring out. The carriage proceeded at a neat pace up the island, the hoofs echoing with a sound which made it seem he must be the only man alive in the world at that moment. But finally they came to Broadway and Houston Street, and here there was noise and confusion and lights enough to convince him the city was still populated, and even make it quite difficult to believe anything untoward had happened.

It often seemed astonishing to Joshua that the world was so well supplied with fools, men and women apparently incapable of know-

ing what went on about them even when it concerned them most seriously, who from one day to the next took more notice of the
weather than they did of a financial catastrophe and were more concerned with a bunion than a war. There they were, he thought with
grim anger as he sat peering out at them, as little aware of what had
happened these past few days—and would continue to happen for
weeks and months and probably for years in the future, affecting
each of them adversely and many of them tragically—as was his
four-year-old son Eugene.

Light streamed from every window and bands blared, making
strident and ugly music which they evidently found exhilarating for
they were laughing idiotically, girls and men alike, as they came
swarming from the theaters into a dazzling white light which traveled for blocks. There were bursts of shattering applause from time
to time, for the city was almost insane about actors and actresses and
treated them to vast amounts of clapping and flowers. They stopped
to gape at the shop windows, temptingly arranged with gold and
silver plate, furs, and bolts of satins and velvets. They went crowd-
ing into the concert saloons and dance halls, restaurants and bars,
while here and there among them, omens they refused to notice,
wandered singing minstrels and blind beggars.

Joshua shook his head, finding it incredible they should be so
blithe, so remorselessly gay at this moment when their world had
been toppled over their heads and yet they refused to take alarm, and
insisted upon continuing their old habits, gorging themselves upon
lobsters and oysters, pouring quantities of liquor down their throats,
and pursuing at all hours the trivial pleasures he was convinced held
for most of them the entire and final secret of life itself.

But when the carriage turned into West Twenty-first Street he
found it dark and silent. Most of the houses were unlighted and no
one was to be seen, for few cared to walk the residential streets at
night, and less so than ever now that the Tweed Ring was in disgrace
and many men who had worked for the city had returned to their
earlier occupations of burglary and pocket-picking, safe-blowing and
miscellaneous thievery.

The carriage stopped, and Joshua glanced up to find that the house
was dark. The window boxes on the first two floors overflowed with
pink and purple petunias and red geraniums, an improvement Rose
had made which pleased her inordinately, but he did not doubt she
would find things to please her just as well in the next place she
lived, and he entered the house resolved against letting her overcome
his determination with any of those tricks of pathos she understood
so well.

He found the door to her sitting room opened, even though he had
several times warned her to lock it when she was alone, and crossed
it softly. She was asleep, and he stood for a moment looking at her in
the faint light which came from a wick floating in oil, telling himself

he would be very kindly but very firm, and then noticed with a rather disconcerting amusement that she had strips of brown paper plastered to her temples and the sides of her mouth, and there were oiled white cotton gloves on her hands.

He struck a match to the wall brackets, saying in a stern, clear voice, "Rose, wake up, I want to talk to you," and Rose gave a start, peeled off the triangles of brown paper, stripped the gloves from her hands and hid them under the pillow while she wiped the oil on her nightgown, and sat up.

"Oh," she moaned, and rubbed her fists against her eyes, yawning. "I'm so glad you've come. I've had the most awful dreams all week."

Joshua looked at her with a face intended to express his concern for her, for himself, for all those others who had not yet noticed the disaster, removed his hat and sat in an armchair, glad to find that at least she knew what had happened and had some clues, even if no comprehension, of what his problems must be.

She swung her feet down, after first surreptitiously removing a pair of oiled cotton slippers, and touched the head of the gilt buddha which stood on the night table, making it move and wobble, and for a moment she watched it with a small, secretive smile, then instantly turned her attention to him while Joshua told himself it was, in some ways, a pity he could not afford her for she was the only woman he knew who could find pleasure in inexpensive things.

"You look so serious, Joshua," she murmured. "Is it very bad? Oh, I know it is." She came to him and dropped on her knees, gazing up at him with an expression both submissive and adoring, having in it some wily imitation of the look he had seen upon the faces of child beggars or a dog fawning to be petted or fed. She took his hand and bowed her head over it, stroking it gently and sympathetically, then laying her cheek against it, and in spite of himself Joshua felt that something inside him which had been stiff and taut had begun to soften and melt, sliding downward from where it had become lodged high in his chest, as if it would finally reach his stomach and dissolve there and trouble him no longer. "I went to my fortune teller the minute I heard about it. She says it's bad, very bad, and will get worse." She darted him an inquiring glance and he got up and walked away while she remained kneeling with her fingertips touching the floor, watching as he began to pace about and following his progress with concern and admiration.

"Your profits are safe," he told her gravely. She had given him her share of the poker winnings the men sometimes distributed between her and Tessie, asking him to invest them for her, and he had withdrawn her stocks from the market several months ago so that she would have that much at least should he be unable or unwilling to provide for her and Eugene. "There are twenty-two thousand dollars in your safe-deposit box." He smiled austerely. "Quite a fortune for you, I should think."

"Oh, yes," she whispered. "Thank you." Her face had become alert and her eyes frightened, so that it was plain she knew what he meant to say. "I'm glad you didn't forget. I was afraid you might."

"Not at all," he assured her. "I know how much it means to you. You could live on it comfortably for several years, couldn't you?"

She continued to stare at him, as if fascinated by the sight of something majestic and terrifying, something she had perhaps been expecting to see for some time—his somber, unrelenting face, declaring that he would take care of her no longer. "I don't know," she murmured, and closed her eyes, slowly shaking her head.

But now that he had made such a stout beginning he had no intention of letting her distract him, and so drew himself to his full height and stood with his feet slightly apart and his arms folded across his chest. "Of course you could," he assured her briskly. "Not in New York, perhaps, but then it isn't sensible to live in New York unless you're rich. Middling people cannot afford it. I would give you something in addition, of course. I expect to be generous."

At that, to his surprise and dismay, she slipped to the floor and lay on her side, her eyes opened wide and staring fixedly. She had not fainted but—as he had seen her do when Eugene was sick or she felt in some other way defeated by fear—had once again taken refuge in this animal-like helplessness, simply lying down and relinquishing all volition. And she might, he recalled, lie there indefinitely, motionless and speechless, unless he could coax or threaten her into returning to life, facing up to her problems and discussing them with him sensibly. He began to pace about, gesturing now and then as he seldom did, for it was a habit he despised as unbecoming to a natural aristocrat, and all the while she gazed vacantly and seemed to hear nothing of his argument, even though he expounded it with what seemed to him such incontrovertible logic that he warmed to his own cause as he pleaded it, portraying himself as a man with excessive burdens and responsibilities, harassed by a multitude of claimants, and he then painted her future, describing the peace and repose away from the city, the meeting with a young man and his proposal of marriage, and when he paused and looked down at her again it all seemed to have been accomplished and there was nothing left for him to do but break the lease on this house and walk out of it for the last time.

"No one would ever marry me," she said at last.

"Of course they would."

"A whore can't reform. No one trusts them. You don't trust me." Her voice was light and colorless.

"Of course I do," he replied defensively. "Rose, I wish you would get up."

"I can't."

He began to argue with her, to assure her that she could if she would only try, but he refused to stoop over and tug at her arm or jog her shoulder, and so she continued to lie there. At last, outraged by this irresponsible behavior, he snatched up his hat and cane and gloves, dashed out of the room and down the stairs but paused at the front door, considering whether she might do herself some injury, and when he reached the bedroom door again she still lay on the floor.

"This is absurd," he declared, and felt that in spite of everything he could do she was succeeding in making a fool of him. "I warn you, Rose, if you don't stop this nonsense immediately I'll leave here and you'll never see me again."

"You'll leave anyway, no matter what I do."

He went to stand at the windows and could not, at the moment, think of his next argument, for she had taken him by surprise with this unprotesting despair and he felt very much as he supposed he might have had he kicked a frisky puppy which bounded to the door to welcome him home. All at once he had a ludicrous image of the furniture being moved out, the draymen picking up chairs and lamps and carrying them down the staircase, the cook and the maid and Mrs. Stump putting on their hats and coats and disappearing, until at last Rose must be bundled up like a corpse and carried to her destination. But what that destination might be, if she refused to participate, he could not imagine.

He came toward her once more with a determination to convince and shame her, make her admit her own part in his troubles and offer to leave for the sake of her love for him. "You must believe, my dear, that this is no arbitrary decision, and I haven't made it easily," he began, in a tone which sounded almost wheedling. Then, as he thought of the checks he must sign, panic or not, the shambles down there at the other end of the island, his voice rose angrily. "But I cannot, by Christ, in these circumstances I cannot maintain three households, don't you understand that? The whole country has gone to hell. Banks are closing. Railroads are going into receiverships. Men have lost their jobs and millions more will. People will die of starvation this winter, thousands of them." At that she gave a faint, protesting whimper, as if feeling the pangs herself. "And this is only the beginning. It will go on for years. I can't take care of you any more, Rose, and by God that's the end of it."

At last she sat up, asking in a light, tender voice, "Did you lose very much, Joshua?"

He spun about, to avoid looking at her. "I don't know yet. No one does. There's some hope, while the Exchange is closed, that enough men will be able to reassess their positions to prevent a complete disaster, but a terrible thing has happened and it affects everyone." He whirled again. "You, as well as the others."

She stood gazing at her feet, her arms at her sides. "I've been expecting this. I knew it would happen one way or another, for one reason or another. Tessie was right. How she'll laugh at me."

"What difference does it make if a slut like that laughs at you?"

But he was watching her carefully, for although he had supposed

himself to have long since become immune to the predicaments of
women, and believed they helped to bring about most of the troubles
of which they complained so unceasingly, he felt nonetheless a disturbing and unwelcome sense of sorrow and pity as he watched her,
trying to imagine where she would go, how she would live, and what
would become of the little boy.

"She's my only friend," she reminded him gently.

"You'll make other friends. Rose, for God's sake don't look as if this
is the end of your life. You're young and beautiful, don't forget that."

"I'm not young, Joshua. I'm almost twenty-five." She smiled knowingly, and once again touched the buddha's head and watched it
wobble. "I bought some pills against earthquakes last week. I guess
they weren't any good."

"You know I've forbidden you to take these concoctions," he told
her severely, for she was accustomed to study the newspapers not
for the political or financial news but for the advertisements of patent medicine vendors, and had frequently asked him if he thought
her spell of dizziness or the pain in her chest or leg meant she would
soon be dead.

"What will I tell Eugene?"

"Tell him," said Joshua practically, "that you are moving into the
country so that he can play in the fields and fresh air."

"He won't like it. He loves the city and he's made friends all over
the neighborhood."

"Don't force me to concern myself with these things, Rose. I've told
you what must be done, and we'll attend to the details presently."

She nodded and, after a moment, said, "You look tired, Joshua.
Don't you want to sleep?"

He gave her a suspicious glance, to let her understand that if she
thought she could get him into bed and change his mind there she
was mistaken; but it was true he was tired and this was, after all,
still his house. His bones seemed to ache, his legs and arms were
heavy, he felt as if some poison had entered his bloodstream, and he
had no hope of being able to cross the floor to the bed but thought
he must surely collapse where he stood.

"I think I will sleep for an hour or two," he told her grudgingly,
and she began to smooth the bed while he undressed.

She asked if he would like a little bourbon and water, and hung his
clothes in the wardrobe where they were kept locked against Eugene's marauding curiosity, for not long ago Eugene had thrown
them out the window, a good joke, Rose had thought, although it had
annoyed Joshua.

Joshua fell upon the bed and lay on his back, feeling as if his body
might sink through the mattress and the floor itself. He was vaguely
aware of Rose tiptoeing about, turning off wall brackets and blowing
out the wick, and all at once he had fallen into a profound sleep
from which he did not waken until he heard the shouts of milkmen

and the bakers' carts rattling over the cobblestones bringing fresh bread for breakfast. He started to leap up, feeling that his sleep had been a crime and some new catastrophe must have occurred while he lay there, and saw Rose leaning out the window and gesturing at the delivery boy, and he fell asleep again.

At nine o'clock, ashamed to have been caught in this weakness but feeling much better, he took the first bath he had had for several days and returned to the bedroom to dress, pleased to see that he once again looked like Joshua Ching. As he stood brushing his hair Rose came in, demurely smiling, the expression she had invariably in the morning, as if she returned each night to her childhood and awoke without memories or misgivings to a fresh life she had not yet spoiled, and he replied with a brusque nod but said nothing.

She wore a pink cotton dress printed with flowers, her hair fell loose, and she carried a tray upon which he was glad to see his favorite summer breakfast of melon and a rare filet mignon, poached eggs on anchovy toast, and a pot of coffee. She set a table near the window, carefully folded the three morning newspapers and arranged them side by side, and when he still said nothing but began to eat and read, she picked up a piece of embroidery, an occupation she had adopted recently as a part of her new gentility and which Tessie had greeted with whoops of laughter and the prediction that next she would begin painting on china. She drank a cup of coffee and nibbled at a piece of toast, for once she had discovered that she could expect to eat regularly she no longer had the ravenous appetite of their first dinner at the Maison Doré, and for half an hour neither of them spoke.

Joshua had taught her that he must not be disturbed when he was thinking and she had obeyed that instruction with scrupulous care, so that even now, when she must be frightened and unhappy, she sat quietly, looking as serene and content as she worked at the embroidery as if this were any ordinary morning. He read one paper and then another, trying to find something to give him hope, and by the time he had finished them was surprised to realize that her quietness and her prompt taking up of the embroidery and retiring into her work, even the dress she wore and the ribbon she had tied in her hair, had given him a reluctant but poignant sense of tenderness, and unexpectedly reminded him that she had provided him not only with the pleasures he had wanted but, more significantly, with comfort and reliable peace.

All at once he got up with a great eagerness to be down in the Exchange area once more, as if his presence might be in itself a stabilizing influence. "It's late," he told her curtly. "I slept too long." He looked at her severely, as if she were to blame. "Good-bye."

"Good-bye?"

"I'm in no mood for discussions this morning, Rose." He hesitated, but then kissed her cheek, clapped on his hat and rushed out, not pausing again to speak to her although she ran after him and stood in the doorway as he got into the carriage, telling himself there was probably no great hurry about closing the house.

The lease had been paid through next April and he would make her understand that she must buy no new dresses, learn to manage the shopping so that the cook could not cheat him so easily, and in general embark upon a program of rigid economy until he found out what had happened to all his plans and assets, and at last admitted that she had become what he had never anticipated—a necessary solace; while the little boy was handsome and alert, industrious in his games and play, and it seemed to Joshua he could discover in him evidences of the energy and stubborn determination he considered among his own best qualities. He was not, in fact, eager to part with either of them, and though he would not have liked to think he had come to love Rose Michel as some besotted men he knew loved their mistresses, nevertheless it was true that he had the monogamous inclinations of an active and preoccupied man who refused to wait, whether for a woman or a clerk.

The Stock Exchange opened after ten days and it was found, as William Talbot had predicted, that the only men who had escaped serious damage were those who had withdrawn from the market and locked up their profits so that they were now in a position to oblige their less prudent friends by taking control of their companies. All at once the three million dollars he still owned seemed to Joshua the greatest opportunity he had had, and he regretted only that he had not the resources of Talbot or Cottrell, both of whom immediately began to acquire bargains in real estate and factories.

Lorenzo Flagg, on the other hand, was described in banks and brokers' offices as a dead duck, and Joshua thought that very likely was no exaggeration, even though Flagg continued to insist each time the Corporate Engineers board met to consider how they might best take advantage of this national blight, that in another week or two he would have his affairs in order, and so he continued to tell them as the winter came on.

"We all know the stock market is a school for scandal," Joshua reminded Cottrell and Talbot, for he felt obliged to defend their partner from these outside slanders, even though Lorenzo Flagg had become almost as repulsive to him as Milton De Groot had once been, with the difference that it was not Flagg's smell which roused his disgust but, rather, his habit of objecting to every advance or change proposed by the Corporate Engineers.

Joshua had long ago discovered Flagg's primary weakness, and had stored this information away. There was no urgency about it, for it was not, Joshua thought, the kind of weakness a man might overcome or grow out of, being, in fact, Lorenzo Flagg's own guilty conscience. For Flagg, having laid his fortune through cheating his partner in their California venture, had inadvertently become willing to let another man cheat him, and had begun to hanker after his financial destruction as men sometimes craved their defeat through alcohol or love or by stepping accidentally in the path of an uncontrolled vehicle.

When this became as clear to Joshua as if Flagg had written it on a slip of paper and handed it to him like a stock quotation, he had realized that here was an opportunity of the best kind, and as the years passed Joshua had brought to bear upon Lorenzo Flagg all the tender persuasiveness he could command, leading him into one tight position and then another and, when Flagg called for help, abandoning him there with promises to return laden with proxies enough to rescue him.

When at last Flagg resigned from the Corporate Engineers, Joshua shook his head over newspaper accounts of the disgrace, which stated that Lorenzo Flagg was no longer feared or followed but was now despised by everyone, and ended by saying it was well known in the Street that the boys had got Lorenzo Flagg under and were walking up and down upon his prostrate form.

Flagg accepted his defeat stoically, only reminding them that if he had not discovered that original Ohio charter there would not be today any Corporate Engineers or any Baltimore-Missouri. "After all, gentlemen," he told them, "a charter is three quarters the value of a company."

"We've built something never envisioned in your original charter," William Talbot said. "And it's cost us money and effort to do it. If you can't keep up with us, Flagg, then we must go along without you."

"Of course. But I promise you I'm not through yet. I'll be back."

"We hope so, Lorenzo," Amos Cottrell assured him.

Joshua thought Lorenzo Flagg was no more likely to come back than was Milton De Groot, who had been rumored a year or two before to have gone to California and become a sheepherder. But not four months after the panic De Groot reappeared in the street, and accosted his former friends in their offices and on street corners, dismally croaking of disaster and predicting that it would finally end with every one of them reduced to his condition.

Joshua pretended at first that he did not know him, but De Groot insisted so long, pleading and whining, that Joshua turned and glared at him. "De Groot, if it is you, and so you say, I'm very much occupied, I have no time to gossip on street corners."

But while he had seen the disappearance, for all practical purposes, of Flagg and De Groot and many others he had known less well and in whose lives he had not participated either for good or ill, Joshua had been amused to watch the dexterity with which Hoke O'Neil had survived the catastrophe which had overwhelmed his own world of Tammany.

"It makes no god-damn difference what happens," Hoke told him, "just so you see it coming." He rubbed together the crooked fingers of his right hand. "Feel it or smell it or however you find it out, but don't get caught by surprise. I saw this one coming from a long way off, now didn't I, Ching? I knew four years ago those boys were in trouble with their diamonds and their horses and their brownstone mansions." Hoke liked those words, and mansion in particular he used with delicate scorn, for he believed as devoutly as ever that an Irishman who tried to rise above his natural bog would never be able to kick the mud off his shoes well enough to fool anyone.

When the Boss had first been brought to trial two years ago, Hoke had been among his sympathizers, had attended the hearings and helped to surround him at the end of the day as he sat amid his courtiers, and had shown himself a loyal defender of his fallen chief. And when the jury disagreed, Hoke had declared that the Boss might be Boss no longer but, at least, he could travel and enjoy his prosperity. "Laws are cobwebs which catch only small flies," he told Joshua with an air of wise confidence.

At the next trial, Hoke was again in attendance, and reported that the Boss was tired of the whole farce and did not believe any jury would ever convict him. "But," said Hoke, "I'm not so sure about that any more. Let's hope he stays in California." He did not, and a few months later was brought to trial in what Hoke declared to be the most wanton display of malice ever shown to any public figure.

"Two hundred million dollars," said Joshua severely, for the reports of thievery had swollen steadily, "is a great deal of money to take out of one city's treasury." After these figures had been published, in fact, Joshua had angrily asked Hoke why it was if so much money had changed hands that the Metropolitan Sand and Gravel Company had not got more of it, but Hoke said the figures were exaggerated and, furthermore, there was no use counting lost profits now.

The Boss was convicted this time and sentenced to jail, and Hoke grew maudlin as he described the scene in the courtroom. "Guilty on two hundred and four counts out of two hundred and twenty." Hoke shook his head. "Not a man moved or spoke—and then they walked out and left him there alone. The poor old son of a bitch." Joshua was scornfully amused, thinking this was only Irish superstition and sentimentality and, in fact, when he saw him next Hoke delivered an indignant harangue on the dishonesty of the former city government. "They had no god-damn right to steal that much. Our next man will steal in moderation, and be bloody well sure that everybody else does, too." Hoke, it seemed, had performed the feat of being loyal to the old government and the new one at the same time, although he admitted that it might take a few months to find his proper niche in the reformed Tammany. "But I'll find it, Ching, I'll find it, all right, don't you ever doubt that."

"I'm sure you will, Hoke," Joshua assured him, but was too much occupied with finding his own advantages to take any particular notice of how he went about it. For as soon as money began to be available, he entered into a variety of complex trading maneuvers with Cottrell and Talbot, stitching together the skein of the Baltimore-Missouri out of fragments other men had lost, and although he continued to urge economy on Rose and Suky, and Susan and Ceda, his first terror and pessimism had given way to a steadily increasing conviction of triumph. And he was so engrossed in his several conspiracies that when the news came early in April that Matt Devlin had been killed, it seemed a happening as remote as if he had been told of the death of someone he had never known or met.

He had arrived at the hotel and found Susan and Ceda drinking tea, only one lamp burning in the dusk, and Ceda was crying while Susan sat silently beside her. But none of this was unusual, and he might have gone to change his clothes before going to dinner with no more than his usual brief greeting, if Susan had not spoken to him in a quiet and surprisingly bitter voice, telling him about the letter which had come that day from Marietta; and Joshua paused, considering the news as if he did not quite know what to make of it, and then turned slowly to find Susan watching him with a cynical scorn, as if to see how well she had been able to predict his response.

"I knew something like this would happen to one or the other of them," he said grimly.

"Something like this, Joshua?"

"I tried to talk them out of that crazy notion. What sensible man would live out there if he could make his living here?" He asked the question with honest incomprehension, just as he had asked it of Pete and Matt Devlin long ago, and no answers they had found had satisfied him.

"I wonder, Joshua, if you weren't always a little jealous of Matt?"

"What an absurd idea." He was rather offended she should think he might be jealous of anyone, for jealousy, after all, was a symptom of inferiority, or at least the suspicion of it. "Matt and I were very good friends, I thought."

Ceda lay back on the couch crying helplessly, and although she tried to stop from time to time, she soon began again. Joshua glanced suspiciously at her and then at Susan, who was not crying now but certainly had been, and found himself wondering if either of them would have shown so much grief at his own death, or would they only begin to squabble over his will, a prospect which haunted him at unexpected times as the ultimate indignity to which he must, if his fortunes prospered, be one day subjected—if not by his wife, then by his daughter and son, even his brothers' children, by some hostile survivor.

But even though he felt obliged to protest that he and Matt had been good friends, he knew it was not quite true. They had never quarreled, and their children, with Samuel's and Aaron's, had grown up together, but Joshua had always suspected that neither Matt nor Pete Devlin had quite trusted or respected him. And therefore he could not resist a small feeling of triumph at this news, which seemed one more evidence that his purposes were invincible, and that while others might pass untimely from the world he would not. In a sense, it seemed a kind of punishment upon Matt Devlin for not having given Joshua Ching his rightful measure of admiration and confidence, even having thought, so Joshua imagined, that his business practices were so far beyond ingenuity as to trespass upon dishonesty. But if that was what Matt Devlin had thought of him, at least he would think it no more.

"What about his will?" inquired Joshua, for this, now that he was dead, was the only real interest he still had in Matt Devlin. What did a man who had gone west with some wild-eyed scheme of combatting nature and justifying himself in the course of the contest and who had been, he was willing to admit, uncommonly lucky, what did such a man do about his gains after he could no longer control or enjoy them. "Or did he leave one?"

"He did. Marietta sent a copy to Morgan. Matt had made it out about a year ago, although he'd never mentioned it. It was found in his safe-deposit box—the only thing in it, Marietta said—and he left everything to Morgan."

"To Morgan?" repeated Joshua sharply. "Everything?"

"Of course, there are provisions, but when Matt's share is added to whatever share Morgan had himself, Morgan acquires control of their company, though he's not to act without Pete's agreement. And he's expected to take care of Marietta and Annabel and the two younger boys, but then, he would do that anyway. Why don't you ask Morgan to let you see it, Joshua?" Again she gave him that peculiar smile. "I can't remember all the details."

"But why didn't Matt leave his share, or part of it at least, to Pete? They were the original founders. That would have been more logical."

"Not to Matt, apparently. Anyway, your nephew is now a banker. A western banker, it's true, but still a banker."

"How fortunate for him," mused Joshua, irresistibly drawn to the contemplation of how much this simplified Morgan's ambitions, but then added quickly, "I wasn't speaking of Matt's death, of course. I know how much Morgan thought of him."

"Do you?"

When he saw Morgan, Joshua put on a remarkably long face, while Morgan behaved exactly as Joshua thought Matt would have preferrred—said nothing, accepted all condolences with a curt nod, looked more angry than mournful, and refused to discuss his father's death with anyone, even Suky.

"He's said nothing to you?" Joshua asked her.

"Nothing at all." Suky looked wan and listless, tears dropped when she seemed least to expect it, and she caught them with her fingertips. Suky, like Susan and Ceda and Felice, had put on light mourning, and they all wore black silk dresses embroidered with jet, which gave them a look of distinguished mystery and caused Joshua some further premonitions on his own behalf, as if this were only a re-

hearsal for the main performance of his death. "Now all those summers are really gone," Suky murmured, with such sadness that
Joshua was offended, for Matt Devlin must have somehow represented to her those childhood years and whatever obscure memories
she had kept of them.

Still, it seemed a curious thing they should be so much concerned
at the death of a man they had not seen for many years and would
likely never have seen again, and Joshua advised himself to accept
it philosophically and continue about his business, according Matt
Devlin just about the same measure of grief he would have expected Matt to accord him, had he died first.

But even so it occurred to him from time to time that there was
something uncanny in this sudden and final and accidental disappearance of one he had known long and well, for had Matt died of
one of the western sicknesses, or even one of the natural western
hazards—blood-poisoning or the bite of a rattlesnake or a fall from a
horse—perhaps it would have had its own logic, but this unexplained
killing at the hands of a stranger he found to be disturbing and eerie,
so that finally he was forced to remind himself it was, after all, the
only possible conclusion to Matt Devlin's pursuit of whatever kind of
freedom he had gone west to encounter. For Matt Devlin, he thought,
had been more interested in living, or even in dying, than in success
or money or reputation; and now he was dead at the age of forty-
eight.

He had some curiosity about how Morgan would handle himself
now that he had succeeded to his father's financial strength, but
when he made tentative efforts to inquire, Morgan told him it would
make no difference at all and Joshua soon lost interest in this, too,
for he had not time enough to plan his own life, much less to wonder
how another man would plan his; and early in June, William Talbot
gave him something new to be concerned about.

"If I were you, Joshua, I'd start to look for a buyer for De Groot
Distilleries. The government's a mad dog, there's no predicting who
will be bitten next, and I would not like to see one of the partners of
the Baltimore-Missouri go to jail."

"Our reports have been honest," Joshua told him stiffly.

"That isn't easy to prove when an entire industry becomes involved in scandal."

"I had been thinking of selling it anyway," said Joshua, for he did
not like the notion that he might be made to run from a government
investigation. "I think it's served its purpose."

"Don't wait too long."

De Groot Distilleries had, indeed, served its purpose, even to surviving all the ingenuities of financial torture to which he had subjected it. For during the time it had been in his control, Joshua had
twisted the company into such a variety of painful positions that
without the frantic speculation in whisky, the crop failures in Europe, the industry's practice of defrauding the government of its

revenue taxes and which Talbot predicted would soon end, De Groot Distilleries would long ago have been abandoned by him as a worthless derelict. None of this could have been predicted eight years ago, and yet it had made it possible for Joshua, while describing himself as an investor and a railroad man, to practice and perfect all the manipulative skills most congenial to him, for De Groot Distilleries was just the kind of company he liked best: Someone else had put it up and there it stood, ready for him to take it down.

He had first contrived to disenfranchise the holders of all foreign stock, and having rid himself of these potential meddlers he had let it be known that the company itself was sound and only Milton De Groot was defunct. After that, he watered the stock by one hundred percent, a figure both Samuel and Aaron had thought excessive but which Joshua assured them was safe and then, a few months later, he watered it again. To the surprise of Samuel and Aaron, the stock rose steadily, and Joshua told them in one of his infrequent attacks of candor, "It's an old alchemist's trick I've learned—turning the water to gold."

It had soon become necessary to levy such heavy assessments on the stockholders they could not meet them, their stock was forfeited, and De Groot Distilleries sank so low it was put into a voting trust controlled by Joshua Ching, and, ever since, Joshua had used it as his private treasury, dipping into it for funds to support the Corporate Engineers, and because every now and then he bought shares of his watered stock, the company had a look of financial well-being which concealed from most men its serious ailments.

There were, of course, many men in Wall Street who knew as well as he did that it was more profitable to reorganize a company than to build it, but only a few of them, Joshua assured himself, had his precise and sensitive intuition, his clairvoyant judgment, and his capacity for enduring the long periods of furious exhilaration without succumbing to the temptation of selling too soon. For tamer men invariably began to long for their old calm and contentment, and so missed their best chances, while he found himself as buoyant and energetic and keenly alert at the end of a prolonged negotiation as he had been at the beginning, with perhaps even a heightening of his capacities for fierce concentration.

"I think I've located my man," Joshua told Talbot one day in mid-July, when they were driving uptown to see Felice and Morgan off for the West. Even their Long Branch reservations had been postponed until Dr. Montgomery had decided that Susette, who was now five months old, was old enough for such a trip, and it seemed to Joshua that during the two years he had spent there, Morgan Devlin had contrived—whether by intention or through one of those accidents of personality which were not easy to separate from intention—to affect all their lives far more than a young man twenty-six years old should be able to do.

The day was hot, and the vast glass and metal vault of the station had filled with smoke and steam and sharp smells of burning coal and grease. The yellow wooden coaches shook and rattled along the concourse, making a din through which Joshua had no hope of discussing his plans with Talbot, who would not likely have been listening if he had, for Talbot's face was dour and bitter as he watched Felice kissing Suky good-bye and crying a little, as they promised each other a letter a week, at the least. Still, Talbot was as pleased with his granddaughter as if Morgan were not her father.

Joshua, deep in speculations of his own, stood to one side, letting Coral and Suky, Susan and Ceda and Alvita Hallam, give Felice all the good advice she would be sure to need in the mountains: she must not fail to cut Susette's eyelashes when she was a year old so they would grow long and thick, she must ride two hours each day and read at least three books every week, take good care of her skin in that dry climate; and, in some unoccupied portion of his mind, Joshua idly reflected upon Matt Devlin and his son.

It gave him a sense of grudging and reluctant wonder to study Morgan, as he had done several times, and most particularly since he had inherited his father's share of Devlin Brothers; for, just as Joshua believed Matt Devlin had never approved of him, neither had he approved of Matt, whose appearance he had thought too unruly for a gentleman, and in Joshua's opinion, Matt's expression of somber austerity was all that had saved him from the danger of looking picturesque. And this he thought was true of Morgan, who even had his father's habit of smiling unexpectedly, abolishing for a moment that contemplative severity, and then lapsing back into it. But of course these qualities, which Matt Devlin might or might not have found a blessing to him in life, could plague or serve him no longer and were now the sole possession of his son, a heritage perhaps more significant for his future than his controlling interest in Devlin Brothers.

There was a flurry of kisses and tears, the baby was carried aboard the train by the nurse, and while Felice stood talking to her father, Morgan approached Suky, and Joshua was surprised to see the look of intensity which came onto his face the moment before he kissed her, and even more surprised to see Suky's answering look, at once inviting and artfully submissive, and he fell to wondering what there was here that he might have overlooked.

But now Morgan stepped quickly away, Suky was kissing Felice again, and Joshua told himself it was fruitless for any man to concern himself with the mysteries of other lives, and he grew impatient for them to be gone. The train moved, the wheels grinding and crashing, the little cars shaking as if they would come apart, and while the others were still waving handkerchiefs and calling their good-byes, Joshua and William Talbot set off briskly, Talbot taking up their conversation in the middle of a sentence which had been interrupted half an hour ago.

"—before I would recommend a floating loan of four million. After all, less than ten years ago Elisha Tibbitts was not worth fifty dollars."

"Between two and four million is the best present estimate I've been able to get."

"One million down is the least you must take."

"I agree. But it will take a little time. Tibbitts is one of those men who imagines he must never make a mistake."

During the next few months Joshua continued to practice his arts of persuasion upon Elisha Tibbitts, a man almost as suspicious as himself, while from time to time he reflected bitterly upon those men who came into the Street convinced that the talent and shrewdness required to make a small fortune somewhere else would infallibly make them a large one in New York.

But at last the sale was completed, Joshua turned over to Elisha Tibbitts the books kept by Van Zandt and Ching during the years De Groot Distilleries had been under his management, and Talbot requested that Tibbitts pay him without delay a floating loan of four million dollars he had granted that company only a week ago. This news traveled quickly, causing astonishment and envy and in some quarters virtuous disapproval, and when a little later there were rumors that William Talbot, Joshua Ching and Amos Cottrell had realized five million dollars during the past year by trading in the wake of the Panic, Joshua was pleased to find his early ambitions had been realized and that he might now walk about the financial district with the conviction that his tread made the earth tremble and his glance sent out flashes which caught other men at the heart, causing them to quaver with terror or giddy expectancy of his favor.

Matt Devlin, he thought, might have confounded their imaginations by the style of his dying, but as for himself, Joshua Ching meant to leave a different legacy.

XLVII

The gilded clock, with its legend: Gold Bought Here, overhung the sidewalk again. The building was three stories high, made of rough gray stone with a plate-glass window upon the street, small watchtowers stood at each corner of the crenellated roof, and this miniature castle contained a counting room, three private offices, a golden oak counter where four clerks might work at their ledgers, a directors' room on the second floor, and a fireproof vault with a double steel door.

Morgan entered it stealthily, even taking the precaution of glancing up the street to make sure no one was watching him, and as he began to wander about, touching the counter, observing the maps, smiling a little at the buffalo and ram heads which confronted each other from across the room, it seemed the door would momentarily open and Matt would walk in, and they would sit down and talk over the changes that had occurred in the Territory while he was away.

He glanced into the private offices at the back, finding evidences in one that it belonged to Pete, another had Jonathan's coat hanging on a peg, and he paused in the doorway of the third, for there was nothing in it but a chair and desk, and his sense of dread increased, though he had no more real conviction now that Matt was dead than he had had at the moment he had opened Marietta's letter—or when he had stood alone in the cemetery the day before, staring at that swollen oblong of grass. Gabe Foster, he had been told, had been buried in a distant corner of that same cemetery, as if to prevent the two from renewing their struggle in some earthbound encounter, but neither had Gabe Foster any reality for him.

All at once he went dashing out, surprised and ashamed that six months after his father's death he should be more afraid than ever of the moment when he must sit at that desk and make the first decision—for whether chance gave him then a trivial or an important one, whether it might involve a few dollars or many thousands, he had a sure conviction of being unequal to whatever judgment would be required; and yet just such decisions had seemed a part of the day's simple routine not so very long ago.

He locked the door and set out for Jeremy Flint's office, though it was not yet seven-thirty. During the past few years, Jeremy Flint had become one of the Territory's successful men, and only those who had long memories could recall that ten years ago he had worn a black bearskin overcoat summer and winter, been drunk more often than he was sober, and had driven about on Sunday afternoons in an open hack with the camp's most celebrated madam, Milly Matches.

For Jeremy Flint had made himself a specialist in mining litigation, as well as a very rich man from his several investments, and he and his wife were often away for two or three months at a time, inspecting properties he owned in California and Nevada, or traveling in Europe. No one had recently seen him drunk, and his bearskin overcoat had been given up for a frock coat and gray trousers, and, with a black hat to cover his bald head, he walked ponderously from his office to his home twice a day, his big, clean-shaven face seemingly impassive, but his blue eyes permanently narrowed to a shrewd and steady gaze which frightened all who owed him money and discouraged many who would have liked to.

His office occupied a single room on the second floor of the building he owned, a small, ill-smelling room he had furnished with objects picked up in abandoned cabins, and from its windows he could watch the activity in the streets and was often to be seen standing there, his large, solid body set against the glass, hands in his pockets and a cigar in his mouth, planning, they always imagined, his next victory.

That was where Morgan found him, and Jeremy Flint turned, looked at him sharply for a moment, and came forward to shake his hand. "Irene told me you were back." They talked for a few minutes, avoiding the subject he had come there to discuss, until finally Morgan asked him if there had been any objections to the terms of Matt's will.

"You may find," Flint said, "that Lem Finney doesn't like this arrangement much. He thinks that with your original nine percent and Matt's twenty-six, you've got more than enough to put you in charge, especially when you add Pete's twenty-six and your brothers' combined shares—nine, isn't it? That leaves the rest of us, me and Mercer and Webb—who can be expected to vote with you most of the time—and Finney and Hart and Church and Manzoni, with thirty among us. Not enough by a long way to protect our interests if there was a real difference of opinion." Jeremy Flint looked at Morgan from beneath the hat brim pulled down almost to his tufted black eyebrows which were, Morgan had often thought, the only outward sign that this slow-moving, serious man had the impudence to have married Milly Matches. "In fact," he added, "I know damn well Finney doesn't like it because he's talked to me about it. He can't understand why the percentage wasn't either split with the other three sons, or with Pete, and he's drawn up in his head several arrangements that suit him much better." Jeremy smiled.

"Why was it drawn this way? Did he tell you?"

"Yes, he did. But I didn't think it was anyone's god-damn business but yours. Matt came to see me about a year and a half ago, on April the twenty-third, in fact. He came at night and he came to the house, and he said that he wanted me to draw his will but keep quiet about it unless it was needed. Yes, by Christ, that was his phrase—unless it's needed—as if he might have been talking about a new piece of machinery for the quartz mill. He had it clearly in mind, exactly as it stands now, nothing was changed after it was drawn, and he said he'd had some trouble lately with one of the ranchmen out in the valley who couldn't meet his loan and claimed he'd shoot the first guy who tried to repossess the property. He said he didn't believe the bastard but that he was maybe crazy enough to do it and—just on the chance this bird took a shot at him some day—he thought he'd like to have things tidy. He wouldn't tell me the fellow's name, though, and I don't think he was expecting it, any more than any of us do. A trip toward the west may, as they say, make a man riper and more expansive, but it also makes him more inclined to rely on settling his problems with a Colt. Now, the reason he gave for the kind of division he made was this." Morgan watched him with alert concentration, for this, he knew, had puzzled them all, and Jonathan plainly thought he had been cheated, passed over in favor of his rival. "He said that Devlin Brothers was what he and Pete had built together and that they had agreed never to let it fall apart, and he thought the best way to keep it building—he wasn't a religious man, you know, but this was his particular notion of keeping himself alive, or functioning, at least, once he was gone—the best chance he thought was to put his own share into your hands with the provision that all decisions be made as if you and Pete owned equal shares. Pete has lost nothing during his lifetime, although of course he will have a smaller percentage to leave his children if he has any others, and the responsibility is finally pinned to one person." He pointed his forefinger. "That's you, the logical choice, I should think. Now, your younger brothers may be a little hurt, but that's their hard luck for having come along later." He smiled slightly. "If I was Matt I'd have done the same thing. Pete has no objections, has he?"

"If he has, he hasn't mentioned them."

Lemuel Finney did not tell Morgan what better disposition he thought his father might have made of his assets, but he did, during the board meeting the next day, find so many questions to ask that at last Morgan said, with an air of patient concern, "Lem, I have no intention of trying to change any of our policies. Furthermore, there's a stipulation that I couldn't if I wanted to. Now what the hell bothers you?"

They were in the directors' room, gathered about the long table with its many marks and scratches, evidences of four fires and hundreds of board meetings during which it had been charred by cigars and carved and whittled upon by absent-minded members. They tilted their chairs and hoisted their feet to the table, and to begin the day's business a bottle of whisky was passed from hand to hand while they waited through Jonathan's reading of the minutes and a recitation of the bank's present condition. This was usually the end of the meeting, and after some desultory exchange of news they went their separate ways, for they all belonged to one another's boards and had no wish to offer advice which might be given back to them a day later. But Lemuel Finney, it seemed, was troubled to find this company in the control of a man younger than his own son and whose sober judgment he apparently trusted no better than he trusted Jake's.

"That's what you say, Morgan, but suppose you decided to make a pretty good-sized investment in, say, a silver mine—how could we stop you? Silver mining, they say, affects men in strange ways."

"Lem," said Pete, "if you want to sell your stock, I'll buy it."

"Of course I don't want to sell it. We've been partners in one thing and another ever since we got out here, Pete. But times are bad. We must be careful."

"Morgan will be careful, Lem," Pete told him, and the others began gazing abstractedly at the ceiling, drumming their knuckles on the table or contemplating the ragged ends of their cigars.

"But Morgan is interested in silver," Lem insisted, and all at once

Morgan gave a scornful laugh and slammed his chair onto the floor. "And so, I've heard, are you, Lem."

"I am? Oh, perhaps a little. I pick up something here and there, when it seems a bargain." He rubbed his hands together briskly, smiling.

Morgan stared at him, ready to ask what bargains he had picked up these past two and a half years, but miners were secretive by nature, himself as well as Lemuel Finney, as if their habits of delving into the earth's hiding places communicated itself to their dispositions, and so he only reminded him, "There's no bargain in an undeveloped mine."

"That's true, Morgan. And it's also true that a silver mine cannot be developed without spending money, a great—deal—of money."

"The money I spend won't be yours, Lem," Morgan assured him, as if he had come into contact with a rampaging cat and wished to calm it before it did him some small but nasty injury.

"Now, Morgan, you don't think I was suggesting—" He appealed to them one after another, speaking of his affection for Morgan, his uncle and his brothers, his reverence for Matt Devlin, and was insisting he had intended no slur on Morgan's honesty when the meeting adjourned, and Morgan was all the more eager to get to Butte.

Two days later, at four in the morning, he and Douglas set out. He left Felice in bed, forbidding her to go downstairs with him, for this, after all, was the first of those tests he had described, and he was stubbornly determined to show her just what it would mean to be married to a mining man. He had often thought, with a sense of wry amusement, a little sorrowful, that Felice had only exchanged one tyrant for another, and now, when he told her good-bye, his face was somber, daring her to complain of this life he had brought her to. "You won't be lonely?"

"Of course I'll be lonely."

"You won't be unhappy?"

"Yes, I will."

"You won't hate me for it?"

"I love you, Morgan." She smiled, touching his hair.

He looked at her carefully, pretending not to believe her, and then was out of the room and down the stairs to find Douglas in the kitchen, drinking coffee and nervously snapping his fingers, eager to be on his way.

Douglas was nineteen now and seemed to have grown several inches since he had seen him last. He was husky and broad-shouldered, his hair had turned dark brown, and his earlier tendency to fight upon any pretext he could invent was giving way to an aggressive earnestness. He had spent these past two years traveling about the various camps buying ore and inspecting properties, and had announced the night Morgan arrived that now he was ready to become his business manager. "I have three thousand dollars to invest, I'm a good shot—and I've got a talent for arithmetic." Morgan agreed that these were useful qualifications for a miner, and they had shaken hands.

It was late in the day when they came in sight of the big butte, red and glowing with the last sunlight, surrounded by the wide shadowed valley and distant mountains, and Morgan was caught by a pang of nostalgic admiration for this ominous country which he had never felt for the flower-trimmed platitudes of prettier landscapes.

The nearer they approached the camp, as scattered and misshapen and unpromising as it had ever been, the more exultant he grew, until he was grinning with what he told himself was surely the rapture of a lunatic. For this land would not be cherished with an agrarian's gentleness, but attacked with fervor and violence, blown apart and dug into deeply as they ransacked it for hidden clots of metal, and when it had at last been blighted and tortured into repellent ugliness, would have acquired beauties in their eyes beyond any enchantments of the greenest forests or most tranquil walled gardens. But, surely, whoever could take joy in this destruction must have the enthusiasm of a madman, and there seemed little hope he would ever be able to explain such savagery to Felice.

There were, he had heard, about three hundred people living in the camp now. A hotel had been built since he had been there last, but there was no schoolhouse and no public hall. Many cabins stood empty, few men were to be seen on the streets, and Bruno Favorite's was still the only saloon and grocery store. Morgan sent Douglas to find a place for them to live, any abandoned cabin not too far gone in disrepair, and went into Favorite's, where he found Bruno lurking behind a counter, a morose and peevish expression on his face which changed miraculously at sight of an old comrade. "Devlin!" he shouted, and then murmured, "Heard about your old man, god-damn shame." He reached up to clasp Morgan's shoulder. "How the hell are you?"

He set out a bottle and two glasses to toast Morgan's return, and according to their ritual, they spent a few minutes recalling old pleasures and asking about old friends, tossing down a drink to the memory of those who were known to be dead and shaking their heads over those rumored to have died.

Morgan lowered his voice, glanced suspiciously at the four players, and asked, "You got my letters?"

"I got them." All at once Bruno arranged his face in its caricature of Lem Finney, while he rubbed his hands together in Lem's habitual gesture and even contrived to produce the same sound as if dry leaves were moving somewhere nearby. Morgan threw back his head and gave a loud, angry laugh, then peered sharply at Bruno as if to ask how much he had sold his loyalty for, but Bruno took a backward step and held up one hand in an oath of virtue. "When Bruno Favorite takes charge of a man's business, he can go to sleep and forget about it."

"Okay, Bruno, I'm glad to hear it. Now, what has that little son of a bitch been up to?"

"Nothing much. He's bought a couple of claims and leased some others."

"Which ones has he bought?"

Bruno backed away, reminding Morgan of a moping parrot lifting his claws as he moves restlessly along his perch. "That's not so easy to find out. You know miners, they keep their secrets."

Morgan looked at him for several moments, then all at once leaned both elbows on the bar, crossed one booted leg over the other, and gave a confidential and beckoning gesture of one hand. "Bruno, don't horseshit me."

"I wouldn't do that to an old friend—"

"What do you want?"

Bruno polished the counter more industriously. "I've been here a long time, remember. I'm the only guy who's stayed here winter and summer and kept this keg-house open for the miners' comfort and convenience—and now, by Christ, if there's going to be a strike I'd like to get in on it."

"I gave you five hundred before I left, Bruno. Wasn't that what you asked me for?"

"That's what I asked you for then, but then, you've got to remember, we didn't know they'd changed the bloody law on us. And that's made a hell of a difference—oh, a hell of a difference, believe me."

"I sent you the money to pay that guy for keeping up the representation."

"So you did, Devlin. So you did." Bruno looked more gloomy, and, when Morgan asked if the money had arrived, Bruno sighed and hung his head and peeped sideways at him, nodding. But then, as Morgan's eyes began to glitter as if he might be thinking of strangling his old friend of the early days, Bruno said, "I told you, it's all been taken care of."

"Then what the hell's wrong? I sent the money, you got it, it's been taken care of." Morgan leaned closer and, finally, murmured, "Tell me what you want, Bruno."

"I want two percent of every claim you work."

"For how long?"

"For good." He gazed at Morgan pleadingly. "That isn't much to ask, Devlin, I've been offered more. Oh, don't worry, I didn't take it, didn't even consider taking it for a minute—I wouldn't do that to a guy who was here in 'sixty-six, you know that."

Morgan studied this proposal for a few moments while Bruno returned to his polishing, and then all at once shook his hand for, after all, there was no other way to find out what had happened while he was away, and Bruno might, as he said, be offering him a bargain in information only for the sake of their old friendship.

Bruno hovered behind the bar, whispering, and Morgan listened with sober attention as he began to describe the changes in the camp.

He told him how much each man had made, who had gone away and who had returned, what newcomers there were and what properties they had located, and although it seemed that Bruno Favorite's capacious memory had forgotten no littlest detail, Morgan heard nothing which interested him very much until the four players had left, Douglas had come to tell him where their cabin was, and he and Bruno sat down at the table with a map before them.

And then Bruno told him that Lem Finney had taken a year's option on the claim Amos Muspratt had leased to him for six months, and for which Amos had sent him six hundred dollars as his share of the profits. Morgan was glowering over this fickleness, when Bruno pointed to a claim adjacent to the Muspratt claim which had been bought recently by a prospector named Homer Grimes. At this, Morgan began to swear and leaned back in his chair, shocked and furious, and Bruno ended his recital with the casual remark that although the work of representation had been done on Morgan's claims, the man who had done it had disappeared before he had filed his records with the District Land Office, an oversight Bruno had luckily discovered when a friend was reading through the records several months later and told him the claims he was overseeing had not conformed to the new laws.

"I took care of it right away," Bruno assured him.

"How?"

"Filed in the guy's name, of course. I know the clerk. What the hell, Devlin, who's going to know the difference?"

"Anyone who really wants to find out."

"But who will look for it?"

"Maybe the same guy who put your man up to leaving in the first place?"

Bruno looked as prudishly disapproving as if this immoral notion would never have occurred to him and he was surprised to find Morgan of so suspicious a nature. "Finney couldn't get away with that," he assured him, but then he began to sulk. "I did the best I could, Devlin. I hired the guy, I saw that he did the work. You couldn't expect me to go to Deer Lodge to watch him record it, now could you? I've got my own responsibilities."

Morgan gave a weary sigh, slapped at the table top and stood up. "Okay, Bruno, you've done what you could, but just to be on the safe side I'll relocate the Halloway claim along with the others. And if it comes to court, then you're my witness."

"I'm your witness."

Morgan and Douglas roamed about for several days, finding little evidence of work on Morgan's properties but, perhaps, enough to meet the new requirements, and he was glad to find this terrain was as familiar to him as if he had never gone away, for he had kept it as fresh in his memory as any doting lover might have kept his sweetheart's face and smile.

Amos Muspratt, however, told him that his new partner would

permit no visitors, and so Morgan squatted on the pile of rock Amos
had been accumulating at the entrance to his underground resort for
the past ten years and spent two hours talking to him with an air of
affectionate confidence, reminding him of old days and old loyalties,
even though Amos Muspratt no doubt remembered quite well that in
the old days he had been what he was now, a solitary miner intent
on his work and aloof from young men's diversions.

At last, Morgan thought he had as much of Amos Muspratt's confidence as any man was likely to get, and he casually asked him
how it happened that Amos had sold that claim to Homer Grimes
when he had been trying to buy it from him for years. "Just one reason," Amos told him. "I was up to here in debt."

"But I'd have paid you just as much, Amos, and we wouldn't have
let it go to an outsider."

"You weren't here."

"You knew I was coming back."

"They said you weren't."

"They?" But Amos had nothing more to say, and Morgan decided
it was time to return to Helena for supplies, before one of those early
snows closed the mountain roads.

"Every son of a bitch here thinks he's Cinderella," he told Bruno,
and surveyed with a broad gesture the camp which had had, from
the beginning, an air of inconsequence, as if nothing would ever
come of it. "They're all waiting for December thirty-first when"—he
snapped his fingers—"this turns into Delmonico's, the cabins into
brownstones and the mules trotting horses—and away they go to the
ball. Well, I'll be back in a week or two, that should give me time
enough to get ready for the celebrations."

They stopped at Deer Lodge to study the records in the District
Land Office, and, as Bruno had assured him, the three claims had
been represented, although the handwriting was not the same as
others recorded on that date, so that if a certified copy had been
made before Bruno had inserted his corrections, it would show them
to have gone unrepresented for a year and almost five months. Douglas glanced at Morgan as they stood reading the records, with Morgan making notes of questions he wanted to ask Jeremy Flint, and his
face was hopeful. "There'll be some trouble on New Year's Eve," he
predicted.

Morgan smiled. "Maybe not. I'll have a better idea after I've talked
to Finney."

"And you won't forget to talk to Flora's stepfather?" Douglas had
reminded him of this several times, but even after several promises
he remained anxious.

For Douglas had, rather sheepishly, but with intense pride, told
Morgan his secret. After all these years, he and Flora Pim had fallen
in love, and they wanted to be married as soon as her parents would
agree that she was old enough, and he had promised to plead Douglas' suit with Josiah Webb.

Felice, he was relieved to find, had not been intimidated by this large family, as he had been afraid she might be—for Felice had described herself as having lived alone in her parents' house with her governess and tutors for her only companions, her mother seeming to pass through her world at a distance—but had learned as much of their lore and habits as if she had been with them for years. While she and Lisette, who might often be found laughing or whispering together, had fulfilled Suky's prediction, for Suky had warned Felice that Lisette had formidable charms, when she chose to exert them, and had suggested that Felice would not miss her once she knew Lisette.

Lem Finney showed him a bland face when he tried to discuss Butte, preferring to talk instead of projects their two companies had in Helena, and assured Morgan that if his son-in-law had bought a claim that was no concern of his, while Homer Grimes pretended not even to know what he was talking about.

"Oh, that claim," he finally agreed.

"Do you want to sell it, Homer?"

"The assay reports have been very disappointing. In fact, I'm thinking of calling it the Humbug." But he would think it over, he said, and he was still thinking it over the day they left, so that Douglas, more determined than ever to have some reckless deed to carry back to Flora Pim now that her stepfather had agreed they might be married after her sixteenth birthday, had joyous expectations of trouble on New Year's Eve.

They traveled with a pack train bearing their supplies for the winter—pots and pans, stools and chairs and blankets and panes for two windows, books and ammunition, canned oysters, bacon and flour, molasses and salt and tobacco and whisky—and Morgan had hired a carpenter, for he had not been able to find one in Butte who knew how to build a four-room cabin with a lean-to kitchen he would ask Felice to live in.

And although he had looked at her almost resentfully when he kissed her good-bye, a little jealous to think she might be so well cared for she would not miss him as much as she should, he soon became so engrossed in those riddles the earth propounded that presently Christmas Eve had arrived—a gloomy day, as it turned out, for no one had thought to plan such a celebration as they had had eight years ago, and men wandered the streets and visited from cabin to cabin, or gathered in Bruno Favorite's to stand gazing absently into their whisky glasses, reminding one another of all that was lacking in their lives.

"Not much like the old days, is it?" Bruno asked Morgan, and when Morgan, who had fallen despondent along with the others, made no reply, Bruno turned to Douglas. "You should have been here then, son. Well, of course, you weren't old enough to enjoy it. But those were the times, believe me," and Douglas, convinced that he had missed experiences he could never hope to match, the very

atmosphere having changed in the meantime—all the dashing
women grown old and the desperate men turned flaccid or been
killed—nodded sadly and philosophically. "The West is gone," Bruno
advised him. "The Old West is gone."

"There never was any Old West, Bruno." Morgan sounded surly,
for he could think of no good reason why he should have exiled himself to this forsaken camp, where only an occasional miner prowled
the streets and the wind whistled noisily all day long and all night.

"You were here," Bruno protested. "You know how different it
was."

"We were different, Bruno," Morgan told him and felt that he was,
in fact, drunker than he had meant to be. "And if you'd remember it
the way it was you'd remember it was god-damn lousy. We were so
hungry our guts ached and our teeth got loose. We were poor and
dirty and full of rotgut. Henry Halloway died while Fletcher was
sawing off his feet. Harry York got so fed up he cut his throat one
morning. And we all thought it was a hell of a good joke when Buckshot Carter fed us wolf meat. Those are the old days he's talking
about, Douglas."

"Don't let him prejudice you. They were great days, son, great
days, no matter what this old man says about it."

"Wish I'd been here." Douglas looked wistful, as if his brother's
recital of the winter's horrors had only whetted his appetite for that
grim and distant world where a man must have the bark on if he was
to survive at all, and he confided to Bruno, "In all these years, I've
never shot at anybody. And never been shot at myself, either."

"That's what I told you, son. The Old West is gone."

"Shut up, Bruno. I don't want him going off half-cocked on New
Year's Eve just because you've convinced him every real westerner
gets his man sooner or later." But when they started out, Bruno,
about to be left alone, gave him such a beseeching glance that Morgan smiled, demanding, "Who the hell invented Christmas, anyway?"

By New Year's Eve, Christmas seemed a long time past, and Morgan and Douglas awoke keenly alert, and grew more and more restless as the day went by, although Morgan insisted they must not take
even one drink, for either the nature of the mountain whisky or the
nature of whisky in the mountains was such that no man's judgment
was as clear or his hand as steady once he had encouraged himself
by a glass or two.

"Whatever happens," he warned Douglas, as they sat over the remains of dinner, polishing and cleaning their pistols, "for God's
sake don't fire unless they fire first. It would be a hell of a thing if we
knocked off Lem Finney—Mrs. Finney would never let Mother hear
the end of it."

Douglas laughed greedily, but gave his solemn oath to fire no random shots. They had, by now, rehearsed this a dozen times, stepping
off the distance night after night, cutting and whittling stakes and

tying them into bundles, and had dug up the tree stumps which had defined the boundaries and filled in the holes so carefully that neither Finney nor anyone else would ever be able to point with certainty to where they had been; and there was nothing more to do but to post the relocation notices at midnight.

Douglas ate little but drank several cups of coffee, cast fierce glances about the room and into their shaving mirror, stamped his feet and said it had turned colder, and asked Morgan every few minutes if it was time to leave.

"We shouldn't be too early. I want to get the job done close enough to midnight that there'll be nothing to argue about but whose watch was right."

At a quarter after eleven Morgan got into his buffalo overcoat, Douglas leaped upon his as if upon an animal struggling to free itself, and with the bundles of sticks under their arms they set off for Butte Hill, walking swiftly and silently and passing men going upon similar errands.

They came trotting up the hill, aware of other men scouring about in the dark, and were not very much surprised to discover stakes driven at the corners of the first claim. But when they attacked one they found it to be the size of a fence post and driven so deep that it took them three or four minutes before they could knock it down, Douglas drove their own marker, and they ran on to the next corner, where they had the same struggle.

"They meant these bloody things to stay put, all right. There it goes. Now—quick!"

Douglas pounded the stake in, and they set off, stumbling over rocks and into shallow holes, peering through the darkness, for the hillside seemed to be swarming with men, there were sounds of hushed voices, an occasional angry exclamation, and as they started across Muspratt's claim, a voice called: "Don't try anything here, boys, whoever you are."

"Amos, for Christ's sake, don't hold us up."

"That you, Devlin? Busy night, isn't it?"

They ran on, and were part way across Homer Grimes' adjacent property when there was the sound of a pistol being cocked nearby. Morgan gave Douglas a resounding whack on the shoulders, warning him not to fire, and they dropped to the ground, crawled a little distance, then sprang up and ran on. "You take those corners—I'll take these. They can't hit us in this light."

Morgan had the post clasped between his hands with the same enthusiastic grip he would have been glad to fasten on Lem Finney's throat, heaving it backward and forward, when he became aware that someone stood not far away, a little distance up the hillside. He paused, searching carefully, and went on with the struggle. The post came loose, he kicked it over, drove in his marker and ran for the opposite corner, and found that another man ran beside him, only a few yards away. He had reached the post and was shoving against it with one shoulder when a sonorous voice called, "You're late! It's nine minutes after midnight!" He sent the pole down, and the same voice informed him, "These relocation notices are invalid. We got ours in first."

Morgan spun around, so enraged he longed to find this man, whoever he was, and kill him. "Who are you?" he yelled. "You bloody coward, show yourself!"

The voice replied in a tone of mocking threat, "There are two of us, don't be so hasty."

Morgan struck a match, found that it was eight minutes past midnight, and shouted, "Your watches are wrong, it's one minute past twelve."

The two voices gave hollow sarcastic laughs, so elaborately theatrical that he paused, trying to think who might sound that way if he laughed into a gunny sack, and Douglas came running up the hill, calling, "Everything's okay down there. Where are the bastards?"

A pistol was fired and one of the men screamed, "You clumsy son of a bitch, I told you not to do that!"

Morgan threw back his head and gave a shout of joyous laughter. "What the hell are you doing on my property, Jake Finney?"

"This isn't your property, Devlin. This is an abandoned claim—and we've relocated it."

Morgan started slowly up the hill, and as he moved, the voices slid cautiously away. "Jake, why don't you answer me? Are you ashamed of what you're doing?"

"This is our claim, Devlin. Get off it."

Morgan walked more quickly, convinced that if it was Jake Finney he would not fire and, if he did, would not hit him, and all at once a man scrambled to his feet and started at a run down the hill. Morgan stopped, helplessly laughing, and the first voice yelled, "Come back here, you god-damn coward!"

"Homer Grimes," Morgan called, "are you going to run off and leave Jake Finney to jump this claim all by himself? Come back here and be a man or, by God, we'll have your brother-in-law for breakfast."

"This is our property, Devlin," Jake Finney told him sternly. "You abandoned it. Your man went off without paying the assessment, and according to the Mining Resources Act of May tenth, eighteen seventy-two—"

"Jake, for Christ's sake, don't you think I know that law as well as you do? Now—skeedaddle."

"We'll sue you."

"Go ahead. But for now, get out."

"Colonel Colt made all men equal," called Homer Grimes from a distance.

"Like hell he did. Get out, both of you. Hurry up, now," he added chidingly, and waved his pistol. He had come close enough to recognize Jake Finney, who began to back slowly down the hillside.

"Devlin, don't take advantage of the friendship between our families. We won't permit you to get away with this."

"You have no choice, Jake." He gestured with the pistol again, then suddenly yelled, "Screw out! Beat it!"

Homer Grimes ran on down the hillside, and Jake Finney moved away slowly and silently, only adding when he was out of pistol range, "Don't imagine you've gotten away with this."

Morgan stood grinning with savage delight at the absurdity of this encounter, and at last turned to Douglas who, reluctantly, put his pistol away, asking, "Is that all?" and seemed incredulous this opportunity for heroism and bloodshed had ended so tamely.

"That's all for now. From here on, we litigate with both pistols and attorneys—the Territory's getting civilized. Let's go have a drink with Bruno."

XLVIII

As the elevator crept toward the eighth floor, Hoke O'Neil stood stiffly erect. For elevators, in Hoke's opinion, were a radical novelty and an effete device, and he had a strong inclination toward conservatism in his surroundings, liking best that which he knew, the infested wards where he spent his days amid familiar filth and poverty, and, comfortable as he was among those he knew and distrusted, he had never yet made a foray out of his own world without suffering the constant expectation that he would give himself away, that his face was too Irish and, what was worse, showed the effects of his youthful batterings, that his speech was uncouth and his manners aggressively bad, and so it was not often he left his beloved Bloody Sixth to venture uptown into this menacing atmosphere of luxurious gentility.

He was therefore rather angry to be here, although he was making this trip of his own volition and without having received even the suggestion of an invitation. But still he could not imagine why his sister Betty Mulligan, call herself Allegra Stuart as she might, should come back here after nine or ten years and establish herself even if she could afford it in this great building on Broadway at Twenty-fifth Street, and live in surroundings which it seemed obvious to Hoke could only remind her intolerably of her desolate and hungry beginnings.

At last, after a journey which seemed to have taken most of the morning while they hovered above that deep shaft into which he expected to be plunged at any moment, the elevator stopped, the doors slid slowly apart and Hoke rushed out, and started down the broad, marble-paved hallway, where his footsteps gave forth a bold and disconcerting echo. He paused, listening, and went on, peered at the doors which were not placed side by side as they would be in any ordinary building where men and women lived cooped together, neighbors and enemies impinging upon one another's lives with remorseless and, he thought, comforting intimacy. Not in this place. Here, apparently, those who were rich enough to pay for such surroundings had no affection for their fellow man or no need of his nearness, at least, and preferred to purchase space enough so they could retreat into its center and huddle there at safe distance from any possible outside contacts; why, he could not guess, perhaps from some morbid fear of contamination.

How his sister had got such a notion into her head puzzled and hurt him, for it seemed a slight to himself, as if she had come to believe herself superior not only to men and women he did not know, but to him, too. And perhaps she had. She had ignored the two notes he had dictated to Tessie, for the busy years had given him little enough opportunity to improve either his spelling or handwriting, and he suspected she would presently inform him that she was now Allegra Stuart in fact as well as in her own fancy and that she had no further use for any reminders of her origin which, it happened, was not in remote accord with her history as the newspapers described it.

Hoke had heard of her arrival from Joshua Ching, who had casually remarked one recent night, "Have you seen your sister? She's come back and, as she promised, she's come back a star—the famous English actress, Allegra Stuart."

Hoke had heard nothing either from or about her, and had almost forgotten that it was because of her ambitions to become an actress that he had met Joshua Ching, and so he supposed this must be Ching's notion of a joke. "Come off it," he told him skeptically.

"But she has. I've read about her from time to time the last few years. Hadn't I mentioned it to you? I'd intended to. Anyway, she's here, and in September she'll play Juliet and Beatrice and Lady Teazle. She's come with her maid and her secretary and her French chef, and the papers describe her as a dream of love and beauty—never seen before and never to be seen again. There was a sketch of her in the *Tribune* the other day, costumed for Juliet." Joshua had looked at him with amusement and ironic challenge, as if daring him to go confront this dream of love and beauty, his sister, and ask her how she had accomplished all this in only ten years, or somewhat nearer nine, as Joshua reminded him.

Still, his recollections of their last meeting made Hoke rather uneasy as he paced the hallway. He had gone to Mrs. Gosnell's, expecting to be praised for his generosity in bringing her half the money Joshua Ching had paid him, and had found her room in greater disarray than usual, the parrot Consuelo's cage being carried down the staircase by a drayman, Allegra with her hair still wet from a recent washing and wearing her white wrapper, cramming her trunk with her books and her chinchilla muff and nearly every possession she had, while the poodle Selah barked so incessantly that Hoke had been tempted to kick him.

Before he was able to make his speech, however, she had snatched the money and counted it, licking her thumb as she riffled through the bills, then swept back her wet hair and twisted it into a skein, wringing a few drops from it, and advanced upon him with her eyes glittering and her face white with fury. "Good-bye, Hoke," she had cried, in a tone of denunciation she must have been practicing with her voice teacher. "I won't see you again. I'm leaving for England tonight."

He had shrugged and sauntered toward the door, remarking, "Okay, Betty. Good luck. Let me know if you run out of cash."

"Let you know?" she had screamed. And all at once she had thrown back her head and begun to laugh, that mocking laughter which struck him with astonishment each time he heard it, and as he turned, surprised and offended by the contemptuous sound it had, she had snatched up a hairbrush and flung it at him. "Beat it, goddamn you! Get the hell out of here and don't ever bother me again! Why didn't you take the whole bloody five thousand while you were at it?" She sprang toward him and Hoke, after one incredulous glance, had dashed out and down the stairs and had reached the landing before she appeared above him, glaring wildly and making a gesture with her raised fist. "Beat it, I said," she yelled, no longer concerned for the good opinion of her landlady, and the door slammed.

Hoke had hesitated, wondering if he should go back and offer her another five hundred dollars, but then decided that since she had said she was leaving that night he would not be able to get it to her in time, and he strolled on out, grinning and whistling through his teeth and telling himself that even if she was mad, even if she thought he had cheated her, it was only a woman's unreasonableness, for he had been the important member of the team and without him she would have nothing at all.

And now she was back again, just as she had predicted, famous and rich, judging by the building she lived in with its ponderous elevator and supercilious operator, its exterior of white stone, its columns extending along a broad portico, its carved demons perched high above the street which had grinned maliciously down upon him as he stood studying the façade as if it were a fortress, and she lived somewhere along this broad hallway, gas-lighted in the middle of the morning, stiflingly hot and silent as were these dwellings of the rich with that silence he thought uncanny—for he preferred the noise and din of the slums which never ceased, either in the streets or in the tenements, and gave the constant sense of life being carried on without secrecy or reticence, at every hour of the day and night.

He passed the elevator again, its machinery still grinding and clenching, and at last paused before a door at one end of the hall, the number which had been given him by the clerk after his name had been sent up and, some minutes later, found acceptable. He hesitated, almost expecting that they would resume where they had last seen each other: She would appear at the door in her white wrapper, hairbrush in hand, and demand to know what he was doing here now.

After a moment he pulled the bell and waited, clearing his throat as if in preparation for that speech he had meant to make long ago. Many minutes seemed to pass and he was beginning to grow indignant, when the door opened and a maid in a starched blue uniform with a white apron and cap, and a face as Irish as his own, looked at him questioningly. "Good morning?"

"She's expecting me."

"Miss Stuart?"

"Who else?"

The maid stepped back and Hoke entered a vestibule, as dimly lighted as the hall had been, and as hot. He meant to keep his hat on, but as the maid held out her hand he took it off and clapped it smartly into her palm. "Well? Where is she?"

"Your name, sir?"

"Hoke O'Neil. Brian Mulligan."

"There are two of you?"

"There's one of me, but I've got two names. She can take her pick."

The maid disappeared and Hoke rambled about the vestibule, observing its furnishings with a disapproving eye, shocked to find that his sister, who had lived the early years of her life among the immigrant Irish, should have chosen, even if she could afford it, to live here. It seemed an indefensible disloyalty to her people, and it gave him a bitter pang.

The vestibule looked to Hoke large enough for a drawing room. The walls were covered with blue paper which had a small gold pattern traced through it, and there were several little dark blue and black rugs. The tables were of a style he had not seen before, and he resented that as a further piece of impertinence, for why should she not have the same furniture everyone else had? Even so, he refused to put out his cigar, and presently the maid returned.

"Mr. O'Neil," she began, and Hoke smiled slyly to find she had chosen that name, for she must want to remind him this tie of kinship had first been broken by him. "Miss Stuart was not expecting you and is not ready to receive. Would you care to wait?"

"How long?" Hoke scowled, tapping the cigar ash onto the floor and daring her to take notice of it.

"Miss Stuart will receive you presently, sir."

"Receive me presently?" He grinned. "I'll wait—she can't get rid of me this easy."

The maid led him into the next room, so much bigger than the vestibule that Hoke was finally convinced she had lost her senses and was playing some role far more fantastic than any she performed on the stage, playing, he told himself, the part of Allegra Stuart, and he began to wander about, looking it over with the critical eye of a man about to make an expensive purchase, telling himself that it was too lavish, too strange, too big, too impressive, and not at all suitable for her to live in or him to visit.

He examined the floor with its tiles set in geometric pattern, marveling that anyone who could afford wooden floors, which would neither buckle nor creak, should choose these chilly and slippery tiles which caused him to skid whenever he stepped too quickly onto a carpet. The wallpaper was crimson, with small golden animals stamped upon it, or Hoke assumed they must be animals, although some bore wings and others a single twirling horn.

The windows were hung with striped draperies, not swagged and fringed and ruffled as were all other draperies he had ever seen, but falling straight from what were apparently brass spears stuck up near the ceiling; and the ceiling, as he discovered when he looked up to find what was holding those black and scarlet and brown curtains, had been tortured with carving until it resembled a forest of ornate icicles, painted dark red and touched here and there with gold.

Passing a doorway, he glanced into a dining room, its walls covered with deep red leather, the table a massive oblong with bulging legs, and the chairs with backs so high the tallest man would have appeared to be crouching in them, possibly defending himself. Wrought-iron candlesticks five feet tall held candles apparently meant to last for several weeks, and he paused before a painting which showed three fat pink naked women on a river bank. Prudishly surprised his sister would display such a picture in her living room, and deciding that in any case the women were not to his taste, he continued his ramble. In another room were many books—for she had always been surrounded by books, even when she must borrow them from the library or go without meals to buy them—and it seemed she must have finally acquired all the books she could ever want, for they filled three walls and were piled upon the floor and on the tables.

But nowhere in all this murky splendor could Hoke discover a single tufted or padded chair or sofa, and although he tested with suspicion two or three straight-backed chairs with thin pads of dark red velvet, and sat for a moment at one end of a long couch, he could find nothing upon which he might sit at his ease and supposed the room was not intended to live in but only to display to envious visitors, if, indeed, she knew the kind of visitors who would be envious of such a room.

Passing the fireplace for the third or fourth time and shaking his head as he went, Hoke glanced up and discovered her portrait, stepped back to examine it, and at last was forced to admit she had changed her identity during these past ten years, unless the portrait was itself an entire fiction.

The young woman in the portrait—and he remembered she was now twenty-seven—stood facing him, her head slightly lowered, and gazed at him with such gentle reproval that he was convinced she meant to accuse him, not only of his shabby life, his unscrupulous search for power without concern for the means by which it was achieved, but also to accuse him in some obscure way, against which he could make no defense, of being among those who willfully harmed the innocent.

But surely she had not always had this aura of purity and gentleness, for how could he have forgotten it, and how was it possible for this expression to belong to that girl who had thrown a hairbrush at him as he dashed down the staircase of Mrs. Gosnell's boarding house?

Her hair was dyed that same gilt blond, it fell over her shoulders and down her back, and was covered with a light golden mesh, embroidered with pearls. She wore a dress which looked no more like any dress he had ever seen than this room looked like those with which he was familiar, made of something white and softly glistening, its sleeves so long that her hands were concealed to the fingers, and the folded skirt had a train which disappeared into some hazy landscape of which she might be only the physical emanation. And, though she looked so angelic that Hoke shook his head in chagrined bewilderment, telling himself this could not be Betty Mulligan, her dark eyes shone with a warm ardor, for undoubtedly this was some worldly seraph.

After gazing up at her for a few moments, Hoke began to feel some powerful inclination to sneak out of there and return to the familiar comforts of the Red Onion, where he might spit on the floor and hear, with the impartiality of a god, the pleas of his neighbors to pay their rent, to lend them money for a funeral, to visit a relative in jail, to attend a wake or a wedding or a prize fight. But as he hesitated, yearning for the stability of those places and people he knew so well, he heard her speak, and spun about as quickly as he might have done if a strange voice had spoken in back of him on the street late at night.

"That's my Juliet. What do you think of her, Hoke?"

The voice was hers, somewhat lower than he remembered, and richer, too, resonant and compelling, for although she had spoken quietly the room seemed to fill with the sound, sending a superstitious chill over his back and down his arms. He glanced from her to the portrait, looking with sharp and shrewd and suspicious eyes for the trickery, and she walked toward him, gliding over that slippery floor without a glance at its treacherous carpets, and taking a sip from a coffee cup as she came.

Her hair was dressed high on her head, and had attached to it no coils or fringes, while her dress was quite unadorned, a dress of violet-colored silk, and she wore no jewelry at all. She paused partway across the room, smiling, and as he continued to look at her with his head lowered challengingly, she set the cup on a table. "Why did you come to see me, Hoke?" She was still smiling, but it was not the tender, accusatory smile of the portrait. Indeed, he was sorry to see that she greeted him with distrust and ironic amusement.

"I can't believe it. Is it you?" He squinted, as at a light which hurt his eyes. She laughed softly and the laugh, too, was curiously unsettling, but still he could not decide how she had contrived to make him feel so awkward and so foolish for she was, after all, still only Betty Mulligan, his sister. "Betty?" he inquired, to remind her that this appearance she cultivated of fragility and innocence, these strange and oversized surroundings, the fashionable gown, and even her manner—which was some baffling combination of great lady and pathetic child—all this was, in fact, no more true than the portrait, and she no more Allegra Stuart than Juliet Capulet.

"I haven't been called that since the last time I saw you, skittering down the stairs at Mrs. Gosnell's with my twenty-five hundred dollars. What did you do with it, Hoke? Can you remember?"

She went on gazing at him with that smile of detached amusement until, angry and hurt, he shouted, "Of course I remember what I did with it! I gave it away to people who asked me for it, who needed it a god-damn sight worse than I did—or than you did, either. I gave it to kids who were starving, and to men and women who hadn't eaten enough to satisfy them more than a few times in their lives. I didn't spend it on myself, if that's what you mean. I gave it, by Christ, to the kind of people you know well enough, Betty Mulligan, even if you do want to pretend you come from some high and mighty family. What's that yarn Joshua Ching told me? Your mother was a Spanish lady and your father an English diplomat and you were born in—I forget what the hell he called it—"

"Saragossa. I read it somewhere and always remembered it. But while you're calling me Betty Mulligan, as if it's a dirty word, you might at least not pretend to be a generous friend of the poor. Have you also become a hypocrite, Hoke?"

"I'm a politician, God damn it! And politicians need money?" He stepped close, tapping his chest. "Do you know what I am? I'm the Superintendent of Market Fees and Rents, by God." He nodded briskly and stepped back, waiting to see what she would say to that.

"What do you do?"

"I supervise market fees and rents," he told her, still glaring.

"Well." Allegra gave a light sigh. "I was just having breakfast. Would you like coffee?"

Hoke nodded sullenly and began to stride about the room, for she seemed, although he did not know why, to have an advantage over him, and during the past several years he had come to imagine it was he who possessed all the advantages. Tessie Spooner fawned over

him. Mud Foley obeyed him like a well-trained dog. Even Marquis
McDuff and Oliver Foss had begun to show him some deference. He
was not accustomed to people who did not want or need something
from him and he found this encounter a peculiar one, for in spite of
his prediction to Joshua Ching that she was lucky and would one
day astonish them both and the rest of the world as well, he had
never expected it actually to happen.

She crossed the room to the bell-pull, moving with the stately grace
which was described as being, with her voice, her greatest assets as
an actress. Joshua Ching had told him that in England people went
to the theater only to watch her cross the stage, and that, of course,
was the product of her years in the ballet and the hours she had
spent walking about with a weight on her head. He knew her secrets,
he reflected glumly, or several of them, and yet none of this creaking
machinery could be detected now, for she gave even to him the impression of having emerged exactly as she was, a miraculous and perfect creation of the benign deity Himself, while he knew quite well
she was only the creation of Betty Mulligan, who had first of all fashioned Allegra Stuart in her imagination and then brought her to life.
He looked at her carefully, wondering how long the process had
taken, whether it had happened suddenly or if there had been, as
seemed more likely, a slow and steady accumulation of effects.

The maid who had answered the door appeared, and Allegra asked
her to bring coffee and toast and suggested to Hoke that he sit down.
Hoke glanced around, chose a chair and sat on it, perching with gingerly care upon the edge, and then promptly rose, as if he might have
found himself on something sharp. "Where the hell did you get this
furniture?"

She smiled again, and, it seemed, there was nothing he could say
which she was not prepared to find amusing, for she was talking to
him very much as the ladies in the Mission School had talked and
which had been one of the reasons he had run away. "It's Eastlake,"
she told him kindly. "Neo-medieval," she added, and seated herself
on one of the high-backed chairs, looking so casually comfortable
there, and so decorative, she might have mistaken him for another
man come to do her portrait, and in fact it struck him that each
movement she made, each tone and expression, was as carefully
prepared and studied as if she expected at any moment to find the
room was, after all, a brightly lighted stage beyond which waited a
large and critical and demanding audience. "I brought it from England. I don't think it's become popular here yet, but it will."

He sat down again, crossing his legs, folding his arms upon his
chest, and all at once gave her a conspiratorial wink. "Betty, come
off it. Saragossa. Neo-medieval. Juliet. Eastlake. We're old side-
partners, you know that." He paused as the maid came to set a tray
on the table beside Allegra, waited while she poured the coffee and
brought it to Hoke, who took the cup uneasily, feeling that this ceremony was surely one more test and one he was unlikely to pass with

distinction. He tasted it, found it very hot, blew on it impatiently, and glared at the maid until she left, after which he drank it although it burned his mouth, and with relief put the cup aside. "Remember Five Points? Remember when Ma died—when they carried her up from the street and we kept trying to talk to her but she had nothing to say?"

"I remember everything, Hoke. I remember that the morning it happened she sent us out to play and kissed us both, and there were tears in her eyes, and as we went out I was still trying to make her laugh." She was staring at him with a look of brooding rapture. "It was a long while before I could understand why she did that—but now I do."

"I still don't."

"And you never will. I remember other things, too, and probably I think about them more often than you do. But why should we talk about that, you and I? We're a long way from Five Points—I am, at least. You choose to remain there, for reasons you may understand, although I don't."

"You're damn right I choose to remain there. I'm no patent-leather mick. What's got into you? A Spanish lady for a mother. What the hell was the matter with the mother you had? You ashamed of her—and of me? You sure as hell weren't ashamed of me when you thought I could help you."

"As it turned out, though, it was I who helped you, wasn't it?"

"Like hell it was. If it hadn't been for me you wouldn't have got one bloody nickel out of the deal because you couldn't do him any favors and you know it. What's more, if by some fluke you'd hit on something, Joshua Ching would have cheated you out of the loot one way or another."

"He might have tried."

"Hah! Who were you? A kid, a nobody, a ballet dancer, for Christ's sake. Who would have listened to your story? I know the son of a bitch—we've been thick as two pickpockets these past few years, Joshua Ching and me, and I can tell you that if you're mad because you think I cheated you, just be god-damn glad you got anything at all. If I hadn't been your brother, you wouldn't have got it from me, either."

"Joshua Ching," she murmured, and her smile became whimsical and derisive. "I've thought about him sometimes. And is he a rich man now?"

"With my help, as you might say." Hoke slid down, feeling that the chair had become more comfortable, and gestured expansively. "Five million, maybe eight. Maybe more. You never can tell about these birds. But he's got a knack for landing on his feet no matter what happens and a gift for blarney when he wants to sell you something that'd do an Irishman credit. Got rid of De Groot Distilleries last year just before the whisky scandals broke. He's smart. Builds railroads, too, or if he don't exactly build railroads, he buys up the ones somebody else built when they get into a fix. When you stop and think," he said slowly, "that not even ten years ago we was both broke and Ching was fretting over his first million, it comes as a pleasant surprise to find us all with money enough to burn a wet dog. Don't it?" He studied her a moment longer. "You look good, Betty. All this—" He gave a sweeping gesture. "Your picture in store windows and all the papers, Ching tells me. You married? You got a rich friend?"

At this she threw him a look of such scorn Hoke felt once again that although he had the advantage of being five years older, nevertheless she had acquired that most formidable female weapon, the ability to make a man feel he had made a fool of himself without any help from her. "I don't need a rich friend. I made sixty thousand dollars last year."

He sat up straight, once more thrusting forth his head to get a closer look at this phenomenon, for while that sum had several times passed through his hands in the interests of buying the loyalty of his constituents, he had not imagined that any woman, much less his sister, had ever earned so much. "You earned it, you say?"

"My contract for next year is for seventy-five thousand. I wouldn't have come here for anything less."

He frowned, hurt and puzzled, for it made his own achievements of which he had been overweeningly proud only a moment before, seem insignificant and despicable. As superintendent of Market Fees and Rents he was paid three thousand dollars a year, but this modest salary carried with it, even under the reformed Tammany, opportunities for another seventy or one hundred thousand; and now all this had dwindled in his eyes, for if a woman could do as well what could it possibly signify. "Seventy-five thousand. Jesus H. Christ. For what?"

She laughed, a sound so merry and mocking that for a moment he thought she was pleased by his little joke, and then she began to walk about the room, surveying her domain as she went. "Shall I tell you what the English critics have to say about me? One of them says: 'She possesses an exceptional power of converting romantic and poetic ideals into actual human beings.'" She gave him a whimsical smile, gesturing, as if to say he could believe it or not as he liked, but it was quite true. "Another one says: 'Her demeanor is natural but her feeling intense, and her every action seems spontaneous.' And the most famous one calls me 'that rare and glorious phenomenon, a dramatic genius.' That's why Dyke Ferguson came to London to see me—and that's why he offered me seventy-five thousand dollars for a one-year contract."

Hoke loosened his collar, feeling that the heat was more than he could endure, although she seemed not to notice it. "I'll take your word for it," he told her grudgingly. "But you know as well as I do that a newspaperman will write any damn thing he's paid to."

She laughed. "Of course. And I've paid some of them very well—no actor gets a good review who doesn't. But that isn't why I'm a great star, which I am. That isn't why women cry when I die as Juliet and clap until their gloves split when Lady Teazle is discovered. No, it's because I give them, for at least a little while, a belief that life can be experienced, not only tolerated or endured."

Hoke grimaced. "Tell me just one thing, Betty. Suppose it's true, and you're everything you say you are." He narrowed his eyes, peering at her, for she had that same expression of pathos and tenderness her portrait showed, and he guessed she might be reflecting upon this power she had to move men and women to ecstasies of joy and remorse and imaginary passions they would not otherwise have felt. "Where'd you pick it up?"

She walked away. "Hoke, you can't be such a fool as to ask me that seriously."

"Now, wait a minute there, Betty. Don't get your Irish up. I asked you a simple question."

"There isn't any simple answer. I picked it up, as you say, by doing nothing else and thinking of nothing else for as long as I can remember. I picked it up by working anywhere I could at anything I could, playing old women and young boys and now and then an animal. I toured in the provinces and was scared and discouraged and exhausted for four years, but I kept working and learning and finally I got a chance to perform in London. But my first Juliet wasn't very good, I was too much in awe of her, and then—after another year or so—I realized that we were not two separate people, she and I, but had certain things in common if I would only make her acquaintance, and from then on she caused me no more trouble. She's there whenever I need her, now, and she always will be. Until I start to grow old, but I don't let myself think very often about that. That would spoil everything, wouldn't it?" She looked at him with that sorrowful smile which moved him against all his resolutions, and he found that quite unexpectedly she had made him feel that their common past, those memories they shared, held a terror and a promise of which he had so far been unaware.

"Are you married?" he demanded.

"I was. My husband died."

"Peace to his ashes."

To his horrified astonishment, for Hoke had a reverential superstition about the dead whether he had known them living or not, she burst into ringing, insolent laughter. "He's still alive—but my publicity says he's dead." She glowered, between menace and playfulness. "Don't tell anyone."

Hoke jumped up. "Betty Mulligan, are you a divorced woman?"

"What's the matter with you, Hoke? You've never owned a principle in your life, and you're pretending to be shocked that I've been divorced."

He looked gloomy. "I'm an Irishman. How the hell would you expect me to feel about my sister being divorced?"

"Then cheer up, I'm not divorced. I said it to tease you."

"Where is the guy?" He glanced around. "Not here?"

"We don't live together any more."

"Who was he?"

"An actor. You've never heard of him and never will. An English actor." She smiled maliciously.

"Oh, my God. Betty, you and me will never be respectable."

"But I am."

"How can you be? You're an actress. You know what people think about actresses. And it's usually true." Hoke reflected for a moment on Rose Michel and her history with *The Black Crook* and brief season of boarding with Annie Wood before Joshua Ching had discovered her. "Not that I think it's true about you, of course," he added doubtfully.

"In London I'm not only respectable, I'm friendly with men and women of the best society. Of course, in New York, that doesn't happen, the town's provincial." She gazed through the opened windows, murmuring, "Odd, provincial, pleasant little old New York—or so they say. But I had to come back, to convince myself I wasn't afraid of it any more. I don't expect to like it and I've never liked the Americans, but I intend to make them love me and they will, they will, I promise you." All at once she gave him a look of intent warning. "Hoke, you must never, never—for any reason at all—tell anyone that you're my brother."

"Now, what the hell, Betty? You ashamed of me?"

"No, I'm not ashamed of you, don't ask me that again. But a legend is part of an actress's equipment, like costumes and wigs, and you must admit that as Betty Mulligan who was born in Dublin and brought here when she was three years old to live in Five Points, I would scarcely seem a very romantic figure. For a long time I wasn't sure I could ever become Allegra Stuart. I knew who I wanted her to be, but I was afraid I'd always slide back into Betty Mulligan, and that finally Betty Mulligan would get the better of me. But I am Allegra Stuart now—and I will be for the rest of my life."

"What about your ballet friends?"

"They've forgotten. I'll deny it." She shrugged. "And tell Joshua Ching he's not to mention that he's ever known me."

Hoke sighed, feeling that somehow she had defeated him. "Okay, I won't tell anyone I'm your brother. Well—so long. Just wanted to see how you were getting along." They stood for a moment and looked at each other, their faces subdued and a little sad, and at last Hoke said, "I believe you—you ain't Betty Mulligan any more, even to me. Congratulations. Just tell me one thing. You're happy now, I hope, with all this?"

"Happy?" She seemed more surprised by that question than by

any other he had asked, and she gave him again that whimsical little smile. "Happy? Why, now, Hoke, must I be happy—along with everything else? If I were happy, it would make me superstitious. I'd take it as a bad omen."

XLIX

The house and its callers puzzled the neighborhood. The shades were drawn all day and all night, numerous private carriages drove up, letting out a procession of well-dressed women who went in quickly, and, a few hours later, came out again, often unsteadily, as if stunned or sick. No men accompanied them and so it could not be a house of assignation, and many of the women looked beyond the years when they might have needed an abortionist's services. It was perhaps some kind of saloon for women, or possibly a gambling house, but so long as the ladies did not molest their children playing in the streets, the neighbors were willing to let them go in peace to perdition.

The patrons of the house, however, were sometimes accosted by the children, who would pause in their street games, the little girls marching solemnly backward and forward with their arms linked, singing "Jenny O'Shea," and the boys would look up from their marble shooting, to try to start a conversation with these interesting callers, but usually they were ignored.

"Hello, ma'am, glad to see you again," one of the little girls would call out, boldly putting herself in the lady's path. "How are you today?"

And finally they were rewarded, for one of the three women who had just stepped down from a closed carriage paused, lifting her hand to conceal her mouth. "Do you know me?"

Coral Talbot, halfway up the steps, glanced back at Susan and Ceda, surrounded by the children, and gave the little girl an ominous look which produced mock shudders among her companions. "Don't encourage them."

But it seemed that Susan's uncertainty had been encouraging, for the little girl declared, "I guess I do know you. I see you often enough."

"You've never seen us before, that's ridiculous," Ceda told them, adjusting her veil.

The children laughed derisively but good-naturedly, and, as Coral disappeared, Susan and Ceda hurried up the steps and followed her into the vestibule where Ceda leaned against the wall, breathing hard. "We've been recognized. Those children are spies. I knew this was going to happen. They looked at us peculiarly the other day."

Susan untied her veil, let the neatly uniformed maid take her shawl, and looked at herself in the mirror, a searching and troubled look, as if she were not so much interested in her face as in her future or, perhaps, her character. "Ceda, you are constitutionally incapable of not worrying. Those children are curious, that's perfectly natural. They have no idea who we are."

"Oh, but they do, I know they do."

"Suppose they do?" Coral demanded. "Is there any reason we shouldn't be here?"

Ceda opened her mouth but Susan shook her head warningly, and they went into the drawing room. Gas jets burned at a low flame, and in their faint light the heavy furniture, marble statues, paintings of dead animals lying amid peeled fruit and nut shells and live ones romping with children, produced an atmosphere which Coral had described as imitation gentility and imitation elegance, but it served its purpose well enough.

At one end of the room stood a table laid with warming dishes, plates and silverware, and Ceda lifted a cover here and there, sniffing curiously before she turned to inform Coral and Susan, "Terrapin soup. Deviled crabs. Sweetbreads and peas."

But they had finished lunch less than an hour ago and both Susan and Coral looked offended at the idea of food, and Ceda followed them up a staircase and down a hall where, though she tried not to, she glanced through several opened doorways to see women seated about tables, all devoutly concentrated upon the cards they held, and all in elaborate dresses and hats, as if they had set out on the pretext of making their afternoon calls. In one room there was a young woman lying on a bed, crying softly, while another sat in a chair nearby, glumly staring, and Ceda drew a sigh, for that was the room set aside by the management for those whose luck had been so bad they must recuperate before starting home.

As they reached the end of the hall, the door opened and a woman met them, smiling. "Good afternoon, ladies. I saw your carriage."

Mrs. De Bow was, like her furniture, an imitation of elegant gentility, and they had seen her in so many gowns that it was Coral's opinion she hired them. Today she had on a dress with a tight black top and orange skirt, while at her waist hung her invariable chain from which dangled keys and smelling salts, a penknife and a watch, so that she seemed ready at all times to meet any emergencies of her establishment.

She ushered them into her private apartment and there, at a table, sat two women, one impatiently drumming her knuckles, the other frowning and tapping her chin. "You know each other?" asked Mrs. De Bow, who never introduced her clients by name.

"Certainly," said Coral, and stripped off her gloves and sat down.

Ceda hurried to the window and peeked out, to find that the children were still there. Mrs. De Bow ruffled the cards once or twice and Susan spoke to Ceda. "Have you made up your mind?"

Ceda turned with a meek, apologetic face. "I don't think I'll play today."

Mrs. De Bow smiled. "Would you like something to eat, perhaps? Or maybe you would prefer reading?" she added, for Ceda, although she now came into the house, having grown tired of waiting in the carriage, seldom played, but retired to the library. Susan had said that since Ceda did not enjoy playing and neither approved of gambling nor of the surroundings in which they were doing it, she might better go for a drive, but Ceda insisted it was her duty to accompany her, chaperone her younger and weaker sister in this gathering place of desperate women.

Mrs. De Bow went on shuffling the cards, her hands moving so swiftly that Ceda watched with horrified fascination, knowing that once again, when the time came for them to leave, Susan would be silent and disgruntled, and further in debt to Coral Talbot, who paid her gambling debts and took notes from Susan in return.

Now the five women confronted one another about the table, each studying the others' faces with a shrewd calculation which gave Ceda sickening qualms, for there was nothing in their expressions of the usual feminine concern with the faces of other women, no apprehension that here was a prettier rival, a more inviting mouth, brighter eyes, longer eyelashes, or certain mannerisms enticing to men, but only an impersonal and, it seemed, savage appraisal of weaknesses and strengths, the mood they were in for the day and their possible vulnerability. Ceda slowly left the room as they began to play, Coral cutting the cards in a brisk and businesslike way while one woman was lighting a cigar and asking the maid to bring her a bottle of champagne.

At sight of this parody, Ceda shook her head sadly, murmuring in Susan's ear, "I'll be in the library." But Susan did not glance at her, merely waved her hand peremptorily and picked up her cards, which, as Ceda had observed, were not very hopeful ones.

Ceda roamed slowly down the hallway, passing the door where the girl on the bed lay weeping while her friend patted her hand, and though Ceda longed to go in and sit with them, ask them how they had come to be involved in this treacherous and terrible business, she was afraid of Mrs. De Bow's anger should she be known to have done missionary work among her clients, and so instead she went into the library.

She went immediately to a shelf where she selected Emerson's *Essays,* her solace on these visits and through which she searched for telling arguments to deliver to Susan, but no matter what she found Susan only smiled bitterly when she quoted it and shrugged, unconvinced. Ceda sat down with the *Essays* and gazed about the room, loathing everything she saw, although it was only an ordi-

nary small room with half a hundred or so books and a portrait of
Mrs. De Bow over the fireplace, apparently done when she had been
several years younger and a good deal happier, and as she turned the
pages she asked herself how it could have happened that she sat in
this gambling house for females in the fiftieth year of her life, waiting for Susan to lose money at poker, and presently she brought out a
handkerchief to catch the tears before they stained her gown. The
truth was, of course, that Coral Talbot had tempted Susan and had
slowly led Susan to crave the excitements of these afternoons as a
drunkard craved drink.

It had begun three or four years ago with games of whist at Long
Branch and, after awhile, Coral had suggested that a little money
changing hands would add to the game's pallid interest, a suggestion
to which Susan had readily agreed, as she had agreed when Coral
Talbot later suggested that poker was a more entertaining game than
whist.

"Don't become too friendly with her, Susan," Ceda had warned.
"Don't let her learn anything about us you wouldn't want all the
world to know."

"You think she's a blackmailer, along with everything else you
suspect her of?"

"She hates Suky, that's the worst thing I know about her. If it
weren't for Suky, her character would mean very little to me one way
or the other." For Ceda was as protective of Suky as she had ever
been, and could not bear to think the dried pea beneath the feather
mattress might ever bruise her niece's tender skin. "And you know
well enough what Joshua will say when he learns about this."

"Joshua is a rich man now, after all. He can afford to have me entertain myself with a friendly game now and then, as the men call it."

"These games are no longer friendly, Susan. They are very un-
friendly, and you know it."

"Poker, it seems, gets less friendly as it gets more interesting."

The truth, of course, even though Ceda would not admit it, was
that Susan was enjoying not merely the excitement of the game,
quite as if she had gone out upon a dangerous adventure in which she
could triumph by her wit and shrewdness, but she was enjoying, perhaps even more, this secret defiance of Joshua.

And Ceda sometimes thought that Joshua had begun to guess
that Susan was misbehaving, for not long ago he had said to her with
an air of somber warning, "A good name is one of the greatest values in life. I hope you have no intention in your malice toward me of
doing anything to jeopardize it. If you have, Susan Ching, please remember it's your name, too."

Susan refused even to discuss this with Ceda, saying that Joshua
warned them all from time to time, it being one of the few firm
principles he still had, and she would not even admit that this was a
wicked thing to say about him. She was almost as difficult with Suky,
even to arguing with her about the portrait just completed by Augus-

tus Adams, whose way with fabrics and jewels and the textures of skin and hair was such that to be painted by Augustus Adams had become for many women an ambition as great as any they had ever been obsessed by. Suky was dissatisfied with the portrait, while Susan insisted it was an exact likeness. Perhaps he had made the hair a little blonder and the skin gleamed as if it were oiled, but these were improvements, after all.

"Is that your opinion, Mama?"

"It isn't an exact likeness at all, Susan," Ceda had objected. "Suky is quite right to be disappointed. She is much more beautiful. Don't you agree, Mr. Adams?"

Augustus Adams looked unhappy. "Mrs. Van Zandt is much more beautiful. But you must not blame the artist, madame. This is the most beautiful portrait I have ever done—Mrs. Van Zandt, herself, exceeds my talent."

"Ah," declared Ceda, and cast a triumphant glance at Susan.

Suky, however, took no notice of Augustus Adams' groveling, but indicated another portrait, still on the easel. "There," she told him gently, "is the most beautiful portrait you have ever done, Mr. Adams. Who is she?"

"Oh, that one, Mrs. Van Zandt?" he inquired uneasily. "Why, that is—"

"You know quite well it's Allegra Stuart, Suky," Susan told her. "We saw her only recently in *Twelfth Night*, and a few months ago as Juliet. Yes, Mr. Adams, that is a magnificent portrait. I quite agree."

"But then," he began apologetically, "Miss Stuart is an actress. A very great actress, as you know, and she is able to create whatever portrait of herself she chooses."

Suky looked at Miss Stuart a moment longer. "I'm not very sure what you mean by that, Mr. Adams. However, since you believe my portrait is the best you can do, I will accept it, naturally." She extended her hand to him, smiling. "Thank you." And Mr. Adams, surprised, held up a gold watch she had given him, snapping it open to read the inscription, and bowed to her deeply.

"Thank you, Mrs. Van Zandt. Thank you, thank you."

They went out and Ceda took Suky's arm. "How generous of you, dear. When he charged five thousand dollars for that miserable picture."

"But how did it happen he did so much better with Miss Stuart?" inquired Suky. "The expression he gave her, that rueful little smile, almost like the waif he did."

"Perhaps he is best with waifs," Susan suggested. "You must find an artist, Suky, who has no taste at all for waifs."

These encounters between Susan and Suky, which only Ceda seemed to perceive as encounters, had come more often as time went by and they might, she thought, be attributed to Joshua's increasing dependence upon Suky.

Not long ago, in fact, Suky and Joshua had emerged one night from what Susan called their conference room—the conservatory, where they often retired to the privacy of its dim blue light and moist fragrances, spurting fountains and baskets of orchids—to inform Steven that he and Leticia Marble would be married on the third of June, at eight o'clock, in the First Presbyterian Church, that there would be eight hundred guests at the church and one thousand at the reception, and they would leave that same night for a six-month tour of Europe.

"How efficient," said Susan admiringly. "I feel as if it's over and done with and there's nothing more to think about."

"After all, Mama," said Suky, "these things do not attend to themselves."

For, as Ceda had tried to tell Susan, she had been for some time willfully abdicating her position and authority, but Susan coolly replied, "It wouldn't make any difference whether I tried to participate or not. They would do exactly as they intend, quite as if I weren't there. In fact, Ceda, I often have the notion nowadays that I may have begun to grow invisible. Look at me carefully, and tell me the truth. Can you see me as clearly as you could before?"

That had puzzled Ceda for a moment, during which she gazed at Susan doubtfully, wondering if this was Susan's way of telling her that her eyesight was failing, and then all at once she began to cry, for Susan made it seem that not only was the situation a hopeless one but that she no longer cared if it was.

And Steven, too, who had never been very friendly with his sister, although they had never quarreled, each living from early childhood as if in a separate house with separate parents, seemed to know that for the time being, at least, he was on probation, as if held under suspicion of possessing irremediable defects which must sooner or later become evident. Even so, it was Suky who had discovered his bride for him.

One night she had remarked to Joshua, "I met a charming girl yesterday at Alvita Hallam's, a second cousin of hers, Leticia Marble, Hiram Marble's oldest daughter. Very pretty, very well educated, she's just come home from three years in Europe with an aunt—her mother is dead—very agreeable, and not quite eighteen. She has one younger sister, and no brothers."

Joshua looked at her intently. "I know Hiram Marble. Let me think about it for a day or two."

Not long after that, Alvita Hallam introduced them at one of her evening receptions, and Steven, who exercised a powerful spell upon most young girls, confounding them with his gallantry and indifference, cast the same spell over Letty Marble, who whispered to Suky, "Oh, your brother is so dignified, so serious, so thoughtful. Most young American men are so frivolous." She rolled her eyes deprecatingly.

"Steven is never frivolous," Suky assured her.

"Such a relief."

Ceda had never learned what, exactly, had happened after that, although she understood by now that marriages were not so simply arranged where money was involved on both sides—or even on one side—as she had once supposed. However it had been done, the formal announcement had gone out and, ever since, there had been calls to make and parties to attend and dances to chaperone; while Joshua seemed in such good humor to have acquired the Van Zandts, the Talbots with their many relations, and now Hiram Marble, that Ceda had a terror of Susan's vice being discovered which pursued her in various guises, awake and asleep, giving her headaches and spells of trembling, making her sigh frequently and mope at the dinner table until Joshua, who preferred to ignore sickness, suspecting that it was usually imaginary, at least with women, had finally inquired if she wanted to see a doctor. Ceda had looked at him guiltily. "Oh, no, Joshua," she had pleaded. "Oh, no."

"I understand," Joshua had mysteriously replied, and said nothing more about it.

She had begged Susan to stop going to Mrs. De Bow's until the wedding was safely over, but Susan said she saw no reason to be bored for three or four months only because Steven was getting married. "The preparations have nothing to do with me, Ceda."

"But people think they do."

"It would never occur to Joshua to suspect me, don't you know that? He's quite sure I'd never dare do anything he disapproves of."

"It's wrong, then, to take advantage of his faith in you."

"Faith in me, Ceda, has nothing to do with it. He imagines I'm afraid of him."

"Someday, Susan, oh, someday, someday," Ceda told her, murmuring it like a refrain even when Susan was not present.

The afternoon passed slowly, she could find no advice in the *Essays* to give Susan she had not given her before, and she felt, as she always did in this house, that she was surrounded by evil and secrecy and that unseen spies were present, recording angels, perhaps, or merely sleuths from a detective agency. And the quiet sounds which reached her seemed more than usually sinister, the clicking of the roulette wheel, the voices of the women placing their bets, the door opening and closing every few minutes, and when at last Susan and Coral Talbot appeared, it was almost dark. Susan was looking, as she usually did after these sessions, tired and morose, all the eager excitement with which she had approached the game was gone, and even before Ceda had spoken, she shook her head to silence her.

"We're ready to leave, Ceda."

To Ceda's surprise, for she had forgotten them, the children were still there, the boys kneeling over their game of marbles while the little girls were skipping rope or gossiping. Coral and Susan and Ceda, never glancing at them, hurried with determination to Coral's carriage and got in, but not before the little girl who had spoken earlier to Susan had waved her hand and called, " 'Bye, ma'am, see you soon."

Susan sank back, closing her eyes, and Ceda looked at her sadly, while Coral gazed out the window as they drove toward Fifth Avenue. "Beggars, beggars," she murmured absently. "You see them everywhere nowadays." Half the city's population seemed to have taken to begging—deformed men and women, blind or crippled, children in rags, paupers smelling like damp unventilated cellars appeared in every neighborhood, and this mention of beggars by Coral Talbot struck Ceda as peculiarly ominous. And, after a moment, Coral glanced disapprovingly at Susan. "Bad luck again, Susan."

"Yes," Susan agreed humbly. "Bad luck again."

"Susan, I hope this won't inconvenience you, but I've had some losses in the market lately, and I'd like to have what you owe me." Susan looked as if she had been slapped but Coral, it seemed, did not notice this and, presently, they stopped before the hotel. "Good night," said Coral pleasantly, and her footman leaped nimbly back onto his perch, while Ceda supported Susan as if she might collapse on the sidewalk.

Susan drew away and spoke to her severely. "Ceda, don't you dare begin to cry. Leave me alone and, whatever you do, don't start preaching at me or making any more of your damned predictions. I'll ask Joshua to give me some advice on the market."

"That's a very good idea," Ceda agreed admiringly. "Ask Joshua for a point."

Joshua, however, looked at Susan, when she made her request, with a quizzical expression. "A point, Susan? How often have I told you to keep away from the market? Don't meddle in it. Neither preachers nor women are good speculators, I won't let them in my office."

A few days later Susan tried to broach the subject again but, as Ceda observed, silently now, Susan had spent so many years cultivating Joshua's ill will she could scarcely hope to find it miraculously converted into good. Joshua refused to talk to her about it and, the third time she brought it up, forbade her to mention the stock market to him ever again.

"What will you do, Susan?" Ceda asked her timidly.

"I don't know. I owe Coral Talbot nearly eleven thousand dollars."

Ceda gasped, then quickly covered her mouth with both hands. "That's a great deal of money."

They talked it over from time to time and Ceda offered to pawn some of her jewelry, but Susan smiled scornfully at this. "You know very well, Ceda, that Joshua would notice it immediately. He regards whatever he gives to anyone else as his own property. Perhaps," she added sorrowfully, "my luck will change."

Susan continued her visits to Mrs. De Bow's, grimly running the children's blockade; for no matter how she tried to conceal herself behind layers of veiling, they seemed able to penetrate her disguise and insisted upon greeting her as an old friend, never impertinent, it was true, merely greeting her when she arrived and waving good-bye to her when she left, and this in itself seemed to Ceda a sinister sign, for she believed the children must have sensed that Susan did not belong here, that Susan was on a desperate course, that Ceda, whom they ignored, was not a participant, and that Coral Talbot, whom they also ignored, was beyond redemption.

"What has your husband said, Susan?" Coral asked her.

Susan looked ashamed. "I have some good points. I should be able to repay you soon."

A few days later, as Susan and Ceda sat late in the afternoon drinking tea, silent and absorbed, no longer discussing the only sub-ject either of them thought about, they heard the outside door open and sat up very straight, Susan carefully placing her teacup on the table, for it could only be Joshua, returning at an hour much earlier than usual. In another moment he stood in the doorway, his gloves on, his hat in his hand and still holding his cane. He now laid these aside and, as Ceda watched him with terrified fascination, stood slowly removing his gloves. Finally he spoke, in a very low voice. "William Talbot tells me you owe his wife more than twelve thou-sand dollars."

Susan remained where she was, her hand extended over the tea-cup, perhaps with the feminine instinct to protect her possessions, even if she could not protect herself. "Yes."

"Talbot talked to me this afternoon. The money is hers, part of her inheritance, and it makes no difference to Talbot if she squanders what was left to her, she's been doing it for years. But now she must meet her commitments with her broker, and she asked him to give her the money, since you would not."

Ceda saw with despair that Susan's look and manner had now re-markably changed, from the moment, in fact, that Joshua had begun to speak. For although during the past several weeks she had grown increasingly subdued, as if her defeat at the card table had infected her entire personality, now her eyes were gleaming and there was a smile upon her mouth which looked almost triumphant. "I couldn't, after all."

They watched each other silently, and at last Joshua said, "I've paid it."

"Thank you."

Joshua entered the room slowly, walked toward her slowly, and stood with his arms folded across his chest and his feet apart, look-ing, Ceda noticed, exactly as he did in Augustus Adams' portrait which hung over the fireplace behind him, creating the uncanny im-pression that two Joshua Chings stood in the room accusing Susan of mischief. "I know why you did it, Susan," he told her quietly. "I probably know better than you do. You've been searching for a long time for a way to get even with me—for what, exactly, I don't know.

And, as time has passed and none of your devices has seemed to work very well, you've become more inventive."

Susan was still smiling, and her face had the same knowing expression it had in Augustus Adams' portrait hanging beside Joshua's, though neither of them seemed aware of this mimicry of themselves but were as entirely concentrated upon each other as they had ever been in the days of their courtship. Indeed, Susan seemed not at all to suspect that it was now only a matter of time, only waiting for Joshua to declare his punishment, but that in effect life for Susan Ching—and even for Ceda Morgan—as they had known it until now, was over.

"As you like to say, Joshua," Susan said, in a softly beguiling voice, "if not victory, at least revenge." Ceda gasped warningly, but Susan was quite beyond her reach.

"Revenge for what, Susan?" Joshua asked her reasonably.

"So many things."

"You're a damned fool."

"After all, Joshua, isn't this better than if I'd had an affair with another man?"

"That wouldn't have troubled me at all, if you'd been discreet about it."

Ceda watched them helplessly, for it seemed they were enjoying as much privacy in this encounter as if they had been in bed together, and she prayed for the gift of those few words which would instantly dissolve the bitterness and tension which seemed to flow through the room, obliging her to remain in the same taut and rigid position, for fear of colliding with it. Joshua stood with his legs spread wide, as if to balance himself against the force of his rage, and in his face Ceda was able to see that now, as she had guessed might one day happen, he had come to hate Susan. At this Ceda began an uncontrollable trembling, for she had never been able to accept the idea that anyone she knew felt actual hatred, and the idea of hatred roused in her vague but terrible apprehensions of violence and disaster, cataclysmic scenes with bloody endings. At any moment, she expected, this hatred would burst out of Joshua and batter the room apart, and she and Susan would lie among the debris.

It therefore seemed to Ceda a miraculous blessing when Joshua continued to talk in the same quiet voice, pitched so low it was not easy to hear him. "Listen to me, Susan. You listen, too, Ceda," he advised her, and Ceda became instantly attentive and obedient, hoping to buy with her humility a bit of lenience for them both. "You will do no more gambling, of course. Let me tell you now that from this time on whenever you leave the house it will be reported to me. When someone comes here, I'll know that, too. I'll trust no longer to your good judgment or your pride or even your self-respect, because you've convinced me very well that you have none." Susan smiled. "I've consulted Dr. Montgomery about you, Susan. He thinks you may be suffering a form of hysterical insanity."

"You have consulted—"

"Of course. No woman who is entirely in her senses loses twelve thousand dollars she doesn't own playing poker. It's Dr. Montgomery's opinion that you need either a long trip abroad, in the company of someone qualified to take care of you, or a rest of several months in surroundings more soothing than these. I haven't decided yet which it will be. But let me warn you both that if anything is said about these plans—which I've made only with your welfare in mind, Susan—between now and June third, I'll pack you off before the wedding, no matter what lies I'll have to tell to explain your absence."

He turned, crossed the room briskly, as if he had concluded a delicate business conference, took up his hat and placed it upon his head as he stood with his back to them, then picked up the gloves and cane and, although he paused a moment longer, continued on into the vestibule and they heard the door close quietly, at which Ceda slipped to the floor, her eyes rolling backward as she fell.

Ceda had what Susan had always told her was the bad habit of fainting whenever she was unpleasantly surprised or badly frightened. The curious phenomenon, which Ceda had not explained, was that although she was unconscious for a greater or lesser period of time, she also knew what was going on about her, what others were saying and doing, and had indeed a weird sense of being aware of what would happen at the instant after her own death. And now Susan glanced down at her, mumbling impatiently, "Oh, Ceda, you fool, what are you doing that for?" and knelt beside her, chafing her wrists, and when Ceda uncertainly lifted her head and looked at her, said, "You are not to mention this to Suky or to anyone else, ever."

Their visits to Mrs. De Bow's came to an end, for they were aware that Joshua, true to his promise, was having them watched, but Susan seemed to think Joshua's threat to put her in a nursing home or send her abroad was more to Joshua's discredit than hers.

And the next time the two familes had dinner together, Coral Talbot suggested they play a game of whist, the exact words she had used in the beginning and, to Ceda, as impudent and heartless a reminder of her success in having irreparably damaged Susan as anything the serpent himself might have said as he lounged by, watching Eve's departure from the garden. Susan, however, seemed to take it as a species of humor she understood and nodded slightly, so that in another moment Coral and Susan, Ceda, who was peremptorily summoned by a glance from her sister, and Harriet Ching were seated at a table, Coral shuffling the cards almost as dexterously as Mrs. De Bow had done, while Joshua sat across the room talking to William Talbot.

"I have never," Ceda later told Susan, "been so astounded at a woman's effrontery as I was by Coral Talbot's. I can only say, Susan, that Joshua is a more tolerant man than I had supposed."

Susan laughed. "Ceda, you would have been a perfect wife—what a shame you wouldn't marry. You're so easily frightened. Men say they want a great many things in a wife, beauty and money and charm, but what they really want is a woman they can scare without too much trouble."

In spite of Joshua's warning, he seemed in high spirits as the wedding day came nearer, and this gave him a look of power and pride which, Ceda reflected, might have been attractive to many women, and yet was not to Susan. That these two people refused to love each other seemed to Ceda the essential mystery in all the secret relations men and women shared, and she congratulated herself she had remained single, for however humiliating the position of a maiden lady might sometimes be, it seemed preferable to these baffling glimpses she had been afforded all her life of the troublesome and disastrous effects of passion.

Nevertheless, Ceda was able to be sentimental and optimistic about love and marriage when she observed its tender beginnings, as if in the first green leaves of early spring she could not or would not remember that there would also come summer, fall, and winter. The greenery would remain as it was, fresh and succulent, promise without fulfillment, yearning without completion, curiosity without knowledge, and she was beamingly pleased whenever she saw Steven and his fiancée together, for Steven seemed to be in love with this girl, and she plainly adored him.

"They are perfectly suited," Ceda told Susan and Suky. "Steven tall and blond, Letty petite and dark. Steven dignified and quiet, she vivacious and quick. And, fortunately, she's not a strong-minded woman. I know they'll be happy."

"She's clever, isn't she?" Susan asked Suky. "A woman must be clever, however young she is, to have interested your father so much. What does she say to him, do you suppose?"

"She says nothing," Suky told her. "She has nothing to say, actually. She's a very simple young girl, after all."

And because Letty Marble was a very simple young girl, Suky had undertaken the arrangements for the wedding, almost as if she were, ten years later, planning the wedding she would have had, had she been allowed to marry Frederic Hallam. "It breaks my heart," Ceda told Susan. "Every detail, every gown, the flowers, the colors, the bridesmaids—and no other bride could ever possibly look as Suky would have looked."

For all Ceda's misgivings, the wedding day came, and Susan awoke confident and gay, as she had not been for a long while. She appeared unceremoniously in Ceda's room to ask her opinion about changes the dressmaker was still making, and late in the afternoon they went to Suky's house as they had done on all important past occasions, for a final conference.

The three women sat in Suky's dressing room and while they talked Mr. Ducarcel darted about, waving hot tongs and flourishing curls and twists of hair as he constructed another of his elaborate coiffures, of which he guaranteed that no two were ever exactly alike.

It had been almost eight years since he had begun arranging Suky's hair, and during all that time she had shown him such tender concern and paid him so generously that in a sense Mr. Ducarcel had fallen in love with her and felt as happy while dressing her hair as he ever did, clucking in self-admonishment when he could not make it behave as he wished, cooing and whispering advice to himself, congratulations or warnings, while he worked. "There, there, that's it. That's exactly as it should be, is it not, Mrs. Van Zandt? This time we have it, do we not? Did you know that Lady Haldane has had her hair dyed that new color for the wedding tonight?"

"She has? What new color?"

"That new blond—that very bright, very golden blond. The actress began it. You know the one I mean. Allegra Stuart."

Suky picked up a mirror to look at the back of her head. "Yes, I know. But I don't like it. Do you?"

"Oh, no, madame, not at all. It's—too—bright. But it's a great rage just now. Golden-blond hair with dark brows and eyelashes." He gestured quickly, as if applying these cosmetics to his own brows and eyelashes. "They imagine that if they imitate her tricks they will look like her, or maybe they imagine they will turn into her." He laughed merrily at this notion. "It's very effective, of course, but only on her—on the others it's dreadful, garish, wrong. But why can't they look at themselves and see that? Ah, no," he said sadly, "they cannot. Very few of them can. You, madame." He bowed to Suky. "And a few others. Mrs. Talbot. A very few others. What most of them want is only a face, any face, a face to be noticed by, and they don't care if it's their own or not." He spread his hands and shrugged, suddenly clapped his equipment into his satchel, bowed to Susan and Ceda, made one more deep bow to Suky, who smiled at him briefly, directly and confidingly, and dashed from the room on his way to his next appointment, for this wedding had him as busy as a New Year's Day.

"I've been to the church this morning," Suky told Susan and Ceda. "The decorations are installed. I've been to Letty's, and the decorations are in place there. I've talked to the confectioner again and the musicians—and now I think I'll sleep for an hour or two."

They kissed her sympathetically, assuring her that no one else could have done what she had done, or done it so tactfully, for there had been no quarrels among the bridesmaids, not even tears or pouts, and at the door Susan turned. "But who is going to talk to poor little Letty? That's the one thing we've all forgotten."

"I talked to her," said Suky. "This morning."

There could be no doubt that Suky had arranged for her brother and Letty Marble one of the prettiest weddings anyone had seen, and when they arrived at the church a little before eight o'clock, Ceda sensed the same excited anticipation among the guests there might have been at the first performance of a famous actress. The walls had been concealed almost to the roof with white wooden lattices

crawling with white roses, their bloom at its most complete, ready
to drop their leaves and turn yellow in a few hours but, for the moment, having a fragrant and suggestive perfection, and the room
glimmered with hundreds of white candles, warming those who sat
nearest them on this hot June night and scorching a few of the roses.

Ceda saw with pride that Philip Van Zandt's three sisters had
come, and there they sat, wearing old-fashioned dresses and old-
fashioned caps, and as Ceda looked at them she marveled at Suky's
persuasiveness but did not concern herself with how it had been
done, only sighed, and told herself that in the end a wedding somehow put everything right and their time of troubles was over.

The music became louder and more triumphant, and as the guests
rose at this signal, Annabel Devlin, who had arrived nearly a year
ago with her brother Robert to attend school, came pacing slowly
forward with Letty's sister, Nancy, and both little girls were casting
sideways smiles, demure and, Ceda thought, apprehensive, as if they
suspected themselves to be intended for some ritual sacrifice. They
were followed by the bridesmaids in white tulle gowns, each with a
sash and satin slippers in a different pale color, their hair streaming
down their backs and wreaths of white roses circling their heads,
twelve remarkably pretty girls, for Suky had suggested to Letty that
it was preferable to slight a friend's feelings and select a pretty
bridesmaid she scarcely knew than to allow old friendships to mar
the effect of her wedding, and this same advice had apparently been
followed by Steven in choosing his groomsmen, among whom walked
his cousin Robert Devlin—the handsomest man in either family, so
Ceda thought.

Steven paced solemnly with Letty's aunt and now, at last, to the
accompaniment of pleased murmurs, Letty came slowly forward on
her father's arm, and Ceda, against all her resolutions, began to
cry, for Letty was wearing, though she did not know it, the dress
Suky had long ago designed for her own wedding, a dress she had
often described to Ceda and had now exactly reproduced, only changing the hoop skirt to a small bustle. But it was still the same white
moiré gown, long-sleeved and high-necked; the same diamond star
was in Letty's hair; there was the train so long it seemed it might
not enter the church and, when it did, was carried by two page boys
in dark blue velvet suits who were, Ceda observed with sad irony,
Suky's own son Joshua, and little Jeffrey Hallam.

As Letty passed them, Ceda noticed with approval that her bouquet of white camellias and orange blossoms trembled and that she
cast Suky a shy, grateful smile, and at this Ceda lost all ability to follow what was happening, shut her eyes and struggled so intensely
with her urge to weep loudly, longing more than any other time in
her life to wail and sob, forsake altogether her usual polite and timid
tears, that when at last she was able to compose herself the bridal
party was leaving the church and, as Mendelssohn's *March* thun-
dered until the roses quivered and a few began to shed their petals,

the ladies had begun to rustle about, searching for the fans and reti-
cules they had buried in their laps, and Ceda was gratified to hear
them babbling their admiring approval of Suky's production.

By the time Ceda reached the vestry the bride and groom were
driving off, to the accompaniment of ringing bells, and when she arrived at Hiram Marble's house a crowd had gathered, policemen were
pushing them back, and a parade of guests streamed across the Brussels carpet. Inside the house, where the furniture was hidden by the
flowers, and musicians, hidden within the flowers, played on all
sides, she at last discovered Susan and they embraced as if in forgiveness for many mutual recriminations.

They sat at the bride's table, and while the cake was speared and
taken aside to be cut, Ceda listened in a dazzled rapture to the healths
being proposed and, each time, took a sip of champagne and eventually grew reckless enough to toss off several glasses. Presently the
bride was opening the first quadrille with Steven's best man and
Steven was dancing with the first bridesmaid, his cousin Evelyn.
Ceda then saw Joshua ask Susan to dance and disappear with her
into the kaleidoscope, and at this proof of her own belief in the magical properties of a wedding, Ceda was again captured by emotion
and might have been unable to recover but for Robert, who stood
there asking her to dance with him.

In a little while the bride was gone, Steven followed soon after,
and Ceda, who did not feel adequate to struggling through the crowd
on the stairs, leaned out an opened window in time to see Letty and
Steven disappear into the carriage. It rattled away, followed by satin
slippers and bags filled with rice, and when one of the slippers
landed upon the carriage roof a cheer went up from the sidewalk
crowds, and Ceda, deeply sighing, turned to find Joshua standing beside her.

"Ceda," he said, and smiled at her with mock seriousness, "Will
you dance with me?"

Ceda gave him a coquettish look. "There's no one, Joshua, I would
rather dance with. And no other man here tonight as handsome as
you are." For there was no doubt in Ceda's opinion that Joshua at
that moment, with his white-blond hair and beard, his well-tailored
clothes, his grave and gracious manner, was as impressive as the
portrait Augustus Adams had painted of him, and she felt a swelling pride as he sped her about the room. "Everything was perfect,
wasn't it?"

"Everything," he agreed. "Thanks to Suky."

"Oh, I'm so glad you know how much she did."

"Of course I know, Ceda," he replied, for surely it was absurd to
suppose he would not be aware of Suky's many contributions to all
their lives.

There was not, Ceda afterward thought, a clue of any kind, for
the evening passed in a bewildering succession of waltzes and qua-
drilles, champagne and lobster, wilting flowers and crushed skirts,

high voices and laughter, which seemed to her more stimulating than anything she had ever experienced before, and she went to bed convinced that Suky had a genius for creating an atmosphere and coercing others to share it which was greater than even her extravagant adoration had suspected, and although later she was ashamed to admit it, even to herself, she slept very well, and dreamed of nothing she could ever remember.

Most certainly she was visited during the few hours left of the night by none of her premonitions, no warnings, no disturbing and inexplicable fears, and yet Ceda awoke feeling that something had gone fatally wrong and lay for a few moments trying to remember if anything had happened the night before to make her uneasy now, but could remember nothing at all. And then, as she heard sounds of loud rapping, she got out of bed, seized a dressing gown and hurried to her bedroom door, forgot that she always locked it and had a momentary panic that someone else had locked her in, and ran down the hallway, crying Susan's name.

The door of Susan's room was opened and Ceda stopped still, for there, with his back to her, stood Joshua, dressed in the black frock coat and gray trousers he wore to his office, gloves on his hands, his hat and cane held together, and across the room was Susan in her nightgown, so that apparently she had been taken by surprise and leaped up, as if to defend herself. While between them and approaching Susan slowly, like a man who tries to catch a wary animal or a terrified child, was Dr. Montgomery, and as Ceda stared at them, telling herself that this must be the dream she had failed to have, Dr. Montgomery approached a little nearer to Susan, repeating her name in a coaxing tone, and Susan darted aside, crying, "No, Joshua, oh, no, please—"

L

The night was so hot that in spite of the noise from the streets, the shouts and singing and perpetually exploding firecrackers, Allegra had opened every window in the dining room, and still the men were wiping their faces and the women's hair clung in tendrils to their foreheads and necks, and only Allegra looked as if this heat was a matter of indifference to her, one more American nuisance she had learned to endure.

She sat at the head of the table, with Dyke Ferguson at the opposite end, and all the while they were proposing toasts—drinking to their hostess, to the nation's hundredth year, to the American Revolution, to the Philadelphia Centennial, to Washington and Lincoln and General Grant, to their wise manager, to peace everlasting, to a successful fall season, to recovery from the hard times the country was so inappropriately suffering on this historic date—Allegra watched them with a skeptical smile, thinking they were like so many children at a birthday party, although, as it happened, the birthday was their nation's.

She looked around at these eighteen permanent members of the company, her friends and enemies distributed more or less evenly among them, and told herself that in the year she had been playing with them she had learned their secrets, their weaknesses and strengths, and congratulated herself that however they had resisted her in the beginning, now, when she invited them to a dinner or a reception, they came with as much eager humility as if the invitations had gone out from their reigning sovereign. Not, however, she reminded herself, because they were any the less resentful of the English actress' power, or even of her importation to their native soil.

"You are all," Dyke Ferguson had told them when he announced that Allegra Stuart would join their company for as long as he could persuade her to stay, "beginning to take yourselves for granted. I predict that Miss Stuart will stimulate you." And this, there was no doubt, had been an accurate prediction.

They had gossiped in the green room after Dyke Ferguson had made his announcement and, according to his custom, abruptly left them to chew it over at their leisure; and even before Allegra Stuart had arrived in America they had chosen sides for and against her, giving Tamzene Twining one team and Allegra Stuart the other.

"That's Ferguson for you," Anthony De Forest had told them. "The man's a dictator and we're his humble subjects."

"Why an English actress?" the second old man asked plaintively.

"Snobbery, what else?" replied Tamsie Twining.

"Booth said there's never yet been an American actor take any money out of England. Why the hell should they come here and get rich on us?"

"They refuse to see our plays and our stars are ignored by them. I'm damned if I'll play with an Englishwoman."

"English and Spanish," Tamsie said, wiggling one forefinger. "An odd combination."

But because Tamzene Twining, during her four starring years in Ferguson's Broadway Theater, had often been as dictatorial as Ferguson himself, Allegra had arrived to find that she had her own following, including the first old woman, who had explained to Allegra the several secrets of the company. Tamzene Twining, she said, was secretly married to Anthony De Forest, and De Forest, whose large straight nose and powerful chin and glaring blue eyes were assets at least equal to his acting ability, had originally been named Patrick Runkle.

"Wait, De Forest," Ferguson had told him, for he was notorious among his actors for the enjoyment he took in torturing them, and they thought his sallow, saturnine face and occasional reluctant smile a fair enough description of his character. "Wait until you try *Macbeth* with her."

"I would prefer," Anthony De Forest had stiffly replied, "to play that with Tamsie."

Ferguson laughed and gave him a look of incredulous pity. "Tamsie—Lady Macbeth? Now, Runkle, for God's sake."

This use of his own name, which Ferguson resorted to whenever he thought his star was bumptious or unruly, had its usual subduing effect, for he lived in dread that someday it would be publicly known that Patrick Runkle was what he had been christened, and the name had come to seem to him more loathsome, more absurd, and more unsuitable to Anthony De Forest than any other name could possibly have been. He would have preferred to have been called anything else and yet there it was, Patrick Runkle, his detested secret.

Some of the legends had changed by now and new ones had been added to the company's lore, and there could be found among them those who believed that Allegra Stuart and Anthony De Forest had become lovers, that Tamsie Twining knew it and was searching for some suitable revenge, or that the English actress and De Forest despised each other and her lover was no one but Ferguson himself. But however they disagreed about these details they had agreed, friends and enemies alike—not after her first rehearsal, for she merely spoke her lines, somewhat indifferently and with an air of ironic amusement, but after her first performance as Juliet—that she was an actress.

"I know exactly when it happens," the second old man had told them, after they had studied her performance for several nights. "It's the 'Amen.' You can feel it coming, the audience feels it coming, and when she finally says it and looks at the Nurse, they know that Juliet has become a woman." He shook his head, baffled with admiration. "The god-damnedest business I've seen in a long time. Then they sigh—you heard that? And then, of course, they start to applaud. Well, there you are. English or not, she's an actress."

"My Juliet," said Tamsie defensively, "was always hampered by my height. But she's so little, no more than five feet three. She can never do Lady Macbeth."

"Lady Macbeth," the second old man reminded her, "is a monster, not a giant."

But Lady Macbeth had not been in Allegra Stuart's contract and, so far, she had refused to play it and said she would as soon play Shylock—or sooner. And so they pestered her about it, glad to have discovered her weakness, since she seemed to know theirs so well and took such a delicate, remorseless advantage of her knowledge, until a general clamor for Lady Macbeth now seemed to come at her from every side, not from her enemies only, but even from her friends and admirers.

Joist Barringer had written two articles urging her to play Lady Macbeth, and Benjamin Burnish had taken it as a subject for one of his editorials. Joshua Ching, who had sought her out in the green room, where she sat on a castoff throne of King Lear's, perching there like a small court jester in the red tights and doublet she wore for Rosalind, had later come to call at her apartment, bringing a basket of plums for the parrot Consuelo, and he had begun to badger her, too, as if their early acquaintance gave him some proprietary interest in her career. Even Philip Van Zandt had reminded her, with some possessive pride, that it had been at his suggestion she had gone to England and his suggestion, too, that she wear lavender dresses, which were beginning to be as much copied as her gilt-blond hair. And, perhaps because he thought she was now committed to pay superstitious attention to any new advice he might give her, Philip had remarked that it was time she play Lady Macbeth, if only to put a stop to nasty gossip that she was afraid of it.

"But I am afraid of it," she told each of them. "It terrifies me, I can't do it, I won't do it, and there's nothing more to say about it." Still, they went on pestering her, these devoted subjects of her newly conquered territory, and insisted it was the least she owed them in return for their immoderate adoration.

And, she wryly reflected, not one of them would have believed her had she told them she kept a bitter conviction that it was this country, with its alluring promises, which had destroyed her mother, caused the death of her older sister, and somehow disposed of her father, for she believed he must long ago have been buried in a pauper's grave, as men were who were found dead in the streets and whose bodies no one claimed—or he might, of course, have been given to one of the medical students who came begging at the city coroner's office. But when she had spoken of this to Hoke, he shrugged. "Forget it," he advised her.

Hoke, who was thirty-three now, had developed a toughness and ferocity, an abiding look of suspicion and grim shrewdness, which made it easy for her to believe that he was, as he said, a power in the ward and a man to be reckoned with all over the city; a man very much, she supposed, like that other Tammany ward leader who had, long ago, paid the costs of their mother's burial.

"You're the practical Irishman, Hoke," she told him. "I'm the other kind."

Hoke grinned. "What you mean is, you couldn't crack my skull with a knuckle-duster. Don't worry, I get a dark blue spell myself now and then. But I work it off—give somebody a poke, slap my girl a couple of times, throw some money at the kids outside my door, or go to a funeral. Nothing like another guy's funeral to take your mind off your troubles. Forget it," he advised her again.

"How did it happen, I wonder, that you became an American—and I have no country at all?"

"You became English," he reminded her.

"No, I didn't become English. I thought I might, I even tried to, but I could no more become English than I could become American. I suppose my real country is the green room." She smiled ruefully. "Hoke, when I die, it's going to be in a strange land, far away from everyone I know. I don't want any mourners, and I want my grave to be unmarked."

At these words, spoken in a serious confiding voice, as if she was making him the executor of her will, Hoke sprang up defensively. "For Christ's sake, Betty, what the hell ails you? It's a sin to talk like that. It's worse—it's asking for trouble." But then, when she gave that joyously mocking laugh, and looked at him with her eyes glittering with sorrow or anger, he threw his hands wide and shook his head, as if it grieved him to find her so impious.

But she was still liable to being taken by surprise, invaded by feelings of unworthiness, and it happened when she expected it least, just as it had on the day she had arrived at Augustus Adams' studio half an hour early, and immediately approached the two children she found there, to begin talking to them with an air of beguiling candor, seeming to have turned herself into a child at that moment, for these were the Van Zandt children and their mother must be in the dressing room.

She was still talking to them several minutes later, and by that time they were old friends, for she had shown them a variety of imitations—Mr. Adams and his housekeeper as well as several ladies whose portraits stood about the wall—when Susan Van Zandt came out of the dressing room with her maid and, without glancing at Allegra, left the studio. The children promptly bid her good-bye, saying wistfully that they hoped to meet her again soon, and when the door had closed Allegra stood gazing at the floor, until all at once she turned to Augustus Adams with a merry little smile. "Don't look so distressed, Mr. Adams, I didn't expect you to introduce us. I know how afraid Americans are of meeting even their social equals."

"Oh, but Miss Stuart, please believe me, Mrs. Van Zandt did not see you, she would never—"

"Mr. Adams," she told him sharply, "don't apologize to me." But she took care not to be early again.

And, in fact, she was angry with Betty Mulligan for having prompted Allegra Stuart to arrive early, for she had heard Mrs. Van Zandt's maid discussing the next appointment, and must have known well enough that her curiosity could accomplish nothing but her own embarrassment—a possibility against which she ordinarily took such precautions, providing herself with sycophants and idolaters, carefully selected and diligently encouraged, that she would not have believed there were any essential parts of Allegra Stuart still left unprotected.

Her dinner parties and receptions were attended by the city's influential men, and some of them brought their wives. Wherever she went, whether driving as she did each afternoon in her claret-colored landau, with her coachman and footman, Jagger and Buxton—who had become celebrities in their own right—dressed in claret-colored livery to match the carriage, or riding her handsome black horse, Bouche Dhu, she was recognized and greeted, almost reverentially, for it seemed they were not sure how much of her was Allegra Stuart and how much was Juliet or Rosalind. Flowers and gifts arrived each day at the theater and at her apartment. Her photographs were in shop windows, her name was printed in large letters on fences and walls and upon the rocks which littered the empty lots of upper Fifth Avenue, and it was truthfully said the English actress had taken the town.

And yet it had begun to seem that the only way she could keep all this, which some days she enjoyed as much as she had once expected to, and other days despised as she had never imagined she might, was to give in to them and agree to Lady Macbeth. For sooner or later, at every rehearsal, each night in the green room, or even now, when she was entertaining this troupe of American Indians, as she privately called them, Lady Macbeth's name was sure to be spoken, and she had begun to dread it and to wait for it as once, long ago, she had dreaded and waited for that first call to London.

For here they sat, eating the food prepared by her French chef, exclaiming over the gold mesh basket full of fruits which proved to be ice cream, toasting their country's birthday with the best champagne, and just as she had expected, Anthony De Forest got to his feet, rather unsteadily, and raised his glass, announcing in a voice so deep and vibrant that when he let it ring through the theater the women in the audience felt its effects in chills over their arms and breasts, "To your success, Miss Stuart, in *Macbeth!*"

As if this was a well-rehearsed signal, the others stood, lifting their glasses and facing her, and only Dyke Ferguson did not move but sat watching her from the opposite end of the table, and his thin face, with its long narrow nose and black brows and mustache— diabolical enough, his company thought, even when his humor was at its unusual best—seemed more than ever to challenge and scoff. "To *Macbeth!*" they cried, and had no sooner drunk the toast than all of them began to talk at once.

"No Shakespearean actress is complete without Lady Macbeth," Tamsie Twining said, though she had never played it, either, and Allegra gave her a smile, at once sympathetic and derisive.

"I know."

"That most terrible test of any genius," the first old man reminded her dolefully.

"I know."

And, the next moment, there was a sound of band music approaching, new explosions of giant firecrackers and rockets, and they sprang up, shouting "The parade! The parade!" and rushed off to the living room, while Allegra and Dyke Ferguson still sat, looking at each other down the table's length.

Ferguson was, it sometimes seemed, the only American she had failed to conquer, for although he had given her the pedigreed poodle Mio when she had signed the contract in London, once she arrived he had shown her no more deference than he did any other member of his company, and that was little enough.

He paid them lower wages, so they said, than another manager would have. He demanded that they submit themselves to his tyranny and he punished the smallest insurrection swiftly and mercilessly. He criticized them constantly and praised them seldom, broke his promises without explanation or apology, bullied them through each rehearsal and glowered at them from the wings as if each performance was expected to be a catastrophe; and yet, when it was not, when the women were waving handkerchiefs and ushers were marching down the aisles bearing huge bouquets, he had little to say, merely looked strongly and warningly at each one as they came from the stage, and when the last had filed by him, retreated to his office and was not seen again until the next day.

There, in that little room under the stairs of the stage entrance, half beneath the street level, which they must pass on their way in or out, they supposed he was plotting against them; and when occasionally he summoned one of them, they crept sheepishly down to confront him, expecting to be baited or ridiculed or denounced. But still, with all his faults, they insisted he was a great manager and defended him from other detractors, and even the stars did not complain about the cubbyholes they had for dressing rooms, the stinking air and harsh lights, the extremes of heat and cold, for that part of the theater was never comfortable; and possibly thought that without this crowded and littered hideout they would never be able to achieve what they did once they appeared upon the stage itself, so many pet wizards kept in cages and sent out at intervals to perform their tricks, only upon the condition they return immediately to their kennels until the time came for them to perform again.

It even seemed that they clung superstitiously to every indignity Dyke Ferguson could invent for them, for Ferguson's Broadway Theater was, after all, the place where people came for their serious entertainment, attending it with a sanctimonious and dutiful air, and they would not join another company no matter how many complaints they made to one another, but were, perhaps, a little proud of having the cruelest and most domineering manager in town.

For a few moments, while the others clapped and yelled and the sounds of the band came steadily nearer, until the drums were booming as if the paraders had entered the building itself and might dash it to pieces with the force of their patriotic fervor, Allegra and Ferguson continued to face each other. "Why won't you play it?" he asked her finally. "You're only giving them what they want by refusing."

"And suppose I play it badly? Isn't that what they really want?"

"You won't play it badly, I'll see to that."

"I can't bellow and rant and splash blood around. I can't do it, I can't—" She was leaning forward, ready to give the table a smack with her fist, but some strangeness in his smile, something which seemed more than usually malevolent, made her ashamed and she sat back, began to pleat the napkin and could not look at him again.

"Remember," he said, "what Sarah Siddons thought about Lady Macbeth."

Allegra still did not look at him but went on pleating the napkin, and murmured, "A slight, delicate, alluring blond woman, full of fire, but exquisitely feminine."

"Yes," he whispered, and she gave him a surreptitious glance, but then looked quickly away from those brilliant black eyes. "She could never play it that way—" Allegra nodded, feeling herself grow more humble, more contrite, and listened with an almost painful attentiveness for what he would say next. "But you can. You have all those qualities."

She looked at him pleadingly. "I do?"

"You know that."

She sighed. "Sometimes I forget."

But then she went into the living room, where she slipped between De Forest and the second old man and hung at the window, watching the marchers parading by, waving torches and lanterns, while around her the company was singing, Tamsie Twining was crying, they were embracing one another and dancing dementedly about the room, and someone had begun to bang out "Hail, Columbia" on the piano.

Coveys of rockets soared into the black sky like sheaves of wheat, bursting into golden showers, and flags hung from numberless poles as far as she could see in either direction. Every office building and house in the city appeared to be lighted—and it was not difficult to imagine that so they were lighted all across the nation. But this frantic celebration only reminded her, more painfully than ever before, of that Fourth of July when the ladies of the Mission School had taken the children to the rooftop to show them the fireworks, and she had imagined they were showing her no man-made wonders but the heaven where, they had said, her mother lived.

Presently Ferguson appeared beside her, saying nothing, only watching her, and she hurried to greet new guests who had somehow struggled through the crowd, and after that kept at a safe distance from him, for Ferguson, it was said, could have convinced Anthony De Forest to play Little Eva.

They were soon gathered about Benjamin Burnish, to hear him tell them, in his soft, regretful voice, that this frenzy was all very well in its way but they must not forget the country was at this moment suffering the worst financial pangs it had ever known, and was more dishonest and corrupt than even the famous American cosmetic of hypocrisy was able to conceal. "The truth of it is, my friends, we should be in national mourning today." He sat in the middle of a long sofa, a small man with a ruff of fine blond hair circling the top of his head and forming tufts upon his pink cheeks, closing his hands and seeming to polish his nails nervously together as he spoke, and they grew obediently quiet and reflective, for the city and much of the country was accustomed to listen respectfully to Ben Burnish—of whom it was said that he was one of the nation's philosophers, a man who had lived long enough to know that however bad things might be they would soon be much worse. "From one end of the country to the other there is poverty and gloom, and the elections this fall will do little to improve our situation. This man Tilden can, if he is elected, perhaps even if he is not, plunge the country into civil war again. We may, I warn you, be at war before many more months have gone by."

Tamsie Twining clasped her hands, sighing. Ferguson sat watching Burnish with the same sober, distrustful look he showed his actors as he stood in the wings, and now and then nodded, as if in approval of the worst accusations Ben Burnish might make. All of them, in fact, looked so remarkably penitent that Allegra was pleased to see how greedy they were for punishment, even to Hoke and his two friends, Oliver Foss and Marquis McDuff, who stood glumly staring at Benjamin Burnish.

"We exist in a moral anarchy," said Burnish. There were more guilty glances exchanged. "But the people are finally beginning to grow tired of suffering so that rich men may become richer and corruption may flourish among their legislators with no more than token objection. Grant, thank God, we will soon be done with." There was some applause, and Ben Burnish, benignly smiling, held up one hand to silence them. "We've had Babcock and Belknap and General Schenck, the Mulligan Letters and Blaine, the Crédit Mobilier and the Whisky Ring, and Beecher and Tilden. Not to mention Boss Tweed, who found his way out of our papier-mâché jail, though Tammany has embraced us again—and we may hope for no better mercy than it has shown us in the past."

"But, Ben," Allegra said softly, "Americans love everything big. Now they can say that their officials are the world's greatest rascals." They laughed, meekly accepting this insult from the English actress.

"We can indeed, my dear," Ben Burnish assured her. "And, for once, we wouldn't be exaggerating. What reason have we for pride tonight—either in our city or in our nation? Was this what our forefathers intended? And yet Wagner has composed a march for our Centennial, and France has sent the hand of their proposed Statue of Liberty." He looked around brightly. "Are we not absurd? I must go." He spread his small hands and rose from the couch, turned to Allegra and made her a ceremonious bow. "My dear, when are we to expect Lady Macbeth from you?"

"Sometime this winter."

They began to applaud, although Ferguson scowled as if he suspected she might have taken advantage of an attentive and excitable audience, and Ben Burnish kissed her as tenderly as if he kissed a child. "You see? We do have something to look forward to. Good night, my friends, good night."

And as Allegra walked to the door with Ben Burnish, they began to argue about his diatribe, some declaring it was unjust while others insisted his criticism had come nowhere near the ugly truth, and interrupted their arguments to remark, as if they could not get over the surprise, "She's going to do it after all. And she told me only last week she never would." But Dyke Ferguson kept his suspicious distance and had nothing to say about it even when he thanked her for the evening's entertainment.

A few days later, as if in fulfillment of Ben Burnish's worst predictions, news came of General Custer's defeat. Flags flew at half mast and windows and doors were hung with black crape. The streets fell surprisingly still and, in the midst of this gloom, Allegra retired into her apartment and spent several days alone there, refused to see anyone, ate little, grew languid with the heat, and gave herself up to morbid speculations, not upon the tawdry condition of American morality, but upon her own heedless promise to play this part she dreaded.

She moped and hung at the windows, gazing down at the street traffic and across at the black-draped buildings, and found some scornful amusement in thinking how well the city's mood fitted with her own despondency.

In a white wrapper, the third successor to the one she had worn at Mrs. Gosnell's, the superstitious garment into which she retreated whenever she had a sudden spell of feeling poor or must prepare a new part, she rambled from one room to another, barefoot and with her hair hanging loose, and recited aloud the Second Player's speech.

She had memorized *Macbeth* long ago, but now she copied it through, and then copied it through again, and from time to time she wandered about, stared at herself in a mirror, nibbled indifferently at whatever food was served, quarreled with the parrot and slept erratically, and at last got up in the middle of the night to have out with herself the problem of the sleepwalking scene.

But she grew so terrified by the sound of the lines and by her shadow cast upon the walls, that when the parrot gave an unexpected squawk she shrieked and ran from the room, stumbled over the barking poodle, who followed her about the apartment yapping at her bare heels, and at last sat down on the floor in a fit of delirious laughter.

The theater was closed for the summer months, and she ignored the first note Ferguson sent, summoning her to his office. When he wrote again, she pleaded that she was ill with some American malady whose nature her doctor could not diagnose, and began with frantic industriousness to read Scottish history, to study her collection of costume plates, to comb and arrange her assortment of wigs, and then all at once she was surprised and indignant at this cowardice. She sent Richard Peterson to Ferguson with a message that she would be there the next morning, and even though she lay awake most of the night, she arrived looking as candid and blithe as if she had been all along with the others of the company, attending the races at Long Branch.

She ran down the steps to the stage door, gaily greeted the old janitor who was its guardian, and rapped at the door of Ferguson's office, expecting he would throw it open with a relieved cry of welcome. She waited for some moments and was becoming more and more indignant, tapping her foot and making faces at the janitor, when he opened it a crack, a little farther, and at last gestured at her to come in.

The little room was furnished with a desk which had appeared in one of his productions as a table and been discarded when it did not please him, four chairs which had been similarly acquired, and several photographs which must have been hung long ago and forgotten, for the clothes were old-fashioned and the faces unknown to her. And Ferguson, she was pleased to see, looked as tired as she felt, and was even more sallow than usual. He had taken off his coat, unknotted his cravat, his shirt was wet through, and as he stood wiping his face she was struck very agreeably by the notion that this man was no more terrifying than any other and that she might, at last, be able to force him to show her the respectful awe she deserved and had not been able to exact.

"Where have you been?"

"Home."

"Why?" He glared at her.

"I was sick. No. I was scared. I was trying to study."

"That's a god-damn lie."

"Don't swear at me, Mr. Ferguson," she yelled. "I was home—I was alone—and I was trying my damnedest to feel my way into that part and I can't do it. I'll spoil it, I tell you. I'll spoil your production. De Forest will laugh at me and so will Tamsie, and so will everyone else. Ben Burnish will pity me, Joist Barringer will turn against me, you'll hate me—and I'll most likely kill myself." She threw her arms wide in a furious gesture, and it all seemed to have come true as she spoke.

"You're not confident," he said softly. "That's good, I despise confident performers. I can't work with them."

"You despise all performers. You have no respect for us. We're your cattle, no better than senators to a millionaire." She gave him a sharp glance. "Isn't that so?"

"You've resisted this part for a long time. And yet it's obviously essential that a Shakespearean actress play it, or admit she's incapable of it. What are you afraid of?" He was watching her with that uncanny concentration he gave to all of them and which she, like the others, feared and resented, and had begun to depend upon.

She placed her hands on the desk and leaned across it. "What am I afraid of? Shall I tell you? I'm afraid of the moment when that damned little call-boy, Tap Doyle, will come sidling up to me there in the green room and whine in my ear, 'The stage waits, Miss Stuart.'"

She turned her back and leaned against the desk, and he finally said, very gently, "You must trust me. We'll work together, I'll support you, I won't let you fail. I won't let you belittle either one of us."

She did not turn but stood thinking of what he had said, and the words had begun to seem as beguiling as any she had ever heard from a lover. And when at last she turned to look at him, she was surprised by the remarkable change in his appearance these past few moments, for where she had seen a look of cruelty and menace, now she saw strength and power and, in fact, to her increasing admiration, Dyke Ferguson seemed so remarkably transformed she warned herself she must take care not to fall in love with him the way inexperienced actresses were always falling in love with their managers and leading men.

She sat down, bowed her head and folded her hands, and murmured in a kind of intoxicated rapture, "Oh, thank you, thank you. I believe you. I trust you."

L I

Morgan talked to Joshua in his new offices, where he appeared nowadays like a reigning prince amid his setting of marble counters, plate-glass windows, frescoed walls and ceilings and carved walnut screens to keep out the press of eager callers. There were huge safes, some of which stood invitingly open, giving a view of their contents, neat piles of bills and arrangements of stocks and bonds and contracts, all displayed as tastefully as if someone had been going to paint a picture of them, but Joshua was no more eager to share them with Morgan than he had been two years ago.

"You say you'll pay three percent, Morgan, but of course you may not be able to. That would mean that you must make a large profit very quickly and, as you say, the leads you've explored so far have only gobbled up whatever you've put into them and opened their maws for more. One hundred and fifteen thousand dollars gone in two years," he said, and leaned forward to examine once again the figures Morgan had set before him. "Only a bonanza will set you right again."

"That's what I think I have. But it needs further development."

"That's what you think you have," said Joshua, gently chiding, for it was obvious he thought his nephew was only one more example of a western man driven mad by the size of the landscape. "I hope so, naturally. But then why doesn't Devlin Brothers make the loan?"

"They've loaned me everything we can afford for speculation right now, and twenty thousand more in private loans from Pete and my brothers and Lisette's husband." Morgan smiled. "To be truthful, sir, we're a little conservative for silver mining."

"Ah," said Joshua, and Morgan got no more consolation from him.

When he met with Hallam's loan board he rattled off statistics, displayed maps and charts and photographs of the shaft houses and the silver mill he had recently completed, showed them ore samples, and read aloud an article written by Billy Church—who had taken Homer Grimes' place as editor of the *Helena Post,* after their New Year's Eve encounter—which described the Yellow Medicine as the most promising property on Butte Hill, with one million dollars presently in sight.

"And yet," Felice's great uncle, Gilbert Lacey, reminded him, "this same property made you a profit of only five thousand dollars last year."

"Yes, sir," Morgan agreed. "Only one other property did as well."

"And you're only down to eighty feet," said Roger Hallam.

"As I explained, sir, we began to find water there, and no one's been able to afford the pumps and hoisting machinery to get below the water line."

While they went on talking, seemingly determined to turn him inside out and examine his guts at their leisure, as if he were some bird or animal being studied for financial omens by this band of ancient priests, Morgan listened almost indifferently and fell to thinking of Felice, whose second child would be born in another week or two, and then his thoughts wandered, as they invariably did these days, to Lemuel Finney, left free by his absence to prey upon his claims at will.

Finney was often in Butte, and whenever they met he pretended the New Year's Eve episode had been only a little joke men could appreciate, even if the women did not. For Rachel had gone to Lisette —after Homer had confessed that he and Jake had not been chased by a gang of ruffians, drunk and recklessly firing their pistols, but only by Morgan and Douglas Devlin—and had begged her to make Morgan give up the claim to avoid trouble between their two families. Lem Finney, however, did not pretend a man gave up a claim for any such reason, and he had filed suit against Morgan in Deer Lodge.

"It's yours for the time being," was the way Lem put it.

"That property belongs to me, Lem, and has ever since 'sixty-six. Zack Fletcher and I took it over when the owner died—he willed it to us."

"But you didn't maintain the cost of representing, Morgan. You apparently got busy or stayed east too long. Or perhaps you didn't know the laws had been changed. We got the word while you and that Englishman were on your way east, as Pete or anyone else can tell you. I'm sorry about it, of course, for your sake, but when I found the representation work had not been done, you must admit it was only natural that I should send Jake and Homer to relocate."

"I left a man to work it, Lem."

"You did?" Lem reared back, peering up at Morgan. "Then what happened to him?"

"He collected the money from Bruno Favorite and set out to enter the costs—but it seems he never got to Deer Lodge." Morgan bent down, peering at Lem, and his eyes shone brightly. "I'd like to know what happened to him myself, Lem. Grizzly bear got him, do you suppose?"

"A prospector, that's what the guy was, and an unreliable bunch of bastards they are, too. Never hire a prospector, Morgan, that's been my experience. They'll drop a pick and disappear just like that." Lem snapped his fingers, and thoughtfully added, "Or, of course, your friend Bruno Favorite might have decided to keep the representation costs himself. Six hundred could seem like quite a sum to him, I imagine."

Morgan smiled tolerantly, for he had no doubt that Jeremy Flint knew, as he promised, how to keep that suit out of the courts for an indefinite time, and, in the meanwhile, he hoped to buy Amos Muspratt's adjoining claim. But there, again, he met Lemuel Finney, who had the same ambition, and Morgan had begun to wonder if it might be true, as Irene Flint had said, that a friendship with the Finneys was as comfortable as the attachment of a cocklebur to your winter underwear.

For now that the prospect of a boom was in the air, Amos had grown more suspicious than ever, and was to be found all day long and half the night seated on a heap of rock at the opened throat of his mine, entertaining men who wanted to buy his property. But when Morgan had offered him twenty thousand dollars, he gave him a crafty smile, to let Morgan know that Amos Muspratt was no tenderfoot.

Sooner or later, though, as Morgan and Lem Finney knew quite well, Amos would be deep enough in debt to sell this property, which was believed by several men to be one of the camp's most valuable claims, and Morgan had a persistent nagging fear—while he was journeying east, while he pondered the copper exhibits in Philadelphia, even while he sat answering questions put to him by the Hallam loan board—that at that same moment Lemuel Finney was persuading Amos to sign his contract.

For there was Amos, squinting as he read the clauses, and there was Finney, urging him with the devil's own eloquence. And, while Morgan longed to shout a warning that Amos could hear across the continent, Amos was letting Finney guide his hand over the paper, and Finney, once the deed was done, was beaming and crisply rubbing his hands together, while Morgan began to sweat with the intolerable conviction that all this had actually happened while he sat here palavering with the loan board.

"And you are still," Gilbert Lacey reminded him, "more than three hundred miles from a railroad." Morgan smiled, accepting the blame for this disadvantage, and knew when the meeting adjourned that they would loan him nothing, and so he went to Suky saying he would leave the next day, and find the money somewhere else.

"But where, Morgan? If you could find it somewhere else, you wouldn't have come here, would you?"

They were in the conservatory, that dim room with its blue lights and dripping water and smell of moist earth, which had returned in his memories as often as if something wonderful or disastrous had happened to him there, and while they talked he paced about, peering into baskets of orchids and fern.

She had had many questions to ask him about Felice, although Felice wrote to her once or twice every week, and all the while he was describing, with a waxing enthusiasm which seemed a little defiant, even to him, his happiness with Felice, Suky watched him with a cool and skeptical curiosity, which all at once had him yearning to take hold of her roughly and shake her a time or two, until that look of faint disbelieving amusement had disappeared. All this, of course, he blamed on Lisette.

"Be careful of Suky," she had whispered, when he came to tell Felice good-bye, for she had been with Marietta for the past few weeks. "She likes best whatever she takes away from someone else." He had looked so honestly shocked at this that Lisette gave a mocking laugh. "Oh, Morgan, you never did have any sense of humor where Suky is concerned. That air she has of spirituality and tenderness—as if she's just discovered a little hurt bird in the aviary. Do you believe all that?"

He had always supposed that he did, and yet it was true that a part of his uneasiness now came from some new suspicion that Suky had grown jealous of Felice, and he had a curious sense of peril, as if all those prohibitions which had kept them virtuous had been weakened by his marriage to Felice and might, indeed, be quite destroyed by only the simplest gesture; and so he took care to keep his distance from her and to talk only of that which might most reliably remind him of where his new loyalties lay.

As he described Felice's first and only visit to the Yellow Medicine, he avoided looking at Suky, only glanced at her obliquely now and then, for she sat with one leg crossed over the other, leaned back against the white wicker sofa with both arms clasped behind her head, and found himself at the mercy of his imagination which, with no trouble at all, could lay Suky flat upon that same couch and put himself on top of her. The Yellow Medicine, no doubt, was a safer place for him to be at that moment, and as he walked back and forth with his hands thrust deep in his pockets, talking a little louder than necessary, for the sound of his own voice distracted him and kept him listening, lest some unintended words be spoken, he was soon tramping about his underground domain of alleys and alcoves where he went poking about for telltale signs of silver or copper, roaming through the stinking dark passages in search of his fortune and future power, and Suky could not follow him there.

The story, as he told it, had some necessary embellishments, for he wanted Suky to see the Yellow Medicine as it would perhaps look next year, not as it did now—a little shack standing beside an opened shaft, furnished with a lopsided table and a bunk covered with a buffalo robe. Felice, he told her, when she was asked if she wanted to go down in the mine, had showed an alert, bright graciousness, like a girl asked for her first waltz at the first great ball of her life, and confidingly gave him her hand. He had lifted her into the bucket and begun to crank the windlass, and as she disappeared Felice had given him a little wave and a reassuring smile, and just so he waved to Suky now and got an answering smile which seemed so treacherously seductive that he made for the other end of the conservatory and finished his description from there.

The air in a mine, he admitted, was damp and smelled foully, of what, he preferred not to say, and the darkness suggested a limitless penetration into the earth which could draw them forward on a long journey from which they would never find a way back; and Felice had given a deep sigh of relief when her visit was over and she started back up to the earth's surface.

"You're thinking that that's a hell of a way for a man to make a living, aren't you?" he demanded of Suky, as he had demanded it of Felice. And then he had leaned down, murmuring to Suky as he had to Felice, "You're right, it is. But it's a great way to make a fortune."

Suky laughed, though he guessed it did not honestly amuse her, and so he went on to a lyric description of their first Christmas dinner in Butte, when he and Felice, in full evening dress, sat down to a dinner served by the maid Nelly Flowers, and toasted each other in champagne.

"You're happy, Morgan, aren't you?" Suky inquired softly.

"Of course!" he declared, and launched promptly upon the subject of Susette, and now he made no pretense of modesty or reason, for Susette, after all, was a small rare treasure any man would be awestruck to own.

While Susette was still a baby, during the months he had been in Butte and Felice had lived with Marietta, he had approached her at each return with a sense of wonder and dismay, had carried her about in his arms and, when no one else was present, engaged her in philosophical speculations about the world she was to live in, telling her some of the good and some of the bad, giving her wise advice and soliciting hers in return. But then, much sooner than he expected, she had begun to walk and talk and, after that, he took care not to let her catch him at such foolishness, for fear she might make fun of him. She was two and a half years old now, and she behaved toward him with an artful combination of impudence and ingratiation, and had sometimes a way of laughing which seemed so mockingly wise that he had become persuaded, never before having studied a young female with such intense concentration and bedeviled fascination, that they were born with all the knowledge they would ever acquire, miniature but complete women with nothing more to learn, who had only to permit themselves to be transformed from tiny sorceresses into full-grown ones.

"I can't tell you," he said to Suky, at the end of this rhapsodic tirade, and now he stood beside her, for Susette seemed an adequate barricade to have raised between them, "what she means to me."

He looked at Suky shrewdly, and she gazed up at him for several moments before she smiled, saying, "I think I know, Morgan."

At that—for it seemed he had clumsily dumped out all their secrets, his and Felice's, and they lay scattered about for Suky to examine, one by one, as he had seen her examine her jewelry, searching, he had always supposed, for the flaws she expected to find—he went dashing away, muttering excuses as he went but paying no attention to whether or not they were reasonable ones, and he did not see her again for several days.

Then late one afternoon he went to her, for the Hallams had astonished him only a few hours before by agreeing to loan him fifty thousand dollars and, far from being grateful, he meant to insist that Suky explain to him why they should have changed their minds.

She was just setting out to drive in the Park, and although he hesitated when she asked him to come along, at last he climbed in. The day was clear and agreeably cold, the first day of October, and as they went circling through the Park they passed little Gothic castles where children were drinking milk and eating cookies, riding the carousel and pushing one another in swings. Rowboats and omnibuses plied the lakes, disturbing fleets of swans, and, from their hilltop, the Irish squatters and their dogs and goats gazed down at this daily pageant and enjoyed the afternoon concert of band music. Some of their shanties were extensive structures, pieced together of boxes and barrels, and they had lived there for many years, an aristocracy of ragpickers, fighting off occasional sorties made by policemen trying to drive them from this perch where they might unloose catcalls and debris upon respectable citizens taking the air below.

Morgan paid no attention to the squatters or the children in their carousels, and cast Suky an aggrieved sideways look each time she tried to draw his attention away from the subject of the Hallam loan, and what it was that had caused them to change their minds.

"It isn't enough?" she suggested.

"After all, I asked for two hundred thousand, and they'd turned it down." He caught her hand, intending to squeeze her fingers until she told him the truth.

"Perhaps they went over your maps and estimates again."

"I've got no right to that loan, Suky, and you know it."

"Your property isn't worth that much?"

"You know what I'm talking about. Why did they give it to me? Tell me the truth, I warn you—because I know, anyway."

He was glaring at her, and it was a moment before he noticed that their carriage had stopped in a confusion of traffic, just as a little girl jumped out of a nearby carriage—so swiftly and unexpectedly that coachmen reined in their horses for fear of trampling her—and ran across the road.

Women's voices cried out in alarm, men shouted at her to take care, and Morgan was out of the carriage at a bound, and, with several other men, halfway across the road in pursuit of the little girl, who carried an armful of red roses and darted expertly out of the grasp of each rescuer until, all at once, she stopped in the midst of the bridle path, with a party on horseback cantering straight toward her, and while a pandemonium of shrieks broke on all sides, the party stopped in its tracks and the child approached a young blond woman in a gray habit, riding a handsome black horse.

The little girl lifted her armful of roses as high as she could, the blond woman leaned down, tenderly smiling, and gathered them into one arm, then touched the child's cheek and spoke to her softly. The little girl made her a deep curtsy, bowing her head, and went scampering back to climb into her own carriage, leaving her rescuers strewn about the roadway, foolishly grinning.

The little girl waved, the woman kissed the tips of her fingers, and all at once she and her party were cantering on their way while the child and her nursemaid drove off, and Morgan, exchanging sheepish laughs with two or three other men, returned to Suky's carriage. The woman, he heard them telling one another, had been Allegra Stuart, no one else, for there was no one else with that gilt-blond hair or that smile or, for that matter, no one else capable of causing such an impromptu melodrama merely by going for an afternoon ride, and as he climbed into the carriage to sit beside Suky again, Morgan was saying eagerly, "That was Allegra Stuart, wasn't it? What a graceful thing to see." He turned, as if he wanted Suky to agree that they had happened upon something extraordinary, this child's tribute to the actress who, only a few nights before, had played a Lady Macbeth which had caused the students in the audience to draw her carriage back to her apartment house themselves.

But Suky did not share his excitement and, indeed, she looked ironically amused. "Surely you don't think it just happened, Morgan?"

He scarcely heard this, for they had been in the audience at that first performance of *Macbeth*, and ever since he had been wondering about her. "How beautiful she is," he said, talking with absentminded enthusiasm, as if to himself. "On the stage, of course, it's impossible to tell what a woman really looks like." Suky gave him another glance, as if he might have lost his wits, but he went on, full of wondering admiration, never asking himself if he was perhaps a

little glad for this chance to show some of the resentment he felt at
being obliged to accept Suky's help. "And she has the same smile
in real life that she had at the end of the performance." This made
him laugh, as joyously as if at some marvelous discovery, and he demanded, "Well, after all, why shouldn't she? She's the same woman."
He shook his head again and his face grew puzzled and reflective.
"That smile," he said, "that gentle, whimsical, remorseful smile."
He fell silent, thinking of the smile, and finally asked, "Where does
it come from? What does it mean?"

"I have no idea," said Suky.

This, of course, might have been only a coincidence, happening
upon Allegra Stuart and her young admirer; but then, three nights
later, he saw her again. It was late at night, nearly three o'clock, and
he had gone with Suky and Philip and Lord and Lady Haldane to one
of the balls which, he found, New Yorkers were not yet tired of
giving, and after it they had stopped at Dorlan's.

This restaurant on Fulton Street had been a part of the city's
tradition for fifty years or more, and each night was crowded with
fashionably dressed men and women, seated at bare scrubbed tables
eating oyster roasts and oyster stews and raw oysters sprinkled with
lemon juice. Ballet girls often came in to see the women's clothes
and jewelry, and while they sat enviously gawking, the men were
glad of an opportunity to gawk at them. The place was noisy and
crowded, and cooks were dancing about their fires, shoveling oysters
on and off the coals with an irresistible rhythm, as if nothing could
stop them now, for they were in the throes of an ecstatic ritual, carried quite out of themselves by the heat and the flames and the smells
of the cooking oysters.

Morgan sat enjoying the gay confusion, for he liked these gathering places of the city where men and women were so much less well
concealed than they imagined, and was so preoccupied in sorting
through the pretty faces that he, like most of the others, did not see
Allegra Stuart until she was seated at a table not far away, and then
he found her there with a sense of shocked and pleased surprise, as
if he had encountered someone he had been hoping to meet without
any expectation that it would happen.

How she had contrived to enter unnoticed this roomful of people
watching one another as avidly as any sportsman might watch for
the animal he wishes to shoot, was a mystery in itself—but there she
was, talking to the others at her table, and she seemed quite unaware
she had been discovered. Men turned, frankly interested, but the
women studied her furtively, as if they would at last unravel her secrets.

She was with Joist Barringer, who had written three articles on her
Lady Macbeth, which Morgan had read with an unusual interest.
The small pink man was Benjamin Burnish, and, of course, they
could all recognize Tamzene Twining, whose effulgent beauty
seemed to suffer some peculiar diminution beside her. The other

man was Anthony De Forest, who had played Macbeth as a bombastic lout, nervously defiant of his loving and merciless queen, and had insisted upon conducting a contest with her as to whether he should become King of Scotland, or she.

Morgan sat watching her with a kind of transfixed curiosity, for he had seen her on the stage three times during the three weeks he had been there and had taken the trouble to make a collection of various expressions and tones and gestures by which she gave, beyond the footlights, a unique grace to the idea of a woman. Her features, he found, now that she was so near, had a slight irregularity, and this created an unexpected piquancy, but although he was hoping to see the smile she had shown the little girl, that smile was not, it seemed, in her repertoire tonight.

And then, to his surprise, she looked directly at him. He quickly smiled, but her face was serious and, he thought, a little defiant, as if she meant to ask what right he had to stare at her, and, obediently apologetic, he glanced away, only to find that Philip was not only smiling at her but was receiving in reply a vague little smile, and it occurred to him that Philip might possibly know her.

For he was unaccountably eager to meet her, to study her, as it were, at closer range, examine at his leisure that quality she had of pathetic radiance, and ask her how it happened that although she was his own age, twenty-eight, she had made so much better use of those years than he had. All he wanted, he told himself, was the opportunity to ask her how she had done it, and why, and once she had told him he would be quite satisfied to go back to poking about in the Yellow Medicine, a little wiser than he had been, for he fancied that her answer might give him a clue to some puzzles in his own nature he had not yet solved.

He went the next night with Suky and Philip and the Hallams to see *The School for Scandal,* and sat there paying little attention to the play, bored when she was off the stage and keenly alert the moment she appeared, and when the intermission came he muttered to Philip that he would like to meet Miss Stuart. Philip smiled slightly, as if to say he had been expecting to hear that, and Morgan felt once again an urgent longing to smack his fist into Philip Van Zandt's face, the same longing he suspected Philip of harboring toward himself.

But nothing of the kind happened and they made their way along the dark passages beneath the stage, to find that although the green room was crowded and there was an air of festive conviviality, as if they had happened into a masquerade where the women wore tall white wigs and panniered gowns, the men ruffled lace at their throats and wrists, and bulging calves made of inflated rubber, Allegra Stuart was nowhere in sight.

They saw Tamzene Twining, her face and shoulders and hair powdered chalk white, smiling at herself in the mirror, and Anthony De Forest exercising his lower jaw. There was the second old man do-

ing a dance step, humming to himself and snapping his fingers. The
soubrette had taken off her wig and held it at arm's length, rearranging the curls, but although Morgan and Philip peered in every direction, Allegra Stuart was not there, and in a moment the call-boy was
at the door, shrilly whining, "First music over, everybody to begin!"

Morgan and Philip were on their way back along the hallway, with
the traffic passing them swiftly on every side, when Allegra appeared
ahead of them out of some other corridor and passed them by, so
preoccupied she seemed not to hear Philip's greeting. Morgan
shrugged, prepared to take the disappointment with stoic philosophy,
when she turned and stopped, smiling at Philip as they approached,
and holding out her hand. "I thought I recognized you." She scarcely
glanced at Morgan as Philip introduced him, but hurried away and
disappeared again. The music sounded more loudly, footsteps went
rushing by, and her voice called to them from the darkness, "Come
to my reception tomorrow night—you, too, Mr. Devlin."

Philip laughed softly. "You see?"

And, once again, Morgan felt that urgent craving to knock Philip
down, and assured himself with sullen jealousy there was some history between those two, for he could read it in Philip's smile and,
even more plainly, in Allegra Stuart's pretense of not recognizing
him.

He left Suky's house the next night a little after eleven and walked
the several blocks to Allegra Stuart's apartment house, for, of course,
anyone who read the newspapers knew where she lived. He went up
in the slowly crawling elevator with three other men in evening dress
and all of them marched down the hallway in solemn silence, their
heels cracking upon the marble floor, and found forty or fifty men
and women gathered in small groups about her drawing room. But,
once again, he could not find her.

This time, however, he was not so much disappointed as relieved,
for although he was eager to see her he had some dread of it, too, and
was glad to ramble about her apartment, examining at his leisure its
strange furniture, the several pictures and two portraits of her—one
as Juliet and one as Rosalind, and he stood for some moments trying
to decide which he liked best—and to make a surreptitious survey of
her guests, finding many among them he recognized from newspaper
sketches or cartoons, and others he had seen on the stage.

By the time he had been there half an hour Morgan was surprised
to find that he felt as much at home as if this place belonged to him
and the guests were his own. He joined one group and then another,
frowning thoughtfully as he listened to Benjamin Burnish issuing
warnings and premonitions of contemporary mischief-making, and
nodding with sly amusement when one of the city politicians, a Mr.
O'Neil, piously assured Joist Barringer, "Reform is at home in Tammany Hall. After all, its birthplace is Tammany."

And, before very much longer, he was so comfortable, had become
so well acquainted, not only with her house but also with her guests,

that it seemed when she did finally arrive it would be his duty to greet her and invite her in and, if he could, put her at ease.

He was still talking to Joist Barringer and Hoke O'Neil, who had fallen into political argument, when he saw her across the room, coaxing a famous Italian tenor to sing, and the man was flexing his fingers and arms like a boxer preparing to step into the ring while the guests were sitting down, fixing appreciative smiles on their faces, and all at once the tenor's voice rang through the room, startling them into a respectful silence.

But although Morgan made a conscientious effort to listen, and applauded more vigorously than anyone else each time the tenor paused, he scarcely heard him, for she sat not far away and he watched her with such concentration it seemed he must know by now as much about her, or a great deal more, than she would be willing to tell him. Still, she had taken no notice of him, and possibly had not even seen him.

It was some time later when he encountered Joshua Ching in the dining room, pacing about the table, but Joshua only recommended the claret and went on. Morgan stacked a plate with a supply of food he had no hope of eating and found a table, where, as he ate and talked to another man, he might watch her sitting between Joist Barringer and Ben Burnish, absently strumming a guitar as she listened to them, and smiling a little, as if she might be thinking of something else.

All at once, for he still supposed she had not seen him, she looked directly at him, a serious, questioning look without the trace of a smile, and he sprang out of his chair and bowed ceremoniously, then sat down again and began earnestly talking to his companion, his ears burning with shame, convinced that anyone could look at him and see that he was helplessly bewitched but too bashful even to go near her.

She began to sing then, very softly, as if she did not intend it for everyone in the room, a song called "The Irish Immigrant's Lament," and he listened, leaning eagerly forward, for it seemed she would send him some important message in that music.

> "I'm very lonely now, Mary,
> For the poor make no new friends—"

The message, if it was one, eluded him, or perhaps she was only mocking Mr. O'Neil and his ferocious friend, McDuff, and the several other Irish immigrants among her guests, and yet her voice had sorrow in it, and a rich pathos which made them sigh and shake their heads.

> "But, oh, they love the better still
> The few Our Father sends."

She bowed her head over the guitar for a moment, while all about the room the Irish immigrants were loudly blowing their noses, and Morgan was so enraptured at this spontaneous display of her power to do whatever she liked with a roomful of people, that she had disappeared into the dining room while he still sat gazing at the empty place she had left on the sofa. Carrying his plate, as if to convince whoever noticed his swift and distraught passage that he was a hungry man in pursuit of something to eat, he found her standing near the windows talking to the city's Superintendent of Market Fees and Rents. He approached them with that same menacing and desperate air, and then paused when they looked at him, for he could think of nothing to say. After a moment, however, he set the plate down with an air of great decisiveness, announcing, "Miss Stuart, I'm Morgan Devlin, we met last night—"

"I know."

He stepped back, disconcerted. "You do?"

"You're Joshua Ching's nephew. You come from—" She gestured vaguely.

"From Montana Territory. But this is where I was born—on East Fourteenth Street. I lived here until I was fifteen." He scowled, dissatisfied with himself, wondering why he should be giving her this miscellaneous information, and both she and Mr. O'Neil were watching him with curious smiles, as if waiting for what details of his history he would tell them next. and at that he began to grow angry, asking himself why she could not understand that he had come to her with an urgent message and that it was to her interest to wait a little until he got hold of himself, show him some of that sympathy she knew so well how to convey when she was on the stage, and not cheat herself of the admiration and longing and confusion he had brought her.

"So long," said Mr. O'Neil, and Morgan turned to him beseechingly.

"I'm sorry if I interrupted you, I only wanted to speak to Miss Stuart for a minute—"

"Take your time," Mr. O'Neil advised him, and when he had left them Morgan found himself more timid and ashamed than ever.

He had had some intention of explaining himself to her, telling her about the Yellow Medicine and the old Halloway claim, and whatever else might convince her he was decently occupied, but now it seemed that he had only a few leases upon shallow holes dug into a mountainside so distant it would sound no more impressive than if he bragged to her of being the architect for a town of prairie dogs.

"I wish you wouldn't smile at me," he told her pleadingly. "You make me feel like a fool. I'm acting like one, I know—I admire you, that's why." He caught hold of her arm and turned her to face the windows, saying, "Look—" as if he would show her something she had never seen before, and they stood gazing silently across the housetops to the river, where the masts were gathered like hundreds of matchsticks, pitched this way and that, and lanterns from the sidewheelers spread colored lights upon the water. "When can I see you?" he asked, so humbly he was afraid she would laugh, but she said nothing, and now she was not even smiling. "May I call tomorrow?"

She still did not look at him, and he waited, growing more anxious and more concerned, until finally she said, "I'm going to drive in the Park at three o'clock. Would you like to come?"

L I I

During the drive Morgan was as vigilant as a hunter in a dense forest, looking on all sides for Suky—although he knew quite well she did not drive until four o'clock—even contriving excuses to glance out the back window to see if she might be bearing down on them from that direction. But, though he remained bolt upright and nearly rigid during the entire hour, at last they stopped before Allegra's apartment house and he sprang out and stood beside the carriage, watching to see that she made no misstep, and she flashed by him and walked swiftly away, as if she had decided to dismiss him here on the sidewalk. Now that he had survived the drive, however, he had no intention of letting her get away from him, and he ran after her and opened the door, jostling the doorman aside, and followed her into the lobby.

"Please let me come upstairs. I want to talk to you."

"You've talked to me for an hour. You didn't have very much to say."

"I told you last night, it's because I'm in awe of you." Then he demanded, truculently, "What difference does it make whether or not I have very much to say?"

And, as if this logic had convinced her, she smiled and he followed her into the elevator, they walked down the hallway without speaking and entered her apartment which, he found, looked much larger now that no on else was there—and more imposing, too, somewhat like a medieval castle with broad, empty spaces and strange, uncomfortable furniture—and, with a nod, she sent him into the library and disappeared.

He walked around the room, arguing with himself, for he could not imagine how he came to be there. The questions he had meant to ask her disgusted him now with their impertinence, and he observed the titles of the books with a skeptical eye, asking himself if she bought them to read, or only to make an impression on besotted admirers like Morgan Devlin. He was standing by the fireplace, frowning over her handwriting, for she had written her name on the flyleaf of every book, studying the broad strokes for clues to whoever Allegra Stuart might be, hidden behind Lady Macbeth and Juliet and Rosalind, when he found her beside him, tossing a match into the fireplace and resting one elbow on the mantelpiece as she turned toward him, slightly smiling.

"You have a constant stream of callers," he told her, quoting from one of Joist Barringer's articles which, indeed, he had all but memorized. "I suppose they'll be arriving any minute now?" He looked rather bitter over that possibility.

"I suppose they will," she agreed. "I'm very capricious, though. Sometimes I see them and sometimes I don't. They like that, you know."

Her poodle came prancing into the room, paused as he discovered a stranger, and then dashed buoyantly to her side, while she stooped to pet him and introduced him to Morgan. A bell rang, footsteps crossed the drawing-room floor, and Morgan glanced at her accusingly. But she sat down and he heard the steps recross the drawing room, clattering upon the tiles and muffled as they passed over the rugs, and although he waited for whoever would walk in next, no one did.

He grinned at her, looking almost obsequiously grateful, and knelt to coax the dog to him, and began to discuss her horse with as much enthusiasm as if he meant to make her an offer for him.

She still said nothing, and as he heard himself running on he began to marvel at his extensive knowledge of highbred horses, until at last she remarked that the horse was named Bouche Dhu, and added, "That's Scottish for Black Muzzle." And then, as he took this information with a show of solemn interest, she grew thoughtful again, stroked the poodle, and he had the impression she was thinking of the part she would play that night and had possibly forgotten he was there.

All at once he leaned forward and began to talk with great earnestness and intensity, determined to tell her who he was, to peel out of the stranger's skin and let her decide what she thought of him, and when she made no interruption, asked no questions and offered no comments, but only continued to watch him with a kind of contemplative curiosity, he grew more confident and more recklessly voluble, more eager for her approval and even rather defiant, for, if she decided against him once she had heard what he had to say, then he was prepared to bundle together his schemes and ambitions and carry them out of her sight, once and for all.

He began with the Italian tenor, and went on to Ben Burnish's political theories and some of his own; he skimmed out to the Territories where he gave her a brief résumé of that life, describing the cosmopolitan character of their little cities, mentioning Indians and wild animals and road agents and other exotics likely to be of some interest to an Englishwoman, referred to Felice and Susette, more for the sake of his conscience than because he had any real hope she cared whether or not he was married, and at last he described Butte Hill, his own Yellow Medicine and the Halloway claim, and the dispute he was having with Lem Finney.

He had been talking for several minutes when she smiled at him again, murmuring, "Silver and copper and gold." At each word, a clear picture of that metal appeared before him, heaped in shining bars of unusual beauty, though it had never occurred to him before that he admired these minerals for any aesthetic reason. "That's what interests you, is it?"

He grew defensive. "Yes, that's what interests me. But not because I'm a miser, which perhaps you think, and not because I necessarily want to become rich. It interests me, to be truthful, because it's as likely as not to defeat you, no matter what you do. And because there's a very nice adjustment in mining between a man, his character, the earth itself, and his relationships with other men who want the same thing he does. And a mine is a separate world. An ugly world, stinking and treacherous, something a woman doesn't understand—and yet it has a mystery and a privacy that's peculiarly fascinating to many men."

"And, perhaps, you're hoping to leave a few footprints?" She smiled, and he saw for the first time some trace of that whimsical remorseful quality for which he had been waiting.

"Perhaps," he admitted, and all at once was wondering, quite optimistically, if it might be possible to make her fall in love with him. And this notion, which would have seemed preposterous until that expression had returned to her face, gave him a suddenly renewed confidence in the persuasiveness of concentrated masculinity.

"But sand is a fickle preservative," she reminded him. "Like the stage. Tell me—what do you know about me? What has Philip told you?"

Rather sorry that she should have changed the subject, for he had begun to sense an unusual warmth flowing between them, as if she was not so inaccessible, after all, but a woman like other women, as submissive and wanton as any of them, if only she was not taken too much for granted in the beginning, he told her, "I don't know anything about you—that you're English and Spanish, you were born in Saragossa—"

She laughed softly, shaking her head in wonderment at this tenderfoot from the Territories who knew no better than to believe what he read of an actress' publicity. "Philip didn't tell you how he happened to know me?"

"Of course not." He scowled, not so much in defense of Philip as to let her know he was a gentleman, a man she could trust, for he would not think of listening to idle gossip about her.

"And Joshua Ching? Has he told you how he met me?"

"He has not." Now he began to grow angry, for he had been imagining that Allegra Stuart was his own discovery, that other men knew her only as Rosalind or Lady Teazle, while he had penetrated those disguises and was well on his way to removing her others, too.

She sighed, marveling, he supposed, at the ways of men, who sometimes talked too much and sometimes not at all. "He didn't tell you how long he's known me or where he saw me first—or who I am?"

"What difference does it make? I've seen you do Juliet, and Lady Teazle, and Lady Macbeth. That interests me more than all the convents you were brought up in and the seven languages you speak."

"I hope so." She stood up, scattering the dog from her skirt so that he sprang to the floor and bounded across the room. "But I know them both so well—your uncle and Philip Van Zandt—and, in a way, everything that's happened to me has depended on them." He began to look gloomy, anticipating some tale of her past life he would not like to hear much better than he had liked hearing Nella Allen's story. "Not that they did me any intentional favors, either one of them." She strolled about, pausing now and then to look at a book title, then examined her portrait as Rosalind, and as she strolled she began to talk, in a voice so low that he listened with an eager anxiety, as if these confessions must reveal to him everything that was hidden behind the legend of Allegra Stuart. "To begin with, I'm not English and Spanish, I'm something much worse—I'm Irish." He laughed appreciatively at that little joke and she glanced at him sideways, smiling slyly. "My name isn't Allegra Stuart, either. It's Betty Mulligan."

"Betty Mulligan," he repeated solemnly. "A very pretty name."

She raised one eyebrow, warning him not to make fun of her and not to be too polite, or she would stop right there, tell him nothing more. "My brother is Hoke O'Neil."

"Hoke O'Neil?"

"The Superintendent of Market Fees and Rent." She turned her back on him and stood watching herself in the mirror. "You met him here last night."

"Oh, yes, of course. I remember him very well." He thought of Mr. O'Neil, pugnaciously telling Joist Barringer that Tammany Hall was the home of political reform, and as he remembered Hoke O'Neil's twisted nose and fingers, his puffed right ear and the scars on his forehead and jaw, the ivory toothpick he had flourished after dinner, he saw all at once quite a different background for Allegra Stuart from the one he had imagined. "And so there never were any convent schools in France," he said, rather sadly.

She was still standing before the mirror, and had begun to rearrange her hair, and as she removed hairpins and slid them back again, seemed as unself-conscious as if he had come to her dressing room after the performance. "No, but I do speak seven languages—or parts of them, at least, but that's only because I'm such a mimic. I went to the Mission School after our mother died—killed herself, out of despair, I suppose, at ever being able to bring up two children in Five Points. Hoke ran away from the school, but I stayed, and that's where I got my education. There, and in other places, later on. But not in any convents."

His face inadvertently showed pity and guilt, as if he might have some complicity in these crimes the Americans had committed against her family, but all at once she gave him a smile, so gay and candid, and touchingly droll, that he sprang up impulsively and went to her, not sure what he meant to do, though it seemed he must comfort her. But she retreated across the room, making a little gesture to keep him from following her.

"I was in the opera ballet for five years, that's where I learned to listen to other actors—you can always tell, if you know what to look for, when an actress has begun at the bottom. I learned to walk there, too, and so I suppose I shouldn't be too resentful that half the time I didn't have enough to eat. And I might be there yet, if it hadn't been for Philip Van Zandt and your uncle." She lowered her head, watching him, and it seemed these memories made her morbid, and rather defiant. "Now and then, when I needed money for my elocution teacher, I used to dance at men's banquets—you know, jump naked out of a papier-mâché pie and go skipping up and down the table a few times." She waited a moment to see how he would take this and, in fact, he looked embarrassed, quite dumfounded at the notion of Allegra Stuart capering about naked before a few hundred strange men.

"You must have been," he told her gallantly, "the prettiest thing any of them had ever seen."

She took this with an indifferent shrug. "Maybe I was. Anyway, that's where I met Philip, and oh, my God, but I was in love with him for awhile. He promised me all kinds of things, but all he ever gave me was an imitation Paisley shawl. And something else—something else I couldn't keep." She frowned, and looked away, and he thought she might begin to cry, but then she gave him another quick look, bright and intense. "You know what I'm talking about?"

"Yes, I think so. I'm sorry."

She began to stroll back and forth, the poodle at her heels. It had grown quite dark, but for the firelight, and as he watched her wandering about he felt that she had forgotten he was there, that he was spying on her when she imagined herself to be alone, a child or a mythical princess, singing to herself the recital of her trials and sorrows. "I was in love with him, until Joshua Ching told me he was meeting another woman in the same room, and making love to her on the same bed where he made love to me—a Mrs. Talbot." She paused, for he had given a start. "That surprises you?"

He made an expansive gesture. "Why, no, not at all. Or, rather," he admitted, "it does surprise me. As it happens, Mrs. Talbot is my wife's mother." This way of referring to her, as if their relationship was the merest accident, would, he hoped, put Coral Talbot into a less compromising position to himself than if he had called her his mother-in-law.

But even so, Allegra laughed, a sound full of provocation and bitterness. "Your wife's mother. Well, I'm not surprised. Then of course you can guess that I met Joshua Ching because he found out that I knew Philip. He's a very economical man, your uncle—I doubt if there's ever been anyone he couldn't find a use for." She was smiling so enigmatically that Morgan grew alarmed, for by now he was ready to believe she had only pretended to tell him her secrets, when in fact she had been learning his, and there was nothing he was more eager to conceal than his guilty memories of Coral Talbot. All at once, in a tone of light-hearted mockery, she raised her voice, declaiming: " 'She was a harlot and he was a thief, but they loved each other beyond belief.' " He gave an outburst of laughter, and she tilted her head to one side. "Are you sorry I've spoiled your illusions about your relations?"

"I didn't have as many illusions about them as you might imagine."

"Or about Allegra Stuart?" But before he could invent a proper answer, she said, "You must go away now, or I'll be thinking of you when I shouldn't. I have to be at the theater at seven o'clock." In the vestibule she turned, smiling up at him, but just what it was that amused her now—the bewilderment he could not conceal, or these several ironic mishaps of her own life—he could not guess. "You see how accidental life is?"

"Can I see you tonight?"

"No. I'm busy." Her poodle sat on the floor, watching him warily, as if he might be about to bark and send him off.

"Tomorrow?"

"What for? I only fall in love nowadays with men who can help me." But he looked so embarrassed at that, ashamed to be told he could be of no use to her, she took pity on him. "Will you take me to a German beer garden tomorrow afternoon?"

"I'll take you anywhere you like. You'll attract a great deal of attention at a place like that."

She laughed delightedly, clapping her hands, and seemed as eager for the excursion as if it were an entertainment quite unknown to the rest of the city's population which would, as usual, occupy Sunday by eating a great deal, dozing through long sermons, reading the newspapers to which Americans were addicted as other nations were addicted to wine or garlic or limburger cheese, taking naps and, finally, worn out with boredom, go to bed with the conviction that at least they had not sinned through enjoyment.

"Wait until you see me," she told him. "I've been there before. I go other places, too, but I've never been recognized when I didn't want to be. When it comes to disguises I could give lessons to the street beggars. I'll see you at four o'clock, on the corner—that one." She opened the door, motioning him out, for he was not at all eager to go. "Don't follow the wrong woman." She laughed, and the door closed softly.

He stood outside the apartment house, wondering if it might be that while he had been plotting to have her fall in love with him he had inadvertently fallen in love with her, but after a moment he confidently assured himself no such thing was possible and set out to walk back to the hotel, where he sat down to write the letters he had been neglecting.

Still, he was not eager to go to Suky's house for dinner, as he usually did on Saturday nights when, by tradition, all members of the family gathered, for he was sure that Suky or anyone else would be able to look at him and see this unusual preoccupation as plain on his face as if he had carefully written the information across his forehead. And so he sent a note to Suky, telling her he was on his way to Baltimore to meet their latest ore shipment, and began to wonder how he would contain his impatience until the next day.

While he ate breakfast he talked to strangers about the country's desperate political condition, wandered through the lobbies, read the newspapers and tinkered with a model for a new stamp mill, and grew more and more restless and discontented as he stared out at the gray sky and heavy rain which seemed sure to spoil their plans, and was unreasonably joyous when, a little after one, the rain stopped, though the sky grew no lighter. And promptly at three-thirty he stood on the corner she had indicated, smoking a cigar and hoping she had not forgotten all about him.

He tramped up and down, pretending that he was trying to keep warm, and expected he would be driven away for loitering. He was approached by several beggars and three whores, and when it was five minutes to four he decided she had never intended to make any such excursion and was, no doubt, peeking out her window at that moment and laughing at him.

In another few minutes a young girl came toward him, walking with a sprightly bouncing step, swinging her reticule and glancing about with such eager inquisitiveness he decided she was either another whore or an Irish parlormaid dressed in her finery and on her way to meet her beau, some blunt-nosed young footman she would presently marry and spend the rest of her life berating for his drunkenness. She wore an old-fashioned sealskin coat with a tear in the hem and so much too large for her that it must have been the gift of her mistress, and as she lifted her skirts to keep them out of the sidewalk puddles, he saw that she wore black and red striped stockings and laced black boots. Her hair was the color of cinnamon and looked like nothing so much as a mass of burnt straw, pinned carelessly on top of her head; and as she passed him, veering over to come quite near, she smiled, showing her teeth and closing her eyes, and spoke to him in a thick brogue. "Sure, and it's me all right. Come along, come along, or have you changed your mind?" She beckoned him with her thumb as she went on.

Morgan caught up with her and she linked her arm through his, smiling at him again, this new smile which changed her face, giving her the lively and inconsequential appearance of so many of the immigrant Irish girls who answered doors and served dinners and wheeled baby carriages all over the city. She looked, in fact, as frivolous and wild as any little biddy he had seen, and she looked several years younger as she walked swiftly along, clinging to his arm with a kind of feminine desperation, talking gaily about what a treat they would have, telling him she wanted to walk for the day was a fine one, or nearly so, and she could look at the people they passed, adding in an undertone that usually she could not because they were looking at her.

They passed Madison Avenue, where a few brownstone houses alternated with vacant lots, and went on to Fourth Avenue which, that far north, was lined with stables and tenements where chickens went clucking about the muddy yards, and by the time they reached Lexington Avenue he had stopped being concerned that Suky or Coral Talbot or anyone else he knew would have strayed so far east. At almost the same time, the moment he felt quite safe from discovery, he also stopped worrying about his several obligations and became as irresponsible as she was pretending to be, telling himself that he was now a tourist, someone who has lost his problems only by being in a foreign country where his ordinary character, because it was unknown, has ceased to exist. And, as she chattered along, sometimes using the brogue and sometimes not, he found he had grown as comfortable and as affectionately patronizing as if she were in fact the little Irish parlormaid she had admitted to being today.

As they got farther south she began exchanging insults and obscenities with the urchins who came pestering them for coins, and her vocabulary was so extensive they either drew off to survey her suspiciously, or burst into surprised laughter and followed them for a block or two. "I've been everywhere in this town," she confided. "Wherever I live I must see everything. Otherwise, I'm so protected nowadays I'd lose all sense of reality—I'd forget who I am. Once," she murmured, "I went down to Chambers Street dressed like a bootblack." She pitched her voice to a nasal whine. "Care to have your boots blacked, sir?" She laughed merrily. "I made a dollar and fifty-seven cents in three hours, what do you think of that? Someday I'll show you myself as a bootblack—dirty face and arms and bare feet and a wig that looks as if the dog's been chewing it. I have other disguises, too, you'll see." She was talking, between her exchanges with the children who scampered along beside them, as if they were two old friends who often made these excursions together, and seemed to believe as much in the veracity of her Irish parlormaid as she believed in Rosalind or Lady Macbeth.

They passed ragmen with their pushcarts and clanging bells, and old-clothes men with a dozen hats piled on their heads. She paused to examine the popular ballads which hung from strings on railings, and he bought her a few pages which she crumpled together and thrust into her reticule. From time to time, the elevated train rattled overhead, scattering sparks and ashes and hot oil down upon those who cowered against the walls, and, each time, she huddled in his arms until it had passed, then looked up with an inquisitive smile, seeming to ask if they had survived that catastrophe, and they went on.

Farther downtown the street was so densely crowded they could make only slow progress, and here they passed one slovenly hotel after another, alternating with dance houses and saloons, where young whores carrying black bottles of gin went in and out the slatted doors in such numbers it seemed there might be, as some reformers estimated, ten thousand of them in the city. Clangorous music brayed from every doorway, and on all sides they heard Chinese and Spanish and Italian, spoken by men and women in their native dress. Deformed beggars approached them, pointing to empty eye sockets, withered and red, or displayed festering lumps upon their necks or heads, and there were some who had neither arms nor legs but lay upon the sidewalks like misshapen melons, covered with rags.

He kept close hold on her now, but she neither cringed at sight of the maimed beggars, complained of the stenches, nor drew away from the hands which reached out and tried to catch hold of them—as if to remind them that they were young and healthy and owed them something in exchange for those advantages—but every now and then she glanced up at him, asking what he thought of all this, and he heard her give a light sigh.

At last they entered a building as big as an auditorium, and were instantly enveloped by voices and laughter and waltz music and the smells of German food. A band played on a balcony at one end, the vast arched roof was covered with frescoes and imitation vines, and long tables were crowded with German families, singing and gossiping, taking their Sunday dinner. She made her way deftly across the sanded floor, moving between the tables as if she knew exactly where to find a place for them, and near the far end of the room she gestured at two seats where they might sit facing each other across the table.

The room was hot and she let the coat fall back, showing that its lining was threadbare and torn, and she gave an impatient gesture of tucking away loose tendrils of her cinnamon-colored wig. Her dress was striped black and white, the stripes running every which way, and it had long sleeves, very wide at the wrists and surrounded by crumpled white ruffles. The bustle, as he noticed when she twisted about, craning her neck to see who was in the balconies, was decorated with ruffles and black velvet bows, a humorous little bustle which, no doubt, was the parlormaid's especial pride.

She pushed up the loose sleeves, leaned her elbows on the table top, and gave him a long list of the food she was going to eat, apparently inspired by the quantities of sausages which lay steaming upon piles of sauerkraut carried by waiters who careened past at a perilous rate, and while he gave their order she began talking in German to the woman who sat beside her, praising her nursing baby so effusively the woman grinned and blushed and her husband, gruffly modest, beat the table in time to the music until the plates clattered and the beer steins jumped.

Then, the moment the waiter was gone, she signaled Morgan that she wanted to dance and was halfway across the room before he could catch up with her, weaving her hips as she went, and attracting nearly as much attention as if she had not bothered with the disguise, after all. He watched her moving swiftly along, admiring this sensual new walk, studying her narrow waist and straight back, rising from the ingeniously bunched skirt with a kind of youthful and touching pride, and the tendrils of the cinnamon-colored wig curling on her bare neck gave him a longing to put his mouth there which became a poignant and almost painful yearning.

At the dance floor she turned, lay both hands on his shoulders, as they danced in the concert-saloons, he took hold of her waist, and they went bounding about among the other dancers in a strenuous polka, and all the while she watched him, smiling that parlormaid's smile and occasionally gave her head such a shake it seemed the wig would topple off. She cavorted about as enthusiastically as if she were still in the opera ballet; the polka was followed by a mazurka and the mazurka by a schottische, and soon he was grateful for the training he had had in these exercises during the hours he hung about the Bella Union, waiting for Ula Malloy. Then, without a word, she started back to their table and he went after her in desperate haste, convinced she was as capricious as she had said and might take the notion to disappear before he could catch her.

But she sat at the table, picking at the sausages and sauerkraut, the potato pancakes and slabs of stinking cheese, sipping the beer, and looked so reflective and troubled he expected to hear that she had had enough of beer gardens and parlormaids, and enough of him, too. She still said nothing, once or twice she smiled, perhaps to reassure him, for he suspected he might be looking as anxious as he felt, and all at once he discovered a ravenous appetite and began to eat with greedy impatience.

"Do you know why I told you all that yesterday?" she asked him finally.

"Because you wanted to. Why you wanted to, doesn't matter, does it?"

"Yes, it does. It does to me. I told you because you were beginning to fall in love with Allegra Stuart—weren't you? I could see it happen," she added, as if to warn him she had the evidence and there was no use trying to fool her. "And all at once I got to worrying about Betty Mulligan."

But it seemed by now only an accomplished fact she stated, not the mere possibility he had mistaken it for yesterday, or half an hour ago, and he said, "You're right, of course. I am in love with you," and went on eating as resolutely as if he intended to undertake a long and hazardous journey and must be well nourished for it.

"I knew it, I can tell. Because it happens quite often, you know. There are several men in love with me right now."

"I should think so," he agreed, still eating with unappeased hunger, and watching her with a rapt intensity. "Everyone you know. Why wouldn't they be?"

She began tapping off her conquests on one finger after another. "Joist Barringer is in love with me, but he isn't my lover. Anthony De Forest was for awhile, but *Macbeth* finished that. Dyke Ferguson." She shrugged. "And two or three Englishmen." She gave an impudent laugh, watching to see if she had made him jealous; but jealousy, it seemed, was drowned for the moment in admiration and desire, and now she leaned forward and began talking in a low voice, urgent and conspiratorial. "But the only one I love is Ferguson—shall I tell you why? Because he's the greatest manager in America, the greatest manager I've ever known, though so help me I hate to admit it—and no star is ever as important as the manager. If it hadn't been for Ferguson, I would never have tried *Macbeth*." She sat back, as if the thought of all she had endured to play that part made her gloomy, and shook her head, sighing. "And if he weren't in Europe now, looking for someone to take my place when I leave next May, we wouldn't be here. Do you know—he wants to marry me?" She raised her eyebrows at this incredible piece of information and immediately became the parlormaid again, fiddling ineffectually with her wig, for whatever strands she pinned up quickly came undone.

"And are you going to marry him?" For somehow this news of a possible marriage was more disturbing than all her talk of lovers, for lovers could not interfere with his own plans, and a husband might.

"I can't, I'm married. But I probably wouldn't marry him anyway, I was married long enough to have become suspicious of it." She leaned on the table, beckoning, as if to draw him a little nearer, and looked all at once like her portrait as Rosalind. "You're curious about me, aren't you?"

Morgan made a deprecating gesture, ready to protest against such a frivolous reason for his admiration, and then grinned, for her smile was quizzical and a shade accusatory and he thought it would do him no good to lie. "I wouldn't call it curiosity."

"Of course you are. You're curious, and so you want to be my lover. Do you deny it?"

"No, I don't deny it. I want to."

"A man thinks he never knows anything about a woman until he's made love to her, but that's not always so. It depends on the man—and on how she feels about him."

"I know," he agreed, and supposed she meant to tell him he could find out nothing, whatever he might persuade her to let him do, for she did not love him. Still, the moment struck him as a crucial one, not to be lost, and he stood up, got her into the coat as efficiently as if she were a doll or a child, and hurried her across the room, thrusting a bill at the waiter, and guiding her resolutely when she turned to protest that she wanted something more to eat, and had not danced enough to satisfy her.

It had grown dark and the lamps of the street vendors glimmered along the sidewalk, and, before she could object that she wanted to walk, he hailed a cab and pitched her into it. And there she sat far in the corner, withdrawn and silent, as if she were alone and caught up in a contemplation of all the disappointments of her lifetime, and Morgan fell to asking himself why he should be convinced that his failure or success with Allegra Stuart was to show him the pattern of all future failure or success, and yet he had the conviction, and it grew stronger. But how he might have come by these dark and secret vices of superstition, he could not explain.

A little farther along they passed one of those sights which had become usual in the city these past few years—a group of men who had taken the garbage barrels from in front of several houses, strewing their contents over the sidewalk, and broken the barrels up to make a fire at the corner of a vacant lot, and there they stood, on this chill October night, warming themselves at the flames and looking, Morgan reflected, like nothing so much as a gang of hobgoblins making ready to broil some unwary human captured from the earth above.

They watched the men, and she murmured, "How ugly it is—it gives me a gnawing at the heart. There's too much sorrow in the world, too much, too much." She looked at him reproachfully. "How silly it is to pretend to be gay, or try to laugh. Why did I do it this afternoon, I wonder? Was it to impress you?" He said nothing and they rode on, jolting about on the hard seat, and fell silent again.

"What are you going to do tonight?" he asked her finally. "See your friends?"

"I have no friends." She gave him another reproving glance. "Only votaries." She turned her head aside. "But I have some enemies who keep me company."

This made him uneasy, as if her enemies must necessarily be his own, and it was his duty to find and punish them. "You have enemies? You must imagine it."

"Oh, no, not the kind I have. I know just who they are, too—shall I tell you? One I was married to, one is a stranger, and one pretends to be a friend." She turned to him, but now the Irish parlormaid was gone and she looked subdued and inconsolable. "That isn't much to complain of, I suppose—since life never makes any of us as happy as we think we deserve."

The hack stopped and once more she was out of it before he had moved, so that he went sprinting after her and got into the elevator only in time, forcing the doors apart with both hands, and though he turned to her with a pleading look, she stared sullenly at her feet.

At the eighth floor, she once again hurried out and went running down the hall, her heels giving out clicking taps and his own booted feet striking a ponderous echo as he raced after her, took the key, and unlocked the door. The vestibule had one light burning, there was a light or two somewhere beyond, and he supposed the apartment might be empty, the servants gone out on Sunday night. She let him remove her coat, but when she started away again he caught her by the shoulders and held her fast, while she quickly protested, "I won't fall in love with you."

This denial turned him as joyous and exultant as if it had been no warning but an admission, and he began to kiss her. "Yes, you will. You will—you have."

L I I I

All the while they traveled across the country, rattling along in the overheated little yellow trains, scrambling for meals in crowded restaurants once they got too far west for dining cars, pitching about in stagecoaches while Humphrey Scannell looked increasingly disconsolate and suffered new symptoms from western food and western water and western whisky, Morgan had shown him as much solicitude as if he were a dying invalid left in his care, and nearly as much tenderness as if he were a beautiful woman. But, it seemed, there were men intended by nature to go west and men intended to stay at home, and Humphrey Scannell would not be beguiled into finding interest in the landscape, he would not shoot at distant antelope from the train windows, and he gazed with a mournful eye at mirages, as if to prove he was not so much a tenderfoot as to find anything extraordinary in the sight of towns and herds of cattle upside down, or vast blue lakes where a moment ago green fields had been.

In Helena, Morgan gave him into Jonathan's charge to house and feed him for a day or two, and warned his brother never to let him out of his sight but to keep him entertained, even if he could not impress him, for Humphrey Scannell was the type of tenderfoot determined to despise whatever he saw on the frontier. Even so, Scannell grudgingly remarked to Morgan when they met early the next morning at Devlin Brothers where he sat amusing himself with their gold scales, the first acceptable toy anyone had so far found for him, "You seem pretty well fixed here, Devlin, all things considered. What do you need the Hallams' money for?"

Morgan laughed heartily, exchanging sharp, fierce glances with Jonathan over Scannell's head, and gave him a whack across the shoulders so violent that Scannell sprang up, ready to defend himself against this rude western affection, and Morgan laughed again to reassure him. "Wait until we get to Butte, Scannell. This camp's well developed." He went out quickly. "Don't forget—you're having dinner with us tonight at my mother's house. Come before six and I'll introduce you to my nineteen-day-old son."

He had gotten Marietta's telegram the day he left New York, and, unbelievable as the news had seemed when he contemplated it, once he saw the baby he discovered that he was now a seasoned husband and father, glad to have him, but not at all so nonplused as he had been by Susette, and he even thought it likely a son would be more interesting once he had grown into a boy. The baby was named William, but he had left it to Felice to tell that to her father.

He had been born, as it happened, on the same day Morgan had gone with Allegra Stuart to the beer garden, and although he expected this coincidence would give him some guilty qualms once he confronted Felice, he was surprised to find that instead there seemed a mystic bond between those two events, although not one he was eager to unravel. He smiled at Felice with all the confidence of a virtuous conscience, held her in his arms very gently, and found he had been able to persuade himself that the distance between Felice, here in Helena, and himself with Allegra Stuart in New York, was in reality a distance in time so great that his feelings for these two women might have been separated by many years. This reasoning occurred to him as somewhat too simple to be honest, but he thought he might better accept what he could not bring himself to regret.

Susette, however, asked where he had been and what he had been doing, and all the while he was explaining the duties which had kept him away she sat on the floor, singing softly to herself and stroking the cat Shekel, now become a staid and sleepy dowager whose descendants lived in cabins and stores and ranches all over the mountains. And when he finished the recital she gave him a wisely confidential glance, as if she knew there was a lie here somewhere but was not sure exactly where it lay hidden. At that, he knelt and clasped about her wrist a bracelet of woven gold, with two hearts dangling from it, and watched while she examined it, turning her hand to set the hearts swinging to and fro, but still he could not be sure he had bought her complete forgiveness.

Even so, he was no sooner out of sight of Felice and Susette and seated in the crowded coach beside Humphrey Scannell, when he fell to thinking again of Allegra Stuart.

As they went rocking and pitching along, ore samples and whisky bottles were passed from hand to hand, while Humphrey Scannell sat with a look of stupefied resentment and, as the hours passed, his skin turned from white to yellow and from yellow to green, until at last he was forced to hang out the window, with Morgan keeping a grip on his belt and smiling absently into the face of the man who sat opposite him, their knees entangled, their booted feet shifting about to gain an advantage, remembering the last time he had seen her, hurrying down that same unlighted corridor where, five days earlier, Philip Van Zandt had introduced them—and as she reached the end of it Allegra had turned, waved once to him, and disappeared.

"Think about me sometimes, won't you?" she had asked, and when he started to protest that she must see him again, whispered. " 'Bid me farewell,' " reminding him of those last words of Rosalind's she had just spoken from the stage; and the next day he was on his way with the Hallams' geologist.

He had thought about her, and indeed could not keep her out of his thoughts, and by now it seemed likely he would be thinking of her for all the rest of his life, singing "The Irish Immigrant's Lament" as a lesson in irony to her guests, playing Lady Teazle or Lady Macbeth, or lying naked beside him when he awoke on Monday morning in her bedroom, leaning on one elbow and watching him with a contemplative curiosity which turned to laughter when he saw her and sat up, momentarily baffled by these strange surroundings.

All at once she was out of bed and had slipped on a white flannel wrapper, crossed the room on tiptoe, and with a flourish whisked away the cloth which covered Consuelo's cage, demanding, "What brought you here?"

The bird, not at all taken aback, retorted, "Bad company, by God!" and she rewarded him with several slices of apple which he seized with greedy ill nature and fell to muttering over, until she warned him he must be civil or be banished to the kitchen and that, she said, was purgatory to him, for the chef was his mortal enemy.

She came back and stood gazing at Morgan, drew her hair away from her face and twined it about the top of her head and then let it go again, and all the while seemed to be studying his history and his character and, he did not doubt, making more discoveries about both than he ever had. In another few moments he expected she would begin to regret what had happened, or would coax him to make her some promises, and he began to wonder which ones he could make with the least dishonesty. But, instead, she kissed him lightly and went out, saying she would bring their breakfast.

She set the table near the fireplace and was for a few minutes absorbed as a child playing with dishes, then stood back, clasping her hands and smiling at the pretty arrangement she had made. "There it is. My favorite breakfast." Her favorite breakfast, he was disappointed to find, was a silver rack filled with crisp toast, a terrine of *pâté de foie gras,* and a bottle of champagne. But then, of course, she might think the breakfast was not only something to eat for hunger's sake, but a way of celebrating the discoveries they had made last night.

When they sat down, she once again fell silent, although now and then she glanced up and smiled, fed the dog two or three crackers soaked in champagne but took only a few sips herself, and left most of her favorite breakfast to Morgan, who ate it eagerly, and he began to think she was waiting for him to leave—speak a few appropriate words, and go away.

But before he had quite finished the *pâté*, drunk the last of the champagne, or decided how he must make his way out of her bedroom, she leaned back, stretched her arms above her head and her legs out straight, tensing and relaxing her muscles like an awakening cat, drew her knees up to her chin, folding her arms across them, and began to watch him steadily, until finally, to defend himself against that bold curious gaze, he laughed aloud.

"I was thinking about you," she admitted. "What is it that sends so many of you Americans west?"

He grinned, relieved she had asked a question he could answer, for he was still expecting to be called upon to explain his ready infidelity, and the absence of that remorse which, she must be thinking, was the least he might protest. "We don't go west for the scenery, I can promise you that—except maybe for an occasional tenderfoot, and he soon finds out the scenery is too damn much for him and leaves. We go, or most of us do, to find the same thing you find in the theater."

"You go to find your antagonist, the one you fear enough to respect." She smiled. "Is that it?"

"I think so."

"But life is the only real antagonist, haven't you found that out yet?" She cocked an eyebrow at him, and then, like a busy housewife reminded of her chores, she gathered the plates and silver upon the tray and carried it out, ushering the poodle ahead with a nudge of her bare foot, and Morgan decided once again that she had given him the signal to leave. She would have callers, he supposed, later in the morning, and he imagined she must have a complicated formula to follow in getting ready for her performance that night. But he still sat there, staring with quite a gloomy face and prepared to plead his case with her, when the door opened and closed and the next moment she was beside him, waiting to be kissed.

Before she left for the theater, a little after six, they stood in the library, drinking coffee, and she fell into another spell of reflective silence, until all at once she said, "I'll act for you tonight. Will you be there?"

"Of course."

"It isn't good for me, but I'll do it."

This, he supposed, was her way of saying good-bye to him. But even so, he waited for her when the performance was over with a curious feeling of anxiety and sadness, and when she came off the stage and found him there she looked as much surprised as if she met some stranger who was determined to stop her, and walked quickly away, saying, "Think about me sometimes, won't you?" And so he had, with a far deeper sense of loss than she might have expected, so that even now, as he held onto his captive geologist lest he go bouncing out prematurely, he had a conviction that somehow his adventure with Allegra Stuart had set into motion a whole series of rewards which would now move irresistibly forward to be claimed by him.

As they approached Butte, the driver rose to his feet, lashing his horses' backs, swearing and exhorting, the coach picked up speed, and Humphrey Scannell threw Morgan one last agonized pleading glance and sank into his corner seat, his eyes shut fast and sweat streaming over his face, and even after the coach had stopped and the other passengers went scrambling out, he still lay there, and paid no attention as Morgan jogged his arm, gently urging him to get out and have a look at this mountain metropolis, see for himself the wonders they had accomplished.

The camp did not, it was true, look any neater than it had two or three years ago. The streets were still heaped with manure and littered with garbage, and trash dumps burned on vacant lots all over the city. But Bruno Favorite's was no longer the only saloon, there were four hotels, wooden sidewalks were sheltered by striped awnings, and there were several new boarding houses and carpenter shops and law offices, a foundry and a blacksmith's shop, and the opera house would soon be ready for its first performance. Piles of lumber and stone stood before dozens of partly built houses, and the merry sound of hammers and saws cheered citizens and visitors alike, for no one might hold himself aloof very long from the energizing effects of a western boom.

Morgan found that his new house was not so nearly finished as he had expected, and he and Humphrey Scannell settled in adjoining rooms at the Hotel de Mineral, for he wanted to keep Scannell under his constant surveillance lest he be seduced by Lemuel Finney, overhear rumors about his own activities he thought improper for Scannell's ears, or possibly fall into intimate conversation with Amos Muspratt. He kept, therefore, a close and jealous guard upon him, first under the pretense of hospitality and solicitude, and then, as Scannell become more at ease, Morgan developed an extraordinary respect for his opinion and would not so much as enter the Yellow Medicine without sending Scannell down first so that he might question him about seams and fissures, timbering and hoists and water levels, and found so many nuances to each question that Scannell never mentioned he had answered those same questions three days ago.

The Yellow Medicine now had a whim-house, an ore-shed, and a shaft-house; the barrel had been replaced by a hoisting works driven by a fifteen-horsepower steam engine; several tons of ore lay at the mouth of its shaft, and Morgan surveyed it with pride, for it had begun to look as a mine should, a clutter of cabins like a miniature city above the ground and, down below, a black warren of alleyways and alcoves forming a net which spread into the earth on three levels and which employed eighteen men on three shifts a day every day of the week. And it made its own contribution of reassuring noise to the increasing din, for certainly men grew optimistic in a silver camp in proportion as the camp grew noisier, and when a tenderfoot could not sleep but lay awake listening to the roar of the underground blasts, starting up out of a half-sleep when the building quivered and his bed shook, covered his ears to shut out the piercing whistles and prayed for even a few minutes' respite from the steady drumming of the stamps, dropping upon the ore day and night, then, indeed, the camp might be said to be well under way.

Morgan led Humphrey Scannell to Favorite's Saloon twice a day and sometimes left him there in Bruno's custody, while he went about the business he could not attend to with Scannell at his elbow. He inspected Lem Finney's new quartz mill, and congratulated Jake Finney on his recent marriage to Anna Grace Burgess, though Lisette had told him that Erma Finney had delayed for three years this marriage to the girl who had once kissed Homer Grimes. He patted the sides of the separating pans with familiar affection, whistled admiringly as the ore came pouring down the chutes, rocked on his heels and hummed as he watched the machinery run through its complicated dance, and all the while felt his flesh crawl with a crueler jealousy than he harbored toward Philip Van Zandt.

But when he tried to wheedle Jake into telling him how much it had cost, Jake grinned slyly and led him outside. And he had no better luck with Homer Grimes when he sneaked back a few days later, thinking Homer might be easier to pry free of his secrets.

"No one knows that but Mr. Finney," said Homer virtuously.

"You won't be shipping to Baltimore any more, I suppose?"

"We certainly won't. And we'll do custom work, at forty-five dollars a ton."

Morgan laughed. "Not mine, you won't. Anyway, I'll be making some improvements in my own equipment during the winter."

"Good luck," said Homer, and Morgan longed to pick him up and throw him against the side of the building, but gave him a cordial smile and walked away.

He also paid several visits to Amos Muspratt, but only when he knew Humphrey Scannell was safely closeted with Bruno Favorite, listening to tales of the early days. For Amos Muspratt, like some other miners who had no money but knew their claims to be rich, had been so captured by the enthusiasm of the past several months that he had bought hoisting machinery and installed it while Morgan was away, and it was Bruno's advice that Amos Muspratt was now in debt to a Salt Lake City bank for seven thousand dollars.

"And so far as that poor son of a bitch is concerned," whispered Bruno, "it might just as well be seven million."

Amos Muspratt had always looked to Morgan a man designed by nature to give other men fine opportunities, and this had made him remarkably patient with Amos over the years, while he tried to persuade Amos that a miner who could not afford to work his claim and would not let another man work it was something in the nature of a national calamity, no more patriotic than if he had taken part in the Crédit Mobilier, the Tweed Ring, the Black Friday attempt to corner the nation's gold, or any of the other devices by which men seemed as determined to wreck the nation as to develop it.

But Muspratt had a miner's stubborn reluctance to relinquish a piece of ground on which he had spent hard physical labor, and when he came up to meet Morgan at the top of the shaft, it seemed that Amos regarded him with more suspicion than ever.

"I haven't found what I was looking for," he told Morgan, who squatted on his heels, rummaging absently among the rocks underfoot and hoping to find some evidence among them. "Maybe it's true the ores don't hold to the deep."

"Maybe it is, Amos. But you must be down three hundred feet by now?" He watched Amos carefully, but got only the same weary sigh and suspicious glance.

"Three hundred feet? Christ Almighty, Devlin, there isn't a shaft that deep on the whole hill."

"Do you want to sell us what you have? We'll ship it east for you at twenty-five percent."

"Maybe I'll try Finney's new mill. They say it's the best we've got, and he was here the other day looking for business."

"At forty-five dollars a ton, Amos?" Morgan inquired, politely surprised a man so wise as Amos Muspratt would consider such a foolhardy agreement. "It scarcely pays you to hoist it at that rate. Well, Amos, I'm glad to see you're getting along so well." He gave him a reassuring smile which appeared and disappeared almost before Muspratt had detected it, leaving only the suggestion that it was Morgan Devlin who was his true friend, not Lem Finney, no matter what Lem Finney might say about it. He started down the hillside, but then turned, as if some remarkably clever idea had just occurred to him. "Amos—how about twenty-five thousand, cash?"

"But why my claim?" Amos asked him plaintively. "Why, old Phineas Pease has twenty-five claims better than this one, and he's giving them away. Go buy up the whole batch, why don't you?"

"You know why I want yours, Amos," and he pointed, to Muspratt's left, at the old Halloway claim, and to his right, where two claims of his own lay on the far side of the one Homer Grimes had patented three years ago. "It's the only economical way there is to work this damned low-grade ore. And, after all, Amos, someone should work it—you'll agree with that, I hope?"

Amos sighed, shrugged, and disappeared down the shaft, and Morgan told Bruno, "If I didn't want that property myself, I'd feel sorry for the poor old bastard."

Humphrey Scannell was still there after three weeks, creeping into narrow crevices, going up and down in ore buckets, and peering at streaks upon the walls, and Morgan was beginning to feel he had been condemned for some obscure crime to carry an incubus about on his shoulders and might never be able to throw him off. When Scannell was shown a vein of silver five feet wide, he found fault with it for not being seven; when he was told the camp now had several good copper prospects, he remarked that these metals should not be indiscriminately mingled; and when Morgan pleaded with him to recommend a loan which would let him go below the water line, Scannell shook his head, saying, "The ores become poorer, Devlin, the nearer you approach the water line. The most ignorant miners I've talked to are agreed on that."

"He may be right," Bruno said, although not in Scannell's hearing.

"He isn't, though," Morgan assured him. "I'm a better geologist than he is."

In the hope of sending him on his way, Morgan and Douglas and Bruno began to tell him tales of epidemics, men carried off by typhoid and pneumonia, and described reports of such deaths in the *Helena Post.* They stood about at the end of the day and exchanged the latest tragedies, sighing over old friends who had died or who presently lay near death, and Scannell listened with an anxious face. "This happens every year, you say?"

"Every year. Regular as clockwork."

"If a man survives the first winter," said Bruno, mopping the bar with his habitual weaving motion, "he's got a better chance the next year. It's the pilgrims who cash in first."

"I'll agree the climate's peculiar," said Scannell, and they laughed with loud appreciation.

"Peculiar is the word for it." Douglas nodded. "An eighty-degree change in one day is average."

"But what the hell, we live in Butte to make money," Morgan told him philosophically. "We didn't come here for our health."

"No, no, of course not," Scannell agreed, and three days later announced that his inspection had been completed. "I'll recommend eighty thousand, that's the best I can do with a clear conscience. A man in my position cannot afford mistakes."

Morgan saw him off on the stage for Corrine, sitting on top of the coach this time, for Scannell had declared he would prefer being pitched into a ravine to suffering that seasickness again, and, during the last few minutes before it left, Morgan plied him with promises of everlasting affection and respect, clasped him heartily about the shoulders, and stood watching as the coach disappeared into a cloud of its own making, exchanging one last farewell wave. Then he turned, his face showing a kind of ferocious joy, as crafty and triumphant as if he had won a great sum at poker, and ran most of the way to the Yellow Medicine with all the eager excitement of a man parted too long from a woman he loved, returning to her at last without the presence of spying and envious bystanders to spoil his pleasure.

"Thank Christ," he told Douglas, "the son of a bitch is gone. Now let's get to work."

He was still waiting to hear from Frederic Hallam when Amos Muspratt told him sadly that he would sell him his claim for thirty thousand dollars in gold. Morgan gave a mock start. "There isn't another claim in camp that's sold for anything like that, Amos."

"Finney offered me twenty-eight. He'd go to thirty, I think—don't you?"

"Amos," Morgan asked him, "would you do that to an old friend? Give me a month and I'll have it for you."

"My bankers won't give me a month."

"Give me a week, then."

Amos smiled, curious and skeptical. "Where'll you get it? You've spent a lot of money lately, it seems to me," he added reproachfully, for he could not understand how it was that other men were able to borrow money when he could not.

And, of course, this was the first puzzle which every miner must solve, for silver was more expensive to mine than gold, and copper was more expensive still, and it was Morgan's belief, which he shared with Muspratt and a few others, that the big butte was made of copper, a vast block of it thrust up out of the earth, covered over with silver and, as a kind of frosting, scattered with gold, an ingenious natural camouflage, Morgan told himself, as if he and nature had collaborated upon this scheme for deceiving less perceptive men. The gold, or most of it, had been scraped off by now, and he thought the Yellow Medicine would produce silver enough to let him go down to where the copper lay in Muspratt's claim for, if he found it there in the quantities he expected, he was convinced it must cross the country like a great underground dike, rising and falling, approaching the surface and then crawling deeper, and that one day he would encounter it in the Yellow Medicine and in his other claims.

Terrified that Amos would break his promise, he rode to Helena and went to call on Irene Flint. He arrived late in the afternoon and dashed up to Jeremy Flint's three-story brick house, where the shades were usually drawn, either to discourage visitors or because this former madam still preferred to live by artificial light, passing an iron chamois with yellow glass eyes which lay on the lawn, and Fong Chong opened the door but closed it again without letting him in.

During the past seven years Irene Flint's original reputation for cleverness had been very much enhanced, for she now owned parts of several well-paying claims and had an uncanny faculty for selling only those shares which their owners later wished they had sold themselves, and Morgan had heard various men say that although they had tried to take some natural advantage of her feminine ignorance and gullibility this was not possible, for she would appear unexpectedly at the mine shaft, whether in summer or winter, and demand to come down and see what they were about, whereupon she would descend in the bucket, carefully holding her train in one hand, wearing a French hat and carrying her parasol, and insist upon removing ore samples which she would herself select.

She had, in fact, the successful speculator's intuition as to when the right time had come to buy and when it was time to sell, but what was the exact source of her knowledge she did not say, and so she was becoming a kind of seer to whom they went, not only when they wanted her to invest in their properties but even before they bought them, and there was a growing superstition that Milly Matches in her reincarnation of Irene Flint was possessed of visionary faculties. For that reason there was an urgent scramble going on for her favor, even though Irene made no claim to supernatural capacities and had laughed gaily when Morgan told her how widespread the superstition had become, for it might be heard nowadays in any camp in the mountains.

"I know something about minerals, it's true," she admitted. "But I judge the man when I invest, not his property. If the man is sound, then the property doesn't make much difference—because if one fails him he'll get another, and then another, until he finds what he needs."

"You make no mistakes?"

"I make mistakes, but I don't talk about them, and other people forget. And then, it's true that I don't make very many." She smiled at him, shrugging. "Why should I? I don't enjoy failure. Neither do you."

Morgan was not inclined to attribute to Irene Flint those occult talents which some men did, and had noticed that whenever he had brought her assay reports or accounting sheets she stared at them with an impassive gaze which told him plainly she did not read them, but he had nevertheless an honest respect for her shrewdness and her knowledge of this treacherous business in which they were both interested, and she had told him long ago that he must never give up a valuable property for lack of money without coming to her.

Now, after what seemed a long time, Fong Chong opened the door again, and beckoned him in. The living room looked somewhat different, for Irene quickly grew tired of her surroundings and was constantly buying new furniture and rugs and bric-a-brac, none of which pleased her for long. This time, the furniture was made of some golden-brown wood, thickly padded with violet silk plush, dangling much fringe and many tassels. There were the usual numbers of low stools and hassocks to circumvent, and he was obliged to duck beneath a conch shell which hung from the center chandelier with long ivy tendrils trailing from it, and as he went stepping nimbly around these hazards, crossing a carpet decorated with fringed banana leaves amidst which lurked a leopard and various birds of gaudy plumage, Irene Flint came toward him in a purple moiré gown, splendid enough for a reception.

She accepted his deferential kiss, and sent Fong Chong to bring a bottle of champagne while she stood beside the fireplace, carefully but deftly rolling a cigarette, and they discussed for a few minutes the recent Territorial gossip. Lem Finney's new house was nearly done, and this in itself was a minor social revolution, for it challenged the other men to build something to equal or surpass it. Pete was talking about building, although Jenny declared they had no need of a bigger house, and Irene said that she and Jeremy had consulted an architect on their trip to the Centennial and would begin to build during the winter. The Harts, the Manzonis, the Webbs, the Churches, and several others would soon begin building, for the prospects of another boom and the developing cattle business had restored their earlier optimism and convinced them that all the old original dreams would presently come true.

"I saw Zack Fletcher a few weeks ago," she added. "He's moving the Cross Eye to the Sun River range."

Irene and Morgan raised their glasses, and sat down to discuss various properties in Butte. When he gave her a sample of chalcocite, she did not spit on it as a man would have done, but sprinkled it with champagne, then held it beneath a lamp and turned it carefully as a jeweler with some rare gem, sending the green sparks darting. They had discussed Amos Muspratt's claim before, but this was the first sample he had brought to her, and as she glanced at him questioningly, Morgan smiled, admitting, "It wasn't easy to get."

"How much does he want?" She whistled softly to hear Amos Muspratt's figure, frowning and shaking her head over the cupidity of these miners, for Irene Flint was known to prefer a bargain.

"But," said Morgan, as quietly as if Fong Chong might be lurking about, spying for Lem Finney, "he says Lem's offered him twenty-eight."

"We can't let that happen, can we?" She returned the ore to him.

Morgan held it in his hand, and as he talked, describing his plans for the Yellow Medicine, he glanced at it from time to time, turning it to catch the play of colors. "There wouldn't be any immediate profit. I have no intention of putting in an expensive reduction works until I know what's there—and until I've protected that lead with other properties. I'll spend the winter sinking shafts and running tunnels, and if I find what I expect to, I'll go east again, and the next time I think I can get a loan that will let us begin serious work. But the town's full of buyers right now, they come in on every stage, they'll buy anything on the market and then turn around and sell it the next day, and I hate like hell to see good properties going to strangers."

"Or to friends?" suggested Irene. "Let me see that again." As he laid it on her palm she cupped her hands about it as if to warm them by its inner heat, closing her eyes and rocking gently back and forth. Morgan frowned, taking care not to be caught smiling at Irene Flint in the throes of her magic rites, for she might have begun to believe in the superstitions about herself, after all, or perhaps this was the means she had used to set them going in the first place. "And why is it you're so sure Scannell and the other experts are wrong?" She did not open her eyes but continued rocking, and as Morgan began a technical explanation which, he was sure, she would not understand, she nodded now and then and listened, he thought, with very much the expression of sublime contentment which came over Susette's face whenever he sang for her the lullaby Dancing Rabbit had taught to Lily Jones.

"It's true the ores become impoverished near the water line, but that's caused by the oxidation of sulphides and silver, and a rise and fall in water in the vein fissures during dry and wet seasons." Irene smiled and hummed softly to herself, encouraging him to go on. "I'll take a prospect on some well-defined fissure that carries good milling ore in the outcrop and sink below the water level and—" He snapped his fingers and Irene opened her eyes to find him smiling at her, not mockingly, but as if to say they both knew something of the art of humbugging, and as she returned the ore sample she drew a long sigh.

"I'll give you twenty. Can you get the rest of it from your family?"

"I'm sure I can."

"I won't charge you interest on this one, I'd prefer to take a ten percent partnership in your company. After all, I've invested sixty-three thousand with you by now." Irene, unlike other vest-pocket bankers, never needed a ledger to refresh her memory, but maintained in her head a most intricate, and accurate, system of bookkeeping.

Amos Muspratt took leave of the claim where he had spent most of his days and nights for eleven years, and the *Helena Post* described the change of ownership as the most important transaction in Territorial history, declaring that what the country needed were more men who could make circumstances—a statement which Amos complained was a slur upon his industriousness. And when, a few weeks later, Morgan boarded up the shaft and the *Helena Post* announced that the property had been found to be worthless, after all, Amos went charging distractedly about the camp, declaring that if anyone had been cheated it was Amos Muspratt, not Morgan Devlin who had bought, for thirty thousand dollars, a property which would one day make him two or three millions.

Morgan avoided him when he could, ducked hastily down an alleyway when he saw him on the street, sidled out of Favorite's when Amos came in, but when Muspratt cornered him, as he did from time to time, Morgan told him soothingly, "Amos, you know god-damn well that mine isn't worth anything. I don't hold it against you, for Christ's sake, I'd have done the same thing myself if some damn fool had offered me that much money."

"Sell it back to me, then."

"What would you do with it?" Morgan inquired gently.

"Sell it to some guy who'll work it, not sit on it the way you're doing. Sell it to someone who would let me have a fair share in it. Why should the discoverer always be the guy who gets screwed?"

Morgan nodded, squinting and staring thoughtfully up the street. "Maybe you're right, Amos. Maybe I should sell it to one of these pilgrims who keeps nosing around." He became brisk, laying one hand on Muspratt's shoulder in a comforting gesture. "No hard feelings, Amos? We're still good friends, aren't we?" Amos puckered his lips, as if at some sour taste in his mouth, and Morgan made his escape, for Amos' continuing passion for that claim made him uneasy, and he only regretted he could not discover a way to capture the entire hill, ride upon it with an invading army of lawyers and bankers and seize it for his own.

For everyone agreed it was only a question of time until this silver and copper camp in its isolated roost on top of the Rocky Mountains would become a city of millionaires, with another city below the ground, two or three times as big as the one they could see. Bruno and Morgan often stood in the doorway of Favorite's Saloon, gazing out over this camp which changed as they watched it, and Bruno would point to the new whim-house on Finney's Buckhorn mine and to the several other structures which, it seemed, had appeared since the last time he looked out. "Those gallows frames are getting thick as pins on a lady's pin cushion. Sure gives the place a hell of a lot of style it didn't have before, doesn't it?" They watched the passing of a train of ore wagons, and when it had gone by, Bruno said, "All we need now is—"

Morgan took up the refrain, repeated every day in the Territorial newspapers: "Transportation and works for the reduction of our ores."

But they did not wait for it to happen. The loan from the Commercial Trust came late in December and Morgan hired six more men, began to build a branch office for Devlin Brothers, and bought an interest in Ralph Mercer's proposed newspaper, the *Butte Independent.* Lem Finney was completing an office and bank building. Jeremy Flint had established an office in Butte. Green Troy had sold his Casino and moved there—without Nola Malachy—and intended to build a hotel and become a respectable citizen, something, Irene Flint told Morgan, for which he had never ceased to hanker. And early in January the opera house was opened by a performance of the Charles Baxter Dramatic Company, which had returned to the mountains from time to time, although never when Morgan had been there, and he and Bruno went to see Fan Moffat in *Camille.*

She was, he was glad to find, as pretty as she had been five years ago, even though she still played Camille with zestful good health and many sidelong glances at the audience, as if she wanted to let them understand she did not believe any woman with ordinary common

sense would sell her horses and jewelry to maintain such a vapid
lover as Charles Baxter, whom she seemed likely to overwhelm with
her vehemence and skepticism. When she went into her decline in a
long white dress which showed her smooth shoulders and full
breasts, loudly coughing each time she was prompted, Fan gave
Morgan a sly glance, and when at last she unfastened her dark red
hair and let it slowly unravel, in the way many of them remembered
so well, there was applause as enthusiastic as any he had heard for
Allegra Stuart.

Bruno, looking dazed, whispered that he must meet her, and they
found her in the green room, sighing heavily, as if Camille's death
had exhausted her, but then smiling as she accepted her admirers'
compliments and, to reward them, she leaned her head to one side
and shook out her hair.

She greeted Morgan with as much surprise as if she had never
guessed who it was she had been smiling at, and she summoned him
to one side where she scolded him for having married another girl.
She pouted and laughed, shrugged and spread her fingers before his
face, sighed and laid her hand upon her breasts, and gave for a
minute or two a demonstration of her old charms, and then she whispered, "I'm sick and tired of this life, I want to marry a rich man."
She gazed at him with a sad and tender look, very pretty, and quite
comical, for she was no more pathetic now than she had ever been.
"Is it true everyone here will soon be rich?" She studied him carefully, rather like a miser contemplating his horde, he thought.
"You've got to help me."

"Shall I introduce you to one of my partners?"

Her eyes sparkled eagerly. "Where is he?"

Morgan indicated where Bruno Favorite lurked, half out of sight
and, it seemed, grown self-consciously aware of his defects for the
first time. "That midget?"

"He'll be a rich man one of these days."

"But he'll still be a midget." She shook her finger at him. "Find me
someone else."

A few days later she stopped him on the street to ask what he had
done in her behalf, and when he said that Bruno Favorite was ready
and eager to marry her, Fan stamped her foot and walked away, but
turned and smiled forgivingly, and the next Sunday morning she
came to the office where he and Douglas sat discussing their plans for
the concentration works they would build later in the year.

She was wearing a dress in the new style, fitted so tight from her
neck to her knees that it seemed likely she must, as some authorities
recommended, have tied her knees together so as not to split the
seams. And when Morgan introduced her to Douglas, she gave him
her hand, touched his hair with maternal familiarity, and told him
how much he had grown since she had seen him last; but then Douglas stiffly informed her he was a married man now with a son nine

months old, and at that Fan gave a cry of despair and sat down. "But you were only a little boy," she told him reproachfully.

"That was a long time ago, Miss Moffat," Douglas assured her, and he left, only giving Morgan a last meaningful grin.

Fan continued to sit there in her Sunday finery, staring morosely at the floor, and at last she sighed more heavily than she ever had over the death of Camille. "I'm getting old." Morgan laughed deprecatingly, and all at once, with a humorously crafty expression, Fan approached him and he watched her with a wary eye and, at the same time, watched the door, for Sunday was a day of business like any other day. "But I've kept my figure, shall I show you?"

She unfastened her dress, showing him her breasts, and Morgan backed away, looking quite shocked, and protesting, "Fan, for God's sake." At that she began to laugh, and went on laughing until she fell into a chair, while he frowned sheepishly, mumbling, "I remember," and tried not to look at her.

The door opened and he spun around to find Amos Muspratt standing there, looking puzzled and alertly interested as Fan sprang up with an indignant cry, turned her back to fasten the dress, and walked out without a glance at either of them. And Morgan, taking this as a narrow escape from another infidelity, welcomed Amos as an old friend, though now that he was there Amos had nothing to say and fell to shambling about the office and scratching his beard while Morgan pretended to go over some reports which lay on his desk.

Finally Amos turned, holding forth his hands in a gesture of supplication, and asking in that querulous voice which had lately become habitual with him, "Devlin, is it true you've got a secret crew down there—six men, on day and night shift?" Amos cocked his head sideways, and gazed at him aggrievedly. "Would you do a thing like that to an old friend?"

"I don't know where you heard that, Amos, but I swear to God it's not true. I got gypped on that deal and you damn well know it. Maybe I'll work it again someday, and maybe I won't, but what I want you to do, Amos," he told him with such extraordinary kindness that Amos looked even more distrustful, "is to keep the hell away from that property and leave me alone."

LIV

Lemuel Finney's new house was three stories high with a ballroom on the top floor—a French chateau crossed with a minaret and a

Gothic cathedral, the whole painted a dark brown. For the day was past when any three-room cabin could be called a mansion, and a mansion nowadays needed three storys, cupolas and balconies and porches pitched about it, and no fewer than twelve rooms; while Irene Flint had surprised them with the news that she and Jeremy were building no ordinary mansion but an octagonal one, and that to be equipped with an observatory tower.

Still, this was the first such house to be completed, and even after it had been put on display at a New Year's Day reception and several dinner parties, the members of the Ladies Study Group scarcely heard Countess Manzoni's argument as to whether or not the death of Mary of Scots had been justified, being all the while wistfully engrossed in admiring Erma Finney's new possessions—her Turkish carpets and double lace curtains, stained-glass windows and leather-bound books—and could not resist rehearsing their botany as they pointed out glass lilies and morning glories on the chandelier, for it reminded them that not many years ago they had lived so primitively that Jenny Devlin's wax bouquet had been a cause for envy among them.

By the end of the year, some of them would have moved into their new houses, by next year the others would follow, and only Jenny said that the house she had satisfied her.

But then Jenny was a greater riddle to them now than she had been when Andrew Danforth had first brought her to the mountains, a beautiful and rather wild-looking young woman, serious, intense, and more commanding than she had seemed to know. Some of her friends thought that Jenny cultivated disaster, but others defended her as a victim, not so much of her own beauty, as of some magnetic attraction she seemed to exert upon unhappiness which, infallibly, sought her out.

Her daughter Leila, who had shown promise of growing up to rival her mother's beauty, had died so suddenly, and—for all that children died easily in the mountains—so unexpectedly, that some of them had been inclined to wonder what Jenny must have done to cause this blight upon her life. For even the most devoted mother was not likely to be wearing deep mourning nearly four years later, still covering her face with a crape veil whenever she appeared in public and turning it back only in private gatherings, and, even then, almost reluctantly, as if she had grown accustomed to using it as a shield.

"Jenny will be forty years old this year, after all," Erma Finney reminded them. "Not that she isn't still beautiful, but if you had known her, as I did, when she first came to Bannack—and it was as if something extraordinary had happened, the first time you saw her —then you would understand why she isn't so eager to put off mourning."

"Nonsense, Erma," Irene Flint objected. "Jenny is a beauty and always will be a beauty. It isn't vanity that makes her wear mourning, it's grief. Why should you look for another reason?"

"She's told me, Irene, that she hates to be stared at."

"But not because she isn't beautiful. She hates to be stared at because she is."

"I pity her," Cornelia Bream said sadly. "More than anyone I've ever known."

"You do?" asked Erma. "I pity Pete. After all, Pete has lost not only his daughter, but his brother, and less than a year apart. He's the one who suffers most keenly, he's simply not as melodramatic as Jenny. But he's changed, especially since Matt's death, until sometimes I find it difficult to believe he's the same man I knew in Bannack."

Erma resented Irene Flint's defense of Jenny, for when she became interested in a puzzle and longed to solve it, Erma could not easily reconcile herself to the possibility that she might never succeed. She had been Jenny Danforth's first friend, the first woman Jenny had known in Bannack, and Erma believed she was entitled to Jenny's confidence or, if Jenny would not give it, then she was entitled to make what she chose of Jenny's secrecy and reticence.

For Jenny was too skilled at deception to have learned the art only since she had lived in the mountains, and Erma had concluded that her misdeeds were by no means confined to the years she had known Jenny, but she must have come to Bannack with them trailing all about her. Her fascination, as Erma saw it, had its source in Jenny's unusual knowledge of misbehavior for, even from the beginning, Jenny's white skin, her green eyes and narrow mouth with its sullen underlip, her thick black eyebrows and straight black hair had made her look too sensual, too contemptuous, too proud and, what was more, too tantalizing, for any woman who had no history.

And indeed, that history had been accumulating ever since, until Erma now observed with a wry interest that Jenny went several times a week to the cemetery where Leila and Matt had been buried only a few yards apart, for surely this was an excessive morbidity, unless Jenny found the place congenial to her own vindictive conscience.

Erma passed there now and then, and she often saw Jenny seated on one of the small black iron chairs which gave the place the air of an outdoor parlor, where the living and the dead might hold their receptions. But one day she stopped her buggy part way up the hillside, surprised to see a woman kneeling beside Matt Devlin's grave marker, her black crape gown and veil spread all about her, and was the next moment more surprised still to realize the woman was not Marietta, but Jenny. Erma waited, curious to see how long she would remain there, kneeling above him in that undignified and compromising position, and when Jenny had not moved after two or three minutes, Erma drove smartly on up the hill, but as she approached the top, Jenny glanced around and sprang to her feet, maneuvering the awkward costume easily, and turned to confront her.

"Good morning, Jenny." Erma smiled, seeking Jenny's confidence. Jenny said nothing, only stood looking at her, though the veils covered her face and Erma could not see what expression Jenny might be hiding or even if she might, as Erma thought, be crying. Erma climbed down and approached her slowly, hoping to reach her before Jenny ran away as, in the absence of witnesses, she might very well do. But Jenny stood quite meekly, and, as Erma came near, said, "I noticed some weeds beginning to grow." She held out her hand, showing Erma that it was true—she had a small bouquet of early summer weeds—and then she said it was late, Marietta was expecting her, and she drove away, rattling off down the hillside in very much her old defiant and reckless style.

It was not easy to take Jenny by surprise, for Jenny seemed to be ready for surprises at every hour and upon all occasions. She was always dressed, as if that was the way she got up in the morning; her hair was always smoothly brushed and arranged, and it seemed she always had something to do. Whenever Erma stopped, at ten in the morning or two in the afternoon or, when Pete was away, at nine or ten o'clock at night, she found Jenny occupied, reading or painting, and she must have completed hundreds of water colors by now, or she was sewing or cooking or working in the garden.

And until three years ago she might also have been found playing the piano, but now she refused to play with Pete at parties and left him to play alone or, more often, to look embarrassed and tell them he was not musician enough without an accompaniment to drown out his mistakes. Even when they pleaded with her she still refused, saying in her light and rather high voice, which was sometimes melodious as a song and other times flat and toneless, almost a chant, that she did not play any more and would not play, and at last they had come to feel it was a forbidden subject.

But then Morgan returned with his bride Felice, and apparently no one thought to tell her there was a prohibition on music. During Felice's first stay with Marietta, they attended no parties and so the subject never came up, but by the time Morgan went east to the Centennial, the first two years of deep mourning were over and Felice and Marietta attended dinner parties and small receptions, where there was no unreasonable gaiety but food to eat and things to talk about which interested them all and, sometimes, a little music, but no dancing.

And then one night at Blanch and Floyd Hart's house, when there had been some twenty guests for dinner, the clamor went up for music, and almost before Pete was asked to play, Felice was skimming across the room and, like a child at her teacher's recital, she sat very straight at the keyboard, waiting for silence. Felice's playing had none of the tentative quality of Jenny's. She made no mistakes she must disguise, but played as authoritatively as if this were her life's chosen work, and while she played she watched Pete's face with a steady seriousness, and whenever he glanced at her, she gave him an affectionate and encouraging smile which Erma found almost poignantly sad, and perhaps some of the others did too, for an unusual hush fell over them.

They played a few Chopin nocturnes and etudes, they played Matt's favorite hymn, "There Is a Green Hill Far Away," and they played the song Jenny and Pete had played the night before Morgan and James Gordon had left for New York, "Come All Ye Fair and Tender Ladies," so that they must have worked the program out between them, and whether or not Felice knew what story that program had told, Erma was sure she did.

Afterward, Pete and Felice stood side by side, Pete holding his fiddle like any concert violinist, and Felice made a curtsy, first to their audience and then to Pete, who gave her in his turn a ceremonious bow, smiling all the while as if at the success of their conspiracy. Lisette put her arms about her sister-in-law, held her close for a moment and kissed her cheek, and Erma heard her whisper, "Thank you."

The next morning, following one of her infallible spells of intuition, Erma set out for Jenny's house before ten o'clock and was not surprised, as she approached the front door, to hear the sounds of piano music but not, of course, the sound of an accompanying fiddle. She paused, listening, and then tapped at the door too gently to be heard above the music, opened it and went in, saying, "Jenny, how nice it is to hear you playing. I'm so glad."

But Jenny disappointed her again and, this time, more deeply than before, for she had been so sure of coming upon tracks too fresh for Jenny to cover over. Jenny did not move, though she stopped playing and let her hands fall into her lap, and as Erma walked toward her Jenny gazed at the sheets of music and seemed to be thinking of something else, or might have been waiting for her to leave. Erma stood beside her and, finally, Jenny glanced up, then smiled a little and shrugged. "I don't play any more, Erma. I haven't for years."

"But you were playing, Jenny. I heard you."

"No, I don't play any more."

Erma did not argue this, for she knew Jenny would win the argument by silence, but after a moment Erma laid one hand on her shoulder, touching her gently, for Jenny was easily startled, and saying softly, "The past is powerful, isn't it, Jenny?"

Jenny made no movement, not even an inadvertent grimace, and presently she stood up, easing away from Erma's hand on her shoulder, crossed the room, and went into the vestibule where she disappeared from Erma's sight, until Erma followed her and found her standing before the gold-framed mirror, looking at herself with a peculiar absorption. Erma watched her, wondering if Jenny found the same barrier there that she did, for Jenny's light green eyes had always seemed to Erma to defy penetration into that secret place which eyes were supposed to give admission to, and then she said, in a tone of sorrowful sympathy, "We all change, Jenny."

Once again, Jenny moved away. "I wasn't thinking about that."

She glanced at the door, but Erma ignored that hint and began to wander about the house. She strolled through the living room, then crossed the hall into the dining room and was headed toward the kitchen when Jenny began to follow her, as if she might be a shop-lifter. All at once Erma paused, observing with a look of surprised interest, as if she noticed it for the first time, the glass globe which had housed the bouquet of wax flowers, roses and fuchsia, mock orange and lilac, reviving their memories of gardens once achieved in earlier homes, at a time when they were still congratulating one another upon a good dandelion crop. The globe stood where it always had, in the middle of the sideboard with silver candlesticks on either side, containing nothing but its own emptiness, suggesting that someone was taking the trouble to preserve a vacuum.

Erma frowned, pondering this, and then asked, "What became of those wax flowers you used to have, Jenny?"

"I threw them out."

Erma glanced at her, for surely Jenny knew she would remember quite well having seen them at Matt Devlin's funeral and never again, but Jenny smiled vaguely, showing no antagonism to these questions but rather the kind of bland expressionless face which Erma thought only the most experienced criminals might present to their inquisitors. "What a pity," said Erma, and went on toward the kitchen. "They reminded all of us of so many things."

Jenny's kitchen was clean, everything in order, those things put away which usually were and those things on display which were usually on display. The curtains had been recently laundered. A vase of wild violets stood on the window sill. The stove was still warm and the oven door opened, and a fresh-baked yellow cake cooled on a rack on the kitchen table; and Jenny now asked Erma if she would have a piece of the cake and a cup of coffee, and Erma agreed that, for the sake of their old memories of Bannack, she would, even though she had just finished breakfast.

She sat at the kitchen table, and while Jenny went about her prep-arations Erma studied the room carefully, but could find nothing amiss. Erma had always wondered at how it was that Jenny, if Jenny was what she thought her to be, should have this instinct for scrupulous housewifery, for this seemed to Erma not at all in keep-ing with Jenny's character as a merciless woman, in search of perpetual excitements.

Jenny sat across from her and they sipped the coffee and spent a few minutes discussing the newest gossip which, in fact, never seemed to interest Jenny very much, perhaps because that which she herself caused was so much more interesting, and Erma reminded her of the first yellow cake she had made in Bannack, with four Salt

Lake City eggs which had cost Dr. Danforth three dollars each. "Sometimes," said Erma, "I think of those days and it makes me sad. We were all so much happier than." Jenny looked at Erma across the coffee cup, and her eyes moved quickly sideways, avoiding Erma's direct questioning gaze, but she did not answer. "Remember the dress you wore to the first ball? Green taffeta, with a white linen collar tied with a black velvet bow. I admired it so much."

Jenny laughed, rather self-consciously. "I'd forgotten it."

"Pete had broken his ankle and couldn't dance."

"Yes," Jenny agreed.

She asked if Erma wanted more coffee and poured it, but she made no effort to escape, so that Erma thought she was perhaps ready to talk to her. "Don't you miss the pretty clothes and bright colors, Jenny?"

"I never think about them. No, I don't miss them."

"But they were so becoming, and seemed so much a part of you. Why, even Marietta has given up crape. How much longer will you wear these things?" She gestured, and Jenny glanced down at her dress, so densely black it refracted no light but seemed to capture and absorb it.

"All the rest of my life, I suppose."

"Oh, Jenny. Even the children don't like it."

"I'm sorry, but I don't think I could wear anything else. I've tried once or twice, but it feels wrong to me."

This notion, that a dress might feel wrong to Jenny when she had so many serious misdeeds to her record, struck Erma as peculiarly immoral. "That garnet ring—you never wear it any more, either?"

"I don't wear any kind of jewelry, Erma." She indicated her left hand. "Just this."

"But surely, Jenny, if you and Pete should have another child, you wouldn't wear mourning any longer?"

"We won't."

"You should, Jenny. For Pete—and for yourself."

"Erma, I'm afraid I can't discuss this with you."

"Of course not," Erma agreed eagerly. "But your well-being concerns me very much, Jenny. It always has." And certainly Jenny must know the truth of this.

"Thank you," said Jenny, and Erma was surprised that she should smile a little.

"But I do hope you won't mind if I ask why you don't want Pete to build a new house, now that everyone else is building?"

"This house is all we need," said Jenny, with such matter-of-fact simplicity that Erma was silent, thinking of how to answer her.

Jenny had changed nothing during the years they had lived there, quite as if she believed that each object and its position in the house was significant, a literal part of what had happened to them. The center table was still covered with the scrapbooks she had made for Leila; the Paisley shawl she had worn in Bannack was thrown across

the piano; Leila's room, as Erma had noticed whenever she went upstairs, still contained her dolls and dresses and the copy of *Aesop's
Fables* they had read to distract her during her sickness. The living-
room furniture had been re-covered, it was true, but it had been recovered with the same dark red damask, just as the draperies had
been replaced with identical ones of blue damask, and even the
plants were the same, tended so carefully by Jenny that not one had
died.

"I don't want to leave here. This is where I expect to spend the
rest of my life."

"But Pete has told Mr. Finney that he has an architect in New
York drawing plans for your new house. There was an article about
it in the *Post* the other day." Since this was Ralph Mercer's paper and
the interview had been given by Pete, Jenny could scarcely pretend
it was only another example of irresponsible western reporting, but
Jenny shrugged.

"Pete may change his mind. Nothing has been decided."

Jenny stood looking down at her until Erma, reluctantly admitting
that this was not to be the day, after all, began fussily gathering
gloves and reticule and silver-rimmed glasses—temporarily laid
aside so that Jenny would not feel she was under too close scrutiny—
all the while insisting that she was late, she had stayed too long, she
must be on her way, and Jenny smiled with tolerant patience, dismissing her.

Jenny sent her ahead and, once again, kept close on her heels, but
even so Erma contrived to circle the parlor table, picking up a few
shells from the blue glass bowl and examining them, touching the
dream book which lay beside it, and paused to gaze at the tambourine,
on a shelf near the vestibule mirror. But Jenny ignored her attention
to these keepsakes and presently they were in the vestibule and Erma
was thanking her for the yellow cake, kissing Jenny on the cheek, and
then all at once she gave a gesture of surprise and touched Jenny's
hair, parted down the center and wound into a coil fastened low on
the nape of her neck. "Why, you've changed back to your old style,
Jenny. How did that happen?"

Jenny was still smiling but, Erma thought, her eyes looked greener
and shone more brightly, for Jenny had always had an unusual abhorrence of questions, a suspicious trait in itself. "It's less trouble,
and I don't like the new styles."

And though she remembered quite as well as Jenny did having
heard Matt Devlin remark that it was Jenny's most becoming style,
Erma decided this was not the time to mention it, for Jenny, she had
often thought, had only a precarious hold on her temper at best and
Erma had no wish to provoke a quarrel which might cost her, once
and for all, the opportunity to hear Jenny's confession and advise her
as to discipline and atonement.

It was some time, though, before she happened upon the solution,
and then she found it in the course of her own duties. In January,

Erma was elected president of the Ladies Study Group, an honor she had had before but without having quenched her appetite for public office, and it became her responsibility to assign to one member each month a subject for discussion, and so it seemed to her a providential coincidence when she found, in a list of such subjects, the title: Has the Fear of Punishment, or the Hope of Reward, the Greater Influence on Human Conduct? For now Jenny might explain to all of them—Marietta too—just what it was that punishment signified to her and why the hope of reward, whether here or in some other place, had been of such small importance to her.

When the day finally came—and it seemed to Erma to be a day of great importance, the culmination of many years during which she had studied this question of punishment and reward and Jenny Danforth—she found some trouble in concentrating her attention on the Countess Manzoni's report of the trials of the Scottish queen, and when she announced that next month's paper would be read by Jenny Devlin, Erma found her throat quite dry, and she was unable to look at Jenny, as she had meant to do, but spoke too rapidly, so that Cornelia Bream had to ask her to repeat the title.

"I said, Cornelia, 'Has the Fear of Punishment,' or the Hope of Reward, the Greater Influence on Human Conduct?' "

"Oh, yes, thank you." Cornelia glanced apologetically about, but Fong Chong had begun to pass among them with tea and cakes and there was for several minutes a babble about the house, the chandelier, the Turkish carpets and the stained-glass windows, but not a word about punishment, fear, or the hope of reward.

It seemed to Erma they drank more cups of tea than they usually did at a meeting of the Study Group, whether because the subject of today's paper had made them thirsty or whether to give them a better opportunity to study the parlor's contents, and Erma grew increasingly eager to have them leave, for, as she had seen from a glance Jenny had given her, Jenny meant to stay and talk to her. And Erma was convinced there was no longer any way that if Jenny once began to talk she could stop.

At last the women were putting on coats and hats and buffalo boots, for the day was cold and a recent snowfall had left the houses deeply banked, and from the hilltop where the Finney house stood, the town appeared to be only a spattering of yellow lights separated by deep mazes where paths had been shoveled between icy walls. Wood smoke hung over the valley, and at five o'clock it might have been midnight.

Even now, the women took their leave with unusual slowness. But, Erma noticed, each time the door opened and another woman left, Jenny was still there, dawdling about, looking at book titles and paintings, talking to Mrs. Flint and, when Irene left, to Marietta and Lisette and Georgina until they left, and when Erma ushered Rachel out, for it had been Rachel's intention to stay for dinner, Jenny was still standing near the bookshelves, pretending to read.

"Why, Jenny, I thought you'd gone," Erma told her, taking care to sound neither too pleased nor too disappointed that she had not. "Would you like another cup of tea?"

Jenny shook her head, and as Erma approached she stood quite straight and confronted her with a look of such defiance that Erma was rather taken aback, for Jenny, it seemed, was no more ready now to ask for help than she had ever been. "I'm not sure that I care for this subject, Erma. It's a little large, isn't it—even for the Ladies Study Group?" Jenny gave her an ironic smile, as if to say they both knew how absurd the Study Group was—only a way of passing time in this god-forsaken land.

"You have some objection to the subject, Jenny?"

"I can't discuss it." Jenny's skin had that peculiar white opacity which had always meant she was either sick or enraged, and her eyes shone with such a menacing flare that it seemed only natural prudence which kept Erma from approaching any nearer.

"You can't discuss it?" Erma repeated, mildly surprised, and puzzled. "But why, Jenny? It's something we all think about."

"But we can't talk about it." Jenny passed her swiftly, almost running, seized her coat and boots, and was opening the door, when Erma stopped her.

"Don't do that, Jenny, don't do anything foolish because you're angry with me. Put on the boots, the snow is deep. I mean to help you," she added gently.

Jenny whirled around, crying in a fierce, high voice, "Leave me alone, Erma Finney, God damn you! Stop following me, stop thinking about me, stop tormenting me!"

"Why, Jenny," Erma said softly, for the tirade, though she had expected it, was a disappointment, not at all what she had been hoping for, and Jenny was pulling on the boots with frantic haste, as if she must get out of there before some catastrophe was let loose between them. She was bent over, the veils from her hat falling over her face to lie in a crumpled heap on the floor, and her body trembled so that Erma frowned and sighed and shook her head in pity; and then took hold of the trailing ends of the veil, lifting them so that she could see Jenny's face. "Who do you wear this for, Jenny? For Leila—or for him?"

Jenny leaped up, snatching the veil away as forcefully as if Erma had been struggling with her for possession of it, and lifting her hand as if she meant to strike her; but then, when Erma confronted her, daring her to do it, Jenny backed away, and was out the door and part way down the steps when Erma called, "Take care, Jenny."

Jenny ran on, though a shudder passed across her shoulders at hearing from Erma Finney the same words she had herself spoken to Matt only a few days before his death, and which had, in spite of all she could do to drive them away, returned at unexpected times, waking her at night, catching her unprepared during the day, until they had at last come to seem to her the summation of her own guilty responsibility—those two words of warning which were no warning at all.

At the bottom of the steps someone approached her in the darkness and a hand took hold of her arm. Jenny gave a start, but it was only the young boy who took care of Lem Finney's horses, come to help her down the sloping, icy walk to her buggy. Jenny let him help her, leaning on him slightly as she moved hesitatingly along, but then all at once she was shocked by the thought that he did not help her because the ground was covered with ice but because she was old, feeble and infirm, and so she seemed as she went creeping timidly forward, reduced from the proud, confident movements of her youth to this tottering and unsure caricature. And at that she gave a movement which jerked her arm free of her young guide's hand, and spoke to him sharply. "Never mind. I don't need your help."

She clambered into the buggy and took the reins from him with a stern face, into which he gazed with a beseeching smile, not, she thought, the sign that even a young boy could respond to her beauty, but only the reflection of his fear that she might report him to Mrs. Finney and cause him to lose his job.

She gave him a nod, but no reassuring smile, and started slowly down the hillside, intending to pass through the main part of town and, perhaps, stop to ask if Pete was ready to ride home with her.

As she drove, the anger slowly disappeared, and she was as surprised that she should have threatened Erma Finney as she once had been to realize she had told Pete that she was in love with Matt. How it was that these things should happen, without her will or intention, was an eternal puzzle, one she no longer had any hope of solving, for each one partook of that sense of wonderment and unreality which had accompanied all the most painful acts of her life.

And she had no very good explanation for why she should have lost her temper on this day, when she knew quite well that Erma had been on her trail since the first day they met, for Jenny had been accustomed to tell herself that Erma Finney was her cross to bear, a whimsical penance assigned her by some malevolent but prankish deity, and had supposed she was so much preoccupied by the real task she had set herself—to search out every trace of selfishness and sensuality, whether her own or his, which had killed Matt Devlin—as to be safely beyond the reach of Erma Finney's trifling notions of sin and repentance.

Still, the picture of herself raising her hand to strike Erma was so deeply humiliating that for some moments she rode with her fingers spread before her eyes, shaking her head over this alien woman who had once been Jenny Danforth, a stranger she could scarcely remember.

And Matt, she sometimes thought, if he were alive today, would not recognize her, and would not love her, either, or perhaps he had loved her no longer on the day of his death.

Pete had not loved her for many years, and yet no one else seemed to guess this and she was not sure that even Pete did, or, if he did, he took care to conceal it.

"The old woman was right after all, wasn't she?" Jenny had asked him not long ago.

"What old woman?" Pete, she thought, had become a more accomplished liar than she these past few years, for he seemed honestly puzzled. "What old woman are you talking about, Jenny?"

"The old peddler woman—what was her name?"

"Mrs. Honeybone."

"She passed by here the other day. Of course, she hasn't stopped since that time you ran out waving a pistol at her—" Jenny laughed, as if this was some cherished family joke. "Don't you remember?"

"Now that you remind me of it. That was a long time ago, Jenny."

"Not so very long ago. It was, let me see—" She pretended to be counting the time. "It was eight years ago next March—and everything she predicted has come true."

Pete began to walk about the room, as if by that means he could ward off whatever she meant to say. "It hasn't come true at all, you've forgotten what she said."

"I haven't forgotten—how could I? She predicted I would die a sudden and violent death." Pete turned and looked at her, and she smiled slightly. "Well, I did."

"Jenny, for God's sake!" Running his hands across the sides of his hair, Pete went on, hurrying back and forth while she watched him with seeming curiosity, her head tipped sideways. "You know the poor old woman's out of her mind."

"What if she is? What difference does it make who tells you the truth?"

But just as often as she became convinced Pete Devlin knew how his brother had died, that either he had hired Gabe Foster to kill him, or had killed him himself, Jenny took pity on Pete and longed to make him some reparation for having been the incidental victim of her love for Matt.

Not long before Matt's death he had begun to sleep in Leila's room, and he had not come back to her since, and Jenny, having none of Erma Finney's conviction that desire and pleasure might be easily forsaken, had noticed that since the panic there had been a number of remarkably pretty young whores in town, the secret, she did not doubt, of Pete's uncomplaining patience. Now and then she looked covertly at them as they drove by, two or three girls in an open carriage, expensively dressed, gaily laughing over whatever young whores could find to laugh at, and wondered which of them would be most appealing to Pete or if, perhaps, he behaved nowadays like an Oriental potentate, making his choice according to his momentary whim.

Each morning, however, before she did anything else, Jenny made Leila's bed and removed any evidence he might have left, shirt studs or cigar ashes, books or magazines or a whisky bottle, and restored to their proper places all of Leila's toys and dolls. Even so, she was not satisfied, and more than once during the morning returned to make sure her reproduction of Leila's room was exact, and she suffered much anxiety lest she overlook some bit of evidence, for it seemed of great importance to conceal their separation.

A few days after Matt's funeral, as convinced of Pete's complicity as Erma was of hers, Jenny had said, "I don't believe Zack Fletcher knew Gabe Foster—I don't believe he'd ever seen him before."

Pete looked politely incredulous. "You don't?"

"I do not. I think he made it up for Lisette's sake, to protect her from thinking her father had been killed by an enemy. Because then, of course, she must spend the rest of her life wondering who that enemy could have been." She watched him skeptically, for she sometimes told herself that here they were, Jenny Danforth and Peter Devlin, an adulteress and a murderer, two great criminals; but then it seemed just as certain they were the victims of a disastrous series of accidents. "That wasn't Gabe Foster."

Pete's eyes narrowed slightly, as if he were giving the possibility his serious consideration, and, after a moment, he spread his hands and said, "Nevertheless, a dead man was there. What difference does it make whether or not his name was Gabe Foster?"

She never mentioned Gabe Foster again, and by now it seemed that Matt's death might, after all, have been only an accident, an aftermath of the Civil War itself, for many men had been killed here in the mountains by the continuing bitter feuds of that conflict they could not relinquish.

Pete had not admitted, either, that he had come into the house when she and Matt were together, and had looked at her with such challenging suspicion when she made a tentative effort to question him that she drew back quickly, thinking she had blundered, just as she had on that Christmas Eve when she told him she was in love with Matt—a weapon which had seemed so sharp, had entered so easily and stealthily, it had taken him as much by surprise as if she had pierced him physically by some deft surgical maneuver.

Pete had baffled her, she could not love him or hate him, and because this sense of isolation was sometimes terrifying, Jenny spent more time than ever before with Marietta. She arrived at Marietta's house at any hour of the day, just as Erma arrived at hers, and as Erma studied her, so she studied Marietta, searching for her secrets with a devoted care; and at last, after long observation, Jenny remarked one day, "The difference between us, Marietta, is that you still have someone to work for."

Marietta glanced at her curiously. "You have Pete."

"That isn't what I meant. I was talking about young children. Someone who needs you."

"You don't think Pete needs you?" At that Jenny fell into retreat, protesting and defending until Marietta said, "I know, Jenny. I know what you meant."

The concerns of Marietta, her children and grandchildren, became so much Jenny's concerns that she had an occasional sense of ironic amusement at the thought that she lived nowadays in a harem, surrounded by other women and young children. For she was as interested as any of them to read the latest letter from Marietta's sister, Susan Ching, making a long journey through Europe with Ceda. When Morgan's son was born, in Marietta's house, she was there to help where she could. When Lisette's children, Polly and Frank, had measles and then whooping cough, Jenny took the little girl home with her and kept her until she was well. She made calico eggs for them at Eastertime—and this trick she had learned once and forgotten until Leila was born, had become so famous Jenny thought it likely that in time she might be known only as the Mrs. Devlin who made yellow cake and calico Easter eggs.

And then one day Jenny had looked at Marietta, sitting at the breakfast table beside Lisette, in a full flood of sunlight, reading Annabel's latest letter aloud, and been taken by a sense of alarmed surprise to realize that Marietta—who had never once talked to any of them about Matt's death but had taken her grief and locked it away, a treasure no one else might observe—had once again contrived to fashion some happiness out of her sorrows. Jenny watched her for a moment with an acute jealousy, for Marietta's skin in the sunlight was fresh, her hair glowed a dark brown, still untarnished, and as Marietta glanced up, questioningly, Jenny looked away, for more than anything else she dreaded to lose Marietta's friendship. Guiltily, she tried to recall what Annabel's letter had been telling them, as if she might be questioned and have to confess she had been thinking of other things, thinking, in fact, that her own love for Matt, so violent and so unhappy, was after all quite meaningless, and his real devotion must have been to Marietta.

Annabel was now twelve years old and had been away for nearly two years, and she sent them reports of everything that happened in the Van Zandt household, or her interpretation of what happened, and other reports of her school work and her school friends. She was studying Latin and Greek and geometry, fancy work and plain sewing, French and ballroom dancing and, when she was in New York, her cousin Suky provided her with a private tutor in elocution.

Annabel's two best friends were Nicola Craig and Nancy Marble, both of them fourteen, an advantage which caused Annabel some distress. "Nancy," she told them, "is awfully jolly and looks much younger than she is. As for Nicola, she might not be so ugly if she didn't have such awful red hair."

"She's growing up," Lisette said. "She has rivals."

Marietta went on reading. "Even so, these two girls are very silly and talk about nothing but beaux and bows, engagement, lovely, Charley, bonnets, Gus, parties, splendid fellow, ribbons, trains, engaged, and so on and on, until midnight." Lisette clapped her hands and exchanged a smile with Marietta, perhaps remembering the day Annabel had been born, when she had been banished from the house to wait in Nella Allen's cabin until she was sent for. "But Nancy and I have been invited to spend the summer with Nicola's parents at Saratoga, if you say I may, and if Cousin Suky gives her permission."

Jenny participated in the plans for Annabel's summer and showed as much concern as Lisette about how many new dresses Annabel should have, and only occasionally she was a little amused to realize she was not shamming this interest—she felt it, she had taken Matt Devlin's family for her own; and she told herself that hypocrisy had been disastrously simple, as they had foreseen long ago, for only Erma Finney seemed determined to force salvation on her, and even she might be less zealous from now on.

As Jenny approached the crowded part of town, the buggy lurching slowly along the frozen ruts, she was still repeating to herself, Has the Fear of Punishment, or the Hope of Reward, the Greater Influence on Human Conduct? She smiled, slowly shaking her head, and then sighed to think of Erma Finney, confronting her as bravely as if she had threatened to kill her, and asked herself, in a whisper, "Shall I go back? Shall I tell her I'm sorry?"

She looked out at the snow-laden rooftops, blackened with soot, and was so engrossed in this decision—one moment ready to start back, the next as defiant as if Erma sat beside her, reminding her of all her faults—that she was astonished to discover she had come to a halt in a tangle of buggies and carts and men on horseback, that she was surrounded by a restless mob of yelling men, and, glancing around, she found they had converged to watch two hurdy-gurdies who had gotten into a fight. One girl had captured a handful of blond curls and was shrieking like a banshee, and as the other seized her dress and gave a mighty yank the girl's breast was laid bare, bouncing and quivering as she leaped about and made haste to cover it with the curls, which were promptly snatched away by the other and flung into the street.

Such fights were a common sight on the streets, for a few drinks of the mountain whisky set all their rivalries loose, but the men enjoyed each new one best, and were gleefully yelling their advice, while the girls, inspired by this enthusiastic audience, were kicking each other's shins, scratching faces and shoulders and necks, their sharp nails leaving long red welts; and then all at once the presence of a disapproving outsider was discovered, a hush fell as a murmur passed over the men, and nudges and sheepish looks were cast upward at Jenny, who glared down upon them as if she had caught them mistreating the two girls themselves.

"Evening, Mrs. Devlin."

"Let the lady pass, for Christ's sake, get out of the way."

And Jenny, her face burning with shame—for the two girls, for the men, for herself and for Erma Finney—went dashing away as the yelling began again, louder and more lunatic than before. She glanced around indignantly and was, for a moment, ready to turn back and make them stop the fight, but then it occurred to her that Pete might be among them, enjoying this sight of two women making themselves publicly ridiculous, and so she tore on in a raging fury, greater than any she could remember, and passed through the town at such a perilous speed she caused some of that same alarm and consternation among the pedestrians which had accompanied her passage years before.

Part
V

L V

By the time Susan and Ceda had been traveling through Europe
for several months, accompanied by Susan's nurse and chaperone,
Joshua was able to admit, though only to himself, that his resentment
and animosity toward Susan—the product of a long accumulation, a
kind of garbage dump he had allowed to grow over the years—had
temporarily deprived him of his judgment. For he had expected to
spirit Susan away as neatly and with as little trouble as if he dismissed an insubordinate clerk or a careless maid, and, but for Suky,
he would have proceeded with his plans, in perfect working order on
the morning after Steven's wedding, for conveying Susan out of his
life and into a nursing home, after which he had expected to see
her only on infrequent visits.

Ceda's terrified cry when she had entered the room had surprised
and irritated him, for he had given no thought to Ceda at all, and he
told her to go to her room and not come out until she was sent for,
as if she were only a troublesome child he had forgotten to lock in
the closet.

But Ceda had disobeyed him, for the first time, and instead of going to her room had gone to bring Suky. When Suky arrived half an
hour later, Susan was no longer crying and running frantically about

the room, but lay silent under the influence of a morphine hypodermic.

Suky came in quietly, was discovered first by Dr. Montgomery, who looked quite chagrined at sight of her, and Joshua confronted her with a challenging and angry expression, loudly demanding, "What are you doing here?" For she was, as it happened, the very last person he would have hoped to see at that moment.

Suky glanced at him, seemed to think the question was not worth answering, and passed him quickly to bend over Susan, kissing her cheeks, smoothing her hair, and then walked swiftly by him again, her eyes filled with tears, murmuring, "Let me talk to you, Papa—please."

At that, for the first time, it occurred to Joshua he might have embarrassed himself, for Suky had never given him any such look before, having in it some tragic implications which seemed all at once to pass from her awareness to his own, and he had followed her meekly, though still determined to have his own way.

It seemed all the more embarrassing because he had never, in any business dealings, permitted either resentment or affection to influence him but had combined as readily with an enemy as a friend, and as readily destroyed a friend as an enemy, all with the utmost confidence and serenity. Still, his mind had grown murky on this issue of finding a suitable punishment for Susan and it was Suky who had saved the awkward situation, not only by suggesting that he send Susan and Ceda to Europe for a year or two, but by asking him, "Have you thought what this will do to all of us?" As he began to reply indignantly that it would do no harm and, furthermore, he did not care if it did, she had added, "Then everything I've been trying to accomplish is absolutely meaningless." And, recognizing that Suky had given him the chance to make a magnanimous gesture for her sake, he had agreed to the European trip, though not without muttering that the nursing home was nevertheless where Susan belonged.

When they left a few days later, Susan had not yet thanked Suky or indicated she was aware of having been saved from anything more unpleasant than a tiresome excursion into the suburbs, and Suky, who had his own inclination to exact payment for each favor done, surprised Joshua by not seeming to expect her mother's gratitude; and so he was convinced that the nursing home, where he had meant to leave Susan for the rest of her life while he distributed stories of his poor wife's lost reason, might have been a catastrophe, spoiling many of his own ambitions and all of Suky's.

By the end of the year he could read Susan's letters with negligent interest, and whenever he thought of the nursing home it was with only a rueful wistfulness, as a small boy might contemplate setting fire to the house of a cranky neighbor or pushing his teacher in the path of a runaway horse—an impractical scheme more suitable for daydreaming than for actuality; but it still seemed to him a natural enough thing for a man to want to be rid of a troublesome wife, and the world had provided so few ways it might conveniently be done.

Before very long, he was congratulating himself upon having had the wit never to have told Suky that more than once he had been obliged to defend her against Susan. "Don't make the mistake," he had advised Susan after one of her earlier insubordinations, "of thinking that because I'm not a noisy man I must necessarily be a meek one."

Susan had laughed at that, saying, "I'd as soon accuse you of being meek, Joshua, as I would Suky."

"Any woman who is jealous of her daughter should have the grace, if she hasn't the judgment, to conceal it."

"You call it jealousy. I call it objectivity."

"There's no such thing as objectivity toward your own child." And, even that long ago, he had added, "Never forget you may need her good will one day," an accurate prediction, as things had gone, though Susan had scoffed at the notion then.

Nor had he mentioned a discussion he had chanced to overhear, perhaps a year and a half ago, when he had entered the apartment quietly, and, when he heard Ceda protest, "You mustn't say that, Susan," had remained silent and listened.

"Why mustn't I say it, for heaven's sake? Of course he has a mistress, he must have. You know, or at least you can guess, that Joshua and I have kept each other at arm's length for some years now, and Joshua, after all, isn't yet senile."

"Susan, Susan—how can you use such a word about him? Such a dreadful, dreadful word."

"The thought of him being senile shocks you more than the idea that he keeps a mistress?"

"Not at all. Not one more than the other, dear Susan. But, oh, please don't think such things about the man we all depend upon."

"We can continue to depend on him, no matter what I think. I'm his wife, you're his sister-in-law. He can't very well turn us out to peddle matches."

"But Joshua is generous to us—very, very generous. And as for his mistress, if he has one, you must try to bear it with a humble spirit. Since he is the breadwinner," Ceda added in a tone of deep piety.

Joshua had never let them know he had overheard that conversation—and others just as seditious—for he considered himself too magnanimous even to admit he had been eavesdropping. And whenever he began to chafe about it, reciting Susan's long history of skepticism and ingratitude and her final escapade with Coral Talbot at Mrs. De Bow's gambling house, he told himself that Susan was not worth his annoyance, for she was an insignificant detail of his life, and congratulated himself that he had made a better success of keeping separate two households than several men he knew who were tormented by their wives' jealousy and tantrums, and the tears and pleadings of their mistresses.

For Rose Michel and Eugene had become stable fixtures of his life; not, he thought, because of conscience or sentimentality, but because each had something to give him which seemed valuable.

Eugene had Joshua's affection and—a more difficult achievement—he also had his respect. For he was deferential without being humble, answered promptly each question Joshua put to him, and showed a dignity and an independence which sometimes caused Joshua to regret he could not trade Steven for him.

Most of Eugene's activities and interests were by now outside his home and he spent his leisure playing in the streets with neighborhood friends, and whenever Joshua came to see Rose in the late afternoon there was Eugene, dashing merrily about, playing baseball or old cat, marbles or shinny or follow-the-leader, and Joshua was pleased to see that usually Eugene was the leader. "Good afternoon, Mr. Ching," he would call with a joyous friendliness which, for the moment, relieved Joshua's mind of whatever had been troubling him, and then went on with his game. But Joshua had not yet decided whether the boy was a natural aristocrat like his father or only his mother's child, attractive to look at but with no destiny before him— for destiny itself was a distinguishing mark, and most of the human race, he thought, was born to none at all, merely the endurance of their days and little more.

This, indeed, seemed to be the predicament of Eugene's mother, just as it was, he thought, the predicament of every woman he had ever known but Suky and Allegra Stuart.

Joshua had continued his habit of arriving at odd and unexpected hours, and so he knew that Rose spent her time as she had when he first met her, arranging her hair and making up her face, and one afternoon he walked into her bedroom to find her hanging over a wash bowl and wearing a white woolen wrapper, wringing out her wet hair which she had just dyed a bright blond—and this unintended caricature of his first meeting with Allegra Stuart at Mrs. Gosnell's boarding house caused him to stand dumfounded for several moments before he barked, "Rose, what the hell are you doing?'

She gave a jump and covered her head with a bath towel before she turned to face him, looking confused and embarrassed, with the slight, guilty smile she showed whenever she was afraid of having displeased him. "Why, Joshua, I wasn't expecting you so early."

"So I see." He walked closer, and although she tried to duck away, he led her to the window and caught hold of her chin while he examined her face. She had drawn kohl around her eyes, blackened her eyebrows and changed the shape of her mouth, and now she presented to him her own variation of Allegra Stuart's wistful and knowing look, as if, having practiced it, she could not forego giving him at least one performance. "Wash your face," he told her. "And see what you can do to get your hair back to normal before dinnertime."

She had made other improvements, too, or at least she meant them for improvements, and so they often seemed to him, for, unlike Susan, Rose had never given up trying to please him. He often saw her studying books of etiquette, and when she found something there which baffled her, she asked him for an explanation, just as Eugene sometimes asked his advice about the multiplication table. And she had gradually acquired several very pretty new mannerisms and gestures, tones and phrases, copied no doubt from women she admired on the stage or saw driving in the Park or shopping at Stewart's, so that he found her a good example of his belief that women were natural mimics who, given a model, would by instinct produce such an accurate facsimile of the original it was almost impossible to detect the falsification.

Her gentility occasionally collapsed before Tessie Spooner's impolite hoots, but she took it up again as soon as Tessie left the house, and he discovered her one day as Tessie had predicted, seated in the parlor painting a china plate with as much diligence and anxious concern as if she had been employed in a factory, and when he praised her work she had produced a steady supply of plates with roses on them.

She had a piano teacher, though she practiced sporadically, and she continued her attempts at embroidery, surprising him with various gifts—bedroom slippers with more of her roses, and suspenders with a design of trailing ivy. Other times, he found her gossiping with Tessie Spooner and bickering with the dressmaker, playing with her poodle Frou Frou and chatting with her canaries, and Joshua reflected that if only a woman had time to spend on herself and some money, she could devise more entertainments upon that single theme than he could discover for the development of his railroads. When she could think of nothing else to do she went to sleep, whether in the middle of the morning or after dinner, and it seemed to Joshua that in this life she lived, when she was not acting her part for him, she was no more resourceful than a dog.

Each time she suspected, or was told, that Joshua was thinking, her manner became that of the sympathetic mother of a small boy who is busy at his hobby of jigsaw carving, and she began to tiptoe about, glancing at him furtively from time to time as if the effort of thinking might have alarming effects, placed cigars and brandy beside him—from which Joshua concluded she did not take his thinking quite seriously and perhaps imagined it was only an opportunity for him to sit in silence smoking and drinking—and if his silence lasted more than a few minutes, she left the room and he would find her asleep or trying on hats.

It was true, however, that if she had seemed clever he would have been offended and suspicious, for that was not the purpose he had acquired her for; and yet she had been clever enough to have kept alert his interest in her sensual accomplishments, so much more skillful than any roses she painted upon china or embroidered upon suspenders.

Nor did Joshua ask himself whether she was happy, but supposed that a girl who would otherwise be walking the streets, long ago turned out of any fashionable whorehouse because of her age, if not some sickness she would have acquired, must be reasonably happy to think of what she had avoided.

But these women—Rose, as well as Susan and Ceda, and excepting only Suky—were the furniture of his life, for as he grew richer, as his name began to be known and reckoned with not only in that small town of Wall Street where he had spent most of his life, but in more distant cities, just so did his dedication to this monument of Joshua Ching increase; and, of course, what had rescued Susan had not been Suky's pleadings, but a belated recognition that a wife in a nursing home for the mentally disturbed would be an unsightly crack in the monument which might finally break it apart.

The Baltimore-Missouri had grown into an influential skein, stretching as far north as Wisconsin, south into Arkansas, and rambling through other states between the Mississippi River and the Missouri, and he and Cottrell and Talbot continued to add to it, whenever they could force some smaller company into bankruptcy or a receivership, with as much pleasure as Suky added a new bracelet or necklace to her collection.

It was described on a large map behind his desk where his visitors might observe it in wonderment, and where he could, many times during the day, pace up and down before it, studying by what method he might acquire a trunk line only fifteen miles long in the southern part of Illinois which would disconcert a small monopoly in that neighborhood. Even during the past four years, while the country's condition grew steadily worse, they had been able to expand, perhaps more rapidly than if the times had been prosperous, for heavy assessments were more painful to bear now, and stockholders might more easily be coerced into forfeiting their holdings, while the suspension of dividends or even the rumor of suspension was often all that was needed to bring onto the market quantities of stock in a company they could use.

Joshua seldom left his office during the day and was no longer eager to be seen at Delmonico's with a table of prosperous brokers, but preferred to let other men seek him out where he sat at his desk eating a squab and talking to whoever sat opposite him, with very little awareness that he was eating and none at all that the other might be hungry.

But, however little attention he paid to the squab, his concentration upon his visitor was absolute, and he had perfected his habit of asking questions which took other men by surprise, having seemed to penetrate their words to discover the meaning they had hoped to hide, until they were convinced it was futile to conceal anything from Joshua Ching for he knew everything anyway, and their best chance of gaining his good will or, at least, not antagonizing him, was to oblige him in every way they could. They came to him in great numbers nowadays, bringing their gifts—points and gossip and information, some of it useful and some of it not, but sifted rapidly by Joshua and put into instantaneous combination with everything else he knew—and by now he had acquired a system of espionage which made him smile at his early dependence upon Spinnage and Achroyd as a mature man might smile to remember his first timid flirtation.

Some of them came to him for advice, some came because he paid them, and some came only for the prestige of being able to say they had talked to Joshua Ching the day or the week before, for he was known in the Street as a man with nerve, as well able to endure punishment as to inflict it, and when he had achieved that accolade he began to see that the legend of Joshua Ching and the accomplishments of Joshua Ching were one and indivisible.

They did not, as he knew, speak of him with affection and he would have been alarmed if they had, for men, he thought, felt affection only for their inferiors. He had no objection, either, to being hated, whether by Milton De Groot or Lorenzo Flagg or Abijah Everest or any of the others he had helped to their own disaster, and felt as well able to defend himself from their petty attacks as if he had been dressed in a suit of full armor while they were naked and armed with paper wads.

There was very little flattery in the legend of Joshua Ching, and he approved of that, too. He was never described by his enemies or admirers—and there was something of each in almost everyone who knew him—as a builder, a man who was helping to construct the nation, but, rather, they had come to expect that in a catastrophe, when the country was collapsing into one of its periodic shambles, Joshua Ching would be found picking over the debris and rescuing for himself bits and pieces which had no apparent use left in them.

It was his characteristic, they said, to discover a method where there was none, to locate a weakness in what had seemed a strong structure, so that he could give it a deft kick and bring it down about its surprised owner's ears, to manipulate men against their wishes and even without their knowledge and, in fact, Joshua was pleased to know that he had become a kind of archfiend who strode about the Street in his frock coat and silk hat, knocking helter-skelter with his cane all the little houses built by earnest pigmies, after which he would, with another stroke of his cane, give a sudden gesture, whereupon those bits and pieces would fly into place, taking form as a far more imposing structure and, this time, his own.

The nervous and squeamish and tremulous period of his life, when he had watched other successful men with envy and hatred, bewilderment and murderous jealousy, seemed to have passed once and for all, a kind of sickness from which he had made a miraculous and complete recovery. There seemed to be no ends he might not finally achieve, and no disaster he might not overcome but that of his own death. Although he preferred not to consider or clearly to recognize that Joshua Ching must one day end as other men did; for it would have been easy enough to believe he had grown beyond that ignominy, as he had grown beyond others.

But there was Steven, back very soon, as it seemed to Joshua, from his six-month European honeymoon, describing his meeting in Florence with his mother and aunt; and before much longer it was obvious that Letty was pregnant.

When Steven had first started to work for Van Zandt and Ching, more than five years ago when he had come home from Germany, and Joshua had outlined the kind of menial tasks he might expect, explaining, "Clerks are too stupid for this work. Your uncles Samuel and Aaron are occupied with other things, and my time cannot be wasted on such details," significantly adding, "Eagles do not catch flies," Stevens had nodded smartly, and agreed, yes, sir. But then, he expected to be an eagle himself one day.

It sometimes occurred to Joshua that he had heard nothing from Steven for fifteen years or more but "Yes, sir," and yet it was true that was all he wanted to hear.

Now and then, and he was inclined to blame Steven for this, too, he paused at his work, vaguely troubled to hear the chimes of Trinity Church, and reflected that for thirty-five years he had spent his days and many of his nights within sound of those bells which had sometimes rung very clearly and sometimes, when he was unusually worried, seemed not to have rung for several days or weeks. But the sense of puzzled concern, never very explicit, was soon gone, for just as he despised men who submitted themselves to happiness or unhappiness, so he despised those who were apprehensive of time, and preferred to take the sound of the Trinity chimes for a reminder of what he had yet to do, rather than of what he had done so far.

That was why, during the past year, he had begun to drive each day past those three vacant lots on the west side of Fifth Avenue at Forty-fourth Street; and now, all at once, it seemed he must share this secret with someone, and of course he could share it only with Suky.

He therefore went to Suky's house, as he often did in the early morning, to spend a few minutes with young Joshua and Sarah before they began their studies with Mlle. Fourier. It was Philip's habit to leave at seven-thirty, just before Joshua usually arrived, but on this morning Philip was still there and apparently they were in the midst of a quarrel, for he heard Philip inquire, "Have you ever wondered, Susan, what it will be like when you walk into a ballroom to find that people are looking at some other woman?" Whereupon Suky, who seemed to think the best medicine for Philip was laughter, gave forth a peal at which Joshua marveled, for he supposed it must be the worst fear she had. "Or don't you look that far ahead?"

"How far ahead do you look, Philip?"

"Only as far as I need to."

"Be sure you know how far that is," she told him, and Joshua smiled, for of course Philip did not look as far ahead as he needed to or he would not constantly be begging her to loan him money—to pay a gambling debt, a market loss; one petty financial disaster and then another seemed to be his lot, and each time he asked of her only the favor that she help him this once, and not mention it to his father-in-law.

Joshua tapped, opened the door, and they both turned, alertly smiling. Suky wore a morning dress of pale blue silk, and apparently Philip's remark had been prompted because she was standing before the mirror, looking at herself. But at sight of Joshua, Philip kissed her deferentially and Suky glanced at Philip from the corners of her eyes, giving that slow smile of conspiracy she had had as a little girl and never lost, and Philip left them.

Suky, Joshua had often thought, would have made a brilliant courtesan or a famous actress, if she had not happened instead to be born Susan Ching, Joshua Ching's daughter, and he sometimes made comparisons between Rose Michel, who was presently borrowing her mannerisms from Allegra Stuart, and Suky, who imitated no one and never had but was as inventive as he was himself, possessed of a life she shared with no one else but lived within her own feelings and imagination which, if these could be looted, would doubtless produce wonders to astonish them all. And Suky, what was more, never acted from a negative conviction but assumed that in one way or another she must eventually prevail, just as he did.

She had apparently been working, before Philip had appeared, at her writing desk, an eighteenth-century French table elaborately inlaid with tortoise shell and mother-of-pearl, where she sat each morning and wrote with a gold pencil in the engagement book she kept with meticulous care. But Joshua had never been invited to read it, and the desk had various secret drawers and compartments, a species of furniture she liked to collect, though whether as a precaution against Philip's curiosity or his own furtive interest, or possibly because she shared his prudent distrust of everyone, Joshua did not know or care, for he was glad to see how reluctant she was to leave anything to chance.

"Come for a drive with me," he told her. "I have something to show you."

Suky never doubted that his surprises would be pleasant ones, and now she threw on a cloak and went tripping down the stairs, as eager for the surprise as when she had been a little girl, for it was a great part of Suky's charm that with all her strange and somewhat awesome beauty, she could look as appealing and innocently provoca-

tive as Sarita herself. "What can it be," she was murmuring. "Whatever can it be?"

The day itself made him glad to have chosen it, for the sky was
clear and clean, and the leaves had just begun to open so that a green
mist seemed to lie all along the Avenue. As they drove, now and then
passing someone they knew, whereupon Joshua gravely lifted his hat
like a statesman accepting praise from strangers and Suky inclined
her head, they talked of young Joshua's progress in riding and Sarah's
in French, of a play they had recently seen, of news from Susan and
Ceda, and Joshua found himself growing more expansive with the
influence of the May morning and more eager to display his surprise.

But first he said, "Did you know there's been some talk that I'm to
serve on the board of directors of the Hallam bank?"

Suky looked rather doubtful, and sorry to be diverted from the
surprise, since this could scarcely be it. "Have you accepted?"

"So far, of course, it's only a rumor."

Suky seemed to understand what he meant by that—that there
was as yet no rumor at all, but he would like to hear one—for she
gave him the same slow, sideways glance she had earlier given Philip,
asking, "Oh?"

Joshua was not inclined to believe that love, in that bright, urgent
form Suky had long ago described to him, had ever existed between
Suky and Frederic Hallam or, indeed, between Suky and anyone at
all; but she had something he thought more valuable than the
ability to love; she knew how to counterfeit it, as he had seen on the
night of Steven's wedding when he had glanced at Suky just as she
was approaching the dance floor with Frederic Hallam. She was walking a little ahead, looking downward as she sometimes did, as if she
were thinking of other things and might have forgotten where she
was, and then she turned, laying her hand on Frederic's shoulder, and
looked up at him with a smile which Joshua remembered yet. For
her expression was at that moment a mingling of submissiveness and
regret, yearning and admiration, something so complex and so delicate he had instantly understood that Frederic Hallam, Suky's con-
queror and victim, would agree to whatever she might ask of him,
and it seemed little enough for Frederic Hallam to put Joshua Ching
on the board of the Commercial Trust.

With that attended to, Joshua spoke to Huggens. "Turn south and
stop in the middle of the block."

The three lots, like all vacant lots everywhere in the city, were
littered with rocks and tin cans, heaped with ashes and refuse,
roamed by dogs and cats and an occasional goat strayed that far
south, and surrounded by a partly collapsing fence upon which was
painted in white letters the advertisement: Balm of a Thousand
Flowers.

"There they are." Joshua nodded. "One, two, three—from there to
there."

Suky leaned forward. "These belong to us?" She glanced at him, with that admiration which came to her face at each new gift, each coup, whatever he did that enhanced them both. "How long have you had them?"

"For several years." But there seemed no reason to tell her he had let them go as a part of the marriage contract with Philip, and had been obliged to find a way to get them back again.

"Several years?" she asked reproachfully, but then leaned forward again, partly closing her eyes and tipping back her head as she did when she examined a new picture. "I wish I'd known about it sooner." She studied them a little longer and then began to talk, in a soft voice, which grew more and more rapturous. "I think we should build two houses, one at either end, and connect them with a picture gallery that faces the street, with a closed garden behind it, where we would give the most superb entertainments. They should be very much alike, but not identical, in the style of a French chateau, and I'd have nothing but old French furniture. There would be a small theater for the children, a billiard room for you and Philip, of course a library in each house, and I'd have pictures by new artists, as well as the old ones. The first reception will be a *fête champêtre*—with dancing." She glanced at the sky. "And we'll give it on just such a night as this will be, only a little nearer to June, because that's when people feel happiest." She turned to him eagerly. "When does the work begin?"

"In a year or two, I hope."

"A year or two? But, Papa, it will take at least two years. Don't you think I should begin making inquiries about an architect? Alvita Hallam told me not long ago that they're planning to build."

"Talk to her, if you like, but it isn't easy to raise money nowadays, and this will cost a great deal. I only wanted you to begin to think about it."

The houses would cost, with their furnishings, or so he had calculated, nearly two million dollars, for if he intended to buy the joys of snobbery for himself and Suky—and no other members of the family had their keen appreciation of all its possible nuances—he must make sure these joys would not be corrupted by misgivings that grander houses, more elegantly furnished, existed a little farther down the street. And he could not afford this yet, although in another year or two, if all went well with the country or even if it did not, he should be able to, for he had other plans maturing.

The Corporate Engineers, according to the predestined fate of all construction companies, was about to be liquidated, leaving in its wake the Baltimore-Missouri, a large network, if rather a weak one in some of its strategic spots, and Joshua had been for some years studying the progress of other roads, their owners and their owners' idiosyncrasies, for he knew he must one day control a series of roads which, as every railroad man hankered for, terminated in Chicago.

He considered each in turn, discarded one for one reason and another for some different reason, and had decided at last that he would own the Chicago-Central, and after that whenever he saw its present owner, Nicholas Craig—for they often attended the same balls and receptions—he looked at him almost as suspiciously as if he had reason to believe that Nicholas Craig loved the same woman he did, but then smiled at him with a proper mixture of cordiality and indifference, and made no attempt to seek him out.

When Nicholas Craig had first made his appearance in Wall Street, not long after the War, and established the brokerage house of Craig and Craig with money he had made as other men did during those times—selling something worthless to the government and using his profits to speculate in government notes, then loaning those profits to the government at high interest rates—Joshua had noticed him as he noticed every new arrival in what he had begun to think was his private realm, and was hopeful that Nicholas Craig would soon disappear.

Craig was a big, heavy-boned man, who looked both fierce and joyous, whose hair was carrot-red, and whose habit of laughing immoderately whenever he heard bad news struck Joshua as a species of lunacy against which he must be on his guard. He had not liked Nicholas Craig's vigorous red hair, either as it sprang up from his scalp or curled upon the backs of his fingers and wrists, nor had he liked the aura he gave off of being a man who expected to succeed, in one way or another. And indeed Joshua had catalogued him as a shoddyite—not one of the most flagrant examples, perhaps, for he had no diamonds stuck in his teeth and, for all his appearance of barbarous energy, he had a soft, deep voice and an accent he might have picked up by spending a year or two at an English school, and it was said his wife was one of the city's most beautiful women, although Nicholas Craig could not be satisfied even in those days with only one beautiful woman.

Joshua, who was shrewdly receptive to the smallest details of his surroundings, even when he seemed most preoccupied, had kept the same watch over Nicholas Craig's career that he kept over the careers of half a hundred other men, and during those times when a man was thought lucky to survive in Wall Street for five years, Nicholas Craig became known as one who had learned the art and mystery of Wall Street trade and, they admitted, he practiced it in a most slashing way. It had never happened that Joshua had encountered Nicholas Craig in a clique or a corner, their rivalries had not coincided, and Craig had apparently been content with getting rich from his market maneuvers, or so Joshua had supposed, until, a few months after the Panic, Nicholas Craig had taken Joshua and everyone else by surprise when it became known he had bought control of the Chicago-Central.

After that, Nicholas Craig and his Chicago-Central was a plan Joshua kept lying about where he would be reminded of it from time to time—as Rose was reminded to paint another china plate or begin a new pair of slippers—and he was sure that one day fate would give him a convenient excuse for pretending to discover a sudden friendship for Nicholas Craig, and, just as he expected, it did.

For Joshua chanced to hear, one night after dinner, a conversation between Suky and Annabel Devlin, and according to his usual habit he heard only the sentence which had some significance for himself when Annabel told Suky, "Nicola says her father owns a railroad, the Chicago-Central, I think it is."

The next time he met Nicholas Craig, they talked about the girls' summer plans, and not long after that, Joshua invited him to have dinner at Rose Michel's house with Benjamin Burnish, Mr. O'Neil, Mr. McDuff, and Senator Stirt—a roster of guests he thought likely to interest Nicholas Craig, who might find some advantage to knowing any one of them. Nor was Nicholas Craig likely to mistrust a dinner given at Rose Michel's house, for he had Rose Michels of his own and made no secret of them—an opera singer had borne him an illegitimate child, so Joshua had heard, and he maintained two separate establishments apart from his home—but then Nicholas Craig was just forty years old and, what was more, he had cultivated a reputation for spending money lavishly and now must live up to it.

As the guests Joshua invited to dine at Rose's house had become more important, or the old ones grew more powerful, and he weeded out those who did not, he had hired a French chef and a French waiter, and the food he served and the wines he had stored in the cellar and garret were not inferior to what was served in his other world, a few blocks to the south, centered in Suky's house and ramifying from there in directions manipulated and discovered by her. Mrs. Stump had evolved from Eugene's nurse into an efficient housekeeper, for Rose continued as helpless as before when confronted with butchers or menus or parlormaids, and all his threats of economizing after the Panic had passed off harmlessly, leaving Rose the inadvertent beneficiary of a generosity he could not avoid.

The table was a welter of crystal and china and silver, burning candles and gold baskets of Jacqueminot roses. The young women were pretty and well-dressed and seemed demure, for it had been several years since Joshua had permitted any pandering at Rose Michel's house. The guests were sated on oysters and roast quails and charlotte russe with strawberries, had drunk liberal supplies of Joshua's best champagne, and Joshua was pleased to see Nicholas Craig grow comfortable as a cat, listening with a look of contented amiability to Ben Burnish's description of the national ills, although he had begun with the city as a kind of political hors d'oeuvre, remarking that between the time of Tweed's first trial and his extradition from Spain, he had paid his lawyers half a million dollars and little good they had done him—for now the Boss was left to mope in Ludlow Street jail, waiting for his old friends to come to his rescue by paying his six-million-dollar fine.

Joshua watched Hoke with amused curiosity, but Hoke looked as blandly unconcerned, paring a cigar, as if he had never heard of

William Tweed or his Ring or Board of Aldermen. Hoke had long since given up his tiger's head badge, his diamond stickpin had been made into a ring for Tessie Spooner, and it was not often he brought his ivory toothpick into play, although he still protested he would never become a patent-leather mick or move out of the Bloody Sixth—a wise enough decision, Joshua thought, for Hoke O'Neil was a hooligan and would always be a hooligan, whatever disguises he must adopt, and his present disguise was that of City Coroner, an appointment he had received the year before.

Much of Hoke's pride in his new office, so Joshua guessed, was the opportunity it gave him to swagger before his sister, until her recent departure for England, for in spite of Allegra's bitterness over the division of that first five thousand dollars, there was a strong camaraderie between them, grown out of the early life they had shared in the tenements—and very snobbish Joshua thought them to be, too, about their shabby beginnings.

Now, while Ben Burnish reminded them of Tweed's many crimes against his fellow citizens, Hoke stuck the unlighted cigar between his teeth and gloomily observed, "Politics is a game where losers lose all."

"Not all losers, Mr. O Neil," Ben reminded him. "Reform is in the air, gentlemen. Not only here, but throughout the land."

"We've had reformers before," Hoke told him and leaned forward, pointing one crooked finger accusingly at Ben. "What you don't seem to get, Burnish, is that this reform you talk about is always in the air. And it always goes right back into the same rat hole it came out of."

Ben Burnish smiled, forgiving him the sins he was too ignorant to know he committed, and turned to Joshua and Nicholas Craig. "From now on, you public benefactors can expect to be called scoundrels by an increasing proportion of your ungrateful beneficiaries." Joshua gave him a bland, tolerant smile, for he heard Ben's dinner-table diatribes with the same condescending amusement he felt for government investigations, unsuccessful brokers, and unlucky businessmen of all kinds. But Nicholas Craig was frowning at his plate and appeared to be uncertain whether to defend himself or seem too innocent to resent the accusations. "How have our railroads been built?" Joshua and Nicholas Craig gazed at him impassively, waiting to hear how the nation had been strung together. "By construction companies, haven't they? And how do these construction companies function? Very simply, in this way—supplies and equipment go into them at one price and emerge upon the cost statements of the completed road at twice the original value, or more." Ben Burnish pursed his lips and opened his eyes wide, while Joshua and Nicholas Craig went on smiling. "That, in itself, is an evil, but unfortunately it's only a beginning. If the roads were sound, if they were safe, if they were operated in the interests of the communities through which they pass, we might be able to pretend the cost was not too high. But the roads are rotten when they're built, and before they are rebuilt many lives are lost."

"Still," Joshua told him reasonably, "the nation needed the roads, asked for them, and got them. And America presently has the best railroad system in the world. You must admit we've done some good, Ben, in spite of ourselves."

"The cost doesn't alarm you? Political corruption of local and state and federal government on a scale never imagined even fifteen years ago. Stockholders swindled, farmers defrauded, labor paid starvation wages. Who keeps the consciences of the men who do these things?"

"You do, Ben, don't you?"

"This will change, it will change, mark my words. Men are beginning to suspect that the arrangements for their misery were not, after all, made in heaven." Ben lowered his voice, as if to tell them a secret. "And yet, for everything we've said tonight, there are men who are growing so rich, and at such a rate, that in a few years what we call great fortunes today will seem little better than a schoolboy's savings. Did you know that?"

"I've heard of it," Joshua admitted. "I have heard of it."

All at once Nicholas Craig threw back his head and gave a loud laugh, causing Ben Burnish to turn to him in surprise. "Didn't anyone tell you, Burnish, that railroads are built for profit, not for patriotism?"

"Ah," Ben agreed, "but was it necessary to make profits of seventy-five or eighty percent?"

"The public don't give a damn what the profits are," Hoke assured him, "so long as the bloody newspapers don't put it into their heads they should."

"But they will care—they will care."

"With your help, Ben?" suggested Joshua.

"I would hope so."

"Now will you tell me," Hoke demanded, when Ben Burnish had left, "just who the hell put the burr under his tail?" And Joshua was reflecting that one day he must buy the *New York Journal* and muzzle Ben Burnish before his editorial harangues had done real damage.

But the *Journal* was not presently for sale, so that by the time Benjamin Burnish had joined the other papers in a general cry for the investigation of the books of the Corporate Engineers, Joshua was obliged to pretend that he and his partners would welcome a Congressional investigation as an opportunity to display their books to the public gaze. "We've nothing to hide, Ben. If they call us, we're ready, any time at all."

Talbot, however, found these threats, which persisted despite his frequent visits to Washington, one more example of Congressional perfidiousness for they had, after all, spent more than two million dollars in Washington during the nine years since the Corporate Engineers had been chartered. "I have no intention of subjecting myself to the kind of humiliation they caused the Crédit Mobilier."

"None of us has, William," Amos Cottrell told him soothingly.

Joshua suggested that a fire break out in the Corporate Engineers offices, but when he discussed with Hoke the starting of the fire and some means of preventing it from being put out too soon, Hoke reminded him that fire was not a reliable agent of destruction, for the books of the Tweed Ring had been burned and their charred remnants discovered, and all the Boss's troubles might be traced to that.

"The poor old bastard," Hoke said. "None of us has even got guts enough to go visit him, cheer him up on his deathbed. Now ain't that a hell of a note?"

"I suppose it is, Hoke. But what are we going to do about the books?"

Hoke's solution pleased Joshua and, when they heard of it, also pleased Amos Cottrell and William Talbot, for it eased their minds of any fear they might make one of those appearances before a Congressional committee, so insulting to a businessman and, sometimes, so disastrous, for several members of the Crédit Mobilier were sick and others were dead of the disgrace. It was Hoke's plan to borrow the best safebreaker he knew from his friend, the warden of the prison where Batty Dunn had lately been confined, and after Batty Dunn had removed the most strategic books, he would set fire to the offices and those books which were rescued would be found to be beyond deciphering. As a further precaution, Joshua and Hoke visited a junk dealer, Joshua examined the books to be sure Batty Dunn had made no substitutions, and watched them ground to a gray pulp which would presently be converted into flour sacks and newspapers, Ben Burnish's *Journal* among them, perhaps.

Tweed died only a week or two later, alone in jail with a servant for his last companion, and his funeral cortege of eight carriages attracted little attention as it passed through the streets, putting so gloomy a finish to the Boss's career that Hoke became even more despondent, as if he had found there some foreboding of his own future. "The guys he helped all let him down," said Hoke. "Me, too."

"Any help he gave you, or anyone else, was incidental," Joshua reminded him, and found some grim amusement in the sight of Hoke's hard face grown piously melancholy.

"Maybe. But a few years ago he'd have had the god-damnedest funeral this town ever saw. Now that crappy little send-off he got yesterday." He looked at Joshua sharply, and remarked, with the same melancholy look and another deep sigh, "Tessie and me are getting married next week." Joshua smiled slightly, supposing Hoke intended some joke, some morbid Irish commentary on weddings and funerals and other such foibles of the human race, but Hoke, it seemed, was not joking. "What the hell," he said, and now looked both sheepish and truculent. "I'm used to her. Anyhow, I'm the City Coroner, and a guy in my position is expected to have a wife."

Joshua promptlv declared that the wedding would be performed in Rose's drawing room, by Judge Azariah Gill, and he would give the reception, and, although Hoke objected that he wanted no ceremonies that were r ot necessary, Joshua insisted he could not let his old friend Hoke O'Neil, Coroner of the City of New York, get married without a celebration.

"Invite The Doctor and Tom Geigan and Patsey Higgins and Mickey Shannon," said Joshua, and went on, giving Hoke a list of the men who had, from time to time, been useful to the Metropolitan Sand and Gravel Company, De Groot Distilleries, the Corporate Engineers, or Joshua Ching. "Invite McDuff and Mud Foley and Oliver Foss—all your friends," he added magnanimously.

Hoke grinned. "They ain't friends, they're confederates. I got no more friends than you have, Ching."

"Invite all your confederates, then."

When the day came the parlor was crowded with pink roses which stood in vases on the floor and on tables, festoons of pink tissue paper were looped across the ceiling, champagne was chilling in tubs of ice, and a cake had been delivered from Delmonico's which was nearly three feet high. A fiddler and a banjo player had been secreted in the dining room behind a stand of rented palms, although Rose had been unable to devise a hiding place for the pianist, and they were picking at their instruments while Rose ran back and forth, criticizing everything, scolding the dog and locking him up, inspecting Eugene in his kilts and black velvet jacket, and when Tessie arrived she fell upon her with kisses and frantic compliments. But Tessie was pensive and subdued, even seemed rather baffled, and indeed looked so little like what Joshua thought of as Tessie Spooner that from time to time he glanced at her, thinking that perhaps it was some other girl Hoke was marrying after all, while Hoke's expression was grim and almost angry and he plaintively remarked to Joshua, "I feel like poor old Danny Deever must have felt the night before."

When Judge Gill took up a position before the fireplace, Hoke signaled Tessie and she followed him with seeming reluctance, hanging her head while the ceremony was read and mumbling her responses, though Hoke barked his in a loud voice. Rose stood beside Joshua, and he glanced at her once to find her staring at the carpet while tears ran steadily down her face, not from any sentimentality over her friend's wedding, as Joshua knew, for Rose had heard the news with a look of shocked incredulity he thought would have been more appropriate to news of Tessie's death. But the moment Hoke had slid the ring onto Tessie's finger and while they both stood gazing at it with puzzled frowns, Rose sprang forward and flung her arms about Tessie, crying, "Oh, Tessie, you're married!"

A waiter came in bearing a tray of champagne glasses, and, at almost the next moment, Hoke's confederates began to arrive, eight or ten broad-shouldered men in black frock coats and trousers, troop-

ing in as if they might have marched there from Five Points in
a group, accompanied by their girls, pretty young whores very gaily
dressed, and Joshua braced himself grimly, recalling that these
men amused themselves on Sunday afternoons by raping women
they found picnicking with their families in isolated areas of Central Park, broke up political meetings by setting fires under the
candidate's buggy horse, plied the streetcars as pickpockets, crawled
into brownstone basement windows at night, and he thought it unlikely they would be able to celebrate the City Coroner's wedding
without some general calamity which it disgusted Joshua to think
he had made the arrangements for himself.

They lined up along the walls, as if they suspected the presence
of enemies, glanced continuously about with threatening and resentful looks, and as they shook hands with Rose and Joshua and muttered their congratulations to Tessie and Hoke, seemed overwhelmed
by a sullen self-consciousness. The girls teetered backward and forward, gawking at the furniture, giggled and whispered to one another
and seized the champagne glasses eagerly, tossing them off with
sighs of relief, and apparently expected that in the magic potion
their salvation would be found.

By the time they had been there for fifteen or twenty minutes and
the musicians were playing loudly and commandingly, the men
were still backed against the walls, watching Hoke carefully but
covertly, as if to take the clues for their behavior from him. Joshua
and Judge Gill stood apart, having nothing to do with this motley
invasion, and talked in undertones about the recent signs of business improvement. Tessie was smiling uncertainly at her friends,
and might never have seen any of them before, while Rose was gulping champagne behind Joshua's back and watching alertly lest he
turn and catch her.

All at once Rose clapped her hands, bringing the men up smartly,
as if in response to a policeman's club beating the pavement in a
call for help. "What the hell's the matter? This is a wedding, not a
wake!"

There was an outburst of embarrassed laughter and Joshua turned
to survey her with disapproving surprise. She stood alone in the
center of the room and now she twirled slowly about, closing her
eyes and smiling, throwing her arms wide and, as Joshua stared at
her, she went floating across the room to Hoke and asked him to
dance with her.

Hoke hesitated, but then seized her with determination about the
waist, Rose put her hands on his shoulders, and they went capering
about the room, shoving the furniture aside as they went, while
Hoke shouted at his friends to join them. They glanced questioningly
at Joshua, who smiled, as if this was exactly what he had intended
when he invited them here, and as the dancing became general he
stepped up to one of the girls and asked her to dance with him, hoping, as he passed Rose, that he might give her a discreet warning

frown, but this proved impossible for she seemed no longer aware
that he was in the room. Whenever he tried to catch her eye she was
looking in another direction, and when he approached her as she
stood eating as if she were starving and drinking champagne as if
this was one time she would have all she wanted, she deftly escaped
him, circled the table and disappeared back into the dancing with
Marquis McDuff.

The floor had begun to shake with their stamping feet, the chandeliers swayed and the gas flames flickered, and the party had suddenly become such a success that Joshua remarked to Judge Gill
they would no doubt spend the night and refuse to leave in the morning, though still nothing had happened to which he might object;
there were only his own misgivings of what they would do after several more glasses of champagne. Tessie had lost her earlier demure
manner and was flashing her wedding ring beneath her friends'
noses with mocking impudence and freely predicting she was the
only woman in the room who would ever wear one, but, so far, she
had not flashed it at Rose, who ignored her, pretending the celebration was her own.

By now Rose was passing from one partner to another and flirting
impartially with all of them, throwing her head back and arching
her neck, laughing into their faces, as no doubt she had done when
she and Tessie worked for Annie Wood. The men and girls sang as
they danced, and Rose sang so loudly her voice rang in Joshua's
ears with a triumphant and defiant stridency, and Joshua watched
her with increasing amazement, for here, of course, was the Rose
Michel she took such care to conceal from him. After a time he
turned his back, refused to look at her, and talked to Judge Gill
in the vestibule while he considered what her proper punishment
would be.

He was hovering between banishment for life and a six-months'
probation, when there was a scream and he strode into the living
room to find Rose with one hand fixed firmly in Tessie's hair, and
before Tessie could escape Rose had slapped her across the side of
the face with a force that sent her staggering and caused several
other girls to cry out in sympathy.

Hoke moved swiftly between them, gave Tessie a smart shove,
signaled his lieutenants with a jerk of his head and they went
streaming past Joshua; the girls trotted obediently after, making
no thanks or apologies as they left, although as Hoke stood at the
door, like a teacher getting his pupils out of a burning building, he
nodded confidingly to Joshua, and Judge Gill disappeared in their
wake.

The clearing of the room had been accomplished so swiftly that
Joshua felt some astonishment to find they were gone and Rose
stood alone in the middle of the floor, littered now with tissue-paper
festoons they had dragged from the ceiling, the furniture shoved to
the walls and several chairs overturned, oyster shells stacked upon

tables and tossed on the carpet, while the musicians peeked inquiringly from behind the rented palms. Joshua started forward, meaning to shake her or in some way bring her to her senses and give relief to his own rage, when all at once she began stamping her feet and sobbing, clenching her fists in the unself-conscious fury of a young child who sees its birthday party become a shambles.

"Rose!" he called loudly.

"I hate her, I hate her, I hate her!" Joshua dashed for the door, snatching his coat and hat from the iron antlers and, as he went out, Rose was still yelling. Tessie had forgiven her that performance some weeks before Joshua did, and then only because he had been forced to admit that a desolate jealousy, too deep to be reached by reason, or controlled by her newly acquired habits of dignity, had, for the moment, overwhelmed her.

L V I

During the past two summers they had rented a house in Long Branch, set back on a lawn decorated with crescent and star-shaped beds of flowers, a house like others on that street, with wide porches, multiple layers of roofs, window boxes filled with geraniums which were a sharp red against the brown shingles, and there the Chings and their neighbors—the Talbots and Hallams, the Haldanes and Cottrells and the families of Joshua's two brothers—were isolated from the crowds of the big hotels and might spend the summer together, fashionably invisible.

The house was dark inside, shadowed in the daytime when the shades were drawn against the heat, and lighted by candles at night, the only way, so Suky said, to make the owner's taste in furniture— black walnut with red plush—more or less tolerable. There was a library in the Gothic style, made ominous by stained-glass windows which, however, fascinated the children when the sun came through them, sending rays of blue and green and red upon their clothes and faces. There were long narrow hallways, steep staircases, and eight bedrooms which had required a diplomat's nicety to assign, for Susan and Ceda had come home last winter.

And no sooner had they arrived than they were set to work at various charities, visiting hospitals and poor missions, organizing homes for seamen's widows and intemperate females—a species of occupation Ceda found congenial, although Susan accepted it with whimsical indifference and correctly interpreted it for what it was, a way Joshua had found of making use of two otherwise useless women and taking some credit to himself for their good deeds. Still, after a year and a half abroad, Susan was anxious to be back and had written several pleading letters, complaining that she and Ceda had been to every museum, visited every church, explored every ruin in England and on the Continent, not only once or twice, but three times, and could endure this homelessness no longer. She had even, it seemed, begun to yearn to see Joshua again, but that lasted only until she saw him, though Susan did not mention this even to Ceda and told herself she had, whatever else, been chastened into a model hypocrite.

Once they were settled in the Long Branch house, Susan found that it was Suky who instructed the servants, planned the meals, wrote the guest lists, decided which hops and ball they would attend, consulted with Joshua and the architect on the plans for two houses Susan was surprised to learn they would start to build in September, and, in fact, they had been there less than two weeks when Susan told Ceda the summer promised to be interminable. "We're obsolete, Ceda, you and I."

"Susan, whatever do you mean? Suky is trying to make things easier for you. She knows you must be tired."

"Must I?"

"Well, aren't you?"

Breakfast was served at eight, lunch at two, and dinner at eight, and, from early Monday morning until Friday night, Joshua and Philip and Steven were in the city, Robert Devlin was working as a clerk in Aaron Ching's law office, and they were a household of women and children and three young girls, for the second week in June Annabel came home from Miss Mayberry's Academy and brought her two best friends, Letty's sister Nancy, and Nicola Craig, to spend the summer.

Suky and Letty met them at the train and they came scrambling off it, laughing excitedly and racing along the crowded platform to arrive at the carriage heaving their chests and panting to catch their breath, quickly clutching one another's hands as they came to an abrupt stop and gazed up at Suky, who smiled at them from the shadows of a white silk parasol. Annabel introduced Nicola, Suky smiled at her tenderly and told her how glad she was to have her there, and they climbed into the carriage, chattering about their trip, about their examinations, and about the bliss of being relieved of all the burdens and duties Miss Mayberry had laid upon them.

"Up at six-thirty to say your prayers."

"Ten minutes exercise with dumbbells—what does she think we're going to be, coal heavers?"

"Breakfast at seven."

"And make your own bed."

"Oh, how lazy I'm going to be this summer, may I, Cousin Suky?"

"Of course, darling."

Nicola Craig was staring at Suky with frank dismay and whispered to Annabel, "You said she was beautiful, but she looks like a goddess." She found Suky watching her, and lowered her eyes. "I didn't mean to be rude, I'm sorry I whispered. You look like a goddess, Mrs. Van Zandt."

"Nicola," Nancy protested. "I'm surprised at you, what terrible manners you have."

"I can't help it," said Nicola humbly. "She took me by surprise."

"I apologize for my guest, Cousin Suky, but she's been spoiled. She's an only child and her father gives her everything she wants." Annabel glanced sideways at her. "He does, Nicola, doesn't he?"

"Just about," Nicola agreed comfortably.

Suky and Letty smiled with grown-up charity at their gawkishness, their uncontrollable enthusiasm over brass bands playing on hotel lawns, elaborately gowned women passing in carriages, and the slow-moving parade along the boardwalk above the ocean. They talked together eagerly and earnestly over whatever caught their attention, laughing unexpectedly and often, though it was not easy to tell what had amused them, and were obviously members of a secret society, cultists and fanatics devoted to their mutual solidarity.

Suky, watching them, told herself that in only a little while, so much sooner than they imagined, they were going to discover the difference between the world as they supposed it to be and the world as it was, and at that moment she had no pity to give them. Her thirtieth birthday had been on the Monday just past and now, as she looked at them, sitting across from her and bouncing about, craning their necks and pointing their fingers and scolding one another, she felt an irresistible envy and resentment, thinking not of that present day, but of ten years from then, for Annabel was thirteen and Nancy and Nicola were not quite fifteen.

But the next moment she was telling herself they were absurdly young, incomplete and unfinished, and their dark-blue school uniforms with white muslin collars and cuffs and black pinafores gave them a gaucherie which made her smile, for they were, after all, only pretty children. Nancy was dainty and vivacious, like her older sister, with hair that was almost black and clear blue eyes, and all her movements were quick and light as a dancer's; while Annabel, Suky found, had changed once again during the past few months. Her earlier shy reticence had given way to a kind of impudent humor, and she seemed as self-centered and vain as if she had become the heroine of her own world at last.

Nicola was the tallest and the nearest to being a woman, with full breasts and a small waist, and her legs in their black cotton stockings showed tapering calves and thin ankles, while her feet were narrow and graceful even in laced black boots. Her face, Suky thought, was rather odd, having a wide forehead and high cheekbones, very large and intent green eyes, and her white skin was densely freckled. Her hair, carrot-red like her father's, was coarse and almost straight and hung to her waist, and yet with all these defects her expression acquired a surprising sweetness whenever she smiled which made her seem temporarily beautiful, and she had an energy and conviction which made her unintimidated even by the fact of being not yet fifteen years old.

She stared at Suky with what appeared to be a worshipful hostility for several moments at a time, then pretended to forget her and gestured with very long-fingered hands as they talked about the women passing in other carriages and on the boardwalk, exchanging comments which were shrewd and malicious, and they seemed keenly aware that they must still wear their hair long and their skirts short, be courteous to their elders and silent in the presence of men, overcome with awe whether they were nor not.

"When is the first hop, Mrs. Van Zandt?" Nicola asked.

"This Saturday night."

The three girls exchanged rapturous glances, and they drove into the driveway. Suky told them where their rooms were, two together on the third floor so they could gossip as much as they liked, and they went galloping up the staircase, catching at one another's hair as they went, and Suky and Letty exchanged glances, shaking their heads, for surely they had never been so young or so silly, while Suky murmured, "Oh, that hair."

Nicola came down to dinner in a green dress Suky thought made a glaring contrast with her hair, which turned quite orange in the candlelight, and all at once the men became alert and interested as she looked each one straight in the eyes for a moment before she curtsied and bent her head, glancing obediently down as Miss Mayberry had drilled her to do. Philip looked amused; Steven seemed surprised; Robert thrust his jaw forward and quickly adjusted his black satin cravat; and Joshua advanced and began talking to her in a manner at once grave and bantering, as if he had immediately understood that this young girl regarded herself as a woman and expected to be treated like one. While Nancy and Annabel, observing all this, reminded each other of Nicola's flirtatiousness the year before at Saratoga.

"And she wasn't even fourteen then, so imagine what she'll be like this summer," whispered Annabel.

Nicola's little triumph ended almost immediately, and although it was not quite possible to tell how it had been done, Suky kept them concentrated upon her by some legerdemain which Nicola watched in silent bewilderment, for she had been turned back into a child, and that was what she was expected to be until the summer was over; and Nicola seemed to accept quite meekly this punishment for her premature pride.

The three girls were constantly together, running through the house on their way to ride on the beach or go swimming, dashing up to their rooms, either laughing and chattering as they had on the day of their arrival, or whispering and mumbling, jerking one another's arms, nudging and pinching and, whenever they thought there were no grownups around to observe them, behaving not at all as Miss Mayberry had taught them to do.

After lunch they lolled about in the shoofly they had been delighted to discover at one side of the house, a platform stuck up in the branches of the willow trees just broad enough for the three of them and reached by a narrow staircase twisted around the trunk, and there they were remote from their alien elders, peering down at them and peeking into the second-floor bedroom windows, although Nicola had been disappointed to find that Mrs. Van Zandt's room was on the other side of the house and so there was no chance of catching a glimpse of her when she was off guard, having her hair dressed or taking a nap or doing whatever she did when she was not making a public appearance. For Nicola had remarked that everything Mrs. Van Zandt did was done as if she had a large audience of strangers watching her.

At the table they sat silent and rigorously eschewed all communication with one another, gazed at their plates and ate daintily and became confused and red-faced if one of the men spoke to them, as though that was the last thing they had expected or were prepared for, and even Nicola, made suddenly conspicuous by a question from Philip or Joshua, gave a beseeching and maidenly smile, ducked her head and mumbled in an undertone, and seemed overcome with relief when the talk turned away from her, as if at the escape from some awesome threat or danger.

They gave at all times the impression of longing to escape to their rooms, to their horseback riding, to the shoofly, anywhere at all out of the glaring illumination they seemed to feel thrown upon them by a grown-up eye, and they might have been, Suky thought, prisoners of the household, rather than guests.

And they were equally aloof from the younger children, Sarita and Joshua who, indeed, seemed no more interested in them but regarded them with a superior and rather scornful tolerance, and disapproved of their laziness. For to them the summer was no time of leisure, and their Grandfather Ching, though now and then he took them driving, had made it plain there was no reason to waste several months only because they had moved to the seashore.

Sarita practiced the piano and studied French and painting with Mlle. Fourier, while young Joshua fenced with an instructor who came twice a week from the city, boxed with another instructor, rode with another, and was about to begin to learn to shoot with another, so that this summer was no different from any others they could remember and they wondered at the big girls in their shoofly, wasting whole afternoons. The children glanced up at them with amused condescension when they passed under the platform, as brisk and businesslike as their grandfather himself, and having long since acquired the poise and discipline and graciousness of little monarchs, nor did they ever seem self-conscious or even aware of being admired wherever they went for their charm and their manners.

Twice during the summer Sarita and Joshua were permitted to attend a Grand Hop, and there they went circling about together with the gravity and decorum for which they had become famous, dancing every dance together with the fidelity of lovers, even though now and then Suky's eyes met her daughter's and she found Sarita watching her with a direct and thoughtful gaze, as if she might be waiting to take her place, wear her clothes, put up her hair and dance with someone other than her brother. But then, it was true Suky imagined that everyone wished to be in her place.

The three girls and the young boy and his sister ignored one another or, when they spoke, their greetings were perfunctory, as became the relationships between those of widely separated generations. The girls emerged each day after lunch, bearing with them all the equipment they required for their siesta in the branches, an assortment of blue and purple cushions, a basket of fruit—apples and grapes and oranges they were permitted to have and a box of candy they were not—and Nicola invariably produced a mirror from her pocket which was passed about as first one and then another fell into reverie at sight of her own face, for it seemed that each believed herself to be the keeper of some special pride or fatal flaw.

Nicola, reclining against the willow's thick trunk, with a cushion behind her head and another at her back, looked down, studying Sarita, and as she disappeared, Nicola advised them, "That little girl will be a greater beauty than her mother one day." She raised both arms and lifted the yellow-red hair, airing her neck. The day was hot, and as the summer drew on they went less often to swim or ride on the beach, remained in their third-floor room when it rained, practicing smiling and putting up their hair, and when the weather cleared inhabited the shoofly as a private bastion, from which they passed judgment on the world. "I could read her future if she'd let me see her palm, but I doubt if she would. She's too clever. Have you ever looked into her eyes?" Nicola pulled at the outer corners of her own eyes, tugging them upward, though this only made Annabel and Nancy laugh scoffingly, for she could scarcely have looked less like Sarita. "She's deep. She knows what she wants."

Nancy lay on her stomach, peering down through the cracks in the floor of their perch, watching the bees as they moved over the flower beds. "Sarita is nine years old, Nicola," she told her languidly. "What a silly idea to say she knows what she wants. You don't even know what you want, and you'll soon be fifteen."

"Yes, I do," Nicola murmured, and stared abstractedly away, as she did whenever she wanted them to pry answers out of her. "I know exactly what I want, and I have, for as long as I can remember."

Annabel gazed up through the branches, and seemed not to have heard Nicola's latest boast. And neither of them asked Nicola what

she wanted, for they had privately assured each other that this
friend of theirs was lacking in feminine mystery, as crude and
simple in her character as in her appearance, no more subtle at
heart than she looked.

Nancy picked up the mirror, and after a minute or two, seemingly
reassured, laid it aside. For all their many consultations with that
small round glass garlanded by china flowers, none of them ever
told the others if what she saw there pleased or displeased her, but
each seemed convinced she would one day discover in it her life's
future history, come upon it quite by accident as she stared at the
unknown face confronting her, sometimes with a puzzled expression, other times defiant or coaxing, proud and confident, and, only
a moment later, troubled and uncertain, causing a long-drawn sigh.

Every so often, when it was determined their supplies were becoming depleted, one of them would slip down the staircase and
around to the back of the house, enter the kitchen stealthily and
wheedle the cook into making them a pitcher of lemonade, and perhaps use her time to even better advantage by stealing a piece of
cake intended for dinner, and return, running and looking over
her shoulder, to climb up again breathless and triumphant; and they
would fall upon the new treasures with greed and competitiveness,
slapping at each other's hands, filling their mouths until they could
not talk, and lie down again, exhausted by the intensity of the adventure, to fall whispering and confidential, for much of their discussion
was not legitimate, as they knew. The had been told often enough,
by their parents, by their nurses and governesses, by older brothers
and sisters, by aunts and cousins and by Miss Mayberry, that young
girls should never concern themselves with the activities of their
elders nor should they ever, ever at all, speculate upon grown-up
life which would come their way soon enough as it was. But it happened they were interested in almost nothing else.

And Nicola had expressed some opinions on grown-up life which
not only would have horrified her elders but which horrified her
friends, for Nicola had a way of misinterpreting everything she saw
or heard and passing on to them her own conclusions as being nothing more or less than the ultimate truth. Only recently, in fact, she
had told them that Alvita Hallam's husband was in love with Annabel's cousin and that she, furthermore, was in love with him, something so obvious to anyone with two good eyes that Mrs. Hallam
must surely be a fool if she did not know it. Nicola called Mrs. Van
Zandt "she" and, however often they corrected her, still called her
"she," as if for this summer at least all the women in the world had
found their concentration in Susan Van Zandt, the object of Nicola's
relentless study and the subject of her perpetual speculations.

Annabel and Nancy had leaped upon her viciously, pinching her
arm and pulling her hair, hissing in her face that she was a wicked
and ungrateful girl to say such a thing about her hostess, but Nicola
defended herself, refused to apologize or recant, and told Annabel

it was time she realized her relatives were no different from anyone else's, for Nicola was fond of describing the various well-concealed scandals in her own family which she had discovered through her habit of eavesdropping in unexpected places, and to which she attributed whatever small education she had rather than to Miss Mayberry's Select Female Academy.

"You're a liar, Nicola Craig, a liar, a liar."

"Why, Mrs. Hallam is Cousin Suky's best friend in all the world."

"What's that got to do with it?" Nicola looked at them with her green eyes wise as a cat's, and nearly as wicked, and impatiently concluded, "I can't explain these things to you. Either you see them or you don't."

"You see what isn't there."

"On the contrary," said Nicola, who had copied from some earlier idol a haughty tone with which she occasionally intimidated them, "I see what is there. All right, then, I won't tell you anything else." But, of course, she did, and without being asked, for Nicola had little capacity to keep her own counsel, must say to them everything that came into her head, and yearned day and night to astonish them with her worldliness.

"You say you know what you want, Nicola?" Annabel ran a finger-tip across her eyebrows, the same definite and distinguishing eyebrows which belonged to every member of her family. "Would you like to know what Nicola wants, Nancy?"

"Not particularly."

There was some animosity among them at the moment, although it was not easy to be sure what it was about, only a vague feeling that Nicola was of the type of female who enjoyed making her conquests among the men who belonged to her friends; Nancy and Annabel had exchanged glances of surprise and disapproval when they had seen Nicola dancing with Robert at last Saturday night's hop and smiling at him as slyly as if she must be telling him one of her disreputable secrets.

"Did you see that?" Nancy had whispered. "I don't trust her."

"Neither do I. We'll watch her."

And they had watched her ever since, although Robert had returned to the city and would not be back again for another week, and had agreed, during a confidential moment they had contrived, that however she had looked at Robert was exactly the way she looked at the miscellaneous young men in lavender gloves, at Joshua Ching and Philip Van Zandt, Joshua's brothers and their sons, and Steven, and every man who came to the house.

"I'm afraid," said Annabel, "our friend is a flirt."

"She'll ruin her reputation," said Nancy glumly, ashamed to admit she was concerned about Robert, for Nancy had no special claims on Robert but, after all, she had seen him first, two years ago at her sister's wedding to Steven Ching.

"I wish we hadn't asked her."

"I'm glad we did. I might as well know the worst."

And now Nicola was going to describe her future, whether they wanted to hear it or not, but first she opened the candy box and peered into it, finally selected a chocolate cream—the most dangerous sweet of all, so Suky said, the surest to ruin both teeth and complexion—bit out a piece and began to hum ecstatically as she chewed it, and recrossed her long narrow feet, stuck into low-cut slippers which showed them very well. "First of all, I'm going to be a great beauty."

Annabel gasped, and Nancy turned over as if she had been stuck by a pin. "With that hair?"

"And all those freckles?"

"And those pink eyelashes?" Annabel shook her head. "Nicola, you must be hitting the pipe."

"What does that mean?" Nancy inquired uncertainly.

"It's a saying we have in the mountains, it means smoking opium, having pipe dreams." Annabel closed her eyes, weaving to and fro.

Nicola selected another chocolate cream and licked her fingertips daintily once she had disposed of it. "First of all," she repeated, "I'm going to be very beautiful. A woman's life isn't worth living otherwise. Haven't you noticed the way men look at her—as if all of a sudden they had a good sharp pain right there." She jabbed at her ribs, and gazed away through the tree's surrounding drapery. "I'm going to marry a foreigner—and live abroad. I'll be very fashionable, and very, very cruel. Men will suffer over me."

Annabel seized her wrist, saying fiercely, "Nicola Craig, I had no idea you were so vain."

Nicola withdrew her hand slowly but with a hard and steady pull. "Of course I'm vain. It's half the pleasure a woman has, don't you know that yet?"

Annabel and Nancy glanced at each other, shaking their heads, as if to ask what they should do about this friend of theirs, this travesty upon womanhood itself. "You may be surprised, Nicola. Suppose it's men who are cruel to you instead?"

Nicola laughed softly. "We'll see. Of course, I've heard they must be a little cruel—just enough, not too much. I wonder if it's true?" She glanced from one to the other, and her green eyes looked as if she might, indeed, become as cruel as she was ambitious to be. "Wouldn't you like to know what the secret is?"

Annabel and Nancy looked at her for a moment, frowning, until all at once Annabel leaped to her feet. "I'm ashamed of you, Nicola Craig!"

Nicola laughed. "You're as curious as I am, and you know it."

Annabel ran down the steps and Nicola hung over the platform's edge gazing at her, her red hair falling over her face and almost within reach of Annabel's grasp. "If my cousin Suky heard you talking like that she wouldn't let us have anything to do with you."

"Your cousin Suky," whispered Nicola, leaning so far over the platform she seemed ready to slide across it, "is too much concerned with herself to think about us."

Nancy crept softly down the steps and for a moment she and Annabel stood together, looking up at Nicola, but all at once Nicola jumped to her feet, ran down to join them, kissed them both and burst into laughter, taking their hands and asking gaily, "I was only joking, you two silly little girls, couldn't you tell? I didn't mean a word of it, not a word. You believe me, don't you, Nancy?" Nancy looked at her hopefully but distrustfully, and Annabel frowned. "Don't you, Annabel? Oh, now, please, let's not have a fuss when we're all such good friends." She touched Nancy's chin, trying to make her look at her. "Aren't we?"

The questions had not been answered, for Annabel and Nancy were regarding her suspiciously, when the carriage turned into the driveway, bringing Suky and Susan and Ceda back from an afternoon of making calls. And all at once, as if afraid to confront these grown-up challengers, they turned and went dashing into the house, pretending they had not even seen them arrive, and came downstairs to dinner demure and subdued, quite unusually meek and ladylike, for their quarrels made all three of them eager to display their virtues.

The days grew hotter, often there was no wind at all along that street, and there was a spreading ease as the summer expanded, to which only Mr. Ching and young Joshua and Sarita seemed impervious, still going briskly about their duties while, up in the shoofly, Nicola and Nancy and Annabel fanned themselves incessantly, pinned their hair on top of their heads for relief, and pestered the cook for sherbets and lemonade. The house was dark all day long, the shades kept drawn, and the smells of the flowers which arrived every other day from New York were so thick and heavy that Nicola said she would remember this hot summer for all the rest of her life, whenever she smelled roses and tuberoses.

"And I'll think of you both," she added generously, giving them one of her unexpected sweet smiles, then peered into the mirror, touching the freckles carefully, as if they might come off on her fingers. All at once she set the mirror down sharply, leaned back against the trunk, pushing her sleeves to her shoulders and folding her arms behind her head. "Maybe I'll be living in London then, and sometimes I'll wish for an afternoon like this."

She closed her eyes and began to talk about Europe, rather as if she were reminiscing, telling them stories of the life she had lived, and described for herself such brilliant friends, abject lovers, and envious rivals, that all at once Annabel and Nancy, who knew a way to subdue her whenever she became too arrogant, began to chant:

"Redny, redny, fire on top,
All the rednys come flipperty-flop!"

They scooted down the steps before Nicola could catch them, for the rhyme invariably sent her into a rage, made her stamp her feet and, sometimes, she began to cry, as she did now, so that presently they climbed back up, and as Nicola wiped her eyes and blew her nose, glancing from one to the other with an aggrieved reproachful face, they settled down peaceably together, for they were sometimes a little ashamed of teasing Nicola about her red hair which, after all, was not her fault.

Even after several weeks had gone by, Nicola had been able to arrange no private conversations with her hostess, but got from her only the same serene, impersonal smile that Suky gave to servants and children not her own and to whoever else was of no interest to her; and this, it seemed, set Nicola to brooding on new ways to attract attention to herself.

There was a portrait of Suky in the drawing-room, recently completed by Augustus Adams, and Nicola could not pass it without stopping, and was sometimes found alone in the room with the portrait, her arms behind her back, her feet spread wide in an ungainly posture, quite lost in the contemplation of it. Suky was wearing a black velvet riding habit, sleek and austere, with a wide white linen collar; most of her hair was concealed by her high black hat, from which a blue scarf floated in a billowing cloud such as only Augustus Adams could paint, and she had a baffling smile, sensuous and suggestive, which seemed directed at someone off to one side of the green fields which surrounded her.

"He sees her the way I do," Nicola confided, when Nancy and Annabel asked what she could possibly find in the portrait to fascinate her so unreasonably. But Nicola, for all her scrutiny of the picture, was unable to reproduce that smile, could not make it fit her face, and she had no better luck when she tried to copy the way Suky walked.

There was a new fashion, and for the past year or two women who had been for many years inhabiting portable cages of one shape or another, had stepped forth almost as if naked in dresses which fit tight to their bodies from neck to knees, and all the defects or advantages they had been concealing were secret no longer. Hair was drawn high and pinned close to the head, without the dangling curls and fringes which had previously distracted attention from necks and foreheads; and no one, it seemed, had been more intended by nature for these new styles than Suky, whose slender, long-waisted body was so subtly curved and molded that Nicola, peering down from the shoofly to watch her getting in or out of the carriage, scowled resentfully, shook her head, and as Suky drove away ran her hands over her own body, as if testing her figure against Suky's, and complained, "I'm just too big—everywhere."

"We've tried to tell you that, Nicola."

"But the way she walks," said Nicola, who almost never heard an insult, and she fell to pondering, until at last she began to describe a pattern with her fingers, slightly moving her shoulders, and, as if she had fallen into a trance, descended slowly from the shoofly and began to parade up and down, back and forth, copying, as she supposed, Suky's characteristic slow and sinuous walk, swinging her hips like a pendulum until at last Nancy and Annabel began to shriek with helpless laughter, Nicola slapped her hands together, and while they still shrieked she ran indoors, locked herself in her room and would not speak to them for several hours.

But she went on imitating Suky's walk, and, as Annabel and Nancy predicted, she kept it up until one day Suky turned unexpectedly and Nicola, almost as red as her hair, sprang toward her, caught hold of her hand and begged her forgiveness with as much passion as if she had been caught stealing some valuable possession which, in fact, was the next thing she did.

For a parasol of Suky's was presently found to have disappeared, that same parasol she had carried the afternoon she had met them at the train, more than six weeks ago—white silk covered with black lace, with a carved pink coral handle—and even after all the servants had been interviewed and the house searched, it was still missing until Annabel, who had glanced accusingly at Nicola when the first news came of the parasol's disappearance, recovered it from the bottom of Nicola's trunk and Suky found the two girls struggling for possession of it, ready to tear it apart, but then they caught sight of her and dropped it on the floor, retreating to the other side of the room.

Suky glanced first at the parasol as it lay at her feet, and then at Nicola and Annabel, for both girls looked so wretchedly confused it was not easy to guess which was the culprit. "Where did you find it?" she asked them gently.

Nicola bowed her head, letting the tears run down her face in splashing drops, and Nicola's tears were another trick she had—they ran so freely that it seemed likely they might purchase her forgiveness for any misdeed at all. "It was in my trunk. I didn't really mean to steal it—I only wanted to have something of yours, Mrs. Van Zandt."

"But why didn't you ask me for it, Nicola? Please take it—I want you to have it."

Nicola seized the parasol, giving Annabel a diabolic smile, and after that she carried it shamelessly about wherever she went, even sitting in the shoofly with the parasol opened and casting its magical shadows upon her face, as they had earlier been cast upon Mrs. Van Zandt. But even the possession of the parasol had not reconciled her to what was obviously true; that so far as Mrs. Van Zandt was concerned they were too young, all three of them, to be very interesting to her that summer.

"Why doesn't she pay more attention to us?" Nicola asked them crossly, and twirled the parasol's handle, clutching it fast, as if she still expected she might be asked to give it up. "Sometimes I think she forgets we're here until she sees us at the table."

"She's got better things to think about," Annabel assured her.

But even so Nicola proclaimed that she adored Mrs. Van Zandt, and would exchange the greatest experience of her future life if she might look like her for just one Saturday night hop.

A few days later Annabel accused Nicola of having created a disturbance over Robert only to attract attention to herself. For on the Saturday after the episode of the parasol, the carriages returned from Monmouth Park and the party came streaming into the house, quite gaily discussing their afternoon at the track, to discover a commotion in the library where Nicola and Nancy and Annabel surrounded Robert, standing embarrassed and defensive before these three young females. And as Suky entered the room Nicola whirled about, defiant and surly, crying, "It isn't true, Mrs. Van Zandt! They find something wrong with everything I do." Her voice rose to a shrill pitch. "They don't like me any more and—" She ran across the room, loudly declaring, "I'm going home!" She passed Joshua and Philip and Steven, leaving a heavy fragrance of young sweat and cologne, and rushed up the staircase.

Suky turned to Annabel. "Why did you slap her?"

"She was kissing Robert."

"No, Annabel," Robert protested. "She wasn't. I wasn't. We were talking."

"We sent her in to get—another cushion," Annabel amended, having nearly betrayed their pantry thefts. "And when she was gone too long we came looking for her. And there she was." She pointed at Robert, who had stayed in the library that afternoon to study, or so he had pretended.

"Young girls," Suky told them, "often see things that don't really happen."

She followed Nicola upstairs and Nicola reappeared after an hour or two, still sullen, but with a glitter of malicious triumph in her eyes, to announce to Annabel and Nancy that Mrs. Van Zandt had begged her not to leave and had, furthermore, given her another present, a little gold watch, engraved inside with her name and the year, so that she would remember this summer always. "And I want you to know, Annabel, that I did not let your brother kiss me."

"He didn't try. Nicola Craig, you're fast. And you know what happens to girls who are fast."

"I know what happens to them. They get married young."

After that they were too excited about the picnic to quarrel, although Nicola complained she could not understand why it must be postponed again, only because Annabel's brother Morgan had not arrived, and Annabel told her, "We're waiting so they can celebrate their birthdays together. That's what they always did when they were young. I've heard my mother and my big sister talk about it."

Nicola raised her eyebrows. "Really?" She smiled down her nose at this sentimental custom. "But after all, they're not young any more." Then, on a Saturday afternoon so hot that Annabel and Nancy had left the shoofly and gone to their rooms where they had fallen asleep, tired out by the heat, he arrived and Nicola came on tiptoe to wake them, saying "I've just met your brother Morgan." She closed her eyes in a mock swoon.

Annabel went running out of the room in her petticoat, dashed back for a wrapper, and was crying with homesickness as she rushed down the stairs, for Annabel had not seen Morgan for nearly two years and it seemed that he, more than Robert, made her long for her life in the mountains and for her family. Joshua Ching had decided it was disgraceful for a relative of his to have been shot to death, even by accident, and so Annabel's father was said to have died of a mountain fever and Annabel, who had obediently repeated this tale to her school friends, had at last begun to wonder if her own memory might be at fault.

When she came back, some time later, she was quiet and subdued, as if the orgy of weeping she must have enjoyed downstairs had done her good, and she splashed cold water on her face while Nicola lay on the bed, drawing patterns over the spread with one forefinger, and finally asked, with an air of skeptical curiosity, "Where do you get these brothers, Annabel?"

Annabel mumbled through the towel, "And I have two more, just as good-looking."

They went downstairs at a quarter of eight, and as they entered the drawing room, Nicola hesitated in the doorway, drawing herself to her full height and thrusting her breasts forward, while Annabel whispered to Nancy, "This will give her something else to think about, at least."

Their entrance caused no commotion, however. The men stood together drinking bourbon and water, talking of railroads and mines, predicting that after the nation-wide disasters following upon the September Panic of five years ago America was now at the beginning of its greatest expansion, and at a glance from Suky the girls settled all in a row on the sofa, folded their hands in their laps, pressed their feet together, and looked raptly intent, gazing steadily at the men, who apparently did not know they were there. While Sarita and young Joshua, who had finished their dinner an hour before, watched the girls for a few minutes with supercilious amusement and, growing bored with their elders, began a game of chess.

"Silver," Mr. Ching remarked to his nephew, "is a poor man's metal. The best financial thinkers have never liked it."

"We haven't only silver—we have just as much copper, or more, and in fact a few of us are beginning to think the whole hill is made of copper."

"But copper, Morgan, hasn't proved its industrial usefulness yet. It may in time, I agree. I hope so for your sake, naturally."

Nicola nudged Annabel. "If I was married to him, I wouldn't let him go traveling alone."

"Don't be silly, Nicola, she trusts him. Anyway, how can she travel when she's going to have a baby?"

Nicola now turned her attention to Suky, who stood across the room with her mother and aunt, talking to them in the murmurous voice which Nicola strained her ears to hear. Suky had on one of those close-fitting dresses, made of sapphire-blue silk with a high neck and long sleeves, there were several strands of pearls about her neck, and she held the little gold scent-box she often carried, so saturated with tuberose perfume that it was easy to know when she had recently passed through the house. "Look how she stands. Look at that waist."

"Hush, Nicola. Mind your own business."

The picnic was announced for the next Sunday afternoon at three o'clock, the men went back to the city on Monday morning, and the three girls spent the day trying on dresses, until Nicola at last gave a despairing wail and flung hers across the room. "No matter what we wear we can't compete with her!"

"No one expects us to," Nancy reminded her, but Nicola sat glaring at herself in the dressing-table mirror, comparing her own crudities—her carrot-red hair and malevolent green eyes, her vehement gestures and wide shoulders and ripe breasts—with Mrs. Van Zandt's discreet coloring and symmetrical proportions, and Nicola's face, they thought, grew quite sinister with jealousy, so cruel and predatory it was difficult to believe she was only a fifteen-year-old girl; and indeed, at such times, they were a little afraid of her, although she had never done anything more desperate than to tear her dress or break some favorite possession of her own.

Nicola was unusually quiet for the next day or two, she told them no tales of her future life, gave them no advice out of her supply of forbidden lore, and then on Wednesday morning, as they went pacing single file about the breakfast table with their arms folded behind their backs to remind them to stand straight for the rest of the day, Nicola announced, "Your brother is back, Annabel."

"He's not coming back until Friday. He told me he was going to Baltimore, and then to New York."

They paced on, counting as they went, and after another turn, Nicola said, "Then he changed his mind—because I saw him this morning."

"You did not."

"Where did you see him?"

"Coming out of her room." Nicola sat down and spread the napkin across her lap, lowering her eyes with a virtuous expression. "At a little after six o'clock." She glanced up, looking almost ferocious with the power of this triumph. "He had on a sack suit with a checkered coat, and he ran down the stairs and out the front door," and she gave a little whistle, indicating the speed with which he had passed.

Nancy leaned toward Nicola. "And what were you doing prowling around the house at six o'clock in the morning, Nicola Craig?"

Nicola gave them her most menacing smile. "I was going to the bathroom."

Annabel did not argue with Nicola, but when the women sat down at the lunch table she asked her cousin Suky where Morgan was, here or in Baltimore, and was told that he was in New York.

"Why do you ask?" Suky inquired.

"No reason," said Annabel, and after a moment murmured in an undertone, "Hitting that pipe again, Nicola?"

Morgan was, to their surprise, wearing a sack suit with a checkered coat when he arrived on Friday night, but since every man in the country owned at least one such suit, that did not prove Nicola had seen him on Wednesday morning and, if she had, Annabel assured her that Morgan and Suky adored each other, had always adored each other, and there was no reason why he should not come out of Suky's room at whatever hour he chose; and Nicola admitted that this reasoning was logical, so far as it went.

At three o'clock on Sunday, as the afternoon was approaching its steadiest and most insistent heat, they set out for the picnic site, nearly sixty men and women and children, riding in open surreys hired from the Stetson House, and jogged along Ocean Avenue in a lively parade, finally turning off onto a rutted, dusty road which carried them past small farms where dogs ran after them, and grimy children stood gaping at the immaculate children who gazed down at them with an air of gentle reproach, as if to ask why they were not themselves dressed like miniature ladies and gentlemen instead of standing there with dirty bare feet, picking their noses and scratching their uncombed heads.

But even now Nicola, whose hair was blowing about while she grabbed at it as if at a swarm of butterflies, was asking, "Where are they? I haven't seen either of them all day."

"I've told you a hundred times, Nicola—they went ahead to make sure everything was all right."

"Did they go alone? Didn't anybody go with them?"

Ceda, seated in front with Susan and Mrs. Talbot, glanced inquiringly around, and at that they lapsed into their private language, a species of pig Latin they imagined unintelligible to everyone but themselves.

After nearly two hours they could hear again the sound of the ocean, left some distance back to go winding through small woodlands and past well-tended fields, and here the caravan stopped, the children clambered down excitedly, the young boys and girls went running after them, and the men stayed behind to help the women in their struggle with blowing skirts and veils. Beyond an embankment covered with tufts of grass and creeping vines, they discovered a natural enclosure protected from the strong winds, where carpets lay strewn about and cushions were piled against the trunks of stunted seashore pine, torches flared in the softening late sunlight, and, at a table laden with silver dishes and baskets of fruit, waiters in Delmonico's livery were opening baskets and laying out food on platters filled with ice. A little distance away a platform had been built for dancing, covered by a canopy of knotted silk ribbons, and at sight of all this Nicola went to Suky with an ecstatic and wheedling expression, saying, "Oh, but you're wonderful, Mrs. Van Zandt. I want to be like you when I grow up. Would you mind very much?"

"Don't be impudent, Nicola," her mother told her, for the Craigs had come down from Saratoga only for the picnic and, while Suky might think of it as a birthday fête for herself and Morgan, to Joshua it was only one more overture in his seduction of the Chicago-Central.

Nicola had brought the white silk parasol, but after studying Suky's black riding habit with its white linen collar, the black silk hat and blue veil blowing about her just as it did in Augustus Adams' portrait, she gave the parasol to her mother and told Annabel, "She makes the rest of us look like overstuffed sofas."

"Very Oriental, Suky," Coral Talbot remarked, and surveyed the encampment carefully, perhaps searching for something which had been forgotten, but, it seemed, nothing had.

All the while she was eating and chattering with Annabel's cousins and their friends, Nicola maintained her vigilant watch, so that when Frederic Hallam and Morgan, having quickly disposed of their appetites, set off together to walk up the beach, it was Nicola who noticed it and nudged Annabel, grimacing. Annabel shrugged, and when the men had been standing there for several minutes, two darkened silhouettes facing each other against the red sky, Nicola whispered, "They're going to fight a duel." Annabel laughed aloud at that and Nicola muttered that if Annabel did not care what happened to her brother there was no reason why she should, either, but she kept an eye on them all the same.

Nicola was humming to herself over the vanilla mousse, which had come out of its mold looking like a little castle, when music began to play from somewhere in the distance, and as they all looked at one another wonderingly, four musicians approached across the dunes, playing as they came. In a moment the platform was crowded with dancers, the women's skirts swaying heavily in the strong winds, and for some time Nicola and Annabel went swirling past each other in waltzes too fast to give Nicola a chance to say anything at all. Nevertheless, there they were still, Morgan and Frederic Hallam, though they could scarcely be seen as the remnants of sunset disappeared.

"Just you wait," called Nicola cryptically, as she sped by with Robert, and over his shoulder she pointed her forefinger at Annabel and pulled the trigger.

By now Annabel had begun to look alarmed, almost convinced that at any moment shots would ring out and one man or both would topple over dead; and then there they came, walking back, and could be seen, when they reached the light of the torches, to be smiling and talking quite amiably, much more like two men who have just concluded a satisfactory business arrangement than rivals ready to fight over a woman. Annabel gave Nicola a mocking smile, and in another moment Morgan and Suky passed them, dancing together, though neither was smiling or talking, and their faces were so serious that Nicola remained hopeful the danger was not yet passed.

But no disasters occurred, the party grew increasingly gay as they danced in the light of flares shot up across the dunes like a perpetual shower of falling stars, and concluded at last with them riding back at midnight beside the ocean, which came slamming onto the beach, and because the three girls were asleep long before they reached home, they could not even remember how they got to their rooms.

They slept through breakfast and arrived in the kitchen at eleven o'clock to plead the cook's leniency for that one morning, and then, because the house was extraordinarily still, the men gone back to the city several hours before, and no one to be seen but Letty and the baby, they climbed up to the shoofly to rest, for the excitement of the picnic had left them languid, and they lay on the platform, gazing up at what could be seen of the sky through the willow's dark strands, sometimes sighing or yawning, and were for some time the quietest they had ever been together.

"I know something I won't tell," mused Nicola at last, and chewed reflectively at the ends of her hair. But Nancy and Annabel might have been asleep, for all the curiosity they showed, and so Nicola shrugged and yawned deeply, stretched her arms above her head and spread her fingers wide, and had nothing more to say until they climbed back to the shoofly after lunch and settled themselves once again amid the blue and purple cushions. And now Nicola looked quite unscrupulously pleased, for Mrs. Van Zandt had not been at the lunch table and was reported as being tired. "And I'll bet I know why, too," murmured Nicola.

"Why, why?" demanded Nancy, for now that lunch was over she was wide awake.

"You'll say I made it up." Nicola spread her skirts and gazed long into the china mirror. "No?" she asked, although they had said nothing. "Promise?" She looked at them shrewdly. "Well, then—he was saying good-bye to her again—this morning. I saw him come out of her room, a little after eight."

"Spy," whispered Annabel.

"You promised," Nicola warned her.

"Take it back, Annabel, I want to hear the rest."

Annabel did not take it back, but watched Nicola with a smile of incredulous, and rather scornful, amusement, and Nicola went on. "He came running down the stairs, and as he passed her portrait he went like this—" Nicola curled the fingers of her right hand, kissed the tips, and opened her hand in a gesture of good-bye, and then she drew in a long breath and began once more to reminisce about her future life, saying softly, "Someday I'm going to be just like she is. You wait and see."

LVII

The plans were completed at last, the carpenters and stone masons hired, and work began on Pete Devlin's house. During the first few months Jenny took no interest in it; but then she began to visit the house, and all during that winter and spring and on into the early months of summer she could be seen climbing about the skeleton structure in her entangling black dress and veil, and the workmen turned sheepish in her presence, thinking she came there to catch them at some dishonesty or carelessness.

The sight of Jenny moving up and down those staircases which seemed to rise without support from one story to the next, and stepping across the wide-spaced floor boards with no apparent giddiness or distrust, became so familiar to passers-by that more than one child was reproved for saying that the house was haunted—the ghost had moved in and taken possession ahead of the family.

But Jenny was less reconciled to the house than she pretended, and when she met Pete there unexpectedly one day, asked what he was doing, as if he had no right to go poking about her house. They had greeted each other politely, their best refuge nowadays, and stood a few moments in what would be the living room, while Pete explained that he had come to discuss some details with the carpenters and Jenny smiled at him skeptically. "You seem to find such pleasure in this house, Pete."

"Shouldn't I?"

"Houses have no meaning, only people."

"Houses have meaning to people, though," he reminded her gently.

Jenny was still waiting, though she scarcely realized it, until some event, some accident or disaster, should give him over into her custody; but when it came, she did not recognize the beginning of it until much later, perhaps because the series of events was so startling, and so terrifying, not only to her but to everyone else, that there had been no possibility of thinking coherently about anything at all. And she was even more surprised that for several days she, like the others, had been willing to imagine the past had been drowned in the flood itself—just as some years before many people had believed, and had said, they were purified by the fire, whatever it had cost them in money and terror—while Pete had emerged from the disaster a hero, having behaved in the midst of crazy excitement and real dangers with a recklessness and bravado which had attracted their astonishment and admiration.

It began as another summer afternoon storm, the kind they expected almost every day, violent and brief, turning the streets into muddy creeks which were quickly dried by the hot sun. Pete was standing outside Finney and Son's new building, talking to Lem. Lisette and Rachel and Georgina, with Jacob's wife, Anna Grace, had driven by not long before, on their way to a meeting of the French Class at Irene Flint's house, waving gaily as they passed, and the streets were crowded as they usually were at three o'clock, with women on shopping errands and men dashing about or standing idle, gossiping and whittling.

Morgan was in the East, on another of his pilgrimages to the Commercial Trust, and Lem was curious to know the news, for although they were rivals in Butte they were partners here, and Lem was obliged for his own sake to wish him success. And when Pete said that Morgan had scarcely had time to get there, much less to convince a board of eastern bankers, Lem squinted through his square-bowed spectacles as if he might be wondering what truth was concealed behind this evasion.

"It's the same old story, isn't it, Pete? The same thing we've been up against all along—money and transportation. But still, they're coming, aren't they? Against their wills, the bastards are coming our way." He glanced up curiously, and Pete did too, as a few pelting drops struck with unusual force upon their hats and shoulders and into the dust-laden street.

Pete smiled, agreeing, and Lem asked him, though the rain began to fall more heavily and men were moving indoors, about Jeremy Flint's latest devices in the Deer Lodge court, for whenever they talked about the old Halloway claim and the litigation it had led them into, they always pretended to be discussing a case which involved men unknown to them. "What I can't understand, Pete, is why Morgan doesn't do more with that Halloway claim. He spends everything on the Yellow Medicine."

"Wait until he gets the Yellow Medicine properly underway, Lem. You know the saying, it takes one mine to run another."

They laughed in recognition of this truth, and, the next moment, there were long peals of thunder, rolling one upon another, the clouds gathered swiftly, and the sky turned dark. Pete started at a run, waving to Lem, who called, "Come to Butte with me, Pete, see for yourself what's going on there nowadays."

"One of these days, Lem—when I get time."

"That's what you've been saying for four years!" Lem yelled, for by now the thunder was roaring steadily and the rain fell so heavily it was not possible to see for a distance of more than a few yards.

The street was a blurred pageantry of dashing horses and men yelling and waving their hats in a sudden attack of savage glee. Women were climbing out of their buggies and running into the nearest buildings, where they stood with men who had sought refuge, all peering from doorways and windows, and still hoping, as they did when taken by surprise in the mountains, that this time the surprise would be a pleasant one, offering something of that agreeable excitement found in prize fights and bull-whackers' contests, but not very often in the climate.

But in another two or three minutes they were glancing at one another uneasily, for the windows were streaming sheets of water impossible to see through, and whenever a man ventured out he was struck by water pouring from the roof with such violence that he retreated inside again, while the street had become a shallow river fed by water running off the hillsides.

Pete stood in the doorway of Devlin Brothers for two or three minutes, expecting that it would presently stop like any other summer storm, and then, as if by some common agreement that this was no ordinary storm but a cloudburst, men appeared in the street, distractedly yelling. Pete turned to Jonathan. "I'm going to find Jenny. Lisette and Georgina and Marietta must be at Irene Flint's by now, but I want to be sure. You go to the school, see that the kids are all right, and you"—he gestured at two of the clerks—"get everything you can up to the second floor."

He had to force his way through the crowd in the doorway, for some of them supposed he was trying to push them outside, and then he started off at a run. The thunder continued to roll, and between flashes of lightning it could be seen that the sky had turned ominously green, as in some unreal twilight.

By the time he reached the bottom of Elm Street, he was sinking at each step as if into a quicksand, floundering helplessly against the rain's beating attack, and he staggered part way up the hillside, but then told himself he would not find Jenny there and stumbled back down again to stand peering through the density of water and darkness, listening intently, and feeling as alien to this watery world as if he had discovered himself deep in the ocean.

Logs and timber came tumbling along, striking against his legs, and in another burst of lightning he saw a stalled buggy, and imagined he could hear a woman's voice, shrieking with anger.

As he got nearer, he saw that the buggy was their own, its wheels mired and the horse rearing and trembling as Jenny lashed at him, screaming in a voice of uncontrolled fury which, sometime later, Pete remembered as the most uncanny sound he had ever heard. And when he reached her and hung onto the side of the buggy, trying to keep his footing against the swift waters, she stared down at him as if they were strangers meeting unexpectedly in some imaginary land, and still went on lashing the horse and shrieking with no seeming awareness of what she was doing. Pete seized the reins and, at last, calmed the animal enough that he was able to pull the buggy, and so walked beside her to Jeremy Flint's house, where he lifted her out, though she still had nothing to say to him and gave him only a glance of terror and rage, then contrived to slip away and go rushing up the steps. The door opened, Marietta and Irene Flint appeared, and Jenny was out of his sight, leaving him to feel that that encounter had been, in some way, the most honest they had ever had.

He found the main streets flooded to a depth of nearly two feet, women had climbed onto chairs and counters, and the streets carried a hurtling raft of boxes and loose timber which moved by with steadily increasing speed as the yellow water poured off the hillsides. Men were at work pulling and shoving the boxes and lumber aside to make way for the rushing water, and Pete plunged into the work with an appearance of ferocious glee, shouting orders which were obeyed unhesitatingly, for they had been waiting for someone to assume responsibility, help them to save themselves from what now seemed a disaster certain to wipe out the camp more completely than any fire had done.

Pigs floated by squealing piteously, and crates of cackling chickens sailed along. Now and again, as the men worked, one of them was knocked down by the force of the water and must be rescued; another was caught against a building behind an accumulating barricade of lumber, and set free by Pete and Ralph Mercer. Outhouses careened by, got jammed into the barricades, and were chopped to pieces by men wielding axes. The sky continued dark, the rain fell with relentless force, and as the streets became estuaries the water rose to six or seven feet in the gulch, and rooftops were crowded with women staring in stoical fury, all their worst premonitions of this mania for westering come true.

When the storm had lasted for an hour, it was suddenly over. The sky cleared swiftly and the sun appeared, dazzlingly bright and very hot, making them look up with astonishment and disbelieving gratitude, but it was several hours before the water pouring down the hillsides had streamed through the town and found its way into the creek, leaving a wake of destruction which looked, during those first hours, more complete than any earlier damage done them by fire.

Pete made his way back once again to Irene Flint's house, inquiring as he went for news of the other parts of town, stopping to help move furniture out of flooded houses and office buildings, and was so peculiarly joyous in his manner, with an air of fierce encouragement and defiance, that he seemed a kind of religious fanatic arrived not only to announce that this was retribution for their sins but to assure them it was also their salvation.

And they agreed that during the height of the storm Pete Devlin had been seen in so many different places, taking no thought of himself but dragging men out of danger, tearing the barricades apart with his hands, and had been so active and so fearless, so resourceful and so unselfish that they began to salute him quite obsequiously and several men took him aside privately to thank him, while to each Pete listened silently and gravely, smiled a little by way of polite reply, as if to assure them he did not expect their gratitude or deserve it and, giving them a light pressure on the shoulder, nodded his head and went on.

After a few days the street had dried, the chickens which had not drowned had been recaptured and the pigs restored to their owners, the barricades of lumber and boxes dismantled, the mud carried out of houses and offices, and there was a general washing of furniture and clothing, while once again the men, if not the women, began to congratulate one another that it might have been worse, and agreed they were lucky it had rained hardest over the main part of town for, otherwise, the houses on the hillsides would have been washed away. The children had been safe in the schools, and all in all they agreed that there had been a measure of providential luck in this newest catastrophe.

"What if it had happened at night?"

"Suppose it had rained as hard as that over Oro Fino?"

They gathered in groups on street corners, glad to feel the hot sun, and most of them decided that between fire and floods they preferred floods. But then, two or three weeks after the flood there began the visitation of some mysterious sickness which might or might not be typhoid. Georgina and Lisette, with their children, were sent to stay with Felice in Butte, but although Pete tried to persuade Jenny and Marietta to go with them, they refused to leave, and Marietta added that Dr. Chaffinch was not sure what might be the nature of the sickness, while the newspapers had not even mentioned it.

Pete reminded them, however, that the Territorial papers preferred to print only cheerful news or news of general disasters: masquerade balls and strawberry festivals, new mines and concentration plants, fires and floods, that was what life in the mountains was made of if the *Helena Post* and the *Mountain Enquirer* could be believed. And Pete smiled as he told them this with a smile both whimsical and secretive, for ever since the flood there had been some curious change in him which Jenny had not been able to solve. It almost seemed he had come to have a new opinion of himself or, at least, had been reconciled to the old one.

A few days after Lisette and Georgina, with the four children, had left for Butte, Marietta and Jenny stopped in the late afternoon to inquire for Pete and were told he had gone out a few minutes earlier, saying he would be back in half an hour. "Shall we wait for him?" Jenny asked Marietta. "Or leave a note?"

"Why not stop at the Emporium and see what came in on the new shipment? Tell Mr. Devlin not to go home, because we're going to have dinner tonight with Mr. and Mrs. Church and we'll be back at six o'clock to drive there with him."

They walked on, smiling and nodding to acquaintances, pausing now and then to chat for a few minutes, and found the Ladies Emporium crowded with customers, turning through newly arrived bolts of English and Scottish woolens.

Marietta found a dark red and black plaid she said would make a pretty dress for Susette, and while Jenny talked to Cornelia Bream, she took it to the doorway to examine it in the light. She stood for a moment, folding it between her fingers, and glanced up to see Pete walking toward her, scowling as if he must be thinking of something which had enraged him, and staring straight ahead as he moved slowly and uncertainly along, so preoccupied, or so angry, that he did not see her. Marietta watched him carefully, glancing about to find Jenny, for, it occurred to her, Jenny should not see him now if he had, as it seemed, had too much to drink.

One of the clerks approached her and all at once Marietta thrust the bolt of cloth into his hands and went to meet Pete, speaking his name softly, and when he still did not see her she stopped directly in his path, putting her hands against his arms and asking, "Don't you recognize me, Pete?"

A man passing by glanced at Pete and smiled understandingly, but Pete looked down at her with a bewildered expression and he was, she saw now, not angry, but baffled and tired. His upper lip was smeared with dried blood, his nostrils had a caking of blood about their rims, as if he had wiped it away hastily and not washed his face, and several dark drops stained the front of his shirt. His forehead was wet with small beads of moisture which had dampened the hair at his temples, and he looked at her for a moment silently, his black eyes shining with unusual brilliance. "Of course I do, Marietta," he said at last.

Jenny appeared in the doorway, and then came quickly forward. "I wondered what was the matter with you this morning," she murmured, as if this were part of a conversation which had begun between them privately and which might now be concluded without Marietta or anyone else either hearing them or guessing what they might be talking about.

"I'm all right," he said, almost truculently. "Off my feed a little. Tired. That's all."

"How long have you been feeling this way, Pete?"

Pete grinned, shaking his head. "You're not a doctor, Marietta, and I'm not sick. Now, I know women love to have patients, but I'm afraid I'm going to disappoint you. I just saw Ray Chaffinch and he says a bloody nose in this altitude isn't unusual, happens to him every so often, and not to begin pampering myself."

"Do you want to go to the Churches' tonight?"

Pete stared at the sidewalk, studied the matter with apparent seriousness, and finally said, "I have some work to finish. Give Reba my apologies."

He bowed, first to Jenny and then to Marietta, with a ceremoniousness which seemed either playful or mocking, put his hat back on and set out with brisk determination, but had gone only a few yards

when he staggered slightly, set himself right again, and as he reached
Devlin Brothers turned to find them still watching him. He grinned,
waved his arm, and disappeared.

"He's sick."

Jenny shook her head. "He's drunk."

"Pete doesn't get drunk."

"He did today. He took a drink this morning before breakfast, and
then told me he wasn't hungry."

Marietta turned to her. "Jenny, what are you thinking about? He's
your husband, he's sick, and you pretend he's done something to
offend you."

Jenny stared at her, more astonished by this show of temper from
Marietta, the intense glowing of her eyes, than by Pete's uncertain
walk or the blood on his face and clothes, and she retreated into
an eager humility. "You know him best, Marietta. What shall we
do?"

Marietta looked at her a moment longer, as if at someone she
neither knew well nor trusted, and they walked slowly back toward
Devlin Brothers, where they hesitated near the door, and all at once
Pete came out and greeted them as if he had not seen them for a long
while. He had washed the blood from his face, his shirt front was
wet where he had tried to scrub out the stains, and he asked them
politely and almost gaily if they had some business with him today.

"Pete—come with us. Come home."

Pete laughed, deprecatingly. "I'm a busy man, Marietta. There
are two men in my office right now, and others waiting." He gestured,
showing them how many men were in there waiting for him. "For
God's sake, don't try to make me believe I've had it."

"You see?" said Jenny to Marietta, with a little smile of triumph.

After a few moments they left him standing there in the doorway,
still smiling at them, leaning against the jamb with one booted foot
crossed over the other, and for the next three or four days he continued to insist there was nothing wrong, he had no fever, Dr. Chaffinch was too busy to bother with trifles, until one morning he did
not appear at breakfast. Jenny had heard him moving about in Leila's room during the night, going downstairs and coming back up
so slowly that for a time she had wondered if he might collapse there
on the staircase, but had refused to go out to ask if he needed help,
telling herself that since he had been so full of bravado, had refused
to admit he might be sick, now he must come to her.

When she had eaten breakfast and heard no further sounds she
began the housework as if he had left, rushing at it with an unusual
vigor, and all the while she listened intently, expecting that momentarily he would call her. He did not, though, and it was almost noon
when she knocked at the closed door of Leila's room, and felt her
heart begin to beat with a peculiar urgency, as if something for
which she had waited many years was now about to happen, and
without her volition, or his.

After a long pause, he answered, "Come in."

She opened the door and stood for a moment, letting her eyes grow accustomed to the darkness, for the shades were drawn and the windows closed, and noticed a smell of blood and vomit with the same finicking disapproval she would have felt had the offense been committed by a stranger. The bed was in such disarray he must have been turning restlessly throughout the night, and his face had an expression of dull stupor, although his black eyes glittered with such intensity she felt as if some powerful, and quite unjust, accusation were being directed at her.

"Shall I send for Dr. Chaffinch?" she asked, as politely as though he had wakened with a slight cough and might like to have a mustard plaster on his chest.

Pete nodded, sighed heavily, and as she turned to leave without coming any farther into the room, he held forth one hand and might have been asking her to reassure him, lie to him perhaps, or express concern, at least. But as she only looked at him and made no move to approach the bed he sighed again, murmuring, "I know what it is without him telling me. Have him send a nurse, if you can find one. You go and stay with Marietta."

Jenny smiled. "What a thing to say. I'll take care of you, you know that." She added, as she closed the door, "Don't get out of bed again, stay where you are."

She went quickly down the stairs and stood for a moment looking into the vestibule mirror, consulting herself with a perplexed and thoughtful expression until at last she gave a slight inadvertent shrug, put on the hat with its long veil, and spent some moments arranging the folds. And all the while she had a sense of estrangement from her own body and thoughts, from the man who lay waiting for her to bring him help or, since Dr. Chaffinch would bring no real help and they knew it, bring him at least an illusion that his sickness was under consideration, and the estrangement was so complete that it seemed she was only going for a drive, to call on Marietta or Erma Finney, or perhaps to see if the carpenters had begun to work again on the house.

It took some time to send a neighbor child in search of the boy who cared for their horses and, once he was found, it then took some time longer to hitch up the buggy. But Jenny did not grow impatient, only wandered about examining her gardens, one for cutting flowers, the other for vegetables, and was serenely picking off wilted leaves when the boy showed her the buggy, standing ready in the street. She smiled at him, saying, "Thank you, Tommy," and then realized she was not even sure his name was Tommy, who might have been the last such boy they had had.

Jenny was convinced—as she had been when she had first found Leila sick—that Pete would die, and thought she might die herself, and this seemed to have in it an inherent logic and justice, for it was what she would have arranged if some impartial fate asked her to suggest a fitting punishment for Jenny Danforth and Peter Devlin. And she decided, as she drove to Dr. Chaffinch's office, keeping the horse to a deliberate pace, for there seemed no reason to hurry only because he had finally admitted that he was sick, that she would treat him exactly as she would have treated any stranger who might have fallen sick in a place where there was no one but herself to care for him.

Dr. Chaffinch was not in his office and she drove about looking for him, so that almost two hours had gone by before they climbed slowly toward the stone and white clapboard house and, as they entered the front door together, the Doctor was saying softly, "It may not be typhoid. We're not sure even of those cases where the patients have died. It's a very difficult disease to diagnose, as you know." He reminded her, as he had done during Leila's sickness, that as the widow of a doctor she knew that a doctor was helpful mostly because sick people imagined he was.

"What else could it be?" inquired Jenny reasonably, removing the crape veil and smoothing the sides of her hair, and she led the way toward the staircase, deftly rolling back her sleeves as she went. She saw very clearly, as she imagined, all that was to happen between herself and Pete, and even felt a sense of eagerness to have it begin. Therefore, she was surprised and disappointed and even rather angry when the door to Leila's bedroom opened and closed and Marietta appeared at the head of the stairs, causing them both to stop still, as if they must ask Marietta's permission to see the patient.

"You've been a long time getting here, Dr. Chaffinch."

"I came as soon as I was found, Marietta."

Marietta moved aside and Dr. Chaffinch continued on up, but as Jenny still hesitated, wondering at the expression on Marietta's face, somber and accusatory, Marietta came slowly down and stood on the step above her. Jenny had an inclination to back away, but that seemed so absurd an impulse, as if she had some reason to be afraid of Marietta, that she faced her instead with a remarkably guileless and inquiring expression. "Yes, Marietta?"

"I got here only a few minutes after you'd left. I knew he was sick, and I knew that eventually he wouldn't be able to pretend that he wasn't. Why did you leave him alone?"

"To get the Doctor," Jenny whispered, innocent and surprised at the accusation.

"Why didn't you send someone else?"

"Who could I send?"

"The room was filthy. The bedclothes were stained with blood and vomit. The slop jar was full. And when I got here he was out of bed, trying to get to the bathroom." She continued to whisper, her face close to Jenny's, and she seized Jenny's arm in a grip so tight that Jenny winced. Marietta gave her a quick, rough shake. "Pete Devlin may die, you know that. And if he does, neither you nor I will have let him feel that he was neglected, that we didn't love him well enough to care for him, whatever it costs us, whether or not it kills us both. Do you understand me?"

Marietta's face had a bitter intensity Jenny would not have expected her to be capable of and, for a moment, she gazed back at her in stupefied bewilderment, as if Marietta had slapped her hard enough to knock her into a brief unconsciousness, and told herself how plain it was now that Marietta had always hated her and yet, how cleverly she had hidden it, only for the sake of preserving the others, once Matt was dead. Jenny gazed at her in a kind of mesmerized fascination, asking herself who ever would have thought she had so much will, that little, soft woman, who had always before looked gentle as a morning in early summer, until finally she heard herself saying, in a pleading urgent voice, "You mustn't stay here, Marietta. It's dangerous. I'll take care of him."

Marietta smiled and the smile seemed to Jenny a sinister one, as if Marietta had meant to let her know she did not trust her to care for him alone. "I'll stay, Jenny, you'll need my help. I'm not afraid." She smiled again, asking, "Are you?"

"Of course not. My life isn't so precious to me any more."

Marietta turned slowly, picking up her skirts, and gave Jenny a glance from over her shoulder. "Neither is mine."

Jenny followed Marietta up the stairs, bewildered and chastened, and filled with a longing to serve not Pete but Marietta or, rather, to serve Marietta through Pete, as if by demonstrating to Marietta her humility, showing her that she would risk her own health to make Pete comfortable, she would at last win what she had supposed until that moment she had always had, Marietta's affection and forgiveness. Though how she could have let herself believe that Marietta had accepted the destruction of her life with patient charity, seemed to Jenny now the greatest mystery of all, stranger far than her own love for Marietta's husband.

Marietta tapped at the door and she and Jenny waited until Dr. Chaffinch opened it and stood before them in his shirtsleeves, his face serious but communicative. Pete lay propped against pillows, his arms at his sides, and once again Jenny noticed his thin, long-fingered hands, the palms turned upward as if in surrender. But he wore clean pajamas, his hair had been combed, the windows were opened and the stiff white curtains moved with a breeze, the bed linen was clean, and Jenny saw with a shock of jealousy that his eyes turned beseechingly to Marietta, and that when Marietta went to him, taking one hand and tenderly touching his hair, he smiled up at her and looked for a moment as eager for her love and protection as if he were not a man fifty-three years old, but a very young boy.

Jenny, rather sorry for herself that at this important and significant moment she should have been replaced by Marietta, stood looking at Pete and Marietta with a suspicious, hostile face, although she was not aware of it until she glanced at Dr. Chaffinch and found him watching her with curious surprise. And, feeling that she had betrayed herself, answered all the questions he might ever have asked himself about them, she went toward the Doctor, smiling as if he were a cherished guest, and began talking to him with the intention of regaining the control she had lost, giving him to understand that she loved Pete and that she would not be put aside, even by Marietta.

"It isn't serious, is it, Dr. Chaffinch?" she inquired naïvely and pleasantly, for it seemed the only possible excuse she could have in the opinion of any one of them for her earlier behavior—this natural feminine conviction that a strong and healthy man, her husband, could have only some minor ailment which would pass in a day or two.

"I'm afraid I can't say that yet, Jenny. We don't know."

"We don't know, we don't know," repeated Jenny chidingly, and went to stand beside the bed opposite Marietta, who did not look at her or at Dr. Chaffinch, but only at Pete. "What do you prescribe, Dr. Chaffinch?"

"I'm afraid to prescribe anything at all, just now. Only rest and quiet, quiet, most of all," he added, looking at Jenny. "If it should be—"

"Typhoid, Doctor," Pete told him brusquely. "Say it. That's what you think, isn't it?"

"I'm not sure. But if it is, some doctors recommend cold baths."

"You don't, Dr. Chaffinch," Marietta said positively.

"I've never been sure they did any good. And the patient suffers greatly from them."

"Even so," asked Jenny, "if they might help?"

"I've seen that, I remember it too well," Marietta said. "Pete's first wife, Dr. Chaffinch, died of typhoid, so did their son. The cold baths did them no good, they were brutal and exhausting, and if you recommend them I'll get another doctor."

Jenny left the room as if she had been dismissed, and stood in the vestibule, tracing her forefinger carefully along the antlers of the stag's head and staring at herself in the mirror, seeing her face as pale and almost as drawn as Pete's, while once more she asked herself how it could be possible she had misunderstood Marietta so completely.

She heard Dr. Chaffinch's footsteps and turned, but stood silent until he reached her. "Tell me the truth now, Doctor."

"He told you the truth. I think it's typhoid. He wants you to leave the house. It's highly contagious, as you know."

"I won't leave, you know that. But Marietta must. I can take care of him."

Dr. Chaffinch smiled. "If it is typhoid, Jenny, you will be grateful to have help. And she's a very resourceful woman who does not lose control of herself in an emergency." He nodded, and left the house.

Jenny began to dread her next encounter with Marietta, for it seemed that all at once and through no fault of her own, the benevolent lies, the necessary pretenses, the hard work, as she interpreted it, they had both given to keeping intact whatever had been left them after Matt's death and, perhaps most important, her dependence upon Marietta, had been obliterated.

She stayed in the kitchen during the afternoon, preparing dishes she knew Pete had enjoyed the few times he had been sick enough to lie in bed for a day or two—a delicate chicken custard, a rice pudding, small sandwiches of raw beef—and all the while, as she studied this new phenomenon of Marietta Devlin, she was eerily aware of the stillness in the house, a kind of stillness she had never before noticed when she had been there alone, for this silence seemed to have in it the prediction of future silences.

She heard few sounds from upstairs, only occasionally Marietta's steps moving softly about, as if he might be sleeping and she did not want to disturb him, and finally Jenny mixed an eggnog, laced it well with brandy, and carried it upstairs. She found Marietta seated beside the bed, reading, while Pete lay with his eyes closed, his face flushed, his head turned to one side in an attitude which took her by surprise, for it gave him an appearance of such abandonment of the effort of living that for an instant she remembered a man she had seen lying on the floor of a half-built shed, hanged by the Vigilantes the night before.

"Marietta, I have supper ready. Won't you come down and eat with me?" She whispered the words, pleading with Marietta, ingratiating and humble.

"I don't think he should be left alone, Jenny. He's quiet now, but his nose began bleeding again not long ago."

"Shall I bring you a tray?"

"You eat first, and while you stay with him, I will." Marietta looked at her candidly and directly, her face as clear and artless as it had ever been, and Jenny retreated meekly back to the dining room where she ate little and without appetite, wondering if she might be catching the disease herself.

During the next few days Jenny continued to behave cautiously and almost timidly, as if she had intruded into Marietta's house and might be put out at any moment. They did not see each other often, and although Jenny was suspicious of this at first, taking it as a punishment, she finally persuaded herself it was only because they were both incessantly busy for, as Dr. Chaffinch had predicted, their tasks multiplied as the disease progressed, and however much they did they could not catch up with what needed still to be done.

Marietta had asked Dr. Chaffinch not to tell anyone that Pete was sick, to pretend he had gone away for a few days, and she said to Jenny, "We don't want the house filled with women. Of course," she added, and smiled ironically, "it's unlikely they'd come if they thought it was typhoid."

They did not mention again, either to the Doctor, who came twice every day, or to each other, that Pete might die, but pretended the sickness would run its course, he would recover, and their lives would be as they had been before.

Pete had little to say when Jenny was in the room, although she often heard his voice and Marietta's, low and secretive, it seemed to her, when she was not with them. But whenever Jenny tried to coax him to talk to her, he replied listlessly and indifferently, turned his head away and would not look at her, and seemed ashamed of his weakness and resentful that she must perform such tasks for him.

Irene Flint came to the house one afternoon, rapping loudly and peremptorily. Jenny was with Pete and Marietta was downstairs, for although Jenny had begged her not to help with the cooking or any of those household tasks which had become seemingly endless, when all along she had prided herself on her easy efficiency, Marietta had paid no more attention to that than she had to Jenny's first request that she leave them alone. As the rapping was repeated, Jenny ran to the top of the stairs to see Marietta standing at one side of the window, where she could not be seen by whoever was outside. The doorknob rattled, for ordinarily the house was unlocked. "Who is it?" Jenny whispered, feeling an unaccountable terror, as if they were under attack.

"Irene Flint. I'll talk to her."

Jenny hesitated, but as Marietta opened the door and Irene Flint confronted them, she rushed down and squeezed past Marietta to stand with Irene on the porch, as if they were concealing something shameful and Irene must not be permitted to learn what it was.

"I've just heard about Pete. I want to help you."

"You can't help us, Irene," Jenny told her, and looked quite excited, as if Irene might force her way into the house. "And you mustn't come here. It's dangerous."

Irene smiled at her tolerantly. "Let me come in—let me talk to you." She looked from Jenny to Marietta. "You're both exhausted."

"No, Irene," Jenny protested, her voice high and nervous. "We're not or, if we are, it doesn't matter. Please, oh, please, go away and don't come back. Leave us alone."

Irene raised her eyebrows, as if marveling at this distraught behavior. "I'm not afraid of it. I took care of Jeremy Flint when he had typhoid—years ago."

Marietta shook her head. "No, Irene. You must believe us. We don't want help and we don't want anyone to know about it."

"But I'm afraid they do."

"Then tell them not to come here," Jenny cried. "Tell them not to bother us, please," and she put both fists to her temples, closing her eyes and shaking her head.

"Tell them not to bother us," Marietta repeated softly.

Irene stood a moment longer, then turned slowly and Jenny darted back into the house as if she had escaped some danger, looked swiftly at Marietta, and ran back up the stairs, panting with an unexplainable fear, and apparently Irene did as they had asked for they had no more visitors, although Dr. Chaffinch said that Pete's sickness was now known in the town and that he was inquired for constantly.

Each day Pete submitted himself silently to the Doctor's examinations, lying on his back, his body rigid and motionless as the Doctor's fingers pressed his belly, searching for pain or tenderness, and replied to his questions with a sullen defiance, as if by denying the symptoms he could deny the disease or, Jenny suspected, deny everything but his own death, which she imagined she could sense him preparing to accept; and she believed that while he lay there he was engaged in argument with himself and had determined he would take his leave of them without betrayal or admission—the final injustice, she told herself as she watched him, wondering at the stoicism this man was able to show under what the Doctor assured her was terrible and increasing pain, and he came gradually to seem as strange and unknown to her as Marietta had become.

But although she felt a deep resentment as she saw him preparing to cheat her, she did not dare question him and was almost afraid to speak to him, so fearful had she now become of Marietta.

Jenny had insisted that since the Doctor thought it not wise to leave him alone, she would stay with him at night and Marietta during the day. But then she found herself unable to sleep, and lay alert and vigilant, listening to their voices, hearing Pete's frequent cough, and trying to imagine what was happening in that room where Leila had died five years ago—much longer ago, as it seemed, than anything that had ever happened in either of their lives. He was, Jenny thought, a pathetic and absurd sight as he lay there, this tall, black-haired man surrounded by a little girl's toys and clothes, and occasionally she found him with the copy of *Aesop's Fables* he had read aloud to Leila lying opened beside him.

As Jenny lay in bed, every sound which came from the other room represented a mystery, something private and secret taking place between Pete and Marietta, so that even when she knew Marietta was reading to him, or that he had suffered another attack of diarrhea and Marietta was carrying the slop jar into the bathroom, returning with warm water to wash him as tenderly and impersonally as if he were a child who had soiled himself, that she was rinsing cloths in ice water to cool his forehead and face—for the fever grew worse in the late afternoon when the room was hot and airless, the sun burning through the drawn shades with a steady fury that made Jenny weak and nauseous—even while she knew there was nothing happening beyond those simple and remorseless requirements of the sickness itself, she was compelled to reinterpret each sound, and became more and more convinced that Pete was telling Marietta the secrets of their lives together during the years since Leila's death, perhaps even the secret of Matt's death.

From time to time, unable to lie there any longer, Jenny would get out of bed and move across the room as stealthily as if she knew there was a burglar in the house, and cross the hall to stand in the opened doorway, until either Pete or Marietta discovered her there.

Marietta might be bent over him, combing his hair very carefully because of the intensity of headache, although he refused to accept Dr. Chaffinch's prescription of morphine, and she would ask, "What's the trouble, Jenny?"

Jenny would answer vaguely, still watching them closely. "I thought I heard a sound of some kind, I must have been dreaming," and she would leave them again, go back and usually fall sound asleep for a short time, but always she was afraid that something of crucial significance would take place between them while she slept or that Pete might die without her knowledge, a possibility which terrified her, even though her conviction that he was going to die did not.

Marietta had become her enemy, Pete's guardian, and Jenny felt a continuous sense of horrified disbelief at what she believed was her discovery of Marietta's disloyalty to Matt. And then, one morning when Jenny had come from a night of sitting beside him—for she remained in the chair near his bed throughout the night, staring into the darkness and afraid to close her eyes lest she fall asleep and lose some valuable clue—having passed Marietta in the hallway where they murmured only a few words like two soldiers changing guard duty, Marietta inquiring if he had been able to sleep and Jenny replying she could no longer tell if he was sleeping or awake, the expression on Marietta's face left her so astonished that she went to the mirror, as if she might find in her own face the explanation of what it had meant. Jenny looked at herself for several moments, suspicious and slyly thoughtful, and at last, satisfied with what she had discovered, smiled at herself as at a fellow conspirator. For Marietta, she was convinced, knew and had always known how Matt had died, and was now so tender with Pete because she had accepted Matt's death as retribution for the harm his disloyalty had done to all of them.

"Of course," Jenny whispered, "of course she knows it. That explains everything. But why did I never think of it before?"

Jenny turned away, so sure she had found the solution that for a time she wandered about, dazed and weak, wondering if she might be going to faint, and believed that her own guilt and mourning had come to an end.

The conviction seemed less clear when she saw Marietta next, but she told herself this was only because of the dependence she had come to feel upon Marietta, and her own absurd and nearly insane invention of Marietta as a saint. They met in the kitchen where Marietta was unpacking the groceries which the delivery boy left outside the door, taking back with him a list of what he was to deliver the following day as if they were playing some dangerous game, and Jenny, not wanting to give away her new-found secret knowledge, smiled ingratiatingly at Marietta and asked what she could do, as if it was Marietta's house rather than her own. "He doesn't want to eat," Marietta said, "but the Doctor says he must, and I think we might be able to persuade him to drink some beef tea. I'm going to make some anyway."

"Let me do it, Marietta. You've done too much, you're looking tired."

"There'll be time enough to rest."

But although Jenny gave her a questioning glance, expecting that now they would discuss what all three of them knew was inevitable, Marietta said nothing more but went on with the preparation of the beef tea, and presently Jenny tied a scarf about her hair and began to sweep the living-room floor as industriously as if there had been a party there the night before.

The idea of Marietta's treachery continued to strike her as something so new, so monstrous, so indicative of her own innocence in which she had never before believed, that during the next day or two it occupied her more completely than the prospect of Pete's death, for his sickness no longer seemed entirely real to her but had become only a series of tedious, disgusting chores, to be performed with no more awareness of their nature than she could avoid. She was brisk and efficient as she bathed him, laid a cold compress on his forehead, changed the bed linen by rolling him onto one side and then the other, but was no longer able to believe that this shrunken stranger whose fierce black eyes restlessly watched her face, was her husband, or had ever been.

One night, when there had been another attack of diarrhea and Jenny was washing him, as prudishly revolted as a schoolgirl, though she took care to keep her expression grim and aloof, she glanced at him inadvertently and found that he was smiling slightly, a smile so singular, derisive and knowing, that it made her heart beat with an expectation of what he would say to her now.

"For a man to die this way, stinking like a pig and helpless as a baby, takes away whatever small dignity he might ever have had— or thought he had." He spoke slowly and with difficulty, for during the past day or so a crust had begun to form upon his lips, sores which looked like so many little boils. Jenny completed her task of cleaning him, and spread the sheet up to his shoulders. "Doesn't it, Jenny?"

She tossed the cloth into a basin. "You're not going to die, Pete."

"Of course I am." He watched her a moment longer. "I was just lying here thinking, Jenny." She looked at him, quickly alert. "Do you know what I was thinking about? Would you like to know?"

"Of course."

"I was thinking what god-damn good luck it is we won't have to spend the next twenty years wondering which of us will die first." He laughed softly. "That's what I was thinking about—are you disappointed?" But then he turned his head aside, closing his eyes. "Put the light out, please."

Jenny bent to blow it out, sat quietly in the straight-backed chair and waited, supposing he had only begun whatever it was he intended to say, but after several minutes during which he remained silent, only restlessly picking at the top of the sheet as he had lately begun to do and turning about in the bed, she spoke softly. "Pete?" She waited, but he did not answer, and in the morning seemed dull and lethargic and gave no indication that he remembered having spoken to her at all.

Jenny told Marietta he had begun talking to her the night before, wondering if Marietta would now tell her what it was they said to each other while Jenny lay trying to sleep during the hot afternoons. Marietta did not look at her, but only asked, "He did? Was he clear?"

"I've forgotten what he said. The Doctor told us he might become delirious." She gave her a wheedling look. "He talks to you, though. I hear him. What does he say?"

"He talks about the past, Jenny. Before we came out here. He talks about the days when Matt and I were first married, and he was courting Lorena."

"But not about me?"

"Do you want him to talk about you?" Marietta looked amused and, Jenny thought, rather scornful.

"Surely," Jenny said, growing troubled and reflective, for he might even now have escaped her, "if he's as sick as Dr. Chaffinch believes, he should have something more to tell us than that."

Marietta whirled around. "What do you want him to tell us?" she demanded and, once again, dismayed and frightened by this strange Marietta, Jenny shook her head and retreated.

"I don't know. It only seems he would tell us something—"

There were small pink spots appearing now on his abdomen, and at sight of these Dr. Chaffinch drew back, as if at some surprising discovery, while Pete lay sweating and silent, holding fast to the headboard with his clenched hands while the Doctor probed at his belly, but although the Doctor looked at him questioningly from time to time, hoping to get his admission of intolerable pain and to be told where it was keenest, Pete seemed to be challenging him to display his medical knowledge, if he had any, to tell him what was wrong, not ask him. The Doctor's fingers touched the spots carefully, pressing lightly, and they disappeared but sprang out once again as he removed his hand.

"That does it," Pete said to him. "You can't pretend any longer you don't know what it is."

"No. It's typhoid. But you'll get well, Pete—it takes time. Be a little patient. You never were a very patient man."

Pete smiled. "How much time have I left?"

"Why, a long time, Pete. Many, many years."

Pete returned his arms to his sides and his white fingers lay on the cotton spread, thinner than ever, the black hairs looking crisp and artificial on his knuckles, and he glanced at the two women, standing side by side at the foot of the bed, his eyes passing thoughtfully from Jenny to Marietta and back again to Jenny, and at last he nodded, sighing.

"How much time has he?" Jenny asked, when she and Dr. Chaffinch had reached the front door.

"He may not die."

"Doctor, don't lie to me."

"You're reconciled, Mrs. Devlin?"

Pete grew increasingly restless, found it more difficult to eat as the crusts covered his gums and teeth and tongue, swallowed with difficulty, and was finally unable to avoid crying out when the Doctor probed at his belly. He plucked continuously at the sheet or gathered folds of it together in his fingers, picked at the sores on his mouth and did not appear aware that Marietta was blotting the blood with a damp cloth, but lay as if stupefied, and then one afternoon he looked up at her as suddenly and challengingly as he had at Jenny. Marietta, hovering above him, paused as Jenny had, surprised to see his look of ferocity and determination, as if by some vast effort of will and intent he had dragged together his resources, dwindling and dispersing from day to day, and he spoke to her in a low, decisive voice. "Jenny was in love with another man, did you know that?"

Marietta touched with the damp cloth the corners of his mouth where he had made the blood appear again, murmuring, "Hush. Don't talk. Sleep."

He seemed to obey her for a few minutes, lapse off into sleep or unconsciousness, but then opened his eyes again. "What did I say?" He seized her hand. "What did I say to you just then, Marietta?"

She smoothed his hair. "You said that Jenny looked so tired you were troubled about her."

He smiled, this time with a wise and crafty look, an expression she had never seen on his face before. "No, Marietta. That isn't what I said. You didn't hear me correctly. Or you didn't want to hear me correctly—which was it?"

"Don't talk, Pete—please don't. Sleep."

But a few hours later he came back to it again, although this time he lay with his eyes closed, and seemed to be talking to himself. "I thought when I married her that she loved me. Now, I don't think she ever did. I must have failed her, or maybe it was only that I was the wrong man—she wanted someone else." He lay silent for some time, and at last drew in a long, deep breath. "There were so many signs, I'm not sure now what they were, but people give themselves away. It's impossible to conceal any strong feeling, however you try." He opened his eyes and looked at her. "Did you know that, Marietta? Did you?" She said nothing, and he sighed. "I must have known it from the first."

"The Doctor doesn't want you to talk, Pete."

He nodded, fell silent for a few minutes, and then said, "Finally, I began to despise myself—and I was sure he despised me, too." He gave a sudden, wildly imploring look, his black eyes shining, breathing more quickly, and was once again tearing anxiously at the sheet. "I tried to warn him in every way I could—but I couldn't make myself talk to him about it. How in hell could I? You understand that, Marietta, don't you?" She turned quickly, but he caught hold of her wrist. "Listen to me, Marietta. Hear what I have to tell you." He went on, still holding her fast, and began to talk with great eagerness and intensity, as if he must be breaking a vow he had made to himself. "Listen to me. Let me tell you how it happened. I never meant to kill him, I swear to you I didn't, Marietta—I think I wanted him to kill me."

Marietta bent toward him, taking his face between her hands. "You don't know what you're saying, Pete, you're delirious." Her tears fell onto his face and she wiped them away, whispering, "Don't talk any more, I beg of you, lie still, be quiet, be quiet—" She sank slowly down, kneeling beside the bed with her head bowed, and Pete began to stroke her hair, as if to give comfort or reassurance, or a benediction, but seemed not to know she was crying, and all the while he talked went on staring at something remote, from that room, or from that hour.

"He wouldn't fire. He stood there—waiting—and I fired once over his head, and the second time, I fired straight at him. Gabe Foster came running up out of nowhere, some guy neither of us had ever seen before, yelling and shooting as he came, and I turned and shot him almost accidentally—I was never that good a shot. Matt was a hell of a lot better, you know that. He could have killed me so easily —I've never stopped wondering why he didn't." His voice grew tender, and his hand went on caressing her. " 'Get out of here, Pete,' he said to me. 'Beat it, for Christ's sake. Don't let them find you here.' He lay there on his belly and I tried to turn him over, but he wouldn't let me. The last thing he said was, 'Forgive me.' " He looked down at Marietta, reflectively murmuring, "Forgive me." After several minutes, Marietta raised her head, and now he seemed to be asleep. But then, as she covered her face with her hands, he looked up at her. "So help me God, I killed him." He sighed deeply. "I don't want to see Jenny again."

Marietta nodded, and after awhile, when he lay with his eyes closed, took the pitcher and went to the bathroom, and as she returned Jenny opened the door of her bedroom. Marietta paused, looking at her for a moment, then went into Leila's room and shut the door.

LVIII

The celebration began several days early and by the morning of the Fourth most of the men were drunk, the mines and mills were closed or running with skeleton crews, there had been fist fights and random shootings and a variety of accidents, and even the dogs seemed to have caught the fever and ran about barking noisily until they were kicked into silence, while the women stayed indoors and tried to keep the younger children away from the main part of town where men lurched along, rambling from saloon to saloon, congregating into knots and separating again, and quarreling over their places in the parade.

The town had been decorated in a style they thought suitable to the liveliest young city of five thousand in the world, as they regularly described it to be. Flagpoles lined the business streets, and a forest of evergreens had been nailed to the fronts of houses and saloons and office buildings. Flags blew briskly and Chinese lanterns danced about, patriotic bunting festooned windows and balconies, and out in the valley a racecourse had been staked, where in midafternoon the men who took pride in their horses and riding skill would test themselves.

Farmers and their families had arrived the night before, and the citizens were amused to see these rustics in their wagons gazing in astonishment at brick warehouses and office buildings. There were many visitors from Helena, come to participate in the revel, for their own town had begun to preen itself on its civilization, but Butte still rejoiced in its newness and masculinity, and let no holiday pass without excitement and disasters enough to convince them the next morning that whether they could remember it or not, the day had been a glorious one.

Morgan appeared at the Yellow Medicine before six o'clock and spent an hour there, warned his foreman Shang Oliver to be sure it was kept guarded all day and all night, and rode out to inspect the copper reduction plant they were building. He stopped next at the office of the *Butte Independent*, where he read Billy Church's description of the parade, the picnics and horseraces, the splendid display of the fireworks and the ball which had lasted until dawn, all minutely described before any of it had taken place for, as Billy explained, by the end of the day he would be as drunk as anyone else. And then, as Morgan approached Devlin Brothers, he saw Douglas staring up at their flagpole, which had been the tallest pole in town the night before, but now the tallest stood a hundred yards down the street, in front of Finney and Son.

Morgan stopped beside Douglas, gazing up at their flag, until all at once Douglas realized he was there and turned with a look of fanatic rage. "When I catch Jake Finney I'm going to knock every god-damn tooth out of his head."

"Leave the son of a bitch alone."

Morgan walked into the building and Douglas followed him, as ready to fight him as Jake Finney, until Morgan turned, grabbed him by the shoulder, swore into his face and then, helplessly laughing, threw one arm about him and suggested they have a drink, toast their own flagpole, and forget the Finneys for one day.

Douglas grew calmer under the influence of two drinks, but while Morgan was reading the mail Douglas disappeared and he did not see him again until the parade began at eleven o'clock, when he discovered him across the street, with the procession between them, glaring ferociously and chewing a cigar, for Douglas had always thought a holiday lost unless he could find someone to fight with. Morgan tried to get his attention, he waved his hat and shouted his name, and then Lem Finney's voice spoke in his ear, greeting him with that deference he had shown ever since Pete's death almost a year ago had put Morgan in complete control of Devlin Brothers.

Lem was bland and polite each time they met, whether here or in Helena, at a social occasion or on the street, but before the conversation ended they would find themselves discussing the old Halloway claim, which only recently had once again been awarded to Morgan on a technical error which Lem insisted was imaginary; and now he brought the subject up again.

"Jeremy Flint, after all, could convince a jury a hyena's asshole was a daisy, but that doesn't make it one, now does it, Morgan?" Morgan grinned, and Lem ruefully added, "I've always been a little hurt that after all the years our families have been friends—and your father and uncle and I came up the river together in 'sixty-two, just seventeen years ago next month"—and Lem lowered his eyes and gazed at his boots, as if to commemorate the event—"that you and Douglas should have treated Jacob and Homer the way you did that night." He glanced up inquiringly, his blue eyes as clear and shrewd as they had ever been, and though his small face had become somewhat withered and pinched, it was still lively and genial and crafty.

Morgan laughed as jovially as Lem, thrusting his hands into his pockets and rocking on his heels. "You never give up, Lem, do you?"

"No, I never give up. If one thing doesn't work I try another, and if that doesn't work—"

Morgan made a magnanimous gesture, offering him the street, the city itself, all the Rocky Mountains if he wanted them. "Try whatever you like, Lem."

"I will, Morgan, I promise you." Lem smiled, nodded, and they went in opposite directions, with Morgan furiously scowling and asking himself how it could be that Lem Finney should have the conceit to imagine he might take away the Halloway claim or anything else that Morgan Devlin either owned or fancied, and the scowl did not disappear until a hand caught his arm and he found Bruno Favorite in his path, inviting him to come inside and have a drink.

Favorite's Saloon stood in its old location, but the former dark little grocery store was now a spacious stone building with a golden oak bar, mirrors and polished glasses and a hired bartender, and Bruno no longer hovered almost out of sight, peering across the counter as he swiped back and forth a dirty and stinking rag, but had emerged in frock coat and silk hat to stand at the door, pointing out the city's ancient landmarks, so rapidly disappearing, to visitors who came flocking in on every coach, although they usually flocked out again a few days later, discouraged to have found that in Butte as in every other new community earlier arrivals had preempted the best locations, owned the most favorable water and mill sites, and held fast to all the likeliest properties.

"When we get rich," Bruno confided, "I'm going to retire and live like a gentleman. I hope you'll do the same."

"I'll have to keep working to support you, Bruno. You've got expensive tastes." He indicated the watch chain, dangling gold nuggets, which was draped across Bruno's high, round belly. "Next thing I know you'll be hankering for diamonds."

"Suppose I do? I'm the guy, remember, who practically kept the camp open single-handed, when everybody else got discouraged. You, too," he reminded Morgan.

"You're the guy, Bruno, who kept the god-damn joint alive," and, hearing his own solemn voice making this pronouncement, Morgan reminded himself he must stay sober enough to watch Susette ride by in the parade, for she had been up when he left that morning, wearing her silver crown and ready for the parade to begin.

Morgan and Bruno edged their way along, searching for an opening through which Bruno might see the parade. A freight wagon painted red and white and blue rumbled by, bearing the town band, and that was followed by a wagon crowded with forty-one little girls, dressed in white and draped with state flags, who blushed and ducked their heads at the approving roar which followed their passage. But all the while Bruno was complaining that he could see nothing, not the band wagon or the Goddess of Liberty, and in fact no one in this city he had founded and sustained would give him so much as a peep at their Fourth of July parade.

At last Morgan helped him to scramble onto the roof of a livery stable, and made for himself a place where he might peer over the heads of other men as a troop on horseback, wearing frock coats and parts of Civil War uniforms, went by in a cloud of dust which made them nearly invisible, and as he saw Susette in the distance, approaching on the palomino gelding he had given her for her fifth birthday, a hand clasped his arm and a woman's body pressed confidingly against him.

Supposing this must be some accident of the crowded street, he

pretended not to have noticed it, and as Susette drew nearer he began
to scowl with concentration, determined to have no such distractions
on his mind, but the woman's breasts moved against his back, her
thighs pressed his leg and, for all his stoic determination, he was unable to resist glancing around, and then he discovered Fan Moffat,
pretending to be too engrossed in the parade to know he was there.
He turned resolutely away, but her breasts and thighs still pressed
against him and her hand held his, while Morgan, thinking it was
surely his duty to struggle with her for possession of his hand, felt
his face burning with shame, as if Fan's misbehavior would be immediately detected by Susette and denounced before all the town.

Fan Moffat had become Fan Troy more than a year ago, to the
disappointment of Bruno Favorite and her other admirers who
would never again see Camille in a white nightgown, her long red
hair trailing on the floor beside her deathbed, expiring with an occasional knowing glance at the audience.

Bruno had tried for several months to persuade her to marry him,
but then one day she married Green Troy in the private dining room
of the Hotel de Mineral and left for a European honeymoon, carrying
an armful of red roses and riding out of town on the roof of the
coach. When they returned, Fan unpacked a number of French
gowns and began to give receptions in their new house, and at the
first one she whispered to Morgan, "Please make your wife be nice
to me. I want everyone to like me."

And, by now, there had been so many newspaper articles about
Mr. and Mrs. Troy, their charities and their entertainments, her
charm and his money, that if Mrs. Troy had ever been an actress it
was not remembered against her and indeed was scarcely remembered at all, and in another year or two her old identity would have
been entirely lost in her new one, just as surely as the old town was
disappearing and a new one taking its place.

But here she stood, leaning against him, and they were hemmed
in on all sides, so that Morgan distractedly wiped his forehead and
face with a handkerchief and then began to wave it, signaling to
Susette, as if she might save him.

Susette rode slowly by, seated on a blanket which bore in large
silver letters the legend Prospects of Butte, and at sight of her he
was so overcome with joyous pride that he quite forgot Fan Troy, and
shouted Susette's name in a voice which sounded as if it came out of
a megaphone. And as Susette's dark eyes searched him out and
found him and she smiled, he felt some crazy impulse to burst into
tears and drew a long breath to save himself, marveling as he often
did that everything sentimental and slavish which had ever been
hidden away in the crevices of his character Susette could summon
forth only by a glance and one of those enigmatic smiles, interpreted
by him as showing a phenomenal and eerie comprehension of the
adult world.

Susette was now a dainty and lively child, with the same earnestly serious manner her mother often showed, though she also had her own mysterious enchantments which kept him perplexed and so eager for her good will that he told himself wryly he courted this little girl more diligently than he had ever courted Felice.

"Your office is empty," Fan murmured. "I just passed it."

He bent down, whispering with an air of mock conspiracy, "I've got to take Susette to her mother," and then set off, glad enough to have made his escape, for he counted Fan among those renegade women who exercised such a mystical charm over him.

It was not easy to persuade Susette there was nothing more to being the Spirit of Butte than that, but at last she agreed to perch on his shoulder, and while he made his way through the dense traffic back to the Hotel de Mineral, Susette held fast to her silver crown and acknowledged each compliment with a gracious little smile.

He found Felice on the hotel verandah with Flora, and he looked at her intently for a moment, as he did each time he had been away, whether for a few hours or a few days or for several weeks, as if to convince himself she had not changed, she loved him as much as before, and once he was satisfied of that he saw them start home in Felice's carriage and began to proceed from one saloon to another, buying drinks for friends and strangers as he went, and falling into deep conversation about the prospects of Butte which, he was told with many maudlin compliments, had been so touchingly portrayed by his daughter.

Early in the afternoon he was seized by an impulse which sent him dashing up to the Yellow Medicine, as anxious as if someone might have removed this valuable hole during his absence and sunk it somewhere else.

The Yellow Medicine had frequent visitors nowadays, but they were seldom permitted to descend the shaft and he assumed with each an attitude of impatient boredom and gloom, saying that the property was not doing as well as he had hoped, that the vein was pinching out and he doubted there would be paying ore below the water line. After that, they were not eager to invest in a property its owner described so pessimistically and went to talk to Lem Finney or someone else, and Morgan would give a nervous snap of his fingers as the intruder walked away, convinced he had rid himself of a dangerous pest, hop nimbly into the cage and slip back down into the darkness.

"Anyone been around here this morning?" he asked Shang Oliver, and stared at him suspiciously, although Oliver had been his foreman for five years and on most days he trusted him as well as any miner ever trusted a foreman.

"Not a damn soul."

"The town's full of strangers," Morgan warned him. "They're crawling all over the hill."

"I know it."

"Keep your eye peeled," Morgan advised him, and, remarking

that he would soon be back, descended into town to discover that a man had fired his pistol at random and struck a small boy who had died a few minutes later and that even now a crowd was forming, in brisk western fashion, to take the man way from his custodians and hang him; for a lynching, several men were heard to say, was just what this celebration lacked and must have. But presently they lost interest and dispersed, for the man had, after all, stolen nothing, and the boy's death had been accidental.

After another hour or two, he remembered his promise to take Felice and Flora to hear Lem Finney's speech, and ran most of the way home, but found only the maid there with William and the baby Peter, who had been born a few weeks after Pete's death. The maid, a young girl who was the most recent of several they had imported from the East, told him they had left half an hour ago, and he found them in the auditorium where Lem Finney, even as Morgan came sneaking to his place beside Felice, was fixing the spectacles upon his nose and raising his hands to silence them.

But the hall soon began to seem intolerably hot, Lem Finney's public-speaking voice sounded shrill in his ears, and Morgan fidgeted and pulled at his collar and at last, giving Felice an imploring glance, he went sneaking out again and returned to the streets to find a dog fight in progress and several men gathered to bet on it.

The fight did not interest him but he watched it idly for a few minutes, wondering where it was he had meant to go when he had left the hall, and was relieved to see Bruno Favorite come along with word that it was time to set out for the race track, and as they strolled toward the valley Bruno talked of the Sunday afternoon when they had raced Lily Jones, sighing and shaking his head, for even the horses were slower nowadays, Bruno declared, and a man wasted his money betting on them.

Bruno had provided a bottle of whisky as a precaution against his disappointment, and he and Morgan sat on the grass passing it back and forth from time to time and watching the races, placing bets and collecting them, until Morgan had another attack of alert awareness, glanced about as challengingly as if he had been told of some nearby menace, and realized he had finally gotten as drunk as he had ever been. He thereupon left Bruno without a word and walked swiftly to the Yellow Medicine, where he found fault with whatever he saw and threatened to fire the entire crew and, after that, a little ashamed of himself, he went into a restaurant and ate a great deal of food, and when he left was feeling almost sober enough to go home and ask Felice what time she wanted to leave for the ball.

Instead, however, he stopped to have a drink and there he heard news of another catastrophe, a little girl, one of those who had ridden in the car of state, had been killed in a street accident, and several men he talked to were crying bitterly over the tragedy, describing her crushed legs and body, and so he went dashing home to be sure the accident had not happened to Susette, instead. Susette, however, was eating dinner with William and her cousin James, and gave him what he took to be a critical look, whereupon he left promptly, thinking that she disapproved of seeing him drunk and would say so if he lingered about.

"I'll be back," he told Felice, who was in the bedroom arranging Flora's hair. "What time do you want to go?"

He was off again, before she had answered him, feeling slightly puzzled as he heard them laughing, for it must be they were making fun of him for looking so stupidly drunk as no doubt he did, and he was sorry to have given them the opportunity. But it seemed by then that only another drink would sober him up, and he presently found himself crowded against a bar, engaged in profound discussion with a man he had never seen before, one of those pilgrims who appeared in Butte nowadays hoping to fall accidentally into a fortune. Before very long he and the man began to argue, the argument grew louder, for the pilgrim was skeptical about the prospects of Butte and his skepticism acted upon Morgan as a mortal insult so that he rushed outside, escaping this time from his own impulse to fight the pilgrim or, indeed, almost anyone at all.

By now it was nearly dark and there were few women on the streets where the men went rambling up and down in groups, turning abruptly from time to time to change their course like so many fish in the wake of a leader, although there was no leader, and Morgan rambled along with them as the darkness fell, until a weak, spraying comet was set off from the fireworks stand, causing a groan of disgust and shouts of derisive laughter. The young man in charge of the display asked them to be patient, bear with him, and a blob of fiery blue flame leaped uncertainly into the air, hesitated and collapsed, descending in a faint shower which disappeared amid more groans and protesting howls.

All at once Morgan set out with an air of great purposefulness and a conviction that he knew at last what it was he had meant to do from the moment he had awakened that morning. He had tried many times to remember the nature of this important and elusive errand, and now that he finally had, he went striding toward the big butte, climbed swiftly to its top, and stood at last looking down over the camp where yellow lights shone from every building and bonfires had been lighted along the main street, and from that vantage point it seemed he was able to survey the past and the future alike, and one was as clear to him as the other.

He stood rocking back and forth, his head swimming agreeably, his teeth clenched in a savage and triumphant grin intended only for himself, watching the occasional flares which sprouted over the camp, yellow or white or blue, and felt a surging pride and confidence, arrogance and vanity and self-congratulation so great that it seemed he had become a colossus bestriding the camp, the Rocky Mountains themselves—an invincible giant inspecting his many achievements, only now at their best beginning. As he stood there,

Morgan lost awareness of time while he contemplated this spec-
tacle of himself, for never before had the vision been so clear or
seemed so inevitable as at that moment, when he felt a powerful
and riotous conviction that he could knock down a great tree with
his fists, open up the earth with his bare hands and tear out its secrets, kick apart mountains with his booted feet, or perform any
other acts of destruction or creativity, for he was, in himself, complete and entire, doomed or destined to conquest; and as he wallowed
gratefully in his own significance and strength, still with that same
evil grin on his face, he felt a rising cruelty and contempt for other
men.

For there in the town below, and on all the surrounding hillsides,
were the mines, spreading beneath the ground in a web of passageways, a growing city which would one day have enclosed whole
forests, swallowed and digested the entire production of great
foundries—and, perceiving all this, he swept off his hat and bowed
low, acknowledging the fireworks, uncertain fountain though they
might be, but nevertheless got up by a grateful citizenry for the purpose of celebrating on this night Morgan Devlin's future achievements.

He turned, surveying his domain, the city below and the mountains beyond, spinning slowly and unsteadily and with one leg
crossed awkwardly over the other, until at last he staggered and
caught his balance, swearing. The next moment he heard a slight,
discreet cough and saw, not far away, that another man stood there
and might have been there for several minutes—and if he had been
talking to himself, as he thought quite possible, then of course this
interloper had heard him.

Morgan's hand inadvertently touched his pistol, and he heard Lem
Finney's voice inquire, "Is that you, Morgan?"

Subdued and ashamed, he mumbled, "Hello, Lem, didn't know
anyone else was around," and was trying to guess if he had been saying for Lem Finney's amusement the words he had said to himself.
Morgan started slowly toward him, thinking that this was the best
opportunity he had ever had or would likely ever have to kill Lem
Finney and be done with him once and for all, but by the time he
reached Lem, his hands were in his pockets and he was smiling with
the expression of knowing skepticism which it seemed came automatically to his face at sight of Lem Finney.

They stood side by side for a few moments, and presently another
spray of yellow and blue light went lobbing over the horizon. Finney
drew in a deep breath and Morgan, glancing at him, remarked, "Good
speech today, Lem," although he had not heard what Lem was saying even during the few minutes he sat in the hall pretending to
listen.

Lem nodded, and Morgan studied him surreptitiously in the faint
starlight, asking himself what Lem Finney had been doing up there
and when he had arrived and if he had recognized him and kept silent,

hoping to catch him in something foolish or dishonest, perhaps trying to sneak down the Buckhorn shaft and take advantage of the town's preoccupation to bore out a few samples he might study at his leisure. Or perhaps Lem Finney had had some such predatory intentions himself toward the old Halloway claim and had been waiting for him to leave. But before Morgan had made the accusation, he reminded himself that although he was drunk, Lem was not, and so they continued to stand side by side, each waiting for the other to leave first, until Morgan said, grinning slyly in the darkness, "You know, Lem, I wonder if maybe we weren't both thinking about the same thing?"

"I was thinking," said Lem, "that this whole god-damn hill is made of copper, and that all of it belongs to me—or will, one of these days." He smiled. "Is that what you were thinking?"

Morgan gave a shout of laughter, and they started back down, but as they reached the crowded streets he remembered with a horrified shock, as if he had committed some atrocious crime, that the ball was in progress and he had forgotten to call for Felice, and he left Lem Finney and went sprinting along, weaving and darting among the groups of drunken and noisy men, and as he neared the hall he collided with a woman who stepped into his path, caught her in his arms to save them both from falling, and found that here was Fan Troy again, petulantly asking where he had been all day. "No one will miss us now, Morgan."

He stepped back and stared at her blankly, unable to guess what she meant, then took hold of her shoulders and moved her out of his path, whispering, "I'm too drunk," and ran on, quite desperately anxious by now about Felice.

Bonfires burned outside the hall, pine torches flared, and men and women in evening dress, many of them strangers to the town or so changed by their clothes that they seemed to be, were streaming through the doors, while some couples hung about outside, resting or escaping from the heat.

The fiddles were squeaking and the floor so crowded with dancers that as Morgan searched anxiously for Felice, their whirling began to make him dizzy, and he blundered into their midst, walking among them and glowering whenever a spinning couple knocked into him. He found her at last, seated at the far end of the room with Flora, and they both glanced up in surprise to find him hovering there, asking what had happened, for Flora was crying bitterly.

"We're all alone!" Flora accused him, and covered her face with her wet handkerchief.

"I'm sorry, I'm sorry." He touched Flora's hair but she would not stop crying and, after a moment, he forced himself to confront Felice, his expression questioning and sheepish, for it was only when Felice looked at him that he was sometimes ashamed of his vanity and arrogance and made her silent promises he would soon break. But to his astonishment, Felice was smiling, and even seemed rather amused by this disheveled celebration. "I'm sorry," he repeated stubbornly, determined not to let her put him off so easily, for he owed her an apology, or many apologies, and she was not to avoid hearing at least one. "I didn't realize it was so late."

"But you don't know what happened, Morgan," Flora wailed. "Douglas got into a terrible fight with Jake Finney, just grabbed him by the collar and hit him in the eye right in the middle of the dance floor and then, as if that wasn't enough, he got mad at me when I tried to make him stop. Oh, the whole day has been ghastly—please take us home!"

And Morgan, made instantly aware of his responsibilities, thrust out his chest, tried to look protective and pompous and more sober than he felt, and, taking each of them by the hand, gently raised them to their feet, kissed Felice on the cheek, murmuring, "I'm drunk as a fiddler's bitch, please forgive me," and steered them carefully toward the door, past the speeding couples who went by at a furious gallop.

L I X

When Pete Devlin's house, as they called it still, was completed, Jenny moved into it. But she was so listless that it required the efforts of almost every woman she knew, and took several weeks to accomplish; and while her friends abandoned their own responsibilities, Jenny wandered about with a detached and disconsolate air from one room to another, drove back and forth between her two houses, and asked them many times, "But what will I do here?"

The house—which they agreed was the finest mansion in the Territory, bigger and more impressive than either Lemuel Finney's or Jeremy Flint's—was no doubt too big for a woman alone, and yet they thought it Jenny Devlin's plain duty to live in it as Pete had meant her to do.

There were twelve rooms and many chimneys, a deep verandah, a porch on the second floor and a balcony on the third, opening from the ballroom, and it stood at the crest of a slope where by next summer a green lawn and clustering shrubs would have replaced the sagebrush and dandelions which grew there now. A low stone wall hemmed the property, and in deference to Jenny's belief that no house was complete without a fence, a handsome iron picket fence surmounted the wall, twined with luxuriant iron vines and iron flowers, and soon to be overgrown with blue morning glories.

It was, her friends agreed, a house to envy, and had it belonged to her six or eight years ago they would have envied her the possession of it and bemused themselves with imagining the life a woman like Jenny Danforth would live in such a house. Now, of course, they knew what life she would live there.

For during the two or three weeks it took them to move her from one house to another, there was no closet they had not surveyed, no drawers which had not been ransacked, and certainly no possibility that Jenny could have spirited past them any secrets at all; nor had even Erma Finney suggested that she was trying to, for Jenny had seemed as indifferent to the inspection of her personal possessions as she was to the new chairs and sofas and draperies; so that she was, by now, something in the nature of a public property and her years of aloofness had finally left her nothing, as they thought, which had not been examined.

There was some slight disappointment that nothing had been found which might properly have been called a secret—only some early water colors, a box made of seashells which contained the garnet ring she had not worn for some time and a spray of cedar, so old and dry it dropped apart when Erma picked it up, remarking that it must be the one she had worn the day she married Pete, or perhaps even earlier, at that first Christmas ball in Bannack. There were a few other keepsakes, a dream book, a black domino and tambourine, recognized by all of them and, confirming the rumors, Leila's silver brushes and combs, toys and dresses and gold locket, and—the one curiosity which Marietta told them was no curiosity at all, but a gift from Matt—an ornate pearl-handled pistol, engraved with the year of Leila's birth. "Pete had wanted a son," Marietta explained. "The pistol was ordered before she was born."

And so, after all, it was possible to pick through Jenny's belongings, as they had always yearned to do, without discovering anything which interested them, and this thorough search had left them disillusioned, for now it seemed the legend of Jenny Danforth must have been their own invention and Jenny herself a lonely woman, beginning to grow old, whose life had been no more interesting to her than any other woman's. There was even a general feeling, which no one expressed, that they were all a little poorer now for having deprived themselves of curiosity and suspicion, and they were inclined to blame this on Jenny, who should not have given them such freedom to investigate her paltry treasures.

Even so, none of them abandoned the project but continued to work at it with as much dedication as if Pete had left them this request in his will which, as they knew, had been drawn to Jenny's benefit, for he had left her everything he had, with only the provision that if she married again her share was to remain with Devlin Brothers. But Jenny, though she might now count herself to be worth more than a quarter of a million dollars, most of it invested in properties expected to become much more valuable, had shrugged that off, too, saying that Morgan must take care of it for her.

Finally, late one afternoon in the middle of May, they untied the scarves from their heads, removed their aprons and turned down their sleeves, and stood admiring their work.

"But where is Jenny?" Irene Flint inquired. "I haven't seen her since we had lunch, have you?"

Lisette ran through the dining room into the kitchen, where Fong Chong was washing dishes, then up to the second floor, calling Jenny's name as she went, and was caught by a sudden fear, for it had occurred to her that if Jenny ever decided to commit some act of melodrama, she would save it for some such moment. But when she reached the end of the hall on the second floor the door opened and Jenny came out, closing it softly behind her and looking questioningly at Lisette, and all at once Lisette was convinced that Jenny had deceived them after all and had hidden something behind that closed door, though she knew quite well it was an impossible feat when ten or twelve women had been over the house from floor to floor and room to room since early in the morning; and, of course, it meant only that she distrusted Jenny more with each new disaster in their lives, however innocent of their troubles Jenny might seem to be.

"They're getting ready to leave," Lisette told her eagerly, ashamed of her distrust. "There's nothing else to do, not one single thing, I promise you." She ran down and paused on the landing, beside the tall stained-glass window, and as Jenny reached her Lisette took hold of her hands, looking at her intently. "Were you hiding from them? Do you want me to say you have a headache?"

Jenny smiled again, surprised at such a suggestion. "Of course not, Lisette. I went in there to put something away, and I looked out, and there was Mrs. Honeybone. She's followed me here."

"That old peddler woman? Why, Aunt Jenny, she wanders all over town every day. She follows everyone, if they wanted to imagine that she did."

"No, not the same way. She hates me."

"Is she there now?"

"She was, just a moment ago."

Lisette opened the window a crack and peeked out, to see Mrs. Honeybone in her dusty black wrap and white kerchief, standing in the road with her legs spraddled, squinting at the house. Lisette shut the window softly, turned to Jenny with a quick, fierce look, and rushed down the stairs and out the door, taking Mrs. Honeybone by surprise as she flung her skirts toward her like a woman scattering chickens, crying, "Get away from here, get away, do you hear me? Quick!"

She started down the stairs and Mrs. Honeybone waddled off while Lisette watched until she turned the corner, as if it was her responsibility to guard Jenny from the various threatening influences which surrounded her, and she ran back to find Jenny thanking the women for their help with a little speech.

"You've all been so kind, I can't tell you how appreciative I am.

I could never have done it without your help, Marietta, Erma, Blanche, Margaret—all of you." She looked from one to another pleadingly, as if surprised by some unexpected emotion. "Thank you," she murmured humbly, and the women were kissing her cheek and wishing her happiness in her new home, but as Jenny's eyes filled with tears they began to leave, seeming eager to escape, and while Jenny stood on the porch and watched with a wistful face, they started off, Marietta and Erma in one buggy, Irene Flint in another, Georgina and Rachel in another, waiting for Lisette, who was still in the house dawdling about.

Each of them waved good-bye while Jenny stood there, a forlorn, anxious expression on her face now that she saw them going back to their own lives from which she had successfully lured them during the past several weeks, and when Lisette came out, drawing on her gloves, Jenny turned to her beseechingly.

"You're not going, too?"

Lisette looked at her seriously, and all at once the house seemed to her as large and formidable, as empty and depressing as it must seem to Jenny, and she was eager to be away from it. "I've got to, Aunt Jenny. I have so many things to do, so many things I've been neglecting."

"You won't forget me? You'll come to see me?"

Lisette turned from the bottom of the steps. "Of course we won't forget you. I'll come tomorrow afternoon, may I?"

"Oh, Lisette," Jenny protested. "You've never asked me before."

"I'll never ask again, I'll just come."

Lisette gave her a glowing smile, meant to convince her she loved and trusted her, and then before Jenny could stop her again she ran down the steps and the buggy set off at a quick trot, with Georgina beginning to talk about James Gordon's invitation even while they were waving to Jenny, still watching from the porch.

James Gordon had reappeared a year ago, with the announcement that he had returned to help develop the country, just as he had promised. He had been, in the meantime, on various expeditions, following his favorite hobbies of adventure and commerce, but neither in Alaska nor in Africa had he found country which pleased him so well as a site his old friend Zack Fletcher had discovered for him not a fair day's ride from White Sulphur in the very heart of the Territory, a primeval paradise, he declared it to be, and stocked with every animal a man could want to shoot—deer and elk, mountain sheep, bear and beaver—its streams leaping with trout and its open spaces overgrown with grass so rich it made his mouth water to look at it.

Sir James admitted to having read several of the new books which were being published in England describing the great western beef bonanza, where a man could not avoid, whatever stupidities he might commit, making yearly dividends on his capital of at least twenty percent. For, it was said, he might run vast herds over unfenced public lands, turning them loose to thrive on bunch grass more delicious than a dinner at Delmonico's; the weather was so benign and reliable that without making any provision at all for his animals he would lose no more than ten percent of his herds—an insignificant loss which would be replenished by the spring increase; an investment of one hundred and fifty thousand dollars would in two years be worth a million and a half and, furthermore, a man might live like a medieval lord, surrounded by thousands of acres which were not his own but might as well be, spending his days as a gentleman should, riding and hunting, while his vassals, an unruly but hard-working crew of young men who could be discovered in Texas and lured north for forty dollars a month and some cans of tomatoes, would attend to the real business of ranching, in itself a picturesque but ephemeral way of life, so that the manuals urged those who wished to sample it to hurry west before the settlers—those men of little imagination but great tenacity—should encroach upon these natural preserves and turn them into farms as they had long since done throughout the Middle West.

And, Sir James said, he thought there was just enough truth in all this that he was willing to gamble a hundred thousand or possibly two on the venture, for Fletcher had assured him there was no use beginning with less, the days of buying a few cattle from the immigrants and building a herd had disappeared with the placers, and ranching nowadays, like a silver mine, required capital and hard work, though Sir James was confident he would find someone else to perform the hard work. Not, however, Zack Fletcher, who had herds of his own to tend.

Ever since the invitation had come, asking them to bring their children and spend two or three weeks or a month, Georgina had coaxed Lisette to go with her to see how this Englishman lived who had transported himself to the wilderness with his chef and his valet, his Oriental carpets and his wine cellar, his antique furniture and dinner clothes, and, when Lisette remained stubbornly resistant, Georgina reminded her that the children, her own Matt and Cissy and Lisette's Frank and Polly, expected to go and could not be disappointed.

"I have so much to do," Lisette objected. "Ralph's away."

"What's that got to do with it? Please?"

Finally, near the end of July, they gathered one early morning at the coach station with the four children. Lisette was unusually quiet and seemed to be still half asleep, but when the driver came swaggering along with a bottle in his hand and Georgina whispered they should never have come—for it was obvious they would have another of those calamitous trips for which the coaches were famous, would probably be tipped over, perhaps tossed into a river or forced to get out and walk, while the men passengers swore savagely and helped set the coach upright or pushed it up a mountainside—Lisette became brisk and optimistic, took charge of the children and smiled at the men, wheedling the best seats from them, and pointed out the sights to the children as they went swaying and tossing along, while the driver's whip cracked methodically and the men drank from flasks they brought more and more frequently out of their pockets.

After a time the passengers lapsed into sullen and stupefied silence, the driver careened from one side of the dusty roadbed to the other while those inside were sent into fits of coughing and choking, and whenever they heard the driver let out a yell to announce their arrival at a stage station, they climbed out, stiff and dizzy, and while the horses were changed hobbled up and down for three or four minutes to relieve their aches and then climbed docilely back at the driver's command, to spin about as if they had been locked into a gigantic top.

Georgina sat with her eyes shut and her teeth clenched, now and then casting an imploring and apologetic glance at Lisette, but Lisette smiled at her gaily, petted the children to keep them quiet, served them a lunch from a picnic basket while the other passengers ate green biscuits and rancid bacon at the stage station, and became merry and confident, for she had finally convinced herself that if she met Zack Fletcher somewhere on this trip the fault would not be hers.

She had seen him only twice since that morning more than five years ago when he had come to tell her he had recognized the man found dead with Matt—once, when she was driving with Felice and he had ridden beside them for a block or two, talking about his cows and covertly watching her as if to learn if she hated him, and she had been so stricken by shame that her face burned and tears came to her eyes, and Zack had quickly ridden off. Then one day, not so very long ago, he had come into the office of the *Helena Post* to complain about an article describing him as a cattle baron, and Lisette had stood half-hidden by the presses, listening, until he discovered her there and retreated in confusion, slamming the door as he went.

But that encounter in the chill, darkened living room, however unwillingly she might have shared the privacy of flesh and sinew, had not ended in the release of pleasure, but left her with a hungering and a discontent which would not be persuaded away by any logic, nor soothed by all the promptings of other loyalties. And she had never since been convinced that she knew Lisette Devlin, or even Lisette Mercer, as well as she had supposed.

James Gordon lived, as he had promised them, in what he called a hunting box, and but for the ledger spread out on the living-room table where Sir James kept careful account of the animals he was slaughtering, the various heads nailed to the walls, and the barns and bunk house for his hands, there was no reason to think they were in the midst of what Georgina reminded Lisette was still Indian territory, where two thousand hostiles were said to be roaming at will.

After they had been there a week, spending the days hunting and riding and fishing and going to sleep at nightfall, none of them were any longer concerned about the Indians, and one night at dinner, having drunk three glasses of champagne, Lisette declared that this was the life for her, she would never again be happy cooped up in town.

"You wouldn't like it very long, Lisette," Georgina reminded her.

"Oh, yes I would, Georgina. I know what I would like and how long I would like it."

"You understand, of course," Sir James told them, "that this is an Englishman's idea of a ranch. If you want to see the real thing, why then we must visit the Double Key."

"Oh, no, we won't," Lisette protested. "We'll stay right here." But even then the children were clamoring to see the Double Key, and Lisette, marveling that children had such unerring instinct for danger, forbade them to talk about it.

A day or two later, as she stood on the balcony outside her bedroom in the late afteronon, she heard men's voices down below, quietly talking, and all at once realized that one of the voices was Zack Fletcher's. As shocked as if she had not known the Double Key was in the vicinity, and feeling her heart begin to beat at a disconcerting speed, she pressed her palms to her face, asking herself what she must do now. Then all at once this agitation struck her as comical, and she hung across the railing trying to hear what they said, and leaned so far she was in some danger of toppling over.

They were not talking about her, however, but about she-stock and bulls and yearling calves, bragging as if the whole countryside belonged to them, visualizing thousands of cattle and still other thousands pushing in from the west and south and east—all the cattle in the nation, apparently, which would come bawling onto the vast eastern plains once the government penned the Indians in smaller reservations and the railroads made it possible to get the cows to market without walking the profit off on the way.

They had extravagant praise for the native cow, a hardy and resourceful animal, partaking of the characteristic virtues of her owner, and they showed almost as much contempt for Mexican and other inferior bulls as they did for soldiers and whisky peddlers and Indians, and Zack was telling Sir James of the troubles he had with poor Lo. "They come off the reservations with guns and ammunition they've bought from the whisky peddlers, and massacre our cows. We got three of the bastards not long ago—Tango got one and I got one and Andy Stinger got one and we left them there to rot, without their balls or hair, to show their friends we bloody well mean business."

"I say, upon my word," remarked Sir James, and Lisette told herself this man was a more perfect barbarian than even she had imagined.

But when she stood in the doorway a moment later, hoping to

see Zack Fletcher choke on his cigar when he found her there, they still sat with their arms folded and their feet on the railing, studying the distance through half-closed eyes, and seemed lost in the contemplation of those hazards Zack had encountered in his movement toward the east, out of the sheltering valleys and protective hills and onto the great plains where men and animals were exposed to new dangers.

"By God, Gordon, but they'll come up practically into your corral in broad daylight and cut out whatever takes their fancy—those sons of bitches are ready to pack off everything excepting a grizzly bear and a red-hot stove." Zack rose to his feet and turned slowly, as if he had known all along she was there, removing his hat and making her a bow which might have looked polite enough to James Gordon but which Lisette perceived to be mocking and ironic, saying, "Why, good evening, Mrs. Mercer, I was just asking for you."

They shook hands, observing each other warily, and Lisette told herself Zack Fletcher had begun to think very well of himself, for that touching humility he had once shown seemed to have been beaten into submission as ruthlessly as if he had taken a stick to a dangerous dog, and his pride had sprung up with a formidable assurance.

He wore black boots and trousers, a leather vest decorated with Indian beadwork, there was a black silk handkerchief tied around his neck, and very likely he had put on this formal equipment in her honor, although, after their first greeting, he ignored her as she had meant to ignore him, only giving her small, shrewd glances which another man would not notice, darted out swiftly from beneath his blond eyebrows while his head was bent, or even when he appeared to be looking in another direction. And, when he asked them to visit the Double Key, he gave the invitation to Georgina and the children, telling them he lived in country so beautiful it was impossible not to be made happy or drunk by it, even when you were thinking of other things.

Lisette sat at the dinner table looking rather sullen and trying to explain to herself how he had contrived to take charge of them, for even when he told them there was room enough in his house if they did not mind sleeping two in a bunk, had no objection to eating with his riders, and would not be disturbed by the cries of his pet mountain lion, adding, "I'm never just sure when I've been away a few days who'll be there when I get back," it only seemed to make them more eager to see for themselves this primitive life.

And so, at four-thirty the next morning, they set out on horseback, followed by James Gordon's coach carrying their baggage, and when they stopped for lunch Sir James approached the river and deftly drew forth several trout in quick succession, while Zack built a fire and soon had the coffee smoking and the fish cleaned and into the frying pan. The children, by now, had fallen into some communal ecstasy, given themselves over to Zack Fletcher and his passion for this rich, wild country, and might, Lisette thought, be lost to her and Georgina forever.

But she could think of no way to protest against what he was doing, capturing her children and Georgina, leading her against her will into his encampment, and when lunch was over Lisette complained that she had a headache and would ride in the coach, and she took Polly and Cissy with her, though the little girls objected that they had no headache and did not like the coach.

Zack gave her a glance of surprised amusement as she sat staring petulantly out the window, as if he would remind her of how scornful she had always been of women who pleaded their illnesses, or even had them, but the others went galloping off, waving good-bye, and Lisette clung to the tug-strap, while the children were soon asleep, so that it seemed she had been abandoned, condemned to this rico-cheting prison for some misdemeanor she had long ago forgotten or had not yet committed. All the while she was busy fending off baskets and suitcases, and jostling about on the wide seat, she pitied herself for being dragged in this fashion to the enemy camp, a place she gloomily foresaw would be as crude and as dangerous as its owner; and so it seemed to be when she got her first glimpse of it late in the afternoon, a low fortress of sod-roofed log buildings sur-rounding an open court where no blade of grass, nor any bush or flower, was seen to grow.

Over the doorway hung a pair of antlers with a human skull impaled on one prong, and this amulet, she told herself, must surely be the house crest. Tin cans lay in a heap at the rear of one wing, and it seemed they had contained the staple of his diet, for she saw no vegetable garden or hen coop. Benches and stools and chairs, with the bark still on them, stood in a row along the verandah, and the river carved its banks so near the house it seemed likely to flood it during high water. Two or three hundred yards away stood several other buildings, barns and bunk house for the twenty or thirty hands he had said he kept during the summer, and Lisette was obliged to admit that it might be true, as the *Helena Post* had said, that Zack Fletcher was a baron and his Seventy-Six Cattle Company one of the Territory's most successful.

All at once the little girls were out of the coach, their brothers ap-peared from nowhere to claim them, and the four ran off, screaming and chattering, and disappeared before she had recovered her senses enough to stop them. The coach door stood open but she hesitated to get out, for it seemed she was being watched by curious and critical eyes, and this premonition sent a chill down her back. And, when the door slammed back against the wall, she gave a start, but then laughed with embarrassment as Zack Fletcher came swiftly to-ward her, looked questioningly at her for a moment, and said sharply, "You're not sick, stop play-acting."

Lisette followed him meekly, and they entered a room so dark that, at first, she could see nothing. But after a moment the room began to grow visible, and it seemed to be very large, for its edges receded into shadows which might contain yet other dimensions, and its walls were hung with animal hides and animal horns and animal heads, so dense a population it would have been easy to imagine she had happened into a cave where any one of these beasts might momentarily spring forward to attack. There was little furniture, only some benches and stools and rough-surfaced tables, a wall bunk covered with a buffalo robe, several tall iron candlesticks, and a center table littered with a variety of musical instruments, mouth organs and banjos and guitars, almanacs, a game of checkers, several decks of cards and three kerosene lamps. Rifles hung on a rack above the stone fireplace, and, in fact, the room looked even more like an arsenal than a cave. The air was pungent with the smells of animals and human sweat, leather and the oil used to condition the weapons, and a haze of dust and cigar smoke hung there like a palpable substance.

His dog now heaved himself up from beside the fireplace, a great animal of no clear breed, shepherd and collie and perhaps some wolf, to judge him by his appearance, smelling strongly of his venturesome habits and indiscriminate diet, and Lisette leaned down and timidly stroked him. The dog, Zack told her, was named Rocks, and the cat, occupying a thin patch of sun which had penetrated the panes where it crouched with its paws curved under its body, its tail wound protectively about its front paws and its slanted eyes nearly shut, was Kibosh.

There were four young men gathered at the far end of the room and as Zack spoke their names they grew confused, removed their hats and mumbled, "Good day, ma'am," and seemed even more apprehensive of her presence than she was of theirs, although they looked, she thought, like a fierce set of pirates, thin and hard-faced suspicious young men, no more than twenty or twenty-two—but for one who was perhaps near thirty. The oldest, Zack explained, was Andy Stinger, his foreman. Next to him stood Tango, but she heard no more names, for all her attention was now upon an Indian she had discovered seated in a corner behind the young men. Zack saw her watching him, and told her in a confiding undertone that she was not to be alarmed for he was an old chief, full of honors and disillusionment, Left Hand, who came sometimes to live with him for a few weeks when he got hungry on the reservation; and at that Lisette gave Zack a sudden look of entreaty and despair and was ready to beg him to rescue her from this terrifying place, when he grinned with malicious understanding and crossed the room, saying, "Come along."

She followed, glancing uneasily at the young men who stood together, rolling cigarettes and muttering with what seemed a sinister air of conspiracy, and they entered a narrow hallway, its walls hung with more guns and more animal hides, from which a series of little rooms opened, not one of them equipped with a door, only hung with canvas or an Indian blanket, and when Georgina stepped from one of these cubicles Lisette ran to her, crying, "Oh, Georgina, you're here!" But then she stopped, for Georgina seemed surprised, and Zack was smiling.

"Are you ready?" Zack inquired, and Lisette found he had asked this mysterious question not of herself, but of Georgina.

"In just a minute."

"Will you take care of her?" he asked, again of Georgina, and Lisette had an instant's morbid recollection of tales she had heard of white women captives given over to the squaws for torture.

"Of course," agreed Georgina, and took her hand, drawing her forward along the corridor, and Zack returned down the long hallway and disappeared.

"Thank heaven he's gone," Lisette whispered. "How can we get out of here?"

"Get out of here?" repeated Georgina, and looked at her curiously. "Here's your room." Georgina pushed aside a canvas curtain to show her a cell, equipped with a bunk, a lopsided table holding a basin and pitcher, a mirror on one wall and several hooks on another. "We're going riding."

"Riding? You've been riding all day, Georgina. Where are the children?"

"Outside somewhere. They won't lie down. All but Cissy, she's fast asleep. Won't you come with us?"

"Of course I won't. I can't stand this place—those herders of his, where did he ever find them? That old Indian and that great ferocious dog. Even the house cat looks wild. What kind of food will he expect us to eat—oh, I can just imagine." She rolled her eyes.

Georgina regarded her seriously for a moment, then reached out to lay her hands against Lisette's cheeks which were, in fact, hot and flushed, and spoke to her tenderly. "Why, honey, you're sick, you've caught something. But I know it isn't serious, just go to bed and sleep for an hour or two, and you'll be all right." Georgina had removed Lisette's hat as she talked, and was now turning down the bed and beating the straw mattress, while Lisette cast a yearning glance toward the bunk but shivered as she thought of lying between blankets not yet deloused from the last Indian who had worn them.

And yet she was eager to hide there and determined that once she had crept into that safe place they would not coax her out again until it was time to leave. She began slowly to undress, sighing, and feeling that she was, in reality, feeble and ailing, and discussed seriously with Georgina what she might eat without doing herself harm. And then, for her suitcases had not been sent in, she lay down in her chemise upon what she was relieved to discover were clean white sheets, made of coarse muslin and unironed, but smelling, nevertheless, as if they had been dried in the sun, and as Georgina bent to

kiss her she looked up with a piteous face, as if to inquire whether
or not she was likely to last through the day.

"We'll be back before dark. Go to sleep now. You'll be all right
when you've had a nap."

"Will I?" She lay listening to Georgina's footsteps passing down
the hallway, the opening and closing door, and then she was alone,
staring perplexedly at the ceiling and asking herself how it could be
that after living for fifteen years in the mountains she should have
turned as squeamish and distrustful as she would expect her cousin
Suky to be.

The riddle, she thought, might solve itself while she slept, but she
could not sleep, and presently she scrubbed the window pane with
her fist, finding a view of the hills and mountains, which seemed to
have receded with the declining afternoon, and not a hundred yards
away the pet mountain lion, which she had hoped was only a creature
of Zack Fletcher's imagination, prowled back and forth in a flimsy
cage which looked scarcely strong enough to hold Kibosh.

She frowned and shook her head, telling herself she would not try
to guess why a grown man should keep a pet mountain lion, and lay
down again, but after a few moments she heard boys' voices shouting, the mountain lion gave a terrifying scream, and she saw through
her peephole Frank and Matthew, with another boy, a little older,
who wore an ammunition belt and pistol, running around the lion's
cage and brandishing their fists. She rapped at the window but they
dashed off in the other direction and disappeared, joyously laughing,
though the older boy turned once and drew his pistol, cocked it at
the screaming cat, but then apparently decided not to shoot it, after
all.

She lay down, more dumfounded than before, asking herself what
kind of place this was, where even the children went fully armed and,
furthermore, who did such a child belong to, for Zack had made no
mention of him. A neighbor, she decided, if there were neighbors in
this country where she had seen no houses since they had left James
Gordon's that morning, and she shook her head again, sighing.

Presently she heard the sound of running hoofs, apparently a great
many animals galloping together, and decided that Zack was taking them out to inspect his property. But they could not be seen
through the window, where she had only a view of the nervous lion,
the darkening hills, and a red glow which lay on the packed earth,
reflecting a sunset she longed to see if only she dared get out of bed.

Sometime later, as she was propped on her elbow with her nose to
the pane, waiting for someone or something to show itself out there,
she heard softly moving footsteps and turned to see a young Indian
girl push the curtain aside and set her two suitcases down.

"What do you want?" Lisette demanded.

The girl did not answer and, while Lisette watched her, she opened
the suitcases, hung up her clothes, and tumbled out hairbrushes

and jars of cream and powder onto the table top. She looked no more
than fifteen or sixteen, with a flat nose and deeply folded lids, and
her black hair, cut off straight at her shoulders, swung to and fro
as she moved. She wore a stained red calico dress and a bright shawl,
the center part of her hair was painted red and there were red spots
the size of a dollar on either cheek, and Lisette told herself that no
doubt she might pass among her own people for a pretty girl. But
she was not more than five feet tall, with round arms and short legs,
and, squaw-fashion, she wore nothing beneath the dress, so that at
every movement her heavy breasts quivered and her buttocks
shifted, and Lisette watched her disapprovingly, thinking it was
easier to explain why she was at the Double Key than to guess for
what purpose Fletcher might be keeping the mountain lion.

Lisette asked her name but the girl gave her a quick, shy glance,
and was gone again. And all at once Lisette sprang out of bed and
began to dress, defiantly telling herself she was not sick and would
not be treated as if she were, she would go out and inspect this place
and see for herself what kind of life Zack Fletcher lived here with
his tame Indians and pet mountain lions and hired desperadoes.

She stood before the mirror, smoothing pomade on her lips and
brushing powder on her face, and smiled at herself, reassured, then
struck a pose as she examined the fit of her riding habit, drew on her
gloves and set out with confidence, but was dismayed to find that
this bravado left her the moment she ventured into the hallway, and
she paused, furious to think she should be experiencing for the first
time all the pangs of a tenderfoot, that cowardly species she heartily
despised.

Nevertheless, she strode along, making more noise than necessary
with the heels of her black boots and switching at the air with her
riding crop, cautiously opened the door and peeked into the big room
and, when she was sure it was empty, entered it boldly and began
to stroll about, regarding everything she saw with a disparaging eye.
"He might as well be living a thousand years ago," she said aloud,
should anyone care to hear her opinion and repeat it to him, "in some
peat bog or lake village."

But now that she had progressed this far without being set upon
by his mountain lion or attacked by his cat Kibosh, neither scalped
by the old Indian nor molested by the evil-looking young men he
employed, she went outdoors with the intention of becoming so familiar with this sinister place there would be no way he might surprise her when he got back.

The sun was down, leaving layers of blue and purple at the horizon, but the long summer twilight had only begun, there was much
light left in the sky and the air was still and hot, stirring just enough
that the cottonwoods along the river kept up a continuous murmuring sigh, rattling their leaves together with a soft and scratchy sound.
A remarkable quiet had fallen, and as she stood wondering which
direction to take, a mouth organ began to play, sobbing and quaver-

ing over some mournful melody she did not recognize, and she turned eagerly, expecting the musician to appear, but the sound grew fainter and then stopped, as if whoever was playing had either walked away or lost interest in the tune.

Lisette left the shelter of the courtyard and turned around slowly, but even though she saw no one she nevertheless felt there was a population surrounding her; she had a sense of unseen life, watching eyes, activity, as if some menacing interest was being taken in her.

With sudden resolution, she set out to visit the mountain lion. But when she came nearer and found it tearing a rabbit to shreds, and it turned to stare at her with glittering eyes as if it might demolish her by a glance, then gave a shriek like the cry of a woman in pain or despair, Lisette began to run and did not stop or turn until she was some distance away, but by then it had set upon the rabbit again and was no longer interested in her.

She wandered on, sniffing curiously at the air, and caught the smells of searing meat and baking bread. She heard again the sound of the mouth organ but now, she thought, the quavering had been exaggerated into a kind of mocking laughter, and once again it faded into the distance and stopped. Wanting to find someone she could talk to, feeling that if she could discover some friendly or at least not hostile man or woman or child, even a pet she was not afraid of, she would be less uneasy, she walked to the kitchen door and looked in.

There, with his pigtail hanging almost to his heels, was the Chinese cook, presiding with energetic authority over a cookstove with a great smoking kettle upon it into which he was throwing chunks of meat passed to him by the Indian girl who stood silently beside him. The old Indian, wrapped in his blanket in spite of the heat, sat cross-legged on the floor, and Lisette, suddenly queasy at the smells of the food and the recklessness with which they were handling it, the stacks of unwashed dishes and pails of garbage, backed hastily away, and began her search again.

In the blacksmith shop she found a man at work, and she stood in the doorway watching him for several minutes before he noticed her and removed his hat. "Good day, ma'am."

Lisette smiled wistfully, hoping that he would invite her in. "Where did they go? Mr. Fletcher and the others?"

"I guess they went out to look at the country, ma'am."

"You don't know when they'll be back?"

"Around suppertime, I would think."

He began to hammer once again, and as if that had been a signal of dismissal, Lisette turned and started slowly away. As she got farther from the blacksmith shop, there was the sound of the mouth organ, coming this time from a different direction, so that whoever was playing it must be wandering about as she was, and yet why this person, probably a child, would not show himself and speak to her she could not understand, for surely even a child could recognize a lonely and bewildered guest.

She thought of going back to the house, perhaps reading an almanac since there had been no other books in sight, or trying to pick out a tune on the banjo which might lure the elusive musician into appearing and give her a companion until the others returned, and she had begun to walk more quickly, as if this plan must be carried out immediately, when there was a sharp cracking report nearby, as of a pistol shot off, and she stopped still, all her earlier fears and distrust of this eerie place with its hidden sounds of music, its unsympathetic animals and silent Indians and Chinese, justified. She stood motionless, waiting. There was another cracking report, and ahead of her in the dust a thin black strip appeared, wriggling, then slowly withdrew, sliding by her with the motion of a lethargic snake which she turned to watch, glancing up in astonishment as a woman's voice gave a shout of laughter.

The report had come from no pistol but was the crack of a bullwhacker's whip, which now was drawn slowly away until at last it disappeared inside the opened door of the barn and a slender figure stood there, grinning and giving her a genial salute. "Hi. Did I scare you?"

Lisette supposed, for a moment, that this was one of those surly young men she had met, but then found it was no young man after all who stood plying the whip with a flexible motion of her wrist, as if she were angling for trout, but a woman dressed in black trousers and knee-high black boots, a green and pink checkered vest over her white shirt, and a broad-brimmed black hat beneath which her short brown hair swung with as much flexibility as if it were independently alive; and now she put the mouth organ to her lips and blew a few notes of that same quavering melody.

She stuck the harmonica into her vest pocket, tossed the whip aside, and came sauntering forward while Lisette watched her as steadily as she might have watched someone she knew to be insane. When she was no more than four or five feet away she stopped, peered at Lisette, and remarked, "For a respectable woman, you've got sand."

Lisette smiled and, to her surprise, the fears were gone and she could not even imagine where they had come from in the first place, for the sight of this old friend and enemy she had never met—though she had spent much time studying her picture, had torn it in half but then, after a year or two, pasted it together again—seemed all at once to have restored her courage. "Did you take me for a pilgrim, Lily Jones?"

Lily opened her eyes wide. "You know me?"

"You sent me a picture of yourself, don't you remember?"

"Oh, no, I didn't, I sent my picture to your brother. Fletcher might've sent his to you."

Lily's body was as thin and pliant as it had been when the picture

was taken, although her brown skin looked crisp and parched and
creases fanned out at the corners of her eyes, as if she had some
habitual grimace of squinting against strong sunlight. But she had
still her abounding health and vitality and as she tipped her head
sideways, her hair flapping against her shoulder like a heavy silk
fringe, she grinned mischievously and, as if she had been appraising
a dog or a horse, told Lisette, "You're pretty, all right, just like he
said." Whether he was Morgan or Zack Fletcher, however, she did
not explain.

Lisette had nothing to say to that, but started toward the house.
Lily took a cigar from one vest pocket, a match from another, raised
her right leg and drew the match swiftly along her buttock, and with
the cigar between her teeth and both hands in her pockets she came
strolling along beside her, as companionable as a young boy out
for a walk. She asked Lisette what she thought of the Double Key
and why she had not gone riding with the others, but, when she got
no reply, was not at all disconcerted but went on talking in a voice
so light it seemed a comical contrast to all this determined bravado.

"Anything you'd like to know about Fletcher before he gets back?"

"Of course not!" Lisette gave her a quick, angry glance, but encountered Lily's sly grin and gleaming green eyes, looking at her
sideways.

"We're old friends. Old friends," Lily solemnly assured her. "I
know all there is to know about him."

"I'm not interested in Zack Fletcher—or in what you know about
him."

Lily gave another shout of laughter and remarked in a low, confidential tone to some invisible companion, "You heard what she
said, didn't you?"

They crossed the courtyard, and although it was Lisette's intention to return to her room, she paused in the doorway, aware of
Lily watching her with that same sly, challenging smile, and instead
sat in one of the lopsided chairs, while Lily sat not far away, tilting
her chair against the wall and resting one booted foot upon her knee.
Presently she drew a flat bottle from her pocket, whimsically inquired if Lisette would have a drink, and took a swallow, and Lisette
grew hopeful she had intimidated this famous female desperado
who rambled the western half of the continent with the easy familiarity with which Lisette strolled about her own living room.

"I've tried to picture you to myself sometimes," Lily told her, "and
now I can look at you just as if I'd known you all these years. That's
funny, isn't it?" Lisette continued staring across the courtyard, as
disdainful as if she had been trapped by a loquacious fellow passenger in a railway train and, after a moment, Lily, who kept a frank
and steady watch upon her, pushed the hat back from her forehead
and inquired, with a naïve interest, "You're still in love with
Fletcher, aren't you?"

Lisette sat up as if someone had jabbed a forefinger hard into the small of her back. "Don't say that to me," she commanded. "You don't know me, and you have no right to say such a thing."

Lily turned down the corners of her mouth, and once again spoke to her invisible companion. "She sure shows war, don't she?"

"Why don't we both keep quiet until they come back?"

Lily tilted the chair at a yet more precarious angle, took another long swallow, and began to whistle, and she went on whistling for several moments until at last she said, "Okay. It's none of my town."

The dog Rocks came shambling along and lay beside Lily, who reached out her foot to caress the back of his neck. The cat appeared, hissed at the dog, and lay at the far end of the verandah, and from time to time Lily and Lisette batted their hands at a troublesome fly. After a few minutes the Indian girl crossed the courtyard, making more of those pigeon-toed tracks which Lisette had noticed wherever she went, and seemed not to know they were nearby until Lily greeted her. At that she turned, startled, looked from one to the other, replied with the same word, and ran off. "That's Red Bead," said Lily.

Lisette glared at her, daring her to tell her anything more about Red Bead.

"She's a Crow," Lily presently added, as if this would be sure to interest Lisette. "He bought her three years ago for a couple of ponies, not very good ones, either, but then Fletcher could teach the Yankees something when it comes to the art of peddling whatever's not needed at home. His woman of convenience," said Lily, tapping the ash from her cigar and keeping a watch on Lisette from the corners of her eyes. "And you can see for yourself—she's prettier than the average squaw, though she sure as hell doesn't smell any better." Lisette continued to sit very straight, trying to pretend she had been stricken deaf, and Lily went on, as if talking to herself or to some old and trusted friend. "Men like Indian women—do you want to know why?"

"I do not."

But Lily smiled at that, with humorous indifference. "That's a damn lie—you want to know, all right, and I'll tell you. They're like dogs, meek and trained to obey, and they're willing to work. Oh, they work like hell and they never complain and they don't have much to say because they don't give a damn about talking to a white man, even if they love him. How?" asked Lily abruptly, mimicking the girl's reply. "Hah?" she added. She bowed her head, making a sign with her forefinger. *"Mita kola.* That about does it. Maybe they've got one or two others for the hay, or maybe they keep still there, too. Anyway, you asked me about Red Bead, and that's it—anything else you'd like to know?"

"Nothing else."

"The old Indian is Left Hand, a Blackfoot chief, not that it's worth much to him any more. The Chinese cook is Chee Shum. I'm Lily Jones, everybody's heard of me by now, and the kid is my nephew, Johnny Lawler." And, as Lisette glanced at her, she seemed inordinately pleased to have produced this little surprise. "Eleven years old last May, and by God if he's not a full-grown man. Swears in two languages, tends his own business, reads sign like an Apache, and plays a good game of poker. Chews tobacco some, but lately he prefers cigars." Lily winked, proud of this precocious relative.

Lisette was staring at her, more shocked by Lily's recital of her nephew's accomplishments than she had been to learn what she had guessed the moment she saw her—that Red Bead was Zack Fletcher's woman of convenience. "But what's become of his childhood?"

"How the hell should I know? What kid wants a childhood?" Lily continued to watch her with the same look of keen inquisition and a contemptuous amusement, as if Lisette's concern for the boy's childhood only proved that respectable women had no proper set of values, and all at once she snapped her fingers. "Here they come."

A slight smoky gathering of dust could be seen far out on the plain, and presently there emerged from it a group galloping forward; a boy's high voice sent up a Rebel yell which was instantly answered by Lily, throwing back her head and giving a cry which made Lisette fold her arms about herself, shuddering.

Lily looked around, her green eyes sharp and hard. "Going to tell him about my little joke with the whip?"

"Of course not. Do you think I'm afraid of you?"

"Going to tell him I told you about Red Bead?"

Lisette smiled. "You're not nearly as fierce, Lily Jones, or even as independent, as you like to pretend, are you?" Lily looked as disconcerted as if her deepest integrity had been called into question. "If you want to know the truth, I feel a little sorry for you."

Lily bounded to her feet. "Sorry for me, for Christ's sake? I'll be a son of bitch if that's not a respectable woman's insult for you!" She gave the railing a kick, and turned on her heel. "You can go to hell, Mrs. Mercer." Her green eyes were malevolent as the mountain lion's, she threw the cigar away, spat across the railing and, making an obscene gesture beneath Lisette's nose, stamped into the house and slammed the door, and Lisette, surprised by this easy victory, burst into laughter and ran to meet the others.

Zack came walking swiftly toward her, his face anxious, as if he thought she was running to him for protection from the several dangers he had left her to encounter alone. But Lisette passed him by and caught hold of Polly and Frank, kissing the little girl and trying to look into Frank's face, to learn if he was now as eager to be rid of his childhood as Lily Jones' nephew, and when he blushed and tried to draw away as if he were being punished in full view of his friends she let him go, giving a rueful little laugh at this first public rejection by her son, and strolled back arm in arm with Georgina, talking gaily with James Gordon and refusing even to acknowledge Zack's presence so that he trailed along, looking puzzled and chagrined, and seemed to have guessed that Lily Jones had betrayed his secrets, bandied his vices about and taken advantage of his absence to make a fool of him, for so Lisette's occasional smile, cryptic and full of insolence, seemed to say.

The dinner gong rang, and Lily appeared in the doorway, looking sullen and aloof, and, when Zack beckoned her aside, seemed distrustful and reluctant to go, but he marched her briskly out of the courtyard, talking to her as they went while Lily waved her arm in gestures of violent protest, loudly declaring, "Not a god-damn thing, Fletcher, so help me God—not a single god-damn word."

L X

Charitable ladies had dispensed baskets in the poor wards, to the Five Points Mission and the lunatic asylum, everyone had been to church at least once, and the whores were murmuring their compliments, mischievously whispering, "How are you, my dear?" as they passed men in top hats and sealskin coats, gravely escorting their wives. Itinerant musicians wandered against the traffic, clinging stubbornly to the wrong side of the street and whistling in piercing tones which made Allegra thrust her fingers into her ears as she stood on tiptoe, trying to catch, now and then, a glimpse of Ferguson's New Broadway Theater. But she would not cross the street to get a nearer view, and had turned shy and reluctant, talking about it very much as she might had she come with him to view some relic of the ancient past, a temple where people no longer worshipped and where, by now, it was difficult to believe they ever had.

"Isn't it beautiful, though?" she asked. "A little Georgian mansion."

And so it seemed to be, for it was made of red brick trimmed with white marble, a line of white pillars filed across the façade, and beneath the cornice stood a marble figure, gazing downward with a sad and bewitched smile, indicating with her opened hands the stone masks of comedy and tragedy which stood on either side of her. The smile, so Allegra had been told, though not by Ferguson, was like her own, but the statue was too small to be seen from the street, and there was no way to reach it from inside the building, and so if Dyke Ferguson had meant this as his private tribute, he might keep the secret as long as he liked.

"A thousand seats?"

"Twelve hundred," he told her impatiently, for she had kept him standing there nearly half an hour and, of course, she knew the number of seats as well as he did. "Come, I've got to show it to you."

"No, no, not just yet, a little longer—oh, please. A revolving stage?"

At that he began to drag her along, and when they found themselves stranded amid horsecars and hacks and carriages, she clung to him as if they had fallen into turbulent water. But then he dashed on, and once again she tried to escape as he stood trying the keys, but presently he threw the door open and thrust her inside, locked it and struck a match, and found her standing meekly beside him, shivering.

"Well, here we are." She gave him a glance, resigned and whimsical. "Let me see it."

"Follow me," he told her, mysteriously whispering, and started along the corridor. The lighted candle went bobbing ahead and she crept after him, sniffing the fresh paint and new wood like an animal familiarizing itself with this strange place first of all by smell, and he led her slowly forward until, all at once, he turned, taking hold of her fingers as she moved toward him with the dazzled expression of someone in a trance, and she stepped onto the stage. "Don't move," he cautioned her again, still whispering, as if they were two robbers broken into a deserted house. "Wait." The candle disappeared, and Allegra, giving a faint, protesting cry, covered her face with her hands.

But then the theater filled with light and she moved cautiously toward the footlights and peered down, expecting to find him hidden there, spying on her. "Dyke!"

"Here I am!" he shouted. "Can't you see me?"

She searched for him, looking through the haze of light and out into the empty theater, a large box lined with crimson brocade where rows of gilt chairs upholstered in crimson velvet curved one beyond another in slowly rising arcs. The crystal chandeliers shed an uncertain radiance, shaking prisms of light which swam before her eyes as she slowly bent her head and began a curtsy, sinking at last so far that her forehead touched one knee, and she murmured in a reverent voice, "Oh, thank you—thank you."

"That's better," she heard him say, from somewhere quite near, and rose swiftly, to find him watching her with that familiar sardonic smile, as if he knew she would follow him anywhere now, and she shrugged and smiled in reply, for she ought to have known better than to imagine she might subdue Dyke Ferguson, the actor's best friend and worst enemy, the man who understood how to make them perform better than they knew how to do, and who asked in return only their perfect subjugation and absolute devotion.

They descended from the stage hand in hand and he led her up the aisle, slowly pacing on the crimson velvet carpet, a monarch leading his consort, or the groom his bride, and all the while she was deep in wonder over this elegant little theater which, once she set her foot upon the stage with an audience facing her, would become all her own, and Dyke Ferguson as insignificant as the call-boy

Tap Doyle. She smiled into the rows of gilt chairs as she passed them,
a smile at once confident and appealing, and a touch melancholy,
for after all, even those future triumphs would soon be gone, and
the audience could almost be seen to rise and file away, to bestow
its compliments somewhere else. He left her there to sit alone in a
box, her coat thrown over the chair back, as if she waited for herself
to appear and please her or not, and he told her to stay just where
she was, for he had other marvels in store.

But once he was gone she leaned on the velvet rope and sat gazing
down at the lighted stage, watching a procession pass across it—
Lady Teazle, giving a merry and taunting laugh, Lady Macbeth, distractedly washing her hands, Rosalind skipped nimbly by—and she
nodded in recognition to each, saluting in turn Viola and Juliet and
Imogene, for Ferguson did not intend that any lesser ladies should
parade those boards and was as adamant as he had ever been against
cup-and-saucer plays and imported French melodramas, would
permit no Camilles and no Frou Frous to desecrate his temple, but
meant to insist as he always had that rich New Yorkers accept the
bill of fare he designed for them.

She sat for several moments, watching herself, so clear an apparition that she became wholly lost and absorbed in it, and at last
found him standing on the stage looking at her with the same alert
concentration he showed whenever she inadvertently caught his
eye during a performance, staring at her skeptically and with some
malevolent humor, as if he expected that in another moment she
would make a fool of herself; and this glimpse, which she tried to
avoid but which somehow or other she got once or several times
during each performance, now made her start slightly and give a
deprecating little laugh.

"I was daydreaming," she admitted, ashamed to have been caught.
"What are you going to show me now?"

"Stay right there," he warned her, and was gone again.

Now she sighed and fidgeted, then smiled at some imaginary companion with the look of anticipatory spite she had seen women give
their escorts while they waited for her to appear, and enjoyed for a
minute or two the luxurious sense that now it was she who was to
be entertained, who might sit in judgment, permit herself to be
moved or bored, to yawn or applaud as the fancy took her. For the
pleasures of displaying herself had diminished and, quite often
nowadays, she resented the performances she gave as she might have
resented being forced to make a gift to someone she suspected was
her enemy, or who would at least not appreciate its value or be
touched by the effort it had cost her.

Ferguson was not in sight, though she heard a clattering from
somewhere offstage, and she lay her head upon her arms and found
herself surprised by an attack of loneliness which made her wonder
how it was she had let him persuade her to come back to America,
this treacherous country in which she had never been able to dis-

cover the virtues, or the advantages, which were so obvious to her brother. For as the City Coroner, Hoke O'Neil seemed to believe it was his decision which marked the city's citizens for life or for death, and his judgment which determined whether they had died honorably or disreputably. A married man, she had found him this time, and the father of a baby girl he described as second-crop Irish, a little squalling creature he had named Brenna who would one day, no doubt, grow up to celebrate this country with native enthusiasm.

The theater fell silent, and she began to wonder if Ferguson had gone off and left her alone, locked in for the night with her sins of pride and display, to contemplate them at her leisure in their true environment. This made her laugh, and the sound rang out with such startling authority that she listened, and was about to make the experiment again when the stage began to revolve, the empty stage disappearing, slipping around out of sight, and there slowly emerged in its place the set for the last act of *Romeo and Juliet*, the tomb, the stone steps leading down to the vault, pillars which seemingly rose to an indefinite height, and Allegra jumped to her feet, applauding and laughing with excitement.

Ferguson walked onto the stage and looked at her gloomily, as if no amount of praise could repay him, and then he flung off his coat, sent his hat spinning, and began to rush about, pulling levers and hauling ropes, whipping the sea-cloth into a foaming froth. The next moment, snow showered down, settling in his hair and upon his shoulders, wind howled and whistled, rain poured in steady streams, lightning streaked and thunder roared, and at last he stood wiping his wet face and shaking his head as if he had surprised himself by these exertions, for he ordinarily moved nothing, not so much as a prompting table, and thought that for a manager to be seen doing any such work would diminish his authority.

"There you are. Everything is more modern, more beautiful, more efficient, and more god-damned expensive than it is in any other theater in the world."

Now he led her back to the green room and there, quite as she had expected, she recognized the old furnishings, the list of rules by which he governed their lives, in the theater and out of it, and she stood looking at herself in the same mirror where she had so often examined costumes and wigs, just before she went onto the stage, and where now she examined Allegra Stuart in her purple velvet gown with its mink collar and the lilac velvet hat decorated with white silk roses; but then she found him looking at her with a somber face, as if to ask what had come over her, to stand there thinking of other things than Ferguson's New Broadway Theater.

For, as she now discovered, there was another Allegra Stuart in the room, the portrait Augustus Adams had completed just before she had gone to Europe, and she approached this stranger slowly, for at first glance she did not think she liked her.

Lady Macbeth's hair hung across her shoulders and breasts, and she had a look of rapturous pride Allegra had thought even then was more suggestive of insanity than ambition, although Ferguson and Augustus Adams had assured her no one would ever see that portrait without recognizing the link there was between them. Her arms were raised above her head, her fingers spread wide in the effort of holding the golden crown, and she appeared to emerge from a mist so wet that even the skirt of her green-gray dress dragged at her body and clung to her legs, for it was Augustus Adams' contention that he had incorporated into the canvas the moist chill of the Scottish highlands, and shown Lady Macbeth as a physical part of her country.

Allegra walked nearer to study this woman, whoever she was—for this was not the first time she had discovered that she no longer knew some earlier self—and after a few moments she frowned and turned away. "I never once played it right." She made an apologetic gesture, as if the criticism had come from him. "Maybe I can do better this time."

"It will hang here as long as you're playing here—and when you leave, I'll put my next star's picture there."

"I know."

For it was Ferguson's belief that she should marry him, and he expected that once she did Albert Montague would remain, as he had for the past eight years, silent and obscure.

Montague came to call on her from time to time in London and she always felt obliged to see him, for some superstition persisted that he might, even now, give her some valuable clue to a part that had lately dissatisfied her. He would pace back and forth, assuring her his own provincial company was more successful than ever and that he was in London only for the purpose of discussing the terms for bringing it in the following season. Then, having outlined these good fortunes, he would criticize the performance she had given the night before and find as much fault with the way she looked, her voice and her gestures, as he ever had when they lived together, and would not leave until he had rehearsed her in a crucial scene or two and made her perform it to his satisfaction.

"I could scarcely believe," he would tell her severely, "that you would have forgotten what I took so much care to teach you."

He plainly believed he had come only in time to save her reputation and that without him her Lady Teazle would have degenerated into frivolity and her Juliet become a mawkish adolescent. And, each time, he left her wondering if perhaps it was true, or at least partly true, for it was much less easy for her now than it once had been to convince herself that neither Albert Montague nor anyone else had been significant to the development of Allegra Stuart, who had sprung into being only out of the miracle of her own nature which had at last demanded to be born.

But to whatever excessive degree she sometimes thought herself addicted to her work, and however she was occasionally surprised and made somewhat sad to discover one more evidence that everything in her life existed only in relationship to what would happen when next she walked onto the stage, she knew that to Albert Montague and Dyke Ferguson, the two men who pretended to love her best, this was in fact the sign of her superiority over those other women who frittered themselves away on the paltry concerns of their own lives, while she devoted herself to portraying the lives of women who had been imagined by great men and who were therefore, so they said, more real than any real woman could hope to be.

She followed Ferguson through the maze of dark hallways, which still lacked those combined fragrances of sweat and dust and stale air without which she would never be able to feel quite at home in a theater, and stopped before a door where she could vaguely see her name printed in black and gold letters. He made a menacing gesture, for it seemed that each new wonder he showed her only made him that much more resentful, and sent her in.

The room was bigger than any dressing room she had ever had, and he had furnished it with Turkish carpets and Moorish banners and hangings of striped silk; there were carved screens and pierced metal lamps, a red silk canopy swung from crossed spears over the divan, and Saracen weapons decorated the walls. Allegra gave a whoop of delight, made a running leap and landed in the middle of the divan, where she lay smiling at him with a mockery of suggestive passion, until at last she folded her arms behind her head, gave him an ironic sideways glance, and remarked, "My portrait comes down when I'm gone—and Tamzene Twining moves into my cozy corner."

He jumped up, swearing as he did only when she resisted his advice about a scene, and dashed out of the room and she heard him rattling down the hallway, still yelling. "You damned, contrary bitch, you Irish slut, you mercenary, unappreciative—" and he went on muttering until she could hear him no longer. But presently there were sounds of crashing and slamming and she ran toward the stage, terrified he might destroy what he had built even before she had enjoyed her first triumph there.

Ferguson's rages, however, were violent but brief and, she suspected, very well controlled, for like an accomplished actor he was able when he was angry to seem larger than he ordinarily did and could show such ferocity and cruelty and vindictiveness that his company trembled before him like children, terrified of this ability he had to humiliate them before each other, and even more by his ingenuity in discovering their weaknesses. And now, far from thrusting down the pillars as she had been afraid he might do, she found him dashing about in a frantic excitement, peering through the footlights, dragging pieces of equipment around to judge their effect, and as he caught sight of her standing timidly at the edge of the stage he swept out his arm in a wave of command, and she walked slowly forward.

"Stand here. Right here." He pushed her into the position he had indicated, warned her not to move, and appeared a few moments later near the back of the theater. "Now, I want to hear you talk— it just occurred to me that the other day I thought I noticed an echo in this section." He snapped his fingers. "Say something!"

"All right."

"Talk. Talk to me, for God's sake. Whatever comes into your mind." He cupped his hand to his ear in an unconscious caricature of an old man, very deaf, screwed up his face in earnest concentration and bent toward her, waiting.

Allegra drew in a deep breath, linked her hands, and spoke very softly. "Thank you, ladies and gentlemen."

Ferguson leaned forward, deafer than ever. "What was that?"

She raised her voice, and it filled the theater. "Thank you, ladies and gentlemen."

"That's better. Go on."

"And now, may I tell you that I have received your applause for the last time."

"What's that?" demanded Ferguson, taken aback, and he stood peering at her, trying to guess what kind of trick she meant to play on him.

"I came to you a stranger," she said, in that rich, commanding voice which made audiences listen to her carefully lest she take advantage of their inattention to tell them something of deep personal meaning which, if they missed it, would be irrevocably lost. "And now I feel as if I had known you all of my life."

He was warier than ever now, had nothing to say, but stood watching her and, presently, she saw out there neither Dyke Ferguson nor anyone else she knew, but the audience itself, that vast animal which was sometimes obedient and humble, sometimes defiant and remote, waiting for her to tell them what she had contrived to learn of those secrets, whatever they might be, small ones or large, which lay at the center of existence itself. For she had convinced them that if only they paid her close attention she would whisper her secrets, or perhaps demonstrate them by some movement or gesture, and so they watched her in rapt fascination and believed her to be more priestess than performer, and, catching their belief, she lost awareness of herself until the sound of applause, coming at the end of some sustained action or long speech, affected her as a stunning surprise, striking with the force of a physical blow.

"After tonight," she went on, speaking slowly, and with a look of sorrowful entreaty, "I shall never act again, and, since we must part from one another forever, please let me say that your love and generosity has been the best part of my life—and that whatever may become of me, it is comforting to know that the art of which I am

a humble representative will remain as long as human nature exists."
She paused, opening her hands and bowing her head. "God bless you
all." She stood for some moments without moving, until Ferguson's
voice, peculiarly strident, rang across the empty theater.

"For Christ's sake, what was that all about?"

She glanced up, gaily smiling. "My farewell speech," she told him,
and seemed quite blithe and indifferent. "Did you like it? I may add
something or other—or maybe I'll leave it as it is. But I like the ending, because people always cry when someone says 'God bless you' to
them in public." She put one finger to her lips and pondered that for
a moment. "Do you know why?"

Ferguson came sauntering down the aisle, his hands in his pockets, and stood with his feet spread wide. "You'll never make a farewell speech."

"Of course I will—everyone does. Sometimes I think it's the most
important performance an actor ever gives. They forget everything
else, but they always remember your farewell speech."

"And when is this farewell speech to be made?"

She shrugged. "I'm not sure yet, but I'll know when the time
comes. I'll know when they've had enough of me, and I only hope to
God I'll know it before they do. After that, I can die any time."

He disappeared into the orchestra pit and, in a moment, stood at
the edge of the stage, watching her furtively and scowling, as if he
might be trying to think of some suitable punishment for what she
had done, taken his triumph and turned it into an exercise in morbidity and fatalism, those Irish flaws in her character he had not
been able to rub out, either by pleading or ridicule; and finally he
asked, "Why must you talk so much about dying?"

"Because I'm trying to get used to the idea. I don't want to be taken
by surprise. You remember what happened to poor Lemira," she told
him in a melancholy voice. "She lived to be ugly and old and finally
died of hydrophobia when her poodle bit her." Her face was transformed by a demonic smile. "It's a great art to know just how and
when to die, isn't it?"

And, by then, he was too disconcerted to expect anything more
from her in the way of extravagant gratitude for his Christmas
present, although he remained suspicious of further snares until the
night the theater opened and then, when she came off the stage,
gravely shook her hand and seemed moved nearly to tears, for he
looked even more derisive than usual. But, it was true, he was as
wary as she of demonstrative affection, afraid it would upset this
delicate balance between manager and star, so that each time they
found themselves in bed together it seemed they had only been
caught up in an accidental lust, without history or future, and, later,
they had some tacit agreement to pretend it had not happened.

"And if I couldn't be one of these women you admire so much,"
she whispered, as she passed him, "what would you think of me
then?"

Half an hour later she saw him lurking near the doorway, and gave him a frank and affectionate smile and a quick salute, as if she had only seen him for the first time, and went back to shaking the hands which were held toward her eagerly, filled with a happy confusion and excitement which convinced her, at least for the moment, that the Americans, whatever she might think of them, were her greatest admirers.

"All my old friends," she kept repeating, whether the friend was Joist Barringer or Benjamin Burnish or Philip Van Zandt. "How good it is to see you again." And she listened with a slight, doubtful smile, as if she might not deserve their compliments. But it seemed to be true that however often she had run away, nevertheless she collected her friends and even her enemies with discrimination and kept most of them as permanent acquisitions, until at last the enemies were, by some alchemy of time and her own nature, transmuted into friends.

Even Joshua Ching walked up and kissed her tenderly, as if the years they had known each other had turned her at last into a talented favorite niece, and stepped back to observe her with a smile which told her they had seen good times and bad together, and were finally comrades. "We've all been waiting for you to come back."

"You have?" Then, glancing about to see where Ferguson was, she whispered, "Tell me about your nephew."

"He's out in the Territories, digging up silver and copper."

"Still digging up silver and copper." She tapped her finger against her chin and shook her head, as if she would have expected him to have had enough of it by now. "And they say there's a boom going on in America?" She spoke the word with a soft, explosive sound, rising on her toes and spreading the fingers of one hand.

"They say there is."

"The most prosperous year in the past generation, Ben Burnish tells me."

"It seems a good beginning," Joshua admitted.

But this, Hoke assured her, was only Joshua Ching's native caution, for he was now said to be among the country's rich men, and was presently building two mansions to live in—for one was no longer big enough to hold him.

Hoke had come to her house on East Fourteenth Street near Fifth Avenue, a little buff-colored house built in 1830, resembling a Greek temple with its pillared portico, though someone had added a fanciful black iron balcony across the front of the second story—all of it in the embrace of the gnarled and writhing wisteria vines for which she had bought it, looking eagerly forward to the weather's change when thick purple sprays of blossom would cover portico and balcony alike and, in the back, overgrown honeysuckle and wild climbing roses would, if she could restrain the gardener, give her garden that atmosphere of accident and neglect which had pleased her so well in a house she had rented once in Italy.

Inside, however, there was a delicate harmoniousness which, at first glance, put Hoke on the defensive just as her mock castle had done, and he strolled about the drawing room, with its swimming light filtered through mauve silk curtains, nudging chairs with the toe of his polished black boot, and scowling at pictures. "No more neo-medieval? No more Eastlake?" He glanced at her sharply, reminding her he had remembered the words. "What's it this time?"

"Eighteenth-century Venetian."

"Holy Jesus." Hoke shook his head disapprovingly. "Venetian."

The small drawing room was hung with mauve silk, its gilt and ivory furniture upholstered in soft shades of mauve and lilac, and it seemed that she had found in this house a new variation of her old liking for close and intimate quarters, walls not too far apart, staircases which did not alarmingly drop away—indeed, something of the same comfortable sense of being sheltered which she had achieved in her quarters at Mrs. Stuart's and even in Mrs. Gosnell's boarding house, where her room had been crowded with the piano and trunk, her one presentable dress hanging on a wall peg, library books piled on the floor, her poodle Selah—buried in Rome with a suitable epitaph—and the squawking parrot Consuelo, the most faithful follower of them all, for he had come to live with her in this house, too.

"I like it better than the last one," Hoke told her. "Not so big, not so scary. Still," he added, "it takes a little getting used to. Money," he said, rubbing his fingers together suggestively. "This cost a potful."

"Well?" she asked him, and crossed one leg over the other, idly swinging her foot and fiddling with her hair as she smiled at him. "Suppose it did? My contract this year is for one hundred thousand."

He stared at her distrustfully for several moments, but then sat down and took out his ivory toothpick, a staff upon which even nowadays he was occasionally obliged to lean. "One hundred thousand?" He squinted, peered at the pictures on the wall, most of them too indefinite for his taste, at the vases of lilacs, many more lilacs than anyone needed, and told her with an air of sympathetic confidence, "That's not so much—when you think how Joshua Ching's managed to pile up about forty million by now, more or less. Of course, he's had to skin a lot of skunks doing it. With my help."

But Hoke was proud of her and asked if he might bring his wife to meet her, quickly assuring her that Tessie did not know he had a sister. "You don't need to worry about me, Betty. How do you think I got to where I am, if it wasn't by being able to keep my mouth shut?"

Hoke brought his wife to her dressing room one night, and Tessie shook Allegra's hand without daring to look her in the eye, mumbling a few words Allegra did not ask her to repeat, and stood about for a few minutes frowning perplexedly as she gazed at the weird furnishings of this great actress' dressing room, and seemed quite relieved when Hoke ushered her out; nor did he bring her again, although he came often himself, with Marquis McDuff or Oliver Foss, Judge Gill or Senator Stirt, or some other politician.

For Allegra had come back with a supply of new habits, and she no longer gave lavish entertainments or let herself be gawked at in public, riding in Central Park or eating oysters at Dorlan's, but was snobbish and seclusive, convinced she was now too significant to too many people to be easily accessible. And, for some reasons which were mysterious even to her, she made it more and more difficult for them to see her at her new little house, where, she insisted, she must have time to rest and read and replenish herself and not be plagued by callers at every hour of the day and night.

She loitered about her dressing room, though, serving supper and champagne and forming a kind of club in her own behalf which soon acquired a reputation for its exclusive, if miscellaneous, membership, and for its good cooking, brought there each evening just as the audience was leaving the theater and served by her maid Edana with a flourish of antique silver and French china, wine coolers and big linen napkins; and while her guests ate she strolled about, wearing her white flannel wrapper, sitting with one and then another and, so it seemed, having an important and secret conference with each of them. But when it came time to leave, she usually left alone, dressed in some outlandish disguise, jumped into the hack she had kept waiting—for her own claret-colored landau was too well known—and left them there still talking and eating, to discover for themselves that she was gone. And not even Dyke Ferguson dared ask what might be the purpose and meaning of this behavior, or even if there was one, for fear of spoiling her next performance, so that she often sat alone in the hack, dressed up like a Haymarket whore in a red wig and pink satin gown, and smiled gleefully to herself, amazed and pleased to find she was now so powerful.

Not everyone she had expected to see in America, however, had so far put in an appearance, and for several weeks she riffled through her letters, looking for one which had been mailed in the Territories.

She was eager to show him her house, and she knew what she would serve him for dinner—caviar, and quail in aspic—and sometimes when she passed through the dining room, where pale yellow silk hung at the French windows looking into the garden, she could see them sitting there, and she would smile tenderly, practicing the smile she meant to give the first time she saw him. She had trouble with that smile, though, and spent much time in perfecting it, even trying it occasionally on Rosalind or Juliet, to see how a larger audience would respond to it.

"Why, you're here," she would say, walking into her drawing room when she came home from the theater. "I thought you were out in the Territories—digging up silver and copper."

Edana occasionally overheard her, but this did not embarrass either of them, for Edana was accustomed to hear voices about the house whenever her mistress was at work on a new role as, Allegra assured her, she was now.

Or, if he should come a little later in the year, once her garden was as tangled and snarled with greenery as a month or two of a New York summer could make it, then she would put on a new dress she was saving, white lace with a lavender satin sash, and they would go into the garden, where now, on cold March days, she strolled the paths scattered with white pebbles and paused to admire those fragments of sculpture she had set into wall niches here and there.

The one she liked best, all that was left of a Roman warrior, his broken face and helmeted head and powerful shoulders, set her to thinking about him, too, and she would examine it lightly with her fingers, remembering the impression he gave of volatile enthusiasm, and the sudden attacks of shyness, so much at variance with his ardent and confident manner and, for that reason, all the more touching. But what she remembered best, and had these past two and a half years, was not the way he looked, and not anything he had said to her, but some strange confusion left in her heart of tenderness and cruelty, fear and joy, yearning and defeat, by which she might recognize a love she would keep all her life; and she counted this as only one more of the whimsical misadventures of her own precarious disposition.

Or he might not come at all, and perhaps this would be her proper punishment for having fallen in love with an American, since she had known as well as anyone else that once an American man set himself the task of getting rich, he thought of nothing else until that had been accomplished.

Then, one day in April, there was delivered to her house a crate which was found to contain a chair—or Edana said she supposed it must be a chair, for there was no other explanation possible for such a contraption. Allegra had it sent into the drawing room and went to look at it, finding that not only Edana but her secretary Richard Peterson, the poodle Mio, her French chef, and the other members of the staff had gathered there, too, to study this freak of western fancy, which had composed with malicious humor and ingenuity a back and arms and legs of the great curving horns of Texas steers, with a broad seat covered with polished black leather. They stood for some moments, quite silent, as if its strangeness had made them suspect it of being alive or dangerous, and watched warily as she walked around it, tapping her lips thoughtfully and humming to herself.

At last Edana spoke to her in a confidential whisper. "I wouldn't go near it, madame, if I was you."

But Allegra delicately touched the horn points to test their sharpness, and then, though they murmured in protest, she sat down and smiled at them. "It's very comfortable. Put it in the library, I'll use it for a desk chair. Where's the card?"

"There was no card, madame," Edana assured her. "You wouldn't expect a card to come with a thing of its kind, would you, madame?"

L X I

Zack stood leaning against the wall of the Yellow Medicine's shafthouse, looking out over the town which fell away below him, as from an inclined terrace, and could find little to remind him of that camp where he and Morgan had lived for two years. But of course that had been almost thirteen years ago, an aeon or longer as the West counted time, whole civilizations rising and perishing in less than a decade, and one building itself upon the debris and abandoned artifacts of another, populations appearing and disappearing as if their life spans had been reduced to that of flies or beetles, preserving by the mysterious methods of lost civilizations their early mythical heroes, their ancient festivals and religious lore, reposited with men like Bruno Favorite and Amos Muspratt, or the wise women of the tribe, Lily Jones and Queen Victoria Butler.

For here was a new city, with little left for him to recognize and, very likely, few men left in its new population who would recognize him. They had looked like strangers, every one, as he passed them, men with red noses and buffalo caps down over their ears, sending forth frosty clouds with every breath, for the weather had turned fiercely cold, the streets had frozen during the night and icicles as big as swords hung from the eaves of log and brick buildings. They strode by him with western purposefulness, dashing back and forth across the streets, and Zack told himself that none of these men had been here in that distant age and they had no interest in those who had, but probably thought of them, if they ever did, as being by now either despicably old or dead, as such early pioneers must surely be.

The camp was not, it was true, anything more beautiful than it had been, but there was more of it, and it had drawn away from the old town in the gulch to build upon higher ground. He had passed several one-story brick buildings, though the favored architecture was still a log cabin with a false front, and the houses were, as before, scattered about in the random fashion of western towns, each owner regarding himself as a community, intact within his own property and having no obligations to his neighbors. And on every street, before half-finished buildings, stood piles of fresh lumber, evidence that this town was no longer a victim of that common frontier malady with caused men to see cities where there stood only two shacks and a water tower.

But the most noticeable change had to do with the mines themselves, the structures which looked like big barns that housed the
machinery, the heaps of waste ore on the dumps which had grown
like a monstrous excrement, reminding him of their own earlier
modest off-scourings, and hillocks were forming of gray-green refuse and black slag around the mine shafts. And, thought Zack, as he
stood listening to the steady pounding of the stamp mills, the hammering and sawing, the shrieking whistles and muffled reverbera-
tions of the underground blastings, all those sounds which accompanied the forcible separation of the earth from her treasures—
this was the camp they had abandoned in disgust because the placers
had played out.

The camp was still known as a silver camp, but Lisette had assured him that copper was there in even greater abundance, and
that it was copper which would make her brother rich. And, while
Zack listened skeptically, offended to hear her praising another man,
she had gone on to brag that Morgan would be one of the most powerful miners in the country, for he had the equipment most necessary to a successful mining man—tenacity and resourcefulness, as
well as infinite patience, relentless energy, and the ability to take a
large gamble after a very cautious reconnoitering.

"He has a bank, too," Zack had reminded her. "And rich eastern
friends. And maybe that's even more important equipment for a
mining man to have."

But then, as Lisette asked, "Still jealous of my family, Zack?"
he looked sheepish, and admitted that Morgan would have found
some other solution if those had been lacking.

"The guy's my friend, for Christ's sake," he had protested.

And now here he stood, waiting for his friend, whom he had not
seen since that morning eight years ago when he had gone ashore at
Cow Island to meet Left Hand, waving good-bye to Morgan and
James Gordon as the *Shiloh* moved out again into the current. He
had come, full of humility and angry self-righteousness, to deliver
a speech he had rehearsed so often it seemed he would begin to recite it the moment Morgan appeared, open his mouth and announce
that Lisette was going to divorce Ralph Mercer and marry Zack
Fletcher—whether she wanted to or not.

Or it might be he would look at Morgan and something in his face
would so powerfully remind him of Matt Devlin the speech would
remain unsaid—and that might be the greatest favor Morgan could
do him today, for otherwise he would find himself involved in an
endless conspiracy to defend her from himself, never to let her know
anything about him which might startle or dismay her, and, in fact,
he would be forced to spend his energies from then on keeping all
the mice out of the parlors, however harmless the creatures might
be.

It was his lifelong superstition that the worst damage a man
could do himself was to fall in love with a respectable woman and

let her find it out, and during the past several months he had accumulated evidence enough that this was no superstition but only the merciless truth.

Thinking of how he had lately gone sneaking into Ralph Mercer's house, after an hour or more of waiting for the right opportunity, the moment when no women of the neighborhood were about and the children were in school, approaching it with his heart beating fast and his mouth dry, as disgusted with himself as if he were going there to commit some petty thievery or other misdemeanor too trivial to take pride in, he grew morose and surly, and sadly wondered what had happened to Zack Fletcher, whom nowadays he scarcely knew.

For nothing had been the same for him since that morning she had appeared at his breakfast table, looking, he thought, almost cruelly gay after she had ridden there in a sullen solitude, and sat down to eat with six or eight of the men who were not that day working on the range, chattering merrily while the men buried their chins deep in their necks or sat mute, and then demanded that he take her to see the cows and creeks he had shown the others the day before. And, from that morning until this, he had been occupied with inventing lies about himself, about the way he lived today and the way he had lived yesterday, and all this in spite of his agreement with the Sioux belief that the man who lies is a weakling.

They had ridden for several minutes, with Zack keeping a furtive watch on her, for she seemed remarkably vivacious and frolicsome, and all the while she was talking about what a glorious morning it was, the bird songs and brisk wind and hot sun, promising another blazing day, he had marveled at this show of feminine inconsistency and decided that as a sex they were given to emotional sleight of hand, a whole series of flashing displays of their peculiar and inexplicable temperament, showing first their gift for obstinacy, then a little surprise of tears and vapors, a sudden change to ebullience and laughter and now, confounding him completely, these alert, ardent glances and sparkling smiles.

Perhaps, he thought, she understood quite well what she was about, or it might be she had no idea at all, and although he had guessed even that early how this ride must end, he watched her eagerly for the pleasure it gave him to look at her, and complimented himself upon the virtuous gesture he intended presently to make, take her back to where Georgina and the children must, about this time, be sitting down to the breakfast table—only he would delay it a little longer for the perverse enjoyment it gave him, this conviction that he could at any moment command his senses with the perfect confidence that the command would be obeyed.

In another minute he was quite surprised to hear himself speak to her sharply. "Why didn't you go east with your husband?"

"How could I leave the children?"

Zack smiled slyly. "They've got relatives all over the Rocky Mountains—but you couldn't leave the children."

"What's troubling you, Zack? Would you be more comfortable if I had gone to Albany? It was only for a few weeks, after all."

And then, as he had been expecting, the catechism began, and no matter what he said she gave another mocking laugh, as if asking some third person to listen to him and tell her how much truth there was in it.

"How pretty that little squaw is, isn't she?" His face began to burn but he had nothing to say, and hoped that was the end of Red Bead. "She's sixteen years old? Or is she fifteen?"

"I guess so."

"And she's been with you for three years?"

"More or less, I forget."

"You got her for two ponies, not very good ones, at that?"

"They were good enough. No Indian should be allowed to ride a good horse, they spoil them."

"But what does she do?"

"She helps Chee Shum. She makes the beds. She keeps the house."

"And you're in love with her?"

He screwed up his face in an expression of incredulous pain. "In love with her? I took her in as a favor to her old man. The tribes are poor nowadays and Indians are always hungry—they come to get something to eat, and sometimes they stay a hell of a long time. That's all."

"What about Lily Jones?"

"Lily Jones?" he repeated, as if he could not imagine who Lily Jones was. "Lily has been rambling around the West for most of her life, making a damn nuisance of herself wherever she goes."

"What's she doing in your house? She said she's been there for the last three or four months."

"She's making another farewell tour, so help me." He laughed aloud. "She's come back to visit the scenes of her youth, so she says —and about as welcome as a rattlesnake in a dog town."

"But you must be in love with someone, Zack. Who is it? Tell me?" Her voice had turned soft and wheedling and her eyes shone with a lustrous glow. "I'd like to know."

And all at once he was relieved, for if she must talk about love then he was prepared to be as glib as necessary, no more embarrassed than if she had begun to discuss any other abstruse subject in which he took no interest. "It's your notion a man's got to be in love with someone, is that it? He can't just be enjoying himself."

"You were in love with me once—have you forgotten?"

"That's a hell of a peculiar thing to hear you say, Lisette," and he frowned at her disapprovingly.

They rode some distance farther, while Zack, who kept a covert watch over her, found his imagination once again beginning to usurp his judgment, grew more and more fretful under this spell of exuberant femininity, and all at once announced it was time for them to start back. He reined in his horse, consulted the sun, sighted this way and that over the brush-covered plains, and had made up his mind not to look at her again, when she complained that she was thirsty. In an instant he was down and running toward the stream, immeasurably relieved by this small diversion, and almost abjectly grateful for the opportunity to do something for her.

He knelt beside the water, swearing softly and marveling that here he was again, as apprehensive and full of misgivings as he had ever been long ago, then scooped up the water in his hat and turned, trying to think of some suitable apology for offering it to her in that way, and found her walking toward him. She held the hat between her hands and took a swallow or two, and as he was about to tell her they must start back she said that she was tired, she had not slept well last night and she wanted to rest a few minutes, and hearing this it seemed to him the future was decided, all his best resolutions were destined for failure, and he spread a blanket for her beneath a cottonwood, then squatted beside her, resting his buttocks on his heels, and watched her with sober thoughtfulness.

Lisette took off her hat and tossed it aside, ripped away her gloves and unfastened the top buttons of her riding coat, and sat with her back against the cottonwood, gazing out across the empty land, until at last she looked at him with a smile so sweetly sad that he drew back, rebuffed, and she touched his hand. "We hurt you, Zack, didn't we?"

"Who hurt me?" he barked, surprised again by his truculence and defensiveness, and felt that he was watching himself with astonishment and disapproval, but had no control over his behavior.

"All of us. My father. Morgan, I suppose, although he didn't mean to. We were so unified and, it's true, I would never have married you or anyone else if there had been any objection from any one of them. I wanted all of us to be together more than I wanted anything else in the world." She spoke softly but did not look at him, and he watched her with a tender and anxious expression of which he was not at all aware, and rejoiced to find that his feelings of malice toward Matt Devlin had disappeared, leaving a vast sense of forgiveness and charity, a welcome and expansive and generous affection which spread though him as warmly as whisky on a cold day and affected his judgment almost as quickly. "I was in love with you, Zack, but I didn't need you because I had them, and now I don't." She looked at him. "It ended, like that, just all of a sudden, because Gabe Foster mistook my father for a man he hated." She closed her eyes. "My father never said he didn't want me to marry you, but he said other things—and I knew what he meant."

"He was right," Zack told her, and found that he was angry again. "Because the years haven't civilized me much, and aren't likely to." He spread his big square hands, the thumbs long and curving backward, almost at right angles to the palms, then snapped his fingers sharply and decisively and stood up. He walked some distance away, trying to escape this raw and lively craving, and paced back and forth several times, talking in a loud voice and making, now and then, some savage gesture with his fist. "You used to say that if one of you ever married the wrong person, it would do all of you some harm and, by Christ, you were right. And I was the guy you meant, wasn't I?"

"But it happened. Pete married the wrong person."

He walked beside the river bank, glancing at her now and then, wondering if she had any better knowledge of what had happened between Matt and Pete and Jenny than she seemed to have at this moment about herself, for she still sat there, languidly leaning against the cottonwood with her head tipped back and her eyes closed, and all at once he went toward her, determined to drag her to her feet and return her to her responsibilities, but instead he knelt beside her and she opened her eyes and smiled at him, whispering his name as if she had turned it into some magic watchword.

Her fingers curved around the back of his neck, and although as he began to kiss her he was still imagining that in a moment all those promises would come to his rescue, presently he lay upon her, and found her this time so eagerly receptive, taking him with a kind of infuriated need, that when at last he drew away they lay silent for several minutes, and finally began to make preparations to leave, sober and thoughtful now, and a little sorrowful.

And ever since that morning he had expected she would discover his secrets, learn his vices, read them on his face or smell them on his skin, guess with unerring instinct that he still, from time to time, took Red Bead into his bed and wallowed with her as enthusiastically as before.

Lisette, in fact, soon began to exert some curious influence upon him even from a distance, for he had presently decided that he would get rid of Red Bead and put that temptation, at least, out of his way. But he did not do it, after all, and reminded himself that one capitulation would lead to another and that if he began by letting her take away Red Bead, he would end stripped of his individuality and deprived of his power. For Zack liked to think of himself as having discovered, like an Indian, his own strong medicine; and he had found it as they did, through the hardships and accidents and perils of his life, going out alone into the wilderness to search for it in pain and fear, and now he carried it with him, a talismanic bagful of trinkets quite meaningless to anyone else—the skin and stuffed head of a wolf, a few magpie feathers, and some secret ingredient known only to himself—and he preferred to believe that if once he should lose or mislay or even momentarily part from this precious medicine-bundle his own catastrophic end would immediately follow.

This was the mystery and magic of his life, the source of his luck, his health and strength, the power he could exert over other men, and he suspected Lisette had guessed at its existence and had some plan to convince him he could just as well get along without it.

Nor would it do him any good to take her into his confidence, plead with her to let him keep it, for women like Lisette would never believe that a man might trust himself to a bundle of dried sagebrush, and so it seemed his only hope was to deny he was any such superstitious heathen, and to persuade her if he could that he put his faith only in what his eyes could see and his ears could hear. Lily Jones, however, he knew to have these same mystical beliefs, and presently he could imagine that Lily had begun to pity him and was privately predicting he would soon forfeit his inalienable right to his own damnation and, with it, his capacities to succeed in every undertaking.

And then one day, when he and Lily had sat a little longer than the others at the breakfast table, Lily eating with relish her favorite dish of apples and molasses, she said as much; or that at least was the interpretation he gave to her words. Lily had recently spent a few days in Milestown and she came back praising its western spirit and announcing that there, for sure, was the last frontier. "The missionaries are taking over, Fletcher," she told him gloomily, her nose almost to the plate, cleaning up the puddle of molasses with a spoon. "Next thing we know, you'll be a married man." Zack jumped up, slamming his fist onto the table and shouting her name in a threatening voice, and Lily clapped both hands over her ears. "What the hell ails you?"

"Shut up, Lily. You talk too god-damn much."

Lily shrugged. "Come off, Fletcher, you don't scare me. I know you too well. Too well—now don't I?"

"We know each other too well, ma'am," Zack agreed, making her a bow. "Too well, and too long."

Lily leaned back, sighing with contentment, for to Zack's never-ceasing surprise and admiration, Lily's fondness for molasses seemed the one consistent affection of her life. Wherever they had been, in Butte, or when they had left Virginia City, when they had met later in St. Louis and again in Abilene, for they frequented the same border towns and Lily's celebrity made her presence known, Lily Jones had remained faithful only to her passion for molasses. "You're fed up with me, aren't you?" she said now, stretching her legs straight and studying her boots. "You wish I'd get the hell out. Admit it. I've got no feelings."

"Stay as long as you like," he assured her magnanimously, giving a sweeping motion of his hand. He was standing in front of the fireplace, smoking a cigar, and thoughtfully watching Red Bead as she padded about the room, removing the plates, stacking them carelessly but never glancing at him, and perhaps she had forgotten he was there.

"Shall I take him with me?"

"Lily, you're a fraud. You don't want to be bothered with that kid now any more than you did when he was born." He gestured quickly. "Take him if you want to. He's yours, we know that much about him anyway. And that's all we do know for sure, isn't it?"

She grinned, pointing her finger at him. "That's all you know for sure, Fletcher. You like him?"

"Of course I like him. But not because I think he's mine."

"He could be."

"He could be. And then again, he could be somebody else's. That's nothing against him. In fact, it's most likely something in his favor. I'd hate to think of a kid inheriting snake blood from both sides of the family. Leave him here—I'll make a top hand out of him in two years."

"Remind him about me now and then, will you?"

"I'll have to. He won't remember you more than a week, and why should he? His Aunt Lily, a dame who wears men's clothes and smokes cigars, a friend of mine—that's who you are. Now you'd like to change that, maybe, rearrange the past a little because you're getting old?"

Lily picked up a cup and threw it at him, giving a screech of rage, and ran out of the house while Zack laughed with malicious delight at his own cruelty, and at the end of the day when he came back and found her sitting on the verandah steps, snipping at the ends of her hair and studying her face in a mirror, exactly as she had done in Butte, she again leaped up and ran away, giving him a furious glare, and Zack sought her out later in her room to apologize, hugging her and taking hold of her chin to make her look at him.

"Lily, I'm sorry. You know I'm a mean son of a bitch. I was mad, and I took it out on you."

"I'll never forgive you for it, Fletcher."

"You expect to stay young forever? Lily, you still look pretty good."

But, at that, she turned on him and he quickly escaped, laughing again, and felt as if he had to some degree rid himself of his anger against Lisette by teasing Lily, who, in spite of her pretense of scorning the usual devices of women, had an abiding vanity and would not believe she had suffered some effects of the climate she had lived in and the way she had lived, preferring to imagine she looked today exactly as she had when she had ridden into Butte with Gaius Jenkins and Charles Hamilton.

The next morning she was gone, without a word to anyone, her old habit; and one day with no more ceremony she would be back again, her grievances against him forgotten, filled with affection and the craving for sentimental reminiscences—for Lily had arrived rather early at a time when the past pleased her better than the present and when her various friends and lovers had acquired significance only because she had known them long ago. And, he was glad to find, she had left the boy Johnny Lawler.

For in spite of his frequent announcements that he was not to be taken in by her suggestions that he was the boy's father, he had a secret wish to believe he was and could discover several reasons to think it must be true. Johnny was so much as he had been at the same age, so eager to be a grown man, and had so little patience with childhood—which he seemed to be trying to ignore, as he might ignore a trivial but annoying ailment—that Zack thought the affectionate pride he took in him must be the natural result of some recognition of his own flesh and blood. Or, of course, it might be nothing more than his liking for children.

The boy had been with him now for almost five years, ever since Lily had taken Zack to meet him at the St. Louis home of her sister, whose married name was Lawler, and whose child Johnny supposed himself to be; and Johnny went briskly and decisively about his work, was paid a salary which he spent as he chose, could ride and shoot almost as well as Andy Stinger, asked no favors and made no complaints because of his youth, but patterned himself with an uncanny fidelity after the men around him. And for these qualities Zack gave him his honest admiration and friendship. But Lisette, he was sure, would not understand that he could love a boy who might or might not be his own, and would understand even less that it made no actual difference to him whose child he was.

In fact, when he thought of his life as he was accustomed to live it, Zack became more convinced than ever before that Matt Devlin had been right, he would not have been a suitable husband for Lisette twelve years ago and he was a less suitable one now. But that gave him little relief from the attacks of jealousy he began to suffer after Ralph Mercer came back, and, to test himself, he made two or three trips to Helena but neither stopped to see her, nor passed by her house.

He called each time on Irene Flint, for Irene had been his first banker, had loaned him several thousand dollars at various times when he wanted to buy a herd and could not borrow the money from Lem Finney, though Finney was happy nowadays to loan him whatever he asked for. And one afternoon Irene began to talk about the early days, when she had been Milly Matches—an incarnation she often seemed to prefer to her present one—and he had first arrived in the mountains and gone to work for Matt and Pete Devlin; and she spoke, rather vaguely, but with a keen bitterness, about Nella Allen and the harm she had done.

Zack sat there for an hour or two, drinking whisky while she drank champagne and trying to make her tell him what she had meant, but Irene turned canny and reticent, murmured a few cryptic sentences she would not explain, and said that what she knew, or thought she knew, was only a guess. Finally Zack left, puzzled and quite drunk, went strolling down into the main part of town, paused to have another drink, and all at once, convinced that Irene Flint had given him a duty to perform, he went dashing up to Nola Malachy's house and loudly demanded to see the madam, then fell silent and abashed and glanced sheepishly about the parlor, as if fearful of finding someone there who would report his presence to Lisette; Lem Finney, perhaps, for Lem was one of the Tivoli's most faithful customers.

While the maid went to ask Mrs. Malachy if she would see him, Zack hung about, looking sullen and resentful, watched the girls and their patrons and congratulated himself upon his own recent emancipation from such public lechery, although not six months ago a whorehouse had seemed to him as lively and entertaining a place as a man could wish for and, indeed, his own Double Key brand was burned on the door of one in Milestown.

He watched two girls skipping around the room in a jigging step and laughing with the puzzling merriment of whores, laughing at themselves, at their clients, at the respectable world—he had never been able to guess which—and the girls looked so young, had such moist, milky skins, still almost childlike, such clumsy manners when they tried to behave grandly, and such natural boisterousness when they became excited, that he felt someone should take them home to their parents or send them back to their schoolteachers. Still, when the maid told him he might see Mrs. Malachy, he gave an inadvertent backward glance, for the girls had challenged each other to a jigging contest and were beginning to throw off their clothes.

He rapped at the door of Nella's apartment, where he had sometimes called on her with James Gordon after Green Troy had moved to Butte, and she opened it, smiling rather uncertainly. Zack stood for a moment sniffing the air, for she saturated it nowadays with a heavy and cloying perfume, and Nella wandered about the parlor with its Oriental screens and jars filled with pampas grass, its many mirrors and a lithograph called "The Lion's Bride" which always made him smile, for it showed a distraught young girl being carried away upon the back of a thoughtful-looking lion who might have been mystified as to what he should do with her next.

He caught hold of Nella's arm, seizing her chin and forcing her head back, but she closed her eyes and kept them stubbornly shut, and finally he let her go. "What do you smoke that stuff for?"

"I like it." She laughed softly, and seemed abstracted and preoccupied, scarcely aware of him and not at all aware of the stamping feet in the parlor, the banjo and piano, doors slamming up and down the hallway, but gave the impression that she was alone in a world which pleased her as well as those she had described to him long ago, the imaginary countries where even her brother, Rick, was chivalrous and gentle. "One of the girls took poison today—Josie. Do you remember her?"

"Of course I do. Did she die?"

Nella shrugged. "She died. What do you suppose she took it for? She was sick." She sat down and folded her hands over her stomach, and this gave her rather a comical appearance, as if she were

imitating, without any awareness of doing it, the women she must
have seen sitting on their porches along the Missouri River front,
barefoot and smoking pipes, swinging one foot and cupping their
hands upon bellies usually swollen in pregnancy. "Have you seen
Lucy Carter lately?"

Zack frowned. "I've been busy."

Lucy Carter had worked at the Tivoli for a few months, and then,
two years ago, he had loaned her the money to start a whorehouse
in Milestown, and now Lucy was his exclusive property and one
more encumbrance he could not easily slough off. She was twenty-
two years old and a very pretty girl, with the eyes of a fox and an
odd, pointed nose, and she wore a blond wig over her black hair, a
disguise she removed whenever she went outdoors and which she
imagined changed her beyond recognition. She had a drawl he
liked to hear because it made him agreeably homesick, and she pretended, like every other western madam he had ever met, to be the
daughter of a good family which had lost its money in some catastrophe. The catastrophe she blamed for her own bad luck was the
Civil War and she said it was her duty now to love God and hate the
Yankees, though not when they came as customers. And Lucy had
lately been sending him letters, which she wrote in violet ink in an
embellished script in keeping with her pretensions, threatening that
she would come to see him, if he would not come to her.

"Where'd you get that stuff, Nella?" he demanded, for she went on
looking at him with a benign and dazzled smile which enraged him.

"Fong Chong gets it for me. He's the most obliging Chinaman, he'll
do anything you ask, serve tea, run errands—"

"Deliver notes?"

Nella seemed momentarily surprised, but then she laughed,
crossed one leg over the other and began to swing her foot, her satin
shoe hanging free and flopping up and down. "Deliver notes? Oh,
I'm sure he would."

Zack pulled his chair up beside her, and as she sat slowly nodding
and gazing at him with an absent-minded and predatory look, he
hunched forward, his elbows resting on his widespread knees, and
stared at her as if he longed to take hold of her and twist her about
nimbly a time or two, like a jointed doll, and put her to rights again
by some deft maneuver. There was the continuous thumping of the
two girls hopping up and down, and a Rebel yell, which was heard
infrequently nowadays, though it had been common as a coyote's cry
in the early years, rose and hung quavering for some moments, and
faded away. "You've had him deliver notes for you, Nella?"

"I suppose so. Why?"

"Who did he take them to?"

Nella smiled slyly. "Why, Zack, do you think I'd give you a list of
my clients?"

"Pete Devlin?"

Nella thought about this. "Yes, Pete Devlin. Pete came here often the last few years of his life. We became very good friends, Pete and I, we sat and talked, right here, and he took me into his confidence. He hated Jenny—does that surprise you?"

"No, it doesn't, because I don't believe the whole god-damn story."

"But why should I lie to you?"

"Pete never talked about his private troubles to anyone."

"Zack, you have no idea—I've heard more confessions than all the priests in the Territory."

"And did he confess to you that he killed Matt?"

Nella got up and walked away. "Matt Devlin was killed by Gabe Foster. You told me that yourself. He mistook Matt for Jim Lowry, and shot him. Isn't that what you said?"

"That's what I said. But it isn't true, Nella, because I found out a couple of years ago that Foster had shot Lowry and killed him before he ever came to the Territories, so he certainly didn't mistake Matt Devlin for him." Zack beckoned to her, but Nella came no nearer, only stood across the room watching him with a defiant and distrustful face. "Fong Chong, I've heard, used to deliver notes to Pete about his wife and Matt. Now, suppose you tell me, Nella, who wrote the notes?"

"I have no idea who wrote them. Why blame me? Why should I have wanted to hurt them? They were good to me—for awhile." All at once Nella looked brightly pleased, as if she had solved a difficult puzzle and would be praised for it. "Mrs. Honeybone must have written them. That's who it was, Zack—only a crazy woman would do a thing like that."

"Only a crazy woman, or a vindictive one."

But all at once he was disgusted with himself, for the notes Fong Chong had told Irene Flint about might, it was true, have been written by Mrs. Honeybone, or by Erma Finney, or by any one of Jenny's envious friends, but certainly not by this passive young woman who had never had the will or even the inventiveness to act either in her own behalf or against another, always allowing decisions to be made for her and waiting, neither hopeful nor despairing, but willing to accept whatever was done to her or for her.

And so he mumbled some apologies and left, to make his way out as stealthily as if he were leaving a burglarized house, pulling his hat low in the hope he might conceal himself under it, and found that the young whores had flung their clothes about the parlor and were completely naked, sweating and panting but, as he went out, still jigging relentlessly up and down.

He walked for some distance, growing sober in the cold air, wondered why he should have wanted to make Nella admit some complicity in Matt Devlin's death, and shook his head wonderingly, sorry he had been drunk enough to go there.

He had intended to leave that night, but he got into a conversation with a man who had just arrived in the Territory with money to spend on cattle and awoke the next morning in the St. Louis Hotel, baffled and melancholy, and it was only after he had lain there for some minutes, reminding himself that he was a busy man nowadays and must keep moving only to stay where he was, that he ate breakfast and hurried away, glancing fearfully along the street as he went and expecting at any moment to catch sight of Lisette.

And now, as he stood waiting at the shaft of the Yellow Medicine, he heard the cage grinding its way back to the surface, no doubt bringing Morgan to meet him, and he yawned and stretched his arms wide, a habit by which he recognized his body's effort to put him at ease, and told himself morbidly, "Here I am, she's broken the medicine—it's all up with me."

He was staring off in the other direction as if he could not hear the machinery, when Morgan's voice spoke in his ear. "Why, I'll be a son of a bitch, it's Fletcher," and they were shaking hands and grinning at each other sheepishly, mumbling and muttering and looking almost painfully pleased at this meeting.

"Long time," Zack suggested.

"How the hell are you?"

"Thought I'd take a look at my property. You wrote me I had a piece of it."

"You sure have." Morgan gave him a light poke in the chest. "You damned old bastard, what took you so long to get here?"

"Been busy," Zack told him meekly, adding, "with my cows."

He smiled by way of apology, and was surprised to discover no suspicion in Morgan's face, no hostility or accusation, and either he knew nothing at all about what had happened between him and Lisette, or he knew and approved of it. And this happy thought caused Zack to glow expansively, until they got into the cage and he reminded himself that he was becoming as much addicted nowadays to pipe dreams as Nella Allen.

They started down, more swiftly than Zack had expected, so that for an apprehensive moment it seemed he had left his stomach behind, and as they descended into the darkness Morgan was explaining the workings with a passionate enthusiasm, bragging, Zack thought affectionately, as he himself liked to brag about his herds, even though the noise of the hoisting machinery made it almost impossible to hear what he said.

They passed a large timbered room, or so it appeared to Zack as it rushed by him, with candles flickering on every side as if surrounding an altar where men, naked above the waist, their bodies white and vaguely glistening, were shoveling ore into bins, and they continued on into the darkness farther down.

The cage came to a bouncing stop and they stepped out and started off along a corridor, passing other men drilling or pushing loaded cars to the shaft, and every few feet Morgan paused to examine the torn faces of the stopes and to pick up ore samples, fondling them and showing them to Zack as if each were some rare specimen of a precious stone. There was a roaring from somewhere nearby, the slick ground trembled and Zack had a momentary apprehension of a cave-in, for he did not like the feeling of a mine and felt a superstitious dread surrounding him when he was in one, as if he had descended into the devil's own realm and could expect him presently to appear and ask which torture he preferred for that day or millennium, and had never yet gone down into one without a conviction that it was the last he would see of daylight.

But to Morgan, plainly enough, this darkness, as full of smells as if they had happened into an underground outhouse, where indistinct but frequent roarings of explosives and the rattling of falling rocks caused Zack every now and then to give a sideways leap; with its patches of blazing powder which might, for all he knew, be the beginning of one of those most terrifying of all disasters, a fire in a mine; with its deep silence periodically disturbed by the chatter of power drills—all these mysteries and intricate details were to Morgan the source of his strength and fulfillment, the same feeling, Zack supposed, which came over him whenever he looked across a green valley to see his herders driving cattle and congratulated himself that his dominion was endless.

"I've got thirty-four men here," Morgan told him. "We take out fifteen tons a day, sometimes more, and we're capitalized at ten million—that doesn't mean we've got anything like it yet, of course," he added, grinning again. "I've spent six hundred thousand and made that much back, but it's gone." He snapped his fingers, and seemed proud of this wasteful extravagance. "Not a dime of it left, I'll have to go east again this summer. I'll show you my new mill, sixty stamps, Zack, think of that, when you remember what it was like that first winter. Sixty stamps make a sound like a roaring surf, the most beautiful god-damn noise you ever heard. When I started to build it they thought I'd lost my mind and said I'd lose my shirt, but I've almost got it back." He turned and put one hand confidentially on Zack's shoulder. "There's never been another mining area like this in the world."

"But," objected Zack, "you've got no weather down here. There's no day or night or winter or summer."

This, however, seemed to Morgan a petty fault to find with the Yellow Medicine, and he went on describing his plans to go below the water line, down to four or five hundred feet or even to eight hundred or a thousand, and it seemed he was ready, if only the ores held to the deep as he expected, to penetrate into the earth's very core and settle for himself that geologist's conundrum, whether it contained eternal fires or an eternal flood.

At last they emerged into the sharp, cold air, where Zack cast a watchful backward glance as the cage dropped out of sight again, and as they walked Morgan was telling him that first they would get a drink, then he would take him home to have lunch and see Felice and his children, and after that they would visit the old Halloway claim, inspect his sixty-stamp mill, his reverberatory furnace, his chemistry laboratory and his smelter, and only when all these things had been done would they call on Bruno Favorite, who would not turn him loose before midnight.

Zack protested that he had not the time, he must be on his way, and as he and Morgan entered one of the sixty saloons which had sprung up where only Favorite's had stood five years ago, Zack was giving his share of the Yellow Medicine to Morgan and assuring him that if he was willing to spend his time in those stinking holes he was welcome to whatever he found there, but as for himself he preferred to remain above ground as long as possible. At this, however, Morgan threw back his head, heartily laughing, and steered him up to the bar where he kept a grip on his arm, as if Zack might otherwise carry out his threat and bolt away before he had done with his boasting.

"I wouldn't trade my herds for the best silver mine in the Territory," said Zack positively, when they had finished the first drink. "Somehow the smell of cow shit suits me better than whatever the hell it is you've got around here."

They touched glasses, drank quickly, filled them again and fell into deep discussion, muttering into each other's faces like two conspirators, Zack about his Seventy-Six Cattle Company which ran two outfits, the Double Key and the Cross Eye, nearly two hundred miles apart, confiding that he had made a profit of sixty percent a year for the last several years, and Morgan talking of Lem Finney's suit against him in the Deer Lodge courts which he whispered would soon be decided in his favor once and for all. Then abruptly Morgan set down his glass, and announced that it was lunchtime.

Zack, suddenly embarrassed at the prospect of entering Morgan's house, of seeing Felice and his children—for he was not able to picture Morgan with children, a comfortable family man, and preferred to keep himself in ignorance of this part of his friend's life lest it once again stir up the old feelings of envy and resentment—now began to back away, protesting that he had only dropped in to renew acquaintances, and was out on the street, still protesting, as Morgan ushered him along, holding him firmly by the elbow and telling him that he could not go until he had seen his children.

"You're Bill's godfather, for Christ's sake, didn't I ever write to tell you that?"

He gave that same joyous, hearty laugh again, wrapped one arm forcibly around Zack's shoulders as they continued walking, and Zack found himself carried along in a kind of dazzled anger and admiration, telling himself grimly that if Morgan now began to describe to him the joys of married life and fatherhood, the advantages of having a beautiful and willing wife, if he began to talk to him of the superior delights of these virtuous pleasures and the resulting benefit to a man's character, then, Zack promised himself, he would knock him down right on this same street corner.

But Morgan delivered him no such preachments, only continued to urge him along and, as they walked swiftly up the hillside, was telling him that Susette would be six years old next month, that William was three and a half, and that the baby, Peter, had been one year old last October. "My God, Fletcher, you can't go away without seeing them."

Zack, somewhat taken aback, asked suspiciously, "You named the youngest one for Pete?"

"Yes, Felice wanted to. She loved Pete, and she pitied him. After Jenny stopped playing the piano, Felice used to play his accompaniments, and she kept hoping that one day Jenny would surprise them all and play with him again. But of course, if she ever meant to, she waited too long."

And now it occurred to Zack, as they approached the house and Morgan pointed it out in the distance, a two-story brick house with white fretwork about its roof and windows, that Morgan had invented Felice and the three children, the house belonged to someone else, and that in fact Morgan was leading him into a trap where he would first accuse him of his crimes with Lisette and next, in good western tradition, they would lock their hands and empty their pistols into each other's faces.

Morgan went dashing ahead, suddenly eager for whatever encounter he was to have there, telling him that this was a new house, the third they had lived in in Butte, and disappeared inside while Zack stood, contemplating it carefully and making unfavorable comparisons between its snug, neat appearance and his own sprawling headquarters, littered with animal hides and weapons. And then, drawing a deep breath, he ran into the house as if on the trail of a runaway horse, and surprised Felice in Morgan's arms, so that he would have turned and run back out again but she came quickly to him, looking so young and so defenselessly happy that he could think of no apology to make and tamely relinquished his coat to her, let Morgan whip the hat from his head, and discovered a little girl standing in the doorway, watching him and smiling, as if she knew quite well what a surprised face he would show at sight of her.

When Susette was introduced she made him a curtsy, looked at him directly but briefly, and then dropped her eyes with no semblance of shyness but a sure instinct for coquetry. Her brother, as blond as Jonathan, though his eyes were dark, approached Zack briskly, bowed and called him Mr. Fletcher and asked how he did, and Zack bent low to shake his hand. A maid in a flowered cotton dress brought him the baby Peter, and Zack, glancing questioningly at Morgan, took the baby and walked back and forth with him a few times while the infant gazed up at him, frowning, until at last Zack returned him to the maid and once again glanced at Morgan, shaking his head wonderingly.

"They're yours," he said, uncertain whether it was a question or a statement, for he felt that in reality these beautiful children had nothing to do with Morgan Devlin but must have been stolen by him and were being kept here as hostages.

Susette approached and regarded him thoughtfully, until Zack began to grow uneasy, and then she said, "Mr. Fletcher, I know all about you." Zack blushed at this news, and she added, "You're my father's best friend, aren't you?" She smiled again and Zack looked at her with anguished admiration, for she reminded him of Lisette, had her same dark eyes, the same narrow upper lip and swollen lower lip, the same delicate and vital femininity, and at last he gave a heavy sigh.

"I hope I am, Susette."

And as William approached and began to question him, asking how many head he ran and how many herders were required in the summer and if he had been attacked recently by Indians, Zack grew more and more gloomy, for the little girl and her two brothers, Felice and the house and its handsome furnishings and smells of good food in preparation, had made him and Morgan strangers again, so that he began to reply slowly and evasively and to examine his drink as if there might be some reason to distrust it, gave from time to time an inadvertent sigh, as if overcome by some terrible exhaustion, and grew increasingly nervous and absent-minded and almost distractedly eager to escape.

LXII

"There's more to this," Ceda said, when Felice's letter came early in April, "than just wanting to take the children to Europe." And before very much longer Ceda began to report dreams of commotion and violence—though the dreams were not clear and she could not tell for certain who was involved in them, whether people she knew or strangers. "I only hope," she told Susan, "there won't be any trouble between Suky and Lisette. After all, they haven't seen each other for sixteen years."

"Why should there be trouble? They were children then, they're grown women now."

And, in fact, Suky had immediately altered her own plans so that she and Sarita might sail on the same boat with Felice and Lisette and their two daughters, for Suky was going abroad as Joshua's emissary to buy furniture and rugs and fabrics and pictures for the new houses.

Morgan had gone on to Baltimore, and when they arrived with Robert at the end of the second week in May, the reunion was so fraught with tears and kisses, laughter and compliments, that Ceda was convinced that if her dreams predicted trouble it would not, at least, be between her two favorite nieces. The real purpose of the trip to Europe, however, remained as obscure as ever, for neither

Felice nor Lisette had any very good reasons to give, only that Morgan had decided it was time for them to make the pilgrimage.

Suky insisted they move out of the Fifth Avenue Hotel and into her house, and whenever Ceda saw them Suky was praising Lisette for one thing or another, her beautiful figure, her smile, her thick brown hair, predicting that Mr. Ducarcel would create a masterpiece once he got hold of it, and she even fastened her own favorite jewels on Lisette, a generosity which puzzled Susan until Ceda reminded her, "After all, the members of Joshua Ching's family cannot be seen nowadays without suitable jewelery—and Felice has her mother's."

They had scarcely arrived when Suky took them to see the houses, which had now been in the process of being built for more than a year and a half, and, with the three little girls, they went wandering about the vast hallways and from room to room, passing numbers of workmen who stood upon scaffolds painting frescoes and carving garlands of flowers and fruits upon moldings and door jambs, while Suky explained that this room would be furnished in the style of Louis XV and that in the style of Louis XVI, and Susette and Polly remarked to Sarita that it smelled mouldy, just as Aunt Jenny's new house had, but now that she lived there the mouldy smell was all gone. And although Suky did not mention the cost of anything, Sarita confided to her cousins that before it was complete her Grandfather Ching would have spent more than two million dollars.

No sooner had she whispered that secret than Joshua Ching bore down upon them in his frock coat and winged collar and Ascot tie, fragrant and sleek, and Lisette and Felice ran to meet him while Joshua, kissing the young women and their children, looked disconcerted at this evidence of passing years and told Susette he had seen her when she was so small he could have picked her up in one hand, some information which Susette received with a doubting smile.

He inquired solicitously for all his western relatives, murmuring his approval at whatever they told him while he gave instructions to various workmen. Then, directing Suky to overlook nothing that would make their visit more agreeable, he sped on his way and Suky said it was time to begin the shopping, for both Lisette and Felice had brought long lists, given them by everyone they knew.

In Tiffany's Suky hovered for several minutes over a pair of diamond and sapphire earrings before she had them sent home for her father's inspection, while the children entertained themselves by selecting the jewels they would wear to their first ball and fell into argument about whether or not it was permissible for a young girl to wear anything but white. "In Paris," said Sarita, "no one wears anything but white. It's only the English and Americans who wear bright colors in a ballroom."

"I'll wear whatever is most flattering to me when the time comes," Susette decided.

"And I," said Polly, who was a quiet, reserved, rather stately little girl, quite different from her volatile mother, "will wear something that shines."

"You can't wear brocade or satin, Polly!"

"It will be tulle or gauze, but it must shine. Like frost, or frozen rain."

"I see," said Sarita mysteriously.

Late each afternoon they drove to the Park, and while Susette and Polly gave each other vigorous shoves in the swings which sent them higher and higher, Sarita swung back and forth as languidly as if she were being tended by her first beau, and their mothers strolled the paths or sat in one of the little red pagodas, decorated with spires and ornate black fretwork, and seemed to be discussing matters of deep importance which were found, however, if one of the children ventured near enough to listen, to be only more gossip about clothes and what they would wear to the ball that the Nicholas Craigs were giving for their daughter, Nicola.

Suky's gown had been made by Worth, but she set her own dressmaker to work on new gowns for Felice and Lisette and Annabel, and she oversaw each fitting, talking to the dressmaker as she talked to Mr. Ducarcel or the architect, with light, vague gestures and a few words and glances at Mrs. Randolph, who had survived in the household almost since Suky's marriage because she was able to understand her cryptic signals and interpret them correctly. The children gathered for each fitting, imitating Suky's look of thoughtful concern, although they sat quietly and did not offer their advice but only occasionally whispered to one another with anxious faces when they discovered a mistake, and then, when the mistake had been corrected, clasped their hands and leaned back in their chairs with sighs of relief.

It seemed, in fact, that Suky could not do enough for her cousin, and on the day before the ball she gave a ladies' lunch, so that Lisette would not feel a stranger among these friends and relatives of herself and Felice.

The dining room, with its white brocade walls and blue velvet carpet, was lighted by candles, bouquets of lilies of the valley filled bowls from one end of the table to the other, white roses and tuberoses stood in silver vases on the sideboard, and tight knots of white rosebuds, carrying streamers of white and blue satin ribbons, lay on each napkin, filling the room with that overpowering fragrance people had come to associate with Suky's house. The rooms were just warm enough for a comfortable bath, the food might have seemed too rich, or too daintily presented, if it had been served to them somewhere else, and there was a species of seduction at work here which soon had them at its mercy—just as it caused their husbands, when they were present, to expand, and to look more and more fatuously pleased, even though they could never remember later what it was that had so befuddled them.

The lunch began at one-thirty and by two-thirty had progressed only to the salad, having disposed along the way of hot bouillon drunk with cooled sherry, roast oysters with sauterne, braised filet of beef with champagne, then on to chicken croquettes with more champagne, until by the time they confronted the salad they had stopped discussing sinister rumors of the return of the bustle, and begun to talk about their friends.

Coral Talbot began it by telling them she had heard of a man they all knew who had put his wife in an institution so that he could marry a girl younger than his daughter, and that the woman had been there for two months before his children could persuade him to let her out, and all the while she talked Coral was stroking the pink plume that curled over the crown of her dark green velvet hat and smiling. "Oh, it's quite true, I assure you, I didn't invent it."

"Preposterous," Jemima Haldane objected. "Such things don't happen."

Coral smiled at her. "Oh, yes, they do."

"I've heard that story," Suky agreed. "He's the same man whose wife pretended to mistake him for a burglar and beat him with a horsewhip—we've all heard about that, and so it's not very surprising if he wanted to get rid of her, is it?"

"It could scarcely have been the same man," remarked Coral, although she did not explain what she meant by that, and Jemima was assuring them that no one they knew would take a horsewhip to her husband.

"It must have been some ballet girl."

They went on to talk of this domestic tragedy and that one, wives humiliated and humbled, governesses brought in not to teach the children and parlormaids who spent very little time in the parlor, opera singers and actresses, but all this had happened at a safe distance, the invaders had entered houses up the street somewhere, not their own. And then, when they had finished the dessert and were rinsing their fingers in warm water perfumed with peppermint, Alvita Hallam reminded them: "It's unjust for us to repeat such stories, even if they were true—and many times they aren't."

"But the world is unjust, Alvita." Coral smiled, shrugging over the world's injustice. "The world is always unjust."

"Yes." Christine Craig was turning the rings on one finger and then another and studying the lights that came from them. "And it's true," she said thoughtfully, "there are these women who exist on the edges of our lives—and who sometimes do us more harm than we would like to imagine."

"Not only those women on the edges of our lives," said Coral Talbot. "There's a woman we all know who has been for many years in love with her best friend's husband—and he with her." She gestured. "Of course, a well-known woman of fashion can always get away with what an unknown cannot."

Felice, who had sat unnaturally straight and quite rigid, as if she had become almost afraid to move for fear of knocking over one of

Suky's precious goblets or vases or in some way disturbing this perfectly set table, now said, though not to her mother, "I think all this is only our imagination. Even beautiful women are not always so sure of themselves as they seem—and it's very easy to become suspicious of anyone we love and depend upon."

And, as if this had banished the stories, they left the table, talking of other things. In the vestibule, as they were kissing Suky and thanking her, they met Sarita and her friends, eight or ten little girls who had been mimicking their mothers at a lunch party of their own, and who instantly stopped their chattering and fell into grave silence at sight of their elders, dropped them dutiful curtsies, and then clustered together again as they ran down the stairs, eagerly whispering.

Susan and Ceda drove Coral Talbot home and when she left them, with a smile of unusual brilliance, as if she must be pleased with her afternoon's mischief, Ceda turned to Susan. "That woman's effrontery will be the death of me some day!"

"What's the matter with you, Ceda? She wasn't talking about us —I wonder who it was?" Susan, who had lately shown a tendency not so much to forgive Joshua for what he had meant to do, as to pretend it had never happened, seemed calmly indifferent; and, Ceda thought, this might be the best, or possibly the only, resolution of that unhappy episode. "Things of that kind happen all the time. Everyone knows it, but no one admits it. There's Jemima Haldane, for example, married to a nonentity and still calling herself Lady Haldane—and all her friends pretending she's entitled to it."

"That's only because of her father's money, Susan. They wouldn't pretend anything of the kind if Amos Cottrell were poor, or even in moderate circumstances."

Susan was gazing out the window, smiling to herself. "But who is the woman who horsewhipped her husband? I must ask Suky. Where could she have heard such a thing? And why did she never tell us about it?"

It was Susan's intention to ask Suky about this the moment she entered the house the next night, but she found such confused excitement—such running up and down stairs and in and out of bedrooms where ball gowns lay strewn across beds and hung from chandeliers, while even the maids had caught the infection and bustled about with unaccustomed energy, poking their noses into every doorway, bringing their dinners to them on trays as if they were so many invalids—that she could find no opportunity for a private word with Suky.

Mr. Ducarcel was at work on Nancy's hair, with Suky strolling by from time to time to correct him gently if he began to stray into error, whereupon Mr. Ducarcel slapped at his forehead as if to demolish himself for such criminal misinterpretation and flew at his work again, moving about his subject with the darting motions and abrupt pauses of a hummingbird at a flower.

Sarah and her cousins had been permitted to stay up, and each took her mother's toilette for her particular assignment, overseeing every detail with ruthless attention, finding fault with the way the maids were powdering shoulders, whispering to Mrs. Randolph that she must make one adjustment or another, offering their praise and criticisms to Mr. Ducarcel, and, by the time the men began to arrive at eleven, had reached a pitch of overwrought ecstasy which had them quite intoxicated.

Joshua and Steven came in first and found the women swarmed about the dressing table where Suky, in a white tulle gown, was bent over Lisette and fastening around her neck, with as much tender flattery as if she hoped to sell it to her, the diamond and sapphire necklace which Joshua had given her at the birth of his first grandchild. And as Suky secured the clasp, she and Lisette were regarding each other in the mirror, their heads close together, smiling as if each might have taken this opportunity to decide the old rivalry in her own favor.

For several moments no one noticed that Joshua and Steven had arrived, being so intent on this crucial encounter between the two cousins, and then Joshua remarked, "I've always thought that women spend the most important part of their lives in public," and they turned to find him looking jovially sardonic.

Annabel spun around, showing him her dress and the wreath of white roses Maxine had made for her hair, the pearl bracelet Suky had worn to her own first ball, anxiously inquiring, "What do you think of us?" and the others watched him alertly, as if his opinion would have some prophetic effect, but before he had answered Morgan walked in, dressed in evening clothes, smelling of hair tonic and Hungary water, and abruptly paused, as if inclined to back away from this barrage of rampant femininity.

Felice approached him, saying they had begun to wonder if he was still in Baltimore, and Morgan apologized, as awkwardly as if he had something to conceal, explaining that the ore shipment had been delayed, but took care not to meet Suky's eyes for fear she would know he had delayed so long because he had not wanted her to ask him any questions about Lisette. He was, in fact, so uneasy that when Philip walked in he shook his hand eagerly, and nearly forgot for the moment that it was his enemy who had arrived.

The maids brought wraps, perfume was sprayed on hair and gowns, and Suky was talking to everyone with her blithe, impersonal manner of gathering together all the disparate elements and arranging them as deftly as a bouquet, sending Annabel and Nancy off with Maxine. Susan and Ceda left together, and at last Morgan confronted Lisette, who had kept out of his way until all at once she was there before him, in a dress of bright yellow tulle with her hair in some intricate arrangement and Suky's diamonds at her ears and throat, and he found himself mumbling like a young boy making his first efforts at praising a pretty woman.

"I don't hate you, Morgan," she whispered.

He backed off a little, but then caught her hands, fervently protesting, "I know you don't."

She went out, her arm about Felice's waist, and Felice, in her ruby-red dress, wearing her mother's jewels, and with her dark hair drawn off her face and twisted into high coils in the Japanese style, fastened with jeweled pins, smiled at him over her shoulder, looking so beautiful and strange and inaccessible that he felt once more the sense of shocked wonder and dismay which had accompanied his first recognition that he was in love with her.

Suky came walking toward him, but he pretended not to see her and went dashing down the stairs and drove off with Joshua Ching, then fell into a gloomy silence as he told himself that even though Lisette had said she did not hate him, she surely did, and it might even be he deserved it.

Ever since the night she had taken him upstairs to Jenny's empty ballroom, as if she had a great secret to tell, set down the candle and stood there before him in that big room with its black shadows and red draperies, talking to him about her love for Zack Fletcher, she had been quick-tempered and moody, then gay and affectionate, as she had been after Matt died, for it had always been true of Lisette that unusual troubles and unusual excitements intensified all her natural characteristics. He had sat in one of the little gilt chairs which lined the wall, his arms crossed, suspicious even before she had said a word, and watched as she began to hum and went waltzing alone up and down the room's length, disappearing into the shadows at the far end and then whirling toward him again, smiling as she went by, but the smile was uncertain, almost beseeching, and all at once he knew what she had to tell him and was only surprised it had not occurred to him long ago.

She began to talk to him then about needs which surpassed duty, dark longings she could not define or understand, and other such mystical notions as tried his patience until he turned to her with a face full of fury, demanding, "If you think you must marry him, then why the hell didn't you marry him in the first place?"

"But you know why I didn't."

"Then, by Christ, you're not going to marry him now. Have you talked to Ralph?"

"I thought you would."

"I will not. And neither will you."

He would never have suspected Lisette of having these insidious and powerful yearnings, and least of all toward Zack Fletcher, and yet she stood with her hands over her face, sobbing, until all at once he left her, telling her to stay there until she was fit to be seen again, he would find an excuse for her. She followed him to the stairs, stamped her foot and slammed the door after him, then opened it again to say she hated him, and had scarcely spoken to him from that night to this. But she had finally agreed, after much pleading by

Felice, to spend the summer in Europe, and that famous antidote to inconvenient love would, he hoped, be successful with Lisette.

As Joshua's carriage approached West Fifty-fifth Street, they fell into a line of traffic moving so slowly that Morgan and Joshua got out and began a struggle to penetrate the crowd of onlookers that had gathered in spite of the light spring rain, to have their say on gowns and jewels.

The ball was being given in Nicholas Craig's stables, a three-storied brick building with a marble front and mansard roof, where he kept a variety of carriages and stabled horses said to be worth more than two hundred thousand dollars, in mahogany stalls with brass fittings and cement floors and, according to the newspapers, every other convenience a horse could want. On the second floor was the ballroom, with two fountains in the center, one of them spouting champagne and the other eau de cologne, its walls hung with crimson damask, and on the third footmen in gold and silver livery milled about prepared to serve a midnight supper, so that all in all the stables of Nicholas Craig were thought to be one of the city's most authoritative demonstrations that a successful American might nowadays cause medieval monarchs to wince at his splendor, even as some of Craig's conservative friends winced.

Nicholas Craig and his wife stood near the top of the staircase, urging their guests to wear their dominoes, for it would be a great disappointment to Nicola if this was not, as they had promised her, a masked ball. Christine Craig looked, as she usually did, beautiful and tired and rather anxious, while her husband, wearing evening clothes more perfectly tailored than Marquis McDuff's, resembled a more or less benevolent demon as he shook their hands, grinning with pleasure and pride at the prospect of another triumphant evening in store for himself. The orchestra was tuning its instruments behind a screen of ferns and wired orchids, and the guests who had arrived strolled up and down, greeting friends and staring at strangers with the condemnatory curiosity for which American women were known; but so far, in spite of the several hundred invitations that had gone out, the room was almost empty, while the street was blocked with carriages and women were refusing to get out until the rain stopped.

But when the orchestra struck up a march the women left their carriages, clutching at gowns and cloaks, and the staircase became so crowded they must mount like penitent pilgrims moving toward their shrine, martyred and dissatisfied with Nicholas Craig, who had obviously invited everyone he had ever heard of, and yet they entered the ballroom with brave smiles, to tell Christine and Nicholas Craig that even if their dresses were torn to shreds, people liked a crush and would remember it always.

Nicola, who had been warned that she must not begin to dance until all of her friends had partners, was making introductions and giving orders, shaking her finger in the faces of young men and warn-

ing them they were not to drink too much, for she would tolerate no
rowdiness at her party. Every so often she ran to the top of the staircase to see who was arriving, and she caught hold of Morgan's arm
as he reached the top, drawing him aside and telling him, quite
distractedly, "I'm Nicola Craig, this party's being given for me and I
met you two years ago at Long Branch. Where are Annabel and
Nancy?"

She looked no more sedate than when he had seen her last, lolling
about in the shoofly, and indeed seemed more than ever at the mercy
of her own ruthless energy. Her hair was as red and her eyes as
green, her paper-white skin was still covered with freckles, and,
when Morgan assured her they would be here any minute now, she
smiled at him with that surprising sweetness which a smile gave her
face, and whispered, "I'll dance with you. Go around this way, so my
parents won't see us—I'm supposed to wait until everyone's here."
She ran ahead of him to the floor, and closed her eyes as his arm
encircled her waist.

She danced for a few moments without looking at him or speaking,
but then glanced up quickly, to catch him smiling at her. "You don't
remember me, do you?"

"Yes, I do."

"Of course, I've grown up since then."

"You were quite grown up two years ago."

She leaned back, studying him, and then burst into laughter as
he frowned, rather embarrassed, for it seemed she knew what it was
he had remembered about her, and the next moment she was gone,
dashing away to talk to Annabel and Nancy, and the three of them
stood wagging their heads in serious conference.

Then she was back again, and as they danced she continued to
watch for interesting newcomers, but every now and then gave him
another of those quick and remorselessly searching glances, which
convinced him the illusion he had had on the mornings he had left
Suky's room that someone was hanging about the hallway had been
no illusion, but Nicola Craig. "There'll be a few surprises before this
night is over," she told him, and then gasped, covering her mouth
with one hand. "Oh!" and she stopped so suddenly that he stumbled
into her. "There she is—Mrs. Van Zandt. Good-bye, forgive me, I've
got to look at her up close."

The room had now become so crowded that many dancers were
forced to retreat to the edges of the floor and look on, and Nicholas
Craig was congratulating himself that whatever happened tonight
there was no way this could avoid being one of the best-remembered
entertainments in some time, for the women were either pretty or
had been so much improved by their gowns and jewels and hair-
dressers that they seemed to be, the men were a credit to his success
and influence, and that crucial ingredient of expectancy and excitement—something which could neither be predicted nor arranged

but must be left to chance with the hope that it would materialize when the time came—could be felt with as much definiteness as if he could reach out his fist and snatch up a handful of it. And, he told Christine, they might as well begin to enjoy themselves, for their responsibilities had been discharged and any of the miscellaneous mishaps of a large number of people gathered together for excitement and challenge, any drunken men or flurries of hysterical tears, any quarrels between young men or between husbands and wives, need not concern them.

Most of the guests had put on their domino masks, and under that influence there was a steadily heightening gaiety. The music seemed to grow louder and to increase its tempo as, in fact, Nicholas Craig had directed the musicians it must do. There was continuous traffic up and down the staircases and in and out of the supper room, numbers of guests went to inspect the horses, and when the message that it had begun to rain hard passed swiftly over the ballroom, there was general laughter, for the gowns and coiffures had arrived intact and it made no difference how they left.

Once Nicola had run off to look at Suky, Morgan danced with Ceda, with Susan, and then went to claim Lisette, who seemed so lively tonight, and so impartially flirtatious, that he congratulated himself the fit over Zack Fletcher had been a temporary one and was now passed off harmlessly.

But as they began to dance the vivacity disappeared, she fell silent, and he watched her with as much brooding concern as if she were his sick child, until finally he asked, "You're not unhappy?"

"Of course I'm unhappy, Morgan." She shook her head, as if to say he must know better than to ask her such a question, but her smile was tender again, and she seemed as eager as he was to repair the first serious quarrel there had ever been between them. "Did you think it was just a whim?"

"You can't live where Fletcher does, or live the way he does."

"That's what Mr. Talbot told Felice, isn't it?"

Morgan was offended she should suggest he had ever asked Felice to live in any such primitive style as the Double Key, and he defensively assured her, "Felice won't live there always. I expect to bring her back here when I can."

"Please don't talk to me about it any more, Morgan, or I'll begin to cry—and you know that would make Suky furious."

Only a little later he saw her dancing with Philip, and once again her eyes were shining, while Philip was talking to her in that confiding way he had which, for reasons unfathomable to Morgan, seemed to charm every woman he approached, and he kept a furtive watch over them until the dance ended, for he found himself longing once again to pounce upon Philip and extinguish that charm, ravage his face with a few quick blows, punish him once and for all for the blight he cast over his life. But there seemed no very good

excuse for any such impetuous chastisement, and so, directing at
Philip a menacing glare which Philip failed to notice, he went prowling about the edge of the floor in search of Annabel.

He found her talking to three young men, for Nicola and Annabel
and Nancy had taken the precaution against which parents warned
young girls of promising each dance to two partners and some dances
to three, a stratagem believed to have caused many duels or, anyway,
hurt feelings. Morgan approached at a quick stride, looking remarkably grim and solemn, for his mind was still wandering on Philip Van
Zandt and the long history of resentments he harbored against him,
and without a word he whisked Annabel away, calling as she went,
"My brother, please excuse me."

He seized her as authoritatively as if she might be trying to escape,
spun her out onto the floor and held her at arm's length, seriously
studying her, until finally he laughed, hugged her close, and continued to rush her about the room. "I remember the day you were
born."

Annabel, who had perhaps been expecting some extraordinary
compliment, something she had waited a long while to hear, looked
cross. "What a thing to say to me, Morgan."

Nicola Craig passed them, dancing for the second time, so Annabel said, with a man whose brown hair and curling beard and morose
expression gave him an air young girls might think gloomily romantic, for Nicola had an almost sickly expression, as if he filled her
with conflicts and intimations beyond endurance. "That," said Annabel, in a voice of gravest significance, "is Mr. Tash. Alexander Tash
the Second. He's an Englishman, a friend of Mr. Craig's. All the
women are mad for him. He's thirty-four years old," she added. "Is
that too old for Nicola?"

Morgan shrugged, unconcerned about Nicola's plight with the
Englishman, and the next moment glanced about sharply as a blond
woman in a white lace gown sparkling with silver beads, half her
face concealed by a domino, passed them swiftly with Nicholas
Craig, her dark eyes gazing steadily at Morgan as she went, and instantly he spun Annabel about and began to follow them, though
now the woman was talking to Craig, had become brightly animated,
and paid no more attention to Morgan.

"Who is that?" demanded Annabel.

Morgan was looking puzzled and almost shocked, as if at the sight
of someone he had not seen for a very long time and might have expected never to see again, and he frowned. "Allegra Stuart, I think."

"Allegra Stuart? Are you sure? Oh, Morgan, do you know her?
Please introduce me, you must, I want to meet her. There were
flakes of gold sprinkled in her hair, did you see that? There she goes,"
Annabel reported, as Morgan made a turn. "Up to the supper room."

Brusque and businesslike, as if he had just caught sight of a man
who owed him a great deal of money, Morgan returned Annabel to
her Aunt Ceda and, casting a furtive glance over the floor to be sure

no one he knew was watching, made his way to the bottom of the staircase, gave one more stealthy glance at the dancers, and went bounding to the top.

The supper room was as crowded as the ballroom. Men were loitering about watching the women eat, restless and impatient, imagining that more beautiful women were downstairs or that the real excitement of the ball was taking place in another part of the building, and Morgan made his way among them slowly, peering over heads and through sprays of feathers and flowers, feeling as acute an apprehension and nearly as much real fear as if he wriggled along a forest floor trying to approach some dangerous but very valuable beast he hoped to capture.

She was not at one of the supper tables and she was not inspecting the buffet, with its silver platters of food and golden cornucopias spilling fruits, and he moved gently along, wondering if she might have escaped him, until he found her at last in a corner of the room, talking to Nicholas Craig and—as if by some arrangement with the malevolent gods—Philip Van Zandt, who could never have contrived to reach her so quickly without their help.

Morgan stood behind her while she talked to Craig, meekly waiting for her to turn and discover him, and the sound of her rich low voice dissolved in a moment every promise he had made himself. She went on talking, as Philip gave him more and more frequent glances, challenging his right to be there, but Morgan's head was full of fumes now and he stood as in a trance, waiting to be welcomed or dismissed, whichever it was to be.

At last she turned slowly, murmuring, as Craig introduced them, "Yes, I know Mr. Devlin. We met four years ago."

Philip, he was surprised to find, was gone, Nicholas Craig had vanished, and Allegra was laughing softly and shaking her head. "But this isn't at all the way I had planned it. We were going to meet in the green room, or in my garden, and I was going to give you such a smile." She looked rueful. "No, I can't do it, after all. What a pity."

Her eyes watched him, luminous and glinting, and her mouth showed a touch of vagrant humor, but the domino gave him the disconcerting impression that she might not actually be there, after all, and he begged her, "Take that damned thing off, I can't see you."

"But I can see you much better this way."

And then, just as it seemed he was about to tell her something he had been saving all this time, something of such importance to them both it must not be forgotten or lost, he spun around, as if he had heard a spoken warning, searched the room but could find no one he knew and, as he turned back, the tag ends of that important message went slipping away, and he could not even remember if he had meant to be serious or merry, to speak of love, or pretend it had never been mentioned between them.

"Come and dance with me," and he heard himself mumble, as she passed him, "I love you."

She was two or three steps ahead and perhaps did not hear him, and he followed along, casting glares of warning on all sides, for she left a wake of murmuring voices.

At the bottom of the staircase she turned, and almost at the moment he took hold of her she went speeding lightly away from him, leaving him to pursue her about the floor through mazes of sound and confusion, beckoning to him and retreating and, as it seemed, never letting him quite catch her before she surprised him by another mischievous maneuver. But then, as he raced after her, following this labyrinth into which she had taken flight, there went Suky, passing only a few feet away with Frederic Hallam. Suky gave him the same vague, impassive glance she gave a forgetful servant or a misbehaving child, and his smiled disappeared, leaving him with a troubled and guilty and rather resentful expression, for it had been unkind of Suky to spoil their game, and it troubled him not to know what she might have seen on his face.

"Do you know who she is?" Allegra asked him. He started to reply, rather stiffly, that she was his cousin, but found her watching him with a sly smile. "She's an enchanted swan—condemned to spend her life as a rich man's daughter." He grinned, for it seemed an apt description of Suky and she added, "I was jealous of her long before I ever met you."

He had scarcely recovered from Suky's accusatory glance when Annabel reached out to touch his arm, making him start and nearly lose the rhythm of the dance, and he wheeled awkwardly a few times, muttering apologies as he went. Allegra, however, seemed not to notice the difficulties he was beset by, and once they were sailing along smoothly again, she said, as if she had never stopped thinking of Suky, "I'm more jealous of her than I am of your wife, isn't that strange?"

He did not like the sound of that, but before he had decided just what was wrong and how he might correct it, she asked, "Where is she? I want to see her."

He turned, surprised to find he knew exactly where Felice was. "Over there, dancing with Van Zandt, the second time tonight," he added, as if to himself. He watched them critically, seeing that Philip was talking to Felice, that she listened with her head a little to one side, and then looked directly at him across Philip's shoulder and smiled, as if she had not seen him for a long while, and at that he set out for the other end of the room where he found Nicola, but she, at least, was too much engrossed by the dour Englishman to take any notice of him.

"She's very beautiful." Allegra sounded contemplative, drawing conclusions of her own about Felice. "But so romantic—and so frightened."

"Frightened? She isn't at all," Morgan objected.

"She's afraid of losing you."

"It's never occurred to her," he insisted, for although it might be true that Felice had some fears of losing him, he refused to believe it, telling himself that the loss would at least not be a permanent one.

Allegra fell silent, and although it occurred to him that he might have hurt her with that quick defense of Felice he could think of no way to repair it, and became preoccupied with looking for spies in the crowd. There was Joshua Ching, standing with his back to the dancers as if this carnival was of no interest to him, talking to Benjamin Burnish. He caught sight of Susan dancing with Amos Cottrell, and Nancy and Robert together again; and every one of them was so abnormally visible, emerging into such clear focus, it seemed that surely out of the five or six hundred people in the room, three quarters of them, at least, were his relatives.

"And there isn't a damn thing we can do about it," Allegra whispered, and with that she left him and disappeared into the midst of the strolling couples while he stood wondering if he dared follow her. But before he had made up his mind, she was going toward the staircase with Philip, descended it swiftly, and was soon out of his sight.

He turned angrily, convinced that someone or other had contrived to cheat them of the real meaning of this reunion, and decided there was to be no end to his trials on this night, for Coral Talbot now approached him, saying, "Please find William for me, I'm ready to go home."

The next dance began and ended and Morgan did not come back. Coral went to dance with Nicholas Craig, but before that dance was half over Ceda was whispering to Susan that something had gone wrong, something dreadful was happening or would happen soon, for neither Morgan nor Philip was on the floor, and Ceda whispered that she had seen them talking, glowering at each other, just before they went upstairs.

"They've gone to drink, or to smoke."

"I only hope there won't be a scandal." For it was the prospect of scandal, so difficult to avoid, so impossible to repair, which could be detected woven into the fabric of all Ceda's prophetic dreams. "They've never liked each other, I've tried to tell you that." And when Nicholas Craig was seen running up to the third floor and a general restlessness attacked the dancers, Ceda took hold of Susan's arm. "I was right, Susan."

Coral Talbot appeared, but when they asked what had sent Nicholas Craig dashing off like that, she shrugged. "Someone told him there's a locked bedroom on the third floor and two men are fighting, or getting ready to." As she spoke, there was a jarring thud overhead which caused the center chandelier to sway, and several women gave squeals of alarm, as if they thought an earthquake had begun.

"There goes Joshua," Ceda reported.

The three women looked at one another, and then joined the procession which moved toward the staircase. But by the time they reached the top, Craig had unlocked the door and was trying to persuade them all to go back downstairs and begin the dancing again, assuring them it was nothing to be alarmed about, just two high-spirited young men, no bones had been broken, no eyes or teeth knocked out, and then William Talbot approached them with an ominous look, and carried Coral off with him.

A few men had edged their way into the bedroom where Morgan and Philip were putting their coats back on, smoothing their hair, and paying no more attention to each other than if each had been fighting with someone else. "Now what in the hell caused that?" Nicholas Craig asked, and seemed aggrieved they should have chosen tonight to let their antagonisms loose.

Neither of them answered but were for some moments busy retying cravats and buttoning waistcoats and knocking the dust from trouser legs, until finally Morgan told Craig in a low, reasonable voice, "We don't like each other."

This caused some laughter among the bystanders and both Morgan and Philip glared at them, as if solidified by their battle against these outside critics. "It was a question of honor," Philip assured Craig, in the same confidential tone.

At this, however, Morgan was heard to mumble, "You old families can be bloody tiresome about your honor, even after it's gone," and he left the room, passing among the bystanders, who faded away discreetly as so many pickpockets.

The music had begun again and the floor was full of whirling couples, but although it had seemed to him half an hour ago that everywhere he looked he was doomed to encounter some familiar face, now he was able to find only strangers. Suky must have left, and had no doubt taken Lisette and Felice with her, and he went skulking along the edge of the floor, trying to make his way out as inconspicuously as possible and feeling he had committed some nightmare indecency they would never forgive.

He caught sight of Christine Craig in the distance, looking as if she might be about to cry, and started toward her, meaning to apologize, but as he came nearer she hurried off in another direction and Morgan, supposing she was too angry even to let him speak to her, continued on his way, until all at once he found Annabel in his path. "Morgan, why don't you look where you're going? Everything's happened tonight! Robert and Nancy are engaged—and Nicola has disappeared with Alexander Tash. We can't find them, and we've looked everywhere." He tried to take this news with a serious face but, try as he would, could not help smiling at the notion of Nicola Craig run off with the melancholy Mr. Tash, and, by that time, the news of Nicola's disappearance had swept the ballroom and his own bout with Philip was lost in the newer excitement. "Felice is waiting for you downstairs," Annabel told him. "I'm going home with Aunt Ceda."

At the top of the staircase he met Joshua Ching, looking grimly pleased by the night's various surprises. "This is one time," Joshua remarked, "when Nick Craig won't laugh hilariously at the news of a disaster."

Felice was waiting with Steven and Letty, and Morgan hurried her out the door and into one of Brooks' carriages, and as they rode he stared at the wet, empty streets, thinking with some unfathomable resentment against Felice that it had been raining this hard the day he had married her and they had driven back to his hotel, as nervously estranged as they were at this moment, while he had contemplated with terror the prospect of finding himself alone with a virgin who had just become his lifelong responsibility.

But those reflections were soon interrupted by visions of Philip, for they had promised each other to finish the fight as soon as the women were on their way to Europe, and now he saw himself joyously battering the teeth out of Philip's head, breaking in his ribs, even though Philip, as he had discovered tonight, was as fierce and as quick as he was himself, if perhaps not so ready to risk his life for the sake of his real or imaginary pride.

The carriage went bouncing over the cobblestones, making him rock gently to and fro, and he smiled angrily to himself, wandering between dreams of Philip's bloody face, of Allegra Stuart moving away from him as they danced, irresistibly drawing him with her, and Nicola Craig getting eagerly into bed, perhaps at that moment, with the expectation and intent of discovering all the world's secrets at once, and he gave a sudden violent and triumphant smack of his fist into the palm of his hand and turned upon Felice with a savagely challenging grin.

He found her watching him, and her expression was cold and reproachful, a look so unusual for Felice that it enraged him even more. "What ever came over you, Morgan? Why did you do such a thing?"

"Why?" He narrowed his eyes, peering at her in the darkness, and thinking that if he were to tell her the truth it was probably that he hated Philip for being an inveterate poacher upon his own preserves, for hounding him in the past and in the present and, for all he knew, in the future as well, and he loudly declared, "Because I hate the son of a bitch, isn't that a good enough reason?"

LXIII

For a few days she was more than usually capricious, given to fits of melancholy and critical of whatever caught her eye, so that they began to grow wary at sight of her and to ask one another what was ailing the English actress to make her so contrary. Anthony De Forest fell under her displeasure more than once, and she complained to Ferguson about his habit of looking her straight in the eye while he lay dead in Friar Laurence's cell. "Will you tell me how I can be expected to grieve over a dead man who's staring at me all the while as skeptically as a mackerel?"

"I'll attend to it," Ferguson assured her.

Then, only a few nights later, as Anthony was bowing in acknowledgment of some unexpected applause, she gave him a smart kick in the ankle, muttering, "Keep in character." And when the performance ended she turned on him, crying, "If you ever do that again, I swear I'll make Ferguson take the part away from you. No actor who's worth a good god damn takes a call in the middle of a scene."

"But my dear," De Forest assured her, with grave dignity, "everyone does it. What are we there for?"

"Shut up, Anthony, shut up," she mumbled, and ran off down the hallway while they gathered sympathetically together and watched her go.

Sometimes she made her apologies with gifts and lavish demonstrations of affection, or she might pretend not to remember her crotchets, and they concluded she must be in the midst of an unhappy love affair, for certainly nothing else could make a woman so fretful, so vexatious, so uneasy and discontented one moment and so saucy and gay the next; but who this lover might be, they could not guess. Joist Barringer, some said, though others were of the opinion it was Ferguson himself, for they had lately been heard squabbling over Desdemona. But whatever it was that had nettled her, it had no effect on her performances, and so there was no defense for them against her imperiousness.

She strolled about her dressing room, wearing the white wrapper, sat with one caller and then another, but never for long, and now and then she went to the door and looked down the hallway and might have been expecting to see someone who did not come.

Joshua Ching sat there one night talking to Ben Burnish about the Chicago-Central which, he said, was not the strong and healthy road it seemed to be. "In fact, Ben, it's nothing more nor less than a bubble prosperity." And Joshua made a gesture with his fork, pricking that bubble.

"There have been such rumors lately," Ben agreed, and cast a sheepish sidelong glance at Allegra, as if it embarrassed him to have been caught by her, letting Joshua Ching put bees into his bonnet.

Allegra wandered away, uninterested in the Chicago-Central, but presently she was back again, asking, "And did they ever find the Craig girl?"

"They found her that night or, rather, the next morning, at the Hoffman House." Joshua smiled.

"With the Englishman?"

"So it would seem."

"Married?"

"There's a difference of opinion about that—but they've all gone to England for the summer. A marriage is said to be more or less necessary or, at least, advisable." Joshua raised his eyebrows slightly and spread his hands, as if to say these untoward happenings were no fault of his, and yet he seemed abstractly pleased by them.

"Poor Nick." Allegra was smiling wickedly. "What's going to be left of the Chicago-Central when he gets back?"

"That remains to be seen. But Nick Craig seems to be rather careless with all his possessions."

Allegra stood looking at him thoughtfully, her arms folded, tapping her chin with one forefinger. "And your nephew? Has he gone back to dig up more silver and copper?"

"Not yet, I think."

"Not yet," she said, and walked away, retreated behind the screen and there she stood staring at herself in the mirror, hidden from her guests and listening scornfully to their talk, sick of them all and wishing they would leave her alone.

She pulled off her wig and tossed it to Edana, signaling her to come help her, and from time to time she raised up on her toes and peeked over the top of the screen. She intended to dress and leave, walk out as she sometimes did without a word to any of them, but then she saw Hoke sitting beside Joshua Ching and holding Mio on his lap, pulling gently at his ears as he had taught him to expect, and talking in such confidential fashion that she got into the wrapper again, threw the fake Paisley shawl over her head and tied it like an immigrant woman's, and approached them softly, convinced that whatever they were saying, she must hear it.

"I'll do it with a heart and a half, I told him—and you can have the room to yourselves." She leaned down, for Hoke's voice was only a mumble. "Nobody will open the door until one of you gives the word."

"What are you talking about, Hoke?"

She jogged his arm, but Hoke paid her no attention. "The boys said it was like the old days, when a fight between two men was a fight, and somebody could expect to get killed. Five Points was a rough place when I was a kid," he added proudly. "You either learned to fight or stayed indoors." Hoke slapped his thigh, and the dog, disturbed, gave a protesting bark. "We tried to keep it quiet, but the word got around, and by the time Devlin showed up—about five-thirty this morning—the boys were out in force and gave him a cheer when he stepped out of the hack, as much as to say they had money riding on him and he better not let them down."

"Has anyone been hurt, Hoke?" She gave his shoulder a quick shake. "Answer me!"

"Hold it, Allegra, for Christ's sake, it's Ching's relatives I'm talking about, not yours. No one's been hurt, the whole thing fizzled out—more's the pity." He turned back to Joshua, who was concentrating upon a roast woodcock, deftly cleaning the bones and arranging them at the edge of the plate in a tidy heap, and Hoke now flexed his fingers, as if the old urge to fight was making them tingle. "Van Zandt offered the choice of weapons, and your nephew told him he liked knives."

"Barbarous," said Joshua. "I've always thought that once a man goes to the Territories he learns habits that make him permanently unfitted for civilized life."

"Knives," Hoke assured him, "are as good a weapon as any. Each man has his own fighting style." Allegra jogged his shoulder again. "Anyway, the upshot of it was that the minute Van Zandt rode up in another hack they set up a cheer for him, too, whereupon his face turned red as flannel and he said he'd have nothing to do with a fight that was fixed against him. Devlin opened the door and told him, not very loud, 'I knew you were a coward and now you've proved it'—and with that the hack drives off, leaving the biggest bunch of sorry Irishmen you ever saw. But they gave Devlin a cheer for his good intentions and that was that. We had a few drinks and everybody left."

Allegra threw up both hands and promptly retreated behind the screen, shaking her head as she went. But a moment later she was back, shivering, and saying she could not believe such a thing could happen in a country that called itself civilized.

"Neither could Van Zandt. My money was on Devlin—he's quick as a goat on his feet. And he's a mean son of a bitch, like any good fighter has to be," Hoke added, and his eyes were aglitter with reminiscent pride, for it was true Hoke's reputation as a fighter had owed as much to his viciousness as to his skill.

"Is that the end of it?" she asked Joshua. "Or will they fight again?"

"It may not be the end of it, but I don't think they'll fight again. My son-in-law isn't cowardly, but he's prudent, let's say, and this western gallantry probably seems as absurd to him as it does to me."

"It's a god-damn shame," murmured Hoke. "Devlin would have cooked him, for sure."

"And you wouldn't have missed either one of them very much, would you?" she asked Joshua.

"Allegra, my dear," Joshua replied stiffly, passing his plate with its cradle of bones to Edana, "we know each other too well to quarrel, and you've insulted me before."

Allegra shrugged and disappeared behind the screen again, and came out at last wearing a black silk gown with a velvet top, a little ruff of black ostrich feathers about her neck, and a black velvet hat on her gilt-blond hair, smiling rather strangely at them, with a look at once tender and defiant. Edana gave her a bouquet of lilacs, for her admirers had been trained to know this was the flower she preferred, Tap Doyle gathered up the baskets of dishes and hurried out, Richard Peterson set off with Mio loudly barking, and with these harbingers to proceed her and the others to follow she walked

swiftly along the hallways, paused at the door while Peterson gestured the loiterers back, and passed between them with the same
smile, kissing her fingers to them before she got into the hack with
Edana and the poodle, and rode away without so much as telling any
one of them good night.

And this, they assured one another, before they dispersed in their
separate directions, meant that she was concerned about a part—
Rosalind might not have pleased her tonight, or possibly she was
brooding over Desdemona, for she began very early to fret over
each new role and, in fact, once she had agreed to do it, was dissatisfied with it from that moment on, and while they were explaining
what troubled her, Allegra went home to mope.

She woke at ten and lay in bed, drinking coffee and reading, and
now and then cast a furtive glance over the little room with its Venetian furniture, sinuously curved and delicately painted, glowing with
the light of June sun through pale yellow silk curtains. But then
she tossed the book aside and sat with her elbows on her knees and
her chin on her fists, presently reached into a bowlful of jonquils
and drew one out and sat twirling its stalk between her fingers, telling herself she should be too familiar with tragic love in its mimicked form to have any more use for it in real life. It must have worn
out its poignancy with her by now, or so she argued, and surely she
was as ready to accept an unhappy love as a happy love, for she had
always suspected there was no great difference between them anyway—and now it was time to stop this trafficking in resentful pride,
put on her clothes, and go down into the garden for a ramble; but
she still went on sitting there, nibbling at the stalk's end, though
it made a bitter taste in her mouth.

Edana rapped at the door, and when she opened it her face was
flushed and she was as breathless as if she had run up the stairs at
high speed. "He's here, madame."

Allegra, winding a strand of hair about her fingers, smiled ominously. "What are you talking about, Edana?"

"Mr. Devlin is here, madame."

"Oh?" She scowled at Edana, for though Edana knew her secrets
—whether from spying or a kind of affectionate empathy, or both—
she was not to seem to. "Why didn't you say so? Tell him I'll be down.
Tell him," she corrected, "I'm not awake yet. He'll have to wait
awhile."

"Yes, madame."

"Send him out in the garden, and ask him if he wants coffee."

She sat a moment longer, almost as surprised as if she had not
seen him a week ago at the Craigs' ball and had never suspected he
was in town, and then she heard footsteps on the garden path and
crept to the window, where she moved the curtains aside and saw
him talking to Edana. Edana presently disappeared, and he went on,
with Mio following curiously along. At the other end of the garden
he stopped and stood for some moments looking at the battered

Roman warrior, and he was smiling, perhaps in recognition of some fierce part of his own nature which had only the day before been ready to carve up Philip Van Zandt as neatly as Joshua Ching had carved the woodcock.

Then all at once she was brushing her hair and washing her face and scouring her teeth, and began to struggle with a white muslin morning dress, pulling it this way and that until she was nearly as frantic as she had been with her costumes at the opera ballet, when it had been her perpetual nightmare that the performance would begin and end before she was dressed, and it was some minutes before she had it on and the buttons mated to their rightful loops.

She flew about the room, searching for shoes and stockings, listening for the sound of his footsteps, and when she bent toward the dressing table mirror, discovered herself there with a pleased little shock, for this wild spontaneity was becoming, and Augustus Adams must paint her that way. But of course the dress, with its short sleeves and round neck and childish blue ribbons, her hair twisted haphazardly over the crown of her head, with a loose curl falling down the back of her neck, the whole costume, would lose half its effect without that look of intense excitement and subdued dread which stared back at her.

She sprayed lilac perfume on her skin and hair and over her dress until the vapors made her sneeze, then took a fine-pointed brush and outlined her eyelids with black kohl, smeared liquid rouge over her face and scrubbed it in with a sponge, and was for a moment as forgetfully engrossed in putting these touches to the portrait as she ever was in completing Rosalind or Juliet.

But when the footsteps stopped she straightened abruptly, listening, ran to the window to make sure he had not grown so impatient at this delay as to leave, and, casting herself one brief imploring glance, ran down the stairs and stood waiting in the opened doorway of the dining room. His back was toward her as he and Mio once again set out for the far end of the garden, Mio at his heels but ambling along at a desultory gait, as if the heat of the morning had made him lazy and indifferent to his usual joys and he had no heart to go capering after bumblebees or puzzling over small green bugs.

She stood watching him, intent and fearful, for some harm seemed sure to come of this meeting, but at last she smiled, as pleased to have him there as if she had not half an hour earlier been blaming him for his neglect and pitying herself for the sorrows of her whole lifetime, of which this was only the latest and sharpest.

He had been pacing steadily back and forth and might, of course, be as uncertain and nervous as she, and now, as he turned and came walking quickly back, there was a clattering of chimes from a nearby church, and Allegra looked up in wondering surprise. "Why, it's Sunday again."

He kissed her, lightly and carefully, as if he thought she might make some objection, and she stepped away and stood looking at him distrustfully, asking herself how did it happen he should come here whenever he chose, and without so much as a note to precede him, only that peculiar chair in her library, around which Edana still steered a wide path.

"I know they've gone," she told him accusingly. "I read about it in the paper this morning. Is that why you're here?"

He looked unhappy at such a suggestion, and thrust his hands into his pockets as western men apparently did whenever embarrassment got the better of them. "That's not why I'm here, Allegra. I'm here because I ran out of resolutions." He smiled meekly, and seemed not at all confident she would accept this excuse. Then all at once he caught hold of her hand and held it fast, and began to talk to her so pleadingly, with such intensity of determination to be heard, that she listened with a doubtful face, thinking she would not be able to defend herself any better this time. "Do you know where I've been this morning? I've walked all over this bloody town, from Five Points to the Mall and from one river to the other." He gestured broadly, showing her all the territory he had covered. "I've been to Park Row and back again, there's nothing I can't tell you about Canal Street or Second Avenue, I've been up by God since five o'clock—"

"And did you walk through the Bowery, too?" she asked him gently, for it pleased her to think of him distractedly prowling the town while she slept.

"I walked through the Bowery, too."

"And you passed by our beer garden?"

"Yes."

"And so now you're here." She smiled a little, as if she might be ready to forgive him, and then remembered another grievance. "But you haven't been to Ferguson's New Broadway Theater."

"I have," he said reproachfully. "I was there last night."

"And you heard me say: 'To you I give myself, for I am yours'?"

"Yes, of course—I heard it."

"And did you know who I was talking to?"

"I wasn't sure. How could I be?"

She looked at him from the corners of her eyes, suspicious of this murderous savage in his blue lounge suit and dotted bow tie with his black hair neatly combed, giving forth a slight fragrance of eau de cologne, and standing there gazing at her with such a tender humility it seemed he would only be gratified if she found some way to punish him. "I've been walking the world these last few days myself," she told him, "wondering why you didn't come. I haven't been happy."

He watched her steadily, with as much sober gravity as if she might be in some curious peril. "I don't want to make you unhappy, Allegra, surely you know that."

"You don't?" she asked, very softly, as if she had put a question to a shifty witness. "But you have." She caught at a vine, just beginning its summer race to cover the house before autumn, and twined the end of it about one finger, bowing her head and giving it her careful attention. "And, anyway, what difference does it make? Unhappiness comes naturally to me, I'd feel strange without it." She unraveled the vine and let it go, spreading her fingers wide as she gave it its freedom. "I wouldn't feel like myself any more." Something wry in his own nature made him smile at that, and she gave a mocking laugh, joyous and melodic, as a singer might run through a scale or a dancer leap into the air, to show off her skill and grace. She walked to the table where Edana had set out a coffee pot and toast and jam. "Are you hungry? Have you had breakfast?"

"I'm not hungry."

"Neither am I." She poured coffee and handed him the cup, but did not look at him, and was turned partly away, gazing out over the garden as she sipped it. "I have to meet Ferguson at two o'clock. You can stay until then if you like." She glanced around sharply, for he made no objection, only nodded and drank the coffee and set the cup down. "That's a lie," she admitted. "But then, what if it is? We can't expect to tell each other the truth."

He bent over her quickly, but she was out of his path before he could touch her, beckoning him to come for a walk. Mio joined them, once again sniffing at the vines and prancing bemused after butterflies, as if they put him in mind of some magic he had forgotten long ago, and they paced slowly through the garden mazes, saying nothing, not pausing once or looking at each other, and started on another round. The sun was falling full upon them, making his face shine, and although for awhile he pretended not to notice it, at last he took out a handkerchief and wiped it surreptitiously over his forehead and jaw, and was, it seemed, tortured by something, the heat or his bad conscience. For when she began to talk about Philip he scowled and wiped his face again, stuffed the handkerchief away and then whisked it out, as if the day grew hotter with every passing minute.

He turned to her abruptly, full of an eager determination to take her into his confidence. "To be honest, Allegra, I thought he'd back out—and he did." She raised her eyebrows, not so sure there was any such innocent explanation, and began to study with seeming great interest a bush covered with sprays of sweet white blossom, its name and habits quite as unknown to her as had been the flowers she had first seen growing in Mrs. Stuart's garden. And when she gave him an oblique glance, she found that he was smiling reflectively, thinking, perhaps, of Philip's face when the Irishmen standing outside the Red Onion gave him a rousing cheer of welcome. "But I think I taught him to walk softly in flannel socks."

And at sight of that secretive smile, her sympathies were all at once with Philip, for whom she had invented so many and such various punishments even as she hurried to meet him in that house on

West Twenty-fourth Street. She caught hold of a branch, bent it and twisted it, though it was tough and stubborn, and at last broke it off and held the blossoming spray between her hands. "It was all a trick —you never meant to fight him at all, did you?"

"Oh, yes I did," he assured her. "Yes, I did."

"And did you choose the Red Onion so the City Coroner could declare it an accidental death if it should happen to turn out that way?" She had a crafty little smile, but directed it at the flower, not at him.

He looked surprised, quite taken aback she should have seen through that strategy, but then he grinned, and did not seem ashamed of being, as his uncle Joshua Ching had remarked, permanently unfitted for civilized life. "We thought of that. But nothing came of it—and now nothing will. We got it out of our systems, whatever it was."

"Oh, indeed, and you think so, now, do you?" Allegra lapsed into the brogue, and she wagged the flower at him. "Well, and if it was me, I wouldn't be so sure of myself as all that. I know the gentleman better than you do, remember. He won't be forgetting it—and he won't be after telling himself the best man won, either, you may take my word for that." She caught at another flower, something scarlet this time, which grew on a bush near the ground, and she knelt beside it, peeking about under the bushes, and there, in those dark, moist recesses, she found hidden away certain other small flowers, white and purple violets, and some unknown yellow blooms of pungent fragrance which she plucked and smelled. "You won't believe me, will you? Well, then, we won't talk about it any more." She pulled at a few of the violets, and then pushed the damp earth down, poking at it and mashing it with many savage little gestures, and seemed so absorbed in all she had exposed, that mesh of growing things, she might have forgotten he was there. She stood up, sorting the bouquet and putting it together to please her better, and casually inquired, "And are you as rich as Joshua Ching by now?"

At that, he gave the first honest laugh she had heard from him that day, and promptly began to explain to her what troubles he was having, though they seemed, as he talked of them, to be troubles he admired, and perhaps he expected her to admire them, too.

He talked of pioneer shafts and options, of weather and water and leeching out, of red oxide and copper glance, growing all the while more candid and confiding, bending down to look into her face with a questioning anxiety as she continued to fidget with the flowers, adding new ones to the cluster. She stopped here and there, trailing her hands lightly across the bushes, and then sniffed curiously at her palms, to see what scent their leaves had left, and when he paused, as if to ask if she had heard enough of mines and mining, she looked up at him thoughtfully, and might not have been listening at all.

"I think about you sometimes, Morgan," she said, so softly he

leaned nearer. "It's like a favorite daydream, where you're unbelievably happy and unbelievably sad." She looked at him doubtfully.
"Do you know?"

"Of course."

"Of course," she repeated chidingly. "Of course."

"But I do know. I have those same daydreams myself." He reached
out quickly, and his hand passed across her arm, lingering, but
then he glanced furtively at the windows of surrounding houses, his
hand went back into his pocket, and he fell eagerly upon the subject
of wet crushers and dry crushers and ten-stamps and sixty-stamps.
"Butte is no longer a camp of mere prospects—we know by now that
it's one of the world's great mines. Would you believe it, there's no
possible way a man can fail in that camp but through bad management or lack of capital—or giving up too soon. But, of course, to
prove up a copper mine takes several years, and limitless capital."
He watched her with intense seriousness, as if to be sure she missed
nothing of this valuable information. "But do you know, Allegra,
whether it's gold or silver or copper—and however much you
think you may have learned—believe me, there's more art in it than
science, and more superstition than either." She was not looking at
him, but she stood still now and faced him directly, with quite a
solemn face, and he went on. "The ancients, you know, believed
there were metal demons who'd been placed in charge of the mines
to guard the treasures—and I think they may have been right." He
watched her carefully, as if her silence troubled him, and then laid
his hand lightly on her shoulder, asking, "Allegra?"

She still refused to look at him, though he coaxed her, wheedling
and apologetic, and when she did her eyes were full of tears. This
discovery acted upon him as if he had inadvertently done her some
physical harm, and he began to plead with her, begging her forgiveness if it was he who had made her sad, and while he talked she
played with the bouquet, wondering if these tears came from real
pain, or if she had only been tempted out of an actress' irresistible
impulse to act.

She heard all his self-accusations, his promises and propitiations,
with a doubtful smile, more wistful than skeptical, until at last she
looked up at him curiously, whispering, "Time, at last, makes all
things even—or so they say. Do you believe that?"

"No, I don't."

"Neither do I." She went sauntering on, and glanced at him over
her shoulder. "But I have no right to blame you for the accumula-
tions of living, after all." For it seemed the future had been too well
planned—not only for him—and what was left of it for them to inhabit together was not much more spacious than this walled garden.

The day grew steadily hotter and Mio had gone to lie beneath an
arching bush, cooling his belly upon the black, wet earth and casting
them beseeching glances whenever they passed him, but she seemed
unaware of the heat, or of Morgan dripping sweat and wiping his

face, cautiously struggling with his collar as if it might be strangling him, and went on sauntering back and forth, loitering along the paths to examine with a botanist's intent scrutiny everything she found there, just as she did each morning when she came into the garden alone. The bouquet grew larger, for she added to it leaves and branches, ferns and perhaps a few weeds, and each time he reached out, as if the impulse to touch her had overcome his judgment, she turned deftly away, or submitted indifferently to one of those brief caresses, a grazing of his hand across the back of her neck or along her arm.

She talked of Joshua Ching and his rapidly growing wealth, saying that there seemed no end in sight to what he might accumulate and expressed some whimsical pity for the plight of Nicholas Craig, not for his daughter's elopement and reported pregnancy, but for his folly in inviting Joshua Ching onto his board of directors. She told him that Joshua Ching had bought the *New York Journal* a year and a half ago, a piece of information Morgan received with surprise, for it had been a well-kept secret, and that now Benjamin Burnish was his creature and indebted to him for a fine new house he owned. This seemed to give her some cruel amusement, and she went on to say that Joshua Ching, true to his lifelong habit, continued to build upon a firm foundation of destruction. "Unless the bones of his friends and enemies are in the mortar, he doesn't believe it will stick together." She laughed softly and, as if at some unexpected thought, asked, "How long will you stay in New York?"

"As long as I can."

"And how long is that?"

"Four days, or maybe five. I'm not going back because I want to."

"Oh, no, of course not," she agreed. "You're going because you're thirty-two years old and not a millionaire yet." He seemed about to begin an explanation of his various responsibilities, and she held up her hand to ward him off. "So many people depend on you—your board of directors and your partners, your bankers and your family, not to mention all your friends. Oh, you needn't tell me, Morgan," she assured him, looking very wise. "I know it as well as you do. Why, I've never met an American yet who wasn't obliged to get rich for the sake of someone else—it's never for himself he does it, have you noticed that? It's for his country, perhaps for his wife or his children. Sometimes he even gets rich for the sake of his conscience." She gave him a sly little look, which turned him obediently meek, searching for another apology, but all at once she tapped his shoulder and lifted up on her toes to tell him confidingly, "But I know so many ways to corrupt your resolution, I'll make you forget everything else." He smiled, nodding in agreement, and shrugged, as if to admit he was helpless, she might do what she liked with him. "I have an infallible spell," she promised, "you'll never escape from it. There, it's begun to do its work, can't you feel it?" Her hand lay for a moment over his heart. "Any minute now it will be too late for you." She

laughed, glancing sideways to see how he took these predictions, but
although he was watching her with solemn intentness, she sighed,
and held the bouquet to her face, telling him ruefully, "I wish it were
true."

"But it is true. I love you."

She pretended to think about that, then looked up quickly, saying,
"Well, and if you love me, sure it's few enough who would blame
you for it—if they knew. For what else have I done with my life but
study all the ways there are to make people love me?" She cocked
her head sideways, and when he laughed, not so much to humor her,
it seemed, as from some presentiment of sorrow, she gave his hand
a confiding touch. "Will you ride with me now in the Park?"

"If that's what you want."

"And will you have supper with me here tonight?"

"If you want to."

At that, she became merry as a child promised some unusual
favor. "We'll eat here, at this table, it will be cool then, and I know
just what we'll have, too, my favorite summer supper. I won't tell
you now what it is, but I've had it planned for months." He was looking at her so seriously that it seemed her infallible spell must have
begun its work, but Allegra took no notice of this, and as she started
away lifted one finger as in a signal of warning. "Wait for me, won't
you? It won't take long."

She ran down the path, Mio followed her part way, but then returned to lie once again in his shady retreat, and as she dashed
through the dining room she thrust the bouquet into Edana's hands,
saying, "Here—do something with these."

She kicked off her shoes as she entered the bedroom, closing the
door on Edana and telling her crossly that she needed no help, and
ran to the window to look down at him—that unknown intruder into
her garden—and while she watched him she began to undress,
standing on one foot to pull off a stocking, unbuttoning her dress
with the other hand, and was thinking all the while of how she could
contrive to surround and entwine him, even though she knew it could
not be done and, perhaps, should not be done.

She went to the mirror and fell to studying her face, troubled
once again by memories and premonitions, and nodded sagely as she
promised herself, "I'll be wiser the next time." There was a light rap
at the door and she started, as alarmed as if she had supposed herself
alone in the house, then crossed the floor slowly in her bare feet, trailing the dress with her, and opened the door. He had nothing to say,
but after a moment she lay her hand against his face, tenderly smiling. "Let's agree not to blame each other—people spoil half their
pleasures with thinking they don't deserve them."

LXIV

Lily lighted the cigar, put it between his fingers, and sat back, clasping her hands about one knee and watching thoughtfully as he began to smoke. Finally she gave a slow, light sigh, and shook her head. "Fletcher, you're a fool for luck."

"Shut up, Lily."

He lay on his back, dressed in black trousers and a blue flannel shirt unbuttoned over his naked chest, for the room was hot and the fire blazing. A cloth covered his forehead and eyes, but his mouth was set in a savage expression, sardonic and cruel, as if he hated Lily and himself and, when he had time to think about it, hated the rest of the world, too.

"But you are, and you know it. Any other guy would be dead."

"Not me, though—I'm a lucky son of a bitch. I'm not dead, I just can't see."

"You will."

Zack grimaced, squeezing his face into an ugly expression, and gave a sudden swing of his arm, apparently meant to knock Lily off her stool, but Lily leaped up nimbly, dodging, and sat down again, carefully drawing the stool back to a safer distance. "Shut up, you god-damn bitch, I know you came here to crow over me."

"That's a hell of a thing to say to me, Fletcher. I came because I heard about you, I wanted to see how you were getting along."

"Now you know, so why don't you get your ass the hell out of here."

Lily made a comical little grimace. "Touchy as a teased snake." She leaned forward, resting her elbows on her knees, and observed him for some moments with a thoughtful concern. "What were you doing out on the range by yourself, Fletcher?"

"I was looking after my cows—what do you think I was doing?"

"You know this is a bad winter. You should have left those cows to shift for themselves, or sent Stinger or Tango."

"They were over on the Musselshell! I've told you that!" Zack raised up on one elbow, peeled the salt poultice from his eyes as carefully as if he expected the flesh to go with it, and his face was puffed and mottled red, his eyelids swollen like walnuts, and after a moment of trying to look at her he gave a hissing sound, despairing and malevolent, threw himself flat upon his back, slapped the poultice violently across his eyes, and lay straight and rigid, only the muscles along his jaw spasmodically working, as if he must be swearing to himself.

Ever since he had arrived at Gordon's five days before, explaining that he had been on his way down from the Sun River when another storm broke and loudly demanding of Gordon why he had no lamps burning at that hour of the day, Zack had had little to say, only lain with his teeth clenched, silently enduring that pain which was known to be keener than some of the most refined Blackfoot tortures, for it was as if burning hot sand had been scrubbed into the eyeballs and sealed there. And it grew more intolerable from day to day, so that Andy Stinger and Gordon kept their distance, and when it was time to change the salt poultice they begged his permission as respectfully as if they had come to ask him if he was ready to be hanged.

They told him, more than once, that snow blindness was a temporary disability, nothing to trouble an old hand like himself, deprecating it as if he had nothing more serious than a sprained thumb. And while they stood in the doorway, ready to take flight should he come leaping at them, they talked of men they knew who had been stricken blind by the glaring snow and, not three weeks later, could see as well as ever—except, of course, at night; that took a little longer. Zack listened—if he did, and they could not be sure he heard them, for the pain kept him engrossed—but neither answered nor took any notice of this false optimism, and seemed to hate them for trying to comfort him. For if he was to be blind he wanted none of their commiserations, nor their pity, but thought they should despise him as a useless object.

"I say," Gordon had told Andy Stinger, when he arrived with Johnny Lawler, "I don't quite trust him with a weapon, the mood he's in, do you?"

"If you don't trust him with it," Andy suggested, "then you try to get it away from him."

Zack had refused to undress, insisting he would be up in an hour or two and on his way again, and for the first three days would not even surrender his hat or boots, but yelled at them whenever they approached and reached out his great hands as if to seize them and dash them together.

"He's as likely as not to kill himself," Gordon muttered.

"Not Mr. Zack, not by a long way."

And Johnny, gazing thoughtfully at Zack, agreed with Stinger. "Hell, no, not Mr. Zack. Not even if he never saw daylight again."

Johnny Lawler and Stinger set out for Helena to bring a doctor, since it seemed unlikely they would discover one any nearer, although Zack shouted that he needed no doctor, he would cure himself or stay blind, and threatened to leave the house if a doctor set foot in it.

"I say, Stinger," Gordon suggested, when he followed them outside, "you might stop by the *Helena Post*. I wouldn't mention the snow blindness—just give them an account of the storm and see what news you can pick up about the rest of the Territory."

Zack still refused to get into a nightshirt, declared he had never worn such a garment and never would, and would not be buried in one, either, if it came to that, and although at last he kicked off the boots and stuck his bare feet into a pair of beaded moccasins, he would not give up the pistol, and day and night it lay beside him, where he could reach down and put his hand upon it.

Lily got there before Andy Stinger and Johnny Lawler had returned and came bounding into the house one early morning, went stamping about in her buffalo boots, swearing with the cold, and demanded to see the patient, for news of his plight had reached Milestown where, she said, she had meant to spend the winter playing poker with friends who were waiting for their cattle to be driven north. But instead she had sacrificed her comfort and risked her life and now here she was, but first she would have a drink, some ham and eggs and fried potatoes and biscuits, buckwheat cakes with butter and black molasses, and while she ate she talked to James Gordon and, from time to time, shook her head and clucked her tongue.

"But how did it happen to an old hand like Fletcher?" Gordon asked her. "Everybody has known for weeks this is the worst winter in years."

"How did it happen? Maybe he forgot to spit over his left shoulder once." Lily gave him a bitter little smile, for it was not often she would admit that circumstances might outwit men. "That's how these things happen, Gordon. You know that as well as I do."

"Ah, well, I suppose so."

She and Gordon had gone upstairs together and Lily crossed the bedroom on tiptoe, approaching so softly she stood beside him for some moments before he sensed that she was there. And when he did he reached out one hand, groping, closed it about her leg and gave her thigh a smart slap, as if to find out what manner of creature he had got hold of, and she jumped and gave a protesting screech. He asked her why she had come, but before she could tell him, he told her to go away again, or at least get out of the room, let him suffer in peace.

But she took up a position near the door where, from time to time, she ventured to talk to him, gossiping about Milestown and old friends she had seen, and little by little she moved the stool nearer until, by nightfall, she sat beside the bed, and when Gordon's housekeeper brought another salt poultice, it was Lily who stripped off the old one, heated by the fever of his eyes as if it had lain in hot water, and put on the fresh one. All the while, though, Zack lay silent, never once thanked her for her attentiveness but told her, whenever he was reminded of her presence, to leave him alone, and in fact it seemed that Zack Fletcher lying there helpless and blind was not the same man they knew when he was in health but had turned morbid and perverse, hated himself and hated whoever approached him, and was as mutinous and vindictive as if this had been done to him by some spiteful human agency.

The housekeeper brought trays at breakfast time, at lunch, and at dinner, but at the end of five days he still had eaten nothing, only occasionally took a drink, and was, it seemed, as distant from them in this ordeal of pain as if he could not hear their voices, and most of the time seemed to have no awareness of who was with him or where he was. Andy Stinger and Johnny returned, to tell them the doctors had too many patients and one of them would be along when he could, and all at once Zack grew alert, called Johnny to him and clasped his wrist, gently, not seizing it with the hard grip he sometimes used to catch hold of Lily, and spoke to him in a voice too low for the others to hear, beckoning Johnny to lean nearer as he replied, then finally nodded and let him go. Andy Stinger and Johnny were going back to the Double Key, and Lily followed them to the door with her arm thrown companionably about Johnny's shoulders, and quite casually she asked him what it was Fletcher had wanted to know.

"Nothing."

"He wanted to know something. Don't make Aunt Lily mad, Johnny."

"He asked me who I saw, and I told him I didn't see anybody."

Lily frowned, looking at him distrustfully, but finally shrugged, for if there was a secret here it seemed unlikely she would be able to pry it loose, and they left, their faces covered with black masks, to protect them against another such catastrophe as Fletcher had suffered.

Later in the day, as Lily sprawled in one of the armchairs in James Gordon's handsomely furnished bedroom, playing the harmonica and now and then singing in her light but not very tuneful voice a few obscene verses from her old favorite, "Joe Bowers," as if to remind Zack of better days, he began to complain of the heat, for the fire was kept burning steadily. Ever since Johnny and Andy Stinger had returned he had been obsessed by the weather, wanted to know whether or not it was still snowing, and seemed convinced that by now the house was buried to the eaves.

"What's it like outside? If it's as hot as it is in here, then I guess I know where I am, all right."

"Don't worry about that yet, Fletcher. It's cold enough to make a polar bear hunt cover."

"How long have I been here?"

"Five or six days, I guess. How long, Gordon?"

James Gordon sat at a desk working on his records, as he did whenever he was not in the saddle, adding cows and subtracting them, balancing winter losses against expected spring increases, and had lately been remarking that this beef bonanza was not the sure thing he had been led to believe, even though it was true that this part of the Territory had providentially missed some of the winter's worst storms.

"One week tomorrow morning."

Zack's face twisted, as if he had heard that he had been there for several months, a year or two, and he began to swear. Lily watched

him, smiling at some private secret, and presently she approached
the bed, stood over him a moment, and then knelt down and spoke in
a low, confidential tone. "I know why you're so damn interested in
the weather, Fletcher." Zack lay motionless, and it seemed he had
not heard her but must be so absorbed by pain as to have become as
deaf as he was blind, and she whispered, "Take my word for it, she
won't come, I know women better than you do."

Before Lily could move he grabbed her by the hair, shaking her
head with as much gleeful violence as a dog punishing a toy, and he
gave her a mighty whack on the buttocks which sent her scuttling
out of the room, pausing only long enough to brandish her fist at him
from the doorway.

Early the next morning the western sky filled with clouds and the
chinook began to blow, the black wind which soon had the stream
banks overflowing and the eaves dripping; horses galloped about,
squealing and kicking up their heels, Lily threw the bedroom window
open wide, and it was a spring day.

Gordon set out with four of his herders to inspect the farther limits
of his own range and to visit the Double Key, for Zack suffered lurid
visions of his riders driving off every animal that could still walk to
be held over until spring in secret coulees and marked off his books
as frozen to death. "I'll be back in a few days," Sir James said, and
added, as he passed Lily. "Upon my word, this country of yours is a
strange one."

No sooner had he gone than Zack gave a yell of rage, tore off the
poultice and hurled it across the room and sprang to his feet, declaring that he would lie there no longer, but when he blundered into a
chair and saved himself only in time from sprawling headlong, he let
Lily guide him back to the bed and flung himself upon his belly, his
arms and legs thrown wide, and looked so perfectly humiliated that
Lily once again drew her chair near and began to play for him on the
harmonica, a mournful, trembling melody which must have suited
his own desperation, for after some time he began to breathe more
deeply and seemed to have fallen asleep.

She rambled about the house, sometimes picked a book from Gordon's library and fell to reading, quite forgetting her patient for two
or three hours at a time, until she went dashing up the stairs and was
rather surprised to find he had not made an escape. She gave instructions to the cook for elaborate dishes to be prepared for him and ate
them herself, for Fletcher, apparently, had decided to starve himself
to death and end his misery that way. She sat at the piano, picking
out tunes and accompanying herself on the harmonica, went out to
ride for an hour or two, for she was no better able to stay indoors for a
whole day than she had ever been, and sometimes she sat beside him,
smoking a cigar, and when he asked for one she lit it and placed it
between his fingers. Occasionally she talked to him until he told her
to keep quiet, and then she sat watching him with a look of whimsical curiosity, and occupied herself with her own thoughts. And so

she was sitting, late one afternoon, when the bedroom door opened and she glanced around to find a woman standing there, wearing a floor-length mink coat, her face so thickly muffled by veiling that Lily could recognize no one she knew.

Then, as Lisette unwound the veiling and tossed it aside, Lily's eyes turned quite green with disbelieving surprise and she stood up, murmuring, "Well—so help me." She made Lisette a salute, wickedly grinning, and wandered across the room with her hands in her pockets, interested to see what would happen now. But Zack had not moved, and perhaps supposed Lily's remark to be one more of those comments she made to herself nowadays, since he rarely talked to her. Lisette started toward the bed, but then paused, looking at Lily, who stood leaning against the door jamb with one foot crossed over the other and her head cocked to one side, maliciously grinning. "Why, good evening, ma'am," she murmured.

Zack's body stiffened with distrustful attentiveness, and his hands covered his face. "Who is it?" Lisette and Lily looked at each other, and he asked the question again, almost pleadingly. Then he shouted, "Lily, god damn you, tell me who it is!"

Lisette touched his fingers. "I'm here, Zack."

Lily shrugged and threw Lisette one last glance, more sympathetic than derisive, as she went out and closed the door.

His body remained rigid, his hands pressed harder against his face, and when she bent over him he seemed to sense it and turned his head, giving a heavy sigh. "Oh, good Jesus Christ. How did you get here?"

She moved back a step or two, and stood looking down at him and carefully wiping the tears away. "I took the coach to White Sulphur —and then I hired a man to drive me here."

"What a damn fool thing to do." Zack drew his mouth back so that his teeth showed, giving his face a vicious and ugly expression. "Suppose the weather had changed again? Who told you where I was? Johnny?"

"No, I heard Johnny was there, but I didn't see him." She sat on the bed, and as she talked she stroked her fingers across his hands, as if she might coax him to stop hiding behind them. "The papers are full of nothing else. Men have been frozen to death on the range and in the line cabins, the doctors are performing amputations every day —and they say that if there are another two or three bad storms, all the cattle in the Territory may be dead by spring." Her lips brushed the backs of his hands, but although he remained motionless for a little longer, all at once he seized her shoulders, not much more gently than he had taken hold of Lily, and thrust her back.

"Don't stay here, Lisette." His voice rose. "You had no god-damn right to come, no one sent for you! Get the hell out of here, all you damned women! Leave me in peace, won't you!" He turned away, his voice fell to a whisper, and it seemed he would at last admit a truth she could never guess if she did not hear it from him. "I'm badly scooped, Lisette. I'm used up."

After a few moments she leaned across him and put her mouth to his, but although he made no protest, he gave no response, either. And then, in a new attack of torment, he clasped his thumb and forefinger about her wrist and closed upon it with an increasing pressure, until she gave a little outcry and tried to draw away, and at that he smiled and seemed evilly pleased to have given some of his own pain to her. But then he sighed, whispering, "I'm sorry. Don't stay here. I don't know what the hell I'm doing. Go away, Lisette, I beg of you."

"I won't go away." She ran her fingers across his hair. "You know that." She wiped the tears again, taking care to make no sound and not to let them fall upon him, for it seemed pity angered him more fiercely than pain or fear, and then she began to tell him what news she had heard or read of the damage the storms had done, and finally she said, "Nella Allen is dead."

"She killed herself." He spoke so quickly, this might be something he had been expecting to hear. "Did she?" He turned toward her, and then turned away again, as if deeply ashamed of this eagerness to look at her.

"No. Or, at least, no one knows whether she did or not."

And she told him that early one morning, more than a week ago, a buggy with its storm curtains drawn had come rambling into town from the direction of the valley, its horse so covered with frost as to look as if he wore a coat of mail, and had paused here and there until at last its slow and erratic course had begun to make it a nuisance. No one seemed to be driving him, and as it grew lighter and the streets more crowded, men noticed that the buggy's only occupant was a woman, curled up on the seat like a child, fast asleep, and in that weather they took alarm, several converged upon the buggy at once, and a man sprang into it as the buffalo robe which covered her fell off, showing them that she wore only a sleeveless silk gown and had lost one of her low-cut slippers.

Lisette went on to describe how quickly the news had traveled that Nola Malachy had been found, dead and frozen hard as a block of ice, riding through town in her buggy early that morning, until by noon even the respectable women knew that when Billy Church went to interview her girls, he was told she had smoked a pipe or two last night and gone out, she had said, for a breath of fresh air. But whether she might have intended to kill herself or whether she had been too lethargic to know what she was doing, they were unable to explain, and neither could they explain why no one had stopped her but, when he asked, looked at him with blank faces, as if the question itself was not a sensible one. And, for a day or so, no one could talk of anything else as they tried to guess why any young woman, even Nola Malachy, should have discarded her life so carelessly, perhaps by intention.

Two days later, on a cold, brilliant day, her funeral procession had passed through the town, led by gamblers on horseback, wrapped in black cloaks, looking solemn, and followed by a band composed of the faro dealers and gambling hall guards, playing dirge music. Nola Malachy's girls, and the girls from other whorehouses, rode in buggies and gazed glumly ahead, taking no notice of any customers they might find along the sidewalks, curiously gawking. And the hearse was so splendid, glistening black and drawn by black horses decorated with black ostrich plumes, that one child was heard to remark in a shrill little voice, "That's just the kind I'm going to get for my mother." Half an hour later, the procession passed through the main street again, but this time the girls were laughing, the music was lively, the men on horseback went galloping by, and presently the saloons were opened for business and Nola Malachy's parlor was crowded and noisy.

" 'Every hour wounds,' " Lisette murmured. " 'The last one kills.' And now she's dead, that frightened little girl who came to me that first night with Shekel in her arms, hoping, I suppose, to exchange the cat for my friendship." Zack lay silent and motionless as Lisette stroked her fingers along the side of his face, shaking her head. "But I don't believe she meant to die. There've been so many accidental deaths this winter."

"Not hers. She killed herself."

"I'll never believe that. Zack, do you know, I can see her so clearly —so clearly—standing there in the sunlight that first day when we drove into Virginia City, with her blond hair shining like cornsilk, almost afraid to smile at me. What a long, long time ago that seems, doesn't it? Almost seventeen years. But isn't it strange, now she isn't Nola Malachy to me any more, she's Nella Allen—and that's who she'll be for the rest of my life."

"Now that she's dead, you're willing to be friends with her again, is that it, Lisette? You're willing to forgive her for having disappointed you—that's what you mean, isn't it?" Zack's voice rose to a harsh, strident pitch, and his fist slammed upon the bed.

"I don't forgive Nella, I never blamed her. I blamed us."

"Whoever the hell you blamed, it makes no god-damn difference to her now, does it?"

"It makes a difference to me. I loved her a great deal."

"You loved her because you pitied her—don't you know that even now? And you've come here to pity me, haven't you?" He flung his arms wide, striking her across the shoulders, and his face was more diabolic than ever, as if nothing would satisfy him now but to ease the despair through some tyrannical abuse. "Go away from here, Lisette!" He raged at her, grabbed her by the shoulders and shook her hard, looking like a man caught up in some rabid insanity, crazed by pain and the discovery of this sunless world he must now inhabit. He yelled at her to leave him, to get out of the room and out of the house, and then as abruptly as the rampage had begun it ended, he covered his face with his hands and shuddered so deeply that he might have been crying.

"Don't pity me," he warned her.

Lisette walked about the room, stirred up the fire and observed herself in a mirror, and kept a furtive watch over him, for although he now lay rigidly still again, it seemed he might momentarily break into another ranting frenzy and turn all his mortification and wrath against her. He surprised her, though, when several minutes had passed, by giving a kind of furious laugh and beckoning to her, and when she came near he seized her arm as if he had not a moment ago been yelling at her to leave but was terrified she might try to escape him.

"You took the coach to White Sulphur," he said slowly. "But how in hell did he let you go?"

Lisette bent over him, her face brooding and sorrowful. "Ralph didn't let me go. I went while he was in Butte, and I left him a letter."

"You left him a letter," said Zack thoughtfully, and at last he smiled, though the smile was ominous. "And what did you say? That you wanted a divorce—that you wanted to marry me?" He grinned, for this was the argument she would not answer, and he shook her by the shoulders again. "Tell me, Lisette!"

"No, Zack, I didn't. How could I?"

She sat beside him, and the ominous smile stayed on his face, as if it might be permanently fixed there, although as she began to stroke his hair again and then kissed his face and mouth, his expression changed slowly, against his will, as it seemed, until it had become rueful and almost sad. His hands approached her breasts, hesitantly at first, but then his fingers separated the buttons and his palms brushed across her nipples, and all at once he pulled the dress away from her shoulders, muttering as if in recognition of some bitter discovery, "I'm blind as a bat, I'll never be able to look at you again." He held her arms as if he wanted to crush them with his fingers, demanding, "What are you crying for, Lisette? Because I'm such a son of a bitch?"

But as she settled herself upon him, his face turned exultant, his hands covered her breasts, and he moved at a hastening pace, with a seeming frantic eagerness for the pang of deliverance, and once the quickening struggle yielded its balm he still held her fast, then dropped into a repose so deep he seemed to fall instantly asleep; and Lisette, belatedly alarmed, sprang up and ran to lock the door.

A few minutes later, her hair smoothed and her skirts straightened, she emerged into the hallway, glanced once up and down, and walked quickly toward the staircase.

But she paused midway down the stairs, for there stood Lily Jones, leaning upon the bannister and, as it seemed in this dim light, giving her a wisely mocking smile. Lisette ran on down, passed her swiftly and was on her way into the kitchen when Lily caught up with her, humorously asking, "His appetite's improved a little now? He thinks maybe he can choke something down, after all?"

Lisette glanced at her coolly and went on into the kitchen. But when she came out, carrying a tray covered with a napkin, Lily fell into step beside her, crossly demanding, "Now what the hell did you have to come here for? We were getting along all right, pretty damn good, in fact."

Lisette stopped. "What difference does it make to you whether or not I'm here? Are you in love with him?"

At this Lily put on a look of anguished incredulity. "No, I'm not in love with him." She gave a kick at the corner of the rug, then stamped on it sharply. "You respectable women give me a pain in the ass. If you let a guy screw you, it's love. If he gets sick and you're sorry for the son of a bitch, that's love, too. I'm not in love with Fletcher, and what's more I never was in love with Fletcher, does that satisfy you?" She walked off and disappeared into the library, the room where she did most of her sulking or, when the whim was upon her, her sentimental reminiscing.

For the next two days Lily did not so much as rap at the door to ask how the patient was getting on, although whenever she saw Lisette—and Lisette left the room infrequently—Lily smiled at her with secretive malice, and seemed to be expecting that with only a little patience she would soon have the kind of entertainment which pleased her best, two men at war with each other, even if she was not herself the cause of the mischief.

After Lisette had been there for four days, however, Lily seemed reconciled to her presence, and they sometimes fell into brief conversation about Zack, although Lily still did not knock at the bedroom door for, she had discovered, there were either low voices to be heard behind it, or a dense silence which neither she nor anyone else ventured to disturb.

Nearly a week had gone by when Lily came in from an afternoon's ride, looking for strayed cattle with some of Gordon's herders, for the countryside was now opened and bare for miles around, and she sat in the library with a kerosene lamp beside her, drinking a glass of whisky and water and reading her favorite book, *Les Misérables,* so absorbed that she paid little attention when she heard men talking outside, and then the door opened and footsteps went swiftly across the living room. Supposing that this was James Gordon, back from his vigil at the Double Key, she ran to meet him, but stopped in the doorway, for some stranger stood there, a man nearly as big as Fletcher himself, dressed in a buffalo coat with his black hat pulled low, and they confronted each other as warily as two rival burglars, met by chance to rifle the same deserted house.

"I've come to see Zack Fletcher," he told her. "Where is he?"

At that, recognizing Morgan's voice, Lily laid the book upon a table, set her glass with gingerly care beside it, and, remarking as if to herself, "The jig is definitely up," went skittering out of the room.

He dashed up the staircase and started quickly along the hallway, banging at each door, throwing it open and, when he found it empty, closing it again and going on to the next. But the last door opened before he had reached it and Lisette confronted him, though not quickly enough, for he pushed her aside and found Zack standing beside the bed, his legs spread wide and his arms outstretched, as if to catch anyone who tried to get by him, with a smile on his mouth that looked quite demented.

"Devlin? What the hell took you so long? I've been expecting you for days."

Morgan paused, looking at him carefully, for Zack's face was grossly swollen and blistered and his eyes glared somewhere past him, and as he hesitated Zack started slowly forward, flailing about with both hands as he came.

"Devlin? Why don't you answer me?"

Lisette whirled around, whispering, "He can't see you."

"I can see him well enough!" Zack yelled. He was still grinning, and now he spoke in a wheedling voice, low and coaxing. "Answer me, Devlin."

Zack gave a thrusting lunge which carried him forward so swiftly that he seized Morgan about the body, and they were grappled together, hauling and twisting, but then almost immediately Morgan stood motionless, Zack released his hold, and they faced each other, breathing hard and smiling with rather sheepish expressions, for it seemed they could not be sure if the battle had been only a mock one, such as had sometimes entertained them on a Sunday in Virginia City or in Butte, or the beginning of a struggle to kill each other.

Lisette gave a helpless little laugh that sounded like a sob and covered her face with her hands, while Zack edged his way cautiously toward the bed and flung himself upon it, folded both arms behind his head and crossed his ankles, pretending this was the way he liked to take his ease, and seemed ready to play his role of host with casual generosity, for he directed Lisette to bring them drinks and something to eat and added, as she went out the door, that she might take her time about it.

Morgan had thrown the coat and hat aside, and now he sat on the stool which had been Lily's accustomed place, leaning intently forward and gazing anxiously into Zack's face, until Zack, perhaps sensing his look of tender sadness, that pity which terrified him, groped about for the poultice and, when he found it, covered his eyes and forehead, mumbling, "A little too much light." The room, however, was quite dark but for the burning logs, and as he spoke Morgan sighed inadvertently, rested his elbows on his knees and bowed his head, studying the carpet and scowling. At last Zack drew in a long breath and smiled slightly, the same reluctant, angry smile which had appeared on his face each time he had meant to deprecate this absurd accident he had blundered into. "I'm not as good a patient as you were, Devlin. I lie here hating everybody I ever met." He turned his head and rose up slightly, but then lay down again, seemingly convinced that no effort of will would make him see. "What the hell are you doing out here?"

"I came for Lisette."

"You came for Lisette," Zack repeated, and pretended to think this over, amused and puzzled by such an unlikely explanation for a trip so far out of the way in the kind of weather they had been having lately. "Aren't you feeding off your own range?"

"I suppose I am," Morgan agreed, quite humbly.

"Mercer wouldn't come himself; it went against the grain of his Yankee dignity, and so you decided to do the job yourself."

"That's about right."

"Take her with you, then." Zack crossed his feet the other way and folded his arms over his chest, reasonably adding, "If she'll go—and if you ask her to, why, I guess she will."

They fell silent again. Morgan seemed harassed by this task he had set himself, not so equal to it as he might have believed a few minutes ago, and Zack waited with a grim smile, giving him no help, and was obviously prepared to make no objection if she chose to leave. "He won't ever give her a divorce, Zack."

"He won't," Zack agreed, and they might have been talking of the domestic troubles of people he did not know, whose plight did not concern him.

"She asked him last September, when she and Felice got back from Europe."

"She did?" Zack politely inquired, and turned down his mouth, for this was the first he had heard of it. "And he said," Zack reflectively murmured, "that he'd be a son of a bitch if he'd give her up to live with that savage, Zack Fletcher, and let his son be turned into another Johnny Lawler."

"Something like that. He says it's happened to other men to have their wives fall out of love with them and into love with someone else, and he doesn't doubt he can tolerate it as well as the next guy."

Zack smiled with sour appreciation for this Yankee philosophy, but then gave an abrupt, impatient gesture, as if to dismiss the subject from his mind. "Tell me, Devlin, how much of the range is clear?" And Morgan, taken aback, began to tell him where the losses had been most severe, giving him news of whole herds wiped out in the Yellowstone Valley, so that by the time Lisette came in Zack was stating it as his sober judgment that no man belonged in the cattle business who would try to get through a winter in this country with single-wintered stock, or with a disproportionate number of breeding cows or bulls in his herds.

They went on to talk of the winter's disasters, as engrossed as if she were not there, until all at once Morgan sprang up, mumbling that he was late, it was time to be on his way, and he had reached the door and was about to open it when he seemed to remember Lisette, still sitting there beside the bed with her hands folded in her lap, grave as a penitent child. He waited a moment, giving her a chance to speak to him if she had anything to say, but when she did not, he went out, closing the door very softly.

Several lamps had been lighted in the parlor, and before he was halfway across it, Lily Jones came swaggering in from the dining room, ducking her head and smiling almost shyly. "Hi, Devlin. How the hell are you?" She extended her hand and Morgan took it, but as he bent down, to examine this apparition from the past, she ducked her head still lower, and tried to draw away.

"Lily?"

This doubt, however, caused her to give him a hurt, defensive glance. "Sure it's Lily. Do I look so different as all that?"

"But you haven't changed at all," he assured her eagerly.

At that, however, Lily passed the index finger of her right hand across her mouth in the Indian sign for a lie, and her old smile reappeared, humorsome and impudent. "Of course I've changed. Want a drink?"

He looked gratefully relieved. "By God, but I do."

"I thought you might." And, from a table, Lily picked up two glasses, and they clicked the rims together. "That was a good year— here's to it. A good year," she repeated, and gave a smart little nod. "One of the best." For Lily, it seemed, had divided her life into years she liked and years she did not like so well, and the year she had spent in Butte had gone into her medicine-bundle, along with *Les Misérables* and "Joe Bowers," and John Powell's newspaper article.

"One of the best," Morgan agreed, and was surprised to find it was quite true.

"Are you still mad at me?"

"I never was."

"You know, I thought maybe you weren't—because you named the Yellow Medicine for me."

Morgan grinned, admitting the Yellow Medicine had found its name the afternoon he raced Lily Jones and she told him she had come to the mountains with Jenkins and Hamilton in search of that yellow medicine said to cure every ailment which could be cured at all. Lily filled the glasses again, and they stood smiling at each other in a warm access of affectionate nostalgia, wondering at wherever those years had gone to.

"But you sure took off in a hurry," he reminded her. "You've got to admit that." He gave a joyous laugh, recalling, as if it had been the most delightful surprise of his life, the picture of himself and Zack Fletcher, kneeling beside that empty hole where their cache had been buried.

"I'd tell a man," Lily agreed, with such pride that her eyes sparkled and her smile became radiant. "No sooner had you two guys left that morning than I set to work. Of course, I knew where it was all along,

Fletcher didn't fool me for a minute." She threw back her head, laughing, and Morgan laughed with her, until they had both grown quite hilarious over the thievery. "I couldn't help myself," she admitted, when the laughter finally stopped, and added, with an air of solemn confidence, "I'm just a natural-born bunch-quitter."

Then all at once it seemed that this brief hail must be quickly resolved into farewell, before the bravado went out of it, and Morgan was saying that he must be on his way. Lily sauntered along beside him, submitted tolerantly to his cautious kiss, and stood in the doorway, looking almost as forlorn as she had each morning when he and Zack set out for their claims. "So long," she told him in a sad little voice, and then, when he turned to give her a last salute, snapped her fingers, as if remembering something of great importance, and called, "Sorry I never got around to making that China Chilo for you and Fletcher!"

L X V

Rose Michel's thirtieth birthday brought on a worse crisis than Joshua would have believed possible, quite as if she had gone into mourning for someone she loved deeply who was now permanently lost to her, that young Rose Michel he had selected from the ranks of *The Black Crook* chorus.

He might easily have forgotten how old she was, but she reminded him so often that he began to observe her carefully, finding opportunities to catch her in a strong light and refusing to let her back away until he had examined her skin and hair and teeth with as much attention as he had given to Tamarack and Asia before buying them, and finally he told her, "I don't know what you're worrying about, Rose. You're as beautiful as you ever were—you may even be a little improved by maturity." He touched, absently, a line beside her mouth and she winced as if he had slapped her, shrinking away from him with a pleading and guilty look.

"I've done everything I can to get rid of that horrible wrinkle." She scrubbed at it with her wet handkerchief, as if there was still some hope it might wash off. "Men can get as old as they like," she said bitterly, "and no one cares."

She gave him an apologetic glance, but Joshua smiled, no more concerned that he would soon be sixty than he had been to be thirty and, indeed, very much less concerned, for at thirty he had considered himself a failure, a man who was worth not quite forty thousand dollars, had suffered torments of ambition and despair no one else had ever guessed which had raged at him continuously, giving him such morbid self-detestation that he had promised to kill himself if he did not become rich; and now, happily enough, he had. He supposed, in justification to Rose, that had he not been so successful he might be feeling about himself very much as she did, and so he could sympathize with her despair even if it was no longer possible for him clearly to imagine the idea of failure, whether it might be a man's failure in his work or a woman's failure in her beauty.

And so, when the day was finally upon her, November the nineteenth, he promised Rose she might refurnish the house in any style she chose, for now that his two houses and their connecting picture gallery had begun to attract crowds who peeked through the fences to watch their progress, he had no longer any hope of convincing her that he was a poor man in disguise.

During the next several months, however, Joshua went there infrequently, for it annoyed him to see carpenters and upholsterers and paperhangers invading his private retreat and casting him furtive glances as he tramped by them in the morning. His nose disapproved the smells of paste and paint and varnish and the dust which had been stirred up by moving the old draperies and carpets, and he told Rose that with the canaries singing, the dog barking, and a horde of mechanics overrunning the house from top to bottom he preferred to avoid it until the damage had been repaired; and after that he went there only briefly, like a man with a business appointment to keep, and when the business had been transacted he promptly left.

He was troubled by no such fastidiousness, however, when he visited his own houses, as he did each morning, and quite often again at the end of the day, passing among the bystanders who peered through knotholes to watch workmen trundling wheelbarrows up runways and dashing about the scaffolding as nimbly as acrobats, and the bricklayers throwing bricks into place, making thick walls creep slowly upward, enclosing the houses as they went.

Joshua regarded the architect, Samuel Sample, as his own discovery, and was as jealous of the possibility that he might design a house for someone else as he was that Rose might one day let another man get into bed with her. He had met him at one of Allegra Stuart's receptions, and when she had described him as an architect who knew how to design a house of ponderous austerity, the phrase had rung so felicitously in Joshua's ear—for it described his own visions of a house to perfection—that he had noted down the name and laid it away for future consultation, along with the names of men whose railroads or horses he hoped to acquire.

And each day, in the company of Mr. Sample, Joshua crept over incomplete stairways and scaffolding, keeping firm hold on his cane as he scaled ladders and clambered across piles of lumber, inspecting each detail of the workmanship with the same suspicious attention he gave to his business, pointing with his cane to question Samuel Sample about whatever did not please him, and watched with a grim face, keeping his hands folded behind his back, when the architect tried to explain why the dining-room fireplaces would not draw.

There were other mishaps. Slabs of marble fell off the outside. A painter at work on the ceiling of Suky's bedroom, where he was describing clouds swarming with angels or cupids, lost his footing and toppled over two or three paint buckets in his descent, and so the work must be begun again. The paneling for Joshua's library had not arrived from Italy and could not be traced through letters or cables. Chandeliers were bent and smashed, and chairs and sofas were discovered in the warehouse, where Suky had them unpacked for her inspection, to have been broken, some of them beyond repair. And, in fact, there were so many catastrophes that Joshua sometimes had premonitions of malevolent influences at work to prevent him from enjoying this reward of his work, for he might, as things were going, die before it was completed.

But these gloomy fits soon passed off, for he tolerated them no better in himself than in anyone else, and the houses grew steadily before their eyes, until he and Suky began to exchange cryptic smiles whenever they met there, two successful conspirators offering each other this silent salute; and Suky had begun to plan, nearly a year before the intended fête, the guest list and the decorations, the food and the music, and only hesitated to order her gown because the future of bustles was not yet decided.

Rose's house was ready early the following summer, and very pretty he found it to be, with its drawing room hung in pink silk caught up with heavy silk ropes, its padded pink velvet chairs and couches, and its soft Brussels carpet with a pattern of roses and thorny vines, and he was glad to be able to go there again, for the houses would not be done for another year and the apartment at the Fifth Avenue Hotel had long since become only an occasional dressing room to him, a place where he sometimes appeared with the expectation that Susan and Ceda would pretend he was there every day.

And while he waited until he might move into what were described as the Ching houses, for it seemed no one thought to call them the Ching and Van Zandt houses, Joshua was putting some finishing touches to his success, so as to have it handsomely polished, a fitting accessory to the monument itself.

Like many other men—Talbot and Cottrell and Frederic Hallam and Hiram Marble, even Nicholas Craig, before he had gone to England—Joshua found the new large corporations an improvement upon more primitive forms of ownership, and was convinced, as they were, that if they could be let alone for a few years to work out the nation's destiny, there was no reason why the entire country should not be owned and controlled by some few corporations, a concept he admired for its elegance, reducing as it did by those remorseless processes of corporate ownership all that was needlessly complex to its simplest components, working upon men and their institutions with the sublime impersonality of the very stars.

Over the years, Joshua had been able to watch his holdings grow, expanding as rapidly as a tree that was half a weed, and it was said of him now that Joshua Ching was a man predestined to own or control railroads which fell into receiverships, so that any property upon which he cast his eye might almost immediately be seen to blanch, lose appetite, and show a variety of early symptoms of that sickness which would before very much longer send it staggering about in search of compassionate support, and thereupon Joshua Ching would step forward to lend it his arm.

Not a year ago, the Chicago-Central had been a strong and vigorous company, with justifiable pride in its network of roads in the Mississippi and Missouri valleys. Once its owner had gone to England, however, old reports showing the company's defects had come mysteriously to light, reports which appeared not only in the *Journal* but in other newspapers, and this created so much fear and disgust among stockholders they were as eager to be rid of their shares as if they had found the certificates to be nastily contaminated.

Joshua wrote long letters to Nicholas Craig, assuring him that the newspaper accounts meant nothing, the public sales of stock were of no consequence for it was merely changing hands, and sent him so many graphs and charts, so many tables of figures, that Nicholas Craig fell into periods of silence lasting for several weeks while, apparently, he tried to decipher them. But at last Craig was forced to borrow large sums of money and Joshua loaned it to him, explaining that he hoped this generosity might save his own large investment in the Chicago-Central; and he confidently expected that the interest he took for it would be the least of his usury.

On almost any day he chose, Joshua could pick up the *Journal,* or another paper, and read that Joshua Ching's two new houses, with their adjoining picture gallery and garden, would soon be completed, and that when they were a man might pass by and see for himself just what two million dollars would buy in the present market, while, if he should happen to belong to the city's upper ten thousand, he might hope sooner or later to get inside and find out what another eight hundred thousand dollars would do. And Joshua smiled tolerantly, thinking the exaggeration did no harm, for knowing readers would make an automatic discount, while the others could not be expected to differentiate one million dollars from two million dollars.

He could read that six hundred foreign wood carvers and sculptors and painters had worked for two and a half years; that chandeliers as big as a ladies' carriage hung in the reception halls; that the smoking rooms were said to be fit for a Bedouin chief, with their silken draperies and menacing background of spears and antique firearms and silver-handled dirks; and the two conservatories would display one of the finest collections of rare orchids and tropical birds to be found anywhere.

The reporters, Joshua knew, slipped past workmen and guards and wandered about, taking notes and asking impertinent questions, but though he intended to have them swept out with the rest of the debris once he was installed there himself, he regarded it as a necessary part of his business that, first of all, his friends and enemies, his admirers and detractors, his followers and the followers they had collected, be allowed to surfeit themselves on his glory and fall sick of envy.

For the same reason, he not only granted interviews but gave fragments of advice to men who caught hold of him as he came out of his office, poked their heads into the windows of his carriage, or approached him on the few occasions he went to have lunch at Delmonico's.

"Would you stay in or get out, Mr. Ching?" a man would ask, plucking at his sleeve and mentioning the name of the stock and the number of shares he held.

Not very long ago Joshua would have ignored the man, or given him a glare and jerked his arm free, but now he quite often paused, looking at him as if he must be giving the problem his careful consideration, and would at last concede, "The entire art of Wall Street is to know when to get out." Whereupon the other would bow, removing his hat in a gesture of gratitude, and Joshua would drive off, leaving him to discover for himself what meaning there might be to that advice.

He had become more or less invisible nowadays, preferring to be seen only by his own kind, men with money enough for him to respect them, and to leave Joshua Ching to the imagination of those inconsequential others, who might make him up as they liked out of what they heard and read. Whenever he entered the tap room of Bertholp's Hotel, after a brisk trot with Tamarack and Asia, he was invariably sought out by men who had succeeded well enough to be there, but had not succeeded so well as himself, and when they asked him to share his recipe with them, he adopted a manner of gracious gravity. "It has been my experience that half the success of any operator is his ability to make a survey of the market and judge if a fluctuation be final or the prelude to a corner." He would bend his eyebrows slightly to impress this maxim upon them, and walk away.

When he was asked, either by newspapermen or by one of his followers, why he had built a parallel line in Ohio, or a trunk line in Indiana, or some other structure which seemed to them irrelevant in purpose or malicious in intent, he replied each time, and rather severely, "I am, from first to last, an antagonist of the monopolies." For that, he had found, was a statement adequate to explain any harassments of other roads.

Each time a reporter was ushered into his office he found Joshua standing before the window with his feet wide apart, his arms folded across his chest, and his head slightly lowered, and in that attitude which Augustus Adams' portrait had preserved, Joshua would turn slowly and give a reluctant smile before they sat down across the desk from each other. And in describing his career, which he sketched with a few light strokes, Joshua found that he had made no serious errors, committed no felonious acts, taken advantage of no man's trust or misfortunes, but instead owed all his success to three qualities which could not be recommended too often to any ambitious young man.

"Industry, frugality, and the ability to drive a bargain," said Joshua, "are the characteristics no successful businessman can do without. I might also add, tenacity. Above all, he must not divide his interests. Once I had decided that railroads were what interested me, I never thought of anything else from that day to this. Naturally, the ability to sacrifice small pleasures, to give up amusements, and to avoid everything which wastes time—that is the climate a man must live in, if he hopes to succeed in whatever he undertakes to do."

Now and then he was asked if the two new houses would provide such a climate, but these questions were dismissed as frivolous for, after all, there must be some eventual rewards to those years of frugality and deprivation.

Nicholas Craig had been in England for not quite seven months when the condition of the Chicago-Central required that it go into receivership, and the largest stockholder on the board, who was found to be Joshua Ching, was appointed receiver, although he protested that he had had too many receiverships as it was, and the job was a thankless one. "Naturally," he told one of those reporters, "I would expect the control to return as soon as possible to Nicholas Craig."

"And yet, Mr. Ching," he was reminded, "that has not been the history of other receiverships awarded to you, has it?"

"That," Joshua kindly assured him, "has been no fault of mine. The companies were beyond repair before they ever came into my hands." And, of course, it was true enough, and their several histories too tangled by now ever to unravel, so that no one might refute with much confidence whatever statements Joshua chose to make about them.

Nicholas Craig, however, was still president of the company, and when he returned from England, the grandfather of a baby boy, Alexander Tash III, Joshua asked him frequently if he noticed any improvements in the Chicago-Central, for it was being dosed with all those remedies for which Joshua Ching was famous; new stock issues; the conversion of bonds into stock, which caused another alarming fall in the market value; the raising of freight rates; and an inflation of the company's capital structure which grew day by day.

"I predict it will take me just two years," Joshua confided to his brothers, "to turn Nick Craig into my satellite and, after that, he can spin about for as long as he likes."

For Joshua considered that the tactics he had used on Milton De Groot and Abijah Everest and even his old partner, Lorenzo Flagg, had been crude and peremptory, and it suited him better nowadays to smother his victims with the same affectionate consideration he saw Suky showing to Alvita Hallam, for they might otherwise lose their usefulness permanently. And Joshua hoped to find new uses for Nicholas Craig who was, after all, still one of the city's rich men. The world, Joshua had perceived, grew smaller for him as he grew more powerful, and it was no longer so easy to cause an enemy to disappear from his sight once and for all.

By the end of May, the houses were nearly completed, and Joshua congratulated himself he had won the race, beaten the Talbots, who had begun their new house only a year ago, the Hallams, who were just breaking ground, Amos Cottrell and Hiram Marble, and other men he knew, for the millionaires were on a remorseless march up Fifth Avenue, and even before the last of the painters and wood carvers had gone the houses were overrun by a new crew of workmen, converting the plot of muddy ground adjoining the picture gallery into a temporary ballroom, and the servants, under the supervision of a formidable English lady in moire antique, were polishing floors and waxing balustrades.

Each day Joshua went through both houses from top to bottom, found more to criticize than to praise, and paced the picture gallery, glad to know his collection showed him a man of taste and that there were no fakes among them—for Frederic Hallam had sent Suky to his own dealer—reciting as he went: Rembrandt and Rubens, Hals and Holbein, Goya, Vermeer, Fragonard; and it was the Fragonard which Suky loved best, for she had remarked that she wished she might borrow that tender gaiety for their fête.

Workmen and maids came and went on all sides but Joshua was scarcely aware of them, except when he stopped one to point out some fault he had discovered, and just so he might have passed by Susan on that early May morning without seeing her, had she not stepped into his path, looking up at him with a rather ironic smile, as if she might be waiting for what words he would find on this unusual occasion.

And, indeed, it was so unusual for them to meet anywhere alone, even amid this traffic of draymen and carpenters, but with neither Ceda nor Suky in the vicinity, that for a moment they confronted each other in some embarrassment, as if they had met in a hotel out of season, strangers thrown together by the absence of other guests.

Joshua began a cautious conversation, and for a minute or two they discussed the fête as if it were a celebration to take place in a foreign country, a ritual which might be of some significance to the natives, though its meaning to themselves was obscure. And as they talked Joshua grew more expansive, his sense of overbounding generosity took hold of him, and he inquired with an air of bantering joviality, "Well, Susan, and will you be happy in your new house?"

Susan smiled. "My house, Joshua?"

More offended by that, and by the quality of her smile, than by anything Susan had said to him for many years, Joshua bowed and went on his way, marveling at how it was he had married a woman who must have in her nature some flaw she was powerless to correct, for otherwise she would surely have arrived by now at a conviction of triumph and conquest nearly as great as his own; and yet she had no trace of it, only this intractable irony and superciliousness.

The anger did not last long, scarcely until he had reached Rose's house, one more welcome sign that he had eliminated Susan from his awareness almost as successfully as he had hoped to do when he had planned to send her to a nursing home, and as he went up the steps he was telling himself that it became Joshua Ching nowadays to have a little charity for those who had been less fortunate in their lives than he.

That, it happened, was what had brought him here this morning, early enough that he might talk to Eugene before the boy ran off with his playmates to school. For even though Joshua had continued to remind Rose the child was no responsibility of his, young Joshua Van Zandt was to leave for Germany in the late summer to attend those same schools which had worked such wonders upon his Uncle Steven, and this had set Joshua to thinking that there was another boy for whose education he must provide, even though he would then ask himself what possible use Eugene Michel could make of an education if he had one.

Eugene, however, looked by now remarkably as Joshua had at the same age, was similarly tall and blond, had the same manner of curt politeness, was deferential to his elders but never obsequious, and often appeared in the late afternoon with his clothes torn and his knuckles bruised, and explained he was being taught to box by the local firemen, although Joshua suspected that most of his fights were on behalf of his mother's neighborhood reputation. Nevertheless, he was pleased by the boy's aggressiveness, and lectured him now and then on the necessity of winning every fight he got into, warning Rose that she must never try to make him stop fighting, for a boy grew into manhood by his victories over other boys.

"Do you expect him to become a prize fighter?"

"I'm not sure what I expect him to become," Joshua told her. "We'll see where his abilities lie. But thank God he's tough."

"Thank God he is," Rose agreed. "Since he was born on the wrong side of the blanket."

Joshua and Eugene often met in the house early in the morning and passed with only a guarded greeting, rather as if they were two rival suitors, Joshua had thought with satiric amusement, and while he discovered a good deal of Joshua Ching in Eugene Michel on some days, there were other times when he told himself that perhaps his illegitimacy had been to his disadvantage and the boy was more a Michel than a Ching, and he remembered the old saying that a great man has not a great son. And yet, it came to him one day that he could not move into the monument so long as there were tag ends of his life still untied, and so he walked in on this morning after his untimely meeting with Susan and told Rose to send Eugene to him, and go to her room.

Rose looked apprehensive, and perhaps thought the moment she had postponed for nearly fourteen years had finally come, and she and Eugene were about to be ushered out of Joshua Ching's life, and she bowed her head and left the room quickly. Eugene was told to wash his face and comb his hair, straighten his tie and present himself to Mr. Ching, and presently he entered the room and stood waiting while Joshua, pretending not to know he was there, continued to gaze out the window. But at last he turned slowly and found Eugene standing very straight, his face serious and defiant, but still respectful, so that perhaps his mother had told him he must be on his guard against Mr. Ching today.

Joshua nodded and smiled, not very warmly, for he had no intention of letting Eugene imagine he might take some advantage of him, and as they confronted each other Joshua became pleasantly aware of the awesome figure he must seem to this lad, in his handsomely tailored clothes, his hair and beard more white than blond nowadays, his face healthily glistening, his body as lithe and erect as it had ever been, for Joshua believed that a man who would allow himself to become dilapidated only because he had begun to grow old was a fool, and he spoke to Eugene in a low, thoughtful tone. "Eugene, how old are you?"

"I'll be twelve next October third, sir."

"Twelve?" Joshua hummed, as he considered this information. "And have you given any thought to what you expect to do in life— how you mean to make your living, that is?"

"Yes, sir. I have."

Joshua had expected the boy would grow embarrassed, shuffle his feet and mutter that he had not got around to thinking about it yet, and asked him, with a smile of tolerant condescension, "What kind of work interests you, Eugene?"

"I'm interested in railroads, sir."

"Do you want to be a conductor, for example?"

"No, sir. I want to own a railroad and operate it."

"Why?" demanded Joshua, quite sharply, for the boy's confidence was disconcerting, being so far out of proportion to the confidence Joshua thought him entitled to have.

"I want to be a rich man, sir."

At this Joshua made a slight grimace, thrust out his jaw and gently stroked his close-cropped beard, and observed Eugene with as much skeptical curiosity as if he had come into his office and applied for a job. "All young boys want to be rich, Eugene, and they imagine it's very easy to accomplish, but I assure you, it is not. How do you expect to go about becoming a rich man—an owner of railroads?"

"I'm going to become an engineer, sir."

This ambition, so sensible—for it was quite true that future railroad men would need more than the remorseless energy which had been required to get the roads built—caused Joshua to smile more warmly. "You're not lazy, Eugene?"

"No, sir."

"Good enough. Don't be late to school."

Eugene gave him a brisk little bow. "Thank you, sir."

He strode across the room, with very much the same stride Joshua used himself when he was preoccupied or acting the role of Joshua Ching for the benefit of bystanders, and left Joshua thinking that the boy must have some of his own unerring instinct for discovering the country's needs a little before the country itself discovered them, and so he told Rose he would send him away in the fall to a boarding school and give Eugene a chance to demonstrate how resourceful he was, and whether or not he was capable of learning.

The school, he said, would not be the kind where Eugene's family must be too carefully investigated but it would, nevertheless, be a very good school for a boy like Eugene Michel who might have expected that the precarious conditions of his birth would have given him no privileges at all. And Rose, perhaps more from relief than from any wish to have Eugene educated, was so humbly grateful, stroking Joshua's hand as if she had got hold of a religious relic, that Joshua promptly decided he would avoid the house until after the fête, for the invitations were out now, and by tomorrow or the next day Rose would know that Mr. and Mrs. Hoke O'Neil had been invited to the reception.

And because he regarded this first entertainment as a symbol of all his triumphs wrapped into one, the culmination of his whole life's history, he wanted no distractions, but must be free to devote himself whole-heartedly to admiring what Joshua Ching had accomplished in a world where most men came and went unnoticed.

Even so, there were annoyances to get between him and the full enjoyment of his powers, and the latest came as Joshua was dressing to go over to the new houses where, in less than an hour, several hundred men and women would go streaming by to pay him their tributes of astonishment and envy. For Susan came into his bedroom, a territory he would never have expected her to invade, to tell him that his niece Lisette Devlin was to be divorced, and would soon be married to another man. He looked at her, more surprised that Susan should be still in her dressing gown at this hour than he was by whatever she had told him, and asked, "Aren't you going to be with us tonight, Susan?"

"I only have to put on my dress. But Joshua, think what it must mean to Marietta—how humiliated she must be. First, that terrible mystery about Matt's death, and now this."

Joshua was tying his cravat, and for all Susan's tragic look, he continued relentlessly cheerful. "Nonsense, Susan. A divorce in the Territories is no more the same thing as a divorce in New York, than a killing in the Territories is the same—" He left the sentence uncompleted, for Susan had given him such a look that she obviously thought he was making one of his cruel, ironic jokes, the only kind which amused him at all—drawing a parallel between Matt Devlin's death and his daughter's divorce—and no doubt he had been. But he thought it was not so very surprising that Lisette, the daughter of Matt Devlin, should have shown herself to be, like her father, willful and reckless, preferring excitement to responsibility and giving way at last to what she had no doubt convinced herself was an irresistible need of her own nature. "What difference does it make to you?" he asked Susan, and gestured vaguely. "Away out there. Don't be late," he warned her as he left the room.

He found that the houses, so lately ringing with sounds of hammer and saw and the voices of workmen, had now fallen into a preternatural silence, and he went stalking through the entrance hall and drawing rooms of his own house first, then down the picture gallery and into the Van Zandt house, and wherever he went he confronted only stoical young Irishmen, hired for the night, who watched him go by with a kind of indifferent curiosity, and seemed not at all disconcerted by the clothes they had been put into—light buff livery with knee breeches and silk stockings, sparkling buckles on their shoes and white powdered wigs upon their round heads, and some of them were even now turning down the gas lights and carrying long tapers as they marched about lighting candles.

In the temporary ballroom, the biggest summer house Suky had yet designed, with its sides and roof made of close-woven lattices crawling with some thousands of white roses, a man with a brush fastened to one foot and a felt slipper on the other was waltzing over the floor as he had been doing when Joshua passed him that morning, until the floor by now shone so that the dancers might see themselves reflected there as if in the hazy uncertainty of a lake shore after sundown. Candles were being lighted here, too, and Joshua crossed the floor with gingerly caution, to peek through the lattices at the dark sky, for the night was a favorable one, warm and clear and full of stars, and he was able to hear the murmurs of gathering sightseers from beyond the outer walls of the picture gallery, making a sound like the roar of a distant surf, and, hearing that, Joshua was all at once tense and irritable, with something in his belly like a hollow conviction of failure, for it had occurred to him the sightseers might, after all, have no one to look at.

Disgusted with this apprehensiveness, the same he was accustomed to suffer when the market collapsed, Joshua fixed on his face an expression so imperturbably calm, so enigmatic and ceremonious, that no servant or guest, not even Susan or Suky, could have a clue to his misgivings, and he went to take up his position in the entrance hall and surreptitiously consulted his watch, finding it to be just fifteen minutes before ten.

The guests were to enter this house first, and might then wander through the picture gallery and into the Van Zandt house, or dance in the pavilion, and Joshua drew himself to his full height and cast indifferent glances over his handiwork which, he found, now filled him with dread and awe. The hall was vast and round, its ceiling a high dome finished with pale blue enamel, scattered with golden stars which, by some device of Samuel Sample's, had been made to wink. The walls were hung with garlands of white camellias, bouquets of white roses in Chinese vases surmounted Roman pillars, and Joshua told himself it had all in all the appearance of a pagan temple on a day of sacrament or penance, and his dread increased.

Presently he heard Suky's voice and spun about, immeasurably relieved, to see her approaching him, almost running along the picture gallery, as if she must tell him something of great importance, before it was too late. Her white gown drifted with her movements as if she did not wear it but only walked in its midst, her throat and hair and arms sent out showers of sparks from his diamonds, and although she watched him steadily as she came hurrying along, as if to keep him there until she could reach him, her beauty seemed to have escaped the boundaries of face and hair and body and to shed a translucence all about her—and Joshua found himself convinced that whatever Suky participated in could not go wrong for him.

Still, she looked so troubled, and she held forth one hand as she approached, as in pleading, that he stood where he was, stricken into immobility. Now she caught hold of his arm, cast him one more of those pleading glances, and lowered her head, until Joshua touched her chin and, reluctantly, she looked at him.

"What is it, Suky?" He stared at her with a terrified anxiety. "What ever has happened?"

Suky shook her head, and seemed perplexed, ready to cry. "I don't know, Papa, I don't know what it is, but all day long I've had the most frightening feeling, and I have it still—that after tonight I'll never again be sure of what I want."

Susan and Ceda had arrived and they gathered to learn what the trouble was, Steven and Letty were a little distance away, watching, and Philip stood skeptically smiling, for Suky had never yet had any forebodings which Philip was willing to take seriously, and he seemed to think that in the end her father's wealth would solve everything.

But whether Suky was only acting, or whether these fears were real ones, he had no chance to discover, for at almost the next moment she looked across his shoulder and smiled, and Joshua found his brothers Samuel and Aaron approaching with their wives and children. He gave Suky one more questioning glance, but she was shaking their hands and laughing, and as he became aware that the musicians had begun to play—not the resounding march he would have preferred but some music chosen by Suky—the gaiety and lightness of the music turned him quite buoyant.

Susan stood beside him and they greeted their guests all in a line, passing them hand over hand from Joshua to Susan, from Susan to Ceda and Suky, from Suky to Philip, and from Philip to Letty and Steven, and after that they were free to wander at will, through all the floors of both houses, and might even peek into closets and bathrooms and pantries, for Joshua meant them to know he had no secrets hidden here, not yet.

Samuel and Aaron confided in undertones that several hundred bystanders had gathered and there was a parade of carriages so dense that even Brooks could not untangle it, bogus invitations were being flashed, and there had been more diamonds and more Worth gowns in sight than anyone had seen for a long time.

But before Joshua could pass this news along, the procession was coming in his direction, a trooping horde of smiling faces, rows of teeth, white shirt fronts and half-naked breasts, and, for all his cordiality, their owners might have been taken apart and reassembled and he would not have noticed the difference. The music grew louder as the voices strove to drown it out, perfumes and the fragrances of bouquets carried by the women saturated the air until it seemed he might suffocate, and from time to time, out of those rows of teeth, those disconnected mouths and eyes, those necklaces and shirt fronts, a familiar face would materialize before him and, with a sense of shock, he would realize that someone he knew had just passed by, and could only hope he had called them by name.

Amos and Mrs. Cottrell had gone in, Lord and Lady Haldane seemed to have passed him, Alvita and Frederic Hallam paused for a moment, as Joshua observed that during the two years since Roger Hallam's death, Frederic's body had grown more solid and his expression increasingly grave, until he had begun to take on an air of invincibility, an earnest, willful man, seeking limitless power. And, thought Joshua, if there was anything at all left in Frederic Hallam's life which still gave him intimations of some more light-hearted world, it could only be Suky—and perhaps those paintings he was said to love beyond everything else.

Nicholas and Christine Craig had gone by, though not with their daughter, for she was still in England. Tessie and Hoke O'Neil came in with Judge and Mrs. Azariah Gill, Marquis McDuff stalked by with Senator Stirt, and it presently occurred to Joshua that almost everyone he knew or had ever met was here tonight, but Rose Michel and Milton De Groot.

He was vaguely surprised to see Morgan Devlin with his sister Annabel and the Talbots, until he remembered that yesterday or the day before he had met him coming out of the conservatory with Suky, and they had chatted for a few minutes about the Butte mines.

And as Morgan paused now to shake his hand, he gave Joshua a smile which seemed to have something peculiar in it, though the smile was gone before he could identify its nature, so that Joshua watched to see what would happen when he approached Suky but could discover no unusual signs in their greeting—but then, Morgan had that trick of solemn impassivity his father had been able to practice at will, creating the impression that here was a man devoutly serious and, at the same time, poised for violence, as Philip had discovered the summer before.

But even they were shaking hands with an appearance of perfect cordiality, and Joshua turned his attention to the Van Zandt sisters, quite old ladies they looked to him tonight—though they were not as old as he—in their white satin caps, and as he bowed over their hands, murmuring that he was glad to see them, yes, very glad to see them, Joshua was reflecting with more pleasure than anything else had given him tonight that from now on the Van Zandt women might attend his receptions or not, as they chose, and neither he nor anyone else would notice their presence or their absence.

LXVI

Zack Fletcher sat watching his prisoner who crouched in the lower bunk and greedily scooped tomato pulp out of a can with his fingers, never taking his eyes off Zack as he ate it, for Homer Grimes had been held captive in this line-cabin for several days, ever since he had glanced up one early morning as he sat at his desk in the editorial offices of the *Mountain Enquirer* to see Fletcher standing in the doorway, holding his pistol rather negligently, and as Homer braced himself against his chair, too scared to speak or yell for help, Zack had given a nod of his head and a gesture of the pistol, saying, "Come along, Grimes."

He had ridden through town with him, but it was so early there was no one about whose attention Homer might hope to attract, and as they reached the open highway, where bull-whackers walked beside their trains, giving now and then a pop of the whip which made Homer glance over his shoulder into Zack Fletcher's malevolent face, they began to gallop and kept it up hour by hour, at a pace which seemed only agreeable to Fletcher, though Homer could soon imagine that his bones had come loose from their sockets, his skeleton was unhinged at every critical point of connection, and that he would presently fall apart, leaving himself strewn along the trail. But he did not dare complain, for he knew quite well why he was there, and was too much preoccupied with wondering where Fletcher was taking him and what he meant to do with him once he got him there.

They passed a coach, bound for White Sulphur, so that Homer could guess he was being taken to the Double Key headquarters farther east, and now and then a man on horseback nodded as he passed them. Once Zack stopped and spent several minutes discussing the Territory's winter losses and the expectation of making it up by the spring increase of calves, replying to the other's questioning that he could see pretty well by now but was still blind after sundown and probably would be for several months more, and at that he laughed, quite fiercely, and gave Homer a swift, terrifying glance, remarking, "As it turned out, I was god-damn lucky."

In the middle of the day they stopped and Zack took his ease beneath a cottonwood, drank from a flask but offered no such refreshment to his captive, and set Homer to work bringing water from the creek, lighting a fire, brewing coffee and frying bacon, and when Homer ventured to observe that the day was a pleasant one, as fine a day as he had seen, Zack gazed at him as if to tell him he might as well enjoy it for he would not see very many more such days and Homer fell silent, more discouraged than despairing, for it was always his expectation that someone would eventually come to his rescue.

They galloped through the afternoon and into the night, slept for a few hours and set out again, and when Homer found himself at last before one of those line-cabins which were scattered about the range, where a herder might spend the winter or pass a few nights or weeks, it looked as welcome to him as if Fletcher had led him back home and left him there with Rachel.

The cabin was so small that Fletcher seemed to fill it up himself, and it contained only two bunks, a three-legged stool and a lopsided table. Zack ordered him to step out of his trousers and kick off his boots, threw them out the door, and with such swiftness and dexterity that Homer felt he was watching all this happen to someone else, crossed his wrists behind his back and tied them together, bound his ankles, then toppled him onto the bunk and turned as he was going out the door to remark, "Stay right there, Grimes, until I come back."

The door slammed shut, there was a sound of a padlock being snapped together, and Homer heard both horses go whispering off across the grassy sod, for neither had been shod and they traveled almost soundlessly, and was for some time quite peaceful, thinking he had got out of this scrape better than he might reasonably have expected to do.

By the time the padlock was snapped open again, making his heart begin to beat at a sickening rate, for he had heard no sounds of approaching horses and had been dozing, the cabin was hot, the air stinking, and his mouth and throat so dry, his belly so anguished, that he had begun to mumble to himself, sometimes praying and sometimes swearing.

Zack untied him, with the same uncanny dexterity, but before Homer had properly flexed his muscles or massaged his arms and thighs, Zack gave a sharp snap of his fingers. "I haven't got much time, Grimes. Get some water, clean this place up—get at it, you son of a bitch," and Homer was obliged to walk gingerly over the turf in his stockinged feet, carrying water from the creek in two cans, until he had washed out the cabin, swept it thoroughly, and was rewarded with a can of tomatoes.

He had only begun to protest that he was still hungry, he could not endure this torture another day and night, when he was trussed up again and flung onto the bunk and his captor had disappeared without any comment at all; and so it went, for one day and another, until a week had gone by and then, for whatever mysterious reasons, Zack Fletcher decided to proceed to the second phase of his punishment, and he began to talk to him.

" 'It seems,' " Zack read from a newspaper clipping, " 'that some of our cattle barons are beginning to take the epithet a little too seriously, and what was intended only as a humorous compliment has become a way of life for more than one of our ranchmen.' " Zack cocked his head sideways, looking at Homer as if to ask where he had heard those words before, but as Homer only gazed at him, seeming puzzled, he went on. " 'We all know that these gentlemen occupy whatever land takes their fancy. We know they declare war as it suits them, and declare it upon the enemies of their choice. We know that Indians and whisky peddlers are shot by them at sight, and that if a baron's stock should chance to freeze to death over a bad winter it is not the winter he blames but some lone herder he calls a cattle rustler, and that herder goes the way of Indians and whisky peddlers.' " Zack folded the clipping and slipped it into his shirt pocket, puffed at his cigar until the room was clouded with its smoke, and nodded. "Go on, Grimes. What comes next?"

"I don't know, sir. What does?"

"You wrote it."

"Oh, no, sir."

"Who did?"

"I don't know, sir."

"Lem Finney?"

"Not Mr. Finney, sir, I can assure you of that. My father-in-law never meddles with the *Mountain Enquirer*."

Zack stood up, Homer watched him beseechingly and then, with the suddenness Homer had come to expect, he was flung at length upon the bunk, tied about the wrists and ankles, and Zack was out the door, saying, "I'll give you a couple of days to search your memory." Homer shouted that he could not last two days on only one can of tomatoes, and the unshod pony galloped softly away, leaving him to reflect upon the sins which had brought him here, the article it had given him so much satisfaction to write, though Lem Finney had forbidden him to write any more of similar nature, whether about Zack Fletcher or some other man.

By now it seemed that he should have objected to being taken into captivity, for if only he had given a loud yell as they were passing through town someone, surely, would have come to his rescue—or perhaps they would have recognized his captor and would have preferred to invoke the ancient wisdom of the mountains which decreed that one man must never interfere in the business of another. Likely enough, Homer at last decided, once Zack Fletcher had decided to capture him, there was no way he could save himself; but why he had not been rescued became each day a greater puzzle.

For while he lay flexing his fingers and toes to keep them from losing feeling, Homer could see the sequence of events as plainly as if he had been present when they took place: When he had not appeared at home for the midday dinner, Rachel had gone to her mother's house. Erma Finney and Rachel had then gone to the offices of the *Enquirer* and been told that Mr. Grimes had not been seen that morning. Lem Finney was in Butte, and so a telegram had been dispatched which had brought a reply that he was down to the two-hundred-foot level of the Buckhorn and that Jake would be along in a day or two. Jacob had arrived, three days later, to find his sister hysterical, and by then everyone in town and all over the mountains would know that Homer Grimes, Lemuel Finney's son-in-law, had disappeared without a trace; or perhaps there would be one brave man among those indifferent deliverers of milk and ice, those drunken and profane bull-whackers, stupefied by marching interminably at the flank of an ox, who would have told them that he had been seen leaving town in the company of Zack Fletcher.

And yet he listened all day long, when he did not fall into one of those uncontrollable dozes, and half the night, but heard only the bark of the coyote, the songs of the birds, and occasional rainstorms, sometimes mixed with hail which pounded the cabin as if it were under bombardment and terrified him worse than Zack Fletcher's sudden appearances did.

In fact, by now, he was glad to see Fletcher, greeted him eagerly, and went about scrubbing and sweeping the cabin with great energy. But Zack ignored his greetings and stood outside, refusing to enter until the stink was gone, peering off into the distance and smoking a cigar, and once the cabin was clean they again sat face to face, Homer on the bunk, and he was each day so immersed in this increasingly wondrous experience of the can of tomatoes, the entire can for him alone, that he did not care very much what would happen next.

Zack removed the clipping from his pocket and began to study it, and as he did Homer observed that the muscles along his jaw began spasmodically to flicker, as if with a rage he could scarcely control, and Homer sighed and rolled the tomato can out the doorway, sincerely wishing he had not thought it his duty to defend the honor of his former master, Ralph Mercer, in the *Mountain Enquirer*.

And presently Zack took up reading to him where he had left off two days before, while Homer listened, smiling to reassure Zack that these words were not his own. " 'One of our cattle barons, who was not so very long ago a man of no particular account among us, now claims one hundred and twenty-four thousand head.' " Zack looked at him swiftly. "Where'd you get that figure, Grimes?" Homer spread his hands, and Zack went on. " 'Even if the figure is considerably padded, there is good reason to believe he may have as many as one hundred thousand head running on three different ranges, and it is said he has that many more in southern states. It has also been said, though not in his hearing, that all this great herd is the progeny of a single steer, brought north by him eight or ten years ago from his native state of Missouri.' "

Zack slipped the paper away, stood up slowly, approached him slowly, and, in another moment, Homer found himself bound faster than ever before, this time with his wrists and ankles fastened together and his back bowed into an arc, and at the discovery that he was bent in the perpetual act of clasping his toes with his fingers, Homer gave a howl, mournful as a coyote's, and the padlock snapped shut.

When he was released, late the next afternoon, he lay moaning, massaging his ribs and back, and declared that he would prefer to be shot dead than spend another twenty-four hours in that position. At last, he opened his eyes and saw that Fletcher sat across from him, watching him with no pleased smile for his sufferings, but only a mild curiosity, as if he might be wondering how quickly a man like Homer Grimes, who had always been cared for by other people, would collapse of fear and pain.

" 'And now,' " said Zack, " 'this same baron has seen fit to run off another man's wife. He cut her out of the herd one day and trotted her off to his pasture, while her husband was away from the Territory, and there he keeps her, even though she is not marked with his brand. It is the position of the *Enquirer* that this kind of rustling must be stopped before it takes on epidemic proportions, and no man with a pretty wife can go east to attend to his family business without the fear that he will return to find his corral empty. In the public interest, therefore, we have reported the crime to you, and now it is to be hoped that a rope, a telegraph pole, and the young men of Helena will attend to the rest.' "

Zack paused, not looking at Homer, who watched him warily and had nearly forgotten not only the pain in his muscles and joints, but had forgotten the terrible thirst and the hunger which had seemed something permanent in his life; for Zack Fletcher, he now perceived, had brought him here to kill him, would do it when the whim was on him, and Homer Grimes would be left in a grave shallow enough for wolves to scratch in, and that premonition made him shudder and cry out in a piteous voice.

"Please believe me, Mr. Fletcher, I didn't write that article."

"You're the editor, Grimes."

"I didn't see it, oh, believe me, sir, I didn't see it."

"Ralph Mercer had to save your life two or three times on the trip out here, because you were such a god-damn clumsy tenderfoot. He put you to work on his paper, you married the friend of his wife, and you show your appreciation by making a laughing stock of him and defaming his wife."

"No, I didn't," said Homer feebly.

Zack leaned forward, spreading his knees and resting his elbows on his thighs, and sat for a few moments observing Homer Grimes who, at last, humbly asked if he might have his can of tomatoes. Zack nodded, watching while he opened it and began to eat, taking out a chunk of the pulp which did not interest him very much, but then, as he ate one tomato and another, his hunger returned, grew ravenous, his thirst set upon him like a sudden feverish attack, and he gobbled the tomatoes and poured the juice down his throat and was, for the moment, content. He cast another glance at Fletcher, still watching him, and at that Homer pressed one hand to his chest, for it seemed the tomatoes might rise into his gorge and burst out of him in a torrent.

"You say you didn't write it, Grimes, but some son of a bitch wrote it, you'll agree to that, won't you? And when I catch him—what do you suppose I'm going to do to him?"

"I can't imagine, Mr. Fletcher. But you've got a right to do something."

"I've got a right?" Zack laughed, deprecating this trivial endorsement. "I've got a duty, Grimes, as I see it. A man who would write a thing like that about his employer's wife, not only doesn't deserve to live, he deserves to die a death that would do credit to a Sioux' ingenuity, now don't he?"

"No doubt about it."

"How, just for example, would you begin, if you were to catch the guy who wrote something like that about your wife?"

Homer was about to decline to enter into any such bloodthirsty conversation, but Zack's expression, at once whimsical and venomous, convinced Homer that the insults—or the insults Zack fancied —to his position as a cattle baron, and to Lisette Mercer, might have driven him temporarily insane. And so, thinking to humor him, Homer began to consider what his own most fitting punishment might be and they were, for awhile, bandying about various suggested tortures—plucked toenails and pierced eyeballs, wrapped entrails and little campfires kindled upon bellies and chests and groins which might warm the torturer while it toasted his victim crisp and black as a marshmallow.

All at once Homer became aware of what they were discussing, gave a long moan, as if he felt the first heat upon his belly, the first tug at a toenail, and collapsed upon the bunk, where he was this time tied in the reverse direction and left there, with Fletcher's warning to make good use of his time until he came back, for he would expect some livelier suggestions when he did.

"Kill me right now," Homer wailed, once the door had been shut and padlocked, and listened as the horse's hoofs went brushing across the high grass, then began to sob, for the pain this time was sharp and continuous, and his backbone was sure to snap before he was set free; and when next he found himself unloosed it seemed he must have been unconscious for many hours or days.

"Well, Grimes," Zack said, in that same curiously tender voice, as if he had a sick child or a sick animal on his hands and was wondering what he should do for it first, "where do we begin?"

"I don't give a damn," Homer mumbled, and was a moment later shocked to hear himself so tamely giving up his life, but then upon reflection it seemed to be true enough, and he repeated it. He lay staring at Zack's boots during a long silence, and Homer supposed he was expected to be preparing himself for the ordeal, but his several pains made this a matter of indifference to him so that he fell into a stupor from which he was aroused by the sudden motion of Fletcher's feet, the sound of a woman's voice, and he looked up to find Fletcher facing the open doorway with his pistol in his hand; and his rescuer had arrived at last. For there stood Lisette, looking at Homer with incredulous pity and disgust, and looking next at Fletcher, with nearly the same expression.

Fletcher slipped the pistol out of sight, perhaps ashamed she had caught him with it, and Lisette gazed from one to the other, as if she was not quite sure which of them was tormenting the other, and finally asked Zack, in a wondering voice, "What are you doing to him?"

Zack looked defensive, annoyed that she had caught him, and scowled, twisting his face into one of those fearsome expressions which Homer thought came so naturally to the face of Zack Fletcher. "I'm talking to him," Zack replied, with the stubbornness of a young boy caught by his teacher in the act of mistreating an animal he does not intend to relinquish.

"What are you keeping him here for?"

Zack sat down again, as if to dismiss her from the cabin. "I'm going to cut his balls off, when I get around to it."

Homer whimpered at that and pulled the buffalo robe about him, wrapping it Indian fashion, and appealed to Lisette, listing his complaints as if he had been an unwilling guest in a badly run hotel. "I was brought here by force and I've been here, as near as I can make out, for ten days—or maybe twelve." He gazed at Lisette where she stood in her black riding habit, the blue silk scarf on her hat drifting with a little breeze, and as he talked, Homer was thinking that she looked almost as she had at that Fourth of July picnic, fourteen years ago, when she had distributed her flirtations between Ralph Mercer and Jacob Finney and, all the time, kept watching for someone who was not there—Zack Fletcher, as he realized now. "I've been bound hand and foot, helpless as a trussed ox on a spit, and in all this time I've had not one thing but canned tomatoes—not a thing to eat or drink for nearly two weeks but canned tomatoes, Mrs. Mercer."

"Don't call her Mrs. Mercer, you son of a bitch," Zack yelled, and Homer retreated within the buffalo robe, pulling it over his head.

Lisette spoke to him gently. "Go away, Homer."

"Away?"

"Go home."

Homer looked uncertainly at Zack, who seemed not to have heard her, taking charge of his prisoner, dismissing him before his punishment was completed or, if Fletcher had been serious, before it had even been fairly begun. "Can I go, Mr. Fletcher?"

"Go ahead. Beat it. But if you tell your father-in-law where you've been, by Christ I'll bring you back here and, next time, I'll stake you out and toast you like I promised."

Homer got up, still wrapped in the buffalo robe, and petulantly demanded, "Where are my trousers and boots?"

"I threw them out there somewhere, see if you can find them."

Homer tipped his hat as he passed Lisette, though she gave him a smile so humorsome and mocking that he suspected she had rescued him not for his own sake but for Fletcher's, and while he went prowling about in the tall grasses, they stood talking in low voices, and watching each other with that intent concentration which might be found on the faces of lovers who have not once had enough of each other. He was offended to think they had forgotten him so soon, isolated as they seemed to be within the privacy of their greedy longings, and this convinced Homer that Rachel's misgivings about Lisette had been quite justified; for her predictions had all come true, and none of them had been able to prevent it.

At last Homer returned, walking awkwardly in the boots, which seemed some unnatural handicap he had put on, threw the buffalo robe on the cabin floor, but, as Zack glared at him, quickly spread it over the bunk, made the cabin tidy as he had been accustomed to do each day, and asked if he might leave. Lisette was smiling again, that sly, whimsical smile she never failed to show him, and Homer, thinking they were by now eager to be rid of him, spoke up boldly.

"I'd like to borrow one of the horses, sir. It's quite a journey, after all." Not far away, Fletcher's horse Skewball was grazing, in the company of the horse Lisette had ridden, and that animal took his fancy, for it was a black gelding, big and shining and immaculately groomed, looking more like a lady's pet than a ranch workhorse. Its ankles were dainty, its eye bright and rolling, and its entire appearance so brilliant that Homer, who felt he was surely owed something for the torments he had suffered, approached the horse and stroked him admiringly. "I'd like to borrow this one, sir."

But Zack, rather as he had been expecting, gave one of his unpleasant bursts of laughter, and advised him, "Screw out, Grimes, before I change my mind."

"You're not very far from the coach station, Homer," Lisette told him, and, hearing these words from the wife of his former master, Homer bowed and set off.

He started to walk in the direction Zack had pointed, although now it was beginning to grow dark, the sun had fallen, and he had some private intention of sneaking back to the cabin to spend the night. He glanced about, when he dared to, but although the horses were still grazing, neither Fletcher nor Mrs. Mercer was to be seen, and must have gone into the cabin, showing him plainly enough that they had no more concern for his opinion than if he were still, in fact, the son of Mercer's butler. He walked on, but all the while his imagination was busy with those two, taking their lawless pleasures and no doubt enjoying them all the better for that reason, and when at last he saw them riding away at an easy pace, he began to loiter about, waiting until they should have disappeared.

Lisette was making some gestures, and Homer supposed he could hear her describing to Fletcher what dreadful things would have followed if he had done any harm to Lemuel Finney's son-in-law, for Mr. Finney, he supposed, was as formidable to everyone as he was to him; and Lisette was, in fact, telling him something of the kind.

They had begun to quarrel about it even while Homer was still searching for his trousers, for Zack was angry that she had sneaked up on him and ordered his captive about as if she were ordering a servant to shine a pair of shoes. "You had no god-damn right to come out here, Lisette. And how the hell did you find me, anyway?"

Lisette smiled at him impudently. "I guessed."

They were both aware of Homer, prowling up and down, beating his way through the tall grasses as if he floundered in a jungle, and although each seemed to know the other was eager for him to leave, as if this unexpected encounter had created some new urgency, they nevertheless fell to arguing, as they had done before, about whether or not Lisette had the right to interfere in what he was doing, only because she believed it was wrong. "Did Johnny tell you where I was? I've taught that little bastard to keep his mouth shut, and by Christ—"

"It wasn't Johnny, don't blame him! You've been leaving so often about this time, and after Gordon brought the papers yesterday, it was easy enough to guess where you were going, and I followed you."

"What's Homer Grimes to you, Lisette? You wouldn't care if I peeled off his hide and hung it on a peg on the wall, and you damn well know it." He seized her arm. "Tell me why you came out here— tell me who you were trying to protect."

"There—he's found the other boot."

And, as if there was no more to be said about Homer Grimes, Zack pointed the direction he must take, and when Homer had gone some distance they entered the cabin and lay down upon that same bunk, Lisette closing her eyes and giving a shudder which traveled through her body, and a sigh of such intense feeling that he was each time alarmed by it, until the pressure of her arms, and her voice, distractedly whispering, abolished concern and hesitancy, and he was once more filled with the longing to propitiate her, soothe her misgivings, and convince himself his anger was only a luxury he allowed himself, whenever the terror overcame him that one day he would lose her again.

They came out to find it was nearly dark, and as he helped her to mount Pasha, the handsome black gelding which had taken Homer Grimes' eye and which was his wedding gift to her, even though they did not know when that wedding would take place, Zack spoke to her severely. "I warn you, Lisette, keep him at a walk."

Lisette smiled, as if to say she would humor his whims. "After all, I rode until two months before Frank was born, and six weeks before Polly was born."

"But this one," Zack told her sharply, "is mine."

And it was true that now he expected her to forget she had ever been married to another man, or had borne him children over whose absence she grieved, however little she might have to say about it— for they were in the East now with Ralph's mother and, so Ralph had assured her, she would not see them again. It even seemed Zack could find more reasons nowadays to mistrust her than ever before, so that whatever she said—as he rode along in that blackness which settled before his eyes with the falling of the night—he would promptly interpret as having in it some present or future danger to himself.

What other reason, he was asking himself, was there for her to have come out here, pretending to be concerned about what harm he might do Homer Grimes, but the obvious one that the child was unwelcome to her, she had lost Polly and Frank because of it and she wanted to be rid of it so that she might return to that life she would not have left of her own free will.

As they rode, quite slowly, it seemed he was dependent on her to lead him, and he fell meek and silent, ceased to argue his right to do Homer Grimes some harm for what Homer Grimes had done to them, and was once again overcome by a despairing conviction that when the sun rose he would not be able to see its light, for this nightly visitation of darkness he had endured for nearly four months seemed at such times a permanent blindness, retaliation not for the crimes he had committed, perhaps, but for the tame surrender he had made of his medicine-bundle.

For he tried, in every way he could imagine, to distract her from what he supposed she might be thinking and feeling nowadays, and was sometimes taken by such an anguished yearning for her happiness that he had some fears of babbling away as incoherently as he must have done when he lay in James Gordon's bedroom; though when he asked Lisette to tell him what he had said to her then, she smiled, sometimes touched his face with that characteristic gesture for which he had long ago envied Morgan—or even Nella Allen, anyone she loved or pitied—and assured him she could not remember.

"You were more or less delirious, Zack, it wasn't easy to understand what you said."

"You've got no right to keep it to yourself," he told her sullenly.

"I'm not keeping it to myself. I don't know."

Well, he thought, whatever it had been, the words had made no real difference and she would not be here now if it were not for this child in her belly, conceived while he lay in a terror of perpetual darkness, on one of those days or nights when the only relief he could find from the pain of the snow blindness he found in a lust so powerful it sometimes left them more despairing than consoled.

But no sooner had she left Gordon's, seemingly upon an impulse as irresistible as the one which had brought her there three weeks before, than Zack had detested himself for having forgotten, however briefly, that Lisette was less likely to please herself than she was to try to interpret the wishes of other people—those others who were meaningful to her, at least.

Even so, once he went back to the Double Key and began trying to learn how he might live with the blurred vision he had recovered, he promptly began to make those concessions he had determined he would never make, and began with what he still thought to be the inconsequential matter of Lisette's potential or real jealousy of Red Bead. He spent some days considering whether or not he should send Red Bead back to her people, but reminded himself that an Indian girl sent home by a white man might expect to be as abused by the squaws and molested by the bucks as if she were no member of the tribe but a captive, and decided instead to give Red Bead to Johnny Lawler, a gift Johnny might not appreciate at its full value just now, though he soon would. Next he divested himself of Lucy Carter, and after that felt so remarkably cleansed that he traveled to Helena to borrow money to invest in a herd which would make up the losses he had suffered on the Sun River range, but even then would not admit the real purpose of the journey was to see Lisette.

Lem Finney and Jake were away, he had never borrowed from Devlin Brothers, and he went to see his most amenable banker, Irene Flint, and there he borrowed fifty thousand dollars.

"I think the spring count will show a twenty or thirty percent loss on the Sun River range," he told her, and watched Irene carefully as he talked, wondering what she had heard or guessed, and why she had given him no clues. "But it may not be that high, because there weren't many bulls or cows among them. The guys that got it worst are the ones who believe you can breed on a large scale in this climate, but they won't think so again after this winter."

"They may," said Irene. "If a man's an optimist, he pays no attention to any contrary evidence."

She smiled, and Zack was quickly alert to what he suspected was a mocking amusement of his own predicament—for there was no subject and no conversation in which he could not discover concealed references to Lisette Devlin and Zack Fletcher, as if he worked in his head a perpetual anagram, finding her name hidden in the most unexpected places, scrambled together with his own in such a way that it seemed they had no privacy left but were known for their misdemeanors throughout the mountains and from one end of the Territory to the other, a private pleasure unluckily turned into public property.

"I'm no optimist," Zack assured her grimly.

"A man who's been as successful in trading cattle as you have?"

Zack scowled, clenching his big fists together, and told her, with the air of one who confides a precious secret, "If I'd been an optimist I'd be no better off than I was when I first came to this Territory—"

"And asked Matt and Pete Devlin for a job."

At that, as if Irene had given him some disastrous insult, he leaped to his feet, slammed his hat upon his head, and dashed across the room, loudly declaring, "So long, Irene, thanks for the loan, you'll get it all back in a few months, you know that." He paused in the doorway, then turned and stared at her with an accusatory face, but Irene continued to smile, the tolerant smile of a madam who has learned long ago that emotion should never interfere with pleasure, and so he had believed himself. "You take me for a damn fool, don't you?"

Irene shook her head. "No."

He looked at her, trying to decide what sinister meaning there was in that word, and thought it was time to get out, before he heard something he did not want to hear, whatever it might be. As he crossed the vestibule, she said, "Lisette Mercer asked me a few days ago if I'd seen you," and Zack paused to consider that information, his face crafty and suspicious, then went out and stood for a moment before the Flints' big octagonal house, with its iron deer upon the winter-dried lawn, its observatory where, it was said, Jeremy Flint amused himself by locating stars in his telescope and his wife took the information and conjured with it, advising him as to his conduct of mining trials and investments.

And this, he thought, was probably as true as the rumor that Mrs. Honeybone's curse was an infallible one and whoever had once come under its malefic influence must expect a slow and gradual withering of his life, just as children expected her curse would wither an arm and make it useless. For although Mrs. Honeybone might have cursed Jenny and so brought about that gradual withering of her life they had all seen take place, she had not written any notes to Pete Devlin because Mrs. Honeybone, he had discovered, could neither read nor write her own name; and so it might be that her baleful influence upon Nella Allen, beginning that day he had seen Mrs. Honeybone shake her fist at Nella as she passed her, was as likely a beginning as any for those various accidents which had left a wake of sorrow and loss.

Smiling a little at these outlandish notions, Zack set out at a rapid gait to walk through the town. He had dressed as he did only when he meant to borrow a large sum of money—in a black frock coat and black broadcloth trousers, a black silk cravat and soft white hat—and in this sober uniform of the successful cattleman he approached Lisette's house, glanced furtively about, and stepped inside as she opened the door, eager to escape from the brilliant light he supposed to surround him there on her porch.

But he found that the two months elapsed since she had left Gordon's had made them quite strange to each other again, and he looked at her carefully, examining her dark red silk dress, and noticed that Matt's ring was still on the little finger of her right hand, and this convinced him she had made no decision he would want to hear.

They stood facing each other across the center table with its litter of albums and lamps and books and a variety of knickknacks which, in one form or another, held some mystic appeal for every woman he had ever known but Lily Jones, and she had for such treasures the same contempt he did.

"You're well now?" Lisette asked him, and her face grew tender and sad.

"Not quite."

"But you will be soon?"

"I don't know."

"Yes, you will—I've talked to Dr. Chaffinch."

"What the hell does that bastard know about it?" It had been Dr. Chaffinch, in fact, once he arrived at Gordon's, who had carried Lisette away with him, though she refused to admit the Doctor had influenced her. Lisette smiled, indicating that she knew well enough what it was he held against Dr. Chaffinch, then shrugged and sat on the couch before the windows, reminding him of the part that piece of furniture had played in their history, and Zack braced his legs against the table, as if to prevent himself from moving toward her by this large and heavy barrier he must shove before him if he did. He peered at her through the dim light, for the room swam hazily before his eyes. "You got a warm welcome when you came back here, did you, Lisette?"

Lisette crossed her ankles, smoothed her skirt, and twirled an earring thoughtfully, and finally she gave a low and, he thought, infuriating laugh. "What a question to ask me."

"Nothing's changed—has it?"

"Oh, yes it has," she assured him, and she went on smiling at him and twirling the earring.

Ever since she had left Gordon's, Zack had been able to work himself into a state of near derangement by thinking of the years she had lived with Ralph Mercer, the two children she had borne him, her return to his house where, he supposed, she had also returned to his bed, and when he had galled himself to the limit of endurance he then remembered Matt Devlin's stubborn attachment to Jenny Danforth and blamed Lisette for having her father's same selfish sensuality.

"He hasn't asked you for a divorce, though, has he?"

"No, and he won't. I've told you that."

"He forgives you because he loves you so god-damn much he's taken leave of his senses, is that it?"

Lisette still smiled, and it occurred to him she had something she was concealing, but the only clue she would give him was this tempt-ing and rather unscrupulous smile. "He hasn't forgiven me, and I don't suppose he loves me any more—but how can he punish me as much as he thinks I deserve if he lets me go?"

"What crap. He's got even less self-respect than I gave him credit for."

"That's the way it seems to you, Zack, but it isn't the way it seems to him."

"How has he treated you, these past couple of months?" he in-quired, very softly. "The same way he did before you went out there to Gordon's?"

Lisette glanced away, she sighed, she murmured that perhaps he had, perhaps he hadn't, how could she guess what such a question meant, and at last gazed at the floor with a face as sullen and stub-born as a badgered child's. "No."

He raised his voice and made a violent gesture. "Answer me, Li-sette! You know what I'm talking about!"

"If you want to know where he sleeps, he sleeps in another room. But then he had, since last September."

Zack looked even more suspicious, but at last smiled wryly, and it seemed to give him some cruel amusement to think of a man so be-sotted with pride as to relinquish his natural pleasures only because his wife had left him for a week or two. "Since last September," he re-peated, and thought that over, raising his eyebrows and twisting his mouth into a grimace which showed his humorous contempt for any such man.

There was a stroke of the door knocker and he whirled around, ex-pecting to see Ralph Mercer come marching toward him, but Lisette went to open it, murmuring, "Rachel and Georgina—we're going to lunch at Anna Grace's." She touched his arm as she passed him and glanced around with that same teasing conspiratorial look, as if to say he had not discovered her clue, and now it was too late for her to tell him, he must puzzle it out for himself.

Georgina's face had an eager inquisitiveness, while Rachel seemed nearly as suspicious of Zack as he was of her, and he moved rapidly across the room, taking a circuitous path, giving them a last gesture with his hat, and was out the door as they glanced at one another in wondering surprise, as if to ask where the apparition had come from and where it had disappeared to.

Rachel approached Lisette where she stood before the mirror, putting on her hat, and they observed each other warily until Rachel said, "We've been friends for a long, long while, Lisette, haven't we?" Lisette was not satisfied with the hat, she adjusted it this way and that, and every now and then she darted a mutinous look at Rachel, but Rachel seemed not to notice the warning, and went on with a conversation they had started the day before. "I'm doing my best to protect you. I deny everything, whatever I hear about you—and then

I find him here." Lisette turned quickly, but she still said nothing. "We can't live only for ourselves, don't you know that?"

Lisette moved so swiftly away that she left Rachel still gazing at the space she had occupied. "You have no idea what you're talking about, Rachel."

"Please, please, Rachel, Lisette—" Georgina implored them. "Don't quarrel—"

"You'll destroy yourself, Lisette. You'll never be spoken to again by a decent woman." She tried once more to approach Lisette, and once more Lisette set off in full flight, to the other end of the room.

"Leave me alone, Rachel, I warn you."

"We'll be late," murmured Georgina. "We're late now."

But neither Lisette nor Rachel heard her, and Lisette said, "It's so hard to know when we're right and when we're wrong, isn't it, Rachel?"

"It isn't hard at all, Lisette."

Lisette smiled at her, sorrowfully. "But have you ever had someone you loved do something you'd always believed was wrong—and still love them anyway?"

Rachel frowned, but then declared quite positively, "No, I haven't. And if that happened—I wouldn't love them any more."

"You haven't changed, Rachel, have you—not in all these years. You still think exactly what you thought the day we went to call on Jenny Danforth on our way home from school, and you peeked into her letter box, and were so disappointed to find it empty. Don't you remember?"

Rachel was not disconcerted to be reminded of this, and she told Lisette with an air of tolerant kindness, "Perhaps I haven't changed, Lisette. But then, perhaps there's been no reason why I should."

Lisette smiled vaguely, for this argument was unanswerable, and they set out for Anna Grace's. As they drove, all three of them watched the streets attentively, as if they expected to find Zack Fletcher still lurking about, and Rachel was reminding her, "I've had to endure a great deal from you, Lisette, all these years."

And then, only a few weeks later, the news traveled through town that Ralph Mercer had gone east again, taking the children with him this time, to put them in school, so he said, and when Rachel went to confirm this she found the house locked and silent and it soon became known that Lisette had gone to James Gordon's and, a few days later, to the Double Key, and so got beyond reach of Rachel's commiseration.

But no sooner had she arrived than Zack was attacked by the uneasy expectation that Lisette would begin to hate him now, blaming him for all she had lost, her children and her respectability, and sourly told himself he was not so sure which was more precious to her.

Nevertheless, he began to build a new house for her, a vast two-storied structure with fireplaces big enough to burn half a tree at once, and Lisette was planning to furnish it with mirrors and feathered Indian headdresses, stuffed heads of buffalo and elk, robes and rugs of the black bear and the grizzly and wall hangings of silver fox and mink, all to be lighted with some half-hundred candles, and it seemed she was delighted by the prospect of living amid this primeval splendor.

When he and Andy Stinger rode out to hunt and fish, she insisted upon going with them, although he made her sleep after lunch in some shady place where he would spread a blanket. She wrote his business letters, and began to keep his books. The house was cleaned, as it had never been before, and Chee Shum was persuaded to change some of his cooking habits. She asked no questions about Johnny Lawler, and had apparently concluded that Johnny's habits were firmly fixed at the age of thirteen and that it was useless to try to separate him from his cigar, his profanity, his liking for pet mountain lions, or his dangerous amusements, and when Johnny harnessed an unbroken bronco to a wagon and climbed aboard, Lisette never seemed to doubt he knew what he was doing.

Most curious of all, it seemed that she and Red Bead had struck up a friendship, or whatever kind of friendship might be possible between two women who had nothing to say to each other but only smiled when they met, and he sometimes found them together, laughing as if they understood the same jokes, and Red Bead now and then appeared in a white woman's gown or a hat with flowers on it which she wore, as Indians liked to do, as an embellishment to her tribal dress.

All this was so mystifying to Zack that from time to time he must try to goad her into quarreling with him, expecting that in the quarrel he would force her to confirm the several suspicions he harbored against her. But Lisette had a way of answering his argumentative overtures with one of those smiles, wanton and knowing and a little defiant, which had been so provocative to him long ago, and so she evaded him until one morning when she showed him a letter from Morgan, mailed nearly a month ago in Albany and delivered by Gordon's foreman the day before, telling them that Ralph still refused to give her a divorce.

Full of a murderous rage at this news, although he had been expecting it, he went dashing out into a hard June rain, swearing to himself and looking so preternaturally evil and vindictive that whoever saw him made haste to get out of his way, and even the dog Rocks disappeared into one of the outbuildings. He strode across the muddy courtyard, would not pause though he heard her footsteps splashing along behind him, and only stopped when she caught hold of his arm and stood before him, wearing Johnny's yellow slicker and hat.

"Zack?" she asked him, and sounded as if she was about to cry. "It was mailed four weeks ago. Maybe he's changed his mind."

Zack bent toward her. "You don't want a divorce, do you, Lisette? You want to go back to him—just as soon as you can."

"But I never can—you know that."

She clutched at the collar of the slicker, to keep the rain from pouring off the hat's brim and onto her neck, and he glanced about to find who was watching them. No one was in sight, they were surrounded by the pelting rain and some eerie ring of silence, the barns and hide-houses might have been empty, and the sky was so dark that the distant fire of the blacksmith's forge looked as if it existed independent of any surroundings, a blazing heat miraculously sustained in the midst of this drenching rain.

"You're still in love with him." He gave her a light, hard shake. "You don't want him to divorce you. Tell me the truth, Lisette!"

Johnny Lawler ran by them with a whoop of greeting, and Zack abruptly released her, looking sheepish, for Johnny had given him a questioning look and no doubt thought this was a strange enough place to choose for a quarrel, and a strange enough morning for it, too.

Lisette was talking to him, though the hat's brim concealed her face, so that he bent nearer, cocking his head sideways as he listened. "One day, a year or so ago, I've forgotten just when it was, I realized that I didn't seem to know Ralph any more, and that I wasn't even sure I ever had." She gave him an oblique upward glance, and then lowered her head again. "The only thing I can't understand about it is that I was quite happy with him. Isn't that strange?"

Zack nodded, and the anger had miraculously disappeared. "I know," he told her tenderly, and was surprised that it seemed to be true. "Go back in the house, Lisette. Put on dry clothes. Try to sleep. Don't run," he warned her, as she started off, and when she had disappeared he went on and soon fell into step beside Andy Stinger, discussing the work they would do that day, and now and then he shook his head, marveling at whatever it was that came over him, without any warning at all, to turn him as wild and vicious as if something had threatened his very life.

He was often away, sometimes for a day or two, occasionally for more than a week, traveling to the Sun River or the Yellowstone, and when he arrived in Milestown to receive a shipment from Nebraska, he heard that the government had at last rounded up some two or three thousand hostile Indians, taking them conveniently at a time when their ferocity had been tamed by hunger and despair, and was now preparing to send them away for their crimes to live in malarial country, and from their encampments along the river the squaws set up a continuous, dismal howling, never resting from it day or night.

The town was full of disgruntled ranchmen and wolfers and buffalo hunters, telling one another that the American government, as usual, had done them this favor too late. And when the Indians were loaded aboard steamers and, still howling, disappeared around a bend in the river, passing the railroad crew as they went, some of them gave the hostiles a genial wave of farewell, while others took firm hold of their own hair and were glad to find it still in place.

Zack and Andy Stinger started back to the Double Key, drinking from their pocket flasks and toasting the departure of Rain-in-the-Face and his band, and were surprised to find that now the danger was out of the way, it seemed something would be lacking in this life, for, they admitted, it scared them to see civilization creeping steadily nearer.

"When the country gets safe," said Zack, with a remarkably gloomy face, "the reformers arrive."

He was still despondent, and more or less drunk, as they approached the Double Key headquarters, so that when Johnny rode out to meet them, galloping at top speed and yelling as he came, as if he brought news of a battle won or lost, some new war declared or the house burned down, and beckoned Zack aside with furtive frowns, Zack received the news that Jeremy Flint had filed Ralph Mercer's divorce proceeding in Deer Lodge, where it had been dated several months back, with a kind of stunned disbelief. He scowled at Johnny as if he could not understand what he was talking about, what kind of foreign gibberish he might be babbling, and sharply reprimanded him for bouncing about in his saddle and waving his arms, until at last Johnny sat still and straight, and turned down his mouth in a cynical grimace, and at that Zack gave a burst of joyous laughter.

He beckoned Andy Stinger to join them, mumbling that they were to travel back to Milestown and find a justice of the peace and bring him to the Double Key, and he scowled as he gave these directions, not liking to admit either to Johnny or to Andy Stinger what purpose he had for a justice of the peace, and sent them off, telling Johnny to give him a little notice, ride ahead, for he did not want to be taken by surprise when they returned with their quarry.

Lisette, he supposed, would now do what all women did when it came time to get married—put on a new dress, decorate the house with flowers, appoint some professional mourners or celebrants to attend her, and acquire that expression of apprehensive sobriety which he dreaded. And, indeed, he drew a melancholy parallel between the Indians' recent loss of freedom and his own.

She surprised him again, however, for she would not be married indoors, would have no witnesses but Andy Stinger and Johnny, would wear no new dress but her black riding habit, and insisted upon setting out very early, scarcely after sunup, to meet them somewhere on those broad prairies where, as she said, they intended to spend their lives.

"After today," she assured him, "everything will seem different," and he heard those words with morbid misgivings, for no doubt she was quite right.

Johnny and Andy Stinger met them first, pointing back to where

the justice of the peace, who had come this long way as their unwilling hostage, rambled along at his leisurely pace, and Zack sent
them on their way and raced to catch up with Lisette, for against all
his warnings she went galloping ahead and, when he caught up with
her, reached out to place her hand in his with a gesture so confiding,
so tender, that it melted all his grudges against her, the tears swam
into his eyes, and he was as relieved to be told he was now a married
man as if he had awakened from drugged sleep to learn he had survived a desperate operation.

Dr. Chaffinch appeared at the Double Key a few days later, summoned by Zack who was wondering how he might keep him there
for the next five months, and Zack walked with him among the outbuildings for an hour or two, arguing and protesting, at one time
caught hold of him with a gesture so threatening an onlooker might
have supposed he was about to choke him, and at last sent him to
see Lisette who asked, in a whisper, what the trouble was.

"Your husband wants you to stay in town with your mother and
Jenny."

"And have Erma Finney and Rachel and everyone else looking at
me to see how big I am? I won't do it, Dr. Chaffinch, I've told him
that."

"Then he wants you to stay in Butte with one of your brothers."

"No. I'm going to stay here."

Dr. Chaffinch looked at her gravely. "My dear, I only hope your
life won't be too unhappy. You're married to a violent man. I suppose you know that."

And when he left her a few minutes later there Zack was again,
leaning against the side of the house with his arms folded and a cigar
in his mouth, as surprised to find Dr. Chaffinch coming out his front
door as if he had never seen him before, and once again he walked
along with him, this time with one arm wrapped about his shoulders,
though ordinarily he distrusted a doctor as he distrusted a lawyer or
a banker. "I'll pay you a thousand dollars for every week you spend
here."

"But surely you understand, Mr. Fletcher, that I have other responsibilities. And it isn't necessary, you must believe me. Your wife
is quite strong, quite healthy, it will be a routine case, as her others
have been."

Zack stopped in his path and peered down at him. "When will you
see her again?"

"I'll come back on the first of August, though even that isn't necessary."

Dr. Chaffinch started away, eager to escape, and Zack let him go,
but then all at once he came riding up beside him again, smiling ingratiatingly, and began to discuss the latest news of the Territory,
quite as if they were strangers who had met midway to the next
town. And, in fact, he soon had the Doctor so beguiled that when they

parted several miles farther on, Chaffinch was as concerned to reassure and console him as if it was Zack Fletcher, not Lisette, he had come out here to see.

Zack touched his hat as he turned to start back, and he was still smiling benevolently. "I'll meet you right here, you old son of a bitch, on the first of August—not one day later." He gave a brief meaningful nod. "And I warn you, be on time."

LXVII

The midafternoon sun warmed the porch, and Jenny and Marietta, seated on a wicker couch, occasionally nodded or waved to someone passing along the street, but no one stopped or ventured to come near, for Morgan was with them and so it must be a family council, called out there because of the fine October day which had become, toward noon, warm as summer, but much more precious.

Even Erma Finney, driving with Rachel and her daughter-in-law, Anna Grace, had passed them by for the first time anyone could remember, only giving a formal smile perhaps meant to show them she had heard the news and was sympathetic, and Jenny had bitterly remarked that Erma would no doubt be willing to forgive Lisette now, or at least to pity her. For Lisette's baby had been born a month earlier than Dr. Chaffinch had predicted, while Zack was away, and the little girl was dead by the time he and Dr. Chaffinch got there.

The Doctor had returned to tell Marietta and Jenny a tale of having been blamed by Fletcher for the child's death, and of finding the Indian squaw who had attended Mrs. Fletcher, with her breasts and face streaked with blood where she had clawed at her flesh, as a squaw would mourn for her own child, hiding in one of the outbuildings and expecting Fletcher to kill her for her own hapless participation.

And, as Dr. Chaffinch had confided, looking as if he had not yet got over the shock of those four days he had spent at the Double Key, there was nothing that man might do which could surprise him, for Fletcher was more savage than any Indian he knew, and Lisette, the Doctor said, had saved them both, the little squaw, and himself, though Fletcher had at last relented enough to shake his hand when he took his leave, and had confided, "I'm building a house in Helena, not far from Pete's—our next child will be born there."

Dr. Chaffinch had sighed, as if to say that was the predicament Lisette had got herself into, and had left Marietta and Jenny sitting, as they had throughout his recital, quite silent.

And so Morgan had been this afternoon, hunched over in his chair and staring at the floor, as if he was ashamed to have them look at him, until all at once he gave his knee a violent slap, declaring, "By God, it's my fault! I shouldn't have let her stay there at Gordon's." He looked at Marietta, narrowing his eyes as if to find if she blamed him as he blamed himself. "I had some damn fool idea that it was her decision to make—and she wanted to stay with him."

He went pacing back and forth along the broad verandah, where Jenny and Marietta spent so much time nowadays, amid its green wicker couches and chairs, covered with embroidered cushions, shadowed by the gaily striped awnings and furnished with plants enough for a conservatory—ferns in hanging baskets, palms, and screens of ivy trailing from the window boxes on the second floor— with books and magazines to occupy them when they were not talking, tea to drink and cakes to eat and to dispense when some neighbor stopped there for a few minutes. And, each time he had seen them during the year since Marietta had moved into Jenny's house, he watched them with a kind of furtive curiosity, a little guilty at those thoughts which came trespassing, for even now he could scarcely believe they were so companionable, or so resigned, as they seemed.

Jenny still wore mourning black, but Marietta wore silk dresses in dark colors, wine-red or purple, with white organdy collars, and perhaps it was because of these becoming clothes that nowadays it was Marietta who seemed the younger, although she was, he remembered, nearly fifty-two, seven years older than Jenny. Or the secret might be in Marietta's smile, not as spontaneous as it had once been, and yet, however much pathos he thought he could find in it, that smile had a warm luster unlike any other he knew. While Jenny looked more restless than ever, even though she now had that restlessness carefully confined, and her brilliance had been so dimmed that while she was still described as a beauty, the legend was that newcomers to the mountains must have seen her in full bloom—before sorrow had done its work on her—ever to appreciate Jenny Danforth's spell.

And as Morgan glanced at them while he went pacing about, he marveled again at this seeming harmony and serenity, as if all misgivings and all pain had been transmuted into a need for companionship, a sharing of the past, even though they never, so far as he knew, spoke of it. They had found new interests, a new ritual for their lives, and their friends professed to discover some deep lessons in the tranquillity of these two lonely women, barricaded behind their books, preparing all the favorite dishes of everyone they knew, so that whoever was invited to a dinner party at Pete Devlin's house spent much time speculating first upon what good things they would have to eat; and it seemed they had even turned their frequent visits to the cemetery into a species of occult holiday, for they went there at every time of year and had made of it a pilgrimage they discussed first, and then set out upon bearing cushions and blankets, perhaps a

book or two, and a basket of gardening tools, for they did not trust
the caretaker to keep the three plots as they should be kept.

Morgan had seen them there sometimes, though for his own part
he avoided the place, and had as much superstition about it as if
he were a very young boy confronting the mystery for the first time,
a horror he could not lose at this retreat of life into the earth
where, each day, he himself went wandering in search of hidden
veins of treasure.

And now, Lisette's child was dead, the child she should never
have had, he thought, for its birth had cost her not only the sorrow
of that loss, but the loss of Polly and Frank, though he blamed himself for that, too, thinking he should have found, during those hours
he and Ralph had argued until they were ready to pitch into each
other with fists and heels, some way to convince him to give the
children back to her; but he had not. He might, of course, hold Zack
Fletcher responsible, but Zack still seemed to him a stranger arrived
from a strange land, the outsider who had at last carried her away
with him, and so it was not Zack he blamed for having taken her, but
himself for not having found the way to prevent it.

"She'll never be happy with him," he told Marietta and Jenny. "It
was more natural for her to be Ralph's wife."

"I'm not sure that's true," said Jenny, but she spoke very softly,
and seemed to be afraid of offering a contrary opinion.

They fell silent again, until at last Marietta said, "These things
aren't the product of anyone's plan or will, Morgan, and Lisette's
been so wonderfully fortunate all her life. She's still young—she'll
have other children."

"It isn't the same," said Jenny slowly, gazing off toward where the
neighborhood children had begun to organize their after-school
games, "it isn't the same, losing a child who's only a few hours old,
as it is to lose a child you've taken care of." Marietta and Morgan
looked at her, for this was the first time she had mentioned Leila in
so long they had supposed that she never would again, but then
Jenny held out her hand to them, looking surprised and apologetic
to realize she had said it. "Oh, please don't misunderstand what I
meant by that."

"I didn't."

"Marietta?" She turned to her anxiously.

"I know what you meant, Jenny."

Marietta gave him a letter, one which had come a few days ago
from her sister, and he read that Susan was now quite accustomed to
living in the Louvre, as she called the houses on Forty-fourth Street,
that young Joshua had left for Germany in September, and that a man
named Nicholas Craig had named his trotting-horse stud Joshua
Ching, and at this Morgan laughed aloud, remarking, "That's real
fame." But then he went on to read that Suky's pregnancy kept her
often in bed nowadays, and at that he felt his face grow burning
hot, hastily folded the letter and returned it to Marietta and an-

nounced that he must be on his way; for although he had known some weeks ago that Suky was pregnant, and had asked himself if this child was possibly his own, to be reminded of it in the presence of Jenny and Marietta seemed to fix the guilt upon him without any doubt, and he was ashamed to have sat there talking in the furious way he had about his responsibilities to Lisette, when it seemed he had little enough responsibility for himself.

"Won't you stay and have dinner with us, Morgan?"

"I can't." He stood with his back to them, staring across the street, where his eyes showed him a blurred vision of houses shimmering amid red flecks, and he gazed at those houses until his vision at last found its focus, and then turned, hoping by then to give some impression of composure. "I've got to get back. We've just opened a new level in the Yellow Medicine—we're down to four hundred feet." He smiled eagerly, hoping to divert them from the other subject, and went on to describe the rich coppper vein he had found, trusting that his evident distraction would seem only what was natural for a man who had lately happened upon a vein of copper assaying at 40 percent. "We're going to christen the old Halloway claim next week," he told them, and his sorrow and concern for Lisette, even his qualms about Suky, momentarily gave way before that passion which had lately seized every man who had been in Butte these past few years, and was beginning to infect the newcomers as well. "Jonathan and Georgina are coming—make the trip with them." He caught hold of their hands, appealing to them urgently. "Or come with the Flints. Will you promise? You've both got to be there."

They looked up at him, then glanced at each other uncertainly, as if to ask whether or not they dared leave this house, this town, for even a few days, for it might be they would return to find some of those memories had vacated the premises, fled away once and for all, and they would never be able to persuade them back again. And seeing those questioning, doubtful smiles, which he could interpret quite well, Morgan relinquished their hands. "Maybe you'll change your minds?"

"Maybe we will, Morgan," Marietta told him, but seemed to know as well as he did that they would not make the trip. She walked to the edge of the verandah, and as he stood on the steps below her, Marietta touched the side of his face, gently caressing it in that same gesture which was so characteristic of Lisette whenever she wanted to offer comfort and which, by what had seemed to him an extraordinary coincidence, was Allegra Stuart's gesture, too. "Don't look so tragic, Morgan. We learn to accept everything, don't you know that?"

She smiled, but he could not answer, only gave them a brisk wave and dashed away, then turned once to look back at the house, set there amid bushes turned yellow and red by early frost. They were preparing to go back indoors, Jenny carrying a tray with the teapot and dishes and Marietta a basket of fern, and as they disappeared he broke into a run, turned the corner and went sprinting along full of

angry sorrow which, nevertheless, presently gave way to an intense
eagerness to be prowling about those underground workings, speaking to each man as if he and no other knew what might be the nature
of that ultimate secret he had hidden down there, dropping from one
level to another in the cage which flashed so swiftly by that an unaccustomed eye saw only darkness and vague, half-naked figures, but
would never guess that here was a second city growing steadily in the
earth, like a rudely drawn hieroglyph of many dimensions—for there
were now at least twenty such mines in the neighborhood of his own.

He had, in fact, spent so much time down there these past several
years that it was the upper world which looked strange to him now,
and whenever he traveled away from the camp, the absence of nox-
ious smells surprised him, while he listened continuously for the
rumbling blasts, the whistles shrieking at all hours of the day and
night, and felt some vague, indefinable disturbance in failing to detect them, as if the world might have begun to go awry.

He was often in the small laboratory he had built near the Yellow
Medicine, and there, amid his collection of alembics and retorts, be-
clouded with fumes which sent Felice and Susette retreating in dismay should they stop to pay him a visit, he mixed chemicals with
the enthusiasm of a medieval alchemist, expecting one day to find
the perfect solvent. He appeared at every hour at the smelters and
the mills, having learned to materialize in the midst of the workmen
with an uncanny stealth, and found fulfilling joys in whatever per-
tained to the resolution of this riddle.

The fierce heat of the roasters, the gigantic stamps pounding the
ore, grinding and gnashing it into a pulp, jiggling it about and whirling it to drive off the sulphur, those great furnaces which cast forth
their molten streams and which so often required a patient tinkering to set them to working again, all seemed to him marvels of beauty
and ingenuity, and he was as resentful as anyone else that outsiders
should have begun to covet those properties they had dismissed only
recently as not being worth a prudent man's investigation.

There were two lines of coaches constantly arriving and departing,
bringing in those who had read the newspaper accounts of the camp's
flourishing present and dazzling future, and they appeared at the
mine shafts where, most often, they were met by men who refused
them entrance to their treasure houses and told them plainly that the
days of easy money in this camp were over. The days of easy money
had never existed at all, but they were regularly invoked in reproving
greedy strangers who were told of that recently disappeared golden
age of every western town. And thus discouraged, most of their visitors boarded the next coach, only to be replaced by others who came
clambering down from their perches on the coach's top or crept out
of the confinement of its interior to lurch about for a few moments
until they recovered their balance, overcame their vertigo, and, taking sight of a gallows frame, went in prompt pursuit of its owner.

As the fame of the mineowners' properties grew, so did their arrogance, and they told one another they must protect themselves from these outside exploiters, lest they find themselves in colonial bondage to Wall Street.

"Even the most prejudiced pilgrims," they liked to say, with sly scornful smiles, "have begun to see the light."

Rumors were rife on street corners and in saloons. Stock of the most respected mines was put upon the market in niggardly quantities, for it was now worth ten or even twenty times its original value. Several mines had gone below the water line and found the ore got richer the deeper they went, and so that superstition had been laid away. Men who went east looking for money brought it back, and this made them wary, for eastern capital had the bad habit of waiting too long, and then expecting to take the rewards of another man's work; and, in fact, there was such enthusiasm that the earlier optimism was agreed to have been, surprisingly enough for a mining camp, quite modest, for it seemed there was nothing more they might wish for but time, and a railroad—and the railroad was finally on its way.

Lemuel Finney and Morgan Devlin, who owned the camp's two newspapers, were given most of the public credit for the mines' rapid development, although Morgan had another sycophant in Bruno Favorite, who assured each man he talked to, "It was none other than my partner, Morgan Devlin, who fired the first gun to awaken the eastern capitalists. Where was Lem Finney, gentlemen, during the winter of 'sixty-five?" Most of them could not answer this question, so Bruno told them that Lem Finney had been in Last Chance, during that crucial winter, digging up gold.

"Lem Finney is a smart man, I don't say he's not," Bruno would tell them as he stood outside his saloon on a clear day, dressed in the frock coat and silk hat he had planned for himself long ago, fingering the watch chain dangling gold nuggets big enough to have foundered a less sturdy midget. "He's smart, he's mean as a snake, and he's rich. Don't misunderstand me," Bruno would add, with a look of mystery upon his doleful face.

While he smoked one fragrant cigar after another, Bruno told the pilgrims tales of the old days in Butte which, by now, had traveled far and wide throughout the mountains, and when those tales had been told, he would conclude, rubbing his hands together and producing that same crisp sound of dry leaves chafing against each other which was so characteristic of Lem Finney, "Oh, Lem Finney's a smart son of a bitch, there's no taking that away from him. But take my partner, Morgan Devlin. Now, there's a man for you. Came to this Territory when he was fifteen years old, and without any help from anybody, with not a damn thing to fall back on but his own pluck —muscle—brains—and enterprise, Morgan Devlin has become the owner of some of the most valuable properties in the Territory, not to mention the director of our most substantial banks, here and in Helena, the owner of our only reliable newspapers, and in another

four or five years he will be worth more millions than you would care
to count, gentlemen."

Morgan, hearing these tales at second-hand, took Bruno aside one
day. "All my pluck and muscle wouldn't have meant a god-damn
thing, Bruno, if my father and Pete hadn't been successful, you know
that."

Bruno shrugged. "You think so?"

"And my brains and enterprise wouldn't have sunk a single shaft
if I hadn't had friends with money enough to help me out when I
needed it. You know that, too."

"Maybe," Bruno conceded reluctantly.

"Then what the hell do you tell them these lies for?"

"They like it. Besides," he murmured confidingly, "I believe it myself by now." And, it was true, he had a deep and honest mistrust of
Lem Finney for not having been with them during the disastrous
winter of 'sixty-five, from which he derived all later events.

"First time they give me a testimonial banquet," Morgan told
him, "I want you to be toastmaster," and he clasped Bruno's shoulder affectionately, for he had some sentimental superstitions of his
own about that first winter and its continuing influence upon their
lives. "That is, if Lem doesn't shoot you first."

Bruno frowned and pouted, not liking the joke, for however
often Morgan assured him that it was all in his imagination, Bruno
continued to insist he had been shot at from ambush on his way to
testify at Deer Lodge, and he often suspected even now that his life
was in danger from various strangers he saw lurking about town,
hired by Lemuel Finney to get rid of Morgan Devlin's most valuable
witness.

Lem Finney, however, had offered Morgan his congratulations on
the court decision, adding, "But you know as well as I do, Morgan,
that my certified copies of the Deer Lodge records prove that claim
was unrepresented by you for one year and four months and
twenty-eight days, while I had a four-man crew at work. The truth of
it is that Bruno Favorite let you down—he forgot all about you
while you were gone, and only remembered his duties when you
came back." Lem peered at him through the square-bowed spectacles. "Where is that man he says he had at work? You've been looking for him for more than seven years and haven't found him yet.
Perhaps he never existed but in Bruno Favorite's imagination—
have you thought of that?"

"Or perhaps he's dead, Lem?" Morgan suggested, but Lem deprecated this, though he smiled to let Morgan know he understood his
meaning quite well.

"There was no such man around that claim when I first saw it,
Morgan. Still, it's yours now, and I wish you luck. I could never go to
war against Matt Devlin's son," and, as he did each time he mentioned Matt's name, Lem lowered his eyes and gazed at his boots.

With the same piety, Lem had denied that it was Fletcher who had been described by his son-in-law as a rustler of cattle and married women, for Homer Grimes had come back from his captivity in pathetic condition, with a tale to tell of terror and suffering at the hands of that fierce ruffian, Zack Fletcher. The man he had actually described, Lem Finney privately assured Morgan, was a ranchman who lived in the Judith Basin, and Finney had reminded him that once men came to live in the Territories they grew lawless and violent, while the women gave way to their habitual restlessness which, in more settled communities, they submerged in a pensive martyrdom; and Morgan had been obliged to admit that he might be telling the truth, for such defections by wives were by no means unusual this side of the Missouri River.

For all the good will between their two families, however, Morgan did not invite Lem Finney to attend the christening party he was giving on the four-hundred-foot level of the old Halloway claim, at midnight on the second of November, partly because he suspected that Finney, once down there, would not leave before he found a way to work some mischief, but perhaps even more because he was still cautious and wary, afraid he might yet be tricked or deceived and that even as Irene Flint spoke the words of benediction, his vein of copper would disappear, streak away into the earth like some powerful serpent, never to be located again.

Jonathan and Georgina arrived several days early. James Gordon appeared next, sheepishly apologizing that his neighbor Zack Fletcher was not back from Cheyenne and so could not attend the christening of this property in which he still owned, for all his disclaimers, a five percent share. Irene and Jeremy Flint came in on the afternoon stage, which crossed the bridge with a roar of running hoofs and drew up before the Hotel de Mineral to discharge its usual number of dazed and shaken pilgrims, and Morgan sprang forward like a relieved lover to hand Irene down, while Jeremy, grown ponderously heavy these past years through maintaining his reputation as gourmand and gourmet, threatened the driver with his cane and declared he would put the company out of business.

"What time do you want us?" Irene asked.

Morgan glanced about, for nowadays all strangers looked suspicious to him, and bent down, murmuring, "Twelve-thirty tonight. The shifts will have changed, and it's as quiet then as it ever is. Wait until you see what I've found," he added, with a look of meaningful warning, and felt once again that dreadful excitement and terrifying buoyancy which signaled to him each new triumph, or failure.

They began to arrive a little after midnight, but found no one to greet them when they stepped from the cage, so that they gathered together, the women in their bright silk dresses and long mink coats, laughing with somewhat more gaiety and confidence than they might have shown at an ordinary evening reception, while only

Irene Flint seemed not at all disconcerted by knowing they had descended so far into the earth, and only Bruno Favorite looked as if he
might be in his natural element.

"Four hundred feet below the surface of the earth," said Sir
James, in a subdued reflective tone. "I say."

A rat scampered by them and crawled into a crevice, lurking there
and peering down at them, while Felice held onto Flora to keep her
from running away, and the next moment Morgan appeared from
some corridor, kissed the women and shook the hands of these several men who had loaned him money, and suggested that they put on
the linen dusters he had provided.

"But that would only spoil the party," Fan Troy protested, and
while they were agreeing with one another that it was better to look
festive, even if their gowns must be thrown away, Billy Church set
it down in his notebook that the ladies had attended this historic
occasion wearing French gowns of scarlet silk and green taffeta,
purple moire and black and yellow striped satin, and their finest
diamonds, their white kid gloves, and their thinnest silk slippers.

Morgan then fell into low and seemingly conspiratorial talk with
Joe Butts and Shang Oliver, hatching schemes they preferred not
to hear, and the general conversation grew louder, they laughed
more often, but still kept a wary watch over that pantomime taking
place between the three accomplices. And then, their fate having
apparently been decided for them, with no questions asked about
whether or not they were prepared for the worst, should it happen,
Oliver and Joe Butts were gone, dissolved back into those same dark
passageways, and Morgan was addressing them in soothing tones,
assuring them there was no cause for fear, for he could read their
misgivings upon their faces, so rueful and apprehensive now that
there was no longer any hope of escape, and then he took Felice into
his arms and pressed her head against his chest, and raised one hand
in some signal or warning.

There was a flash, a muffled explosion, the ground shuddered, and
they heard a rattle of distant falling rock as the passageway filled
with smoking dust, sending them into fits of coughing, the men
swore, and as the dust slowly settled they looked about at one another with expressions of pleased surprise, for they were still there
and, unless Morgan was deceiving them, no catastrophe had taken
place.

"You see?" he asked them comfortingly, and smiled, to reassure
them further. "That's all there is to it. Come along." He nodded, beckoning to Irene Flint, took her by the hand, and they set off together,
leading the procession.

Each was now supplied with a lantern and they moved forward
in single file, traveling along behind Morgan and Irene, who led
them at a slow ritualistic pace through these silent black mazes,
where soot-blackened figures lurked against the walls, shyly watching as the women went by.

Morgan and Irene were murmuring to each other in the distracted voices of lovers ransacking unpremeditated joys, full of impatient ardor as their fingers grazed the exposed vein of copper which writhed across the wall, thrusting upward from beneath their feet, coiling the length of the corridor, and twisting out of sight into the level above them, until at last Irene gave him an imploring ecstatic glance, whispering, "Iron and copper pyrites, oh, my God." From time to time she paused, rummaging among the debris, selected some fragment which caught her fancy, and, thrusting it into her reticule, let him take her hand again.

The others, obediently following, were solemn and had little to say, the women seemed perplexed, more dazed by the nature of the mine itself than infatuated with its treasures, while the men came pacing at their heels, taking due and serious notice of everything they saw, though only James Gordon had any comments to make about it, and he occasionally remarked, "I say, upon my word."

At last they reached the end of their march, a small chamber, filled with fumes and dust and a murky light, where men were at work like so many half-seen phantoms, wielding their picks at a merciless rate, and all at once had torn a hole from that working into the next, whereupon other faces appeared and grinned at them. The women, disconcerted, gathered near the doorway of this chamber which seemed to be lined with nests of diamonds, clusters of crystal, blazing blue and green and purple, sparkling like some underground fire in the flare of lanterns and candles, and agreed it was surely a creation of the demons which had been uncovered here, for nothing natural or familiar was to be found in it.

Irene Flint now had hold of a champagne bottle, presented to her by Morgan, who had drawn it from a washtub filled with ice and bottles and glasses, and bearing it in her right hand like a club she approached the ragged opening which gave entrance into the old Muspratt claim, drew back her arm and struck a mighty blow against the doorway, announcing, "I christen thee—Milly Matches!"

Morgan and Douglas were filling glasses, the miners from the Muspratt working came forward to receive their share, and a toast was proposed by Bruno Favorite to his partner, whose pluck, muscle, brains, and enterprise had achieved what the camp's most intoxicated visionaries had said could never be done, while Billy Church approached Mrs. Flint with his notebook opened to inquire, "What does Milly Matches stand for, ma'am?"

"You've never heard of Milly Matches?" she asked him incredulously.

"No, ma'am."

"Well, then," said Irene, "I'll tell you about her." The others fell into deferential silence, and Morgan and Douglas passed among them, pouring champagne. "Milly Matches lived in Bannack that first winter of 'sixty-two, when there were no more than four or five hundred white men in the Territory, and not fifty white women. Morgan

wasn't there, though his father and his uncle were, and so were
Mr. Flint and Mr. Troy. They say she was a hurdy-gurdy—or maybe
she was something else—but whatever she was, she was very beautiful, with hair like a flaming match and blue eyes, and the miners
loved her, though not for her beauty, as it happens. They loved her
because when there was an epidemic of typhoid, Milly Matches
helped to nurse the sick men." Irene glanced around at all those serious faces, and although her smile was a shade ironic, at last she
nodded, remarking, "Which was damn brave of her, when you think
of it, because most of the respectable women wouldn't risk their
health."

"What happened to Milly Matches, ma'am?"

"What do you suppose? She caught typhoid fever." Irene
shrugged. "She died."

"Oh, I say," Sir James objected. "Caught typhoid fever and died."
He gave that a moment's philosophic reflection. "Still, she has her
monument, doesn't she?"

"She has her monument," Irene agreed, flung her glass against the
wall, Jeremy pitched his after it, and there was for a moment or two
a steady explosion of popping glasses before they all went trooping
out, waving good-bye to the miners, then hurried along the corridor
and were hoisted up so swiftly they stepped out of the shaft-house to
find, with the sense of disbelieving astonishment which overcame
every visitor to the mines, that the night was bright, the stars were
many, and seemed so near Bruno Favorite made a gesture as if to
pluck one. And then they saw that Amos Muspratt stood not far
away, his face greedy and more than usually resentful, although
Morgan greeted him with a magnanimous smile and went to shake
his hand.

"Glad to see you, Amos."

"Quite a little spree you've been having for this time of night. But
what would anyone be doing down in that worthless old hole?"

Morgan bent over Muspratt with a serious, confidential air. "You
know, Amos, this may surprise you, but I decided to have one more
try and, by God, would you believe it, I think there may be something there after all?" He seemed whimsically surprised by this
unexpected good fortune, and Amos, looking like a man overtaken by a sudden queasiness, turned and left them, walking away
down the hillside with thumping strides and flapping his arms as
he went, as if he might be asking himself questions he could not
answer.

The opening of the Milly Matches, collateral descendant of that
first worthless claim in Daylight Gulch, was greeted throughout the
camp as a general achievement, shedding something of its luster
upon every one of them, and only Lem Finney, when he offered Morgan his congratulations, had the look of one who suspects his rival
may have crept into his bedroom during his absence. But when
Morgan tried once again to buy Homer Grimes' Humbug, so incon-

veniently located there between the Milly Matches and the Yellow Medicine, Lem raised one hand in protest at such an unbusinesslike proposition, declaring he had refused fifty thousand dollars and sixty thousand, and now he refused seventy-five thousand.

"I don't need money, Morgan, you know that. At least, not that kind of money. Anyway, who knows how far that vein you've found may reach? Right through the old Muspratt claim and into Homer's?" Lem gave his hands a brisk rubbing. "After all, Morgan, you've got enough right now to keep you busy for some time."

The railroad arrived a few days before Christmas, as likely a present as any of them could want, and just what they had been hankering for these twenty years. And yet, as some few hundred of the camp's citizens gathered late on a cold night at the still uncompleted depot, they stamped their feet and swung their arms, huddled in their buffalo coats, and grumbled because it had kept them waiting so long.

Milestown had been reached not long ago and, although Helena was still isolated, the Butte mines would be opened from now on, the days of shipping ore by wagon freight for several hundred miles and of walking the profit off cattle by trailing them great distances to market, had ended. But it should have ended long ago, they told one another, and so there was much bitterness among them now about the greed of the railroad company, and many jokes about its stupidity.

"A hell of a long time they've taken to get here."

"They should have been here three years ago."

"Three years, my ass. Five years."

The train approached them at tentative speed, its whistle shrieking steadily as it bore down upon them, lighting the darkness as it came and looking, after all, small and inconsequential, not so impressive as the blue freight wagons for which there was, all at once, a collective pang of nostalgia as someone began to sing a verse of the bull-whacker's song, "Joe Bowers." It was taken up here and there in the crowd and then dropped, as they went on to complain of the cupidity of the railroad company and, most particularly, of Lemuel Finney, who was said to have profited handsomely from his friendship with the company's officials, and who was even now aboard that train with some forty or fifty of them, while they stood here in the stinging cold.

"We were too god-damn eager for it, they knew they had us by the balls."

"They'd have done it sooner or later, without our help."

"It was more to their interest than ours. After all, they'll get rich hauling our ore."

They fell momentarily quiet as the little engine, pulling a string of yellow cars, came to a stop beside them and its passengers peered through the lighted windows, pressing their faces to the panes, as if wondering what outpost they had reached.

"Come on out," someone yelled. "What the hell are you guys ashamed of?"

At this, as if to demonstrate that they had nothing at all to be ashamed of, a score or more of men, in silk hats and frock coats, and Lem Finney among them, emerged onto the platform with its drapery of patriotic bunting and milled about there for a few minutes, seeming more confused than disappointed that no cheers had greeted them, no brisk band music played, and when Lem Finney stepped forward, he was met not by applause but by an outburst of sullen laughter.

"The son of a bitch is going to make a speech," Bruno Favorite protested.

"Not to me, he isn't," Morgan said, and as Lem began to speak there was a general movement of dispersal and an unenthusiastic cheer went up but died away on the air.

"Ladies and gentlemen, we are gathered here tonight to welcome to our city the great Utah and Northern Railroad—"

"Glad you finally made it."

"A hell of a big favor you guys have done us."

They drifted away, slipping off into the darkness with slow stubbornness, while Lem Finney pleaded with them to pay their respects to the officials of the Utah and Northern. But by then the platform was all but deserted, men were dissolving back into the town, entering saloons and hotels, or setting out on horseback to ride the distance into Butte City.

"One thing's for sure," Morgan remarked to Bruno and Douglas, as they exchanged nods with men passing by, "you meet everyone you know in Butte nowadays—and everyone has come to stay. The town's on the map."

And the change, it seemed, had come with that same bewildering swiftness by which a chinook could dissipate a heavy snowfall: Inside the earth the shafts reached deeper, the drifts went farther, spreading a web of passageways where men worked day and night, and by now the mines employed so many hands that there were always enough men off-shift to keep the streets and saloons and gambling houses crowded. Ore wagons rumbled through the streets at every hour, and the smoke from the smelters had begun to grow dense and oppressive, breathing the stench of sulphur and arsenic over them, killing their trees and bushes.

Tall smokestacks and ore roasting in heaps in the open filled the air with the smell of rotten eggs and garlic, floating in dense white clouds that stung their eyes and made them cough, while from those vast, barnlike structures which surrounded the mine shafts came shrieking whistles that rent their ears with a hideous music, and jolting blasts caused the earth to tremble, rattled dishes and broke windows; and yet there was a general agreement that if a man owned a good lead, knew his business, was persistent and energetic and had his fair share of the American mania for work, there was no possible way he could fail.

In the summer, clouds of dust swirled over the town, settling in their hair and on their clothes, crept under windowsills and doors, and when it rained they sank in mud over their ankles. In winter the buckling wooden sidewalks were coated with ice which made a treacherous footing, sending them skidding and toppling into heaps of rubbish or ponds of muddy ice. But they never complained of these inconveniences, and assured one another that such mishaps were of no consequence in a camp which now had at least twenty mines which were the wonder of the world and new ones opening up every day, and they demonstrated at all times an aggressive loyalty to this mountain perch.

They were lofty with strangers, looked at them with skeptical amusement as being neither hardy enough for the life, nor deserving of its special and peculiar pleasures, known only to those who had seen the town when it was no more than a cluster of shacks strewn at random through the valley and over the hillsides.

Nor had they any objection to being told their city was ugly, but boasted quite freely of what they had done to spoil the countryside— once rather beautiful, in its strange, gloomy fashion, with its surrounding dark buttes, under shadows by midafternoon, its air of being lonely and haunted by some alien spirits hostile to man and all his works, as though it might have been left over from some earlier creation, forgotten when the world was redesigned, and abandoned just as it had first erupted there.

"It's ugly," they announced, even before the accusation had been made, "but not half as ugly as it will be, when once we get these mines to working properly."

And so, rather than make apologies for the devastation they had accomplished so far, they deprecated it, saying it was only a paltry beginning, no more than a modest clue to the hideous landscape they would produce in a few more years, and suggested they come back when the Milly Matches and the Buckhorn, the Yellow Medicine and the Humbug and all their neighbors, had come nearer to completing this ravishment they had now only fairly begun.